THE ROUTLEDGE HANDBOOK
OF FICTION AND BELIEF

The Routledge Handbook of Fiction and Belief offers a fresh reevaluation of the relationship between fiction and belief, surveying key debates and perspectives from a range of disciplines including narrative and cultural studies, science, religion, and politics. This volume draws on global, cutting edge research and theory to investigate the historically variable understandings of fictionality, and allows readers to grasp the role of fictions in our understanding of the world.

This interdisciplinary approach provides a thorough introduction to the fundamental themes of:

- Theoretical and Philosophical Perspectives on Fiction
- Fiction, Fact, and Science
- Social Effects and Uses of Fiction
- Fiction and Politics
- Fiction and Religion

Questioning how fictions in fact shape, mediate or distort our beliefs about the real world, essays in this volume outline the state of theoretical debates from the perspectives of literary theory, philosophy, sociology, religious studies, history, and the cognitive sciences. It aims to take stock of the real or supposed effects that fiction has on the world, and to offer a wide-reaching reflection on the implications of belief in fictions in the so-called "post-truth" era.

Alison James is Professor of French at the University of Chicago. Her research interests include the Oulipo group, the contemporary novel, theories and representations of everyday life, documentary literature, and questions of fact and fiction.

Akihiro Kubo is Professor of French Literature at Kwansei Gakuin University. His research interests focus on twentieth-century French literature and theories of literature.

Françoise Lavocat is Professor of Comparative Literature at the Université Sorbonne Nouvelle. She received an honorary doctorate in Humane Letters from the University of Chicago, and is a member of the Institut Universitaire de France as well as a member and section chair in the Academia Europaea.

THE ROUTLEDGE HANDBOOK OF FICTION AND BELIEF

*Edited by Alison James, Akihiro Kubo,
and Françoise Lavocat*

NEW YORK AND LONDON

Designed cover image: Getty

First published 2024
by Routledge
605 Third Avenue, New York, NY 10158

and by Routledge
4 Park Square, Milton Park, Abingdon, Oxon, OX14 4RN

Routledge is an imprint of the Taylor & Francis Group, an informa business

ISBN: 978-0-367-63515-2 (hbk)
ISBN: 978-0-367-63517-6 (pbk)
ISBN: 978-1-003-11945-6 (ebk)

DOI: 10.4324/9781003119456

Typeset in Times New Roman
by codeMantra

CONTENTS

Contents

FIGURES AND TABLES

Figures

Tables

CONTRIBUTORS

Nicolas Baumard is Director of Studies at the CNRS and Professor at the Ecole Normale Supérieure – PSL University in Paris. His work aims at understanding how cognitive and behavioral adaptations selected over the course of human history (e.g., moral sense, exploratory preferences, romantic love) can inform the structure and dynamics of social and cultural phenomena: social norms, religious beliefs, political institutions.

Anne Besson is Full Professor in Comparative Literature at Artois University (Arras). Her research fields include science fiction and fantasy genres, expansive fictional universes (cycles and serials, derivative texts, media adaptations), theories of fictionality, narratology, and the new media culture. Her latest book is dedicated to political uses of SFF (*Les Pouvoirs de l'enchantement*, Vendémiaire, 2021). She has also (co)edited some twenty collections including the *Dictionary of Fantasy* (2018) and *Dictionary of Imaginary Middle Ages* (2023), and coordinated two MOOCs on fantasy and on science fiction.

Emmanuel Bouju is currently Professor of Comparative Literature at the Université Sorbonne Nouvelle, Director of the CERC, and an honorary Senior Member of the Institut Universitaire de France. He has been a visiting professor at Indiana University in Bloomington and Harvard University. His publications include *Réinventer la littérature: démocratisation et modèles romanesques dans l'Espagne post-franquiste* (with a préface by Jorge Semprún, 2002), *La transcription de l'histoire. Essai sur le roman européen de la fin du vingtième siècle* (2006), *Fragments d'un discours théorique* (2016), and *Épimodernes. Nouvelles "leçons américaines" sur l'actualité du roman* (2020)—to be published in English at Palgrave-MacMillan.

Olivier Caïra is Lecturer in Sociology at the University of Paris Saclay and a member of the narratology team of the CRAL (EHESS, Paris). He works on leisure industries and the experience of fiction, particularly in the fields of cinema and games. His publications include *Définir la fiction: Du roman au jeu d'échecs* (Paris: Editions de l'EHESS, 2011), "Fiction, Expanded and Updated," in John Pier (ed.), *Contemporary French and Francophone Narratology* (Columbus: Ohio State University Press, 2020), and *Le Cerveau comme machine - Génies et surdoués à l'écran* (Geneva: Georg Editeur 2020, with a foreword by Barry Levinson).

Claude Calame is Director of Studies at the École des Hautes Études en Sciences Sociales in Paris (Centre AnHiMA: Anthropologie et Histoire des Mondes Antiques); he was Professor of Greek Language and Literature at the University of Lausanne. He also taught at the Universities of Urbino and Siena in Italy, and at Yale University in the United States. In English translation, he has published *The Craft of Poetic Speech in Ancient Greece* (Cornell University Press 1995), *The Poetics of Eros in Ancient Greece* (Princeton University Press 1999), *Myth and History in Ancient Greece. The Symbolic Creation of a Colony* (Princeton University Press 2003), *Masks of Authority. Fiction and Pragmatics in Ancient Greek Poetics* (Cornell University Press 2005), *Poetic and Performative Memory in Ancient Greece* (CHS – Harvard University Press 2009), *Greek Mythology. Poetics, Pragmatics and Fiction* (Cambridge University Press 2009), and most recently, in French and soon in English (Cambridge University Press), *La Tragédie chorale. Poésie grecque et rituel musical* (Les Belles Lettres 2017).

Aboubakr Chraïbi is Professor of Arabic Middle Literature, a literary category whose concept he has developed, at Inalco – Paris. He has worked extensively on the relationship between narrative and religion in premodern Islam. Currently, his research concerns the Arabic manuscript corpus of the *Thousand and One Nights* and its variations from a perspective that combines philology and narratology; he also works on the treatment of characters in fiction. Recent publication (2022): "Études de genre et population fictionnelle des *Mille et une nuits: nouvelle approche*." *Quaderni di Studi Arabi* 17, no. 1–2 (December): 246–76.

Nicolas Correard has been Maître de Conférences (Associate Professor) in Comparative Literature at Nantes Université since 2009. A specialist in Menippean satire, early modern satirical fictions, and their impact on the history of ideas, he co-edited *Quand l'interprétation s'invite dans la fiction* (2014), *Fictions animales* (Atlande, 2022), and a special issue of the journal *Dix-septième siècle* on the influence of Lucian of Samosata (no. 286, 2020/1). Recent articles include studies on Lucian of Samosata's influence on early modern unbelief, the relationship between the practice of literary paradox and heterodoxy, and the aesthetics of dissimulation in the Renaissance.

Gregory Currie teaches philosophy at the University of York. He is a fellow of the British Academy and of the Australian Academy of the Humanities. Educated at the LSE and the University of California he has taught in Australia, New Zealand, and the United States. He is the author of a number of books including *The Nature of Fiction* (CUP, 1990), *Narratives and Narrators* (Oxford University Press, 2010), and *Imagining and Knowing* (Oxford University Press, 2020). He is completing a book titled *The Agency in Art* (Oxford University Press, 2024). He is editor in chief of *Mind & Language*.

Ève de Dampierre-Noiray is currently Senior Lecturer in Comparative Literature at the Bordeaux-Montaigne University. Her research work focuses on twentieth- and twenty-first-century European and Arab literature (in French, Arabic, Italian, and English), in particular, the critique of colonial representations; the power and challenges of fiction in a postcolonial context; contemporary Arabic poetry (Mahmoud Darwich's poetry, twenty-first-century Egyptian and Syrian poetry); and translation. Her other publications include her essay *De l'Égypte à la fiction* (Classiques Garnier, 2014, prix D. Potier-Boès de l'Académie Française 2015); her work on Darwich, Char and Lorca, *Formes de l'action poétique* (with C. Boidin and E. Picherot, Atlande, 2016); her handbook on Mahmoud Darwich's translations *Dans une rime de bois* (PUB, 2023) and, as a translator, Abdulrahman Khallouf's poetry collection, *Happiness Is a Bee Stinging Me at the Hip*, translated from Syrian Arabic (Alidades, 2022).

Markus Altena Davidsen (b. 1981) is University Lecturer in the Sociology of Religion at Leiden University, the Netherlands. His research interests include non-institutional religion and the pragmatics of religious narratives, and he has published widely on fiction-based religions, especially Jediism and Tolkien spirituality. For his doctoral dissertation, *The Spiritual Tolkien Milieu: A Study of Fiction-based Religion* (2014), Davidsen was awarded the Gerardus van der Leeuw Dissertation Award from the Dutch Association for the Study of Religion. As editor, he recently published *Narrative and Belief: The Religious Affordance of Supernatural Fiction* (Routledge, 2018).

Edgar Dubourg is a PhD student at the École Normale Supérieure – PSL University in Paris. He takes an interdisciplinary evolutionary approach to the study of fictional stories. He is interested in how cognitive adaptations and adaptive sources of variability impact both the universality and the variability of cultural preferences for entertaining items such as movies, novels, or video games.

Anne Duprat is Professor of Comparative Literature at Université Picardie-Jules Verne and a senior member of the Institut Universitaire de France. Specialized in the theory of fiction, she has published several essays on early modern European literature. Her publications include *Histoire du Captif. Un paradigme littéraire, de l'Antiquité au XVIIe siècle* (2023), *Vraisemblances. Poétiques de la fiction en France et en Italie* (2009), and a co-authored translation of Cervantes' theatre in French (*Théâtre barbaresque*, 2022). Her current project ALEA "Figures of Chance" (2020–2024) brings together specialists in the history and theory of literature, historiography, aesthetic philosophy, and epistemology around the representations of chance in European art (sixteenth to twenty-first century).

Jean-Paul Engélibert is Professor of Comparative Literature at the University of Bordeaux Montaigne and Co-director of the Plurielles research unit. For the past ten years, his research has focused on utopias, dystopias, and fictions of apocalypse, and more generally on the political imagination of the modern and contemporary novel. He has notably published *Apocalypses sans royaume. Politique des fictions de la fin du monde, XXe-XXIe siècles* (Classiques Garnier, 2013) and *Fabuler la fin du monde. La puissance critique des fictions d'apocalypse* (La Découverte, 2019), and edited with Raphaëlle Guidée "Utopie et catastrophe. Revers et renaissances de l'utopie," special issue, *La Licorne*, no. 114 (2015).

Heather Ferguson is Professor of Psychology at the University of Kent. Her research broadly examines the cognitive basis of social communication, including the time-course of integration, the underlying neural mechanisms, and the extent to which constraints from world knowledge and context compete to influence social interaction and pragmatic language comprehension. This work has received generous funding, including a European Research Council grant examining social communication across the lifespan, and multiple Leverhulme Trust grants that link social behavior directly to language and development. Recently, she has been collaborating with philosophers and film studies experts to run empirical studies that test how art influences social wellbeing and open-mindedness.

Jacopo Frascaroli is Postdoctoral Research Fellow in the Department of Psychology at the University of Turin. He earned his PhD in Philosophy at the University of York in 2022 as part of the Leverhulme-funded interdisciplinary project "Learning from Fiction." Jacopo's work brings together aesthetics, philosophy of mind, and cognitive science. His PhD thesis "Art and Learning: A Predictive Processing Proposal" explores the potential of predictive processing as a general framework for the study of the arts and aesthetics. Jacopo is currently editing a theme issue on the same topic for *Philosophical Transactions of the Royal Society B.*

Stacie Friend is Reader in Philosophy at the University of Edinburgh. Her research is at the intersection of aesthetics, language, and mind, especially as these pertain to our engagement with fiction. She is currently the President of the British Society of Aesthetics and an Editor of the philosophy journal *Analysis*, as well as the Director of the interdisciplinary research project "Art Opening Minds: Imagination and Perspective in Film," funded by the Templeton Religion Trust.

Kris Goffin is passionate about research that combines philosophy and psychology and provides knowledge about socially relevant topics such as racism, sexism, and other forms of discrimination. He has done research on implicit bias (such as implicit prejudices and stereotypes), emotions, moral psychology, aesthetic experiences, and various interactions between these topics. His research thus focuses on philosophy of cognitive science and mind, emotion theory, moral psychology, and aesthetics. He is a currently Postdoctoral Researcher at UAntwerp and KULeuven, doing interdisciplinary research on implicit bias. Before this, he held postdoctoral positions at Birkbeck College and the University of Geneva.

Kayleigh Green is PhD Researcher at Birkbeck College, University of London. A recipient of a Leverhulme Trust studentship (2018–2021), her research is at the intersection of philosophy and cognitive psychology, currently focusing on the rationality of reading and the experimental use of fiction as a tool by which to reduce discriminatory attitudes toward marginalized groups. To empirically investigate her research questions, Kayleigh conducts psychological experimental studies, interpreting the data output using both philosophical and scientific frameworks of reference. She previously worked on the Leverhulme Research Project "Learning from Fiction: A Philosophical and Psychological Study".

Sarah Hammerschlag is the John Nuveen Professor of Religion and Literature, Philosophy of Religion, and History of Judaism at the University of Chicago Divinity School. Her research thus far has focused on the position of Judaism in the post-World War II French intellectual scene. She is the author of The Figural Jew: Politics and Identity in Postwar French Thought (University of Chicago Press, 2010) and *Broken Tablets: Levinas, Derrida and the Literary Afterlife of Religion* (Columbia University Press, 2016), the editor of Modern French Jewish Thought: Writings on Religion and Politics (Brandeis University Press, 2018), and co-author of *Devotion: Three Inquiries in Religion, Literature and the Political Imagination* (University of Chicago Press, 2021).

Paul L. Harris is a developmental psychologist with interests in the development of cognition, emotion, and imagination. After studying psychology at Sussex and Oxford, he taught at the University of Lancaster, the Free University of Amsterdam, and the London School of Economics. In 1980, he moved to Oxford where he became Professor of Developmental Psychology and Fellow of St John's College. In 1998, he was elected as fellow of the British Academy. In 2001, he moved to Harvard University where he teaches developmental psychology at the Graduate School of Education. His latest book is *Child Psychology in 12 Questions* (Oxford University Press).

Patrick Jagoda is the William Rainey Harper Professor of Cinema & Media Studies, English, and Obstetrics and Gynecology at the University of Chicago. He is Director of the Weston Game Lab, and Co-founder of the Game Changer Chicago Design Lab. Patrick's books include *Network Aesthetics* (2016), *The Game Worlds of Jason Rohrer* (2016), *Experimental Games* (2020), and *Transmedia Stories* (2022). Patrick designs transmedia, digital, and analog games, including the climate change alternate reality game Terrarium (2019), which received the 2020 IndieCade award for the best Location Based and Live Play Design. He is recipient of a 2020 Guggenheim Fellowship.

Alison James is Professor of French at the University of Chicago. Her research interests include the Oulipo group, the contemporary novel, theories and representations of everyday life, and questions of fact and fiction. She is the author of *Constraining Chance: Georges Perec and the Oulipo* (Northwestern University Press, 2009) and *The Documentary Imagination in Twentieth-Century French Literature: Writing with Facts* (Oxford University Press, 2020). She has also edited volumes and journal issues on literary formalism, fieldwork literatures, and nonfiction across media.

Erin James is Professor of English and Affiliate Faculty of Environmental Science at the University of Idaho. Her books include *Narrative in the Anthropocene* (Ohio State University Press, 2022) and *The Storyworld Accord: Econarratology and Postcolonial Narratives* (University of Nebraska Press, 2015), the latter of which won the International Society for the Study of Narrative's (ISSN) 2017 Perkins Prize and was a finalist for the Association of the Study of Literature and Environment's (ASLE) Ecocriticism Book Award that same year. She has also published essays in *DIEGESIS*, *SubStance*, the *Journal of Narrative Theory*, and *Poetics Today*, as well as *Environment and Narrative: New Directions in Econarratology*, which she co-edited with Eric Morel (Ohio State University Press, 2020).

Eva-Maria Konrad is Junior Professor of Methods of Literary Studies at the Institut für deutsche Literatur at the Humboldt-Universität zu Berlin. Her research interests concern the philosophy of literature, literary theory, comparative literature, and German literature from the nineteenth to the twenty-first century. Her publications include *Dimensions of Fictionality. Analysis of a Fundamental Literary Concept* (Paderborn: Mentis, 2014), and "Are emotional responses necessary for an adequate understanding of literary texts?" (2019), in *Debates in Aesthetics* 14, no. 1: 45–59 (as co-author). She is also the co-editor of the special issue on *The Paradox of Fiction* (2018) of the *Journal of Literary Theory* 12 (2) and of the book series *Theorema* (Berlin/Heidelberg: Metzler).

Akihiro Kubo is Professor of French Literature at Kwansei Gakuin University. His research interests focus on twentieth-century French literature and theories of literature. He is the author of *Hyosho-no Kizu, Daiichiji Sekaitaisen kara miru Furansu Bungaku* [*French literature and First World War*] (Jinbun Shoin, 2011) and the translator of Jean-Marie Schaeffer's *Pourquoi la fiction?* [*Naze-Fiction ka*] (Keio Gijuku Shuppan, 2019) and Gérard Genette's *Métalepse* [Metalepsis] (Jinbun Shoin, 2022).

Françoise Lavocat is Professor of Comparative Literature at the Université Sorbonne Nouvelle. She received an honorary doctorate in Humane Letters from the University of Chicago, and is a member of the Institut Universitaire de France as well as a member and section chair in the Academia Europaea. Her publications include *Arcadies malheureuses* (Champion, 1997), *Usages et théories de la fiction* (ed. PUR, 2004), *La Syrinx au bûcher* (Droz, 2005), *La théorie littéraire des mondes possibles* (ed. CNRS, 2010), *Pestes, Incendies naufrages, Écritures du désastre au XVIIe siècle* (ed. Brépols, 2010*)*, *Fait et fiction: pour une frontière* (Seuil, 2016, Del Vecchio, 2020), and *Les Personnages rêvent aussi* (Hermann, 2020). Since 2018, she has been President of the International Society for Fiction and Fictionality Studies.

Loïse Lelevé is Associate Professor in Comparative Literature at Paris Nanterre University. Her research revolves around forgers and forgery in contemporary European fiction, with a special focus on fiction ethics in the "post-truth" era. Her publications in English include the paper "Conspiracy Theories, Storytelling and Forgers: Towards a Paradoxical Ethics of Truth in Contemporary European Fiction" for the *Lincoln Humanities Journal;* or "'Romanzo non vuol dire bugia': Fiction as a Counterfeit and Counterfeiting as an Ethical Challenge in Contemporary Italian Narratives of Paolo Ciulla's Forgeries" in *Deeds and Days.*

Annick Louis is Professor at the University of Franche-Comté and a senior member of the Institut Université de France. She specializes in comparative literature of the nineteenth, twentieth, and twenty-first centuries, with a focus on Latin American and European cultures. Her work proposes an epistemological perspective on literature and social sciences. Her most recent books are *L'Invention de Troie. Les vies rêvées de Heinrich Schliemann* (EHESS, 2020, Louis Barthou Prize of the Académie Française 2021); *Sans objet. Pour une épistémologie du littéraire* (Hermann, 2021); *Homo explorator. L'écriture non littéraire d'Arthur Rimbaud, Lucio V. Mansilla y Heinrich Schliemann* (Garnier/Classiques, 2022).

Eliot Michaelson is Reader in Philosophy at King's College London. His work is primarily in the philosophy of language. Together with Jessica Pepp and Rachel Sterken, he has written a number of pieces on online communicative environments, how they have altered our communicative practices, and what they can teach us about the nature of meaning and communication.

Agnes Moors is Professor at KU Leuven and associate member of the Swiss Center for Affective Sciences. She combines theoretical work informed by philosophy with empirical research. Her theoretical work focuses on the comparison of emotion theories, the conceptual analysis of automaticity, the critical analysis of dual-process models, and the development of a goal-directed model for behavior causation. Her empirical work examines the role of goal-directed processes in emotional and (seemingly) maladaptive behavior using experimental, behavioral, and neuroscientific methods. She is the author of *Demystifying Emotions: A Taxonomy of Theories in Psychology and Philosophy* (Cambridge University Press, 2022).

Vera Nünning is Professor of English Philology at Heidelberg University, where she also served as Vice-Rector for international affairs. She has published books on eighteenth, nineteenth, and twentieth-century British literature, and (co-)edited 25 volumes on contemporary literature and narrative theory. Her articles deal with narrative theory, gender studies, cultural studies, and British fiction from the eighteenth to the twenty-first century. Her book *Reading Fictions, Changing Minds* appeared in 2014. She was a fellow in two Institutes of Advanced Studies and is associate editor of three book series. She is currently co-editing *The Palgrave Handbook of Feminist, Queer and Trans Narrative Studies*.

Lionel Obadia, PhD in Sociology (1997), was Associate Professor in Ethnology at the University of Lille (1998–2004) and is Full Professor of Anthropology (since 2004) at the University of Lyon, France. He also teaches in other French universities (EHESS, EPHE, SciencePo). He is a specialist of anthropology of religion, Asian religions, and globalization. His works focus on hybridization and cultural/religious transfers. He has conducted fieldwork in France, Europe (on Buddhism in the West), Nepal (on Buddhism and Shamanism), the United States and Israel (on Jewish messianism), and South India (in Auroville). His research now explores the relationships between religions and digital technologies.

Julie Orlemanski is Associate Professor of English at the University of Chicago. She is the author of *Symptomatic Subjects: Bodies, Medicine, and Causation in the Literature of Late Medieval England* (University of Pennsylvania Press, 2019) and articles in numerous journals and edited collections. She is the co-editor of the *Norton Anthology of English Literature, Eleventh Edition* (forthcoming 2023), and she also co-edits *postmedieval: a journal of medieval cultural studies*. Her current research concerns, variously, fictionality, prosopopoeia, the early Cistercians, and the use of modern concepts to study premodern cultures.

Nicholas D. Paige holds the rank of Professor in the Department of French at the University of California, Berkeley. He is the author of *Technologies of the Novel: Quantitative Data and the Evolution of Literary Systems* (2021, supported by a Guggenheim fellowship), *Before Fiction: The Ancien Régime of the Novel* (2011, awarded the 2013 ASECS Gottschalk prize), and *Being Interior: Autobiography and the Contradictions of Modernity* (2001). He is also the translator of Lafayette's 1670 novel *Zayde: A Spanish Romance*. His articles have appeared in journals such as *Representations, Poétique, Modern Language Quarterly, PMLA, Revue d'histoire littéraire de la France, New Literary History,* and *Poetics Today*.

Thomas Pavel, born in Bucharest, Romania, earned a Doctorat 3e cycle at the University of Paris-3. He is Emeritus Professor in Romance Languages and Literature, Comparative Literature, and the Committee on Social Thought at the University of Chicago. Earlier he taught at Princeton University, the University of California, Santa Cruz, the University of Québec in Montreal, and the University of Ottawa. His books include *The Poetics of Plot* (1985), *Fictional Worlds* (1986), *The Spell of Language* (2002), and *The Lives of the Novel* (2015).

Ayse Payir is Researcher at Boston University. Her work focuses on the development of natural and supernatural thinking from early to middle childhood. After receiving her undergraduate degree in Psychology from Yeditepe University in Istanbul in 2008, she moved to the United States and studied Developmental Psychology for her master's at New York University (2008–2010) and for her PhD at the University of North Carolina at Greensboro (2010–2016). Prior to her position at Boston University, she worked as a researcher at Columbia University.

Jessica Pepp is a Burman Fellow and Researcher in Theoretical Philosophy at Uppsala University, Researcher at the University of Oslo, and Docent at the University of Turku. Her research interests are mainly in the philosophy of language and mind, focusing especially on questions about linguistic reference, intentionality, and various forms of insincerity. She is PI of the Swedish Research Council project "New Frontiers of Speech: Philosophy of Language in the Information Age."

James Phelan, Distinguished University Professor of English at Ohio State University, has devoted his research to thinking through the consequences of conceiving of narrative as rhetoric. Since 1993, he has been the editor of *Narrative* and co-editor of the *Theory and Interpretation of Narrative* Series at the Ohio State University Press. His recent publications include *Somebody Telling Somebody Else* (2017), the co-edited volume *Fictionality in Literature: Core Concepts Revisited* (2022), and *Narrative Medicine: A Rhetorical Rx* (2023). In 2021, he received the Wayne C. Booth Lifetime Achievement Award from the International Society for the Study of Narrative.

Isabelle Ratié is Professor of Sanskrit at the Université Sorbonne Nouvelle (Paris) and a senior member of the Institut Universitaire de France. Her research bears on the history of Indian philosophy. A recipient of the Friedrich Weller prize, she has authored or co-authored six monographs and numerous articles and co-edited two collective volumes. Her latest books include *Utpaladeva on the Power of Action* (Harvard University Press, 2021), based on her recent discovery of lost chapters of a major medieval philosophical treatise by the Kashmirian philosopher Utpaladeva, and *Qu'est-ce que la philosophie indienne?* (Gallimard, 2023), co-authored with Vincent Eltschinger.

Philippe Roussin is Senior Researcher at the CNRS and a member of the Centre de recherches sur les arts et le langage (CNRS-EHESS). He was Visiting Professor in French Studies at Wadham College (Oxford University) from 2013 to 2016. From 2017 to 2021, he was the coordinator of the international research network "Literature and Democracy: Theoretical, Historical and Comparative Approaches (XIXth-XXIst Centuries)." He is the author of *Misère de la littérature, terreur de l'histoire. Céline et la littérature contemporaine* (Gallimard, 2005). He has recently co-edited, with Mohamed-Salah Omri, *Literature, Democracy and Transitional Justice. Comparative World Perspectives* (Legenda, 2022).

Markus Rüsch is Full-time Lecturer at Kyoto Women's University and received his Dr Phil. from Freie Universität Berlin in Japanese Studies. His research interests are Aesthetics of Religion, Buddhism and Literature, and Buddhism and Ethics. His recent publications include *Argumente des Heiligen: Rhetorische Mittel und narrative Strukturen in Hagiographien am Beispiel des japanischen Mönchs Shinran* (2019); and "Biography as Interreligious Dialogue: The Case of Modern Biographies on Shinran" (*Journal of World Buddhist Cultures*, 2022).

Marie-Laure Ryan is an independent scholar based in Colorado. She is the author of *Possible Worlds, Artificial Intelligence and Narrative Theory* (1991), *Narrative as Virtual Reality: Immersion and Interactivity in Literature and Electronic Media* (2001), *Avatars of Story* (2006), *Narrating Space/Spatializing Narrative* (2016, with Kenneth Foote and Maoz Azaryahu), *A New Anatomy of Storyworlds: What Is, What If, As If* (2022), and *Object-Oriented Narratology* (forthcoming 2024, with Tang Weishen), as well as over 100 articles on narratology, media theory, and digital culture. In 2017, she received the Wayne Booth Life Achievement Award from the International Society for the Study of Narrative. Her website is at www.marilaur.info and she can be reached at marilaur@gmail.com.

Barbara Selmeci Castioni has held various teaching and research positions at the Universities of Lausanne, Basel, and Fribourg since defending her doctoral thesis at the University of Neuchâtel on the relationship between fictional literature and sanctity in seventeenth-century France. She has published some forty articles, co-organized a dozen international colloquia, and participated in several editions of texts. Her main fields of research are the relationship between literature and religion (1600–1830), the history of the press, and illustrative engraving.

Rachel Sterken is Associate Professor of Philosophy at the University of Hong Kong. She works primarily at the intersections of philosophy of language, semantics, ethics, and social philosophy. Most of her research to date focuses on generic language, conceptual engineering, fake news, communication with artificial intelligences, among other topics. She is Research Director of Concept Lab Hong Kong and the AI&Humanity Lab, and Affiliated Researcher of the Musketeers Foundation Institute of Data Science, all at the University of Hong Kong. She is currently Principal Investigator of the Norwegian Research Council funded project "Meaning and Communication in the Information Age."

Adam Toon is Senior Lecturer at the University of Exeter. His work focuses on topics in philosophy of science and philosophy of mind. He is the author of *Models as Make-Believe: Imagination, Fiction and Scientific Representation* (Palgrave Macmillan, 2012) and *Mind as Metaphor: A Defence of Mental Fictionalism* (Oxford University Press, 2023).

Lena Wimmer is Postdoctoral Scholar at the University of Freiburg. After completing a PhD in Psychology at Heidelberg University in 2015, she worked as research and teaching associate at the University of Duisburg-Essen, as research fellow at Bangor University (funded by the German Research Foundation (DFG)), as research associate at the University of Kent, and as substitute professor at the University of Kassel. Taking a cognitive psychology perspective, she investigates the preconditions, processes, and outcomes of reading fictional literature; effects and mechanisms of dispositional mindfulness and mindfulness-based interventions; and verbal and thinking skills of autistic people.

Alok Yadav is Associate Professor of English at George Mason University. He is the author of *Before the Empire of English: Provinciality, Nationalism, and Literature in Eighteenth-Century Britain* (2004). His essay in this volume extends a discussion begun in "Literature, Fictiveness, and Postcolonial Criticism" (*Novel* 43 no. 1 [2009]). His current work centers on an online project on *Anthologies of African American Writing*.

Henrik Zetterberg-Nielsen is Professor at Aarhus University and was visiting professor at Tampere University in 2014–2018. His research has attempted to contribute to conversations about mainly three areas of narrative theory: first person narration, unnatural narratology, and fictionality. His current project is on human sexuality and the roles of imagination and fictionality in human sexual practices and preferences. Sample publications include "The Impersonal Voice in First-Person Narrative Fiction", "Ten Theses about Fictionality" with James Phelan and Richard Walsh (in *Narrative*, January 2015), and *Fictionality and Literature – Core Concepts Revisited* (edited with James Phelan et al.) in 2022 at OSU Press. He heads the research group Narrative Research Lab (http://nordisk. au.dk/forskning/forskningscentre/nrl/intro/) and the "Centre for Fictionality Studies" (http://fictionality.au.dk/).

Lisa Zunshine is Bush-Holbrook Professor of English at the University of Kentucky, a Guggenheim Fellow (2007), and author/editor of twelve books dealing with various aspects of cognitive science, literature, and culture, including, most recently, *Getting Inside Your Head* (JHUP, 2012), *The Oxford Handbook of Cognitive Literary Studies* (2015), and *The Secret Life of Literature* (MIT Press, 2022).

INTRODUCTION

Alison James, Akihiro Kubo, and Françoise Lavocat

Belief and Make-Believe

This handbook takes as its point of departure a philosophical conundrum: the conceptual and concrete entanglement of fiction and belief. The human ability to simultaneously believe and not believe, or indeed to simultaneously make something up and believe in it, has long been the subject of commentary. The Roman historian Tacitus, in his *Annals* (V.10), suggests that humans can at once invent a story and believe it: *fingebant simul credebantque* ("they coined and credited [the tale] at the same time"); glossing this quotation, Francis Bacon observes: "he that will easily believe rumours will as easily augment rumours [...]: so great an affinity hath fiction and belief" ([1605] 1893]). Bacon, of course, is using the term "fiction" in the pejorative meaning of "lie" or "untruth," and his phrase suggests what we might call cognitive dissonance. However, this knitting together of belief and invention takes a more positive meaning in Samuel Taylor Coleridge's famous phrase on the "willing suspension of disbelief for the moment," which characterizes our attitude toward the "shadows of the imagination" (Coleridge, [1817], 2014, Chapter 14, 2: 208). More recently, theories of fiction as a form of "pretense" (Searle, 1975) or "make-believe" (Walton, 1990) also imply the production of something which mimics, performs, or resembles belief. Fiction then implies a "distinctive cognitive attitude": "not belief, not entirely unlike belief" (Schroeder and Matheson, 2006, 21).

On the side of "not belief," it seems clear that we do not posit the actual existence of fictional entities. Yet, it also seems obvious that works of fiction contain explicit or implicit propositional content that has an impact on our beliefs and plays a significant role in shaping our understanding of the real world. We assume that fictions reliably improve or expand our knowledge of certain historical facts, for instance, as when we acquire an understanding of Russian history by reading Tolstoy's *War and Peace* (1869; see Currie, 2020, 151). We learn a great deal about the First World War from war novels such as Henri Barbusse's *Under Fire* (1916) or Erich Maria Remarque's *All Quiet on the Western Front* (1928). These novels are also believed to have had an important influence on anti-war public opinion during the war and into the 1930s. In some cases, novels have played decisive roles in the formation of national identity, as is the case for the Filipino novelist José Rizal's *Noli Me Tángere* (1887). If fictions have influence on both an individual and a collective scale (see James, Kubo, and Lavocat, 2023), it follows that they can also have a negative impact, conveying false or harmful beliefs. If fiction had no cognitive value, who would care about racial or gender stereotypes represented in fiction? Recent debates on the rewriting of classic texts, especially books for children, show that

DOI: 10.4324/9781003119456-1

the fear of fiction's dangerous influence is pervasive (Taylor, 2023). Yet, claims that fictions transmit beliefs have also met with strong skepticism, whether from philosophers and literary theorists (Landy, 2012, 10) or from scientists who have not found the empirical evidence to confirm such an influence (see Edgar Dubourg and Nicolas Baumard's contribution to this volume).

Two main questions emerge here: that of our belief *in* fictions and that of the effects *of* fictions on beliefs external to them. This handbook addresses the connection between fiction and belief from these two points of view. First, the issue of our belief in fictions concerns the internal credibility of fictional worlds and the nature of our emotional and cognitive investments in non-existent characters and events. Second, the question of the effects of fiction asks how our beliefs about the real world may be altered by fiction, whether directly or indirectly, temporarily or permanently. The contributions to this volume offer theoretical arguments for or against such effects while also engaging with the available empirical evidence on the persuasiveness of fiction. What cognitive attitude is involved in our reception of fiction, and what epistemic value can fiction have? What kinds of beliefs do we form in reading or consuming fictions, and how are these beliefs connected to knowledge? Do we learn facts from fiction, and what care should be taken in doing so? Does fiction aim to persuade us to adopt certain beliefs, and by what means? Our aim is to take stock of current debates on the relationship between fiction and belief from a broad interdisciplinary and comparative perspective, offering insights from philosophy, narrative theory, literary studies, media studies, religious studies, history, cognitive sciences, and sociology.

Belief, Knowledge, and Credulity

Belief itself has often been subject to suspicion, set on the side of opinion (*doxa*) as opposed to knowledge (*episteme*). Thus, in Plato's *Theaetetus*, Socrates objects to the identification of correct belief or right opinion (*orthe doxa*) with knowledge, since people can be persuaded by orators and lawyers to adopt correct judgments without possessing knowledge (201b–d). Providing an account (*logos*) for a true belief seems to offer a more assured path to knowledge (*Theaetetus*, 201d–210b), so that since Plato, philosophers have often defined knowledge in terms of "justified true belief"; however, this definition has also been contested (e.g., Gettier, 1963). Belief is a core concept in epistemology, but can also be framed as an ethical issue: what ought we to believe? What constitutes adequate evidence for our beliefs (see Adler, 2002)?

As Lisa Zunshine shows in her contribution to this volume, belief is an imprecise term that covers both intuitive and reflective mental stances. Moreover, we tend to essentialize beliefs as inherent qualities held by others, which determine their behaviors—but not our own. In other words, we impute credulity to other people or peoples. Bruno Latour has argued that belief is what we, supposing ourselves to be modern, attribute to others (and thus subject to iconoclastic critique) in the context of a colonial or anthropological encounter, while believing ourselves to be in possession of the objective facts (Latour, 2009). We might add that beliefs—and by extension credulous attitudes—are also what we often ascribe to people in the past. When asking whether the ancient Greeks believed in their myths, Paul Veyne points out that the very terms of the question involve post-Enlightenment assumptions about our own exclusive access to the truth (1988, 112–13), whereas mythology can involve a complex combination of belief and non-belief (84). Kendall Walton suggests that ancient myths functioned both as fiction and as nonfiction: "many myths may never have been straightforward truth claims, and even if they were, they may have been fiction all along" (Walton, 1990, 95). Recent approaches in cognitive science have also suggested that we overestimate the gullibility of others, when in reality most people successfully operate within a framework of "epistemic vigilance" (Sperber et al., 2010) or "open vigilance" (Mercier, 2020, 31) when deciding whom to trust and what to believe.

These debates are related to fiction in a number of respects. Perennial fears about the influence of fiction on beliefs (and actions) rest on the assumption that certain people or groups of people (women, children, premodern or "non-modern" peoples) are especially susceptible to confusing reality and imagination. Relatedly, fiction itself is frequently associated with modern skepticism, doubt, and unbelief. For instance, it has been suggested that the development of fiction in the West is symptomatic of a retreat from religious belief, with fictional models replacing "wornout mythical explanations" (Pavel, 1986, 132). Accounts that associate fictionality with the so-called rise of the novel in the eighteenth and nineteenth centuries postulate a complex modern attitude that responds both to secularization and to the forms of representative monetary instruments involved in credit economies (Poovey, 2008, 110). Thus, Catherine Gallagher argues that "modernity is fiction-friendly because it encourages disbelief, speculation, and credit" (2006, 345). Although these views can and should be disputed (see Fludernik, 2018 as well as Julie Orlemanki's contribution to this volume), it is clear that a reflection on belief offers insight into the historically variable understandings of fictionality. This is particularly true, as shown by the contributions in Part III of this volume, when we consider fictionality in relation to religious beliefs. Françoise Lavocat also affirms that we can observe different types of correlation between practices of fiction and religious belief (Lavocat, 2016, 231–33).

To return to one well-known account of the relationship of belief and fiction, Coleridge's notion of the "willing suspension of disbelief" has been extended to refer to a generalized tolerance for all fictionality, and to the temporary abandonment of the real world that allows readers to engage with the fictional entities of an imaginary world. Yet Coleridge's formulation from 1817, describing his contribution to the co-authored *Lyrical Ballads* of 1798, aims more specifically to account for the poet's ability to awaken "poetic faith" in supernatural beings—in opposition to the "things of every day" that are Wordsworth's specialty ([1817] 2014, 2: 208). This notion of poetic faith draws on Coleridge's theory of the primary and secondary imagination, the primary being understood as "the living power and prime agent of all human perception," and the secondary as "coexisting with the consciousness will, yet still as identical with the primary in the *kind* of its agency, and differing only in degree, and in the *mode* of its operation" ([1817] 2014, 1: 205–06; emphasis in original). Coleridge's well-known negative formulation on the suspension of disbelief has as a positive corollary the willing production of belief in objects of the imagination. We should also note that Coleridge's account of "poetic faith" retains a significant religious dimension, entailing the effort to "transfer [...] a semblance of truth" (208) to supernatural events and agents. Does such poetic or fictional faith inevitably impinge on our beliefs about the real world—and even about those "everyday" things which, according to Coleridge's account of Wordsworth, we cannot actually see or understand without the help of poetry?

Imagining and Believing

Coleridge's definition of "poetic faith"—or, as it is usually reframed, faith in fictions—draws explicitly on Enlightenment debates over knowledge and imagination. It also lies under the shadow of skepticism, casting our engagement with fiction as at once a symptom of generalized doubt (the attitude of "disbelief" is initially assumed, especially when it comes to supernatural beings) and as the willed overcoming of this doubt. In this skeptical vein, Hume had argued that

> The sentiment of belief is nothing but a conception more intense and steady than what attends the mere fictions of the imagination, and [...] this manner of conception arises from a customary conjunction of the object with something present to the memory or senses.
>
> ([1748] 1999, 5.2.13)

Hume is not speaking here specifically of literary or poetic fictions, but rather of what Jean-Marie Schaeffer (2020, 131), in an analysis of Hume, calls "cognitive fictions": mental representations that are either pre-reflexively generated or consciously constructed. In his analysis of these cognitive fictions, Hume describes a basic imaginative competency that offers us the ability to form a conceptual picture of the world. Subsequently, it is embodied experience and memory that generate belief, conferring greater power on conceptual objects that would otherwise remain figments of the imagination. Schaeffer claims that recent experiments in cognitive science confirm Hume's view on the lack of clear-cut internal (or ontological) difference between types of representation (Schaeffer, 2020, 137–38).

Still, says Hume, we cannot simply *choose* to believe any combination of ideas; belief lies in "some sentiment or feeling" that "depends not on the will, nor can be commanded at pleasure" (Hume, [1748] 1999, 5.2.11). Imagination is free, then, but belief depends on a complex set of conditions. Kendall Walton puts the point more bluntly: "Beliefs, unlike imaginings, are correct or incorrect. [...] We are not free to believe as we please. We are free to imagine as we please" (1990, 59). Unsurprisingly, the distinction between imagining and believing remains for many contemporary philosophers a defining criterion for fiction: fiction communicates imaginings, whereas nonfiction communicates beliefs (Abell, 2020, 9–10; Currie, 2020, 17–18). Others, however, dispute this view, arguing that belief and imagination are not incompatible and that there is in fact possible interaction between fiction and pre-existing structures of belief (Friend, 2008, 2014; Matravers, 2014, 92). According to Jean-Marie Schaeffer, the phenomenon of fictional immersion is not to be confused with the commitments involved in belief: "Immersion accedes to representations *before* they are translated into beliefs. Their translation into beliefs homologous with those that would be 'normally' induced by representations fictionally mimed is blocked at a superior cognitive level, that of conscious attention" (Schaeffer, 2010, 163). Nevertheless, when analyzing Hume's account of the unitary nature of our mental representations, Schaeffer insists both on the difference and on the "reciprocal permeability" of our attitudes to fiction and our commitments to facts (Schaeffer, 2020, 143). Artistic fictions (following Hume once again) involve a complex intentional attitude in that they are "contaminated" by reality—that is, by the kind of liveliness or intensity that characterizes objects of belief—yet at the same time do not actually gain the support of belief (Schaeffer, 2020, 141). Returning to Schaeffer's claim that mental "blocks" prevent us from believing in fictions, Françoise Lavocat (2020) points out that literary and cultural history offer numerous counterexamples. In *Fait et fiction* (Fact and Fiction, 2016, 224–27), she argues that fiction puts belief into play, in two senses: first, it exposes us to a cognitive conflict between belief and disbelief that is intrinsic to the operations of fictional immersion and emersion; second, it projects a possible world that may interfere with or problematize our ordinary systems of belief.

This inference also moves in the other direction; that is, our beliefs about the real world, about the beliefs of the author, or about the author's community shape our understanding of the imagined worlds projected by fictions. Approaches to this question include David Lewis's analysis of the "collective belief worlds" that provide the proper background to our understanding of truth in fiction (Lewis, 1978, 44). Walton develops Lewis's account in his description of the principles that determine which fictional truths imply which others: the "Reality Principle" (RP) is a strategy of "making fictional worlds as much like the real one as the core of primary fictional truths permits" (Walton, 1990, 187), while the "Mutual Belief Principle" (MBP) "directs us to extrapolate so as to maximize similarities between fictional worlds and the real world not as it actually is but as it is or was mutually believed to be in the artist's society" (195). Both principles, although they may be in tension, have a place in our practices of reading. Another version of the Reality Principle is Marie-Laure Ryan's "principle of minimal departure" (Ryan, 1980, 406), which "means that we will project upon the world of the statement everything we know about the real world, and that we will make only those adjustments which we cannot avoid." The question here is that of which beliefs external to the fictional world are necessary to give that world coherence and meaning. Imagining cannot happen without belief.

Models, Facts, and Emotions

Given these mechanisms of immersion and world-building that involve a reciprocal interaction between fiction and belief, in what ways can fiction be said to change our minds (Nünning, 2014)? The cognitive value of fiction, for some, does not come from the direct transmission of beliefs but rather from its capacity to train the mental capacities (Landy, 2012) or from its links to forms of behavioral modeling that favor learning (Schaeffer, 2010, 41–108). Thought experiments can be considered as fictional models that allow us to clarify or test hypotheses (in this volume, the contributions by Adam Toon and Anne Duprat explore this connection between fiction and scientific models).

Aside from this modeling function, however, fictions can convey ordinary empirical facts about the real world, either directly or via inference, since they generally contain a mix of referential and non-referential elements. This is especially so if we consider that fictions often resemble the real world or overlap with a community's beliefs about the real world (Currie, 2020, 157–60). Stacie Friend (2014) notes that readers are not generally careful about forming beliefs from fiction, even if they ought to exercise caution. Indeed, some psychological studies have found the opposite: rather than more carefully vetting information we find in fiction, we are likely to believe even blatantly false statements in a fictional context (Gerrig and Prentice, 1991). This empirical finding has been attributed to a lack of systematic cognitive processing, or to the process of "transportation" and identification involved in our encounters with fiction (Schreier, 2009, 332–33). Even if it has proven difficult to corroborate such studies (see Wheeler, Green, and Brock, 1999), the concern remains that our usual modes of "epistemic vigilance" (Sperber et al., 2010) may function differently, and perhaps less effectively, when we interpret fictions.

Literary scholars and philosophers often suggest that the effects of fiction on our beliefs stem mainly from its axiological dimension, and from our emotional and empathetic engagement with the experiences of characters—an engagement that is especially prevalent in traditional media such as literature, theater, and cinema (Lavocat, 2020, 26). The nature of these emotional responses has given rise to many discussions on the nature of our belief in fiction. The "paradox of fiction" has attracted philosophers and theorists who investigate the relation between belief and emotional response provoked by fictional beings or situations (see, in this volume, Eva-Maria Konrad). In his seminal article, Colin Radford formulates the question in terms of three propositions which make sense individually but become inconsistent as a set: (1) We feel genuine and rational emotions for objects which we consider as fictional; (2) Emotions, if they are genuine, presuppose the belief in the existence or the reality of the objects which cause them; (3) We believe that these objects are purely fictional, i.e., we do not believe in them. For Radford, this paradox shows that our emotional reactions caused by fictional works are "irrational" (Radford, 1975), but many other solutions have been proposed by philosophers and theorists. While "make-believe" or "pretense" theories of fiction affirm that the emotions we feel are not genuine emotions but "quasi-emotions" (Walton, 1978), "thought theories" argue that our emotions can be caused by the "thoughts" or "mental representations" without belief (Carroll, 1990; Lamarque, 1981).

Whether we experience genuine emotions or quasi-emotions, our empathetic engagement with fictional characters has been credited with deploying and enhancing our theory of mind (Nünning, 2014; Zunshine, 2006), and thus helping us make sense of human experience—both our own and that of others. From a psychological point of view, Keith Oatley (1999) suggests viewing fiction as a "cognitive and emotional simulation" that gives us insight into our own emotions and experiences. In Martha Nussbaum's work on the ethics of fiction, fiction is considered to have a stronger effect on belief than nonfiction, precisely because it appeals to our emotions and thus more powerfully allows us to develop ethical understanding. Fiction involves our beliefs about what matters in human life (Nussbaum, 1990, 18).

Fiction and Fictionality: State of the Field

Fictionality studies today can be divided into several main trends. One favors a semantic conception of fiction as a world with its own ontological features, taking into account reference (Lavocat, 2016; Pavel, 1986; Ryan, 1991). Another develops a "rhetorical" approach: in the wake of Wayne Booth's conception of literary fiction as "the art of communicating with readers" (Booth, [1961], 1963, xiii), it envisions fictionality, more broadly defined, "as a resource used to communicate and persuade" (Nielsen, Phelan and Walsh, 2014; Walsh, 2007). Other accounts emphasize the pragmatic distinction between factual and fictional discourse, depending on contexts of communication and publication and the associated cognitive attitudes adopted (Caïra, 2011; Schaeffer, 2010). A variant of this pragmatic tendency consists in emphasizing the institutional contexts and social practices that allow fictional communication (Abell, 2020).

Reconciling some of these approaches (2012), Stacie Friend proposes considering fiction and non-fiction as genres (in the sense that Kendall Walton in 1970 speaks of "categories of art"): as clusters of characteristics that are not necessary and sufficient, but standard, counter-standard, or variable. Thus, the fact that fiction appeals to the imagination, and contains non-referential characters, is a standard feature (i.e., expected by the reader), but not only can a factual text also appeal to the imagination, but a fictional artifact can contain referential characters.

The study of fiction and fictionality has rapidly been developing in the direction of transmedial and interdisciplinary domains of study, looking beyond narratology's traditional preoccupation with literary fiction. Examples include the *Handbook of Narratology* (Hühn, Pier, Schmid, Schönert, 2009) and expanded as the online open-access *Living Handbook of Narratology* (2014–2019), with articles organized around key concepts. Tobias Klauk and Tilmann Köppe's *Fiktionalität: Ein interdisziplinäres Handbuch* (2014), focuses on theories of fictionality and psychological and historical aspects of fictionality, as well as the question of the boundary between fiction and nonfiction. The latter question is also studied in depth, from a transhistorical and comparatist perspective, in Françoise Lavocat's book-length study *Fait et fiction: pour une frontière* (2016). Monika Fludernik and Marie-Laure Ryan's handbook devoted to *Narrative Factuality* (2020), in addition to revisiting the question of the fact-fiction boundary, also explores the use of narrative to convey reliable information across media.

In this volume, several of these current tendencies are represented, and they imply different understandings of the relationship between fiction and belief. Semantic and pragmatic approaches address the question primarily in terms of plausibility, play, fictional immersion, imagination, and commitment to characters (see, in this volume, Thomas Pavel and Marie-Laure Ryan). Rhetorical approaches focus on narrative strategies, which can make fiction an extremely effective tool for emotional and ideological manipulation (see James Phelan and Henrik Zetterberg Nielsen). For the proponents of the semantic approach, especially in analytic philosophy of fiction, the articulation between fiction and belief poses a problem of both logic and pragmatics (Currie, 2020, Chapter 9; Friend, 2014; Matravers, 2014). It may even be understood as a paradox (as in Radford's famous "paradox of fiction"). For proponents of the rhetorical approach to fictionality, on the other hand, there is no contradiction in the fact that fictions are the vehicle of information (whether true or false) and that they transmit beliefs.

Volume Overview

Our handbook continues the tendency toward interdisciplinary and cross-media expansion of the field of fictionality studies, embracing forms of fiction from hagiography to video games. It offers an overview of existing scholarship while also aiming to advance the study of the epistemological implications and cognitive effects of fiction. It combines theoretical articles with empirical case studies and strives to encompass a diverse range of cultural domains and geographical areas.

Part I: "Believing in Fiction: Philosophical and Theoretical Perspectives," presents contemporary research on the relationship between literature and belief in the fields of literary theory (especially narratology), analytic philosophy, and the philosophy of science. It focuses on the question of how we believe in fictions, or how fictions may shape beliefs, while also considering how fiction favors an exploration of belief as a philosophical and social issue. Philosopher Stacie Friend, starting from the widely accepted opposition between fiction related to imagination and nonfiction associated with belief, advocates for a theory that recognizes the numerous links between fiction, imagination, and belief. Nicholas Paige then examines Coleridge's famous phrase on the "willing suspension of disbelief." He locates this expression that has become a commonplace in Coleridge's religious and philosophical thought, and traces its genealogy from Antiquity as well as its astonishing posterity up to the present day—with inevitable deviations from the historical meaning of the phrase. Paige sets out to explain the remarkable plasticity of the formula.

The following three chapters define fiction through games (Marie-Laure Ryan), emotions (Eva-Maria Konrad), and characters (Thomas Pavel). Marie-Laure Ryan asks under what conditions a game can be considered as fictional and whether it can be factual (she answers this question in the negative). In Ryan's view, suspension of disbelief and fictional immersion are inseparable. The question of the role of emotions in this process then arises. Eva-Maria Konrad, returning to the debate sparked by Radford's paradox of fiction, analyzes how emotional engagement with fictions affects beliefs and vice versa. She proposes that we understand the relationship between fiction and emotions as an "affective-hermeneutic circle." Thomas Pavel considers what it means to "believe in" a character and shows that this belief involves several degrees, in which the question of plausibility comes into play. He argues that despite the exaggerations and idealization involved in novelistic representation, the reader recognizes in the characters concrete characteristics of human situations that enrich his or her daily experience.

The next two chapters detail some of the difficulties involved in believing (in) characters. Does fictional narrative affect beliefs in the same way if the narrator is found to be unreliable? Jim Phelan, without denying the possible risk of a reader adopting the erroneous or morally reprehensible point of view of an unreliable narrator, argues that readers who are aware of the rhetorical games of fictionality enjoy the complexity of unreliable narration. It is precisely this dual perspective that readers are invited to adopt that offers them worthwhile views of the actual world. Lisa Zunshine shows that the issue of belief in real life is delicate and confusing, subject to manipulation and illusion; she points out in particular that we are always ready to consider others as more credulous than ourselves. Fictional texts often represent embedded belief situations, which may (but do not necessarily) resemble those of the real world. In any case, readers delight in the depiction of these sophisticated processes, which may eventually allow them to revise their interpretations of tricky belief situations in the real world.

The relationship of fiction to scientific methods (including thought experiments) is the subject of the last two chapters. Adam Toon reflects upon the relationship between science and fiction, which are apparently quite distinct, the former being dedicated to making people believe, and the latter to pretending to believe. However, the relationship between science and fiction is closer than it seems, especially when it comes to model systems. In this context, scientists are also engaged in make-believe to gain a better understanding of the world. Finally, Gregory Currie, Heather Ferguson, Jacopo Frascaroli, Stacie Friend, Kayleigh Green, and Lena Wimmer return to the long-running debate about learning (whether relevant or misleading) through fiction. They ask to what extent fiction provides thought experiments. The authors bring counterarguments to most of the proposals available in the critical literature on the relationship between fiction and belief, notably the arguments of plausibility and immersion as conducive to belief shaping. They argue that experimental research has shown both an effect of fiction on belief and the opposite.

This question is taken up from another perspective in the second part of the volume, "From Fiction to Belief: Social and Political Effects." This section focuses on the role of fiction in its varied forms (from watching series to playing games to virtual reality) in shaping everyday social practices as well as social identities and interactions. The assumption that fiction influences social representations is rarely denied, since it is so widely accepted. This supposed impact of fiction generates intense political debate, particularly surrounding issues of gender, race, and ethnicity. However, this section opens with a chapter which questions the impact of fiction on belief, from an evolutionary perspective and based on experimental data. Edgar Dubourg and Nicolas Baumard endeavor to explain why the idea of the power of fiction is false yet remains popular and widely accepted.

The other chapters in this section support the opposite view. Vera Nünning analyzes the impact of gender stereotypes, especially in children's literature. From a psychological perspective, Kris Goffin and Agnes Moors look at how fiction transmits, but can also deconstruct, gender biases. Ayse Payir and Paul L. Harris also examine, from a psychological perspecive, the effects on children of early exposure to fictional stories. In particular, they examine whether religious upbringing influences children's perception of fictionality or their beliefs about what is possible in reality.

In the following two chapters, Patrick Jagoda and Olivier Caïra address the issue from a game-studies perspective. Jagoda analyzes the borderline case of "Alternate Reality Games" (ARGs) showing that their fictionality facilitates the production of beliefs by allowing a negotiation of the status of events and privileging the co-creation of the game world. Caïra, who is more skeptical about the ability of fiction to influence beliefs, argues that the interactive nature of games is largely opposed to an immersive attitude and thus to the production of beliefs. These two contributions on games therefore present divergent views.

The following three chapters have in common that they address the issues of trust, credulity, and credit. Jessica Pepp, Rachel Sterken, and Eliot Michaelson attempt to distinguish fake news from fictional news—the latter of which is not intended to deceive and has an aesthetic purpose. Philippe Roussin, noting that trust in public speech is the pillar of democracy, analyzes a novel by Melville (*The Confidence-Man: His Masquerade*) as an illustration of what literature can teach us in this respect. Emmanuel Bouju and Loïse Lelevé show that literature itself is based on credit in the sense of trust and debt, and that the effects of literature on beliefs follow from this. The authors consider that contemporary literature offers a powerful tool for analyzing present political crises.

Henrik Zetterberg-Nielsen and Anne Besson start from rather different theoretical assumptions (Zetterberg Nielsen defends a rhetorical approach while Besson favors a pragmatic and theoretical approach to contemporary fiction as a constellation of worlds). However, both examine the uses of fiction in the context of political struggle. Zetterberg-Nielsen considers fictionality, as it appears in political memes and commentary, propaganda images and Hollywood blockbusters, as a formidable tool of disinformation and manipulation, thanks to the way it mobilizes emotions. Besson is interested in the way in which today's youth mobilizations borrow slogans, settings, and characters from the genres of fantasy and science fiction, demonstrating the capacity of these fictions to offer keys to understanding and modes of action on the world. Alok Yadav, for his part, shows how literary fictions can be scrutinized for their perpetuation of colonial ideologies, while postcolonial fictions correct the biases of historiography and the gaps in the archives.

The last three chapters in this section consider the potential of fiction to predict the future and to engage people in action to avoid probable future catastrophe, particularly in the context of climate change. Anne Duprat analyzes the French army's use of anticipatory fiction to predict, forecast, and prepare for future wars, and traces the history of the emergence of probability in fantasy literature.

Jean-Paul Engélibert examines the rise of dystopia as a literary genre with a heuristic scope, based on belief in the relevance of its analysis of the current situation and the plausibility of its predictions. To conclude this section, Erin James's chapter examines the case of "cli-fi" fiction, both on the side of those who warn of the urgency of acting to mitigate the effects of climate change and on the side of the skeptics (whose success, particularly Michael Crichton's, has been devastating in its effectiveness against ecological theses). She notes in both cases the use of referential paratexts that aim at and succeed in accrediting the fiction. Finally, she suggests that texts that do not deny their status as make-believe may offer more promising paths to pro-environmental behavior.

The relationship between fiction and belief for religions is a sensitive but fruitful question. To what extent do religions accommodate fiction, and to what extent are fiction and religious belief in conflict? Religions exploit, control, or prohibit fictions in very different ways. Part III, "Fiction and Religious Belief," attempts to understand this complex relation between fiction and religious belief in both traditional world religions and recent religious phenomena, even if the focus on belief as the defining feature of religion can also be contested; religion can also be defined primarily in terms of practice and the differences between "belief" and "faith" must also be taken into consideration. The first chapter of this part analyzes religious phenomena (to use Émile Durkheim's phrase) under their two dimensions: belief and rites (Durkheim, [1912] 1995, 34). Claude Calame examines Greek myths from a pragmatic perspective and argues that myths are fictional discourses which nevertheless generate belief by their performative virtue. The next chapter deals with medieval Latin Christendom. Julie Orlemanski refutes the idea that fictionality is lacking in this premodern era and shows the close relationship between fictional discourses and authentic discourses such as historiography or religious doctrines.

In the following two chapters, Nicolas Correard and Barbara Selmeci Castioni examine the emergence of religious skepticism from the Renaissance to the eighteenth century. Correard, analyzing the literary corpus from Erasmus to Wieland, proposes that fictionality has contributed to the rise of religious unbelief. Selmeci Castioni traces the process whereby the genre of hagiography shifts from the religious regime into the aesthetic regime and thus becomes literary fiction in the seventeenth century.

Markus Rüsch also deals with hagiography in the following chapter, drawing on his research on Buddhism in Japan. After a brief presentation of the literature about Shinran, one of the most important Buddhist monks in the Heian era, Rüsch focuses on a hagiography written by a contemporary novelist and examines how its fictional devices such as direct speech and detailed information generate religious belief. After this chapter, Isabelle Ratié gives us a broad perspective on ancient and early medieval India. She points out the affinity for fiction found in both Buddhist and Jaina traditions and analyzes the functions of fictionality from the religious point of view.

The following two chapters are devoted to Arabic and Islamic literature. Both Aboubakr Chraïbi who studies the premodern period and Ève de Dampierre-Noiray who investigates modern and contemporary literatures emphasize the complex attitudes toward fiction that characterize the Islamic tradition. Chraïbi analyzes fictional works written during the first two Arab-Muslim dynasties (Umayyad and Abbasid), such as *Kalîla and Dimna* and the *Thousand and One Nights*, showing how they were often defictionalized by religious discourse and had to fit into official histories. Religious and political authorities placed obstacles in the way of overt fictions, fearing competition with the Koranic narrative. Dampierre-Noiray, for her part, emphasizes the modern emergence of fiction as an autonomous notion. Fiction is, nevertheless, still subordinated to moral or political purposes, with some contemporary exceptions. The political and religious implications of fiction are also the subject of Sarah Hammerschlag's study of Jewish fiction. She considers Philip Roth's *Operation Shylock: A Confession* (1993) as representative of the use of contemporary metafictional techniques as political and religious strategies.

The final two chapters deal with the phenomenon of religions generated by fictions. Markus Altena Davidsen, analyzing the uses of fantasy fiction for religious purposes, claims that these neo-paganisms which he calls fiction-based religion, such as Jediism, can be considered serious religions. Lionel Obadia examines the fake, fiction, parody, and invented fictions which have developed as non-conformist forms of religion. In particular, he examines the (re)invention of the sacred enabled by digital technology.

While it is by no means possible to conflate religious phenomena and attitudes toward fiction, the last section shows how the history of religions and the history of fiction have been intertwined in sometimes surprising ways, as well as how their relationship has been transformed by changes in the media landscape in the twenty-first century. More broadly, by taking our belief-like investments in fiction as a point of departure for their critical reflections, the contributors to this volume invite us to reflect on the cognitive, emotional, and social mechanisms that determine belief or disbelief in representations. In the era of conspiracy theories, fake news, and the widespread circulation of digital memes, it has become particularly urgent to offer a wide-reaching reflection on the implications of believing in fictions, or of using fictions to influence belief.

Works Cited

Abell, Catharine. 2020. *Fiction: A Philosophical Analysis.* Oxford: Oxford University Press.

Adler, Jonathan E. 2002. *Belief's Own Ethics.* Cambridge, MA: MIT Press.

Bacon, Francis. (1605) 1893. *The Advancement of Learning.* London, Paris, and Melbourne: Cassell & Company.

Booth, Wayne. (1961) 1983. *The Rhetoric of Fiction.* 2nd ed. Chicago, IL: University of Chicago Press.

Caïra, Olivier. 2011. *Définir la fiction: du roman au jeu d'échecs.* Paris: Éditions de l'EHESS.

Carroll, Noël. 1990. *The Philosophy of Horror: Or, Paradoxes of the Heart.* New York and London: Routledge.

Coleridge, Samuel Taylor. (1817) 2014. *Biographia Literaria.* Edited by Adam Roberts. 2 vols. Edinburgh: Edinburgh University Press.

Currie, Gregory. 1990. *The Nature of Fiction.* Cambridge, MA: Cambridge University Press.

Currie, Gregory. 2020. *Imagining and Knowing: The Shape of Fiction.* Oxford: Oxford University Press.

Durkheim, Émile. (1912) 1995. *The Elementary Forms of Religious Life.* Translated by Karen E. Fields. New York: The Free Press.

Fludernik, Monika. 2018. "The Fiction of the Rise of Fictionality." *Poetics Today* 39, no. 1 (February): 67–92. https://doi.org/10.1215/03335372-4265071

Fludernik, Monika, and Marie-Laure Ryan. 2019. *Narrative Factuality: A Handbook.* Berlin: De Gruyter.

Friend, Stacie. 2008. "Imagining Fact and Fiction." In *New Waves in Aesthetics*, edited by Kathleen Stock and Katherine Thomson-Jones, 150–69. Basingstoke: Palgrave Macmillan.

Friend, Stacie. 2012. "Fiction as a Genre." *Proceedings of the Aristotelian Society* 112, no. 2, part 2: 179–209. https://doi.org/10.1111/j.1467-9264.2012.00331.x

Friend, Stacie. 2014. "Believing in Stories." In *Aesthetics & the Sciences of Mind*, edited by Gregory Currie, Matthew Kieran, Aaron Meskin and Jon Robson, 227–48. Oxford: Oxford University Press.

Gallagher, Catherine. 2006. "The Rise of Fictionality." In *The Novel*, edited by Franco Moretti, vol. 1, 336–63. Princeton, NJ: Princeton University Press.

Gendler, Tamar Szabó, and Karson Kovakovich. 2006. "Genuine Rational Fictional Emotions." In *Contemporary Debates in Aesthetics and The Philosophy of Art*, edited by Matthew Kieran, 241–53. Oxford: Blackwell Publishing.

Gerrig, Richard J., and Deborah A. Prentice. 1991. "The Representation of Fictional Information." *Psychological Science* 2, no. 5: 336–40.

Gettier, Edmund L. 1963. "Is Justified True Belief Knowledge?" *Analysis* 23, no. 6: 121–23. https://doi.org/10.1093/analys/23.6.121

Hühn, Peter, John Pier, Wolf Schmid, and Jörg Schönert. 2009. *Handbook of Narratology.* Berlin: De Gruyter.

Hühn, Peter, Jan Christoph Meister, John Pier, and Wolf Schmid. 2014–2019. *Living Handbook of Narratology.* https://www.lhn.uni-hamburg.de/node/138.html.

Hume, David. (1748) 1999. *An Enquiry Concerning Human Understanding.* Edited by Tom L. Beauchamp. Oxford: Oxford University Press.

Klauk, Tobias, and Tilmann Köppe. 2014. *Fiktionalität: Ein interdisziplinäres Handbuch.* Berlin: De Gruyter.

James, Alison, Akihiro Kubo, and Françoise Lavocat. 2023. *Can Fiction Change the World?* Transcript no. 29. Cambridge: Legenda, Modern Humanities Research Association.

Lamarque, Peter. 1981. "How Can We Fear and Pity Fictions?" *The British Journal of Aesthetics* 21, no. 4: 291–304.

Landy, Joshua. 2012. *How to Do Things with Fictions.* New York: Oxford University Press.

Latour, Bruno. 2009. *Sur le culte moderne des dieux faitiches: suivi de Iconoclash.* Paris: La Découverte.

Lavocat, Françoise. 2016. *Fait et fiction: pour une frontière.* Poétique. Paris: Seuil.

Lavocat, Françoise. 2020. "Immersion fictionnelle, médias, croyances." *Recherches. Revue de didactique et de pédagogie du français*, no. 72 : 9–31. https://www.revue-recherches.fr/wp-content/uploads/2022/07/009-031_R72_Lavocat.pdf.

Levinson, Jerold. 2006. *Contemplating Art: Essays in Aesthetics.* Oxford: Oxford University Press.

Lewis, David. 1978. "Truth in Fiction." *American Philosophical Quarterly* 15, no. 1: 37–46.

Matravers, Derek. 2014. *Fiction and Narrative.* Oxford: Oxford University Press.

Mercier, Hugo. 2020. *Not Born Yesterday: The Science of Who We Trust and What We Believe.* Princeton, NJ: Princeton University Press.

Nielsen, Henrik Skov, James Phelan, and Richard Walsh. 2014. "Ten Theses About Fictionality." *Narrative* 23, no. 1 (December): 61–73.

Nünning, Vera. 2014. *Reading Fictions, Changing Minds: The Cognitive Value of Fiction.* Heidelberg: Universitätsverlag Winter.

Nussbaum, Martha. 1990. *Love's Knowledge: Essays on Philosophy and Literature.* New York: Oxford University Press.

Oatley, Keith. 1999. "Why Fiction May be Twice as True as Fact. Fiction as Cognitive and Emotional Simulation." *Review of General Psychology* 3, no. 2: 107–17.

Pavel, Thomas G. 1986. *Fictional Worlds.* Cambridge, MA: Harvard University Press.

Plato. 1997. *Complete Works.* Edited by John M. Cooper. Indianapolis/Cambridge: Hackett Publishing Company.

Poovey, Mary. 2008. *Genres of the Credit Economy: Mediating Value in Eighteenth- and Nineteenth-Century Britain.* Chicago, IL: University of Chicago Press.

Prentice, Deborah A., Gerrig, Richard J., and Bailis, Daniel S. 1997. "What Readers Bring to the Processing of Fictional Texts." *Psychonomic Bulletin & Review* 4: 416–20.

Radford, Colin. 1975. "How Can We Be Moved by the Fate of Anna Karenina?" *Proceedings of the Aristotelian Society* Supplementary Volumes, 49: 67–93.

Ryan, Marie-Laure. 1980. "Fiction, Non-Factuals, and the Principle of Minimal Departure." *Poetics* 9, no. 4 (August): 403–22.

Ryan, Marie-Laure. 1991. *Possible Worlds, Artificial Intelligence, and Narrative Theory.* Bloomington and Indianapolis: Indiana University Press.

Schaeffer, Jean-Marie. 2010. *Why Fiction?* Translated by Dorrit Cohn. Lincoln: University of Nebraska Press. First published as *Pourquoi la fiction?* (Paris: Seuil, 1999).

Schaeffer, Jean-Marie. 2020. *Les troubles du récit.* Vincennes: Thierry Marchaisse.

Schreier, Margrit. 2009. "Belief Change through Fiction." *Grenzen der Literatur*, edited by Simone Winko, Fotis Jannidis and Gerhard Lauer, 315–37. Berlin: De Gruyter.

Schroeder, Timothy and Carl Matheson. 2006. "Imagination and Emotion." In *The Architecture of the Imagination: New Essays on Pretence, Possibility, and Fiction*, edited by Shaun Nichols, 19–29. Oxford: Clarendon Press.

Searle, John R. 1975. "The Logical Status of Fictional Discourse." *New Literary History* 6, no. 2: 319–32. https://doi.org/10.2307/468422.

Sperber, Dan, Fabrice Clément, Christophe Heintz, Olivier Mascaro, Hugo Mercier, Gloria Origgi, and Deirdre Wilson. 2010. "Epistemic Vigilance." *Mind and Language* 25, no. 4: 359–93.

Sullivan-Bissett, Ema, Helen Bradley, and Paul Noordhof, eds. 2017. *Art and Belief.* Mind Association Occasional Series. Oxford and New York: Oxford University Press.

Tacitus. 1937. *Annals, Books 4–6, 11–12.* Vol 4. of *Tacitus.* Translated by John Jackson. Loeb Classical Library. Cambridge, MA: Harvard University Press. https://www.loebclassics.com/view/tacitus-annals/1931/pb_LCL312.151.xml.

Taylor, Derek Bryson. 2023. "Roald Dahl's Books Are Rewritten to Cut Potentially Offensive Language." *New York Times*, February 20. https://www.nytimes.com/2023/02/20/books/roald-dahl-books-changes.html

Veyne, Paul. 1988. *Did the Greeks Believe in Their Myths? An Essay on the Constitutive Imagination.* Translated by Paula Wissing. Chicago, IL: University of Chicago Press.

Walsh, Richard. 2007. *The Rhetoric of Fictionality: Narrative Theory and the Idea of Fiction.* Columbus: Ohio State University Press.

Walton, Kendall. 1978. "Fearing Fictions." *The Journal of Philosophy* 75, no.1 (January): 5–27.

Walton, Kendall. 1990. *Mimesis as Make-Believe: On the Foundations of the Representational Arts.* Cambridge, MA: Harvard University Press.

Wheeler, Christian, Melanie C. Green, and Timothy C. Brock. 1999. "Fictional Narratives Change Beliefs: Replications of Prentice, Gerrig, & Bailis (1997) with Mixed Corroboration." *Psychonomic Bulletin & Review 6*, no. 1: 136–41. https://doi.org/10.3758/BF03210821

Zunshine, Lisa. 2006. *Why We Read Fiction: Theory of Mind and the Novel.* Columbus: Ohio State University Press.

PART I

Believing in Fiction

Philosophical and Theoretical Perspectives

1

BELIEF, IMAGINATION, AND THE NATURE OF FICTION

Stacie Friend

We use the term "fiction" in at least two different ways. In the first, fiction contrasts with truth or reality. For example, we might say that Santa Claus or Zeus are fictions, or that the politician's speech was fiction from beginning to end. In the second, fiction contrasts with nonfiction. We classify novels, short stories, many films, some ballets, and so on, as *works of fiction*, and histories, biographies, newspaper articles, documentaries, and so on, as *works of nonfiction*. In the first sense, fiction seems to be precisely what we should not believe, or should not believe *in*. But the situation is not clear-cut when distinguishing between representational works. Some works of fiction are about real individuals and events, while some works of nonfiction are false. Is there anything general to say about the relationship between belief and works of fiction? In what follows, I consider the implications of several accounts of the nature of fiction for answering this question.

The most popular philosophical definitions of fiction today offer a direct answer. According to these theories, fiction and nonfiction are distinguished by the attitudes they invite: whereas nonfiction invites belief, fiction invites imagining. I discuss these theories, as well as other accounts that answer the question more indirectly. In the final section, I consider reasons to be skeptical that fiction and nonfiction can be defined via the contrast between imagining and belief.

Before proceeding, a few clarifications are in order. First, the philosophical theories I consider emerge from the analytic or Anglo-American tradition, which has also influenced—and to a lesser extent, been influenced by—discussions of the topic in narratology. Second (and relatedly), I will not closely examine arguments from other disciplines for the view that no distinction can be drawn because all narrative, insofar as it must select and structure events, is ultimately fiction. There have been many rebuttals of this "panfictionalist" position (e.g., Lavocat, 2016; Ryan, 1997).[1] The important point here is that the distinction between fiction and nonfiction is a distinction within the domain of *representations*, and all representation is selective.[2] It is both impossible and pointless to represent every aspect of a situation, a point Lewis Carroll makes vividly when he imagines a map whose scale is one mile to one mile.[3] I, therefore, assume that a distinction is possible.

Precedents

The starting point for several theories of fiction is a focus on the *language* of fictional works, whether in terms of its meaning or structure or use. All such theories face the obvious objection that fiction, like nonfiction, is not limited to written texts (Walton, 1990). However, I will set this concern aside

DOI: 10.4324/9781003119456-3

here, so as to describe the implications of these accounts for the role of belief. Consider the opening lines of Chimamanda Ngozi Adichie's *Half of a Yellow Sun:*

> Master was a little crazy; he had spent too many years reading books overseas, talked to himself in his office, did not always return greetings, and had too much hair. Ugwu's aunty said this in a low voice as they walked on the path.

> *(Adichie, 2017, 3)*

These lines mention three individuals—Master, Ugwu, and Ugwu's aunt—all of whom were invented by Adichie, along with the scene. The names thus do not refer, and the sentences are not true. But none of that is surprising; works of fiction are typically about things that do not exist and events that never happened. Such observations motivate a *semantic* distinction according to which nonfiction contains truths and refers to real entities, whereas fiction does not—or more generally, that nonfiction is about the real world and fiction is about "fictional worlds."[4] If this were right, then it would be a mistake to believe (or believe in) anything represented in a work of fiction.

However, most theorists agree that semantic definitions cannot be right. Many works of fiction refer to real individuals, places, and events. Adichie's novel refers to Nigeria and the Nigerian Civil War, and all the characters in Hilary Mantel's *Wolf Hall* are real historical individuals. On the other side, many works of nonfiction are about what does not exist. Physics textbooks describe ideal gases and frictionless planes, while reams of serious literary criticism have been written about fictional characters. Moreover, falsity does not a fiction make; the author of a biography who deceives readers about her subject does not thereby write fiction.[5] Indeed, some works of fiction are more accurate than some works of nonfiction. A comparison of, say, Geoffrey of Monmouth's twelfth-century *History of the Kings of Britain* with any of Gore Vidal's novels about United States history is sufficient to demonstrate this fact.

Now, many theorists deny that ordinary referring terms, such as *Nigeria* or *Thomas Cromwell*, refer in fictional contexts.[6] According to this view, although the place and person existed, the relevant fictions are not about them; instead, they are about fictional characters for whom the real individuals are models. However, even if this were true—which in my view it is not (Friend, 2019)—this still would lend no backing to a semantic distinction. It would be the fictionality of the work that cut off reference, rather than the converse. Of course, we *expect* to find fictional characters and events in fiction, and we expect works of nonfiction to be true. Still, these expectations do not generate necessary and sufficient conditions for a distinction.

A different linguistic approach focuses on the formal features of texts. For example, the use of unmarked indirect speech in the passage from Adichie's novel might be indicative of fictionality, alongside the more well-known device of free indirect discourse, exemplified in this passage from George Eliot's *Middlemarch*:

> Dorothea was in the best temper now. Sir James, as brother in-law, building model cottages on his estate, and then, perhaps, others being built at Lowick, and more and more elsewhere in imitation—it would be as if the spirit of Oberlin had passed over the parishes to make the life of poverty beautiful!

> *(Eliot, [1872] 2000, 21)*

Some narratologists (notably Hamburger, 1973) have offered *syntactic* definitions of fiction based on such constructions, insofar as they seem to reflect a necessarily invented scenario: inside views of someone's thoughts from a third-person perspective. Like invented characters and situations, this fictionalized access to the mind seems to exclude belief.

Now, philosophers take it as an article of faith that a work of fiction could be indiscernible from a work of nonfiction (e.g., Currie, 1990; Davies, 2007; Lamarque and Olsen, 1994; Searle, 1975). Of course, we can usually tell the difference (Lavocat, 2016). Still, the syntactic approach seems to draw the lines in the wrong place. Hamburger explicitly contrasted first-person homodiegetic narratives with "fiction proper," relegating them to the domain of "pretense"; this would exclude many paradigmatic fictions, like Nabokov's *Lolita* or Grass's *Tin Drum* from "fiction proper." Furthermore, there are plenty of fiction authors, like Ernest Hemingway, who avoid such constructions, and plenty of nonfiction authors, like Simon Schama, who embrace them. So syntactic definitions do not provide necessary or sufficient conditions for distinguishing the categories.

If fiction cannot be distinguished from nonfiction semantically or syntactically, as philosophers typically take for granted, perhaps the distinction is *pragmatic,* turning on what authors *do* with the language—more specifically, the speech acts they perform. Authors of nonfiction, it is widely agreed, engage in *assertion*: they make claims put forward in a serious way, with a commitment to truth and the aim of being believed. If sentences in fiction were also assertions, then authors would be engaged in systematic deception, since they know what they write is false. Yet fiction is not deception. Margaret Macdonald (1954) thus argued that authors of fiction are engaged in the *pretense* of assertion, so that assessments of truth or falsity are irrelevant and belief is not intended (see also Searle, 1975).[7] In different terms, "the author ... does not seriously stand behind the assertions of his narrative" (Genette, 1990, 765).

Defining fiction in terms of pretend assertion does not seem promising. First, on any plausible reading, "pretend assertion" cannot mean that authors engage in robust games of make-believe; it just means that authors pen their words without the intention to be taken seriously. But this conception is too weak to distinguish fiction from other activities like hypothesizing, imitating, joking, speculating, and so on (Currie, 1990; Genette, 1993). Moreover, if authors were systematically pretending to tell the truth, presumably they would try harder to write works indiscernible from nonfiction; in this respect, Hamburger is right that much fiction cannot plausibly be described as pretense.

Second, many works of fiction do contain assertions which we are meant to believe. These are often indirect, as when Orwell portrays the consequences of Stalinism through the plot of *Animal Farm* or when Dickens condemns the treatment of the poor through multiple characters. But direct assertions also appear in fiction. Elizabeth Gaskell begins *Mary Barton* with "There are some fields near Manchester, well known to the inhabitants as 'Green Heys Fields,' through which runs a public footpath to a little village about two miles distant" ([1848] 1996, 5). Henry James's *The Portrait of a Lady* opens, "Under certain circumstances there are few hours in life more agreeable than the hour dedicated to the ceremony of afternoon tea" ([1881] 2009, 19). These look like straightforward assertions. Notice that denying this conclusion on the grounds that the statements appear in a work of fiction is begging the question; one already has to determine which works are fiction before the denial is possible.

For these and other reasons, most philosophers today reject definitions of fiction that rely on appeal to truth and reference, syntactic structure, or pretend assertions. Although none of the theories explicitly mentions belief, all imply that belief is not the appropriate response to fiction. It is this dimension of the accounts that is reflected in many current philosophical theories.

Contrasting Attitudes

In offering theories of fiction, most philosophers today focus on the responses that readers (or more generally, audiences) are invited to adopt. The motivating idea is that nonfiction invites *belief* whereas fiction invites *imagining* or (equivalently) *make-believe*. Within the relevant literature, the contrast between belief and imagining is usually treated as a contrast in *attitudes* toward the contents of representations, distinguished by their functional roles in cognition (see Liao and Gendler, 2019). When we believe, say, *that there are burglars in the house*, this proposition gets integrated into our mental representations of how things (really) are and can motivate action, such as calling the police. If we merely imagine that there are burglars, we do not integrate the proposition with the rest of our beliefs, and we do not act in the same way. In this sense, the relevant theories take fiction to be defined in opposition to belief.

Before describing some of these theories, I want to consider a related notion frequently associated with fiction: the *willing suspension of disbelief*. This phrase, coined by Coleridge in his *Biographia Literaria*, originally concerned "supernatural" or "romantic" elements in a story, which would have to be imbued with enough of "a human interest and a semblance of truth" that readers would temporarily set aside their ordinary skepticism ([1817] 2009, 270).[8] The basic idea was that if a writer succeeded in creating a sufficiently absorbing narrative, readers would go along even with unrealistic or implausible content—that is, content that they would never normally believe.

However, the phrase has come to have a broader connotation, according to which any fiction, not just the unrealistic, requires readers to suspend their disbelief in the characters and events of the story itself. Despite the ubiquity of the phrase, it is not entirely clear what "suspending disbelief" means in this sense. Do we temporarily *believe* what we are reading? Although this position has been defended (Suits, 2006), it looks false; after all, we do not act as if we believe what we read. Do we adopt an attitude of indecision regarding the truth of the story? Again, this appears implausible. Not only do we *know* (and therefore believe) that the characters and events are not real, but our emotional and other responses to fiction presuppose this knowledge. As Eva Schaper puts it, to suspend the knowledge that Hamlet is unreal would be to adopt "an attitude so naïve or childlike as scarcely to be describable in terms of … being genuinely moved by fictional events and characters" (Schaper, 1978).

The claim that fictions invite imagining is not subject to the same worry, since imagining something we do not believe is not just unproblematic; it is the paradigm case. In what follows I describe some prominent versions of this account, beginning with Kendall Walton's theory, which originated this approach.

Walton (1990) defines a work of fiction as a work whose function it is to act as a prop in certain games of make-believe. For Walton there is a continuity between children's games, for which the props might be toy cars or action figures, and the games prompted by fictions. Works of fiction *prescribe imagining* their content, and imagining as prescribed is participating in the game of make-believe authorized by the work. The appeal to games entails a normative element: some moves are licensed while others are not. If I felt like it, I could imagine Dorothea and Casaubon performing in a Broadway musical, but this would be an inappropriate response to *Middlemarch*. Walton proposes that it is the function of prompting imaginings that distinguishes fiction from nonfiction. A work's function may be determined in various ways depending on our social practices, for instance by the author's intention, how the work is normally treated, and so on.

Walton's theory has been subject to numerous criticisms. Many theorists, while agreeing that fictions invite imagining, reject the articulation of this idea in terms of games of make-believe. They also deny that something normally treated as fiction—for example, the Greek myths today—thereby counts as fiction, insisting that genuine fiction requires the *intention* to invite imagining. Whatever we say about these issues, a larger problem is that Walton's category of fiction turns out to be much broader than our ordinary notion (Friend, 2008). Many works of philosophy, such as dialogues between fictional characters or arguments containing thought experiments, so qualify. The same holds for any vividly told nonfiction narratives, which invite us to imagine what it was like for people to live in different times and places, to undergo wonderful or horrible experiences, to feel this way or that, and so on. For Walton all pictures invite imagining that we are seeing their subjects face to face, but some pictures look like nonfiction, such as journalistic photographs. More generally, paradigmatic nonfictions invite various forms of imagining that are compatible with belief, including the experience of mental imagery, the simulation of others' emotions, imagining perceiving or experiencing events, and the mental representation of the "world of the story."

None of this is a criticism of Walton, who is not interested in the ordinary distinction between fiction and nonfiction (1990, 70). His aim is instead to delineate an explanatory category of works that prompt imagining and make-believe, however we pre-theoretically classify them.[9] For anyone interested in the ordinary distinction, though, Walton's category is too expansive. One reason is that the sorts of imagining listed above are all compatible with belief. So, when theorists appeal to imagining to distinguish between fiction and nonfiction, they invoke imagining what we do *not* believe. This is exactly the approach taken by *fictive utterance* theorists (who, despite the name, often apply the account to non-textual fictions like films as well. See, e.g., Carroll, 1997; Currie, 1999).

Fictive utterance theorists, like theorists who invoke authorial pretense, maintain that works of nonfiction are assertive. Most fictive utterance theorists assume a "Gricean" analysis of assertion, according to which assertion involves a reflexive intention: the speaker intends their interlocutor to believe what they say in virtue of recognizing that very intention.[10] In parallel, they adopt a reflexive explanation of the speech act—or more generally, the creative act—that characterizes fiction-making. According to Currie, for example, fictive utterance involves a *fictive intent,* in which the speaker wants the audience to make believe or imagine certain proposition *P*, and to do so at least partly as a result of their recognizing the speaker's intention that they make believe *P* (1990, 31). To exclude cases where an author invites audiences to imagine a true story, Currie proposes an additional criterion in his definition of fiction: "a work is fiction iff [if and only if] (*a*) it is the product of a fictive intent and (*b*) if the work is true, then it is at most accidentally true" (46). Other fictive utterance theorists (e.g., Davies, 2015; Stock, 2017) agree that fictions are the product of fictive intent, though they differ in how they constrain what is to be imagined, and often allow that we imagine what is non-accidentally true. The key idea across all such theories is that the content of nonfiction—what is to be believed—is determined by what really happened, while the content of fiction—what is to be imagined—is determined by the creative acts of authors.

Advocates of this approach acknowledge that their criteria are problematic when applied to whole works. We have already seen that authors of fiction can make assertions that invite belief and that authors of nonfiction can invite us to imagine what does not exist. Many works of fiction also treat what really happened as a constraint, for instance, if their overall purpose is to convey certain truths (as with Sinclair in *The Jungle*), while many works of nonfiction contain invented material we are not supposed to believe. For example, the "New Biographers" of the early twentieth century, such as Emil Ludwig, André Maurois, and Lytton Strachey, deployed devices borrowed from fiction, such as narrating their subjects' thoughts, but this was considered a new form of the nonfiction genre rather than a kind of fiction. Similarly, anyone familiar with the conventions of Classical Greek and Roman history knows that speeches and battle descriptions were invented. Tacitus's *Annals* and *Histories* are full of stylized speeches and vivid battle scenes, the contents of which readers are not supposed to believe. More recently, the 2014 documentary series *Cosmos: A Spacetime Odyssey,* presented by the astrophysicist Neil deGrasse Tyson (like its predecessor, the 1980 series *Cosmos: A Personal Voyage,* presented by Carl Sagan) places deGrasse Tyson within the "Ship of the Imagination" so that he can travel the universe to get close to various phenomena, such as (*per impossibile*) black holes.

Consequently, fictive utterance theorists typically give up the ambition of defining fictional *works* in favor of defining fictional *parts*.[11] Currie (1990) focuses on "fictional statements," which are individual sentences, while Davies (2015) and Stock (2017) define longer stretches of discourse falling short of full works, labeled "fictional narratives" or "fictions," respectively (for films, scenes or images are typically invoked).[12] On these views, a work such as Tacitus's *Histories* may include fictional statements, fictional narratives, or a fiction without itself being a work of fiction. But there is no formula for getting from the parts to the classification of the whole. Advocates of this approach tend to dismiss the question of how to classify whole works, maintaining that the right explananda for a theory of fiction are the smaller units defined by fictive intent.

There are certainly some cases in which we are apt to describe a part of a representation as fiction or nonfiction, such as scientific and philosophical discussions that include thought experiments or works that divide fairly sharply between factual and invented material, such as Tolstoy's *War and Peace* and Melville's *Moby Dick*. However, this is not true of most works that include both invitations to believe and invitations to imagine. For instance, in *The Jungle* the horrific conditions in the meat-packing industry are experienced and related by fictional characters. Similarly, in *One Day in the Life of Ivan Denisovich*, Solzhenitsyn conveys the brutal reality of the Soviet gulag through a composite character undergoing a fictional sequence of events. The movie *JFK* mixes real footage with fictional material seamlessly to put forward Oliver Stone's account of the assassination, whereas the BBC documentary series *Walking with Dinosaurs* is constructed entirely of CGI dinosaurs whose activities are narrated in the style of nature programs. Notice that the classification of such works is not at all controversial. No critic has suggested that *The Jungle, Ivan Denisovich*, or *JFK* is nonfiction, or that Tacitus's *Histories, Cosmos,* or *Walking with Dinosaurs* is fiction. This is at least partly because their authors clearly intended them to be (non)fiction. Fictive utterance theorists, though, take no account of such classificatory intentions.

It might seem a merely verbal quibble whether to focus on fictional parts or fictional works. However, it is only at the level of works that the contrast between fiction and nonfiction becomes significant to interpretation and criticism. When Edmund Morris's *Dutch: A Memoir of Ronald Reagan*, the only authorized biography of the former president, was published in 1999, it provoked controversy over the use of a fictional narrator—a fictionalized version of Morris himself, with fictional family and friends—to relate what was otherwise a closely researched, accurate story (Friend, 2012). But this was not due to any disputes over which parts of the text were to be believed and which merely imagined; it was because some parts were to be merely imagined that the controversy arose. This makes sense only insofar as the *work as a whole* was classified as nonfiction. The use of a fictional narrator in nonfiction was provocative and noteworthy, by contrast with its use in a work of fiction.

Needless to say, it matters to us whether we are supposed to believe or merely imagine different statements or passages in works of fiction and nonfiction. Someone unfamiliar with the conventions of Classical history, for example, would be in danger of forming false beliefs. But distinguishing between what we should and should not believe is different from knowing how to approach the work as a whole.

Institutional Accounts

There are two alternative approaches put forward by philosophers participating in the current debate. Some agree that an appeal to imagining rather than belief is relevant to defining fiction, but they make this appeal at the level of *practices* or *institutions* rather than at the level of works and their parts. Others reject the project of defining fiction in terms of a contrast between cognitive attitudes altogether. I discuss these approaches in this and the next section.

Peter Lamarque (2014) proposes a theory of the first kind.[13] For Lamarque, fiction and nonfiction are distinct practices governed by particular conventions. The conventions of the fiction practice may vary, but they are unified by the authorial intention that the audience adopt the "fictive stance," which means imagining or making believe "that it is being informed about particular people or objects or events, regardless of whether there are (or are believed to be) such people or objects or events" (Lamarque, 2014, 20). The fictive stance is directed at the whole work, and it is consistent with some elements of a work also counting as assertions. By contrast, authors of nonfiction take on the "commitments of assertion," including factual accuracy, proof, and argument (97). Again, the appropriate stance is directed at the work as a whole, and it is consistent with elements of the work also being imagined.

Lamarque is certainly correct that authors and readers participate in different practices and adjust their ways of producing or consuming works according to the relevant conventions. But it is doubtful that our responses to works in each category consist of uniform psychological attitudes. One reason is that the conventions governing the practices of fiction and nonfiction change over time and across genres. We have seen that it was once conventional for historians to make up speeches and battle descriptions, but this is no longer acceptable. More recently, providing "inside views" of real individuals' thoughts via free indirect discourse has shifted from being a sure sign of fictionality to a convention within certain genres of nonfiction, like New Journalism. So, works of fiction and nonfiction might invite a mix of different attitudes, depending on the particular genre.

Catharine Abell (2020) proposes an institutional account of fiction that avoids some of these concerns. According to Abell, fiction institutions are defined by systems of rules or conventions. The rules are designed to provide "equilibrium solutions" to a "coordination problem": namely, the problem of coordinating with others in the communication of imaginings. Compare a system for the regulation of driving on public roads. Such a system allows drivers to coordinate the movements of their vehicles with each other simply by following the same set of rules, for example, by driving on the specified side of the road, stopping at red lights, and so on. The rules mean that drivers do not need to figure out each other's intentions or desires to resolve the challenge of coordinating.

Abell claims that, like shared use of roads, the communication of imaginings poses a coordination problem. The problem is how authors can produce a work that prompts readers to imagine the same content as the author, when we typically have no independent access to the specific intentions of authors with respect to the meanings of their works. By contrast, she says, the communication of beliefs in nonfiction is constrained by how the world is and our understanding of what people typically believe in various circumstances. Imaginings are in these respects unconstrained, prompting the need for a system of conventions to enable their communication from author to reader. Such conventions will be of the form "*if an agent produces an utterance of type Z, imagine X*" (Abell, 2020, 35). Rules of this kind enable us to determine, for example, that when we confront a metaphor what we should imagine will have a different content than the literal, or that when Shakespeare has a low-born character speaking in eloquent blank verse, we are to imagine that the character actually speaks as such a person ordinarily would.

On this view, a work counts as fiction so long as it bears the right relation to a fiction institution, which means (roughly) that the author intends her audience to respond to the work as a whole in conformity with the rules of the institution, and the content of the work is at least partly determined by the rules of the institution (Abell, 2020, 37). This definition allows that works of fiction can invite a variety of different responses, including some responses that do not conform to the standard rules. So, the fact that works like *Moby Dick* and *The Jungle* invite belief in much of their content does not exclude them from the domain of fiction, insofar as the authors intended readers to recognize the fictional conventions that still apply to them and to respond accordingly. Indeed, Abell allows that a work of fiction could be entirely, intentionally accurate, citing Helen Garner's novel *The Spare Room*. So long as Garner intended readers to respond to the work in conformity with a practice of fiction, and the content of at least some of the work is determined by that practice, it counts as fiction.

For Abell, imagination plays a direct role in defining fiction institutions, but only an indirect role in classifying works of fiction. Her theory is thus flexible enough about the features of particular works to accommodate many cases that pose a challenge to fictive utterance accounts. However, it is questionable that the existence of fiction practices or institutions should be explained by reference to a special problem of coordinating imaginings as opposed to beliefs. First, there is little reason to think that authors of fiction must imagine the content of their works in order to produce them, or that the aim of fiction generally is to get readers to experience just the same imaginings as authors (John, 2021). Second, it is a mistake to think that the interpretation of fiction is totally unconstrained by what is true or real. For works to be interpretable at all requires at least some shared assumptions about the real-world background (Friend, 2017). Relatedly, even if there is a problem about communicating imaginings, it is unlikely that it is substantially different from problems posed by communicating beliefs. Works of nonfiction do not consist solely of assertions meant literally, and readers often rely on conventions—such as the conventions of Classical history—to determine what to believe.

A different challenge to Abell's theory emerges when we examine the ways that practices of fiction and nonfiction change over time. Consider when the first examples of New Journalism were produced in the 1960s by writers like Tom Wolfe or Gay Talese; or when Truman Capote wrote the first "nonfiction novel," *In Cold Blood*, in 1965. Capote insisted that he had created a new literary art form, one which deployed the conventions of fiction in a (putatively) entirely factual report. Suppose that this is true. It seems that Capote intended readers to conform to a fiction practice in responding to the book's stylistic features, and for the content (including many passages in free indirect discourse) to be partly determined by conventions of that practice. But despite meeting Abell's criteria, *In Cold Blood* is not a work of fiction. It is instead a work of nonfiction that was groundbreaking in its use of devices traditionally associated with the novel. It thereby helped to *create* a new nonfiction genre, now called "creative nonfiction," which is taught by journalism schools.[14]

Despite these concerns, there is something right about the idea that fiction and nonfiction works are parts of practices or institutions of producing, consuming, disseminating, and criticizing representations. It is less clear that these practices can be defined in terms of invited imaginings.

Skeptical Approaches

Taken together, the objections discussed in the last two sections have led some philosophers to argue that fiction and nonfiction cannot be distinguished by differences in invited attitudes. Stacie Friend draws this conclusion on the grounds that works in each category standardly invite a mix of belief and imagining. Derek Matravers's (2014) skepticism is more radical: he denies that there is any interesting distinction between fiction and nonfiction and prefers to dispense with the notion of imagination altogether.

I have argued (Friend, 2008) that attention to the history of fiction and nonfiction practices demonstrates that there is no conception of imagining as opposed to belief that can distinguish between works of each type. Many works of nonfiction invite imaginings, including imagining what has been invented (as in Tacitus's *Histories*), while many works of fiction invite belief, including cases where this is the main purpose (as in Sinclair's *The Jungle*). I propose instead that fiction and nonfiction are *genres*: that is, ways of classifying representations that guide appreciation, so that knowledge of the classification plays a role in a work's correct interpretation and evaluation (Friend, 2012, n.d.). On this Genre Theory, the criteria offered by other theories—including the invitation to imagine or believe, but also the kinds of syntactic and semantic properties described in §1—should be understood as *standard features* of the genres, rather than as definitive of them.[15] Standard features are those that we expect works in a genre to have, but they do not provide necessary and sufficient conditions for classification.

I argue instead that classification relies on a combination of non-essential standard features and *categorial features,* which are features that explicitly concern categorization, such as the author's intentions with respect to categorization and established practices of classifying works. For example, Tacitus's *Histories* count as nonfiction because he intended to write nonfiction history within an established practice recognized by his audience, who were aware of the relevant conventions. To the extent that intention matters, what matters here is Tacitus's intention to write history, rather than any intentions regarding the attitudes readers should take to different passages. I claim that the classification of works as fiction or nonfiction has a variety of cognitive effects, discovered empirically, in virtue of the expectations (standard features) associated with each category. These effects are not uniform and cannot be reduced to a contrast between belief and imagining.

I do not deny that the practices of fiction have something to do with imagination. I propose, however, that the connection lies on the side of producers of fiction rather than consumers, suggesting "that the existence of those practices we associate with fiction can be explained at least partly by the purpose of allowing authors to use their creative imaginations," specifically to invent what would not be permissible according to contemporary conventions of accuracy for nonfiction (Friend, 2008).

There are several objections that can be raised against the Genre Theory. First, the theory is underdeveloped. On the one hand, insofar as I insist that there are no necessary or sufficient conditions for classification, it remains unclear whether there is anything that genuinely unifies the categories of fiction and nonfiction (Carroll, 2015). In this way the theory seems to be little more than a "family resemblance" account, describing a variety of different features, changing and shifting over time, of the works that we take to be fiction or nonfiction (Stock, 2016). On the other hand, the role played by categorial features and the appeal to creative imagination as motivating fiction practices suggests an account of stable institutions that evolve over time (Lamarque, 2014; Stock, 2016). However, the account does not say enough about how these institutions themselves might be unified. Second, the theory seems to render the distinction between fiction and nonfiction too fragile and too insignificant. If nonfiction authors can just as easily make things up as fiction authors, it seems as if there is no justification for criticizing inaccurate nonfictions. And if there is nothing substantive that characterizes fiction and nonfiction, then it is hard to see how the categories can do any genuine explanatory work.

Now, my Genre Theory is clearly motivated by skepticism that any more substantive definition will be able to capture our variegated practices of fiction and nonfiction. Another response to that skepticism is to give up on the project of fiction altogether—not because "everything is fiction" but because the distinction between the categories does no explanatory work. This is Matravers's (2014) view.

Drawing on a range of psychological studies of narrative comprehension, Matravers argues that classification makes no difference to our cognitive engagement with representations. This is because our basic response to understanding *any* narrative is to construct a "mental model," a complex, dynamic mental representation of the characters, situations, and sequences of events. Knowing that a work is fiction or nonfiction, says Matravers, has no bearing on how we do this. Moreover, whether the narrative is fiction or nonfiction, the mental model will contain some representations we treat as candidates for belief and others we do not. Matravers rejects the assumption that the content we do not believe thereby counts as "imagined," describing it simply as represented or included in the model. (If imagining as a concept has any role to play on Matravers's account, it is in the more classic sense of experiencing imagery which, as noted above, is not exclusive to fiction.) Matravers proposes that the more fundamental distinction is between *confrontations*—perceptions of events in egocentric space in which direct action is possible—and *representations,* which allow us to cognize events outside our egocentric space, excluding direct action. There are differences of degree among representations—for instance, in how detailed and imagistic they are—but there are, for Matravers, no substantive differences in kind related to the fiction/nonfiction distinction.

Matravers's attempt to set aside imagining (apart from imagery) as a useful concept is problematic. For example, there seems to be a significant difference between representations of what really happened and representations of what is merely imaginary, even if we cannot act directly in either case (Lamarque, 2016). This is so regardless of whether the representations appear in works of fiction or nonfiction. Moreover, the distinction between confrontations and representations may not be as sharp as Matravers supposes. Lamarque offers as an example a situation in which someone tells you that there is a bear behind you. This is a representation which, like many other kinds of testimony, generates action.

Another concern is Matravers's assumption that if fiction and nonfiction cannot be distinguished by a contrast between imagining and belief, then there can be no differences in how we engage with works in each category. This is an empirical claim, and there is reason to think that it is false. For example, several studies support the view that we process the same text differently depending on how it has been categorized. We seem to remember far more of the exact wording and detail when we believe a text is fiction (Hendersen and Clark, 2007), but make more inferences using background knowledge—thereby constructing more elaborate mental models—when we believe it is nonfiction (Zwaan, 1994). Our affective responses seem to differ (Humbert-Droz et al., 2020; Sennwald et al., 2015; Sperduti et al., 2016). Our brains even exhibit different activation patterns while reading, depending on the way a text is labeled (Altmann et al., 2014). So, *contra* Matravers, it looks like knowledge of the category does affect engagement. This suggests that even if the confrontation/representation distinction is important, as it surely is, we may still have reasons to distinguish between fiction and nonfiction representations.

Conclusion

The proposal that the distinction between fiction and nonfiction can be drawn by appeal to the contrast between imagination and belief has generated a lively debate within philosophy. Although there are many objections to the position, an alternative has yet to attract the same consensus.

Still, the lesson that emerges is that any theory of fiction must take into account the many ways in which fiction interacts with belief. It is widely agreed that we acquire all sorts of beliefs from fiction: "The average person's knowledge of law firms, emergency rooms, police departments, prisons, submarines, and mob hits is not rooted in real experience or nonfictional reports. It is based on stories" (Bloom, 2010). Philosophers argue about whether such beliefs amount to knowledge, while psychologists study the persuasive powers of fictional works (see the chapter on Learning from Fiction in this volume). Moreover, many practices of fiction are *designed* to impact our opinions and attitudes, from didactic children's stories to alternative histories to political novels. For example, both philosophers and psychologists have claimed that fictions can reduce prejudice, in part by changing stereotypical beliefs (e.g., Johnson et al., 2013; Nussbaum, 1997; but see Goffin and Friend, 2022, for an opposed view).

Nor are any of these observations in tension with the claim that works of fiction invite imagining. It is by *imagining* the made-up characters and events of a work like *The Jungle* or *Nineteen Eighty-Four* that our beliefs about the real world are affected. Furthermore, theorists who propose that fiction enhances our moral or intellectual capacities usually focus on the ways in which works engage our imaginations. Such capacities include those relevant to the acquisition of belief, such as the ability to conceptualize alternative scenarios or to be open to new evidence and experiences.[16] Only theories of fiction that recognize these interrelations between fiction, imagining, and belief are likely to be successful.[17]

Notes

1 The term is Ryan's.
2 This point is emphasized by Lamarque (2014, Chapter 2).
3 This example, from Carroll's story "Sylvie and Bruno Concluded," is owed to Paloma Atencia-Linares.

4 For example, about "possible worlds" in one sense or another (see, e.g., Doležel, 2000; Lewis, 1983; Ryan, 1991).
5 For a contrary view, see Deutsch (2000).
6 In analytic philosophy, versions of this view are defended by e.g., García-Carpintero (2015, 2019), Kroon (1994), Lamarque and Olsen (1994), Macdonald (1954) and Motoarca (2014). In literary studies and narratology, see e.g., Furst (1995), Genette (1980), Pavel (1986) Ricoeur (1990) and Riffaterre (1990).
7 Macdonald is the first to put forward this view, though Searle developed and popularized it. Note that the proposal is better understood as an account of the language within works of fiction, rather than as a definition of fiction. However, for present purposes I go along with the standard interpretation.
8 On the history of Coleridge's phrase, see Nicholas Paige's contribution to this volume.
9 Schaeffer's (2010) appeal to the *ludic feint*, influenced by Walton, has a similarly broad scope.
10 García-Carpintero (2013) proposes an alternative fictive utterance account deploying a different conception of assertion.
11 Walsh (2007, 2019) also focuses on particular utterances, but this is in the context of a radically different construal of fictionality as a rhetorical device in communication.
12 Currie (2014) has since revised this position.
13 This theory develops from Lamarque and Olsen's (1994) earlier view, but Lamarque more clearly distinguishes his later account from other fictive utterance theories.
14 Some philosophers deny that *In Cold Blood* is clearly nonfiction (Davies 2015; Stock 2011). Friend (2012; n.d.) argues that it is.
15 This notion of *standard features* originates with Walton (1970), whose account of "categories of art" is the model for Friend's theory.
16 Whether fiction can improve such intellectual capacities is an empirical question that has gone largely untested, however.
17 I am grateful to the editors of this volume for helpful comments on a previous draft. This research was funded by the Templeton Religion Trust Project Grant TRT-2021-10476.

Works Cited

Abell, Catharine. 2020. *Fiction: A Philosophical Analysis*. Oxford: Oxford University Press.
Adichie, Chimamanda Ngozi. 2017. *Half of a Yellow Sun*. London: Fourth Estate.
Altmann, Ulrike, Isabel C. Bohrn, Oliver Lubrich, Winfried Menninghaus, and Arthur M. Jacobs. 2014. "Fact vs Fiction: How Paratextual Information Shapes Our Reading Processes." *Social Cognitive and Affective Neuroscience* 9, no. 1 (January): 22–29.
Bloom, Paul. 2010. *How Pleasure Works: The New Science of Why We Like What We Like*. New York: W.W. Norton.
Carroll, Noël. 1997. "Fiction, Non-Fiction, and the Film of Presumptive Assertion: A Conceptual Analysis." In *Film Theory and Philosophy*, edited by Richard Allen and Murray Smith, 173–202. New York: Oxford University Press.
———. 2015. "Fiction." In *The Routledge Companion to Philosophy of Literature*, edited by Noël Carroll and John Gibson, 359–71. New York: Routledge.
Coleridge, Samuel Taylor. 2009. *Biographia literaria*. Auckland: Floating Press.
Currie, Gregory. 1990. *The Nature of Fiction*. Cambridge: Cambridge University Press.
———. 1999. "Visible Traces: Documentary and the Contents of Photographs." *Journal of Aesthetics and Art Criticism* 57, no. 3 (Summer): 285–97.
———. 2014. "Standing in the Last Ditch: On the Communicative Intentions of Fiction Makers." *The Journal of Aesthetics and Art Criticism* 72, no. 4 (Fall): 351–63.
Davies, David. 2007. *Aesthetics and Literature*. London: Continuum.
———. 2015. "Fictive Utterance and the Fictionality of Narratives and Works." *The British Journal of Aesthetics* 55, no. 1 (January): 39–55.
Deutsch, Harry. 2000. "Making Up Stories." In *Empty Names, Fiction, and the Puzzles of Non-Existence*, edited by T. Hofweber and A. Everett, 17–36. Stanford, CA: CSLI Publications.
Doležel, Lubomír. 2000. *Heterocosmica: Fiction and Possible Worlds*. Baltimore, MD: Johns Hopkins University Press.
Eliot, George. 2000. *Middlemarch*. 2nd ed. New York: W.W. Norton & Company.
Friend, Stacie. 2008. "Imagining Fact and Fiction." In *New Waves in Aesthetics*, edited by Kathleen Stock and Katherine Thomson-Jones, 150–69. New York: Palgrave Macmillan.

———. 2012. "Fiction as a Genre." *Proceedings of the Aristotelian Society* 112: 179–209.

———. 2017. "The Real Foundation of Fictional Worlds." *Australasian Journal of Philosophy* 95, no. 1: 29–42.

———. 2019. "Reference in Fiction." *Disputatio* 11, no. 54: 179–206.

———. n.d. *Matters of Fact and Fiction*. Oxford: Oxford University Press.

Furst, Lilian R. 1995. *All Is True: Claims and Strategies of Realist Fiction*. Durham, NC: Duke University Press.

García-Carpintero, Manuel. 2013. "Norms of Fiction-Making." *The British Journal of Aesthetics* 53, no. 3 (July): 339–57.

———.2015. "Is Fictional Reference Rigid?" *Organon F* 22 (Suppl. issue 1): 145–68.

———. 2019. "Singular Reference in Fictional Discourse?" *Disputatio* 11, no. 54: 143–77.

Gaskell, Elizabeth. 1996. *Mary Barton: A Tale of Manchester Life*. New York: Penguin Classics.

Genette, Gérard. 1980. *Narrative Discourse: An Essay in Method*. Translated by Jane E. Lewin. Ithaca, NY: Cornell University Press.

———. 1990. "Fictional Narrative, Factual Narrative." *Poetics Today* 11, no. 4 (Winter): 755–74.

———. 1993. *Fiction and Diction*. Translated by Catherine Porter. Ithaca, NY: Cornell University Press.

Goffin, Kris, and Stacie Friend. 2022. "Learning Implicit Biases from Fiction." *Journal of Aesthetics and Art Criticism* 80, no. 2 (Spring): 129–39.

Hamburger, Käte. 1973. *The Logic of Literature*. Translated by Marilynn J. Rose. Bloomington: Indiana University Press.

Hendersen, Deborah J., and Herbert Clark. 2007. "Retelling Narratives as Fiction or Nonfiction." *Proceedings of the 29th Annual Cognitive Science Society*. Austin, TX: Cognitive Science Society, 353–38.

Humbert-Droz, Steve, Amanda Ludmilla Garcia, Vanessa Sennwald, Fabrice Teroni, Julien Deonna, David Sander, and Florian Cova. 2020. "Lost in Intensity: Is There an Empirical Solution to the Quasi-Emotions Debate?" *Aesthetic Investigations* 4: 460–82.

James, Henry. 2009. *The Portrait of a Lady*. Oxford: Oxford University Press.

John, Eileen. 2021. "Catharine Abell. *Fiction: A Philosophical Analysis*." *Journal of Aesthetics and Art Criticism* 79, no. 4 (Fall): 514–17.

Johnson, Dan R., Daniel M. Jasper, Sallie Griffin, and Brandie L. Huffman. 2013. "Reading Narrative Fiction Reduces Arab-Muslim Prejudice and Offers a Safe Haven from Intergroup Anxiety." *Social Cognition* 31, no. 5 (October): 578–98.

Kroon, Frederick. 1994. "Make-Believe and Fictional Reference." *Journal of Aesthetics and Art Criticism* 52, no. 2: 207–14.

Lamarque, Peter. 2014. *The Opacity of Narrative*. London: Rowman and Littlefield International.

———. 2016. "*Fiction and Narrative*, by Derek Matravers." *Mind* 125, no. 498 (April): 616–19.

———, and Stein Haugom Olsen. 1994. *Truth, Fiction, and Literature: A Philosophical Perspective*. Oxford: Clarendon Press.

Lavocat, Françoise. 2016. *Fait et fiction: pour une frontière*. Poétique Paris: Seuil.

Lewis, David. 1983. "Truth in Fiction." *Philosophical Papers*, 1: 261–80.

Liao, Shen-yi, and Tamar Gendler. 2019. "Imagination." In *The Stanford Encyclopedia of Philosophy*, edited by Edward N. Zalta, last revised Winter 2019. https://plato.stanford.edu/archives/win2019/entries/imagination/.

Macdonald, Margaret. 1954. "The Language of Fiction." *Aristotelian Society Supplementary Volume* 28, no. 1 (July): 165–84.

Matravers, Derek. 2014. *Fiction and Narrative*. Oxford: Oxford University Press.

Motoarca, Ioan-Radu. 2014. "Fictional Surrogates." *Philosophia* 42, no. 4: 1033–53.

Nussbaum, Martha C. 1997. *Poetic Justice: The Literary Imagination and Public Life*. Boston, MA: Beacon Press.

Pavel, Thomas. 1986. *Fictional Worlds*. New ed. Cambridge, MA: Harvard University Press.

Ricoeur, Paul. 1990. *Time and Narrative, Volume 3*. Translated by Kathleen Blamey and David Pellauer. Chicago, IL: University of Chicago Press.

Riffaterre, Michael. 1990. *Fictional Truth*. Baltimore, MD: Johns Hopkins University Press.

Ryan, Marie-Laure. 1991. "Possible Worlds and Accessibility Relations: A Semantic Typology of Fiction." *Poetics Today* 12, no. 3 (Autumn): 553–76.

———. 1997. "Postmodernism and the Doctrine of Panfictionality." *Narrative* 5, no. 2 (May): 165–87.

Schaeffer, Jean-Marie. 2010. *Why Fiction?* Translated by Dorrit Cohn. Lincoln: University of Nebraska Press.

Schaper, Eva. 1978. "Fiction and the Suspension of Disbelief." *British Journal of Aesthetics* 18, no. 1 (Winter): 31–44.

Searle, John R. 1975. "The Logical Status of Fictional Discourse." *New Literary History* 6, no. 2 (Winter): 319–32.

Sennwald, Vanessa, Florian Cova, Amanda Garcia, Patrizia Lombardo, Sophie Schwartz, Fabrice Teroni, Julien Deonna, and David Sander. 2015. "Is What I'm Feeling Real?" Unpublished manuscript, University of Geneva.

Sperduti, Marco, Margherita Arcangeli, Dominique Makowski, Prany Wantzen, Tiziana Zalla, Stéphane Lemaire, Jérôme Dokic, Jérôme Pelletier, and Pascale Piolino. 2016. "The Paradox of Fiction: Emotional Response toward Fiction and the Modulatory Role of Self-Relevance." *Acta Psychologica* 165 (March): 53–59.

Stock, Kathleen. 2011. "Fictive Utterance and Imagining." *Aristotelian Society Supplementary Volume* 85, no. 1: 145–61.

———. 2016. "Imagination and Fiction." In *The Routledge Handbook of Philosophy of Imagination*, edited by Amy Kind, 204–216. Abingdon: Routledge.

———. 2017. *Only Imagine: Fiction, Interpretation and Imagination.* Oxford: Oxford University Press.

Suits, David B. 2006. "Really Believing in Fiction." *Pacific Philosophical Quarterly* 87, no. 3 (September): 369–86.

Walsh, Richard. 2007. *The Rhetoric of Fictionality: Narrative Theory and the Idea of Fiction.* Columbus: Ohio State University Press.

———. 2019. "Fictionality as Rhetoric: A Distinctive Research Paradigm." *Style* 53, no. 4: 397–425.

Walton, Kendall L. 1970. "Categories of Art." *Philosophical Review* 79, no. 3 (July): 334–67.

———. 1990. *Mimesis as Make-Believe: On the Foundations of the Representational Arts.* Cambridge, MA: Harvard University Press.

Zwaan, Rolf A. 1994. "Effect of Genre Expectations on Text Comprehension." *Journal of Experimental Psychology: Learning, Memory, and Cognition* 20, no. 4: 920.

2

THE "WILLING SUSPENSION OF DISBELIEF"

The Long History of a Short Phrase

Nicholas D. Paige

In one sense, the history of what has become the go-to phrase in English for describing the mental state of consumers of fictions is not long at all: Samuel Taylor Coleridge had no forerunners when in Chapter 14 of the *Biographia Literaria* of 1818 he defined "poetic faith" as the "willing suspension of disbelief." But in another sense, the history can be considered essentially coterminous with the entire tradition of Western mimetic speculation since Aristotle—one riff among many on the idea that something like belief, however attenuated or modulated, is involved when we read novels and epics or watch tragedies and movies. The primary aim of this chapter is to show how Coleridge's phrase plugs into this tradition of "belief talk" and insinuates itself into common parlance, at least in English. A second aim, more methodological, shadows the first, and involves the assumption that certain variations of belief talk—be it Coleridge's or others'—mark a decisively new (or modern) understanding of fiction or fictionality. Instead, I argue that the belief idiom, already present in Plato and Aristotle, is simply built out over time: from the Renaissance on, thinkers have taken up the sketchy, sometimes marginal remarks of the Classical tradition, smoothing and systematizing where possible while introducing competing conceptualizations and ways of speaking as necessary. This process of enrichment—which characterizes so much human activity—has not stopped to this day.

Coleridge on Dramatic Illusion

It is seldom recognized that at its inception, Coleridge's proverbial formulation does not occur as part of a general phenomenology of novel-reading or theater-going (Garratt, 2012, 756; Kivy, 2011, 99–100; Paige, 2011, 209n14). Coleridge did have thoughts about such matters, as we will see, but the passage of the *Biographia Literaria* that is suspended disbelief's origin is concerned with the much more specific issue—a delicate issue, in Coleridge's day—of supernatural subject matter.

Recounting his collaboration with William Wordsworth on *Lyrical Ballads* (1798), Coleridge describes the conceptual ambition of the collection. Both friends shared a basic commitment to "two cardinal points of poetry"—"the power of exciting the sympathy of the reader by a faithful adherence to the truth of nature, and the power of giving the interest of novelty by the modifying colors of the imagination" (Coleridge, 1983, 2: 5). Cardinal points indeed, or poetological commonplaces: Coleridge is working, here, a widely shared opposition between two paths to readerly involvement, one that arguably can be traced back to Aristotle's thoughts about the relation between verisimilitude (or probability: *eoikhè*) and surprise (or wonder: *thaumaston*).[1] But they are also cardinal points in

DOI: 10.4324/9781003119456-4

28

that they are poles, polar opposites, because verisimilitude ("truth to nature") and surprise ("novelty") are felt to be mutually incompatible: the verisimilar tends to not be surprising and the surprising tends not to be verisimilar. The project of the *Lyrical Ballads* is to prove "the practicability of combining both" (5). Wordsworth would work the subjects of "ordinary life" that can "be found in every village" (6); his task, obviously, was to move such subjects to the pole of surprise—"to give the charm of novelty to things of every day" (7). This would come via a defamiliarization of the quotidian: Wordsworth was to strip away the "film of familiarity" that keeps us from really seeing "the loveliness and the wonders of the world before us" (7). This wonder, this novelty, was "a feeling analogous to the supernatural" (7). Meanwhile, Coleridge was to take the symmetrically opposite tack, treating "incidents and agents ... supernatural" (6) in a manner that would seem emotionally real: his job consisted in "the interesting of the affections by the dramatic truth of such emotions, as would naturally accompany such situations, supposing them real" (6). Thus the "two cardinal points" would be finessed in such a way as to produce both a supernaturalized nature and a naturalized supernatural.

It is in this context that Coleridge invents his formula. The "semblance of truth" that he was attempting to generate for his supernatural subject matter would achieve "that willing suspension of disbelief for the moment, which constitutes poetic faith" (6). Wordsworth didn't have to worry about the suspension of his reader's disbelief because the kind of true-to-nature subject he chose wouldn't generate disbelief in the first place. The only other passage in the *Biographia* where Coleridge uses terms similar to those in his famous phrase confirms the importance of the supernatural context. Shakespeare's characters, Coleridge writes, are able to "bribe us into a voluntary submission of our better knowledge, into suspension of all our judgment..., and [to] enable us to peruse with the liveliest interest the wildest tales of ghosts, wizards, genii, and secret talismans" (217–18). Echoing the "dramatic truth" that he declared as his aim in the *Lyrical Ballads* project, the poet speaks now of "a *dramatic* probability" imparted to "characters and incidents border[ing] on impossibility" (218).[2] Coleridge is careful to avoid qualifying our adherence as belief.

> The poet does not require us to be awake and believe; he solicits us only to yield ourselves to a dream; and this too with our eyes open, and with our judgment *perdue* behind the curtain, ready to awaken us at the first motion of our will; and meantime, only, not to *dis*believe.
>
> *(218)*

All the components of the better known, more concentrated formulation of Chapter 14 are present—the supernatural context, plus the terms "voluntary," "suspension," and "disbelief"—along with some other details, such as the dream analogy and the helpful stipulation that a negated disbelief is not the same as belief pure and simple.

This link between suspended disbelief and the supernatural has been all but forgotten as writers and scholars of all stripes have rushed to take the phrase as a general explanation for how we experience fiction. But if the link is crucial for understanding the deeper background to Coleridge's coinage, as I will show, it is also true that our common misconception is perhaps not so wide of the mark. For Coleridge had long been interested in the more general problem of belief in fictions (especially though not exclusively the theater), and it turns out that many of his formulations in this context are congruent with the phrasing in the *Biographia*.[3] The most extensive discussion occurs in the notes for the 1808 lectures on poetry. There, Coleridge attempts to distinguish between our reaction to a landscape painting and a staged forest scene. Neither, he says, truly deceives us, but the stage nevertheless aims at a kind of illusion that the painting does not. The staged forest produces an "*analagon* [analogue] of deception, a sort of temporary Faith which we encourage by our own Will" (Coleridge, 1987, 1: 130). An illusion that is close to deception but not quite: one can feel Coleridge struggling with the fuzziness of the distinctions, as when he first writes that the aim of the stage is "to deceive," only to cross it out and substitute "to produce illusion" (130). Be that as it may, in addition to the mention of "faith" and "will," the poet comes up with a formulation anticipatory of the suspension of disbelief's double negative when he stipulates that the illusion consists "not in the mind's judging it to be a Forest but in its remission of the judgement that it is not a Forest" (130). In a rewritten version of this passage, Coleridge scuttles the idea of remission—quite reasonably qualified by one scholar as "suspension by any other name" (Marshall, 2020, 25)—and defines the goal of the theater as the production of "a sort of temporary Half-Faith, which the Spectator encourages in himself and supports by a voluntary contribution on his own part" (134). But in a later letter—from 1816, a year in which he was working on the *Biographia Literaria*—"remission" has become full-blown suspension: "the true theory of Stage Illusion" must derive from "a voluntary lending of the will to this suspension of one of it's [*sic*] own operations," that of judgment "concerning the reality of any sensuous impression" (Coleridge, 1959, 641–42). There is seemingly little conceptual daylight, therefore, between the way Coleridge conceives of dramatic illusion tout court and the reader's processing of unbelievable subject matter.

To what extent is the willing suspension of disbelief an innovation over previous descriptions of the way we relate to literature? Surprisingly, the question has hardly been posed. Some noted scholars have proceeded with the assumption that Coleridge's phrase is the sign of an epochally novel understanding of literature or art more generally. Such is the case for Catherine Gallagher, for whom Coleridge is a kind of triumphant endpoint to her account of what she holds to be the eighteenth-century "rise of fictionality"; Michael McKeon has treated the formula as convenient shorthand for a distinctively "modern" aesthetics (Gallagher, 2006, 347–49; McKeon, 1987, 128). Others have pointed to specific Enlightenment "forerunners" to whom Coleridge may plausibly be indebted (Bormann, 1972, 56–60; Chandler, 1996, 39–40; Kauvar, 1969, 91–94). And specialists of Romanticism have looked more to Coleridge's contemporaries, especially to German writers such as A. W. Schlegel, from whom Coleridge was wont to crib (Burwick, 1991). Such references may be more or less illuminating depending on the case, but the basic problem with measuring the novelty of Coleridge's phrase is that the latter is very difficult to disentangle from the entire Aristotelian tradition of thought about verisimilitude: commentators had for many centuries glossed the issue of belief, posed by Aristotle in parts of the *Poetics*.

Early Modern Belief Talk

Italian Renaissance commentators tended to elaborate on the passage in *Poetics* 9 (1651b) where Aristotle speaks of historically attested characters as superior to invented ones precisely on account of the automatic belief they inspire. Francesco Robortello, in the first of the major commentaries on the *Poetics*, offers this restatement: in order to feel the "major passions" that are pity and fear, the audience must

> know that the thing actually happened in such and such a way. Thus if a tragic plot contained an action which did not really take place and was not true, but was represented by the poet himself in accordance with verisimilitude, it would perhaps move the souls of the auditors, but less. … If verisimilar things move us, the true will move us much more. Verisimilar things move us because we believe it to have been possible for the event to come about in the way specified. True things move us because we know that it did come about in the way specified.
>
> *(quoted in Weinberg, 1961, 392)*

Robortello thus proposes—and his variance with respect to Aristotle is probably minimal—two types of belief: one, inferior, produced by a verisimilar treatment of invented subjects and characters, and a second, more prized belief, deriving from historical conviction. Based on the summaries of

Renaissance poetological discourse provided by Bernard Weinberg, we can safely conclude that such a reading was anything but unusual for the day.

To be sure, this type of credence does not equate precisely with dramatic illusion as Coleridge speaks of it. Yet, it is part of a tangle of discursive strands that are impossible to separate: they make up the belief talk that over the following centuries were reworked and expanded in France and Great Britain.[4] Some of these strands posit a belief that arises out of the experience of poetry or drama, and that can be enhanced by proper handling on the part of the poet. Thus, in 1583, Orazio Ariosto writes of gaining the audience's credence by "weaving a series of events (even if invented) as verisimilarly as possible, endowing the persons introduced with appropriate characters, [and] making them express thoughts fitted to the circumstances" (quoted in Weinberg, 1961, 936). The pursuit of belief impels other theorists to begin to elaborate practical suggestions. Thus, in a 1598 treatise, Angelo Ingegneri reasons that if actors are going to be speaking Italian, it's more verisimilar if the play is set in Tuscany as opposed to Cyprus; similarly, the temporal span of the represented action ideally should be in real time, for "that belief whence the passions are aroused" is more efficaciously produced "the more the [things of the play] approximate the truth" (quoted in Weinberg, 1961, 1090).[5] And already in 1543, Bartolomeo Cavalcanti offers an early articulation of what has become known as the "fourth wall" principle: avoiding the direct address of the audience,

> The actors must represent things as the persons whom they simulate would do them among themselves and not let it appear that these are things that are narrated or simulated; for this brings displeasure to the spectators and removes belief from the plot.
>
> *(quoted in Weinberg, 1961, 920–21)*

Was belief for these thinkers total? Generally not. Certainly, some were more doctrinaire than others: against even Aristotle, Luigi Castelvetro, for example, held that invented characters could not hope to solicit any credence at all.[6] But in most formulations the aim was always producing *more* belief, suggesting then a kind of sliding scale whose unattainable asymptote is perfect illusion. Thus, in the words of Ingegneri,

> If those who perform the plots could make the spectators believe that those stages upon which they perform them were really those cities and those lands where the plots are imagined to have happened, they would most willingly do so.
>
> *(quoted in Weinberg, 1961, 1101)*

And even commentators who willingly speak of belief don't hesitate to hedge and to qualify: "If we wish to concern ourselves with persuading the spectators that the thing represented is really true," writes Orazio Ariosto, "it will no longer suffice to make the stage-settings of boards ... but entire cities will have to be founded" (quoted in Weinberg, 1961, 936). Belief, then, seems like the right word for these writers, at the same time it is not *quite* the right word. Thus Francesco Buonamici:

> Verisimilitude in represented things consists in assuring that the parts of the action are linked and that they bend the soul of the spectator to believe that things happened in this way; but the effect of verisimilitude on the spectator is never strong enough—unless he is an imbecile—for the thing representing to be mistaken for the thing represented.
>
> *(Buonamici, 1597, 111)*

Like others cited above, Buonamici seems to regard belief as something that arises from plot as opposed to stagecraft—thus his reference to the linking of actions. But he is careful to add that belief is not a kind of superstitious delusion, and the logic, in these accounts, was almost always of a the-more-the-better variety. Belief was less a toggle switch than a volume button, and the more poets could turn it up—can the music ever be too loud?—the more effect they would produce on their audience.

How far is this from Coleridge? About two centuries and all the ramifying developments such a span implies. Let's now work forward and back along that path, taking a cue from Coleridge's thoughts in the 1808 lectures. For there he gives explicit coordinates for the "dream" theory he was working out, one designed to thread the needle between the Scylla of "French Critics" who hold "Stage-Illusion" to be an "actual delusion" and the Charybdis that is Samuel Johnson, who "den[ies] it altogether" (Coleridge, 1987, 1:135). The latter reference is plain. In his 1765 preface to Shakespeare, Johnson attacks the neoclassical unities of time, place, and action, founded on "the supposed necessity of making the drama credible" (Johnson, 1968, 76). "Supposed": Johnson strenuously disagrees.

> It is false, that any representation is taken for reality. […] The truth is that the spectators are always in their senses, and know, from the first act to the last, that the stage is only a stage, and the players are only players.
>
> *(76–77)*

Who the "French critics" may be is less clear. As we'll see, some eighteenth-century French critics purveyed accounts of illusion that were easily as mitigated as Coleridge's own. But most probably Coleridge is thinking generally of the neoclassical doctrine that Johnson dates to "the time of [Pierre] Corneille," that is, the first half of the seventeenth century (Johnson, 1968, 75).

It is true, as Johnson says, that the neoclassical unities—and other fabled "rules" for which the French are still famous—were justified in order to secure the credence of spectators (see notably Forestier, 2003). But it is much less clear that the French held any faster than the Italians to dramatic belief as complete delusion. On the face of things, Jean Chapelain's reasoning in an early articulation of the so-called 24-hour rule, written in 1630, might appear to tend in such a literalist direction. Chapelain there declares that while the imperative behind all poetic representation is "to be so perfect that no difference is detectible between the thing imitated and the thing imitating," theater is especially up to the task because the medium "hides" the person of the poet, thus better "overwhelm[ing] the imagination of the spectator and guid[ing] him without obstacle to the credence in the representation that he is supposed to maintain" (Chapelain, 2007, 223–24). Easily recognizable, here, is the influence of the Renaissance commentaries of the Italians, where the unities were first discussed before their systematic uptake by the French. We might also detect in Chapelain's formulation the implication of sliding-scale belief, given that theater is said to prompt *more* belief than narrative, but admittedly Chapelain does not put much pressure on the idea of credence—perhaps because his short letter was as much a polemical document as it was a work of theory.[7]

At any rate, while rehearsing the need for belief, subsequent French theorists let some of their doubts show, the best example being a particularly contorted passage in the most important theatrical treatise of the period, François Hédelin d'Aubignac's *Pratique du théâtre*, published in 1657 though probably composed starting in the late 1630s. The sentence occurs in a discussion of the necessity of temporal restriction—for if a lot of time passes in a play, we would expect to see the players eat, drink, and sleep, and since we don't, the artifice will be obvious. D'Aubignac then writes,

> I certainly realize that theater is a kind of illusion, but spectators must be tricked in such a way that they don't imagine they are being tricked, even though they do know it; while they are being tricked, their mind must not be aware of it; but only when the mind reflects on it.
>
> *(2001, 317)*

A lot in the passage is obscure, starting with the first "but," which doesn't seem to follow from the concession of the opening ("I certainly realize"), and the use of the word "illusion" in the apparent sense of the theatrical experience is both historically rare in this period and unusual in d'Aubignac's text (where it typically refers to elements of the stage set). Still, even without elaborate parsing, we can see d'Aubignac's hesitations: spectators must not imagine (*imaginer*) they are being fooled even though they know (*savoir*) that they are being fooled; their mind must not be aware of (*connaître*) the trickery, though they are aware of it if they reflect (*faire réflexion*; during or after the spectacle is not clear). One scholar has aptly called this messy surfacing of d'Aubignac's own doubts a classic case of fetishistic denial (Harris, 2014, 56). But no psychoanalysis is necessary to hazard that the multiplication of countervailing verbs stems from an attempt, however involuntary or repressed, to grapple precisely with the problem that Coleridge held doctrinaire "French Critics" incapable of seeing.

And on both sides of the Channel that grappling became much more explicit in the eighteenth century, where the word "illusion," something of a hapax in d'Aubignac, becomes integral to belief talk. Some seek to dispel recourse to belief and illusion entirely. Such is the case for Johnson, but much earlier for the abbé Dubos, who in an extremely influential treatise of 1719 reasons that while "it is true that everything we see at the theater conspires to move us, nothing there is an illusion for our senses, since everything is displayed as an imitation" (Dubos, 1719, 620–21). As we see here, and as is clear in Johnson as well, these accounts are not designed to argue for a disabused spectatorship or an early Brechtian *Verfremdungseffekt*. Rather, they provide models for explaining audience adhesion—which should be as strong as possible—as something other than a kind of belief (usually through some sort of theory of passionate identification, whose history is also a long one). Yet Dubos and Johnson are outliers, and despite their visibility they do not change the fact that most commentators prefer to tweak the belief–illusion model rather than give it up. Marmontel's widely known article "Illusion" in the *Encyclopédie* is noteworthy for its attempt to refashion the understanding of the term under pressure from Dubos's skepticism. For Marmontel accepts that people know they are in the theater, and that "complete" or "full" illusion (the adjectives come back repeatedly) is impossible and moreover undesirable, in that (and here he follows Dubos) it would chain us to tragedy's negative emotions and foreclose any experience of pleasure (Marmontel, 1777). Marmontel opts then for what he calls "half-illusion" (Marmontel, 1777, 561). According to this model, which Marian Hobson has dubbed "bimodal," two thoughts can be present to the mind at once: on the one hand, we know we're in a theater (and can say to ourselves "What acting!"), while on the other, we really think we are watching real events unfold (Hobson, 1982, 47–49). Yet, even the bimodal model ends up getting pulled back toward the side of illusion: Marmontel further maintains that the two thoughts aren't quite symmetrically present, in that it's the illusion of reality that should predominate over the consciousness of fiction—according to the now centuries-old commonplace that stronger illusion makes for greater impact on the soul of the artwork's percipient. Theorists found it decidedly difficult, therefore, to get away from the idiom of belief and the related, newly popular "illusion": whatever refinements and stipulations were necessary when using the terms, they continued to make sense to writers of the period.

Beyond the *Incredulus odi*

And the terms made sense for Coleridge further down the line, in the early nineteenth century. Besides Johnson and the "French Critics," Coleridge left us some other coordinates for his thinking about dramatic illusion, in the form of manuscript annotations to Richard Payne Knight's *Analytical Inquiry into the Principles of Taste*, which, appearing in 1805, was fresh scholarship as the poet was preparing his 1808 lectures. Most of Coleridge's marginalia occur in Knight's long chapter on the sublime and pathetic. There, Knight vigorously dissents from Edmund Burke's proposition—which is in complete congruence with Aristotelian thought since the Renaissance—that "the nearer tragedy approaches the reality, and the further it removes us from all idea of fiction, the more perfect is its power" (cited in Knight, 1805, 314). Knight instead aligns himself with Dubos and Johnson, both of whom he quotes more than once, arguing that the fact that "all the distress of dramatic fiction is known and felt, at the time of its exhibition, to be merely fiction" does not preclude the excitation of "real and complete … sympathies" in the spectators" (327). But Coleridge will have none of either of these opinions. On the one hand, pace Burke, any "fits of forgetfulness and deception" one may have during a performance are unsustainable; on the other, contra Knight, "the fact [is] that we *know* the thing to be a representation, but that we often *feel* it to be a reality" (Coleridge, 1992, 405–06). Coleridge returns repeatedly to the distinction between knowing and feeling; thus, when Knight opines that "Fiction is known to be fiction, even while it interests us most," Coleridge interjects, "This is false[;] it is not *felt* to be fiction when we are most affected" (Coleridge, 1992, 408; Knight, 1805, 354). Even though Knight does not dispute that real emotions are excited by literature, this is not enough for Coleridge, who is unwilling to relinquish an illusion model, even if the illusion is now one of feeling rather than knowing. Granted, he reasons, one "species of delusion" is impossible in the playhouse, that of the representation being taken for a reality; but "another species of delusion" must "occasionally [be] superinduced," otherwise "I do not see how it is possible that we should be affected to the degree to which a fine tragedy exquisitely represented does affect us" (3:406). These are of course annotations, and one should expect them to be inchoate. But they show—as do the final lectures, already described—that Coleridge was fully committed to an explanation of aesthetic adhesion elaborated in terms of belief and illusion.

These earlier engagements with the tradition of thought on belief are, at any rate, banal; they leave us far from what Coleridge is remembered for. How did he hit upon the idea of coming at the problem from the other side—from the side of disbelief suspended, as opposed to belief induced? It is here that the supernatural context of the famous phrase needs to be recalled, for it helps explain Coleridge's modification of the customary idiom. "Disbelief" was most widely used in religious discourse, as a neighboring term for atheism. But it also figured as a descriptor for a modern state of mind—for the rational, non-superstitious worldview that in Weberian parlance would come to be known as disenchanted. This acceptation lent itself easily to the grand narrative of neoclassicism, as when Hugo Blair, in his *Lectures on Rhetoric and Belles-Lettres* (1783), writes that "the disbelief of magic and enchantments" led to the abandonment of romance fiction and its replacement by a more rational novel (307). Not that Spenser and Shakespeare, Ariosto and the *Arabian Nights*, need to be consigned to the dustbin of literary history: such enchanted poetry made sense as a product of a more superstitious era, and it could still be enjoyed even without the belief that audiences of the before times may have invested in it. But writing in such a way *now* was impossible. Thus Richard Hurd, whose *Letters on Chivalry and Romance* (1762) vigorously defends the reading of the enchanted canon, nevertheless, concedes that it cannot be a model for today's serious writers: "I would advise no modern poet to revive these faery tales in an epic poem" (101).

Coleridge's part of the *Lyrical Ballads* project thus went against prevailing neoclassical logic. In that, he found himself in the same boat as practitioners of the gothic, whose creations were routinely chastised via a phrase from Horace's *Ars Poetica* (line 188): *incredulus odi*, or, literally, "disbelieving, I hate." Horace had used the words to explain the spectator's rejection of actions too horrible for contemplation—his chief example was Medea's infanticide—and counseled the apprentice poet to steer clear of such subjects. But in the eighteenth century, Horace's line proved useful when critiquing contemporary writers who attempted to take the supernatural seriously. Horace Walpole's *Castle of Otranto* (1764) was initially greeted with favor by the *Monthly Review*, whose reviewer didn't seem entirely convinced that the novel was a translation of a medieval original but was willing to play along. But then Walpole brought out a second edition six months later, admitting authorship and further stating prefatorily (in arguably proto-Coleridgian terms) that his novel was an attempt to blend "common life" and "probability" with "the great resources of fancy" (Walpole, 1996, 9–10), and by this point the same reviewer would have nothing to do with the book:

> When, as in this edition, the *Castle of Otranto* is declared to be a modern performance, that indulgence we afforded to the foible of a supposed antiquity we can by no means extend to the singularity of a false taste in a cultivated period of learning. [...] *Incredulus odi* is, or ought to be, a charm against all such infatuations.
>
> *(quoted in Sabor, 1987, 72)*

Some three decades later, with the gothic novel in full swing and spinning off into stage adaptations, a reviewer of a contemporary play censures the ghosts, again via Horace: "We would interdict the production of any *new* spectre on the stage. This 'reign of terror' is over: 'incredulus odi.' In a modern play, ghosts cannot be tolerated" (quoted in Cleary, 1995, 201–2n39). And indeed, Coleridge himself, reviewing Matthew Lewis's *The Monk* in 1797, doesn't hesitate to trot out Horace's injunction as proof that a work so improbable can scarcely pretend to impart a moral lesson (Coleridge, 1995, 59).[8]

But of course, this was just one interpretation of the classical poetological inheritance: others marshalled different passages to argue that an impossible premise could nonetheless be the starting point for a psychologically verisimilar work. Notably, *Poetics* 24 (1460a) contains a section in which Aristotle lauds Homer for having "taught other poets the right way to purvey falsehoods" (Aristotle, 1987, 60). The argument is less than clear, but the philosopher seems to suggest that an action that follows logically from another action will have the effect of validating the first action in the listener's mind, and shortly thereafter, Aristotle advises that any irrationality should be kept "outside the plot-structure," giving the example of Oedipus's perplexingly having no knowledge of how his father had died (60). Translating the *Poetics* in 1789, Thomas Twining homed in on these obscure comments as particularly in need of interpretation. Discounting André Dacier's opinion that Aristotle was simply advising an "artful intermixture" of history and invention, Twining argued that Aristotle was really talking about cause and effect. His gloss, which introduces remarks on the enchantments of Homer, Ariosto, and Shakespeare, contains some remarkable Coleridgian echoes.

> The Poet invents certain extraordinary characters, incidents, and situations. When the actions, and the language, of those characters, and, in general, the *consequences* of those events, or situations, as drawn out into detail by the Poet, are such as we know, or think, to be *true*—that is to say, poetically true, or *natural*; such, as we are satisfied must necessarily, or would probably, follow, if such characters and situations actually existed; this probability, nature, or *truth*, of representation, imposes on us, sufficiently for the purposes of Poetry. It induces us to *believe*, with hypothetic and voluntary faith, the existence of those false events, and imaginary personages, those ἀδύνατα [impossibilities], ἄλογα [irrationalities], ψεύδη [lies]—those marvelous and incredible fictions, which, otherwise managed, we should have rejected: that is, their improbability, or impossibility, would have so forced themselves upon our notice, as to destroy, or disturb, even the slight and willing illusion of the moment.
>
> *(Aristotle, 1789, 486)*[9]

Whether Coleridge read Twining's commentary matters little. Certainly, Twining's phrasings are intriguingly close to the language Coleridge uses when discussing both "Stage-Illusion" and the suspension of disbelief made possible when the supernatural is properly handled. But the wider point is that Coleridge's language, though innovative, is nonetheless perfectly congruent both with the reprocessing of the classical canon that took place in the Renaissance and then in subsequent neoclassical discourse, especially when it involved the irrational or the supernatural. Perfectly congruent, yet of course different: mitigated belief is replaced, in one genial stroke, by crossing out the disbelief of the *incredulus odi*. All the other material—from the voluntary and temporary nature of the operation to the idea of a faith that is peculiarly poetic—is either standard-issue or a light addition to the tradition.[10]

The Success of a Turn of Phrase

Does the "willing suspension of disbelief" represent a light-bulb moment, the ushering in of a new way of relating to literature—if not modern "aesthetics" itself? Or might it be simply a nice turn of phrase, a felicitous but otherwise anodyne tweaking of an inherited, endlessly nuanced commonplace? Most surely the latter. Coleridge's formulation seems to have attracted no followers over the rest of the century: a simple Google n-gram search suggests that occurrences of the phrase before 1900 are found only in reprints of the original passage in the *Biographia Literaria*. The same search strongly suggests that its independent afterlife—that is, its uncoupling from its immediate context— is attributable to George Saintsbury's phenomenally popular *History of Criticism*, published at the opening of the twentieth century. In his account of the *Biographia*, Saintsbury qualifies Coleridge's coinage as "one of the great critical phrases of the world" (1904, 208n1). The suspension of disbelief is not yet, in Saintsbury, all-purpose shorthand for the experience of fiction: it is invoked only when the critic is discussing the successful overthrow of the rationalistic "Neo-Classic dynasty," and it is taken, therefore, as the hallmark of a "modern" sensibility (8).[11] While this narrative of rupture is unjustified for reasons I have explained, the importance of *History of Criticism* lies in its transformation of the "suspension of disbelief" into a slimmed-down, detachable unit, or just possibly cliché: Saintsbury doesn't hesitate to drop the epithet "willing," anticipating the casual use that has slowly dominated the more complete citation of Coleridge (see Figure 2.1). And detachable the phrase has proven. It figures as the title for a whole chapter of Norman Holland's widely read study on reader response; Victor Nell's equally remarked monograph on the same topic uses it as a useful placeholder for the general phenomenon of readerly absorption (Holland, 1968, 63–103; Nell, 1988, 56).[12] And many scholars invoke it as consensual common ground, even when their understandings evidently diverge from Coleridge's.[13] Needless to say, in everyday parlance the phrase has even detached itself from its author: "During one week in 1997, Coleridge's biographer Richard Holmes recorded seven separate uses of the phrase in newspaper articles and radio programs variously describing films, books, drama, and scientific theories. None mentioned Coleridge" (Tomko, 2016, 1).

Figure 2.1   Frequency of occurrences of the phrase "willing suspension of disbelief" (solid line) and the truncated "suspension of disbelief" (dotted line).

But just as his dissatisfaction with people like Johnson and Knight spurred Coleridge to reformulate earlier commonplaces, (dis)belief talk has, over time, been both reformulated and—more often—rejected by scholars interested in pursuing other conceptual idioms. If some philosophers continue to find the suspension of disbelief worth keeping around (Galgut, 2002, 190–99; Schaper, 1978, 31–44), the title of Kendall Walton's article "Appreciating Fiction: Suspending Disbelief or Pretending Belief?" suggests a veering away from Coleridge's novel formula, back toward "belief," but now understood as a kind of play ("make-believe") that bears little relation to the tradition Coleridge was working with (Walton, 1980, 1–18).[14] Colin Radford and Michael Weston's seminal exchange on readers' paradoxical involvement with the fates of characters they know to be made up quotes the phrase (without attribution) before concluding that disbelief and belief are beside the point (Radford and Weston, 1975, 71–72). And generally literary and narrative theorists have followed this drift away from belief talk, into idioms of "pretense" or "immersion" (see e.g., Schaeffer, 2010). Nonetheless, as this handbook suggests, belief talk—and Coleridge's famous contribution to it—may still have a future.

Of course, it's possible to take a specialist's approach to Coleridge's willing suspension of disbelief. One might, then, try to approach it via an internal study of the poet's oeuvre: "poetic faith," for example, could be related to Coleridge's personal theology (Tomko, 2016, 65–107), or the epithet "willing" to his idea of the creative imagination (Burwick, 1991, 191–229). Or we might try to integrate the phrase into the philosophical system Coleridge was developing in dialogue with the German Idealist tradition (Marshall, 2020; McFarland, 1987, 114–45). Such approaches would plausibly end with the assertion of the historical importance of his thought, of which the four words under study would be the tip of the iceberg. Yet, no matter how the scholar may try to weave the phrase tightly back into the full texture of Coleridge's work, its subsequent success would not have been possible if its use had such a high barrier to entry. I have preferred to view the willing suspension of disbelief as part of the steady proliferation of discourse around human reactions to the mimetic representational practices characteristic of the West since the Greeks—part, then, of a constellation of easily transmissible, endlessly ramifying commonplaces building out over time. Certainly, Coleridge offers a striking riff on the traditional idiom of belief, and it is not given to everyone to coin a phrase of such endurance. Most likely, however, the phrase has acquired a life of its own precisely because its meaning is relatively modest; it turned out there was an intuitive appeal in speaking of crossed-out disbelief. But other ways of speaking have long had and still have competing appeal, and modern scholars, continuing the build-out Coleridge was part of, have introduced new terms—"games," "contracts," "immersion," "make-believe."

David Hume, reviewing Bernard de Fontenelle's attempt to account for the paradoxical pleasure viewers take in tragedy, found his predecessor was on to something. "This solution seems just and convincing," wrote Hume in his 1757 essay "Of Tragedy," "but perhaps it wants still some new addition, in order to make it answer fully the phaenomenon, which we here examine" (189–90).[15] Additions ever wanting, we ever rededicate ourselves to expanding the discursive edifice our forerunners have built up in hope of explaining the effects of art.

Notes

1 See the discussion of the seemingly vengeful statue of Mitys in *Poetics* 9 (1452a).

2 Here and elsewhere, emphasis is always in the original text.

3 All the relevant passages from Coleridge's oeuvre are exhumed already in the first scholarly article on the suspension of disbelief (see Morrill, 1927, 436–44). For the purposes of this chapter, I will not attempt to differentiate between belief in literature read from belief in drama performed. The fact is that Coleridge's treatment both suggests and erases medium specificity, and in this, Coleridge doesn't differ appreciably from the Aristotelian tradition he inherits.

4 It bears noting that these belief idioms circulate alongside (and sometimes intersect with) idioms of passionate contagion and identification: all are ways of grappling with the various ways we can be "hooked"—to use Rita Felski's term—by art (Felski, 2020).

5 In his *Poetica d'Aristotele vulgarizzata e sposta* of 1570, Luigi Castelvetro lays down similar rules.

6 "We cannot imagine a king who did not exist, nor attribute any action to him" (quoted in Weinberg, 1961, 504).

7 Chapelain was responding to an earlier text in which the aging playwright Alexandre Hardy rejected the increasingly modish Aristotelian constraints; see Chapelin, 2007, 66.

8 For further remarks on the poetological difficulties posed by the marvelous and the gothic, see Paige, 2011, 174–79, 188–96.

9 In an interesting echo of Coleridge's marginalia to Knight, Twining goes on to maintain that the syllogism identified by Aristotle makes it so that the reader "*feels* the truth of the premises" (486). As an aside, Twining appears to have been the first to intensively use the expression "dramatic illusion."

10 It is commonly held that the willed nature of our involvement is an innovation that Coleridge developed from A. W. Schlegel, who spoke of "voluntary surrender": "no other critic before Coleridge [save Schlegel] had expressed the idea that the submission to illusion is voluntary" (Morrill, 1927, 441n13). But Twining's language suggests that the drift toward "willingness" may not have any need for a specifically Romantic imagination. Already in 1668, John Dryden had written of "the belief of fiction" as follows: "reason suffers itself to be so hood-wink'd [...] but it is never so wholly made a captive, as to be drawn head-long into a perswasion of those things which are most remote from probability: 'tis in that case a free-born subject, not a slave; it will contribute willingly its assent, as far as it sees convenient, but will not be forc'd" (Dryden, 1966, 18). While one critic has called this an "early and striking statement of the phenomenon Coleridge would call the 'willing suspension of disbelief'" (Carlson, 1984, 115), it might be more accurately said to be a then-idiosyncratic slant on neoclassical belief talk.

11 Saintsbury says explicitly that although the willing suspension of disbelief "derives of course from Aristotle, [...] the advance on the original is immense" (3:208n1).

12 Another scholar in this field has argued for rewriting the phrase as "the willing construction of disbelief" (Gerrig, 1993, 240).

13 "The basic rule of dealing with a work of fiction is that the reader must tacitly accept a fictional agreement, which Coleridge calls 'the suspension of disbelief,' " writes Umberto Eco, thus quietly grafting onto Coleridge the idiom of "contract," doubtless of much more recent facture (Eco, 1994, 75). Paul Ricoeur's use of the phrase is also mediated by the idea of a contract (see Ricoeur, 1985, 271).

14 Gregory Currie, whose theory of fiction also privileges make-believe over belief, offers a gloss on Coleridge: "'the willing suspension of disbelief' is best understood as an operation of the mind whereby we suppress our *occurrent* disbelief in the story" (Currie, 1990, 8n9). Both Walton and Currie are content to leave the phrase unattributed.

15 Fontenelle's *Réflexions sur la poétique*, which Hume is commenting, were published in 1747 but probably written in the late 1690s.

Works Cited

Aristotle. 1789. *Aristotle's Treatise on Poetry.* Translated by Thomas Twining. London: Payne.

Aristotle. 1987. *The Poetics of Aristotle.* Translated and with commentary by Steven Halliwell. Chapel Hill: University of North Carolina Press.

Aubignac, François Hédelin d'. (1657) 2001. *La pratique du théâtre.* Edited by Hélène Baby. Paris: Champion.

Blair, Hugo. 1783. *Lectures on Rhetoric and Belles-Lettres.* Vol. 2. London: W. Strahan and T. Cadell.

Bormann, Dennis R. 1972. "The Willing Suspension of Disbelief: Kames as a Forerunner of Coleridge." *Communication Studies* 23, no. 1 (Spring): 56–60.

Buonamici, Francesco. 1597. *Discorsi poetici nella accademia fiorentina in difesa d'Aristotile.* Florence: Giorgio Mare Cotti.

Burwick, Frederick. 1991. *Illusion and the Drama: Critical Theory of the Enlightenment and Romantic Era.* University Park, PA: Pennsylvania State University Press.

Carlson, Marvin. 1984. *Theories of the Theater: A Historical and Critical Survey, from the Greeks to the Present.* Ithaca, NY: Cornell University Press.

Chandler, David. 1996. "Coleridge's 'Suspension of Disbelief' and Jacob Bruckner's 'Assensus Suspensione.'" *Notes and Queries* 43, no. 1 (March): 39–40.

Chapelain, Jean. 2007. *Opuscules critiques*, edited by Alfred C. Hunter and Anne Duprat. Geneva: Droz.

Clery, E. J. 1995. *The Rise of Supernatural Fiction, 1762–1800.* Cambridge: Cambridge University Press.

Coleridge, Samuel Taylor. 1959. *Collected Letters of Samuel Taylor Coleridge.* Edited by Earl Leslie Griggs. Vol. 4. Oxford: Clarendon.

Coleridge, Samuel Taylor. (1818) 1983. *Biographia Literaria, or, Biographical Sketches of My Literary Life and Opinions.* Edited by James Engell and W. Jackson Bate. Princeton, NJ: Princeton University Press.

Coleridge, Samuel Taylor. 1987. *Lectures on Literature 1808–1819.* Edited by R. A. Foakes. Princeton, NJ: Princeton University Press.

Coleridge, Samuel Taylor. 1992. *Marginalia.* Edited by H. J. Jackson and George Whalley. Vol 3. Princeton, NJ: Princeton University Press.

Coleridge, Samuel Taylor. 1995. *Shorter Works and Fragments.* Edited by H. J. Jackson and J. R. de J. Jackson. Vol. 1. Princeton, NJ: Princeton University Press.

Currie, Gregory. 1990. *The Nature of Fiction.* Cambridge: Cambridge University Press.

Dryden, John. 1966. "A Defence of an Essay of Dramatique Poesie." In *The Works of John Dryden*, edited by John Loftis, Vol. 9, 3–22. Berkeley: University of California Press.

Dubos (Abbé), Jean-Baptiste. 1719. *Réflexions critiques sur la poésie et sur la peinture.* Paris: Jean Mariette.

Eco, Umberto. 1994. *Six Walks in the Fictional Woods.* Cambridge, MA: Harvard University Press.

Felski, Rita. 2020. *Hooked: Art and Attachment.* Chicago, IL: University of Chicago Press.

Forestier, Georges. 2003. *Passions tragiques et règles classiques: essai sur la tragèdie française.* Paris: Presses universitaires de France.

Galgut, Elisa. 2002. "Poetic Faith and Prosaic Concerns: A Defense of 'Suspension of Disbelief.'" *South African Journal of Philosophy* 21, no. 3: 190–99.

Gallagher, Catherine. 2006. "The Rise of Fictionality." In *History, Geography, and Culture*. Vol. 1 of *The Novel*, edited by Franco Moretti, 336–63. Princeton, NJ: Princeton University Press.

Garratt, Peter. 2012. "Moving Worlds: Fictionality and Illusion after Coleridge." *Literature Compass* 9, no. 11 (November): 752–63.

Gerrig, Richard J. 1993. *Experiencing Narrative Worlds: On the Psychological Activities of Reading.* New Haven, CT: Yale University Press.

Harris, Joseph. 2014. *Inventing the Spectator: Subjectivity and Theatrical Experience in Early Modern France.* Oxford: Oxford University Press.

Hobson, Marian. 1982. *The Object of Art: The Theory of Illusion in Eighteenth-Century France.* Cambridge: Cambridge University Press.

Holland, Norman N. 1968. *The Dynamics of Literary Response.* New York: Oxford University Press.

Hume, David. 1757. *Four Dissertations.* London: A. Millar.

Hurd, Richard. 1762. *Letters on Chivalry and Romance.* London: A. Millar.

Johnson, Samuel. (1765) 1968. "Preface to Shakespeare." In *Johnson on Shakespeare* (pp. 59–113), edited by Arthur Sherbo. New Haven, CT: Yale University Press.

Kauvar, Gerald B. 1969. "Coleridge, Hawkesworth, and the Willing Suspension of Disbelief." *Papers on Language and Literature* 5, no. 1 (January): 91–4.

Kivy, Peter. 2011. *Once Told Tales: An Essay in Literary Aesthetics.* Chitchester: Wiley- Blackwell.

Knight, Richard Payne. 1805. *An Analytical Inquiry into the Principles of Taste.* London: T. Payne and J. White.

Marmontel, Jean-François. 1777. "Illusion." In *Supplément à l'Encyclopédie ou dictionnaire raisonné des sciences, des arts et des métiers*, vol. 3, 560–562. Amsterdam: M. Rey.

Marshall, Tom. 2020. "Coleridge's Epoché: Phenomenology and the Suspension of Disbelief." *Essays in Romanticism* 27, no. 1 (April): 23–40.

McFarland, Thomas. 1987. *Shapes of Culture.* Iowa City: University of Iowa Press.

McKeon, Michael. 1987. *The Origins of the English Novel, 1600–1740.* Baltimore, MD: Johns Hopkins University Press.

Morrill, Dorothy I. 1927. "Coleridge's Theory of Dramatic Illusion." *Modern Language Notes* 42, no. 7 (November): 436–44.

Nell, Victor. 1988. *Lost in a Book: The Psychology of Reading for Pleasure.* New Haven, CT: Yale University Press.

Paige, Nicholas. 2011. *Before Fiction: The Ancien Régime of the Novel.* Philadelphia, PA: University of Pennsylvania Press.

Radford, Colin, and Michael Weston. 1975. "How Can We Be Moved by the Fate of Anna Karenina?" *Proceedings of the Aristotelian Society, Supplementary Volumes* 49: 67–93.

Ricœur, Paul. 1985. *Le temps raconté.* Vol. 3 of *Temps et récit.* Paris: Seuil.

Sabor, Peter. 1987. *Horace Walpole: The Critical Heritage.* London: Routledge and Kegan Paul.

Saintsbury, George. 1904. *A History of Literary Criticism and Literary Taste in Europe from the Earliest Texts to the Present Day.* Vol. 3. New York: Dodd, Mead, and Co.

Schaeffer, Jean-Marie. 2010. *Why Fiction?* Translated by Dorrit Cohn. Lincoln: University of Nebraska Press.

Schaper, Eva. 1978. "Fiction and the Suspension of Disbelief." *British Journal of Aesthetics* 18, no. 1 (Winter): 31–44.

Tomko, Michael. 2016. *Beyond the Willing Suspension of Disbelief: Poetic Faith from Coleridge to Tolkien.* London: Bloomsbury.

Walpole, Horace. (1764) 1996. *The Castle of Otranto: A Gothic Story.* Edited by W. S. Lewis and E. J. Clery. Oxford: Oxford University Press.

Walton, Kendall L. 1980. "Appreciating Fiction: Suspending Disbelief or Pretending Belief?" *Dispositio* 5, no. 13/14 (Winter-Spring): 1–18.

Weinberg, Bernard. 1961. *A History of Literary Criticism in the Italian Renaissance.* Chicago, IL: University of Chicago Press.

3

THE FICTIONALITY OF GAMES AND THE LUDIC NATURE OF FICTION

Make-Believe, Immersion, Play

Marie-Laure Ryan

Even before fiction became established as a theoretical concept, its oppositional relation to belief was acknowledged in formulae such as "the poet nothing affirms and never lies" (Sir Philip Sidney) or [poetry requires a] "willing suspension of disbelief" (Samuel Taylor Coleridge). Both formulae are negative: the poet does not express beliefs, and readers ignore their actual beliefs in the non-existence of the creatures of the poets' imagination. So what does the poet do instead of expressing beliefs, and why do readers take interest in non-existing creatures? In the 1970s and 1980s, when the advent of ordinary language philosophy and more particularly of speech act theory launched a wave of inquiries into the nature of fiction, answers were formulated in terms of concepts strongly suggestive of games and of a playful attitude toward fictional representation: non-seriousness (Austin), pretending (Searle), make-believe (Walton, Currie). In this chapter, I explore the connections between games, play, and fiction in three sections. The first discusses the make-believe approach to fiction; the second analyzes the notion of immersion as expression of the user's mode of participation in the fictional game of make-believe, assuming this is a valid way to define fiction; and the third asks under what conditions games can be considered fiction.

Make-Believe

The original association of fiction with games of make-believe appears in Kendall Walton's seminal book *Mimesis as Make-Believe: On the Foundations of the Representational Arts* (1990). As the title indicates, Walton's ambition goes beyond the definition of "standard," i.e., literary fiction, the focus of previous philosophical attempts at definition (Searle, Lewis). Through the notion of make-believe, Walton proposes a media-transcending theory of fictionality.

> In order to understand paintings, plays, films, and novels, we must look first at dolls, hobby-horses, toy trucks, and teddy bears. The activities in which representational works of art are embedded and which give them their point are best seen as continuous with games of make-believe. Indeed, I advocate regarding these activities as games of make-believe themselves, and I shall argue that representational works function as props in such games, as dolls and teddy bears serve as props in children's games.
>
> *(1990, 11)*[1]

DOI: 10.4324/9781003119456-5

Walton uses the example of children playing a game in which they pretend that stumps are bears as model for literary fiction and pictorial representations. If the poles of literature and painting can be adequately explained by a common definition, all artistic hybrids of language and image—film, comics, theater, video games—will be automatically covered by the account. The game works like this: children decide among themselves—this is a highly social activity—that they are in a wilderness full of bears. Every stump in the (real) forest counts as a bear in the game, even the stumps of which the children are not aware, so that if they discover a new stump, there will be one more bear in the game world. It follows that the players have no complete knowledge of the game world: it contains surprises for them, but the more they play the game, the more they learn about its world. Once a bear has been discovered, the rules of the game allow some activities and prevent others: since a bear is a dangerous animal, players can try to capture it, shoot it, or flee from it, but they cannot pet it or put a saddle on its back. By declaring stumps to be bears in the game, the children confer upon them the status of "props in a game of make-believe." Since this game does not have rules for winning or losing, its point lies in the richness of the imaginative activity inspired by the pseudo-bears; this activity is a source of pleasure, and it can be said to be autotelic, despite the numerous educational advantages that psychologists ascribe to play (as well as to reading fiction).[2] Walton uses the term "fictional truths" to refer to the imaginings authorized by the rules of the game. Thus, "there is a dangerous bear near you and you are in danger" is a fictional truth in the game world if there is a stump next to the player, but "there is a cuddly toy that you can take to bed with you" is not. Here is Walton on fictional truths:

> When it is "true in a game of make-believe," as we say, [that Fred runs away from a bear], the proposition [that he runs away from the bear] is *fictional*, and the fact that it is fictional is a *fictional truth*. In general, whatever is the case "in a fictional world"—in the world of a game of make-believe or dream or daydream or representational work of art—is fictional.
> *(1990, 35; I changed the example to make it fit with the game I am discussing.)*

A noteworthy feature of this passage is that the concept of fictional truth encompasses not only games of make-believe and representational works of art (and literary fictions, though Walton omits to mention them here), but also dreams and daydreams. If dreams and daydreams produce fictional truths, then a fictional truth is simply a proposition contemplated by the mind that is not true in the real world. But this spontaneous activity cannot be considered a "game of make-believe," because it lacks rules, and it lacks a prop that triggers these rules. The fictionality of dreams and daydreams is simply their imaginary, non-existing character, and this leads back to the common but informal conception of fictionality as untruth, as expressed in this statement: "the fiction that the earth is flat." If the notion of fictional truth is to do more than designate that which is not true in the real world, it must be connected to props. A prop in a game of make-believe is an object—doll, canvas, text, stump—whose function, according to Walton, is to prescribe imaginings by generating fictional truths. "Props are generators of fictional truths, things which, by virtue of their nature or existence, make propositions fictional" (37). Thus, I would erase "daydream" and "dream" from the above list of situations that create fictional truths, and limit the concept to the case of a communicative situation involving more than one participant, and resting on rules that are agreed upon by all sides. It is only in such conditions that fiction can be considered a *game*.

What then is the general rule that ties together all the games of make-believe that use a prop? Though Walton does not formulate it explicitly, I would suggest that this rule is "taking something for something else." Consider the following examples.

1 In the children's game of make-believe, the stumps are taken as bears.
2 In playing with dolls, the doll is taken as a baby.

3 In a theatrical performance or a film, an actor is taken to be Hamlet.

4 In a painting, splotches of color on a canvas are taken to be a ship or as a couple strolling by the ocean.

5 In a literary fiction, the proposition "Anna Karenina threw herself in front of a train" is taken to refer to true facts.

The nature of the convention that links the left to the right side is, however, not the same in all cases. In (1), the connection is a matter of mutual agreement; if one of the children decides to sit on a stump and pet it, she is breaking the rule of the game or maybe initiating another game. In (2), as Walton observes, the prop is not tied to a single game, but to whatever game the children may decide to play: feeding the baby, putting her to bed, spanking him. The manufacturers of the doll facilitate these games (and thus stimulate the imagination) by creating an object that bears an iconic resemblance to a baby, but it is only when it is used in a game that the doll becomes a baby in make-believe: the rest of the time it is only a three-dimensional image of a baby. In (3) convention and iconicity both play a role: the actor is cast as Hamlet by the production team, speaks the lines attributed to Hamlet in the play, and usually dresses in a way compatible with the spectator's idea of what Hamlet looks like. Iconic resemblance is the sole source of meaning in a "game" (4) if this is indeed a game: it is because the painting looks like a ship that spectators perform operations such as identifying the hull, the sails, the crew—all activities which Walton regards as contemplating fictional truths. This is a matter of semiotics, not of mutual agreement. Semiotic considerations do not work for (5): we cannot say that the reader assumes that in the fictional world Anna Karenina threw herself in front of a train by virtue of the semantics (i.e. symbolic meaning) of the sentence "Anna Karenina threw herself in front of a train." The sentence could be either nonfiction or fiction, depending on whether it appears in a report in the newspaper or in a novel, but its semantics, its mode of signification remains constant. It is by virtue of a contract between reader and author that it is taken to denote fictional truths, that is, make-believe facts.

Note, however, the asymmetry between (4) and (5). All visual representations, in order to be identified as that which they represent, rely on iconicity; therefore, if (4) is a game of make-believe by which spectators pretend to see a ship, so are all pictures with identifiable content.[3] By contrast, verbal texts can be either fictional or not depending on a pragmatic rule independent of their mode of signification. This paradoxical situation is not an oversight but Walton's intended thesis: "The reader will notice that I have left no room for nonfictional depictions. Pictures are fiction by definition (works of fiction when they are works)" (351). While there is an "as if" at work in all five examples, the "as if" of (4) does not qualify it, in my view, as a game of make-believe, if by game one understands a behavior governed by rules agreed upon by all participants. Admittedly, the painter of a ship would probably want the painting to be recognized as a ship, though it is mere blotches of paint, but this recognition does not depend on the spectator's awareness of the painter's intent, as it would when deciding whether a verbal utterance aims at truth or at fictional truth. Yet, even if the relevance of Walton's concept of game of make-believe is not as wide as he suggests, make-believe offers intriguing insights into the working of standard (i.e., culturally recognized) forms of fiction.

But what exactly is make-believe? For Walton, make-believe is the opposite of belief; it is a fake kind of belief. He distinguishes belief from imagining in the following way: "Imaginings aim at the fictional as beliefs aim at the true" (41). Derek Matravers has objected to this formula by observing that factual texts, which ask to be believed, also prompt imaginings; in fact, it would be difficult to decide if a text is worth believing without first mentally contemplating the situation that it describes. According to Matravers, "All narratives are prescriptions to imagine" (2014, 18); therefore, a prescription to imagine is not an invitation to play a game of make-believe. There is no make-believe involved when I ask you to imagine what the world will be like if the global temperature rises by 2 degrees, but there is certainly an invitation (prescription?) to imagine. The distinction between fiction and factual texts could perhaps be saved by saying that in fiction, imagining is an end in itself, while in factual texts, it is subordinated to making a decision about the truth of the text.

Another way to conceive make-believe is to regard it, following Searle, as pretense: we pretend that we are facing a ship when looking at a ship picture, that John Smith is Hamlet, that "Anna Karenina committed suicide" is true. This is the "regarding something as something else" that I mention above. But this view runs into problems when fictional statements are true: reading *War and Peace*, we do not pretend that Napoleon invaded Russia, we know that it is true, both of the fiction and the real world. Fictions are representations constructed on the basis of statements that can be either true or false in the real world, but are all true in the fictional world. Make-believe, then, could be conceived as the "regarding as true of an alternate (that is, fictional) world."

Worth noting here is the recourse to the concept of fictional world. While this notion seems intuitive to most readers, philosophers aiming for maximally economical, and non-ambiguous formal definitions are wary of it, because of its vagueness. Gregory Currie, who has also proposed a theory of fiction based on make-believe (1990), rejects it outright as a violation of Occam's razor; world is not a formally definable concept, and it is unworthy of a logical approach. His definition replaces "in the world" with "in the fiction," that is, in the work:

> Anything that is true in the fiction is available for the reader to make-believe. A large part of playing a game of fictional make-believe is to work out what is true in the fiction, and hence what is appropriate to make-believe.
>
> *(1990, 70–71)*

Walton frequently mentions fictional world, because the concept makes his task much easier (it makes more intuitive sense to say that a fictional truth is something that is true in a fictional world rather than in a "work" as Currie has it), but he is almost apologetic about the concept. A fictional world for Walton is not some kind of place or space, but a collection of fictional truths: "To speak of a fictional world is, in part, to speak of the class or cluster of fictional truths belonging to it" (1990, 62). Speaking of the world of a fiction is thus a shortcut for speaking of everything that is true in it, though defining what is true, whether of a world or of a work, has turned out to be a thorny problem. A phenomenological, rather than strictly logical conception of fictional world would say by contrast that a world is much more than a collection of propositions and their logical or pragmatic entailments, it is a representation constructed by the mind on the basis of the text (the prop) as well as on life experience and general knowledge, a representation that is much larger than the sum of its parts. When I imagine fictional characters, I do more than imagining the propositions that describe them, I imagine them as material bodies, surrounded by an environment, located in space and time and tied to other entities by networks of relations: this environment and these relations fully deserve to be called a world, and since this world is produced by a fiction, rather than being the one we inhabit, it is a fictional world.

Insofar as it acknowledges the global nonfactuality of a representation, describing fiction as a prop in a game of make-believe is a formal account that looks at the fictional world from the outside. It does not tell us what it is like to play the game, to experience the fictional world from the inside. For a phenomenological account of this experience, let us turn to the concept of immersion.

Immersion

Walton does not use the concept of immersion in relation to fiction, nor, to my knowledge, did anybody until Jean-Marie Schaeffer in his 1999 book *Pourquoi la fiction?* (*Why Fiction?* English translation 2010). Yet Walton's ambition to explain the experience of "being caught in a story" (1990, 6) anticipates current interest in the phenomenon of immersion. Other metaphors under which immersion (itself a metaphor) has been studied are "being lost in a book" (Nell, 1988), "entrancement" (also Nell), and "transportation" (Gerrig, 1993). The notion of aesthetic illusion, popularized in the visual arts by Ernst Gombrich, can also be regarded as a precursor of immersion (Wolf, 2014).[4] Yet, it is to digital technology, more specifically to virtual reality (VR), that immersion owes its current popularity as a way to capture the fictional experience. In the early 1990s, when VR was just a twinkle in its developers' eyes, it was conceived as "an interactive immersive experience generated by a computer" (Pimentel and Teixeira, 1993, 11). The metaphorical basis of immersion means absorption in a liquid element that differs from the user's normal environment; immersion, therefore, involves the replacement of the world, or reality, inhabited by the user with an alternate reality. The oxymoron of virtual (= non-real) reality refers to a computer simulation of non-existing or distant objects or environments that makes the user experience them as if they were real and present. The disappearance of the computer from active consciousness is, therefore, the basic condition of immersion. When trying to capture the exact nature of the experience, VR researchers often rely on literary comparisons, such as "being in an engrossing book," or Coleridge's already-mentioned idea of "suspending disbelief" (Pimentel and Texeira, 1993, 15). This idea of suspending disbelief suggests that immersion is the result of a deliberate attitude rather than an illusion. VR researchers Mel Slater and Maria Sanchez-Vives argue, however, that the disappearance of the medium is never complete: users only experience the presence of simulated objects when they remain aware in the back of their mind that they are perceiving a computer-generated image. In real life, we take the presence of the environment that surrounds us for granted and we do not reflect on it; in VR, by contrast, the experience of presence should become a cause of wonder and a potential source of pleasure. As Janet Murray writes: "It is in fact this double consciousness that makes VR so thrilling—our sense that the virtual world seems so real despite our knowledge that our feet are still planted in this world" (2020, 19).

Similarly, though fictional immersion consists of the feeling of inhabiting another world, it cannot be complete, for this would mean the loss of the ability to distinguish textual worlds from the real world. The danger of complete immersion has been illustrated by Don Quixote, who immersed himself so deeply in romance novels that his brain "dried up to such a degree that he lost the use of his reason" (Cervantes, 1994, 58). Just as aesthetic illusion does not produce real illusion, but only an illusionist effect—an illusion of illusion—immersion can only remain an aesthetic experience if the experiencer remains aware of dealing with a representation.

As a type of attention, immersion is very difficult to define. Schaeffer considers the experience to be a "black box," triggered by "cognitively impenetrable" "pre-attentional primers" (2005, 238) that evade introspection. Some mental processes conducive to immersion can nevertheless be identified. Users must be able to rely extensively on their life experience in their construction of the fictional world, or on their familiarity with the world of other texts of the same type. In the case of verbal texts, immersion depends on the ability to form mental imagery; once again, this ability depends chiefly on life experience, but it can also derive from the reader's familiarity with certain generic landscapes, such as that of fairy tales. To follow the evolution of narrative worlds, users must be able to construct the so-called situation models (Zwaan, 2005) of the states of affairs represented in the text, and to produce a dynamic simulation of the narrated events by regularly updating these models. Insofar as situation models are independent of the exact wording of the text, they support the idea that immersion requires the disappearance of the medium or at least its bracketing out from consciousness. The experience of immersion may involve the phenomenon of motor resonance, through which the textual representation of the gestures of characters activates in the brain the same neural processes as the physical performance of these gestures in the real world (Speer et al., 2009).

Victor Nell, a psychologist who has studied immersion by interviewing passionate readers, stresses the effortlessness of the experience. Immersed readers slip easily into fictional worlds. The experience is hampered by difficult materials because "consciousness is a processing bottleneck, and it is the already comprehended messages … that fully engage the receiver's conscious attention" (1988, 77). This explains the popularity of long novels and multi-media franchises: having already performed the groundwork of building the fictional world, the mind can easily return to it, using the "already comprehended messages" as stepping stones. Poetry and short stories by contrast are anti-immersive, because as soon as readers have performed the necessary work to build their world (if indeed one can speak of world in the case of poetry), they are expelled from it until they re-read the text, a common, almost mandatory task with poetry. This notion of easy accessibility is not necessarily to the taste of literary critics, who may regard immersivity as the trademark of popular, or "genre" literature. As Nell writes: "Indeed, the richness of the structure the ludic reader creates in his head may be inversely proportional to the literary power and originality of the reading matter" (1988, 77–78). The more difficult a text, the more difficult it is to bracket out distracting stimuli from the external world.

The term of immersion can be understood either as intense concentration, or as a mimesis-based experience. In the concentration sense, you can be immersed in playing a concerto, in improving your golf swing, or in solving a rock-climbing problem. In the mimetic sense, immersion presupposes a representational work that constructs a world in which users relocate themselves imaginatively, and whose evolution they simulate mentally. Non-mimetic games, such as chess, only involve the concentration kind, while non-interactive narrative media such as verbal storytelling, theater, and film only involve the mimetic kind. But the two kinds are not incompatible with each other: in a mimetic computer game, players can be both immersed in a fictional world and deeply absorbed in the kind of actions that enable them to progress in the game. The fusion of the two types of immersion is made possible by the players' identification with an avatar, which gives them the sense that it is *me* who performs actions and solves problems. This identification, which transports the player into the game world as an active and individuated member, rather than as a mere point of view as in standard narrative, explains the unmatched power of mimetic computer games to create immersion.

As a dominant type of mimesis, especially in fiction, narrative offers various types of immersion (Ryan, 2015). Here are three particularly powerful forms. *Spatial immersion* is a model of space that enables audiences to follow the movement of characters and to attribute various symbolic meanings to different areas, and a sense of place that invites them to slow down their reading in order to take in the atmosphere, the mood, the sensory richness of the current setting, all that contributes to its imaginative presence. It is the need for spatial immersion that makes readers choose novels that take place in a certain location, and that inspires computer game players to explore the game world. *Temporal immersion*, an experience that can also be called narrative tension (Baroni, 2007), resides in the burning desire to find out what happens next, and it covers the three fundamental narrative experiences of suspense, curiosity, and surprise (Sternberg, 1992). *Emotional immersion* is the power of narrative to inspire affective reactions to the characters, such as feeling vicariously happy when good things happen to characters one likes and sad when bad things happen to them, or conversely, happy when bad things happen to the villain and spite when he succeeds. The phenomenon of emotional immersion has inspired what is known in the scholarly literature as the fictional paradox (cf. Chapter 4 in this volume): do non-existing characters inspire genuine emotions or only simulated (or fictional ones), and how come negative emotional responses such as pity for characters do not spoil the pleasure of fiction? The emotions we feel for fictional characters are not only of a different quality than the ones we feel in real life, it is also questionable whether fiction provides as rich a variety of emotions as real life: though readers may like certain characters, there is no fictional equivalent to being in love with a human being. While the emotions inspired by standard narratives are directed at the characters, computer games where the player must deploy skills also create self-directed emotions, such as triumph, pride, or dejection, depending on how the player succeeds in the game.

Is mimetic immersion specific to fiction? If we think of it in terms of experiencing a non-existing, text-produced world as if it were real, it certainly is. But if we think of it in terms of the intensity of the imaginative experience inspired by a representation, it is not. We can certainly be emotionally, spatially, and temporally immersed in a representation of the real world. Every representation creates a world-image; in the case of fiction, this world-image is largely autotelic; we engage with it for its own sake. In the case of nonfiction, of factual narrative, we use this representation to gather knowledge about the real world. Both fictional and factual representations require imagining, and there is therefore no reason the world-image projected by a factual text could not be immersive. This is the opinion of Kendall Walton:

> Some histories are written in such a vivid, novelistic style that they almost inevitably induce the reader to imagine what is said, regardless of whether one believes it or not. (Indeed, this may be true of Prescott's *History of the Conquest of Peru.*) If we think of the work as prescribing such a reaction, it serves as a prop in a game of make-believe.
>
> *(1990, 71)*

Walton does not use the concept of immersion, but it is clear that he regards make-believe as an immersive experience. The *History of the Conquest of Peru* is a prop in a game of make-believe because of the vividness of the reader's act of imagination. I think, however, that it is wrong to make this vivid imagining dependent on make-believe because it does not necessarily involve pretending that the false is true. In contrast to VR immersion, narrative immersion is not always based on "something passing as that which it is not."

We may in fact ask if fiction is intrinsically immersive. Knowing that the world represented by a work does not exist is detrimental, rather than conducive to intense involvement, because our lives are tied to the affairs of the real world and we have, therefore, a vested interest in these affairs. As Françoise Lavocat suggests, "It could be narration, rather than fiction, which leads to immersion, simulation and transportation, while fiction, on the other hand, leads to distance and disbelief" (2016, 73; my translation).[5] The immersivity generally attributed to fiction may thus come from the fact that most fictional works are narrative, rather than being due to fictionality *per se*. But fictional narratives have an immersive advantage over nonfictional ones, because they are not limited to reporting the knowable and documentable, and they can use a wider variety of narrative techniques that enhance the presence of their world to the imagination. If we combine the distinct immersive advantages of factual and fictional narratives, we get the genre of creative nonfiction, or true fiction, which narrates basically true facts through the techniques of fiction. It is currently one of the most popular genres of writing.

Not only is immersivity not restricted to fiction, it is not necessarily a feature of fiction. I am not thinking of those fictions that try, but fail to immerse—a matter of artistic achievement—but of those that deliberately reject immersion. If the disappearance of the medium from active consciousness is a prerequisite of immersion, as the VR model suggests, then immersion is incompatible with self-reflexivity. But drawing attention to the signifiers and to the status of the text as a representation has been one of the dominant pursuits of postmodernism, not only in literature but in other media as well. A prominent example of this anti-illusionist stance is the French New Novel, as represented by Alain Robbe-Grillet, who in his manifesto *For a New Novel* (1965) rejects plot, a factor of temporal immersion, and characters, a source of emotional immersion, approving only of description because it promotes the visibility of *écriture*.

If factual representation can be immersive, and fiction non-immersive, one is entitled to ask whether there is a special relation between fiction and immersion. I suggest there is, though this relation is not binding. Deliberately non-immersive fictions are parasitic upon immersive fictions. They want to break the game of make-believe—but this presupposes that the game exists in the first place. Postmodernism is the product of a late culture that is obsessed with novelty, but feels that immersivity has been exhausted by realism; anti-immersive self-reflexivity represents, therefore, the only opportunity left for formal innovation. If we exclude deliberately anti-immersive, aggressively self-reflexive forms of fiction, the relation between knowledge and immersivity is inverted in fictional and factual narratives. The primary goal of factual narrative is to produce knowledge, and its immersivity, when present, is an extra bonus. With fictional narrative, on the other hand, immersivity is primary, and producing knowledge is an extra bonus. Non-immersive factual representation is still useful; non-immersive fiction is a failure, unless it teaches something interesting about itself through self-reflexivity. Therefore, fiction has a special relation to immersion.

Games and Fiction

The make-believe conception of fiction regards children's improvised games of pretense as the urform and as the essence of fictionality, modelling on these games its analysis of the more culturally recognized types found in literature, film, theater, and comics. Within this theory, it makes no sense to ask: are games of make-believe fiction, since their fictionality is presupposed by the definition. But the family of games is large and diverse. This raises the question of whether all games should be regarded as fiction, or only some of them—just like some, but not all verbal narratives and films are fiction.

To debate the fictionality of games, I propose to invoke the classificatory system outlined by French sociologist Roger Caillois, who distinguishes four types of games and two forms of play. The four types of games are *agôn* (competitive games, like chess and football), *alea* (games of chance, like roulette), *mimicry* (dramatic acting, or pretending to be pirates), and *illinx* (seeking dizziness, disorder, and vertigo, as in base jumping or riding a roller-coaster). But the categories are not mutually exclusive; *agôn* combines with mimicry in avatar-driven computer games while competitive games can be decided in part by the throw of a die, as in Catan or Monopoly. In addition, Caillois distinguishes two kinds of play that form the opposite poles of a continuum. At one end is free improvisation, turbulence, and gaiety, which he calls *paidia*; at the other end is submission to "arbitrary, imperative, and purposefully tedious conventions." "This latter principle is completely impractical, even though it requires an ever-greater amount of effort, patience, skills, or ingenuity. I call this second component *ludus*" (2001, 13). *Paidia* games are often called sandbox games; they offer tools to the players for inventing their own scenarios, they do not have winners or losers, and they have a strong affinity for the mimicry category; in fact, I doubt that *paidia* can be non-mimetic. They are not without rules, but as Walton's stumps-as-bears example demonstrates, the rules are freely chosen by the players, and they prescribe that something should pass as something else, thereby enforcing mimeticism. The idea of *ludus* has been further sharpened by Bernard Suits when he defines games as "the voluntary attempt to overcome unnecessary obstacles" (Suits, 2014, 43). These games have a precise goal, in contrast to *paidia* games, such as putting a ball into a net in soccer; but the rules prevent easy ways to reach this goal, prescribing instead difficult ones: in soccer, you must control the ball without using your hands (except for the goalie). In contrast to *paidia*, *ludus* games have rigid winning or losing conditions. Of the four kinds of games distinguished by Caillois, mimicry is the most obviously fictional, since it corresponds to Walton's games of make-believe. Similarly, *paidia* has greater affinities for fiction than *ludus*. I believe that all *paidia*-based games are fictional, but only some *ludus* games are. Here is why.

In order to be fiction, games must communicate something that could be, but is not believed. As prescriptive artifacts whose purpose is to propose specialized forms of agency—agency different from the pursuit of practical goals of everyday life—games rely on rules, but rules are not the kind of thing that can be true or false, believed or not-believed; rather, they are "in effect" or "not in effect": for instance, the rules of chess are in effect within the game of chess but not in everyday life nor within the game of go.[6] In the case of chess, the rules tell the players what actions are possible, and nothing else: players do not try to imagine the fear of the queen as the king is being checked.[7] When game rules offer nothing to the imagination, when the game goals are purely abstract (such as putting a ball into a net) rather than being states you would want to pursue in real life, they do not induce make-believe.

For a game to induce make-believe, and therefore to be fictional, the actions of the player must count as the performance of a recognizable type of real-world action. In other words, the game must be mimetic.[8] When I swing a tennis racket or move a piece in chess, I do nothing more than swinging a racket or moving a chess piece. In an improvised game of make-believe, by contrast, putting a doll in a crib counts as putting a baby to sleep, and running away from a stump counts as fleeing from a bear. In a video game, manipulating the controls can counts as rescuing princesses, killing dragons, opening doors with keys, casting spells on enemies, traveling through a world, equipping one's avatar with a sword—the list is endless. In an abstract video game like *Tetris*, manipulating controls also counts as something else, namely making a shape fall into a space where it will fit snugly with other shapes, but this something else has no practical equivalent in real life. Killing dragons admittedly does not occur in real life either, but if dragons existed and threatened people, then killing them would have practical significance, while making a shape fall into a space where it fits snugly with other pieces only has meaning because of the conventions of a game.

An early attempt to invest games with mimetic content was to decorate game boards, especially the boards of dice games played on monocursal labyrinths, such as *Chutes and Ladders* or what is known in French as *Le jeu de l'oie*, according to narrative themes. From *The Path to Good Life and Heaven* represented in the ancient Indian versions of this game, to the seventeenth-century *Labyrinth of Ariosto*, which represented episodes of the poem *Orlando Furioso*, to the nineteenth-century *Game of Life*, decorated games boards injected narrative interest into a set of rules devoid of strategic interest because they allow few or no choices. I call these games pseudo-fictions, because the narrative themes of the board do not affect gameplay: as Katie Salen and Eric Zimmerman have shown, they are all based on an abstract algorithm that consists of adding or subtracting randomly chosen numbers (determined by the throw of the dice) until one of the players reaches a certain total (corresponding to the number of the last square) regardless of the board decorations. *Labyrinth of Ariosto* could, however, be regarded as a prop in a game of make-believe, and therefore as a fiction, to the extent that it invites the players to impersonate the characters of Ariosto's poem and to recite parts of it when they land on certain squares. In this case, the abstract board game is only a pretext for engaging in make-believe, and the players do not care about who is the first one to reach the final square.

The fictionalization of games received an enormous boost from computer technology. If computer games are so popular, it is because they create a multisensory fictional world and engage the player—whether or not he or she identifies with an avatar—in an activity that affects the development of this world. Abstract computer games, like Tetris or PacMan to some extent,[9] have become exceedingly rare since the technology was sufficiently developed to produce realistic game worlds. Whether mimetic computer games rely on a scripted narrative content, as in what Jesper Juul calls games of progression, or allow players to create their own stories, as in simulation games like The Sims, each playing of the game produces a new set of fictional truths. But computer games are not the only ones that lure players with mimetic content and invite them to a game of make-believe; table-top role-playing games have been called by Olivier Caïra "les forges de la fiction" (cf. Chapter 16 in this volume), the breeding ground where fiction is being collectively produced through an interaction between the game master, the players, the rule book, and the throws of the dice. Similarly, strategic war games, a genre developed in the nineteenth century, simulate military operations both real and imaginary by means of props, dice, and a rulebook.

I have suggested that games can be either fiction or nonfiction, depending on the presence or absence of a mimetic dimension. But nonfiction is not necessarily non-mimetic; it includes factual representation, which shares mimeticism with fiction. The question now arises of whether games can be factual representations. Aren't war games based on real battles? Isn't there a genre of computer games, known as "serious games" (Bogost, 2010), that attempts to arouse awareness of real-world issues, such as environmental damage and colonialism for *When Rivers Were Trails* (2019) or transgender experience for *Dys4ia* (Ensslin, 2022)? Moreover, doesn't the metaverse of *Second Life* allow real-world communication, such as public lectures where supposedly true facts are offered for belief? My answer is that games can be either fictional or not, but they cannot be factual. Serious games are like didactic novels: they try to make a point about the real world, but by means of invented characters and situations. They don't say "this happened," but "this could happen, so draw some conclusions." Moreover, insofar as each playing of the game generates different fictional truths, it does not reveal individual facts, but only possibilities.[10] As for the *Second Life* example, I would say that *Second Life* is not really a game in itself but a set of tools for creating a wide variety of worlds and social encounters, some of which are games and others are not. In some of these encounters, players pretend to be their avatars, and they build a space that promotes make-believe. In others, they conduct the affairs of the real world, and the function of the avatars is not to let participants pretend to be somebody else, but simply to represent them, just as participants are represented by their picture in a Zoom meeting.[11] When *Second Life* public events deal with the communication of facts, they are no longer games. Thus, games may be either fictional or nonfictional, depending on whether they are mimetic or abstract, and they can be "based on facts," like novels, but they are never factual in the way documentary films and historiography can be. Just as we can learn some facts from realistic novels (for instance, to take an example from Currie [2020], learn from *War and Peace* that the French aristocracy spoke French), we can do so from some games, especially from "serious games," but this is a matter of fishing out isolated pieces of information, rather than granting belief to the game as a whole.

Notes

1 This view is echoed by Jean-Marie Schaeffer: "I am convinced that one cannot understand what fiction is if one does not take as a starting point the fundamental mechanisms of 'doing-as-if'—of ludic feint—and of imaginative simulation, of which the genesis is observed in the games of role-playing and the daydreaming [*rêveries*] of early childhood" (Schaeffer, 2010, xii).

2 On the benefits of play, see D. W. Winnicott (edited by Tuber, 2008) and Sutton-Smith (1997); on the benefits of fiction, see Oatley (2011).

3 Does this claim extend to photography? In a 1984 article, Walton describes photography as a "transparent medium" that facilitates vision, just as glasses or telescopes do. According to this view, we see people or landscapes through photos just as we see stars through a telescope, without make-believe. Photos are, therefore, not fictional.

4 It is worth noting that in an article defining aesthetic illusion, Wolf regularly resorts to the idea of immersion: "Aesthetic illusion consists primarily of a feeling, with variable intensity, of being imaginatively and emotionally immersed in a represented world and of experiencing this world in a way similar (but not identical) to real life" (2014, 270).

5 Lavocat rejects this interpretation, but I find it very plausible, at least as far as narration is concerned.

6 This restriction of rules to the domain of the game, which is separate from the domain of real life, explains why I do not agree with Jesper Juul's (2005) claim that video games are "half real" combinations of real rules and a fictional world. If game rules were real, they would apply in everyday life, which they obviously do not.

7 I remember a computer game called Battle Chess that showed vivid battle scenes whenever a piece was taken. It taught children nothing about chess strategy because all they did was let their pieces be captured in order to watch the video. In other words, they treated the game as fiction.

8 An alternate conception of fictionality, which does not require mimeticism and, therefore, accepts abstract games like chess as fiction, is offered in Caïra (2011).

9 Some people regard the shapes that pursue PacMan as characters, more specifically as monsters, because they have names, but they lack individuality. The famous Heider and Simmel experiment (1944) has shown that people tend to narrativize the movement of abstract shapes by attributing intention and, therefore, characterhood to them; if this is the case, there may be no such thing as abstract games.

10 Similarly, simulations are not factual representations, even though they can provide useful information for the real world, because facts concern what has already happened, while simulations deal with the possible.

11 In fact, *Second Life* meetings can be regarded as a precursor of Zoom, and they have been eclipsed by it.

Works Cited

Austin, J.L. 1962. *How to Do Things with Words*. Cambridge, MA: Harvard University Press.

Baroni, Raphaël. 2017. *La Tension narrative: suspense, curiosité et surprise*. Paris: Seuil.

Bogost, Ian. 2010. *Persuasive Games: The Expressive Power of Videogames*. Cambridge, MA: MIT Press.

Caillois, Roger. (1958) 2001. *Man, Play and Games*. Translated by Meyer Barach. Urbana: University of Chicago Press.

Caïra, Olivier. 2007. *Jeux de rôle: les forges de la fiction*. Paris: CNRS.

Caïra, Olivier. 2011. *Définir la fiction. Du roman au jeu d'échecs*. Paris: Editions EHESS.

Cervantes Saavedra, Miguel de. 1994. *Don Quixote de la Mancha*. Translated by Walter Starkie. New York: Signet.

Currie, Gregory. 1990. *The Nature of Fiction*. Cambridge: Cambridge University Press.

Currie, Gregory. 2020. *Imagining and Knowing: The Shape of Fiction*. Oxford: Oxford University Press.

Ensslin, Astrid. 2022. "Videogames as Complex Narratives and Embodied Metalepsis." In *The Routledge Companion to Narrative Theory*, edited by Paul Dawson and Maria Mäkelä, 411–22. London: Routledge.

Gerrig, Richard. 1993. *Experiencing Narrative Worlds: On the Psychological Activities of Reading*. New Haven, CT: Yale University Press.

Heider, Fritz, and Marianne Simmel. 1944. "An Experimental Study of Apparent Behavior." *The American Journal of Psychology* 57, no. 2 (April): 243–59.

Juul, Jesper. 2005. *Half-Real: Video Games Between Real Rules and Fictional Worlds*. Cambridge, MA: MIT Press.

Lavocat, Françoise. 2016. *Fait et fiction: pour une frontière*. Poétique. Paris: Seuil.

Matravers, Derek. 2014. *Fiction and Narrative*. Oxford: Oxford University Press.

Murray, Janet. 2020. "Virtual/Reality: How to Tell the Difference." *Journal of Visual Culture* 19, no. 1: 11–26. https://doi.org/10.1177/1470412920906253.

Nell, Victor. 1988. *Lost in a Book: The Psychology of Reading for Pleasure*. New Haven, CT: Yale University Press.

Oatley, Keith. 2011. *Such Stuff as Dreams: The Psychology of Reading Fiction*. New York: Wiley.

Pimentel, Ken, and Kevin Teixeira. 1993. *Virtual Reality: Through the New Looking Glass*. New York: Intel and Windcrest McGraw Hill.

Robbe-Grillet, Alain. (1963) 1965. *For a New Novel: Essays on Fiction*. Translated by Richard Howard. New York: Grove Press.

Ryan, Marie-Laure. (2001) 2015. *Narrative as Virtual Reality 2: Immersion and Interactivity in Literature and Electronic Media*. Baltimore, MD: Johns Hopkins University Press.

Salen, Katie, and Eric Zimmerman. 2004. *Rules of Play*. Cambridge, MA: MIT Press.

Searle, John. 1975. "The Logical Status of Fictional Discourse." *New Literary History* 6, no. 2 (Winter) : 319–32.

Schaeffer, Jean-Marie. 2005. "Immersion." In *The Routledge Encyclopedia of Narrative Theory*, edited by David Herman, Manfred Jahn and Marie-Laure Ryan, 237–39. London: Routledge.

Schaeffer, Jean-Marie. 2010. *Why Fiction?* Translated by Dorrit Cohn. Lincoln: University of Nebraska Press.

Slater, Mel, and María V. Sanchez-Vives. 2016. "Enhancing Our Lives with Immersive Virtual Reality." *Frontiers in Robotics and AI* 3, article 74. https://doi.org/10.3389/frobt.2016.00074.

Speer, Nicole K., Jeremy R. Reynolds, Kheena M. Swallow, and Jeffrey M. Zacks. 2009. "Reading Stories Activates Neural Representations of Perceptual and Motor Experiences." *Psychological Science* 20, no. 8 (August): 989–99. https://doi.org/10.1111/j.1467-9280.2009.02397.x.

Sternberg, Meir. 1992. "Telling in Time II: Chronology, Teleology, Narrativity." *Poetics Today* 13, no. 3 (Autumn): 463–541.

Suits, Bernard. 2014. *Grasshopper: Games, Life and Utopia*. 3rd edition. Peterborough, ON: Broadview Press.

Sutton-Smith, Brian. 1997. *The Ambiguity of Play*. Cambridge, MA: Harvard University Press.

Tuber, Steven, ed. 2008. *Attachment, Play and Authenticity: A Winnicott Primer*. Lanham, MD: Jason Aronson.

Walton, Kendall. 1984. "Transparent Pictures: On the Nature of Photographic Realism." *Critical Inquiry* 11, no. 2 (December): 246–77.

Walton, Kendall. 1990. *Mimesis as Make-Believe, On the Foundations of the Representational Arts*. Cambridge, MA: Harvard University Press.

Wolf, Werner. 2014. "Illusion (Aesthetic)." In *Handbook of Narratology*, edited by Peter Hühn, Jan Christoph Meister, John Pier and Wolf Schmid, 270–87. Berlin: De Gruyter.

Zwaan, Rolf. 2005. "Situation Model." In *The Routledge Encyclopedia of Narrative Theory*, edited by David Herman, Manfred Jahn and Marie-Laure Ryan, 534–35. London: Routledge.

4

FICTIONAL EMOTIONS AND BELIEF

Eva-Maria Konrad

Our engagement with fictions not only has a considerable effect on our emotions, but arguably also affects, challenges, and improves our beliefs. These two observations are more often than not considered and reflected on apart from each other, whereas the following chapter makes a point of discussing the conjunction of beliefs and emotions with regard to fiction.[1] This relation will be regarded as one of reciprocal influence, resulting in the following leading questions: are certain beliefs prerequisites for our emotional engagement with fictions? And does our emotional engagement with fictions have an effect on our beliefs, especially with regard to understanding and learning something about these fictions, about ourselves, and about the real world?

After a preliminary paragraph addressing the definitions of central concepts, the second section will focus on the influence of certain beliefs on our emotional engagement (or better: on the possibility of our emotional engagement) with fictions. The last section will work in the opposite direction, attending to the influence of our emotional engagement with fictions on our beliefs. Though all subchapters will be informed by a philosophical perspective and, therefore, by a consistent methodology, the objects as well as the scope of the two main sections differ significantly. The second section will concentrate on the "paradox of fiction" and, therefore, on a long-lasting and extensive, but widely known discussion with a very concrete object in its focus. The subject of the last section, however, is not a similarly prevalent issue of research, nor is the section focused on a single problem. Therefore, the presentation of the debate concerning the well-known "paradox of fiction" will be kept rather short, whereas considerations on the influence of fictional emotions on our beliefs—a question that so far lacks a systematic account—will be more extensive.

Preliminary Remarks

Since the concepts of fiction, belief, and emotion are at the center of this chapter, each of them is in need of clarification. First of all, when addressing fictions, the main object of the following considerations will be fictional literature, though most of what will be said is applicable to other fictional genres and media as well. But what, then, is *fictional* literature? Does it differ from factual literature on the grounds of syntactic, narratological, referential, ontological, or pragmatic characteristics? And who is the decisive authority who assigns fictionality to artefacts—the author, the text, the reader, or an institution? After years of discussion, there is still no consensus on these questions. Nevertheless, over the last twenty years, the discussion has developed a tendency toward institutional and pragmatic

DOI: 10.4324/9781003119456-6

theories that consider fictionality to be a practice guided by certain rules that both authors and readers are aware of and usually stick to. The most prominent advocates of this view are Peter Lamarque and Stein Haugom Olsen, who claim that an "utterance is fictive (in the fictive mode) not in virtue of being made up, or of having a made-up content, but in virtue of its role or purpose" (Lamarque and Olsen, 1994, 18). Therefore, they argue, "*the fictive dimension of stories (or narratives) is explicable only in terms of a rule-governed practice, central to which are a certain mode of utterance (fictive utterance) and a certain complex of attitudes (the fictive stance)*" (Lamarque and Olsen, 1994, 32; emphasis in original; cf. also Köppe, 2008, 25; Olsen, 1981). With regard to the concept of fictionality, this will be the controlling idea in this chapter as well.

Concerning the concept of emotion, heated discussions have been conducted as well, but

[o]ne general insight granted by most contemporary theorists is that emotion involves (1) physiological, (2) evaluative, (3) motivational, and (4) phenomenological components. Although the extent to which these components are necessary or sufficient for emotion is highly contended, few would deny that each has a role to play.

(Adair, 2019, 1061f; cf. also Konrad, Petraschka, and Werner, 2018, 194f.)

When you feel overwhelmed by joy because of your toddler's first steps, your body starts to release endorphins, you appraise these first steps as an important leap toward autonomy (of your child as well as of yourself), you might feel inclined to hug and kiss your child and call your husband, and you might feel like this is one of the best feelings you have ever had. Still, it is important to note that each of the four aspects represents a gradual dimension (your body can release endorphins in greater or smaller quantities, etc.), so that even "two experiences of the same emotion-type may differ dramatically" (Friend, 2022, 262) with regard to all of the four dimensions listed by Heather Adair.

Against this background, the following considerations will focus on "fictional emotions," that is on emotions that are directed toward fictions (or fictional entities). It is important to note that speaking about "fictional emotions" does not imply that these emotions are different (in general or in kind) from our "normal" emotions. There are huge debates on this topic (cf. Friend, 2022), but the concept of "fictional emotions" itself remains neutral on the subject.

Last but not least, the concept of belief will be taken to be a propositional attitude (i.e., an attitude toward a proposition) with three important qualities. First, it has a rather close connection to the concept of truth, as the term "belief" usually refers "to the attitude we have, roughly, whenever we take something to be the case or regard it as true" (Schwitzgebel, 2019). Second, to believe something "needn't involve actively reflecting on it [...], [n]or does the term 'belief', in standard philosophical usage, imply any uncertainty or any extended reflection about the matter in question" (Schwitzgebel, 2019). And third, a belief is usually considered to be a gradual issue as well as a cognitively relatively stable attitude (cf. Friend, 2014, 232, 238).

The Impact of Beliefs on Fictional Emotions

This section is guided by the question of whether certain beliefs (or the lack of them) play a decisive role for the possibility of our emotional engagement with fictions: Are certain beliefs (or certain kinds of beliefs) necessary for responding emotionally to fictions? The most prominent discussion dealing with this issue is the debate on the so-called "paradox of fiction." This paradox consists of three *prima facie* equally plausible premises that can't be all true at the same time:

Premise 1: We have genuine/rational emotions toward fictional entities.
Premise 2: To have a genuine/rational emotion toward an entity, we must believe that this entity exists.
Premise 3: We do not believe that fictional entities exist.

The origin of this paradox is Colin Radford's article "How Can We Be Moved by the Fate of Anna Karenina?" (1975), which, together with Kendall L. Walton's paper "Fearing Fictions" (1978), initiated an extensive debate that has meanwhile experienced several turns. While Radford is taken to argue that all three premises are true and that "we are irrational, inconsistent, and incoherent in being moved" (Radford, 1995, 75) by fictions (which means to maintain the paradox), numerous attempts have been made to question and refute one (or more) of the three premises and, therefore, to solve the paradox.

Among efforts to refute premise (1), Walton's account of quasi-emotions is the most prominent.[2] He argues that the emotions we experience phenomenologically during an artistic encounter resemble our emotions in everyday circumstances very closely, but that they are unique in one regard: whereas our bodily as well as our affective responses directed toward fictional objects (characters, situations, etc.) are very similar, if not identical, to our bodily and affective responses directed toward real entities (objects, people, situations etc.), fictional emotions run in an "offline mode" (cf. Walton, 1997, 43). In other words, they lack the motivational component of our everyday emotions. A person watching a horror movie usually does not "flee the theater, call the police, warn his family" (Walton, 1978, 7), but remains more or less calmly in her seat. According to Walton, the reason for this "abnormal" behavior is that fictional emotions are not caused by beliefs, but only by make-beliefs: the movie-goer Charles knows that he is not *actually* endangered by the approaching green slime and that the object of his fear, the slime, is only fictional. Charles only *imagines* to be genuinely afraid of the slime and to fear it, and therefore, this make-belief does not cause fear, but "only" quasi-fear. If fictional emotions are quasi-emotions in this sense, premise (1) is invalidated.

Other accounts try to weaken premise (3), with two strategies being the most salient: one way to undermine premise (3) is to argue in the wake of Samuel Coleridge's adage of a "willing suspension of disbelief" that during the process of receiving fiction we actually *do* believe in the existence of fictional entities (situations, etc.), or at least we do not disbelieve in their existence (cf. Yanal, 1999, Ch. 7; Suits, 2006). According to these approaches, then, it is not true that we do not believe that fictional entities exist—at least not *while* we are reading—and therefore, premise (3) can be dismissed. Proponents of a second prominent strategy, on the other hand, advocate a realistic theory concerning fictional entities: they claim that fictional entities actually do exist—not as material entities, but, for example, as contingent abstract objects or artefacts (Novitz, 1987; Reicher-Marek, 2014; Thomasson, 1999).

For years now, however, the most prominent way to dissolve the paradox of fiction has been to challenge premise (2). As Robert Stecker summarizes already in 2011,

> now virtually no one accepts (2). For one thing it is far too strong. This can be seen when we recall that we can pity people who lived in the past and who no longer exist. We can pity those who will live in a hypothetical future. We can also feel emotions about states of affairs that we know have not been actualized and may never become actualized such as fear for the next big earthquake in the Midwest. In such a case we do not believe that the object of emotion exists. Finally, we seem to be capable of irrational emotions such as those that are brought on by phobias, where we may know that we are in no danger yet are still afraid.
>
> *(Stecker, 2011, 295)*

If, as this line of argumentation goes, a belief in the existence of objects is not a necessary condition for our having genuine emotions toward them, then premise (2) is wrong. Therefore, the puzzle has seemed to be solved for more than ten years now.

Amazingly enough, however, the debate on the paradox of fiction and the questions related to it is still ongoing.[3] The reasons can be seen in recent developments in at least three different areas. First, progress in (neuro)psychological research in emotions in general as well as in the way we experience fictions brought new outcomes to light that were incorporated into the debate on the paradox of fiction and had a considerable impact on it. A new era of interdisciplinary research between (neuro)psychologists and philosophers seems to have begun, and promises to find new problems as well as new solutions with regard to the issues the paradox is concerned with (cf. Cova, Garcia, and Sennwald, 2014; Sperduti et al., 2016). Second, the development of new media and, accordingly, new areas of research about them also lead us to ask old questions anew. Interactive fiction, for example, has challenged the idea that fictional emotions lack a motivational component. When we play videogames (especially virtual reality games), we obviously interact with the objects and characters in the fictional world (cf. van de Mosselaer, 2018). Adding interactive fictions to the picture is, therefore, a challenge as well as an asset to the seemingly solved paradox of fiction. Third, there has been a tendency in recent years to go back to the roots and to take a closer look especially at the initial papers of Radford and Walton once again. This resulted in surprising new findings: for one thing, it has been argued that neither Walton nor Radford have ever espoused cognitivism—and, therefore, never defended premise (2) after all (cf. Dos Santos, 2017; Friend, 2022). For another thing, it turns out that Walton is not completely consistent in his statements on the genuineness of quasi-emotions either. In "Fearing Fictions," he seems to contrast genuine emotions with quasi-emotions and emphasizes, "I don't mean that there is a special kind of fear, make-believe fear, which [the movie-goer] Charles experiences. What he actually experiences, his quasi-fear feelings, are not feelings of fear" (Walton, 1978, 22). In his later paper "Spelunking, Simulation, and Slime. On being Moved by Fiction," on the other hand, Walton argues that fictional emotions *are* genuine, but that they are of a different *kind* than "normal" emotions because of their "offline mode":

> It goes without saying that we *are* genuinely moved by novels and films and plays, that we respond to works of fiction with real emotion. [...] My negative claim is *only* that our genuine emotional responses to works of fiction do not involve, literally, fearing, grieving for, admiring fictional characters.
>
> *(Walton, 1997, 38)*[4]

So either the quasi-emotions we experience during a fictional encounter are no genuine emotions at all or they *are* genuine emotions, but of a different kind than "normal" emotions. In view of these recent developments, there seems no end in sight for the discussions on the paradox of fiction.

The Impact of Fictional Emotions on Beliefs

In complete contrast to the debate on the paradox of fiction, research on the question of whether and how fictional emotions can have an impact on our beliefs is rather scarce. Of course, for several decades, there has been an enormous output of publications on the relation between works of fiction and knowledge, and the debate on fictions and emotions is almost equally extensive. These two fields of investigation, however, rarely intersect, and there are reasons for this: the discussion on literature and knowledge concentrates in large part on the conveyance of propositional knowledge, and since fictional emotions are not available in propositional form and do not immediately result in propositional knowledge, the impact of fictional emotions on beliefs is not in the direct focus of this ramified debate. *If* emotions are addressed in these contexts, research is mostly concerned with the question of how fictions can improve and refine our emotions—and therefore, with an emotional education through fictions, but not with an acquisition of new beliefs. So, instead of focusing on the impact of fictional emotions on beliefs, current research on fictional literature is predominantly concerned either with fictional emotions, but not with beliefs, or with beliefs, but not with fictional emotions.

Nevertheless, some of the most topical discussions in today's research *could* be paraphrased in terms of a relation between fictional emotions and beliefs. Parts of the debate on empathy and fiction, for example, could be interpreted as a discussion on the acquisition of practical knowledge or knowledge by acquaintance by reading fiction. If one goes through the monographs and papers, however, it is inevitable to conclude that this context is almost never established (and sometimes even explicitly refuted) within the research on empathy and fiction.[5] Since an ascription of concepts and contexts that are atypical to the respective discussions does not seem meaningful and should be avoided, this section tries to map the field by characterizing some of the most prominent (and, at the same time, paradigmatic) accounts that have actually given thought to the influence of fictional emotions on our beliefs—beliefs about the fictional text itself, about ourselves (especially about our emotions and higher-order beliefs about our beliefs), and about the real world. For this purpose, this section is structured by the three different kinds of knowledge acquisition these approaches focus on: knowledge by acquaintance (or "knowledge what it is like"), practical knowledge (or "knowledge how"), and understanding (that is, in a sense, propositional knowledge or "knowledge that").

Two final remarks should be added: First, this chapter cannot delve into the controversial issue of the relations of these types of knowledge.[6] It only assumes that there *is* a relation and that, therefore, any acquisition of practical knowledge or of knowledge by acquaintance either is or results in an acquisition of propositional knowledge (and that is: of beliefs) as well. Second, it is important to note that the chapter continues to speak of "knowledge" only to simplify matters, but not to determine that all alterations of beliefs have to result in knowledge. Some of the presented accounts make this strong assertion, but others only have a mere improvement of the epistemic status in mind that lacks the conditions of truth and justification. In this sense, an alteration of beliefs caused by fictional emotions is obviously a gradual matter.

Accounts claiming that our emotional engagement with fictions provides knowledge by acquaintance mostly imply the following two premises: first, we can only get to know the phenomenal quality of an emotion by actually experiencing the emotion; second, the phenomenal quality of emotions toward fictional entities and the phenomenal quality of emotions toward real entities do not differ from each other (at least not in decisive ways) (cf. Feagin, 1996, 6). If one approves of these assumptions, the thesis immediately suggests itself that by engaging emotionally with fictions, we can gain knowledge about what it is like to have a certain emotion, about what it is like to be in a certain situation, and also about what it is like to evaluate an object emotionally.

One prominent approach that is in accordance with this line of argument is the one Dorothy Walsh offers in her *Literature and Knowledge*. Walsh's core idea is that by reading literary art we acquire knowledge "in the sense of realizing by living through" (Walsh, 1969, 101). Our engagement with literature entails, according to Walsh, not only the experience of something given, but more importantly also a realization of what it is like to experience this given—a moment of self-reflection. Literary art's genuine quality is, therefore, to "provide [...] us with experience of experience" (Walsh, 1969, 124), with an "inside view" (Walsh, 1969, 117) of what it is like to have a certain experience.

As Walsh's focus on the concept of experience already indicates, her arguments heavily rely on an emotional engagement with fictions—and even more than meets the eye. First, most of her examples deal with fictional emotions. When she illustrates her concept of "experiencing in the sense of living through," for instance, she refers to pain: "Pain is experienced as phenomenally subjective; it is 'in me.' [...] Thus, I know more than that I am in pain, I know more than the pain, I know what it is like for me to suffer this pain" (Walsh, 1969, 102f.). Second, and more importantly, Walsh explicitly includes emotional engagement with fiction in her theory when she states in her concluding remarks that

> what literary art presents is designed to elicit a full response, sensuous, intellectual, and emotional, not separated but interfused. It is this fullness of presentation and fullness of response that accounts for the sense of immediacy. Knowing by living through is distinguishably different from knowing through the process of inference, and the sense of its being lived experience is associated with this, for, however much any particular realization may involve an emphasis on the sensuous, or the intellectual, or the emotional, this is only a matter of emphasis.
>
> *(Walsh, 1969, 138)*

These considerations were and continue to be influential and have elicited the development of a number of related approaches either in the wake of or in critical analysis of Walsh's account.[7] One of them is presented by Susan Feagin who argues in her *Reading with Feeling* that one of the most salient values of our engagement with fiction (and of our appreciation of fiction) is the way it improves a mental capacity she calls "affective flexibility" (Feagin, 1996, 238): This

> stretching is accomplished [...] through exploring different affective directions. One way is to have a new emotion [...]. Another way to do the stretching is to experience familiar emotions in response to new things. And finally, a third way is when one has an experience that one identifies as an emotion or feeling but which one had not individuated as such before.
>
> *(Feagin, 1996, 200)*

Although, in general, Feagin is less interested in the cognitive merits of fictional literature than in its effects on "the affective side of our minds" (Feagin, 1996, 242), her account resembles Walsh's in its concentration on experiential knowledge gained by simulating what it is like "to be a certain sort of person or to live through a certain type of situation" (Feagin, 1996, 111). When reading fictional literature, one empathizes with a fictional character, that is, "one 'shares' an emotion, feeling, desire, or mood of that character. The 'sharing' [...] is done through a simulation" (Feagin, 1996, 83). By simulating mental processes and activities in this way, one acquires "knowledge what it is like." As a consequence, according to Feagin, her simulation account not only demonstrates how reading fictional literature can enlarge our affective repertoire, but it also "helps to show that imagination can serve epistemic purposes, precisely because it provides a bit of conceptual apparatus—the notion of simulation—for distinguishing imaginal activities that count as knowledge from those that do not" (Feagin, 1996, 111).

Alongside accounts that concentrate on knowledge by acquaintance when considering fictional emotions' impact on our beliefs, there are other approaches that focus on fictional emotions' influence on our practical knowledge. One of them is Tilmann Köppe's "theory of emotion-based practical learning processes" (Köppe, 2008, 198).[8] Köppe's core idea is that fictional literature can influence processes of practical reasoning in different respects, and that practical reasoning can in turn result in a manifestation of practical knowledge (cf. Köppe 2008, 203). In other words, Köppe considers practical knowledge to be "the result of successful practical reasoning" (Köppe, 2008, 157).[9] But what is successful practical reasoning? As Köppe elucidates, it implies two necessary conditions: a reliable epistemic ground based on theoretical knowledge and an evaluative statement resulting in action-oriented intentions (cf. Köppe, 2008, 159). With reference to Patricia Greenspan and Martha Nussbaum (cf. Greenspan, 1981, 1988; Nussbaum, 2001, 2004), Köppe considers emotions to be among the most prominent (and with regard to fictional literature most relevant) ways of reacting evaluatively to objects or circumstances. According to Köppe, therefore, fictional literature can lead to an acquisition of practical knowledge by its influence on processes of practical reasoning—and, that is, on our affective evaluative statements.

Köppe thinks of this influence basically in terms of a "guidance of our attention" (Köppe, 2008, 180):[10] If we want to evaluate what is good and right for us, we have to be able to get a correct idea of the action situation we are in. The better our ability to perceive and observe the characteristics that are action-relevant, the more and the better the data that influence our evaluation—and, therefore, the better the result of our judgement. As maintained by Köppe, literature serves as a playing field or practice area in this respect (cf. Köppe, 2008, 190): In accordance with Martha Nussbaum, he is of the opinion that reading fiction "cultivate[s] our ability to see and care for particulars" (Nussbaum, 1990, 184)—and that means, among other things, that by reading fictional literature we train and exercise our ability to develop and interpret situation-related emotions. In this way, our emotional engagement with fiction improves our practical reasoning (and therefore leads to practical knowledge) by its impact on three different levels of judgements: It can not only affect, modify and improve our evaluation of (1) the fictive world, but also of (2) certain aspects of the real world, and (3) of our pre-existing beliefs about ourselves (cf. Köppe, 2008, 162). As Köppe emphasizes, his theory hereby also helps to explain common intuitions with regard to our engagement with fictions, as, for example, that the kind of knowledge one can gain by reading fictional literature is similar to the kind of knowledge one can acquire by living through real situations (cf. Köppe, 2008, 200): one can only get to know the phenomenal dimension of an emotion by having the emotion—an intuition lying at the heart of Walsh's account.[11]

A different debate that also immediately relates to fictional emotions' impact on practical knowledge is the discussion on the influence of our imaginative involvement with fictions on our moral lives. Peter Lamarque, for example, argues that one should think of this impact not in terms of moral lessons stated or implied by works of fiction but as moral visions expressed in it: "A competent reader might hope to learn from the literary work not by formulating a derived moral principle but by acquiring a new vision or perspective on the world" (Lamarque, 1995, 244). This new perspective is the result of the synergy of two elements, namely an internal and an external perspective on the fictional text: "Under the internal perspective, fictional characters are imagined to be fellow humans in real predicaments, objects of sympathy and concern, similar to ourselves in many respects" (Lamarque, 1995, 247). It is obvious that with regard to the internal perspective, fictional emotions play a decisive role. The internal perspective, however, is guided by the external perspective on the text—"an awareness of modes of representation [that] dictates the kind of involvement appropriate from the internal perspective" (Lamarque, 1995, 248). Which fictional emotions are adequate is, therefore, according to Lamarque, not only dependent on the presented content, but even more on the presentation of the fictional content itself. For this reason, "a different kind of moral appropriation will be available under different thematic interpretations of a work" (Lamarque 1995, 249).[12]

David Novitz's account on the connection of fiction, emotion, and knowledge, on the other hand, is much broader than the approaches mentioned so far. He advocates the opinion that "there is no one way in which we learn from literary works of art. There is, rather, a *pot-pourri* of ways, a veritable medley of methods, for acquiring beliefs, knowledge, skills, and values of one sort or another" (Novitz, 1987, 142). According to Novitz, we can, therefore, gain all kinds of knowledge by reading literature: knowledge that, knowledge how, as well as knowledge what it is like. He claims, however, that although the debate often concentrates on the acquisition of propositional knowledge, "a good deal of what we learn from fiction is practical rather than propositional or attitudinal" (Novitz, 1987, 119). Accordingly, Novitz focuses particularly on practical knowledge (in the sense of strategic and conceptual skills) and empathic knowledge (in the sense of experiencing what it is like to be in certain, often demanding situations) that fictional literature can afford. In all this, he considers emotions to play a central role: If we want to learn from fiction, we have to understand it—and one "can properly understand fiction [...] only if one is in a position to be appropriately moved by the fate of its characters" (Novitz, 1987, 87). A necessary "condition of being appropriately moved by, and so understanding, fiction [is, in turn], that one should respond imaginatively to it" (Novitz, 1987, 87).[13] This idea has far-reaching implications: Novitz considers our emotional engagement with fiction not only to be a necessary condition for a proper understanding of fiction, but also a necessary condition for learning "about our world from fiction" (Novitz, 1987, 130)—a view that closely resembles Jenefer Robinson's.

Jenefer Robinson's perspective on the influence of fictional emotions on our beliefs is less concerned with learning than with understanding (which can be explained as knowledge gained by the act of comprehending and therefore—at least partly—as propositional knowledge).[14] Robinson is convinced that

> if we do arrive at beliefs about what we have read after we have finished reading, those beliefs depend essentially upon the emotional experience of reading the novel. [...] [I]t is only through an emotional experience of a novel that one can genuinely learn from it.
>
> *(Robinson, 2005, 156)*[15]

So, fictional emotions play an important role in the acquisition of an understanding of works of fiction and thus enable us to come to an interpretation of the works. In other words, fictional emotions significantly influence our beliefs about (the meaning of) the works of fiction that arouse these emotions.[16]

Robinson offers three arguments to support this claim. First of all, she argues that fictional emotions direct the readers' attention to significant passages of a work of fiction:

> The emotions function to alert us to important aspects of the story such as plot, characters, setting, and point of view. Especially in reading the great realist novels of the Western tradition, our emotions can lead us to discover subtleties in character and plot that would escape a reader who remains emotionally uninvolved in the story.
>
> *(Robinson, 2005, 107; cf. also 108, 111; cf. similarly Elgin, 2008)*

Second, Robinson repeatedly claims that emotional responses toward fictional characters and events also provide "an important source of data" (Robinson, 2005, 125; cf. also 116, 122) adding to the information the works explicitly present: "[O]ur emotional reactions to a novel are [...] a means of filling in the gaps [in the sense of Wolfgang Iser's 'Unbestimmtheitsstellen'], and hence also an important part of *understanding* the novel" (Robinson, 2005, 125). Third, she comes up with a logical deduction following the premise that emotion processes in real life basically work the same way as emotion processes in the context of fiction: "[U]nderstanding character is relevantly like understanding real people, and [since] [...] understanding real people is impossible without emotional engagement with them and their predicaments" (Robinson, 2005, 126; cf. also 105, 128), an emotional engagement with fictional characters is necessary for an adequate understanding of them. Due to the fact that Robinson is also convinced that "understanding characters is a *sine qua non* of understanding the works in which they figure" (Robinson, 2005, 131), emotional engagement becomes a highly relevant factor for understanding (and then interpreting) works of fiction.[17]

But this is not the only kind of influence of fictional emotions on our beliefs that Robinson concentrates on: As she emphasizes, fictional emotions can also teach us about life itself. Though this " 'sentimental education,' an education by the emotions" (Robinson, 2005, 156) does not necessarily entail the development of beliefs immediately, Robinson considers it at least to be possible that it has an impact on our beliefs in a second step: as a result of the emotional experiences readers have while reading, they are "led to reflect on them and to discover their significance. [...] [I]f all goes well, [they] eventually reach understanding and acquire new beliefs" (Robinson, 2005, 159). This impact of fictional emotions on our belief system can actually be very profound and long-lasting:

> if my emotional reactions to the novel are strong enough, then they in turn may become encoded in emotional memory, making new connections between affective appraisals and bodily responses (somatic markers) and influencing my thoughts and beliefs long after I have finished the novel.
>
> *(Robinson, 2005, 116)*

Conclusion

The different suggestions and solutions presented in the last two sections prove that the relation of fictional emotions and beliefs poses a serious challenge for anyone who tries to explain the influence of one on the other. Nevertheless, I am convinced that to get a fuller picture of our actual practice with works of fiction, it is necessary to unite the perspectives of these two sections and not to take only one direction of impact into account, but to reflect on the *reciprocal* influence of fictional emotions and beliefs. Proceeding from Robinson's considerations on a cognitive monitoring of our emotional responses to fiction, one could argue that, more often than not, fictional emotions and beliefs constitute an "affective-hermeneutic circle": Our initial emotional response to, say, a certain character in a fictional text is primarily guided by the information the text has offered so far as well as by our prior (partly stereotypical) knowledge of and emotional experience with real people and with other literary characters similar to the one in question. As we go on reading, we gather more information on this character—her background, her motives, her wishes, hopes, and fears—and, therefore, get to know and understand her better. This might force us not only to adjust our emotional response to the character, but also to become more aware of what is apparently emotionally significant to us, of how our emotions get triggered by certain character traits or situations and maybe even of certain prejudices that caused our initial emotional reaction—a process that will indubitably affect our beliefs about the real world as well. Our adapted emotional response as well as our more reflected (or even changed) beliefs might, then, enable us to perceive ignored details and aspects of the character and of the story that we were unaware of in light of our initial reaction. Maybe our incipient sympathy or antipathy tempted us to overlook some traits that didn't fit into our first image of the character and her situation and that our attention is directed to only now. In this way, an adjusted emotional response can lead to an even better understanding of the character and, therefore, of the text as a whole—and, once again, also of ourselves, and of our outlook, disposition, and mindset. The deepened understanding of the character as well as of ourselves emerging from these new insights might incite us to an altered emotional reaction once again, and so forth. In other words, one could argue that an adjustment and improvement of our fictional emotions always goes hand in hand with an adjustment and improvement of our beliefs—about the work of fiction, about ourselves and about the real world.

Notes

1 This chapter is not concerned with the relation of emotion and belief in general. The question of whether beliefs are a component part of emotions themselves (and issues related to this discussion) will not be addressed.
2 It should be noted that Walton's paper does not respond to Radford's earlier article, but seems to have originated independently. Nevertheless, in the discussion on the paradox of fiction, Walton's considerations are usually regarded as a refutation of the first thesis of the paradox anyway.
3 For a comprehensive bibliography of papers on the paradox of fiction published between 1975 and 2018, see Konrad, Petraschka, and Werner (2018).

4 Cf. also Stecker (2011, 298, Fn. 7): "For Walton, Charles's quasi-fear consists of the physiological changes in his body and the phenomenal state they engender. It does not consist in Charles's fearing the slime in his imagination, or as Walton puts it in *Mimesis*, his fictionally being afraid of the slime. But it is all too easy to forget this and start thinking of quasi-fear as the latter."

5 Gregory Currie, who explicitly relates empathy and belief with regard to fictions, is one of the few exceptions. Cf. Currie (2020, 153): "[F]ictions might affect things other than beliefs. There is fiction's supposed capacity to enlarge our skill or know-how; many deny that this enhancement of practical knowledge need involve change in belief (Nussbaum, 1990). I'm happy to grant that change in empathic abilities is possible without change in belief, but it is often likely to result in changed beliefs: your sharpened empathic powers are likely to lead you to new thoughts about the lives of others. So fictions that affect empathy are likely to affect belief as well."

6 Cf. Klein (2005, 525): "Whether the reduction of one form of knowledge to another is ultimately successful is an area of contention among epistemologists."

7 Walsh's emphasis on "[k]nowing by vicarious living through" (Walsh, 1969, 129) could be seen as a trailblazer for the actual debate on literature and empathy. In addition, her statement that artists "can evoke the imaginative experience of apprehending things in a certain valuational perspective" (Walsh, 1969, 131) is highly compatible with views like those of Martha Nussbaum or Patricia Greenspan, who think of emotions in evaluative terms (see below). For critical assessment of Walsh's theses (and of the idea of acquiring knowledge by acquaintance through fictional literature in general) cf. Lamarque/Olsen (1994, 370–78).

8 "Theorie gefühlsbasierter praktischer Lernprozesse" (my translation).

9 "Praktisches Wissen ist das Resultat gelungener praktischer Überlegungen" (my translation).

10 "Aufmerksamkeitssteuerung" (my translation).

11 Köppe, therefore, also shares Walsh's opinion that emotions entail a self-reflexive element: "They [fictional emotions] are not only evaluative statements on certain objects they are directed to, but they are an (implicit) comment on my own capacity of experience, my needs and my dispositions of value as well" (Köppe, 2008, 200f.; my translation of "Es handelt sich nicht nur um wertende Stellungnahmen zu bestimmten Gegenständen, auf die sie gerichtet sind, sondern in ihnen liegt sozusagen auch ein (impliziter) Kommentar über meine eigene Erlebnisfähigkeit, meine Bedürfnislage und meine Wertdispositionen."). Cf. in this manner also Smuts (2014, 134).

12 Martha Nussbaum is another prominent thinker who is concerned with the ethical dimension of our engagement with fictions. Nussbaum argues "that certain literary texts (or texts similar to these in certain relevant ways) are indispensable to a philosophical inquiry in the ethical sphere: not by any means sufficient, but sources of insight without which the inquiry cannot be complete" (Nussbaum, 1992, 23f.). Nevertheless, Nussbaum is keen to demonstrate the "richness of the connections between emotion and judgment" (Nussbaum, 1992, 42), not the connections between emotion and belief.

13 For criticism on Novitz's concept of imagination and his "romantic theory of knowledge" (Novitz 1987, 3) cf. Lamarque (1989) and Carroll (1990).

14 For a discussion on the conceptual localization of "understanding" within the field of propositional and practical knowledge see Currie (2020, Chapter 5).

15 Robinson applies her claim particularly to "realistic novels, plays, and films" (Robinson, 2005, 106).

16 Robinson is not completely consistent in her formulations concerning the extent of this impact, however. There are weaker wordings where she only asserts that "our emotional responses to novels, plays, and movies help us to *understand* them, to understand characters, and grasp the significance of events in the plot" (Robinson, 2005, 105). Elsewhere, Robinson promotes a much stronger claim: "[N]othing else can do the job that emotions do. Without appropriate emotional responses, some novels simply *cannot* be adequately understood" (Robinson, 2005, 107; cf. similarly Miall, 1989; Novitz, 1987). For critical assessment of the strong thesis see Feagin (2009) and Konrad, Petraschka, and Werner (2019).

17 It is important to add that, according to Robinson, fictional emotions don't fulfil their educational function detached from all other contexts. She repeatedly insists that a cognitive monitoring of our emotional responses to works of fiction plays a crucial role in the process of understanding and interpreting as well: "When we respond emotionally to some incident in a story, there is an initial unthinking or instinctive appraisal [...], which fixes attention and produces a physiological response and is then succeeded by cognitive evaluations of the incident. There is then likely to be extensive reappraisal in the light of succeeding events in the novel. When we *reflect* about our experience of the novel, one of the things we are doing is engaging in *cognitive monitoring* of our earlier responses. Finally, when we have reflected enough so that we think we have made sense of the incident in the light of preceding and succeeding events in the novel, we may report on our reflections about our experience of the work by offering an *interpretation* of the work as a whole" (Robinson, 2005, 122f.; cf. also 115–17; 134f.).

Works Cited

Adair, Heather V. 2019. "Updating Thought Theory: Emotion and the Non-Paradox of Fiction." *Pacific Philosophical Quarterly* 100, no. 4 (December): 1055–73.

Carroll, Noël. 1990. "Review of Knowledge, Fiction & Imagination, by David Novitz." *The Journal of Aesthetics and Art Criticism* 48, no. 2 (Spring): 167–69.

Cova, Florian, Amanda Garcia and Vanessa Sennwald. 2014. "Is What I'm Feeling Genuine? Fiction vs. Reality". Unpublished manuscript.

Currie, Gregory. 2020. *Imagining and Knowing: The Shape of Fiction.* Oxford: Oxford University Press.

Dos Santos, Miguel F. 2017. "Walton's Quasi-Emotions Do Not Go Away." *The Journal of Aesthetics and Art Criticism* 75, no. 3 (Summer): 265–74.

Elgin, Catherine Z. 2008. "Emotions and Understanding." In *Epistemology and Emotions*, edited by Georg Brun, Ulvi Doğuoğlu and Dominique Kuenzle, 33–50. Aldershot: Ashgate.

Feagin, Susan L. 1996. *Reading with Feeling. The Aesthetics of Appreciation.* Ithaca, NY and London: Cornell University Press.

Feagin, Susan L. 2009. "Affects in Appreciation." In *The Oxford Handbook of Philosophy of Emotion*, edited by Peter Goldie, 635–50. Oxford: Oxford University Press.

Friend, Stacie. 2014. "Believing in Stories." In *Aesthetics and the Sciences of Mind*, edited by Greg Currie, Matthew Kieran, Aaron Meskin and Job Robson, 227–48. Oxford: Oxford University Press.

Friend, Stacie. 2022. "Emotion in Fiction: State of the Art." *British Journal of Aesthetics* 62, no. 2 (April): 257–71.

Greenspan, Patricia C. 1981. "Emotions as Evaluations." *Pacific Philosophical Quarterly* 62: 158–69.

Greenspan, Patricia C. 1988. *Emotions and Reasons: An Enquiry into Emotional Justification.* New York: Routledge.

Klein, Peter D. 2005. "Knowledge, Concept of." In *The Shorter Routledge Encyclopedia of Philosophy*, edited by Edward Craig, 524–32. New York: Routledge.

Konrad, Eva-Maria, Thomas Petraschka, and Christiana Werner. 2018. "The Paradox of Fiction – A Brief Introduction into Recent Developments, Open Questions, and Current Areas of Research, including a Comprehensive Bibliography from 1975 to 2018." *Journal of Literary Theory* 12, no. 2 (September): 193–203.

Konrad, Eva-Maria, Thomas Petraschka, and Christiana Werner. 2019. "Are Emotional Responses Necessary for an Adequate Understanding of Literary Texts?" *Debates in Aesthetics* 14, no. 1: 45–59.

Köppe, Tilmann. 2008. *Literatur und Erkenntnis. Studien zur kognitiven Signifikanz fiktionaler literarischer Werke.* Paderborn: Mentis.

Lamarque, Peter. 1989. Review of *Knowledge, Fiction & Imagination*, by David Novitz. *Philosophy and Literature* 13, no. 2 (October): 365–74.

Lamarque, Peter. 1995. "Tragedy and Moral Value." *Australasian Journal of Philosophy* 73, no. 2: 239–49.

Lamarque, Peter, and Stein Haugom Olsen. 1994. *Truth, Fiction, and Literature: A Philosophical Perspective.* Oxford: Clarendon Press.

Miall, David S. 1989. "Beyond the Schema Given. Affective Comprehension of Literary Narratives." *Cognition and Emotion* 3, no. 1: 55–78.

Novitz, David. 1987. *Knowledge, Fiction & Imagination.* Philadelphia, PA: Temple University Press.

Nussbaum, Martha. (1990) 1992. *Love's Knowledge: Essays on Philosophy and Literature.* Oxford and New York: Oxford University Press.

Nussbaum, Martha. 2001. *Upheavals of Thought: The Intelligence of Emotion.* Cambridge: Cambridge University Press.

Nussbaum, Martha. 2004. "Emotions as Judgments of Value and Importance." In *Thinking About Feeling: Contemporary Philosophers on Emotions*, edited by Robert C. Solomon, 307–35. Oxford: Oxford University Press.

Olsen, Stein Haugom. 1981. "Literary Aesthetics and Literary Practice." *Mind* 90, no. 360 (October): 521–41.

Radford, Colin. 1975. "How Can We Be Moved by the Fate of Anna Karenina?" *Proceedings of the Aristotelian Society, Supplementary Volume* 49: 67–80.

Radford, Colin. 1995. "Fiction, Pity, Fear, and Jealousy." *The Journal of Aesthetics and Art Criticism* 53, no. 1 (Winter): 71–75.

Reicher-Marek, Maria E. 2014. "Ontologie Fiktiver Gegenstände." In *Fiktionalität. Ein interdisziplinäres Handbuch*, edited by Tobias Klauk and Tilmann Köppe, 159–89. Berlin and Boston: de Gruyter.

Robinson, Jenefer. 2005. *Deeper than Reason: Emotion and its Role in Literature, Music, and Art.* Oxford: Oxford University Press.

Schwitzgebel, Eric. 2019. "Belief." In *The Stanford Encyclopedia of Philosophy* (Winter 2021 Edition), edited by Edward N. Zalta. https://plato.stanford.edu/archives/win2021/cite.html.

Smuts, Aaron. 2014. "Painful Art and the Limits of Well-Being." In *Suffering Art Gladly: The Paradox of Negative Emotion in Art*, edited by Jerrold Levinson, 123–52. New York: Palgrave Macmillan.

Sperduti, Marco et al. 2016. "The Paradox of Fiction: Emotional Response Toward Fiction and the Modulatory Role of Self-Relevance." *Acta Psychologica* 165 (March): 53–59.

Stecker, Robert. 2011. "Should We Still Care about the Paradox of Fiction?" *British Journal of Aesthetics* 51, no. 3 (July): 295–308.

Suits, David B. 2006. "Really Believing in Fiction." *Pacific Philosophical Quarterly* 87, no. 3 (September): 369–86.

Thomasson, Amy. 1999. *Fiction and Metaphysics*. Cambridge: Cambridge University Press.

Van de Mosselaer, Nele. 2018. "How Can We Be Moved to Shoot Zombies? A Paradox of Fictional Emotions *and Actions* in Interactive Fiction." *Journal of Literary Theory* 12, no. 2: 279–99.

Walsh, Dorothy. 1969. *Literature and Knowledge*. Middletown, CT: Wesleyan University Press.

Walton, Kendall L. 1978. "Fearing Fictions." *The Journal of Philosophy* 75, no. 1 (January): 5–27.

Walton, Kendall L. 1997. "Spelunking, Simulation, and Slime." In *Emotion and the Arts*, edited by Mette Hjort and Sue Laver, 37–49. Oxford: Oxford University Press.

Yanal, Robert. 1999. *Paradoxes of Emotion and Fiction*. University Park, PA: Pennsylvania State University Press.

5

FICTIONAL CHARACTERS
AND BELIEF

Thomas Pavel

Reflection on literary fiction, its referential power, and its ability to persuade is particularly fruitful when it focuses on characters. Their social positions, feelings, and actions most often are borrowed, sometimes remodeled, from the actual world. Invented actors and situations always remain in touch with the general features of human life.[1] Their plausibility, therefore, is a crucial element in our understanding and appreciation of literary works. The following chapter will examine how various stages of literary reception contribute to this process and suggest that both plausibility and belief may vary between maximal and minimal intensity. Terms like "fiction" and "literature" will only refer to works that embody the results of literary imagination.[2]

Imitation and Reception

Consider Amy Dorrit, the main character in Dickens's *Little Dorrit*. What does it mean to *believe* her? For the first readers of this long novel, which was published as a serial between 1855 and 1857, as well as for its present-day readers, who often need to take a break and resume reading hours or days later, it means, at first, to follow the tacit guidelines of the fictional game which require them to immerse themselves—as spectators rather than as actual participants—in the novel's "story-world"; that is, to become familiar with its characters, starting with the main ones, and to remember that, since they all play various roles in this literary entertainment, as much as their existence, their passions, and their actions resemble those often seen in the actual world, these characters' life, Amy Dorrit's included, cannot be understood as literally true in the actual world.

Dickens's narrative, however, is *reliable*: told in the third person by an author/narrator who believes in the importance of his statements, underlines the coherence of the story, and relentlessly points to its psychological and social relevance, *Little Dorrit* expects its public to trust what it reads.[3] Accordingly, readers can assume that, although fictional, Amy Dorrit, as well as the other characters, are easy to remember, given that their family links, physical features, and moral attitudes are explicitly or implicitly stated. In the list of characters that opens the novel, Dickens informs us that Amy Dorrit, nicknamed Little Dorrit, is "the daughter of Mr. William Dorrit, a shy, retiring, affectionate little woman" (Dickens, [1857] 1963, xxvi).

The novel, therefore, helps its readers remember its characters, including Amy Dorrit, as well-established participants in its story-world. At her first appearance in Book I, Chapter 5, Little Dorrit's face is described as "pale [and] transparent [...], quick in expression, though not beautiful in feature,

DOI: 10.4324/9781003119456-7

64

its soft hazel eyes excepted" (53). In the next chapter one meets her father, Mr. Dorrit, a respectable inmate at the Marshalsea debt prison, soon followed in Chapter 7 by the narrative of Amy's birth and childhood in the same prison. During this long novel, readers discover Amy Dorrit's self-effacement, her generosity, and her deep devotion to her father, despite his being "a shy, irresolute man, but a strong assertor of the 'family dignity'" (xxv), as the list of characters sarcastically describes him. Amy Dorrit, in other words, has a fictional *personality*, which allows readers to remember who she is throughout the novel.

Both fictional and easy to recognize within the novel's reliable narrative, Amy Dorrit belongs to a specific environment, which Dickens, the author, intended to depict as significantly similar to his own and his initial readers' country, England, about ten to fifteen years before the publication of the novel, that is, before the prison of Marshalsea was closed in 1842 and imprisonment for debts ended in 1844. Within this context, readers could assess the plausibility of the story and of the characters' actions, Amy Dorrit's included. The specific fictional approach, the genre to which the work belongs, and the artistic method employed by the author shape the *framework* of the story. Reliable narratives like *Little Dorrit* tell plausible stories that happen in a well-defined social and historical context close to the actual world inhabited by its readers. Such realist stories aim at presenting the world as it is and at bringing to light the historical and social reasons *why it is so*.

Characters and their plausibility are important because narrative literature, be it realist or not, most often focuses on close relations that bring human beings together: love, family, alliances, or rivalries within communities and beyond their borders, that is, aspects of life that readers can easily identify and whose human verisimilitude they are ready to evaluate. Whereas realism depicts individual characters whose life-paths necessarily take the wider social and historical forces into account, not every single character, main or secondary, displays the most typical features of the surrounding society. Amy Dorrit's father is a self-important failure, her sister Fanny a "proud and ambitious" go-getter, and her brother Tip "a spendthrift and an idler" (both defined as such in the characters' list, xxv–xxvi), but Amy herself is deliberately presented as an exception, as a unique person, significantly different from her milieu. As the author states:

> What her pitiful look saw, at that early time, in her father, in her sister, in her brother, in the jail; how much, or how little of the wretched truth it pleased God to make visible to her; lies hidden with many mysteries. It is enough that she was inspired to be something which was not what the rest were, and to be that something, different and laborious, for the sake of the rest. Inspired? Shall we speak of the inspiration of a poet or a priest, and not of the heart impelled by love and self-devotion to the lowliest work in the lowliest way of life!
>
> *(71)*

In other words, human beings may well imitate each other given the similar conditions within which they and those around them spend their time, and yet originality, personal choices, the need to be different, and what Dickens calls "inspiration," an impulse no one knows where it comes from, are often decisive.

In the same way, the main male character, Arthur Clennam, illegitimate son of a passionate, but socially unaccepted love affair, believes that his mother is the "hard, stern, austere" Mrs. Clennam, whom Arthur's father had to marry for financial reasons and at whose request Arthur's actual mother was never allowed to see him, an interdiction so painful that she soon died. Mr. Clennam, unable to stand his legal wife's temperament, left for East Asia taking his son with him. Back in London after his father's death, Arthur, already in his early forties, does not quite know how to lead his life, but, in contrast with his weak father and stern (step)-mother, he is always honest and kind. As reliable as the narrative attempts to be, as plausible as the characters and their stories might appear thanks to the novel's realist method, the two main characters are deliberately portrayed as *exceptions.*

Plausibility, therefore, could be described as a *variable*, which depends both on the creative method, realism in this case, and on the *range* of likelihood chosen by the author. In this novel, the likelihood of Amy's personal features and of both Amy's and Arthur's behavior is close to the limit of plausibility or of probability. If one asked several readers "how many people like Amy and Arthur have you met in actual life?," the most frequent answers would probably be "very few" or "none." Although these readers may have noticed a certain similarity between Amy, Arthur and their own acquaintances concerning, say, Amy's shyness or Arthur's gentleness, they are unlikely to find the *maximal* intensity of her eagerness to serve and protect and of his inner, silent wounds. And yet, by making the characters memorable, such features attract the novel's readers. They believe Amy Dorrit or Arthur Clennam despite these characters being, to a considerable extent, unbelievable.

How is this possible? What kind of belief is involved in such cases? Are they (fictional) exceptions? Are they, on the contrary, quite frequent, perhaps signaling a rule of literary fiction? This issue is related to the crucial question of mimesis, of imitation, in art and literature. According to Socrates's well-known argument (Plato, *Republic*, 10, §596–98), to represent a bed, an artist needs to look at a real bed and paint a similar one on the canvas. Similarly, to paint someone's portrait, the artist must look at this person and capture his/her specific traits in the painting. In poems and narratives, to imitate would thus mean to observe how individuals feel and act and to describe them in literary works. However, Socrates wonders, since the actual bed copies, embodies the form or idea of bed produced by the divinity, whereas the painting copies the copy of this same form or idea, wouldn't the imitation by the artist be too far removed from the initial production of the object, that is, from its truth?

The answer came later, formulated by Plotinus, in his treatise "On Intelligible Beauty," *The Enneads*, 5.8, where he remarks that the sculptor Phidias

> Did not produce his statue of Zeus according to anything sensible, but grasping what he would be if Zeus wanted to appear before our eyes.
>
> *(Plotinus, 2018, 611)*

Way beyond imitation, the statue of Zeus incorporates and irradiates the greatness of the father of gods, stimulating viewers to believe in him, to respect and venerate him.

"Incorporate" and "irradiate" are also requirements of verbal art, as Plato's *Phaedrus* suggests. In this dialogue, Socrates distinguishes between on the one hand genuine knowledge and on the other hand the "divine madness" which, as he explains, moves our immortal soul through prophecy, religious rituals, poetry, or erotic impulses (*Phaedrus* §244b–45a). Coming from the Muses, from high above, poetic madness, allied with reason, could lead the soul on the right heavenly path. Without going into the details of Plato's and Socrates's arguments, it is enough to notice that they help turn our critical attention from the artist to the viewer's, the listener's, and the reader's reception. They are those who look, listen, or read the artwork, they vibrate to what it offers, and believe what it shows.

Transport, Participation

To describe the readers' grasp of artistic plausibility and their belief in fictional characters, let's now follow the stages of artistic reception.

First, attending the fictional game, being touched by the "divine madness" Socrates spoke about, could be called transport, in both senses of "transportation": that is, "transit" from the actual world to the fictional one, and "rapture," "elation," the state of mind this movement brings about. For the earliest English readers of *Little Dorrit*, this transport kept them in their own country, where they had to cross only a small chronological distance, from the late 1850s to a couple of decades earlier. Present-day readers of the novel, however, must travel all the way from their place and time to England and the long forgotten first half of the nineteenth century. Both kinds of readers also experience the artistic and ludic excitement of finding themselves among unknown people, most of whom are caught in difficult situations.

Since the distance that spectators and readers of fiction must cross and the nature of the territories where transport leads them varies considerably, let us briefly consider the kinds of fictional territories where this travel, this transit takes them. The most disorienting such places are those found in literary works inspired by *myths*. When the public lands in the world of Aeschylus's trilogy *Oresteia* or of Seneca's *Thyestes*, the frequent supernatural interventions as well as the scandalous violations of the closest blood links signal that readers/spectators are *not* in their home-world. The same is true about Aeschylus's *Prometheus Bound*, Sophocles's *Oedipus Rex*, and most neoclassical tragedies that much later rewrote Greek mythology. Homer and Virgil's epic poems, the ancient Indian *Mahabharata*, Ferdowsi's *Shanameh*, the *Persian Book of Kings*, the *Mabinogi* Welsh tales, the Irish *Tain*, the Islandic *Sagas*, some of the Arthurian romances, in particular Wolfram von Eschenbach's *Parzifal*, also belong here.

In Aeschylus's trilogy, the public witnesses Orestes murdering his own mother, Clytemnestra, and hears the god Apollo assert that men, not women, are crucial for children to be born. In Seneca's tragedy, spectators witness the repulsive rivalry between Atreus and his twin brother Thyestes. Similarly, in the *Saga of the Volsungs*, the Northern god Odin's visit to humans, the female characters' ability to turn into birds or simulate other women's faces and bodies, or beautiful Signy's cruelty to nine of her brothers and her adulterous links with Sigmund, the tenth one, let readers feel that the fictional transport, understood as transit from the actual world, dropped them in a stunningly unfamiliar place.

Less shocking, yet still distant from the public's everyday life, are stories that, without taking place in the "once upon a time" mythical worlds, or in their slightly tamed version narrated by ballads and fairy tales, still include *some* supernatural elements, usually in harmony with older popular beliefs in the existence of ghosts and the power of magic spells. In Shakespeare's *Hamlet*, the ghost appearance of the dead king of Denmark is at the same time surprisingly unlikely and essential for grasping the main character's moral profile and the progress of the plot.

Yet, almost simultaneously, transport understood as rapture and elation helps readers and spectators sense the inner resonance of what they see or read. Perhaps, who knows, Orestes must indeed avenge the death of his father, perhaps Signy is right to continue the fight against the enemies of the Volsungs, perhaps Hamlet's father could have come back to get justice done. The impulses that lead Orestes or Signy to act might be felt as odd, unfamiliar, yet, to some extent, as conceivable, especially since one can witness them here, now, in this play, in this Saga. How could I mistrust Hamlet's inner struggle, his way of doubting the ghost's call for revenge without, however, fully rejecting it? Perhaps I should remember that these stories include an *as though* meant to modulate the watchers or readers' belief in their plots and characters. Shouldn't I, therefore, just keep watching or reading, to get more familiar with these story-worlds?

The easiest way of reassuring oneself is to remember that Oreste's, Thyestes's, Signy's, Hamlet's, and Amy Dorrit's stories are fictions; some of them, Dickens's for instance, being easier to accept than the ancient Greek, the old Nordic or Shakespeare's. This mixture of shock and willingness to continue the *as though* game leads to the next stage of artistic reception, which consists in leaving aside the initial reservations and tacitly agreeing to observe *attentively, empathically* what goes on in the literary work.[4]

To be attentive means to notice and remember as many aspects of the story as possible, treating as doubtful only those that are presented as equivocal within the *as though* game of the work. In *Hamlet*, for instance, readers/spectators realize that the young prince questions the *truth* of the ghost's testimony, which might be a devilish temptation, but is certain that he *did* see a ghost. Concerning empathy, at this stage readers/watchers of fictional stories allow themselves to feel close to the represented characters and their actions. However difficult it might be for spectators to tolerate the murder of Clytemnestra, they can still empathize with Electra and Orestes's mourning of their father Agamemnon's death. However stupefying Signy's role in the murder of her nine brothers might seem, readers still feel for her devotion to her last brother, Sigmund. By accepting the fictional world's distant ways of being, its social and moral guiding principles, the passions, actions, and debates of its characters, readers/watchers follow and feel the action *as though* they were themselves inhabitants of this world. Given the playful nature of fiction—serious as the issues raised by this kind of game may be—this acceptance is only provisional. It means "let's just say that ...," "let us see where it might lead."

Belief in characters is similar. At this stage, one reads or watches Thyestes's, Orestes's, Signy's, Hamlet's, and Amy Dorrit's actions not unlike a member of a trial jury, who, during the testimony of a witness, conditionally trusts it, knowing well that later it might be suspected and rejected. For the time being, therefore, there is no need to remind the readers/watchers that they all are at the theater or that they are reading a book. Their limited, playful immersion in the story, their special kind of participation goes without saying. It permits observation and compassion, but, like virtually all public games, it forbids the public's intervention. As for genuine belief, the term might be too strong. We make a note of the most important elements of the story, we take them into account, yet something in us still waits.

Recognition

What we wait for is the sense that something in these fictional characters signals, evokes, resembles human features that are present in the actual world where we, watchers/readers, live. As Flint Schier (1986) argued, *iconic* artistic images directly refer to the represented objects, allowing the public to *recognize* them for what they are. This also happens in literary works, where the targets of recognition are first, actual individuals or generally accepted mythical individuals, second, concrete representatives of general social and moral features, and third, typical situations. Although actual individuals are not so frequent, the plays, novels, and films about well-known historical figures do interest readers and viewers by highlighting relevant aspects of past customs, moral perspectives, and political choices. Such works may shed light on specific past periods or reflect on more general features of power and authority. Concerning actual historical plausibility, Shakespeare's *Julius Caesar* (1599) and *Anthony and Cleopatra* (1607) closely follow Plutarch's lives of Caesar and Augustus. In many Renaissance and neoclassical historical plays, novels, and operas, however, characters are simplified and only partially dependent on precise historical knowledge.

In Racine's *Britannicus* (1669) and *Bajazet* (1672), the main characters do belong to the actual Roman and Ottoman history, respectively. Yet, since these tragedies aim at illustrating the tension between political power and erotic impulses, they also include characters and actions that have no explicit historical basis. As Roland Barthes (1964, 24–26) explained, several plots of Racine's tragedies involve authority figures falling in love, each time according to a simple logic which requires that

A has all power over B
and
A loves B who does not love A

The capital letters represent the main characters, A standing for the Roman emperor Nero in *Britannicus* and for the Sultan's favorite Roxane in *Bajazet*, while B refers to Junia, great-granddaughter of Augustus and to the Sultan's younger brother Bajazet. In Nero and Roxane, in other words, spectators recognize two major features: tyranny and erotic impulse, whereas in Junia and Bajazet they detect and recognize decisive resistance. In these neoclassical tragedies, the representative characters and the generality of their social and moral features are more important than the individual, peculiar traits.

Nero, in Racine's *Britannicus*, is both a tyrannical emperor and a young, fickle male who courts and wants to marry Junia, Britannicus's beloved, to show his power and, also, to satisfy a sudden, possibly jealous, whim. Junia, by contrast, has for a long time been in love with Britannicus, with whom she is united by what Barthes aptly calls a "sisterly" affection. Do spectators *believe* Nero and Junia? Yes, in so far as the young male unmistakably represents blind vices, tyranny and lawless eros, whereas the female character displays the virtues of chastity and fidelity, but also because bits of caprice make the tyrant more plausible, while Junia's ability to deceive him brings her closer to actual human beings. Given the plays' emphasis on general representative features, these small idiosyncratic traits make the characters more persuasive.

In his *Phaedra* (1677), based on a mythical story and on Euripides's and Seneca's tragedies about it, Racine uses the same logical scheme: Phaedra, the young wife of the legendary hero Theseus, falls in love with her stepson, Hippolytus, who rejects her advances. Deeply hurt, she lets her confidante tell Theseus that his son has attempted to rape his stepmother. Theseus then asks Poseidon, the god of the seas, to punish Hippolytus. A sea monster kills the young man and Phaedra, desperate, remorseful, commits suicide. Clearly present, the pattern "A has all power over B & A loves B who does not love A" is slightly modified. It is not Phaedra herself who has all power over Hippolytus, but her husband, Theseus, king of Athens. Also, in the original Greek myth and in Euripides's adaptation, the reason why the young man does not accept his stepmother's love is his devotion to Artemis, goddess of chastity, and his rejection of Aphrodite, goddess of love. In the ancient version of the story, the rivalry between the two goddesses leads Aphrodite to ignite Phaedra's love for her stepson. Thus, from far above, the goddess of love would either convert the chaste young man to her own worship or punish his refusal. In Racine's play, by contrast, the rejected Phaedra almost dies of pain when she finds out that her stepson is in love with another woman. Anger and jealousy motivate Phaedra's revenge.

The seventeenth-century viewers/readers felt that the ancient story and Euripides's play asked them to travel too far away. Belonging to another time, acting according to an outlandish set of customs and values, the Greek goddesses could not easily win their trust. Their sense that the work was written long, long ago might have calmed the shock of finding out about Aphrodite and Artemis's rivalry and their using mere mortals to fight against each other. But because recognition was not easy to achieve, seventeenth-century French adaptations tried to moderate the difference between the characters' motivations in the original story and the actual customs of the recent public. French writers took, therefore, advantage of the old myths' flexibility, given that ancient Greek writers themselves often revised these myths to get a slightly more plausible version, as one can see by comparing Orestes's late reunion with his sister Electra in Aeschylus's *Libation-bearers*, Sophocles's *Electra*, and Euripides's *Electra*. Similarly, neoclassical tragedies modified the legend of Phaedra and Hippolytus to make sure that it did not offend the prevailing good manners at the time and that the public's belief in the characters' plausibility would be easier to achieve.

This is why in Racine's *Phaedra*, Hippolytus, far from rejecting any kind of erotic attraction, as he does in Euripides's version, is in love, a pure, respectful love, with young Aricia, who answers his feelings. In this tragedy, spectators could thus recognize not only Phaedra's guilty passion, but also the ideal, noble feelings that unite Aricia and Hippolytus, closely resembling the unbreakable links between Theagenes and Chariclea in Heliodorus's *Ethiopian Story*, a Hellenistic novel written more than a half-millennium after the Greek tragedies cited above and whose neo-platonic and Christian resonances fascinated seventeenth-century readers and writers, Racine included. This play, one might therefore say, *civilized* Hippolytus, by transforming the proud, chaste lonely adorer of Artemis into a loyal, faithful disciple of chaste love.

Plausible versus Memorable Characters. Resonance

The desire to bring story-worlds closer to their readers' actual world shaped several literary and artistic movements and genres, including the late eighteenth- and early nineteenth-century Romantic efforts to take history and cultural geography into account, the persistent nineteenth- and twentieth-century realist and naturalist ambition to show life *as it is* and *why it is so*, and the rise of the novel as the most popular literary genre. Thanks to Johann Gottfried Herder's insights, critics and writers ceased to consider that literary plausibility and the public's belief in literary works and their characters always followed the same paths. Born in the ancient Mediterranean world, Greek tragedy, Herder argued, was the product of a culture very different from the Northern European one which hosted Shakespeare's theater. In each case, a work's plausibility and the public's opportunity to believe its characters depended on the links with the surrounding time and culture. To tame, to civilize an old legend meant to betray its original meaning, especially when the works it inspired had been written long ago and far away. The world being so diverse, the first task of readers and writers was to discover and revere the past of their own culture. Concerning the cultures of foreign, distant peoples, the public had to learn to appreciate their specificity. The Realists pushed farther the fragmentation of the world into "slices of life." Since each short period, each country, each region, each social class, each profession was assumed to have its own peculiarities, the task of realist literature consisted in understanding and describing each of them. Naturalists agreed, often insisting on the most unattractive aspects of the "slice of life" they selected and of its characters.

An admirer of realist achievements, Henry James took narrative literature, especially the novel, very seriously. In *The Art of Fiction* ([1884] 1948), he expressed his surprise that some literary critics condemn "any story which does not more or less admit that it is only a joke" (55). He strongly asserted that "the only reason for the existence of a novel is that is does compete with life" (56). Belief, therefore, is essential, and its success requires that the differences between the story-world and the actual world be minimal. By contrast, Robert Louis Stevenson's answer, *A Humble Remonstrance* ([1884] 1948), argued that no art competes with life.

> Man's one method—he continued—whether he reasons or creates, is to half-shut his eyes against the dazzle and confusion of reality.

Not unlike arithmetic and geometry, Stevenson wrote, the arts

> turn away their eyes from the gross, colored, and mobile nature at our feet, and regard instead a certain figmentary abstraction. [...] Our art is occupied, and bound to be occupied, not so much in making stories true as in making them typical; not so much in capturing the lineament of each fact, as in marshalling all of them towards a common end.
>
> *(90)*

The novel, he concluded,

> is not a transcript of life, to be judged by its exactitude; but a simplification of some side or point of life, to stand or fall by its significant simplicity.
>
> *(100)*

In Stevenson's view, literary situations, characters, and actions never "transcribe" actual life. They simplify and exaggerate "some side or point" of reality, over-coordinate its various aspects, and often add improbable elements to emphasize what should be recognized, even though these additions might reduce plausibility.

Stevenson's position is more persuasive, since, as we have seen, central figures of a literary work rarely display features that are *both* recognizable and plausible. Why would one be interested in characters whose features and actions can be easily predicted? Plausible to some extent, most often the *representative* features of literary characters can be recognized precisely because they are rare, unusual, therefore striking and memorable. It is difficult to take Amy Dorrit's devotion to her imperfect father, her silent, deep love for Arthur Clennam, her ability to protect him from the sad story of his origin, as "a transcript of life," to use Stevenson's terms. Yet, these features signal her generosity and her discretion so well that readers recognize them without being troubled by their implausibility. Quite the opposite: Little Dorrit's overstressed virtues could make readers realize that although such perfection looks beyond actual possibility, it can at least be conceived and narrated.

Conversely, Emma, the main character of Flaubert's *Madame Bovary* (1857), marries a kind, honest, but not very smart medical practitioner in a provincial French town and dreams of a beautiful, passionate life in high society. She gets into two extra-marital liaisons, both disappointing, purchases too many luxury objects and clothes, and ends up owing a large debt. Unable to pay, she commits suicide. Shocking but not always plausible, her faults and her end make her difficult to forget. Her character and her fate might seem unlikely to occur in actual life, but thanks to Flaubert's art, they are recognizable and, especially, conceivable, given that readers may both sympathize with Emma Bovary and be irritated by her actions.

Realist writers like Dickens and Flaubert use only a certain amount of implausibility, well surrounded by persuasive images of social and political reality which contrast with Little Dorrit's incredible kindness and Emma Bovary's dreamy self-promotion. In a slightly different way, the personality of Jean Valjean, the central figure in Victor Hugo's *Les Misérables* (1862), was initially shaped by a social system where actual needs do not count, only legal property does. Arrested, judged, and condemned for having stolen a loaf of bread for his hungry nephews, the young Valjean spends many years in prison. When he comes out, bitter and defenseless, a charitable bishop hosts him. During the night, Valjean steals the bishop's silver cutlery and runs away. Police catch him and bring him back to the bishop's residence, but the saintly man claims that he himself gave Valjean the cutlery as a gift and invites him to take the silver candlesticks as well. This gesture moves Valjean so deeply that for the rest of his life he would always give, help, sacrifice himself. Is this pattern of action plausible? Would readers literally believe them? Quite unlikely, especially in the overdramatic situations imagined by Hugo. Do readers recognize Valjean's magnanimity? Are they happy to believe it as a desirable ideal? Undoubtedly. Valjean's actions are so dazzling that readers can neither miss their greatness nor refrain from believing in the ideal they point to.

We might thus distinguish between, on the one hand, the characters' features, actions, and psychological details that trigger immediate recognition, and, on the other hand, the representative types, moods, and more complex psychological factors and conversions that are to some extent recognized right away yet are fully understood only later.

As for the values and ideals that reign over the represented world, often they are the object of an immediate tacit insight, whereas an explicit, arguable identification takes place later, sometimes much later. This last stage of viewing/reading fictional literature, coming after transport, participation, and recognition, could be called *resonance*, since it lets the work and its characters vibrate, often for a long time, within one's heart and mind.[5] At this point, the viewer's/reader's attention and memory go back and forth, compare what goes on with what happened earlier, take discoveries into account, assimilate surprises, foreshadow what would happen next, and respond to the denouement. Both heart and mind host the work's resonance during reading, a few days later, and sometimes much later, tacitly assessing the resemblance between fiction and actual life, at the most concrete level, as well as at the level of higher values and exemplarity.

Models and Warnings

To *believe* a character's profile and actions thus means to appreciate, first, their possible or real links to actual life, second, their plausibility as representatives of human qualities, individual or collective and, third, their impact as value models or as warnings. The following examples are meant to illustrate how characters and plot appeal to readers' trust, either by joining forces or by going in opposite directions.

Heinrich von Kleist's novella *Michael Kohlhaas* (1808), which takes place in the sixteenth-century Saxony and Brandenburg, two kingdoms belonging to the Holy Roman Empire, narrates the conflict between Kohlhaas, an honest horse dealer, and the Junker Wenzel von Tronka, who shamelessly abuses him. At each stage of the conflict, the corrupt network of local nobility prevents Kohlhaas from getting justice. Because the legal system in place fails to help, Kohlhaas, now "a freeman of the Empire and the world, subject to God alone" (Kleist, [1810] 1978, 143), calls for a general rebellion against Junker von Tronka, defeats the Saxon troops and, calling himself "the emissary of the Archangel Michael," establishes "the seat of our Provisional World Government" at a local castle. When Martin Luther intervenes in person, Kohlhaas accepts a truce, but … I'll let the readers who don't know this story find out what follows and add that one can rarely find a literary character as both *believable* and *implausible* as Kohlhaas. In addition, some of the events narrated in the second half of the story require a new "transport" into a story-world closer to that of fairytales. Kohlhaas himself remains as fascinating as before, but from this point on readers might at the same time believe *him* and take the story with a grain of salt.

In Henry James's *The Beast in the Jungle* (1903), John Marcher, the main character through whose eyes the story is told, does not necessarily appear as fully plausible. Given his unusual self-obsession and his inability to pay attention to those close to him, he might be seen as a warning rather than a model for the story's readers. A reserved, solitary member of the London elite, Marcher encounters May Bartram at an elegant luncheon followed by a visit to a private art collection. Both remember their first meeting, several years before, when Marcher did let her know his deep secret: the conviction that his future would include an unpredictable but major event or revelation, a "Thing" that would involve no action, no effort on his part, no effort to win a distinguished place in the world. As he puts it, he would

> Have to meet, to face, to see [it] suddenly break out in my life; possibly destroying all further consciousness, possibly annihilating me; possibly, on the other hand, only altering everything, striking at the root of all my world and leaving me to the consequences, however they shape themselves.
>
> *(412)*

Could it be love? May Bartram asks him, but Marcher makes clear that amorous attractions are too prosaic to mean something for him. If she wants to watch the "Thing" with him, he suggests, she will know more. She accepts the invitation and, from then on, the two would continually see each other. It soon becomes clear for readers, but not for Marcher, that May Bartram is ready to be his if only he understood and answered her love, which he does not. The denouement opens his eyes, alas, too late, his blindness warning readers about the dangers of self-absorption. Can readers *believe* John Marcher and his story? Not very likely, if the criterion is everyday plausibility. It works, however, as a superb *parable* of egotism, loneliness, and inability to love.

Things Fall Apart by Chinua Achebe (1958) takes place in late nineteenth-century Nigeria, before and after the beginning of colonization. Okwonkwo, the main character who belongs to the fictional clan of Umuofia, aims at being a strong male, courageous, ambitious, fully devoted to the established beliefs and rituals, unwilling to accept that different kinds of life could replace them. Three kinds of white English-speaking men settle in the region: at first, Pastor Brown, a gentle Christian priest who starts a church and a school, then, when he falls sick and passes away, the much stricter, intolerant Pastor Smith takes over, and soon the new colonial administration imposes its own laws that do not take into account the traditional way of life. Okwonkwo tries in vain to convince his fellow clan members to resist. The colonial district commissioner comes to take the rebellious Okwonkwo to court, but he already has committed suicide.

Okwonkwo's character and the novel's plot are deeply moving, both at the historical and the moral level. Without overpraising every detail of the Ibo old way of life, Achebe makes readers sense what it meant for Okwonkwo to *belong* fully, unconditionally, to his community. The main character, as well as his son Nwoye do disagree with some of the ancient customs of Umuofia and with some of the decisions pronounced by its frightening Oracle. Yet, whereas the young Nwoye betrays the clan by going to Pastor Brown's school and converting to Christianity, Okwonkwo remains fully committed to Umuofia's independence and to the energetic, masculine ideal that has shaped his life. Readers admire him, deplore his death, and *believe* him without having to agree with every single action he takes.

Conclusion

To conclude, believing in a fictional character involves several layers of awareness and commitment. It could signal the viewers'/readers' acceptance of the fictional game, their at least partial if not, sometimes, full readiness to agree with the states of affairs, the characters, and actions the *as though* imagines. At the next level, viewers/readers are invited to recognize the fictional characters' features and evaluate their plausibility, either as concrete human features also present in the real world or as increased, even exaggerated, manifestations of physical and moral properties as well as of admirable or unworthy ways of acting. After the detour through fiction and the visit of its story-worlds, the public inevitably returns to everyday life. By believing the fictional characters' ideals and deeds, their advances and roundabouts, the multiplicity of examples they offer, each leading to its own conclusion, viewers/readers become ready to sense and evaluate their own, actual world.

Notes

1 Concerning the referential and formative power of literature, this chapter is in deep debt to Umberto Eco (1979), Gregory Currie (1990), Kendall Walton (1990), Peter Lamarque and Stein Haughom Olsen (1994), John Gibson (2007), Jean-Marie Schaeffer (2010), and Joshua Landy (2012).
2 This chapter continues my earlier work on fictionality (1986) and relies on Marie-Laure Ryan (1992 and 2022), Ruth Ronen (1994), Lubomir Dolezel (2000), David Herman (2002), Thomas L. Martin (2004), Emma Kafalenos (2006), Olivier Caïra (2011), Françoise Lavocat (2016), Bohumil Fort (2017), and Alice Bell and Marie-Laure Ryan, eds. (2019).
3 See the studies of narrative rhetoric by Phelan (2004) and Walsh (2007).
4 On empathy and literature, see Keen (2010) and Chandler (2013).
5 Rosa (2019) examines this notion from a sociological point of view.

Works Cited

Achebe, Chinua. 1958. *Things Fall Apart*. London: William Heinemann.
Barthes, Roland. 1964. *On Racine*. Translated by Richard Howard. New York: Hill and Wang.
Bell, Alice, and Ryan Marie-Laure, eds. 2019. *Possible Worlds Theory and Contemporary Narratology*. Lincoln: University of Nebraska Press.
Caïra, Olivier. 2011. *Définir la fiction. Du roman au jeu d'échecs.* Preface by Jean-Marie Schaeffer. Paris: Éditions de l'École des Hautes Études en Sciences Sociales.

Chandler, James. 2013. *An Archaeology of Sympathy: The Sentimental Mode in Literature and Cinema*. Chicago, IL: The University of Chicago Press.

Currie, Gregory. 1990. *The Nature of Fiction*. Cambridge: Cambridge University Press.

Dickens, Charles. (1857) 1963. *Little Dorrit*. With an introduction by Lionel Trilling. Oxford: Oxford University Press.

Doležel, Lubomir. 2000. *Heterocosmica. Fiction and Possible Worlds*. Baltimore, MD: John Hopkins University Press.

Eco, Umberto. 1979. "*Lector in Fabula*. Pragmatic Strategy in a Metanarrative Text." In *The Role of the Reader: Explorations in the Semiotics of Texts*, 200–260. Bloomington: Indiana University Press.

Fort, Bohumil. 2017. *An Introduction to Fictional Worlds Theory*. Frankfurt/New York: Peter Lang.

Gibson, John. 2007. *Fiction and the Weave of Life*. Oxford: Oxford University Press.

Herder, Johann Gottfried. (1773) 2008. *Shakespeare*. Translated and with an introduction by Gregory Moore. Princeton, NJ: Princeton University Press.

Herman, David. 2002. *Story Logic: Problems and Possibilities of Narrative*. Lincoln: University of Nebraska Press.

James, Henry. (1884) 1948. "The Art of Fiction." In *Henry James and Robert Louis Stevenson. A Record of Friendship and Criticism*, edited by Janet Adam Smith, 53–85. London: Rupert Hart-Davis.

James, Henry. (1903) 1951. "The Beast in the Jungle." In *The Portable Henry James*, edited by Morton Dauwen Zabel, 270–325. New York: Viking.

Kafalenos, Emma. 2006. *Narrative Causalities*. Columbus: Ohio State University Press.

Keen, Susanne. 2010. *Empathy and the Novel*. Oxford: Oxford University Press.

Kleist, Heinrich von. (1810) 1978. "Michael Kohlhaas." In *The Marquise of O--- and Other Stories*, translated by David Luke and Nigel Reeves, 114–213. London: Penguin.

Lamarque, Peter, and Olsen Stein Haugom. 1994. *Truth, Fiction and Literature: A Philosophical Perspective*. Oxford: Clarendon Press.

Landy, Joshua. 2012. *How to Do Things with Fiction*. Oxford: Oxford University Press.

Lavocat, Françoise. 2016. *Fait et fiction: pour une frontière*. Poétique. Paris: Seuil.

Martin, Thomas L. 2004. *Poiesis and Possible Worlds: A Study in Modality and Literary Theory*. Toronto: University of Toronto Press.

Pavel, Thomas G. 1986. *Fictional Worlds*. Cambridge, MA: Harvard University Press.

Phelan, James. 2004. *Living to Tell About It. A Rhetoric and Ethics of Character Narration*. Ithaca, NY: Cornell University Press.

Plato. 1961. *Collected Dialogues*. Bollingen Series LXXI. Princeton, NJ: Princeton University Press.

Plotinus. 2018. *The Enneads*. Edited by Lloyd P. Gerson. Cambridge: Cambridge University Press.

Ronen, Ruth. 1994. *Possible Worlds in Lierary Theory*. Cambridge: Cambridge University Press.

Rosa, Hartmut. (2016) 2019. *Resonance. A Sociology of Our Relationship to the World*. Translated by James C. Wagner. Cambridge: Polity.

Ryan, Marie-Laure. 1992. *Possible Worlds, Artificial Intelligence and Narrative Theory*. Bloomington: Indiana University Press.

———. 2022. *A New Anatomy of Storyworlds. What Is, What If, As If*. Columbus: Ohio University Press.

Schaeffer, Jean-Marie. (1999) 2010. *Why Fiction?* Lincoln: University of Nebraska Press.

Schier, Flint. 1986. *Deeper into Pictures. An Essay on Pictorial Representation*. Cambridge: Cambridge University Press.

Smith, Janet Adam, ed. 1948. *Henry James and Robert Louis Stevenson. A Record of Friendship and Criticism*. London: Rupert Hart-Davis.

Stevenson, Robert Louis. (1884) 1948. "A Humble Remonstrance." In *Henry James and Robert Louis Stevenson. A Record of Friendship and Criticism*, edited by Janet Adam Smith, 86–100. London: Rupert Hart-Davis

Walsh, Richard. 2007. *The Rhetoric of Fictionality: Narrative Theory and the Idea of Fiction*. Columbus: Ohio State University Press.

Walton, Kendall. 1990. *Mimesis as Make-Believe*. Cambridge, MA: Harvard University Press.

6

FICTIONALITY, THE ZONE OF GENERIC FICTION, AND THE ALLURE OF UNRELIABLE NARRATION

James Phelan

Frances Ferguson has famously claimed that "free indirect style is the novel's one and only formal contribution to literature" (159). Free indirect style, aka Free Indirect Discourse (FD), is indeed a remarkable phenomenon, but unreliable narration would like a word.[1] Consider just a half-dozen examples from the tradition of Anglo-American fiction. Here's Samuel Richardson's Pamela in *Pamela or Virtue Rewarded* (1740):

> My master continues to be very affable to me. As yet I see no cause to fear any thing. Mrs. Jervis, the housekeeper, too, is very civil to me, and I have the love of every body. Sure they can't all have designs against me because they are civil.
>
> *(47)*

Here's Mark Twain's Huck Finn in *Adventures of Huckleberry Finn* (1884):

> I studied a minute, sort of holding my breath, and then says to myself: "All right then, I'll go to hell"—and tore it up. It was awful thoughts and awful words, but they was said.
>
> *(201)*

Here's Charlotte Perkins Gilman's character narrator in "The Yellow Wallpaper" (1892):

> There are things in that paper that nobody knows but me, or ever will. Behind that outside pattern the dim shapes get clearer every day. It is always the same shape, only very numerous.

And it is like a woman stooping down and creeping about behind that pattern. (1397)
Here's William Faulkner's Jason Compson in *The Sound and the Fury* (1929)

> Once a bitch always a bitch what I say. (180)

Here's Toni Cade Bambara's Sylvie in "The Lesson" (1972):

DOI: 10.4324/9781003119456-8

Back in the days when everyone was old and stupid or young and foolish and me and Sugar were the only ones just right, this lady moved on our block with nappy hair and proper speech and no makeup.

(85)

Here's Sandra Cisneros's character narrator in "Barbie-Q" (1991):

So what if our Barbies smell like smoke when you hold them up to your nose even after you wash and wash and wash them. And if the prettiest doll, Barbie's MOD'ern cousin Francie with real eyelashes, eyelash brush included, has a left foot that's melted a little—so? If you dress her in her new "Prom Pinks" outfit, satin splendor with matching coat, gold belt, clutch, and hair bow included, so long as you don't lift her dress, right?—who's to know.

(16)

I—and, I'm sure, you—could go on for pages and pages adding examples. But even these six nicely illustrate the following general points, all of which I'll say more about below.

As I quote these examples, I assume that you will recognize their unreliability, but examining them points to a working definition of the technique. Unreliable narration in fiction occurs when the perspectives of the character narrator and the implied author—about what happened and/or about how to interpret and evaluate what happened—diverge. Since an implied author has greater authority with readers than a character narrator, the implied author's perspective carries more weight and readers deem the narration to be unreliable. This account also leads to a working definition of reliable narration: telling in which the perspectives of the character narrator and the implied author converge.

As the working definition indicates, narrators can be unreliable in different ways, or, in other words, there is more than one kind of unreliability. Pamela's naïve reasoning is radically different from Sylvie's cynical judging. Furthermore, different kinds of unreliability can interact and overlap. Gilman's character narrator's unreliable interpretation of her environment leads to her unreliable report that there is a woman-shaped figure behind the wallpaper. In other words, narrators can be unreliable reporters, unreliable interpreters, and/or unreliable evaluators.

Recognizing the different kinds of unreliability helps to clarify the relation between unreliability and belief. Although it would be possible to say that all kinds of unreliability involve judgments about belief—"readers don't believe a narrator's reports, interpretations, or evaluations"—I think we add precision to our theoretical account by making finer discriminations among the kinds of unreliability. Thus, I propose to link each kind with a different cognitive concept: unreliable reporting with belief, unreliable interpreting with understanding/perception, and unreliable evaluating with (ethical) judgment. To put it another way, sometimes authors guide readers not to believe a narrator's reporting (as with the assertion by Gilman's character narrator that there's a woman behind the wallpaper); sometimes authors guide readers to recognize a narrator's misunderstanding or misperception (as with Pamela's take on her situation), and sometimes authors guide readers to recognize a narrator's ethical misjudgments (as with Sylvie's claims about Sugar and herself in relation to everyone else).

It's also worth noting that the boundaries between the kinds of unreliability are not rigid and that a single narrative statement can be unreliable in more than one way. For example, the unreliable reporting of Gilman's character narrator follows from her misunderstanding of the wallpaper, and Sylvie's unreliable evaluating goes hand-in-hand with her unreliable interpreting of her situation.

Authors of different identities across a time span from at least the so-called rise of the novel to the contemporary period have been drawn to unreliable narration, and they have marshaled the technique in the service of a wide range of effects. Twain uses Huck's unreliable evaluation of his decision as a way to increase Huck's appeal to readers. Faulkner, by contrast, uses Jason's unreliable evaluation of Caddy to increase readers' distance from him.

Unreliable narration frequently sits cheek-by-jowl with reliable narration. Cisneros's character narrator reliably reports the condition of her fire-damaged Francie but unreliably denies that it matters. Thus, a narrator who is unreliable about some things may be reliable at others.

To these observations based on the examples, I add two others that stem from the popularity of unreliability among storytellers. First, while the default assumption governing narrative communication is that narrators are reliable until proven otherwise, experienced readers of character narration have come to expect unreliability, especially in literary fiction. Second, unreliability has spread beyond prose fiction to other genres and other media, most notably, memoir, film, and graphic narrative (both fictional and nonfictional).[2]

All these points are worthy of further investigation from a variety of perspectives, individually or in combination, including formal, literary-historical, and ideological. My perspective in this essay is philosophical-rhetorical, and my overarching question is why writers and readers of generic fiction are so drawn to unreliable narration. My short answer is that the frame of fictionality separating generic fiction from nonfiction, a frame that establishes what I call the zone of generic fiction which contains fictional narratives of all kinds, makes the complex communicative exchanges of the technique simultaneously *appealing, consequential*, and *safe* for both authors and their audiences. The rest of this essay provides the longer answer. Furthermore, since unreliable narration is a subtype of character narration, I will offer reflections on the more general technique, which also includes the subtype of reliable narration.[3] Again briefly, authors and audiences are drawn to all character narration because it is appealing and consequential. In practical terms, however, when the character narration is reliable, they do not worry about safety, because the technique does not pose the same potential ethical threat to authors and narrators as unreliable narration. I begin the longer answer with some necessary background on my ways of conceiving both fictionality and narrative as rhetoric and then expand what I've already said about a rhetorical view of unreliability. Once those frames are in place, I return to the why question.

Fictionality as Rhetoric in the Universe of Discourse

My version of a rhetorical approach to the universe of discourse focuses on how rhetors (speakers, writers, etc.) seek to achieve certain purposes in relation to target audiences.[4] This focus on tellers and their means, purposes, and audiences leads me to identify four macro-genres of discourse: nonfictionality, fictionality, lying, and blurring. Here are working definitions of these macro-genres along with some additional commentary.

Nonfictionality is discourse in which a rhetor directly reports on, interprets, evaluates, or otherwise engages with actual states of affairs in order to influence an audience's response to or understanding of the actual. The default settings for nonfictional discourse are sincerity and reliability. As you read this essay, you take for granted that I am expressing what I actually believe, that I want to be accurate, and that I hope to be insightful about unreliable narration.

Fictionality is discourse in which a rhetor intentionally and non-deceptively uses invention, projection, or some other departure from direct reference to actual states of affairs in order to influence an audience's response to or understanding of the actual.[5]

Fictionality, in other words, is an indirect way of intervening in an audience's understanding of or response to the actual. In this view, then, fictionality and nonfictionality are not binary opposites but different means to the same ends of having effects in the real world. Furthermore, rhetors often turn to fictionality when they believe that the devices of indirection can lead to more effective interventions.

Lying and blurring are best understood in relation to fictionality and nonfictionality. Lying is discourse in which a rhetor deceptively uses invention or some other departure from the actual in order to directly intervene in their audience's understanding of the actual. A liar typically does not want their deception exposed.

Blurring is discourse in which a rhetor blends or plays with the lines between fictionality and nonfictionality in order to intervene in their audience's understanding of the actual. The rhetor does not expect the audience to sort their text into neat bundles of fictional and nonfictional statements but instead to recognize the blurring/playing with the line. Authors of autofiction such as Karl Ove Knausgaard in *My Struggle* and J.M. Coetzee in *Boyhood, Youth, Summertime* are notorious blurrers.

These understandings of the macro-genres have several important consequences for my purposes here.

These understandings situate generic fictions such as the short story, the novel, and the fiction film as a subset of the larger domain of fictionality. In addition, generic fictions are clearly marked zones in which rhetors can give free rein to their imaginations and invent or project whatever they think can help them achieve their purposes of indirectly intervening in the actual. I use the term "zone" to indicate the force of the frame of fictionality, the way that, in suspending the referentiality of nonfiction, it licenses invention. As for indirect interventions, they range widely across the zone. Gilman's story indicts the nineteenth-century rest cure. Bambara's story itself offers a lesson about how Black adolescents may react to learning about income inequality. And so on. Indeed, just about any well-known fiction generates a plethora of thematic readings that testify to its efforts to intervene in the world. Audiences flock to the zone of fictionality precisely because they know that the characters and events they read about are imaginative inventions and projections and thus that the larger narratives are extended thought experiments. As a result, generic fictions, using any narrative techniques, can be both consequential (the indirect interventions) and safe (the imaginative thought experiments).[6]

By distinguishing fictionality from generic fictions, this approach helps us recognize the pervasiveness of fictionality outside the clearly marked zone of generic fiction—in advertising, in political campaigns, in what-if and counterfactual scenarios, and more. Recognizing that pervasiveness in turn helps us recognize that fictionality and nonfictionality often exist side-by-side in any given discourse, and that rhetors and their audiences easily shift back and forth between them. In other words, global nonfictions may contain local instances of fictionality, and generic fictions local instances of nonfictionality. Authors can use such juxtapositions in a variety of ways. For our purposes here, one of those ways stands out. Authors of generic fictions may signal a character narrator's unreliability by having them distort local nonfictionality. For example, an author may situate a character narrator in a well-known nonfictional city such as New York and then use the character narrator's erroneous description of its geography to indicate their unreliability.[7]

Within the zones of generic fiction, authors have the liberty to represent narrators or characters using all four modes of discourse. Within the boundaries of a fictional storyworld, the default mode for narrators and characters is nonfictionality, a phenomenon that makes reliability the default for character narration. But the author can signal that the intra-fictional nonfictional discourse is unreliable. Thus, for example, when Gilman's character narrator claims that there is a figure behind the wallpaper, she makes a nonfictional claim within the storyworld. The character narrator is neither lying nor fictionalizing— but she is unreliably interpreting the appearance of the wallpaper. In other words, she believes her claim, but Gilman's readers do not. See also principle #4 in the next section on Narrative as Rhetoric.

Just as rhetors and audiences can easily negotiate shifts between nonfictionality and fictionality outside the zones, so too can they within them. In Chapter 3 of *Huckleberry Finn*, for example, Twain has a lot of fun with Huck's inability to recognize and participate in Tom Sawyer's use of fictionality as he leads Huck and other boys in his game of "robber." Twain's fun depends on his assumption that his audience will recognize that Tom is engaging in fictionality, while literal-minded, nonfictionality-bound Huck is unable to follow Tom's shift into fictionality. After what turns out to be their last game,

Huck says, "I reckoned [Tom] believed in the A-rabs and the elephants, but as for me I think different. It had all the marks of a Sunday-school" (41–42).

Furthermore, authors of generic fiction can show both narrators and characters lying or playing with the lines between fictionality and nonfictionality—without violating the broader boundaries of their marked-off zones of fictionality. Indeed, as noted above, when fictional narrators lie, they are engaging in one kind of unreliability (typically misreporting). And when they play with the lines between fictionality and nonfictionality, they may also be playing with the lines between reliability and unreliability.

This approach clearly distinguishes fictionality from lying. When a simple lie (e.g., an assertion that something happened when it did not) or a more elaborate deception (e.g., a fraudulent memoir) gets uncovered, that uncovering does not transform the lie into a fiction. Instead, the lie remains a deceptive use of nonfictionality, but its deception has been revealed. Thus, when an author signals that a character narrator in a generic fiction is lying to their narratee (rather than misreporting something they believe to be the case), that lie does not mean they construct a fiction-within-a-fiction. Instead, the author uses the lie to signal that the character narrator is an ethically deficient unreliable reporter.

Narrative as Rhetoric

I move now from this rhetorical take on the universe of discourse to a rhetorical take on narrative. For the purposes of this essay, I highlight five key principles.

Principle 1: Narrative is a way of knowing, that is, a means of coming to terms with human experience, and a way of doing, that is, a means of moving an audience to feel, to think, and even to act differently. As the default rhetorical definition has it, narrative is somebody telling somebody else on some occasion and for some purposes that something happened. (I label this definition a default because I recognize that sometimes particular narratives deviate from it, as, for example, when someone tells somebody else that something is happening, will happen, might happen, won't happen, should happen, and so on.) This conception means that the ethos of the somebody telling, including their credibility, is a key aspect of narrative communication. More generally, the focus on tellers, audiences, occasions, and purposes highlights the idea that narratives are always shaped (sometimes well, sometimes poorly, and sometimes in-between) in the service of their tellers' rhetorical actions. Authors who employ character narrators give their narration a major role in that shaping (for further discussion of this view, see Phelan [1996, 2017, and 2023]).

Principle 2. By conceiving of narrative as rhetoric, the approach reconceives the traditionally understood relations among tellers, audiences, and the elements of narrative. Since the rise of structuralist narratology in the 1960s, most narrative theory has viewed narrative as a structure built out of elements of story and elements of discourse, and, thus, centers those elements in the task of interpretation. Rhetorical theory, however, subordinates those elements to the author-audience-purpose nexus, regarding them as resources that authors may or may not deploy depending on their purposes in relation to target audiences. To put this point another way, rhetorical theory identifies the two constants of narrative, author(s) and audience(s), and the variable resources that enable their exchanges: occasions, paratexts, narrators, narratees, characters, events, character-character dialogue, narrative techniques (including reliable and unreliable narration), time, space, and so on. In this view, in any given pair of narratives, an author will use multiple resources, but not necessarily the same ones and not necessarily in the same way. Unreliable narration, then, is a resource that authors may use in some ways but not in others—or not at all—depending on their purposes.

Principle 3. The model conceives of the author as the agent responsible for the shaping of the narrative. While I find it useful to refer to this agent as the implied author in order to distinguish them from the biographical author whose agency gets expressed in many other actions in their life, I have no quarrel with those who find the term unnecessary and prefer to refer to the author.[8] The key point is that there is an authorial agent whose activity shapes the text in one way rather than countless others. As the working definition of unreliability has it, the technique relies on this authorial agent's perspective diverging from a character narrators.

Principle 4. Rhetorical readers are those members of the actual audience who seek to join the author's target audience (also called the authorial audience).[9] The authorial audience and the "implied reader" are synonymous terms; rhetorical theory is less shy about who is doing the implying. In fiction, rhetorical readers also seek to join the narrative audience, an observer position within the storyworld from which the characters, events, and narration are seen as real. The narrative audience, in other words, is not aware that these elements exist within the zone of fiction. Consequently, the narrative audience regard nonfictionality as the default macro-genre of narration. For example, they take Gilman's character narrator's claims about the wallpaper as a sincere expression of what she perceives.

The narrative audience is distinct from the narratee, the narrator's addressee. The narrative audience is a role that actual readers take on, while the narratee is an intratextual element that the narrative audience can observe. Richardson's narrative audience has access to Pamela's letters to her parents, her narratees. Authors can set up a variety of relationships between narrative audiences and narratees, but I will not get into those details here.[10]

The narrative audience is nested within the authorial audience and that nesting explains the double consciousness involved in reading fiction: in the narrative audience we can feel real emotions for characters, while simultaneously remaining tacitly aware in the authorial audience that they are invented. (Reading nonfiction does not generate double-consciousness; thus, there is no narrative audience in nonfiction.) Authors rely on this double-consciousness as they use unreliability to generate a wide range of effects. If readers didn't regard Huck Finn in one part of their consciousness as an autonomous actor making his own ethical decisions, they would not respond so strongly to his decision to go to hell. If readers didn't simultaneously recognize Twain's perspective on his invented character, they would not tune in to Twain's purposeful critique of both slavery and Christianity.

Principle 5. In most narratives and especially in generic fictions, the default definition applies to both the author's and the narrator's rhetorical actions. This double application is especially relevant to character narration, where the author contains within a single text two different somebodies (author and character narrator) telling to at least two different audiences (authorial audience and narratee) for at least two different purposes. We can thus use the metaphor of tracks of communication to describe the two rhetorical actions, one going from narrator to narratee, the other from author to authorial audience/rhetorical readers. In reliable narration the tracks typically converge, while in unreliable narration they diverge.

A Rhetoric of Unreliability

In presenting my versions of fictionality as rhetoric and narrative as rhetoric, I've touched on various aspects of my rhetorical take on unreliability. In this section, I'll consolidate and expand upon those points as part of an overall summary of my understanding of the technique.[11]

I begin by reinforcing principle #5 of narrative as rhetoric: effective character narration in fiction involves an author using a single text to show two distinct tellers addressing two distinct audiences for at least two different purposes.

As for the telling itself, authors use narrators to perform three main functions: reporting, interpreting, and evaluating. Thus, we can identify three axes of narrative communication, with each axis corresponding to one of those functions: the axis of characters, events, time, and space (reporting); the axis of reading or construing (interpreting); and the axis of ethics (evaluating). Consequently, authors and character narrators can converge or diverge along each of these axes. Their divergence yields the three main kinds of unreliability: misreporting, misinterpreting, and misevaluating. We can be even more fine-grained and identify three additional kinds of unreliability for narration that is as good as far as it goes but stops short of being fully adequate: underreporting, underinterpreting, and underevaluating. Thus, the rhetorical approach identifies six types of unreliability. (I do not distinguish three more kinds with the prefix of "over" because I find that the effort to separate, say, "misevaluating" from "overevaluating" or "overvaluing," does not have a significant payoff. In other words, I acknowledge the "over-" but include it in the "mis-.")

Authors can vary the convergence and divergence of the two tracks of communication over the course of a narrative. They can set up convergence with the reporting and divergence with the interpreting or evaluating. And they can set up convergence of a function in one passage and divergence in another. In other words, identifying one passage of unreliability is not sufficient grounds for arguing that there is unreliability all the way down.

Unreliable narration can have effects on author-narrator-audience relationships that range across a spectrum from deeply estranging to strongly bonding. Jason Compson's unreliability is estranging because it consistently increases the ethical and affective distance between him and Faulkner's rhetorical readers. Huck Finn's unreliability is typically bonding because it closes the affective and/or ethical distance between him and Twain's rhetorical readers. When Huck decides to tear up the letter to Miss Watson, for example, he judges himself as a sinner, while Twain uses the trajectory of Huck's relationship with Jim to signal that Huck makes the ethically superior choice. The power of both Gilman's "The Yellow Wallpaper" and Bambara's "The Lesson" depends to a large degree on their use of bonding unreliability. As Gilman traces the character narrator's gradual dissociation of identity, she closes the affective and ethical distance between the character narrator and her rhetorical readers. As Bambara shows Sylvie resisting the lesson about inequality that Miss Moore teaches her and her friends, Bambara increases rhetorical readers' positive affective responses to her.

Rhetorical readers do not assess unreliability in relation to some hypothetical alternative of objective narration. All narration is subjective because it all involves a narrator's perspective. Judgments about reliability then are judgments about the relation between two subjective perspectives, the author's and the narrator's. Again, when those perspectives converge, we have reliable narration, and when they diverge, we have unreliable narration.

There is no 100%-guaranteed-or-your-money-back method of determining unreliability, because it is a kind of irony: someone *implies* to somebody else that the surface statement (or set of statements) is not to be taken at face value. In standard irony, the teller implicitly says to the audience, "I know that you know that I don't stand behind this statement." In unreliable narration, the implied author covertly says to rhetorical readers, "I know that you know that I do not endorse this report/interpretation/evaluation."

Nevertheless, even though there is no comprehensive list of textual strategies we can consult to determine (un)reliability, authors have over the years developed a repertoire of such strategies. Here are seven commonly used ones[12]:

Inconsistency. Narrators who say one thing about X on p. 2 and then say something else about X on p. 10 that doesn't square with what they've said on p. 2 are unreliable in at least one of those places.

Use of faulty logic. Pamela's "they're so civil, therefore, they don't have designs on me" is a clear example.

Departures from culturally accepted ways of reporting, interpreting, and evaluating. Faulkner frequently signals Jason's unreliability in this way, especially along the axis of ethics.

Telling about things that are either impossible or highly implausible within the rules governing the storyworld. Gilman uses this strategy with her character narrator.

Failure to connect the dots of the telling. Often a character narrator will report a pattern of some kind and either fail to recognize the significance of that pattern or misinterpret it. Bambara's Sylvie consistently fails to recognize the method behind Miss Moore's efforts to instruct Sylvie and her friends about the ways of the world.

Signaling that a narrator's desire for something to be so overpowers their recognition that it is not, cannot, or will not be so. Cisneros's handling of the last line of "Barbie-Q" is a good example.

Using a narrator's tics or what poker players call "tells" to signal unreliability. Two common tells are the use of particular phrases or sudden swerves from one kind of language to another. As these examples indicate, authors frequently signal these tells by reference to either general linguistic norms or to the narrator's more common way of telling.

Why Unreliable Character Narration?

I turn now to unpack and elaborate on the short answer to the question of why writers and readers of generic fiction are so drawn to character narration in general and to unreliable narration in particular. The frame of fictionality separating generic fiction from nonfiction, which means that readers know they are entering a realm of invention, makes the complex communicative exchanges of character narration and unreliability simultaneously *appealing* and *consequential*; in addition, this frame makes unreliable narration *safe* for both authors and their audiences. I see four main reasons for the appeal:

Reason 1. The zone of generic fiction. As noted above, the zone gives free rein to the exercise of the human imagination. There is something appealing to an author in the challenge of not only creating a character clearly distinct from themself but also fully occupying that character's distinct perspective with every sentence of their narrative. Similarly, there is something appealing to readers in the challenge of simultaneously occupying the double perspective of the author and the character narrator.

Reason 2. The continuity of identity between experiencing-I and narrating-I. An author's choice to tell through the perspective of a participant in the narrative action, whether as protagonist or secondary character, has major consequences for author-narrator-audience relationships—and some of these are not possible with non-character narration. Not surprisingly, these consequences arise from the dual roles indicated by the term "character narrator." Previous narrative theory has wisely separated the roles in its common use of the terms "narrating-I" and "experiencing-I." But this separation runs the risk of diverting attention from the continuity between the roles, a continuity that makes possible generic fiction's most intimate sharing between tellers and audiences of what I'll call the experiences of *being-there* (via character narration in the present tense) and *having-been-there* (via character narration in the past tense).

To clarify this point, let's conduct a thought experiment with two steps: (a) re-reading the first three passages I quoted in the introduction, reproduced below, and (b) considering my renderings of them as non-character narration via internal focalization and Free Indirect Discourse.[13]

My master continues to be very affable to me. As yet I see no cause to fear any thing. Mrs. Jervis, the housekeeper, too, is very civil to me, and I have the love of every body. Sure they can't all have designs against me because they are civil.

Pamela noticed that her master continued to be very affable to her and that Mrs. Jervis, the housekeeper, was also very civil. Indeed, Pamela felt that everyone in the household loved her. Their civility made her confident that not all of them could have designs on her.

I studied a minute, sort of holding my breath, and then says to myself: "All right then, I'll go to hell"—and tore it up. It was awful thoughts and awful words, but they was said.

Huck studied a minute, holding his breath, and then thought "All right then, I'll go to hell" and tore up the letter. He viewed his thought as awful and final.

> There are things in that paper that nobody knows but me, or ever will. Behind that outside pattern the dim shapes get clearer every day. It is always the same shape, only very numerous.
> And it is like a woman stooping down and creeping about behind that pattern.

She thinks that there are things in that paper that only she knows now and forever. She sees the dim shapes behind the outside pattern becoming clearer every day. She perceives it as essentially the same shape, even as it has many variations. She thinks it resembles a woman stooping down and creeping about behind that pattern.

This thought experiment, I believe, yields several significant results. First, the renderings largely preserve the information about the character's perceptions and actions, but they seriously reduce the being-there and having-been-there effects for readers of the originals. The mediation of the non-character narrator adds another layer to rhetorical readers' perceptions of the characters and their experiences, and, in so doing, it eliminates the feedback loop between narrator and character that is central to that intimate sharing. To illustrate via just one of the examples, Twain constructs Huck's decision to go to hell as the most significant having-been-there moment in the novel. Both its significance and its intimacy depend on the continuity and the subsequent feedback loop between Huck the narrator and Huck the character. Twain uses Huck's narration as part of his characterization of Huck, just as he uses Huck's actions to inform his audience's understanding of Huck as narrator. The roles coalesce here, as Huck the narrating-I misevaluates Huck the experiencing-I's decision, and that convergence is crucial to the power of this climactic moment.[14]

Reason 3. The complexity and efficiency of character narration and the even greater complexity and efficiency of unreliable narration. The results of the thought experiment again provide supporting evidence. Richardson uses Pamela's statement "Sure they can't all have designs against me because they are civil" to simultaneously convey the intersection of her naivete with her faulty logic and to suggest that the intersection itself follows from her desire to have the situation be as she describes it. My narrator's statement "Their civility made her confident that not all of them could have designs on her," is, at best, a pale imitation of Richardson's communication, one that is especially weak on conveying Pamela's desire.

For his part, Twain uses Huck's "It was awful thoughts and awful words, but they was said" to convey the solemnity, significance, and finality that Huck attaches to his decision. My "He viewed his thought as awful and final" flattens those nuances into a relatively unappetizing pancake. Gilman uses the present tense unfolding of the character narrator's direct perceptions to show her hallucination-in-progress, her move from seeing dim shapes to configuring those shapes into the figure of a woman. Because the non-character narration filters the character narrator's perceptions, the in-progress evolution of them is less apparent.

Reason 4. The doubled perspective of character and implied author. Telling from and listening to the perspective of a participant in the action distinct from the author is appealing because perspective-taking is so central to human experience, and because character narration in fiction automatically doubles perspective. Once an author chooses to write from the perspective of someone else, they must also work out their own relation to that perspective: do they endorse it as reliable or diverge from it in whole or in part, rendering it unreliable? And how do they signal their position to their readership?

Mikhail Bakhtin's general account of the relations between narrators and authors applies with special force to the relations between character narrators and their authors.

> Behind the narrator's story, we read a second story, the author's story; he is the one who tells us how the narrator tells stories and also tells us about the narrator himself. We acutely sense two levels at each moment in the story; one, the level of the narrator, a belief system filled with his objects, meanings, and emotional expressions, and the other, the level of the author who speaks (albeit in a refracted way) by means of this story and through this story.
>
> *(1981, 314)*

Rhetorical readers, then, are in the position of simultaneously taking in these two levels and negotiating the relationships between them. When the two levels are mutually supportive, or, to use my earlier metaphor, when the two tracks of communication converge, readers face one kind of appealing challenge. When the levels/tracks diverge, readers face another, even more complex, but still appealing challenge. Right after Huck narrates his crucial decision and his resolution to stick by it, he narrates his next step: "Then I set to thinking over how to get at it and turned over considerable many ways in my mind; and at last fixed up a plan that suited me" (201). Rhetorical readers remain attuned to the two levels that Bakhtin describes, noting Huck's report, Twain's tacit confirmation of its accuracy (Twain relies on the principle that the default is reliable narration), as well as Twain's using the statement for further revelation of who Huck is (a self-reliant planner) and how he tells the story: Huck withholds the details of the plan from his narratee, a move that means Twain simultaneously withholds them from his readers. In short, lots going on. But, as my previous commentary on Huck's unreliable account of his crucial decision indicates, that passage is even more layered, complex, challenging, and rewarding.

I see two main, interrelated reasons why character narration and unreliable narration are consequential. Since the reasons are interrelated, I'll list them together: the frame of fictionality itself and the freedom for both invention and indirection in the zone of generic fiction.

As noted above and as I'll further substantiate below, fictionality's purpose is to indirectly intervene in the actual world, and rhetors often turn to fictionality precisely because they believe that they can make more effective interventions than they could with the directness of nonfictionality. Thus, even as rhetorical readers experience the appeal of the doubled perspectives of character narration, they read for authorial purposes. In other words, it is not just that the doubling of perspective provides a complex take on the intimate sharing of being-there and been-there effects but it's also that both authors and rhetorical readers have an interest in the answer to "so-what" questions about that take on the sharing. At the same time, the zone of generic fiction licenses authorial experimentation with the indirections of double-perspective narration, and thus enhances the technique's capacity to contribute to effective interventions.

Gilman's "The Yellow Wallpaper" dramatically illustrates these points. Gilman's ability to immerse her rhetorical readers in the character narrator's slow unraveling provides powerful being-there effects and remarkable bonding unreliability. But more than that, in reading for purpose(s), rhetorical readers recognize that she marshals these effects in order to make her cases against the rest cure in particular and the operations of the patriarchy in late nineteenth-century America more generally. As for the greater license provided by fictionality, we know that Gilman's story arises out of her own experience of a postpartum psychosis, although not one that led to her completely losing touch with reality. If Gilman were to write a nonfictional account of that experience, she would be constrained in a way that she is not in the zone of generic fiction. In "The Yellow Wallpaper," Gilman takes advantage of the freedom conferred by the zone of generic fiction and traces the character narrator's devolution to the point where she has completely lost her own identity, is unable to recognize her husband, and is reduced to crawling around their rented house:

> Now why should that man have fainted? But he did, and right across my path by the wall, so that I had to creep over him every time!
>
> *(1403)*

Gilman marshals this bonding unreliability in the service of this heart-breaking yet extraordinarily effective ending, one that contributes significantly to her critiques of the rest cure and of the patriarchy behind it.

As for why unreliable character narration is safe, I see two main reasons, one that also helps explain why it is appealing, and one that also helps explain why it is consequential. It's worth returning to the point that in fiction, safety is more of a concern for unreliable than for reliable narration. It's not that reliable narration in fiction can never be dangerous, but rather that the dangers posed by reliable narration are similar to those posed by nonfictionality: is the rhetor's discourse in the service of some ethically or politically reprehensible position? Thus, if an author constructs and endorses a fictional character narrator whose interpretations and evaluations are governed by an ethically defective ideology (e.g., racism, sexism, able-ism, homophobia, and/or other possibilities), the situation is not all that different from one in which, say, a politician gives voice to that ideology on the campaign trail. In both cases we lay the dangers—and the deficiency—of the rhetorical action at the feet of the rhetor responsible for advancing the ideology: the politician and the author (not the reliable character narrator or their narration). If we judge Twain as endorsing Huck's sometimes derogatory comments about Black people (and his use of the n-word), we also interpret Twain as using dangerous reliable narration.

With unreliable character narration, authors sometimes invite their rhetorical readers to experience the being-there and have-been-there effects deriving from taking on the perspectives of deeply flawed character narrators. To draw on our examples, Gilman asks her readers to take on the seriously distorted interpretive perspective of her character narrator, and Faulkner ask his readers to take on the seriously distorted ethical perspective of Jason Compson. To move beyond the examples I have been considering, Vladimir Nabokov in *Lolita* requires his readers to take on the reprehensible ethical perspective of a pederast, and Jonathan Littell in *The Kindly Ones* asks his readers to adopt that of a Nazi perpetrator. In taking on these perspectives, readers run the risk of either succumbing to despair (in the case of Gilman) or becoming complicit with the ethically distorted perspectives. Because the risks are real, there's no guarantee that actual readers won't be harmed in these (or other) ways. But rhetorical readers can avoid the risks because (1) they know that such character narrators are inventions contained within the zone of fiction, and thus are not doing their damage in the actual world, and (2) their perspectives are framed within those of their authors, and, thus, rhetorical readers see not just with them but also beyond them. This seeing beyond takes us back to the importance of authorial purposes. In each case, the author implicitly promises their rhetorical readers that taking on the double perspective will lead them to some worthwhile insights about the actual world. There is of course no guarantee that an author will fulfill that promise, but the history of literature demonstrates that countless authors do.

In conclusion, then, a rhetorical conception of fictionality, with its emphasis on how rhetors use their imaginations to indirectly intervene in the actual world, helps explain how reliable and unreliable character narration in fiction works and why authors and readers are so drawn to these techniques. Character narration is itself a sophisticated rhetorical phenomenon and unreliable character narration adds another layer of complexity—and opportunity—to author-audience communication. This complexity makes unreliable narration appealing, consequential, and safe. In sum, unreliable character narration demonstrates the power—and wonder—of fictionality, the generic zone of fiction, and the human imagination.

Notes

1 Wayne C. Booth introduced this term in 1961, and it is now part of common parlance. This essay follows in the tradition of Booth's attention to narrative as rhetoric. Not all theorists of unreliable narration take this rhetorical approach. Indeed, there have been extensive debates about whether to locate the source of unreliability in the author's relation to the narrator, in the narrative text itself, or in readers and their ways of construing textual phenomena, including the effect of various kinds of positionality (historical, social, personal) on such construals. I have made a case for the explanatory power of the rhetorical approach in Phelan (2005, 2017). But I don't regard the other positions as invalid; instead, they are rooted in different ways of interpreting texts. The collections by D'hoker and Martens and by V. Nünning provide excellent essays representing a diversity of views.

2 Many of the general points about character narration in fiction also apply to nonfiction narratives. In Phelan (2005), I have written about Frank McCourt's extensive use of unreliability in his Pulitzer Prize-winning memoir, *Angela's Ashes*. But a full discussion of unreliability in nonfiction is the subject of another essay.

3 A note on terminology: narratologists, influenced by the groundbreaking work of Gérard Genette, often use the terms "homodiegetic narration" to refer to telling by a narrator who is also a character in the story and "heterodiegetic narration" to telling by a narrator who is not a character. I find it more reader-friendly to use the terms "character narration" and "non-character narration."

4 My conceptions are deeply influenced by related work on fictionality as rhetoric, especially Walsh (2007), my collaboration with Walsh and Nielsen in 2015, and my further collaboration with multiple scholars in *Fictionality in Literature: Core Concepts Revisited* (2022).

5 Again, the rhetorical view is not universally accepted. In narratological circles, the dominant alternative is an ontological view that sees fiction and nonfiction as binary opposites rooted in the difference between invention and referentiality. This ontological view underlies the development of Possible Worlds Theory, which views fictional worlds as clearly distinct from the actual world, even as they can share some features of the actual world. See, for example, Pavel and Ryan. See also note 6 about John Searle's speech act approach.

6 This rhetorical view is significantly different from John Searle's view that fictional discourse is non-serious. In Searle's view, authors within the generic zone only pretend to perform illocutionary acts. These descriptions imply a hierarchy in which nonfictional discourse ranks above fictional discourse. A rhetorical approach rejects that hierarchy.

7 It is possible that the author may not realize that the narrator is erroneously reporting the geography. In that case, the narration is not unreliable but what I call deficient, because the error is unintentional. See the discussions of deficient narration in Chapters 10 and 12 of *Somebody Telling*.

8 Booth (1961) also introduced this term. Narratologists have long debated how best to define the term and indeed its general utility. See Phelan (2005), Kindt and Muller (2006), A. Nünning (1997), and the special issue of *Style* edited by Brian Richardson.

9 Not all actual readers want to be rhetorical readers and that's a good thing. Different ways of reading can generate different valuable knowledge about literary texts.

10 For some of those details, see Copland and Phelan (2022).

11 In this section, I distill longer discussions in both Phelan (2005, 2017). The latter discussion also explicitly theorizes reliable narration.

12 This list slightly modifies the one in Phelan (2023) and uses different examples.

13 I acknowledge that my renderings are not the only ones possible, but I have tried not to make mine tendentious.

14 I do not claim that character narration is an inherently superior technique, just that its appeal is different from non-character narration. Authors often find that the layering provided by a non-character narrator better serves their overall purposes.

Works Cited

Bakhtin, Mikhail. 1981. "Discourse in the Novel." *The Dialogic Imagination*, edited by Michael Holquist, translated by Caryl Emerson and Michael Holquist, 259–422. Austin: University of Texas Press.
Bambara, Toni Cade. 1972. "The Lesson." *Gorilla, My Love*, 85–98. New York: Random House.
Booth, Wayne C. (1961) 1983. *The Rhetoric of Fiction*, 2nd ed. Chicago, IL: University of Chicago Press.
Cisneros, Sandra. 1991. "Barbie-Q." In *Woman Hollering Creek and Other Stories*, 14–16. New York: Vintage.
Coetzee, J. M. 2012. *Scenes from Provincial Life: Boyhood, Youth, Summertime*. London Penguin.
Copland, Sarah, and James Phelan. 2022. "The Ideal Narratee and the Rhetorical Model of Audiences." *Poetics Today* 43, no. 1 (March): 1–26.

D'hoker, Elke, and Gunther Martens. 2008. *Narrative Unreliability in the Twentieth-Century First-Person Novel.* Berlin: De Gruyter.Faulkner, William. (1929) 1984. *The Sound and the Fury.* New York: Vintage.

Ferguson, Frances. 2000. "Jane Austen, Emma, and the Impact of Form." *Modern Language Quarterly* 61, no. 1 (March): 157–80.

Gammelgaard, Lasse, Stefan Iversen, Louise Brix Jacobsen, James Phelan, Richard Walsh, Henrik Zetterberg-Nielsen, and Simona Zetterberg-Nielsen, eds. 2022. *Fictionality in Literature: Core Concepts Revisited.* Columbus: Ohio State University Press.

Genette, Gérard. 1980. *Narrative Discourse: An Essay in Method.* Translated by Jane Lewin. Ithaca, NY: Cornell University Press.

Gilman, Charlotte Perkins. (1892) 2007. "The Yellow Wallpaper." In *The Norton Anthology of Literature by Women: The Traditions in English*, edited by Sandra M. Gilbert and Susan Gubar, 3rd ed., 1392–402. New York: W.W. Norton.

Kindt, Tom, and Hans-Harald Muller. 2006. *The Implied Author: Concept and Controversy.* Berlin: De Gruyter.

Knausgaard, Karl Ove. 2013–19. *My Struggle.* 6 vols. New York: Farrar, Strauss, and Giroux.

Littell, Jonathan. 2010. *The Kindly Ones.* New York: Harper.

McCourt, Frank. 1996. *Angela's Ashes.* New York: Scribner.

Nabokov, Vladimir. (1955) 1989. *Lolita.* New York: Knopf.

Nielsen, Henrik Skov, James Phelan, and Richard Walsh. 2015. "Ten Theses about Fictionality." *Narrative* 23, no. 1 (January): 61–73.

Nünning, Ansgar. 1997. "Deconstructing and Reconceptualizing the Implied Author: The Resurrection of an Anthropomorphized Passepartout or the Obituary of a Critical Phantom?" *Anglistik. Organ des verbandes deutscher anglisten* 8: 95–116.

Nünning, Vera, ed. 2015. *Unreliable Narration and Trustworthiness.* Berlin: Walter de Gruyter.

Pavel, Thomas. 1989. *Fictional Worlds.* Cambridge, MA: Harvard University Press.

Phelan, James. 1996. *Narrative as Rhetoric.* Columbus: Ohio State University Press.

Phelan, James. 2005. *Living to Tell About It: A Rhetoric and Ethics of Character Narration.* Ithaca, NY: Cornell University Press.

Phelan, James. 2017. *Somebody Telling Somebody Else: A Rhetorical Poetics of Narrative.* Columbus: Ohio State University Press.

Phelan, James. 2023. *Narrative Medicine: A Rhetorical Rx.* New York: Routledge.

Richardson, Brian, ed. 2011. "Implied Author: Back from the Grave or Simply Dead Again?" Special issue, *Style* 45, no. 1 (Spring).

Richardson, Samuel. (1740) 1980. *Pamela; or, Virtue Rewarded.* London: Penguin.

Ryan, Marie-Laure. 1992. *Possible Worlds, Artificial Intelligence, and Narrative Theory.* Bloomington: Indiana University Press.

Searle, John. 1975. "The Logical Status of Fictional Discourse." *New Literary History* 6, no. 2 (Winter): 319–32.

Twain, Mark. (1884) 2004. *Adventures of Huckleberry Finn.* 2nd ed. Edited by Gerald Graff and James Phelan. Boston, MA: Bedford-St. Martin's.

Walsh, Richard. 2007. *A Rhetoric of Fictionality.* Columbus: Ohio State University Press.

7

BELIEF IS A MESS. THAT MAKES IT GOOD FOR FICTION. (A PERSPECTIVE FROM COGNITIVE LITERARY THEORY)

Lisa Zunshine

Think of a fictional character who believes in something—for instance, a religious tenet or a political ideology—and whose faith is true, deep, and pure, uncomplicated by doubts, untainted by tacit considerations of cost and benefit, and unwavering in its constancy. You may have a hard time coming up with many examples of such uncompromisingly true believers. They are just not very exciting, narratively speaking. In contrast, a character whose outward manifestations of faith belie inner conflict radiates social complexity of the kind that fiction can't get enough of.

Here, for instance, is Martin, a priest protagonist of Daniel Kehlmann's novel *F*, performing the Eucharist while thinking that one has to be "deranged" to actually believe that the wafer becomes "the body of a crucified man." What awes Martin is not the miracle of transubstantiation but the power of the social. As he sees it, it is people's beliefs about other people's beliefs that make the sacred ceremony work:

The altar boy pours water over my fingers, the organ sounds the hymn, I lift the chalice with the Host. It is a moment of drama and power. You could almost think these people actually believe that a wafer is transubstantiated into the body of a crucified man. But of course they don't. You can't believe any such thing, you'd have to be deranged. But you can believe that the priest believes it, and the priest in turn believes his congregation believes it; you can repeat it mechanically, and you can forbid yourself to think about it. *Holy, holy, holy.* I chant, and actually feel surrounded by a force field.

(2013, 38)

The social dynamic of belief depicted in Kehlmann's novel—which is to say, people's tendency to behave as if they believe something not because they actually believe it but because they think that other people do, which in turn, causes those other people to behave as if they do—is a real and fascinating phenomenon studied by cognitive psychologists and anthropologists (see, for instance, Mercier, *Not Born Yesterday: The Science of Who We Trust and What We Believe*). So is, too, the other aspect of this scene, which is that "beliefs are often an occasional and elusive consequence of ceremonies rather than their foundation" (Boyer, 2013, 351).[1] We shall turn to those studies in due time, but first let us consider several other fictional examples of conflicted belief, similarly driven by intricate social reasoning but reflecting different psychological dynamics.

DOI: 10.4324/9781003119456-9

88

Lawrence Kramer, a protagonist of Tom Wolfe's *The Bonfire of the Vanities*, works as an assistant District Attorney in the Bronx. The reason that he chose this job over a better paying one in the private sector is personally meaningful and even heroic: "He, Kramer, would embrace life and wade up to his hips into the lives of the miserable and the damned and stand up on his feet in the courtrooms and fight, *mano a mano*, before the bar of justice" (2010, 35–36). Although this appealing credo and the system of progressive beliefs underlying it are repeated several times in the novel, both by Kramer and by his boss, the District Attorney Abe Weiss ("Doesn't it make you feel good to use your talents for something that means something?" [533]), the actual emotional reality of his daily life may be better characterized as managing his *cognitive dissonance*. This is a term used by psychologists to describe the discomfort arising from our awareness that we hold conflicting beliefs. One way of minimizing this discomfort is to try to convince ourselves that we actually believe in something that we didn't think we believed in, something that we merely wanted other people to think that we believed in.

In Kramer's case, far from feeling good about using his talents for something that means something, he is routinely "assailed by Doubts" (41) about his mission, which seems to consist of "the eternal prosecution of the blacks and Latins" (111). To make matters worse, he also has to live with the knowledge that he has recently ratcheted up his prosecutorial zeal against yet another Black defendant, not because he passionately believed in his guilt, but because he wanted to impress and seduce a pretty juror. This particular example of cognitive dissonance comes to a head when he meets with his old college friends, tells them how he won the case, and notices them "giving him the look you give someone who turns out to be a covert reactionary … something awful." At this moment, Kramer no longer remembers that he "sank" the guy because he wanted to sleep with the jury member. Instead, he feels indignant that he has "to defend himself against a bunch of intellectual trendies in a trendy bistro in trendy fucking Soho," people who have no idea of what it is like to be an assistant DA in the Bronx (256). The only person, he thinks, "who understood how brilliant he had been, who understood the righteousness of the justice he had wrought" (257) is the pretty jury member. Behold the triumph of self-deception in service of tamping down cognitive dissonance: Kramer succeeded in getting a harsher sentence for the defendant solely to impress the girl, but now he seems to sincerely believe that he did it for "righteous" reasons, and that the girl can, in fact, vouch for the objective truth of his beliefs. To quote from research on cognitive dissonance, Kramer engages in "motivated forgetting of information that does not align with the lie" (Polage, 2017, 633).

On a different occasion, Kramer is acutely aware that he is making himself believe in something that may not be true. He is doing what in his circles is called "lighting up the witness," which is to say ignoring signs of the witness's unreliability in order to bolster a case. As he puts it,

> [This witness] was not likely to be known as a pillar of probity—and yet he was the only star witness you had. At this point you were likely to feel the urge to light him up with a lamp of truth and credibility. But this was not merely a matter of improving his reputation in the eyes of a judge and jury. You felt the urge to sanitize him for yourself. You needed to *believe* that what you were doing with this person—namely using him to pack another person off to jail—was not only effective but right. This worm, this germ, this punk, this erstwhile asshole was now your comrade, your point man in the battle of good against evil, and *you yourself wanted to believe* that a light shone round about this … organism, this former vermin from under the rock, now a put-upon and misunderstood youth.
>
> *(447; emphasis added)*

Kramer's reasoning here (made to seem all the more compelling because of how it implicates the audience) exemplifies yet another feature of our social psychology. Being aware of a cognitive bias does not make us less vulnerable to it. In fact, thinking that, when it comes to cognitive biases, "forewarned is forearmed" is a cognitive bias in its own right. Kramer knows that he is manipulating his belief (i.e., minimizing his cognitive dissonance) in a way common among people in his profession, yet he cannot stop.

What are literary scholars, or cognitive literary scholars, such as myself, to make of writers' interest in fake, tortured, conflicting, incoherent, self-serving, etc., beliefs? Approaching works of fiction from this perspective—that is, noticing how they model a variety of complex social patterns involving belief—may lead one to assume that fiction has some kind of special relationship with the concept of belief and/or with the research on this topic. At the very least, writers seem to be uncannily good at representing, or even anticipating, insights of psychologists.

Are they, in general? Cognitive literary critic Patrick Colm Hogan suggests that they are, and that this becomes apparent when one looks at authors who are removed in space or time from contemporary psychological studies and whose texts thus could not have been influenced by them. As he sees it, the processes at work in such texts

> are largely unselfconscious, a matter of implicitly understanding patterns in human relations and conveying that implicit understanding representationally, which is to say, through the depiction of situations that manifest the patterns—usually in a heightened or more salient form than we would encounter in everyday life.
>
> *(2019, 26)*

This chapter takes as its starting point Hogan's argument about writers implicitly understanding patterns in human relations and representing them in a "heightened" form, and discusses one particular type of this heightened representation. I focus on belief because the fundamentally fraught nature of this social phenomenon—that is, its dependence on public performance and its susceptibility to (self-)deception—makes it a particularly inviting (though by no means the only) object for a fictional, i.e., heightened representation. The way I see it, belief is a social morass, and that makes it good for fiction. Wading through it allows writers to pursue a particular set of literary goals. And while the results sometimes align with insights of psychologists, we should not take it as evidence that a wish to illustrate a psychological insight was what drew writers toward these troubled waters.

It so happens that the novels that I look at in this chapter, such as *F* (2014) and *The Bonfire of the Vanities* (1987), do not fit the criteria suggested by Hogan, because they are not removed in space and time from contemporary psychological studies. Hence, I should make it clear that it is irrelevant for my purposes whether or not either Kehlmann or Wolfe have ever had any documented interest in such studies. My subject here is specifically literary opportunities opening up for writers who portray characters with conflicting or incoherent beliefs. To talk about these opportunities, I begin by discussing cognitive and social instabilities of the concept of belief. I then show that writers intuitively exploit such instabilities to generate the kind of subjectivity that we have come to associate with fictional subjectivity.[2] As Wolfe put it in a later-day "Introduction" to his novel, the "concept of the heart at war with the structure of society" is at the core of creative writing (2010, xx). There may be a good reason, then, why creative writers would gravitate toward belief with its built-in chasm between what is publicly performed and privately felt, especially when that private feeling itself is reflective and unstable.

Intuitive and Reflective Beliefs

In its everyday use, the term "belief" is strikingly imprecise. It covers an array of mental stances that have little in common. For instance, I "believe" that if I am hit by a heavy object, I will get badly hurt.

This means that when I find myself in an environment in which heavy weights are moved around, such as a gym or a construction zone, I behave in such a way as to avoid having one dropped on me. I do so *intuitively*, that is, without contemplating who first introduced me to this idea, and when; without regularly bolstering my conviction by recalling incidents of other people who have been hurt this way; and without wondering if other people around me share this belief.

I also "believe," given that I am writing this in summer 2022, during the Russian war against Ukraine, that Putin's Russia is a fascist dictatorship.[3] This belief is *reflective*. That is, I know when I started believing this and which political analysts and historians have shaped my thinking. I am also aware that, in the early days of the war, I found myself constantly gathering evidence that supported this belief, as if getting ready to defend it against those who would argue with me.

Here is yet another kind of reflective belief. Imagine that I have one friend who regularly talks to me about the Christian concept of the Trinity and another, who talks to me about String Theory. While I do not really understand either of these two concepts, I can, nevertheless, engage in conversations about them, e.g., about their history and cultural roles, or about my respective friends' involvement with them. What this means is that I "believe" in the Trinity and String Theory as things that exists in other people's minds. In other words, I meta-represent my beliefs: thinking about them is contingent on my reflecting on their sources and/or on the circumstances in which I formed them, as well as on their relative compatibility with my other beliefs. For instance, I believe in String Theory more than I believe in the Trinity because it feels more compatible with what I think of as my scientific outlook on the world, even though, ironically, it is easier for me to talk about the Trinity than it is to talk about String Theory.

The concept of intuitive and reflective beliefs was first articulated by philosopher and cognitive scientist Dan Sperber. According to Sperber, we treat beliefs that we hold *intuitively*, that is, without reflecting or even being "capable of reflecting on the way we arrived at them or the specific justification we may have for holding them" (1997, 68), as data. We let them circulate among our mental databases without restrictions: serving as inputs for other inferences and influencing a wide variety of behaviors. (For instance, my intuitive belief in gravity underlies a truly untold range of my actions.) In contrast, *reflective* beliefs are "not freely used as premises in inference" (69) because they are subject to constraints that restrict their movement among the mental databases, constraints that may involve our awareness of the circumstances in which we acquired them and/or the contexts in which they obtain (e.g., my friend Mary told me about String Theory; the Trinity is a Christian doctrine).

The difference between intuitive and reflective (that is, metarepresentational) beliefs is not absolute. As Sperber puts it, it "should even be possible that some contents be believed both intuitively and reflectively by the same individual at the same time, each belief playing a different role in the believer's thinking and behavior" (81). For example, to quote cognitive anthropologist and evolutionary psychologist Pascal Boyer,

> We all have physical intuitions, which … help us to predict the trajectory of the ball that bounced on the floor. We can also entertain reflective thoughts about the fact that a ball in motion contains momentum or force.
>
> *(2013, 352)*[4]

Moreover, the capacity to entertain reflective beliefs plays

> A major role in the development and transmission of cultural representations, allowing concepts and ideas that are only half-understood, or that are well understood but only within the context of explicit theories, to stabilize in a human population and to expand the range of thoughts that can be entertained, way beyond what would be possible on a strict intuitive basis.

In other words, "much of culture, from religion to science, is made of reflective concepts and beliefs" (Sperber, 1997, 83).[5]

Why Your Belief Is Intuitive While Mine Is Reflective

For the purposes of the present argument, I am interested in the *social* aspect of the fact that we use the same umbrella concept, belief, to think about a wide variety of mental stances. It seems, for instance, that when it comes to judging *other people's* beliefs, it comes easy for us to consider them as intuitive or at least as more intuitive than ours. Of course, we don't call them intuitive in the sense outlined by Sperber. Instead, we think of those beliefs as "true" or "real," a characterization which may stem from our evolved cognitive predisposition to essentialize abstract concepts, such as power, love, belief, race, etc., that is, to think of them as having non-visible, deep, "supposedly inherent qualities" which "make them the thing that they are" (McIntosh, 1998/1999, 562–63).[6] Thus, because we essentialize beliefs, we think of them as causing specific behaviors. In reality, beliefs are not defined by any essential qualities, and the causality often goes in the other direction: "beliefs follow the behavior, rather than the other way around" (Mercier, 2020, 261).

Hence, we may assume that when other people engage in an effortful and time-consuming ritual associated with a particular religion or political ideology, their behavior is caused by or expresses their true belief in the tenets of that religion or ideology. We may assume it even while knowing that when we ourselves engage in that ritual, our own belief in those tenets is reflective rather than intuitive; for instance, that we may be more predisposed toward it in a particular social context; that we may append it with qualifiers indicating the relative degree of our certainty; or that we may participate in an involved ritual hoping to *attain* the kind of true belief that we know we lack.[7] Generally, we may be less ready to attribute to other people, or social groups, the same kind of ambivalence, complexity, and reflectivity about their beliefs that we are aware of in ourselves or in our in-group.

Observe that I use the pronoun "we" to talk about the general tendency, but there may also be some individual differences in the readiness with which "we" see others' behavior as caused by intuitive beliefs. Consider, for instance, research on attributional complexity, i.e., "the motivation to understand human behavior, along with the preference for complex explanations of it" (Castano et al., 2020).[8] According to social and cognitive psychologist Emanuele Castano and his colleagues, long-term exposure to literary fiction, but not to popular fiction, positively predicts attributional complexity (which, I should add, does not automatically translate into any kind of moral goodness)[9]. This opens interesting questions about cultural and personal contexts in which a specific individual may be more or less disposed toward ascribing intuitive beliefs to other people or groups, but I will not address these questions in this chapter.

So, what does it mean to say that it is often the *social* aspect of our experience of belief that reveals one of its important features, which is that, in our everyday use, reflective beliefs of others are often treated as intuitive beliefs? To start with, this may explain why it comes to us as a surprise that thinking that gods are real is "an exceedingly rare intuition" even in the cultures that are organized around religious sentiments.[10] To put it differently, when we observe a community in which gods are prominently present in everyday discourse and in ritual, we take this presence of reflective belief as an expression of intuitive belief on the part of the members of the community. Because they talk about it so much, they must surely believe it! However, as Boyer puts it,

> The more we know about our evolved psychology, the more we understand why most people, at most times, in most situations will *not* consider their gods real, in the sense of having a definite intuition that the gods are actually there … This of course may seem surprising, as a *reflective* notion of superhuman agency, and its involvement in human affairs, is so pervasive

in human cultures, indeed probably one of the most easily acquired pieces of socially transmitted information. But [this] paradox is mostly an artifact of our folk understanding of "belief," which gets in the way of a proper understanding of mental states. We cannot really understand why a successful cultural notion describes an exceedingly rare intuition as long as we confuse intuitive mental content with explicit reflections.

(2013, 354–55)

Let us consider briefly a couple of other cultural contexts in which other people's potentially reflective beliefs are treated as intuitive, in contrast to our own, which are given, as it were, the benefit of the doubt, i.e., allowed to remain reflective. As cognitive anthropologist Hugo Mercier, who works with gullibility and vigilance, points out, there seems to be a fascinating contradiction between the fact that people are actually not gullible and their willingness to believe that other people are. Rumors about others' gullibility are "intuitively compelling" and as such are likely to spread and "become culturally successful, even when they are wildly unrepresentative." Crucially, the idea that other people are gullible "provides post rationalizations for actions or ideas that have other motivations"; for instance, an argument about gullible masses can be used to explain why they "couldn't be trusted with political power, as they would be promptly manipulated by cunning demagogues bent on wrecking the social order" (2020, 163–64).

As a literary historian, I am familiar with a version of this claim as applied to fiction and its alleged corrupting effect on readers. This is to say, on readers *other* than those who issue the dire warnings, for they themselves are, apparently, immune. They know, for instance, that reading Goethe's *The Sorrows of Young Werther* (1774), a novel about a young man who kills himself over unrequited love, will have no dangerous effect on them. Other people, however (e.g., young people, women, children, racialized others, as well as people from the past) must be more vulnerable. Thus, back in the eighteenth century, German writer and art critic G.E. Lessing feared that reading *Werther* "might induce young people to imitate its suicide ending." The same fear was expressed by Goethe himself and by others (perhaps those standing to increase their social capital or to reap financial benefit from the rumor about the emotional power of the story).[11] This sentiment would later become the foundation of the so-called Werther Effect, or the widespread perception that there was, in fact, a suicide epidemic following the publication of the novel. In reality, there seemed to have been altogether only three cases, so "contrary to popular belief … a suicide epidemic did not arise after all" (Thorson and Öberg, 2010, 69–70).

Still, the belief in the power of fiction—over *other* people, that is—dies hard. In fact, it doesn't die at all. Today, it may take the form of thinking that reading fiction is "morally improving." As philosopher and literary critic Josh Landy puts it,

Human nature is a strange thing. We know how blissfully immune we are to influence from artworks whose underlying worldview departs from our own (am I really likely to become a con-man after watching *The Sting*? an advocate of whaling after reading *Moby Dick*?), and yet we carry on assigning films and novels and plays and poems to friends we consider in dire need of inner change. "Read this," we say, "it will make you see things differently" (by which of course we mean "it will make you see things my way"). Perhaps we give a copy of *Candide* to one who is laboring under the delusion that God works in the world. Perhaps she returns the favor by forcing us to read some C. S. Lewis. The two of us end up, like the positivist and the priest in *Madame Bovary*, as firmly entrenched in our positions as we ever were before. We should all just come out and admit it: "morally improving" is merely a compliment we pay to works whose values agree with ours.

(2008, 70)

Because we suspect that others' intuitive beliefs can be easily manipulated—for instance, when a honey-tongued demagogue or a compelling book comes their way—we underestimate the role of reflective beliefs in shaping people's behavior.[12] Generally, applying our notion of belief—by which we mean, more often than not, *intuitive* belief—to situations featuring complex social behavior can be misleading, for a variety of locally specific reasons. To give one example (and one I only mention here briefly but have discussed at length elsewhere [see Zunshine, 2022, 113–21]), explaining people's behavior in terms of their beliefs is also extremely fraught in communities subscribing to the "opacity of mind" model (See Robbins and Rumsey, 2008). In such communities, one cannot talk about mental states, including beliefs, of other people, unless they have explicitly stated them themselves, in which case one can safely repeat those statements.

Given how problematic the idea that you can explain people's complex social behavior by their underlying beliefs is, we may even be better off retiring the concept altogether. What keeps it alive—as, for instance, in Western liberal democracies, in which the notion of people's real beliefs is integral to cultural discourse—is the combination of specific historical factors and the quirks of our cognitive architecture (See Zunshine, 2022, 121–39).[13]

What are those quirks?

Why Belief Is Not *Really* There: The Cognitive Illusion of "Mindreading"

Here are possible cognitive reasons why, under certain historical circumstances, the notion of belief as a cause of complex behavior can retain its cultural plausibility. One fundamental feature of human social cognition is that we make sense of our own and of other people's observable behavior in terms of invisible mental states, such as thoughts, desires, intentions, and, yes, beliefs—a phenomenon known as "mindreading," "theory of mind," or "folk-psychology" (see Apperly, 2011; Boyer, 2018; Sperber, 1997). For instance, during a faculty meeting I see my colleague quickly glancing up at another colleague, right after some remark made by the chair, and I immediately construct the first colleague's behavior as caused by a particular thought or intention vis-à-vis the second colleague in relation to what the chair has just said. In reality, however, my colleague may have been thinking about something completely unrelated or may have jerked up her head as a result of a neck spasm.

This is to say that the unceasing attribution of mental states that we engage in in our daily social interaction means neither that our mindreading intuitions are *correct* (quite often they are wrong), nor—and this is perhaps most important—that the thoughts and feelings that we thus intuit are *actually there*. Instead, what *is* there is our cognitive adaptation for explaining behavior as caused by mental states, an adaptation that has a long evolutionary history and that we are stuck with as a social species, for better or for worse.

The key point here, specifically concerning our notion of belief, is that, along with other mental states, it is an artifact of our cognitive architecture. We cobble together beliefs, our own and other people's, as we move along, in order to navigate our social environment.[14] And because beliefs are thus fundamentally ontologically unstable, they are subject to perpetual second-guessing, faking, and manipulation.

Ways in Which Belief Is a Mess

Let us sum up the ways in which the concept of belief is a mess, so that we can talk (in the next section) about why it may be good for fiction. First of all, many of our beliefs, especially those that are socially meaningful and thus *interesting* (as opposed, for instance, to our belief in gravity, which is intuitive and also socially boring) are reflective. This is to say that they are embedded in specific social contexts; come with various tags pointing to their sources as well as with qualifiers indicating degrees of one's certainty in their content, and are open to change/revision.

Second, because our socially meaningful beliefs are reflective, they are ridden with possibilities for cognitive dissonance. Like Lawrence Kramer from *The Bonfire of the Vanities*, we may think that we sincerely believe in something, only to be faced with the fact that our actual behavior contradicts what we thought we believed in, or is perceived by other people as contradicting what they or we thought we believed in. To minimize cognitive dissonance arising from such situations, we may lie to ourselves and others and engage in "motivated forgetting of information that does not align with the lie" (Polage, 2017, 633). This process is responsive to intricate social nuances and fraught from top to bottom.

Third, we entertain an essentialist view of belief. This means that we think that "true" belief is characterized by certain essential qualities and are thus prepared to interpret external behavior, that of others and our own, as manifesting those qualities (while in reality essences do not exist, and the essentialist thinking is itself an artifact of specific features of our cognitive architecture). It also means that we think that beliefs cause behavior, while in reality it is often the other way around.[15]

Fourth, we tend to think of other people's beliefs as more intuitive, or at least less reflective, than ours. When *I* spend three hours at a house of worship, reciting prayers, moving my body in unison with other bodies, and sharing a ritual meal, it is because I value the community offered by this congregation. However, when I observe *you* engage in the same activities, I think (or suspect enviously) that you are moved by an actual faith, or, in any case, by a greater degree of faith than I know myself to possess. Recall that Lawrence Kramer is willing to grant the District Attorney the belief in the value of what they do in the Bronx County Building, which he cannot grant to himself anymore. He is humbled by the size of his "Doubts" (257), but he has no way to gauge those of his boss.

Which brings us to the fifth point. Faced with communal pressure, we may "perform" our beliefs for the benefit of others. But the very fact that we know that we can do it, also opens the possibility that we would suspect that others are also faking their beliefs. So, on the one hand, we may think that others' belief is less complicated and more intuitive than others, but, on the other hand, we may also be open to a position of radical skepticism regarding any kind of "real" belief on the part of others. To put it differently, our belief in other people's intuitive belief is itself a reflective belief and as such it is open to change and revision.

Finally, note that I have considered these five points separately, in order to keep the discussion manageable. In practice, however, they are not neatly isolated. There are plenty of social contexts in which several or all of these dynamics come together and influence each other: performing one's reflective belief; minimizing cognitive dissonance between one's behavior (as observed by other people) and what one thinks of as one's "real" belief; perceiving others' belief as more intuitive than one's own (i.e., integrated without source tags or with weak source tags) and thus more open to manipulation than our own; expecting that some essential qualities of people's belief would come through in their behavior, yet also knowing that behavior can be performed precisely to meet this kind of expectation, and thus fluctuating in one's assessment of other people's beliefs.

This is the kind of mess that our daily grappling with "our folk-psychological understanding of 'belief'" (Boyer, 2013, 355) offers to fiction. What does fiction do with it?

Why This Mess Is Good for Fiction

First, I must restate the general point that I made in the opening of this essay. Looking at literature, one finds numerous vivid illustrations of insights that have been explicitly articulated by social and cognitive psychologists. This should not be taken as evidence of fiction aiming at accurate representation and thus being, in effect, a species of social science. Fiction has its own goals, quite different from those of psychology, even if we do need cognitive psychology to become aware of the building blocks intuitively used by the writers to achieve those goals.

Having discussed these issues extensively, most recently in *The Secret Life of Literature* (2022), I offer here only a brief summary that will serve as the context for my present argument that belief, with its built-in social messiness, is good for fiction. (I am aware that this argument will leave unanswered larger questions about cognition and fiction, such as, for instance, how the sociocognitive patterns that I describe change across different genres and media, and how specific cultural pathways may contribute to our enjoyment of those patterns. While space concerns make it impossible to do justice to those important questions here, readers are invited to follow up on them in my book, available for free through the MIT Press's Open Access Program at https://direct.mit.edu/books/oa-monograph/5288/The-Secret-Life-of-Literature.)

For over 4,000 years, writers have been experimenting with our cognitive adaptations for "mindreading" by constantly devising new social contexts that let their audiences imagine the complex mental states of characters and, in some cases, of narrators and implied authors/readers. The complexity of those mental states arises from their *embeddedness* within each other: mental state within mental state within yet another mental state. For instance, in the Eucharist scene from Kehlmann's novel, Martin *thinks* that the priest *believes* that his congregation *believes* in transubstantiation, which is a third-level embedment of mental states. Writers can use a wide variety of extremely subtle but also not-so-subtle stylistic means to recursively embed mental states within each other on this high level. Without being consciously aware of doing so, they constantly cast about for new social contexts conducive to this kind of high sociocognitive complexity. And when it comes to their audiences, reading complex intentionality into a text—which is to say, intuitively expecting fictional subjectivity to be constructed as a series of complex embedments, explicitly spelled out or merely implied—has become our standard experience of fiction and literature, that is, of novels, plays, and narrative poems, but also of some ostensibly non-fictional texts, such as memoirs concerned with imagination and consciousness.

This is the basis for my present argument that belief, much of it being cognitive illusion, is good for fiction. As a social mess—subject to cascading mistaken assumptions, to performance and manipulation, as well as to deception and self-deception used to minimize cognitive dissonance—belief provides numerous opportunities for conjuring up situations conducive to complex embedment of mental states.

Thus, it is not a coincidence that, in order to follow Martin's musing about his parishioners' beliefs, we (readers) have to process complex embedments such as, "you can *believe* that the priest *believes* … [that] his congregation *believes*" in transubstantiation (38; emphasis added). Similarly, it is not a coincidence that various soul-searchings of Lawrence Kramer of *The Bonfire of the Vanities* depend on constant high-level embedment. For instance, when it comes to describing the concept of "lighting up the witness," Kramer *knows* that he *wants* to *believe* that his witness has been *misunderstood* (i.e., thought of as something other than he is) by others.

Just so, we need to process numerous complex embedments of mental states in order to be able to follow Kramer's attempts to minimize the massive cognitive dissonance which arises when his own "Doubts" about his job receive what seems to be a painful confirmation from his former college friends, who look at him as at "a covert reactionary … something awful." For instance, we know that Kramer is *mortified* to *realize* that they *think* that his *beliefs* have undergone a terrible change. We also know that to deal with his mortification, he starts *feeling angry* about them *judging* him while *not knowing* what it *feels* like to be an assistant DA in the Bronx. Moreover, when Kramer begins to think that the only person who truly understood "the righteousness of the justice he had wrought" (257) was the pretty juror, we know that he is deceiving himself. In this moment, rich with dramatic irony,[16] mental states of the implied reader become an integral part of the embedment. The implied reader *knows* that Kramer now *believes* in his own *righteous anger*, which is to say that Kramer seems to have *forgotten* that he had only *wanted* the pretty jury member to *think* that he *believed* in the righteousness of his case in order to impress her.

Or consider Kramer's conversation with District Attorney Weiss shortly after they arrest the rich Wall Street trader Sherman McCoy on charges which, as Kramer knows, are not 100% convincing (hence his earlier endeavor to "light up the witness"). Weiss—whose office nickname is Captain Ahab, after Melville's character, obsessed with the Great While Whale—talks rapturously about finally nailing his Great White Defendant and thus sending "a helluva good signal" to minority New Yorkers, showing them that Weiss and his office "represent *them* and they're a part of New York City":

Weiss gazed down 161 Street like a shepherd upon his flock. Kramer was glad no one but himself was witnessing this. If more than one witness had been on hand, then cynicism would have reigned. You wouldn't have been able to think about anything other than the fact that Abe Weiss had an election coming up in five months, and 70 percent of the inhabitants of the Bronx were black and Latin. But since there was, in fact, no other witness, Kramer could get to the heart of the matter, which was that the manic creature before him, Captain Ahab, was right.

"You did a great job yesterday, Larry," said Weiss, "and I want you to keep pouring it on. Doesn't it make you *feel good* to use your talents for something that means something?"

(533; emphasis in the original)

To make sense of this passage we must process several complex embedments—without being consciously aware of it. For instance, we know that Kramer is *imagining* other people *thinking* that Abe Weiss only *pretends to believe* in justice (which is to say, *wants* people to *think* that he *believes* in justice), while in fact he only cares about the election. We also know that Kramer is *glad* that, in the absence of the cynical witnesses, he can afford to *forget* about those other *motivations* of his boss. As implied readers, we may also be expected to observe how Kramer minimizes his cognitive dissonance. That is, we *know* that Kramer *wants* to *believe* that Weiss is *sincere*—because that would mean that he, Kramer, is sincere, too—and that he temporarily manages to achieve that elusive comforting belief: "the heart of the matter … was that … Captain Ahab was right." We are also left with lingering doubts about Weiss's sincerity. That is, we *wonder* if, like Kramer, Weiss desperately *wants* to *believe* in what he claims to *believe*, or if he indeed believes in what he professes.

Observe the intricate multidimensional interaction among the intersubjective dynamic created by the embedments; our essentialist biases; and our expectation that other people's beliefs may be more intuitive than ours (or less reflective than ours). Here is one way to describe this interaction. When we wonder about Weiss's sincerity (thus processing a complex embedment of mental states), we tacitly assume that there is such a thing as a "true" belief (an essentialist assumption), and we are prepared to consider the possibility that Weiss is neither faking it, nor minimizing his own cognitive dissonance, which means that he may just be capable of the "true" belief, which is to say, the kind of *intuitive* belief, of which a character to whose mind the novel gives us direct access (i.e., Lawrence Kramer) is not capable.

Let me pause here and clarify several points. First, I didn't attempt to list *all* possible complex embedments that make the passages above what they are (i.e., an ironic commentary on "the heart at war with the structure of society" [Wolfe, "Introduction," 2010, xx]). Nor do I claim that, were you to articulate mental states structuring those passages, you would come up with the same set of thoughts, feelings, and intentions of characters and implied readers that I did. In fact, I am sure that yours would be different from mine. But however different they might be, the relationship *among them* would be the one that I describe, which is to say that mental states would be embedded on at least the third level, that is, mental states within mental states embedded within yet other mental states. First-and second-level mental states simply will not capture adequately the sociocognitive complexity conjured up by those scenes.

Second, given the specific style of *The Bonfire of the Vanities*, many of the complex embedments that I listed above are explicit, that is, they are more or less explicitly spelled out in the text. This may give you an incorrect impression about the prevalence of explicitly spelled-out embedments in fiction in general. In fact, the opposite is often the case. Fiction depends to a large degree on implied complex embedments, that is, on the attribution of complex mental states that are not spelled out (or even mentioned) in the text and that we have to read into it in order to make sense of the action.[17]

Third, although a lot of what is happening in those passages involves belief, I don't want you to think that belief is uniquely or exceptionally important for embedment. One valuable quality of belief is that it plays well with others. Deception, self-deception, shame, embarrassment, self-consciousness, hypocrisy, etc., are good for fiction, because they all depend on attribution of mental states embedded on a high (i.e., at least third) level (Zunshine, 2022, 158–62). Belief integrates well with all those troublemakers, as long as it is not any kind of actual true belief—a boring state of mind, unprofitable for fiction. (That is, for fiction as we know it: a powerful imaginative engagement with the social mind of the reader.) At its best, belief brims with the promise of essentialist assumptions, doubt, fakery, and failure,[18] and that's the way we like it.

Conclusion: Fiction Models Belief in Its Own Way

If there is one take-home message offered by this essay, it is this: *fiction models belief by means other than representing accurately real-life dynamics involved in belief.* For instance, we may come across a situation, in a work of fiction, in which a character wrongly assumes that another character's belief is more intuitive and less reflective than her own. Or we may come across a situation in which a character minimizes her cognitive dissonance about her beliefs by first lying and then engaging in a "motivated forgetting of information that does not align with the lie." Or we may read a story in which people behave as if they believe in something not because they actually believe it but because they think that other people do, which in turn, causes those other people to behave as if they do.

All such fictional situations correspond nicely to a variety of cognitive biases and other psycho-social dynamics described by psychologists. However, I do not believe that locating such situations in fictional texts and confirming their real-life truth value is a meaningful literary-critical endeavor. Fiction turns to the fraught phenomenon of "belief" to generate complex embedments of mental states. It may so happen that, in the process of generating such embedments, it will accurately reflect some real-life dynamic, but then, again, just as often, it may not. The former representation will not be more intrinsically valuable than the latter, certainly not from any kind of aesthetic perspective.

Let me illustrate this idea with a brief example from my earlier work. Studies by social and cognitive psychologists have shown that "people in weaker social positions engage in more active and perceptive mindreading than people in stronger social positions" (Snodgrass, 1985, 149; see also Vignemont, 2007). Some fictional texts accurately reflect this dynamic by portraying characters of lower social standing (which can be corelated with class, gender, race, or age) as better mindreaders. They do it by means specific to literature, which is to say by depicting characters in weaker social position as capable of embedding mental states on a higher level than their social superiors (Zunshine, 2022, 65–87). Other texts, however, *invert* the real-life dynamic. They portray characters in weaker social positions as not capable of keeping up with their "betters'" high-level embedment. It can be argued that such misrepresentations of the real-life dynamic serve particular ideological agendas of the authors, but that's a different issue (Zunshine, 2022, 87–98). What is important here is that fiction is not obligated to depict accurately sociocognitive patterns which characterize actual social interactions.[19] Both following *and* inverting those patterns allow writers to construct complex embedments of mental states, and this is what they are (intuitively) after.[20]

Just so, the same work of fiction may feature one character who attributes to another an intuitive belief that she later discovers to be reflective, and another character who follows the opposite trajectory, that is, who attributes to someone a reflective belief that later turns out to be more intuitive than she expected. To single out the former situation and to celebrate its consilience with some published psychological studies would miss the point about what both of those situations offer to the writer in terms of generating the complex social subjectivity that we have come to associate with fiction, that is, a subjectivity that depends on mental states embedded on a high level.

To conclude, complex embedment of mental states in fiction is the ontological instability of "mindreading" writ large. Belief is an active and versatile contributor to this instability. To return to Hogan's observation that writers implicitly understand patterns in human relations and portray them in a heightened form, we can expect that representations of belief will continue to play an important role in the construction of fictional subjectivity as we know it, a subjectivity that rivets readers' social minds by intensifying and reimagining real-life mindreading patterns. Belief is too much of a mess in real life to pass on an opportunity to explode this mess on page or stage.

Notes

1 Compare to Marquez (2018, 277).

2 For a discussion of why readers may actually enjoy literature's intensification of real-life sociocognitive patterns, see Zunshine (2006 and 2022 e.g., 109–12) ("Distal and Proximate Causes of Complex Embedment in Literature").

3 For a discussion of "rashism" or "ruscism," see Snyder (2022).

4 For a further discussion of beliefs that are simultaneously reflective and intuitive, see Mercier (2020, 261).

5 For a recent review of intuitive and reflective beliefs in the context of a dual-processing model, see Baumard and Boyer (2013).

6 See also Zunshine (2008, 44–48).

7 Compare to Dilley's discussion of "the training of thoughts practiced by early Christian monks" (2017, 14–15).

8 Importantly, Castano et al. observe that the construct known as attributional complexity "further includes the presence of meta-cognitive elements in the process through which explanations are reached, and the tendency to infer abstract attributions, both for internal and external factors" (n.p.).

9 "Literary texts," as Landy puts it, "can make us more finely aware and more richly responsible. But they will only do so if we want them to" (2008, 81).

10 For a detailed discussion, see Luhrmann (2012).

11 As Thorson and Öberg (2010) observe, it was "expressed in the programme booklet of Manet's opera *Werther*, which was staged at the Royal Opera in Stockholm in 1997. It was, furthermore, stated twice during the radio broadcast of the opening night of the opera" (70).

12 See, for instance, Mercier (2020, 32–34) and Xavier (2018, 272–73) on propaganda, as well as Schulmann (2022, 13:17–14:50) on beliefs of people with Soviet experience.

13 See Zunshine (2022, 121–39).

14 Zunshine (2022, 138).

15 For a discussion, see Hogan (2019, 232).

16 For a discussion of dramatic irony as "a prototypical implied third-level embedment," see Zunshine (2022, 13).

17 For a detailed discussion of implied embedments, see Zunshine (2022, 13–19).

18 On the importance of failure for literary imagination, see Spolsky (2015).

19 Of course, real life is not obligated to faithfully follow those patterns either.

20 For a discussion of whether or not writers are aware of their practice of embedding complex mental states, see Zunshine (2022, 39–43).

Works Cited

Apperly, Ian. 2011. *The Cognitive Basis of "Theory of Mind."* New York: Psychology Press.

Baumard, Nicolas, and Pascal Boyer. 2013. "Religious Beliefs as Reflective Elaborations on Intuitions: A Modified Dual-Process Model." *Current Directions in Psychological Science* 22, no. 4 (August): 295–300.

Boyer, Pascal. 2013. "Why 'Belief' Is Hard Work: Implications of Tanya Luhrmann's When God Talks Back." *HAU: Journal of Ethnographic Theory* 3, no. 3 (Winter): 349–57.

Boyer, Pascal. 2018. *Minds Make Societies: How Cognition Explains the World Humans Create.* New Haven, CT: Yale University Press.

Castano, Emanuele, Alison Jane Martingano, and Pietro Perconti. 2020. "The Effect of Exposure to Fiction on Attributional Complexity, Egocentric Bias and Accuracy in Social Perception." *PLoS ONE* 15, no. 5 (May 29). https://doi.org/10.1371/journal.pone.0233378.

Dilley, Paul C. 2017. *Monasteries and the Care of Souls in the Late Antique Christianity: Cognition and Discipline.* Cambridge: Cambridge University Press.

Hogan, Patrick Colm. 2019. *Sexual Identities.* New York: Oxford University Press.

Kehlmann, Daniel. 2014. *F (a Novel)*. Translated by Carol Brown Janeway. London: Quercus.

Landy, Joshua. 2008. "A Nation of Madame Bovarys: On the Possibility and Desirability of Moral Improvement Through Fiction." In *Art and Ethical Criticism*, edited by Garry Hagberg, 63–94. Hoboken, NJ: Blackwell.

Luhrmann, Tanya. 2012. *When God Talks Back: Understanding the American Evangelical Relationship with God.* New York: Alfred E. Knopf.

Márquez, Xavier. 2018. "Two Models of Political Leader Cults: Propaganda and Ritual." *Politics, Religion & Ideology* 19, no. 3: 265–84.

McIntosh, Janet. 1998/1999. "Symbolism, Cognition, and Political Orders." *Science & Society* 62, no. 4 (Winter): 557–68.

Mercier, Hugo. 2020. *Not Born Yesterday: The Science of Who We Trust And What We Believe.* Princeton, NJ: Princeton University Press.

Polage, Danielle. 2017. "The Effect of Telling Lies on Belief in the Truth." *Europe's Journal of Psychology* 13, no. 4 (November): 633–44.

Robbins, Joel, and Alan Rumsey. 2008. "Introduction: Cultural and Linguistic Anthropology and the Opacity of Other Minds." *Anthropological Quarterly* 81, no. 2 (Spring): 407–20.

Schulmann, Ekaterina [Шульман, Екатерина]. 2022. "Patriotic Upbringing: Indoctrination of Schoolchildren" ["Патриотическое Воспитание: Индоктринация Школьников"]. Интервью каналу@Редакция Алексея Пивоварова. Video. April 25. https://www.youtube.com/watch?v=ZSZFGqv05xo&t=1s.

Snodgrass, Sara E. 1985. "'Women's Intuition': The Effect of Subordinate Role on Interpersonal Sensitivity." *Journal of Personality and Social Psychology* 49, no. 1 (July): 146–55.

Snyder, Timothy. 2022. "The War in Ukraine Has Unleashed a New Word." *The New York Times*, April 22, 2022. https://www.nytimes.com/2022/04/22/magazine/ruscism-ukraine-russia-war.html.

Sperber, Dan. 1997. "Intuitive and Reflective Beliefs." *Mind & Language* 12, no. 1 (March): 67–83.

Spolsky, Ellen. 2015. "The Biology of Failure, the Forms of Rage, and the Equity of Revenge." In *The Oxford Handbook of Cognitive Literary Studies*, edited by Lisa Zunshine, 34–54. New York: Oxford University Press.

Thorson, Jan, and Per-Arne Öberg. 2010. "Was There a Suicide Epidemic after Goethe's Werther?" *Archives of Suicide Research* 7: 69–72. Published online: November 30, 2010. https://doi.org/10.1080/13811110301568.

Vignemont, Frédérique de. 2007. "Frames of Reference in Social Cognition." *Quarterly Journal of Experimental Psychology* 61, no. 1 (January): 1–27.

Wolfe, Tom. (1987) 2010. *The Bonfire of the Vanities.* London: Vintage Books.

Wolfe, Tom. 2010. "Introduction: Stalking the Billion-Footed Beast." In *The Bonfire of the Vanities,* ix–xxx. London: Vintage Books.

Zunshine, Lisa. 2006. *Why We Read Fiction: Theory of Mind and the Novel.* Columbus: Ohio State University Press.

Zunshine, Lisa. 2008. *Strange Concepts and the Stories They Make Possible: Cognition, Culture, Narrative.* Baltimore, MD: Johns Hopkins University Press.

Zunshine, Lisa. 2022. *The Secret Life of Literature.* Cambridge, MA: MIT Press. https://direct.mit.edu/books/oa-monograph/5288/The-Secret-Life-of-Literature.

8

FICTION AND HISTORIOGRAPHY

Annick Louis

Although often viewed as differentiated or opposed discourses, fiction and historiography have always been entwined. Such opposition allegedly arises from the fact that fiction does not seek to achieve belief whereas historical discourse aims at belief and veracity, as historiography refers to a scholarly activity considered as imparting knowledge. At the same time, it is widely accepted that fiction is neither true nor false, even if the question of truth and that of belief cannot be entirely separated.

Traditionally, in Western culture, the debate revolved around the relationship between narrative and history. In the twentieth century, though, this conversation took on a new dimension, as the discussion around the relationship between fiction, narrative, historiography, and belief took center stage, replacing the question of the relationship between narrative and history (Anheim, 2010). The debate has not been settled yet, although different disciplines (literary studies, history, sociology) have provided concepts and theories aiming to solve it these last two or three decades, in the context of the consolidation of a transnational culture (Topuzian, 2017). The numerous debates concerning the boundaries between historiography and fiction have highlighted the fact that the essential problem is how to determine that representations are fictional.

A pragmatic perspective will be adopted here, which considers that the notion of fiction does not reference a form of organization of representations, but rather the epistemic attitude adopted toward representations, whatever their mode of organization. Therefore, analyzing the epistemic attitude of the sender and the receiver toward these representations, and more precisely determining what kind of relations they will establish between these representations and their referential beliefs, is essential (Schaeffer, 2020). In the case of narrative representations, the subset of referential beliefs concerns the events and actions that animate entities that partake in what is presented as reality. Yet, the ability to determine whether a story is a fiction or a historical account does require investigating the issue of belief. Therefore, taking into consideration theories of fiction is crucial to exploring the relationship between fiction and historiography, and to understanding how they generate belief. In fact, fiction can be considered as a genre whose scope transcends literature, as it includes various artistic languages (García, 2017; Schaeffer, 2020).

Historical Reminder: The Positivist Paradigm versus the Process of Writing

According to the Aristotelian tradition, the production of fictions through the double activity of *mimesis* and plot (*muthos*) is not separated from knowledge operations. However, the advantage of poetry

DOI: 10.4324/9781003119456-10"

over history stems from its being more philosophical and mobilizing names and subjects from history. In addition, in poetry each part of the composition is subordinated to the whole, while history is forced to make sense less intelligible because it accounts for actions and events scattered across time. The opposition, therefore, is not situated between fiction and non-fiction; it falls between genres which, in their rhetorical definitions, produce forms of unequally accomplished knowledge (Aristotle, 1451b, 27–32; Calame, 2012). The contradictions of the dominant Aristotelian rhetorical-poetic model in Western culture manifest themselves in the early modern period, which had long been considered an era of harmonious relations between literature and history by theorists such as Roland Barthes (1984) and Hayden White (1978). Recently, Françoise Lavocat (2020) has shown that between the sixteenth and the eighteenth centuries, the variety of positions and the abundance of debates provoked by the conflictuality of thought on the relationship between history and fiction highlight their rivalry and the attempt at mutual appropriation. Lavocat also points out that Corneille considered that belief made emotion possible, because a fiction that respects historical facts is more easily believed; Corneille also identifies what Aristotle calls an "impossible belief" in false versions of history (97).

In the nineteenth century, two opposed tendencies coexist. On the one hand, Augustin Thierry's paradigm establishing that fiction must inspire the new historical writing, also endorsed by Jules Michelet; on the other, the lack of problematization of narrative—what De Certeau calls the "ivresse statisticienne" ("statistical rapture") (1975). The role of the historian evolves, as scholarly history became prominent in most Western countries; by the end of the century, the works of the previous generations—such as Michelet, Renan, Taine or Fustel de Coulanges—are considered literature. The rejection of a historiographic tradition based on a rhetorical approach that privileged literary style, by then considered incompatible with scientific rigor, leads to a process of "scientization" and "professionalization" of history; historians such as Charles-Victor Langlois and Charles Seignobos in France and Leopold von Ranke in Germany advocate for a strict account of facts. According to the positivist paradigm, narrative is devoid of epistemic significance, and thus, is neither problematized nor relevant. However, historians of the two coexisting tendencies conceive their work as connected to the past by means of the archives (Anheim, 2019).

In the early twentieth century, with the establishment of social history, the literary dimension of history was disqualified with the mobilization of new arguments, and narrative was brought to trial. The *École des Annales* openly criticized narrative history; rejecting narrative, event, chronology, and individuality implies that narrative is, therefore, not specifically analyzed as a literary form, and at the same time the rejection of "histoire-récit" (history-narrative) was substantiated even more with the quantitative and serial "turn" performed by this social science history. If the *École des Annales* had no consideration of the scriptural forms whatsoever, similarly, the historiographical scene in the 1970s circumscribed the approach to the question of the writing of history to repudiating "histoire-récit," thus overlooking any autonomous problematization of the literary dimension of history writing (Lepetit, 1996; Schöttler, 2010). However, in this context of a prevailing quantitative history, some works proclaimed the theoretical legitimacy of narrative: Paul Veyne's *Comment on écrit l'histoire?* ([Writing History] (1971)), Michel de Certeau's *L'écriture de l'histoire* [The Writing of History] (1975), Hayden White's *Metahistory: The Historical Imagination in Nineteenth-Century Europe* (1973). Thus, in the 1970s and 1980s, the distinction between history and fiction reconfigured a debate that had so far concerned historians only, challenging social history in its scientific ambitions. Effectively, a major shift in historiography determined that writing would no longer be perceived as a secondary operation of communication. Of particular importance in this context is the so-called *linguistic turn* that rehabilitated the role of language and narrative in social sciences, by questioning a dominant approach to history, mainly empiric, anti-theoretical and attached to the idea of objectivity (Cannadine, 2002; Revel and Loriga, 2022; Rorty, 1967).

Paul Veyne proposed to conceptualize history as a narrative, laying the foundation for an epistemology of history. History, he asserted, is not scientific; it is nothing but a narrative, yet a true narrative, a sort of "true novel." History devises plots that are very unscientific combinations of material causes, ends, and coincidences. In history, explaining is nothing more than how the story builds itself into an understandable plot. Michel de Certeau conceives historical practice as a practice of writing. History is a narrative which is to be referred to a locus of enunciation, to a technique of knowledge, linked to the historical institution. Considering the locus of the historiographical operation allows to resituate historical discourse in the contemporary moment of its production. Historical practice thus depends on the structure of the society that establishes the conditions of the telling, the latter being neither legendary nor devoid of relevance (Dosse, 2010). De Certeau was one of the first historians to claim that writing is not an accessory aspect of the historian's work while upholding that history is a scientific activity. He argues that the scriptural staging of historiographical operation has its own characteristics: chronological order, textual completeness, the attempt to give a true content in the form of a narrative, the massive presence of metaphors and the fragmented or layered structure of the historical text that includes parts constituted by the archives and the documentation disseminated in quotations, references, and notes. As a result, historical discourse produces a reality effect that builds up reliability.

Concurrently, the Anglophone narrativity current, too, argued that writing and narrative were by no means mere devices. By postulating narrative as a specific feature that distinguishes history from the natural sciences, it also operated an epistemological reversal on the question of the narrative in history by claiming that narrative is a cognitive tool and a specific form of explanation in history (Delacroix, 2010). According to Hayden White, historical content cannot be disconnected from its discursive form; rhetorical tropes prefigure historical discourse, determining argumentative and narrative choices. History can be defined as a form of fiction production that is indistinguishable from other types of fiction; in order to avoid the relativism that this position may entail, Hayden White distinguishes between events (which pre-exist the historian) and facts (which are discursive phenomena). This progressive dissolution of events as history's main object challenged the distinction between realistic discourse and fiction, leading, according to White, to a new form of representation founded on a fictionalization of the past. Historiography's nature is literary, but not neutral; behind the objectivity of historians, we can identify the political connotations of history (Revel and Loriga, 2022, 235–58; White, 1987).

In the 1980s and 1990s, Paul Ricoeur's work on narrative identity, as mobilized by historians, was marked by their negative reactions to Hayden White's fictionalist theses, as well as by negationist provocations, and the revival of the debate on the question of narrative in history. Historians such as Lawrence Stone, Roger Chartier, Carlo Ginzburg, and Arlette Farge pointed to the radical difference between narrative (and even literary resources) and fiction. Denouncing the relativism and skepticism of the positions that claimed to embody the *linguistic turn*, Ginzburg (1991) and Chartier (1998) argue for the establishment of principles of narrative organization of the writing of history and point out that narrative had never disappeared from the writing of history, as historical narratives strive to be the reconstruction of a past that was. Arlette Farge for her part integrates the voices of those that history has written out of its official narrative (Farge, 1974, 2010). Her attention to the textual, narrative, and syntactic procedures whereby history states its regime of truth leads her to re-appropriate the conclusions of narratological scholarship, particularly those developed in the Anglophone world.

Overcoming the Opposition between Fiction and Knowledge

Drawing on previous developments, one may conclude that in the 1990s, the debate on the implications of the *linguistic turn* led a number of historians to reflect on their own practices. At the same time, the belief that the form of the discourse adds nothing to the content and that writing is not a theoretical problem remained a widespread opinion within the discipline (such as Gertrude Himmelfab or Armando Momigliano). Nevertheless, over the last twenty years, we have witnessed a simultaneous development of the theories of fiction and a return to the hybridization and combination of fictional and historiographic discourse in a substantial number of works that blur the boundaries between fiction and non-fiction. Some of these works, such as Emmanuel Carrère's *L'Adversaire* (*The Adversary*, 2000), have had a significant social impact and have given rise to controversies.

Gérard Genette's *Fiction et diction* (1991) reignited the debate around the status of fiction. Genette undertakes his exploration by first attempting to define the difference between fictional and factual narratives, setting out from the assumption that factual and fictional narratives present textual characteristics allowing them to be differentiated (located at different levels). This hypothesis relates to the tradition initiated by Käte Hamburger ([1957] 1986) and taken up by Ann Banfield (1982) and Dorrit Cohn (1999). For Genette, fiction and poetry are both "distinctively literary" (the former by its theme and the latter by its forms), while the literariness of non-fiction prose such as memoirs is "conditional" (and likely to be valued as such only in certain circumstances and because of specific formal features). In other words, Genette's view is that fiction is constitutively literary, whereas other forms, such as non-fiction, essay, and autobiography, are subject to the contingency of not being literature. One can recognize, in this stance, the heritage of structuralism, but Genette's approach implies also that the boundaries between fiction and non-fiction are to be clearly established in order to prevent readers from confusing fictions and facts in a context where the negationist movement was gaining momentum and in order to prevent them from being induced to believe false versions of history (1980).

An important turn in the conception of fiction occurred at the end of the 1990s, when it started to be considered as an anthropological fact, defined according to its inscription in reality—a turn that could be grounded in cognitivist theories that were imported into the human and social sciences. In the continuity of analytic philosophy as well as thinkers as Kendall Walton (1990), Jean-Marie Schaeffer in *Pourquoi la fiction?* (1999; translated as *Why Fiction*, 2010) argued that fiction does not constitute a risk, in the sense that it does not remove the subject from the world; on the contrary, it plays a fundamental role in the process of human knowledge. Fiction, therefore, appears as a specific mode of knowledge shared by humans. Setting Aristotle against Plato, Schaeffer updates the Aristotelian argument according to which *mimesis* would be specific to humankind and might be traced back to childhood. Drawing on Searle's (1984, 1992) and Walton's works and on the findings of cognitive psychology, he comes to the conclusion that fiction is a "shared ludic feint" ("feintise ludique partagée") and pinpoints the mental capacity to distinguish fiction from illusion, which we all have practiced since childhood. This definition resonates with the "art for art" stated by Emmanuel Kant, and earlier studied by Schaeffer, because fiction appears as a purpose in itself that promotes the cultivation of the mental powers for sociable communication (Schaeffer, 1992). Once fiction was legitimized because appertaining to the framework of human practices, there remained the question of the distinction between fictional and referential narrative, to which Schaeffer returns in *Les troubles du récit* (2020), where he proposes a reflection driven by and oriented toward cognitivism. Pretense is brought center stage, and the attempt to differentiate the two types of narrative is postulated from human mental capacity. Dwelling on the issue of cognitive immersion, he argues that the specificity of the fictional narrative lies in this type of mental pretense: each fiction is the result of a process of mental pretense, but each pretense does not produce fiction, because to produce fiction the degree of immersion must have a specific feature. Fiction is a framed activity; contrary to the referential narratives, it is constructed in such a way as to maximize its power to induce immersion. Thus, the hypothesis of fiction as a cognitive capacity of humans, a cultural conquest according to Schaeffer, allowed him to redefine its status as no longer based on textual elements but on the cognitive attitude the texts and the readers engage with.

Simultaneously, especially from the twenty-first century onward, one witnesses a development of new media and artistic currents that rely on the blurring of the boundaries between fiction and non-fiction by setting up complex links to new technologies. The wide-ranging character of the phenomenon led Françoise Lavocat to review contemporary theories and uses of fiction in *Fait et fiction* and to take a stance whereby she advocates for the boundaries for literary and artistic fiction (2016, 52). She opposes the loosening of those boundaries since there is a risk of erasing the specificity of fiction, and placing it on the same level as truth, by means of an instrumentalization of the techniques of the narrative in various fields. It is thus a question of conceiving the specific territory of literary and artistic fiction, yet not rejecting the fact that its borders are porous and unstable. Lavocat contends that "fiction insists," and that it withstands the attacks inflicted upon it. Her conclusion is that the emergence and the generalization of non-fiction from the 2000s should not lead exclusively to a consensus on the hermeneutic fecundity of the "knowledges of literature": it is also necessary to adopt a certain critical lens, and to be cautious with respect to the contents and ideologies of these narratives—or "docu-fiction" (this is how the trend is styled in the mainstream media).

The attempts at theorizing fiction were made at a time when humanities and social sciences renewed their interest in literary narrative and in particular in fictional narrative, which opened up new perspectives, leading some disciplines to embrace the anthropological conception of fiction (Anheim and Lilti, 2010; Fléchet and Haddad, 2018; Heinrich and Flahault, 2005; Nora, 2011; Revel, 1995). One category of narratives in particular attracted attention from historians for the blurring of the boundaries between fiction and history. On the one hand, in the 1970s and 1980s, in countries where state violence and social control prevailed, some of these fictions took on the task of accounting for what history does not tell. In such cases, fiction allows for conveying individual experiences in contexts of persecution or extermination (*Recuerdo de la Muerte* [Remembrance of Death] by Miguel Bonasso, 1988; *Temporada de huracanes* [Hurricane Season] by Fernanda Melchor, 2017). In Europe, in narratives coping with the repression of left-wing militants of the 1970s, which opposed the legitimacy of democracy, fiction denounced the flaws of the law (*Das Verschwinden des Philip S.* [The Disappearance of Philip S.] by Ulrike Edschmid, 2013). On the other hand, a certain number of contemporary artistic works have challenged the pact of the historical novel, by taking the liberty of distorting historical events in fictions. If the foundational pact of the historical novel can be defined as abiding by the global historical events and the fictionalization of individual aspects of historical characters, one of the key issues of contemporary works is to put to the test the border separating history from individual stories. Among others, let us quote: *La literatura nazi en América* [*Nazi Literature in the Americas*] (1996) by Roberto Bolaño, *Anatomía de un instante* [*The Anatomy of a Moment*] (2009) by Javier Cercas, *HHhH* by Laurent Binet (2010). At the same time, authors such as Svetlana Alexievitch, who was awarded the Nobel Prize for Literature in 2015, questioned the boundaries between journalistic narrative, autobiography, and fiction in books such as *Boys in Zinc* (1992) or *Chernobyl Prayer* (1999), which use narrative techniques at several levels of the story.

Most of these narratives produce an "inquiry effect," a "documentary effect," or a "historiography effect"; they may mobilize an "I" that engages an autobiography, an autofiction, or the biography of another that echoes one's own. Yet, the real, the document, the archive, the investigation incorporated into the narrative may derive from real archives, and be, therefore, authentic documents (such as in W.G. Sebald's *Austerlitz,* 2001, or Rodrigo Rey Rosa's *El material humano* [*Human Material*], 2009). However, archives may also be forged or fictional (partially or entirely), as in works such as Julio Cortazar's *Libro de Manuel* (1973), Javier Cercas's *Soldados de Salamina* (*Soldiers of Salamis*) (2003), or Philippe Artières's *Vie et mort de Paul Gény* [Life and Death of Paul Gény] (2013); some of these narratives show the political dimension of works based partly on false archives that induce belief (as in Cercas's case according to Delage, 2022 and Lauge Hansen, 2018). At any rate, their incorporation into the framework of a literary narrative, fictional or non-fictional, alters their status—which remains to be defined. The "inquiry narrative" is a contemporary trend that can be described in the following terms: a narrative adopting the form of the inquiry, incorporating documents, archives, historical events, and other materials inscribing the referential, often in its raw material form, among which some mobilize documents, but others propose a fictional incorporation of documents, or fictional documents. If the origins of the "evidential" or "indiciary" paradigm can be located in the nineteenth century (Boltanski, 2012; Ginzburg, 1980; Kalifa, 2010), the "inquiry narrative" has become popular in the first two decades of the twenty-first century, combining historical, family, journalistic, and historiographical inquiry (Coste, 2017; Demanze, 2019; Louis, 2020; Piégay, 2019; Zenetti, 2019). It characterizes a broad international artistic movement, both fictional and non-fictional, which legitimizes the literary narrative as being endowed with a truthful dimension and the position of the narrator as exposing the truth of historical events.

Belief in Formal and Rhetorical Contemporary Experiments

As literature experimented with new narrative forms to narrate social and historical experience, it aroused the interest of historians and of specialists from other disciplines such as sociology and anthropology. As a result, fiction became the object of a specific investment. Some historians as well as readers sought in it not a resource but a mode of production of knowledge. At the same time, the specialization of the social and human sciences resulted in a quest for new audiences through innovative narrative experiments, particularly among historians, publishing works blurring the boundaries between historical writing canons and literary fiction, challenging disciplinary writing. Thus, development of theories of fiction and some historians' formal experiments were contemporaneous. Among other examples, we can cite *The Lost* by Daniel Mendelsohn (2006), which, in spite of being a non-fiction narrative, uses literary and fictional narrative resources (as the structure shows, particularly because the climax is situated at the end of the narrative, but also in the literalization of the relationship between places and memory, and the coexistence of narrative levels that imbricate the family history and the Bible); *Histoire des grands-parents que je n'ai pas eus* [*A History of the Grandparents I Never Had*] and *Laëtitia* by Ivan Jablonka (2012, 2016), the former being an academic work turned into an investigation that recalls the detective genre, the latter attempting to reconstruct the life of a femicide victim mobilizing both detective story and fictional techniques; *Le petit X. De la biographie à l'histoire* [Little X. From Biography to History] (2012) by Sabina Loriga, which proposes an interpretation of the individual in history based on fictional novels; Patrick Boucheron's *Léonard et Machiavel* [Leonardo and Machiavelli] (2013), which tells the story of the "connivance" of Leonardo and Machiavelli, challenging the absence of sources, by combining the historical method and literary imagination. These historians propose narratives situated halfway on the spectrum ranging between history and literature, which often stage the "I" of the historian, which, as it introduces his own individuality, history, and opinions, introduces literary techniques, and also adopt a narrative mode that corresponds to the inquiry. We find the same literary resources in some of the fictional works mentioned above: an "I" that acquires a certain thickness and an inquiry, often corresponding to the detective novel (Cercas, Haenel). Emmanuel Bouju, in *La Transcription de l'histoire dans le roman européen* (2006) has suggested that historiography's exploration of territories that were so far exclusively literary is a response to the way contemporary historical literature mimics the historiographical scene, by exposing the resurrection of the past as an investigation mobilizing the collection of testimonies, archives, and the critique of sources.

Among these literary works, those concerning in particular the Second World War and the Holocaust spark controversies. It was the case of *Les Bienveillantes* [*The Kindly Ones*] by Jonathan Littel (2006) and *Jan Karski* by Yannick Haenel (2009), although some other subjects have sometimes aroused debates among academics, for example *Civilizations* by Laurent Binet (2019) (Lavocat

2019). Thus, the publication of Eric Vuillard's *L'Ordre du jour* (2017; translated as *The Order of the Day*) provoked a dispute with Robert Paxton (2018), whereas the same author's earlier work *Conquistadors* (2009), which relies on the same fictional treatment of history but deals with a historical subject that does not appear to be very controversial in France, i.e., the conquest of America, was acclaimed as a novel while restoring the emotions of history. Vuillard's novel was accused by Paxton of being devoid of veracity. According to the historian, Vuillard's version of the relationship between German industrialists and the National Socialist Party does not reflect historical facts, which induces readers to believe a false version of history.

Thus, we can say that debates are partly sparked by the conviction that a fiction which presents itself as if it were dealing with historical events, but which does not respond to the conventions of the traditional historical novel, can create belief, and even replace the beliefs generated by historians, defining therefore a competition between historical knowledge and literary knowledge.[1] In such cases, historical events are considered to be falsified and literary works accused of being implausible, giving rise to controversies. For instance, in spite of their differences, such was the case of three novels published and widely discussed in France in the 2000s (Barjonet, 2022: 199–218): Littel's *Les Bienveillantes* [*The Kindly Ones*]—fictional "memoirs" of the fictional character Maximilien Aue, who narrates his participation as a perpetrator in the massacres of the SS on the Eastern front; *Jan Karski*—relating the experience of the Polish militant who endeavored to alert the Allies about the extermination of the Jews, and *HHhH*—the story of "Operation Anthropoid," initiated from London and executed by three Czechoslovak paratroopers, with the objective of assassinating in Prague Reinhard Heydrich, deputy governor in Bohemia-Moravia. Published between 2006 and 2010, these works, which fictionalize events or historical figures of the Second World War, were accused of falsifying history (Lanzmann argued that Haenel's novel contradicted historical truth by imposing a retrospective moral judgment [2010]; the writer defended himself by asserting that literature can denounce politics and even replace it [Haenel, 2015]), of being implausible (see Viart, 2006, on *Les Bienveillantes*), of "deconstructing" history (see Rastier, 2019, also on *Les Bienveillantes*). The blurring of the boundaries between fiction and history produced in such cases is problematic only if, in a given society, the fictionalization (or literalization in some cases, for not every literary narrative is fictional) of historical events is considered as falsification, and if the capacity of fiction to generate beliefs and convictions (including historical ones) competes with the transmission of what historians have established as truths (in educational and specialized institutions, and through the media). Paradoxically, some historians, such as Annette Wieviorka, have claimed that literature is more effective than historical accounts in capturing the experiences of individuals (2002, 77). For instance, Heather Morris's best-seller *The Tattooist of Auschwitz* (2018) has been criticized for creating a false version of events and inducing readers to believe it in spite of recent, thorough academic research on Auschwitz.

What one ought to address is therefore why the treatment of history proposed by some novels and historical works appeared disputable. One answer is that they can be considered as mimicking the "historiographical gesture," for they explore what history fails to apprehend, as if they were outside of history, while offering a link to the past in the service of a specific interpretation, and thus toying with the "powers of literature," as well as with the boundaries between fiction and history (Giavarini, 2018; Guidée, 2013). For others, who liken them to negationism, some of these literary works do not take account of the achievements of the historical discipline (Boucheron, 2011; Lanzmann, 2010; Wieviorka, 2010). As we have shown so far, the reactions of historians and critics illustrate that any deviations from writing protocols established by the historical discipline are still hard to accept, even when the works explicitly present themselves as fiction; simultaneously, when fiction appropriates historical documents or testimonies (as in *Jan Karski*), it undoubtedly alters their meaning. But when the novels are in line with what has been established in history, they leave themselves wide open to criticism—for not offering that "*je-ne-sais-quoi*" "extra flavor" readers expect from fiction. Thus, works such as *Robespierre, derniers temps* by Jean-Philippe Domecq (1984), a book in which the writer reflects on what literature can contribute to history, have been praised for their historical accuracy and the interpretation they offer of the period covered. In other words, these debates highlight a certain anxiety about the fact that literature (fiction in this case) and social and human sciences may have a complementary relationship, while being competing discourses at the same time.

The use of the first person singular in the narrative and of the "récit-enquête" ("inquiry narrative") by historians such as Jablonka has generated many controversies. Some point out that this device seems to ignore what De Certeau (2002) called "the fiction of historiographic discourse," which designates the paradox in the historiographic operation: it is characterized by displacements and reclassifications of documents that historians deal with, and, on the other hand, writing is only a production of difference, because the questions and the analysis of historians are always anchored in the present. Thus, historiographic writing is a fiction of reality whose object is an absent body. However, the criticisms were essentially directed at the fact that this practice of a form of non-fiction is partly grounded in a personal auctorial status, and on the academic symbolic capital of the authors, sometimes acquired in the course of the debates mentioned. Adopting a narrative and explanatory form that corresponds to that of ethno-historical inquiry sometimes implies renouncing properly scientific inquiry, while exhibiting one's results as if they indeed derived from a scientific process (Le Caisne, 2017). These were the terms of the debate that the publication of Ivan Jablonka's *Laëtitia ou la fin des hommes* (2016) provoked, raising questions about the grounds of credibility. Philippe Artières, one of the few contemporary French historians to be critical of Jablonka's work, argues that the position adopted by the narrative calls into question the responsibility of the historian, because the authority of the narrator does not derive from scientific inquiry but from Jablonka's position in the academic world (2016). However, we must not forget that this was already the case in Patrick Modiano's *Dora Bruder*: the staging of the "I" in fact overshadows the investigative work which, as we know, was carried out by the historian Serge Klarsfeld (Hilsum, 2012).

At this point, it is appropriate to examine the conception of literature used in these works and debates. Indeed, literature appears as a specific form of knowledge, while the analysis is based on the separation between the literary sphere and the other fields of writing and narrative, and thus, in a sense, isolates literature from social productions, even if it explicitly postulates that literature speaks of the social (Giavarini, 2018). By making of literature an object of analysis of their discipline, historians, and sometimes other scholars, appear to legitimize a specific conception of literature, which, most of the time, is consistent with that established by literary national institutions, and recognizes exclusively the literary canon without taking into account its contexts and the situation of the texts at the time of their writing, publication, and circulation. An ontological conception of literature, according to Schaeffer, means that the canonized time of literature implies the negation of historical time (2011). As a result, some authors of documentary novels are sometimes considered as having depicted historical events in a more accurate manner than historians, but without being considered as historians. Rodolfo Walsh's *Operación masacre* [*Operation Massacre*] (1957) may be considered as an epitome: the book does not conform with conventions of American non-fiction, but by blurring the boundaries between fiction and non-fiction, it establishes a historical truth, turning a minor Argentine historical event into History.

Nevertheless, literary writing is no historiographical operation, even when it borrows its narrative or writing strategies from historiography or imitates rhetorical conventions and acknowledged methods of historical writing. Literary writing and fiction are different sorts of operation, whose specificities vanish should they be confused with historiography. Undoubtedly, however, the adoption of this narrative mode in fiction and in literary narrative produces a specific effect and projects onto the text a demand for historical truth: the reader expects that the area of the fiction that refers to historical events or characters will abide by the social and disciplinary consensus on the given historical events, or at least that it will not deviate from them, lest it should be accused of falsifying history. In other words, the "historiographical gesture" entails a "way of reading" (Ludmer, 2010), even if the narrative does not match the achievements of the historical discipline. Nevertheless, the reader assumes that the narrative's intention is to present a historical truth, which often conceals the possibility of understanding its ideological stakes.

If the inquiry is a method, it is also a discourse composed of verbal and narrative techniques, which must be analyzed as such. The unprecedented success of fictions built on this narrative mode stems partly from the fact that they appear as original novelty (Zenetti, 2019). What Cercas has called "the fictionless novel" (2009) is actually a novel that presents itself as deprived of fiction, since today the formalization of its features allows for a mimesis of the genre (Delage, 2019). Also, it appears as a novel that exposes a historical truth ignored until then, especially by history, or one which history could not account for and was unable to tell. One can return, from this perspective, to Wieviorka's reading of Cercas (2016): for the historian, the archival fiction combines three conditions: the search for historical truth, democratic political engagement, and the ethics of investigative writing as a form of literary justice. The historian Patrick Boucheron considers "the fictionless novel," and not the historical account, to be the genre which does not have to relinquish anything and thus manages to totalize the historical narrative, because history must comply with disciplinary protocols (2011). However, he does not elaborate on what exactly history must give up that "the fictionless novel" can preserve. Some historians (such as Jablonka, Wieviorka, Boucheron) seem to assume that the use of the "inquiry narrative," especially when adopting historiographical rhetoric and protocols, necessarily rests on the achievements of the historical discipline, yet can also produce historical falsification. Let us also point out that these debates also raised the question of the institutional positioning of social-scientific research, because some of these historians partake in prestigious networks, either before or after their contributions to these debates, which play a role inducing belief.

Toward a New Cognitive Approach to Fiction and Historiography?

Hence, nowadays, the question of what separates fiction from historiography is as acute as ever, and concerns belief in particular. The appropriation of narrative and fictional modes of the novel by historians and the use of writing conventions drawn from the historical discipline by fictional literature has resulted in a renewed necessity to consider reflexivity of practices and to make explicit linguistic, literary, and rhetorical choices. And more precisely, each field must clarify how it determines the sort of relations it will establish between these representations and the referential beliefs it shares, or, in the case of narrative representations, the subset of referential beliefs regarding the events, actions, and animated entities that are part of what the receptor considers the reality.

These considerations lead to the question of how a written text generates belief. Answering this requires a consideration of the question of genre. Any given work is pluriaspectual, i.e., is a complex semiotic object in which characteristics of different levels (pragmatic, semantic, syntactic) interact (Schaeffer, 1989). The distinction established by Schaeffer between auctorial and lectorial genericity contributes to the discussion on the relationship between fiction and historiography (2006, 101). Auctorial genericity corresponds to acts of choice, imitation, and transformation of texts and traditions existing at the time of production of the work. Lectorial genericity, on the other hand, refers to later classifications and affinities with texts and types of texts that do not exist at the time of the work's production, or are unknown to the author. These operations of attribution of genericity do not distort the identity of the text, but enrich it; they underline, however, the fact that generic conventions play a central role in the creation of belief, because what readers and/or authors recognize as conventions enable them to situate texts in generic terms and, therefore, determine the degree of belief that readers can assign to the narrative.

In addition to genre, two elements seem to be key factors when considering the blurring of writing protocols and the circulation of writing and narrative techniques between fictional and historiographical discourses: on one side, what one could call the "apparatus of readability," which includes the "paratext" (Genette, 1987) and the context of production and edition, as well as the institutional and social insertion and uses of the texts (Louis, 2018), and on the other side, the epistemic attitude of the reader toward these discourses. In order to determine that a set of representations is a piece of fiction, it is therefore necessary to analyze the epistemic attitude of the sender or the receiver toward these representations (Schaeffer, 2020). More precisely, it is necessary to determine the sort of relations they will establish between these representations and their referential beliefs, or, in the case of narrative representations, the subset of their referential beliefs that concern the events, actions, and animate entities that are part of what they consider to be the reality.

Thus, we can argue that today the circulation of rhetorical and generic conventions and writing protocols between fictional works and historical discourse has clearly resulted in a new conception of fiction, which also alters our relationship to belief. This development, which concerns specialized reflections as much as the social and cultural fields and the debates in the public sphere occurring over the last two decades, has led to the idea that, although fiction and historiography are discourses with different objectives and aiming at different contextual insertions, they have overlapping zones in which regimes of truthful belief arise. Among a variety of examples, we can refer to Ricardo Piglia's novel *Respiración artificial* [Artificial Respiration] (1980), in which he presents a meeting between young Hitler and Kafka as a historical event in order to explain the origins of fascism and of military dictatorships in Argentina; we can also recall Titaua Peu's *Pina* (2016), a novel that gives as historical a referendum in favor of Tahiti's independence, or Roberto Bolaño's *Estrella distante* [*Distant Star*] (1996), where history and fiction are so intricately intertwined that it is extremely challenging for the reader to tell them apart. In these cases, a reader that is unaware of the details of the events can be led to believe that they actually took place, as the reception of these works has proved. This by no means implies the adoption of a panfictionalist attitude (Ryan, 1997), nor a defense of this position, nor does it entail the widening of the field of fiction to the point of considering that the concept is equivalent to that of discourse, representation, and narrative, thus eliminating the specificity of the category of fiction. Nevertheless, the existence of contact and superimposition zones between historical discourse and fiction implies a new attitude toward both. Moreover, this does not entail that one can gain identical knowledge or gain knowledge by means of the same processes from a historical account and from a work of fiction. Following Schaeffer, let us argue that the space of belief and the space of imagination implement structurally identical cognitive mechanisms. His hypothesis, which takes up Hume's idea of the existence of a "unique code," implies that factual narrative and fictional narrative harness the same cognitive resources despite their difference in pragmatic status—provided that one understands pragmatic status as a positioning in the real world that is always cultural and historically situated. One must acknowledge as well that the ability to recognize rhetorical and writing protocols is culturally and historically defined. It can thus be inferred that cognitive attitudes evolve and situate us today in a new relation with respect to how fictional and historical narratives are perceived.

Nevertheless, as recalled above, the hybridization of methods, conventions, and protocols of writing stemming from literary fiction as much as from historians' works have highlighted the close relationship between writing techniques and belief. This movement seems to suggest that a new cognitive approach is emerging, allowing the hypothesis of a "suspended reading" between fiction and non-fiction. Yet, exhibiting this hybrid character of the works would not necessarily result in the creation of new beliefs intended to replace, contradict, or corroborate the achievements of the historical discipline. The risk of inducing beliefs contrary to what the scientific community considers to be historical truths exists, however. Only the positioning of the reader in reality ensures the avoidance of this kind of effect, but the latter may be oriented by the apparatus of reading, in particular by the editorial forms and media interventions of the authors, editors, and critics. Let us emphasize that if the particularity of the work of art is its polysemic character, it is nonetheless essential to recognize the conventions, protocols, and resources of writing employed by the historical discipline for what they are. In other words, these are writing and narrative techniques whose ideology is by no means predetermined, being neither progressive nor reactionary. Acknowledging this conventional character of writing history and fiction reduces, and even removes, the risk that a work that blurs the boundaries between fiction and historiography will induce belief, either true or false.

Note

1 See Emmanuel Bouju and Loïse Lelevé's discussion of this issue in their contribution to the present volume.

Works Cited

Alexievitch, Svetlana. (1992) 2017. *Boys in Zinc*. Translated by Andrew Bromfield. London: Penguin.

Alexievitch, Svetlana. (1999) 2016. *Chernobyl Prayer*. Translated by Anna Gunin and Arch Tait. London: Penguin.

Anheim, Etienne. 2010. "Philosophie et histoire." In *Historiographies I. Concepts et débats*, edited by Christian Delacroix, François Dosse, Patrick Garcia and Nicolas Offenstadt, 562–76. Paris: Gallimard/Folio.

Anheim, Etienne. 2019. "Science des archives, science des histoires." *Annales. Histoire, sciences sociales* 74, no. 3–4 (September): 505–20.

Anheim, Étienne, and Antoine Lilti, eds. 2010. "Savoirs de la littérature." Special issue, *Annales* 65, no. 2 (March–April).

Aristotle. 1922. *Poetics*. Translated by S. H. Butcher. London: MacMillan and Co. http://classics.mit.edu//Aristotle/poetics.html.

Artières, Philippe. 2016. "Ivan Jablonka, l'histoire n'est pas une littérature contemporaine." *Libération*, November 6, 2016.

Banfield, Ann. 1982. *Unspeakable Sentences: Narration and Representation in the Language of Fiction*. Boston, MA: Routledge and Kegan.

Barjonet, Aurélie. 2022. *L'ère des non-témoins. La littérature des 'petits-enfants' de la Shoah*. Paris: Kimé.

Barthes, Roland. 1984. "Le discours de l'histoire." *Le bruissement de la langue*, 163–77. Paris: Seuil.

Binet, Laurent. 2010. *HHhH*. Paris: Grasset.

Bolaño, Roberto. 1996. *La literatura nazi en América*. Barcelona: Seix Barral.

Boltanski, Luc. 2012. *Enigmes et complots. Une enquête à propos d'enquêtes*. Paris: Gallimard/Essais.

Bolaño, Roberto. 1996. *Estrella distante*. Barcelona: Anagrama.

Bonasso, Miguel. 1984. *Recuerdo de la muerte*. Buenos Aires: Era.

Boucheron, Patrick. 2011. "On nomme littérature la fragilité de l'histoire." *Le Débat* 165 (May–June): 41–56. DOI: 10.3917/deba.165.0041.

Boucheron, Patrick. 2013. *Léonard et Machiavel*. Paris: Verdier.

Bouju, Emmanuel. 2006. *La transcription de l'histoire, essai sur le roman européen*. Rennes: Presses Universitaires de Rennes.

Calame, Claude. 2012. "Vraisemblance référentielle, nécessité narrative, poétique de la vue. L'historiographie grecque classique entre factuel et fictif." *Annales. Histoire, sciences sociales* 67, no. 1 (January–March): 81–101.

Cannadine, David, ed. 2002. *What Is History Now?* London: Palgrave MacMillan.

Carrère, Emmanuel. 2000. *L'adversaire*. Paris: P.O.L.

Cercas, Javier. 2003. *Soldados de Salamina*. Barcelona: Tusquets.

Cercas, Javier. 2009. *Anatomía de un instante*. Barcelona: Montandon.

Chartier, Roger. 1998. *Au bord de la falaise. L'histoire entre certitudes et inquiétudes*. Paris: Albin Michel.

Cohn, Dorrit. 1999. *The Distinction of Fiction*. Baltimore, MD: John Hopkins University Press.

Coste, Florent. 2017. "Propositions pour une littérature d'investigation." *Journal des anthropologues* 148–49: 43–62.

De Certeau, Michel. 1975. *L'écriture de l'histoire*. Paris: Gallimard.

De Certeau, Michel, Dominique Julia, and Jacques Revel. (1975) 2002. *Une politique de la langue. La révolution française et les patois: l'enquête de Grégoire*. Paris: Gallimard.

Delacroix, Christian. 2010. "Écriture de l'histoire." In *Historiographies II. Concepts et débats*, edited by Christian Delacroix, François Dosse, Patrick Garcia and Nicolas Offenstadt, 731–43. Paris: Gallimard/Folio.

Delage, Agnès. 2019. "Javier Cercas historien. Pour une approche critique de la fiction d'archive contemporaine." *Littérature, discipline littéraire et archives*, Fabula.org, April 2019.

Delage, Agnès. 2022. "Democracy without Justice: The Paradox of Literary Justice in the Work of Javier Cercas." *Literature, Democracy and Transitional Justice Comparative World Perspectives*, edited by Mohamed-Salah Omri and Philippe Roussin, 106–32. Transcript 19. Oxford: Legenda/Modern Humanities Research Association.

Demanze, Laurent. 2019. *Un nouvel âge de l'enquête. Portraits de l'écrivain contemporain en enquêteur.* Paris: Corti/Les Essais.

Domecq, Jean-Philippe. 1984. *Robespierre, derniers temps.* Paris: Seuil.

Dosse, François, 2010. "Récit." In *Historiographies II. Concepts et débats*, edited by Christian Delacroix, François Dosse, Patrick Garcia and Nicolas Offenstadt, 862–76. Paris: Gallimard/Folio.

Edschmid, Ulrike. 2013. *Das verschwinden des Philip S.* Berlin: Suhrkamp.

Farge, Arlette. 1974. *Délinquance et criminalité: le vol d'aliments à Paris au XVIIIe siècle.* Paris: Plon.

Farge, Arlette. 2010. "Marginalités." In *Historiographies I. Concepts et débats*, edited by Christian Delacroix, François Dosse, Patrick Garcia and Nicolas Offenstadt, 491–502. Paris: Gallimard/Folio.

Flahault, François, and Nathalie Heinrich, eds. 2005. "Vérités de la fiction." Special issue, *L'homme*, no. 175–176 (July–December).

Fléchet, Anaïs, and Élie Haddad, eds. 2018. "L'écriture de l'histoire: sciences sociales et récit." Special issue, *Revue d'histoire moderne & contemporaine* 65, no. 2 (April–June).

García, Victoria. 2017. "Teoría (y) política de la ficción." *Badebec. Estudios críticos* 13: 212–39.

Genette, Gérard. 1987. *Seuils.* Paris: Seuil.

Genette, Gérard. 1991. *Fiction et diction.* Paris: Seuil.

Giavarini, Laurence. 2018. "Histoire, littérature, vérité. Sur la littérature comme geste historiographique." In "L'écriture de l'histoire: sciences sociales et récit," edited by Anaïs Fléchet and Élie Haddad, Special issue, *Revue d'histoire moderne & contemporaine* 65, no. 2 (April–June): 8–96.

Ginzburg, Carlo. 1980. "Signes, traces, pistes. Racines d'un paradigme de l'indice." *Le débat* 6 (November): 3–44.

Ginzburg, Carlo. 1991. *Il giudice et lo storico. Considerazioni in margine al proceso sofri.* Turin: Einaudi.

Guidée, Raphaëlle. 2013. "L'écriture contemporaine de la violence extrême: a propos d'un malentendu entre littérature et historiographie." In *Littérature et histoire en débats*, fabula/Les colloques. http://www.fabula.org/colloques/document2086.php./

Haenel, Yannick. 2009. *Jan Karski.* Paris: Gallimard.

Haenel, Yannick. 2015. "Que ces fripouilles lisent des romans!" *Charlie Hebdo*, no. 1199, July 15, 2015.

Hamburger, Käte. (1957) 1986. *La logique des genres littéraires.* Translated by Pierre Cadiot. Paris: Seuil.

Hilsum, Mireille. 2012. "Serge Klarsfeld/Patrick Modiano: enjeux d'une occultation." In *Cahier de l'Herne* no. 98: *Patrick Modiano*, edited by Raphaëlle Guidée and Maryline Heck, 187–91. Paris: Éditions de l'Herne.

Jablonka, Ivan. 2012. *Histoire des grands-parents que je n'ai pas eus.* La Librairie du XXIe siècle. Paris: Seuil.

Jablonka, Ivan. 2016. *Laëtitia ou la fin des hommes.* Paris: Le Seuil.

Jeannelle, Jean-Louis. "Les littératures factuelles." *Fabula.* http://www.fabula.org/atelier.php?Litt%26eacute%3Bratures_factuelles.

Kalifa, Dominique. 2010 "Enquête et 'culture de l'enquête' au XIXe siècle." *Romantisme* 3, no. 149:3–23.

Lanzmann, Claude. "Jan Karski, un faux roman." *Marianne*, January 23, 2010.

Lauge Hansen, Hans. 2018. "Victimas y victimarios. Trauma social y representación de víctimas y victimarios en la novela española de memoria." *Passés futurs*, August 29, 2018. https://www.politika.io/en/notice/victimas-y-victimarios-trauma-social-y- representacion-victimas-y-victimarios-novela-espanola.

Lavocat, Françoise. 2016. *Fait et fiction.* Paris: Seuil.

Lavocat, Françoise. 2019. "Contrefactuel et eutopie – à propos de *Civilizations* de Laurent Binet." *AOC* media – Analyse Opinion Critique, *AOC*, October 2.

Lavocat, Françoise. 2020. "Le conflit entre histoire et fiction: le XXe siècle au miroir du XVIIe siècle." In *Faktuales und fiktionales Erzählen II. Geschichte – Medien – Praktiken*, edited by Hanna Häger, Dustin Breitenwischer and Julian Menninger, 83–101. Baden-Baden: Ergon.

Le Caisne, Léonore. 2017. "*Laëtitia* ou la fin de l'enquête scientifique. À propos de: Ivan Jablonka, *Laëtitia ou la fin des hommes*." *Revue d'histoire moderne & contemporaine* 64, no. 1: 175–85.

Lepetit, Bernard. 1996. "Les Annales. Portrait de groupe avec revue." *Une École pour les sciences sociales. De la IVe section à l'École des hautes études en sciences sociales*, edited by Jacques Revel and Nathan Wachtel, 31–48. Paris: CERF/Éditions de l'EHESS.

"L'Histoire saisie par la fiction." 2011. Special issue, *Le Débat* no. 165 (May–August).

Little, Daniel. 2020. "Philosophy of History." In *The Stanford Encyclopedia of Philosophy*, Winter 2020 edition, edited by Edward N. Zalta. https://plato.stanford.edu/archives/win2020/entries/history/.

Littel, Jonathan. 2006. *Les Bienveillantes.* Paris: Gallimard. Translated by Charlotte Mandell as *The Kindly Ones.* New York: Harper Collins, 2010.

Loriga, Sabina. 2011. *Le Petit X. De la biographie à l'histoire.* La Librairie du XXIᵉ siècle. Paris: Seuil.

Loriga, Sabina, and Jacques Revel. 2022. *Une histoire inquiète. Les historiens et le tournant linguistique.* Paris: EHESS/Gallimard/Seuil.

Louis, Annick. 2018. "Leer una revista literaria: autoría individual, autoría colectiva en las revistas argentinas de la década de 1920." In *Laboratorios de lo nuevo. Revistas literarias y culturales de México, España y el Río de la Plata en la década de 1920*, edited by Rose Corral, Anton Stanton and James Valender, 27–53. Mexico City: El Colegio de México.

Louis, Annick. 2020. "Les séductions de l'enquête." In *Ce que les artistes font à l'histoire*, edited by Oliver Abel, Thomas Hirsch and Sabina Loriga. Special issue, *Passés Futurs, Politika*, no. 8 (December). https://www.politika.io/fr/notice/seductions-lenquete.

Ludmer, Josefina. 2010. *Aquí América latina. Una especulación.* Buenos Aires: Eterna Cadencia.

Melchor, Fernanda. 2017. *Temporada de huracanaes.* Mexico City: Random House.

Mendelsohn, Daniel. 2006. *The Lost. A Search for Six of Six Million.* New York: Harper Collins.

Morris, Heather. 2018. *The Tattooist of Auschwitz.* London: Harper.

Nora, Pierre. 2011. "Histoire et roman: où passent les frontières?" *Le débat* 165, no. 3 (May–June): 6–12. Doi: 10.3917/deba.165.0006.

Paxton, Robert. 2018. "The Reich in Medias Res." *The New York Review of Books*, December 6.

Peu, Titaua. 2016. *Pina.* Tahiti: Au vent des îles.

Piégay, Nathalie. 2019. "Nouveaux usages de l'enquête." *Critique* 870, no. 11: 981–95.

Piglia, Ricardo. 1980. *Respiración artificial.* Buenos Aires: Pomaire.

Rastier, François. 2019. *Extermination et littérature. Les témoignages inconcevables.* Paris: PUF.

Revel, Jacques. 1995. "Ressources narratives et connaissance historique." *Enquête*, February 1, 2007. http://enquete.revues.org/document262.html.

Rey Rosa, Rodrigo. 2009. *El material humano.* Barcelona: Anagrama.

Ricoeur, Paul. 1983. *Temps et récit. Tome I: l'intrigue et le récit historique.* Paris: Seuil.

Rorty, Richard. 1967. *The Linguistic Turn. Recent Essays in Philosophical Method.* Chicago, IL: University of Chicago Press.

Ryan, Mary-Laure. 1997. "Postmodernism and the Doctrine of Panfictionality." *Narrative* 5, no. 2: 165–87.

Ryan, Mary-Laure. 2010. "Mondes fictionnels à l'âge de l'internet." In *Les arts visuels, le web et la fiction*, edited by Bernard Guelton, 66–84. Paris: Publications de la Sorbonne.

Schaeffer, Jean-Marie. 1989. *Qu'est-ce qu'un genre littéraire?* Paris: Seuil.

Schaeffer, Jean-Marie. 1992. *L'art de l'âge moderne. L'esthétique et la philosophie de l'art du XVIIIe siècle à nos jours.* Paris: Gallimard.

Schaeffer, Jean-Marie. 2010. *Why Fiction?* Translated by Dorrit Cohn. Lincoln: University of Nebraska Press. Originally published as *Pourquoi la fiction?* Paris: Seuil, 1999.

Schaeffer, Jean-Marie. 2011. *Petite écologie des études littéraires.* Paris: Thierry Marchaisse.

Schaeffer, Jean-Marie. 2020. *Les troubles du récit. Pour une nouvelle approche des processus narratifs.* Paris: Thierry Marchaisse.

Searle, John. 1984. *Minds, Brains and Science.* Cambridge, MA: Harvard University Press.

Searle, John. 1992. *The Rediscovery of the Mind.* Cambridge, MA: MIT Press.

Sebald, W.G. 2001. *Austerlitz.* Berlin: Hanser.

Schöttler, Peter. 2010. "Annales." In *Historiographies I. Concepts et débats*, edited by Christian Delacroix, François Dosse, Patrick Garcia and Nicolas Offenstadt, 25–41. Paris: Gallimard/Folio.

Topuzian, Marcelo. 2017. "Introducción: entre literatura nacional y posnacional." In *Tras la nación. Conjeturas y controversias sobre las literaturas nacionales y mundiales*, edited by Marcelo Topuzian, 9–65. Buenos Aires: EUDEBA.

Veyne, Paul. 1971. *Comment on écrit l'histoire.* Paris: Seuil.

Viart, Dominique. 2006. "Les Prix, 'Sismographe de la vie littéraire.'" Interview with Claire Devarrieux, *Libération*, November 8, 2006.

Vuillard, Eric. 2017. *L'ordre du jour.* Paris: Actes Sud. Translated by Mark Polizzotti as *The Order of the Day.* New York: Other Press, 2019.

Walsh, Rodolfo. 1957. *Operación Masacre.* Buenos Aires: Sigla.

Walton, Kendall. 1990. *Mimesis as Make-Believe: On the Foundations of the Representational Arts.* Cambridge, MA: Harvard University Press.

White, Hayden. 1973. *Metahistory: The Historical Imagination in Nineteenth-Century Europe.* Baltimore, MD: The Johns Hopkins University Press.

White, Hayden. 1978. "History and Literature." In *The Writing of History: Literary Form and Historical Understanding*, edited by Robert H. Canary and Henry Kozicki, 3–40. Madison: University of Wisconsin Press.

White, Hayden. 1987. *The Content of the Form: Narrative Discourse and Historical Representation.* Baltimore, MD: The Johns Hopkins University Press.

Wieder, Thomas. 2010. "Polémique autour de Jan Karski." *Le Monde*, January 25, 2010.

Wieviorka, Annette. 2002. *L'ère du témoin.* Paris: Hachette.

Wieviorka, Annette. 2010. "Faux témoignage." *L'Histoire* 357 (January): 30–31.

Wieviorka, Annette. 2016. "Javier Cercas, la quête de vérité." *L'Histoire,* no. 427 (September). https://www.lhistoire.fr/portrait/javier-cercas-la-quête-de-vérité

Zenetti, Marie-Jeanne. 2019a. "Les angles morts de l'enquête." *En attendant Nadeau*, July 16, 2019. https://www.en-attendant-nadeau.fr/2019/07/16/angles-morts-enquete- zenetti/.

Zenetti, Marie-Jeanne. 2019b. "Un effet d'enquête." *Ateliers Fabula.* https://www.fabula.org/ressources/atelier/.

9
FICTION AND SCIENTIFIC KNOWLEDGE

Adam Toon

Introduction

What has fiction to do with science? Setting aside the stories of H.G. Wells or Jules Verne, the answer seems to be "not much." At first glance, science and fiction would appear to have entirely different aims. After all, science aims to discover the truth. In contrast, fiction seems to be relatively unconcerned with truth. Instead, it aims to be profound, moving, satirical, or perhaps just entertaining. We also seem to take a different attitude toward the products of these activities. If presented with a scientific theory, we are invited to believe what it says. We are invited to believe that the world contains atoms, electrons, or black holes. If presented with a novel (or play, or film), we are invited not to believe, but to make-believe. We are invited to imagine or pretend that the world contains unicorns, Sherlock Holmes, or Mickey Mouse. Given these differences between science and fiction, associating the two looks like a serious mistake, which can only lead to confusion. Indeed, it might even seem dangerous, liable to encourage all manner of worrying threats to scientific authority, from Creationism to "post-truth" politics (Giere, 2009; see also Appiah, 2017).

These concerns are certainly not to be taken lightly. The term "fiction" is ambiguous, and its use in some contexts can be highly charged. Any simple declaration to the effect that science is fiction (or involves fiction, or is like fiction, etc.) runs the risk of generating more heat than light. If we want to draw parallels between science and fiction, we must make clear exactly what we are saying, and what purpose it serves. In this chapter, I will examine three strands of thought that, in one way or another, seek to understand science by looking to fiction. As we shall see, each of these strands draws on fiction in different ways and for different theoretical purposes. The first strand uses a technical notion of fiction taken from the work of Hans Vaihinger; the second compares our talk about theoretical entities to talk about fictional characters; and the third compares scientific models to works of fiction. None of these ideas seek to undermine science or reject outright its claim to discover truths about the world. Taken together, however, they do suggest that the quest to discover the truth is not as far removed from the activity of telling stories (or putting on plays or making films) as we might like to think.

Fictions

Our first notion of fiction comes from Hans Vaihinger and his classic work *The Philosophy of "As If"* (1924). (The original German edition was published in 1911.) Vaihinger distinguishes between

 DOI: 10.4324/9781003119456-11

hypotheses and *fictions*. A *hypothesis* is a claim about the world, whose truth we wish to determine. In contrast, for Vaihinger, a *fiction* is a statement that is false, and known to be false by those who use it. Vaihinger also distinguishes between scientific and unscientific fictions: a *scientific* fiction is one that proves useful; an *unscientific* fiction is one that does not. It is no surprise that science is full of hypotheses, of course. We expect scientists to make claims about the world, and check if they are true. At first glance, however, it is difficult to see why science should involve fictions. If science aims to discover the truth, why would it find any place for statements that are known to be false? Why should there be any scientific fictions?

One reason that science involves fictions has to do with discarded hypotheses. There are many theories that we once thought were true but now know are false. Vaihinger gives the example of the Ptolemaic system, which takes the earth to be at the center of the cosmos. Once, this might have been a hypothesis, at least for some of its proponents. Indeed, it might even have been taken to be true. Nowadays, of course, we know that it is false. And yet, we can still use the Ptolemaic system to predict the positions of the planets in the night sky. If we do so, we have a fiction, in Vaihinger's sense: we have a set of statements that are false, and known to be false, but which are still useful for some purpose. (In fact, early astronomers' attitude toward the Ptolemaic system is a matter of debate. Duhem [1906] argues that it was commonly understood as a sort of fiction, including by Ptolemy himself. For critical discussion, see Lloyd [1978] and Rosen [2005].) In a similar manner, we still use Newtonian mechanics to design airplanes and build bridges, even if we know that, strictly speaking, it is false, and has been superseded by quantum mechanics or relativity theory.

Some fictions are thus discarded hypotheses—claims that we now know are false but still keep on the books for certain purposes. This is not the only way in which fictions can arise in science, however. Even more important is their role in modeling and idealization. Consider the billiard ball model of gases (Hesse, 1966). This model allows us to understand the behavior of a gas by treating its molecules as a collection of tiny billiard balls whizzing around randomly in a container. The model involves several hypotheses about gases. For instance, it claims that gases consist of molecules, that the temperature of a gas depends on the kinetic energy of its molecules, and that these molecules exert pressure when they collide with the walls of the container. Along with these hypotheses, however, the model also involves various simplifying assumptions. For instance, it assumes that molecules only act upon each other in collisions and that, when they do collide, they do so perfectly elastically, without losing any energy. In reality, we know that the situation is more complicated: molecules do exert forces on each other between collisions, and their collisions are not perfectly elastic. And so, these assumptions also count as fictions, in Vaihinger's sense. They are statements that are false, and are known to be false, but which are still useful for certain purposes.

Why do we invoke these fictions? Why make assumptions that we know to be false? Because reality is complicated. In most cases, we can only hope to make sense of it by introducing a whole host of simplifications or idealizations. Otherwise, we would scarcely know where to begin. If we tried to take account of each and every aspect of the behavior of each and every one of the countless molecules that make up the gas, our task would be impossible. On the other hand, if we make our simplifying assumptions, we can begin to see how to turn our problem into a more familiar and tractable one—i.e., describing the behavior of a set of billiard balls (or, speaking more precisely, a set of simplified and idealized billiard balls). In some cases, it is possible to bring our assumptions a little closer to reality. For instance, we can introduce an equation to account for the forces that molecules exert on each other between collisions. And yet, even if we do this, fictions will remain. For instance, we will probably still assume that, like billiard balls, molecules are hard and spherical, even though we know this is false. It is important to emphasize that this is not somehow a failing of the billiard ball model in particular—if it is even a failing at all. In fact, the situation that we find here is the norm in science, rather than the exception. As Nancy Cartwright (1983, 158) puts it, "a model—a specially prepared, usually fictional description of a system under study—is employed whenever a mathematical theory is applied to reality."

The use of fictions, in Vaihinger's sense, is therefore widespread in science. Indeed, in an influential article, Arthur Fine (1993, 16) writes:

> Preeminently, the industry devoted to modeling natural phenomena, in every area of science, involves fictions in Vaihinger's sense. If you want to see what treating something "as if" it were something else amounts to, just look at most of what any scientist does in any hour of any working day.

Fine's article helped to recover Vaihinger's ideas for contemporary debate in philosophy of science and has inspired much recent work on fictions in science (e.g., Suárez, 2009). Vaihinger's own interests extended far beyond science, however. In his view, fictions can be found in many domains of human thought, including mathematics, metaphysics, ethics, law, and theology. In a recent, and similarly wide-ranging, discussion, Kwame Anthony Appiah (2017, 127) characterizes Vaihinger's central ideas as follows: "first, that in idealization, we build a picture—a model—of something that proceeds as if something we know is false were true; and second, that we do so because the resulting model is useful for some purpose." In the case of scientific modeling, our purpose is usually to predict or control the behavior of some part of the world. In other cases, fictions might serve very different purposes. For instance, an atheist might use religious doctrines to guide their ethical views, even if they take those doctrines to be false. Fictions are "useful untruths" (Appiah, 2017, 1), and their usefulness can take many different forms, from managing the world to "manag[ing] our selves" (2017, 26).

Let us accept that science is full of fictions, in Vaihinger's sense. What should we make of this? Does the role of fictions pose a threat to science? The first point to emphasize is that much of what I have said so far would come as a little surprise to practicing scientists. The scientists (or engineers) who use Newtonian mechanics to build a bridge know that, strictly speaking, Newton's laws are false. But they also know that these laws are well suited to the job of building bridges, and that if they tried to use quantum mechanics instead, they wouldn't get very far. Similarly, scientists who build a model are usually perfectly well aware that it involves various simplifications or idealizations. Indeed, an important part of their work consists in selecting the right assumptions for the task in hand. For instance, physics or chemistry textbooks will normally list the simplifying assumptions involved in the billiard ball model. They will also explain the range of circumstances in which these assumptions are likely to lead us astray (e.g., at high pressures, when the interactions between molecules outside collisions become increasingly significant). From this perspective, to say that science involves fictions in Vaihinger's sense is simply to point to a familiar fact about scientific practice.

And yet, once we reflect on the role of fictions in science, we see that it challenges many of our ordinary ways of thinking about scientific knowledge. Consider the hypothesis that gases consist of molecules. Suppose we ask: do we know that this hypothesis is true? After all, we can't see molecules. Philosophers of science who are *realists* (and no doubt many scientists too) would say that we do know that this hypothesis is true. In fact, we know that gases contain molecules precisely because of the success of the billiard ball model (and other models like it). There are two standard realist arguments here. The first is *inference to the best explanation* (Lipton, 2004). According to inference to the best explanation, we should infer the hypothesis that would, if true, provide the best explanation for the evidence. For instance, if the hypothesis that gases contain molecules provides the best explanation for their behavior, we are entitled to conclude that this hypothesis is true. The second realist argument is the *no miracles argument* (Putnam, 1981). It also takes the form of an inference to the best explanation. According to the no miracles argument, if a hypothesis is successful (e.g., if it provides true predictions), the best explanation for its success is that it is true. And so, we should conclude that the hypothesis *is* true. If it weren't true, says the realist, its success would be a miracle.

These realist arguments have considerable intuitive force. Taken together, they underlie the confidence that many of us feel in the scientific worldview. The difficulty is that, despite their undoubted appeal, both arguments start to look more problematic once we reflect upon the role of fictions in science. After all, to say that our theories involve fictions, in Vaihinger's sense, is to say that they are false! For instance, our hypothesis that gases contain molecules was part of the billiard ball model and we know that, strictly speaking, this model is false. This immediately raises a host of questions. Can false theories explain things? Intuitively, many feel that only true theories can explain. And yet, if science is full of fictions, then insisting on truth means that we risk finding that it has explained very little. (For further discussion, see Bokulich, 2012; de Regt, 2015.) Even if we allow that false theories can explain, this seems to cause trouble for inference to the best explanation. It told us to infer that our best explanation is true. And yet now we see that even our best explanations are typically false. The no miracles argument also starts to look less compelling (Fine, 1993). It said it would be a miracle if a false theory gave true predictions. And yet now we see that even our most accurate predictions usually come from false theories.

Fictionalism

The widespread role of fictions in science, therefore, seems to cause trouble for standard arguments for scientific realism. One way to respond to these worries is to abandon realism. There are many different forms of anti-realism. Historically, an important form of anti-realism was *logical positivism*. Positivists tried to rid science of talk about unobservable entities, like molecules or electrons, by reducing claims about unobservable entities (also called *theoretical statements*) into claims about observable ones. For instance, a positivist might try to reduce claims about the behavior of molecules in a gas into claims about its pressure or temperature, which we can check using instruments. Nowadays, this task is widely thought to be impossible. Despite the positivists' best efforts, it seems that science simply cannot do without talk about unobservable entities. A more popular form of anti-realism today is Bas van Fraassen's *constructive empiricism* (1980). Unlike the positivist, van Fraassen concedes that scientists make claims about unobservable entities, and that there is no way to do without them. It is simply that, unlike the scientific realist, Van Fraassen says that we shouldn't believe these claims. Instead, we should remain agnostic: we should continue to use theoretical statements for various purposes (e.g., to make predictions about the observable world) but suspend judgment regarding their truth.

Van Fraassen's position is often described as a form of *fictionalism* (e.g. Kalderon, 2005b; Rosen, 1994). Van Fraassen (1980, 35–36) also refers briefly to Vaihinger when developing his approach. There are certainly similarities between Van Fraassen's view and Vaihinger's. Both authors emphasize that statements can be useful, even if they are not true or taken to be true. There are also important differences, however. The first is that, for Vaihinger, fictions are false, and known to be so. Van Fraassen does not say that theoretical statements are false; he simply says that we should suspend our judgement. In his view, the appropriate attitude to take to these statements is not disbelief, but agnosticism. The second important difference between Vaihinger and Van Fraassen's views is more subtle and contested. We've seen that the idea that science uses fictions in Vaihinger's sense would come as little surprise to scientists themselves. In contrast, it seems likely that scientists would object to Van Fraassen's take on things. For many scientists, theoretical statements are hypotheses that, in some cases at least, we have reason to think are true. They might, therefore, be reluctant to follow Van Fraassen's advice and remain agnostic. (For discussion of whether constructive empiricism is at odds with scientists' views, see Rosen, 1994; Van Fraassen, 1994.) Still, it is important to emphasize that, although he urges caution regarding theoretical statements, Van Fraassen does not seek to undermine the authority of science. For the constructive empiricist, science is still a rational enterprise, which aims to discover the truth about the observable world, and often succeeds in doing so.

Fictionalist approaches have been developed in many fields, including philosophy of mathematics (e.g. Field, 1980; Leng 2010; Yablo, 2002), the metaphysics of modality (e.g. Rosen, 1990), moral philosophy (e.g. Joyce, 2001; Kalderon, 2005a), and philosophy of mind (e.g. Demeter, 2013; Toon, 2023; Wallace, 2022). In each case, we find a predicament like the one concerning unobservable entities in science. Our discourse seems to talk about certain entities that, for whatever reason, we find problematic: unobservable entities, Platonic objects, possible worlds, moral properties, mental states, and so on. We find that we cannot avoid talking about such things. And yet we also find it difficult to commit ourselves to their existence. Fictionalism seems to offer a middle way: keep talking about unobservable entities (or Platonic objects or possible worlds or moral properties or mental states, etc.), because such talk is useful, or even indispensable; just don't believe it—either because you think it is false, or because you want to remain agnostic. It is common to distinguish between *hermeneutic* and *revolutionary* fictionalism (Burgess, 1983; Stanley, 2001). Hermeneutic fictionalism aims to interpret a discourse as it is: it claims that the discourse is already fictionalist in spirit. Revolutionary fictionalism aims to reform the discourse: it says our existing discourse isn't fictionalist but should be. In these terms, many (though not all) of Vaihinger's views on science are (arguably) hermeneutic, while Van Fraassen's are (arguably) revolutionary. In contrast, Vaihinger's views on religion as a useful "myth" are more likely to count as revolutionary, at least to many followers of those religions.

Vaihinger's notion of fiction is a technical one, which seems far removed from our ordinary use of the term in connection with novels, plays, films, and the like. Fiction in this ordinary sense need not be false, of course. Most novels (or plays or films) are full of true, often quite humdrum, facts about people, places, and events. Even if there is no Sherlock Holmes, much of what we read in *The Hound of the Baskervilles* is perfectly true: it is true that Baker Street is in London, that phosphorous emits an eerie glow, and that Dartmoor can be a dangerous place to go walking at night. And, of course, many will argue that fiction can reveal deeper truths too—about human nature, perhaps, or our relationships with others (for a helpful overview of this debate, see Gaut, 2003). It is also debatable whether ordinary fiction need be useful, in Vaihinger's sense. Isn't fiction often wonderfully lacking in purpose? At first glance, fictionalist views like Van Fraassen's might seem equally distant from the world of novels, plays or films. And yet fictionalists often draw parallels with ordinary fiction. Typically, these parallels are concerned not so much with works of fiction themselves—the text of a novel, for instance, or a performance of a play—but with the way that we talk about these works.

The fictionalist's central idea is that we can talk about certain objects (e.g. unobservable entities in science) without committing ourselves to their existence. It is here that the fictionalist sees a parallel with ordinary fiction. After all, don't we talk about fictional characters without committing ourselves to their existence? If we say, "Holmes lives at 221B Baker Street," we are not claiming that there is a real, flesh-and-blood detective who lives on a certain street in London. And yet we can still talk meaningfully about Holmes and what we say can be right (e.g., "Holmes lives at 221B Baker Street") or wrong (e.g., "Holmes lives at 222B Baker Street"). The fictionalist suggests that we might understand talk about problematic objects in a similar manner. Consider theoretical statements in science. According to the fictionalist, if we say, "electrons are negatively charged," we are not (or should not be) claiming that there is a real, subatomic particle that has this property. And yet we can still talk meaningfully about electrons and what we say can be right (e.g. "electrons are negatively charged") or wrong (e.g. "electrons are positively charged").

Is this analogy successful? One worry is that fiction itself is far from straightforward. There are significant debates among philosophers of fiction about the correct way to understand our discourse about fictional characters. For instance, *realists* about fictional characters think that our discourse about them commits us to their existence: they think we need to grant that Holmes exists in some sense (e.g., as a non-existent or abstract entity) to make sense of the way that we talk about him (e.g. Meinong, 1960; Thomasson, 1999). *Anti-realists* about fictional characters deny this (e.g. Russell, 1956; Walton, 1990). The mere fact that there is such a debate suggests that the fictionalist's analogy might not provide such an easy way to avoid ontological commitment. Another worry is that, when we look at fictionalist analyses more closely, we can find that the analogy with fiction plays a fairly limited role. For instance, fictionalists often claim that talk about fictional characters avoids ontological commitment because it has an implicit "story prefix". On this analysis, our statement about Holmes is short for "In the Holmes stories, Holmes lives at 221B Baker Street." This analysis is disputed by some philosophers of fiction (e.g., Walton, 1990). Even if we assume that the analysis works, however, the reason it works might have little to do with fiction *per se*. As Gideon Rosen points out,

> The story mentioned in a story prefix need not be a literary fiction, nor for that matter, any sort of fiction in the usual sense. [It] can be *any representation whatsoever*: a story, a scientific theory, or a metaphysical speculation. The basic point is unaffected: so long as you are not independently committed to regarding this representation as true, when you assent to "In F, P" you incur no obligation to assent to "P" by itself.
>
> *(1990, 331–32; emphasis in original)*[1]

Models and Fiction

Our final strand of thinking about science and fiction also focuses on models and idealization. Unlike Vaihinger, however, it does not operate with its own, technical notion of fiction. Instead, it suggests that we can understand the practice of scientific modeling by looking to fiction in the ordinary sense of novels, plays, and films. To see how this is supposed to work, it will help to consider the contrast between *physical modeling* and *theoretical modeling*. Imagine that an engineer wants to build a new airplane. One way to test her designs would be to build a scale model. For instance, she might build a scale model of the plane's wing and put it through tests in a wind tunnel. By finding out about the properties of her scale model, the engineer hopes to find out about the properties of the plane itself (e.g., how much lift its wings will generate). This is an instance of *physical modeling*, since the engineer's model is an actual, physical object (e.g. a two-meter long wing built out of balsa wood or fiberglass). Now recall the billiard ball model of gases. This is a case of *theoretical modeling*. Unlike the engineer, the scientists who use this model do not build an actual, physical object to serve as their model. Instead, they simply write down a set of equations and assumptions. As we've seen, real gases do not satisfy these assumptions. In fact, *no* actual, concrete object satisfies all the assumptions made by the billiard ball model of gases. Even ordinary billiard balls are not perfectly spherical, and will lose some energy when they collide.

Despite the obvious differences between physical and theoretical modeling, we find that scientists often talk about the two activities in similar sorts of ways. The engineer finds out about the properties of her airplane by first investigating the properties of her scale model. Likewise in theoretical modeling, it is said, scientists find out about the world by first investigating the properties of a simplified or idealized version of it, called a *model system*. For instance, the model system of the billiard ball model is a set of tiny, perfectly spherical billiard balls that obey the scientists' assumptions. This isn't a real collection of billiard balls that the scientists can set up in the laboratory, of course. Their model system doesn't exist in the way that the engineer's scale model does. And yet, scientists still talk as if they can use this model system in a similar manner to the engineer's scale model. First, they apply Newton's laws to investigate the properties of their simplified and idealized model system. Next, they use what they have learned to find out about the more complex behavior of molecules in a gas. In fact, a considerable part of scientific practice seems to involve constructing model systems, learning about their properties, and (if we are lucky) using these model systems to understand the real world.

Once we look at theoretical modeling in this way, it can start to seem like a rather odd and surprising sort of activity. On the face of it, we might expect scientists to be concerned with describing the world as it is. And yet, when we look more closely, we find that scientists spend a lot of their time talking about things that don't exist, like collections of tiny, perfectly spherical billiard balls whizzing around in imaginary containers. The reason they do this is familiar from our discussion of Vaihinger, of course. The real world is complicated. To make progress, we need to start by investigating something simpler and more tractable. In the case of physical models, this seems straightforward, at least in principle. If our model is a physical object, it is easy to see how we might go about investigating its properties: we might put it in a wind tunnel, measure how it reacts under different conditions, take videos of different test runs, and so on. Theoretical modeling is more puzzling. After all, it looks like there is no object for us to investigate! There are no actual, concrete objects to serve as our model systems. As a result, theoretical modeling raises various questions. What exactly are scientists doing when they construct a theoretical model? How can they talk about systems that don't exist or learn about their properties? And how can learning about systems that don't exist tell us anything about the real world?

To answer these questions, some philosophers of science have suggested we should compare scientific models to works of fiction. There are two different versions of this approach: *indirect fiction views* and *direct fiction views* (for more on this distinction, see Toon, 2016). Indirect fiction views compare the equations and assumptions that scientists write down when constructing a theoretical model to passages about fictional characters. Consider this passage from J. B. Priestley's novel *The Good Companions:*

> Somewhere in the middle of this tide of cloth caps is one that is different from its neighbours. It is neither grey nor green but a rather dirty brown. Then, unlike most of the others, it is not too large for its wearer but, if anything, a shade too small, though it is true he has pushed it back from his forehead as if he were too hot—as indeed he is. This cap and the head it has almost ceased to decorate are both the property of a citizen of Bruddersford, an old and enthusiastic supporter of the United Football Club, whose name is Jesiah Oakroyd. He owes his curious Christian name to his father, a lanky weaving overlooker who divided his leisure, in alternating periods of sin and repentance, between *The Craven Arms* and the Lane End Primitive Methodist Chapel, where he chanced to hear the verse from First *Chronicles*, "Of the sons of Uzziel; Micah the first, and Jesiah the second," the very day before his second son was born.
>
> *(Priestley, 1929, 4)*

When he wrote this passage, Priestley was not describing a real, flesh-and-blood citizen of Bruddersford and supporter of United called Jesiah Oakroyd. There is no such town, no such football club, and no such person. And yet, once Priestley has written this passage—and the many other passages that make up the novel—we can talk meaningfully about Jesiah Oakroyd. In fact, we often talk about fictional characters as if they *were* real, flesh-and-blood people: we might say that Jesiah Oakroyd is a working man, supports United, and wears a brown flat cap. The indirect fiction view sees a parallel here with theoretical modeling. When scientists write down their equations and assumptions, they are not describing an actual, concrete object. There is no such object. And yet, once the scientists have written down their equations and assumptions, they can talk meaningfully about their model system. In fact, they often talk as if it were an actual, concrete object, whose behavior they can investigate.

According to the indirect fiction view, then, when scientists write down their equations and assumptions, they are doing the same sort of thing as an author describing a fictional character. Just as Priestley asks us to imagine a fictional citizen of Bruddersford who wears a flat cap, so scientists ask us to imagine a collection of tiny billiard balls whizzing around in a container. In the same way that Priestley conjures up Jesiah Oakroyd, so scientists conjure up their model system. Scientists' subsequent talk about their model system is to be understood in the same way as talk about fictional characters. Crucially, fictional characters have properties that go beyond those explicitly stated in the text. We assume that Jesiah Oakroyd has blood in his veins and needs oxygen to survive, even if Priestley never bothers to say as much. Likewise, model systems have properties that go beyond those specified in scientists' initial equations and assumptions. This explains how scientists can learn about their model system. We learn about the real world by comparing our model systems to the world. A key problem for this view arises when we ask: what exactly *are* model systems? We've seen that they are supposed to be like fictional characters. But what are fictional characters? As we've noted already, philosophers of fiction are divided on this question. Realists about fictional characters think they exist in some sense (e.g., as non-existent or abstract entities), while anti-realists deny this. Similar disagreement exists over the nature of model systems. Some authors are realists about model systems (Contessa, 2010; Thomasson, 2020; Thomson-Jones, 2020), some are anti-realists (Frigg, 2010), and some remain neutral (Godfrey-Smith, 2006). None of these alternatives is without difficulties, however (Friend, 2020; Thomson-Jones, 2007; Toon, 2012).

The *direct fiction view* hopes to avoid these problems with fictional characters. To do so, it proposes a different analogy between models and works of fiction (Toon, 2010, 2012; for a related approach, see Levy, 2015). Rather than comparing scientists' equations and assumptions to descriptions of fictional characters, it compares them to works of fiction that represent real people, places, and events. Consider the following passage from the historical novel *Q* by Luther Blissett, the Italian writers' collective:

> The prophet of Münster passes through the Ludgeritor and leaves the city behind him, escorted by a dozen men. No one else has been able to follow him: everyone has his role in the Plan. We crowd on to the city walls. The bishop prince's camp is clearly visible a short distance away, slightly blurred by the mist rising from the damp earth. We see them advancing towards the embankment dug by the bishop's mercenaries. There is commotion in their ranks, they take aim with their hackbuts. Matthys gestures to his men to stop. Matthys walks on alone. (2003, 230).

Unlike Priestley's description of Bruddersford and Jesiah Oakroyd, this is not simply a description of a fictional town and its inhabitants. Instead, it represents a real town, Münster, and a real person, Jan Matthys, the leader of the Münster rebellion. More specifically, it represents Matthys' fateful actions in Münster on Easter Sunday, 1534. Some of what the novel asks us to imagine about Münster, Matthys, and the rebellion is true (e.g. that the rebellion was led by Anabapists, that Matthys was captured and brutally executed) while much of it is made up by the authors (e.g. that the events were closely followed by a mysterious Catholic spy named *Q*). The direct fiction view sees a more appropriate parallel here for theoretical modeling in science. Like historical novels, scientists' equations and assumptions ask us to imagine the world in a certain way. Some of what they ask us to imagine is true (e.g., that gases consist of molecules, that they collide with the walls of the container), while some of it is false (e.g. that these molecules are spherical, that the collisions are perfectly elastic).

The indirect fiction view claims that scientists represent the world indirectly, via model systems. In contrast, the direct fiction view claims that scientists represent the world directly, by asking us to imagine things about it. There are no model systems. There are simply equations and assumptions that scientists write down, norms that govern their interpretation, and the imaginings that they prescribe. Why do scientists talk as if there were model systems? Toon (2012) argues that they are engaging in make-believe. The scientists are pretending—they are "going along with" the model to tell us what it asks us to imagine. For instance, suppose that a scientist using the billiard ball model to predict the behavior of a gas remarks that "the molecules collide elastically." According to the direct fictions view, the scientist is not describing a collection of fictional molecules; she is telling us to imagine this about the real molecules. On this view, we learn about a model by tracing out the implications of our initial equations and assumptions. For instance, we learn that if we imagine that gas molecules only act upon each other in collisions, collide elastically, and so on, then the pressure of the gas will be proportional to its temperature. In this way, the direct fiction view hopes to provide a deflationary analysis of theoretical modeling, which does without the need to posit model systems. Its critics feel that these hopes are in vain and that we still need model systems to make sense of theoretical modeling and the way that scientists talk about it (Thomasson, 2020; Weisberg, 2013).

How does recent work on models and fiction relate to the other strands of thinking about science and fiction that we considered earlier? It shares Vaihinger's interest in modeling and idealization, of course. Unlike Vaihinger, however, it tries to understand these aspects of scientific practice by looking to works of fiction in the ordinary sense. In this respect, work on models and fiction resembles fictionalist views like van Fraassen's constructive empiricism, which also see parallels between theoretical claims in science and our talk about fictional characters. The scope of this analogy is more restricted, however: for authors on models and fiction, the analogy applies only to scientists' claims about model systems, not all theoretical statements. The reason is that, unlike van Fraassen, work on models and fiction is not motivated by worries about the status of unobservable entities, like molecules or electrons. Instead, its central aim is to make sense of the practice of modeling, although the direct fiction view also hopes to achieve this in a way that it metaphysically parsimonious. Whether or not it is ultimately successful, such work brings philosophy of science closer than we might expect to debates in philosophy of fiction.

Conclusion

On the face of it, science and fiction seem to ask us to adopt different attitudes: science asks us to believe what it says, while fiction asks us to engage in make-believe. As we have seen, however, matters are not quite so straightforward. Many statements we find in science are what Vaihinger calls *fictions*. We use these statements to manage the world, but we do not believe them. Anti-realists like van Fraassen urge us to adopt a similar attitude to all theoretical claims: we should use statements about unobservable entities to make predictions or build machines, but we should not believe them. Some authors see a parallel here with our talk about works of fiction. Recent work on models and fiction develops this parallel further. On this view, it is not only that scientists do not believe their idealizations and assumptions; they are also engaging in make-believe. Like novelists or playwrights, scientists often ask us to imagine the world in a certain way so that we can understand it better.

Further Reading

Vaihinger's classic work on fictions is *The Philosophy of "As If"* (London: Routledge, 1911/1924). Recent discussions and applications of Vaihinger's ideas include M. Suárez (ed.) *Fictions in Science* (London: Routledge, 2009) and K. A. Appiah, *As If: Idealization and Ideals* (Cambridge, MA: Harvard University Press, 2017). The key source for van Fraassen's constructive empiricism is *The Scientific Image* (Oxford: Clarendon Press, 1980). On van Fraassen's view as a form of fictionalism, see G. Rosen, "What Is Constructive Empiricism?" *Philosophical Studies* (1994). P. Godfrey-Smith, "The Strategy of Model-Based Science." *Biology and Philosophy* 21 (2006) and R. Frigg, "Models and Fiction." *Synthese* 172 (2010) endorse the indirect fictions view. A. Toon, *Models as Make-Believe: Imagination, Fiction and Scientific Representation* (Basingstoke: Palgrave Macmillan, 2012) and A. Levy "Modeling Without Models." *Philosophical Studies* (2015) both develop versions of the direct fiction view.

Note

1 My thanks to Stacie Friend for many helpful and illuminating discussions on the relationship between fiction and fictionalism.

Works Cited

Appiah, Kwame Anthony. 2017. *As If: Idealization and Ideals*. Cambridge, MA: Harvard University Press.
Bokulich, Alisa. 2012. "Distinguishing Explanatory from Nonexplanatory Fictions." *Philosophy of Science* 79, no. 5 (December): 725–37.
Burgess, John P. 1983. "Why I Am Not a Nominalist." *Notre Dame Journal of Formal Logic* 24, no. 1 (January): 93–105.
Cartwright, Nancy. 1983. *How the Laws of Physics Lie*. Oxford: Clarendon Press.
Conan Doyle, Arthur. (1902) 2003. *The Hound of the Baskervilles*. London: Penguin.
Contessa, Gabriele. 2010. "Scientific Models and Fictional Objects." *Synthese* 172, no. 2 (January): 215–29.
Demeter, Tamás. 2013. "Mental Fictionalism: The Very Idea." *The Monist* 96, no. 4 (October): 483–504.
De Regt, Henk W. 2015. "Scientific Understanding: Truth or Dare?" *Synthese* 192, no. 12 (December): 3781–97.
Duhem, Pierre. (1906) 1969. *To Save the Phenomena: An Essay on the Idea of Physical Theory from Plato to Galileo*. Translated by Edmund Dolan and Chaninah Maschler. Chicago, IL: University of Chicago Press.
Field, Hartry H. 1980. *Science without Numbers*. Princeton, NJ: Princeton University Press.
Fine, Arthur. 1993. "Fictionalism." *Midwest Studies in Philosophy* 18: 1–18.
Friend, Stacie. 2007. "Fictional Characters." *Philosophy Compass* 2, no. 2: 141–56.
Friend, Stacie. 2020. "The Fictional Character of Scientific Models." In *The Scientific Imagination: Philosophical & Psychological Approaches*, edited by Arnon Levy and Peter Godfrey-Smith, 102–27. Oxford: Oxford University Press.
Frigg, Roman. 2010a. "Models and Fiction." *Synthese* 172, no. 2 (January): 251–68.
Gaut, Berys. 2003. "Art and Knowledge." In *The Oxford Handbook of Aesthetics*, edited by Jerrold Levinson, 439–41. Oxford: Oxford University Press.
Giere, Roland N. 2009. "Why Scientific Models Should Not Be Regarded As Works of Fiction." In *Fictions in Science: Philosophical Essays on Modeling and Idealization*, edited by Mauricio Suárez, 248–58. London: Routledge.
Godfrey-Smith, Peter. 2006. "The Strategy of Model-Based Science." *Biology and Philosophy* 21, no. 5: 725–40.
Hesse, Mary. 1966. *Models and Analogies in Science*. Notre Dame, IN: University of Notre Dame Press.
Joyce, Richard. 2001. *The Myth of Morality*. Cambridge: Cambridge University Press.
Kalderon, Mark Eli. 2005a. *Moral Fictionalism*. Oxford: Clarendon Press.
Kalderon, Mark Eli. 2005b. "Introduction." In *Fictionalism in Metaphysics*, edited by Mark Eli Kalderon, 1–13. Oxford: Oxford University Press.
Leng, Mary. 2010. *Mathematics and Reality*. Oxford: Oxford University Press.
Levy, Arnon. 2015. "Modeling Without Models." *Philosophical Studies* 172, no. 3 (March): 781–98.
Lewis, David. 1978. "Truth in Fiction." *American Philosophical Quarterly* 15, no. 1 (January): 37–46.
Lipton, Peter. (1991) 2004. *Inference to the Best Explanation*. London: Routledge.
Lloyd, Geoffrey E. R. 1978. "Saving the Appearances". *The Classical Quarterly* 28, no. 1: 202–22.
Meinong, Alexius. 1960. "The Theory of Objects." In *Realism and the Background of Phenomenology*, edited by Roderick Milton Chisholm, 76–117. New York: Free Press.
(Original work published 1904)Priestley, J. B. 1929. *The Good Companions*. London: William Heinemann.
Putnam, Hilary. 1981. *Reason, Truth and History*. Cambridge: Cambridge University Press.
Rosen, Gideon. 1990. "Modal Fictionalism" *Mind* 99, no. 395 (July): 327–54.

Rosen, Gideon. 1994. "What is Constructive Empiricism?" *Philosophical Studies* 74, no. 2 (May): 143–78.

Rosen, Gideon. (2005). "Problems in the History of Fictionalism." In Fictionalism in Metaphysics, edited by Mark Eli *Kalderon, 14–64.* Oxford: Oxford University Press.

Russell, Bertrand. (1905) 1956. "On Denoting." In Logic and Knowledge, edited by Robert Charles Marsh, 41–56. London: George Allen and Unwin.

Stanley, Jason. 2001. "Hermeneutic Fictionalism." Midwest Studies in Philosophy 25: 36–71.

Suárez, Mauricio. 2009. *Fictions in Science: Philosophical Essays on Modeling and Idealization.* New York: Routledge.

Thomasson, Amie. 1999. *Fiction and Metaphysics.* Cambridge: Cambridge University Press.

Thomasson, Amie. 2020. "If Models Were Fictions, Then What Would They Be?" In *The Scientific Imagination: Philosophical & Psychological Approaches,* edited by Arnon Levy and Peter Godfrey-Smith, 51–74. Oxford: Oxford University Press.

Thomson-Jones, Martin. 2007. "Missing Systems and the Face Value Practice." http://philsci-archive.pitt.edu/archive/00003519.

(Longer manuscript version of Thomson-Jones [2010].) Thomson-Jones, Martin. 2010. "Missing Systems and the Face Value Practice." *Synthese,* 172, no. 2 (January): 283–99.

Thomson-Jones, Martin. 2020. "Realism About Missing Systems." In *The Scientific Imagination: Philosophical & Psychological Approaches,* edited by Arnon Levy and Peter Godfrey-Smith, 75–101. Oxford: Oxford University Press.

Toon, Adam. 2010. "The Ontology of Theoretical Modeling: Models as Make-Believe." *Synthese* 172, no. 2 (January): 301–15.

Toon, Adam. 2012. *Models as Make-Believe: Imagination, Fiction and Scientific Representation.* Basingstoke: Palgrave Macmillan.

Toon, Adam. 2016. Imagination in Scientific Modeling. In *The Routledge Handbook of Philosophy of Imagination,* edited by Amy Kind, 451–62. London: Routledge.

Toon, Adam. 2023. *Mind as Metaphor: A Defence of Mental Fictionalism.* Oxford: Oxford University Press.

Vaihinger, Hans. 1924. *The Philosophy of 'As If': A System of the Theoretical, Practical, and Religious Fictions of Mankind.* Translated by Charles Kay Ogden. London: Routledge.

Van Inwagen, Peter. 1977. "Creatures of Fiction." *American Philosophical Quarterly* 14, no. 4 (October): 299–308.

Van Fraassen, Bas. 1980. *The Scientific Image.* Oxford: Clarendon Press.

Van Fraassen, Bas. 1994. "Gideon Rosen on Constructive Empiricism." *Philosophical Studies* 74, no. 2 (May): 179–92.

Wallace, M. 2022. "Mental Fictionalism." In *Mental Fictionalism: Philosophical Explorations,* edited by Tamás Demeter, Ted Parent and Adam Toon, 27–51. London: Routledge.

Walton, Kendall. 1990. *Mimesis as Make-Believe: On the Foundations of the Representational Arts.* Cambridge, MA: Harvard University Press.

Weisberg, Michael. 2013. *Simulation and Similarity: Using Models to Understand the World.* Oxford: Oxford University Press.

Yablo, Stephen. 2002. "Go Figure: A Path through Fictionalism." *Midwest Studies in Philosophy* 25: 72–102.

10

LEARNING FROM FICTION[1]

Gregory Currie, Heather Ferguson, Jacopo Frascaroli,
Stacie Friend, Kayleigh Green, and Lena Wimmer

The idea that fictions may educate us is an old one, as old perhaps as the view according to which they distort the truth and mislead us.[2] While there is a long tradition of passionate assertion from both sides of this debate, systematic arguments are a relatively recent development, and the idea of empirically testing these ideas is particularly novel.[3] Ideally, the debate will be a cross-disciplinary one. Interpretive studies of literature, drama, film, and other media of fictional presentation give us a sense of the depth and significance of particular works, as well as providing reflection on more general questions about genre, style, and reception. Psychologists have recently begun to study the cognitive and other effects of exposure to fiction. Philosophers have a role to play in clarifying concepts, distinguishing in a fine-grained way between hypotheses, and constructing and assessing arguments. These three activities don't correspond neatly to discipline boundaries. Philosophers have offered interpretations of particular works, often in the cause of arguing for the cognitive richness of the work in question. In a few cases, we find collaboration across the disciplines (Wimmer et al., 2021a, 2021b, 2022).

Our aim in this chapter is to provide some clarity about what is at stake in this debate, what the options are, and how empirical work does or might bear on its resolution.

What Is in Dispute?

Those who think we learn from fictions do not claim that we learn from all fictions, and will probably agree that fictions are sometimes a potent source of error and ignorance. For those who think that fictions do influence people's opinions, the problem is to identify situations where that influence counts as learning and to describe the factors that make that a more or less likely outcome.[4] It will be evident from this that anyone skeptical of the power of fiction to enable learning cannot simply point to the many examples of fictions which manifestly lack this capacity; that will be agreed to by all parties. Nor is wholesale skepticism about learning from fiction—that no one ever learned anything from any fictional work—plausible; at the very least we learn about what characters and events the author has chosen to describe.[5] What is likely to be questioned is a kind of easy-going optimism which takes it as obvious that exposure to the right kind of fiction (whatever that is taken to be) will give us valuable knowledge of the world and the people in it. It is not unreasonable to ask for evidence and argument to support such a claim, and to point out that establishing that someone learned something from a particular fictional source may be rather difficult.

DOI: 10.4324/9781003119456-12

While some, notably Dr. Johnson, have suggested that learning from fiction requires the fiction in question to exemplify morally correct principles, recent commentators do not identify potential for learning with advocacy of any particular moral stance; a common view now is that cognitively rich and insightful fiction is unlikely to be overtly didactic.[6] The case for learning from fiction has largely drawn on traditionally canonical authors and genres: tragic drama, the realist novels of the nineteenth century, and their modernist successors. In line with contemporary revisionism about the canon, those concerned with this issue now seek examples in a culturally wider class of works.[7] The debate has also taken in other media, notably through a focus on film as a medium of fictional presentation.[8] Here philosophers have been active in debating whether film has a distinctive capacity for philosophical instruction. We will not have space to focus here on this specialized aspect of the more general debate.

Knowledge, Reliability, and Fiction

This is a contribution to a volume concerned with fiction and belief. Certainly, much learning involves change of belief, but this is by no means all the learning there is, or so many assume. Learning may also involve the acquisition of skills, the refinement of our capacities, the gathering of new experiences. These things are rarely insulated from belief change but it would be controversial to say that they are nothing more than alterations to belief. And in discussions of fiction, these other forms of learning are prominent; it is said that fictions refine our empathic abilities, make us more attuned to other perspectives, and allow us to glimpse experiences distant from our own.[9] We will at some points touch on these matters. It will also be necessary to ask whether some apparent changes in belief might actually be something else.

People believe many kinds of things: that God exists, that the coat you are wearing is red, that $2 + 2 = 4$ and that kindness is valuable. Beliefs differ greatly in their significance and in the extent to which they can be tested. But for any belief we can ask: Is that true? And we can relatedly ask: Would it be better if you changed your belief? Not every change of belief is learning; you have not learned anything by coming to believe that the earth is flat. What more is required? One answer is: your new belief must be knowledge, and that means it must be true; you can't *know* that the earth is flat when it isn't. But philosophers have convinced themselves that true belief does not generally amount to knowledge; something you read in your horoscope can be right but the horoscope did not give you knowledge though it gave you true belief. Why not? It was once thought sufficient to say that the horoscope did not give you any rational grounds (any "justification") for your belief. Most philosophers now think that this is not right.[10] On one formulation of the worry, one may have a true, justified belief but still be right "by accident" in a way which denies you the status of knowing what you believe. Subsequent work has often emphasized the idea that knowledge depends on the reliability of the process by which you came to believe; a reliable process does not always yield the correct result, but when it does that is no accident.[11] We turn to the issue of reliability in fiction directly.

To speak of fictions as reliable sources of true beliefs may seem paradoxical, since fictions are most often thought of as trading in stories that are not true and telling us of characters that do not exist. In fact, many of us treat fictions as reliable on some topics; indeed, there are cases where a work of fiction is among the best, most reliable source one could have. The best way to learn what is said in a novel may be to read it yourself, and the best way to learn about the qualities of an author's style may be to read their works. Those skeptical about learning from fiction have not denied this; their skepticism focuses instead on claims that fiction helps us to learn things about the world beyond and independent of the work itself. However, cases of learning about the fictional work (or its maker) from the work itself are of some interest for us because they are often cases where the reliability of the source—the fiction—can be independent of the reliability of the author. The author may have quite unreliable views about their own style; views that a careful reading of the works themselves would undermine. When we consider the prospects for gaining knowledge of the world beyond the fiction, the question of the author's reliability is important, as we shall now see.

Hilary Mantel's three novels focusing on the life of Thomas Cromwell have probably shaped the views of many on the events and personalities of the Tudor court. People who did not know before reading *Bring Up the Bodies* that Anne Boleyn was tried and executed for, among other things, treason, may well come to believe it after. This does not seem an unreasonable way to acquire this particular belief; the work belongs to the genre of historical fiction, a standard feature of which is fidelity to the known major events of the period. But while Mantel's writings might be relied on to, as she puts it, "closely track the historical record,"[12] a reader who came to believe that Boleyn was as malign a person as Mantel represents her would be in a much less secure position. On questions of motive and character the historical record is equivocal in this case (as in many others) and anyway Mantel, like other historical novelists, asserts the right to speculate on matters of motive. It might turn out that the novel's representation of Boleyn's character is correct, but a reader who accepted it as truth would arguably not have acquired a *reliably* true belief.[13]

Reliance on the Author

Learning from others is most often discussed in epistemology under the heading of "testimonial knowledge," a topic which has seen a great deal of philosophical attention in the last two decades.[14] Testimony, where one is simply told something, contrasts with argument, which provides you with a reason, though not always a conclusive one. Of course, in many cases, the provision of reasons is itself partly a matter of testimony; I may cite the fact that I have seen footprints in support of the proposition that there is a lion outside but you have only my word that I have seen them; it is a rare argument that is completely independent of testimony. While philosophers differ over the fundamentals of testimony, there is general agreement that in many situations it is reasonable to depend on it for one's knowledge. Is this what is happening in the case of Mantel and the last days of Anne Boleyn? Perhaps not. She was probably not seeking to *tell* these facts to her readers; she may have assumed that they would know this already, or not cared one way or the other. Learning about Boleyn's execution from *Bring Up the Bodies* illustrates one way to learn that depends on someone's reliability but does not amount to testimonial learning. This happens in other kinds of cases, as when I judge that it's raining outside because I see you take an umbrella when leaving the house. You were not telling me anything, but my believing there is rain makes sense only so long as I think you are reliable on that topic.

In fiction we do sometimes find a practice of outright assertion, or something close to it. Many things said by Victor Hugo in *Notre Dame de Paris* were intended to inform readers about the history and present state of the Cathedral, and were influential in shaping subsequent restorations. There are also cases where there is, we may suspect, an intention to communicate an opinion but only by rather indirect means. Jerrold Levinson notes that "Ibsen would not have written [*An Enemy of the People*] as he did if he had not meant to advocate a certain position about the perils of majority thinking and the herd instinct."[15] While there are statements put in the mouths of characters in that play that conform to this position, there are also statements from characters that contradict it. Overall though, the play seems designed to make following the dictates of individual conscience the more attractive option. If something like what Levinson suggests was not his aim, we may think, Ibsen would have written a different sort of play. To have grounds for thinking that an author is advocating a position you don't have to find outright assertions of that position from them; it is enough to think that an intent to advocate in this way explains, at least in part, the shape of the work itself.

Fictions as Reasons

You may recognize, or think you recognize, an intent in Ibsen's play to communicate the value of individual conscience. What might persuade you that what is communicated is true, or at least worth serious consideration? If this is straightforward testimony you may resist persuasion. While testimony on factual matters can seem a reasonable source of knowledge, it is often thought much less acceptable in such moral matters as the value of conscience.[16] In morals it can seem, at the least, unacceptably passive simply to follow another's opinion. Anyway, thinking of a fiction like Ibsen's play as a case of testimony misses an important feature of the play itself. The play is not merely a means by which Ibsen communicates his opinion; it provides, or seeks to provide, a reason of sorts for believing what is communicated, or at least for giving it greater weight than one otherwise would.

How might a fiction such as Ibsen's play provide reasons? In at least two ways. One is by providing an argument for some favored position, expressed by one or other character. Another way opens up when the play transforms an abstract moral view into a concrete scenario that purports to show *why* this is the right position, or at least why it is a position worth taking seriously.[17] On this view, Ibsen shows us a way in which people acting from a self-regarding or short-sighted perspective are apt to arrive at positions with manifestly unacceptable consequences. Importantly, the aim may not be to persuade us of the truth of the moral position but to help us guard against its violation. It is sometimes noted that, when asked for the "message" of some fiction we often can do no better than a platitude: we end up saying that *The Third Man* tells us not to support our friends when they do evil things—perhaps the headline message of Ibsen's play is comparably hard to disagree with.[18] But learning can be a matter of being reminded, in a vivid way, of something we knew but might be tempted to ignore. Fictions that remind us of these things can be epistemically valuable not because they change belief but because they help to connect belief more effectively to action.[19]

We see now a variety of functions that a fictional work can fulfil in the learning process. One is simply to serve as the vehicle of expression for an idea. Another is to provide reasons in favor of that idea, ones that are stated or implied by its characters. A third is to add persuasive power to the idea by rendering it concrete, showing how ideas and attitudes have practical consequences.

This final claim faces an obvious objection. Surely, all Ibsen does is provide us with a story concerning imaginary people in imaginary situations; their behavior can no more persuade us of the rightness of a view than imaginary observations can persuade us of the correctness of a scientific theory. In both kinds of cases only real instances will do. On reflection however, it is not obvious that only real events can tell us anything informative. For example, we often want to know what *might* go wrong with some plan; waiting to find out what *does* go wrong gives us no way to avoid a potential disaster. Instead, we try to construct an imaginative scenario—one that hasn't happened—which conforms to the plan but in which things do go wrong; that way we can revise the plan before it is too late. Fictions sometimes does this. The film *Fail Safe* (1964) purports to show how, given the control measures in place at US bomber Command, an accidental nuclear attack on the Soviet Union could still occur. If the film's narrative fairly represented these controls and their vulnerabilities, one might then have grounds for believing nuclear war more likely than one previously did. As a matter of fact, it is widely accepted that the pathway to the attack portrayed in this film depends on mischaracterizing the actual procedures in place.[20] Still, the general point holds: a fiction might, through imaginative yet realistic scenario construction, tell us something interesting.

Fail Safe investigates a well-defined and specific mechanism which depends in part on automatic systems and partly on human decision. It is not difficult to see whether it truly represents a way for the plan in place to fail. But fictions are more commonly appreciated for their exploration of processes much less clearly delineated. Martha Nussbaum highlights the way in which Henry James' *The Golden Bowl* traces the steps on the way to an understanding between Maggie Verver and her father

Adam, finding a crucial moment in Adam's image of her as a "sea creature." James is among the most admired novelists for his psychological insight, with this late novel regarded by some as a high point. But whatever the novel's literary merits, we do not seem to have a way to check that James' scenario conforms to a plausible model of human behavior. Might the detailed interactions James describes so carefully be unrealistic? The work's literary qualities may make it hard to judge; James' late style makes for difficult reading, absorbing cognitive resources that might otherwise be focused on assessing the psychological plausibility of the events he describes.[21] We may wonder, similarly, whether what Ibsen is doing in *An Enemy of the People* is creating a rhetorical environment likely to promote agreement with his moral outlook, without providing us with any good reasons for doing so. We are familiar with the tactic of making a certain outlook or perspective attractive by having it represented by characters who are attractive or likeable, but where their attractiveness or likability gives no real support to the outlook in question.[22] Fictions, with their occasions for heightened emotions, plot twists, and vividly drawn characters are, arguably, inherently unreliable environments for evaluative learning because we are not well able to segregate our responses to what is incidental and rhetorical from what is germane to the issue.

However, we should not overestimate the rationality of other, nonfictional, modes of communication when it comes to evaluative matters: are not our ordinary attempts to change people's moral outlooks similarly rich in rhetorical trappings? Where, in any case, is this supposed divide between rhetoric and moral argument? Only stern rationalists in morals see no place for the activation of sentiments in moral persuasion; what has come to be called the "Humean theory of motivation" insists that belief alone never motivates and that desire is essential (Smith, 1994). Fictions may sometimes go to excess in this direction but we can find fictions where this is avoided. And fiction has the advantage that it allows for disengagement and reflection (especially so in the novel) that may help us avoid being carried along by the authoritative tone of a present speaker.

So far we have spoken of learning from fiction as if it were a special kind of learning, distinct from that provided by more conventionally authoritative means such as textbooks and lectures. But some have sought to find a closer connection between fiction and the systematic inquiry we find in science and philosophy. The idea is that fictions sometimes provide *thought experiments*, a practice well established in science and philosophy for advancing research and which involves imagining a scenario rather than actually observing it. Occasionally, these thought experiments have a somewhat literary feel to them, as with the story of Schrödinger's cat which (on one interpretation of quantum mechanics) is simultaneously alive and dead until observation resolves the contradiction. In philosophy, thought experiments are often invented in order to support or undermine claims in moral philosophy, metaphysics, and elsewhere. For example, the now famous "trolley experiment" first suggested by Philippa Foot prompts us to explore the acceptability, in varying circumstances, of sacrificing one life in order to save many.[23]

There has been some enthusiasm for the view that novels, dramas, and films may provide reliable pathways to belief by shaping sometimes rather elaborate thought experiments.[24] The claim here need not be that thought experiments in fiction prove anything—this will be admitted concerning thought experiments in other areas. The claim need only be that they are capable of adding to the reasons, if not always for believing a proposition, then at least for taking it seriously.

Notably, however, there is growing opposition to thought experiments at least as they occur in philosophy; these are the ones most similar to those we might identify in novels, dramas, and films since they often involve human characters in morally charged situations. On this view, philosophical thought experiments are apt to be highly misleading because of the strain they put on our cognitive resources. For example, they ask us to extend our judgement from ordinary to extraordinary cases, something it is said we cannot reliably do.[25]

Others, however, don't dispute the usefulness of at least some thought experiments in science and philosophy, but insist that the complex works of literature so often appealed to by those who say we learn from fiction are not comparably reliable. Thought experiments in science and philosophy succeed best when they focus exclusively on a single precisely characterized problem, avoid rhetorical elaboration, subplots, and nonessential details, and allow a sustained (often brief) act of imaginative engagement with the events described. The novels and dramas so often valued for their capacity to instruct us are often bewilderingly complex in construction, with a plethora of surprising events and vivid characters designed to evoke emotions from mild amusement to hatred; the best-regarded novels sustain these sorts of complexities over days and even weeks of attentive reading. All this greatly increases the concern we may have that our cognitive resources are, in the context of a thought experiment, pushed beyond the bounds of reliability.[26]

Knowledge, Reasonable Belief, and Understanding

We have focused so far on whether and how we can get knowledge from fiction. In at least two ways this may be too narrow a formulation. First of all, the process of learning, where it focuses on belief, should surely have as its target the idea of belief improvement, and not every improvement in belief results in knowledge. If I used to believe the earth is flat and am told it is spherical that seems like dramatic improvement even though the earth is not, strictly speaking, spherical. We must be careful not to set standards for learning from fiction that we would not apply in other areas; fictions able to improve belief would surely add to the case for learning from fiction. But the problem with a focus on knowledge is not only that it may be too demanding; in some circumstances knowledge will not be enough. The thought here is that one may have knowledge but lack what we might call "understanding," something likely to be emphasized by those who say that the value of fiction lies in its capacity to make us wiser. On this view one may know a certain proposition—know that it is true—but lack understanding of it.[27] In some respects, the desired understanding may consist simply in more knowledge: knowledge, for example, of what explains it or caused it to be so, knowledge of its actual or likely consequences. But an emphasis on understanding also moves us into an area flagged earlier for investigation: skills and abilities. Understanding an event is said sometimes to involve being able to judge how things would be if that event had occurred in a slightly different way, or what would have to have happened for the event not to have occurred at all. It is far from clear that having this ability resolves neatly into knowing facts of various kinds, though it will involve such knowledge.

Encouraged by this thought we may see a close connection between fiction and skills, abilities and habits of various kinds. Thus, Elaine Scarry (2012) speaks of "the capacity of literature to exercise and reinforce our recognition that there are other points of view in the world, and to make this recognition a powerful mental habit." As well as helping us to recognize other perspectives, fiction is sometimes said to acquaint us with the experiences of the people who have them (see e.g., Putnam, 1978, 83–96; Walsh, 1969). We are said, for example, to gain from literary and filmic representations some knowledge, limited no doubt, of what it is like to be caught up in tragic events, to be exposed to extremes of deprivation, to be socially marginalized—all experiences we may well want not to undergo but which we think it would be good to know more about. It is far from clear that this kind of knowledge consists merely in coming to have certain true beliefs.

To this it may be objected that while we may feel, as the result of reading a novel, that we have a sense of what some experience would be like, we have no idea whether we are right—only actually having that experience would let us know that. Believing that we know something is no guarantee that we do. True, you may one day have that experience, and conclude that you were right in thinking that fiction had given you some prior acquaintance with it. There are two important questions to ask about that. One is philosophical and highlighted in our earlier discussion: why would this be anything other than a lucky accident? What reason do we have for thinking that we can mimic human responses to a complex situation purely on the basis of description of that situation? The second draws on the psychology of memory: can we be confident that we are recalling the imagined experience in such a way that it could (reliably) by compared with the actual current experience? This is, of course, an empirical question and one not easy to answer given that there is disagreement among psychologists of memory about the nature and extent of its proneness to error.[28] Our next section takes up the issue of the relevance of empirical studies to the question of what and how we learn from fiction.

Empirical Perspectives

The contributions of philosophers, critics, and literary theorists to the debate about learning from fiction have so far been notable for their lack of engagement with systematic empirical inquiry. The underlying assumption seems often to be that our own experience with fiction provides support for the view being advocated; friends of learning from fiction are often happy to testify to its effects on their own cognitive development. Such testimony is not worthless, but we can no more rest content with it than we could with assurances from school pupils that they learned French very well. In schools we have exams, and in the area of more practical skills we have equally objective measures; we are able to tell with reasonable accuracy whether a plumbing apprentice can mend pipes effectively. Do we have anything comparable to support claims about learning from fiction?

There is some evidence. But the search is at an early stage and there are difficulties in the way of getting the data we would most like to have. Much current research exposes people to brief passages of fiction followed immediately by a battery of tests, whereas the claims traditionally made on behalf of fiction concern the cumulative benefits of extensive and varied reading. Studies that addressed such claims directly would be costly in participants' time and commitment and would take decades to complete. Another difficult question concerns causal direction: are people more empathic because they read extensively in fictions that calls on empathic skills, or do they gravitate to fictions of this kind because of their prior capacity and enthusiasm for empathy?

In recent years, there has been quite a lot of small-scale research into the effects of fiction, much of it focused on aspects of social cognition: our ability to understand and respond fluently to the thoughts, desires, and feelings of others. There are established psychological tests used to measure people's empathic capacities, as well as their ability to comprehend the mental states of others (a major component in so-called "theory of mind" or "ToM"), and these tests are typically applied immediately after reading. Results have been mixed and in some cases only very small effects have been found.[29] Replication of some apparently positive results has been hard to achieve, and where improvements on empathy and ToM-related tasks have been found it is often unclear how long the results last.[30] Indeed, large and lasting effects on skills and abilities from one episode of reading would be surprising, so the current absence of strong evidence for a fiction-effect should not discourage researchers from conducting more fine-grained or more long-term studies. In relation to change over time, we may distinguish between the inculcation of skills and attitudes, such as one's capacity for empathy and hospitality toward immigrants, where significant change tends to be slow and incremental, and straightforward cases of change in factual belief which are sometimes instantaneous; I start believing it is raining as soon as I see the rain.

When it comes to acquiring factual beliefs from fiction the experimental data is somewhat mixed. One study suggests that fictions in various media can be successful in promoting factual belief, though retention is fragile (Brodie et al., 2001); there is also evidence that fictions may produce false beliefs quite easily (Appel and Richter, 2007; Marsh and Fazio, 2006). Concerning evaluative attitudes, evidence has been found for the effect of fiction on attitudes to out-groups, medical treatment, and negative stereotypes.[31] The effects described in these studies would be seen by most people as positive, since they involve transitions to less prejudiced and more inclusive attitudes. But Kris Goffin and Stacie Friend (2022) suggest a number of reasons why fictions may also increase bias.[32]

Studies of fiction's effects on beliefs and attitudes are one aspect of a larger field of study: the persuasiveness of messages. Until fairly recently, work in this area was dominated by studies of advertising and other areas where the message is said to be "overt," contrasting with the implicit or covert messaging of fictional stories. Gerrig's articulation of the idea of "narrative transportation", the process by which a reader is "taken to" the world of the story, eventually returning to the real world in some way cognitively changed, provided a framework for thinking about the effects of such messages (1993). The idea was taken up in an influential study (Green and Brock, 2000) which suggested that degree of transportation is a strong determinant of the cognitive effects of narrative, but that whether the narrative in question is read as fiction or as nonfiction makes very little difference. Why should degree of transportation make a difference, while thinking the work is fiction rather than nonfiction seems not to? It is said that readers who are more transported are less likely to be "vigilant" in their reading: less prone to consider the material critically and more likely to believe what they might otherwise reject. But a study by Prentice and Gerrig (1999) suggests that fictionality (the quality of being—or being regarded by the reader as—fiction) may actually reduce vigilance; participants told that the story they were reading was fiction were more likely to accept on its basis such false claims as "mental illness is contagious" than were those who read it as nonfiction.[33] It remains an open question whether, at least in some circumstances, recognition that a work is fiction does dampen the effect of reading on belief.

We may also ask: did subjects in Green and Brock's experiment really change their belief? Note that reader's opinions were tested immediately after reading. People's greater willingness to endorse the idea that the world is dangerous might simply be an effect of the extent to which they were emotionally moved by the story (emotional involvement being a significant feature of transportation). We are familiar, after all, with the way emotions color the way the world seems, sometimes for quite brief periods. A related query asks whether we are here failing to distinguish between belief in the ordinary straightforward sense and what we have called "attitude" or an evaluatively tinged way of seeing the world, something often responsive to emotion but not identical to it. To say that the world is a dangerous place might in some contexts—an academic seminar on risk—be a purely factual judgement, but in ordinary communication it is more likely to be an expression of pessimism rather than a factual assessment. Still, neither possibility nullifies the interest of Green and Brock's experiment. The result indicates an effect of storytelling on our way of seeing the world, if only a temporary one. And whatever the effect of fiction-reading in this case is, it appears not to be less than the effect of taking the story to be fact.

Limitations and Summary

We have simplified in various ways. For example, we have considered the effect of fiction on belief in terms of an encounter between an individual learner and a single work. As theorists of cultural evolution emphasize, learning in humans is often the product of multiple sources; if fictions change our beliefs they do so as contradicted or reinforced by other sources, against a background of approval or disapproval from authorities and peers, as mediated by our own biases and assumptions. A proper study of the role of fiction in shaping belief will have to accommodate these factors.

Another simplification is that we have focused here on the effects on belief of broadly realist fictions: narratives with plausible human characteristics in naturalistic settings. This ignores a range of important cases: many operas, fantasy literature of certain kinds, absurdist drama, experimental novels, and short fictions. Questions raised above, such as whether readers are able to determine the psychological plausibility of plot developments, can seem irrelevant to such works, yet one would hesitate to say that they have no interesting capacity to restructure our beliefs.

What we have done is to focus on a range of arguments, many of them underdeveloped in the existing literature, which suggest how more conventional fictions might change belief, attending especially to the positive changes we call learning. We also outlined the more obvious objections that might be brought against these proposals. Finally, we reviewed the highlights of a growing literature intended to find experimental evidence for (or against) fiction's capacity to change belief and other cognitive processes.

Notes

1 The authors acknowledge the generous support of the Leverhulme Trust, under grant RPG-2017–365: Learning from fiction: A philosophical and psychological investigation.
2 Plato's view of the moral and cognitive value of fiction was pessimistic (see *Republic* books II, III, X); Aristotle was more positive (*Poetics*, 1448b 13–19, 1451a 38–1451b 12, *Rhetoric*, 1371b 4–10). Later commentators with broadly positive views, often focusing on Shakespearean drama, include Dr. Johnson (see below note 4).
3 Early in the contemporary debate was Walsh (1969); see also Goodman (1976), Novitz (1987), Carroll (2002), Young (2003); Gibson (2007). Particularly influential has been Nussbaum 1990; for criticism of her position see, e.g., Kalin (1992). For negative views about learning from fiction, see Stolnitz (1992), Diffey (1995). Lamarque and Olsen (1994), while not disputing the possibility of learning from fiction, argue that to value a work of art as a work of art is not to value it for its truth or the knowledge it imparts. Currie (2020) combines philosophical and empirical arguments to mount a case that is largely (but not wholly) skeptical of claims about the educative effects of fiction. Dubourg and Baumard, in this volume, are especially skeptical. Useful introductions to the debate are Gaut (2003), Gibson (2008). An early experimental investigation of the impact of fictional information on real-world beliefs was Gerrig and Prentice (1991). Other important studies prior to the last decade are Prentice, Gerrig and Bailis (1997); Marsh, Meade, and Roediger (2003); Appel and Richter (2007).
4 Note that readers are often unaware, or reluctant to admit, that they are susceptible to persuasion by fictional media (Dill, 2009; Golan and Day, 2008), though they may judge others more susceptible than themselves. (Douglas, Sutton, and Stathi, 2010; Golan and Day, 2008). Hans and Dee note the contribution of police and crime fiction to the general pool of lay legal knowledge (1991, also Glasser, 1988; Haney and Manzolatti, 1980). Bloom says as much about our understanding of hospital procedures, submarines, and crime (2010, 167). Children seem particularly susceptible to this phenomenon: reading anthropomorphic literature, for instance, appears to increase their attribution of human-like properties to such entities as stones, whales, birds, and trains (Hopkins and Weisberg, 2016, 62, 63).
5 But see Dubourg and Baumard, in this volume: "for the moment, it is more reasonable to conclude that fictions don't impact beliefs".
6 For Johnson, see contributions to his twice-weekly periodical *The Rambler*, anthologized in Johnson (1977), ed. Bate. A theme of Johnson's was that (then) contemporary realistic fiction, unlike the fantastical tales of earlier times, was apt to invade the opinions, and the morals, of readers and so writers must guard against making immorality seem attractive (see Johnson, 1977: 11–12).
7 For a useful anthology of writing from the seventeen-century writers influential in canon construction to contemporary works of criticism and revision see Morrison (2005).
8 On film, see essays by Livingston (2006), Wartenberg (2006), and Smith (2006). See also Smith (2017). For an interesting empirical study of the effects of film on attitudes, see Butler et al. (1995).
9 See, e.g., Nussbaum (1990, 280): "the reader of Proust's novel comes to know his or her own love through a very complex process, one that involves empathic involvement with Marcel's suffering." Psychologist Keith Oatley and colleagues claim that "engaging in the simulative experiences of fiction literature can facilitate the understanding of others who are different from ourselves and can augment our capacity for empathy and social inference" (Mar and Oatley, 2008, 173). John Gibson (2008) emphasizes the importance of fiction for providing us with opportunities to experience the lives of others.
10 Edmund Gettier's (1963) very brief paper, and one of the most cited in philosophy, crystallized these doubts, though they are visible in earlier work by Bertrand Russell and others.
11 Alvin Goldman's (1967) is an early statement of the view.

12 Reith Lecture 1, June 13, 2017. https://www.bbc.co.uk/sounds/play/b08tcbrp.

13 At least for the case of film viewing, there are institutions that seek to track fictional deviations from reality; see e.g., https://www.historyvshollywood.com/. We are grateful here to Françoise Lavocat.

14 Coady (1992) has been influential in reviving interest in the epistemology of testimony. For slightly earlier work, see Fricker and Cooper (1987). Lackey and Sosa (eds.) (2006) is a collection of essays on the topic. For the place of testimony and testimony-like exchanges in fiction, see Friend (2014); Stock (2017); Ichino and Currie (2017).

15 Levinson (1996, 225).

16 See Hills (2009). For a more positive view of moral testimony, see Jones (1999). See also Hopkins (2007).

17 See Nussbaum (1990, 139–40) for the claim that a fiction (in this case Henry James' *The Golden Bowl*) may provide a "persuasive argument" for something "for which a philosophical text would have a hard time mounting direct argument." On whether narratives, fictional or otherwise, can provide arguments see Olmos (2017); Schultz (1979); Hunt (2009). On whether narratives can constitute explanations, Velleman (2003) is critical of the idea while Carr (2008) defends it.

18 See again Stolnitz (1992); also Carroll (1998).

19 Noël Carroll (2000, 368–69) says that "what art teaches us generally is not new maxims and concepts, but rather how to apply them to concrete cases." This way of thinking about learning in the moral sphere is strongly influenced by Aristotle's emphasis on phronêsis or practical wisdom in the Nicomachean Ethics. Related ideas are taken up in section "Knowledge, Reasonable Belief, and Understanding" below.

20 It might be argued that the film's cognitive value survives this observation about inaccuracy, depending instead on its vivid portrayal of the thought that "If the system does fail, these are the terrible consequences," combined with the surely plausible thought that *some* failure is a realistic possibility. Perhaps *Dr. Strangelove*, with its satire sometimes bordering on absurdity, makes this point more effectively because it allows us to turn aside from interrogating the detailed realism that *Fail Safe* aims for.

21 The idea that more demanding fictions leave us less capacity to scrutinize their implicit empirical claims is controversial. Some research suggests that stylistic ease or difficulty in fiction has no statistically significant effect on credulity and degree of belief change (Marsh and Fazio, 2006, 1145).

22 Psychologists refer to the "halo effect." For example, a person judged physically attractive is disproportionately likely to be rated as intelligent. The first empirical study was due to Edward Thorndike (1920).

23 See Foot (1967). Another noted thought experiments in philosophy is Hilary Putnam's (1975) "Twin earth scenario" which suggests that the contents of our thoughts depend on the external environment. Among many in the physical sciences are Newton's "bucket experiment" intended to show the absoluteness of rotational motion, and Einstein's "lift" experiment, used to show that light rays are bent in gravitational fields.

24 See e.g., Elgin (2007), Green (2017).

25 See e.g., Machery (2017). Tamar Gendler (2004) argues that thought experiments do have a distinctive, though fallible, capacity to provide justifications for our beliefs.

26 See Egan (2016), Currie (2020), Section 8.4.

27 See Hills (2016). Against this Paula Sliwa (2015) argues that understanding is not a different category from knowing.

28 For a recent review of findings and opinions, with some rather positive conclusions about memory's reliability see Brewin et al. (2020).

29 See the meta-analysis by Dodell-Feder and Tamir (2018).

30 See Kidd and Castano (2013) for an empirical study claiming evidence for the effects of fiction on empathy. For a failure to replicate their study, see Panero et al. (2016). For a response see Kidd and Castano (2017, 2018). See also Samur, Tops, and Koole (2018).

31 On evaluative attitudes, see Vezzali et al. (2015); on medical treatment, Green (2006); on negative stereotypes, Kaufman and Libby (2012).

32 See also Kris Goffin and Agnes Moors' contribution to the present volume.

33 For discussion and references see Friend (2014).

Works Cited

Appel, Markus, and Tobias Richter. 2007. "Persuasive Effects of Fictional Narratives Increase Over Time." *Media Psychology* 10, no. 1: 113–34.

Bloom, Paul. 2010. *How Pleasure Works: The New Science of Why We Like What We Like.* London: Bodley Head.

Brewin, Chris R., B. Bernice Andrews, and Laura Mickes, L. 2020. Regaining Consensus on the Reliability of Memory. *Current Directions in Psychological Science* 29: 121–25. https://doi.org/10.1177/0963721419898122.

Brodie, Mollyann, Ursula Foehr, Vicky Rideout, Neal Baer, Carolyn Miller, Rebecca Flournoy, and Drew Altman. 2001. "Communicating Health Information through the Entertainment Media." *Health Affairs* 20, no. 1: 192–99. https://doi.org/10.1377/hlthaff.20.1.192.

Carr, David. 2008. "Narrative Explanation and Its Malcontents." *History and Theory* 47, no. 1: 19–30.

Carroll, Noël. 1998. "Art, Narrative and Moral Understanding." In *Aesthetics and Ethics: Essays at the Intersection*, edited by Jerrold Levinson, 126–61. Cambridge: Cambridge University Press.

Carroll, Noël. 2000. "Art and Ethical Criticism: An Overview of Recent Directions of Research." *Ethics* 110, no. 2: 350–87. https://doi.org/10.1086/233273.

Carroll, Noël. 2002. "The Wheel of Virtue: Art, Literature, and Moral Knowledge." *The Journal of Aesthetics and Art Criticism* 60, no. 1: 3–26.

Coady, C.A.J. 1992. *Testimony: A Philosophical Study.* Oxford: The Clarendon Press.

Currie, Gregory. 2020. *Imagining and Knowing: The Shape of Fiction.* Oxford: Oxford University Press.

Davison, W. Phillips. 1983. "The Third-Person Effect in Communication." *Public Opinion Quarterly* 47, no. 1: 1–15.

Diffey, T. J. 1995. "What Can We Learn from Art?" *Australasian Journal of Philosophy* 73, no. 2: 204–211.

Dill, Karen. E. 2009. *How Fantasy Becomes Reality: Seeing Through Media Influence.* New York: Oxford University Press.

Dodell-Feder, David, and Diana Tamir. 2018. "Fiction Reading has a Small Positive Impact on Social Cognition: A Meta-Analysis." Journal of Experimental Psychology: General 147, no. 11: 1713–27. https://doi.org/10.1037/xge0000395.

Douglas, Karen M., Robbie M. Sutton, and Sofia Stathi. 2010. "Why I am Less Persuaded Than You: People's Intuitive Understanding of the Psychology of Persuasion." *Social Influence* 5, no. 2: 133–48.

Eco, Umberto. 1979. *The Role of the Reader: Explorations in the Semiotics of Texts.* Bloomington: Indiana University Press.

Egan, David. 2016. "Literature and Thought Experiments." *Journal of Aesthetics and Art Criticism* 74, no. 2: 139–50.

Elgin, Catherine. 2007. "The Laboratory of the Mind." In *A Sense of the World: Essays on Literature, Narrative, and Knowledge*, edited by John Gibson, Wolfgang Huemer and Luca Pocci, 43–54. London: Routledge.

Fazio, Lisa K., Sarah J. Barber, Suparna Rajaram, Peter A. Ornstein, and Elizabeth J. Marsh. 2013. "Creating Illusions of Knowledge: Learning Errors That Contradict Prior Knowledge." *Journal of Experimental Psychology: General* 142, no. 1: 1–5. https://doi.org/10.1037/a0028649.

Foot, Philippa. 1978. "The Problem of Abortion and the Doctrine of the Double Effect." In *Virtues and Vices*, 18–32. Oxford: Blackwell. Originally appeared in the *Oxford Review*, no. 5 (1967).

Fricker, Elizabeth, and David E. Cooper. 1987. "The Epistemology of Testimony. *Proceedings of the Aristotelian Society*, supplementary volumes 61, no. 1: 57–106.

Friend, Stacie. 2014. "Believing in Stories." In *Aesthetics and the Sciences of Mind*, edited by Gregory Currie, Matthew Kieran, Aaron Meskin and Jon Robson, 227–248. Oxford: Oxford University Press.

Gendler, Tamar Szabó. 2004. "Thought Experiments Rethought—and Reperceived." *Philosophy of Science* 71, no. 5: 1152–63.

Gerrig, Richard J., and Prentice, Deborah A. 1991. "The Representation of Fictional Information." *Psychological Science* 2, no. 5: 336–40.

Gettier, Edmund L. 1963. "Is Justified True Belief Knowledge?" *Analysis* 23, no. 6 (June): 121–23.

Gibson, John. 2007. *Fiction and the Weave of Life.* Oxford: Oxford University Press.

Gibson, John. 2008. "Cognitivism and the Arts." *Philosophy Compass* 3, no. 4: 573–89.

Glasser, Ira. 1988. "Television and the Construction of Reality." *Applied Social Psychology Annual* 8: 44–51.

Goffin, Kris, and Stacie Friend. 2022. "Learning Implicit Biases from Fiction." Journal of Aesthetics and Art Criticism 80, no. 2: 129–39. https://doi.org/10.1093/jaac/kpab078.

Golan, Guy J., and Anita G. Day. 2008. "The First-Person Effect and its Behavioral Consequences: A New Trend in the Twenty-Five Year History of Third-Person Effect Research." *Mass Communication and Society* 11, no. 4: 539–56.

Goldman, Alvin I. 1967. "A Causal Theory of Knowing." *Journal of Philosophy* 64, no. 12: 357–72.

Goodman, Nelson. 1976. *Languages of Art: An Approach to a Theory of Symbols.* Indianapolis, IN: Hackett.

Green, Mitchell. 2017. "Narrative Fiction as a Source of Knowledge." In *Narration as Argument*, edited by Paula Olmos, 47–61. Cham: Springer.

Green, Mitchell, and Timothy C. Brock. 2000. "The Role of Transportation in the Persuasiveness of Public Narratives." *Journal of Personality and Social Psychology* 79, no. 5: 701–21.

Haney, Craig, and John Manzolatti. 1980. "Television Criminology: Network Illusions of Criminal Justice Realities." In *Readings on the Social Animal*, edited by Elliot Aronson, 125–36. San Francisco, CA: Freeman.

Hans, Valerie P., and Juliet Dee. 1991. "Media Coverage of Law—its Impact on Juries and the Public." *American Behavioral Scientist* 35, no. 2: 136–49.

Hills, Alison. 2009. "Moral Testimony and Moral Epistemology." *Ethics* 120, no. 1: 94–127.

Hills, Alison. 2016. "Understanding Why." *Nous* 50, no. 4: 661–88.

Hopkins, Emily J., and Weisberg Deena Skolnick. 2016. "The Youngest Readers' Dilemma: A Review of Children's Learning from Fictional Sources." *Developmental Review* 43: 48–70.

Hopkins, Robert. 2007. "What Is Wrong with Moral Testimony?" *Philosophy and Phenomenological Research* 74: 611–34.

Hunt, Lester. H. 2009. "Literature as Fable, Fable as Argument." *Philosophy and Literature* 33, no. 2: 369–85.

Ichino, Anna, and Currie Gregory. 2017. "Truth and Trust in Fiction." In *Art and Belief*, edited by Sullivan-Bissett, Bradley, and Noordhoff, 53–83. Oxford: Oxford University Press.

Johnson, Samuel. 1977. *Selected Essays from the "Rambler," "Adventurer" and "Idler."* Edited by W. Jackson Bate. New Haven, CT: Yale University Press.

Jones, Karen. 1999. "Second-Hand Moral Knowledge." *Journal of Philosophy* 96: 55–78.

Kahneman, Daniel. (2003) 2011. *Thinking Fast and Slow*. London: Penguin.

Kalin, Jesse. 1992. "Knowing Novels. Nussbaum on Fiction and Moral Theory." *Ethics* 103, no. 1: 135–51.

Kaufman Geoff F., and Lisa Libby. 2012. "Changing Beliefs and Behavior through Experience-Taking." *Journal of Personality and Social Psychology* 103, no. 1 (July): 1–19. https://doi.org/10.1037/a0027525.

Kidd, David Comer, and Emanuele Castano. 2013. "Reading Literary Fiction Improves Theory of Mind." *Science* 342, no. 6156 (October): 377–80. https://doi.org/10.1126/science.1239918.

Kidd, David Comer, and Emanuele Castano. 2017. "Panero et al. (2016): Failure to Replicate Methods Caused the Failure to Replicate Results." *Journal of Personality and Social Psychology* 112, no. 3 (March): e1–e4.

Kurzban, Robert, Angela Duckworth, Joseph W. Kable, and Justus Myers. 2013. "An Opportunity Cost Model of Subjective Effort and Task Performance." *Behavioral and Brain Sciences* 36, no. 6: 661–726. https://www.cambridge.org/core/journals/behavioral-and-brain-sciences/article/an-opportunity-cost-model-of-subjective-effort-and-task-performance/8EB5B3A090D390C92891C703EC420A51

Lackey, Jennifer, and Sosa Ernest. eds. 2006. *The Epistemology of Testimony*. Oxford: Oxford University Press.

Lamarque, Peter, and Stein Haugom Olsen. 1994. *Truth, Fiction, and Literature: A Philosophical Perspective*. Oxford: Clarendon Press.

Levinson, Jerrold. 1996. "Messages in Art." In *The Pleasures of Aesthetics*, 224–41. Ithaca, NY: Cornell University Press.

Levy, Neil. 2011. "Resisting 'Weakness of the Will.'" *Philosophy and Phenomenological Research*, 82, no. 1: 134–55.

Livingston, Paisley. 2006. "Theses on Cinema as Philosophy." *Journal of Aesthetics and Art Criticism* 64: 11–18.

Machery, Edouard. 2017. *Philosophy Within Its Proper Bounds*. Oxford: Oxford University Press.

Mar, Raymond A., Keith Oatley, Jacob Hirsh, Jennifer dela Paz, and Jordan B. Peterson. 2006. "Bookworms Versus Nerds: Exposure to Fiction Versus Non-Fiction, Divergent Associations with Social Ability, and the Simulation of Fictional Social Worlds." *Journal of Research in Personality* 40, no. 5 (October): 694–712. https://doi.org/10.1016/j.jrp.2005.08.002.

Mar, Raymond A., and Keith Oatley. 2008. "The Function of Fiction Is the Abstraction and Simulation of Social Experience." *Perspectives on Psychological Science* 3, no. 3 (May): 173–92. https://doi.org/10.1111/j.1745-6924.2008.00073.x.

Marsh, Elizabeth, and Lisa K. Fazio. 2006. "Learning Errors from Fiction: Difficulties in Reducing Reliance on Fictional Stories." *Memory & Cognition* 34, no. 5: 1140–49.

Marsh, Elizabeth J., Michelle L. Meade, and Henry L. Roediger III. 2003. "Learning Facts from Fiction." *Journal of Memory and Language* 49, no. 4 (November): 519–36. https://doi.org/10.1016/S0749-596X(03)00092-5.

Morrissey, Lee. 2005. *Debating the Canon: A Reader from Addison to Nafisii*. New York: Palgrave Macmillan.

Novitz, David. 1987. *Knowledge, Fiction and Imagination*. Philadelphia, PA: Temple University Press.

Olmos, Paula, ed. 2017. *Narration as Argument*. Cham: Springer.

Panero, Maria E., Deena Skolnick Weisberg, Jessica Black, Thalia R. Goldstein, Jennifer L. Barnes, Hiram Brownell, and Ellen Winner. 2016. "Does Reading a Single Passage of Literary Fiction Really Improve Theory of Mind? An Attempt at Replication." *Journal of Personality and Social Psychology* 111, no. 5 (November): e46–e54. https://doi.org/10.1037/pspa0000064.

Prentice, Deborah A., Richard J. Gerrig, and Daniel S. Bailis. 1997. "What Readers Bring to the Processing of Fictional Texts." *Psychonomic Bulletin & Review* 4, no. 3 (September): 416–20. https://doi.org/10.3758/BF03210803.

Prentice, Deborah A., and Richard J. Gerrig. 1999. "Exploring the Boundary Between Fiction and Reality." In *Dual Process Theories in Social Psychology*, edited by Shelly Chailen and Yaacov Trope, 529-46. New York: Guilford Press.

Putnam, Hilary. 1975. "The meaning of 'meaning.'" Minnesota Studies in the Philosophy of Science 7: 131–93.

Putnam, Hilary. 1978. "Literature, Science and Reflection." In *Meaning and the Moral Sciences*, 83–96. London: Routledge & Kegan Paul.

Samur, Dalya, Mattie Tops, and Sander L. Koole. 2018. "Does a Single Session of Reading Literary Fiction Prime Enhanced Mentalising Performance? Four Replication Experiments of Kidd and Castano (2013)." *Cognition and Emotion* 32, no. 1: 130–44. https://doi.org/10.1080/02699931.2017.1279591.

Scarry, Elaine. 2012. "The Literacy Revolution: Poetry, Injury and the Ethics of Reading." *Boston Review* 37: 66–70.

Schultz, Robert A. 1979. "Analogues of Argument in Fictional Narrative." *Poetics* 8, no. 1–2: 231–44.

Smith, Michael. 1994. *The Moral Problem.* Oxford: Blackwell.

Sliwa, Paulina. 2015. "Understanding and Knowing." *Proceedings of the Aristotelian Society* 115, no. 1: 57–74.

Smith, Murray. 2006. "Film Art, Argument, and Ambiguity." *Journal of Aesthetics and Art Criticism* 64, no. 3: 33–42.

Smith, Murray. 2017. *Film, Art, and the Third Culture.* Oxford: Oxford University Press.

Stock, Kathleen. 2017. "Fiction, Testimony, Belief, and History." In *Art and Belief,* edited by Sullivan-Bissett, Bradley and Nordhoff, 19–41. Oxford: Oxford University Press.

Stolnitz, Jerome. 1992. "On the Cognitive Triviality of Art." *The British Journal of Aesthetics* 32, no. 3: 191–200, https://doi.org/10.1093/bjaesthetics/32.3.191

Sullivan-Bissett, Ema, Helen Bradley, and Paul Noordhoff, eds. 2017. *Art and Belief.* Oxford: Oxford University Press.

Thorndike, Edward L. 1920. "A Constant Error in Psychological Ratings." *Journal of Applied Psychology* 4, no. 1: 25–29.

Velleman, J. David. 2003. "Narrative Explanation." *The Philosophical Review* 112, no. 1: 1–25.

Vezzali, Loris, Sophia Stathi, Dino Giovannini, Dora Capozza, and Elena Trifiletti. 2015. "The Greatest Magic of *Harry Potter*: Reducing Prejudice." *Journal of Applied Social Psychology,* 45, no. 2: 105–21. https://doi.org/10.1111/jasp.12279

Walsh, Dorothy. 1969. *Literature and Knowledge.* Middletown, CT: Wesleyan University Press.

Wartenberg, Thomas E. 2006. "Beyond Mere Illustration: How Films Can Be Philosophy." *The Journal of Aesthetics and Art Criticism* 64: 19–32. https://doi.org/10.1111/j.0021-8529.2006.00226.x

Wimmer, Lena, Friend Stacie, Currie Gregory, and Heather Ferguson. 2021a. "Reading Fictional Narratives to Improve Social and Moral Cognition: The Influence of Narrative Perspective, Transportation, and Identification." *Frontiers in Communication. Language Sciences* 5. https://doi.org/10.3389/fcomm.2020.611935.

Wimmer, Lena, Heather Ferguson, Gregory Currie, and Stacie Friend 2021b. "Testing Correlates of Lifetime Exposure to Print Fiction Following a Multi-method Approach: Evidence from Young and Older Readers." *Imagination, Cognition and Personality* 41, no. 1: 54–86.

Wimmer, Lena, Stacie Friend, Gregory Currie, and Heather Ferguson. 2022. "The Effects of Reading Narrative Fiction on Social and Moral Cognition: Two Experiments Following a Multi-method Approach." *Scientific Study of Literature* 11, no. 2: 223–65.

Young, James O. 2003. *Art and Knowledge.* London: Routledge.

11

DO FICTIONS IMPACT PEOPLE'S BELIEFS? A CRITICAL VIEW

Edgar Dubourg and Nicolas Baumard

The idea that fictions impact beliefs is as old as literary theory. In *The Republic* (Book 2, section 357) for instance, Socrates already argued that the City should control the content of poetry. It is during youth that the most lasting opinions are formed, and in order to educate the future citizens who will participate in the life of the city, it appears necessary to control the stories on which society's moral principles are based. Thus, Socrates argued, stories by poets Homer and Hesiod should depict the gods and heroes as role models. Conversely, the episodes of the *Iliad* exposing the lamentations of Achilles should be censored because they depict the heroes in postures that are unworthy of the courageous man the City must create. Around the same time, in China, Confucius compiled writings about strikingly similar concerns in the *Classic of Poetry* (*Shijing*), tackling the dire consequences of *poetic misrepresentations* (i.e., fiction) on people's moral beliefs and, ultimately, on socio-political institutions (see Cai, 1999; for a parallel between Plato's and Confucius' visions of fiction, see Schaeffer, 2010, Chapter 1).

This opinion is not limited to Plato and Confucius. Many philosophers and politicians have expressed similar concerns regarding literary characters. Two thousand years after Plato, Rousseau criticized theater for making people laugh at good and virtuous characters in the *Letter to M. D'Alembert on Spectacles* (1758). Later on, the idea that fictional content influences people's beliefs gave rise to a wide range of rather similar concepts, such as (1) the concept of "bovarysm," coined by French philosopher Jules de Gauthier in 1857, and accounting for the way real people supposedly try to imitate the fantasized life of fictional heroes and heroines (Gaultier and Buvik, 2006); (2) the concept of 'external mediation' in René Girard's theory of human mimetic desire (Girard, 1992); (3) the concept of anti-mimesis, stating that artistic and fiction experiences influence real life, and captured by Oscar Wilde's famous statement that "Life imitates Art far more than Art imitates Life" (Wilde, 1891); or again (4) the idea of fiction as a "moral laboratory" or as a "teaching instrument" (Hakemulder and Hakemulder, 2000; Scalise Sugiyama, 2021a).

The idea that fictions can change people's beliefs is also widespread outside academic circles (see Shirley, 1969, for a study about people's belief that fictions change their beliefs). This is manifest in how people have long dreaded the potential negative consequences of fictions on beliefs for society. From the moral panics about the harmful effects of fictional romantic novels in eighteenth-century England to the moral condemnation of video games in most societies today (Markey and Ferguson, 2017; Vogorinčić, 2008), many have socially condemned the consumption of fiction, for fear that

141   DOI: 10.4324/9781003119456-14

people would adopt inaccurate or dangerous beliefs. People do seem to take fictional narratives as opportunities for learning, teaching, and social control. The use of fiction takes multiple forms in modern humans' life. For instance, reaching adulthood, people might read fictional stories to their children for educational purposes, and keep on reading literary fictions because they feel that it makes them smarter or more insightful.

The magnitude of this belief is observable in its concrete and serious consequences on fiction-making: we could enumerate a great number of ways fiction producers are constrained because of it (e.g., censorship). 'Bowdlerisation' is one example: this term was created after Thomas Bowdler censored Shakespeare's thirty-seven plays, by omitting or transforming parts considered immoral. This expurgated edition of Shakespeare was more in line with Victorian values and became, on average, more popular than before. Similarly, in today's China, the China Film Administration has been exercising its power to ban or edit many foreign movies, according to the alleged impact of their content on Chinese citizens' beliefs. For instance, very recently, *Lord of War* (2022) was shortened by 30 minutes: the final scenes, when the rather immoral character comes through with no punishment, were cut and replaced by text screen summary stating that he confessed to all his crimes and was sentenced to life in prison.

Such efforts of control and sometimes censorship are made precisely because fiction is considered a powerful tool to impact people, notably through education. The association between entertainment and education has been coined 'edutainment' by recent research (Anikina and Yakimenko, 2015; Singhal, 2004) and is currently being investigated by policymakers. For instance, a TV series tackling HIV and the problems raised by risky sexual behaviors was used to inform Nigerians about the disease and its treatment. At first sight, it seems that such interventions are effective: one study finds strong effects of the exposure to this fictional TV series on people's knowledge about the treatment and about the sources of transmission of HIV (Banerjee et al., 2019). Considering, for instance, the urgency of the ecological transition, and if such effects are generalized, policymakers could use climate fictions in educational programs to raise awareness and prompt sustainable behaviors. However, for policymakers to invest in such programs, they need to be sure that the intervention is effective, and more so than an alternative.

In all, this view that fiction can be used to change others' beliefs has been institutionalized for so long and is so well anchored in our daily lives that one might not easily realize that it is merely a hypothesis. In recent years, scientific theories, grounded in evolutionary and cognitive research, have proposed multiple explanatory models. Notably, it has been argued that people selectively retain relevant and accurate information from fictional stories (Nakawake and Sato, 2019; Scalise Sugiyama, 2021b; Schniter et al., 2018, 2022; D. Smith et al., 2017; Sugiyama, 2001) or that fictional stories allow us to simulate and, therefore, "experience" new situations, notably by taking the perspective of a fictional protagonist (Bloom, 2010; Gottschall, 2012; Mar and Oatley, 2008; Scalise Sugiyama, 2005; van Mulukom and Clasen, 2021; see Dubourg and Baumard, 2022, for a review of the evolutionary literature; see Best, 2021, for a review of the psychological literature). Both hypotheses, therefore, make the prediction that fictions can effectively change people's beliefs, and even that this effect is precisely why fiction emerged in human cultures.

The idea that fictions impact beliefs is thus strongly entrenched in philosophy, in literary theory, in public policy, in behavioral science, as well as among the lay people. But is it true? Here, we will argue against such a view. First, we will review empirical studies testing the hypothesis that fictions impact beliefs: such recent empirical evidence challenges the hypothesis that fictions do impact beliefs. Then, we will propose an explanation as to why this idea that fictions impact beliefs can be widespread and seemingly intuitive even if it is wrong.

A Critical Review of the Empirical Evidence

Mixed Empirical Findings Do Not Clearly Support the Main Hypothesis

A large number of studies have tried to empirically test the hypothesis that fiction consumption caus-ally impacts beliefs, some relying on correlational evidence, others aiming at estimating the causal ef-fects through pretest-posttest designs (e.g., Green and Brock, 2000; E. J. Marsh et al., 2003; Mulligan and Habel, 2013).

In correlational studies, researchers survey people about their beliefs and their preferred kinds or genres of fiction. Then, they test whether people holding more such or such beliefs also consume more such or such fictional genres. In statistical terms, they test whether both measures significantly correlate. For instance, Hefner and Wilson (2013) find that people who report watching romantic comedies more also report having more romantic ideal beliefs.

In pretest-posttest studies, researchers study the differences in beliefs of people before and after they are exposed to a specific piece of fiction. For instance, Howell (2011) studied how people's be-liefs about climate change were impacted by the movie *The Age of Stupid*, by statistically comparing participants' beliefs before and after they had watched it. The film had an impact on people's concern about climate change and viewers' agency, for instance. However, such effects did not persist after ten to fourteen weeks (see Section 'Testing the Stability of the Effects').

In some of them, but not all, they adopt a quasi-experimental design, assigning participants ei-ther to a test group (i.e., participants read or watch the fiction that is supposed to change people's belief) or to a control group (i.e., participants read or watch something unrelated, or some fiction that does not include aspects hypothesized to change people's beliefs). Then, they compare the difference between before and after the experimental conditions (difference in difference). In Riley's study (2017), students from Uganda were assigned to two conditions: in the test condition, they watched an aspirational movie featuring a role model, while in the control group, they watched a placebo movie (i.e., a movie that is not relevant to the test). The treatment significantly increased students' math performance at an exam, compared with the control. However, there was no effect on any other subjects than math.

In all, there seems to be mixed evidence to support the main hypothesis that fictions impact be-liefs. Some studies find significant effects (e.g., Butler et al., 1995, on the impact of the movie *JFK* on conspiracy beliefs; Prentice et al., 1997; Wheeler et al., 1999, on the impact of short stories on beliefs; Diekman et al., 2000, on the impact of romance stories on beliefs about safe sex; Mutz and Nir, 2010, on the impact of crime drama on the belief that the justice system is functional; Mulligan and Habel, 2013, on the impact of the movie *Wag the Dog* on the belief that president has launched a fake war; Kretz, 2019, on the impact of romance movies on the belief in soulmates). However, some do not find significant effects (e.g. Schofield and Pavelchak, 1989, on the impact of the movie *The Day After* on the belief that a nuclear war will occur; Green and Brock, 2000, on the impact of the short story "Murder at the Mall" on the belief in a just world; Hefner and Wilson, 2013, on the impact of romance comedy movies on romantic ideal beliefs; Nera et al., 2018, on the impact of a TV show episode on conspiracy beliefs; Petterson et al., 2022, on the effect of fictions with animals on concern for animal welfare).

Other kinds of analyses in media studies focused on the effect of fiction exposure on the *salience* of beliefs. Maybe fictions don't impact beliefs but put some of them high "on the agenda." Chances are that some become hot discussion topics when they are represented in a very popular fiction. For instance, a movie about a nuclear war had a great impact on the salience of and information about nuclear war (but not on people's belief—see Feldman and Sigelman, 1985). However, in another study, the impact of political fiction series (i.e., *Borgen*) on the public agenda was very small: the hypothesis that there was a causal relation between the topic of an episode and the saliency of the topic after its release was dismissed by the authors (Boukes et al., 2022). In all, there is also mixed evidence for this agenda-setting effect of fictions on beliefs.

We have summarized this literature, stating that there is mixed evidence to support the main hypothesis that fictions impact beliefs. However, there *are* some significant results. But do these results really tell us anything about the *causal* impact of fictions? As it is well known, "correlation does not imply causation" (this fallacy is also known by the phrase *cum hoc ergo propter hoc*: "with this, therefore because of this"). In the following section, we discuss several statistical and experimental flaws. That is, we point to reasons why some studies find that fictions do impact beliefs, even if such effects don't actually exist.

Methodological Problems Cast Doubt on the Robustness of the Significant Effects

The "Third Variable" and "Self-Selection" Problems in Correlational Studies: Differences between People Explain Both What They Believe and What They Like

A wealth of studies tested correlations between fiction exposure and beliefs (e.g., Buttrick et al., 2022, on the correlation between the consumption of literary fiction and complex beliefs about the world; Kretz, 2019, on the correlation between the consumption of romance movies and the belief in soulmates; Hefner and Wilson, 2013, on the correlation between the consumption of romantic comedy movies and romantic ideal beliefs; Scrivner et al., 2021, on the correlation between the consumption of horror movies and the belief that one is prepared to face a pandemic; Mumper and Gerrig, 2017, for a meta-analysis of the numerous studies studying the correlation between fiction reading and level of Theory of Mind). Such correlational studies had the objective to support the hypothesis that fiction consumption causally impacts beliefs.

However, it is not legitimate to deduce a cause-and-effect relationship between two events or variables solely on the basis of an observed association between them. Such correlations between fiction consumption and beliefs would be indicative of a plausible causal process only if they hold after accounting for *all* other factors that cause both beliefs and fiction consumption. The correlational studies presented here often control for standard demographic variables: we then know that the correlations they find are not due to differences between people's age, gender, education, or social status. But that is obviously not an exhaustive list of how people differ from each other. What if another variable could explain both what people overall believe and what fictions they consume?

This is known as the "third-variable" or "omitted variable" problem. For instance, childhood socio-economic status might have a causal impact both on what people believe *and* what fictions they prefer. Or maybe personality traits are great causal forces on both dimensions. Then, the correlations can be explained in such terms: some people resemble each other in what they believe and in what they like *because an unspecified causal factor accounts for how both dimensions vary.*

This is also sometimes referred to as a selection bias, but here it underlies the same idea: in such correlational studies, the participants in the treatment group, that is, those who decided to watch or read some kind of fictions, *selected* this activity by themselves and therefore somehow chose to be included in the "test group." In econometrics, the umbrella term for this is "endogeneity bias," because the correlations one finds are *endogenous* to the tested population (i.e., in statistical terms, the explanatory variable is correlated with the error term capturing all the variance that has *not* been specified in the model, hence also the omitted variable). Again, the problem is the same: the characteristics of the people which caused them to read or watch some specific kinds of fictions might cause them to hold some specific beliefs.

For instance, people vary in the extent to which they are open to new experiences and overall curious. This is captured by a personality trait called "Openness-to-experience" by personality psychologists. Researchers developed a questionnaire to compute a "score" which approximates people's level of Openness-to-experience (Costa and McCrae, 1992; McCrae and John, 1992). There is robust empirical evidence that this score correlates with (1) the extent to which people hold the belief that humans hold diverse values (DeYoung, 2015; Feist and Brady, 2004; Matz, 2021; McCrae, 1993), and with (2) what fictions they prefer consuming (e.g., fantasy and science fiction; Dubourg et al., 2022; Nave et al., 2020). Therefore, both variables are correlated, making it seem like fantasy fiction *causes* changes in people's belief, whereas such correlation might be explained by personality differences between people causing variation in both variables.

The "Trust-Calibration" Problem in the Self-Reporting of Beliefs: Participants
Intuitively Trust Scientific Experimenters to Tell Them Accurate Information

Most of the studies used self-reporting to measure people's beliefs, that is, they directly asked people what they believed. In pretest-posttest studies, such questions were asked while participants took part in a scientific experiment, sometimes online, sometimes in the lab. Such questionnaires have recently been contested in many scientific fields, because they are considered as *not ecologically valid*: participants in experimental settings are known to respond to them in ways that are sometimes inconsistent with what they believe or how they behave in real-world settings (Osborne-Crowley, 2020).

Notably, the setting of a scientific experiment is likely to influence what beliefs people report holding, because of the presence of an experimenter: we expect participants to believe more easily conveyed pieces of information in this specific setting because it was delivered by a trustworthy and competent source (i.e., a scientist). It makes it hard to be confident about such measurements of changes in people's actual beliefs after an experimental intervention, in ways that would be externally valid (i.e., that would still be valid outside of the experiment; Andrade, 2018).

For instance, Prentice and her colleagues (1997) asked participants to read a fictional text in which they included blatantly false information (e.g., "Most forms of mental illness are contagious"). Then, in a trivia quiz taking place just after the reading, participants were likely to answer consistently, even when the answers were obviously inaccurate. Chances are that participants took the content of this text at face value because it was presented by a scientific experimenter, even if it was presented as fictional.

It seems as if the evaluation that a scientist is a good source to revise one's beliefs was more powerful than the identification of the fictional status of the text. This interpretation of such results is consistent with a cognitive approach to information-sharing in humans, whereby people intuitively, unconsciously, and yet carefully calibrate their trust to the source of the information before adopting a new belief (Mercier, 2017, 2020).

The "Social-Desirability" and "Hypothesis-Guessing" Biases in Experimental
Settings: Participants Want to Please the Experimenters
and Report Beliefs That Fulfill This Goal

In the latter case, participants follow what they (wrongly) take as an expert's opinion: fiction loses its fictional status because it is presented by a scientist. There is another case where the reporting of belief is biased: when such beliefs are thought of to be socially evaluated: then, participants likely succumb to the *social-desirability bias* (i.e., when participants orient their responses to be viewed favorably by others, notably by the experimenters; Krumpal, 2013, for a review).

For instance, when experimenters ask if their participants intend to engage in anti-nuclear behavior (after a movie about a nuclear war), they globally report that they do, and more so after the movie (Schofield and Pavelchak, 1989). We argue that they report such a belief because they understand that this response would be judged positively, and the fiction exposure simply makes this idea more salient. If this is true, it is as if the movie was saying: 'The appropriate belief to report is that everybody should engage in anti-nuclear behavior'. The same could be said about the finding that students who read passages of Harry Potter related to the issue of prejudice (*versus* any other passages) reported being more tolerant about immigrants (Vezzali et al., 2015).

Sometimes, to be judged positively by someone, we don't report beliefs that are objectively socially desirable, but we report beliefs that we think our interlocutor expects. Experimental participants might do just that: this is called the *hypothesis-guessing bias*. It happens when the participants guess what the experimenters want to test: then, they are likely to respond accordingly. This is arguably the case in all pretest-posttest studies analyzing the effect of fictions on beliefs: experimenters show some topic-specific fictional content and then ask participants questions about this very topic. Participants can easily guess what would please the experimenter and unconsciously respond accordingly.

The Problem of Accuracy in Identifying the Source of One's Beliefs: Participants Do Not Always Know or Remember Where Their Beliefs Come From

Some studies explicitly ask participants whether they believe they learn new information or change their worldviews because of fiction consumption: in general, they do believe that fictions impact their own beliefs. However, it does not necessarily mean that it is accurate: people can be wrong about the origin of their own beliefs.

For instance, some people explicitly report that they read romance with the objective to learn new things about love from fiction (Hefner and Wilson, 2013). The hypothesis that romance is primarily thought of as a way of learning leads to the prediction that people unhappy about their relationship or relationship status should enjoy more and read more romance fiction (to learn how to fare better). In a recent paper, van Monsjou and Mar (2019) tested just this very prediction. Their results from their empirical study show that it is actually the other way around: people who already fare better in romantic relationships enjoy reading romance fiction more. This result supports the hypothesis that some people are just more psychologically prone to having romantic relationships, which makes them both more successful at romantic relationships and more likely to consume romance fiction.

The Problem of Direct versus Substitution Effect: People Consuming Fictions Change Their Behaviors without Changing Any Belief

Some recent studies in economics have tried to overcome such methodological problems by using more ecologically valid paradigms. In so-called natural experiments, researchers use the fact that some external arbitrary factor leads to differences in exposure to fiction in some close areas. This resembles random assignments in intervention studies (see DellaVigna and La Ferrara, 2015, for a review). It overcomes all the previous problems because (1) nobody is asked to report anything (so that there is no more social desirability or trust calibration biases) and (2) the *availability* of a fiction in a given location is exogenous (so that there is no self-selection or endogeneity bias).

To take a concrete example, La Ferrara and her colleagues (2012) wanted to estimate the causal effect of consuming fiction on women's fertility choices. Their hypothesis was that exposure to emancipated female characters would inspire women to delay pregnancy. To test this causal hypothesis, the researchers needed to find a context where the availability of a fiction appears as an "exogenous" variable, so that it does not depend on people's individual choice to be exposed to them. They used the fact that access to the television network that hosted the TV show took time, and people in some parts of the country had access to it before others. Which regions came first was argued to have no link whatsoever with women's fertility and can thus be seen as a random treatment allocation process with regard to it. The researchers could then compare fertility measures in regions where people could watch soap operas with regions where they couldn't (yet), because the network provider had not yet established access. In other words, the variation in delay of network distribution served as a randomization process that split the population into a treatment and control group. To measure fertility choices, they used administrative data from the government census. This strategy allowed them not to use self-reporting questionnaires and directly measure people's behaviors. Their evidence suggests that coverage by the television network which airs soap operas has a causal impact on the decrease in the probability of giving birth.

With this robust paradigm, some studies found significant effects of fictions on beliefs. For instance, Jensen and Oster (2009) show that, in rural India, exposure to television shows (in regions where it was possible to be exposed to them because of the availability of cable TV) alters people's beliefs about women's autonomy. The timing of changes in people's beliefs is aligned with the introduction of cable, so it seems not likely that they are due to a third variable. In this case, changes in beliefs and behaviors after exposure to fictional content are likely caused by the acquisition of consequential real-life information (e.g., women who work and are financially independent *actually exist* in the real world) that either change people's perception of social norms or make people more optimistic and raise their agency, that is, their willingness to act and have an impact on their life.

However, this literature in economics has recently been aware of and vigilant about a crucial bias in such natural experiments. It could be the case that the effect of fictions on behaviors is not caused by a direct effect on people's beliefs or even on people's cognition, but by a substitution (indirect) effect, captured by the intuitive idea that while people are consuming fictions, they are not doing anything else (DellaVigna and La Ferrara, 2015). To take one example from DellaVigna and La Ferrara's article, if soap opera becomes more culturally successful, then the effect of soap opera must be considered "with respect to the activities that it substitutes, like meeting with friends in a social context." Therefore, an effect of fictions on any life outcome, if significant, might not be the consequence of a change in belief at all.

Dahl and DellaVigna's study (2008) show a concrete example. They investigated the question of the impact of movies with violence on violent crimes in the United-States. To do so, they exploited the day-by-day variation of the release of movies with violence, and their popularity, in movie theaters, from 1995 to 2004: it shows a strong exogenous variation of violent movie exposure over time. They also retrieved the number of reported assaults and intimidation for a given day from the National Incident-Based Reporting System (NIBRS). After controlling for some potentially confounding variables (e.g., seasonality, rainy weather), they find that, over the nine years covered by this study, the "amount" of exposure to violent movies significantly *decreases* the number of assaults the very same day. Is this due to a decrease in one's violent beliefs after having been exposed to fictions with violence, that is, to some sort of catharsis? The study shows that this is not the case. First, there was no delayed effect of fictions on violent behaviors: researchers observed no effect of exposure to violent movies on the number of assaults or intimidation in the days after exposure. Second, and more importantly, the decrease of violent crimes caused by exposure to violent movies was significant within a specific time frame during the day, between 6 pm and 12 am, that is, when people go to the movies. The most likely interpretation is, therefore, that violent movies *attract* people that could otherwise be violent in the real world. That is, "violent movies lower violent crime because they reduce the allocation of time to even more pernicious activities," such as drinking at bars or wandering around at night (DellaVigna and La Ferrara, 2015). The net effect of violent movies can be computed: they lead to a decrease of 1,000 assaults per weekend, on average. However, this is not due to any cognitive changes in people's beliefs, but to the effect of voluntary incapacitation: the only explanation that fits the statistical observations is that people who have a more violent temper self-select into movies with violence (more so than other movies) and are, therefore, incapacitated from committing crimes.

More generally, to understand the impact of fiction consumption on beliefs, such findings urge us to consider the activity it is likely to be substituted for, what economists call the "next-best alternative activity." The question, therefore, should not be "Do fictions impact our beliefs?" but "Do fictions impact our beliefs *more than the alternative activity?*"

What Can Be Done to Overcome These Problems?

Testing the Stability of the Effects

To overcome the problems we have just reviewed, some researchers implement new methodologies. Notably, experimenters started to measure the *temporal stability* of what they assumed was an actual change in belief, by asking again the same questions to the same participants a few weeks later (i.e., test-retest design).

To our knowledge, the handful of studies that tested the stability of the effects with such a test-retest design were inconclusive. They typically find significant results when comparing people's beliefs before and directly after the exposure to the fiction. However, and crucially, this statistical significance always disappeared when comparing people's belief before and some weeks after fiction exposure (Brodie et al., 2001; Howell, 2011; Schneider-Mayerson et al., 2020; Strange and Leung, 1999).

Such results support the hypothesis that people didn't actually change their beliefs after having read or watched a fictional story, but rather *reported* beliefs that were consistent with what they had *just* read or watched (for the reasons we listed in the previous section). After a time (in the afore-mentioned experiments, between three weeks and two months), they return to reporting their actual beliefs from before the exposure to the fiction.

Comparing Effect Sizes

The effect size is the measure of the magnitude of the effect. While a *p*-value (i.e., a number calcu-lated with a statistical test that describes the likelihood of observing such results under the assumption that the null hypothesis is true) indicates whether an intervention works, an effect size indicates *how much* it works. Moreover, an effect size is independent of the sample size, whereas a *p*-value can reach significance with enough individuals even if the effect is very, very small.

It is paramount to report effect sizes when studying the effect of fictions on beliefs, notably be-cause one needs to compare the impact of fictions on beliefs with the impact of the activity it substi-tutes on beliefs. For instance, to argue that horror movies make people less prosocial, one would need to prove that it makes people even less prosocial than the activity it substitutes, which is likely to be meeting with friends: are people less prosocial because they watched horror movies, or because while doing so they didn't talk with their friends and benefited from this effect?

Reporting effect sizes is also important to compare the size of effects of different variables, and inferring which variable contributes 'more' to the observed effect. In Smith and Apicella's article (2022), Hadza hunter-gatherers were given the dictator game (i.e., after having received money, par-ticipants decide whether and how much money they want to give to another participant). The control group heard a control story before the game, while the test group heard a prosocial story. People from the test group did give more in the dictator game. However, the effect was small, and the amount of money transferred was more strongly correlated with other variables, such as marital status or region of residence.

Replicating the Findings

Reproducibility is a major principle in science according to which the results from scientific studies should be achieved again to be verified, using the same methodological paradigm, but usually performed by other researchers. The replicability crisis is an ongoing methodological crisis in many scientific fields, and notably in medicine and psychology: results of many studies are impossible to reproduce (Ioannidis, 2005; Open Science Collaboration, 2015).

The most well-known example in the matter at hand is the question of the impact of literary fiction on Theory of Mind, that is, the cognitive capacity to understand others' mind (Zunshine, 2006). First, Mar and his colleagues (2006) found correlational evidence of an association between fiction exposure (compared with non-fiction exposure) and social ability. To measure people's lifetime exposure to literary fiction, they used the Author Recognition Test (ART), which asks people to recognize classical authors' names in a list.

Then, Kidd and Castano (2013) found significant (yet small) effects of literary fiction (compared to popular fiction) on advanced tests of Theory of Mind (e.g., RMET; Baron-Cohen et al., 2001), in pretest-posttest experiments with control conditions, and controlling for the participants' previous exposure to fiction (using ART as a control variable). Black and Barnes (2015) also found a significant yet small effect of literary fiction using a within-participant design (again, compared to popular fiction), but using different controls (e.g., narrative transportation). In another study, they also looked at the effects of TV drama (compared to documentary) on Theory of Mind and found significant results (Black and Barnes, 2015). In 2016, Kidd and Castano replicated their own findings from 2013, with success. Such results would suggest that a one-time and brief exposure to literary fiction could immediately enhance social cognitive skills.

However, this is not the full story. Researchers tried to reproduce and extend such results. Djikic and her colleagues (2013) failed to find an effect of literary fiction (compared to essays) on Theory of Mind. An important article from 2016 was the first close replication attempt of Kidd and Castano's original findings. It was performed by three different research groups. They failed to find that reading literary fiction improves Theory of Mind (Panero et al., 2016; see Kidd and Castano, 2017; Panero et al., 2017 for a discussion). Another close replication again failed to replicate Kidd and Castano's results (Samur et al., 2018). Other conceptual replications did not find any association between lifetime exposure to literary fiction and social cognitive skills (Wimmer et al., 2021), nor between single short exposure to literary fictiona and social cognitive skills (Lenhart and Richter, 2022). A meta-analysis reported significant but small effects comparing exposure to fiction and exposure to non-fiction (Mumper and Gerrig, 2017). And a recent study performed a *p*-curve analysis (i.e., a statistical test aimed at looking for publication biases) and partially explains why apparently so many studies find significant effect: because papers with significant effects are more likely to be published (Quinlan et al., 2022). Finally, a recent study used for the first time a randomized control methodology, randomly assigning participants to a test group (where they had to read fiction 45 minutes a day for four weeks) or two control groups (where they had to read non-fiction 45 minutes a day for four weeks, and where they had to not engage in any reading for pleasure). Fiction readers did not outperform non-fiction readers or participants who did not read on any social outcome (Dodell-Feder et al., 2022).

The debate is not over, but most importantly, it highlights the necessity to wait for close replications before making any causal claim following single experiments. It seems more parsimonious, in light of the reviewed empirical evidence, to conclude that there is no specific immediate effect of fiction exposure on Theory of Mind. Future research should replicate such findings with other media (see Rathje et al., 2021 for theater; Castano, 2021 for movies) but also carefully design studies to test predictions that are theoretically grounded. As we have seen, some studies compared highbrow fiction exposure with lowbrow fiction exposure (e.g., Castano, 2021; Kidd and Castano, 2013), while other studies compared fiction exposure with non-fiction exposure (e.g., Black and Barnes, 2015; Mumper and Gerrig, 2017). The theoretical assumptions behind such tests are not at all similar. Besides, the former design has been criticized because of the lack of strong demarcation between literary and popular fiction. We argue that the latter suffers from the same flaw: fictionality is a continuum, as evidenced by literary naturalism, the recent emergence of hybrid genres such as autofiction or docufiction, or the success of realistic "inspired-from-real-facts" movies.

Using Behavioral Measures

Another way to work around the methodological problems we reviewed would be to actually measure, neither beliefs, nor intention to behave, but actual behaviors. The main cognitive function of beliefs is to orient future action. We assume that, when they ask whether people change their beliefs about, for instance, nuclear wars, safe sex, justice, or climate change, after some fiction exposure, what researchers really want to know is whether people actually engage in anti-nuclear behaviors, use more condoms, act more morally, or dedicate more effort to fight climate change. That is, the main question is not "Do people hold different beliefs?" but "Do people behave differently?"

This apparent subtlety is actually crucial, because, as we have seen in the previous subsection, people can report holding specific beliefs *even if they do not actually believe in them*, for social reasons (e.g., pleasing the experimenter) or epistemic reasons (e.g., waiting for the belief to be more strongly confirmed to act according to it). (On this point, see also Lisa Zunshine's contribution to the present volume). A cognitive approach to belief explains this oddity: humans can hold beliefs in a cognitive 'meta-representational' format (Sperber, 2008) so that they have no practical consequence whatsoever on behavior or on other beliefs (Mercier, 2020). Again, this is very useful, in order not to act on any belief we might encounter. Crucially, it means that not all beliefs lead to changes in behavior.

For instance, when people answered the trivia quiz after reading a fictional story with inaccurate information (Prentice et al., 1997), some answered (obviously, wrongly) that chocolate leads to losing weight, because this information was included in the story. However, we argue that this belief is held in a meta-representational format: after the test, participants are not likely to actually eat chocolate with the objective of losing weight.

To take a second example, in a classical study, people were interviewed before and after having seen the movie *JFK*. Immediately after, more people reported believing in the conspiracy hypothesis that multiple agents were involved in the Kennedy assassination and its cover-up (Butler et al., 1995). First, this belief was reported under the direct influence of the broadcast and this study didn't check the stability of this reported belief. As we have seen, it may very well not last much longer. But, even more importantly, it is a self-reported statement of a belief that should not be very consequential in behavioral terms: we argue that participants are not likely to change their future *actions* in accordance with this new reflective belief.

This discrepancy between belief and behavior has been put to light with randomized controlled trials. For instance, one study tested the impact of a fictional movie with relevant information about the national antipoverty program in India (Ravallion et al., 2013). Two months after the movie, participants from the control villages were more likely to believe that employment had increased or that economic opportunities had improved. Yet, it was not objectively the case: an objective measure of employment showed no gain on average between the two conditions. Likewise, in Tanzania, students who were incentivized to watch an edutainment show about business believed more than others that entrepreneurship is interesting. However, the show had in fact a negative effect on actual investment in learning: there was a negative treatment effect on exam performance (Bjorvatn et al., 2020; see Barsoum et al., 2022, for a similar study in Egypt). We hypothesize that such negative effects are not direct consequences of fiction consumption, but indirect *substitution* effect (i.e., people who are watching TV series are not studying).

The fact that we can hold beliefs in a format that prevents them from impacting any other belief or behavior urges further research to directly study the *behavioral* consequences of fiction exposure, not just changes in self-reported beliefs.

Conclusion: The Impact of Fictions on Belief Remains to Be Demonstrated

Mixed results and methodological flaws make us more inclined to reject the hypothesis that fictions impact beliefs, because of the lack of sound empirical evidence in favor of it. First, studies testing the impact of fiction on beliefs show no consistency in the significance of the effects. Second, because correlational studies cannot account for everything that differs between participants, they cannot make causal claims, and this is captured by the saying that "correlation does not imply causation." On another note, pretest-posttest studies, because they investigate changes in beliefs and use self-reporting surveys, are particularly subject to some experimental flaws, derived from the fact that people trust the experimenters, want to appear desirable, and are likely to guess (rightly or wrongly) what the experimenters are testing. Such flaws cast doubt on the external validity of the significant results. The stability of such effects seems to be challenged: when participants are re-tested some time after the test, they show no stability in their response, and instead return to reporting what they believed before the fiction exposure. Finally, some natural experiments in economics find significant, but yet small effects. It could be the case that fictions do impact some beliefs, when people have no strong priors (e.g., information about HIV treatment in a fiction), and in the context of a highly realistic fiction (e.g., soap operas).

Therefore, considering such mixed results, we argue that the burden of proof now lies with those who hold that fictions do have an important impact on our beliefs. It seems more probable, in the face of this critical review, that fictions have no effect, or small effect on some specific beliefs under particular circumstances.

If It Is Wrong, Why Is the Idea that Fictions Impact Beliefs So Widespread?

Why do people believe that fictions impact beliefs? The first reason is simply that they confound correlation and causation. People rightly observe that people consuming such or such kinds of fictions are also more likely to hold such or such beliefs, and wrongly infer that there is a causal process happening. For example, meeting a fan of horror movies who holds the belief that real people are overall dangerous and malicious, we would easily conclude that he watched too many horror movies and *therefore* acquired this belief. However, as we have seen, a more parsimonious explanation is that people's broad personality causes both what people believe and what fictions people consume (in the latter example, a high score on the Big Five trait Neuroticism).

Maybe the most consensual findings in personality psychology is that human psychology universally varies along five dimensions, and therefore as many "personality traits" (i.e. the Big Five): (1) Openness-to-experience, basically capturing how tolerant and curious one is, (2) Conscientiousness, measuring how meticulous and farsighted one is, (3) Extraversion, which is about how energetic, enterprising, and positive one is, (4) Agreeableness, capturing how empathetic, cooperative, and warm one is, and (5) Neuroticism, capturing the extent to which one experiences intensively bad feelings such as fear, anxiety, or anger (McCrae and John 1992, for an introduction of the Big Five personality traits; Durkee et al., 2020: a study of this Big Five Model of human personality across 115 nations). Longitudinal studies have consistently shown that personality traits are extremely stable across an individual's lifespan. They vary a little according to people's age, but much of this variation is due to universal patterns (Damian et al., 2019; Fraley and Roberts, 2005; e.g., all humans become lower in Openness-to-experience as they age; Helson et al., 2002; H. W. Marsh et al., 2013; and all humans increase in Agreeableness and Conscientiousness in young adulthood: this is known as the maturity principle of developmental psychology; Bleidorn et al., 2013, 2020). Moreover, the effects of specific life experiences on personality are very small (Bleidorn et al., 2018). Finally, such personality traits are flexible in response to socio-cultural long-lasting conditions that were relevant in humans' ancestral environments (e.g., the amount of resources; Baumard, 2019; Boon-Falleur et al., 2022).

Evolutionary theory posits that personality traits vary between humans and not so much across the lifespan because they are considered as evolutionary behavioral niches that lead to some adaptive benefits (Nettle, 2007; Smaldino et al., 2019). This theory predicts that personality traits are partly genetically inherited. This idea is captured by common observations that children's character resembles their parents or grandparents. From twin studies, adoption studies, and recent advances in genomic studies allowing to map the entire human genome, we know that such personality traits are indeed partly genetically inherited (Penke and Jokela, 2016). We can actually compute the level of influence of genes on personality and personality stability, independently of life-events: it accounts for at least half of the explained variance (Bouchard and Loehlin, 2001; see Briley and Tucker-Drob, 2014, for a meta-analysis of longitudinal behavioral genetic studies of personality development).

On the one hand, such personality traits make some beliefs (and not others) more appealing and more acceptable to people (Langston and Sykes, 1997). For instance, being higher in Openness-to-experience leads one to be more exposed to, and more easily accept, the belief that human cultural thoughts are highly diverse, and therefore be more tolerant of differences (DeYoung, 2011, 2015; Feist and Brady, 2004; McCrae, 1993). Being higher in Agreeability makes one hold more complex beliefs about others' intentions and thoughts (i.e., Agreeability is associated with socio-cognitive Theory of Mind; Nettle and Liddle, 2008). Being higher in Neuroticism makes one more sensitive to frightening beliefs (Kumari et al., 2007). And being low in Neuroticism leads one to be more exposed to or more easily accept the belief in a just world (Golparvar et al., 2014).

On the other hand, scores of personality traits significantly predict what fictions people enjoy to consume (see Michelson, 2014, for a theoretical essay and a review on the links between the Big Five model and fiction consumption). It has been tested with a sample of 3.5 million participants, with their Big Five scores and the movies they liked on Facebook: scores of personality traits are significantly associated with the genres of such movies (Nave et al., 2020). For instance, people who are higher in Openness-to-experience were significantly more likely to "like" fantasy or science fiction movies on Facebook and people higher in Neuroticism were significantly more likely to "like" horror fictions. In a recent study, we have shown that, more specifically, people who enjoy movies with imaginary worlds are higher in Openness-to-experience (Dubourg, Thouzeau, de Dampierre et al., 2022). Many other studies investigate the links between personality traits and fictional content features.

This consistently explains why people believe that fictions impact beliefs: because both variables are associated but for reasons that have nothing to do with a causal process. Beliefs and preferences for fictional content correlate largely because of people's cognitive predispositions, notably their personality, which appears not to change much during their life.

Conclusion

In this chapter, we first reviewed the empirical literature testing whether fictional narratives, be they movies, novels, or fictional short stories, impact people's beliefs. There is mixed evidence supporting this hypothesis, with some statistically significant and some statistically insignificant results. We consider that this inconsistency greatly challenges the hypothesis. Furthermore, we reviewed methodological problems that could very well account for the significant results such studies find: participants are likely to report beliefs that they don't actually hold, for a variety of reasons that have to do with the experimental setting and the way human cognition works. Studies that try to overcome such problems by implementing a test-retest design found no effects.

Therefore, for the moment, it is more reasonable to conclude that fictions *don't* impact beliefs. This statement has big implications on current hypotheses aiming at explaining the very origin of fiction in human cultures. It actually challenges the dominant hypothesis which posits that fiction emerged by natural selection precisely because of its effect on beliefs. We proposed an alternative: the "entertainment technology" hypothesis (Dubourg and Baumard, 2022). This hypothesis offers an explanation as to why people believe that fictions impact beliefs even though it is not the case: both producers and consumers benefit from this inaccurate but positive belief in many ways.

We can easily imagine why people might disagree with such a claim: one might consider that fiction loses some merit or nobility if it has no effect on people's beliefs. However, our framework does not see fiction consumption as some useless or pointless human activity, quite the contrary: it focuses on the wide range of emotions that fictional stories can and do evoke and proposes social advantages that people can derive from their consumption, other than the ones to adopt or update their beliefs. Moreover, this view puts fiction in a different light. Because successful fiction captures our attention by appealing to our preferences, desires, and emotions, fiction is a magnifying glass of the human mind. Through the study of fiction, then, we can gain a richer and deeper insight into the human mind and the human experience.

Works Cited

Andrade, Chittaranjan. 2018. "Internal, External, and Ecological Validity in Research Design, Conduct, and Evaluation." *Indian Journal of Psychological Medicine* 40, no. 5 (September-October): 498–99. https://doi.org/10.4103/IJPSYM.IJPSYM_334_18.

Anikina, Oksana V., and Elena V. Yakimenko. 2015. "Edutainment as a Modern Technology of Education." *Procedia - Social and Behavioral Sciences* 166 (January): 475–79. https://doi.org/10.1016/j.sbspro.2014.12.558

Banerjee, Abhijit, Eliana La Ferrara, and Victor H. Orozco-Olvera. 2019. "The Entertaining Way to Behavioral Change: Fighting HIV with MTV." NBER Working Paper No. 26096. National Bureau of Economic Research. https://doi.org/10.3386/w26096.

Baron-Cohen, Simon, Sally Wheelwright, Richard Skinner, Joanne Martin, and Emma Clubley. 2001. "The Autism-Spectrum Quotient (AQ): Evidence from Asperger Syndrome/High-Functioning Autism, Males and Females, Scientists and Mathematicians." *Journal of Autism and Developmental Disorders* 31, no. 1 (February): 5–17.

Barsoum, Ghada, Bruno Crépon, Drew Gardiner, Bastien Michel, and William Parienté. 2022. "Evaluating the Impact of Entrepreneurship Edutainment in Egypt: An Experimental Approach." *Economica* 89, no. 353 (January): 82–109. https://doi.org/10.1111/ecca.12391.

Baumard, Nicolas. 2019. "Psychological Origins of the Industrial Revolution." *Behavioral and Brain Sciences* 42: e189. https://doi.org/10.1017/S0140525X1800211X.

Best, John. 2021. "To Teach and Delight: The Varieties of Learning From Fiction." *Review of General Psychology* 25, no. 1 (March): 27–43. https://doi.org/10.1177/1089268020977173.

Bjorvatn, Kjetil, Alexander W. Cappelen, Linda Helgesson Sekei, Erik Ø. Sørensen, and Bertil Tungodden. 2020. "Teaching Through Television: Experimental Evidence on Entrepreneurship Education in Tanzania." *Management Science* 66, no. 6 (June): 2308–25. https://doi.org/10.1287/mnsc.2019.3321.

Black, Jessica E., and Jennifer L. Barnes. 2015a. "The Effects of Reading Material on Social and Non-Social Cognition." *Poetics* 52 (October): 32–43. https://doi.org/10.1016/j.poetic.2015.07.001.

Black, Jessica E., and Jennifer L. Barnes. 2015b. "Fiction and Social Cognition: The Effect of Viewing Award-winning Television Dramas on Theory of Mind." *Psychology of Aesthetics, Creativity, and the Arts* 9, no. 4 (November): 423–29. https://doi.org/10.1037/aca0000031.

Bleidorn, Weibke, Christopher J. Hopwood, and Richard E. Lucas. 2018. "Life Events and Personality Trait Change." *Journal of Personality* 86, no. 1 (February): 83–96. https://doi.org/10.1111/jopy.12286.

Bleidorn, Weibke, Christopher J. Hopwood, Mitja D. Back, Jaap J.A. Denissen, Marie Hennecke, Markus Jokela, Christian Kandler, Richard E. Lucas, Maike Luhmann, Ulrich Orth, Brent W. Roberts, Jenny Wagner, Cornelia Wrzus, and Johannes Zimmermann. 2020. "Longitudinal Experience–Wide Association Studies—A Framework for Studying Personality Change." *European Journal of Personality* 34, no. 3 (May): 285–300. https://doi.org/10.1002/per.2247.

Bleidorn, Wiebke, Theo A. Klimstra, Jaap J. A. Denissen, Peter J. Rentfrow, Jeff Potter, and Samuel D. Gosling. 2013. "Personality Maturation Around the World: A Cross-Cultural Examination of Social-Investment Theory." *Psychological Science* 24, no. 12 (December): 2530–40. https://doi.org/10.1177/0956797613498396.

Bloom, Paul. 2010. *How Pleasure Works: The New Science of Why We Like What We Like.* New York: W.W. Norton.

Boon-Falleur, Mélusine, Nicolas Baumard and Jean-Baptiste André. 2022. "Optimal Resource Allocation and Its Consequences on Behavioral Strategies, Personality Traits and Preferences." *PsyArXiv.* June 24. https://osf.io/2r3ef, doi: 10.31234/osf.io/2r3ef

Bouchard, Thomas J., Jr., and John C. Loehlin. 2001. "Genes, Evolution, and Personality." *Behavior Genetics* 31, no. 3 (May): 243–73. https://doi.org/10.1023/A:1012294324713.

Boukes, Mark, Lotte Aalbers, and Kim Andersen. 2022. "Political Fact or Political Fiction? The Agenda-Setting Impact of the Political Fiction Series Borgen on the Public and News Media." *Communications* 47, no. 1 (March): 50–72. https://doi.org/10.1515/commun-2019-0161.

Briley, Daniel A., and Elliot M. Tucker-Drob. 2014. "Genetic and Environmental Continuity in Personality Development: A Meta-Analysis." *Psychological Bulletin* 140, no. 5 (September): 1303–31. https://doi.org/10.1037/a0037091.

Brodie, Mollyann, Ursula Foehr, Vicky Rideout, Neal Baer, Carolyn Miller, Rebecca Flournoy, and Drew Altman. 2001. "Communicating Health Information Through the Entertainment Media." *Health Affairs* 20, no. 1 (January-February): 192–99. https://doi.org/10.1377/hlthaff.20.1.192.

Butler, Lisa D., Cheryl Koopman, and Philip G. Zimbardo. 1995. "The Psychological Impact of Viewing the Film 'JFK': Emotions, Beliefs, and Political Behavioral Intentions." *Political Psychology* 16, no. 2 (June): 237–57. https://doi.org/10.2307/3791831.

Buttrick, Nicholas, Erin C. Westgate, and Shigehiro Oishi. 2023. "Reading Literary Fiction Is Associated With a More Complex Worldview." *Personality and Social Psychology Bulletin*, 49(9): 1408–1420. https://doi.org/10.1177/01461672221106059

Cai, Zong-qi. 1999. "In Quest of Harmony: Plato and Confucius on Poetry." *Philosophy East and West* 49, no. 3 (July): 317–45. https://doi.org/10.2307/1399898.

Castano, Emanuele. 2021. "Art Films Foster Theory of Mind." *Humanities and Social Sciences Communications* 8: 119. https://doi.org/10.1057/s41599-021-00793-y.

Clasen, Mathias. 2017. *Why Horror Seduces.* New York: Oxford University Press.

Costa, Paul T., Jr., and Robert R. McCrae. 1992. "Four Ways Five Factors Are Basic." *Personality and Individual Differences* 13, no. 6 (June): 653–65. https://doi.org/10.1016/0191-8869(92)90236-I.

Dahl, Gordon, and Stefano DellaVigna. 2008. "Does Movie Violence Increase Violent Crime?" NBER Working Paper No. 13718. National Bureau of Economic Research. https://econpapers.repec.org/paper/nbrnberwo/13718.htm.

Damian, Rodica Ioana, Marion Spengler, Andreea Sutu, and Brent W. Roberts. 2019. "Sixteen Going on Sixty-Six: A Longitudinal Study of Personality Stability and Change Across 50 Years." *Journal of Personality and Social Psychology* 117, no. 3 (September): 674–95. https://doi.org/10.1037/pspp0000210.

DellaVigna, Stefano, and Eliana La Ferrara. 2015. "Economic and Social Impacts of the Media." NBER Working Paper No. 21360. National Bureau of Economic Research. https://econpapers.repec.org/paper/nbrnberwo/21360.htm.

DeYoung, Colin G. 2011. "Sources of Cognitive Exploration: Genetic Variation in the Prefrontal Dopamine System Predicts Openness/Intellect." *Journal of Research in Personality* 45: 364–371.

DeYoung, Colin G. 2015. "Openness/Intellect: A Dimension of Personality Reflecting Cognitive Exploration." In *Personality Processes and Individual Differences*, edited by Mario Mikulincer, Philip R. Shaver, Lynne M.

Cooper and Randy J. Larsen, 369–99. Vol 4 of *APA Handbook of Personality and Social Psychology*, edited by Mario Mikulincer and Philip R. Shaver. Washington, DC: American Psychological Association. https://doi.org/10.1037/14343-017.

Diekman, Amanda B., Wendi L. Gardner, and Mary McDonald. 2000. "LOVE MEANS NEVER HAVING TO BE CAREFUL: The Relationship Between Reading Romance Novels and Safe Sex Behavior." *Psychology of Women Quarterly* 24, no. 2 (June): 179–88. https://doi.org/10.1111/j.1471-6402.2000.tb00199.x.

Djikic, Maja, Keith Oatley, and Mihnea C. Moldoveanu. 2013. "Reading Other Minds: Effects of Literature on Empathy." *Scientific Study of Literature* 3, no. 1 (January): 28–47. https://doi.org/10.1075/ssol.3.1.06dji.

Dodell-Feder, David, Gloria Liu, Paige Amormino, Elizabeth Handly, and Diana Tamir. 2022. "The Impact of Fiction Reading on Social Outcomes: A 4-Week Randomized Controlled Study." *PsyArXiv*. December 15. https://doi.org/10.31234/osf.io/e4n9v.

Dubourg, Edgar, and Nicolas Baumard. 2022. "Why and How Did Narrative Fictions Evolve? Fictions as Entertainment Technologies." *Frontiers in Psychology* 13: 786770. https://doi.org/10.3389/fpsyg.2022.786770.

Dubourg, Edgar, Valentin Thouzeau, Charles de Dampierre, and Nicolas Baumard. 2021. "Exploratory Preferences Explain the Cultural Success of Imaginary Worlds in Modern Societies." *PsyArXiv*. February 16. https://doi.org/10.31234/osf.io/d9uqs.

Durkee, P. K., A.W. Lukaszewski, C. R. von Rueden, M. D. Gurven, D. M. Buss, and E. M. Tucker-Drob. 2020. "Niche Diversity Predicts Personality Structure Across 115 Nations." *Preprint*.

Feist, Gregory J., and Tara R. Brady. 2004. "Openness to Experience, Non-Conformity, and the Preference for Abstract Art." *Empirical Studies of the Arts* 22, no. 1 (January): 77–89. https://doi.org/10.2190/Y7CA-TBY6-V7LR-76GK.

Feldman, Stanley, and Lee Sigelman. 1985. "The Political Impact of Prime-Time Television: 'The Day After.'" *The Journal of Politics* 47, no. 2 (June): 556–78. https://doi.org/10.2307/2130896.

Fraley, R. Chris, and Brent W. Roberts. 2005. "Patterns of Continuity: A Dynamic Model for Conceptualizing the Stability of Individual Differences in Psychological Constructs Across the Life Course." *Psychological Review* 112, no. 1 (January): 60–74. https://doi.org/10.1037/0033-295X.112.1.60.

Gaultier, Jules de, and Per Buvik. 2006. *Le bovarysme*. Paris: Presses de l'Univ. Paris-Sorbonne.

Gilbert, Daniel T., Douglas S. Krull, and Patrick S. Malone. 1990. Unbelieving the Unbelievable: Some Problems in the Rejection of False Information. *Journal of Personality and Social Psychology* 59, no. 4 (October): 601–13. https://doi.org/10.1037/0022-3514.59.4.601.

Girard, René M. 1992. *Mensonge romantique et verite romanesque* (Nouv. tir). Paris: Grasset.

Golparvar, Mohsen, Amin Barazandeh, and Zahra Javadian. 2014. "The Relationship between Big Five Personality Factors and Belief in an Unjust and a Just World, Beliefs of Justice Compensation." *Clinical Psychology and Personality* 12, no. 1 (September): 61–74.

Gottschall, Jonathan. 2012. *The Storytelling Animal: How Stories Make Us Human*. New York: Houghton Mifflin Harcourt.

Green, Melanie C., and Timothy C. Brock. 2000. "The Role of Transportation in the Persuasiveness of Public Narratives." *Journal of Personality and Social Psychology* 79, no. 5 (November): 701–21. https://doi.org/10.1037/0022-3514.79.5.701.

Hakemulder, Jèmeljan. 2000. *The Moral Laboratory: Experiments Examining the Effects of Reading Literature on Social Perception and Moral Self-concept*. Utrecht: Benjamins.

Hefner, Veronica, and Barbara J. Wilson. 2013. "From Love at First Sight to Soul Mate: The Influence of Romantic Ideals in Popular Films on Young People's Beliefs about Relationships." *Communication Monographs* 80, no. 2 (June): 150–75. https://doi.org/10.1080/03637751.2013.776697.

Helson, Ravenna, Virginia S. Y. Kwan, Oliver P. John, and Constance Jones. 2002. "The Growing Evidence for Personality Change in Adulthood: Findings from Research with Personality Inventories." *Journal of Research in Personality* 36, no. 4 (August): 287–306. https://doi.org/10.1016/S0092-6566(02)00010-7.

Howell, Rachel A. 2011. "Lights, Camera … Action? Altered Attitudes and Behaviour in Response to the Climate Change Film *The Age of Stupid*." *Global Environmental Change* 21, no. 1 (February): 177–87. https://doi.org/10.1016/j.gloenvcha.2010.09.004.

Ioannidis, John P.A. 2005. "Why Most Published Research Findings Are False." *PLOS Medicine* 2, no. 8 (August): e124. https://doi.org/10.1371/journal.pmed.0020124.

Jensen, Robert, and Emily Oster. 2009. "The Power of TV: Cable Television and Women's Status in India." *Quarterly Journal of Economics* 124, no. 3 (August): 1057–94. https://doi.org/10.1162/qjec.2009.124.3.1057.

Kidd, David Comer, and Emanuele Castano. 2013. "Reading Literary Fiction Improves Theory of Mind." *Science* 342, no. 6156 (October): 377–80. https://doi.org/10.1126/science.1239918.

Kidd, David Comer, and Emanuele Castano. 2017. "Panero et al. (2016): Failure to Replicate Methods Caused the Failure to Replicate Results." *Journal of Personality and Social Psychology* 112, no. 3 (March): e1–e4. https://doi.org/10.1037/pspa0000072.

Kidd, David, Martino Ongis, and Emanuele Castano. 2016. "On Literary Fiction and Its Effects on Theory of Mind." *Scientific Study of Literature* 6, no. 1 (January): 42–58. https://doi.org/10.1075/ssol.6.1.04kid.

Kretz, Valerie Ellen. 2019. "Television and Movie Viewing Predict Adults' Romantic Ideals and Relationship Satisfaction." *Communication Studies* 70, no. 2: 208–34. https://doi.org/10.1080/10510974.2019.1595692.

Krumpal, Ivar. 2013. "Determinants of Social Desirability Bias in Sensitive Surveys: A Literature Review." *Quality & Quantity* 47, no. 4 (June): 2025–47. https://doi.org/10.1007/s11135-011-9640-9.

Kumari, Veena, Dominic H. ffytche, Mrigendra Das, Glenn D. Wilson, Sangeeta Goswami, and Tonmoy Sharma. 2007. "Neuroticism and Brain Responses to Anticipatory Fear." *Behavioral Neuroscience* 121, no. 4 (August): 643–52. https://doi.org/10.1037/0735-7044.121.4.643.

La Ferrara, Eliana La, Alberto Chong, and Suzanne Duryea. 2012. "Soap Operas and Fertility: Evidence from Brazil." *Applied Economics* 4, no. 4 (October): 1–31.

Langston, Christopher A., and W. Eric Sykes. 1997. "Beliefs and the Big Five: Cognitive Bases of Broad Individual Differences in Personality." *Journal of Research in Personality* 31, no. 2 (June): 141–65. https://doi.org/10.1006/jrpe.1997.2178.

Lenhard, Jan, and Tobias Richter. 2022. "Does Reading a Single Short Story of Literary Fiction Improve Social-Cognitive Skills? Testing the Priming Hypothesis." *Psychology of Aesthetics Creativity and the Arts.* Advance online publication. https://doi.org/10.1037/aca0000533.

Mar, Raymond A., Keith Oatley, Jacob Hirsh, Jennifer dela Paz, and Jordan B. Peterson. 2006. "Bookworms versus Nerds: Exposure to Fiction versus Non-fiction, Divergent Associations with Social Ability, and the Simulation of Fictional Social Worlds." *Journal of Research in Personality* 40, no. 5 (October): 694–712. https://doi.org/10.1016/j.jrp.2005.08.002.

Mar, Raymond A., and Keith Oatley. 2008. "The Function of Fiction Is the Abstraction and Simulation of Social Experience." *Perspectives on Psychological Science* 3, no. 3 (May): 173–92. https://doi.org/10.1111/j.1745-6924.2008.00073.x.

Markey, Patrick M., and Christopher Ferguson. 2017. *Moral Combat: Why the War on Violent Video Games Is Wrong.* Dallas: BenBella.

Marsh, Elizabeth J., Michelle L. Meade, and Henry L. Roediger III. 2003. "Learning Facts from Fiction." *Journal of Memory and Language* 49, no. 4 (November): 519–36. https://doi.org/10.1016/S0749-596X(03)00092-5.

Marsh, Herbert W., Benjamin Nagengast, and Alexandre J.S. Morin. 2013. "Measurement Invariance of Big-five Factors over the Life Span: ESEM Tests of Gender, Age, Plasticity, Maturity, and La Dolce Vita Effects." *Developmental Psychology* 49, no. 6 (June): 1194–218. https://doi.org/10.1037/a0026913.

Matz, Sandra C. 2021. "Personal Echo Chambers: Openness-to-Experience Is Linked to Higher Levels of Psychological Interest Diversity in Large-Scale Behavioral Data." *Journal of Personality and Social Psychology* 121, no. 6 (December): 1284–300. https://doi.org/10.1037/pspp0000324.

McCrae, Robert R. 1993. "Openness to Experience as a Basic Dimension of Personality." *Imagination, Cognition and Personality* 13, no. 1 (September): 39–55. https://doi.org/10.2190/H8H6-QYKR-KEU8-GAQ0.

McCrae, Robert R., and Oliver P. John. 1992. "An Introduction to the Five-Factor Model and Its Applications." *Journal of Personality* 60, no. 2 (June): 175–215. https://doi.org/10.1111/j.1467-6494.1992.tb00970.x.

Mercier, Hugo. 2017. "How Gullible Are We? A Review of the Evidence from Psychology and Social Science." *Review of General Psychology* 21, no. 2 (June): 103–22. https://doi.org/10.1037/gpr0000111.

Mercier, Hugo 2020. *Not Born Yesterday: The Science of Who We Trust and What We Believe.* Princeton, NJ: Princeton University Press.

Michelson, David. 2014. "Personality and the Varieties of Fictional Experience." *The Journal of Aesthetic Education* 48, no. 2 (May): 64–85. https://doi.org/10.5406/jaesteduc.48.2.0064.

Mulligan, Kenneth, and Philip Habel. 2013. "The Implications of Fictional Media for Political Beliefs." *American Politics Research* 41, no. 1 (January): 122–46. https://doi.org/10.1177/1532673X12453758.

Mumper, Micah L., and Richard J. Gerrig. 2017. "Leisure Reading and Social Cognition: A Meta-Analysis." *Psychology of Aesthetics, Creativity, and the Arts* 11, no. 1 (February): 109–20. https://doi.org/10.1037/aca0000089.

Mutz, Diana C., and Lilach Nir. 2010. "Not Necessarily the News: Does Fictional Television Influence Real-World Policy Preferences?" *Mass Communication and Society* 13, no. 2: 196–217. https://doi.org/10.1080/15205430902813856.

Nakawake, Yo, and Kosuke Sato. 2019. "Systematic Quantitative Analyses Reveal the Folk-Zoological Knowledge Embedded in Folktales." *Palgrave Communications* 5: 161. https://doi.org/10.1057/s41599-019-0375-x.

Nave, Gideon, Jason Rentfrow, and Sudeep Bhatia. 2020. "We Are What We Watch: Movie Plots Predict the Personalities of Those Who "Like" Them [Preprint]." *PsyArXiv*. https://doi.org/10.31234/osf.io/wsdu8.

Nera, Kenzo, Myrto Pantazi, and Olivier Klein. 2018. "'These Are Just Stories, Mulder': Exposure to Conspiracist Fiction Does Not Produce Narrative Persuasion." *Frontiers in Psychology* 9: 684. https://doi.org/10.3389/fpsyg.2018.00684.

Nettle, Daniel 2007. *Personality: What Makes You the Way You Are*. Oxford: Oxford University Press.

Nettle, Daniel, and Bethany Liddle. 2008. "Agreeableness Is Related to Social-Cognitive, But Not Social-Perceptual, Theory of Mind." *European Journal of Personality* 22, no. 4 (June): 323–35. https://doi.org/10.1002/per.672.

Open Science Collaboration. 2015. "Estimating the Reproducibility of Psychological Science." *Science* 349, no. 6251 (August): aac4716-1–aac4716–8. https://doi.org/10.1126/science.aac4716.

Osborne-Crowley, Katherine. 2020. "Social Cognition in the Real World: Reconnecting the Study of Social Cognition With Social Reality." *Review of General Psychology* 24, no. 2 (June): 144–58. https://doi.org/10.1177/1089268020906483.

Panero, Maria E., Deena Skolnick Weisberg, Jessica Black, Thalia R. Goldstein, Jennifer L. Barnes, Hiram Brownell, and Ellen Winner. 2016. "Does Reading a Single Passage of Literary Fiction Really Improve Theory of Mind? An Attempt at Replication." *Journal of Personality and Social Psychology* 111, no. 5 (November): e46–e54. https://doi.org/10.1037/pspa0000064.

Panero, Maria Eugenia, Deena Skolnick Weisberg, Jessica Black, Thalia R. Goldstein, Jessica L. Barnes, Hiram Brownell, and Ellen Winner. 2017. "No Support for the Claim That Literary Fiction Uniquely and Immediately Improves Theory of Mind: A Reply to Kidd and Castano's Commentary on Panero et al. 2016." *Journal of Personality and Social Psychology* 112, no. 3 (March): e5–e8. https://doi.org/10.1037/pspa0000079.

Penke, Lars, and Markus Jokela. 2016. "The Evolutionary Genetics of Personality Revisited." *Current Opinion in Psychology* 7 (February): 104–09. https://doi.org/10.1016/j.copsyc.2015.08.021.

Petterson, Aino, Gregory Currie, Stacie Friend, and Heather J. Ferguson. 2022. "The Effect of Narratives on Attitudes Toward Animal Welfare and Pro-Social Behaviour on Behalf of Animals: Three Pre-Registered Experiments." *Poetics* 94 (October): Article 101709.

Prentice, Deborah A., Richard J. Gerrig, and Daniel S. Bailis. 1997. "What Readers Bring to the Processing of Fictional Texts." *Psychonomic Bulletin & Review* 4, no. 3 (September): 416–20. https://doi.org/10.3758/BF03210803.

Prentice, Deborah A., and Richard J. Gerrig. 1999. "Exploring the Boundary Between Fiction and Reality." In *Dual-Process Theories in Social Psychology*, edited by Shelly Chaiken and Yaacov Trope, 529–46. New York: Guilford.

Quinlan, Joshua A., Jessica K. Padgett, Amin Khajehnassiri, and Raymond A. Mar. 2022. "Does a Brief Exposure to Literary Fiction Improve Social Ability? Assessing the Evidential Value of Published Studies with a p-curve." *Journal of Experimental Psychology: General*. Advance online publication. https://doi.org/10.1037/xge0001302

Rathje, Steven, Leor Hackel, and jamil zaki. 2021. "Attending Live Theatre Improves Empathy, Changes Attitudes, and Leads to Pro-Social Behavior" [Preprint]. *PsyArXiv*. https://doi.org/10.31234/osf.io/feqr8

Ravallion, Mark, Dominique van de Walle, Puja Dutta, and Rinku Murgai. 2013. "Testing Information Constraints on India's Largest Antipoverty Program." *The World Bank*. https://doi.org/10.1596/1813-9450-6598

Riley, Emma. 2017. "Increasing Students' Aspirations: The Impact of Queen of Katwe on Students' Educational Attainment." *CSAE Working Paper* WPS/2017-13.

Samur, Dalya, Mattie Tops, and Sander L. Koole. 2018. "Does a Single Session of Reading Literary Fiction Prime Enhanced Mentalising Performance? Four Replication Experiments of Kidd and Castano (2013)." *Cognition and Emotion* 32, no. 1: 130–44. https://doi.org/10.1080/02699931.2017.1279591.

Scalise Sugiyama, M. 2001. "Food, Foragers, and Folklore: The Role of Narrative in Human Subsistence." *Evolution and Human Behavior* 22, no. 4 (July): 221–40. https://doi.org/10.1016/S1090-5138(01)00063-0.

Scalise Sugiyama, Michelle. 2005. "Reverse-Engineering Narrative: Evidence of Special Design." In *The Literary Animal*, edited by Joanathan Gottschall and David Sloan Wilson, 177–96. Chicago, IL: Northwestern University Press.

Scalise Sugiyama, Michelle. 2021a. "The Fiction That Fiction Is Fiction." *ASEBL Journal* 15 (January): 8–12.

Scalise Sugiyama, Michelle. 2021b. "Co-Occurrence of Ostensive Communication and Generalizable Knowledge in Forager Storytelling: Cross-Cultural Evidence of Teaching in Forager Societies." *Human Nature* 32, no. 1 (March): 279–300. https://doi.org/10.1007/s12110-021-09385-w.

Schaeffer, Jean-Marie. 2010. *Why Fiction?* Translated by Dorrit Cohn. Lincoln: University of Nebraska Press.

Schneider-Mayerson, Matthew, Abel Gustafson, Anthony Leiserowitz, Matthew H. Goldberg, Seth A. Rosenthal, and Matthew Ballew. 2020. "Environmental Literature as Persuasion: An Experimental Test of the Effects of Reading Climate Fiction." *Environmental Communication* 14, no. 1: 1–16. https://doi.org/10.1080/17524032.2020.1814377.

Schniter, Eric, Hillard S. Kaplan, and Michael Gurven. 2022. "Cultural Transmission Vectors of Essential Knowledge and Skills among Tsimane Forager-farmers." *Evolution and Human Behavior*, S1090513822000460. https://doi.org/10.1016/j.evolhumbehav.2022.08.002.

Schniter, Eric, Nathaniel T. Wilcox, Bret A. Beheim, Hillard S. Kaplan, and Michael Gurven. 2018. "Information Transmission and the Oral Tradition: Evidence of a Late-life Service Niche for Tsimane Amerindians." *Evolution and Human Behavior* 39, no. 1 (January): 94–105. https://doi.org/10.1016/j.evolhumbehav.2017.10.006.

Schofield, Janet W., and Mark A. Pavelchak. 1989. "Fallout from *The Day After*. The Impact of a TV Film on Attitudes Related to Nuclear War." *Journal of Applied Social Psychology* 19, no. 5 (April): 433–48. https://doi.org/10.1111/j.1559-1816.1989.tb00066.x.

Scrivner, Coltan, John A. Johnson, Jens Kjeldgaard-Christiansen, and Mathias Clasen. 2021. "Pandemic Practice: Horror Fans and Morbidly Curious Individuals Are More Psychologically Resilient During the COVID-19 Pandemic." *Personality and Individual Differences* 168: 110397. https://doi.org/10.1016/j.paid.2020.110397.

Shirley, Fehl L. 1969. "The Influence of Reading on Concepts, Attitudes, and Behavior." *Journal of Reading* 12, no. 5 (February): 369–413.

Singhal, Arvind, Michael J. Cody, Everett M. Rogers, and Miguel Sabido, eds. 2004. *Entertainment-Education and Social Change: History, Research, and Practice*. Mahwah, NJ and London: Lawrence Erlbaum.

Smaldino, Paul E., Aaron Lukaszewski, Christopher von Rueden, and Michael Gurven. 2019. "Niche Diversity Can Explain Cross-cultural Differences in Personality Structure." *Nature Human Behaviour* 3, no. 12 (December): 1276–83. https://doi.org/10.1038/s41562-019-0730-3.

Smith, Daniel, Philip Schlaepfer, Katie Major, Mark Dyble, Abigail E. Page, James Thompson, Nikhil Chaudhary, Gul Deniz Salali, Ruth Mace, Leonora Astete, Marilyn Ngales, Lucio Vinicius, and Andrea Bamberg Migliano. 2017. "Cooperation and the Evolution of Hunter-Gatherer Storytelling." *Nature Communications* 8: 1853. https://doi.org/10.1038/s41467-017-02036-8.

Smith, Kristopher M., Ibrahim A. Mabulla, and Coren L. Apicella. 2022. "Hadza Hunter–Gatherers with Greater Exposure to Other Cultures Share More with Generous Campmates." *Biology Letters* 18: 20220157. https://doi.org/10.1098/rsbl.2022.0157.

Sperber, Dan. 2008. "Intuitive and Reflective Beliefs." *Mind & Language* 12, no. 1 (March): 67–83. https://doi.org/10.1111/j.1468-0017.1997.tb00062.x.

Sperber, Dan, Fabrice Clément, Christophe Heintz, Olivier Mascaro, Hugo Mercier, Gloria Origgi, and Deirdre Wilson. 2010. "Epistemic Vigilance." *Mind & Language* 25, no. 4 (September): 359–93. https://doi.org/10.1111/j.1468-0017.2010.01394.x.

Strange, Jeffrey J., and Cynthia C. Leung. 1999. "How Anecdotal Accounts in News and in Fiction Can Influence Judgments of a Social Problem's Urgency, Causes, and Cures." *Personality and Social Psychology Bulletin* 25, no. 4 (April): 436–49. https://doi.org/10.1177/0146167299025004004.

van Monsjou, Elizabeth, and Raymond A. Mar. 2019. "Interest and Investment in Fictional Romances." *Psychology of Aesthetics, Creativity, and the Arts* 13, no. 4 (May): 431–49. https://doi.org/10.1037/aca0000191.

van Mulukom, Valerie, and Mathias Clasen. 2021. *The Evolutionary Functions of Imagination and Fiction and How They May Contribute to Psychological Wellbeing During a Pandemic* [Preprint]. PsyArXiv. https://doi.org/10.31234/osf.io/wj4zg.

Vezzali, Loris, Sofia Stathi, Dino Giovannini, Dora Capozza, and Elena Trifiletti. 2015. "The Greatest Magic of Harry Potter: Reducing Prejudice: Harry Potter and Attitudes Toward Stigmatized Groups. *Journal of Applied Social Psychology* 45, no. 2 (February): 105–21. https://doi.org/10.1111/jasp.12279.

Vogorinčić, Ana. 2008. "The Novel-Reading Panic in 18th- Century in England: An Outline of an Early Moral Media Panic." *The Novel* 22.

Wheeler, Christian, Melanie C. Green, and Timothy C. Brock. 1999. "Fictional Narratives Change Beliefs: Replications of Prentice, Gerrig, and Bailis (1997) with Mixed Corroboration." *Psychonomic Bulletin & Review* 6, no. 1 (March): 136–41. https://doi.org/10.3758/BF03210821.

Wilde, Oscar. 1891. *Decay of Lying: An Observation*. London: Oneworld Classics.

Wimmer, Lena, Gregory Currie, Stacie Friend, and Heather Jane Ferguson. 2021. "Testing Correlates of Lifetime Exposure to Print Fiction Following a Multi-Method Approach: Evidence from Young and Older Readers." *Imagination, Cognition and Personality* 41, no. 1 (September): 54–86. https://doi.org/10.1177/0276236621996244.

Zunshine, Lisa. 2006. *Why We Read Fiction: Theory of Mind and the Novel*. Columbus: Ohio State University Press.

12
THE IMPACT OF FICTION ON BELIEFS ABOUT GENDER

Vera Nünning

Though a growing body of empirical research confirms that "fictional literature is associated with a wide range of real-world consequences" (Fong et al., 2015, 283), literary scholars have hesitated to appreciate the social impact of fictional stories (see James, Kubo, and Lavocat, 2023). This reluctance may be due to a perceived link between the social uses of literary works and a didactic conception of literature that reduces fiction to a means of conveying pragmatic messages or ideologies. However, acknowledging the social importance of literature does not necessarily imply a neglect of the aesthetic conventions or the unique features of fiction. Indeed, literary works can have a social impact precisely because of their aesthetic qualities. Empirical studies have shown that the quality of writing influences whether readers immerse themselves in a book and a change of beliefs, attitudes, or self-image occurs (see Green and Carpenter, 2011, 116).

Research on the impact of fiction dates back to the late 1990s, where studies at first concentrated on very specific attitudes or beliefs. Psychologists such as Richard Gerrig and Melanie Green were able to demonstrate the persuasive impact of fiction and could identify the psychological factors that influence the degree of persuasiveness of a story. By now it is well-established that the degree of immersion in or "transportation" into a text, its "perceived realism," and the readers' emotional engagement with the characters are key factors influencing the persuasive impact of a story (see Green and Brock, 2005; Green and Carpenter, 2011, 117f.). Early studies focused on the impact of fiction on specific beliefs of readers, asking, for instance, whether eating chocolate can help one lose weight. Only recently has there been a shift toward the study of more complex phenomena such as gender, which have to be inferred by considering not only the characters' thoughts and opinions but also their appearances and behavior. Thus, many areas of interest are still waiting to be explored.

In the following, I will give an overview of the field and examine how it can be further developed by researchers. First, though gender is entrenched in fictional texts—even animals in children's books are usually gendered—it has to be clarified why it is important to concern oneself with the presentation of gender in literature. Second, I will present the main results of the empirical studies on the impact of fiction. This overview will be divided into two parts: the impact of storybooks on children and that of fictional stories and novels on adults. While the former has brought forth a solid and coherent body of research, the latter has produced results that are suggestive but somewhat contradictory. The last section will discuss possible reasons for a few ambiguities in recent studies and suggest future directions of research.

    DOI: 10.4324/9781003119456-15

Gender Matters

Given the crucial changes achieved in the wake of the second women's movement, one might presume that further examination of gender issues is unnecessary. However, even the growing acknowledgement of LGBTQ+ people and the increasing acceptance of queer forms of life in many parts of the world—not to mention new career opportunities for women—cannot obscure the fact that many goals have not yet been achieved. In a groundbreaking article, Paula England (2010) lists both the achievements and unfulfilled aims of this "uneven and stalled" revolution, and provides convincing hypotheses that explain the continuing inequality between the sexes. Highlighting facts such as the pay gap and stressing that women have only entered a few of the career paths formerly reserved for men, England notes that most people still pursue gender-typical careers (such as women becoming teachers rather than craftsmen or technicians). Gender-untypical job opportunities are only taken into consideration when they offer the only possibility for upward mobility. The reason for the stalling of—or even backlash against—the drive for equality can be found in continuing beliefs in gender essentialism, i.e., the idea that the sexes are innately different, having fundamentally different traits and skills. This gender essentialism contradicts the liberal idea of equal opportunities for everyone, which leads to the co-existence of conflicting developments. On the one hand, women are able to pursue career lines formerly closed to them. On the other hand, they mostly choose fields fitting stereotypical feminine traits, while only few men enter feminine spheres or behave in ways traditionally understood as typical for women (becoming a secretary, being a child carer).

The stability of gender stereotypes can be explained by a variety of factors, perhaps predominantly by the fact that even people who do not explicitly believe in differences between the sexes still think and act according to implicit biases and stereotypes, which "activate specific brain areas that help us identify, interpret, and remember the things we see, hear, and learn about others" (Ellemers, 2018, 282). These cognitive processes may, for instance, be responsible for the differences in parental behavior when communicating with girls or boys, even when parents try to raise their children in a gender-neutral way (see *ibid.*, 280). Perhaps most importantly, gender stereotypes are prescriptive; people do not just think that men and women are biologically hardwired to behave in specific ways, but also that they ought to behave in these ways. People who defy stereotypes tend to be devalued (see *ibid.*, 286).

Psychological studies measuring how far people endorse gender stereotypes often use the BEM Sex Role Inventory (see Kokesh and Sternadori, 2015, 141) that is also employed in the studies on the impact of fiction discussed below. Among the traits considered to be prototypically feminine are affection, nurturing, warmth, and sensitivity to the needs of others, while athleticism, independence, leadership, and ambition are listed as masculine. One might object that such stereotyping does not necessarily imply the depreciation of feminine behavior. After all, warmth is a positive trait, and a woman conforming to the role of an affectionate, sensitive housewife can be held in high esteem by men and women. Yet, as Peter Glick and Susan Fiske (e.g. 2011, 530–32) have demonstrated, in many Western societies there is a co-existence of conflicting attitudes toward gender stereotypes, an "ambivalent sexism." This concept refers to contradictory evaluations of gender-typical traits: "benevolent sexism" signifies a celebratory attitude toward traits and behavior perceived as feminine, while "hostile sexism" refers to an unfavorable evaluation of these same traits. Both attitudes serve to support male predominance and perpetuate unequal relations between the sexes.

Works of literature can both perpetuate and question gender stereotypes; they can undermine or confirm sexist attitudes.[1] Due to the persuasive power of many fictional works, reading literary texts can reinforce or challenge readers' belief in and attitudes toward gender-typical traits. The persuasive potential of fictional stories is dependent on aspects concerning the minds of readers (such as their degree of "transportability") and the features of the narratives (e.g. conventions that engage readers' emotions and induce perspective-taking; Nünning, 2014, 186–247; 2020). Since gender stereotypes are usually not made explicit, and since as a rule readers are unaware of the implicit content of literary works and the fact that literature can change their beliefs, fiction may be a unique means of influencing implicit stereotypes and implicit bias (see Goffin and Moors in this volume). Some facets of fiction's impact on readers' beliefs about gender have already been demonstrated.

The Impact of the Presentation of Gender Stereotypes in Children's Literature

Given that childhood and adolescence are formative periods in which new beliefs and categories are acquired, the presentation of gender stereotypes in storybooks for children is not just an academic issue. The imitation of role models is a crucial part of children's acquisition of knowledge (see Bussey and Bandura, 1999), and since fictional characters and media personalities often function as role models, they can exert a strong influence on the development of young readers (see Cook et al., 2013, 151f.; Coyne et al., 2014, 418). The analysis of the gender stereotypes portrayed in fictional stories for a young audience has, therefore, been a topic of interest and concern for decades, and has produced a large and coherent body of research. The results of this research are quite sobering.

First of all, during the last 120 years, children's storybooks have predominantly featured male characters. This "symbolic annihilation" of females was observed in a study of more than 5,600 books that were published in the twentieth century in the US (McCabe et al., 2011, 218).[2] Though the overrepresentation of male characters in fictional books for children has decreased during the last sixty years, only a very slight decrease could be discerned in books published during the last two decades. What is more, even those storybooks that included female protagonists usually portrayed them as less active and more emotional (see Casey et al., 2021, 12, 15). This imbalance also characterizes the most popular one hundred books sold in 2017 and 2018 (see Ferguson, 2018, 2019). In both years, the bestselling children's books mainly depicted male characters, with a ratio of about two to one. Female characters were far less likely to be among the protagonists of stories, which in itself relegates them to a position of inferiority and restricts their potential for showing complexity, reducing them to stereotypes. Moreover, female characters were less likely to speak—they got 50% fewer opportunities to express their thoughts than male characters. The disparity between female and male characters even increased in bestsellers sold in 2018. "Speaking parts for male characters rose by 19%, while the number of lead roles increased by 9%. Female lead roles dropped by 7%" (Ferguson, 2019, 2).

Second, the presentation of the characters confirmed gender stereotypes that perpetuate the passivity and powerlessness of feminine figures. A study based on the analysis of 150 children's books published in the twentieth century concluded that the depiction of female characters as passive and dependent has not changed during the last fifty years (see Kokesh and Sternadori, 2015, 145). The gender bias in bestsellers sold in 2017 and 2018 is particularly pronounced among the animals that are portrayed in children's books: About 73% turn out to be male, and some of these embody hypermasculinity, for instance, as dragons, bears, and tigers. By contrast, cats, birds, or insects are gendered as female—quite literally as the prey of males (see Ferguson, 2018, 2019). As a rule, female characters in children's literature are presented as passive, dependent, clingy, and emotional, while male characters are active, powerful, and independent. This is not to say that there are no new publications with strong female characters—but unfortunately these were not among the bestselling books.

This preference for stories perpetuating gender stereotypes may be due to authors picking up dominant attitudes, the notion that male characters are more prototypical "than females when categorizing humans" (Casey et al., 2021, 14), or parents buying books they remember from their own childhood. They may also be due to the wishes of children, who like gender-conforming books better than those that deviate from the norm (see Abad and Pruden, 2013, 2). At any rate, it is next to impossible to exactly measure the impact of such books, since they confirm attitudes that are prevalent in society and promoted in other media and even on clothes: 1,444 clothing items showed that boys' t-shirts usually featured animals such as lions and sharks, while girls' clothing sported "small, harmless, domesticated animals" (Ferguson, 2018, 4f.). Bestselling children's books thus support a message that is predominant anyway—a fact which makes it difficult to assess the influence of these books.

It is, however, possible to measure the impact of a genre featuring a type of masculinity that can induce children to change their behavior: male superheroes "are generally portrayed as strong, assertive, aggressive, fast, powerful leaders, and as portraying a muscular ideal body type" (Coyne et al., 2014, 417). After being repeatedly exposed to videos of superheroes, both girls and boys played more often with weapons—a habit that did not diminish after a time period of one year. Moreover, boys (but not girls) showed a higher degree of verbal and physical aggression in their relationships with other children (see *ibid.*, 427). Interestingly, an increased amount of time playing with weapons did not involve a preference for superhero franchises, a finding which suggests that the stories are the driving force changing the behavior of the children (see *ibid.*, 425).

The impact of fictional stories has also been shown in a host of studies that observed the influence of children's books portraying non-stereotypical characters. Repeated exposure to gender-untypical characters changed the young readers' play behavior and their attitudes. After reading such books, children judged play associated with girls as appropriate for boys as well, and in one case children even changed their predilections for future jobs, with 73% of the girls voicing a preference for atypical jobs. However, this effect only occurred after repeated exposure, for at least a few months, and girls who voiced a desire to become a truck driver ultimately said that they would refrain from it, since they wanted to be near their families (see summary of Nhundi in Abad and Pruden 2013). Repeated readings of stories (or book chapters) with an atypical protagonist thus reduced children's endorsement of gender stereotypes, with a particularly strong impact on boys being exposed to non-stereotypical male behavior (see Kneeskern and Reeder, 2020, 1). It has to be stressed, however, that such stories are not representative of children's literature, and non-conforming characters are usually presented as being exceptional (see *ibid.*, 4).

Even rarer are children's books or young adult novels featuring lesbian, gay, or transgender protagonists. Such novels could fulfill an important function, since for young adults identifying as LGBTQ+, role models are often hard to find. In order to gauge the potential impact of the portrayal of queer desire, Christopher Cook and colleagues (2013) analyzed the content of eleven novels published in 2010, all of them award nominees for the Lambda Literary Award, which is awarded to works which explore or celebrate LGBTQ+ themes. The results that emerge from this study are mixed. On the one hand, the novels collectively featured sixteen lesbian characters that embody non-stereotypical traits. The presentation of such a defiance of gender roles might reduce young readers' endorsement of gender stereotypes. On the other hand, many of the characters sported stereotypical traits and behavior as well. Among the gender-related themes that were identified in the novels, three confirmed and three defied stereotypes. Thus, the gender-untypical protagonists asserted themselves, pursued same-sex intimacy, and broke free of constraints (see Cook et al., 2013, 154). This was counteracted, however, by the characters' acting in ways that corroborate stereotypes: Nearly all of the novels described female characters as very emotional, and lesbian desire was correlated with negative feelings. Moreover, within lesbian relationships, one of the female characters usually displayed stereotypical masculine thoughts, feelings, and actions, i.e., "one being active, aggressive, even violent, the other passive and nurturing" (*ibid.*, 163). Thus, while those few books that represent queer identities offer new, less restrictive role models, they simultaneously continue to confirm stereotypes that shed negative light on female characters, with lesbian identity being seen as the cause of internal conflict and emotions such as anxiety or depression.[3]

With gender stereotypes perpetuated even in some novels portraying lesbian characters, it is no surprise that popular young adult novels published between 2000 and 2010 depict a conventional and predominantly negative image of young women as being passive, dependent, and mainly concerned with their appearance. As Jessica Kokesh and Miglena Sternadori found, this rather depressing representation of women was prevalent in ten carefully selected books that included, for instance, Meg Cabot's *The Princess Diaries* (2000), selling over 4 million copies, or Ann Brashares's *Sisterhood of the Traveling Pants* (2001), the first of a prize-winning series of which 8 million books were sold. While homosexuality is presented as a personal weakness and a cause for turmoil in the ten books (see Kokesh and Sternadori, 2015, 146), there are no depictions of loving and equal heterosexual relations either. Since interviews with young readers suggest that the majority believed the books to be realistic and sometimes used them as a guide to determine how to act in a given situation, the five basic types of young women represented in these novels deserve to be pointed out: (a) "The Meanie," i.e., a popular but mean character who does everything to climb the social ladder; (b) "The Wimp," an insecure character who at first suffers from her lack of perfection, until "she is forced to become an ideal woman" (ibid., 148); (c) "Miss Perfection," who has internalized all expectations concerning ideal feminine behavior, (d) "The Rebel," who fights against the restrictions imposed by gender stereotypes, and (e) "The Sticky Willy," who either gives or needs emotional support to such an extent that she is unable to carry on with her own life (see ibid., 146–51). Though not all young readers said that they thought the novels were life-like, they claimed that they identified with some characters and thought of them as friends, which suggests that the books did have a persuasive impact, since emotional engagement or identification with a character correlates with the persuasiveness of narratives (see Green and Dill, 2013, 452f., 456).

These five types of characters as well as others, such as erratic or absent mother figures, indicate that there is some truth to the claim made by Jerilyn Fisher and Ellen Silber (2000) that many novels, soap operas, or girl magazines are still pervaded by character types introduced in fairy tales such as "Snow White" or "Cinderella." These tales influence ideas about moral behavior in relation to gender. They often feature a beautiful, thin, passive, and docile young girl, who is mistreated by a bad stepmother or a witch and suffers silently until she is rescued by the prince, on whom she is utterly dependent—which somehow seems to promise a future relationship of true love. In such stories, relationships between women are characterized by competition (which still features prominently in young adult novels); good mothers are absent, and those (step)mothers that are present embody evil or even demonic desires. Four of the five character types depicted above are easily discernible in Fisher's and Silber's account of fairy tales; the only one that is lacking is the rebel.[4]

A hugely popular representation of the rebel can be found in Suzanne Collins's young adult novel *The Hunger Games* (2008), in which Katniss, the sixteen-year-old protagonist, defies gender norms. When her younger sister is nominated to fight to the death in the "Hunger Games," she volunteers to go in her stead, thus fulfilling the role of the male protagonist in a quest, a genre that shows the hero mastering all adventures, triumphing by mere force of will, courage, and inventiveness in fights in which everyone else would fail, and ends with his coming back as the acclaimed victor, bringing back marvelous treasures or, in Katniss's case, feeding the whole province for a year. In this novel, the male companion takes the role of the (usually feminine) sidekick, being more emotional than Katniss and having to be saved by her twice. Though the heroine sporadically acts as a caretaker, she takes over a role typically reserved for male heroes and has masculine traits. Not only does she skillfully use her bow and kill four people, she does it without displaying any emotions. Though the novel could be valued as providing one of the rare popular examples of a heroine defying gender stereotypes, she is portrayed as an exception to the norm, and mainly shows stereotypically masculine behavior. It is questionable whether such a novel can contribute to the reduction of stereotypes or should be valued as offering a role model for young readers.

Other bestselling series aimed at young readers, such as Stephenie Meyer's *Twilight* series, perpetuate gender stereotypes. The protagonists Bella and Edward conform to traditional expectations: the hero is tall, good-looking, active, protective, and in control, while Bella is subordinate, weaker, less assertive, more insecure, and emotional. This power imbalance corresponds to conservative models of romantic partnerships. The heroine endorses the ideal of true romantic monogamous love, and she is insecure and dependent to a point where it becomes impossible for her to live without Edward—she can be categorized as the typical "Wimp" in the typology proposed by Kokesh and Sternadori. Thus, in their formative years, children are overwhelmingly entertained by storybooks that perpetuate gender stereotypes.

The Impact of Fiction on Adults

The impact that popular or literary fiction written for adults can have on its readers is more difficult to assess than the influence of storybooks on children. There are several difficulties that have to be taken into account. First, beliefs about gender roles are relatively stable for adults. Though many studies have demonstrated the persuasive impact of fictional stories on the beliefs of mature readers, the beliefs examined (such as that eating chocolate helps you lose weight) were more changeable than those about gender stereotypes. The relative durability of gender stereotypes renders it unlikely that a reader will significantly change their outlook after reading just one book.

A second difficulty lies in the fact that the impact of reading fiction is stronger when it is repeated. In order to change their beliefs, even children with much more malleable beliefs had to read several stories or a whole book, preferably over a longer time span. This can be achieved in kindergarten or primary school, where it is relatively easy to ensure that groups of children read the same stories for several months.[5] With regard to adult readers, such a prolonged reading experience is harder to realize—and even if a significant number of adults read several books over a period of months, the impact of the texts would be more difficult to assess since avid readers might consume other novels, films, TV series, etc., with different conceptualizations of gender at the same time.

It may be due to these difficulties that, in comparison to children's literature, there are relatively few studies on the influence of novels on adults' beliefs about gender. The studies that I could find have dealt with the challenges in different ways. Some of them asked participants to read a brief story under laboratory conditions and then tested its impact. Though there was a change in readers' beliefs, this consisted of a small modification. Others have identified participants who read certain genres regularly and analyzed these readers' attitudes toward gender stereotypes in contrast to non-readers or to readers of non-fiction. This, again, is prone to difficulties, partly because it is impossible to determine whether the participants were influenced by their reading, or whether people with specific attitudes toward gender prefer to read certain genres. Moreover, some of these studies produced conflicting or ambivalent results.

In spite of these challenges, there are several studies that suggest reading novels has an impact on adults' beliefs about gender. For example, readers' evaluations of E.L. James's bestselling trilogy *Fifty Shades of Grey* were associated with their (lack of) ambivalent sexism. Lauren Altenburger and colleagues (2016) noted a positive correlation between women readers who rated the book(s) as 'hot' and hostile sexism, and a positive correlation between ratings as 'romantic' and benevolent sexism. In addition, readers who described the book as 'romantic' and 'hot' were likely to hold both hostile and benevolent sexist attitudes. Altenburger and colleagues concede, however, that it is possible that women endorsing benevolent or hostile sexism might have been drawn to read the book. If this was true, the huge popularity of both this trilogy as well as the similar book series *Twilight* and their film adaptations would testify to a rather alarming degree of sexism in contemporary societies.

Using a different approach, Tobias Richter and colleagues (2014) could demonstrate that reading a brief story about a mother shopping and caring for her children had an impact on female readers' self-concept. After exposure to a story featuring a woman conforming to gender stereotypes, many female readers perceived themselves as more feminine (according to the BSRI femininity score). In accordance with similar studies, only readers who had been immersed in the story showed such an effect. Richter and colleagues also argue that assimilation, i.e. adopting features that resemble those of the protagonist, is only one possible reaction to a story. Readers who were similar to the protagonist (mothers with children) did not exhibit a change in their self-concept. This result may be due to the fact that they compared themselves to the character in the story, emphasizing differences rather than the (obvious) similarities (see *ibid.*, 183). The readers' response to stories thus seems to be based on their self-image.[6]

Another direction of research focuses on the impact of reading certain genres, such as romance, mystery, or science fiction. These studies proceed from the hypothesis that fictional worlds are built in a genre-specific way, and that repeated exposure to such worlds can influence readers' attitudes. The wide definitions of genres, which are based on major themes (searching for an ideal partner, trying to find a murderer) pose a problem that may explain some ambiguities of recent research. Nonetheless, some of these studies deserve closer scrutiny.

One of the noteworthy results pertains to the hypothesis that repeated reading of certain genres may convey destructive beliefs about what characterizes an ideal romantic relationship. In 1982, Roy Eidelson and Norman Epstein identified five beliefs that are closely related to gender stereotypes and are involved in problems and the breaking up of relationships, among them the belief that both partners should be able to gauge the other's wishes and feelings intuitively (2), and that there are fundamental, innate differences between the sexes (5) (see Eidelson and Epstein, 1982, 715f.). In 2019, Stefanie Stern and colleagues could show that there is a correlation between preferences for certain genres and destructive beliefs about relationships. Reading "science fiction/fantasy was associated with more realistic beliefs about the way relationships work in the real world" (Stern et al., 2019, 458), with readers being less likely to support four of the five destructive beliefs about romantic relationships than the control group. Romance readers, in contrast, believed in innate differences between the sexes, thus endorsing one of the destructive beliefs.

A positive correlation between reading certain genres and the questioning of gender stereotyping was demonstrated by Katrina Fong and colleagues. Readers of three out of four genres whose impact was studied were less likely to endorse traditional gender roles and more likely to believe in gender role egalitarianism. The genres correlating with these positive effects were domestic fiction, romance, and "suspense/thriller," while "science fiction/fantasy" did not appear to have any effect on beliefs about gender (see Fong et al. 2015, 277, 278). That readers of romances question gender stereotypes conflicts with Stern's findings—a conflict that may be due to the very broad definition of the genres.

The critical distancing from gender stereotypes demonstrated by Fong was confirmed in a study analyzing the relation between literary fiction and psychological essentialism. The latter is connected with stereotyping and prejudice, which in turn is linked to category-based understanding and a lack of individualization. Since literary fiction usually presents complex individualized characters whose traits and attitudes have to be inferred by readers, Emanuele Castano and colleagues hypothesized that "exposure to literary fiction should reduce psychological essentialism" (2021, 2). This hypothesis was confirmed: Readers of literary fiction are less likely to support gender stereotypes than readers of popular fiction or non-readers.[7]

Thus, literary fiction (as studied by Castano et al., 2021), domestic fiction, romance, and 'suspense/thriller' (see Fong et al., 2015) have been shown to correlate with reduced endorsement of (gender) stereotypes. With regard to literary fiction, this can be explained with the presentation of complex characters. When reading literary fictions, readers can expand their horizons and have new experiences as well as come to know a variety of "different personality traits, modes of thinking, attitudes, and intentions" (Nünning, 2014, 301). Many characters we encounter in literary fiction cannot be understood solely by using social categories and (gender) stereotypes. This exposure to diversity, however, is usually not part of reading the types of popular fiction whose effect was studied by Fong and colleagues. That genres such as romance or domestic fiction can correlate with reduced stereotyping may be due to the kind of spontaneous perspective taking that readers have to practice when trying to understand fictional texts. "[T]emporarily adopting characters' perspectives and trying out new modes of thinking or patterns of evaluation" (ibid., 300), alternating between sharing the thoughts and feelings of male and female characters, may partly be responsible for readers' reduced susceptibility to social stereotyping. Having virtual experiences through empathizing or identifying with fictional characters has not only been shown to heighten the persuasiveness of a narrative, it can also have an impact on how we think. In order to assess the persuasiveness of a text and its potential to change readers' gender stereotypes, one needs to take narrative forms into account and evaluate, for instance, the degree to which such conventions enhance the "perceived realism" of a story or induce readers to adopt the characters' perspectives (see Nünning, 2020).

Directions for Further Research

The results of the studies that have analyzed the impact of fictional texts on (young and old) readers' beliefs about gender are substantial and impressive. However, some of the findings on fiction's influence on adult readers are partly conflicting and ambivalent. These difficulties might be ameliorated by the following directions of research that may help to assess the persuasiveness of a fictional text and make it possible to identify stories that better match the research aims than those texts often used in empirical studies.

First, at the time of writing, most studies do not consider formal features of the texts when analyzing the (non)stereotypical content of a story. Nearly all studies restrict themselves to pointing out the gender-(un)typical attitudes, beliefs, and behavior of the protagonist or, at most, list the types of characters that they deem important to the story. However, fictional stories often present a wide range of characters with different personality traits and diverse interpretations of gender roles. Especially in more complex texts, it is necessary to explore the importance of a wide range of characters and, particularly, of modes of writing. Often, there are several characters of seemingly similar weight—just think of Elinor and Marianne in Jane Austen's *Sense and Sensibility*—but, nonetheless, the text encourages readers to favor the perspective of one of them, for instance, by way of focalization (i.e., by using one character as the center of consciousness, through whose eyes we learn about the traits and actions of the other character, which implies that the focalizer's evaluations inform the readers' understanding of the other character). It is also important to consider the strategies that direct readers' sympathy, which induces readers to engage primarily with certain characters and evaluate their traits favorably, while distancing themselves from others. Merely focusing on the protagonist is not enough when trying to assess the gender-specific values embedded in a text. Many texts present both gender-typical and -untypical characters—but it makes a world of difference whether a queer character is presented in a sympathy-inducing or distancing manner. It is thus crucial to take the formal features of a text into account.

Moreover, formal features are important for assessing how fictional stories can potentially reduce harmful biases toward members of outgroups. Some modes of writing prompt readers to engage with and flesh out the thoughts of unfamiliar characters. Using inferences to comprehend opaque behavior and unfamiliar personality traits allows readers to understand the character on a deeper level, and since they use their own assumptions about the way the human mind works, they can, below the surface of obvious differences, discover similarities between the character and themselves. Sharing unfamiliar characters' thoughts can therefore "counter[] the 'similarity bias' and reduc[e] social stereotypes" (Nünning, 2014, 218).[8]

Second, most studies use a rather simple categorization system for novels presenting characters that either confirm or defy gender stereotypes. However, many texts and subgenres cannot be categorized in this way. What is needed is a typology of the presentation of gender in fictional works that goes beyond the opposition of novels that either provide gender-untypical role models or continue to disseminate stereotypes.

It makes more sense to place novels, and possibly certain subgenres, on a scale, with one of the poles signifying the perpetuation of stereotypes devaluing feminine traits, while the other marks a positive non-stereotypical presentation of female characters (see Table 12.1).

Even though this scale does not allow a precise categorization of every novel, such a typology shows "tendencies, penchants, leanings, allegiances" (McMurry, 2019, 19) and recognizes that literary works can present a wide range of beliefs about gender. In order to acknowledge overlaps, one of the categories is reserved for novels which feature a mix of contradictory attitudes toward gender stereotypes. In addition, we have to contextualize and historicize these categories—the heroine in *Jane Eyre*, for instance, was criticized for being too willful and disobedient when the book first appeared, while nowadays readers may be struck by her willingness to play the "Angel in the House" once she has found her cousins and married Rochester. Moreover, this scale highlights that it is problematic to judge the value of literary works on the basis of their attitudes toward gender: not criticizing gender stereotypes does not equal supporting them. This scale renders it possible to evaluate and categorize novels more precisely than by differentiating between traditional, stereotype-confirming, and innovative stereotype-defying works, as well as providing a tool for the selection of novels whose impact can be studied.

Table 12.1 Scale of novels ranging from stereotypes which denigrate women as inferior to men to presenting positive or even idealized images of women as role models

Femi-phobic	*Gender-indifferent*	*Femi-ambivalent*	*Femi-literate*	*Femi-phile*
Presenting (stereotypically characterized) women as inferior to (stereotypically characterized) men	Portrayal of complex male and female characters without positing a hierarchy; neither endorsing binaries nor criticizing them	Presenting a mixture of contradictory attitudes, emphasizing the worth of a few female characters and criticizing some stereotypes, but at the same time endorsing other, gender-typical feminine behavior	Criticizing gender stereotypes and emphasizing the lack of agency and self-expression of female characters	Positive or even idealized portrayal of female protagonists with gender-typical or -untypical traits, presentation of new role models
Kingsley Amis, *Take a Girl Like You* 1960; Angry Young Man Fiction; Hardboiled Crime Fiction	Dave Eggers, *The Every* (2021)	Mary Wollstonecraft, *Mary: A Fiction* (1788); Wilkie Collins, *The Woman in White* (1859–1860)	Charlotte Brontë, *Jane Eyre* (1847), Monica Ali, *Brick Lane* (2003)	Sarah Scott, *Millennium Hall* (1762), Dorothy Richardson, *The Tunnel* (1919); Sue Grafton's Kinsey Millhone Series (female hardboiled crime stories)

Third, the great majority of empirical studies on the impact of fictional stories on beliefs about gender deal with images of women. There are only a few studies on female sexuality (focusing on lesbians), and next to no studies of masculinity, male homosexuality, transgender identities, or gender fluidity. Literary studies on queer and trans characters abound, but these analyses usually do not consider the possible impact on readers. It is to be hoped that this research gap will be closed soon, as the number of novels presenting LGBTQ+ characters is growing. For the purposes of classifying novels whose impact can be studied, we need a scale slightly different from the one presented above; one that maps the presentation of gender as binary and prescriptive on the one end, and the positive portrayal of queer, gender-nonconforming characters on the other (see Table 12.2). The latter sometimes also encourages reflection on gender norms, and may thus reduce stereotyping. The first two categories are identical with the ones presented above, but the other three are different, since it would be problematic to place heterosexual cisgender women in the same category as non-binary, inter, or trans characters.

Again, it has to be stressed that many novels are hybrids, comprising a mix of two or more of the features typical of any given group. But placing novels or subgenres on a spectrum of beliefs about gender in fictional works enables a relatively precise categorization. As the few references to mystery novels show, for example, these works can be placed anywhere on the scale; it just depends on the subgenre and the author. Instead of analyzing the impact of mysteries on beliefs about gender, one should differentiate between subgenres that feature femi-phobic, gender-literate, or even femi-phile attitudes. Placing novels or subgenres on such a scale provides a better basis for the analysis of the impact of fictional stories on readers' beliefs about gender. A selection of works based on these categories may yield less conflicting results than earlier studies.

Table 12.2 Scale of novels ranging from binary and prescriptive gender presentation to positive portrayal of queer, gender-nonconforming characters

Femi-phobic	*Gender-indifferent*	*Gender-ambivalent*	*Gender-literate*	*Gender-transcending*
		Favorable, appreciative presentations of some queer and non-typical characters, while at the same time perpetuating some stereotypes	Favorable portrayal of queer characters; representation of the problems inherent in gender binaries, criticism of gender stereotypes or of the denial of diversity	Favorable, sympathetic presentation of diversity, gender fluidity, and/ or transgender characters; encouraging reflection about gender
		Radclyffe Hall, *The Well of Loneliness* (1928); Jane Eagland, *Wildthorn* (2010)	E.M. Forster, *Maurice* ([1913–1914] 1971); Jeanette Winterson, *Oranges Are Not the Only Fruit* (1993), Val McDermid, Lyndsay Gordon series	Virginia Woolf, *Orlando* (1928); Jeffrey Eugenides, *Middlesex* (2002); Bernardine Evaristo, *Girl, Woman, Other* (2019)

Fourth, as far as literature's influence on beliefs about gender is concerned, one should come up with differentiations more subtle than the rather broad division into "literary fiction" and "popular fiction" on the one hand (see Castano et al., 2021), or into popular genres such as "romance," "science fiction/fantasy," or "suspense/thriller" (Fong et al., 2015, 276) on the other. The division between literary and popular fiction can be fruitful as far as the analysis of their respective impact on cognitive faculties of readers is concerned. There is good reason to believe that literary fiction can reduce psychological essentialism and endorsement of gender stereotypes. These effects can be due to the greater complexity of the conception of characters in literary fictions, while popular fictions often feature types that do not require readers to change or adjust their initial categorization.[9]

With regard to the presentation of gender, such a differentiation between literary and popular fiction is not adequate, however. Many eighteenth- or nineteenth-century classics (i.e., "literary fictions") confirm gender stereotypes and depict female characters, as Virginia Woolf famously asserted, as "Angels in the House" or "fallen women." Indeed, censorship practices rendered it difficult to publish works with protagonists who flout gender stereotypes. At the same time, popular fictions—such as Collins's *Hunger Games*—can feature gender-untypical heroines.

A division into four or even seven types of genres, which adds classics and contemporary fiction to the list (see Black et al., 2017, 7), does not solve the problem either. A genre such as "science fiction" presents a wide variety of worlds where gender stereotypes can be endorsed and gender-typical behavior presented as a model, or, alternatively, questioned, for instance, with the creation of alternatives such as Jael in Joanna Russ's novel *The Female Man* (1970), or hermaphrodites, aliens, or cyborgs (see Fink, 2021, 190). In some science fiction novels, only one gender exists, or the future worlds are peopled with androgynous, gender fluid, or transgender characters. Naomi Alderman's *The Power* (2016) even features a matriarchy in which women adopt masculine behavior and brutally exploit men. Given such a diversity, it is counterproductive to assume that "science fiction/fantasy" either endorses or criticizes gender stereotypes. We need more differentiation with regard to genres in order to get valid results. For the identification of such subgenres, one might use the scales introduced above.

Fifth, in order to assess the importance of the gender-specific attitudes embedded in fictional works, one needs a set of categories that can evaluate the degree of persuasiveness of a given text. Psychological studies often measure the degree of transportability of readers, and a similar assessment should be implemented with regard to the texts that are read. There are some preliminary studies (see Nünning, 2014, 214–40; 2020, 83–88), but these should be refined and tested. Gauging the persuasive potential of fictional texts helps to better understand the impact of bestselling books that reach a large audience. Assessing the persuasiveness of a story is particularly important with regard to texts endorsing gender stereotypes that are read aloud by parents or discussed in schools. The classroom can be a perfect setting for discussing the more troublesome, restrictive implications of texts celebrating stereotypical images of femininity and masculinity, and thus reinforcing gender stereotypes and discrimination against women. The degree of persuasiveness can also serve to assess the degree of the impact a text is likely to have, and thus renders it possible to identify works that can disseminate beneficial attitudes toward gender. Taken together, the five research directions presented above should help to read fiction through a critical lens and make full use of the cognitive and humane potential that literary texts are rightly famous for.

Notes

1 The same holds for the presentation of Black people and racism, as well as corresponding stereotypes and implicit biases. There are many structural similarities concerning the impact of fiction on perpetuating or challenging stereotypes about gender and race.

2 In contrast to many other studies, this study by McCabe et al. is based on a wide range of genres and encompasses books addressed to children of all ages.

3 However, the evaluation and impact of stereotypical behavior of queer characters depends on the audience. While queer people prefer realistic characters that mirror their own experiences (see McInroy and Craig, 2016, 39–41, 43), "normalizing" queer characters and showing their suffering can reduce readers' homophobia. An empirical study of the impact of Brent Hartinger's novel *Geography Club* (2003) on eighth grade students in English art classes demonstrates that the reading of the book, combined with discussions and reading assignments, did lower homophobia and "was effective in significantly reducing homophobia in participants with high pretest homophobia" (Malo-Juvera, 2016, 18).

4 One sub-type of rebel includes the stepmother or enchantress, who can be interpreted as a revolutionary in a patriarchal system.

5 The persuasive effect of these books may have been heightened by the fact that teachers and caretakers discussed them with the children. However, it showed no (or indeed a contrary) effect when parents pointed out that the behavior of the heroes was problematic (see Coyne et al., 2014, 416).

6 One study also demonstrated that reading a story can change readers' self-image (see Djikic et al., 2013). But so far, there is no conclusive evidence for the impact of fiction on readers' self-image.

7 Earlier studies by David C. Kidd and Emanuele Castano that claimed that literary fiction improves readers' theory of mind have been contested—their results could not be replicated (see Panero et al., 2017). Therefore, this study from 2021 may be contested as well, even though it is co-authored by five researchers (without Kidd) and tackles a different topic. This study is not concerned with improvement of readers' social cognitive skills, but with their endorsement of psychological essentialism. Since the 2021 study adds to the findings by Katrina Fong et al. and Stefanie Stern et al., I include it here. However, the arguments put forth in these studies are hampered by the imprecise definition of genres, which I will return to below.

8 See, however, Goffin and Friend (2022).

9 However, genres such as romance or mystery are based on the possible deceptiveness of social categorization, since the suspense is largely due to the effort of identifying at least one character who is not categorized correctly in the beginning (the murderer; the love-interest only pretending to be "Mr Right").

Works Cited

Abad, Carla, and Shannon M. Pruden. 2013. "Do Storybooks Really Break Children's Gender Stereotypes?" *Frontiers in Psychology* 4: 1–4. https://doi.org/10.3389/fpsyg.2013.00986.

Altenburger, Lauren E., Christin L. Carotta, Amy E. Bonomi, and Anastasia Snyder. 2016. "Sexist Attitudes Among Emerging Adult Women Readers of Fifty Shades Fiction." *Archives of Sexual Behavior* 46, no. 2 (April): 455–64. https://doi.org/10.1007/s10508-016-0724-4.

Black, Jessica, Stephanie C. Capps, and Jennifer L. Barnes. 2017. "Fiction, Genre Exposure, and Moral Reality." *Psychology of Aesthetics, Creativity, and the Arts* 12, no. 3 (August): 328–40. https://doi.org/10.1037/aca0000116.

Bussey, Kay, and Albert Bandura. 1999. "Social Cognitive Theory of Gender Development and Differentiation." *Psychological Review* 106, no. 4 (October): 676–713.

Casey, Kennedy, Kylee Novick, and Stella F. Lourenco. 2021. "Sixty Years of Gender Representation in Children's Books: Conditions Associated with Overrepresentation of Male Versus Female Protagonists." *Public Library of Science ONE* 16, no. 12 (December): e0260566. https://doi.org/10.1371/journal.pone.0260566.

Castano, Emanuele, Maria P. Paladino, Olivia G. Cadwell, Valentina Cuccio, and Pietro Perconti. 2021. "Exposure to Literary Fiction Is Associated with Lower Psychological Essentialism." *Frontiers in Psychology* 12: 1–10. https://doi.org.10.3389/fpsyg.2021.662940.

Cook, Jennifer R., Sharon S. Rostosky, and Ellen D.B. Riggle. 2013. "Gender Role Models in Fictional Novels for Emerging Adult Lesbians." *Journal of Lesbian Studies* 17, no. 2 (March): 150–66. https://doi.org/10.1080/10894160.2012.691416.

Coyne, Sarah M., Jennifer R. Linder, Eric E. Rasmussen, David A. Nelson, and Kevin M. Collier. 2014. "It's a Bird! It's a Plane! It's a Gender Stereotype!: Longitudinal Associations Between Superhero Viewing and Gender Stereotyped Play." *Sex Roles* 70, no. 9–10 (May): 416–30. https://doi.org/10.1007/s11199-014-0374-8.

Djikic, Maja, Keith Oatley, and Mihnea C. Moldoveanu. 2013. "Reading Other Minds: Effects of Literature on Empathy." *Scientific Study of Literature* 3, no. 1 (June): 28–47.

Eidelson, Roy J., and Norman Epstein. 1982. "Cognition and Relationship Maladjustment Development of a Measure of Dysfunctional Relationship Beliefs." *Journal of Consulting and Clinical Psychology* 50, no. 5 (October): 715–20. https://doi.org/10.1037/0022-006X.50.5.715.

Ellemers, Naomi. 2018. "Gender Stereotypes." *Annual Review of Psychology* 69 (January): 275–98. https://doi.org/10.1146/annurev-psych-122216-011719.

England, Paula. 2010. "The Gender Revolution: Uneven and Stalled." *Gender & Society* 24, no. 2 (March): 149–66. https://doi.org/10.1177/0891243210361475.

Ferguson, Donna. 2018. "Must Monsters Always Be Male? Huge Gender Bias Revealed in Children's Books." *The Guardian*, January 21, 2018. https://www.theguardian.com/books/2018/jan/21/childrens-books-sexism-monster-in-your-kids-book-is-male.

Ferguson, Donna. 2019. "'Highly Concerning': Picture Books Bias Worsens as Female Characters Stay Silent." *The Guardian*, June 13, 2019. https://www.theguardian.com/books/2019/jun/13/highly-concerning-picture-books-bias-worsens-as-female-characters-stay-silent.

Fink, Dagmar. 2021. *Cyborg werden: möglichkeitshorizonte in feministischen theorien und science fiction*. Bielefeld: transcript.

Fisher, Jerilyn, and Ellen S. Silber. 2000. "Good and Bad Beyond Belief: Teaching Gender Lessons Through Fairy Tales and Feminist Theory." *Women's Studies Quarterly* 28, no. 3–4 (Fall-Winter): 121–36. https://www.jstor.org/stable/40005478.

Fong, Katrina, Justin B. Mullin, and Raymond A. Mar. 2015. "How Exposure to Literary Genres Relates to Attitudes Toward Gender Roles and Sexual Behavior." *Psychology of Aesthetics, Creativity, and the Arts* 9, no. 3 (August): 274–85. https://doi.org/10.1037/a0038864.

Glick, Peter, and Susan Tufts Fiske. 2011. "Ambivalent Sexism Revisited." *Psychology of Women Quarterly* 35, no. 3 (August): 530–35. https://doi.org/10.1177/0361684311414832.

Goffin, Kris, and Stacey Friend. 2022. "Learning Implicit Biases from Fiction". *The Journal of Aesthetics and Art Criticism* 20 (January): 1–11. https://doi.org/10.1093/jaac/kpab078.

Green, Melanie C., and Timothy C. Brock. 2005. "Persuasiveness of Narrative." In *Persuasion: Psychological Insights and Perspectives,* edited by T. C. Brock and M. C. Green, 117–42. Thousand Oaks, CA: Sage.

Green, Melanie C., and Jordan M. Carpenter. 2011. "Transporting into Narrative Worlds: New Directions for the Scientific Study of Literature." *Scientific Study of Literature* 1, no.1 (January): 113–22. https://doi.org/10.1075/ssol.1.1.12gre.

Green, Melanie C., and Karen E. Dill. 2013. "Engaging with Stories and Characters: Learning, Persuasion, and Transportation into Narrative Worlds." In *The Oxford Handbook of Media Psychology*, edited by Karen E. Dill, 449–61. New York: Oxford University Press.

James, Alison, Akihiro Kubo, and Françoise Lavocat, eds. 2023. *Can Fiction Change the World?* Oxford: Legenda.

Kneeskern, Ellen, and Patricia Reeder. 2020. "Examining the Impact of Fiction Literature on Children's Gender Stereotypes." *Current Psychology* 41, no. 3 (March): 1472–85. https://doi.org/10.1007/s12144-020-00686-4.

Kokesh, Jessica, and Miglena Sternadori. 2015. "The Good, the Bad, and the Ugly: A Qualitative Study of How Young Adult Fiction Affects Identity Construction." *Atlantic Journal of Communication* 23, no. 3 (July): 139–58. https://doi.org/10.1080/15456870.2015.1013104.

Malo-Juvera, Victor. 2016. "The Effect of an LGBTQ Themed Literary Instructional Unit on Adolescents' Homophobia." *Study & Scrutiny: Research on Young Adult Literature* 2, no. 1: 1–34.

McCabe, Janice, Emily Fairchild, Liz Grauerholz, Berenice A. Pescosolido, and Daniel Tope. 2011. "Gender in Twentieth-Century Children's Books." *Gender & Society* 25, no. 2 (March): 197–226. https://doi.org/10.1177/0891243211398358.

McInroy, Lauren, and Shelley L. Craig. 2016. "Perspectives of LGBTQ Emerging Adults on the Depiction and Impact of LGBTQ Media Representation." *Journal of Youth Studies* 20, no. 1: 32–46.

McMurry, Andrew. 2019. "Ecocriticism and Discourse." In *Routledge Handbook of Ecocriticism and Environmental Communication*, edited by Scott Slovic, Swarnalatha Rangarajan and Vidya Sarveswaran, 15–25. London and New York: Routledge.

Nünning, Vera. 2014. *Reading Fictions, Changing Minds: The Cognitive Value of Fiction*. Heidelberg: Winter.

Nünning, Vera. 2020. "The Value of Literature for the 'Extension of our Sympathies': Twelve Strategies for the Direction of Readers' Sympathy." *REAL* 36, no. 1 (December): 73–98. https://doi.org/10.2357/REAL-2021-0003.

Panero, Maria E., Deena Skolnick Weisberg, Jessica Black, Thalia R. Goldstein, Jennifer L. Barnes, Hiram Brownell, and Ellen Winner. 2017. "No Support for the Claim That Literary Fiction Uniquely and Immediately

Improves Theory of Mind: A Reply to Kidd and Castano's Commentary on Panero et al. (2016)." *Journal of Personality and Social Psychology* 112, no. 3 (March): e5–e8.

Richter, Tobias, Markus Appel, and Frank Calio. 2014. "Stories Can Influence the Self-Concept." *Social Influence* 9, no. 3 (May): 172–88. https://doi.org/10.1080/15534510.2013.799099.

Stern, Stephanie, Brianne Robbins, Jessica Black, and Jennifer Barnes. 2019. "What You Read and What You Believe: Genre Exposure and Beliefs About Relationships." *Psychology of Aesthetics, Creativity, and the Arts* 13, no. 4 (November): 450–61. https://doi.org/10.1037/aca0000189.

13
IMPLICIT BIAS, FICTION, AND BELIEF

Kris Goffin and Agnes Moors

Introduction

In this chapter we discuss, from a psychological point of view, how fiction can influence implicit biases, such as unconscious racist and sexist attitudes and stereotypes. It might be argued that we learn these attitudes and stereotypes from fiction.

It is well known that many fictional narratives contain stereotypes. Today, many fictions no longer display blatant racist or sexist stereotypes, but several of them still fall prey to more subtle stereotypes. For example, in many contemporary romantic comedies, women are no longer explicitly portrayed as helpless, humble, and subservient, but they are still pictured as overly emotional and primarily dependent on romantic relationships for their happiness (e.g., see the film *Isn't It Romantic*, 2019). For another example, Asian women are often sexualized or exoticized in movies (see the film *Memoirs of a Geisha*, 2005) and Asian men often have an accent and lack emotional depth (see the "Karate Kid" film franchise, 1984–2010). Finally, Black men are still all too often presented as criminals in crime TV shows (e.g., *Law & Order: Special Victim's Unit*, 1999). Indeed, Black men are disproportionally portrayed as wrongdoers and criminals, while the crime solvers and law enforcers are disproportionally White. More indirectly, these Crime TV shows often idealize the justice system and normalize various inequalities and injustices (for an overview, see, Color of Change, 2017).[1] This has come to the foreground, especially since recent problems of police violence and the related unresolved legacies of slavery and segregation in the United States have been the focus of many debates.

Given that many fictions contain stereotypes, the first question we will address in the present chapter is: does fiction teach us implicit bias? A second question we will tackle is whether fiction can help in mitigating these implicit attitudes. Before doing so, we will clarify what implicit biases are and how they are measured, and we will consider mechanisms that plausibly install implicit bias in daily life.

What Is Implicit Bias and How Is It Measured?

Much recent research in (social) psychology has been devoted to how people often unconsciously endorse stereotypes. For instance, one can believe that it would be racist to think that Black men are likely to be criminals, and that racism is horrible. Yet, research indicates that even if one is anti-racist, one can behave in ways that seem to indicate that one does (unconsciously or implicitly) endorse such stereotypes (Banaji and Greenwald, 2013).

DOI: 10.4324/9781003119456-16

In this chapter, we are concerned with implicit social biases. A social bias can be understood as a bias in cognitions about a social group (Banaji and Greenwald, 2013; Saul, 2013). While interacting with members of particular social groups, one's mental processes can be biased. Examples of targeted social groups are race and gender groups, such as Black people and women. There are other cases of bias, which are not directed toward social groups, such as purely cognitive biases (e.g., biases in attention or reasoning), but in this chapter, we only discuss social bias. What makes a social bias implicit is that the individual is not typically aware of the bias. Sometimes it even contradicts their explicit mental states.

The mental states that are involved in social bias can be quite diverse (Holroyd and Sweetman, 2016). Many distinguish between an attitude and a stereotype. An attitude specifies a relation between a social group and a valence attribute (i.e., good or bad, or positive or negative), for instance, a relation between "Black people" and "bad." A prejudice is a negative attitude. A stereotype, on the other hand, specifies a relation between a social group and a non-valence attribute, for instance, a relation between "Black people" and "athletic" or between "Black people" and "criminal." The attributes in stereotypes often have a valence, but they do not simply convey valence like attitudes do. Both negative attitudes toward social groups (e.g., racialized attitudes) and stereotypes can be implicit.

To assess people's social biases, researchers have developed so-called implicit measures. These are contrasted with traditional, explicit measures. Explicit measures directly ask a person, for instance, whether Black people are more dangerous than White people. In implicit measures, on the other hand, a person's mental content is inferred in an indirect way from their behavior.

A famous example of an implicit measure is the Implicit Association Task (IAT), which is a task designed to measure people's attitudes toward social groups (Banaji and Greenwald, 2013; Greenwald and Banaji, 1995; Greenwald, McGhee, and Schwartz, 1998; Greenwald et al., 2009). One example is an IAT which tests whether individuals relate Black and White people with positive or negative valence. The task requires participants to categorize pictures of Black and White people and positive and negative words using the same or a different response. In one phase of the task, participants are asked to press left if they see a Black person or a positive word and to press right if they see a White person or a negative word. In another phase of the task, participants receive the opposite mapping between Black and White persons and positive and negative words. Then words and pictures are shown. What is measured is the speed by which participants resolve this task and the number of errors they make in both phases. If results show that a participant is slower and makes more errors in the first phase, when they have to combine Black faces and positive words, it is inferred that they have an implicit bias toward Black people.

Other IATs measure stereotypes, understood as relations between social groups and other concepts than positive or negative. An example is the gender-career IAT (Banaji and Greenwald, 2013).[2] Here, participants are asked to categorize words referring to male and female categories and words referring to career and family using the same or a different response. In one phase of the task, they have to press left for words referring to female and career and right for words referring to male and family. In another phase, they have to press left for words referring to male and career and right for words referring to female and family. The majority of people tend to be quicker and more accurate in combining male with career and female with family, which suggests that they hold an implicit gender-career stereotype. This is also true of people who explicitly reject these stereotypes (Banaji and Greenwald, 2013; Greenwald and Banaji, 1995; Greenwald et al., 2009).

Another example of an implicit measure of stereotypes is the first-person shooter task (Correll, Park, Judd, and Wittenbrink, 2002). This task is designed to measure whether people implicitly endorse the stereotype that Black men are likely to be criminals and tend to behave according to this stereotype. In this task, participants play a sort of first-person shooter game, in which they have to shoot armed people. Pictures are shown of Black and White people holding objects: some hold a gun, some do not. The task goes quite fast, and it is not always clear which objects the people are holding. The task is, however, to only shoot the people who are holding guns. It turns out that most participants, even those who explicitly reject the stereotype, have a bias in the mistakes they make (i.e., the so-called shooter bias, Payne, 2001): unarmed Black men are more often shot than unarmed White men.

Implicit measures have been criticized. It has been argued, for instance, that it is not clear what these measures actually measure (for an overview and responses to the criticism, see Brownstein, Madva, and Gawronski, 2020) and whether they can meaningfully be called implicit (Corneille and Hütter, 2020). It is also debated what constitutes these biases: unconscious beliefs (Mandelbaum, 2016) or unconscious associations (Gawronski and Bodenhausen, 2011; Strack and Deutsch, 2004). For instance, is it the case that people unconsciously believe that "Black men are dangerous" or do they simply associate Black men with danger? A belief can be understood as a qualified relation between two concepts that is held to be true. An association, on the other hand, points at the fact that two concepts are related without specifying the nature of the relationship. Concepts simply conjure each other up (see De Houwer, 2014), as we will address further later.

A final line of criticism denounces the fact that implicit measures of attitudes toward groups are poor predictors of discriminative behavior (e.g., Kurdi et al., 2019; Oswald et al., 2013). This attitude-behavior gap has led some authors to search for moderators of attitude-behavior relations (e.g., Brownstein et al., 2020; Friese et al., 2008) and others to argue for the measurement of other (more proximal) causes of behavior such as the expected utility of behavior (Moors and Köster, 2022).

How Do We Acquire Implicit Biases?

It has often been suggested that the learning of the attitudes and stereotypes responsible for implicit biases can be framed as a case of evaluative learning or conditioning (De Houwer, 2007; Olson and Fazio, 2001, 2006). Evaluative learning is the phenomenon in which the pairing of an initially neutral stimulus with another, positive or negative stimulus results in a change in the perceived valence (i.e., goodness/badness) of the former stimulus (Baeyens et al., 1992; De Houwer, 2007; De Houwer et al., 2001; Hofmann et al., 2010; Mitchell et al., 2009).[3] For instance, take the stimulus "men with ginger hair." Suppose you initially have a neutral attitude toward ginger men: you do not think ginger men are particularly good or bad. As a kid, however, you were bullied by an irritating ginger boy. In high school, many other people spoke of ginger men as undesirable and ugly losers and treated them accordingly. In your youth, the stimulus "ginger men" is thus repeatedly coupled with other, negative stimuli such as being undesirable, being ugly, and so on. As a result, you may learn that "ginger men" are associated with negative valence. So the initially neutral valence of ginger men shifts toward negative valence because the stimulus is coupled with negatively valenced stimuli. In another example, the initially neutral valence may shift toward positive valence because one sees ginger men, such as Ed Sheeran, being coupled with positively valenced stimuli, such as "nice music" and "likeable guy." Of course, this example does not hold for everyone. If you do not like Ed Sheeran, the effect will not occur.

Evaluative learning is a somewhat different kind of learning than studying for your statistics exam. Evaluative conditioning is something that happens to you, rather than something that you do. Learning that ginger men are positive or negative is the result of being passively exposed to pairings between ginger men and positive or negative other stimuli, not something that you actively try to memorize. Evaluative conditioning is a useful tool to navigate the world, as we automatically learn which things are good and bad for us. The dark side of evaluative conditioning, however, is that it also applies to social groups.[4]

Let us now unpack the mechanisms underlying evaluative learning. As we said before, evaluative conditioning is the pairing of an initially neutral stimulus with another positive or negative stimulus, which results in a change in the perceived valence of the former stimulus. A mechanistic explanation of evaluative conditioning is an explanation of how this change in perceived valence comes about. In line with the aforementioned debate between theorists who believe that implicit attitudes are associations versus theorists who think they are beliefs, there are theorists who think evaluative learning is associative and theorists who think that it is more like learning a belief. The traditional way of understanding evaluative learning is the associative model. When two concepts are paired: "ginger men" and "negative," one learns to associate "ginger men" with bad valence: one learns "ginger men—bad." When one thinks of ginger men, the next thought is "bad." Recently, however, evidence is accumulating that evaluative conditioning might not be merely associative, but propositional (for an overview see Madva, 2016). Instead of learning that two concepts are related in some way, as is the case in a mere association, one learns something about the nature or the quality of the relation between these concepts. One learns, for instance, that "ginger people are bad." Mitchell and De Houwer et al. (2009) argue that all learning is propositional, that is, based on knowledge about propositions understood as qualified relationships rather than unqualified associations. A similar statement has been made by philosophers such as Mandelbaum (2016). We wish to point out that despite disagreement about the details of the various processes underlying the evaluative conditioning effect, there is consensus that the effect itself—a change in liking of an initially neutral stimulus resulting from the pairing of this stimulus with another positive or negative stimulus—is robust (De Houwer, 2007; De Houwer et al., 2001).

Note that evaluative learning is about goodness or badness. In line with the aforementioned distinction between attitudes and stereotypes, we could make a distinction between evaluative learning and other types of relationship learning. Instead of learning the relation between an object and good or bad, we can (by means of the same procedure learn the relation between an object and another concept. Thus, we can learn a relation between "Black person" and "bad," but we can also learn the relation between "Black person" and "dangerous."

Now that we understand the processes involved in the formation of attitudes and stereotypes in real life, we will focus on how this applies to learning attitudes and stereotypes from fiction.

Fiction as a Bias Teacher

Many fictional narratives, such as TV shows, contain stereotypes, often in subtle sometimes in less subtle ways. In the introduction we mentioned some examples: Romantic comedies reinforce gender stereotypes such as women being dependent on romantic relationships for their happiness. Asian women are often objectified and overly sexualized; Asian men often appear as one-dimensional skilled martial artists. Black men often are presented as criminals, while the heroes of the story are often White people.

A good case could be made that we learn implicit attitudes and stereotype from fiction. Indeed, in many articles on implicit bias, it is presumed that popular media are important sources of bias learning and "unlearning" (for an overview, see Dasgupta, 2013). These media not only include fictional TV shows but also news shows and non-fictional programs.[5] In fact, the influence of non-fictional media is more widely studied than that of fictional media (see e.g., Entman, 1994; Payne and Dal Cin, 2015; Roos et al., 2013). The idea that fiction is a bias teacher is often presupposed but not very thoroughly empirically investigated. Nevertheless, it makes sense to think that engaging with fiction is sufficient to learn implicit attitudes and stereotypes. We will discuss this hypothesis.[6]

It has been shown that people can learn relationships between things by merely observing other people. In the evaluative conditioning literature, this phenomenon is described as "observational evaluative conditioning" (Baeyens and Vansteenwegen et al., 1996). Here, learning does not require directly experiencing the stimuli being paired, but occurs when seeing other people experiencing those stimuli. One might understand attitude learning from fiction as a case of observational evaluative conditioning. Maybe our negative attitudes toward a certain social group do not reflect our own negative experiences from interacting with members of this group, but rather stem from the experiences of the fictional characters that we observe. If we are exposed to many fictional Black men holding guns on television, we might learn to associate black men with guns. If we see or read that most fictional scientists are old White men with beards, we might learn to associate the profession of scientist with men and not with women.

Goffin and Friend (2022) argue in their paper for the pessimistic stance that many works of fiction install harmful biases in people. As an example, they discuss the "glass slipper effect" (Rudman and Heppen, 2003), which is an effect that indicates that implicit gender stereotypes as displayed in "Prince Charming" narratives, in which the male love interest is a brave hero who saves the helpless woman, influence one's career aspirations. Rudman and Heppen (2003) argue that these implicit stereotypes are correlated with women being less ambitious.

Goffin and Friend (2022) also referred to the "bias contagion" phenomenon, which is a form of observational learning in which individuals copy biased behavior as seen by others (Weisbuch, Pauker, and Ambadi, 2009). The behavior in question can be extremely subtle, such as standing further away from people of color than from White people in elevators. A number of studies have indicated that bias contagion also works by watching television series (Weisbuch, Pauker, and Ambadi, 2009; Willard, Isaac, and Carney, 2015). By watching characters on TV displaying subtle signs of aversion, such as smiling less toward characters from a specific social group, spectators can copy this subtle aversive behavior. Tragically, however, bias contagion even occurs when TV shows, such as "CSI" and "Grey's Anatomy," actively contra-stereotype their characters and portray women and people of color as having high-level jobs (Weisbuch, Pauker, and Ambadi, 2009). When the actors interacting with these characters display subtle behavior vis-à-vis these characters, such as standing a little bit further away from them, spectators still pick this up, even if only implicitly.

There are also studies on the influence of video games on implicit bias. Saleem and Anderson (2013), for instance, showed that violent videogames with Arab stereotypes and Arab terrorists increased anti-Arab attitudes as measured by an IAT. Moreover, a great deal of research examines stereotypes presented in children's fiction (e.g., Kneeskern and Reeder, 2020; Peterson and Lach, 1990). It is often thought that many social biases are learned at a very young age, and then maintained throughout the rest of life (for an overview, see Dasgupta, 2013).

Another mechanism that may be involved in the learning of biases from fiction is known as Spinozan Belief Formation. Dan Gilbert (1991) distinguishes between two accounts of the acquirement of new beliefs: the Cartesian model and the Spinozan model (referring to the philosophers Descartes and Spinoza). The Cartesian model states that when a person is confronted with a statement or proposition, a first step is to process the proposition or to consider it. A second step is to evaluate the proposition as true or false after evidence in favor or against the proposition is gathered. A person may also suspend judgment if the evidence is deemed insufficient to hold something true or false. The Spinozan view, which Gilbert (1991) himself defends, states that belief formation happens instantly. When a person is confronted with a proposition, the first step is to process and believe it. In a second step, however, one can re-evaluate this belief and then reject it or conclude that it was correct. Here, believing a proposition is the default, which may or may not be overruled in a later stage. On the Cartesian model it takes effort to believe or reject something. On the Spinozan model, on the other hand, it only takes effort to reject a belief. Because people do not always have sufficient opportunity or motivation, they will often hold beliefs they have not critically examined. Empirical support for the Spinozan belief formation hypothesis comes from studies showing that participants seem to immediately believe things they read, even if the text is explicitly presented as fiction (Gilbert et al., 1993). It would take effort to critically examine what we read or to stop believing the things that are offered to us while reading. If this is true, then fiction should not only provide us with relational information, in the form of associations or propositions, but also generate instant beliefs, including those that constitute implicit bias.[7]

One might raise skepticism against the idea that it is fiction that teaches us these biases. One might think that biases live in a society, and that fiction presents a reflection of what lives in that society (see Payne et al., 2017, for a structural account of bias). One could argue that we pick up biases from real-life interactions and pass them on through fiction. Even if it seems plausible to assume that real-life biases find their way into fiction, fiction may in turn select and exaggerate certain stereotypes, thereby creating novel biases in people who never had them in the first place and sustain or enlarge them in people who did. In other words, it may be a two-way street or even a vicious cycle.

Given that we can learn biases from real-life experiences as well as from fiction, the question arises whether fiction is special. Is fiction especially good or bad at teaching biases? Some argue that narratives in particular are better in persuading us to believe something. This idea is referred to as "narrative persuasion" (Busselle and Bilandzic, 2008; Hamby, Brinberg, and Jaccard, 2016). Two factors may contribute to this narrative persuasion. The first is that fiction is often designed to create strong emotional experiences (Busselle and Bilandzic, 2008). The second is that people are less likely to check for accuracy in fiction than in real life (Dal Cin et al., 2004; Prentice and Gerrig, 1991). We discuss each of these two factors in more detail.

Regarding the first point, some authors claim that fiction is persuasive because it elicits strong emotions (Busselle and Bilandzic, 2008; Hamby, Brinberg, and Jaccard, 2016). This should create an ideal circumstance for observational evaluative learning, as positive and negative experiences are essential ingredients of evaluative learning. One might object, however, that fiction produces less intense emotions precisely because we know we are dealing with fiction. Witnessing a crime in real life will evoke much stronger emotions than seeing a crime in a movie. However, the knowledge that what is happening in fiction is not real is often compensated by the use of several strategies such as the use of extreme stimuli, the use of superstimuli, and the use of techniques that foster "immersion." To create an equally strong affective experience in fiction as in real life, the events need to be far more intense or extreme. That is why in movies there is so much horror, tragedy, and violence. You need to present more extreme events than in real life to obtain an emotional reaction of some sort. The same goes for psychological experiments: the more you simulate real life (e.g., in VR) the less intense your stimulus must be. The two positions discussed here—that fiction elicits strong versus weak emotions—focused mainly on the intensity of emotions. It could also be argued that the emotions generated by fiction are of a different kind than the ones generated in real life (Walton, 1990).

In addition to more extreme stimuli, certain forms of fiction also make use of "superstimuli" (Ramachandran and Hirstein, 1999; but see criticism by Gombrich, 2000). Superstimuli are not necessarily more extreme, but they have exaggerated features, which may create affective experiences in the audience. For instance, in cartoons, characters have large eyes and big heads, like babies do, to make sure they are perceived as cuter and elicit more empathy. Finally, works of fiction employ a range of techniques to make sure the audience becomes immersed in the fictional world and empathizes with the fictional characters living in it. This too may contribute to the emotional power of fiction (Visch, Tan, and Molenaar, 2010). We may conclude that depending on the successful use of the discussed strategies, fiction may be more or less effective in eliciting affective experiences that contribute to observational evaluative learning.

Regarding the second factor, some researchers argue that in real life and non-fictional stories, people tend to check whether the facts that are presented are actually true (Dal Cin et al., 2004; Prentice and Gerrig, 1991). In fiction, they are less likely to do this because it is clear from the start that they are dealing with fiction. Paradoxically, however, the fact that people do not engage in fact-checking also makes them more susceptible to uncritically adopt the stereotypes presented in fiction and develop biased attitudes based on them. In other words, they do not necessarily consider the presented stereotypes to be fictional. The argument to support the claim that we gather information without checking is based on the ideas of the aforementioned Spinozan belief formation framework (Hamby, Brinberg, and Jaccard, 2016).

In addition to the factors involved in narrative persuasion, we may speculate that fiction can be especially powerful in generating stereotypes. Creators of fiction make use of various "tropes" or predictable elements in crafting their stories. Fiction presents us with archetypes or caricatures of people such as "the foreigner" or "the professor." Instead of presenting us with real people, we see fictional characters who are one-dimensional. Often these caricatures are problematic because they reflect harmful stereotypes. For instance, as mentioned before, the "Karate Kid" film franchise (1984–2010) portrays Asian characters as martial arts fighters with a thick accent, who also lack emotional depth. Thus, fiction may facilitate observational learning of relational information involved in stereotypes.[8]

In this section, we have presented various ways in which we can conceptualize fiction as a bias teacher. In the final section, we will examine whether fiction can also be a bias remover.

Fiction as Bias Remover

Some argue that fiction can help people to get rid of racist, sexist, and other social biases. If it is true that we can learn biases from fiction, then fiction can be used strategically to unlearn biases.

In the previous section, we have mentioned "narrative persuasion." The idea that fictional narratives are supposedly really good at making someone believe something can be used for the better. One application might be to narratively persuade people to stop (implicitly) endorsing harmful attitudes and stereotypes (Hamby, Brinberg, and Jaccard, 2016).

In fact, this is a very old idea. Psychological researchers have experimented with using fictional stories to re-educate people and save them from their vices and addictions. For instance, Cautela (1971) discussed a story that is supposed to mitigate alcohol addiction. It is a story that makes you imagine in detail a case in which drinking alcohol makes you vomit. It also describes how you feel wonderful if you reject drinking more alcohol. This story is supposed to teach you a negative attitude toward alcoholic beverages and help with alcohol addiction.

Let us focus on the mechanism and procedure that may be behind these kinds of unlearning from fiction. Some have argued that by means of evaluative conditioning, which we have discussed in the beginning of the chapter, we can reduce biases (Olson and Fazio, 2006). Applying this to fiction, we could then argue that by coupling members of certain social groups to positively valenced objects, we can reduce implicit prejudice.

The procedure or phenomenon at stake here is called "counterconditioning." A researcher tries to reverse the outcome of a previous conditioning procedure that led to the initial attitude by using another conditioning procedure that would create the opposite attitude. If the initial conditioning episode paired "ginger men" with negatively valenced stimuli, counterconditioning will entail the pairing of "ginger men" with positively valenced stimuli, with the aim of creating a positive attitude toward ginger men.

There is fair consensus that counterconditioning does not consist of the "unlearning" or updating of a previous attitude, but rather consists of the learning of a new attitude that sits next to the old one (Baeyens, 1988; for an overview see Bouton, 2002). Research thus suggests that the best one can do is to learn new attitudes that contradict the old ones, but this does not mean that the old ones disappear. The old attitudes may re-emerge when the right contextual cues are presented. This would imply that fiction cannot really erase biases through counterconditioning. This thus means that we cannot "unlearn" bias from fiction.[9]

So far, counterconditioning has been targeted at implicit attitudes or prejudices toward certain social groups. One can build a similar case for implicit stereotypes. Counter-stereotype exposure (Dasgupta and Greenwald, 2001) is meant to diminish people's implicitly endorsed stereotypes by confronting them with images and scenarios that reject these stereotypes. We believe fiction can play a role in this. If people are confronted with images or scenarios of scientists who are not old white men with beards, existing gendered and racialized stereotypes of a scientist may be counteracted. However, as is the case in evaluative counterconditioning, it is likely that counter-stereotype exposure will also not automatically lead to the "unlearning" of the old stereotypes (see also Madva, 2017).

Some researchers have argued that intergroup contact is an effective way to reduce prejudice (see Dasgupta and Rivera, 2008). The idea is simple: the more you interact with people from a particular social group, the less biased you become toward members of this social group because intergroup contact creates opportunities for counterconditioning. However, not all interactions turn out to have this effect. Research has shown, for instance, that prejudice is not reduced if there is a power imbalance, for instance, if a person of one social group is serving or obeying a person of another social group (see Anderson, 2010; Dasgupta and Rivera, 2008). The two people interacting have to be each other's equals to some extent.

Fiction could be designed to simulate intergroup interaction among equals: by reading about or viewing screenings with people from different social groups, or by reading about interactions between people from social groups, one can create a fictional intergroup contact. There are some psychological studies that have investigated fictional intergroup contact. In an overview article about experiments testing various prejudice mitigation strategies (Paluck and Green, 2009), the fictional intergroup contact strategy seems to be quite successful. In a number of studies with school children as participants (Cameron and Rutland, 2006; Cameron et al., 2006; Liebkind and McAlister, 1999; Slone et al., 2000), the children were presented with fictional stories in which there was a positive contact between them and children from the same and from other social groups (race, gender, disability). Results showed a positive effect in prejudice reduction. However, this positive effect is only measured by means of self-reports and not by means of implicit measures (Paluck and Green, 2009).[10] Thus, it is unclear whether the results of these studies also apply to implicit prejudices. This could be a topic for further research.[11]

It might also be the case that the true unlearning of biases from fiction is not done by a passive viewing or reading, but by means of reflection and discussion on the fictional narrative. Fiction might stimulate you to reflect on your biases and make you aware that you have these biases (see Fisher, 1998).

These are various ways in which we might mitigate biases through fiction. Some researchers are, however, skeptical of the idea that fiction would be helpful in combatting biases. Goffin and Friend (2022), for instance, argue that the initial conditioning of "bad" attitudes is more likely to happen than the possibility of counterconditioning of these "bad" attitudes into "good" ones.

However, instead of making big optimistic claims like "fiction can help us to unlearn bias" or alternative pessimistic claims like "fiction is more likely to create than reduce bias," it would be better to further investigate the phenomenon of learning implicit bias from fiction through rigorous psychological research. A promising avenue for future research would be to investigate the conditions under which fiction leads to the creation and reduction of biases. More broadly speaking, the question can be raised of what the moderators are that influence whether fiction is better able to teach and/or to reduce biases? Examples of moderators could be the artistic quality of the fictional work. Is good fiction better at reducing biases than bad fiction?[12] Maybe when consumers of fiction think that it is "too obvious" that the author has as an aim to reduce bias, or the creator is "too manipulative," the effect might be absent or opposite.

It is often said that fiction can teach biases as well as remove them. This chapter presented an overview, from a psychological perspective, of several ways that both phenomena might occur.

Notes

1 It is worth noting that in our examples, we mainly focus on the U.S. context, as U.S. visual culture has arguably one of the biggest impacts on Western culture. The psychological claims we make, however, are taken to be universal.

2 The test may be taken online for free here: https://implicit.harvard.edu/implicit/user/agg/blindspot/indexgc.htm.

3 For a good introduction to the psychology of learning, see De Houwer and Hughes (2020).

4 There is debate about whether evaluative learning really is automatic, or whether it requires awareness of the pairings (for a review, see Corneille and Stahl, 2019).

5 Interestingly, many stimuli in an experimental setting are in fact "fictional." In the lab pictures or videos are shown; or one needs to read a vignette. Experiments "in the wild" are rarely done. So, in fact many psychological studies engage with fiction, without explicitly mentioning it.

6 We would like to point out that we are neutral on theories of fiction. The claims of this chapter are meant to be consistent with most theories of fiction.

7 One might think that the Spinozan theory of the mind contradicts the idea that fiction involves "make-believe" (Walton, 1990). This is not necessarily the case. Walton is neutral about the specific subpersonal mental processes that give rise to his theory of make-believe. The make-believe hypothesis states that while engaging with fiction you exercise your imagination. The Spinozan theory would state that if you imagine something, you then consequently also believe that this is the case, but you can always reject these beliefs right after you acquire them. Spinozan theory and make-belief are not necessarily contradictory, but one might think that they form a bit of an awkward pair. However, the Spinozan theory is indeed controversial.

8 Of course, not all fiction has these one-dimensional stereotypes. Fiction can also focus on the complexity of the characters.

9 The fact that counterconditioning does not lead to erasing attitudes but rather to the formation of new attitudes that contradict the old ones can be seen as evidence for the fragmentation of the mind hypothesis. This hypothesis states that people often have contradictory beliefs and attitudes, and in different contexts our behavior is guided by different (and possibly contradicting) attitudes and beliefs (Mandelbaum, 2014).

10 Paluck and Green (2009) mentioned that similar studies done with reading about other cultures or about people from different social groups have no, or a less overwhelmingly positive effect than the studies just mentioned. So the effect is stronger if the fictional narrative describes an interaction between members of different social groups.

11 It might be remarked that although fiction is used in this way in many U.S. schools, the question remains whether this is effective to address deep social inequities.

12 See also Nussbaum (1996).

Works Cited

Baeyens, Frank, Geert Crombez, Omer Van Den Bergh, and Paul Eelen. 1988. "Once in Contact Always in Contact: Evaluative Conditioning is Resistant to Extinction." *Advances in Behavior Research and Therapy* 10, no. 4: 179–99.

Baeyens, Frank, Paul Eelen, Geert Crombez, and Omer Van Den Bergh. 1992. "Human Evaluative Conditioning: Acquisition Trials, Presentation Schedule, Evaluative Style and Contingency Awareness." *Behaviour Research and Therapy* 30, no. 2 (March): 133–42.

Baeyens, Frank, D. E. B. Vansteenwegen, J. A. N. De Houwer, and Geert Crombez. 1996. "Observational Conditioning of Food Valence in Humans." *Appetite* 27, no. 3: 235–50.

Banaji, Mahzarin R., and Anthony G. Greenwald. 2013. *Blindspot: Hidden Biases of Good People*. New York: Bantam.

Bouton, Mark E. 2002. "Context, Ambiguity, and Unlearning: Sources of Relapse After Behavioral Extinction." *Biological Psychiatry* 52, no. 10 (November): 976–86.

Brownstein, Michael, Alex Madva, and Bertram Gawronski. 2020. "Understanding Implicit Bias: Putting the Criticism Into Perspective." *Pacific Philosophical Quarterly* 101, no. 2 (June): 276–307.

Busselle, Rick, and Helena Bilandzic. 2008. "Fictionality and Perceived Realism in Experiencing Stories: A Model of Narrative Comprehension and Engagement." *Communication Theory* 18, no. 2 (May): 255–80.

Cameron, Lindsey, and Adam Rutland. 2006. "Extended Contact through Story Reading in School: Reducing Children's Prejudice Toward the Disabled." *Journal of Social Issues* 62, no. 3 (September): 469–88.

Cameron, Lindsey, Adam Rutland, Rupert Brown, and Rebecca Douch. 2006. "Changing Children's Intergroup Attitudes toward Refugees: Testing Different Models of Extended Contact." *Child Development* 77, no. 5 (September–October): 1208–19.

Cautela, Joseph R. 1971. "Covert Conditioning." In *The Psychology of Private Events: Perspectives on Covert Response Systems*, edited By Alfred Jacobs and Lewis B. Sachs, 109–30. New York: Academic Press.

Color of Change. 2017. "Normalizing Injustice: The Dangerous Misrepresentations that Define Television's Scripted Crime Genre." https://colorofchange.org/press_release/normalizing-injustice-new-landmark-study-by-color-of-change-reveals-how-crime-tv-shows-distort-understanding-of-race-and-the-criminal-justice-system/

Corneille, Olivier, and Christoph Stahl, C. 2019. "Associative Attitude Learning: A Closer Look at Evidence and How It Relates to Attitude Models." *Personality and Social Psychology Review* 23, no. 2: 161–189. https://doi.org/10.1177/1088868318763261

Corneille, Olivier, and Mandy Hütter. 2020. "Implicit? What Do You Mean? A Comprehensive Review of The Delusive Implicitness Construct in Attitude Research." *Personality and Social Psychology Review* 24, no. 3 (August): 212–32.

Correll, Joshua, Bernadette Park, Charles M. Judd, and Bernd Wittenbrink. 2002. "The Police Officer's Dilemma: Using Ethnicity To Disambiguate Potentially Threatening Individuals." *Journal of Personality and Social Psychology* 83, no. 6: 1314–29.

Dal Cin, S., M. P. Zanna, and G. T. Fong. 2004. "Narrative Persuasion and Overcoming Resistance." In *Resistance and Persuasion*, edited by Eric S. Knowles and Jay A. Linn, 175–91. New York: Psychology Press.

Dasgupta, Nilanjana. 2013. "Implicit Attitudes and Beliefs Adapt To Situations: A Decade of Research on the Malleability of Implicit Prejudice, Stereotypes, and the Self-Concept." *Advances In Experimental Social Psychology* 47: 233–79.

Dasgupta, Nilanjana, and Anthony G. Greenwald. 2001. "On the Malleability of Automatic Attitudes: Combating Automatic Prejudice with Images of Admired and Disliked Individuals." *Journal of Personality and Social Psychology* 81, no. 5 (November): 800–14.

Dasgupta, Nilanjana, and Luis M. Rivera. 2008. "When Social Context Matters: The Influence of Long–Term Contact and Short–Term Exposure to Admired Outgroup Members on Implicit Attitudes and Behavioral Intentions." *Social Cognition* 26, no. 1 (February): 112–23.

De Houwer, Jan. 2007. "A Conceptual and Theoretical Analysis of Evaluative Conditioning." *Spanish Journal of Psychology* 10, no. 2 (November): 230–41.

De Houwer, Jan. 2014. "A Propositional Model of Implicit Evaluation." *Social and Personality Psychology Compass* 8, no. 7: 342–53.

De Houwer, Jan. 2019. "Implicit Bias is Behavior: A Functional-Cognitive Perspective on Implicit Bias." *Perspectives on Psychological Science* 14, no. 5 (September): 835–40.

De Houwer, Jan, and Sean Hughes. 2020. *The Psychology of Learning: An Introduction from A Functional-Cognitive Perspective*. Cambridge, MA: MIT Press.

De Houwer, Jan, Sarah Thomas, and Frank Baeyens. 2001. "Association Learning of Likes and Dislikes: A Review of 25 Years of Research on Human Evaluative Conditioning." *Psychological Bulletin* 127, no. 6 (November): 853–69.

Entman, Robert M. 1994. "Representation and Reality in the Portrayal of Blacks on Network Television News." *Journalism Quarterly* 71, no. 3 (Fall): 509–20.

Fisher, Robert. 1998. "Stories for Thinking: Developing Critical Literacy Through the Use of Narrative." *Analytic Teaching* 18, no. 1: 16–27.

Friese, Malte, Wilhelm Hofmann, and Manfred Schmitt. 2008. "When and Why Do Implicit Measures Predict Behaviour? Empirical Evidence for the Moderating Role of Opportunity, Motivation, and Process Reliance." *European Review of Social Psychology* 19: 285–338.

Gawronski, Bertram, and Galen V. Bodenhausen. 2011. "The Associative–Propositional Evaluation Model: Theory, Evidence, and Open Questions." *Advances in Experimental Social Psychology* 44: 59–127.

Gerrig, Richard J., and Deborah A. Prentice. 1991. "The Representation of Fictional Information." *Psychological Science* 2, no. 5 (September): 336–40.

Gilbert, Daniel T. 1991. "How Mental Systems Believe." *American Psychologist* 46, no. 2 (February): 107–19.

Gilbert, Daniel T., R. Tafarodi, and P. Malone. 1993. "You Can't Not Believe Everything You Read." *Journal of Personality and Social Psychology* 65, no. 2 (August): 221–33.

Goffin, Kris, and Stacie Friend. 2022. "Learning Implicit Biases from Fiction." *The Journal of Aesthetics and Art Criticism* 80, no. 2 (Spring): 129–39.

Gombrich, Ernst H. 2000. "Concerning 'The Science of Art': Commentary on Ramachandran and Hirstein." *Journal of Consciousness Studies* 7, nos. 8–9 (August): 17.

Greenwald, Anthony G., T. Andrew Poehlman, Eric Luis Uhlmann, and Mahzarin R. Banaji. 2009. "Understanding and Using The Implicit Association Test: III. Meta-Analysis of Predictive Validity." *Journal of Personality and Social Psychology* 97, no. 1 (July): 17–41.

Greenwald, Anthony G., and Mahzarin R. Banaji. 1995. "Implicit Social Cognition: Attitudes, Self-Esteem, and Stereotypes." *Psychological Review* 102, no. 1 (January): 4–27.

Greenwald, Anthony G., Debbie E. Mcghee, and Jordan L. K. Schwartz. 1998. "Measuring Individual Differences in Implicit Cognition: The Implicit Association Test." *Journal of Personality and Social Psychology* 74, no. 6 (June): 1464–80.

Hamby, Anne, David Brinberg, and James Jaccard. 2016. "A Conceptual Framework of Narrative Persuasion." *Journal of Media Psychology* 30: 113–124. https://Doi.Org/10.1027/1864-1105/A000187.

Hofmann, Wilhelm, Jan De Houwer, Marco Perugini, Frank Baeyens, and Geert Crombez. 2010. "Evaluative Conditioning in Humans: A Meta-Analysis. *Psychological Bulletin* 136, no. 3 (May): 390–421.

Holroyd, Jules, and Joseph Sweetman. 2016. "The Heterogeneity of Implicit Bias." In *Implicit Bias and Philosophy*, edited By Michael Brownstein and Jennifer Saul, 1: 80–105. New York: Oxford University Press.

Kneeskern, Ellen E. and Patricia Reeder. 2020. "Examining the Impact of Fiction Literature on Children's Gender Stereotypes." *Current Psychology* 41: 1472–1485.

Kurdi, Benedek, Allison E. Seitchik, Jordan R. Axt, Timothy J. Carroll, Arpi Karapetyan, Neela Kaushik, Diana Tomezsko, Anthony G. Greenwald, and Mahzarin R. Banaji. 2019. "Relationship Between the Implicit Association Test and Intergroup Behavior: A Meta-Analysis." *American Psychologist* 74, no. 5 (July-August): 569–86.

Liebkind, Karmela, and Alfred L. Mcalister. 1999. "Extended Contact Through Peer Modelling to Promote Tolerance In Finland." *European Journal of Social Psychology* 29, no. 5–6 (August–September): 765–80.

Madva, Alex. 2016. "Why Implicit Attitudes Are (Probably) Not Beliefs." *Synthese* 193, no. 8 (August): 2659–84.

Madva, Alex. 2017. "Biased Against Debiasing: On the Role of (Institutionally Sponsored) Self-transformation in the Struggle Against Prejudice." *Ergo: An Open Access Journal of Philosophy* 4, no. 6: 145–179. https://Doi.Org/10.3998/Ergo.12405314.0004.006.

Mandelbaum, Eric. 2014. "Thinking Is Believing." *Inquiry* 57, no. 1: 55–96.

Mandelbaum, Eric. 2016. "Attitude, Inference, Association: On the Propositional Structure of Implicit Bias." *Noûs* 50, no. 3 (September): 629–58.

Mitchell, Chris J., Jan De Houwer, and Peter F. Lovibond. 2009. "The Propositional Nature of Human Associative Learning." *Behavioural and Brain Sciences* 32, no. 2 (April): 183–246.

Moors, Agnes, and Massimo Köster. 2022. "Behavior Prediction Requires Implicit Measures of Stimulus-Goal Discrepancies and Expected Utilities of Behavior Options Rather Than of Attitudes Toward Objects." *Wiley Interdisciplinary Reviews: Cognitive Science* 13, no. 5: E1611.

Nussbaum, Martha. 1996. *Poetic Justice: The Literary Imagination and Public Life.* Boston, MA: Beacon Press.

Olson, Michael A., and Russell H. Fazio. 2001. "Implicit Attitude Formation Through Classical Conditioning." *Psychological Science* 12, no. 5 (September): 413–17.

———. 2006. "Reducing Automatically Activated Racial Prejudice Through Implicit Evaluative Conditioning." *Personality and Social Psychology Bulletin* 32, no. 4 (April): 421–33.

Oswald, Frederick L., Gregory Mitchell, Hart Blanton, James Jaccard, and Philip E. Tetlock. 2013. "Predicting Ethnic and Racial Discrimination: A Meta-Analysis of IAT Criterion Studies." *Journal of Personality and Social Psychology* 105, no. 2 (August): 171–92.

Paluck, Elizabeth Levy, and Donald P. Green. 2009. "Prejudice Reduction: What Works? A Review and Assessment of Research and Practice." *Annual Review of Psychology* 60 (January): 339–67.

Payne, B. Keith. 2001. "Prejudice and Perception: The Role of Automatic and Controlled Processes in Misperceiving a Weapon." *Journal of Personality and Social Psychology* 81, no. 2 (August): 181–92.

Payne, B. Keith, and Sonya Dal Cin. 2015. "Implicit Attitudes in Media Psychology." *Media Psychology* 18, no. 3: 292–311.

Payne, B. Keith, Heidi A. Vuletich, and Kristjen B. Lundberg. 2017. "The Bias of Crowds: How Implicit Bias Bridges Personal and Systemic Prejudice." *Psychological Inquiry* 28, no. 4: 233–48.

Peterson, S. Bender and Mary Alyce Lach. 1990. "Gender Stereotypes in Children's Books: Their Prevalence and Influence on Cognitive and Affective Development." *Gender and Education* 2: 185–197.

Ramachandran, Vilayanur S., and William Hirstein. 1999. "The Science of Art: A Neurological Theory of Aesthetic Experience." *Journal of Consciousness Studies* 6, nos. 6–7 (June–July): 15–51.

Roos, Leslie E., Sophie Lebrecht, James W. Tanaka, and Michael J. Tarr. 2013. "Can Singular Examples Change Implicit Attitudes in the Real-World?" *Frontiers In Psychology* 4: 594.

Rudman, Laurie A., and Jessica B. Heppen. 2003. "Implicit Romantic Fantasies and Women's Interest in Personal Power: A Glass Slipper Effect?" *Personality and Social Psychology Bulletin* 29, no. 11 (November): 1357–70.

Saleem, Muniba, and Craig A. Anderson. 2013. "Arabs as Terrorists: Effects of Stereotypes Within Violent Contexts on Attitudes, Perceptions, and Affect." *Psychology of Violence* 3, no. 1 (January): 84–99.

Saul, Jennifer. 2013. "Implicit Bias, Stereotype Threat, and Women in Philosophy." In *Women in Philosophy: What Needs To Change*, edited By Katrina Hutchinson and Fiona Jenkins, 39–60. Oxford: Oxford University Press.

Slone, Michelle, Ricardo Tarrasch, and Dana Hallis. 2000. "Ethnic Stereotypic Attitudes Among Israeli Children: Two Intervention Programs." *Merrill-Palmer Quarterly (1982-)* 46, no. 2 (April): 370–89.

Strack, Fritz, and Roland Deutsch. 2004. "Reflective and Impulsive Determinants of Social Behavior." *Personality and Social Psychology Review* 8, no. 3 (August): 220–47.

Visch, Valentijn T., Ed S. Tan, and Dylan Molenaar. 2010. "The Emotional and Cognitive Effect of Immersion in Film Viewing." *Cognition and Emotion* 24, no. 8: 1439–45.

Walton, Kendall. 1990. *Mimesis as Make-Believe: On the Foundations of the Representational Arts*. Cambridge, MA: Harvard University Press.

Weisbuch, Max, Kristen Pauker, and Nalini Ambady. 2009. "The Subtle Transmission of Race Bias via Televised Nonverbal Behavior." *Science* 326, no. 5960 (December): 1711–14.

Willard, Greg, Kyonne-Joy Isaac, and Dana R. Carney. 2015. "Some Evidence for the Nonverbal Contagion of Racial Bias." *Organizational Behavior and Human Decision Processes* 128: 96–107.

14

CHILDREN'S IDEAS ABOUT STORIES AND ABOUT REALITY

Ayse Payir and Paul L. Harris

Well before they go to school and start to read, most children hear a lot of stories. Some theorists have argued that stories are a key framework for the organization of experience (Bruner, 1993). If that claim is true, the types of stories that children are exposed to by the surrounding community, as well as the status attached to those different types of stories, are likely to impact how children conceptualize their experience, especially their ideas about what can and cannot happen in the real world. In this chapter, we begin to explore this possibility by considering four basic questions. First, what types of stories are children regularly exposed to and is there some fruitful way to group them into different genres? Second, when do young children begin to display some sensitivity to the differences between story genres and on what basis might they do so? Third, granted that children differ in the extent to which they are exposed to particular story genres, what is the impact of that differential exposure? In particular, do children assume that what happens in the type of story world to which they are routinely exposed is a useful guide to reality? Alternatively, do they assume that stories reflect only what happens in a non-existent, fictional world? Finally, if exposure to a particular story genre changes children's thinking, when is that change apparent—is it apparent in children's autonomous reflection or is it only apparent in their receptivity to suggestions put to them by other people? We start by discussing young children's exposure to various types of stories.

Early Exposure to Stories

Research on children's acquisition of language shows that they are often told—or overhear—oral narratives. These narratives are not necessarily intended for them but for the engagement and entertainment of a larger circle (Miller et al., 1990). Such narratives are typically a recounting of an actual experience, either an experience that befell the raconteur, the child, or some other person, albeit with selection and embellishment in the re-telling. From early childhood onward, children will also hear recollections by their caregivers of a more straightforwardly biographical nature—family stories largely intended for their ears and interest. In each of these two cases, children might reasonably regard the narratives as mostly true even if, in either case, there can be exaggeration, distortion, or misremembering by the narrator.

Alongside such narratives of recounting and recollection, many children are invited to listen to fictional stories. To varying degrees, such narratives can be supplemented by a dialogue between adult and child with respect to the motives and feelings of the story characters (Lever and Sénéchal,

    DOI: 10.4324/9781003119456-17

2011). Many stories for young children are heavily anthropomorphic, involving animal characters who dress, talk, and act like human beings. In addition, some stories involve quasi-human protagonists, such as fairy godmothers, witches, or giants, who have special powers enabling them to bring about ordinarily impossible transformations. In either case, the stories are regarded as fictional by adults and typically presented as such to children.

Finally, many children are exposed to religious narratives that include an extraordinary or miraculous event: water is turned into wine, the entire earth is flooded, seas are parted, or Jesus is raised from the dead. Such narratives are ordinarily presented as credible accounts of events that once took place.

Summing up, we can plausibly claim that young children are exposed to factual narratives—oral recountings or biographical recollection—and to fictional narratives—stories with anthropomorphic protagonists or fairy tales that include extraordinary transformations. In addition, many—but not all—children are exposed to religious narratives involving ordinarily impossible events. However, to briskly summarize the narrative landscape in this fashion is to beg an important question. To what extent are young children sensitive to the distinction between factual and fictional narratives—and if they are sensitive to that distinction, where do they situate religious narratives in the context of that distinction?

Distinguishing factual and fictional narratives

Children might have some appreciation of the difference between factual and fictional narratives because they often differ in their context and the framing. Whereas oral recountings and biographical recollections are typically delivered in an apparently spontaneous oral mode, fictional stories are often read to children from a book. However, such cues are clearly imperfect indices of whether any given narrative is factual versus fictional. On the one hand, children will sometimes hear about actual events via a written narrative—read to them from a book, newspaper, letter, or text message. On the other hand, they will sometimes hear about fictional events in the context of an oral narrative told by an inventive parent or an appointed storyteller—with no written text to hand. In any case, even when such cues are reliable, they can at best supply external indicators of what is likely to be a factual versus a fictional narrative. Even if young children are sensitive to such indicators, that sensitivity need not be based on any conceptual insight into the radically different status of the factual as compared to the fictional.

Accordingly, it is appropriate to ask when children have a deeper grasp of the fundamental difference between the two primary narrative genres. More specifically, when do they realize that fictional narratives typically describe what has happened to a fictional protagonist and often—but not always—include implausible or impossible elements whereas factual narratives typically aim to describe what has actually happened to a real person?

Various experiments have recently been conducted to find out if and when children are able to make this fundamental distinction. In one study conducted in the USA, children were first probed to check whether they could distinguish between familiar, make-believe characters such as Cinderella or Harry Potter, on the one hand, and familiar, historical characters such as Abraham Lincoln or Martin Luther King, on the other, by placing pictures of such characters into a designated box, one for make-believe characters and one for real characters (Corriveau et al., 2009). Preschoolers ranging from three to six years were quite good at making this distinction—not perfect but certainly competent.

These initial findings showed that young children rapidly appreciate the distinction between make-believe and reality as well as the fact that any given character or protagonist will fall on one side or the other of that basic divide. Next, children were presented with short narratives about various unfamiliar protagonists and asked to decide on the basis of the surrounding narrative elements whether any given protagonist was make-believe or real. For example, they might hear a narrative about a soldier who fought in the Civil War or alternatively about a soldier who fought with a magical sword. Here, a clear age change emerged. Older children—five- and six-year-olds—were able to use the narrative elements as a clue and differentiated accurately between protagonists who were real and protagonists who were fictional whereas younger children—three- and four-year-olds—sorted them unsystematically. A related age change was found when children were asked to explain their sorting decisions. Having judged a protagonist to be real, the older children often referred to actual events mentioned in the narrative: "He fought in the Civil War." By contrast, having judged a protagonist to be make-believe, they often referred to the implausibility of narrative elements: "There's no such thing as a magical sword." Younger children's justifications, by contrast, were mostly unsystematic and did not cohere with their prior sorting decisions. A follow-up study showed that some of the younger children were able to respond more systematically if they were first provided with modest prompts. More specifically, if they were presented with questions about the plausibility of key elements in the narrative (e.g., 'Could someone really have a magic sword?') and answered them accurately, they typically proceeded to categorize the protagonist appropriately.

The systematic judgments and justifications of the older children, together with the receptivity of at least some younger children to prompting, showed that an appreciation of the basic distinction between fictional and factual narratives starts to emerge in early childhood and is well-established by five or six years of age. Children associate fictional narratives with accounts of ordinarily impossible episodes and factual narratives with accounts of realistic episodes. Admittedly, this analysis is ultimately too simple. Not all fictional narratives recount impossible or even improbable events. Conversely, allegedly factual narratives sometimes recount events that could not have actually taken place. Thus, as they get older and more attuned to particular genres, it is likely that children will fine-tune this basic distinction. Nevertheless, despite this important caveat, it is evident that young children do not suffer from a general tendency to confuse factual and fictional narratives. Indeed, they are quite discerning even when presented with narratives they have not previously encountered.

Two additional studies consolidated and extended this basic conclusion. Children's accuracy in categorizing real versus make-believe protagonists proved to be linked to their broader grasp of representational relationships. More specifically, children who realized that various types of representation—not just narratives but also mental states, and even directional sign-posts—may or may not represent how things actually are in the world were better at the story categorization task than children lacking that conceptual insight (Corriveau and Harris, 2015). In addition, as one might reasonably expect in the context of such a conceptual insight, a similar developmental timetable was found in a quite different cultural setting, namely in Iran. Again, children aged five and six years proved able to categorize a story protagonist as make-believe or real, using the real-world plausibility of episodes in the surrounding story as a guide (Davoodi, Harris, and Corriveau, 2016).

In summary, by the time they go to school, young children have typically grasped the fundamental distinction between narratives that are supposed to be true and, as such, recount events that actually happened and narratives that are made up—with no aspiration to historical truth.

The Impact of Religious Narratives

We may now turn to the third question posed in the introduction. Granted the basic distinction between factual and fictional narratives, what status do children ascribe to religious narratives and what impact do these narratives have on children's thinking? As a case study, we consider the impact of differential exposure to religious narratives. For obvious reasons, children differ considerably in their exposure to this particular genre.

Suppose that, consistent with the findings described so far, young children appraise religious narratives with respect to their conformity to, or departure from, everyday causal regularities, and judge them to be factual or fictional accordingly. If that analysis of their appraisal process is correct, children should regard religious stories, especially those that recount a miracle—which, by definition, constitutes a radical departure from everyday causality—as works of fiction about make-believe protagonists. In effect, young children should conceive of religious stories as tantamount to fairy tales.

On the other hand, religious narratives are typically presented to children as accounts of what allegedly happened rather than as entertaining fictions. In principle, therefore, if children have received a religious education and are receptive to the distinctive framing of religious narratives by the surrounding community, they might well regard religious stories as factual narratives about people who once lived rather than as fictional narratives about make-believe characters.

To examine these competing possibilities, Corriveau et al. (2015) presented five- and six-year-olds with three versions—realistic, magical, and religious—of several stories. Like the stories used by Corriveau et al. (2009), the realistic versions included no implausible or impossible elements whereas the magical versions included an ordinarily impossible outcome brought about via magic. The religious versions were similar to the magical stories insofar as they also included an ordinarily impossible outcome, but the outcome was achieved via divine intervention rather than magic. For example, in one story, a character was thrown overboard a ship and was about to be swallowed by a large whale. In the realistic version of this story, the character was saved by his fellow fishermen. In the magical version, he used his magical powers to get away from the whale. Lastly, in the religious version, he was saved by God after praying for several days. To examine the potential impact of a religious upbringing, children from two different backgrounds were compared: secular children, namely those who were attending a secular US elementary school and did not attend any type of religious service with their family, and religious children, namely those who were attending a denominational Christian school, or attending religious services with their family, or doing both.

Consistent with past findings, both secular and religious children claimed that the protagonists in the realistic narratives were real. Also, consistent with past findings, children in both groups claimed that the protagonists in magical narratives were make-believe, although this pattern was somewhat more consistent among the secular children. There was, however, a clear-cut difference between the two groups in their judgments about the religious narratives, with secular children mostly claiming that the protagonists were make-believe and religious children mostly claiming that they were real. Lastly, the justifications that children provided were consistent with their real versus pretend judgments. Children mainly offered reality-oriented justifications for realistic stories and impossibility-oriented justifications for magical stories. Although both groups of children offered religion-oriented justifications for their judgments about religious stories, secular children referred to religion to justify their judgment that the protagonists in these stories were not real, whereas religious children referred to religion to justify their judgment that the protagonists in these stories were real. Further analysis also confirmed that the pattern of judgment was similar within each of the three religious subgroups. Thus, whether religious children had been exposed to religious teaching via their family, or alternatively in their school, or indeed in both contexts, they typically claimed that the protagonists in religious stories were real. By implication, exposure to religious teaching does not have to be massive or even consistent across different contexts in children's lives for it to shift their thinking about the nature of narratives. Moreover, a follow-up study showed that the effect of religiosity could not simply be ascribed to greater familiarity with the content of particular Bible narratives among the religious children. The same pattern emerged when quasi-religious narratives were generated, narratives that included novel miraculous events, such as a parting of the mountains (rather than a parting of the seas) but were not taken directly from the Bible.

How should we interpret these results, especially the differential responding of secular as compared to religious children? Taken together, children's judgments and justifications confirmed that they appraise many narratives by asking how far the narrative events conform to, or deviate from, their understanding of everyday causality. Narratives that conform to everyday causality are regarded as real, and based on this inference, the protagonists associated with those events are also regarded as real. Narratives that deviate from everyday causality are regarded as fictional and the protagonists associated with those fictional events are regarded as make-believe.

But granted this over-arching hypothesis, how can we explain the fact that secular children are prone to treat religious stories as fictional narratives—consistent with the general hypothesis— whereas religious children are more likely to treat them as factual? At least two interpretations of the distinctive stance of religious children toward religious stories appear feasible.

One possibility is that a religious education impacts children's ideas about causation. This hypothesis, echoing the proposals made by Bruner (1993), implies that the framework that children use to make sense of the world depends on the narratives that they have been exposed to. More specifically, exposure to biblical narratives alters children's ideas about the impact of divine power on the course of real-world events. Let us dub this hypothesis the "divine power" hypothesis. Whereas secular children routinely assume that, generally speaking, there are only naturalistic causal agents in the world, religious children come to believe that there are special powers that divine agents can harness to defy those ordinary causal constraints. On this hypothesis, when religious children hear a miracle story, they regard the miracle as something that could actually happen, given the relevant intervention by a divine power, rather than as something that is impossible and, therefore, implausible in the real world. Hence, to the extent that the story does not ultimately deviate from their distinctive conception of reality—which incorporates such divine power—they are likely to judge its protagonist as real.

A more radical hypothesis—what we might call the "unconstrained reality" hypothesis—is that a religious education changes not just children's notions about whether there are agents with a divine power over the course of events but radically undermines their tendency to think in causal terms at all. More specifically, it is possible that repeated exposure to religious instruction, especially religious narratives, encourages children to forego causal analyses of what can and cannot happen. Instead, children might come to think of reality—and the narratives that may or may not describe it—as unpredictable and unconstrained. Given God's omnipotence, anything can happen.

With these two hypotheses in mind, we took a closer look at the ways that secular and religious children think about a range of narrative types, and the extent to which they invoke causal considerations in assessing the status of a given narrative.

Analyzing Narratives in Terms of Their Causal Plausibility

In addition to magical, religious, and realistic narratives, children often encounter a fourth type of narrative, namely "unusual" narratives which recount a sequence of events that is possible in the sense that it does not run counter to any causal laws but is nonetheless very unlikely. Indeed, compelling narratives frequently include a sequence of events that is, strictly speaking, possible but unexpected and dramatic. Consistent with our general hypothesis, we expected children to again rely on their understanding of everyday causality. Thus, to the extent that the story events in an unusual story do not run counter to what children think of as causally possible, they should regard such stories as factual.

To better understand the differences between secular and religious children, we analyzed their causal thinking more thoroughly—especially the extent to which they claimed that a given story was fictional because the story events were causally impossible or was factual because the story events were causally possible. With this analysis, we aimed to differentiate between the "divine power" hypothesis and the "unconstrained reality" hypothesis. The "divine power" hypothesis implies that any differences between secular and religious children should be localized: differences should emerge for stories implying divine intervention but not for other types of stories, including those that include an unusual or improbable series of events. By contrast, the "unconstrained reality" hypothesis, implies that such differences might impact not just religious stories but other story types—insofar as religious children might be more prepared to accept that anything can happen. The two hypotheses also differ in their predictions about the frequency with which children will invoke causal considerations. The "divine power" hypothesis predicts that religious children will invoke causal factors as often as secular children—they will differ only in the frequency with which they endorse rather than reject divine intervention. By contrast, the "unconstrained reality" hypothesis predicts that religious children will invoke causal constraints less often—given their intuitive assumption that anything can happen.

With these goals in mind, children from either a religious or a secular background were presented with stories in one of four different versions: magical, religious, unusual, and realistic (Payir et al., 2021). After listening to a given story, children were invited to make a judgment about whether the story was fictional or factual and also to provide a justification, explaining why they had made that particular judgment. Like the stories used by Corriveau et al. (2009, 2015), the magical stories included outcomes that defied ordinary causal regularities by means of magic. The religious stories also included outcomes that defied ordinary causal regularities, but they were brought about by divine intervention rather than by magic. The outcomes in the unusual stories had no elements defying ordinary causal regularities, but the particular sequence of events was unlikely to happen in real life. Finally, the events in the realistic stories were consistent with ordinary causal regularities and fairly commonplace.

Importantly, the main story outcome was the same across the four-story versions. For example, the protagonist survived falling from a boat into the sea but the causal sequence leading to her survival was different in each story version (e.g., a magic fairy helped her to get back to the boat in the magical story; God helped her to walk on water in the religious story; a passing whale carried her back to the boat in the unusual story; and her friends threw her a rope in the realistic story). Accordingly, if children differentiated among the stories, it was likely to be on the basis of the causal sequence within the narrative, not on the basis of the narrative outcome. To detect possible developmental changes, the study included both younger (five- to seven-year-olds) and older children (eight- to eleven-year-olds) from religious and secular backgrounds. Finally, as a check on the stability of children's judgments, half the children were asked to judge the reality status of the story outcome and half to judge the reality status of the story character. Neither of these two factors—age and type of judgment—affected the overall pattern of results. Accordingly, we focus on the impact of story version and family background.

Figure 14.1 shows how often children judged a story to be a factual as opposed to a fictional narrative depending on these two factors. We first comment on children's pattern of judgment across the four-story versions—irrespective of their background—and then compare religious and secular children—especially in their response to religious stories.

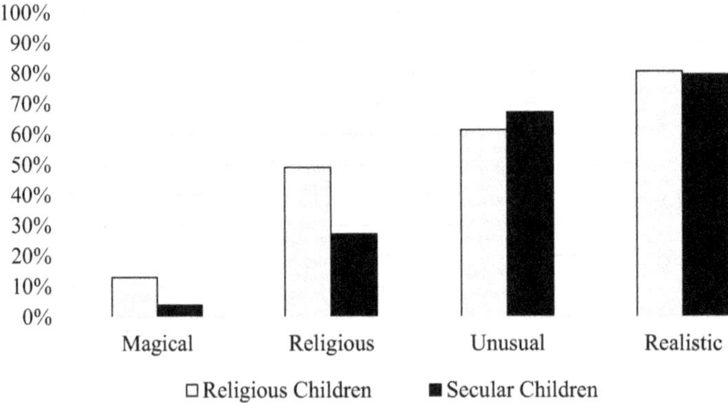

Figure 14.1 Percentage of factual (as opposed to fictional) judgments for each of four-story versions as a function of children's family background (religious versus secular).

At one extreme, children mostly judged magical stories to be fictional. At the other extreme, they mostly judged realistic stories to be factual. Their judgments of religious and unusual stories fell in between these two extremes. They were prone to judge religious stories as fictional—but less often than magical stories. By contrast, they were prone to judge unusual stories as factual—but less often than realistic stories. In sum, a clear rank ordering emerged across the four-story versions, from the most likely to be fictional to the most likely to be factual: magical, religious, unusual, and realistic. This rank-ordering is evident from inspection of Figure 14.1—for both religious and secular children. Moreover, as mentioned earlier, this rank-ordering was robust: it emerged no matter whether we asked children to judge the status of the protagonist, or the status of the story outcome and it emerged among younger and older children alike.

What led children to this stable pattern of judgment? Granted that the stories varied systematically in terms of the causal sequence that had produced the story outcome, we concluded—consistent with our general hypothesis—that children were sensitive to the feasibility of that causal sequence and judged the stories accordingly—with causally anomalous sequences being regarded as fictional and causally feasible sequences being regarded as factual. Children's justifications allowed us to check this interpretation in more detail. Recall that having made a judgment, children were asked to justify that judgment Accordingly, it was possible to analyze the frequency with which children explicitly endorsed or rejected the causal sequence that had been described for a given story.

This follow-up analysis confirmed that children were indeed markedly swayed by causal considerations. For example, in justifying their judgments about magical stories, children often mentioned the causal sequence and almost invariably rejected it as impossible (e.g., "Because she can't walk on water. Magical powers don't make sense"). At the other extreme, in justifying their judgments about realistic stories, children mentioned the causal sequence but almost invariably endorsed it as possible, (e.g., "Because you can have a rope in a boat and you can toss it to someone and they could survive if they were off a boat in a bad storm like she was"). Against this over-arching pattern of causality-based judgments, we can now take a closer look at where the religious and secular children diverged.

Inspection of Figure 14.1 reveals a clear-cut difference for the religious stories. As compared to religious children, secular children were less likely to say that the story was factual—and more likely to say that it was fictional. Again, an analysis of children's justifications cast more light on this difference. When secular children mentioned the sequence of events in the story, they almost always rejected it as impossible (e.g., "Because, well, I don't think anybody could walk on water but I think it's possible that they could swim"). By contrast, children with a religious background were more divided in their thinking. Although some of them referred to the impossibility of the causal sequence (e.g., "God can make some miracles, but he wouldn't be able to do this. You can't make someone walk on water"), others endorsed the possibility of such a sequence (e.g., "Because she prayed to God that she could walk on water and she thought anything was possible and God made that happen").

In sum, irrespective of their family background, children drew a boundary between stories that were consistent with causal regularities or defied those regularities. They typically judged most magical and a considerable number of religious stories as fictional, and in justifying those judgments, they produced a large number of cause-based judgments often referring to the impossibility of the causal sequence described. By contrast, children typically judged unusual and especially realistic stories, as factual, and went on to endorse rather than deny the plausibility of causal sequence. Children's religious background did not override this overarching division between the stories that were consistent versus inconsistent with causal regularities. Nevertheless, children's background did have a localized impact. Secular children rarely endorsed the causal sequence in religious stories whereas religious children were more prone to do so.

What do these findings imply for the two hypotheses introduced earlier? Given that children from secular and religious backgrounds were equally likely to appraise the reality status of the story on the basis of its causal plausibility, we can reasonably dismiss the "unconstrained reality" hypothesis, which asserted that a religious education might undermine children's overall tendency to think in causal terms. The "divine" power hypothesis, on the other hand, is strengthened: secular children were likely to judge religious stories as fictional and to reject the possibility of divine intervention whereas religious children were more prone to judge the story as factual and to endorse the possibility of divine intervention.

At the same time, the findings indicate that secular and religious children are broadly similar in the way that they think about different types of narrative. They think of them as arranged along a continuum ranging from the magical and fictional at one extreme to the realistic and factual at the other extreme. Yet, they differ in their assessment of religious stories. Given their assumptions about the plausibility of divine intervention, religious children are more prone than secular children to "displace" religious stories toward the factual end of the continuum.

Thinking about What Might Have Happened Instead

The "divine power" hypothesis implies that exposure to religious teaching changes the way that children think about the possibility of divine intervention. There are, however, two ways in which that change in thinking might manifest itself. One possibility is that exposure to religious teaching has an impact on children's spontaneous thinking. Religious children might be more prone than secular children to speculate about and propose the possibility of divine intervention. An alternative possibility is that the impact is primarily on children's receptivity to possibilities proposed to them by other people. Counterfactual thinking, in which children engage in "thought experiments" by imagining whether things could have turned out differently if an alternative course of action had been taken (Harris et al., 1996), provides an ideal context for exploring these two issues (Harris, 2021).

Payir and her colleagues presented children attending either secular or religious schools with stories in which a character experienced a negative outcome (e.g., a farmer had a bad crop due to a drought) (Payir et al., 2022). After the presentation of each story, children's counterfactual thinking was probed in two different ways. First, to explore what preventive measures children would generate spontaneously (i.e., without any explicit suggestions from the experimenter), they were invited to speculate on how the negative outcome could have been prevented. Second, to examine children's receptivity to explicit suggestions, the interviewer invited them to consider four potential preventive measures: one consistent with natural causal laws and three that defied those laws, namely (i): a divine intervention via prayer; (ii) a mental intervention via the making of a wish; and (iii) a magical intervention via magical powers. Children judged whether or not each intervention could have led to a change in the outcome and justified their response. Finally, children were invited to choose the intervention that "could have been most helpful" in preventing the negative outcome.

When invited to engage in their own speculation about preventive measures, children rarely invoked supernatural causes. With few exceptions, the alternatives that they generated were consistent with natural causal laws (e.g., "If only he had watered the berries more"). In addition, as seen in Figure 14.2, children's evaluation of the four proposed interventions largely depended on whether these interventions were consistent or inconsistent with natural causal laws. Thus, regardless of their age and family background, children often endorsed the plausibility of the naturalistic intervention but frequently denied the plausibility of the mental and magical interventions. Children's justifications for their endorsement—or lack of endorsement—further solidified these patterns. They often referred to the efficacy of a naturalistic intervention when justifying why it would have successfully prevented the negative outcome (e.g., "Because then the plants would have had more water which would help"). Conversely, they often denied the effectiveness of mental and magical intervention when justifying why these would have brought no change in the outcome (e.g., "Because wishing

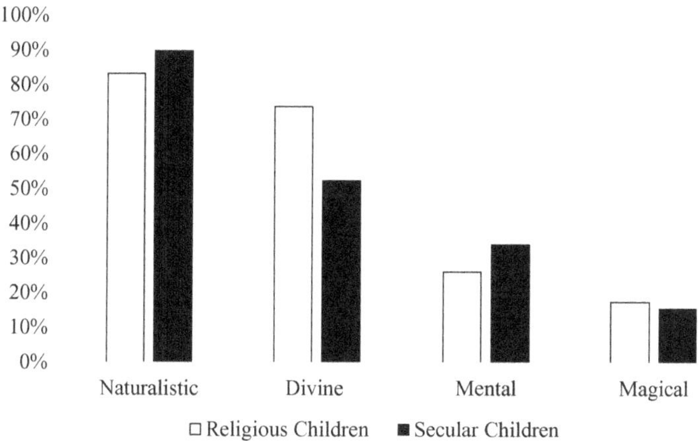

Figure 14.2 Percentage of endorsement for each type of intervention as a function of children's religious background (religious, secular).

won't affect the berries"; "A fairy came out of nowhere … Woo! All the plants grew! I don't think that's likely.").

Nevertheless, children's evaluation of proposed divine interventions did reveal a significant effect of background. Compared to secular children, religious children were more likely to judge divine intervention as plausible and to distinguish divine intervention from the other two non-naturalistic interventions (i.e., mental and magical). Indeed, religious children explicitly endorsed the effectiveness of this type of intervention when justifying why it would have worked (e.g., "Because God would make a storm, a lightning storm!"; "Because God can do almost everything in the world"). By contrast, children attending secular schools were more dubious about the possibility of such an intervention (e.g., "Because it's more of a belief rather than something actually impacting the berries").

Finally, recall that children were invited to choose the particular intervention—among the four with which they were presented (i.e., naturalistic, divine, mental, and magical)—that could have been most helpful in preventing the negative outcome. Children's responses to this question confirmed the conclusions drawn from their judgments and justifications. As expected, irrespective of age and family background, children rarely considered mental and magical intervention to be the best intervention. However, children's background did influence their preference for naturalistic as compared to divine intervention. The children attending secular schools overwhelmingly preferred the naturalistic intervention as the best option, dismissing the divine intervention with little hesitation. The preferences of the children attending parochial schools were more divided. Their best option preferences included the divine, as well as the naturalistic intervention.

In sum, in their spontaneous counterfactuals and their best option preferences, children drew a clear boundary between events that are consistent or inconsistent with ordinary causal regularities, confirming the earlier findings (Payir et al., 2022). When invited to generate counterfactuals about how a negative outcome could have been prevented, children did not spontaneously generate supernatural measures. Even when presented with such preventive measures, they judged the mental and magical measures as implausible and ineffective whereas they judged naturalistic interventions as both plausible and effective. Nevertheless, despite this overall differentiation between natural and supernatural preventive measures, religious children displayed some receptivity to divine intervention. When the interviewer invited them to consider various counterfactual alternatives, they often judged divine intervention as plausible, and they often endorsed this intervention as the best option.

By contrast, secular children were more dubious about its plausibility, and they rarely selected it as the best option.

These findings help to refine the conclusions drawn in the previous section. When left to their own devices, children from secular and religious backgrounds were equally unlikely to invoke supernatural interventions. The paucity of divine interventions in children's spontaneous counterfactual thinking not only helps us to dismiss the "unconstrained reality" hypothesis, it also shows that a religious education does not impact children's self-generated or spontaneous thoughts about causality. Nevertheless, exposure to religion does appear to impact children's receptivity to the idea of divine intervention. Religious children often judged divine interventions to be plausible and, in their justifications, they endorsed its effectiveness whereas secular children had a more skeptical stance toward divine intervention—both in their plausibility judgments and in their justifications. In sum, these findings provide further evidence for a refinement of the 'divine powers' hypothesis. They show that a religious education leads children to accept that divine intervention can change the course of events even if that thought rarely occurs to them spontaneously.

Conclusions

We began our chapter with the claim that narratives serve as a key framework for children to organize their experience (Bruner, 1993). Given this claim, we argued that the different kinds of narratives that children hear in their community, and the consensus surrounding the reality status of these narratives, might impact how children judge what can and cannot happen in real life. The evidence reviewed in this chapter lends support to this claim. Starting from a young age, children understand the fundamental distinction between factual stories about real protagonists and fictional stories about made-up protagonists using the plausibility of the key elements in the story as a guide. Exposure to religious teaching has a targeted impact on this understanding, encouraging children to believe in the power of divine intervention. Nevertheless, it leaves broader aspects of children's causal understanding untouched, given that, like their more secular counterparts, religious children think in terms of a hierarchy of causal likelihood, ranging from magical implausibility through realistic plausibility. We speculate that this hierarchy is a universal—found across all cultures—but needless to say more research is needed to establish this claim.

Our conclusion that children's imagination is reality-based, and in that respect is quite pedestrian, may seem to be at odds with the common portrayal of children as having a weak grasp of the distinction between fantasy and reality, and prone to entertain unusual or magical possibilities (Harris, 2000). After all, if children are very conservative about what is possible and what is not, why do they readily consume children's fiction which involves ordinarily impossible characters, events, and transformations?

Recent findings indicate that young children's supposed preference for such unrealistic or fantastical content might not exist. For example, given a choice between realistic and fantastical stories, four- to five-year-olds do not show a preference for fantastical stories (Barnes, Bernstein, and Bloom, 2015). Similarly, when presented with realistic and fantastical stories and asked how to continue those stories, four-year-olds mostly opt for a realistic continuation, regardless of the story type (Weisberg et al., 2013). Furthermore, even when presented with unrealistic events, young children come up with realistic explanations for them. For example, having judged that it is not possible to have a pet unicorn, six- to seven-year-olds also explain that the person might have "won [it] at the farm in like a different country" (Nancekivell and Friedman, 2017).

In sum, although a great deal of fiction written for children include supernatural elements, there is little indication that children take these elements as real. In contrast with the rich imagination that adults typically attribute to them, children's imagination seems to be grounded in their naturalistic understanding of everyday reality. It needs to be inspired by external input, such as children's stories or a religious education, to entertain more exotic possibilities. This conclusion does not imply that children cannot enjoy fiction with supernatural elements; like adults, children can be absorbed in fiction of every kind, but their understanding of the distinction between reality and fantasy stays intact.

Works Cited

Barnes, Jennifer L., Emily Bernstein, and Paul Bloom. 2015. "Fact or Fiction? Children's Preferences for Real versus Make-Believe Stories." *Imagination, Cognition and Personality* 34: 243–58. https://doi.org/10.1177/0276236614568632.

Bruner, Jerome S. 1993. *Acts of Meaning.* Cambridge, MA: Harvard University Press.

Corriveau, Kathleen H., Eva E. Chen, and Paul L. Harris. 2015. "Judgments About Fact and Fiction by Children from Religious and Non-Religious Backgrounds." *Cognitive Science* 39: 353–82. https://doi.org/10.1111/cogs.12138.

Corriveau, Kathleen H., and Paul L. Harris. 2015. "Children's Developing Realization That Some Stories Are True: Links to the Understanding of Beliefs and Signs." *Cognitive Development* 34: 76–87. https://doi.org/10.1016/j.cogdev.2014.12.005.

Corriveau, Kathleen H., A. L. Kim, C. Schwalen, and Paul L. Harris. 2009. "Abraham Lincoln and Harry Potter: Children's Differentiation between Historical and Fantasy Characters." *Cognition* 112: 213–25. https://doi.org/10.1016/j.cognition.2009.08.007.

Davoodi, Telli, Kathleen H. Corriveau, and Paul L. Harris. 2016. "Distinguishing Between Realistic and Fantastical Figures in Iran." *Developmental Psychology* 52: 221–31. https://psycnet.apa.org/doi/10.1037/dev0000079.

Harris, Paul L. 2000. *The Work of the Imagination.* Oxford: Blackwell.

Harris, Paul L. 2021. "Early Constraints on the Imagination: The Realism of Young Children." *Child Development* 92: 466–83. https://doi.org/10.1111/cdev.13487.

Harris, Paul L., Tim German, and Patrick Mills. 1996. "Children's Use of Counterfactual Thinking in Causal Reasoning." *Cognition* 61: 233–59. https://doi.org/10.1016/S0010-0277(96)00715-9.

Lever, Rosemary, and Monique Sénéchal. 2011. "Discussing Stories: On How a Dialogic Reading Intervention Improves Kindergartners' Oral Narrative Construction." *Journal of Experimental Child Psychology* 108: 1–24. https://doi.org/10.1016/j.jecp.2010.07.002.

Miller, Peggy J., Randolph Potts, Heidi Fung, Lisa Hoogstra, and Judy Mintz. 1990. "Narrative Practices and the Social Construction of Self in Childhood. *American Ethnologist* 17: 292–311. https://doi.org/10.1525/ae.1990.17.2.02a00060.

Nancekivell, Shaylene E., and Ori Friedman. 2017. "She Bought the Unicorn from the Pet Store: Six-to Seven-Year-Olds are Strongly Inclined to Generate Natural Explanations." *Developmental Psychology* 53: 1079–87. https://doi.org/10.1037/dev0000311.

Payir, Ayse, Larisa Heiphetz, Paul L. Harris, and Kathleen H. Corriveau. 2022. "What Could Have Been Done? Counterfactual Alternatives to Negative Outcomes by Religious and Secular Children." *Developmental Psychology* 58: 376–91. https://psycnet.apa.org/doi/10.1037/dev0001294.

Payir, Ayse, Niamh Mcloughlin, Yixin Kelly Cui, Telli Davoodi, Jennifer M. Clegg, Paul L. Harris, and Kathleen H. Corriveau. 2021. "Children's Ideas about What Can Really Happen: The Impact of Age and Religious Background." *Cognitive Science* 4: e13054. https://doi.org/10.1111/cogs.13054.

Shtulman, Andrew, and Susan Carey. 2007. "Improbable or Impossible? How Children Reason about the Possibility of Extraordinary Events." *Child Development* 78: 1015–32. https://doi.org/10.1111/j.1467-8624.2007.01047.x.

Weisberg, Deena Skolnick, David M. Sobel, Joshua Goodstein, and Paul Bloom. 2013. "Young Children Are Reality-Prone When Thinking about Stories. *Journal of Cognition and Culture* 13: 383–407. https://doi.org/10.1163/15685373-12342100.

15

FROM SUSPENSION OF DISBELIEF TO PRODUCTION OF BELIEF

The Case of Alternate Reality Games

Patrick Jagoda

Introduction: Fictionality in the Twenty-First Century

Fiction exceeds the narratives told across the pages of a novel or through the moving images of a serial television program. Critics such as Kendall Walton (1990) and Jean-Marie Schaeffer (2010) have analyzed the importance of fiction beyond fictional texts, especially in the ways that the mode influences humanity at developmental and existential levels—for instance, through activities such as make-believe or faculties such as the imagination. Along similar lines, Henrik Skov Nielsen, James Phelan, and Richard Walsh (2015) identify a widespread cultural dimension of fiction that they call "fictionality." As a mode, fictionality emerges in domains as diverse as politics, technology, and sports. In proposing this category, Nielsen et al. foreground three key moves that characterize it. First, they argue that fictionality is a mode that exceeds fiction as a constellation of genres that appear across media forms. In other words, a fictional discourse can operate in everyday conversation outside of the context of a fictive text that uses broadly recognizable conventions to call for the "suspension of disbelief" in Samuel Taylor Coleridge's famous phrase (62). Second, fictionality is not a matter of circumventing, obscuring, or ignoring reality or the truth. Instead, fictionality can also serve as a generative "means for negotiating an engagement with that world" (63). Third, in exceeding both narrative genres and a mere opposition to the truth, fictionality can be understood as "a fundamental cognitive skill" that allows people to create and communicate without referring to real-world referents (63). In all of these ways, fictionality calls for a *rhetorical* approach to fictive discourse insofar as it asks "how somebody uses particular techniques, strategies, and means to achieve particular ends in relation to particular audience(s)" (63).

While fictionality has both transhistorical manifestations and cultural variations, we have seen an interest in the sociopolitical power of fiction—if not yet fictionality—emerge through late twentieth- and early twenty-first-century media cultures that exist alongside the realm of computation, networked connectivity, and digital interactive games. This curiosity is particularly evident in popular films and television series from the 1990s through the 2010s. Notably, these moving image media do not participate in the rhetoric of fictionality, but do express a fear about fiction as a social and cognitive strategy that exceeds the contained fictional text in closer alignment with Jean Baudrillard's theory of simulation (1994). Though such media can be traced back to earlier films such as *Videodrome* (1983), a thick cluster of films in the late 1990s depict a fictional world that covers over a true world for either an individual or the majority of the world's population. These films, which draw

DOI: 10.4324/9781003119456-18

196

on earlier conspiracy films but with a specific emphasis on digital technologies, include *Abre los ojos* (1997), *The Game* (1997), *The Truman Show* (1998), *The Matrix* (1999), *eXistenZ* (1999), and *The Thirteenth Floor* (1999). Such films stage the dramas of the blurring of fiction and truth through the epistemological and sensory confusion occasioned by media technologies, especially virtual reality and video games. At the most fundamental level, the reality that the protagonist in each of these films occupies is revealed, for one reason or another, to be a fiction. Representations of simulacra or virtual undecidability have continued since that moment with popular films such as *Inception* (2010) and television series such as *Black Mirror* (2011).

Alongside representations of the power of fiction, hybrid reality television and documentary media have harnessed this power by creating elaborate scenarios in which viewers are incorporated into the production of a fiction, but in which one or more people within the production do not understand that what they are experiencing is a fiction. This work, which more precisely explores fictionality as a rhetorical strategy, includes much of the comedic work of Sacha Baron Cohen, including *Da Ali G Show* (2000), *Borat! Cultural Learnings of America for Make Benefit Glorious Nation of Kazakhstan* (2006), and *Who Is America?* (2018), which constructs a fictional frame in order to test the limits of people, both ordinary individuals and public figures, in conforming to normative or discriminatory structures. Even more experimental applications of fictional constructs, which select participants believe to be true or undesigned, include Derren Brown's Netflix specials *The Push* (2016) and *Sacrifice* (2018). In these series, constructed situations condition participants to engage in risky actions that might run contrary to their usual behaviors. Other media have even gone as far as to exclude viewers from knowing about their fictionality or constructedness at all. Here, we might include the found footage conceit of *The Blair Witch Project* (1999) as well as alleged documentaries that might be fictive productions such as *Exit through the Gift Shop* (2010) or *Catfish* (2010). Unlike the fictional works in which the viewer encounters fictionality at a spectatorial remove or critical distance, media objects that blur their status implicate the viewer in the negotiation of fictionality and sometimes cause frustration through their deception. In these cases, the precise line between fiction and documentary is never fully disclosed or confirmed.

In this chapter, I would like to take up a limit case of fictional realities: the Alternate Reality Game (ARG). Admittedly, the ARG remains a much less popular or even recognizable media form than the video game. Fundamentally, an ARG is a narrative-driven experience that includes interactive challenges across both online and offline settings. As one of the earliest designers of these games, Sean Stewart puts it, an ARG has four key formal features. First, the narrative is decentralized and dependent on audience assembly. Pieces of that narrative might exist across social media platforms, websites, and live encounters. Second, unlike a video game, an ARG story is not conveyed via a single screen, medium, or platform. It is "transmedia" in the sense that it might travel from a TikTok video to a Twitch livestream to a live meetup. Third, at least ideally, the audience of an ARG is substantial. A standard multiplayer video game tends to limit the number of players. For example, a cooperative video game like *It Takes Two* (2021) allows for two players or a competitive racing game like *Mario Kart 8 Deluxe* (2017) can accommodate up to eight players via wireless play. Even more expansive video games tend to limit their player counts, for reasons of balance or server capacity. For example, popular games such as *Tetris 99* (2019) limit the player count at 99 and *Fortnite* (2017) allows up to one hundred players per game. By distinction, ARGs attempt to accommodate between several hundred to millions of players to participate in their shared worlds—and indeed may even rely on such numbers for their collaborative worldbuilding. Fourth, Stewart emphasizes the improvisational dimension of ARGs, which invites an audience to co-create a story world and its progression through choices and inventions. As Kim et al. (2009) point out, across these qualities, "the overarching story line ties together all of the elements of an ARG into a cohesive whole," though here a fictional narrative that is not merely composed by the designers but is augmented or fully co-created by the players.

To offer a brief example, one of the earliest examples of an ARG was *The Beast* (2001). The game was produced by Microsoft as a tie-in to Steven Spielberg's film *A.I. Artificial Intelligence*, though was never announced explicitly, *as a game*, when it began. Through clues that were subtly hidden in the film trailer and other promotional materials, participants began to follow a person named Jeanine Salla who was investigating the death of a friend and a conspiracy that surrounded it. The trail led to over forty websites and a series of puzzles. Thousands of players organized on the Yahoo! Group Cloudmakers message board on April 11, 2001, to make sense of this unknown development, and the ARG finished on July 24, 2001. After this time, several notable ARGs attracted from thousands to millions of players, including *I Love Bees* (2004), *Year Zero* (2007), *The Lost Ring* (2008), and *Potato Sack* (2011).

The form of the ARG arguably draws on a longer constellation of historical precursors, including fictional narratives from paranoid postmodern literature to science fiction and mystery films; experimental games and play from Fluxus event scores to the New Games Movement; performance art from Happenings to the Yes Men; and network art from mail art to netprov. Even as this important genealogy deserves greater attention, it is important to note that ARGs are exemplary of both the early twenty-first-century media ecology and the centrality of fictionality within it. Alongside the formal elements that Stewart foregrounds, perhaps the aspect that most centrally characterizes ARGs is the "This Is Not a Game" aesthetic. This line was originally a slogan for *The Beast* itself. Yet, with time, it developed into a hallmark of the form. Unlike a traditional fiction, an ARG does not announce itself *as a game or fictional object*. That is, this experience embeds itself within the media platforms that sustain its narrative in such a way that its status as fiction or reality is unknown. Instead of encountering a start screen, as one might in a video game, the player of an ARG might receive a friend request from someone on Facebook, follow an anomaly on a paper flyer, or discover a strange TikTok video that points to a network of other media. In most cases, these games begin with a so-called rabbit hole that might be viral video or a compelling puzzle that draws potential players into the narrative world. Admittedly, the ARG experience varies among different players. For example, in the early- to mid-2000s, almost no one would have participated in an ARG. By the 2010s, following several widely publicized (if rarely played) ARGs, designers adapted to greater saturation of the form by inventing new methods for defamiliarizing such an experience in order to distinguish it from a composed fiction or game. Over time, the ARG has lost some of its novelty and there are communities of players that pursue such experiences—via online communities such as ARGNet—with full knowledge that they are fictional. Even so, the form remains peripheral or rare enough as to lack that consistency of reception that we might expect of a novel, thereby giving ongoing, if differential, force to the This Is Not a Game aesthetic.

In this chapter, I explore the ARG as an affirmation of fictionality beyond fiction. Unlike a literary or cinematic work of fiction, which engages in a *suspension of disbelief*, ARGs are capable of facilitating a *production of belief*. Such belief might take many forms, including unconscious confidence in the nonfictive status of a piece of media that serves as a rabbit hole, conscious trust in the truth of a scenario or organization at its center, or even a behavioral belief that might spur direct action or response beyond the consumption of a narrative. While most ARGs may capture this belief-producing energy for only a short period, they offer a model for generating bottom-up belief in the form of shared worldmaking and the process of living a fiction (beyond reading or viewing it) *as* an extension of reality. Before returning at greater length to ARGs and what they have to teach us about fiction and belief, I want to think through two other cases that blur fiction and reality, and sometimes even have effects on belief: Method acting and Live Action Roleplaying Games. Both forms can be said to directly inform aspects of the ARG at levels of performance, roleplaying, and gameplay. At the same time, neither form exceeds the suspension of disbelief to the same extent that the ARG is able to accomplish. Ultimately, I contend that thinking alongside ARGs can teach us something valuable about its own historical moment that has been characterized by "post-truth" politics and "fake news" facilitated by algorithmic bias. Despite myriad misuses of fictionality in the early twenty-first century, ARGs provide a model for the potential of fictionality to experiment with new ideas and organize communities to co-create more equitable and just worlds together.

Method Acting and the Fictional "If"

Method acting provides one way of thinking about how an ARG might engage in a production of belief that differs from the more common fictional suspension of disbelief. Method acting names a collective of training techniques derived from practitioners starting with Konstantin Stanislavski and extending to students of the techniques such as Lee Strasberg and Stella Adler. Stanislavski served as the director of the Moscow Art Theater since 1898 where, as performance studies scholar Shonni Enelow observes, he "experimented with a naturalistic theatrical style, instructing actors to ignore the audience and attempting to inspire their belief in the actuality of the scene" (Enelow, 2015, 7). Though a popular uptake of Method acting came to treat it as quintessentially or even overly theatrical and unrealistic, the original technique sought to tap into the authenticity of an actor's feeling within a fictional production. The system was imported to the US and gained greater visibility after the translation of Stanislavski's *An Actor Prepares* in 1936 and especially with Strasberg's Actors Studio space, which he ran from 1951 to 1982.

Enelow (2015) argues that, especially after this importation to the United States, Method acting resonated with key cultural and media dimensions of the 1950s and 1960s—just as I would argue that alternate reality games resonate with the media ecology of the 2000s and 2010s. Enelow situates the rise of Method alongside experimental film, and performance scholar Jacob Gallagher-Ross contends that Method in the United States is indebted to the mid-century role of both image and audio recording technologies, including the naturalistic details captured by cinema (Gallagher-Ross, 2015, 294). Again, at a later moment, I see alternate reality games, as a cultural form, similarly emerging alongside and becoming embedded within the world wide web, video game culture, and the emergence of transmedia storyworlds starting in the 2000s.

Method acting offers an insightful comparison to ARGs because of the blurring it introduces between the real and the fictional. Lee Strasberg, drawing as much from Evgeni Vakhtangov as from Stanislavski, was less insistent that an actor "imagines herself in the same circumstances as her character" than that she "uses her own emotions" to inhabit the character (Enelow, 2015, 10). The fictional production here becomes reliant on the truthfulness or authenticity of the motivation for the performance. Stanislavski was invested in Method as "an art of 'experiencing' " as opposed to older approaches of " 'craftsmanship' and 'representation' " that he found to be more constructed and less genuine (Enelow, 2015, 8).

Method acting sometimes enters into ARG productions where participants might inhabit the world of the experience for weeks or months at a time. In many cases, ARG participants play versions of themselves who find themselves in the middle of a conspiracy or fantastical situation. Nevertheless, from its genesis, though allowing for variations across practitioners, Method acting still belongs to the realm of suspended disbelief. On the one hand, in *An Actor Prepares*, Stanislavski ([1936] 1948) argues that "all action in the theatre must have an inner justification, be logical, coherent, and real" (43). Despite this foundation in emotional reality rather than fictional representation, he also insists on the importance of the fictional and conditional "if" to Method. As he puts it, "*if* acts as a lever to lift us out of the world of actuality into the realm of imagination" (43). Indeed, Stanislavski seeks to avoid a confusion or blurring between reality and fiction. Through his directorial persona in the text, he tells his students, "With this special quality of *if* … nobody obliges you to believe or not believe anything. Everything is clear, honest, and above-board" (44). In addition to differentiating clearly between reality and fiction, the "if" motivates real action but should not be confused with reality. Whereas "truth" is "what really exists, what a person really knows," action on a stage "consists of something that is not actually in existence but which could happen" (121). In other words, the attachment of Method is to a *potential* or *virtual* reality. The actor develops a belief but it is a belief in herself, her collaborators, and an emotional state rather than in the actual truth of the situation. In some ways, this belief parallels what Kendall Walton (1990) calls "the experience of being 'caught up in a story,' emotionally involved in the world of a novel or play or painting," as with the "quasi-fear" a viewer might feel while watching a horror film (6 and 196). In Stanislavski's case, however, belief applies to the performer and not, as for Walton, the reader or spectator.

Though ARGs engage the fictional and conditional "if" in some respects, I will argue that their goal is the production of belief, instead of an instrumental engagement with potentiality that still emphasizes the suspension of disbelief. Before doing so, however, I offer one other brief comparative case: the Live Action Roleplaying Game.

Live Action Roleplaying Games and "Bleed"

Live Action Roleplaying Games (LARPs) are interactive fictional performances in which players roleplay and perform their characters, usually in a shared physical real-world environment. Inspired by tabletop roleplaying games like *Dungeons and Dragons*, as well as improvisational theater, such game worlds are often designed by game runners or designers and populated by players. Unlike ARGs, LARPs do not call their fictional status into question, and invite players to participate knowingly in their constructed worlds. Despite this clear fictional frame, LARPs still risk confusing reality and fiction, a risk and opportunity that this form shares with Method acting. As Strasberg (1987) emphasizes, the Method draws on "affective memory" to create "a real experience on the stage" (113), a state that entails "a fear of losing control" (116).

In LARPs, the inadvertent slippage between reality and fiction is most visible in the phenomenon of "bleed." Arguably, the possibility of lost control over a performance becomes even riskier in LARPs than in Method acting, both because the scenario is fully interactive and dependent on player improvisations, and also because it is usually performed by players who are not professional actors. Though the LARP's "magic circle" of gameplay (to use Johan Huizinga's term) demarcates a space and time that exists outside of everyday life, the boundary of this circle is permeable (10). As game designer Sarah Lynne Bowman (2015) explains, players agree to a series of "social rules" that enable the game to proceed. Such rules may govern the characters in the fictional world, dictating that player 1 is a werewolf and player 2 is a vampire and that they are both in a gothic cyberpunk world rather than a contemporary community center. Moreover, real-world rules might still apply to gameplay—for instance, that players should not touch or hug others without their explicit consent. Beyond this contract, players have a fictional alibi that dictates that the actions of their characters are not actions that the player in the real world has actually taken or even would take (Bowman, 2015).

Bowman argues that even as roleplaying might be seen as "consequence free," in practice, "roleplayers sometimes experience moments where their real life feelings, thoughts, relationships, and physical states spill over into their characters' and vice versa." In other words, the LARP's fictionality can have effects on the players' lives outside of the game in ways of which they might not be fully conscious or of which they are conscious but cannot easily control. Based on her experience as a LARP designer and player, Bowman identifies two key forms of bleed: "bleed-in" and "bleed-out." These types of influence can be experienced as either positive or negative. First, bleed-in happens when "the emotions, thoughts, relationship dynamics, and physical states of the player affect the character." A positive instance of bleed-in might involve a player's real-world background as a medical professional enabling a more detailed improvisation when a character is injured in battle. A negative example might entail a preexisting hostility or rivalry between two players that influences a relationship between two characters who should otherwise be allies or friends within the game's diegesis. Second, bleed-out happens when a character trait or scenario that concerns a character influences real-world player feelings when they leave the game. For example, two players who are married within the LARP might begin to develop feelings for one another outside of the game—or only one of them might experience this type of bleed.

Unlike ARGs, the culture of LARPs foregrounds and enforces lines between in-game play and out-of-game interactions, before, during, and following gameplay. In particular, LARPs rely on explicit "in-game signaling" to minimize bleed (Bowman, 2015). Olga Vorobyeva (2015) lays out a typology of such signals that allow players to move between frames of fiction and reality. These may include a "verbal marker" or "safeword" and "non-verbal markers" such as gestures or facial expressions such as winks. Such tools allow players to dial down the intensity of an interaction or to clarify which elements are fictive and which are not. Bowman also suggests other strategies for transitioning out of a fiction, including "out-of-game socializing," "writing" and journaling, and "becoming immersed in other experiences."

By distinction to LARPs, ARGs rely on the This Is Not a Game aesthetic I mentioned in the introduction. While the experience might include the signs of a designed game, and players might speculate about its origins on message boards or chat platforms, the location of the fictional line or status of the event is usually not confirmed during gameplay. One exception to this rule, which both LARPs and ARGs might have in common, are the use of debriefing sessions—sometimes known as "de-roleing" in LARPs (Bowman). Following days, weeks, or months of gameplay, most ARGs reveal themselves as games after the experience reaches its conclusion. Though this debriefing might be delayed, in comparison to the ongoing frame checks of a LARP, an ARG still enables players to share and process feelings together, and to enter into dialogue with the designers or game runners.

As this brief overview of LARPs suggests, these games enforce a partial suspension of disbelief within a fictional world that encourages immersion but also gives players easy ways to move out of the experience. Like Method acting, beyond the "as if," the LARP does not seek to create belief in the reality or truthfulness of any part of the unfolding scenario.

Alternate Reality Games and the Production of Belief

To give a clearer sense of how an ARG operates, I begin this section with two brief examples from ARGs that I have co-directed and co-designed. Unlike entertainment-focused ARGs such as *The Beast*, both of these ARGs were serious or learning-oriented games. Though I have worked on ARGs focused predominantly on entertainment and artistic goals, I put forward these cases to think more explicitly about the ways that fictional games can generate the production of belief and influence real-world processes. To differing degrees, both cases used a This Is Not a Game aesthetic to blur the lines between fiction and reality.

The first ARG, *S.E.E.D.*, took place in 2014 for a group of primarily Black and brown high school students on the South Side of Chicago. I have written about this game at greater length in another context, but I will offer a brief summary here (Jagoda, 2022). The core of this transmedia experience unfolded both in person on the University of Chicago campus and online for three intensive weeks of gameplay. The narrative premise of the game was that a group of scientists (the Temporal Archivists) at the University had invented a temporal communication device (the titular S.E.E.D.) that opened up a channel for sending and receiving messages to the near future. Instead of merely positing the existence of this device, our design team built an elaborate model of it and used Method-acting-adjacent processes to inhabit the role of Temporal Archivists for three weeks. The purpose of this ARG was to use a speculative fiction format to motivate underrepresented youth to move into STEM fields and to put forward a vision of STEM that was founded in principles of social justice. During the weeks of gameplay, many of the students demonstrably believed in the reality of the S.E.E.D. device and the Temporal Archivists, as they undertook challenges and played games that introduced them to the scientific process, public health, mathematical cryptography, and more. Moreover, during the debriefing session that followed the game, when the designers revealed the constructedness of the preceding weeks, several students admitted their belief in and attachment to the ARG's shared world.

The second ARG, *Cene*, took place in 2022 for middle schoolers in three schools on the South Side of Chicago. This game, which did not announce itself explicitly as a game or fictional experience, also ran for nearly three weeks and took the place of an environmental science and climate change curriculum. In February and March 2022, over 350 middle school students at Bret Harte Elementary, UChicago Woodlawn Charter, and the Laboratory Schools completed over 2,500 team-based quests. The narrative posited another communication channel with a group called the Keepers who were curators of a constellation of possible futures known as the Possibility Space. Even more than *S.E.E.D.*, *Cene* used contemporary media platforms to add immersion to gameplay and diminish the fictional frame. Whereas *S.E.E.D.* relied on live-action interactions and YouTube videos in 2014, *Cene*'s realism came from a different media environment in 2022. The participants interacted with the Keepers via a website but also a livestreaming platform created by media artist Marc Downie. On that platform, we used a glitchy aesthetic and an acting style that drew not on theater or film acting as much as Twitch streamer interactions with their audience to contribute a provisional plausibility to an otherwise science fictional narrative.

In order to think about the real-world effects of ARGs such as *S.E.E.D.* and *Cene*, it is important to delve deeper into the This Is Not a Game aesthetic. This aspect of ARGs can make people uncomfortable, because of the ways it blurs fiction and reality by not confirming to players that they are engaging in a designed experience. As a designer of such games, I am often asked whether my ARGs engage in unethical dynamics by attempting to convince people that their fictions are real. This type of question, while important, often assumes a reductive concept of ethics as a permanent fidelity to transparency. More importantly, this question also produces a false opposition between fiction on the one hand and reality, truth, and belief on the other, instead of acknowledging the ways that fiction can sometimes produce reality, clarify truth, and condition belief in generative ways.

Furthermore, the discomfort with the status of ARGs is not unique to this form and has attached to ideas about fiction for millennia. The Western distrust of fiction is apparent as early as Plato's *Republic* (circa 375 BCE). Arguably the most famous portion of the text, the allegory of the Cave (which directly informs several of the contemporary films I mentioned in the introduction such as *The Matrix*) already constructs a binary between mere fictional and false images versus the true knowledge of the Forms. Briefly, Plato imagines people imprisoned in a Cave in which they can only see shadows on a wall as others pass on a bridge behind them and cast these shadows with real objects. Since the prisoners only see shadows, they mistake these fictional images for the reality of the things themselves. As Socrates puts it in the text, "The realm revealed through sight should be likened to the prison dwelling" (517b1, 211). For Plato, truth can only be acquired by the prisoner who escapes these chains and travels to the surface where they witness the sun and the physical world. Plato's wariness of representation, mimesis, and art recurs in many other places in the *Republic*—not to mention Socrates's focused critique of poetry in the dialogue *Ion* in which he discusses the performance of Homer and Hesiod's works with the titular character, a rhapsode. In the *Republic* and elsewhere, Plato puts forward an early critique of epic poetry and acting—domains that extend most directly to contemporary fiction—as dangerous forms of mimesis and antitheses to philosophy. For him, imitation exploits our susceptibility to deception through the senses and keeps us from the truth that only philosophy can provide.

The anti-mimetic and anti-fictional values described by Plato are essential to a vision repeatedly promulgated by Western culture. Jean-Marie Schaeffer (2010) describes this as "the ambivalent attitude" toward fiction that combines "a mixture of fascination and distrust" surrounding mimesis (2). Versions of this ambivalence have recurred with virtually every new medium or popular artistic form. Beyond poetry, readers of novels in the eighteenth century (particularly women) were frequently treated as causing a variety of psychological, social, and physical harms: escapist self-indulgence, psychological tendencies toward imitation of harmful ideas, wasteful use of time that took away from labor, and physical harm to eyesight (Vogrinčič, 2008). By the twentieth century, similar discourses were extended to new media that became popular during this period. For example, television was criticized for producing escapist fictions, anti-intellectual ideas, addiction, and imitation of harmful behaviors (as evidenced by the common slogan, often used before American death-defying televisual stunts or fictional representations, "Don't try this at home!"). Since the late twentieth century, video games have also been critiqued for promoting violence, sexual perversions, and harmful mimesis that spills over from fiction to the real world—especially since the United States Senate hearings in 1993 that targeted games such as *Mortal Kombat* and *Night Trap*. As Schaeffer puts it, regarding the long-standing ambivalence about fiction, "only the target of the polemic has changed in the course of history" but "the values promoted by Platonic philosophy are the essential base of the vision of the world of Christian Occidental culture" (2010, 6, 14).

In all of these cases, from epic poetry to video games, the fear of a new medium and its fictional immersion yielded widespread moral panics and social critiques. It is not difficult to see, then, why ARGs, with their more layered relationship to fiction, might cause discomfort. Unlike all of these cases, which still explicitly announce the distinction between their fictional representation and the real world—not to mention the cases of Method acting or LARPs which promote greater blurring or immersive intensity but still insist on the short duration of that indistinction—ARGs refuse this distinction altogether, at least during the duration of gameplay. To put this another way, ARGs do not merely *suspend disbelief* but, at least for the period of gameplay, *produce belief* in the reality of the scenario as existing beyond the status of a designed game. Empirically, of course, ARGs went from an experimental and unknown form in the early 2000s, with experiences such as *The Beast* or *I Love Bees*, to a more familiar (if not yet popular) form by the 2010s. As such, players had all kinds of ways to discover and know that they were likely participating in a fictional gameplay experience. Nevertheless, this stabilization of a novel form into a genre was only familiar to a relatively small group of ARG enthusiasts, making a This Is Not a Game aesthetic viable with many audiences, with particular techniques of event conditioning, even in the 2020s. Moreover, even the small possibility that the experience might be nonfictional or indeed not a game was enough to produce a different type of engagement for many participants and a more substantial, if still provisional, belief in the co-created world.

ARGs exemplify a theory of fiction that departs from the idea of fiction as a classification of narrative genres or media forms that depict invented, imaginary, or feigned elements that are announced through either discursive or nonverbal signposts. In many ways, ARGs, even as they are still designed experiences, bring us closer to a theory of fictionality that exceeds the page or screen. As Schaeffer argues, even outside of the rhetorical frame adopted by Nielsen, Phelan, and Walsh, all fiction can be understood in a more fundamental way as a cultural competence and a unique frame on the world. For Schaeffer, Plato's model is one of affective "contagion" that stands in opposition to "rational knowledge" or well-argued rhetorical persuasion (Schaeffer, 2010, 17). Plato, then, reveals an "incapacity to recognize that mimetic 'contagion' *is* a type of knowledge and even in a way a type of knowledge that is more fundamental than that of dialectical reason and rational persuasion" (29–30). Instead of accepting fiction as pre-logical or false, Schaeffer proposes that we "integrate the Platonic point of view (imitation as feint) into the Aristotelian model (imitation as cognitive modelization)" (39). For Aristotle, theatrical mimesis and catharsis can serve to "displace real conflicts toward a purely representational level and to resolve them on this level" (36). In combining Plato and Aristotle's views, we might argue that even as fiction depicts something invented or feigned, this seeming deception can also serve as a basis for how we process, model, and engage reality at a psychological and social level. Indeed, I would add that Plato's own writing, which of course takes place through the persona of Socrates, repeatedly betrays the unique value of fiction. The narrative of the Cave is already an allegory or fiction that serves to animate and teach Glaucon (and the reader) about philosophy, reason, and the Forms. Pedagogical stories show up in other parts of the dialogue as well, including the fictional narrative or myth of the metals that animates the value of the "noble lie" or the Myth of Er that concludes the *Republic*.

Even as all fiction and the expanded field of fictionality can be understood as operating as both feint and cognitive modelization, ARGs more directly experiment with the power that comes with even a temporary belief in, rather than suspension of, a fictional construction. In a sense, this model is evident, even common, if we consider sociopolitical ideology. For example, harmful ideologies such as sexism or racism are essentially fictional constructions, since there is no empirical reason that gender or race should devalue certain human beings and elevate others. In Louis Althusser's famous definition, ideology depends on an imaginary frame insofar as ideology "represents individuals' imaginary relation to their real conditions of existence" (2014, 181). Certainly, imagination and fiction are not synonymous. Fiction involves imaginative capacities on both the part of the writer, designer, or speaker on the one hand and the reader on the other. At the same time, unlike the more open-ended category of imagination, fiction entails specifically narrative and systematic forms of worldbuilding. Even so, ideology arguably relies more on fiction (admittedly fiction that usually incorporates nonfictional components) than on a general capacity for imagination. A political movement like fascism or even more widespread prejudicial position such as anti-Semitism relies on a systematic worldbuilding process made up of personal stories, imagined conspiracies, sustained writings, designed aesthetics, multigenerational socialization, educational curricula, state propaganda, and other texts.

Unlike sociopolitical ideology, ARGs are of course a genre of games or transmedia stories. Yet, by producing belief, however temporary, they invite participants to inhabit their world—one that is composed of designed and fictional elements—while treating constructed elements as naturally occurring aspects of the real world. In other words, the ARG produces an "alternate reality" that integrates itself into the prior, dominant, or consensus reality. In this way, the ARG is both a designed fictional form and an experiment with fictionality. As Nielsen, Phelan, and Walsh (2015) argue, "Fictive communication may invite the reader or listener to map an engagement with representations of *what is not* onto *what is*. This mapping can substantially affect his or her sense and understanding of what is" (68). Schaeffer proposes two precise mechanisms for how such fictive contagion of the real might take place, even in cases when the fictive is clearly marked as such. First, there is "immersion" or "the permeability of the frontiers between fiction and reality" that we see in the case of a commitment by the LARP player to her explicitly signaled fictional scenario that may cause bleed. Second, there is "training" or "the modeling of reality by fiction" that we see in uses of imitation in education, behavior modification, or habit formation that may use fiction to condition reality (20). I am arguing that ARGs, without their clear-cut markers of fictional status, have the potential to achieve even greater degrees of both immersion and training.

ARGs are able to exceed the realm of *make-believe* as conscious pretending and to take on a world making and building power that can *make (a participant) believe* in an alternate reality. The "alternate" that modifies "reality" in "alternate reality game" demands a more precise conceptualization. The alternate is virtual but not in the sense of something not real. As philosopher Gilles Deleuze observes, "The virtual is opposed not to the real but to the actual" (2014, 272). That is, something virtual operates in the realm of differential potentiality prior to any eventual actualization. The fictions that ARGs posit can be understood in just this way. An ARG puts forward a possible or potential world that did not preexist the experience. While related to philosophical discussions of "possible worlds," this approach does not merely entail imagining a world to be possible via logical extrapolation but asks players to act *as* they are living, for the duration of the experience, in that possible world (Ryan, 2014). Here, the distinction between a traditional fiction and an ARG is important. A fictional novel is conventionally read by one person at a time and in silence. This fiction might later be discussed in a reading group or among members of a literature seminar, but the experience of the text tends to be individualistic. An ARG, by distinction, is experienced by a substantial group of players who inhabit that world together for an extended period. The ARG invites and brings into existence a community with shared coordinates and goals who, at some level, alter their behaviors, habits, and beliefs in order to make the potential world real and even actualized for a time. If a novel can be treated as a thought experiment about another world, an idea that possible world theories of fiction explore, an ARG is a material experiment with living in a possible world (Doležel, 1998; Ronen, 1994).

If we return now to Schaeffer's fictive contagion in the context of the ARGs with which I began this section—*S.E.E.D.* and *Cene*—we can see how an ARG might enable contagion that exceeds the fictional worldbuilding of ideology. First, both of these ARGs produced *immersion*, a permeability between fiction and reality, through Method acting, interactive roleplaying, detailed lore, and a refusal to confirm the event's fictionality. For three weeks, in both cases, participants *believed*, at different levels, in a communication channel to the future and the Possibility Space, respectively, without being told that this was only make-believe. Second, both experiences engaged in *training*, a use of fiction to model reality, through the integration of STEM and social justice curricula into gameplay. Both cases yielded intense engagement from the participating youth.

The immersion and training of these ARGs could admittedly have occurred without a blurring of fiction and reality, taking the form of a LARP. However, the added production of belief that we orchestrated elevated the experience from a thought experiment to a temporary experiment in alternative living. ARGs may share qualities of ideology and conventional fiction, but also depart from them. First, ideology relies on false consciousness or at least a conscious reproduction of someone else's sociopolitical project. Second, fiction invites "cognitive modelization," as Schaeffer argues, but largely puts forward an author's linear narrative, even as it relies on readerly interpretation (39). By distinction to both forms, ARGs promote more active forms of collaborative and improvisatory worldbuilding that are designed to depart from pre-authored narrative. That is, in both *S.E.E.D.* and *Cene*, players were invited to roleplay versions of themselves, alter the actions of characters, and determine significant elements of the world that they shared for those three weeks. Beyond prefabricated binary or limited decisions scripted by designers, players made qualitative contributions to the ARG storyworld that gave them a feeling of ownership and investment in this shared project.

After players came out of these two ARGs, and had a chance to debrief and discuss their experience, they still had the memory of at least partial belief in this other world, and the connections they had made with other people during the extended period of gameplay. That world was not merely one in which temporal or dimensional communication devices existed, but also one in which they were taken seriously as future STEM professionals (in *S.E.E.D.*) or innovators who could mitigate the existential threat of climate change (in *Cene*). The belief in another world was also an actualizable belief in their own capacity to engage in a life that was not previously imaginable to them to the same degree, either because of the underrepresentation of Black and brown people in STEM professions or the global and daunting threat of climate chance. For these players, the fictional world of these ARGs was not an imagined possibility but the memory of a material reality that they inhabited together and believed in for several weeks.

Conclusion: The Darker Side of Fictional Worldbuilding in an Algorithmic Era

The possibility that this chapter sketches out in the form of Alternate Reality Games is also a risk. The fear of fictional mimesis is evident as far back as Plato in the fourth century BCE. The risk of mimesis has also been exacerbated in contemporary and non-literary contexts, including infamous psychological studies such as the 1971 Stanford prison experiment—a prison simulation in which volunteers selected to play the role of guards and prisoners began to adopt many of the brutal qualities of those roles. Beyond this threat of behavioral imitation, however, we have seen a more substantial phenomenon emerge in the early twenty-first century with a production of belief rooted in fiction that does not declare itself as fiction. The nineteenth century already saw utopian groups and communes such as the Shakers, Fourierists, and Oneidans, and the twentieth century added intentional communities or cults such as Heaven's Gate, Aum Shinrikyo, and the Rajneeshpuram community that produced unique beliefs and maintained them through the production of alternative cultures. Arguably, most of these groups followed a shared philosophy or (as many would argue) a fiction that most followers came to believe. Regardless, these groups were still largely isolated and limited phenomena. With the emergence of the World Wide Web in the 1990s and the development of Web 2.0 in the 2000s, the nature and scale of global social organization shifted in unprecedented ways. This environment was the one in which ARGs and transmedia storytelling began to thrive. By the 2010s, billions of people were using social media and became subject to proprietary algorithms that could not only collect user data but also feed it back to them in order to shift attitudes and behaviors. This technological transformation correlated with and in many ways accelerated corresponding sociopolitical shifts which produced radical divisions among people.

One of the most visible and prominent cases of what has been broadly called, since the *Oxford Dictionaries* declared it its word of the year in 2016, the "post-truth" era, has been the QAnon conspiracy. Following an anonymous person known only as "Q" (a name that potentially derives from an Italian novel composed by the art collective known as Luther Blissett), this far-right American group, which emerged in 2017, put forward numerous conspiracies, such as a transnational child sex trafficking ring that sought to take down then-President Donald Trump (Frankel, 2021). As several commentators have noted, groups such as QAnon are formally comparable to ARGs with their This Is Not a Game aesthetic, paranoid and conspiracy narratives, and behind-the-scenes puppet masters (Berkowitz, 2020; Jagoda and Schilt, 2020). Indeed, both of these phenomena are made possible by a media ecology in which people constantly move across media platforms and integrate apps such as YouTube, TikTok, Discord, and Spotify into their daily routines. Social scientist Peter Forberg (who also worked as an ARG designer as an undergraduate) has argued that the QAnon conspiracy can "gain coherence for the user in part due to the algorithmic systems that organize content, user experiences that determine participation in environments, and routines through which the user incorporates the internet into daily life" both online and offline (2022, 4). Beyond simple texts or scripts, algorithms that spread fictions as if they were true information can be seen as "weapons" that are "actionable, possessing the power to inflict social harm (e.g., the Facebook group recommendation algorithm is a weapon radicalizing target demographics)" (5). We might even argue that groups like QAnon combine radical political rhetoric at the level of text, including forms of fictionality, with what game studies scholar Ian Bogost calls "procedural rhetoric" that relies on "persuasion through rule-based representations and interactions" like what we see in contemporary video games (Bogost, 2007, viv).

Cults and radical groups such as QAnon point to the dangers of the production of belief, particularly in our contemporary media environment. In light of such cases, we need to develop new approaches to use fictional rhetoric, energy, and creative capacities for less harmful or discriminatory ends. Instead of mobilizing the affective energies of possible followers, as QAnon has done, ARGs suggest a different model in which participants mutually negotiate the status of the event in which they are participating and co-create a world based on their imaginations and discussions. The designed form of the game produces both immersion in an alternate world during gameplay and ultimately, through post-game debriefing or analysis, invites enough critical distance that players can think through how worldmaking occurs in our historical moment. If people once thought seriously with and through dreams and fictional texts, there is reason to think with and through the games of our era of transmedia flows and networked interconnectivity. Though in some ways a marginal case, Alternate Reality Games are exemplary of our contemporary moment of transmedia fictionality. For all of their superficial similarities, ARGs, as I am conceptualizing them, differ dramatically from conspiracies that seek to mobilize human efficacy toward hatred and violence, or cults that marshal belief for the gain of particular leaders. Admittedly, the risk of slippage between these forms remains. These experiences marshall a This Is Not a Game aesthetic to enact a provisional production of shared belief among players. Even so, as I hope I have suggested, ARGs rely on an ethos of improvisatory, collaborative worldbuilding that can use the power of fiction, pedagogically, to both imagine and instantiate worlds that are more playful, equitable, and just.

Works Cited

Althusser, Louis. 2014. *On the Reproduction of Capitalism: Ideology and Ideological State Apparatuses.* London: Verso.

Baudrillard, Jean. 1994. *Simulacra and Simulation.* Translated by Sheila Faria Glaser. Michigan: Ann Arbor: University of Michigan Press.

Berkowitz, Reed. 2020. "A Game Designer's Analysis Of QAnon." *Medium*, September 30.

Bogost, Ian. 2007. *Persuasive Games: The Expressive Power of Videogames.* Cambridge, MA: MIT Press.

Bowman, Sarah Lynne. 2015. "Bleed: The Spillover Between Player and Character." *Nordic LARP* blog: https://nordiclarp.org/2015/03/02/bleed-the-spillover-between-player-and-character/

Davis, Erik. 1998. *TechGnosis: Myth Magic Mysticism in the Age of Information.* 1st ed. New York: Harmony Books.

Deleuze, Gilles. 2014. *Difference and Repetition.* Translated by P. Patton. London: Bloomsbury.

Doležel, Lubomír. 1998. *Heterocosmica: Fiction and Possible Worlds.* Baltimore, MD: Johns Hopkins University Press.

Enelow, Shonni. 2015. *Method Acting and Its Discontents: On American Psycho-Drama.* Evanston, IL: Northwestern University Press.

Forberg, Peter L. 2022. "From the Fringe to the Fore: An Algorithmic Ethnography of the Far-Right Conspiracy Theory Group Qanon." *Journal of Contemporary Ethnography* 51(3): 291–317.

Frankel, Eddy. 2021. "QAnon: The Italian Artists Who May Have Inspired America's most Dangerous Conspiracy Theory." *The Art Newspaper*, January 19.

Gallagher-Ross, Jacob. 2015. "Mediating the Method." *Theatre Survey* 64(2): 291–313.

Huizinga, Johan. 1980. *Homo Ludens: A Study of the Play-Element in Culture.* New York: Routledge.

Jagoda, Patrick with Ireashia Bennett, and Ashlyn Sparrow. 2022. *Transmedia Stories: Narrative Methods for Public Health and Social Justice.* Stanford University Press: https://transmediastories.supdigital.org/cover/index.html.

Jagoda, Patrick, and Kristen Schilt. 2020. "How Alternate Reality Games Are Changing The Real World." *Big Brains Podcast*, episode 59, December 10.

Kim, Jeffrey, Elan Lee, Timothy Thomas, and Caroline Dombrowski. 2009. "Storytelling in New Media: The Case of Alternate Reality Games, 2001–2009." *First Monday*: https://journals.uic.edu/ojs/index.php/fm/article/view/2484/2199.

Nielsen, Henrik Skov, James Phelan, and Richard Walsh. 2015. "Ten Theses About Fictionality." *Narrative* 23(1): 61–73.

Plato. 1992. *Republic.* Translatec by G. M. A. Grube and C. D. C Reeve. Indianapolis: Hackett Publishing Company.

Ronen Ruth. 1994. *Possible Worlds in Literary Theory.* Cambridge: Cambridge University Press.

Ryan, Marie-Laure. 2014. "Possible Worlds." In *Handbook of Narratology.* 2nd ed., edited by Peter Hühn, 726–742. Berlin: De Gruyter.

Schaeffer Jean-Marie. 2010. *Why Fiction?* Translated by Dorrit Cohn. Lincoln: University of Nebraska Press

Stanislavski, Constantin. (1936) 1948. *An Actor Prepares.* Translated by Elizabeth Reynolds Hapgood. New York: Theater Art Books.
Stewart, Sean. 2007 "Alternate Reality Games." *Writer's blog*: https://web.archive.org/web/20070225033452/http://www.seanstewart.org/interactive/args/.
Strasberg, Lee. 1987. *A Dream of Passion: The Development of the Method.* Edited by Evangeline Morphos. Boston, MA: Little Brown and Company.
Vogrinčič, Ana. 2008. "The Novel-Reading Panic in 18th-Century in England: An Outline of an Early Moral Media Panic." *Medijska Istraživanja* 14 Št. 2: 103–24.
Vorobyeva, Olga. 2015. "Ingame or Offgame? Towards a Typology of Frame Switching Between In-Character and Out-of-Character." *Nordic LARP Blog*: https://nordiclarp.org/2015/02/25/ingame-or-offgame-towards-a-typology-of-frame-switching-between-in-character-and-out-of-character/.
Walton, Kendall L. 1990. *Mimesis As Make-Believe: On the Foundations of the Representational Arts.* Cambridge, MA. Harvard University Press.

16
INTERACTIVE ENVIRONMENTS AND FICTIONAL ENGAGEMENT

Olivier Caïra

Introduction: Why Interactivity?

Interactive fictions are the usual suspects in most of today's alerts about people confusing fact with fiction. Since the 1980s, tabletop role-playing games like *Dungeons & Dragons* and video games have fueled many phenomena of "moral panic" (Markey and Ferguson, 2017; Matelly, 1997). The purpose of this chapter is to explain why this fear is intrinsically related to the features of interactivity, and why it has always led to false alarms.

Interacting with a fictional diegesis (characters, objects, places, and/or events) requires the engagement of an extradiegetic being—a player or an artificial intelligence—through various means of action. When we role-play, we become hybrid beings, usually called "player-characters," and this hybridity is *de facto* suspicious if people rely on naïve theories of fiction. Since playing implies intradiegetic agency rather than contemplation, one might think that players actually believe what is happening in their game and risk reproducing their in-game behavior in everyday life.

It is, therefore, important to study the different forms of interactivity according to two major criteria: the level of agency and the type of environment. Precise categories will help us establish why interactive fiction generates more fear than harm. But before entering the field of interactivity, it is essential to explain how the frame of a game is established, by drawing on pragmatic theories of fiction, and how the alarmist discourse on "perfect illusion" was constructed, particularly in the context of theatre.

Fictional Framing, Inferences, and Cross-Checking

In this chapter, "belief" will be used in the narrow sense of "believing what is happening in a fictional diegesis." It is clear that fiction plays a substantial part in shaping our stereotypes and mental representations—which can also be called "beliefs"—but this broader question will not be addressed here. If we "believe what is happening in a fictional diegesis," it does not simply mean that we acknowledge that some propositions are true or false within the diegesis. It implies that we believe that at least some parts of the fictional content are also true outside the diegesis.

As Jean-Marie Schaeffer explained in *Why Fiction?* ([1999] 2010), mimetic fictions proceed from a double logic. On the semantic level, their contents obey the principles of pretense and, in the case of realist works, they are often saturated with information that is also true outside the diegesis. The

DOI: 10.4324/9781003119456-19

particularity of this mode of communication is that, on the pragmatic level, it operates within a pragmatic framework of shared playful feint which creates cognitive "blocks" between the lures that we encounter in the works and our system of beliefs about the world:

> If all the inferences that go from the fictional universe toward the real universe seem to be blocked, this is not true in the reverse direction. The first are blocked because they would end at a contamination of our beliefs concerning what is and what is not the case for fictional representations. In fact, this is only a specific form of a problem [...], that of the necessity of a "motor brake," susceptible of hindering the mimemes from ending at reactive loops, at erroneous beliefs, at phenomena of self-deception or (in the case of dreams) at motor discharges.
>
> *(Schaeffer, 2010, 200)*

Like other pragmatic theorists of fiction (Caïra, 2020; Searle, 1979), Schaeffer shows that the issue of "Truth in fiction" (Lewis, 1978) is a matter of discernment between propositions which can be cross-checked with real-world knowledge and propositions which are only valid in the diegesis. If it is important to draw and to conceptualize a frontier between fact and fiction, it is not to make it impassable but to remain in control of what passes through it (Lavocat, 2016).

Coleridge's "suspension of disbelief" is not a double negative to express a state of belief which would define the fictional stance. What is suspended is not negated. The common feature of fictional frames is to lift the burden of proof which weighs on everyday communication (Caïra, 2011, 2020). It is not only a matter of propositional inferences, but a general suspension of our pragmatic promises and of verifiability, regardless of the medium of our expression. Within the fictional diegesis, anything becomes possible, because what a pragmatic frame does is to change the premises which apply to communication in its boundaries (Bateson, [1972] 2000; Goffman, 1974). As Hollywood studios say in their disclaimers: "The story, all names, characters, and incidents portrayed in this production are fictitious. No identification with actual persons (living or deceased), places, buildings, and products is intended or should be inferred." This does not mean that the whole diegetic content of a fictional work is imaginary, but that the studio—or the individual author—states that any inference or cross-check made from this content to the real world would not be relevant, even when the plot and the characters are clearly based on facts. It is not surprising that these disclaimers appear on many video games today.

Looking for Baltimore Soldiers

Theatrical controversies can help us understand what shapes the contemporary discourse on interactive experiences of fiction. A Shakespearian tragedy is not meant to be interactive, but there is always a risk that somebody in the audience may break the conventional "fourth wall" between the stage and the auditorium. So these controversies gave us a taste of what would happen in contemporary games because they dealt with the only form of contemplative fiction in which anyone could literally burst into the scene and perform significant diegetic actions.

The story is famous. In his essay on *Racine and Shakespeare* ([1823] 2011), Stendhal tells the anecdote of a young soldier in charge of safety in a theater in Baltimore who shot and wounded the actor playing Othello when the Venetian General was on the verge of killing his wife Desdemona. It is supposed to have happened in 1822, and this anecdote became very popular among French intellectuals thanks to Roland Barthes. Antoine Compagnon (1998, 2002), Christine Angot (2015), Françoise Lavocat (2016), Jean-Louis Comolli (2019), and Pierre Vesperini (2021) all quote the story as if Stendhal had reported a fact. Unfortunately, the Canadian historian Michael D. Bristol shows in *Big-Time Shakespeare* (1996) that there is absolutely no trace of such a spectacular event in the

Baltimore, the Maryland, or the East Coast press in general. Furthermore, French academics Sabine Chaouche (2005) and Jean-Yves Vialleton (2016) have shown that there is an "eternal return" of such anecdotes in the history of theater, the main protagonist always being a young man from the country with a military position and—supposedly—a poor cultural level. Stendhal made up the story, but it is constantly quoted as the report of a real event.

Some uses of this anecdote can be disturbing. Christine Angot's article "La belle équipe" was published in the aftermath of the November 2015 terrorist attacks in Paris, in a special series of texts in *Le Monde des Livres* called "Écrire sans trembler" ("Writing without fear"). The French novelist quotes the Baltimore Soldier anecdote as if Stendhal's words were the ultimate guarantee of reliability: "C'est une histoire vraie. Elle nous a été racontée par Stendhal. Les faits sont réels" ("It is a true story. It was told to us by Stendhal. The facts are real"). Then comes a risky comparison between this "true story" and the 2015 tragedy.

> The same thing happened here, amplified, and premeditated. At the Bataclan, on Friday, November 13, a concert by a Californian band, The Eagles of Death Metal, was taking place. They were playing when the soldiers of Daesh fired. As if metal music could pierce their eyes, and that at the Bataclan the scene was not musical and fictitious, but real.[1]
>
> *(Angot, 2015)*

Ironically, Christine Angot criticizes a confusion between "fictitious" and "real" performances on the basis of what is clearly a piece of fake news. Her comparison between Othello and a death metal show is also problematic: how can she label a musical performance as "fictitious"? How can she say that what was displayed onstage was a motive for the attacks when, at the same time, Daesh terrorists were slaughtering people around the Stade de France and in several cafés and restaurants in Paris?

If not all the uses of the Baltimore Soldier anecdote are as problematic as Angot's, this example shows how the discourse on the risk of confusion between fact and fiction can be based on confusing narratives. It may be time to get over those anecdotes and start studying field data and statistics. In the case of theatrical performances, the fact that some intellectuals need to use a two-century old tale to provide an example of this type of confusion speaks for itself: these events simply do not happen in real-life theatres. When violence occurs at a musical show or a sporting event, it is not because the protagonists misread fictitious elements, but because they hate the *real* artists, athletes, or supporters involved in the performance, or the performance itself and what it stands for. If there was any risk of a "perfect illusion"—to use Stendhal's expression—of a confusion between an actor and his character in our societies of extreme risk avoidance, not a single theater would be open today. There are no Baltimore Soldiers.

Whether it concerns video games or tabletop role-playing games, the alarmist discourse has characteristics similar to the anecdote of the Baltimore Soldier. First, it focuses on a protagonist who is defined as young, poorly educated, and culturally very distant from the speaker. Second, it relies on a very loose definition of fiction. Finally, it establishes a relationship of univocal and unconditional belief that leads to violent behavior. This is why most of the scaremongering deals with teenage gamers: they are supposed to be both a vulnerable and a dangerous demographic, and they play games that their parents never knew. It is interesting to see how tabletop role-playing games such as *Dungeons & Dragons* (1974) are encouraged by today's parents because of the same properties that worried those who gave in to moral panic in the 1980s and 1990s: "My teenage kid reads voluminous and incomprehensible books on fictional lore"; "My teenage kid spends dozens of hours locked up with her friends"; "My teenage kid takes pages and pages of notes and spends her time imagining stories in fantasy or science fiction worlds." Since online gaming has become the chief reason for parental concern, the use of rulebooks, the gathering of friends around a table and the exercise of imaginative skills have become positive features of interactive entertainment, for a generation that grew up with *Dungeons & Dragons* without suffering the evils that the late twentieth-century whistle-blowers predicted.

Interacting with Fictional Elements: Three Types of Agency

Why do those prophecies fail so ... predictably? The answer could be found in Jean-Marie Schaeffer's works: because fiction, interactive or not, is not pragmatically belief-oriented as lies and fake news are. But most of these warnings do not concern the pragmatic status of fiction, which they ignore, to insist on two aspects: the possibilities of action offered by games and the immersive properties of interactive environments. To treat these two points in an analytical way, it is necessary to look more closely at the various forms of interactive fiction that have appeared since the 1970s.

The most popular kind of interactivity among academics is the branching narrative you read or create, for example, with a free software like Twine. Scholars often mention it because its "twisty little passages" (Monfort, 2003) looks like a Borgesian "garden of forking paths" and it is interesting to sketch different patterns (lines, networks, trees, hubs ...) and to study how the links between narrative sequences are programmed (Ryan, 2006). This is a canonical form of scenario punctuated by choices that generate branching, but also by random processes or by logical operations that can lead players down a path without asking them any question (for example, when a series of bad decisions leads to an unhappy ending for their character). But one must keep in mind that not all game scriptwriters work with this tool, and that many interactive fictions are not based on such patterns, but on improvisation from an open-ended plot or on "sandbox" environment in which the players build their own plots and challenges. The aim is not to give an exhaustive overview of current interactive fiction media, but to provide two useful typologies to better understand the debates on belief in computer games, board games, live action role-playing games, and tabletop role-playing games.

The first typology is based on *agency*. Interactivity is quite a fuzzy concept, because many commercials have labeled simple navigation devices as interactive. For example, using a DVD/Blu-ray disc or visiting a museum with an audio guide, we are supposed to enjoy an "interactive experience." It is, because we get to choose the order, the language, the tempo, and the number of the sequences we will navigate through, but this is the weak sense of interactivity. The strong sense is based on real agency: interactivity implies leverage, significant diegetic action, most of the time through an avatar, a player/character.

We can identify three levels of agency: *how-*, *what-*, and *why*-interactivity.

- The *how*-interactivity is the weakest one. It only gives you the option of the method you will use to achieve a given challenge. As a player, you have no choice but to succeed but you can decide how you will achieve the challenge. This is the case in many computer games and boardgames. For example, you have to defeat a mafia boss, and what gives you agency is that you can attack his mansion with big guns or sneak into it and poison his grappa, or climb a hill and use a sniper gun, etc. As long as the boss is alive, or every time you fail at killing him, the narrative will remain stalled.
- The *what*-interactivity level provides more gaming opportunities. You are still encouraged to deal with the challenge, but you *can* fail at it or produce unexpected results. The narrative will continue even if you get captured or if you only wound the boss. It is only possible if the game adapts to unexpected events, for example, in tabletop role-playing because there is a human game master improvising right in front of you. It is also the case in live action role-playing games and many computer games based on modular scripts and a large number of subplots.

- The *why*-interactivity gives you a chance to completely leave the tracks of the challenge or to play without any defined challenge. You *can* refuse to deal with the challenge, or you *may* achieve it with your own agenda. You can decide to kill the mafia boss just to take his place and become a bad character. You can choose to seduce someone in the village, to simply wander around, or to run a pizzeria, etc. This happens mostly in tabletop role-playing, if the game master adopts a non-directive attitude—or if the group decides to play without a game master—and in "storygames" like *Once Upon a Time* (1994), since these games are designed to let the participants create their own stories from scratch.

An interesting difference between *what-* and *why*-interactivity is their relationship to fictional genres. In the former, you are free to choose your own goals, but the basic mechanics of the diegesis will not be affected by your decisions. In the latter, your agency is so important that you may even change the genre of the game you are playing. For example, *Once Upon a Time* is a storygame in which most of the cards represent a basic element of the "fairy tale" genre: a sword, a castle, a magical object, a speaking animal, a thief, etc. Other cards display a possible ending for the collaborative narrative which will be improvised around the table. Generally speaking, during the first few games of this game, the groups stick to the fairy tale genre and have a lot of fun developing their own plots. But many players, after a few sessions, start to hybridize this format with other generic conventions: parody, of course, but also noir, espionage, vampire romances, even superhero movies. These genre shifts are much more likely to be seen in smaller groups, as they involve constant negotiation of the playfulness of what is being experimented with. The shift occurs gradually, often as a result of associations of ideas or intertextual nods which occur during the course of the improvisation. During a *Once Upon a Time* session, a player invents a king's seneschal whom she names "Bogad." The player to her right calls out "Humphrey Bogad?"; she smiles and continues to describe the seneschal with many of the features of the American actor (Bogart) in his film noir typical roles: he wears a long coat and a hat, sips strong liquor, and speaks in a drawling voice. When the narrator changes, another player tells of Bogad's meeting with the princess as if she were a femme fatale, and the plot turns to a conspiracy to murder her stepmother. We thus see the hybridization taking place in a regime of shared authorship, without it having really been initiated by an individual proposal or by collective deliberation.

Agency, Engagement, and Belief

The differences between these three levels of interactivity are mainly a matter of technology, communication, and collective expectations. Technology has clearly made it possible to develop all forms of agency in video games, thanks to the storage and calculation capacities of computers, but also thanks to the diversification of human–machine interfaces. However, we will see in the next section that the most important possibilities of action are found in underdetermined environments that are rather poor in terms of technology but rich in the use of natural language. Indeed, the type of communication offered in interactive fictions has a direct impact on agency, as one can only play those actions whose meaning can be processed within the game. This is, in the current state of software technology, the main limitation of video games: no machine is able to process messages in natural language as a human player does. In the same way, many board games exclude analogical instructions—which are by definition equivocal—and only take into account univocal actions: move two squares forward, place a new unit in an area, collect such and such resources, draw a card, etc. Finally, collective expectations determine the choice of interactive fictions actually practiced and the degree of unpredictability that one wishes to experience during a session. Since we are dealing with leisure, there is no overarching authority that could rank the forms of agency in place of the players themselves. *Why*-interactivity is highly valued among tabletop role-playing game enthusiasts, but even within them, the rigidity of a very linear "door-monster-treasure" scenario can be appreciated for its tactical balancing or for the narrative tension it generates.

A low level of agency (*how*-interactivity) does not imply a bad gaming experience. On the contrary, simple challenges can lead to exciting games, as shown by the success of countless sports, racing, fighting, or investigation video games based on this principle. The diversity of methods that can be experimented with creates a strong replay value of the fictional experience, thus the possibility of progressing through repetitive events while testing different tactical choices over the course of sessions. Most boardgames are also based on *how*-interactivity: how to find the culprit, how to develop the most successful civilization, how to terraform a planet, how to complete the Holy Grail quest, etc.

This first typology gives us some valuable elements to understand why engagement in interactive fiction does not generate much belief.

In the case of *how*-interactivity, the artificiality of the agency proposed to us is all the more obvious as it is oriented toward the reiteration of action scripts over the course of the sessions. We are thus strongly solicited by the challenge to be taken up within the game, while being directly confronted with the plurality of methods we can use to achieve our objectives. All of this takes place in a diegetic temporality marked by the cyclical repetition of sequences until success, which has little equivalent in our daily lives.

Why-interactivity places us in a much more powerful position than we normally occupy, as it allows us to change the purposes of our actions, and even to influence the rules of the diegesis and the gender conventions that structure it. It seems difficult to develop beliefs about such malleable fictional content, since it would be a matter of adding credence to diegetic states that we have determined ourselves or that we might choose to modify.

What-interactivity is more in line with the experience of our agency in the everyday world, especially in respect to the passage of time, but it also clashes with the mechanisms that otherwise allow us to develop beliefs. The artificiality of an interactive diegesis inevitably appears to us because it allows us, as extradiegetic beings, to intervene as if we were natives. When we play a ninja or a lawyer in a game, belief in our fictional character's behavior is all the more improbable because the proposed role is foreign to us.

As the game multiplies tricks to make us throw shuriken like the ninja or plead like the lawyer, we become all the more aware of our incompetence to perform those skills and, more fundamentally, of our exteriority to the stakes of the situations proposed. We are not there to serve the Shogun or to clear our client, but to have fun playing these characters.

Character agency is a constant reminder of our extradiegetic nature. In other words, interactivity constantly generates *metaleptic effects*: signs of porosity between the intra- and extra-diegetic levels. A metaleptic effect is not a deliberate metalepsis (Genette, 2004) that an artist would use as a trope. Nor is it a "catalepsis" (Caïra and Hamus-Vallée, 2020), i.e., an accidental break in the referential illusion as seen in cinema when a camera or microphone appears in a shot. It is a consubstantial feature of the interactive experience, just as the presence of the "fourth wall" is an intrinsic part of the theatrical performance.

Interactive Diegesis: Three Types of Environment

These three forms of interactivity can be found in different environments. The most popular ones in academic studies are the determined environments, because anyone can find them as products. Therefore, they are more suitable for content or device analysis, they require less field observations and reports, and they provide a solid common ground for scientific debate. But the overrepresentation of determined environments in the field of research should not obliterate two other forms of diegetic construction: under- and overdetermined environments.

- The *determined environments* are those offered by board games and computer games in their vast majority. All the diegetic elements relevant to the game action are present in the physical game material or in the computer game code, although not everything is always revealed at the beginning of the game. If it is possible to combine elements to craft objects (combining rope and tree trunks to make a raft, mixing four magical ingredients to brew a potion, etc.), this is because these "new" artefacts were already planned by the game developers (the "rope" and "tree trunks" cards are discarded and the "raft" card appears with new sailing abilities for the characters; the ingredients disappear and the potion becomes available onscreen, with magical effects determined beforehand). It is not possible to create objects, places, or characters *ex nihilo* during the game, even if they are supposed to be within reach in the diegesis: grass and stones are generally visible in the game's scenery, but it is impossible to pick them up, just as the windows of buildings are most of the time impossible to open. If you want to change the diegesis ontologically, you have no choice but to stop the game, reprogram the software or enrich the board game material, and then start a new game. The actions that player characters can perform are similarly limited: nothing that has not been determined before the game is possible, even if it is a trivial behavior. For example, the *Mass Effect* video games (2007–2021) allow you to use supernatural powers, explore hundreds of planets, conduct complex investigations, and fight all sorts of alien adversaries, but you cannot perform actions as simple as brushing your teeth, singing a song, or digging a hole in the ground.
- *Underdetermined environments* allow you to dig holes and sing songs, because the diegesis of storygames, and tabletop role-playing games is extremely incomplete, and because all the players around the table agree on a rule of performative expression. There can be a map and many sourcebooks on the table, or a scenery onscreen, but it becomes possible for anything mentioned or described to exist within the fictional frame, as long as no one objects. Some storygames literally start from a blank page and let the players collectively create the storyline during the first few rounds. Here is an example collected during the testing of a game inspired by the American comedy *The Hangover* (2009). As in the film, the player-characters wake up after a very drunken night and find themselves in a compromising situation. The game started with this simple question: "You wake up with a terrible headache, what is your first impression." No other information was provided: no spatial or temporal indication, no instruction as to the definition of the player-characters. Player A said: "Ooooh, I'm feeling so bad, why am I lying on concrete in this hangar?" Player B said: "What is that smell? It is kerosene? Why is it so hot in there?" And player C added: "Hey! Why are we dressed in our underwear? Where's my tuxedo?" This small group improvised a criminal story for several hours, based on the elements described and the questions posed during this brief exposition. Each player added diegetic information, almost with each line: the identity of the hungover partygoers, the purpose of the hangar, the approximate year of the action, etc. Underdetermined environments are not necessarily as sparse in detail as the one being constructed in this example. When used at a role-playing game table, even the densest fictional worlds, such as *Lord of the Rings* or *Star Wars*, become underdetermined, as it becomes possible to embroider invented details into the fabric of the most familiar diegetic elements as the game progresses.
- *Overdetermined environments* are real settings that players use for a fictional purpose, mainly murder parties and live action role-playing games. In this case, you embody your character, most of the time with a costume, so your significant diegetic action is to really move, speak, eat, etc., in this setting. You can also *pretend* to perform more problematic actions, like pretend to sleep, to be paralyzed by a spell, or complain about a wound you didn't get. These games offer many

conventional rules to simulate the practice of magic or combat. The environment being real, you cannot use performative speech to create a hangar or a smell of kerosene as the game progresses, and all the players have to deal with counter-immersive elements, such as a real plane flying over a fictional medieval village, or simply the ringing of a telephone during play.

The plasticity of an interactive diegesis depends not only on the type of agency proposed to us but also on its degree of determination. We can compare the three categories of environments described above to different forms of creation in non-interactive media. Novel writing is a good example of underdetermined diegetic creation: there is no obstacle to the performativity of natural language, whether written or oral. The cinema functions by successive takes on determined environments: a certain rigidity therefore prevails, the changes of diegetic elements not being able to be made as the actors play. Finally, theatre is a typical case of overdetermination of the diegesis, since the whole fictional narrative unfolds live in front of the public, without takes or editing, with a permanent risk of counter-immersion linked to the concreteness of what is played out on stage.

In tabletop role-playing as well as in a novel, a vase will only break if a performative statement indicates that it is so. In stage play or film, a deliberately broken vase will appear in all parts or takes of the same shot, while a vase broken by accident will be replaced identically or removed from the set of scenes where it was supposed to appear. In life-size role-playing as in theatre, the overdetermination of the scenic environment implies that, if a vase breaks, the event must appear as intentional, since it is irremediably part of the diegetic facts imposed on the characters. The weather of the diegesis follows the same principles, for example, if it is to snow:

- In an underdetermined environment, saying that it snows makes it a diegetic element.
- In a determined environment, you ask the developers to add snow on the setting, the board, the screen.
- In an overdetermined environment, you need to hope it snows before you play.

Belief and Fictional Environments

This second typology completes the previous one by giving us keys to the limits of the promise of immersion. While there is no fictional experience without engagement, the phenomenon of immersion is much more difficult to observe. Part of the fieldwork consists in taking it seriously without trivializing it: cultural industries often promise us immersion, and their audiences actively seek it, but it would be wrong to consider it as our ordinary state when faced with works of fiction. On the contrary, it is often described as a rare and precarious state, and therefore linked to particularly memorable experiences.

This scarcity of moments of immersion explains, in supplement to the pragmatic arguments seen above, why there is little to fear from interactive games in terms of confusion between fiction and reality. In addition to the metaleptic effect of our agency in a foreign diegesis, each type of environment generates powerful counter-immersive effects.

Determined environments have seemingly the same immersive appeal as most works of fiction, and indeed many of them are adaptations of novels, comics, or blockbuster films into video or board games. But the quest for immersion in a literary narrative, whether successful or not, is aided by an overall unity of intent between the descriptions, the intentions of the characters, and the progression of the narrative. We never experience the diegetic limits of a novel, since we cannot leave the "scenic railway" of the story. On the contrary, when we are given a character's intentions and freedom of movement, it is inevitable that we will seek to act in unexpected ways: explore places that will not be accessible, interact with objects that will remain inert, attempt to interact with inhabitants of the diegesis who have no script suitable for our concerns. It is particularly the poverty and repetitiveness of the dialogues which, in board games as in video games, have counter-immersive effects: the interface offers only a finite list of sentences, reminding us at each line that we do not really have the floor in the diegesis. Of course, if most of the player's experience is based on racing, combat, or exploration, the limits of the dialogue's interface will not severely affect the game's success, but it will generate engagement without belief.

Underdetermined environments provide a satisfactory answer to the objection of poor dialogue, since they are built on the use of natural language between players. One can, therefore, experience the feeling of being one of the characters in the diegesis who communicates with others in a spontaneous and nuanced way, but the main counter-immersive effect is elsewhere. Indeed, the participants of a role-playing game or of a storygame make the choice to gather around a table (or on an online meeting platform) and to use neither costumes nor scenery. One is thus faced with one's fellow players who are not concerned with formal mimesis, instead of dialoguing with avatars who could maintain a certain illusion of "transport" to the diegesis. This choice of a pen-and-paper practice is not absurd, as it gives the group an unparalleled freedom to navigate the environment and describe what is relevant to the plot. In particular, it is up to the game master to recreate the novelistic "scenic railway" around her group of player-characters, so that the environment never appears too rigid and incomplete. But this is done at the cost of many extra-diegetic exchanges around the table. Here again, one meets players who are passionate and very committed to their hobby, but none of them entertain a relationship of belief with regard to their preferred interactive environments.

Games in overdetermined environments have opposite properties, although they also favor natural language exchanges. When playing a live action role-playing game, the immersion effects seem a priori much more powerful, since one embodies a character instead of interpreting it at a table or in front of a screen. Field observations by Sébastien Kapp (2013) show the importance of direct perception and bodily experiences such as cold or fatigue in the engagement specific to these games. But the link with belief is also lacking here, as the participants measure the gap between the game, their daily life and what their character's life would be all the better as they are the artisans of this "collaborative fictional immersion," to quote the title of Kapp's thesis. For example, they know that the overdetermined environment is only a spatiotemporal "pocket" (a few hectares of forest used for a weekend, for example), and that it is impossible for them to decide, as one would in a tabletop role-playing game or in certain video games, to ride west for two days. Despite their best efforts, it is difficult for them to avoid the metaleptic effects of their own bodies or language habits: Vikings or Gondorians would not have fillings on their molars and would not speak twenty-first-century English.

Conclusion

Even though a large majority of fictional works rely on mimetic representation, mimesis and fiction remain different concepts and should be studied as such. Formal mimesis tends toward make-believe at the semantic level, while the fictionality of works and experiences tells us, at the pragmatic level, that the constraints of proof on messages are temporarily lifted, and that we are, therefore, not asked to believe in their content. This paradox is only apparent, since our skills as producers or receivers of fiction are sufficient to give us the necessary discernment between what circulates in these frames and the premises that apply to everyday life. The discussion of the "Baltimore Soldier" case reminded us that, despite the appetite of some intellectuals for anecdotes featuring supposedly uneducated audiences depicted as victims of a confusion of frames, these colorful narratives are invented stories which, after two centuries of uncritical retelling, could safely disappear from today's academic debate.

Olivier Caïra

This chapter presents two typologies which can be used to study the various forms of engagement in interactive fiction. These categories of player agency and environmental level of definition can help explain why we see so few traces of belief in games, even when the fictional engagement is a very strong one. Character agency has an inherent metaleptic effect: it brings a constant reminder of our extradiegetic nature, our otherworldliness. When we read a book about wizards, we are not characters in the story, so we can aim at fictional immersion as invisible spectators of a narrative which only involves intradiegetic protagonists. But if we play a wizard in the same diegesis, we are constantly reminded that we cannot think or act as one.

The three kinds of environments described above also work as foils in terms of belief. Determined environments are clearly artificial and they limit the scope of our actions to what the game requires. Underdetermined environments give us such a performative power that it is impossible to believe in diegetic elements that we created a few minutes ago. And overdetermined environments are extremely fragile in terms of immersion because they require that we constantly adjust a real setting to our expectations toward a fictional diegesis.

The absence of belief in the content of interactive fictions—even those which generate intense engagement—is more interesting than belief itself, because it shows how skilled we all are when it comes to blocking inferences from fictional frames to other frames of experience, even when their make-believe dimension is particularly strong. Jean-Marie Schaeffer's question "Why fiction?" is more challenging if we consider that belief is neither a condition nor a by-product of fiction.

Note

1 *"La même chose a eu lieu chez nous, amplifiée, et préméditée. Au Bataclan, on donnait, vendredi 13 novembre, un concert d'un groupe californien, The Eagles of Death Metal. Ils étaient en train de jouer quand les soldats de Daech ont tiré. Comme si la musique métal risquait de leur transpercer les yeux, et qu'au Bataclan la scène n'était pas musicale et fictive, mais réelle."*

Works Cited

Angot, Christine. 2015. "La belle équipe." *Le monde des livres*, 20 November 2015.
Bateson, Gregory. (1972) 2000. *Steps to an Ecology of Mind.* Chicago, IL: University of Chicago Press.
Bristol, Michael D. 1996 *Big-Time Shakespeare.* London: Routledge.
Caïra, Olivier. 2011, *Définir la fiction: du roman au jeu d'échecs.* Paris: Éditions de l'EHESS.
Caïra, Olivier. 2020. "Fiction, Expanded and Updated." *Contemporary French and Francophone Narratology*, edited by John Pier, 155–71. Columbus: Ohio State University Press.
Caïra, Olivier, and Réjane Hamus-Vallée. 2020. *Le goof au cinéma: de la gaffe au faux raccord, la quête de l'anomalie filmique.* Paris: L'Harmattan.
Chaouche, Sabine. 2005. *La scene en contrechamp: anecdotes françaises et traditions de jeu au siècle des lumières.* Paris: Honoré Champion.
Comolli, Jean-Louis. 2019. *Cinéma, numérique, survie. L'art du temps.* Lyon: ENS Éditions.
Compagnon, Antoine. 1998. *Le demon de la théorie: littérature et sens commun.* Paris: Seuil.
Compagnon, Antoine. 2002. "Brisacier, ou la suspension d'incrédulité." In *Frontières de la fiction*, edited by Alexandre Gefen and René Audet, 415–26. Bordeaux: Presses Universitaires de Bordeaux.
Genette, Gérard. 2004. *Métalepse. De la figure à la fiction.* Paris: Seuil.
Goffman, Erving. 1974. *Frame Analysis: An Essay on the Organization of Experience.* Cambridge, MA: Harvard University Press.
Kapp, Sébastien. 2013. *L'immersion fictionnelle collaborative: une étude de la posture d'engagement dans les jeux de rôle grandeur nature.* PhD dissertation, École des Hautes Études en Sciences Sociales, Paris.
Lavocat, François. 2016. *Fait et fiction: pour une frontière.* Poétique. Paris: Seuil.
Lewis, David. 1978. "Truth in Fiction." *American Philosophical Quarterly* 15: 37–46.
Markey, Patrick M., and Christopher Ferguson. 2017. *Moral Combat: Why the War on Violent Video Games Is Wrong.* Dallas: BenBella Books.

Matelly, Jean-Hughes. 1997. *Jeu de rôle: rimes? Suicides? Sectes?: Istres, Toulon, Carpentras*. Toulon: Presses du Midi.
Monfort, Nick. 2003. *Twisty Little Passages: An Approach to Interactive Fiction*. Cambridge, MA: MIT Press.
Ryan, Marie-Laure. 2006. *Avatars of Story*. Minneapolis, MN: Minnesota University Press.
Schaeffer, Jean-Marie. 2010. *Why Fiction?* Translated by Dorrit Cohn. Lincoln: University of Nebraska Press.
Searle, John R. 1979. "The Logical Status of Fictional Discourse." In *Expression and Meaning Studies in the Theory of Speech Acts*, 58–75. Cambridge: Cambridge University Press.
Stendhal. (1823) 2011. *Racine and Shakespeare*. Richmond: Oneworld Classics.
Vesperini, Pierre. 2021. "'Trigger Warnings,' quand même Shakespeare ne passe plus." *Philosophie Magazine*, October 19, 2021.
Vialleton, Jean-Yves. 2016. "Les anecdotes sur le comédien classique: pour une approche comparative." *La reserve*. http://ouvroir-litt-arts.univ-grenoble-alpes.fr/revues/reserve/319-les-anecdotes-sur-le-comedien-classique-pour-une-approche-comparative.

17

FAKE NEWS
AND FICTIONAL NEWS[1]

Jessica Pepp, Rachel Sterken, and Eliot Michaelson

Introduction

This chapter is about two things that the term "fake news" has been widely used to talk about. The first is what we will call "fictional news."[2] Fictional news includes the genres of news satire (e.g., *The Daily Show*, *The Colbert Report*) and news parody (e.g., *The Onion*, *The Babylon Bee*, *Weekend Update*). Fictional news was once the main thing that the term "fake news" was used to talk about.[3] Today, fictional news is not what is usually meant by "fake news." Sometime around 2016, a new idiomatic use of the term rose to prominence. This new use of the term refers to a societal phenomenon that is seen as a threat to the epistemic state of individuals and whole societies, as well as a danger for the well-functioning of societies more broadly. Spelling out what this threatening phenomenon of fake news is and how it is different from the non-threatening, or even helpful, phenomenon of fictional news (especially news satire and parody) is not an easy task.

Speaking loosely, we might say that both fictional news and fake news (in the new sense of the term)[4] involve made-up stories. But they seem to be birds of very different feathers. Fictional news is a collection of artistic genres, the works of which may be valuable cultural assets. News satire and news parody, when they are done well, have the potential to entertain and inform consumers, to challenge their assumptions, to deepen their understanding of societal problems and human foibles, and otherwise to improve their epistemic and emotional states. Fake news is not thought to offer these kinds of benefits. Readers of fake news do not learn from it. At best, they recognize its fakeness and ignore it; at worst they are misled and/or spread the fake news further so that it can mislead others. (In the remainder of the chapter, we will use "fake news" in the post-2016 way, and "fictional news" to talk about satirical, parodical, or otherwise fictional works.)

Despite the contrasting evaluative attitudes people tend to have toward fake news and fictional news, it is not as easy to distinguish them as it might first seem.[5] Social media platforms have struggled to limit the visibility of fake news on their platforms without blocking access to legitimate fictional news. Partly in response to these efforts, producers and promoters of fake news sometimes claim that it is instead fictional news (parody or satire).[6] This may be done to evade flagging, blocking, or demotion, or to escape censure after the fact. In this environment, the practical challenge of distinguishing fake news from legitimate[7] fictional news, on the massive scale that is required, is immense. Technical academic work in fake news detection now standardly incorporates some form of satire detection or omission.[8] But behind this challenge lurks a philosophical question: what *is* the

DOI: 10.4324/9781003119456-20

difference between fake news and fictional news? What line is to be tracked by the automated systems that computer scientists are developing?[9] This is our question.

In this chapter, we approach the question via a recently burgeoning literature in philosophy and communications studies about how to define fake news. After a brief discussion of fictional news, we survey various definitions of fake news, highlighting the different ways in which they distinguish fake news from fictional news. A unifying feature is that these definitions appeal in one way or another to the *beliefs* of consumers. Some define fake news as involving intentions on the part of producers to deceive consumers: to lead them to form false beliefs of one type or another. Others define fake news as involving expectations on the part of producers that consumers will be deceived, even if this deception is merely expected, but not intended. According to yet another definition, something is fake news only if it is actually disposed to deceive consumers. Proponents of such definitions distinguish fictional news from fake news by claiming, or implying, that fictional news is *not* intended, expected, or disposed (respectively, depending on the definition) to lead consumers to form false beliefs. So, a strong connection has been drawn between fake news and belief in most efforts to define fake news. We challenge this connection and contend that none of these relations to consumers' beliefs is essential to fake news. We then offer an alternative definition of fake news. The alternative definition seems to face the problem that it does not distinguish adequately between fake news and fictional news, allowing that an item might be *both* fake news and fictional news. Finally, we argue that this challenge is a general one, affecting not only our account of fake news but the others we have surveyed as well. We close by outlining a way to address it by complementing our account of fake news (or, indeed, any account of fake news) with an account of artistic genres.

Fictional News

In order to address the question of what distinguishes fake news from fictional news, we need to give at least a rough characterization of fictional news. This section contains some preliminary remarks in that direction.

By "fictional news," we mean works of art or entertainment that are presented in the *format* of *official news media*.[10] By "official news media," we mean the outputs of the various institutions which, within a given cultural context and time period, are dedicated to the public distribution of news (which we will define, very loosely, as a description of an important recent event or situation) and are publicly accepted as having this function. By "format," we mean the characteristic aspects of official news media that mark them as such. There are a wide variety of such formats across different sorts of media, countries, and time periods. The following are just a few examples:

- The structuring of printed newspaper articles with a headline in large type (and, in many countries, having a characteristic grammatical style), author byline, writing location, and the article itself in columns alongside other articles.
- Online newspaper articles starting with a headline, short summary, and author information, often with an accompanying photo, and the time of last updating noted.
- Televised news featuring an anchor person seated at a desk with television- or computer screen-style graphics behind them that accompanies their reporting, which is spoken in a characteristic cadence.

In today's changing media environment, it might be that various social media formats are formats of official news media. News is increasingly distributed via Twitter and other platforms, both by those who are making the news and by those reporting it, as well as by ordinary observers to whom social media offers a broad and instantaneous platform.[11]

The prominent examples of fictional news that we mentioned in the Introduction (all hailing from the American entertainment landscape) fit this broad definition. *TheOnion.com* has many aspects of the format of an online news outlet. That it is not an online news outlet is evident from the claims made in its articles, which are either absurd in themselves or absurd when considered as news reports from an online news outlet. (For example, a recent headline reads, "12-year-old Job Applicant Asked to Explain 12 Year Employment Gap on Résumé."[12] Another is, "Man Does Good Job Getting Drunk."[13]) The *Weekend Update* segment on *Saturday Night Live* has many aspects of the format of a television news broadcast. That it is not a television news broadcast is evident both from the absurdity of its news reports, the inclusion of audience laughter, and the fact that it is part of a late-night humor show. *The Daily Show* uses many aspects of the format of a television news broadcast, such as the anchor desk with background video screens and interviews with correspondents "on location." Unlike *TheOnion.com* or *Weekend Update*, *The Daily Show* discusses actual news, albeit in a humorous and satirical fashion. But although the news discussed may be real, it is fictional that the discussion is an official news media output.[14]

These common examples of fictional news are works of satire, parody, or both. The parody of official news media can have many functions. It can serve to satirize official news media itself, or to satirize the people, institutions, and societal conditions of the day. Sometimes the parody is not in the service of satire or social commentary, but is simply a vehicle for silliness or a good punchline (as is often the case with *Weekend Update*). It should be noted that the category of fictional news could certainly reach beyond parody, satire, and comedy. Literary, visual, or performing artists might tell fictional stories in the format of a news story, newspaper, or newscast—or an extended series of such items, or in the format of Facebook posts or tweets. Such works would be along the lines of an epistolary novel, only using news format rather than letter format. Moreover, true stories might be fictionally presented in such formats. Thus, works of fictional news might be instances of literary fiction, dramatic cinema, performance art, creative memoir, and many other traditional genres. We are not aware of examples of such works,[15] but they could certainly be created if they have not been already. Again, these would be works of art using the format of official news media as a fictional device.

Fake News

Fake news has been appealed to in explaining electoral outcomes,[16] information resistance, societal polarization, and horrifying violence. Political opponents have hurled the term "fake news" at each other as a term of abuse. Academic studies have sprung up to measure and analyze fake news. Social media platforms have implemented measures to guard against fake news.[17] Some governments have proposed and/or passed legislation that criminalizes fake news, sometimes without providing any clear definition of the term.[18] The explosion of theoretical, practical, and legal activity underscores the importance of arriving at a working definition of the term "fake news." Academics have answered this call, offering up a "cornucopia of definitions" (Habgood-Coote, 2019), which, despite their variation, seem to be circling around the same phenomenon (Brown, 2019; Pepp, Michaelson and Sterken, 2022). In this section, we will provide a non-comprehensive, though representative, survey of this field of definitions, through the lens of our question: what is the difference between fake news and fictional news?

Deceptive Intention Definitions of "Fake News"

One potential answer to our question is that fake news is intended to deceive, whereas fictional news is intended to entertain and (perhaps) enlighten but not to deceive. Many recent definitions of "fake news," which we will call *deceptive intention definitions*, require that a work be produced with some sort of intention to deceive in order to count as fake news. Proponents of such definitions often claim that an important advantage of including a deceptive intention condition is that it distinguishes fake news from satire or news parody.[19]

Deceptive intention definitions of "fake news" vary with respect to (i) the nature of the required deceptive intention and (ii) what else, in addition to the required deceptive intention, is necessary and sufficient for a work to be fake news.

Concerning the nature of the required deceptive intention, some hold that it is an intention to deceive people concerning the *content*, or *subject*, of the work. For example, a report that Politician X was arrested for driving drunk could only be fake news, according to these definitions, if the producer(s) of the report intended to deceive people into thinking that Politician X was arrested for driving drunk.[20] For them to have this intention, the producer(s) must believe that it is not the case that Politician X was arrested for driving drunk. If, instead, the producer(s) of the report had themselves received inaccurate information and/or if they had been sloppy in researching the story, so that they had produced a false report that they nonetheless believed to be true, they would not have produced fake news, according to deceptive intention definitions. Instead, they would have produced excusably inaccurate or perhaps even inexcusably sloppy journalism.[21]

According to other definitions, what producers of fake news must intend to deceive people about is not (necessarily) the content of the report but its *source*, or the process by which it was produced. For instance, Fallis and Mathiesen (2019) require that producers of fake news intend to deceive (at least some) people into believing that the work in question was produced through a standard journalistic process (including, e.g., active inquiry into information of relevance for members of the society, careful verification of information received, transparency about sources, conflicts of interest, and unknowns). Mukerji (2018) requires that producers of fake news must intend to deceive people into believing that the producers were not indifferent as to whether what the work *asserts* is true or false.[22] Croce and Piazza resist the view that fake news must be intended to deceive about the content of the work, but agree that "in a *weak sense* fake news is always asserted with the intention to deceive." The "weak sense" they have in mind is that fake news is always intended to deceive about its source or the attitude with which it is produced. That is, it is intended to deceive people into believing it to be a real news report that is "talking seriously" (2021, 57).

Of course, the fact that a work is intended to deceive in some way or another does not by itself entail that the work is fake news. For example, someone might leave an intentionally deceptive note for their roommate; the note is not fake news. It is easy to come up with many similar examples. Accordingly, there is a general consensus that in order to be fake news, a work must have the form of news, or be presented as news. This is developed in different ways by different authors. According to Rini (2017, E-45), fake news "purports to describe events in the real world, typically by mimicking the conventions of traditional media reportage." According to Pritchard, fake news must be presented as news, which means that the work must be presented as coming from a source of information that is "designed to convey accurate information to others about recent events, where that information is not already widely known" (2021, 52), although it does not come from such a source. Fallis and Mathiesen (2019, 8) also require works to be "presented as news" in order to qualify as fake news. Similar requirements hold for other views.

Broadly speaking, then, deceptive intention definitions agree that for a work to be fake news, it must be presented as news and it must be intended to deceive. Fallis and Mathiesen (2019, 8) add that the work must also have the *propensity* to deceive people as to its source: a faked news report with no hope of fooling anyone about its being real news is not fake news, either, according to their definition. These definitions are often claimed to rule out fictional news from counting as fake news because fictional news, although it may be presented as news, is not intended to deceive its audience, either about its content or about how and with what attitude it was produced.

Non-Deceptive Intention-Based Definitions of "Fake News"

A few recent definitions of "fake news" do not require any deceptive intentions on the part of producers. One example is Axel Gelfert's definition of "fake news" as "the deliberate presentation of (typically) false or misleading claims *as news*, where the claims are misleading *by design*" (2017, 108). This definition does focus on the intentions of producers, but it does not require those intentions to be intentions to deceive. For the claims in a work to be "misleading by design" is not for them to be designed by the producer to mislead people. Rather, it is for the work to be generated and propagated by a method that is known or expected by the producer to result in people being misled, and is deliberately employed in spite of (and without concern for) this likelihood.

Pritchard (2021, 48) argues, against Gelfert's definition, that for a work to be fake news, its producers must intend to deceive consumers about the work's content, even if this is not their only or even their primary intention. This is because, according to Pritchard, getting people to click on things "under the guise of them being news" requires those people to find the claims "at least remotely plausible." Hence, intending to get people to click-through to a work under the guise of its being news entails intending to deceive them about the content of the work. (49) Croce and Piazza reject Pritchard's argument on the grounds that people may well click and share items presented as news, even if they do not believe those works or find them plausible, as long as they have other motivations such as strengthening their political identity or social bonds (2021, 57ff). It is ultimately an empirical psychological question whether believing the claims in a putative news report or finding them plausible is (in general) a predictor of click-through and sharing engagement. But it certainly seems possible for a producer of fake news to have Croce and Piazza's view and, therefore, to intend only for audiences to find the works they produce useful for various social and political purposes. At the same time, they might recognize that the method they use to produce the works (i.e., one which involves no concern for the truth of the claims therein) is likely to result in some portion of the audience being misled. Gelfert's definition is able to classify such works as fake news, even if their producers have *no* intention to deceive the audience, either about the contents of the works or the conditions of its production. As long as the producers expect the works to end up misleading people, but deliberately produce and disseminate them anyway, the resulting works may be fake news.

How does Gelfert's definition rule out various forms of fictional news (such as satirical news) from being fake news, if it allows that even fake news may be produced without intentions to deceive? Gelfert suggests that fictional news does not count as fake news because the producers of fictional news do not deliberately use a means of production that they expect is likely to mislead. For example, writers of articles in *TheOnion.com* presumably do not expect their process of coming up with funny satirical articles to be likely to result in people being misled; thus, they do not deliberately use a misleading method without concern for its misleadingness.

A different deceptive, intention-free definition of "fake news" comes from Grundmann (2020). Grundmann defines fake news as

> News that is produced or selected in general ways such that it has the robust disposition to lead, at the time of publication and under normal conditions, to a significant amount of false beliefs in a significant number of the addressed consumers.
>
> *(2020, 8)*

In this definition, "news" applies to "a process of formation or selection" of works. So for a *work* to be an instance of fake news, on this definition, is for it to be produced or selected by *processes* that are disposed to lead to significant false beliefs among consumers. An individual work produced in this way might turn out (by some accident) to be true, and thus not *itself* be disposed to lead to false beliefs, but it would still have been produced by a process that has this disposition.

Grundmann's definition is, as he puts it, "purely consumer oriented," insofar as what is required for a process of producing and selecting works to be a fake news process is its disposition to affect consumers, not the intentions or other mental states of its producers. In particular, it is the disposition of that production process to lead to false beliefs on the part of consumers. Presumably, the definition would rule out fictional news production processes from being fake news processes because these processes *in fact* lack that disposition. The claim would be that the processes by which fictional news is produced are not robustly disposed to lead to significant amounts of false beliefs. (Notice the difference between this and what Gelfert's definition suggested, that fictional news would be ruled out because its producers do not *expect* their production process to lead to false beliefs, whether or not it is in fact disposed to do so.)

So far, all the definitions we have surveyed seem to define "fake news" in such a way that fictional news is excluded. If one's definition of "fake news" requires fake news to be produced or distributed with the *intention* to deceive its audience about its contents or about the way it was produced, then one would argue that no fictional news is intended to deceive in these ways. If one's definition of "fake news" requires fake news to be produced or distributed with the *expectation* that it would deceive audiences in one way or another, then one would argue that no fictional news is expected to deceive in the relevant way. If one's definition of "fake news" requires fake news to be *actually disposed* to deceive its audience in one way or another, then one would argue that no fictional news is disposed to deceive in these ways.

These claims are not obviously true, and we will challenge them below. But it is certainly tempting to think that what sets fake news and fictional news apart has something to do with deception. Most proposals for defining "fake news" embrace this tempting thought by building a connection to deception into the definition.

Defining "Fake News" without Appeal to Deception

In earlier work (2019), we proposed a definition of "fake news" according to which no sort of deceiving or misleading is essential, whether concerning content or production, and whether actual, dispositional, intended or expected. Instead, we proposed that the defining feature of fake news is a mismatch between the way people treat a work as having been produced and the way it was in fact produced. In particular, fake news is not produced by what we labelled *standard journalistic practices*, but it is *treated for certain purposes* as though it were produced in that way. Our official definition reads: "Fake news is the broad spread of stories treated by those who spread them as having been produced by standard journalistic practices, but that have not in fact been produced by such practices" (69).

By "standard journalistic practices," we refer to an evolving set of practices characteristic of the evolving social institution of journalism. These practices are partly constitutive of journalism, in the sense that works produced using them have a stronger claim to be genuine works of journalism than works produced in other ways. Examples of contemporary standard journalistic practices include: continuous monitoring for new information that is important or relevant for members of a society, careful verification of information received, transparency about sources and conflicts of interest, independence from the individuals and institutions reported on, and proportionality in information gathering and reporting. We think that works produced in accord with a substantial portion of these practices are not fake news, even if they turn out to be false or misleading.[23]

Treating a work as having been produced by standard journalistic practices is not the same thing as *believing* that what the work says is true. Nor is it the same thing as *believing* that it was produced by standard journalistic practices. Let us illustrate this with an example. Suppose a report of outrageous corruption on the part of a politician one dislikes shows up in one's Facebook feed. The report's source might be unclear and its details might seem unlikely, leading one to suspect that it is not genuine journalism (i.e., that it was not produced following a substantial proportion of standard journalistic practices). Nonetheless, later that day one might treat the report as genuine journalism for the purposes of an argument with someone who supports the politician. One might refer to the report as though it were genuine journalism during the conversation. One might even temporarily mentally categorize the report as genuine journalism by, say, including its contents in a mental list of things to be cited as evidence of the politician's unsuitability. In doing so, one might be deliberately crafty, having a keen awareness that one is using fake news to support one's cause. But one might also simply permit oneself to ignore or downplay temporarily the provenance of the report, because it makes it easier to hold up one's side of the argument and, perhaps, because confirmation bias makes it easier for one to suppose that the report, or something close to it, might be true, even if it was not produced through standard journalistic practices. Either way, one is treating the report as having been produced by standard journalistic practices for the purposes of this argument, even though one does not believe that it was so produced.

Of course, it is often the case that people treat a given work as genuine journalism for a certain purpose because they believe it *is* genuine journalism. Our point is simply that the reverse does not hold: there are all kinds of ways to treat a work as genuine journalism without believing that it is. Relying on the work in political arguments is just one example.[24]

We think there are good reasons *not* to build intentions to deceive, expectations of deception, or dispositions to deceive into the definition of "fake news." This is not because we think fake news typically lacks such features. On the contrary, we agree that fake news often has these features. But we also think that works lacking these features can be fake news.

First, let us consider the general idea embraced by deceptive intention definitions, that in order for a work to be fake news, its producer must intend to deceive their audience, either concerning the work's content or concerning how or with what attitude it was produced. If this is right, then works produced sincerely, by people who take themselves to be reporting the truth, cannot become fake news. This does not seem right: suppose that a group of people take themselves to have some sort of clairvoyance concerning what is really going on in the world, and they start a website to reveal the shocking "truths" they "know" to the rest of the world. These people do not really have any such clairvoyance, but they truly believe that they do. If the reports they publish are spread broadly on social media and treated as genuine journalism by those who spread them, then it seems to us that they become fake news.

Pritchard (2021, 56) rejects this judgement and suggests that these works would not be fake news, but rather genuine news that is "epistemically deficient." In Pritchard's view, works produced by a given source count as genuine news as long as that source is "designed to convey accurate information to others about recent events, where that information is not already widely known" (52). (This is the case for our imagined would-be clairvoyants.) He holds that it is important not to assume that genuine news must be produced by standard journalistic practices, because this leaves us unable to countenance genuine news that is epistemically deficient or problematic. That, in turn, raises problems for developing individual and societal responses to fake news, since it makes it more likely that restrictions designed to combat fake news might also impinge on genuine news that is or is judged to be epistemically deficient (64–65).

We agree with Pritchard that this would be undesirable, and we agree that it is important to distinguish between genuine news that is epistemically problematic and fake news. However, we do not think that our definition of "fake news" leaves us unable to do this. On our understanding of "standard journalistic practices," it is perfectly possible for a work to be produced by following standard journalistic practices *to a sufficient degree to qualify as genuine journalism* and still be epistemically problematic.[25] For one thing, there may be no precise cut-off for the degree to which standard journalistic practices must be followed in order for a work to count as genuine journalism. Thus, a work might be produced by a method that deviates somewhat from some of these practices and still count as genuine journalism. The respects in which a method deviates from these practices might introduce unreliability or other epistemic problems. For another thing, standard journalistic practices themselves might not be epistemically ideal (it seems likely that they are not). So even works that have been produced by following these practices very closely might be epistemically deficient in some respects. Thus, building it into our understanding of *genuine news*, or *genuine journalism*, that it is produced by following standard journalistic practices *to a certain degree* does not mean that there is no way to distinguish between problematic genuine journalism and fake news.

Perhaps more importantly, it seems to us that cases like that of the would-be clairvoyants are naturally and intuitively categorized as part of the societal phenomenon that came to be called "fake news" around 2016. Consider the "Pizzagate" affair, which is often cited as a paradigm example of this phenomenon. We are not sure if any account of its origins has been decisively established, but according to Wikipedia, it began with posts on Twitter and 4chan claiming that emails of Anthony Weiner, Huma Abedin, and John Podesta revealed a pedophilia and human trafficking ring with Hillary Clinton at its centre. These were later reported, in news article form, on *YourNewsWire.com*, a website usually described as a "fake news website." Other websites and promoters picked up the story from there. Let us suppose that something like this is correct. According to some reports, Sean Adl-Tabatabai, who ran *YourNewsWire.com*, denied spreading disinformation and insisted that his site was a legitimate news organization.[26] Probably these claims are not sincere, but we cannot see inside Adl-Tabatabai's mind to check. Given this, we ask: what if Adl-Tabatabai *was* trying to reveal to others what he misguidedly took to be true? Would this mean that the Pizzagate story was not fake news after all? We think it would not. Pizzagate is a paradigm case of fake news not because of what was going on in Adl-Tabatabai's mind, but because it was a non-journalistically produced story that became wrapped in the mantle of journalism and was treated accordingly by a substantial portion of its audience. It is for this reason that, although the facts about the states of mind of producers of fake news are almost always murky, we, the various commentators on fake news, both in academia and public life, do not feel that deep insight into their state of mind is needed in order to classify works (such as the Pizzagate story) as fake news.

If we are correct about this, then neither intentions nor expectations to deceive should be part of the definition of "fake news." This lends some support to a view like Grundmann's. But Grundmann's requirement that fake news must be actually disposed to deceive a significant portion of its audience—whatever the intentions or expectations of its producers—is not quite right, either. This is for the reason explained above: as long as a work is treated as genuine news, for various purposes (such as political argumentation or social identification), by a significant portion of those who consume and spread it, it is not clear that those people's actual belief in the work matters very much. In fact, it is empirically unclear how large a portion of those who share fake news online believe the stories they are sharing, and thus it is unclear to what extent these stories are disposed to deceive audiences.[27] But even if much fake news *is* disposed to deceive (significant) audiences, whether it is really fake news does not seem to depend on this (currently unclear) empirical matter. Moreover, it is easy to imagine a situation in which audiences become non-disposed to believe fake news—or, perhaps, to believe *anything* they read online—but continue to use fake news for various political and social purposes in the ways described above.

For all of these reasons, we think it is an advantage of our definition of "fake news" that it does not require fake news to be intended, expected, or disposed to deceive. However, the absence of these requirements from our definition blocks the routes to excluding fictional news from counting as fake news that were open for the other definitions. Our definition seems to imply that some works of fictional news might also be fake news. Fictional news is not produced by following standard journalistic practices. So if works of fictional news are broadly spread by people who treat them as having been produced by following standard journalistic practices, then these works come to be fake news, according to our definition. In the next section, we address this apparent problem for our view.

Fictional News, Fake News, and the Importance of Genre

A famous actual case in which a work of fictional news was broadly spread and treated as genuine news by those who spread it was Iran's Fars News Agency's 2012 republishing of a pretend poll from *The Onion* suggesting that rural White Americans preferred Ahmadinejad to Obama. Presumably, the Fars News article was broadly spread (in Iran) and treated by its audience as genuine news. Allowing that the Fars News article is the same work as the *Onion* article (albeit in translation), our definition of "fake news" implies that the work became fake news once it was broadly spread and treated as genuine news in Iran. This might seem like a problem for our definition. For it is tempting to insist that the *Onion* article is, and remains, *satire*: it is fictional news, not fake news, Fars News' confusion notwithstanding. If our definition says otherwise, so much the worse for our definition.

In response to this, we begin by observing that the Fars News case, and related cases, also present a challenge for definitions of "fake news" that require works of fake news to be intended, expected, or disposed to deceive. The propensity of articles from *The Onion* and (its conservative counterpart) *The Babylon Bee* to lead to false beliefs on the part of significant numbers of readers, even without translation or re-publication, is well established.[28] So it seems that these articles are "produced or selected in general ways such that [they have] the robust disposition to lead, at the time of publication and under normal conditions, to a significant amount of false beliefs in a significant number of the addressed consumers," thus (at least arguably) satisfying Grundmann's definition of "fake news," cited above. Moreover, the fact that their articles are disposed to lead to false beliefs is not something that the producers of these works are unaware of, so it is reasonable to conclude that they are using a method of production that is expected by them to deceive a significant portion of the audience. So, at least arguably, their articles count as fake news according to Gelfert's definition, as well.[29]

Finally, it is not even clear that deceptive-intention definitions of "fake news" exclude all fictional news from being fake news. This is because it is not clear that being intended to deceive disqualifies a work from being satire, parody, or fiction. Suppose that a news satire website publishes a satirical article which is intended to suggest that a certain real politician reacted extremely unreasonably to a real altercation with a member of the public. The article does this by revising the actual details of the case in hyperbolic but (for those following the case) obviously fictional ways.[30] Suppose, also, that the producers and/or publishers of the article do not believe that the politician reacted extremely unreasonably, but they do dislike the politician, and they are aware that the message that the politician reacted extremely unreasonably will play well with their target audience, who also dislike the politician. By changing or exaggerating the details of the case, they do not intend to deceive their audience about what actually happened, but they do intend to deceive their audience about whether what actually happened was an extremely unreasonable reaction on the politician's part. This work would then be intended to deceive about its implied message—a message conveyed by inviting the audience to evaluate the politician's *actual* reaction similarly to how they would evaluate the hyperbolic reaction described. However, this intention to deceive would not entail that the work is not satire. It even seems consistent with the work being satire that its producers intended to make significant portions of their audience believe the hyperbolic details added to the story, or believe that the story was genuine journalism. Indeed, successfully deceiving large parts of one's audience, while leaving room for those who are attentive and in the know to get the joke, is sometimes considered a hallmark of excellent satire.[31]

Quite generally, then, the definitions of "fake news" that we have discussed do not clearly exclude all fictional news from also being fake news. One response to this would be to try to shore up these definitions with additional requirements that would rule out the sorts of works just mentioned from counting as fake news. We suspect that this effort would be in vain, however. For it seems to us that what these cases—actual and hypothetical—suggest is that the categories of fake news and fictional news overlap. The Fars News article, for instance, began as satire—fictional news—and it remained fictional news. But it went on to become fake news as well. At least for a while, it was *both* fictional news and fake news.[32]

If we are right that there is overlap between the categories of fake news and fictional news, then the task of limiting exposure to fake news on social media platforms becomes even more complicated. For, in that case, it might not be desirable to aim to block fake news across the board. Doing so might unduly restrict access to fictional news that has become, additionally, fake news. And, as we noted at the beginning of the chapter, fictional news has an important role to play in society, both aesthetically and epistemically. At the same time, if fictional news that has become fake news should not be blocked, this might seem to give a free pass to *all* fake news. Producers or distributors of fake news need only categorize their works as satire, parody, or fiction, and they will have a legitimate claim to space in the public discourse.

But in fact, although *some* fake news is also fictional news (like the Fars News article), most fake news is not. Not having been produced by following standard journalistic practices does not suffice for a work to be fictional news. Nor, we contend, does a producer's claiming that a work is fiction (or satire or parody) suffice for that work to be fiction (or satire or parody). To set goals for limiting exposure to fake news without restricting fictional news, we need to complement our account of fake news with (the beginnings of) an account of fictional news. Such an account is needed if we embrace the overlap between fake news and fictional news, while seeking to carve out some protection for fictional news that is also fake news. Such an account is also needed if we reject the overlap and aim, instead, to refine the definition of "fake news" so that fictional news will be excluded.

We can start with the kinds of fictional news that the term "fake news" was formerly used to refer to: news satire and news parody. Instances of these genres are currently the works of fictional news most likely to become, additionally, fake news. News satire and news parody are established artistic genres. What it takes to be an instance of one of these genres depends, in part, on what genres are. There are a range of different theories of genre within the philosophy of art,[33] but we are not aware of any on which the producer's *claiming* that a work is of a certain genre suffices on its own for the work to be an instance of that genre. So, the mere fact that creators like Paul Horner and Christopher Blair have publicly claimed that their work is satire does not entail that it is, in fact, satire. On the other hand, a producer's *intention* (whatever they may claim publicly) that a work be of a certain genre is given weight by several theories of genre.[34] And some theories say that a producer's intention that a work perform the function characteristic of a given genre suffices for the work to be an instance of that genre (whether or not the producer has intentions concerning the genre *per se*).[35] But we are not aware of any theories of genre according to which a producer's intention that a work be of a certain genre suffices on its own for the work to be an instance of that genre.

What this suggests—rightly, it seems to us—is that genre membership is not so easy that purveyors of fake news can simply claim, or intend, to be producing news satire or news parody, and thereby make it the case that what they produce is news satire or parody. What they would need to do to produce instances of these genres is a live question, which will be answered differently by different theories of genre. According to some theories, they would need to produce works that exhibit sufficient characteristic features of these genres;[36] for others, they would need to intend to fulfil the characteristic functions of these genres;[37] for others still, the works would need to be part of a tradition of news satire and news parody (through some combination of being influenced by and influencing such works, being intended to be part of that tradition, and being classified by others as part of that tradition);[38] and for yet others still, they might need their works to be accepted as parts of these genres by the communities of aesthetic appreciation that organize around them.[39]

We will not try to settle the question of what it takes for a work to be an instance of a genre in general, or of what it takes for a work to be an instance of news satire or news parody, specifically. To approach that task would require (at least!) another chapter and is further complicated by the rapidly evolving media landscape. However, what our brief discussion suggests is that the effort to understand and combat the phenomenon of fake news goes hand-in-hand with the effort to understand the nature of artistic genre in general, and genres that use the form of news as a fictional device, in particular. Above, we noted that news satire and news parody are not the only genres whose instances might use the device of being presented in the form of news. Works of literary fiction, dramatic cinema, performance art, creative memoir, graphic novels, and many genres of visual art might also employ this device. If such works become prevalent online, it will be important to complement our understanding of fake news with an understanding of the boundaries of many artistic genres. In order to protect these genres while reducing the reach of fake news, social media platforms and other actors will need tools for identifying genuine instances of the genres. These tools should ultimately be based on our best theories of genre.

To round off our discussion of the importance of genre to the separation of fictional news from *merely* fake news, let us consider a worry. Could there be works that are not instances of any established genre, but that use the fictional device of being presented in the form of news and are works of art deserving of protection? This certainly seems possible. New genres can come into existence, and it seems at least conceivable that some works of art neither create a new genre nor belong to any existing one. Would such a work be deserving of protection if it became fake news? It seems that it would, but not because it is an instance of a genre (since we are supposing that it is not an instance of any genre). Rather, it would deserve protection in virtue of being a work of art. This suggests that the true philosophical foundation of an approach to sorting fictional news from merely fake news is a theory of what it is to be a work of art. That question, however, is even more unsettled and controversial than the question of what it is to be an instance of a certain genre. And while such genre-defying cases are conceivable, they are certainly not common. So, for practical purposes, definitions of "fake news" will benefit most by being complemented with a theory of genre. Indeed, theories of the *specific* genres of news satire and news parody are important to incorporate, even if a general theory of genre remains out of reach.

Conclusion

In this chapter, we have tried to answer the question of what differentiates fake news from fictional news. We gave an overview of the recent philosophical literature on the definition of fake news, dividing the various definitions on offer into those that are based on the deceptive intentions of producers and distributors, on the one hand, and those that are not based on such intentions, on the other. Among definitions that are not based on deceptive intentions, we also separated definitions that require an *expectation* that consumers will be misled (exemplified by Gelfert's definition), and those that require a *disposition* to mislead consumers (exemplified by Grundmann's definition). All of these definitions appeal in some way to the beliefs of consumers of fake news, whether by requiring an intention to deceive consumers, an expectation that they will be deceived, or a simple disposition to deceive them. By contrast, the definition we presented does not require intentions or expectations on the part of producers to deceive or mislead consumers. Nor does it require dispositions to be misled on the part of consumers. Of course, it is likely that people are often deceived and misled by fake news—that consuming fake news often induces false beliefs, both about the world at large and about the provenance of the fake news stories themselves. These are important effects of fake news, but not, we have suggested, essential to the phenomenon itself.

Concerning our question of what the difference is between fake news and fictional news, we acknowledged that our definition does not rule out instances of fictional news from being, at the same time, fake news. But we pointed out that it is not clear that definitions of the other types do this, either. We embraced the conclusion that some fictional news is in fact, and at the same time, fake news. Finally, we argued that the fact that the categories overlap means that a useful account of fake news must be complemented with an account of the artistic genres whose instances may become fake news. This will provide a theoretical foundation for efforts to limit the spread of fake news while protecting artistic expression.

Notes

1 We would like to thank participants at the Workshop on Fiction and Belief, Part V, for extremely helpful discussion, and the editors of this volume for invaluable feedback on an earlier draft. Work on this paper was supported by the Swedish Research Council, grant VR2019-03154.

2 We describe in more detail what we mean by "fictional news" in the section entitled "Fictional News".

3 In a survey of academic articles from 2003 to 2017 that used the term "fake news," Tandoc et al. (2018) found that the most common use was to refer to news satire.

4 By the "new sense of the term 'fake news,' " we mean the now most widespread use of the term, to describe an epistemically dangerous societal phenomenon. This use has largely replaced the older use of the term to refer to news satire and parody. We will have much more to say below about what this phenomenon of fake news is. In describing this as a "new sense" of the term "fake news," we do not mean to imply that the phenomenon itself is completely new (see Pepp, Michaelson, and Sterken, 2019), nor that it is the unique such sense (see Brown, 2019; Pepp, Michaelson and Sterken, 2022, *pace* Habgood-Coote, 2019).

5 Horne and Adali (2017) found that, based on certain data sets and isolated characteristics, fake news shares more characteristics with news satire than real news.

6 For instance, the website RealRawNews.com, which is the source of viral fake news stories such as "Military Arrests Bill Gates" (on charges of "child trafficking and other unspeakable crimes against America and its people") (August 1, 2021), offers the disclaimer: "Information on this website is for informational and educational and entertainment purposes. **This website contains humor, parody, and satire.** We have included this disclaimer for our protection, on the advice on legal counsel" (emphasis in original). Another example is America's Last Line of Defense, a network of websites and Facebook pages run by Christopher Blair, which include disclaimers to the effect that they are satire, but are often spread as real news on social media. Moreover, Blair claims to design the stories as much to fool a certain audience as to entertain another (Funke, 2020; Gillin, 2017). An earlier well-known example is Paul Horner, who was behind many viral fake news stories in the 2016 US election, which he claimed were satire (Dewey, 2016).

7 What is required for fictional news to be legitimate? This is a difficult question that we cannot take up here. We think it is a safe assumption that a significant portion of fictional news is legitimate, even if there are also many borderline cases. Indeed, the works of Christopher Blair and Paul Horner, mentioned in footnote 6, may be examples of work that is not clearly legitimate fictional news, but also not clearly fake news, since these works were—if their creators were telling the truth about their motives—intended as satire. However, as will be discussed later on, a creator's intention to create satire is not sufficient for the result to be satire.

8 For a survey of the methods used in fake news detection, see Collins et al. (2020), Sharma et al. (2019), Zhang and Ghorbani (2020), Zhou and Zafarani (2020). For work that explicitly takes up the problem of distinguishing fictional news from fake news, or satire-detection, see, for example: Golbeck et al. (2018), Horne and Adali (2017), Rubin et al. (2015, 2016), Shu et al. (2017), and Thota et al. (2018).

9 Social media companies can use machine-learning algorithms (amongst other detection methods) to distinguish fake news and fictional news using only data sets or features thereof. However, without an accurate benchmark—that meets the descriptive, normative, and societal functions we, as a society, would like such categories to serve—there is no guarantee that the categories picked out, tracked, and shaped by detection algorithms (and their designers and those verifying the data) will serve our aims and needs as a society. Thus, reflection on the categories we as a society want and need is a crucial part of developing this technology, even independently of the development of explainable fake news detection (see Shu et al., 2019).

10 The work on fake news detection mentioned in footnote 5 uses a variety of definitions of news satire, specifically: Horne and Adali (2017) define satirical news as "stories that are from news sources that explicitly state they are satirical and do not intentionally spread misinformation. Satire news is explicitly produced for entertainment." Rubin et al. (2016), following Ermida (2012), characterize news satire as a form of deliberate deception, whereby it is "a genre of satire that mimics the format and style of journalistic reporting" (Rubin et al., 2016, 9) and is "comically extended to a fictitious construction where it becomes incongruous or even absurd, in a way that intersects entertainment with criticism" (Ermida, 2012, 187). Of course, the features used to track such definitions and identify satirical news are fine-grained features of the news stories and/or surrounding context, using natural language processing (NLP), machine learning, and/or other detection techniques. As we note below, our notion of fictional news is broader than the notion of news satire.

11 For more on this changing nature of the official news media, see, for instance, Pepp, Michaelson, and Sterken (2019) and Michaelson, Pepp, and Sterken (2022).

12 https://www.theonion.com/12-year-old-job-applicant-asked-to-explain-12-year-empl-1850168685

13 https://www.theonion.com/man-does-good-job-getting-drunk-1819574952

14 Or so the show's creators have maintained. Questions might be, and indeed have been, raised as to whether the show is best seen as comedy or as journalism.

15 Wes Anderson's film *The French Dispatch* (2021) is in the vicinity, although it is not presented in the format of news media.

16 For example, fake news has played a role in explaining the success of populist candidates in the 2016 US presidential election, the 2017 French presidential election, the 2017 German election, and the 2018 Italian election (Cantarella, Fraccaroli and Volpe, 2023).

17 These include third party fact-checking, community flagging and reporting, and algorithmic detection. For example, Facebook claims to reduce the prominence of stories that have checked out false or been repeatedly flagged/reported in News Feeds. Twitter claims to remove, reduce the visibility of, or label misleading information.

18 Poynter reports that laws specifically prohibiting the creation or spread of "fake news," so called, have been passed or proposed, for example, in Burkina Faso, Cambodia, Croatia, Egypt, France, Malaysia and Russia (Funke and Flamini, https://www.poynter.org/ifcn/anti-misinformation-actions/, retrieved 8 March 2023). According to Poynter, France's law was the first to provide a definition of "fake news," roughly: "Inexact allegations or imputations, or news that falsely report facts, with the aim of changing the sincerity of a vote."

19 See, for example, Rini (2017, E-59), Gelfert (2018, 106), Mukerji (2018, 931–32), Fallis and Mathiesen (2019, 5), and Pritchard (2021, 49).

20 See, for example, Rini (2017), McIntyre (2018, 112), and Pritchard (2021)

21 We elaborate on the boundary between fake news and poor journalism below.

22 Strictly speaking, it is *publishers*, rather than *producers*, who must intend to deceive in this way, according to Mukerji's definition. In addition, it is important for Mukerji that the claims to whose truth the publishers are indifferent—that is, "bullshit," in the sense of Frankfurt (2005)—are *asserted* rather than merely implied. (For more recent accounts of bullshit, see Engel, 2021; Gjelsvik, 2018). Mukerji thinks that if what is strictly asserted in a work is truthful, then strategic omissions or implications designed to mislead do not qualify the work as fake news. Pritchard (2021, 47) disagrees, arguing that "the most effective forms of fake news might well involve no literal falsehood at all," and mislead people instead by leaving out important context or qualification. Jaster and Lanius (2018, 2021) define fake news as "news that lacks truth and truthfulness," where news can lack truthfulness by being "bullshit" in something like Frankfurt's sense. They do not limit fake news to what is asserted, however. It is not clear whether Jaster and Lanius require that producers of fake news intend "to deceive their audience about their attitude toward the truth" (2021, 22, note 10), and thus it is not clear whether their definition should be classed as a deceptive intention definition or not.

23 In contrast, Grundmann's "purely consumer-oriented" account rejects this. He suggests that due to general selection bias in news reporting, even news produced by following standard journalistic practices might be "*slightly* fake news" (2021, 13).

24 Croce and Piazza propose that many consumers and sharers of fake news have the unreflective attitude of "treating a content as settled for the purpose of social recognition." Consumers may have this attitude toward a work whose content they do not believe. Having this attitude may lead to sharing a work widely and "treat[ing the work] as true" in order to reinforce one's social bonds and a sense of belonging to a group (2021, 58–59). The phenomenon they describe seems like another example of treating a work as having been produced by standard journalistic practices (although they explicate it in terms of treating a work as true, rather than in terms of having been produced by standard journalistic practices). On belief and social cognition, see also Lisa Zunshine's contribution to the present volume.

25 See also our discussion in (2019, 76).

26 See, for example: https://www.thedrum.com/news/2017/01/29/man-behind-one-the-biggest-sites-accused-fake-news-former-bbc-worker.

27 Empirical work suggests that belief in the accuracy of a news story plays little role in whether or not consumers choose to share it: false news stories are shared at least as often as accurate news even when those sharing the story could have identified it as inaccurate had they considered the possibility (cf. Epstein et al., 2021; Grinberg et al., 2019; Pennycook, Epstein et al., 2021; Pennycook, McPhetres et al., 2020; Vosoughi, Roy and Aral, 2018). Moreover, consumers' sharing behavior has been found to track features such as novelty (vs. familiarity), emotional evocativeness, engagingness, and whether the content aligns with the political values of the consumer (cf. Chen, Pennycook and Rand, 2021; Pennycook, Cannon and Rand, 2018; Pennycook and Rand, 2019, 2020; Vosoughi, Roy and Aral, 2018).

28 For discussion and some empirical results, see Garrett, Bond and Poulsen (2019).

29 Gelfert claims that the *Onion* story in the Fars News case is *not* a work of fake news, but does not explain how his definition is consistent with this claim. This is also noted by Pritchard (2021, 51).

30 As was arguably the intention behind a 2019 *Babylon Bee* article that was believed to be real by many readers. *Snopes.com* discusses the case here: https://www.snopes.com/fact-check/georgia-lawmaker-go-back-claim/. In the text that follows, we are not suggesting that the writers of *The Babylon Bee* had any of the deceptive intentions that we are hypothetically supposing. All we are pointing out is that if they did, this would not necessarily disqualify the work from being satire.

31 The Onion argued in an amicus brief to the US Supreme Court that the point of parody is to be as close to the real thing as possible, so that it is confusing: Brief of The Onion as Amicus Curiae of Anthony Novak vs. City of Parma, Ohio, No. 22–293 (2022). (www.supremecourt.gov/DocketPDF/22/22-293/242292/20221003125252896_35295545_1-22.10.03%20-%20Novak-Parma%20-%20Onion%20Amicus%20Brief.pdf)

32 In our earlier work, we suggested that, on our account, the Fars News article counts as fake news relative to one region (Iran) or audience, but does not count as fake news relative to another (the United States). (2019, 88, note 37) This approach of relativizing a work's status as fake news to regions or audiences may be a viable way to develop an account on which the categories of fake news and fictional news are, at least in this relativized way, mutually exclusive. The approach we set out here avoids the complications of relativization and illuminates what we now think may be a genuine insight about fake news: that fictionality is no guarantee against it.

33 See Malone (2022) for a useful overview.

34 See, for example, Friend (2012) and Evnine (2015).

35 See, for example, Abell (2015).

36 See, especially, Todorov (1973), Currie (2004) and Friend (2012).

37 See, especially, Abell (2015) and Carroll (1997).

38 See Evnine (2015).

39 This is suggested by Malone's (2022) sketch of a social theory of genre.

Works Cited

Abell, Catharine. 2015. "II—Genre, Interpretation and Evaluation." *Proceedings of the Aristotelian Society* 115, no. 1, part 1: 25–40.

Allen, Richard, and Murray Smith, eds. 1997. *Film Theory and Philosophy*. Oxford: Oxford University Press.

Bernecker, Sven, Amy K. Flowerree, and Thomas Grundmann. 2021. *The Epistemology of Fake News*. Oxford: Oxford University Press.

Brown, Étienne. 2019. "Fake News and Conceptual Ethics." *Journal of Ethics and Social Philosophy* 16, no. 2: 144–54.

Cantarella, Michele, Nicolò Fraccaroli, and Roberto Volpe. 2023. "Does Fake News Affect Voting Behaviour?" *Research Policy* 52, no. 1. https://doi.org/10.1016/j.respol.2022.104628.

Carroll, Noël. 1997. "Fiction, Non-Fiction, and the Film of Presumptive Assertion: A Conceptual Analysis." In Allen and Smith 1997, 173–202.

Chen, Xi (Cathy), Gordon Pennycook, and David G. Rand. 2021. What Makes News Sharable on Social Media? *PsyArXiv* Preprints. https://doi.org/10.31234/osf.io/gzqcd

Collins, Botambu, Dinh Tuyen Hoang, Ngoc Thanh Nguyen, and Dosam Hwang. 2020. "Fake News Types and Detection Models on Social Media: A State-of-the-Art Survey." In *Asian Conference on Intelligent*

Information and Database Systems. Communications in Computer and Information Science 1178, 562–73. Singapore: Springer. https://doi.org/10.1007/978-981-15-3380-8_49

Croce, Michel, and Tommaso Piazza. 2021. "Consuming Fake News: Can We Do Any Better?" *Social Epistemology* 37, no. 2: 1–10.

Currie, Gregory. 2004. *Arts and Minds.* Oxford: Oxford University Press.

Dewey, Caitlin. 2016. "Facebook Fake-News Writer: 'I Think Donald Trump Is in the White House Because of Me.'" *The Washington Post,* November 17. https://www.washingtonpost.com/news/the-intersect/wp/2016/11/17/facebook-fake-news-writer-i-think-donald-trump-is-in-the-white-house-because-of-me/

Engel, Pascal. 2021. "Post-Truth Is an Assertion Crisis." *Revue internationale de philosophie* 297, no. 3: 27–41.

Epstein, Ziv, Adam J. Berinsky, Rocky Cole, Andrew Gully, Gordon Pennycook, and David G. Rand. 2021. "Developing an Accuracy-Prompt Toolkit to Reduce COVID-19 Misinformation Online." *Harvard Kennedy School Misinformation Review* 2, no. 3 (May). https://doi.org/10.37016/mr-2020-71

Ermida, Isabel. 2012. "News Satire in the Press: Linguistic Construction of Humour." In *Language and Humour in the Media,* edited by Jan Chovanec and Isabel Ermida, 185–210. Newcastle Upon Tyne: Cambridge Scholars Publishing.

Evnine, Simon. J. 2015. "'But Is It Science Fiction?': Science Fiction and a Theory of Genre." *Midwest Studies in Philosophy* 39, no. 1: 1–28. https://doi.org/10.1111/misp.12037

Fallis, Don, and Kay Mathiesen. 2019. "Fake News Is Counterfeit News." *Inquiry.* Online first. https://doi.org/10.1080/0020174X.2019.1688179

Friend, Stacie. 2012. "VIII—Fiction as a Genre." In *Proceedings of the Aristotelian Society* 112, no. 2, pt. 2: 179–209.

Funke, Daniel. 2020. "How a Disinformation Network Exploited Satire to Become a Popular Source of False News on Facebook." *Politifact,* The Poynter Institute, January 23. https://www.politifact.com/article/2020/jan/23/one-most-popular-false-news-sites-facebook-part-pa/

Garrett, R. Kelly, Robert Bond, and Shannon Poulsen. 2019. "Too Many People Think Satirical News Is Real." *The Conversation,* 16 August. https://theconversation.com/too-many-people-think-satirical-news-is-real-121666.

Gelfert, Axel. 2018. "Fake News: A Definition." *Informal Logic* 38, no. 1: 84–117.

Gillin, Joshua. 2017. "If You're Fooled by Fake News, This Man Probably Wrote It. *Politifact,* The Poynter Institute, May 31. https://www.politifact.com/article/2017/may/31/If-youre-fooled-by-fake-news-this-man-probably-wro/

Gjelsvik, Olav. 2018. "Bullshit Production." In *Lying: Language, Knowledge, Ethics and Politics,* edited by Eliot Michaelson and Andreas Stokke, 129–42. Oxford: Oxford University Press.

Golbeck, Jennifer, Matthew Mauriello, Brooke Auxier, Keval H. Bhanushali et al. 2018. "Fake News vs Satire: A Dataset and Analysis". In *Proceedings of the 10th ACM Conference on Web Science,* 17–21. *WebSci* 18. https://doi.org/10.1145/3201064.3201100

Grinberg, Nir, Kenneth Joseph, Lisa Friedland, Briony Swire-Thompson, and David Lazer. 2019. "Fake News on Twitter during the 2016 US Presidential Election." *Science* 363, no. 6425: 374–78.

Grundmann, T. 2020. "Fake News: The Case for a Purely Consumer-Oriented Explication." *Inquiry* 6 (September): 1–15. https://doi.org/10.1080/0020174X.2020.1813195

Habgood-Coote, Joshua. 2019. "Stop Talking About Fake News!" *Inquiry* 62, nos. 9–10: 1033–65.

Horne, Benjamin D., and Sibel Adali. 2017. "This Just In: Fake News Packs a Lot in Title, Uses Simpler, Repetitive Content in Text Body, More Similar to Satire than Real News." *Proceedings of the International AAAI Conference on Web and Social Media.* https://doi.org/10.1609/icwsm.v11i1.14976

Jaster, Romy, and David Lanius. 2018. "What Is Fake News?" *Versus* 47, no. 2: 207–24.

Jaster, Romy, and David Lanius. 2021. "Speaking of Fake News: Definitions and Dimensions." In Bernecker. Flowerree, and Grundmann 2021, 19–45.

Malone, Evan. 2022. "The Problem of Genre Explosion." *Inquiry.* Online first. https://doi.org/10.1080/0020174X.2022.2131623

McIntyre, Lee. 2018. *Post-Truth.* Cambridge, MA: MIT Press.

Michaelson, Eliot, Jessica Pepp, and Rachel Sterken. 2022. "Relevance-Based Knowledge Resistance in Public Conversations." In *Knowledge Resistance in High-Choice Information Environments,* edited by Jesper Strömbäck, Åsa Wikforss, Kathrin Glër, Torun Lindholm and Henrik Oscarsson, 106–27. London: Routledge

Mukerji, Nikil. 2018. "What Is Fake News?" *Ergo: An Open Access Journal of Philosophy* 5: 923–46. Pennycook, Gordon, Tyrone D. Cannon, and David G. Rand. 2018. "Prior Exposure Increases Perceived Accuracy of Fake News." *Journal of Experimental Psychology* 147, no. 12: 1865–80.

Pennycook, Gordon, Z. Epstein, M. Mosleh, A. A. Arechar, D. Eckles, and David G. Rand. 2021. "Shifting Attention to Accuracy Can Reduce Misinformation Online." *Nature* 592: 590–95. https://doi.org/10.1038/s41586-021-03344-2.

Pennycook, Gordon, and David G. Rand. 2019. "Lazy, Not Biased: Susceptibility to Partisan Fake News Is Better Explained by Lack of Reasoning Than by Motivated Reasoning." *Cognition* 188: 39–50.

Pennycook, Gordon, and David G. Rand. 2020. "Who Falls for Fake News? The Roles of Bullshit Receptivity, Overclaiming, Familiarity, and Analytic Thinking." *Journal of Personality* 88, no. 2: 185–200.

Pennycook, Gordon, Jonathon McPhetres, Yunhao Zhang, Jackson G. Lu, and David G. Rand. 2020. Fighting COVID-19 Misinformation on Social Media: Experimental Evidence for a Scalable Accuracy-Nudge Intervention. *Psychological Science* 31, no. 7: 770–780.

Pepp, Jessica, Eliot Michaelson, and Rachel Sterken. 2019. "What's New About Fake News." *Journal of Ethics & Social Philosophy* 16, no. 2: 67.

Pepp, Jessica, Eliot Michaelson, and Rachel Sterken. 2022. "Why We Should Keep Talking about Fake News." *Inquiry* 65, no. 4: 471–87.

Pritchard, Duncan. 2021. "Good News, Bad News, Fake News." In Bernecker, Flowerree and Grundmann 2021, 46–67.

Rini, Regina. 2017. "Fake News and Partisan Epistemology." *Kennedy Institute of Ethics Journal* 27, no. 2: E-43.

Rubin, Victoria L., Yimin Chen, and Nadia K. Conroy. 2015. "Deception Detection for News: Three Types of Fakes." *Proceedings of the Association for Information Science and Technology* 52, no. 1: 1–4.

Rubin, Victoria L., Nadia K. Conroy, Yimin Chen, and Sarah Cornwell. 2016. "Fake News or Truth? Using Satirical Cues to Detect Potentially Misleading News." In *Proceedings of the Second Workshop on Computational Approaches to Deception Detection*, 7–17. https://doi.org/10.18653/v1/W16-0802.

Sharma, Karishma, Feng Qian, He Jiang, Natali Ruchansky, Ming Zhang, and Yan Liu. 2019. "Combating Fake News: A Survey on Identification and Mitigation Techniques." *ACM Transactions on Intelligent Systems and Technology (TIST)* 10, no. 3: 1–42.

Shu, Kai, Limeng Cui, Suhang Wang, Dongwon Lee, and Huan Liu. 2019. "dEFEND: Explainable Fake News Detection." In *Proceedings of the 25th ACM SIGKDD International Conference on Knowledge Discovery & Data Mining*, 395–405. https://doi.org/10.1145/3292500.3330935

Shu, Kai, Amy Sliva, Suhang Wang, Jiliang Tang, and Huan Liu. 2017. "Fake News Detection on Social Media: A Data Mining Perspective." *ACM SIGKDD Explorations Newsletter* 19, no. 1: 22–36.

Tandoc Jr, Edson C., Zheng Wei Lim, and Richard Ling. 2018. "Defining 'Fake News': A Typology of Scholarly Definitions." *Digital Journalism* 6, no. 2: 137–53.

Thota, Aswini, Priyanka Tilak, Simrat Ahluwalia, Nibrat Lohia. 2018. "Fake News Detection: A Deep Learning Approach." *SMU Data Science Review* 1, no. 3: 10.

Todorov, Tzvetan. 1973. *The Fantastic: A Structural Approach to Literary Genre*. Translated by Richard Howard. Cleveland: Case Western Reserve University Press.

Vosoughi, Soroush, Deb Roy, and Sinan Aral. 2018. "The Spread of True and False News Online." *Science* 359, no. 6380: 1146–51.

Xichen Zhang, and Ali A. Ghorbani. 2020. "An Overview of Online Fake News: Characterization, Detection, and Discussion." *Information Processing & Management* 57, no. 2: 102025.

Zhou, Xinyi, and Reza Zafarani. 2020. "A Survey of Fake News: Fundamental Theories, Detection Methods, and Opportunities." *ACM Computing Surveys (CSUR)* 53, no. 5: 1–40.

18

TRUST, CREDULITY, AND SPEECH

Philippe Roussin

Trust in politics is traditionally considered a central pillar of democratic legitimacy and stability. Because political trust is considered a necessary precondition for democratic rule, a decline in trust is generally thought to fundamentally put representative democracy at risk. The crisis of democracies is thus measured today by a decline in confidence in those who govern and in the credibility of public speech. Contemporary populism, in America as in Europe, forces us to rethink the relationship between leaders and citizens. It thrives on the discredit of public speech, on the gap between reality and its representation. It is not only an ideology, a strategy, a political offer, but also a political style and a type of discourse, made of expressions, of turns of phrase and syntactic forms (bullying, coarse language, readiness to resort to anecdotes as "evidence") (Moffitt, 2016, *passim*). It seeks to acquire an image of credibility and profoundly alters the political grammar of trust (performers, audiences, stages, and the mise-en-scène of the phenomenon).

This discursive and performative dimension of populism is rarely at the heart of the analysis of political scientists, but literature can provide us with tools to help understand what this style of political discourse consists of, why trust is always fundamentally trust in speech, and what justifies the penchant for credulity that characterizes our linguistic interactions. I will base my demonstration on an analysis of Herman Melville's *The Confidence-Man: His Masquerade,* a great novel, first published in 1857, about trust, credulity, and credit given to others, the reasons for granting or refusing them, their links with truth, and the struggle between charity and prudence, which also incorporates a reflection on the characters of novels and the complex interplay between fiction, trust, and belief.

The philosopher Gilles Deleuze saw in Melville's novel a great book on "the powers of the false" (Deleuze, 1989, 133–34). In an interview given to the *New Yorker* in 2017, Philip Roth recommended its reading on the grounds that "Herman Melville's *The Confidence-Man: His Masquerade* was the right book to read in the days of Donald Trump Potus" (Thurman, 2017). The author of *The Plot against America* (2004) thus considered the fictional character created by Melville as one of the distant ancestors of the author of *The Art of the Deal*. Donald Trump explained in this work to his glory published in 1987: "I don't do it for the money. I've got enough, more than I'll ever need. I do it to do it. Deals are my art form" (3). Several factors, according to the businessman, contribute to the success of the deal: *think big, maximize your options, know your market*:

DOI: 10.4324/9781003119456-21

> Some people have a sense of the market and some people don't. Steven Spielberg has it. [...]
> Woody Allen has it for the audience he cares about reaching, and so does Sylvester Stallone, at
> the other end of the spectrum.
>
> *(Trump, 1987, 36)*

And *get the word out*

> You need to generate interest, and you need to create excitement [...] A little hyperbole never
> hurts. People want to believe that something is the biggest and the greatest and the most spec-
> tacular. I call it truthful hyperbole. It's an innocent form of exaggeration—and a very effective
> form of promotion.
>
> *(39–40)*

Philip Roth wasn't the first to call Donald Trump a conman. As early as 2016, political opponents,
among them other candidates for the nomination of the Republican Party, had already presented him
as a "con artist." He himself reserved the term for contemporary artists: "I've always felt that a lot
of modern art is a con, and that the most successful painters are often better salesmen and promoters
than they are artists" (Trump, 1987, 25).

The Confidence-Man: His Masquerade was a commercial failure and the last novel Melville published. A neologism, the term was coined in 1849 and used in connection with the character Melville
was inspired by. The action takes place on April 1 (*All Fools Day*: by an almost Melvillean oddity,
the book appeared on April 1, 1857) during a journey of 1,200 miles across the United States, from
North to South, along the Mississippi, on a steamer leaving Saint Louis (Missouri) to go down the
river toward New Orleans (Louisiana). The story is reduced to a single day, beginning at sunrise and
ending at midnight, before the steamer reaches its final destination. The novel ends open-endedly. In
the final scene, night has fallen, and after a long discussion with an old farmer, first about the Bible
and then about money, the character of the Cosmopolitan turns off the light in the ship's salon. The
novel ends with the sentence: "Something further may follow of this Masquerade."

Melville's book raises the ethical question of whether trust is just and morally obligatory, whether
it is binding in all cases and constitutes a valid maxim without exception ("as the apostle said to the
Corinthians, 'I rejoice that I have confidence in you in all things' " [Melville, 2006, 53–54]). Should
it, as ethics would have it, be the rule? Should we, when in doubt, nevertheless favor it, while leaving
room for mistrust? Does the general obligation to trust formulated as a principle retain its meaning
and remain relevant in all circumstances? Should the decision to observe this general obligation always be followed? When does morality require preserving trust, and when does it require destroying
trust? When does the trust that consists in counting on benevolence and goodwill come into conflict
with the ways of counting on the reactions and attitudes of others that characterize the actor, the
publicist, the extortionist? Can an ethics of principles support a theory of action? Melville is not
speaking in universalist terms. The book has a specific setting; it considers the question of why trust
has become a source of distrust in the world of money and of the free market society, in "the age of
joint-stock companies" (Melville, 2006, 181) and of the "Wall street spirit" (49), in the society of
Christian missions, slavery, and the frontier at the time when he published the book.

Etymology suggests the close links that exist between trust, faith, fidelity, confidence, credit, and
belief. For Melville and the nineteenth-century reader, *confidence* was primarily a synonym for *trust*.
The word *con* now means a trick or fraud. We have forgotten that it comes from the word *confidence*.
His Masquerade, the subtitle, itself has a double meaning: it conjures up the idea of entertainment in
which the actors are masked, but it also speaks of falsification, dissimulation.

We spontaneously believe the stories we are told, and we trust people not out of credulity but out of necessity. "Without the general trust people have in each other, society itself would disintegrate," wrote Georg Simmel, "for very few relationships are based entirely upon what is known with certainty about another person, and very few relationships would endure if trust were not as strong as, or stronger than rational proof or personal observation" (Simmel, 2004, 177–78). The German sociologist made trust one of the three invisible institutions, along with authority and legitimacy, on which society rests. As Niklas Luhmann writes after him in his classic *Trust and Power*:

> Trust in the broadest sense of confidence (*Zutrauen*) in one's expectations, is a basic fact of social life. In many situations, of course, a person can choose in certain respects whether or not to bestow trust. But a complete absence of trust would prevent him or her from getting up in the morning. He would be prey to a vague sense of dread, to paralyzing fears.
>
> *(Luhmann, 2017, 5)*

Trust is neither faith nor belief. It presupposes a relationship with others. It is only possible between human beings, mediated by a collective norm embodied in an institution. If we believe in the stories we are told, it is, among other reasons, because we trust the source—the author, the interpreter, or the tradition—of the story, and if we trust the source, it is because we are able to trace it back and identify it. In this sense, the trust we place in others and in their words poses the same kind of problems as the predisposition to believe our fellow human beings, which has long been analyzed by the epistemology of testimony. In the modern epistemological tradition, testimony as a legitimate source of beliefs and knowledge is the object of a certain suspicion. A testimony being a content of information transmitted from one subject to another by some mediation, the classical theory examines its validity in the same way as that of any belief whatsoever, questioning the evidence that supports its reliability. In *An Inquiry into the Human Mind on the Principles of Common Sense* (1764), Thomas Reid, on the contrary, makes testimony a principle of common sense, through what he calls the "principle of credulity." The principle of credulity is "a disposition to confide in the veracity of others, and to believe what they tell us" (Reid, 1997, 6.24, 194/196b). According to Reid's philosophy of common sense, testimonies are generally correct and based on reliable mechanisms with which we are endowed by nature and which, as a matter of necessity, we are to take for granted in the ordinary affairs of life. We can trust what we perceive. Eyes do not lie. The remedy for David Hume's skepticism is, therefore, not through rational debate: rather, it consists in the indisputable acceptance of what has always seemed and continues to seem objectively true for us and in the reaffirmation of the normative value in the way people ordinarily perceive the world around them. Reid associated Hume's skepticism with modern urban culture with its increasingly secularized, individualized, mobile, and commercial world dominated, during the mid-eighteenth century, by information and opinion (see Rosenfeld, 2014). Common sense, by contrast, he conceived of as a mental faculty necessary to social life, a source of social cohesion linking the subject to the community, "the degree of judgment which is common to men with whom we can converse and transact business" ([1785] 1997), 424). This differs starkly from a remark by one of Melville's characters to the effect that appearances and behavior are misleading and cannot be considered as guarantees of words: "Life is a pic-nic en costume; one must take a part, assume a character, stand ready in a sensible way to play the fool" (Melville, 2006, 139).

The Economy of Trust

Trust has long been understood as one of the conditions for the marketing of goods and services. It became an important issue with the development of trade in Europe around the tenth century. The historian Giacomo Todeschini has shown how, within the framework of a growing dialogue with the urban elites, Franciscan theology developed a large part of the vocabulary of economics that is still with us today: it became necessary to define the role and social status of merchants as well as their credentials as professionals in economic exchange at a time when cash and money were becoming an everyday reality. The merchants were alternately objects of confidence and mistrust on the part of the official representatives of wealth, in the eyes of whom profit should consist in the disinterested management of a collective patrimony, aiming at the advantage of the community and the expansion of Christianity. Conceived of by the Franciscans as "the common good of the faithful," the market was presented "as a system of relationships based on reciprocal trust and credibility" (Todeschini, 2009, 153).

The question of who could be trusted primarily concerned those "with doubtful reputations"—the poor, the miserable, the delinquents, and those who did not belong to the community of the Church, beginning with the Jewish merchants.

> In fact, it was necessary and actually indispensable for trust to be concretely based on the membership of individuals in well-structured and civically identifiable groups in a way that everyone's identity was defined by belonging to important families, professional corporations, guilds, confraternities, or companies. The recognizable market consisted of these collective subjects, and people who acted in the market in a credible and ethically admissible way had to belong to these groups.
>
> *(Todeschini, 154–55)*

In this world where the market was still a mirror of the community of the faithful, the introduction of external and foreign subjects and of economic behaviors indifferent to religious and civic solidarity created an element of danger for the "logics of mutual recognition" and the "ethical nature of the economic game." There was, therefore, an intimate intertwining between religious faith and economic credibility: "This *fides* (trust, reliability, trustworthiness) depends on the good name that the merchant has […]. It also depends to a great degree on his ability to lead his social life in religiously recognizable terms" (Todeschini, 165).

While the advent of modernity and the increasing complexity of the social order are at the origin of the mutation of economic languages, they did not cause the place and the importance given to trust by the market to disappear. On the contrary, it was promoted to the rank of principle or foundation of political economy. As anonymity and abstraction have taken over from personalized exchange, distance commerce has evolved into practices that are increasingly detached from the traditional supports of trust (personal knowledge, familiarity or belonging to the same community). Confidence changed into a hope of reliability and an expectation of continuity in human conduct. It is now based on an extrapolation from available information. The confidence in "the age of joint-stock companies" and the "Wall Street spirit" becomes a mechanism for reducing risk, uncertainty, vulnerability, and the fruit of rational calculation. It is a way of anticipating the future and directing social time with credit (Rey, 2002, 2014). From this point of view, it is significant that the multiple avatars of the confidence-man in Melville's novel are systematically presented as strangers, unknown individuals without guarantees, offering little that allows for social control: the absence of information about such individuals guides the interlocutor toward trust or mistrust, according to his charitable disposition or his credulity.

The expansion of markets finally gave rise to a new vision of the relationship between the economy and morality. Trust that had mainly been based on moral or cultural considerations was relegated to the rank of a non-rational behavior, and trust became a reciprocally interested relationship based on calculation and the personal interest that governs economic exchanges. The philosophy behind this reformulation of trust is expressed by Adam Smith in his *Inquiry into the Nature and Causes of the Wealth of Nations* (1776): "It is not from the benevolence of the butcher, the brewer, or the baker, that we expect our dinner, but from their regard to their own interest. We address ourselves, not to their humanity but to their self-love" (Smith, 2007, 16).

One will find in Melville's novel the most contradictory views as to the meaning and benefits of the evolution that trust has undergone in modern times. It is one of the incarnations of the confidence-man who explains that "[c]onfidence is the indispensable basis of all sorts of business transactions. Without it, commerce between man and man, as between country and country, would, like a watch, run down and stop" (Melville, 2006, 133). It is a pastor who declares: "Next to mistrusting Providence, there be aught that man should pray against, it is against mistrusting his-fellow-man" (24). It does not seem, according to the character of a misanthrope, that the modern world is able to satisfy the need for confidence: "go lay down in your grave, old man, if you can't stand of yourself. It's a hard world for a leaner" (116). A businessman, finally, has no doubt that he can bring the "spirit of Wall street" into the Christian missions and create a "World's Charity" (51).

Classical Liberalism and Trust

Trust has also been seen by liberal thought as a cornerstone of civil society and the legitimacy of power. We are referring here to the theory of government as *trust*. In *Two Treatises of Civil Government* (1689), John Locke makes trust the bond of society, *vinculum societatis* (Locke, 1953, 183 ff.). He gives it a central place in the social contract by which free men in a state of nature would show trust among themselves and with regard to the sovereign. Trust designates a relationship with leaders (but also with others) which forms the obverse of the obligation. Individuals consent to the majority speaking for the whole of society. Representation is an act of trust. Lucien Jaume, in *Les origines philosophiques du libéralisme* (2010), writes that the project of "a society fundamentally appealing to trust" is at the heart of liberal thought and of the relationship between freedom and law:

> The notion of trust is paramount in a liberal society [...] Trust designates this relationship with leaders (as well as with others) that underlies obligation, and even serves as its precondition. Indeed, trust is what, by vesting such persons with the duties of legislator, enables us to lay store in future laws and thus to prepare for the future obligation. Trust develops and grows more complex through the medium of public opinions [...] The relationship between liberty and the law must thus, in order to be fully understood, be considered as thr relationship between. freedom and trust.
>
> *(Jaume, 2010, 258)*

In this optimistic vision, political trust is not based on reputation or knowledge; it consists in a "gift of credit toward the moral freedom of others"; "the ability of someone to work for our good and not for their personal profit" (Jaume, 2010, 271).[1] Trust in rulers increases trust among members of society. It can never be unconditional and must be regularly maintained. In *Democracy in America* (*II*, 1840), Alexis de Tocqueville worried about knowing what foundations it could rest on in a society where tradition and old hierarchies were no longer authoritative:

> As to the influence which the intelligence of one man has on that of another, it must necessarily be very limited in a country where the citizens, placed on the footing of a general similitude, are all closely seen by each other; and where, as no signs of incontestable greatness or superiority are perceived in any one of them, they are constantly brought back to their own reason as the most obvious and proximate source of truth. It is not only confidence in this or that man which is then destroyed, but the taste for trusting the ipse dixit of any man whatsoever.
>
> *(Tocqueville, 2002, 489)*

A Novel about Trust and Credit

In Melville's novel, the steamer that descends the Mississippi bears the French name Le Fidèle, a clear reference to the old *fides*. It is a reduced model of humanity.

> As among Chaucer's Canterbury pilgrims, or those oriental ones crossing the Red Sea towards Mecca in the festival month, there was no lack of variety. Natives of all sorts, and foreigners; men of business and men of pleasure; parlor men and backwoodsmen; farm-hunters and fame-hunters; heiress-hunters, gold-hunters, buffalo-hunters, bee-hunters, happiness-hunters, truth-hunters, and still keener hunters after all these hunters. Fine ladies in slippers, and moccasined squaws; Northern speculators and Eastern philosophers; English, Irish, German, Scotch, Danes; Santa Fé traders in striped blankets, and Broadway bucks in cravats of cloth of gold; fine-looking Kentucky boatmen, and Japanese-looking Mississippi cotton-planters; Quakers in full drab, and United States soldiers in full regimentals; slaves, black, mulatto, quadroon; modish young Spanish Creoles, and old-fashioned French Jews; Mormons and Papists Dives and Lazarus; jesters and mourners, teetotalers and convivialists, deacons and blacklegs; hard-shell Baptists and clay-eaters; grinning negroes, and Sioux chiefs solemn as high-priests. In short, a piebald parliament, an Anacharsis Cloots congress of all kinds of that multiform pilgrim species, man.
>
> *(Melville, 2006, 16–17)*

The boat will also be compared to a ship of fools. During the day, travelers, anonymous and unknown, get on and off at each stopover. People appear and disappear from the boat. Arrivals, departures, and passages from one place to another create an environment in which all interactions are constrained. *Le Fidèle* is reminiscent of Theseus' boat, the story of which is told by Plutarch in *De viris illustribus*. Here, however, it is not the wooden parts of the ship but the passengers being transported that continually change and are gradually replaced. *Le Fidèle* represents a moving and unstable society that is constantly renewing itself. It receives additional passengers in exchange for those who disembark so that, though always full of strangers, it continually adds to them, as it were, or replaces them with still stranger strangers. The operation raises, in total, the same philosophical concern about the nature of things and their identity: what is *Le Fidèle* loyal to, whom do its passengers trust?

The steamer is the scene of encounters between multiple characters who do not know one another and will never see each other again, travelers without priorities who will not form lasting relationships. It is the setting for philosophical discussions that have trust as their common thread—a disposition that, again, assumes the existence of a familiar and regulated world, of close and lasting interpersonal relationships and of contracts to be honored, of exchanges of views on charity and philanthropy, but also of commercial transactions quickly concluded, with or without success. *Le Fidèle* gathers together a society of strangers and brings together a community of strangers. It is a world in miniature. It evokes both the world of the market, the world of capitalism in its infancy, that of the Frontier and America ante bellum democracy. On board blows "the dashing and all-fusing spirit of the West" (17).

The *Confidence-Man* is a "novel with no plot, no real hero, no progression, no denouement" (Lapoujade, 2010, 1214). It is mainly made up of conversations and dialogues, with the exception of three meta-fictional digressions. It is constructed as a series of sketches in which multiple characters intersect in terms of their number as well as the variety of masks they are suspected of wearing. The first chapter is the only non-dialogue scene in the book: it is organized around three inscriptions and sets the scene. A notice, which is not reproduced in the text, is posted near the captain's cabin. It offers a reward "for the capture of a mysterious impostor, supposed to have recently arrived from the East, quite an original genius in his vocation, as would appear, though wherein his originality consisted was not clearly given" (Melville, 2006, 9–10). The crowd presses in front of the sign as in front of "a theatre-bill." Then climbs aboard, alone, with no porter or friend to accompany him, a mute man in pale-colored clothes carrying no "trunk, suitcase, carpet bag, or package." For these reasons, the crowd is quick to catalog him: "it was clear that he was, in the most extreme sense of the word, a stranger." Confronted with the wanted notice, the mute writes on a black slate which he brandishes above him for all to see: "Charity thinks of no evil." The formula is taken from the description of love in the Epistle to the Corinthians (1 Corinthians 13). Without pleasure, the crowd observes its author, whom it takes for a simpleton of a bizarre and harmless kind. As the crowd gathers around him, nudging him as he passes, the stranger erases and partially corrects his messages, retaining only the word 'charity' throughout as it was writing. He writes successively on his blackboard the following sentences: "Charity has suffered a long time, and is good"; "Charity supports everything"; "Charity believes everything"; and "Charity never fails." A third and final inscription, which receives the assent of the crowd, then appears. It is written on a piece of cardboard that serves as a sign for the hairdresser hung above his cabin, near the captain's office. The sign represents an open razor and carries, "for the public benefit," two words, "not unfrequently seen ashore gracing other shops, besides barbers," "NO TRUST"; an inscription which, comments the narrator summarizing the attitude of the crowd,

> Though in a sense not less intrusive than the contrasted ones of the stranger, did not, it seemed, provide any corresponding derision or surprise, much less indignation; and still less, to all appearances, did it gain for the inscriber the repute of being a simpleton.
>
> *(12)*

The variation of the avatars of trust (faith, belief, credulity, credit) is thus introduced by the "strange trinity" (Blaise, 2018) of the "original genius" whose head is put at a price, the deaf-mute whom the crowd makes fun of, and the riverboat hairdresser who, despite his gruff demeanor and unfriendly message, is perfectly accepted by the crowd of passengers. The identification of the crook, described as a stranger and a "mysterious impostor," will prove to be endless, his apprehension repeatedly deferred throughout the novel. The stranger who in this first chapter makes himself the apostle of the principle of charity will turn out to be its first iteration. In this society of strangers, the confidence-man character is not identifiable, as he never ceases to disguise himself and to metamorphose. He escapes. He is unrecognizable and diabolically takes on shifting appearances: he "ties himself," says the philanthropist (one of his incarnations), "to no narrow tailor or teacher, but federates, in heart as in costume, something of the various gallantries of men under various suns" (137). He is an actor, a good performer who dresses and behaves like Harlequin. Its tricks, its deceptions, its language lead astray. He can make the most contradictory remarks and feign the most incompatible convictions, adapting them to his interlocutor: "Give me your story. Ere I undertake a cure, I require a full account of the case" (99); "My dear fellow, tell me how I can serve you" (138).

The novel continues with a parable-like altercation. On the deck of the boat, a crippled and free Black man is suspected of being a crook disguised as a beggar, "some white operator, betwisted and painted up for a decoy." The text does not say which of the possible causes of the suspicion and defiance of the crowd prevails: apparent infirmity, the color of the skin or the free condition of a Black man. Summoned to prove that he is in good faith and, despite lacking identity papers, above all suspicion, he appeals to the testimony of trustworthy passengers met on the boat. But no witnesses come forward. Oral testimonies, like tangible evidence ("documentary proof"), are matters for caution. Failing to inspire confidence on word or on the faith of certified documents, how can Black Guinea (the nickname given to the cripple) expect to be believed? A young Episcopalian pastor first delivers a sermon on the importance of mutual trust in an attempt to be supportive of Black Guinea. A suspicious one-legged man to whom the churchman asks if he is devoid of any spirit of charity replies tit for tat that "charity is one thing, and truth is another" (22). It is one thing to trust out of charity, another to be lucid. Another character will compare the truth to a ruthless mechanism ("Truth is like a thrashing-machine; tender sensibilities must keep out of the way" [125]). It will be noted that, throughout the discussions and staged exchanges among frontiersmen who are strangers to one another, and, more broadly, in this new American world where "Christian confidence" has become "conditional" confidence, the people located outside the circle of trust traced by the crowd of passengers on *Le Fidèle* are, on the one hand, a free slave, with no master to vouch for him:

"No confidence in dis poor ole darkie, den?

Before giving you our confidence [...] we will wait the report of the kind gentlemen who went in search of one of your friends who was to speak for you.

(24–25).

And on the other, the American Indians "treacherous to the given word," who break treaty promises and are the object of the Pioneer's hatred ("in one breath, he learns that a brother is to be loved, and an Indian to be hated" [151]). The conversations aboard *Le Fidèle* evoke everything in the American political news of the moment, particularly slavery, the Indian wars and the Christian missions.

An avatar of the confidence-man strikes up a conversation with one passenger. This is usually the way chapters begin. Thomas Velasquez writes:

The steamboat becomes a convenient place for all sorts of conmen trying to sell stocks in failing companies or miracle herbal medicine that can cure everything (from cancer to an ordinary cold), or raise money for so-called charities such as the Seminole Widows and Orphans Society, or even simply convince people to give money as a token of trust in their fellows travelers.

(Velasquez, 2019, 2)

The word "trust" appears many times during the forty-five chapters of the novel. The verb *diddle* and its derivatives come after. "To seem" is the most frequently used verb in the novel. The title of Melville's novel suggests the presence of a central character. Throughout the novel, however, just what form he takes is anything but clear. Seven avatars are shown in the first half of the narrative before giving way in the second part to a new, astonishing creature, the extravagantly costumed Cosmopolitan who bears the edifying name of Frank Goodman and could well be the wanted conman, even if other serious candidates (all dressed in white from the first chapter, starting with the deaf-mute) have preceded him. He seems to somehow sum up this apparent cacophony in his curious colorful attire. Melville's book on trust is a "masquerade," an eternal change of costumes. Transaction completed, the character takes another form.

The confidence-man character is not a literary invention of Melville. Such characters were called *diddlers*, after the name of a popular early nineteenth-century comedy hero who was to give rise to the verb *diddle*. The suspicious one-legged man makes the crippled Black man who appears in the novel "some sort of black Jeremy Diddler" (24). The herbal doctor is called thus as well:

Jeremy Diddler? I have heard of Jeremy the prophet, and Jeremy Taylor the divine, but your other Jeremy is a gentleman I am unacquainted with.
You are his confidential clerk, ain't you?"
Whose, pray? Not that I think myself unworthy of being confided in, but I don't understand. (141)

Edgar Allan Poe had seized the word and the notion as early as 1843 in a tale entitled "Diddling Considered as one of the Exact Sciences": "Diddle, rightly considered, is a compound whose ingredients are minuteness, interest, perseverance, ingenuity, audacity, nonchalance, originality, impertinence, and grin" (Poe, 1984, 607). Poe's portrait draws the outlines of a man who puts his own interests before those of others, works on a small scale, and has the creative mind of an inventor who does not allow himself to be distracted. His true motives are usually the last to be revealed.

Fiction and Characters

A book about trust, credulity, and defiance whose hero is an elusive character and an invisible man whom one is never sure of having met, *The Confidence-Man: His Masquerade* also includes a reflection, repeated three times in three interpolated chapters, on what a fictional character is. In the first chapter (chapter 14, "Worth the consideration of those to whom it may prove worth considering"), Melville's narrator questions the need for consistency in the portrayal of the characters, and he concludes that this is a defect:

> [T]here is nothing a writer of fiction should more carefully see to, as there is nothing a sensible reader will more carefully look for, than that, in the depiction of any character, its consistency should be preserved. But this, though at first blush, seeming reasonable enough, may upon a closer view, prove not so much so [...] [I]s it not a fact that, in real life, a consistent character is a *rara avis*? [...] That fiction, where every character can, by reason if its consistency, be comprehended at a glance, either exhibits but sections of character, making them appear for wholes, or else is very untrue to reality [...] No writer has produced such inconsistent characters as nature herself has.
>
> *(Melville, 2006, 75)*

The thesis on the inconstancy of novel characters has its origin in the pages of Montaigne devoted to the inconstancy of human nature (*Essais* II, I, "De l'inconstance de nos actions"). It feeds the remarks on the conflicting aspirations of the reader of fiction. Audiences expect characters to be consistent, when people in real life are not:

> But though there is a prejudice against inconsistent characters in books, yet the prejudice bears the other way, when what seemed at first their inconsistency, afterwards, by the skill of the writer, turns out to be their good keeping. The great masters excel in nothing so much as in this very particular. They challenge astonishment at the tangled web of some character, and then raise admiration still greater at their satisfactory unraveling of it; in this way throwing open, sometimes to the understanding even of school misses, the last complications of that spirit which is affirmed by its Creator to be fearfully and wonderfully made.
>
> *(76)*

The second meta-fictional reflection (chapter 33: "Which may pass for whatever it may prove to be worth") is an astonishing defense of literary *defamiliarization*, since it boldly relies on an unexpected comparison between fiction and religion—which has the consequence of bringing fiction closer to belief: fiction (like religion), explains Melville, must make the link between this world and the other world felt; it is in fact this link between the two worlds:

> [T]he people in fiction, like the people in a play, must dress as nobody exactly dresses, talk as nobody exactly talks, act as nobody exactly acts. It is with fiction as with religion: it should present another world, and yet one to which we feel the tie.
>
> *(187)*

The third comment (in chapter 44) discusses the notion of "original characters." Melville here expresses his skepticism with regard to Charles Dickens, then the most popular of novelists, and his perplexity at the idea widespread among the literary critics of the time that since Fielding, who "made a very considerable addition to the populousness of the world of fiction," the "creations of Dickens are more numerous than those of all the authors that preceded him, from the days of Fielding and Smollet, put together" (*Putnam's Monthly*, 1853, 558–62). He points out that original characters have never been *made* by their authors, but *found* by them. The reader will never have the opportunity to meet them any more than the passengers of *Le Fidèle* who read the search notice were able to meet the confidence-man:

> True, we sometimes hear of an author who, at one creation, produces some two or three score such characters; it may be possible. But they can hardly be original in the sense that Hamlet is, or Don Quixote, or Milton's Satan. That is to say, they are not, in a thorough sense, original at all. They are novel, or singular, or striking, or captivating, or all four at once.
>
> *(237)*

Finally, concludes Melville, there cannot be

> But one such original character to one work of fiction. Two would conflict in chaos. […] But for new, singular, striking, odd, eccentric, and all sorts of entertaining and instructive characters, a good fiction may be full of them.
>
> *(238)*

If there is one, the connection between these interpolated chapters that deal with fiction and the general motif of trust discussed throughout the book is a priori anything but clear. It seems, in any case, to read Melville well, that trust and fiction have in common to be based on social conventions, whereas fiction and belief are tools for connecting worlds.

Trust and Language

In the society aboard *Le Fidèle*, language constitutes the only social institution. It is also the only tool the confidence-man and his avatars have to gain trust, to do business and to close a deal: "Ah, you are a talking man—what I call a wordy man. You talk, talk" (129); "A smart fool always talks well; takes a smart fool to be tonguey" (96). Their skills rely on their ability to speak to get in or out of any situation, manipulating information or their partner. The art of fully controlling the direction of an encounter without the other party realizing it, and all through seemingly innocent conversation, is what makes these characters unique. The beginnings of conversations with strangers are always the most difficult phase of the task. To get a message across, to make people believe, one might assume that clarity is crucial. Melville's approach is quite different. It implements on the lexical level a vocabulary with double meaning, judiciously placed and, on the syntactic level, long sentences placed close to each other, which leads to their negation or to paradox. Throughout the text, we regularly encounter a vocabulary with multiple objectives, one of the meanings of which refers to trust while the second is adapted to the specific situation. The text, Michel Imbert writes, "highlights the semantic floating of the terms which is due to the inflection of a voice; the black beggar pronounces *valuable* 'walloable' (a portemanteau word collapsing *wallow*, *allowable* and *valuable* all into one), 'worthy' becomes 'wordy' ('well wordy of all you kind ge'mmen's kind confidence')" (Imbert, 2012, 17). Melville never stops building sentences that are so many contradictory injunctions: "From evil comes good"; "Distrust is a stage of trust"; "I have confidence in mistrust." The environment offers no means of verification of information, no stability, and no support for travelers. The language used is constantly undermined. The volume of information offered by the narrator is purposely limited.

Speech is a verbal game for dubious purposes. Governed by trade, it is the subject of great mistrust and strong suspicion.

> The transaction concluded, the two still remained seated, falling into familiar conversation, by degrees verging into that confidential sort of sympathetic silence, the last refinement and luxury of unaffected good feeling. A kind of social superstition, to suppose that to be truly friendly one must be saying friendly words all the time, any more than be doing friendly deeds continually. True friendliness, like true religion, being in a sort independent of works.
>
> *(Melville, 2006, 64)*

Two elements are intentionally missing in the novel for speech to be trusted and believed: duration and the responsibility of the interlocutor vis-à-vis what he is saying. Believing the person who speaks and trusting him presupposes being able to recognize in him a commitment to responsibility for what he says. But trust is not only a relationship with others; as we have said, it is a commitment over time and a bet on the future. In a world without a future and without a past of *Le Fidèle*, where time is absent, speech does not produce trust: it is an art of the deal. As for fiction, it seems to borrow from both belief and trust: it is close to belief in that it postulates another world; it is comparable to trust when it asks the reader to give credit to the author.

Note

1 My translation.

Works Cited

Blaise, Marie. 2018. "Melville, l'homme-confiance et le faiseur de nœuds." Fabula / les colloques, "Le coup de la panne. Ratés et dysfonctionnements textuels." http://www.fabula.org/colloques/document5814.php.

Deleuze, Gilles. 1989. *Cinema 2. The Time-Machine*. Translated by Hugh Tomlinson and Robert Galeta. Minneapolis: University of Minnesota Press.

Imbert, Michel. 2012. "L'heure de vérité dans *The Confidence-Man* d'Herman Melville." *Revue française d'études américaines* 133: 8–23.

Jaume, Lucien. 2010. *Les origines philosophiques du libéralisme*. Paris: Champs-essais.

Lapoujade, David. 2010. " 'L'escroc à la confiance' ou l'efficacité du faux." In *Bartleby le scribe, Billy Bud marin et autres romans, Œuvres IV*, by Herman Melville, edited by Philippe Jaworski, David Lapoujade and Hershel Parker, 1214. Bibliothèque de la Pléiade. Paris: Gallimard.

Locke, John. 1953. *Two Treatises of Civil Government*. London and New York: Everyman Library

Luhmann, Niklas. 2017. *Trust and Power*. Translated by Howard Davis, John Raffan and Kathryn Rooney. Cambridge: Polity Press.

Melville, Herman. 2006. *The Confidence-Man: His Masquerade*. Edited by Hershel Parker and Mark Niemeyer. New York and London: W. W. Norton & Company.

Moffitt, Benjamin. 2016. *The Global Rise of Populism: Performance, Political Style, and Representation*. Stanford, CA: Stanford University Press.

Poe, Edgar Allan. 1984. "Diddling Considered as One of the Exact Sciences." In *Poetry and Tales*, edited by Patrick F. Quinn, 607–17. New York: Library of America.

Reid, Thomas. (1785) 1997. *Essays on the Intellectual Powers of Man*. Edited by Derek R. Brookes. Edinburgh: Edinburgh University Press.

Reid, Thomas. 1997. *An Inquiry into the Human Mind* on the Principles of Common Sense. Edited by Derek R. Brookes. Edinburgh: Edinburgh University Press.

Rey, Jean-Michel. 2002. *Le temps du crédit*. Paris: Desclée de Brouwer.

Rey, Jean-Michel. 2014. *Histoires d'escrocs. Tome 3, l'escroquerie de l'homme par l'homme ou the confidence-man*. Paris: éditions de l'Olivier.

Rosenfeld, Sophia. 2014. *Common Sense. A Political History*. Cambridge, MA: Harvard University Press.

Simmel, Georg. 2004. *The Philosophy of Money*. Translated by Tom Bottomore and David Frisby. Third enlarged edition edited by David Brisby. London and New York: Routledge.

Smith, Adam. 2007. *An Inquiry into the Nature and Causes of the Wealth of Nations*. Edited by Salvio Marcelo Soares. Lausanne: MetaLibri Digital Library.

Thurman, Judith. 2017. "Philip Roth E-mails on Trump." *New Yorker*, January 30. https://www.newyorker.com/magazine/2017/01/30/philip-roth-e-mails-on-trump

Tocqueville, Alexis (de). 2002. *Democracy in America*. Translated by Henry Reeve. A Penn State Electronic Classics Series Publication. University Park, PA: The Pennsylvania State University.

Todeschini, Giacomo. 2009. *Franciscan Wealth: from Voluntary Poverty to Market Society*. St Bonaventure: Franciscan Institute Publications.

Trump, Donald with Schwartz, Tony. 1987. *TRUMP, The Art of the Deal*. New York: Random House.

Velasquez, Thomas. 2019. "The Confidence-Man: His Masquerade, or the Promise of 'Something Further.'" *Miranda*, n° 19. Online since October 8, 2019. http://journals.openedition.org/miranda/20354; DOI: https://doi.org/10.4000/miranda.20354

19

LITERATURE ON CREDIT

Fiction and the Fiduciary Paradigm

Emmanuel Bouju and Loïse Lelevé

Credit (in the double fiduciary sense of *credibility* and the *credit that one grants in recognition of a debt*) has served as a touchstone for many attempts at defining the "plasmatic" powers of fiction (its demiurgic, world-building powers; see Cassin, 1986) ever since classical Antiquity, when the question of the "price of truth" and the relation between truth and money became indissociable from that of the relation of language to reality, of sign to referent, of *mythos* to knowledge (Hénaff, 2002). As (false) currency served as a common metaphor for the manipulation of signs outside of any referential purpose, and therefore for a troubled and troubling relation between representation and reality, and model and representation, concepts borrowed from the financial and economic sphere were requisitioned to assess the *value* of fiction in particular, and that of literature in general. Simultaneously, the conflictual relationship between debtor and creditor became a common trope of comedy up until the seventeenth century,[1] thanks, in particular, to the complex web of lies, inventions, and fictions it allowed authors to unfold, and to the parallel drawn between the debtor-creditor relationship and that of the author and their reader or spectator.

The meaning of the credit metaphor, however, has drastically evolved from the eighteenth century onward, when the modernization of the European credit system, coupled with a series of spectacular financial crises, deeply reshaped European societies through what has sometimes been analyzed as a collective trauma (Rey, 2002; Tuduri and Sarthou-Lajus, 2019). Occurring in France, but resonating throughout Europe (Rey, 2011), the collapse of the Law System in the 1720s followed by the brutal depreciation of the assignats at the time of the French Revolution were at the source of a whole new literary representation of finance, credit, and debt, seeking to make sense of the enormous and unheard of consequences of those crises. In the eighteenth and nineteenth centuries, the debt paradigm took a preponderant place in contemporary fiction and was henceforth linked with the problem of *fiducia*, understood "both as trust and as the fact that language can make something come into existence, or make one believe in it" (Tuduri and Sarthou-Lajus, 2019). It is the beginning of the literary representation and elaboration of a complex network involving credit, trust, belief, and suspension of disbelief, and the performative qualities of language, wherein by interrogating the fascinating and terrifying consequence of trust, namely the fact that

Fortune [...] is built on something eminently fragile: the trust someone is granted, a trust that rests, more often than not, not upon any actual reality, but upon what is said, reputation, consideration, fame—in short, upon *a collective make-believe being enunciated*
(Rey, 2011, emphasis in original)

authors actually question the very powers of literature. For, as Rey argues in *Le Temps du crédit*, it is not scientific or political literature, but rather fiction, and especially the novel, that then becomes the choice medium to investigate the unprecedented results of the transformations of capitalism. Thus, the exploration of a new "ethics of debt, deriving from the Aristotelian condemnation of interests and the Catholic criticism of speculation" that "informs nineteenth-century literature" (Péraud, 2011b), and the complex entanglement of moral and fortune it implies (whereby the subject is defined by their own personal *credit*, their net worth depending from the value of their word) goes hand in hand with the new epistemic ambitions of literary realism. According to Rey, only the novel can explore efficiently the ontological and social consequences of redefining beings through their *credit*. So the old "fiduciary framework as an enunciative model" (Péraud, 2008, 222) turns out to be reversed: where, in the Classical Age, the reader was indebted to the author, it is now the latter that begs the former for *credit*—in the same way, Péraud argues, that Raphaël asked Blondet to "credit him with an hour of boredom" in order for him to tell him his life story in Balzac's *La Peau de chagrin* (*The Wild Ass's Skin*, 1831).

This "uneasy fiducia" (Péraud, 2011b), this anxious questioning of fictional value through the lens of trust and belief, not only pervades the nineteenth-century literary production of a social imagery of credit, and with it of a renewed concept of the powers of fiction, as exemplified in the works of Balzac (Péraud, 2011a); it also informs the novels of Dumas, Zola, Valéry, or Gide, in France (Goux, 1984), of Thomas Mann in Germany, or, in the United States, of Melville and his *Confidence-Man* (Rey, 2011).[2] The volatility of the currency sign is compared to the arbitrariness of the linguistic one (Péraud, 2011b), as financial crises are linked to new ways of imagining political, polemical, or fictional forms of commitment with regards to the representation of capitalist impasses or iniquities. This is evidenced recently, for instance, in Italian novels retracing the life of counterfeiter Paolo Ciulla: the 1920s economic crisis that leads the forger to create fake banknotes serves as a prism to investigate that of the transition from lira to Euro in Maria Attanasio's *Il falsario di Caltagirone* [The Caltagirone Counterfeiter] (2007), or the worldwide bankruptcy of 2008 in Dario Fo and Piero Sciotto's *Ciulla, il grande malfattore* [Ciulla, the Great Wrongdoer] (2014).

This article argues, however, that contemporary fiction poses (re)new(ed) challenges to the tried-and-tested mobilization of credit imagery to assess the relations between literature and politics. As demonstrated by Carlo Ginzburg in *Clues, Myths, and the Historical Method* (Ginzburg, 1989), the veridical and referential values of a given narrative traditionally rest upon what he calls an "evidential (or indiciary)[3] paradigm," a sleuth-like mode of investigation and of hunting down traces. Clues of a past and enigmatic event (be it the passage of an animal, the creation of an artwork, a murder, or a childhood traumatic experience) are carefully arranged into an efficient narration that confers meaning to them and thus makes them interpretable. The hunter tracking down a prey, the art historian trying to authenticate a painting, the detective investigating a crime scene, the psychanalyst interpreting symptoms of a repressed event, all build what they present as their *readings* from an evidential paradigm that truly is a narrative device and matrix. And, in turn, both non-fiction and referential fiction have long founded their truth-telling ambitions on the very same paradigm: they endeavor to articulate traces and clues collected from reality into epistemic narratives claiming to offer a specifically literary heuristic perspective on reality. Hence the investigative model pervading nineteenth-century literary attempts to represent and question social and political changes (Kalifa, 2010), or, more recently, a "pragmatic turn" in contemporary fictions that reclaim the scientific methods and benefits of evidence and investigation-based disciplines such as anthropology, history, or sociology (Coste, 2017; Demanze, 2019), aiming at redefining the relations between fiction and scientific literature (Jablonka, 2014). In such writings, readers' trust, or their ability to confer credit on the narrative, is not at stake: such a literature seeks its authority and its epistemic (and, in turn, ethical) value in its open use of the evidential powers of Ginzburg's indiciary paradigm.

There seem to be, however, a superposition of the renewed, anti-fiduciary use of the evidential paradigm in recent referential fiction and non-fiction, and the apparition of what can properly be termed a *fiduciary paradigm*, specific to a whole other part of contemporary fiction, and based on the vocabulary and the key notions derived from the Latin *fides*—considered as a political virtue of commitment: "credit," "confidence" (trust), and ultimately: "belief."[4]

This paradigm explains the title of this chapter: "Literature on Credit," a plastic formulation in that we can read it as: (1) literature seeking "credit" or, to which credit is granted (i.e., that seeks to be credited, that makes a claim for credibility, and that is granted credit at least temporarily); (2) literature that "lives on credit" ("à credit," the French equivalent of "on credit," can be used, as Antoine Furetière pointed out more than four centuries ago in his *Universal Dictionary*, to mean "for pleasure, without utility, without a reason": that is, as a luxury, as a non-fungible share in reality, an unproductive expense); or, if we stretch the sense of the phrase a bit and reverse its connotations: (3) literature that gives credit (as in the banking sense), that creates value, an immaterial profit: a force for the augmentation of reality[5]—thus, a literature that not only draws from the complex relations of fiction and credit from the Antiquity, but profoundly turns around their very terms. Such a literature is not only *credited* by the debtor-creditor relationship of the author and the reader; it *credits itself* by its capacity to establish, question, and reverse this relationship; it claims the paradoxical credit of the unprofitable as a way to seek *more* of reality; it does not ground its truth, its epistemic and ethical value, on its creditable representation or investigation of reality, but *adds* to it. Hence another connection of such a literature to the social sciences: not through the accrediting use of the evidential paradigm and mimesis of scientific methods of writing, but through the investigation of the role of belief in contemporary society. As sociologist Bernard Lahire wrote:

> When beliefs engender as much social energy in a multiplicity of actors that comment, authenticate, appropriate, buy and sell, admire, etc.; when public or private money is directed, or laws made, on the basis of these same beliefs, then belief and magic are not specialized issues anymore. They are central facts that potentially concern the whole of social sciences, from religious history to monetary economics, from political anthropology to art history and sociology.
>
> *(Lahire, 2015, 9)*

There are, therefore, three ways of investigating the links between literature and politics through the notion of credit: seeking credit (credibility); giving credit (as the acknowledgement of a debt); being credited (as the author).

Seeking Credit

We can take as a starting point the (classic) mode of questioning the credibility of fiction, focusing on the specific but representative and enlightening case of historical fiction as a literary engagement: this involves not only the old question of the believability of historical narrative (which is one of our questions here), but also the speculative wager involved in the mobilization of different possible memories of the past. It means taking into account the credibility of thought experiments that involve temporal recomposition such as "presentism" (Hartog, 2016), anachronism, "euchronia," or alternate history (Deluermoz and Singaravelou, 2021), reenactment … as well as the act of make-believe required by narratives that take the form of a "mirror box" (Bouju, 2015),[6] to treat the phantom pain of the lost past, death, and disappearance. Literature is highly familiar with this force and paradoxical virtue of delusion. This counterfeit currency ("fausse monnaie"[7]) of delusion is a provisional credit, granted willfully and knowingly: an acknowledgment of debt looking for a higher truth—even in the case of stories told by unreliable narrators.[8] In other words, literature that highlights its *make-believe* powers as a restorative or compensatory offering in the face of past and present traumas (Hirsch, 2012) knows it presents only an illusion, but it asks for this illusion to be *credited with* actual performative powers, as it *gives itself away* as but a dubious reflection nevertheless able to incarnate, and therefore give meaning to, unshaped, untold, or unacknowledged "phantom" pains. From the credit sought and given, a new, albeit unreferential truth, may emerge.

This addresses the credit that is sought in the limit cases that emerge when the line between fact and fiction (Lavocat, 2016) is conspicuously and provocatively crossed, mostly for political reasons as well as aesthetic ones. This is the case in what could be called the *"istorical* novel"* (Bouju, 2020a, 125–35): that is, eye-witness fiction, linked to the regression from the *histor* of Herodotus—the historian as an inquirer—to the archaic *istor*—the eye-witness. The public, or even polemical, questioning with regard to the trust that should be given to these literary undertakings helps us to measure the level of readerly engagement or recusal which has an effect on the status of the narrative in the political economies of memory and bearing witness, of documentation and the archive. In this regard, *Jan Karski* by Yannick Haenel (Haenel, 2009) can be taken as a paradigmatic example of the polemical and political effects of the use of the *istor* and the make-believe powers of fiction. Though the book is comprised of three parts, of which only the last one is properly fictional, it has been read as a scandalous fictionalization, and therefore falsification, of history, by such prominent figures as Claude Lanzmann and Annette Wievorka (Lanzmann, 2010; Wieviorka, 2010). However, the first-person account, in which the witness fictionally takes charge of the narrative to deliver another truth that was previously unheard and untold because it was inaudible, is carefully framed by two non-fictional others, the first of which is an ekphrasis of Lanzmann's movie showing the real Jan Karski, and the second a biography drawn from Karski's own autobiography,[9] as well as by a falsified quotation by Paul Celan (*"Niemand zeugt für den Zeugen"*, "Nobody testifies for the witness" becomes *"Qui témoigne pour le témoin?"* ["Who testifies for the witness?"], highlighting the transformations at work in Haenel's historiographic recreation). The *istorical* narrative intervenes only *after* the referential accounts, where the documentary ends, when the actual speech of the historical witness has been impeached and rendered useless, and thus when the unreceived message can be redeemed, and artificially revived, through the mirror-box of fiction. Historians such as Wievorka may refuse to *credit* the investigative and compensatory attempt of fiction, but Haenel's narrative very clearly begs its reader to acknowledge *in good faith* the value of the historical truth uncovered by the *istorical* monologue; to *trust* that the fictional reconstitution of the unheard speech of the witness is an effective, ethical, and powerful way to give voice to the narrators of the untold stories of the past that still shape our present. The reading contract is clear, even if the account is manipulated; the *istorical* invention is a bold and polemical one, but it needs to be credited *as such*, and not rejected as a mere falsification, if one is to give justice to the complex enunciative and narrative apparatus of the book (see also Bähler, 2023).[10]

The effect is a credit or discredit (depending on the reader's ethical and epistemic decision to trust in the *istor* and their narrative, or conversely to reject any fictionalization of the past as a mystification) that is proportionate to the fictional *coup de force*, to the momentary surges of authority involved in this usurpation of identity. Such a form of credit, on the part both of the author and of the reader who chooses to grant the credit sought by the fictional narrative, is then also the basis for the recusal of (or resistance to) the contemporary regime of "post-truth"—through a *mise en abyme* of the mechanisms of the politically motivated secret or conspiracy. And it also exposes the necessity of a critical response regarding what gives falsehood an effect of truth—as well as an attempt to expose the socially constructed nature of truthfulness. This shift from the evidential (or *indiciary*) to the fiduciary, from the burden of proof to the audaciously required and freely given credit (provided that a clear and non-manipulatory reading pact is present and respected), seems to be not only true in the literary sphere, but more largely in the social sciences nowadays. It is the case in art history, for instance, where the conceptualization of "post-connoisseurship" methods appears typical of a new criticism of the use of the evidential paradigm (Lenain, 2011; Schwartz, 2014).

Giving Credit (as the Acknowledgment of a Debt)

Credit (as in *credit and debt*, see Kluge and Vogl, 2009) is a notion that sits at the crossroads, or at the superposition of the three languages of economy, politics, and ethics. This makes the "debt narrative" (the fiction novel on credit and debt) the Rosetta Stone of the contemporary novel: a literary and symbolic Rosetta Stone like the one that allowed Champollion to decipher hieroglyphics by comparing three different versions of a single text (the first one written in hieroglyphics—"the language of the gods"—the second one in demotic Egyptian—"the language of documents"—and the third one in Greek—"the language of communication"); three versions of a decree (a statutory order) that settled the credit and debt accounts of the Ptolemaic Priests in Memphis.

This relates to a line of questioning that was revived in fiction, especially European fiction, with the 2008 crisis and the following debate on "odious debt":[11] whereby the aesthetic artefact becomes a means of making the current globalized democratic "crisis" legible, as well as a way to decipher what Annie McClanahan calls the "dead pledges" (literally the *mort-gages* in French) of the "Living Indebted" (McClanahan, 2017). In European novels today, we see that the pressure of (sovereign and individual) debts is quite systematically related to a lack of credibility of (and credit granted to) democracy and the future. This is a crisis of "defuturization," as Joseph Vogl put it in *The Specter of Capital*, placing the emphasis on the way neocapitalism and its "*oikodicy*" captured the very word "future" as a financial product (Vogl, 2013, 241–45, 2014); it is an agonistic conflict between violent probability patterns and fragile possible engagements, linked to the algorithmic articulation of time, and it is a credit crunch of democratic institutions and representations, which forbids the reunification of all social *symbola*.[12] For example, Walter Siti's *Resistere non serve a niente* (Resistance is futile, 2014), an imaginary biographical portrait of a genius in international finance (Tommaso Aricò) who is secretly working for the Calabrian Mafia (the '*ndranghetta*), elaborates on the very form that constitutes the contemporary economy, where the erasing (or unreadability) of the traces of any transaction, and the non-institutional financing of liquidities, allow for the "natural" insertion of mafias into the political texture of our societies and for the perversion of the democratic contract. On a meta-narratological level, however, the novel also represents the compromise of a writer (the fictional *alter ego* of Walter Siti) in the service of a deeper reality, represented metaphorically by his dilapidated house (which was bought on credit). The fact that the novel is "written on credit" creates a "debt to the truth" that the author wishes to repay, and he does so by waging a war of detail and precision against the mob-democracy (Bouju, 2020b).

This meta-narratological level of the "debt narrative" questions the fiduciary links between auctoriality and lectoriality. We find the narratological tradition of "(un)reliability," reconsidered through the intermediary of the "Con Man" motif (narrative force as the manipulation of trust):[13] this has to do with the credit of narrative "confidence" in the pragmatics of fiction, and with the contractuality that questions the legitimacy of the boundary between fact and fiction.

Being Credited

"Give credit where credit is due," as the proverb goes. This brings us to number three: "authorial credit" in the sense of being credited as the author of a text, including in the economic sense of owning the copyright (which translates to French as the "author's rights," *les droits d'auteur*). This means credit as a socialized and political measure of authorship/auctoriality and authority, beyond the fictional screens (which, as we know, are regularly questioned and contested by the law).

There is the principal democratic dimension of "authorizing oneself (literature)," in the double sense of "allowing oneself literature" (as we allow ourselves a luxury) and "authorizing oneself = literature itself": authorizing oneself, giving oneself authority, making oneself an author, an authoritative body able to add to reality, to augment it through the plasmatic creative powers of fiction, against the abuse of political authority. It is a matter of authorizing oneself to pit one authority against another—such that authorship or auctoriality, be it spectral or broken, resists as best it can, through the "weak ties" that it creates, the authority of power and the law as well as the real and concrete violence that they exert.[14]

What we find here is a conflict of authorities that mimics the Archimedes principle: a matter of claiming for oneself an authority whose strength is inversely proportional to that of the adversary. Would the political credit of literary auctoriality be proportionate to the discredit of the political? One thinks, for instance, of the literary representations of past and present Mezzogiorno, past and present Sicily, which have been both a battlefield for clashing conservative and progressist accounts of the social and economic realities of Southern Italy, and a crucible for crucial literary innovations (see Di Gesù, 2003, 2015). The anxiety regarding the very possibility of any actual political progress in the island used to echo, in an author such as Leonardo Sciascia, for instance, a troubled questioning of the actual powers of fiction and imagination, as evidenced in his pseudo-Manzonian diptych *Il consiglio d'Egitto* (The Council of Egypt, 1963) and *Morte dell'Inquisitore* (Death of the Inquisitor, 1964). Paradoxically, such a literary and political disquiet on his part (linked to an existential pessimism) may have been understood to influence his representation of the political struggles of Sicily through a fatalistic prism not that far away from that of Lampedusa (Farrell, 2010; Rosengarten, 1998). Both inscribe themselves, therefore, in a long tradition of a pessimistic representation of the social and political immobilism of Sicily, from Verga to Andrea Camilleri. However, from the 1990s and the 2000s onward, one can see the emergence of a new Southern literature aiming at challenging such representations in order to offer a new image of Sicily as a territory of fundamental political inventions and struggles for emancipation. Women authors such as Maria Attanasio, Silvana La Spina, Maria Rosa Cutrufelli, Silvana Grasso, or Giovanna Giordano have grounded and wagered their auctorial credibility on the very lack of a political one granted to the institutions of the territory they represent and explore. By offering a counter-history and a counter-narrative of Sicily that stages the marginalized and the forgotten (Todesco, 2016), they claim a literary credit based on the very possibility to *accredit* past struggles and present them through their literary depiction. The political discredit of the social and economic infrastructures of the island, and the conservative literature threatening to present them as unavoidable realities, are thus defied through a double gesture by which these writers authorized themselves to write literature, in spite of a *very* masculine literary tradition, in order to authorize and legitimate other political narratives when the existing ones are lacking, misleading, or unjust.

More broadly speaking, the political credit of literature is not necessarily a good sign *per se*. As early a commentator as Tacitus elaborated on the discredit of Roman political rhetoric, which he said became epideictic in proportion to its deflation of truth value (*Dialogus De Oratoribus*). Think of the paradoxical prestige that is the social value of literature under authoritarian regimes. Or, how in democracies right now, the current revival of the credit (the public and political popularity) of literature seems to be in proportion to the discredit of political discourse—at the risk of creating misunderstandings about the nature of literature itself. One can thus debate the political functions of contemporary fiction: should it take place within the realm of "care literature" (see, for instance, Gefen, 2017), a literature that is meant to heal—or should we rather consider, as Iris Murdoch said, that the "greatest art invigorates without consoling"? Alternatively, should we ground literary credit on the prestige of "exposed" literature conceived as performative literature, or prefer a *fiduciary* model that preserves the agency of the reader?

This is a line of questioning that has been singularly revived by contemporary modes of shared authority (*Wu Ming* for example[15]), linked with the notion of the *commons*: in particular in the digital realm (*Creative Commons*, for example).

Conclusion

In a political and cultural moment when words such as "post-truth" and "gaslighting" can be termed "words of the year" by prestigious dictionaries, the problem of the *credit* of fiction becomes a burning one. Age-old questions regarding the value of literature—such as who, or what is to be believed? Who owns the credit found in the text? What political status can we grant to its credibility?—find both a new meaning and a new urgency in contemporary fiction that embraces a fiduciary paradigm. The fact that literature bases its credit on its representation, thematization, or parody of financial credit, false currency, and economic and political collapse, is nothing new. What seems to be specific to a fiduciary, contemporary literature, however, is the trust granted by contemporary authors, and ideally contemporary readers, to the interplay of confidence and interpretation, fictionalization and credit, *fiducia* and make-believe that we find in fiduciary narratives, as a democratic, efficient, and common tool for the political investigation of present realities. The credit of contemporary fiduciary fiction is intrinsically a problematic one: it must be both sought and granted; it challenges its own value and meaning at the very moment it endeavors to build a new auctorial and textual authority. Yet, it is also a powerful means of granting credit both to literature, and to reality as a set of representations the common dimension of which threatens to be lost in the anxieties of the so-called post-truth era and its relativistic *disenchantment*. Contemporary fiction has to authorize itself, or discredit, fictional representations or investigations of reality. The fiduciary paradigm is the very movement by which contemporary fiction conquers a fragile but genuine and heuristic, political, epistemic, and ethical efficiency.

Notes

1 See, for instance, Molière's *Dom Juan*, and the dialogue between Dom Juan and M. Dimanche in Act 4, scene 3.
2 For an overview of the question in British literature, see for instance the works of Mary Poovey (2008).
3 To translate more closely the Italian "*paradigma indiziario.*"
4 This is at least one of the major hypotheses at the center of the literary turn E. Bouju has called *epimodernism* (Bouju, 2020a, 2023).
5 *Auctoritas* referred originally to the act of "augmenting," of authorizing in the sense of "granting additional validity to," of promoting or even creating legitimacy, according to the etymology laid out in the *Dictionary of Indo-European Concepts and Society* by Émile Benveniste (Benveniste, 1969, 148–51), who stressed the importance of the poetic *augere*, its creative significance, and its legal and prophetic dimensions.
6 The "mirror box" is an apparatus used by neurologists to treat the "phantom pain" of amputees: by contemplating the reflection of their remaining member parallel to the missing one and tricking their brain into thinking the reflection is the *actual* missing member, the patient can "move" said member and try and chase the pain away. E. Bouju argues that epimodern historiographical fiction functions as a mirror box, producing make-believe versions of the past that, though ostensibly forged, but *credible and creditable*, can—in fiction, but with actual political power—act upon the traumas and pains of the past.
7 "Counterfeit currency must be *taken* for real currency and for that reason must *give itself (away)* for a genuinely authenticated one" ("La fausse monnaie doit être *prise* pour de la vraie monnaie et pour cela doit *se donner* pour de la monnaie convenablement titrée," [Derrida, 1991, 111]).

8 On unreliable narration, see James Phelan's contribution to this volume.

9 The whole set-up is explicitly described in the very beginning of the book; the partition between fiction and non-fiction is unmistakable.

10 For other approaches of the "istorical" treatment of fictional credit, see also Jonathan Littell's *Les Bienveillantes* [*The Kindly Ones*], *Goetz & Meyer* by David Albahari, and the entirety of the work of Javier Cercas—all the mirrored responses of *El monarca de las sombras* [The Monarch of the Shadows] to *Soldados de Salamina* [*The Soldiers of Salamis*].

11 According to the formal doctrine of "odious debt," as Odette Lienau puts it in *Rethinking Sovereign Debt*, "a fallen regime's debt need not be repaid if it was not authorized by and did not benefit the underlying population" (Lienau, 2014, 9).

12 It may be recalled that the *symbolon* was invented precisely "as a token of agreement" in debt matters. As Marc Shell put it in *The Economy of Literature*: "*Symbola* were pledges, pawns, or covenants from an earlier understanding to bring together a part of something that had been divided specifically for the purpose of later comparison." Such a *symbolon* could be a ring-coin (*sphragis*): one that can easily be broken in two. Or, later, as in Henry's times, when it served "as token of debt owed to the government", it could be in the shape of a "tally stick", with a "stock" and a "stub" (Shell, 1978, 33).

13 On the "confidence man," see the article by Philippe Roussin in this volume.

14 See "Sidelined," Elfriede Jelinek's Nobel Prize speech (https://www.nobelprize.org/prizes/literature/2004/jelinek/lecture/) and Bouju (2020a, 159–70).

15 Not only are the works of this collective of Italian authors very regularly co-authored, they also are published online for free in their original language, under a *Creative Commons* license, thus complying with the political values arbored by the group. Additionally, each work by Wu Ming is also the result of a complex and rich dialogue with their readers on their social media and more particularly on the group blog (https://www.wumingfoundation.com/giap/). The writers openly acknowledge the importance of such contributions and of that form of dialogical creation (for a recent example of a literary thematization of its relevancy, see Wu Ming, 1 2021).

Works Cited

Bähler, Ursula. 2023. "Qui lit vrai et qui lit faux? *Jan Karski* de Yannik Haenel et *HHhH* de Laurent Binet." In *Littératures du faux*, edited by Jochen Mecke and Anne-Sophie Donnarieix, 69–83. Berlin: Peter Lang. https://www.peterlang.com/document/1294488.

Benveniste, Émile. 1969. *Le vocabulaire des institutions indo-européennes. Pouvoir, droit, religion*. Paris: Minuit.

Bouju, Emmanuel. 2015. "A Nest in the Air: Phantom Pain and Contemporary Narrative." In *Being Contemporary: (Un)Timely Essays in French Culture. Homage to Susan Rubin Suleiman*, edited by Lia Brozgal and Sara Kippur, 349–66. Liverpool: Liverpool University Press. https://hal.univ-rennes2.fr/hal-01773814.

Bouju, Emmanuel. 2020a. *Épimodernes. Nouvelles "leçons américaines" sur l'actualité du roman*. Québec: Codicille éditeur.

Bouju, Emmanuel. 2020b. "The Debt Narrative and the Credit Crunch of Democracy." *Differences. A Journal of Feminist Cultural Studies* 31, no. 3: 59–75. https://doi.org/10.1215/10407391-8744497.

Bouju, Emmanuel. 2023. *Epimodernism: Six Memos for Literature Today*. Basingstoke: Palgrave-MacMillan.

Cassin, Barbara. 1986. "Du faux ou du mensonge à la fiction (de *pseudos* à *plasma*)." In *Le plaisir de parler. Études de sophistique comparée*, edited by Barbara Cassin, 3–29. Arguments. Paris: Minuit.

Coste, Florent. 2017. *Explore. Investigations littéraires*. Forbidden Beach. Paris: Questions théoriques.

Deluermoz, Quentin, and Pierre Singaravelou. 2021. *A Past of Possibilities: A History of What Could Have Been*. New Haven, CT: Yale University Press.

Demanze, Laurent. 2019. *Un nouvel âge de l'enquête. Portraits de l'écrivain contemporain en enquêteur*. Les Essais. Paris: Corti.

Derrida, Jacques. 1991. *Donner le temps*. Vol. 1, *La fausse monnaie*. Paris: Galilée.

Di Gesù, Matteo. 2003. *La tradizione del postmoderno. Studi di letteratura italiana*. Critica letteraria e linguistica 32. Milano: F. Angeli.

Di Gesù, Matteo. 2015. *L'invenzione della Sicilia. Letteratura, mafia, modernità*. Lingue e letterature 7. Roma: Carocci.

Farrell, Joseph. 2010. "Sicilies: Tomasi Di Lampedusa and Leonardo Sciascia." In *"Il gattopardo" at Fifty*, edited by Davide Messina, 73–86. L'interprete 99. Ravenna: Longo.

Gefen, Alexandre. 2017. *Réparer le monde. La littérature française face au XXIe siècle*. Paris: Corti.

Ginzburg, Carlo. 1989. *Clues, Myths, and the Historical Method*. Translated by John Tedeschi and Anne C. Tedeschi. Baltimore, MD: Johns Hopkins University Press.

Goux, Jean-Joseph. 1984. *Les monnayeurs du langage*. Paris: Galilée.

Haenel, Yannick. 2009. *Jan Karski*. Paris: Gallimard.

Hartog, François. 2016. *Regimes of Historicity: Presentism and Experiences of Time*. Translated by Saskia Brown. New York: Columbia University Press.

Hénaff, Marcel. 2002. *Le prix de la vérité. Le don, l'argent, la philosophie*. Paris: Seuil.

Hirsch, Marianne. 2012. *The Generation of Postmemory: Visual Culture After the Holocaust*. New York: Columbia University Press.

Jablonka, Ivan. 2014. *L'Histoire est une littérature contemporaine. Manifeste pour les sciences sociales*. La Librairie du XXIᵉ siècle. Paris: Seuil.

Kalifa, Dominique. 2010. "Enquête et 'culture de l'enquête' au XIXᵉ siècle." *Romantisme* 149, no. 3: 3–23. https://doi.org/10.3917/rom.149.0003.

Kluge, Alexander, and Joseph Vogl. 2009. *Soll und haben. Fernsehgespräche*. Zurich: Diaphanes.

Lahire, Bernard. 2015. *Ceci n'est pas qu'un tableau. Essai sur l'art, la domination, la magie et le sacré*. Laboratoire des sciences sociales. Paris: La Découverte.

Lanzmann, Claude. 2010. "Jan Karski de Yannick Haenel: un faux roman." *Marianne*, January 23, 2010. https://www.marianne.net/societe/jan-karski-de-yannick-haenel-un-faux-roman.

Lavocat, Françoise. 2016. *Fait et fiction: pour une frontière*. Poétique. Paris: Seuil.

Lenain, Thierry. 2011. *Art Forgery. The History of a Modern Obsession*. London: Reaktion Books.

Lienau, Odette. 2014. *Rethinking Sovereign Debt. Politics, Reputation and Legitimacy in Modern Finance*. Cambridge, MA: Harvard University Press.

McClanahan, Annie. 2017. *Dead Pledges: Debt, Crisis, and Twenty-First-Century Culture*. Stanford, CA: Stanford University Press.

Péraud, Alexandre. 2008. "Quand l'immatérialisation de l'argent produit le roman. La mise en texte balzacienne du crédit." In *La production de l'immatériel. Théories, représentations et pratiques de la culture au XIXᵉ siècle*, edited by Jean-Yves Mollier, Philippe Régnier and Alain Vaillant, 217–30. Le XIXᵉ siècle en représentation(s). Saint-Étienne: Publications de l'Université de Saint-Étienne.

Péraud, Alexandre. 2011a. "La Comédie humaine comme mise en texte de l'imaginaire social du crédit." In *Les français et l'argent, XIXᵉ–XXIᵉ siècle. Entre fantasmes et réalité*, edited by Alya Aglan, Olivier Feiertag and Yannick Marec, 235–49. Histoire. Rennes: Presses universitaires de Rennes.

Péraud, Alexandre. 2011b. " 'La panacée universelle, le crédit!' (César Birotteau). Quelques exemples d'inscription narrative du crédit dans la littérature du premier XIXᵉ siècle." *Romantisme* 1, no. 151: 39–52. https://doi.org/10.3917/rom.151.0039.

Poovey, Mary. 2008. *Genres of the Credit Economy: Mediating Value in Eighteenth- and Nineteenth-Century Britain*. Chicago, IL: University of Chicago Press.

Rey, Jean-Michel. 2002. *Le temps du crédit*. Paris: Desclée de Brouwer.

Rey, Jean-Miche.l 2011. "Histoires de famille." *Romantisme* 151, no. 1: 11–22. https://doi.org/10.3917/rom.151.0011.

Rosengarten, Frank. 1998. "Homo Siculus: Essentialism in the Writing of Giovanni Verga, Giuseppe Tomasi Di Lampedusa, and Leonardo Sciascia." In *Italy's "Southern Question." Orientalism in One Country*, edited by Jane Schneider, 117–31. New York: Routledge.

Schwartz, Gary. 2014. "A Corpus of Rembrandt Paintings as a Test Case for Connoisseurship." In *Connoisseurship. l'œil, la raison et l'instrument. Actes du colloque des 20, 21 et 22 octobre 2011 à l'école du Louvre*, edited by Patrick Michel, 229–37. Rencontres de l'École du Louvre. Paris: École du Louvre.

Shell, Marc. 1978. *The Economy of Literature*. Baltimore, MD: Johns Hopkins University Press.

Todesco, Serena. 2016. *Tracce a margine. Scrittura femminile nella narrativa storica siciliana contemporanea*. Gioiosa Marea: Pungitopo.

Tuduri, Claude, and Nathalie Sarthou-Lajus. 2019. "La littérature et le crédit. Entretien avec Jean-Michel Rey." *Études* 4257, no. 2 (February): 93–102. https://doi.org/10.3917/etu.4257.0093.

Vogl, Joseph. 2013. *Le Spectre du capital [Das Gespenst des Kapital, 2010]*. Zurich: Diaphanes.

Vogl, Joseph. 2014. *The Specter of Capital*. Stanford, CA: Stanford University Press.

Wieviorka, Annette. 2010. "Faux temoignage." *L'histoire* 349: 30. http://www.cairn.info/magazine-l-histoire-2010-1-page-030.htm?contenu=resume.

Wu Ming, 1. 2021. *La Q di Qomplotto. QAnon e dintorni: come le fantasie di complotto difendono il sistema*. Roma: Alegre.

20

FIFTH-GENERATION FICTIONALITY? FICTION, POLITICS, WAR

Henrik Zetterberg-Nielsen

Introduction and Outline of the Chapter

As stated in many other contributions to this volume, the relation between fiction and belief is not at all straightforward; instead, the concepts seem almost incompatible, since we do not believe in the actuality of fictional events and entities.[1] The relation explored in this section of the book between fiction and politics entails a similar theoretical mystery; independent of which definition of fiction and fictionality you subscribe to, it seems all but clear why the employment of fictionality would be politically efficient and how it could work ideologically to change opinions about the real world. Notwithstanding, fiction and fictionality play tremendously important political roles in everything from contributing to ideas about a "national spirit" and imagined communities, in Benedict Anderson's phrase, to mobilizing for or against religious or ethnic minorities, or for or against wars, to recruiting for the army.

In the present chapter, I begin by briefly presenting a rhetorical approach to fictionality, which seems to me especially fruitful in the context of ideology, politics, propaganda, and fake news. This approach and its distinction between fictionality as a communicative resource and fiction as a generic concept make it possible to examine the political uses fictionality is put to outside as well as in generic fiction. After a section on the relation between propaganda, fake news, and fictionality, the chapter examines three different cases and the ways in which each uses fictionality for political purposes related to war. The first cluster of cases concerns the information wars about Ukraine and Russia's invasion of the country. Here I examine how fictionality is used especially in visual representations to influence perceptions about the events and political realities. Next, I move on to the hit movie series *Top Gun* with most attention to the recent installment, *Top Gun 2: Maverick* (2022), and discuss how the movie propagandistically sells war to the American people through fiction, and which ideas of justice, individuality, courage, and power positions pervade the movie and the world view it projects. Before concluding, I briefly turn to another Hollywood movie of a completely different kind, Tarantino's *Inglourious Basterds* (2009), and explore the complex ways in which it thematizes (anti-)war propaganda in fiction and represents art as also terror, and movies as literally explosive.

Carl von Clausewitz famously viewed war as politics by other means (Clausewitz, [1832] 2008, 28); the three main cases are all about how fictionality serves as a means to war as politics.[2]

DOI: 10.4324/9781003119456-23

Henrik Zetterberg-Nielsen

A Rhetorical Approach to Fictionality and Fiction

The theoretical horizon of this chapter as far as fictionality is concerned is that of rhetorical approaches to the issue in the wake of Walsh's 2007 publication *The Rhetoric of Fictionality*. In 2015, James Phelan,[3] Richard Walsh and I suggested in "Ten Theses about Fictionality," that the reorientation toward a rhetorical approach in the way of thinking about fictionality could be captured by three opening moves. One,

> To distinguish between, on the one hand, fiction as a set of conventional genres (novel, short story, graphic novel, fiction film, television serial fiction, and so on) and, on the other hand, fictionality as a quality or fictive discourse as a mode.
>
> *(Nielsen, Phelan, and Walsh, 2015, 62)*[4]

Two, to "emphasize that the use of fictionality is not a turning away from the actual world but a specific communicative strategy within some context in that world" (62). Three: "to advance a general claim [...] The ability to invent, imagine, and communicate without claiming to refer to the actual is a fundamental cognitive skill" (63). Together these moves help us understand why the employment of fictionality in strategical communication can be a means to accomplish real-world purposes, as we will see below. Together with Simona Zetterberg Gjerlevsen, I have defined fictionality as "intentionally signaled invention in communication" to stress the importance, in our view, of the overtly invented nature of fictional communication (Gjerlevsen and Nielsen, 2020, 23). Richard Walsh, partly in response to this definition, has suggested a relevance-based definition drawing on Sperber and Wilson, and in general, over the last decade, a large number of articles utilizing, expanding, criticizing, and developing a rhetorical approach to fictionality have appeared.[5] The approach is founded on the mentioned key distinction between generic fiction, such as the novel, short story, and fiction film, on the one hand, and the quality of fictionality, understood as a mode of discourse prevalent across genres and media, on the other hand.[6] This implies that, as a communicative strategy that signals invention, fictionality is also prevalent outside fiction as a genre, and is different from most earlier approaches to fictionality, where fictionality has traditionally been investigated as the qualities, characteristics, and affordances of fiction as a genre, which has, in turn, been described by the ways in which it differentiates itself from other genres.[7]

Fictionality in this conception is different from narrative in general, based on the fact that audiences tend to make assumptions about speakers' and writers' intentions, and sometimes question or test the truth-value of some narratives—for instance, historical narratives about the French Revolution—while other narratives do not invite similar responses, because (as is the case with most novels) they are overtly presented as invented rather than true.[8] Therefore, it seems evident that we should not make the mistake of conflating the inevitable constructedness of all narratives with the overt invention of some narratives. Hence, we need the distinction between narrative and fictionality. I will investigate how fictionality inside and outside fiction can intend to inform and misinform even as its invented nature is foregrounded.

Fictionality in the Service of Misinformation?

Questions of propaganda, satire, and fake news are thoroughly entangled in questions about freedom of speech, science, democracy, truth, and knowledge. These questions are increasingly important in an era when new media and information search options contribute to a de-hierarchization of knowledge that complexly runs counter to, but also extends, an enlightenment project. In a landscape in which true, false, and invented stories are used for political and ideological purposes, the concept of fictionality can contribute substantially to guiding our understanding of different communication strategies.

In her 2017 article "Fake news. It's complicated," Claire Wardle distinguishes between seven types of fake news, one of which is "Satire or parody ('no intention to cause harm but has potential to fool')" (Wardle, 2017), whereas the remaining six are different examples of intentionally misleading communication.[9] I wish to argue that the fact that invention is signaled does not justify the conclusion that there is no intention to harm or to deceive. Consider the following two outrageous statements:

1 "Muslims committed 9,000 out of 9,022 rapes in Denmark last year."
2 "The kind, intelligent war hero and professor looked up from his research and thought to himself: 'Are we not obliged as a country to react to the fact that Muslims committed 9,000 out of 9,022 rapes in Denmark last year?' "

It does not seem justified to say that there is an absolute and categorical distinction between the two statements in a way so that the second can never intend to misinform, let alone cause harm. In fact, receivers often react to assumed fictionality with a rejection of the world view, they interpret it to purport. That said, fictionality always requires at least a minimal (and sometimes a very great deal of) interpretation in relation to how it is relevant to understanding the real world.

It is integral to the rhetorical approach, I maintain, that receivers will always make assumptions about intentions. Conceiving a text or speech act as ironic, true, lie, or fictional entails an assumption about the sender's intention. To this approach a concept of communication that does not entail assumptions about intentions is unintelligible. Combining the insights that even fictional artefacts can (be assumed to) aim to misinform, and that receivers always make assumptions about intentions, we can make a heuristic scheme (see Table 20.1):[10]

The scheme does not assume any alleged ontological difference between fiction and non-fiction or between the objects they represent. It does not say that the universe of a novel has to be a specific way, or that non-fiction is always referential. It simply assumes that receivers adjust their attitudes to (what they perceive to be) rhetorically different strategies.

For now, I leave the fourth box open, like Genette's box in *Narrative Discourse Revisited* with homodiegetic narrative in external focalization (Genette, 1989, 121). I will then work my way toward solidifying an approach in which it makes sense to say that receivers sometimes—indeed, often— form the belief that overtly fictional communication is misinforming. Being based on assumptions, such attitudes and beliefs can be, and again often are, agonistic. This means that in addition to forming aesthetical and ethical judgments, receivers will also form judgments about whether or not the work misinforms compared to the takeaway about the real world. In this sense, the question about

Table 20.1 Assumptions about communicative acts

	Assumed signaled non-invention	*Assumed signaled invention*
No assumed intention to misinform	Science, truth, facts, documentaries.	Typical novels, computer games, drama, imagined scenarios, satirical fake news. Movie pictures. Campaigns and advertisements with imaginary scenarios.
Assumed intention to misinform	Lies. Fake news. Deception. Misinformation.	?

misinformative purposes is intermingled with questions about ethically flawed worldviews. I have no intention to obscure the crucial distinction between fictionality and lie, but to examine how and why fictionality is used for better and worse to make arguments and intervene in real-world discussions.

Fictionality in Memes and Perspectival Representations of the Ukraine-Conflict

This section examines the use of fictionality in visual representations of the context and consequences of the Russian invasion of Ukraine.

Language plays a key role in shaping perceptions of conflict, and language is not neutral. In the introduction, I used the expression "invasion" in the context of Ukraine; here "conflict." During the first several months, Russia and most of its media used the expression "special military operation" (специальной военной операции), following Putin's own term on February 24, when he sent Russian troops into Ukraine in a large-scale escalation of the "conflict," which had one major starting point in 2014 when Russia annexed the Crimea (Nikolskaya and Osborn, 2022). Words such as invasion, conflict, operation, even liberation, and war, all aim at designating specific events in the real world but provide different, sometimes incompatible, views on the ramifications and ethical implications of these events.

Images, similarly, to a large degree aim not just to neutrally represent events, but to promote certain frames for understanding their ethics and the drives of the actors.[11] Markus Ojala, Mervi Pantti, and Jarkko Kangas suggest that three major frames can be discerned in media images of the conflict in 2014 and 2015:

> Focusing on three such political framings—the Ukraine conflict as national power struggle, as Russian intervention, and as geopolitical conflict—the present study examines how these are visually reproduced in news images.
>
> *(Ojala, Pantti, and Kangas, 2017, 475 [for more on each framing see 477])*

The authors state that "Photography can be conceived of as the primary visual component in the multimodal process of news framing (Geise and Baden, 2014; Powell et al., 2015)" (Ojala, Pantti, and Kangas, 2017, 475). They add that "Recent research has increasingly acknowledged the influence of news images in the interpretation of wars and conflicts (e.g., Butler, 2005; Roger, 2013; Zelizer, 2004)" (Ojala, Pantti, and Kangas, 2017, 476). The article provides excellent interpretations of many images from four selected journals (*The Guardian, Die* Welt, *Dagens Nyheter*, and *Helsingin* Sanomat) and of the frames they provide, and the findings usefully highlight how "Ukrainian civilians were the single most frequently depicted actor group in visual coverage of the conflict in all newspapers. Table 20.1 also indicates that their representations were overwhelmingly positive, as were those of non-Ukrainian civilians. This is—whether for ethical or political reasons or not—because civilians were typically depicted in roles that tend to generate feelings of sympathy (Chouliaraki, 2008; Höijer, 2004)" (Ojala, Pantti, and Kangas, 2017, 480). The findings in the article about representations of the conflict in 2014–2015 can be replicated when compared to pictures of the conflict in 2022.[12]

However, one very prevalent type of image (and language use) is conspicuously absent from these accounts. That is the group consisting of images intentionally signaling invention in communication, i.e., employing fictionality. These images are not typically depicting civilians but predominantly shape beliefs and perceptions about the major actors in the form of politicians and nations.

A typical, recurring theme in these images employing fictionality is the depiction or prediction of a surprise outcome of the meeting between the major and the minor force (see Figure 20.1):

Drawing on numerous pre-existing scripts in the form of Russia as a large bear and as "red," and on the popular idea that a David is a fan favorite to bring down a Goliath, the image very effectively

Figure 20.1 Image by Polish illustrator Pawel Jonca. @Pawel Jonca.

conveys the "prophesy" that Ukraine (marked by the national colors and seemingly in the shape of a Danish Lego brick) will come out "unharmed" whereas Russia will endure injuries.[13] The image turns the real world assumed probability of the outcome on its head. In reality, if you have superior strength, power, military, and size, odds are you will prevail against a minor, weaker opponent. In fiction, however, it is a very strong convention that the smaller (possibly more agile and/or intelligent) person or army will take out the larger opponent.[14] The image, in part, draws on fictional probability to influence perceptions of real-world possibilities. By means of representing something that is clearly not real but overtly invented, the image conveys a relatively straightforward message about the political situation along the lines of: it is literally and figuratively not going to be the walkover, which (the sender of the image imagines) Russia/Putin imagines. Instead, it will end by hurting Russia more than Ukraine.

The overt fictionality of many images of conflict and war is almost entirely absent from discussions about images in warfare. But fictionality strongly contributes to shaping beliefs about such conflicts. Not only about their outcome as above, but also—as the next example demonstrates (see Figure 20.2)—about villains and ethics:

All of Putin's facial features are made up of war items: bombers, bombs, and corpses. The tragic results of war are thus depicted as directly connected to Putin and to what is on his mind. He literally has a "face of war," and the image may prompt receivers to recall Dali's painting with that very title (see Figure 20.3)

But whereas Dali's painting depicts the victims who make up the face and its features, especially in the form of eyes and mouth, the front cover of Putin represents him as the responsible perpetrator. He even has drops of blood from the corner of his mouth as if he is devouring the human bodies and thus, like a vampire, lives on human blood (Figure 20.4).

Figure 20.2 *Internazionale* 4/10 march 2022, cover illustration by Noma Bar. @Noma Bar. Reproduced by permission of the artist.

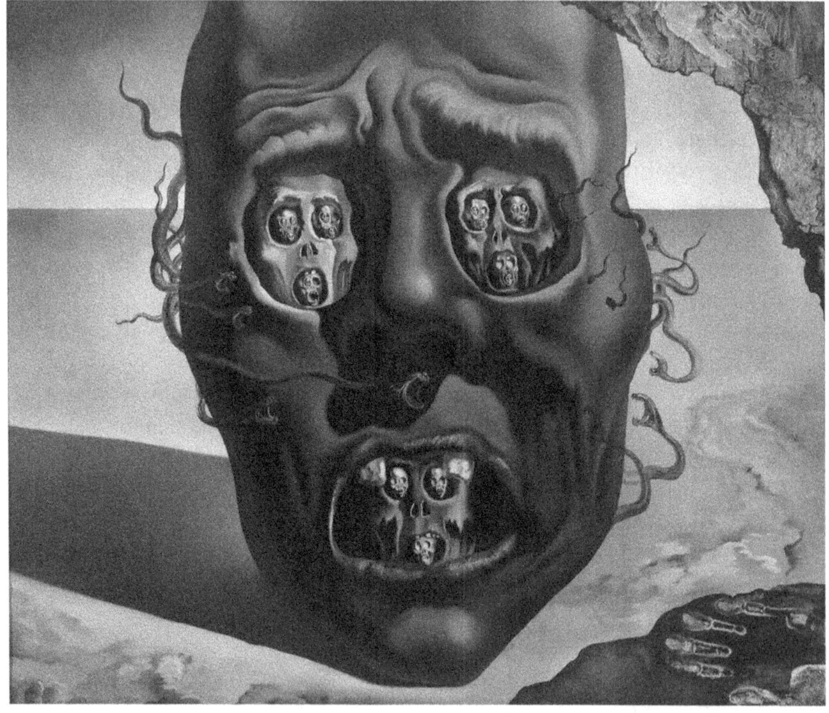

Figure 20.3 Salvador Dalí, *The Face of War*, 1940, oil on canvas, Museum Boijmans Van Beuningen. © 2023 Salvador Dalí, Fundació Gala-Salvador Dalí, Artists Rights Society.

Figure 20.4 Anonymous image attributed to Banksy by Facebook user "Ferocious Dog," March 14, 2022, https://www.facebook.com/photo.php?fbid=518020753013296&set=a.283870476428326&type=3&theater. Apparently adapted from the music video to "Go Bananas" by the Russian band Little Big, YouTube, uploaded by Little Big, November 15, 2019, 0:33, https://www.youtube.com/watch?v=ADlGkXAz1D0

Whereas one would expect a pin prick to destroy a fragile balloon very easily, the image suggests instead that the act of violence causes the perpetrator himself to implode instead. The whole image, including Putin himself, is kept within a Ukrainian color scale. When we see the surprise demise of the aggressor, we witness an overtly fictional representation, since the images clearly and intentionally signal invention. It is part of the communication that receivers understand that they do not witness the real Putin in real action against a real balloon. And this very fact is what makes the image political and turns it into an argument. As a political argument, the image foregrounds certain views and aspects. For instance, that Putin is frailer than the balloon; that he is the aggressor; that Ukraine will prevail against all odds, but that Putin will not, etc. At the same time, it excludes or backgrounds other aspects, including the human suffering, the role of Russia and its parliament in relation to Putin as a person, and the enormous military support from Western countries in the form of high-tech weapons and defense systems to Ukraine, which is only from a certain perspective an autonomous entity. No matter how aesthetically and ethically pleasing such images may sometimes appear, they are highly political and mobilizing and aimed directly at affecting beliefs through fictionality with an efficiency rarely available to non-fictional communication. Through fictionality, Putin is repeatedly cast as a villain. "Villain" itself is a concept shaped to a very high degree by our knowledge of and from fiction. Everyone can probably immediately mention several dozen fictional villains, whereas we rarely tend to think about real-world persons in such terms. Hence fictionality is used to ascribe clear-cut roles to real world actors, making the world more comprehensible and less nuanced, thus making value judgments "simple." The final example in this section depicts Putin as a villain even more directly (see Figure 20.5):

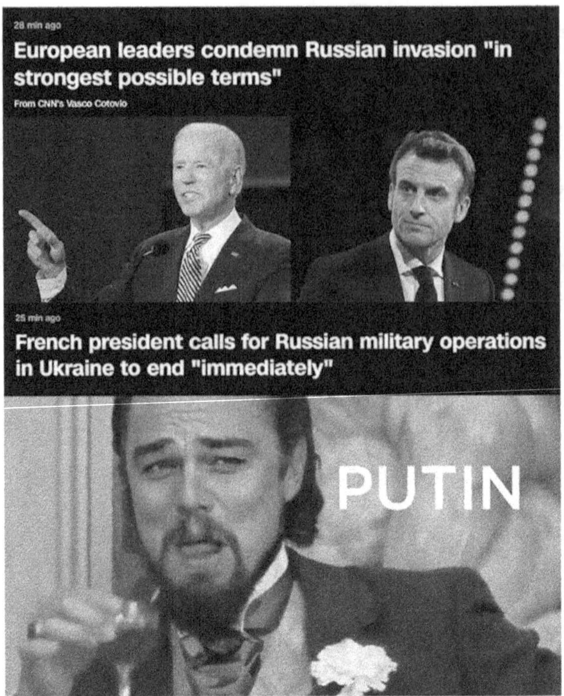

Figure 20.5   Anonymous internet meme. With image adapted from Quentin Tarantino's 2012 film Django Un-chained, posted by user 9GAGGER on the social media site 9GAG on February 24, 2022, https://9gag.com/gag/amgARwj.

At one level, the image depicts Putin as completely unaffected by the accusations and demands, but while doing this it casts him as one of the most inhumane Hollywood villains of all times; Di-Caprio's despicable character Calvin Candie, who in Tarantino's *Django Unchained* is a slave owner without any respect for humanity.[15] The movie supplies a pre-established frame of understanding of a certain character and his traits and personality. It repurposes a popular fiction movie to provide a specific perspective on a conflict that post-dates it by a decade. As for all examples in this section, they are clearly subjective expressions meant to deliberately affect viewers' perceptions of the ethics and motives of nations and individuals as political actors. The examples all have an unambiguous bias toward sympathy for Ukraine, and antipathy toward Putin and Russia. Interpreting them as rhetorical arguments to this effect does not amount to sharing the same bias—or to the opposite. Additionally, all the discussed images are comprehensible from a Western perspective, whereas I lack the insight in Russian contemporary political imagery to claim anything about a potential Russian use of overt fictionality for the purposes of political persuasion.[16]

In the next section, I move from such instances of fictionality outside fiction (albeit often drawing on pre-conceptions modelled on fiction through and through) to propagandistic use of fictionality in relation to war inside a well-established genre of fiction: the Hollywood movie.

Fictionality as War Propaganda in Fiction— The Military-Entertainment Complex

In *Top Gun 2: Maverick*, the most important plot point of all is shaped by the fact that "the enemy" has so-called fifth-generation fighters so advanced that America has lost any and all technological advantage it may have had. This leads to many of the choices and the plot twists and is all-decisive for how the operation to bomb and eliminate a uranium plant on foreign soil can be carried out. The movie is very well-reviewed and extremely effective and has an awe-inspiring audience rating of 99% at *rottentomatoes.com*, meaning that it reaches almost an entire audience and gets their applause, even if this doesn't mean an audience endorsement of the American military, and even if audience members do not even notice the propaganda or the movie's value system. Hollywood creates an imagined community tying together entire Western populations in admiration for American military ability. The movie seems to be irresistible. It is so technologically advanced compared to other means of persuasion by fictionality that one could say that it represents fifth-generation fictionality, giving it an edge over all competitors with less developed engines of fictionality at their disposal. Its precursor *Top Gun* (1986) was a similar blockbuster success. Both movies were made in close collaboration with the Pentagon and the US military (Lau, 2021, 9), which thoroughly influenced the production and plot (Lau, 2021, 10).[17] Both installments led to a huge surge in recruitment to the army and navy.[18] The close relationship between movie creation and the war industry in the United States goes almost all the way back to the very beginning of the former with the very first Academy Award winner for best picture being the war movie *Wings* in 1929, heavily subsidized by the war department.[19] Disney has a similar strong tradition of working with the Pentagon going back to the Second World War.[20] The working relationship between fictionality industries in the form of the motion picture industry and computer games developers on the one hand and military development on the other hand runs even deeper than this. In the articles "All but War Is Simulation: The Military-Entertainment Complex" and "Theaters of War: The Military Entertainment Complex," Tim Lenoir (and in the latter, also Henry Lowood) plays on President Dwight D. Eisenhower's famous warning about the "military–industrial complex" to talk instead about the military-Entertainment Complex (Lenoir and Lowood 2003, 21). This amounts to designating not only the collaborations resulting in movies co-scripted with the Department of Defense,[21] but also the co-developments of technologies of simulation and the recurrence of key researchers across the entertainment-military line. In the very first lines of the latter article, the authors state: "War games are simulations combining game, experiment, and performance. The U.S. Department of Defense (DoD) has been the primary proponent of war game design since the 1950s" (Lenoir and Lowood, 2003, 1) and on the next page: "The U.S. Department of Defense defines a war game as "a simulation, by whatever means, of a military operation involving two or more opposing forces, using rules, data, and procedures designed to depict an actual or assumed real life situation" (Lenoir and Lowood, 2003, 2). This attests to the fact that there is fictionality *in* (preparation for) warfare and fictionality *about* warfare—and to the fact that a movie like *Top Gun Maverick* is a war game. The authors also explain how:

> High-end simulators cost twice as much as the systems they were intended to simulate. Thorpe's idea was that aircraft simulators should be used to *augment* aircraft. They should be used to teach air-combat skills that pilots could not learn in peacetime flying, but that could be practiced with simulators.
>
> *(Lenoir and Lowood, 2003, 11)*

This is exactly what also happens *in* the movie, where the results of simulated practice form the basis of core arguments about if and how the operation can be performed and whether it is necessarily a suicide mission (albeit euphemistically referred to). Additionally, the authors argue that

> Examination of the work and careers of individuals who have participated in both the military simulation community and the entertainment industry suggests paths through which dissemination of research ideas across these seemingly different fields takes place. Consider the example of Dr. Robert S. Jacobs, currently director and president of Illusion, Incorporated. [...] Having

headed up the design team at Perceptronics that worked on the original design of SIMNET, he has been a technical contributor to the majority of later, related training programs. (23) [...] Company founder Stuart Rosen's computer game development experience began at Atari, where he became a program manager and oversaw the Pac-Man conversion for home computers and video consoles. [...] Rosen then moved to Bolt Beranek & Newman Advanced Simulation, where he led the design, development and integration of networked interactive simulation systems for U.S., British and Japanese forces. This included extensive work on the SIMNET project.

(Lenoir and Lowood, 2003, 24)

The article concludes with an example where fictional entertainment and military recruitment are indistinguishable.

On Independence Day, 2002, the traditional summer blockbuster date in the entertainment industry, the US military released its new videogame, *America's Army: Operations*. [...] the game, intended as a recruiting device, is distributed free on the internet. [...] the game is a first-person multiplayer combat simulation [...] On the first day of its release the military added additional servers to handle the traffic, a reported whopping 500,000 downloads of the game. The site continued to average 1.2 million hits per second through August 2002. Gamespot, a leading review, not only gave the game a 9.8 rating out of a possible 10, but also regarded the business model behind the new game as itself deserving an award.

(Lenoir and Lowood, 2003, 36)

But what is it about fictionality—by definition, the overt signaling that something is invented and **not** real that makes it so extremely persuasive and so appealing to masters of war that they are willing to pay billions of dollars to enroll it as a mercenary? This is what *Top Gun Maverick* will exemplify.

The Lessons of Top Gun Maverick

In "Misogynist Films: Teaching *Top Gun*," Tania Modleski convincingly demonstrates how the first installment undercuts female authority in sexist ways:

At one point in Top Gun, Charlie (Kelly McGillis), the love interest who also happens to possess a PhD in astrophysics and to teach at the flight school Maverick (Tom Cruise) attends, chastises Maverick for a move the latter makes in a war game. "What were you thinking?" she asks. Maverick, in time-honored fashion, pulls out the "you weren't there" card. "You don't have time to think up there. If you think, you're dead." Thus is female authority effectively undermined. Indeed, I argue that Charlie is raised so high (given an advanced degree in astrophysics) in order to make her conquest, her fall into the arms of Maverick, her admission that he is a "genius" at flying so much greater. [...] I show a clip that shows how the film visually participates in the abasement of the woman: when Charlie is first introduced by the male instructor (Tom Skerrit) who is in the process of citing her impressive credentials, the film cuts to the lower half of a woman's body wearing a tight skirt and stockings with seams, as if this were a World War II film and not a post-Vietnam one.

(Modleski, 2007, 102)[22]

Although not exactly entirely inclusive, *Top Gun Maverick* is not as sexist as the first one. It makes half-hearted efforts to include somewhat resourceful women in the male narrative in ways that have been updated to try to reflect the changing times. And it has been met with critical acclaim by audiences and reviewers alike rather than with reproach. As Slavoj Žižek writes in the foreword to *Sociology through the Projector* in the context of similarly acclaimed Hollywood productions, *United 93* and *World Trade Center*, such praise should make us suspicious, and we should "ask ourselves what ideological purposes it [the acclaimed styles of the movies] serves" (Žižek, 2007, iix).

The opening images of the movie show "The Navy Fighter Weapons School" and convey a tremendous fascination with engines and planes. The very first words we hear are from a radio announcing that "Today we're looking at some of the hottest weather …", which may lead a viewer to believe that the movie or even the navy would address an updated real-world challenge in the form of climate change. That possible assumption couldn't be more wrong since, after these first words, the movie is one long tribute to fuel-burning engines of all kinds—in water, on roads, and in the air. One of the next images, we meet, is a sign near the school stating, "Use of deadly force authorized" (Kosinski, 2022, 0:04:48). That statement, on the other hand, very accurately announces what follows. The opening conflict of the movie is that cut downs to the military is announced and represented by a clearly villainous figure who believes in the future of robots and unmanned planes, which will make the humans obsolete (Kosinski, 2022, 0:15:09 et passim).

That viewpoint is to be proven wrong in the logic of the movie, according to which cuts are bad, robots are bad, and the real human person is all that matters. In the following, I will examine the reasons for the movies' distribution of sympathy and antipathy and for how it follows and diverts from reality. Paradoxically and logically at the same time, when the movie then later presents encounters with "the enemy," that enemy is completely reduced to something less than human, a faceless figure of simulation repeatedly referred to as "a bandit," whom we are most definitely not invited to imagine as having to "sleep, eat, take a piss." Similarly, the state/nation/country of the enemy is only vaguely hinted at. It is a "threat to allies in the region," evoking the image of America as the protector and big brother who helps keep the peace. Enemy territory is under "Rogue state control," thus placed outside law and international jurisdiction. It is in a state of exception that serves to legitimize the unprovoked, non-retaliatory American attacks, bombings, and homicides on foreign territory in an affirmation of American exceptionalism as a means to greater good. The enemy has the huge advantage of "fifth generation fighters" (Kosinski, 2022, 0:33:16 et passim).

From the point in the movie when the mission and its premises are explained, it is stated repeatedly and beyond the point of indoctrination that the human pilots need to learn, "don't think!" echoing Maverick's words in the first movie, and that it is "the pilot not the plane." Though again, the latter is only made to pertain to acts of personal heroism and flying skills and not in the slightest to loss of life—let alone enemy life, which can be joked about as if in a computer game.[23] The enemy is portrayed as so completely imbecile and idiotic in its lack of ability to recognize the "heroes" and their plans that it amounts to dehumanization in and of itself. The logic leading to the final encounters is that the mission has a chance of success under all circumstances, but the important question becomes if this can be achieved without loss of American life. In that context, the formidable flying skills of the pilots become all-decisive against enemy fifth-generation fighters.

Purposes of Fictionality in *Top Gun Maverick*

Compared to the actual geopolitical situation in the world insofar as the military is concerned, the entire plot of the movie thus revolves around two mutually supportive counterfactual premises. One, that the American military is technologically inferior and outmatched,[24] and two, that the individual, human being and his or her skills on the other hand greatly outweigh technological superiority (and that, therefore, a shift away from person-based combat is an ethical as well as a strategical mistake).[25] Naturally, this raises the critical question: why intentionally use fictionality, and what is the purpose of basing the plot on these two counterfactual premises?

As for the plot line, it helps make the American pilots underdogs whom one can more easily root for. The overriding propagandistic message invites the viewer to believe in a worldview in which America is struggling to keep up materially and technologically (and thus over time must importantly resist any demands for cuts to the military budget) but ethically and personally superior. Consequently, US forces have not just a right but an obligation to intervene across the world.

There are several real-world aims achieved by this. The two most tangible are recruitment and image. Fictionality popularizes and glamorizes army life in several respects.[26] Heroism prevails, while death as war reality is eliminated. War is represented as a game—and one of personal glory at that. In the movie, the two words "You die" are repeatedly used, but every time as the result of a simulation. The "you" who "dies" is still there alive. War is a simulation.

The less tangible and even more important aim is the modelling of an entire worldview building on but going beyond the particularities of this story. Hollywood fictionality is put to use to create an entire belief system about the world and the role of America and Western countries in this world. The Oscar awards effectively participate in exporting such world views across as many countries as possible. From the to me appalling *The Hurt Locker* awarded the Oscar for best picture in 2010 via the, in my view, despicable *Argo* receiving the same prize in 2013, to *Top Gun Maverick* being at the time of writing a prime contender for the 2022 award, the Oscar awards are part of a large engine rewarding mutually coherent and overlapping worldviews and belief systems. *The Hurt Locker*, also highly praised, is directly about the Iraq War and shows the enormous personal cost of traveling to Iraq and dismantling bombs in the most extreme circumstances for an American minor. The main character thus loses the possibility of any kind of normal relationship with family and everyday life at home, and in the end has no other life options or interests left than to continue working in Iraq with the extreme dangers and adrenaline kicks it entails. In that sense, the film is anything but rosy. At the same time, it is entirely affirmative in relation to common American worldviews and images of Iraq. It portrays the American effort in Iraq as self-sacrificing and heroic. Americans, personified by the main character, literally sacrifice themselves to create peace and order in the chaos that the Iraqis have created. The Iraqis are portrayed as bomb makers and terrorists at odds with everyone else and not least with themselves. It is in this chaotic hell of a country that the Americans arrive and selflessly try to bring a modicum of order. There is a very low degree of ambiguity in relation to the distribution of roles, and the film does not complicate matters by asking about other possible motives on either the American or Iraqi side.

Argo in a similar fashion adds other facets to the same picture: the Americans are heroes, and clever, and very unselfish. The Iraqis/Iranians are shouting/non-sensical/chaotic crowds of fanatics, and stupid. CIA and the movie industry are working together in secret to do the best for the world and they do not even need any kind of recognition for it.

In comparison with other forms of propaganda and misinformation, this level of fictionality offers some large advantages as a means of communication. Before summarizing some of these in the conclusion, I will briefly compare it to the very different strategies in an entirely different type of Hollywood movie about similar issues, Tarantino's *Inglourious Basterds* (2009). In comparison, it seems to me that *Top Gun Maverick* is propaganda whereas *Inglourious Basterds* is *about* propaganda.

Hollycaust

Inglourious Basterds, including misspellings of both words of the title, is a film by the provocative and experimental American director Quentin Tarantino (1963–). It is an overtly counterfactual representation of the Second World War, not only because it contains fictitious people, resistance groups, and events, but also because Hitler and a large part of his officers perish during an action against them in a cinema premiere of a propaganda film that the German Propaganda Minister Goebbels has helped set up.[27] The simultaneity of the fictional and the historical is already hinted at in the very first words of the film, which read: "Once upon a time in Nazi-Occupied France" (Tarantino, 2009, 0:01:53). The words draw on a formula we know from fairy tales and at the same time refer to a specific place and a specific time in world history. The film also includes a lot of metafictional elements and does, for example, sometimes stop completely when a new person is introduced, and show us clips from his or her past and prehistory.[28] This is, for example, the case with Hugo Stieglitz, who is freed from prison by the resistance group whose leader, Aldo Raine, is played by Brad Pitt in the film. Hugo Stieglitz is freed to be included in the group that seeks out, kills, and scalps Nazis in Germany.[29] The film's central pivot point is the cinema scene at the premiere of a documentary about Fredrick Zoller, who is in the movie a real person and considered a war hero by the Germans because he killed far more than one hundred people from a tower where he was besieged. Goebbels has produced the film as a tribute and as propaganda, and Zoller plays himself in the film. The film is set to premiere in a cinema owned by the woman Shosanna, who in the film's first scene, which takes place a few years earlier, escapes the Nazis' murder of her family, who were hidden under the floor of a house. It turns out that a large number of top Nazis, including Hitler himself, will be attending the premiere. As a result, two groups independently set about planning an assassination. One plan is drawn up by Aldo Raine's resistance group. It involves a particularly comical attempt to pass as Italian without knowing even a minimum of Italian idioms and pronunciation. Their plan is to bomb and shoot down the Germans in the hall. The plan is, unbeknownst to all parties, drawn up in parallel with Shosanna's; she, together with her African-American lover and employee at the cinema, plans to blow up and burn the theater while the Germans are locked inside. A significant point is that Shosanna's bomb is made of film strips, in the form of nitrate film, which is extremely flammable and explosive, and which has also in real life led to several large fires. In this way, the film stages and juxtaposes film and terror on several levels. As a whole, it is about the relationship between information, terror, propaganda, and film in a way that extends beyond the Nazi era and into the post-war era and our own time. In a sense, the plans of both groups succeed, although a number of people, including Shosanna, die in the process. She cuts her own film into Goebbels' so that it interrupts the German propaganda film "Pride of the Nation" with Zoller in the role of himself in the tower. In her own film, Shosanna tells the audience that they will now be killed by a Jew. At the same time, the incendiary bomb made of the nitrate film is set off, and a powerful fire ravages the hall and the panicked Nazis, who meanwhile are also fired upon and killed from above by men from Aldo Raine's group with machine guns. In the culmination of Tarantino's movie, viewers thus find themselves in the ethically uncomfortable situation of watching Goebbels' propaganda movie with a disgust intentionally evoked by Tarantino by showing the Nazis' applauding Zoller's killing of hundreds of people from the tower while the viewer is at the very same time tempted to himself applaud what seems like justice for the very same appalling German officers in the form of the men from Aldo Raine's group standing on the balconies and shooting down with machine guns on the defenseless people in the hall in a situation spatially and thematically mirroring that of the German documentary as well as the initial slaughter of Shoshanna's family, gunned down by machine guns from above. Similarly, the Germans are literally incinerated in another instance of the punishment mirroring the crime.[30] In this way, the metaphor of an explosive film is literalized, and the viewer is invited to consider the latent violence and terror that is always associated with propaganda and misinformation.[31]

Conclusion

In the chapter, I set out to examine the question of how and to what degree fictionality in and outside fiction can be used to harm and to misinform. As for the question mark in the box in my scheme above for "Assumptions about communicative acts," containing communication where some receivers may assume simultaneous signaled invention *and* assume intention to misinform, the arguments in the article lead me to conclude that this is not a non-existing or even a rare type. However, as mentioned earlier, such assumptions and ethical judgments are agonistic, and probably many viewers of *Top Gun Maverick* are not going to make an assumption that it is misinforming. Conversely, other viewers and critics found that *Inglourious Basterds* in fact is misinforming. Such interpretative differences illustrate the inherent ambiguities of fictionality even when deployed as propaganda. To me, *Top Gun Maverick* intentionally creates a deficient perspective on the world, which the viewer is invited to share with specific real-world aims; whereas *Inglourious Basterds* does not, because I do not personally feel invited by the movie to see it as "inaccurate" or as stating something about the vengefulness of Jews or pushing me to believe or do something, I wish to resist. Rather it illuminates for me some connections between images and reality, as Suleiman states, and also between cinema and ideology, or between fiction and belief, and this seems to me what it is essentially about. A typical form of Hollywood movie (emblematic for how many other movies, novels, and computer games work at some level) is overtly fictional and (mis)informative at the same time. If some receivers find some cultural artefacts misinformative, then that is a critical and interpretive judgment rather than an objective fact. This agonistic subjectivity is not something to try to erase, but instead helps explain why representation matters, and why audiences routinely discuss and like and dislike novels, TV series, and movies based on perceptions on how they represent immigrants, the relation between genders, experts, mental illnesses, etc. A viewer can make the contextual, interpretative judgment about certain fictional narratives that they seem to represent a world view in which African Americans are unintelligent and sexually unhinged (*The Birth of a Nation* [1915]) or in which women are prone to falling in love with their rapists (*Game of Thrones, 365 Days*), or in which Middle Eastern cultures are less coherent and more violent and chaotic than Western ones (*Argo*), or in which the United States is fundamentally a peacekeeping force in the world (*The Hurt Locker, Top Gun Maverick,* and countless others different in some aspects and similar in others). Having potentially made such judgments, receivers have an option to make the judgment (possibly in contradistinction to other people's judgments of the same artefact) that such representations are ethically deficient and amount to misinformation.

Sometimes such assumed misinformation may be attributed to ignorance, lack of knowledge, unconscious stereotyping, or outdated historical assumptions, and sometimes it is attributed to intentional manipulation, propaganda, and attempts to influence beliefs by means of fiction and fictionality.

Fictionality in general, and large-scale subsidized multimillion-dollar fictional enterprises in particular, offer superior advantages compared to misinformation or other means of ideological persuasion. In addition to tremendous affective and emotional appeal through visual and auditory effects, they are shielded from direct attacks of lying or misinformation because they do not claim to inform or be truthful in the first place. Compared to embedded reporting (see Butler, 2005), for example, which can be highly subjective and limited in perspective and controlled by governing forces, Hollywood fictionality is much more effective and without the disadvantages of manipulative real-world reporting. Most other propaganda and misinformation (such as state-controlled news about the front line, the people's support for the war, the size of the army, or the discontent of the opponent) quickly appear comically anachronistic and inadequate compared to the fiction engines of the entertainment-military complex of today. The latter pertains to the perception of entire populations in an all-encompassing world view about geopolitics, rogue states, ideology, race, and religion that is almost irresistible and impossible to place oneself outside of.

Recent fictionality theory can certainly not be credited for having discovered these affordances and forces of fiction, but it does provide new ways to examine and understand it, including revealing some of the specific ways smaller instances of fictionality in memes and pictures form a continuum with larger global fictions, as well as the ways in which fiction and belief are related.

Notes

1 I wish to thank the editors of the volume for thorough, insightful comments, which helped me improve the clarity of my argument here.

2 *"War Is Merely the Continuation of Policy by Other Means"* is the headline to Section 24.

3 Please see Phelan's contribution to part I of the volume. Phelan's overarching focus on narrative as something used by senders to achieve certain purposes in relation to receivers remains a huge inspiration to fictionality theory in general and my own approach in particular.

4 This is a formulation of a point already implied in Walsh (2007).

5 See James Phelan (2015), Paul Dawson (2015), Alexander Bareis (2016), Mari Hatavara and Jarmila Mildorf (2017), Stefan Iversen, Louise Brix Jakobsen, Samuli Björninen and others.

6 See Walsh: "Not that fictionality should be equated simply with "fiction," as a category or genre of narrative: it is a communicative strategy, and as such it is apparent on some scale within many nonfictional narratives, in forms ranging from something like an ironic aside, through various forms of conjecture or imaginative supplementation, to full-blown counterfactual narrative examples" (Walsh, 2007, 7). See also (Nielsen, Phelan, and Walsh, 2015).

7 Fiction theory has a long and varied history in literary studies, philosophy, and related fields. See, for example, Hans Vaihinger's philosophical approach to "as if" (Vaihinger, 2021), Kendall Walton's concept of "make believe" (Walton, 1993), Dorrit Cohn's attempts to identify the "distinction of fiction" (Cohn, 2000), the possible-world theories of Marie-Laure Ryan, Thomas Pavel, and Lubomir Doležel (Bell and Ryan, 2019), and Daniel Punday's investigations of fictionality and postmodernism (Punday, 2009). See also Pavel (1986), Schaeffer (1999), and Lavocat (2016). Walton, Vaihinger, Schaeffer, and Lavocat are noteworthy exceptions to the prevalent tendency to think of fictionality as a quality of genres of fiction.

8 Which is not to say that fictionality theory is alone in drawing this particular distinction which can also be made on other bases (e.g., on pragmatic or ontological grounds).

9 See also Edson C. Tandoc, Zheng Wei Lim, and Richard Ling, who distinguish between types of fake news based on whether there is an "intention to deceive" (Tandoc, Lim, and Ling, 2018, 148). For a similar discussion of the relation between different types of fake news and misinformation in a broader context of story-critical approaches but with no view to the examples in this article, see "Introduction" in *Dangers of Fictionality and Narrative* (Nielsen, 2023). For a discussion of the specifically satirical types of fake news see (Nielsen, 2020).

10 The rough scheme here covers only communicative acts inviting relatively straightforward assumptions as far as invention is concerned. For a description of hybrid forms such as autofiction, etc., see Phelan's suggestion of the macro genre of "blurring" in the current volume.

11 See (Ojala, Pantti, and Kangas, 2017) for an article on the conflict in 2014–2015. For recent social media used in the conflict, see (Rosenblatt and Tenbarge, 2022), and for images in wars, see (Butler, 2005) and (Kirkpatrick, 2015).

12 See, for instance, Farrant (2022).

13 This is following the visual logic of the image of the country as a solid brick, and in no way to ignore the massive human tragedies and crimes against humanity.

14 So much so that audiences were shocked in the episode of *Game of Thrones* "The Mountain and the Viper," which aired June 1, 2014, and was rated as one of the best episodes ever screened, when this failed to happen, and the muscular giant Gregor Clegane literally crushed the skull of his much smaller, much more agile, and much, much more charming and well-spoken opponent Oberyn Martell.

15 The image is one out of many by anonymous creators utilizing the Calvin Candie character to indirectly characterize perceived aspects of Putin.

16 As a general observation based only on personal experience and not on empirical evidence, it seems clear to me that more populistic and totalitarian regimes and politicians rely much more on misinformation and much less on fictionality, and that—as an example—Obama regularly employed sophisticated instances of fictionality across media and contexts, whereas Trump very rarely if ever resorted to such rhetoric.

17 On the relation between the first *Top Gun* installment and American elections, see Pach (2004).

18 See Binoy Kampmark: "The USAF has gone into an enthusiastic recruitment drive, hoping to inject some verve into the numbers. In of itself, this is unremarkable, given a shortage of pilots that was already being pointed out in March 2018. That month, Congress was warned about a shortfall of 10 percent equating to 2,100 of the 21,000 pilots required to pursue the National Defence Strategy. Shortages were also being noted by the US Navy. Recruitment stalls have mushroomed across movie halls. Navy spokesperson Commander Dave Benham is hopeful. 'We think Top Gun: Maverick will certainly raise awareness and should positively contribute to individual decisions to serve in the Navy.' With the film running throughout the country, the Navy's recruitment

goals for the 2022 financial year of 40,000 enlistees and 3,800 officers in both active and reserve components may be that much easier" (Kampmark, 2022). And Alissa Wilkinson: "[…] for the Navy, Top Gun was more than just a movie. It was a recruitment bonanza. Military recruiting stations were set up outside movie theaters, catching wannabe flyboys hopped up on adrenaline and vibes. Others enlisted on their own. Interest in the armed forces, primarily the Navy and the Air Force, rose that year, though it's unclear just how much. Naval aviator applications were claimed to have increased by a staggering 500 percent" (Wilkinson, 2022).

19 See Wilkinson (2022).

20 See Wilkinson (2022).

21 These include: *Air Force One* (1997), *Apollo 13* (1995), *Armageddon* (1998), *Batman & Robin* (1997), *Behind Enemy Lines* (2001), *Black Hawk Down* (2001), *Deep Impact* (1998), *Godzilla* (1998), *The Green Berets* (1968), *I Am Legend* (2007), *Indiana Jones and the Last Crusade* (1989) *Iron Man* (2008), *Iron Man 2* (2010) *The Jackal* (1997), *Goldfinger* (1964), *Thunderball* (1965), *Licence to Kill* (1989), *GoldenEye* (1995), *Tomorrow Never Dies* (1997), *Jurassic Park III* (2001), *The Karate Kid Part II* (1986), *The Next Karate Kid* (1994), *King Kong* (2005), *Last Action Hero* (1993), *The Silence of the Lambs* (1991), *Star Trek IV: The Voyage Home* (1986), *Top Gun* (1986), *Top Gun: Maverick* (2022), *Transformers* (2007), *Transformers: Revenge of the Fallen* (2009), *Transformers: Dark of the Moon* (2011), *True Lies* (1994), *Wonder Woman 1984* (2020), *Wings* (1927) (Underhill, 2013).

22 Modleski has many other examples and also references other movies, which succeed at giving women voices on issues of war (103 et passim).

23 As a correct assessment states: "Hollywood knows how to sell the life of a soldier. Top Gun paints the life of an elite pilot as mostly a real-life video game, with young men competing to top the charts at the academy" (Wilkinson, 2022).

24 In reality, America spends about three times as much as the second largest military, China, and ten times as much as number three, India (World Population Review, 2022).

25 In reality, America strongly resisted and voted against a UN ban of automated weapons such as so-called killer robots, (AFP in Geneva, 2021), and has been conducting drone liquidations in Yemen and other countries systematically through the years since 2001.

26 Thanks to the editors for pointing out that partly or wholly invented stories since the *Iliad* has been used to glamorize war, and that the movie is thus firmly rooted in a long tradition. In this sense it is not special or unique, but Hollywood delivers an engine that makes it possible to reach global audiences in the millions in a very short time span.

27 The movie has been the center of intense critical debate hinging not least on the critics' stance on whether or not the movie is historical enough and testimonial enough to be accused of revisionism and of reversal of the roles of perpetrator and victim. Should one see it in the context of testimony theory and ask, "who witnesses for the witness?" or as so overtly detached from the real history that it is about something else, such as the power of cinema. Ben Walters makes an even-handed case for the latter in "Debating *Inglourious Basterds*" (Walters, 2009, 22). See also Rieder on revenge fantasies in the movie (Rieder, 2011). Susan Suleiman brilliantly lays out the debates about the movie and about how and if it compares to other movies with somewhat similar subjects such as *Schindler's List* and *Life Is Beautiful*, before offering her own ingenious interpretation of the movie and many of its countless references to pre-war-, war-, and post-war movies about race and war. After outlining the stakes, Suleiman ends by taking the stance that "as a film that foregrounds the problematic relation of images to reality, it's 'damn good,' to quote Lieutenant Raine's phrase about Landa's deal with the generals" (Suleiman, 2014, 86).

28 See also Dassanowsky (2012).

29 By having the Americans "scalp" their enemies, the movie plays on a well-known Hollywood racist cliché incarnated by several John Wayne-movies; that indigenous people in America should be combatted because of their savage ways, thus juxtaposing American and German racism as expressed propagandistically in movies.

30 See Suleiman (2014, 74).

31 "I like that it's the power of the cinema that fights the Nazis," Tarantino has said. "But not just as a metaphor, as a literal reality" (Walters, 2009, 20).

Works Cited

AFP in Geneva. 2021. "US Rejects Calls for Regulating or Banning 'Killer Robots.'" *The Guardian*, December 2, 2021. https://www.theguardian.com/us-news/2021/dec/02/us-rejects- calls-regulating-banning-killer-robots.

Bareis, Alexander. 2016. "Randbereiche und Grenzüberschreitungen: zu einer Theorie der Fiktion im Vergleich der Künste." In *Fiktion im vergleich der Künste und Medien*, edited by Anne Enderwitz and Irina Rajewsky, 45–62. Berlin: De Gruyter.

Bell, Alice, and Marie-Laure Ryan, eds. 2019. *Possible Worlds Theory and Contemporary Narratology.* Lincoln: University of Nebraska Press.

Butler, Judith. 2005. "Photography, War, Outrage." *PMLA* 120, no. 3 (May): 822–27. https://doi.org/10.1632/003081205X63886.

Clausewitz, Carl von. (1832) 2008. *On War.* Oxford: Oxford University Press.

Cohn, Dorrit. 2000. *The Distinction of Fiction.* Baltimore, MD: Johns Hopkins University Press.

Dassanowsky, Robert. 2012. *Quentin Tarantino's Inglourious Basterds: A Manipulation of Metacinema.* New York and London: Continuum.

Dawson, Paul. 2015. "Ten Theses Against Fictionality." *Narrative* 23, no. 1 (January): 74–100. https://doi.org/10.1353/nar.2015.0006.

Farrant, Theo. 2022. "20 of the Most Powerful Photographs Taken in the First Weeks of the Russia-Ukraine War." *Euronews*, April 19, 2022. https://www.euronews.com/culture/2022/04/19/20-of-the-most-powerful-photographs- taken-in-the-first-weeks-of-the-russia-ukraine-war.

Genette, Gerard. 1989. *Narrative Discourse Revisited.* New York: Cornell University Press.

Gjerlevsen, Simona Zetterberg. 2016a. "A Novel History of Fictionality." *Narrative* 24, no. 2 (May): 174–89. https://doi.org/10.1353/nar.2016.0008.

Gjerlevsen, Simona Zetterberg. 2016b. "Fictionality." In *The Living Handbook of Narratology*, edited by Peter Hühn. Hamburg: Universität Hamburg. https://www-archiv.fdm.uni- hamburg.de/lhn/node/138.html.

Gjerlevsen, Simona Zetterberg, and Henrik Skov Nielsen. 2020. "Distinguishing Fictionality." In *Exploring Fictionality. Conceptions, Test Cases, Discussions*, edited by Cindie Aaen Maagaard, Daniel Schäbler and Marianne Wolff Lundholt, 19–40. Odense: Syddansk Universitetsforlag.

Hatavara, Mari, and Jarmila Mildof. 2017. "Hybrid Fictionality and Vicarious Narrative Experience." *Narrative* 25, no. 1 (January): 65–82. https://doi.org/10.1353/nar.2017.0004.

Kampmark, Binoy. 2022. "Top Gun: Maverick: The Pentagon Recruitment Drive." *Scoop Independent News*, June 23, 2022. https://www.scoop.co.nz/stories/HL2206/S00042/top-gun-maverick-the-pentagon-recruitment-drive.htm.

Kirkpatrick, Erika. 2015. "Visuality, Photography, and Media in International Relations Theory: A Review." *Media, War & Conflict* 8, no. 2 (May): 199–212. https://doi.org/10.1177/1750635215584281.

Kosinski, Joseph, director. 2022. *Top Gun 2: Maverick (Top Gun: Maverick).* Paramount Pictures. 2 hr., 11 min. Viewed at youtube.com.

Lavocat, Françoise. 2016. *Fait et fiction: pour une frontière.* Poétique. Paris: Seuil.

Lenoir, Tim. 2000. "All But War Is Simulation: The Military-Entertainment Complex." *Configurations* 8: 289–335. https://doi.org/10.1353/con.2000.0022.

Lenoir, Tim, and Henry Lowood. 2003. "Theaters of War: The Military Entertainment Complex." In *Kunstkammer - Laboratorium - Bühne. Schauplätze des Wissens im 17. Jahrhundert*, edited by Jan Lazardzig, Helmar Schramm, and Ludger Schwarte, 432–64. Berlin: De Gruyter.

Modleski, Tania. 2007. "Misogynist Films: Teaching 'Top Gun.'" *Cinema Journal* 47, no. 1 (Autumn): 101–05. http://www.jstor.org/stable/30132003.

Nielsen, Henrik Skov. 2020. "Factuality and Fictionality in Fake News." In *Travelling Concepts: New Fictionality Studies*, edited by Monika Fludernik and Henrik Skov Nielsen, 161–78. Literary and Cultural Studies, Theory and the (New) Media Vol. 3. Berlin: Peter Lang.

Nielsen, Henrik Skov, James Phelan, and Richard Walsh. 2015. "Ten Theses about Fictionality." *Narrative* 23, no. 1 (January): 61–73. https://doi.org/10.1353/Nar.2015.0005.

Nikolskaya, Polina, and Andrew Osborn. 2022. "Russia's Putin Authorises 'Special Military Operation' Against Ukraine." *Reuters*, February 24, 2022.

Ojala, Markus, Mervi Pantti, and Jarkko Kangas. 2017. "Whose War, Whose Fault? Visual Framing of the Ukraine Conflict in Western European Newspapers." *International Journal of Communication* 11: 474–98.

Pach, Chester. 2004. "'Top Gun' Toughness, and Terrorism: Some Reflections on the Elections of 1980 and 2004." *Diplomatic History* 28, no. 4 (September): 549–62. http://www.jstor.org/stable/24914875.

Pavel, Thomas. 1986. *Fictional Worlds.* Cambridge, MA: Harvard University Press. Punday, Daniel. 2009. *Five Strands of Fictionality: The Institutional Construction of Contemporary American Fiction.* Columbus: The Ohio State University Press.

Rieder, John. 2011. "Race and Revenge Fantasies in *Avatar*, *District 9* and *Inglourious Basterds*." *Science Fiction Film and Television* 4: 41–56. https://doi.org/10.3828/sfftv.2011.3.

Rosenblatt, Kalhan, and Kat Tenbarge. 2022. "Ukraine Fights Back on TikTok, Where War Is Fought with Memes and Misinformation." *NBC News*, March 4, 2022. https://www.nbcnews.com/tech/tech-news/tiktok-ukraine-war-misinformation- propaganda-rcna18146.

Schaeffer, Jean-Marie. 1999. *Pourquoi la fiction?* Paris: Seuil.

Suleiman, Susan Rubin. 2014. "The Stakes in Holocaust Representation: On Tarantino's Inglourious Basterds." *Romanic Review* 105, no. 1–2 (January–March): 69–86. https://doi.org/10.1215/26885220-105.1-2.69.

Tandoc, Edson C., Zheng Wei Lim, and Richard Ling. 2018. "Defining 'Fake News'." *Digital Journalism* 6, no. 2 (August): 137–53. https://doi.org/10.1080/21670811.2017.1360143.

Tarantino, Quentin, director. 2009. *Inglourious Basterds*. Universal Pictures. 2 hr, 33 min. https://play.hbomax.com/page/urn:hbo:page:GYg_RZgXeKEiCrwEAAABF:type:feature.

Underhill, Stephen. 2013. "Complete List of Commercial Films Produced with Assistance from the Pentagon." Washington, DC: FOIA.

Vaihinger, Hans. 2021. *The Philosophy of 'As If'*. London: Routledge. https://doi.org/10.4324/9781003091585.

Walters, Ben. 2009. "Debating Inglourious Basterds." *Film Quarterly* 63, no. 2 (Winter): 19–22. https://doi.org/10.1525/FQ.2009.63.2.19.

Walton, Kendall L. 1993. *Mimesis as Make-Believe On the Foundations of the Representational Arts*. Cambridge, MA: Harvard University Press.

Wardle, Claire. 2017. "Fake News. It's Complicated." *First Draft* 16 (February): 1–11. https://firstdraftnews.org/articles/fake-news-complicated/.

Wilkinson, Alissa. 2022. "The Long, Long, Twisty Affair Between the US Military and Hollywood." *Vox*, May 27, 2022. https://www.vox.com/23141487/top-gun-maverick-us-military- hollywood.

World Population Review. 2022. "Military Spending by Country 2022." https://worldpopulationreview.com/country-rankings/military-spending-by-country.

Zetterberg Nielsen, Henrik Pernile Meyer, Maria Mäkelä, and Samuli Björninen. 2023. "Introduction." In *Dangers of Fictionality and Narrative*. Bern: Peter Lang.

Žižek, Slavoj. 2007. "Foreword. Projector in the Heart of the Social." In *Sociology Through the Projector*, edited by Bulent Diken and Carsten Bagge Laustsen. New York: Routledge.

21
USES OF FANTASY FICTION IN CONTEMPORARY POLITICAL MOBILIZATION

Anne Besson

The expansion of fantasy worlds and the role fan practices play in this expansion have become a major cultural phenomenon (Besson, 2015). For the past twenty-five years, the ever-increasing importance, for a very large audience, of science fiction and mostly fantasy universes such as *Star Wars*, *The Lord of the Rings*, *Harry Potter*, and *Game of Thrones*, has been enriched by the involvement and sustained participation of active fan communities. People sharing those worlds—not only "hardcore fans" but a large set of media consumers in our fiction era—relate to them in a special way: ever-present across many media, these worlds are perceived as deeply familiar and foster a strong sense of belonging. More and more, those cultures of fiction are materializing in everyday life in many different forms (from cosplaying to locating platform 9 and ¾ in the real King's Cross Station in London), and political mobilization probably provides among the most interesting examples of this in the last ten years (Besson, 2021, 2023). After providing the necessary context about the contemporary political uses of fantasy fiction, we will address the question of political faith (hope, enthusiasm, commitment): the fictional references, as a new form of propaganda, aim to produce strong feelings of sharing and belonging, and a sense of participation for the audience.

Fiction and Political Mobilization

This chapter will, therefore, focus on this very dynamic use of fantasy fictions in a context of political action (struggles for human rights, campaigns, demonstrations, strikes, etc.). We can mention a few examples for the sake of clarity: in 2010, Palestinian activists dressed up as the Na'vis from *Avatar* (a movie directed by James Cameron, 2009), covering themselves in blue make-up, to protest against the Israeli occupation policy; in Southeast Asia, the Rebellion's recognition gesture from *The Hunger Games*[1]—the three middle fingers extended—was taken up by Thai protesters against the military coup of June 2014, then by Burmese protesters in 2021; the Umbrella Movement in Hong Kong, in 2014 and especially in 2019, took *The Hunger Games* as a predominant model ("If we burn, you burn with us" [Davis and Wasserstrom, 2020]) (see Figure 21.1).

In the famously numerous French demonstrations, placards recently exhibited references to the *Game of Thrones* series, both visual (typography, images, dummies) and semantic ("Winter is not coming anymore" during the Global Climate Strikes in 2018 and 2019; see Figure 21.2), to *The Lord of the Rings* universe ("Hobbits' Strike" or "Sauron will not get our pensions") or the French

DOI: 10.4324/9781003119456-24

Figure 21.1   Hong-Kong, 2019. Photo @Tom Grundy, HKFP.

Figure 21.2   Marche pour le climat, September 8, 2018, Paris. Photo © Fanny Dollberg/*Reporterre*.

Figure 21.3 Pension Law Protest, January 29, 2020, Paris.

Arthurian comedy series *Kaamelott* ("Sire, on en a gros," "Sire, we resent it") during the Pension Law protests of 2019–2020 (see Figure 21.3).

We all have in mind the "Scarlet Handmaids" (from Margaret Atwood's 1982 novel *The Handmaid's Tale*) marching in silence to defend the right to abortion (François, 2023) in the United States (where that mobilization failed to prevent the Supreme Court decision overturning Roe, but contributed to alerting public opinion where abortion rights were at stake), Colombia and Chili (this rights was then won), but also Belgium or Poland; masks and make-up from *The Joker* movie (Todd Philipps, 2019), *La Casa de Papel*, a Spanish TV show that aired on Netflix in 2017, or the Guy Fawkes figure taken up by Anonymous hacker groups because of its previous apparition in *V for Vendetta*, an engaged comic by Alan Moore (1982–1990), and then adapted in a movie produced by the Washowskis in 2005, were also spotted by photographers.

The works chosen as references emanate mainly from an English-speaking sphere (England, the United States, and Canada) that continues to produce globalized successes, and more rarely from Western Europe. Their use, on the other hand, proves to be perfectly international, on all sites of protest: the Handmaids have appeared in the United States but also in Argentina and Poland in 2017–2018; the Jokers, new heralds of a violent and disenchanted urban protest, were photographed at the end of 2019 in Beirut, Lebanon, Spain, and Chile.

One can well imagine the attractiveness, whether it is to arouse the interest of more young people for civic action or to ensure the necessary media and socio-numerical coverage, of what Stephen Duncombe describes as "ethical spectacles": public performances which, while being playful and attracting sympathy, nevertheless aim at a real effectiveness (Duncombe, 124–75). They borrow the finery of the mask (those of Guy Fawkes, of Dali, of the "Scream" of Munch popularized by the series of films *Scream*, by Wes Craven [1996–]) and those of the costumes, like the vast red flaming dress and the headdress hiding the face of the scarlet Handmaids that the women refuse to become when they defend their rights to control their own bodies. These have the double advantage of attracting the eye and protecting those who wear them from social or judicial sanctions. Those women can moreover transmit their role to others, thus limiting the risk of fatigue or wear and tear that is a habitual problem in militancy.

The dressed-up protesters are at once more and less than themselves (brilliant symbols, interchangeable carriers), which can be a pertinent way of designating the individual in a situation of political engagement. The fact that the material vectors of the protest (the costumes and slogans, for example) are borrowed from fantasy fictions, must itself be understood as a contestation of the current reality: it is elsewhere (and tomorrow …) that we can still find reasons to fight and to hope; it is from fictional scenarios and media images that we borrow the symbolic means of resistance.

Fantasy References, Political Context

Such a tendency arises in a context of more and more extreme political polarization: and whether we like it or not, fantasy and SF works and stories are nowadays important parts of the debate (Kyrou, 2020). The "progressive," or subversive, "potential of fantasy" (Baker, 2012) already has a long cultural history, as it is consubstantial with these genres since their origin: their escapism is indeed understood as a reaction to the successive steps of industrial modernization and political threats: George Orwell's *Animal Farm. A Fairy Story* (1945) condemning the Stalinist abuses, or the Star Trek fandom rallying in support of their slogan, "Infinite Diversity in Infinite Combinations" at the very moment of the moral backlash of the Nixon US presidency are some of the milestones on this busy road. Today, fantasy fiction is very widely judged, by a part of its audience at least, by sociopolitical criteria—in terms of values expressed by the story, or the gender and ethnic diversity of the casting of characters, for example (Proctor, 2017). And in the other direction, fiction is more and more believed to affect our way of understanding real facts, as we consider them with the tools of comprehension provided by our shared culture; each new political event can be commented on using analogies with well-known fictions: what situation is it like, what character can be compared to this or that political figure and so forth.

For example, last spring on Twitter, May 4 (usually a Star Wars Day on social networks), "Monsieur Samovar" (@m_samovar), a gay French teacher with 24.3k followers (October 22) wrote about the French elections. He compared the left-wing coalition set up to win the Parliament to the Council of Elrond in *The Lord of the Rings*, where the different people of Middle Earth—Elves, Dwarves, and Men—unite to fight Sauron, Lord of Evil—to put it simply, but this simplicity is precisely the idea: everybody should grasp the point, appreciate the analogy and draw on it in turn, when the real situation is much more complicated by the position of the center-right presidential party (LREM), balancing left and right backers, identified here as supporters of the Evil side, and the fall of the Socialist Party, formerly a dominant force, now angry that it has to suffer the decisions of the more radical LFI, Jean-Luc Mélenchon's party.

> The reactions of LREM to the left-wing coalition's efforts in the legislative elections= the Twitter of Sauron and Saruman when the peoples of the Middle Earth joined forces to go and kick their asses. Blah, blah, blah, the Council of Elrond, a danger for the institutions.[2]

This first message poses an imaginary situation where the opponents, Sauron, Saruman and so on, have their own social networks where they try to make the coalition appear as a "danger for the institutions" of Mordor and thus the stability of the world. The direct analogy (=) between Macron's party and the Evil side of Middle-Earth superimposes the epic and ethically clear stakes of the battle for Gondor with the much murkier electoral strategies of today's politicians, presented as distorting any moral reference points the fantasy work can provide. The numerous "answers" to the message take their turn commenting on and assessing the relevance of comparisons and proposing more of the same fictional examples, for instance, the reply of "Structures minimalistes" (@minimaliste13): "Saruman: I will resign from the White Council if Elves and Dwarves ally."[3] They discuss who are the orcs, the trolls, the elves ("to see elves of the socialist party uniting with LFI's orcs is somehow disgusting"—"with you, the trolls are already here"[4]), and which character Macron would be—not Sauron, more "a Grima who dreams of being Faramir."[5] They mix well-known political quotes with the context taken from Tolkien (if Mélenchon, infamous for saying "I am the Republic," were Gandalf, he would say, "I AM middle earth"[6]).

Pop culture references to fictional situations and characters have become one of the symbolic and semiotic systems shared on social networks to read and write our conflicts. They rely on media franchises such as *Hunger Games*, *Harry Potter*, *Star Wars*, and *Game of Thrones*, which are the core of a wide generational or trans-generational culture—hence their efficiency and attractiveness. They are probably better known to most people, and will undeniably last longer in memories, than the real-life political jolts of the moment. Parody or not, their proper functioning requires both a shared knowledge about the fantasy universe, with different levels of expertise (one can understand or master only some of the references) and shared political values if the game is to go on (in the example above, the general analogy, with its positive association for the left coalition, was not challenged). This association between fictions and political stances in social conversations (loving the universe enough to be able to wittily play with its components and agreeing on a common line of interpretation) produces a sense of community or a feeling of belonging, and encourages political debate and the total reshaping of its traditional forms.

While it is easier and, therefore, more common to signal good feelings—to approve and relay such and such a position on online social media networks—than to translate them into real actions, envisioning a spectrum that goes from participation to engagement allows us to highlight an obvious continuum between the two sets of uses of fantasy references. It is indeed because we first watched, heard of, or discussed *The Handmaid's Tale* or *The Joker* (a film by Todd Philips, 2019) that their eventual transpositions into political events will be able to take on meaning and impact; their ethical and political relevance (what they have to say to us, individually and collectively) has already been established via public discourses, so that their quotation is apt to convey an immediate message, easily understandable by all participants of the previous debate.

This map (Figure 21.4) is the main picture produced by the pro-Ukrainian social network account "Middle-earth of Eastern Europe" (on Twitter, @Me_of_EE), created in June 2022 to post "LOTR russo-ukrainian War memes" (to quote the profile). It superimposes the cartographic style as well as the toponyms of Middle-earth on a map showing a part of Eastern Europe poorly known to a wide Western audience (around central Ukraine, Belarus, Romania, small Moldavia, Poland, etc.). The parallel works because the big picture is quite clear-cut: Gondor is Ukraine, Minas Tirih Kiiv, and Mordor is Russia, of course, Osgiliath standing at the border. It should be noted that the identification between the Russians and the orcs is much older, constituting one of the main possible readings of Tolkien's novel in the context of the Cold War. Russian nationalists then reappropriated this stigma as part of an ironic strategy of "self-hatred" well explained by Eliot Borenstein (2020, 2023).

Beyond that first easy part of identification, the map arouses our interest for the lesser-known locations: for instance, seeing the Evil fortress of Dol Guldur, facing the Lorien, at the North-West of the

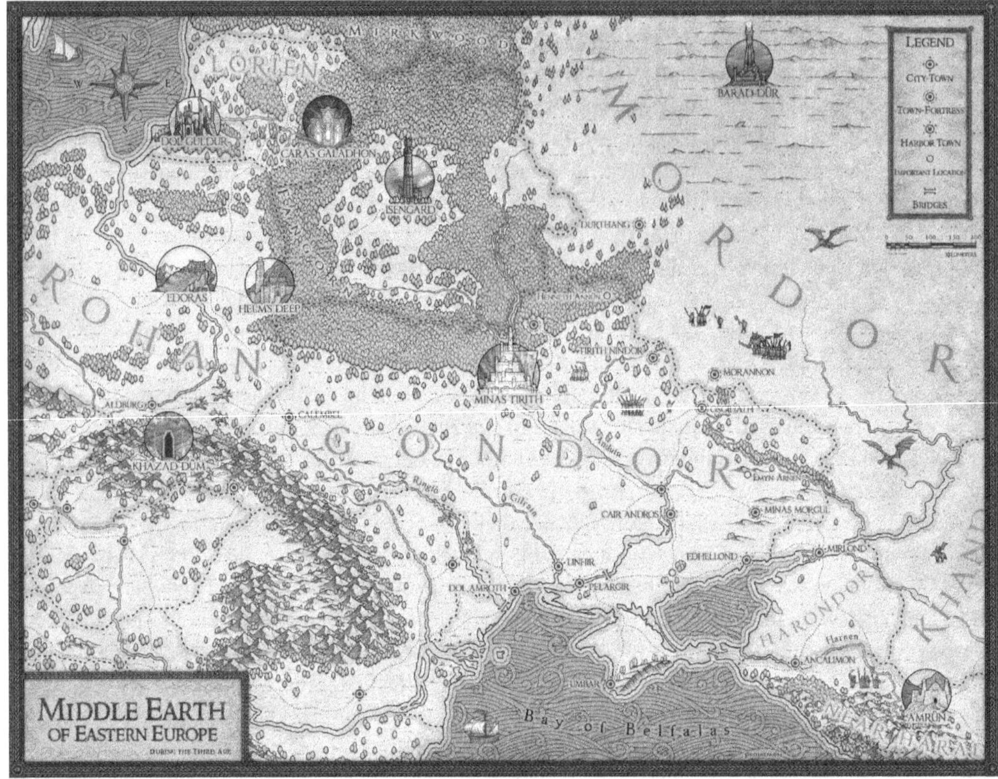

Figure 21.4 Middle-earth of Eastern Europe map, @Me_of_EE, 2022.

semi-fictional map (where the places normally occupied by European countries are literally covered by the imaginary topography) may well lead some to check a real map and discover the Russian enclave of Kaliningrad stuck between Poland (Rohan) and Lithuania (Lorien). The choice of Isengard for Belarus and Minsk draws attention to the position of this country, subservient to Russian policy just as Isengard is a traitor to Gondor. Along the main map, the profile picture underlines the boundaries of "Gondor"/Ukraine so it appears clearly that their shape includes Donbass and Crimea. The fictional counterpart of Crimea is the harbour of Umbar, a place, south of Gondor, which was taken and lost multiple times throughout the wars that ravaged Middle-earth during the Second and Third Ages.

The levels of expertise about the fictional world of Middle-earth and about the Russo-Ukrainian conflict go hand in hand and progress together, the desire to go deeper being triggered by the graphic and hermeneutic appeal of the imaginary map. It is indeed fiction, in the foreground, that attracts us so we take a closer look at reality, that opens us to a better understanding of the geopolitical forces at work—even if, obviously, it is strongly determined by a starting postulate that one would almost come to forget when captured by the fun of investigating the relevance of the real-life fictional counterparts: Ukrainian Gondor occupies the central role of Good in its epic conflict against Evil. To put it bluntly, the game is also propaganda. To depict one's enemy as a monster out of a horrific tale is a very old habit in propaganda drawings; the Prussian invaders, then the Germans, were caricatured as giants or ogres during the European Wars of 1870 and 1914–1918. What has changed today, beyond the sheer scale of online diffusion, is that they are no longer pictures out of a folktales' book, but widely known characters who play precise roles in long, complex stories with disputed allegorical meanings: the cultural thickness the popularization of media conversation has given them.

Communication Strategy and/or Political Commitment

It is on this basis that we must now address the question of political "belief," which we will define as full commitment, or at least interior assent that something is deeply meaningful and has to be done or thought for the greater good. What can be left of it when confronted with fictional references? Following the thesis of David B. Suits (2006), that belief is not "an all-or-nothing affair" but something more contextual and sometimes even contradictory, are fantasy fictions used to raise spirits and to express or symbolize strong political values? Or mostly as a way of mobilizing supporters, in each part of the political spectrum, by claiming the monopoly of an association with the "Good ones," as we have already witnessed in our previous examples; that is, something more akin to opportunism or to strategies of political communication? Clearly, the difference might be thin or just a question of moment and position (what political group, where in the field), but it requires investigation nonetheless to better understand how the two perspectives may work together or against one another.

Appeal, attractiveness, fun, spectacular public performances, are among the expressions we used when describing the uses of fantasy fiction in political action. It was the explicit goal Stephen Duncombe wanted to emphasize in his essay *Dream: Re-imagining Progressive Politics in an Age of Fantasy* (2007); for him, leftist politics, strongly associated with moralism, seriousness, utilitarianism, "all work and no play" (as noted by Richard Gruneau in his introduction to *Popular Culture and Political Practice* [1988, 11]), must reconnect with enjoyment and fantasies. Leaving this field to the right, much more comfortable with "creating reality" or saying what people want to hear (Duncombe, 2007, 1–9), and failing to embrace the creative modes of action of social movements, would mean missing out on the "lingua franca of our time, fantasy and spectacle" (9). Taking up the question of faith as illusion, he claims at the beginning on his reflection: "we need a secular alternative, dreams recognizable for what they are—human constructs of our hopes and desires—but no less powerful for their transparency" (10). This is precisely how fantasy worlds are used, to renew our ability to imagine other spaces of possibility, something that can only be done outside of a reality generally perceived as *deceptive*.

Fantasy references, when used in a political context, aim first of all to focus media attention (social media and traditional media), and thereby to get the audience to rally to the cause. This is political communication: a way of playing with media, taking from media culture to be brought back into it, trying to catch what is likely to work with the audience and to meet the expectations of the media. The goal is for the tagline to be repeated, shared, retweeted, for the signs or the placards to be the most photographed, to raise interest in the terrible competition for attention we well know (Citton, 2014a, 2014b)—and this is easier to do by quoting famous fantasy works than by making actual political claims (see Figure 21.5). The interest such a power can present expresses itself mainly in two different ways.

This need to focus media attention (Grossman, 2022), to be seen, is absolutely crucial for the social conflicts which take place far from the eyes of the Western world. As we have seen during the Hong Kong protests, for instance, activists take great risks and need to publicize their fight against a very powerful state and military censorship: in that context, by using beacons of the Western culture industry, they draw our attention, they make us *care*. Western audiences will be more likely to be witnesses and supporters—we *recognize* their bravery and their sacrifice—because we saw the movie. The effect of such "reality-meets-fiction" moments is very powerful: when Manik Sethisuwan posts a picture of a protester doing the *Hunger Games* sign, #Thailand, #ThaiCoup, in June 2014, with the caption "Our struggle is not fiction. Thanks"; when the posters "That's how it starts" become "This

Figure 21.5   Manik Sethisuwan, Twitter post, @sethiwusan, June 2014.

is not fiction" in the hands of "scarlet handmaids" standing before the stairs of the US Supreme Court in June 2022 after the overturning of the *Roe vs Wade* decision; watching such scenes, hitherto considered to belong to alarmist anticipations, come true right before our eyes produces astonishment and stupefaction. The spectacle is touching and frightening, it has a "last stand" quality that our narrative experience makes deeply moving (see Bruner, 2002 on the influence of narratives on the way we apprehend our lives).

But in a very different way, this kind of fiction-based political communication also triggers feelings of entertainment and pleasure that are very important among younger generations. Closely associated with childhood memories of fun and play (TV franchises and tie-in toys), fantasy references can arouse enthusiasm, revive in us a naive faith in heroism and battles worth fighting for. The youth activists (and among them fan activists, see Jenkins et al., 2016) very well know how hard it is to mobilize a part of their generation on political issues, because of a prevalent sense of helplessness and disinterest for world events among them. The key to reach them could well be the use of fiction, where one can keep a playful distance from one's commitment. Because they are always told that everything is potentially fake and deceptive, nothing has to be taken too seriously—so even fighting for a better world to live in becomes part of a game, very serious when you're in it, but at any moment you can come out and not suffer too much because those strong feelings were embedded in a special fictional time and place.

The media communication here works to allow youth communities to grasp the references, recognize them as theirs and hopefully feel concerned: such effects can be witnessed in the immediate aftermath of *The Joker* movie (a story of social violence suffered and then inflicted) or *La Casa de Papel* (a story of revenge against finance by contemporary Robin Hoods mocking the police).

The latter show, for instance, has put *Bella Ciao*, the famous old song of the Italian resistance fighters at the end of World War II, a hymn to rebellion, a joyful and lively tune, back on everyone's lips.

Each of these two kinds of effect (catching the eyes of an audience bored by dystopian fights in the real world; boosting morale by bringing fun into harsh settings) takes us a step beyond communication, to the fringe of faith. Strong feelings of sharing and belonging, and a sense of participation are involved: the protest song *Bella Ciao* shows this very well, since it is also deeply moving in itself and even more so when we hear it in the TV show, twice at the end of the first season (s. 1 ep. 11 and 13), at a time when the audience has become very close to the characters and wants them to win. When, through the song, the characters bid farewell to their beloveds and leave for an ultimate resistance fight, the audience gets the goosebumps, and the burglary story takes on a deeper resonance. This example, and many others, show that the shared references, when they belong to beloved fictions, produce emotions—are tied to powerful affect.

It is then, perhaps paradoxically, our own stories and history that become bigger, richer, more precious and grander so as to be brought closer to the great stories of our time that are *Star Wars* and *The Lord of the Rings*—stories that, for their fans, touch the heart and raise up the soul. Political faith—hope, enthusiasm, commitment, the desire to change the world or just to put an end to the most glaring injustices—is notoriously fragile and very difficult to maintain, because it crashes up again and again against the reality of fights that are always lost. The revolutionary flame can barely burn in an environment so poor in oxygen as social networks and connected screens: fantasy fables in this context are used as a way to revive that flame via tales of great battles and small heroes who are noble and simple, tragic and touching, whether they win or lose. They are part of an attempt to "take back the narrative" (a very powerful motto of fan communities) on a collective basis.

Fiction and Propaganda

Of course, it is sweet-talking people, playing with their feelings to let them think they are part of something meaningful and bigger; it has to be so, as long as leaders or programs want to mobilize people. Chomsky and Herman famously identified "mass media" playing a "propaganda role" and "manufacturing consent" (2002), and when Duncombe asks his reader to "Imagine an Ethical Spectacle" (2007, 124), he immediately emphasizes the importance of being perfectly aware that "[f]ascism and commercial appear to have cornered the market on the political use of fantasy and the mobilization of desire" (124). In fact, this worry goes back to the very beginning of Fascist movements in the twentieth century, when it was strongly expressed by Walter Benjamin's warning, in 1935, about the aestheticization of politics, to which Marxists were supposed to respond with politization of art (Benjamin, 1969).

The boundary between fiction and propaganda, though necessary to maintain (Lavocat, 2016), is indeed a fine line and a widely addressed question (for instance, as "politics of affect" in Massumi, 2015), as it is one of the known margins of fictionality; rife with hoaxes, fake news, and clickbait, our contemporary media context multiplies gray areas where it is hard to separate submission to lies from the willing suspension of disbelief, or attempts to deceive from "shared ludic feint" (to quote Schaeffer's definition of fiction, 2010, 138–39). In this context, it is interesting to take a last look at the communication strategies of Putin's Russia and Zelenski's Ukraine in the media war they are waging in their current conflict. Their striking differences are indeed symptomatic of a cultural change that has been underway for several decades: on the one hand, "good old" propaganda, taking the form of oversimplified historical memories, appealing glory days (us against the Nazis); on the other, newer fiction-based political communication that is just as simplified: us against Mordor. The parallel with *The Lord of the Rings* that we have already mentioned is present not only in many memes, gifs, and visual content on the networks, but also in official speeches at the highest level of the Ukrainian staff (Leloup, 2022).[7]

Both claims (Ukrainians as nazis, Russians as orcs) are lies and a large part of the audience is more or less aware of it but only one of these shared pretenses highlights its own status as fiction.

This example encapsulates our previous reflections. We find the same choice of fantasy to revive political faith, by prompting the idea of a Good War against Evil. Also, by resorting to this media strategy, Ukraine multiplies the signals of its belonging to the West: it anchors itself in a culture, an entertainment industry, a social world, which turns its back on the anti-capitalist, anti-American ways of thinking typical of the ex-Eastern bloc and then Russia and pro-Russian Ukrainian parties. And finally, an imaginary past is chosen against the historical annexation attempted by Putin ("On the Historical Unity of Russians and Ukrainians," 2021). Neither side wants to give the other an argumentative monopoly: Ukraine also claims the historical roots of its independence, and not only through medieval fantasy, and Russian nationalists symmetrically claim orc identity as a martial badge. Nevertheless, while the New Russia proclaims itself "Most Holy" again and dreams of a glorious comeback in its own history in line with a medievalist imagery of national roots (Victoroff, 2022), Ukraine, in contrast takes a stand on the side of Middle Ages as fantasy, reinvented as a place of freedom and greatness far from any constraint or oppression of the "system"—the latest avatar, coming directly from the United States of the 1960s and 1970s, of our collective representations of the Middle Ages.

References to fantasy fictions are everywhere in contemporary political mobilizations, as they echo a shared imaginary likely to raise spirits and exalt values that are recognized as positive by a large spectrum of political stances. They serve both as visual codes and digital traces in times of crisis, and as reading grids superimposed on the events of the contemporary world; they offer simple keys of access to a complex reality, always oriented from the point of view of groups seeking to assert themselves by relegating their enemies to the side of the Dark Ones. In all cases, community effects are produced, and agreement on hermeneutic codes and their applicability becomes the vector of a commitment which fantasy stories seem the best able to produce today.

Notes

1 Three novels by Susan Collins, 2008–2010, four movies, directed by Gary Ross (I) and Francis Lawrence (II–IV), 2012–2015.
2 "Les réactions de LREM devant les tentatives de l'union de la gauche aux legislatives = le Twitter de Sauron et Saroumane lorsque les peuples de la Terre du Milieu se sont alliés pour aller leur botter les fesses.
Gna-gna le Conseil d'Elrond, danger pour les institutions." Translations are mine.
3 "Saroumane: je quitte le Conseil blanc si les Nains et les Elfes s'unissent."
4 @DanielLattanzio, 5 mai 2022: "Voir les elfes du PS s'allier avec les orques de LFI a quelque chose d'écœurant," and the immediate reply of @lgwnh "Avec vous, les trolls sont déjà là."
5 Monsieur Samovar, 5 mai "Manu c'est à peine un Grima qui se rêverait en Faramir."
6 @mrtn_Axl, 4 mai 2022, "La Terre du Milieu, c'est MOI !!"
7 See a mix of pro-Ukrainian LoTR memes from Damien Leloup'paper: https://img.lemde.fr/2022/04/14/0/0/1800/900/1342/671/60/0/e02d721_1649925720130-montage-ukraine-3-2.jpg

Works Cited

Baker, Daniel. 2012. "Why We Need Dragons: The Progressive Potential of Fantasy." *Journal of the Fantastic in the Arts* 23, no. 3: 437–59.
Benjamin, Walter. (1935) 1969. "The Work of Art in the Age of Mechanical Reproduction". In *Illuminations*, edited by Hannah Arendt, translated by Harry Zohn, 217–252. New York: Schocken Books. https://web.mit.edu/allanmc/www/benjamin.pdf.
Besson, Anne. 2015. *Constellations. Des mondes fictionnels dans l'imaginaire contemporain*. Paris: CNRS Editions.
Besson, Anne. 2021. *Les pouvoirs de l'enchantement. Usages politiques de la SF et de la fantasy*. Paris: Vendémiaire.

Besson, Anne. 2023. "Engagement and Enchantment: Political and Ethical Uses of Fantasy Fictions." In *Can Fiction Change the World?*, edited by Alison James, Akihiro Kubo and Françoise Lavocat, 155–65. Oxford: Legenda.

Borenstein, Eliot. 2020. Articles from the "Soviet Self-Hatred" section of Eliotorenstein website, from "The Fellowship of the Wrong", September 29 2020 to "Orknash Supporting the Home Team", October 3 2020. https://www.eliotborenstein.net/soviet- self-hatred.

Borenstein, Eliot. Forthcoming. *Soviet Self-Hatred: The Secret Identities of Post-Socialism*. Ithaca, NY: Cornell University Press.

Bruner, Jerome. 2002. *Making Stories: Law, Literature, Life*. New York: Farrar Straus & Giroux.

Chomsky, Noam, and Edward S. Herman. (1988) 2002. *Manufacturing Consent: The Political Economy of the Mass Media*. New York: Pantheon Books.

Citton, Yves, ed. 2014a. *L'économie de l'attention, nouvel horizon du capitalisme*. Paris: La Découverte.

Citton, Yves. 2014b. *Pour une écologie de l'attention*, Paris: Seuil.

Davis, Hana Meihan, and Jeffrey Wasserstrom. 2020. "Hong-Kong and the Hunger Games." *The Millions*, January 24, 2020. https://themillions.com/2020/01/hong-kong-and-the-hunger-games.html.

Duncombe, Stephen. 2007. *Dream: Re-Imagining Progressive Politics in an Age of Fantasy*. New York and London: The New Press.

François, Anne Isabelle. 2023. "Feminist Resistance and the Powers of Fiction". In *Can Fiction Change the World?*, edited by Alison James, Akihiro Kubo and Françoise Lavocat, 141–55. Oxford: Legenda.

Grossman Emiliano. 2022 "Media and Policy Making in the Digital Age". *Annual Review of Political Science* 25: 443–61.

Gruneau, Richard, ed. 1988. *Popular Cultures and Political Practices*. Toronto: University of Toronto Press.

Jenkins, Henry, Sangita Shresthova, Liana Gamber-Thompson, Neta Kligler-Vilenchik, and Arely M. Zimmerman. 2016. *By Any Media Necessary: The New Youth Activism*. New York: New York University Press.

Kirou, Ariel. 2020. *Dans les imaginaires du futur*. Chambéry: ActuSF.

Lavocat, Françoise. 2016. *Fait et fiction: pour une frontière*. Poétique. Paris: Seuil.

Leloup, Damien. 2022. "Entre l'Ukraine et la Russie, la Bataille pour l'héritage du *Seigneur des anneaux*." *Le monde*, April 14, 2022. https://www.lemonde.fr/pixels/article/2022/04/14/entre-l-ukraine-et-la-russie-la-bataille-pour-l-heritage-du-seigneur-des-anneaux_6122172_4408996.html.

Massumi, Brian. 2015. *Politics of Affect*. Cambridge: Polity.

Proctor, William. 2017. "'Bitches Ain't Gonna Hunt No Ghosts': Totemic Nostalgia, Toxic Fandom and the Ghostbusters Platonic." *Palabra Clave* 20, no. 4: 1105–42. Online http://palabraclave.unisabana.edu.co/index.php/palabraclave/article/view/1105/pdf.

Putin, Vladimir. 2021. "On the Historical Unity of Russians and Ukrainians." July 21, 2021. http://en.kremlin.ru/events/president/news/66181.

Schaeffer, Jean-Marie. 2010. *Why Fiction?* Translated by Dorrit Cohn. Lincoln, NE: University of Nebraska Press. First published in French as *Pourquoi la fiction?* Paris: Seuil, 1999.

Suits, David. 2006. "Really Believing in Fiction." *Pacific Philosophical Quarterly*, 87: 369–86.

Victoroff, Tatiana. 2022. "Russie." In *Dictionnaire du moyen âge imaginaire. Le médiévalisme, hier et aujourd'hui*, edited by Anne Besson, William Blanc and Vincent Ferré, 383–87. Paris: Vendémiaire.

22

FICTION, BELIEF,
AND POSTCOLONIAL CRITICISM

Alok Yadav

The labels "fiction" and "nonfiction" seem to imply genres of discourse that are appropriately conceived of as opposites, as inhabitants of mutually exclusive domains (one real, one make-believe), and, hence, as strangers one to the other, but it would be more accurate if we thought of them as siblings, with many shared traits, despite their differences, and as co-inhabitants of a shared world. In this essay, I explore some of the facets of the imbrication of fiction with the world of actuality. This imbrication of fictional works with the world of actuality motivates most postcolonial criticism—and, for this very reason, this critical practice has sometimes been chastised as failing to attend to the fictiveness of fiction, as treating works of fiction as though they were historical documents or nonfictional discourses.[1] Here, I seek to show some of the general grounds on which postcolonial criticism proceeds when dealing with works of fiction, how and why it thinks of fiction as existing in an embrace with the world of actuality rather than as busy constructing heterocosms of its own—and why, as a result, this body of criticism thinks fictional works may be scrutinized for the "beliefs" (values, assumptions, outlooks) they embody or communicate. While the discussion offered here is keyed to postcolonial contexts, the implications of most of the discussion apply to fiction in any context.

The Language of Fiction

Almost anything in a literary work can be fictional, but one fundamental limit or constraint on fictionality is the language in which the work is written. However fictional the elements of the work might be—the characters, the action, the setting, the dialogue—the *words* in which these are conveyed are not invented or imagined but are part of the world that the fictional text shares with its readers. This simple but far-reaching fact can seem trivial and predetermined: in the modern West, the assumption has often been that a literary writer will write in his or her native tongue. Even in that context, however, this is an oversimplified assumption (especially in relation to immigrant and other bicultural writers)—but in postcolonial contexts (as also in medieval and early modern contexts in Europe), the choice of the language in which an author writes is itself often fraught and anything but neutral. In postcolonial contexts, the choice of language in which to write involves both the personal acculturation of the writer and what we might call the apparatus of languages that governs the writer's local world, in particular the legacy of European languages enduring from the era of European imperialism and functioning as national languages (languages of wider communication) within the postcolonial polity itself and as languages of international reach on the global stage. There are often grave

DOI: 10.4324/9781003119456-25

286

inequalities between and among language spheres in these postcolonial contexts—not least in terms of the existence of venues for literary publishing and for marketing and circulation of literary works. (Thus, an author like Ngugi wa Thiong'o may have written his later works in Kikuyu, but they circulate, both within Kenya and beyond, in English translation. In India, the Sahitya Akademi seeks, with limited success, to promote the translation of noteworthy literary works written in the more than twenty regional languages of India into English and into other regional languages, but market forces ensure that celebrated works of Indian writing in English get translated into other Indian languages: So, if you look for a Hindi or English translation of Amar Mitra's *Dhrubaputra* that won [a] Sahitya Akademi Award in 2006, you may not find any. But Amitav Ghosh's *Flood of Fire*, published in 2015, is easily available in Hindi translation as *Agnivarsha*. [*Deo, 2012*].

These realities of the world of actuality inescapably color the choice of language used for fictional works and the reception accorded to these works. The author's choice of language imports into the fictional work the burdens borne by that language in the author's world and makes the fictional world a contested ground via the beliefs readers hold regarding that language and its place in their world.

Among African writers, for example, debates about writing in imperial or in indigenous languages have been a central concern from colonial times to the present. This debate has looked different in the different African colonial contexts: "The French and Portuguese with their so-called assimilationist policies discouraged the use of African languages," in contrast to the British, and, not by chance, "literature in African languages arose only in British Africa with the exception of the Belgian Congo" (Westley, 1992, 159). A writer like the Senegalese Léopold Sédar Senghor, a leading proponent of *Négritude* and a critic of assimilationist projects, nonetheless, writes in French and acknowledges, "Je pense en français; je m'exprime mieux en français que dans ma langue maternelle" (1962, 841) ("I think in French; I express myself better in French than in my mother tongue" [2003, 39]); he adds, "nous, écrivains noirs, nous sentons, pour le moins, aussi libres à l'intérieur du français que de nos langues maternelles. Plus libres, en vérité, puisque la liberté se mesure à la puissance de l'outil: à la force de création" (1962, 843) ("we, black writers, feel at least as free within French as within our mother tongues. More free, in truth, since *Freedom* is measured by the power of the tool: by the force of creation" [2003, 41]). But, at the same time, Senghor argues that the French language is no longer purely a possession of the French: it is, rather, "[un] Soleil qui brille hors de l'Hexagone" (a "Sun that shines beyond the Metropolis") and is a vehicle for the expression of *Négritude* and *Arabisme* as much as for French culture (1962, 844; English translation 2003, 41). In opposition to this stance, a writer like Obiajunwa Wali argues that African literatures written in European languages represent a "dead end": the "uncritical acceptance of English and French as the inevitable medium for educated African writing is misdirected, and has no chance of advancing African literature and culture … any true African literature must be written in African languages," he argues; "Literature in Africa would then become the serious business that all literature truly is, reaching out to the people for whom it is meant" (1963, 14). In the South African context, writing in the later 1980s during the apartheid era, Hein Willemse acknowledges the politically motivated rejection of the Afrikaans language by black South Africans (which found expression in the Soweto protests of 1976 and in the paucity of Afrikaans writing by black authors, Willemse himself being an exception) (2003, 228). The Nigerian writer Peter Onwudinjo champions the use of Nigerian pidgin English, especially for a work like his *De Wahala for Wazobia* (2007), viewing pidgin (as he writes in the preface to this poetic work) as "a pragmatic language that employs a peculiar version of the English language while at the same time retaining the idioms, grammar and syntax of the original African language and culture from where the work draws its life blood" and choosing it as the medium for this work in particular because the issues discussed in the work "affect the young people more closely" and because, "outside the lecture halls pidgin is more generally spoken by many Nigerian students and young people" (Emezue, 2009, 6–7). These examples give one a sense of the cultural politics around language use in different African contexts—whether one is dealing with French or pidgin English, Afrikaans, or an African language, such as Yoruba or Wolof or Swahili: given such realities, the fictional works of postcolonial African writers also remain entrammeled in the politics of language simply through their choice of language. For our purposes, it is sufficient to note that whenever postcolonial authors put pen to paper, they place themselves within ongoing cultural debates and dynamics involving the politics of language: in choosing to write in a particular language, they choose an audience, they convey an identity, they adopt a perspective on the world they write about, and they occupy a cultural location within the world of actuality. However fictional the text they produce might be, however attentive or not it might be to the issue of language, it inescapably speaks in a particular idiom derived from the real world shared by its readers and its author. Compared to its nonfictional counterpart, a fictional work is no less (and perhaps more deeply[2]) imbricated in the cultural politics of language and faces assent or dissent from potential readers and occupies a particular cultural space on the basis of its language choices. The people engaged with a fictional work—authors and readers alike—think, feel, desire, and will in a particular language or configuration of languages and the author's choice of language in writing a work of fiction inevitably requires the work to situate itself amid the sentiments, solidarities, and antipathies of the real world, amid the beliefs the readers hold about their world, including, in particular, their beliefs about the politics of language in their world.

So, too, for those postcolonial authors who write in European languages, the degree to which and ways in which they indigenize or nativize the European language they are using is a significant issue. As Chinua Achebe remarks, "The price a world language [like English] must be prepared to pay is submission to many different kinds of use. The African writer should aim to use English in a way that brings out his message best," refashioning it so that it is "able to carry his peculiar experience" (1975, 100). But no matter how fully the European language is indigenized, postcolonial fiction written in such languages inevitably negotiates an internal challenge of translating the (non-europhone) cultural world being presented into the linguistic medium through which it is being presented. These worlds may be fictional, but their expression of thoughts, concepts, emotions, values, associations is inescapably tied to the language(s) through which this expression takes place. This situation produces various lines of stress and problems (and opportunities) of translation within postcolonial works written in European languages. A work like Salman Rushdie's *Shame* (1983) dwells on the gap between the English word "shame" and the Urdu word "sharam," with all the cultural baggage attached to each of them, and, in doing so, it highlights for us the way in which the *language*, the diction of a fictional work inevitably exists and operates on a nonfictional plane. It is a matter not simply of the semantic specificity of words (e.g., *sharam*/shame), each embedded within a given language, but also of "the connotations, cultural salience, and cultural scripts linked to these terms … in [their] speech communities" (Dewaele and Pavlenko, 2004, iii)—that is, the whole set of beliefs, values, norms, and identities associated with and negotiated through these words. It is not just the words themselves, but everything they carry with them, that writers import into their fictions and that make the space of the fictional world replete with the world of actuality.

This inescapable irradiation of the space of a fictional world with the specificities of the world of actuality occurs both at the level of language and discourse (words/concepts, names, idioms, proverbs, jokes, forms of address, figures of speech, songs, legends, myths, etc.) and at the level of "social facts" (statuses, roles, institutions, groups and group relations, histories, etc.) that are embodied in specific terms. The Nigerian writer Gabriel Okara offers an optimistic account of being able "to capture the vivid images of African speech" in English expression, even as he acknowledges all the cultural context, values, and beliefs, and history that are condensed into the words of a particular language: "from a word, a group of words, a sentence and even a name in any African language, one can glean the social norms, attitudes and values of a people" (1963, 15). A fellow Nigerian writer of a later generation, Peter Onwudinjo, points, more cautiously, to the things that cannot be carried over "the cultural/linguistic border" when translating experiences that occur in African worlds into European languages, even indigenized versions of those languages:

> After dealing with ideas that can be taken across the cultural/linguistic border, the African [writer] comes face to face with an array of images, metaphors, idioms, proverbs, witticisms, parallelisms, ideophones, symbols, similes, lyrics and innumerable expressions and nuances that are so delicately and deeply rooted in a particular culture that their meanings disintegrate in foreign expression.
>
> *(Emezue, 2009, 5–6)*

This loss or abandonment of cultural specificity weighs on the choice to use a European language to render a non-European world and, as noted above, the consequences of this choice are felt more acutely in creative expression than in other kinds of writing. For the writer of a postcolonial fiction written in a European language, the fictional world becomes, because of its medium of expression, not less but *even more* tightly bound up with the language-world of the actualities it emerges from, through the politics of cultural translation that it engages with each sentence of its discourse: an indigenous language carries these burdens unconsciously, as it were; the writer's Europhone discourse, by contrast, confronts the challenge of carrying this burden with each word it utters.

The Relations between Reader and Fictional Text

When a reader enters a particular postcolonial fictional world, they enter either as a denizen of what is a culturally familiar world or as a stranger making their way around a culturally unfamiliar world: as in the world of actuality, so, too, in the world(s) of fiction, one is an insider or an outsider: both the fictional world itself and the reader who comes to it bring with them the cultural specificities, differences, solidarities, and antipathies that mark the world of actuality. In "The Burden of English" (1992), an essay concerned with the situation of teaching English literature in a postcolonial context, Gayatri Chakravorty Spivak underlines another aspect of the interconnectedness of fiction and actuality when she asserts that, in teaching a literary work "the goal is at least to shape the mind of the student so that it can resemble the mind of the so-called implied reader of the literary text, even when that is a historically distanced cultural fiction" (2012, 36). Spivak here points to an important aspect of what is involved in reading a culturally distant literary work: though the world the work presents may be fictional, this fictional world is built, as I have argued above, on certain continuities with the known world of the author and their readers: this "known world" is not just a world of material realities, but also a world of common knowledge, of common sense, of attitudes, values, beliefs, interests, identities, roles, sensibilities, assumptions, expectations, ways of doing things, habits, customs, decorums, of known (or even shared) histories, experiences, exigencies, etc. Whether fictional or not, the literary work imposes on the reader the burden of its own outlook on the world (at least in so far as the actual reader seeks to comprehend the ideal reader implied by the work). The cultural knowledge and awareness assumed by the outlook of the fictional work again imbricates the fictional work in the known world shared by authors and readers. The density and specificity of this cultural knowledge and cultural awareness implied (or required) by a literary work will vary from one work to another, but all literary works, however fictional they may be, are bound to the known world through this and (as we have seen) through the very words that compose the text. As a result, the question of address and of audience—the question of whom an author writes for (and, accordingly, how a writer handles the exposition of their subject matter)—have been central issues in postcolonial criticism (and so, too, in discussions of world literature).[3] These are issues that efface or escape, as it were, the fictionality of the fictional work: they force the work, despite its fictiveness, to stand face-to-face and in dialogue with the world of actuality.

I have said that these issues, these entanglements of fiction with the known world, are complications that have confronted postcolonial writers; they are issues that arise whenever we read postcolonial works. But they are also issues that arise whenever we look at "metropolitan" literary works from a postcolonial perspective. In a series of lectures delivered at Harvard in 1998, Chinua Achebe, discussing his study of English literature in 1952 at University College, Ibadan, recalls how his British professor sought to engage his Nigerian students by including Joyce Cary's *Mister Johnson* (1939), a novel set in Nigeria and featuring a Nigerian protagonist: "Though the addition of Cary's novel was well intentioned, the class of Nigerian students expressed unanimous distaste for it," Achebe comments.

> My problem with Joyce Cary's book was not simply his infuriating principal character, Johnson. More importantly, there is a certain undertow of uncharitableness just below the surface on which his narrative moves and from where, at the slightest chance, a contagion of distaste, hatred and mockery breaks through to poison his tale.
>
> *(2000, 24)*

> What … *Mister Johnson* did for me … was to call into question my childhood assumption of the innocence of stories. It began to dawn on me that although fiction was undoubtedly fictitious it could also be true or false, not with the truth or falsehood of a news item but as to its disinterestedness, its intention, its integrity.
>
> *(2000, 33–34)*

This negation of the "innocence" of stories challenges the notion that fiction presents us only with a make-believe world, that it makes no assertions about the world of actuality and thus is not accountable to our views about the world of actuality. When Achebe relates that he and his classmates felt "unanimous distaste" for the novel, he is not suggesting, simply, that they found the novel's handling of its fictional protagonist wanting in generosity: the *contagion* of "distaste, hatred and mockery" that "poison[s] the tale" affects not only the novel's fictional world, but also leaves a bitter taste in the mouths of its young Nigerian readers. The attitudes, beliefs, evaluations communicated in the novel about fictional entities also bleed through the semipermeable membrane of the fiction to impinge on the world of actuality—beginning with how they strike the novel's real-world readers. In the previous section, I emphasized the inescapable continuities of language and of cultural understanding and outlook that bind a fictive world to the world of actuality; here, Achebe points out that however separate, distinct, hermetic a fictional world might be, it nonetheless serves as an oblique commentary that communicates attitudes, beliefs, evaluations about the world of actuality to its readers. And readers can choose to assess this commentary in terms of "its disinterestedness, its intention, its integrity." What I wish to emphasize in Achebe's anecdote is what it illustrates not so much about the internal characteristics of a fictional discourse but about a reading practice, an interpretive practice that understands the fictional discourse as offering an implicit or explicit commentary on some aspects of the world of actuality. The stance of the reader, the mode of uptake of a work of fiction is as important as any features of the discourse of a fictional work for thinking about its relations with the world of actuality. One could, of course, adopt an aestheticizing reading practice that resists drawing any implications from a fictional work about the work of actuality. But the point is that such a stance is not obligatory—and that readers regularly engage with fictions in a different mode.

Achebe adopts a similarly engaged stance in an essay from some twenty years earlier, "An Image of Africa," about racism in Conrad's *Heart of Darkness*, which was originally delivered as a lecture in 1975 and published in 1977. On Achebe's reading, Conrad's novella may "set up layers of insulation" between the account of the African world it presents and Conrad himself by telling the story not directly but via "a narrator behind a narrator."

> The primary narrator is Marlow, but his account is given to us through the filter of a second, shadowy person. But if Conrad's intention is to draw a *cordon sanitaire* between himself and the moral and psychological malaise of his narrator, his care seems to me totally wasted because he neglects to hint however subtly or tentatively at an alternative frame of reference by which we may judge the actions and opinions of his characters.
>
> *(2016, 19–20)*

Achebe sees Conrad's novella as participating in a much broader Western discourse about Africa, a discourse shaped by

> The desire—one might indeed say the need—in Western psychology to set Africa up as a foil to Europe, a place of negations at once remote and vaguely familiar in comparison with which Europe's own state of spiritual grace will be manifest.
>
> *(2016, 15)*

Achebe returns to this theme toward the close of his essay:

> Conrad did not originate the image of Africa which we find in his book. It was and is the dominant image of Africa in the Western imagination, and Conrad merely brought the peculiar gifts of his own mind to bear on it. For reasons which can certainly use close psychological inquiry, the West seems to suffer deep anxieties about the precariousness of its civilization and to have a need for constant reassurance by comparison with Africa. If Europe, advancing in civilization, could cast a backward glance periodically at Africa trapped in primordial barbarity it could say with faith and feeling: There go I but for the grace of God. Africa is to Europe as the picture is to Dorian Gray—a carrier onto whom the master unloads his physical and moral deformities so that he may go forward, erect and immaculate.
>
> *(2016, 23)*

Achebe characterizes this othering of Africa as involving a dynamic remarkably similar in its general mode and function to Edward Said's account of the Western othering of the Muslim East in *Orientalism* (1978), published just a year after the publication of Achebe's lecture. Many Conrad scholars have taken issue with Achebe's account of *Heart of Darkness*, but they have typically not argued that this work of fiction exists as a heterocosm of its own and makes no assertions about the real African world. Rather, they have argued that Achebe mistakes the import of the depiction that is presented: the work means to critique and reject the "image of Africa," the product of "the moral and psychological malaise" of the narrator, that Achebe understands it as embracing. For our purposes, what is important in this debate is that both sides understand this work of fiction as making claims about how we should understand the African world, though they disagree about what those claims are. Both sides of the debate understand Conrad's fictional discourse as existing amid and in relation to a whole array of other (fictional and nonfictional) Western discourses about Africa and, like them, speaking about this world as it has been understood by European observers. Conrad's fictional discourse may give us an imagined world, a world we are asked to make-believe, but to both sides of the debate it matters what the character of this make-believe is: if we are asked to make-believe Africans who are bestial, barely human, lacking in a capacity for articulate speech, motivated by an irrational, unpredictable, inscrutable "frenzy," then, Achebe argues, the crucial thing is not that this is make-believe but that this is dehumanizing make-believe *about* Africa and Africans (2016, 21). Thus, it seems consequential to all parties in the interpretive debate about Conrad's work to examine whether the novel "celebrates this dehumanization" (as Achebe contends [2016, 21]) or critiques it (as Achebe's critics contend). See Moran, 2021 for an overview of these critical contentions.[4]

In an essay on "The Truth in Fiction" (1978), Achebe draws on I. A. Richards' notion of readers' "experimental submission" to the constructs offered to them in a literary work (Richards, 1955, 117), to develop his account of the experience of reading works of fiction. This "experimental submission" to a fiction involves two aspects, a heuristic aspect ("experimental") and an experiential aspect ("submission"). With regard to the experimental, heuristic aspect: we know the work to be a fiction, but we nonetheless try it on as an account of whatever aspect of our world it names or implicates either directly or obliquely through the fiction. Achebe writes,

> What distinguishes beneficent fiction from such malignant cousins as racism is that the first never forgets that it is fiction and the other never knows that it is. ... Malignant fictions like racial superiority ... never say, "Let us pretend." They assert their fictions as a proven fact and a way of life.
>
> *(Achebe, 1990, 148)*

But the acknowledged fictiveness of literary fictions does not insulate them from the possibility of being pernicious—as Achebe's own discussions of *Mister Johnson* and of *Heart of Darkness* show us—just as it does not prevent them from offering us insights about the world, about life, about others, about ourselves, because this fictiveness does not prevent them from speaking about the world of actuality. Such fictions solicit our "experimental submission," that is, our *assent* to their construal of things, but the assent we grant them while reading is "experimental" in the sense that we scrutinize the account offered against our own sense of what is true to life and we discard or critique or make allowances for the account where we find that it falls short, where it seems reductive, where it distorts or falsifies things in unacceptable ways. (There are also, of course, many kinds of non-realism in literary works that we accept, even though we recognize them as artifice.)

But in I. A. Richards' conception, the reader's experience of poetry (or literary fiction more generally) is not only *experimental* but also an experience of *submission*:

> In the reading of poetry we give a fuller and more entire response to the words than in any other reading; ... we include not only an intellectual apprehension of their meanings, but an experimental submission to them, the fullest realization of their varied powers upon us.
>
> *(1955, 117)*

The subject's engagement with their imaginative constructions, their "fuller and more entire response" to them runs the risk of becoming the kind of delusive belief that Achebe distinguishes from "beneficent fiction." Imaginative fictions—works of literature—do not merely inform us, Achebe argues; they transform us "into active participants in a powerful drama of the imagination." They *initiate* us into knowledge rather than merely *inform* us: we encounter ourselves, grapple with ourselves in the course of reading (1990, 144). Achebe gives the example of Tutuola's *The Palm-Wine Drinkard* and comments: "This self-encounter" or "imaginative identification" in the process of reading is "the major source of the potency and success of beneficent fictions":

Things are not merely happening *before* us; they are happening, by the power and force of imaginative identification, *to* us. We not only see; we *suffer* alongside the hero and are branded with the same mark of "punishment and poverty," to use Tutuola's familiar phrase.

(144)

Achebe's account here focuses on the reader's identification with the hero, but whatever the form the engagement with the fiction takes, Achebe's main point is the potency of this engagement, the (experimental) submission it involves.

Both these aspects of fiction entail, for Achebe, a responsibility on the part of fiction that underwrites his critique of *Mister Johnson* and of *Heart of Darkness*, as it does Said's critique of the discourse of Orientalism, and as it does much other postcolonial criticism of literature. R. Radhakrishnan borrows a phrase from Amitav Ghosh's *The Shadow Lines* (1988) to speak of fiction's paradoxical responsibility "to imagine with precision" the fictive world it presents (2012, 659). Likewise, Salman Rushdie, in "Truth, Lies, and Literature" (2018), argues that the task facing fiction writers today is "to do what fiction has always been good at doing—to construct, between the writer and the reader, an understanding about what is real." These various engagements with fiction from a postcolonial perspective, from Achebe and Said to Rushdie, Ghosh, and Radhakrishnan, all speak to the ways in which fictions are imbricated with the world of actuality and the ways in which readers of fiction experience and assess this "understanding about what is real" that is communicated, paradoxically, by the fictive work.

This sense of readers' engagements with fiction's claims on the world of actuality arises, however, not only from analytical or scholarly discussions of fiction but also from the ordinary experiences of readers of fiction. We have already had a glimpse of Achebe's experience as a student in the 1950s reading *Mister Johnson* in school. Let me cite a couple of other examples of readers (writers) reflecting on their early experiences of reading literature to illustrate further the ordinariness of this sense of the imbrication of fiction and reality and some of the forms it can take. The potential illustrations of this phenomenon are endless, but I will refer here to Nadine Gordimer's discussion of this and Simon Gikandi's, as illustrative, like Achebe's, of different postcolonial situations. In "Adam's Rib: Fictions and Realities" (1995), Nadine Gordimer takes up the popular suspicion that writers of fiction are really writing about persons they know and experiences they've had and simply dressing these up as "fiction," that the designation "writer of fiction" is "itself fictitious," that "[t]he writer's imagination is the looter among other people's lives" (1). On this view, the notion of "fiction" is merely an alibi, one that allows a writer to "cannibalize" other people's lives while pretending to invent characters and situations. On this view, the creative imagination is always parasitic on the writer's real world and the lives the writer is aware of, however displaced and disguised these might be in the fictionalized presentation. Gordimer, as a writer of fiction, wishes to push back against this conception, but she acknowledges that, as a young reader herself, during "the radiant reading days of adolescence,… deep in D. H. Lawrence, I went through the local library in fervent pursuit of his circle as real-life counterparts of his characters" (2). Gordimer asks in puzzlement:

Of what possible significance could it have been to me, a sixteen-year-old autodidact living in a small gold-mining town in South Africa, to be told that the mother and Miriam, in *Sons and Lovers*, were Lawrence's own mother and his first love? … What could be added to my understanding of, let alone pleasure in, the Lawrence novels and stories by my becoming privy to the gossip of men and women a world away … ?

(2)

It is Lawrence's fictional characters who have remained with Gordimer all her life (3), but for the young Gordimer, being able "to connect thrilling fictions as a *realizable possibility* with people who actually were alive once" (2–3) allowed her to expand "the restricted context of my own burgeoning, the small variety of people I knew" (2).

Later, speaking as a writer (rather than a young reader), Gordimer reexamines the alchemy by which fiction is created: she suggests that "The writer in relation to real personages is ... like Primo Levi's metamir" ("a metaphysical mirror"), which (as Levi writes) "does not obey the law of optics but reproduces your image *as it is seen by the person who stands before you*" (5; Gordimer is quoting from Levi, 1990, 49, emphasis added by Gordimer). Gordimer acknowledges that the fiction writer works with materials drawn from the world of actuality, but the writer mixes, concentrates, embellishes, modifies, transforms what she draws on; she interprets, responds to, reimagines what she sees: "There simply is not enough *there*, of what can be grasped in a single individual to make a fictional character" (6). Gordimer quotes Joseph Conrad (from *A Personal Record*, 1912) on this subject: " 'What is a novel,' he asks, 'if not a conviction of our fellow-men's existence strong enough to take upon itself a form of imagined life clearer than reality[?]' " (6–7). Resisting any reductive stance (either in the direction of derivativeness from real life *or* in the direction of pure invention), Gordimer adopts a both/and stance regarding the sources of fictional characters: "Imagined: yes. Taken from life: yes" (4). Gordimer's primary focus (in this lecture) is on the *sources* of fiction, but her discussion also continually references people's (including her own) responses to and *reading of* fiction. The imbrication of fiction with the world of actuality occurs in both directions, both in the sources of fiction and in its implications and uptake, both where it comes from and what it offers us and how we take it up.

This latter aspect is given more emphasis in Simon Gikandi's discussion of his first encounter with Achebe's fiction in the early 1970s, when he was thirteen years old (2001, 3). Gikandi recounts how his encounter with *Things Fall Apart* taught him, for the first time,

> That fiction was not merely about a set of texts which one studied for the Cambridge Overseas exam ...; on the contrary, literature was about real and familiar worlds, of culture and human experience, of politics and economics.
>
> *(3)*

If a modernist theory of (Western) literature associates it with the work of estrangement or defamiliarization, Gikandi describes here a very different experience of the "shock of recognition" that occurs for postcolonial and migrant and minority subjects when they encounter a work that evokes, in the right key, aspects of their own experience and cultural worlds they have inhabited but that have remained outside the formal curriculum (or even their own independent reading), when their whole formal education has involved a process of displacement, of acquisition of new worlds but also of estrangement from many aspects of their home worlds. If Gordimer notes her fascination as a teenager with the world of D. H. Lawrence—a world distant from and alien to her own experiences—but emphasizes the role of this fiction in expanding her sense of "realizable possibilit[ies]" in life; Gikandi emphasizes the dynamics of *recognition* and self-recognition that occurs when one sees something resembling one's own experience, one's own life-world given objective form and (as Conrad puts it) "imagined life" in a literary work. Growing up "in the highlands of East Africa," Gikandi was not familiar with the Igbo culture presented in Achebe's novel (for example, to Gikandi and his fellow students, "the yam was as alien as the proverbial apple that opened all English readers" [4]), but the affirmative engagement with African culture in the novel, its ability to articulate, for example, the place of the yam in "a symbolic economy in which material wealth was connected to spirituality and ideology and desire" (4), offered to its African readers of Gikandi's generation a transvaluation of

African culture(s), which allowed Achebe "to shift the idea of Africa from romance and nostalgia, from European primitivism, and from a rhetoric of lack, to an affirmative culture" (8). The significance of fiction for its readers resides, then, not only in the vicarious experiences it provides but in the work it does, through this, on our perceptions and understandings of life-worlds in the world of actuality—and, in particular, on our sense of the cultural value of these life-worlds.

Fiction's Augmenting of Reality

This notion that fiction does work on the world of actuality and that this capacity of fiction is one of its important characteristics in a postcolonial context is brought out from a different direction in Abdulrazak Gurnah's remarks in his 2021 Nobel Lecture on how he committed himself to fiction-writing after his family fled to England after the revolution of 1964 in Zanzibar.

> It was there, in my home-sickness and amidst the anguish of a stranger's life, that I began to reflect on so much that I had not considered before. It was out of that period, that prolonged period of poverty and alienation, that I began to do a different kind of writing. It became clearer to me that there was something I needed to say, that there was a task to be done.
>
> *(2)*

What was this task? Gurnah describes it as an effort to redress the shortcomings, the lacunae, the distortions of the archives of history. Gurnah notes the "brutalities" of the revolution itself—"detentions, executions, expulsions, and endless small and large indignities and oppressions" (2)—and says of his subsequent recollection, from England, of his and others' experiences in that world:

> It was only in the early years that I lived in England that I was able to reflect on such issues, to dwell on the ugliness of what we were capable of inflicting on each other, to revisit the lies and delusions with which we had comforted ourselves. Our histories were partial, silent about many cruelties [in the pre-revolutionary world] (2).

> And then, in the wake of the revolution, it became clear that something deeply unsettling was taking place. A new, simpler history was being constructed, transforming and even obliterating what had happened, re-structuring it to suit the verities of the moment. This new and simpler history was not only the inevitable work of the victors, who are always at liberty to construct a narrative of their choice, but it also suited commentators and scholars and even writers who had no real interest in us, or were viewing us through a frame that agreed with their view of the world, and who required a familiar narrative of racial emancipation and progress. It became necessary to refuse such a history ... a desire grew to write in refusal of the self-assured summaries of people who despised and belittled us.
>
> *(3–4)*

Gurnah goes on to discuss the ways in which, once one is writing, the writing deepens and broadens; it outgrows the motives that first impelled it (4). But the purpose that he describes, the "task" taken up with the pen, is that of using fiction to redress the failings of the nonfictional archive, writing postcolonial fiction to redress the distortions of the colonial archive, writing fiction "truthfully" to give voice to what otherwise remains silent: "to show what can be otherwise, what it is that the hard domineering eye cannot see, what makes people, apparently small in stature, feel assured in themselves regardless of the disdain of others" (4).

The "task" that Gurnah describes in his Nobel Lecture gives fiction a worldly vocation. This vocation is closely related to what has long been recognized as one of the limitations of historiography: E. H. Carr, in *What Is History?* (1962), noted already that the chief challenge facing the critical historian is not the many accidental lacunae in the historical record, but the partial or partisan perspectives from which the historical record is constructed:

> Our picture of Greece in the fifth century B.C. is defective not primarily because so many of the bits have been accidentally lost, but because it is, by and large, the picture formed by a tiny group of people in the city of Athens. … Our picture has been preselected and predetermined for us, not so much by accident as by people who were consciously or unconsciously imbued with a particular view and thought the facts which supported that view worth preserving.
>
> *(1987, 13)*

This is the same issue that Gurnah describes with respect both to pre-revolutionary and post-revolutionary Zanzibar. The remedy that Gurnah finds in the work of a "truthful" fiction is also closely related to the recognition that Gikandi found in Achebe's fiction or that Rushdie suggests is the task of the fiction writer today. It is also what Paul Ricoeur, in "The Function of Fiction in Shaping Reality" (1979), lays out as the specific capacity of fiction, to *add to* and *enlarge* our understanding of actuality through the insights of the imagined lives and imagined worlds presented in fiction. Fiction, Ricoeur argues, gives us a redescription (rather than simply a description) of reality (123) and it is precisely the fact that fiction is not merely a portrait of an already existing reality but the invention of something new that allows it to refer to reality in a new mode (126). A work of fiction is able to arrive at the discovery of other facets of the world of actuality through the process of invention: Ricoeur calls this fiction's process of "productive reference" to reality (127). Fictions are heuristic accounts for redescribing reality (141) and the "experimental submission" that we give them allows us to arrive at the new understandings that Gurnah seeks to attain. There is no guarantee, of course, that a given fiction will succeed in this task, will prove its truth-telling capacity, will garner belief, but this is the task that postcolonial fiction and postcolonial criticism, in their full ambition, set themselves.

Notes

1 One can get a sense of the kind of tension I have in mind in David Punter's remark, in the preface to *Postcolonial Imaginings: Fictions of a New World Order* (2000), that he conceives of "literature in a fashion radically different from most 'postcolonial critics'" (vii). Punter elaborates that what he means by "the literary" is, in part, "a phenomenon of lies and truth, of narratives that wind and twist and go nowhere, of history and trauma endlessly and impossibly rewriting each other; as trace and supplement, without origin, without closure, and thus as the distorted mirroring, the per-version, of the worlds in which it functions" (6). We recognize here a conception of the literary as what resists and exceeds the determinations of the social and the political and thus as tied up with "all that is omitted" (in Punter's view) in some postcolonial approaches to literature (5). Punter's emphasis here falls on literature's difference from and distance from "the worlds in which it functions," but the force and significance of literature, even in his conception, depends on its imbrication with reality as much as on its difference from it. My emphasis in this essay falls on the *inescapability* of the imbrication of literature with reality, but that is a far cry from asserting an identity between the two.

2 The choice of language has regularly been felt to be a more pertinent issue in relation to literary writing than in relation to various kinds of nonfictional and nonliterary writing (e.g., scholarly writing, journalism, administrative records). Creative expression is more closely tied to cultural identities, mores, and manners than is the case with more instrumental kinds of writing and so the choice of language is seen as more significant in this domain. I develop some aspects of this issue in what follows.

3 Graham Huggan, drawing on Anthony Appiah's discussion, argues that Europhone postcolonial writers "recognize that the value of their writing as an international commodity depends, to a large extent, on the exotic appeal it holds to an unfamiliar metropolitan audience" (1994, 24). This critique (that such writing addresses

a metropolitan audience, as much as any local audience, and that this affects the very character of what is written) has its roots in the anti-imperial struggle to forge a national culture and to liberate it from colonial subordination: Frantz Fanon argued in 1959 that "The crystallization of the national consciousness will both disrupt literary styles and themes, and also create a completely new public. While at the beginning the native intellectual used to produce his work to be read exclusively by the oppressor, whether with the intention of charming him or of denouncing him through ethnic or subjectivist means, now the native writer progressively takes on the habit of addressing his own people" (quoted in Allan, 2007, 1). This transnational circulation of postcolonial and world literature complicates—or, for some eyes, betrays—the anti-imperial project, insofar as this "transnational" circulation finds its center of gravity in the metropolitan West, thus reproducing the dynamic that Fanon wished to see dismantled. Even if we are committed to a cosmopolitan horizon (rather than a national one), the cultural specificities and the question of whom a work addresses remain consequential issues.

4 In point of fact, many of the critical responses to Achebe's reading of *Heart of Darkness* do not focus their attention on the depiction of Africa and Africans in Conrad's novella at all (despite it being Achebe's primary focus). Rather, they argue that the novella's main object of critique is European imperialism and that Conrad offers a cynical or indignant view of the self-delusions that propel and rationalize this imperialism. Such a response to Achebe's essay seems to miss the point that Achebe acknowledges that, for some readers (but not for him), this may be the novella's main interest. And, in any case, it is, of course, perfectly possible to critique the self-deluding ideology of European imperialism in Africa as a civilizing mission while still offering, as Achebe contends, a dehumanizing account of Africans—especially if the critique takes the form of suggesting that such a mission, even if it were sincere and not just a cover for rapacious exploitation of the continent, is doomed to failure and risks dragging European civilization into the mire with it. Achebe's analysis suggests that while Conrad may offer a sardonic critique of the European imperial enterprise in Africa, he is neither able to challenge nor seeks to challenge "the dominant image of Africa in the Western imagination" that he inherited from his culture (Achebe, 2016, 23).

Works Cited

Achebe, Chinua. (1964) 1975. "The African Writer and the English Language." In *Morning Yet on Creation Day: Essays*, 91–103. Garden City, NY: Anchor Doubleday.

Achebe, Chinua. (1978) 1990. "The Truth of Fiction." In *Hopes and Impediments: Selected Essays,* 138–53. New York: Anchor Doubleday.

Achebe, Chinua. 2000. *Home and Exile.* New York: Oxford University Press.

Achebe, Chinua. (1977) 2016. "An Image of Africa: Racism in Conrad's Heart of Darkness." *Massachusetts Review* 57, no. 1 (Spring): 14–27. [The essay, in an earlier version, was first published in the *Massachusetts Review* 18, no. 4 (Winter 1977). It is based on the second Chancellor's Lecture, delivered by Achebe at the University of Massachusetts Amherst in February 1975.]

Allan, Michael. 2007. "Reading with One Eye, Speaking with One Tongue: On the Problem of Address in World Literature." *Comparative Literature Studies* 44, nos. 1–2: 1–19.

Carr, E. H. (1962) 1987. *What Is History?* The George Macaulay Trevelyan Lectures Delivered at the University of Cambridge January–March 1961. 2nd ed. Edited by R. W. Davies. London: Penguin Books.

Deo, Pankaj K. 2012. "Bound by Boundaries of Language." *The Tribune* (Chandigarh), October 16, 2012. https://www.tribuneindia.com/news/archive/features/bound-by-boundaries-of-language-604887.

Dewaele, Jean-Marc, and Aneta Pavlenko. 2004. "Introduction." *Estudios de sociolingüística* 5, no. 1: i–v. (Special issue on Bilingualism & Emotions)

Emezue, Gloria M. T. 2009. "The Stimulus of (Postcolonial) Violence: An Interview with Peter Onwudinjo." *Postcolonial Text* 5, no. 1: 1–12.

Gikandi, Simon. 2001. "Chinua Achebe and the Invention of Culture." *Research in African Literatures* 32, no. 3 (Fall): 3–8.

Gordimer, Nadine. 1995. "Adam's Rib: Fiction and Realities." In *Writing and Being (The Charles Eliot Norton Lectures, 1994)*, 1–19. Cambridge, MA: Harvard University Press.

Gurnah, Abdulrazak. 2021. *Writing: Nobel Lecture by Abdulrazak Gurnah.* Stockholm: The Nobel Foundation/Svenska Akademien.

Huggan, Graham. 1994. "The Postcolonial Exotic." *Transition* 64: 22–29.

Levi, Primo. (1985) 1990. "The Mirror Maker." In *The Mirror Maker: Stories and Essays*, translated by Raymond Rosenthal, 47–51. London: Methuen.

Moran, Shane. 2021. "Achebe on Conrad." *Research in African Literatures* 51, no. 4: 82–102.

Okara, Gabriel. 1963. "African Speech… English Words." *Transition* 10 (September): 15–16.

Punter, David. 2000. *Postcolonial Imaginings: Fictions of a New World Order*. Edinburgh: Edinburgh University Press.

Radhakrishnan, R. 2012. "Modern Fiction and Politics." *Modern Fiction Studies* 58, no. 4 (Winter): 659–67.

Richards, I. A. (1934) 1955. *Coleridge on Imagination*. London: Routledge & Kegan Paul.

Ricoeur, Paul. 1979. "The Function of Fiction in Shaping Reality." *Man and World* 12, no. 2 (June): 123–41.

Rushdie, Salman. 2018. "Truth, Lies, and Literature." *The New Yorker*, May 31, 2018. https://www.newyorker.com/culture/cultural-comment/truth-lies-and-literature.

Senghor, Léopold Sédar. 1962. "Le Français, Langue de Culture." *Esprit* 311 (November): 837–44.

Senghor, Léopold Sédar. (1962) 2003. "French, Language of Culture." Translated by Steven G. Kellman. In *Switching Languages: Translingual Writers Reflect on Their Craft*, edited by Steven G. Kellman, 35–41. Lincoln: University of Nebraska Press.

Spivak, Gayatri Chakravorty. (1992) 2012. "The Burden of English." In *An Aesthetic Education in the Era of Globalization*, 35–56. Cambridge, MA: Harvard University Press.

Wali, Obiajunwa. 1963. "The Dead End of African Literature?" *Transition* no. 10 (September): 13–15. https://doi.org/10.2307/2934441

Westley, David. 1992. "Choice of Language and African Literature: A Bibliographic Essay." *Research in African Literatures* 23, no. 1 (Spring): 159–71.

Willemse, Hein. 2003. "The Black Afrikaans Writer: A Continuing Dichotomy." In *Switching Languages: Translingual Writers Reflect on Their Craft*, edited by Steven G. Kellman, 223–35. Lincoln: University of Nebraska Press.

23

CAN FICTIONS PREDICT THE FUTURE?

Anne Duprat

In 2019, the French Ministry of the Armed Forces announced the launch of an innovative strategic research program. A team bringing together officers, experts, and researchers from the University of Paris Sciences et Lettres and fiction creators (scriptwriters, novelists, and graphic novelists) was tasked with imagining several future warfare possible scenarios. The aim was to "make the world of the possible meet with that of the temporarily impossible, to imagine the threats that could put France and its interests at risk by 2060," and thus prepare "the French armed forces to meet the challenges of tomorrow's conflicts" (Red Team, 2021, 10). Of course, only a portion of the scenarios produced would be published; the others—the most plausible ones? or those that had already started to come true?—would remain classified.

On the face of it, the project is not new: the novelistic imagination has always been recognized as having a disruptive power that is very useful for predicting the future. Nor was it invented by the companies that, inspired by the tech leaders of Silicon Valley, boast of looking for these "mad skills" in their potential employees, thanks to which the most creative among them could think outside the box and conceive innovative projects. Capital has always promoted the powers of imagination, associated with audacity and risk-taking. The most recent form of this promotion takes over from the equally condescending and well-calculated esteem that scientific, economic, and political institutions have been pleased to bestow on the visionary gift of poets since the nineteenth century—as does, in Musil's *The Man without Qualities* (1930–1943), the brilliant financier Arnheim inspired by the German industrialist Walter Rathenau. Fiction-makers are exempted from sticking to the truth, which means that they can innovate by escaping the tyranny of the already seen and the already thought. When they offer their contemporaries, who are bound to the present time, a glimpse of what the future could hold for them and suggest new routes toward those contingent futures that still exist only in their imagination, they nevertheless do so on the basis of an absence of guarantee well understood by all: any coincidence with events that would come to pass later could only result from chance.

The social and cultural promotion of creators' faculty of anticipation usually confirms the monopoly of the true, the real, and the useful by the exact sciences on the one hand and by the political and economic powers that rely on their expertise on the other. Who would then think, in order to preserve world peace or avoid an epidemic, of relying on fictions freely imagined by scriptwriters rather than on informed, factual forecasts, based on reproducible calculations and subject to the control of proof? In order to understand how this happened, we should return to the specific problem posed by the credibility of fictions about the future; that is to say, to the ability of fictions, as such, to make reliable predictions.

299

DOI: 10.4324/9781003119456-26

This problem in fact intersects the issue of the credibility of fictions in general, without exactly corresponding to it. We know that anticipation fictions, like all products of the imagination openly presented as such, can be persuasive. However, while the authors who imagine the future are in practice freer to invent than writers who describe the present or recount the past, since the former are not likely to be contradicted, they are all the more responsible in principle for the method they use to produce this description; indeed, it can produce dire effects from the moment it is likely to be believed. Even if it is not accompanied by any exhortation, a convincing prediction implicitly commits its audience to act in order to reach a state presented as desirable or to avoid a fatal prospect.[1] The more one attributes to fictions, alongside other types of discourse and knowledge, the capacity to function as models allowing societies to project themselves into the future and to act accordingly, the greater appears their responsibility in the formation of the representations they propose. Paradoxically, it is the same requirement, disappointed in the latter case, that causes contemporary fiction to be criticized for its inability to contribute—besides scientific forecasts and political warnings—to modifying behaviors as regards a climate change whose effects are increasingly unavoidable (Ghosh, 2016). In both cases, what is being questioned is the capacity of fiction to forecast, and the way in which the credit given to it actually determines our capacity to act.

In order to account for the credibility of anticipation fictions and the effects they can produce, we will begin by recalling, following the lead of many theorists of fiction, that it generally depends on the type of knowledge we think we can draw from the use of fictions, literary or otherwise (Currie, 1990, 2020; Lavocat, 2016; Renauld, 2014). Taking up Pascal Engel's suggestion in this respect, which consists in attributing to fictions a type of learning that is both practical and propositional (Engel, 2013), I will suggest applying this view to the particular case of anticipation fictions. Insofar as, for these fictions, credibility is also expressed in terms of probability, I will briefly describe the link between the historical evolution of the epistemological function that could be attributed to fictions and the transformations of the notion of probability, after the emergence of the modern scientific meaning of the term in France and in England in the 1660s (Hacking, 1975). In light of this history, I will then examine the use that can be made today of the fictional anticipation experiment conducted by the Red Team collective in France since 2019, for an analysis of the credibility of fictions of the future.

Fictions of the Future and Knowledge

What can we know after having seen a film or read a novel, apart from the facts strictly related to the fictional world it unfolds? As Pascal Engel (2013) points out in an analysis of the various existing conceptions of literary knowledge, it has been agreed for more than a century that fictions cannot teach us anything about what is; what they let us know would not be a matter of knowing-what, but of knowing-how (Engel, 2013; Ryle, [1949] 2002). In most contemporary philosophies of fiction (Currie, 2020; Renault, 2015), as for theorists of literary ethics, notably Martha Nussbaum, or for scholars of cognitive approaches to the literary (Cave, 2017; Kukkonen, 2019), the kind of practical knowledge attributed to fictions, whether affective, expressive, or otherwise, is always clearly separated from the idea of propositional knowledge. However, for Engel, one should not dismiss the idea that the practical knowledge delivered by literature can itself have a propositional value. He thus suggests that we understand the knowledge accessed via the quasi-beliefs that fictions arouse in us as a form of indirect practical knowledge: what I know, by reading these books, is *how it is*, not in the sense of a non-propositional practical knowledge, but in the sense of a mode of presentation, a description of a way of doing things that is propositional in the sense that "it can be perfectly encoded in a proposition that is either true or false" (Engel, 2013, 137).[2] While at the end of a swimming lesson we can only legitimately expect to have learned how to swim, by contrast our use of fictions allows us to assemble a series of singular practical understandings that, taken together, do form "a knowledge of generalities, regularities and laws" (137). Thus, fiction teaches us to live by giving us access, beyond the acquisition of techniques and practical skills that increase our capacity to act, to general truths about life and the human soul. These are competencies that increase our knowledge of how the world works.

We can certainly be pleased to see this suggestion take over a motif that has long contributed to the defense of fictions in general in the West—the Aristotelian idea that poetry, more philosophical than history, although it does not belong to science (*episteme*) since it deals only with the particular, nevertheless, provides us with a general knowledge of the laws that govern human behavior in general. This account is, however, of limited use in the case of anticipation fictions. Their very nature is to make claims (a) about what might happen one day, and not about what has always been, and (b) about what the future world itself will be like, and not (or not only) about how humans will behave there. Anticipatory science fiction, in particular the kind that deals with the near future (which is our concern here), describes worlds that are neither actual nor currently possible. However, it asserts under the cover of a convention of fictionality that they could become so in the very near future.[3] This promise differentiates near future fictions on the one hand from utopias, which from the start set up their worlds in the unreal, and to a certain extent from the fictions of very distant anticipation as well, since they are not subjected to the same requirement.

The credibility of near-future fictions must, therefore, be considered from two perspectives which are necessarily linked. On the one hand, we need to understand what makes us actually believe, rightly or wrongly, in the representations of the future given in fictions—sometimes even independently of their degree of plausibility. On the other hand, we can enquire into what makes the fictions themselves believable, that is to say what gives them the ability to inspire this confidence in the double sense of the notion as analyzed by Gloria Origgi. Origgi points out that confidence does not only describe the attitude we adopt toward what we decide to trust, but is also a property of the object in question, which may in itself be more or less reliable. Thus, trust is both, as Hobbes wrote, "a passion proceeding from belief of him from whom we expect or hope for good, so free from doubt that upon the same we pursue no other way" ([1640] 1889, Part I, Chapter 9, §9) and a potentiality that an object has to elicit this passion in us; it is then in itself reliable (Origgi, 2008, 10–13), and in the case of fictions, credible.

Now, the relationship between the subjective and objective values of the trust that can be placed in fictions has a history. We will outline a few of its stages, starting with the emergence of the modern notion of probability in the last third of the seventeenth century, as analyzed in now classic studies by Ian Hacking (1975) and Lorraine Daston (1995). This phenomenon proved to be essential to the promotion, from the eighteenth century onward, of fictions about the future as forms of speculation on the material becoming of the world.

The Rise of Probable Fiction (Eighteenth to Twenty-first Centuries)

We mainly evaluate the credibility of fictions in a scalar way, according to the genre to which a given work belongs (one fiction is thus more or less credible than another, according to the reading contract that governs it) or according to its singular characteristics (within the same genre, a work can be more or less close to the experience that readers have of the world). Yet, the nature of the belief one grants to fiction as such is of course also susceptible to synchronic variations (according to its place in a given culture) and diachronic ones, within the same tradition. One of the transformations undergone by the credibility of fictions in the West turns out to be essential to the rise of the anticipation fiction genre. It is the shift that took place around the 1660s, when the notion of probability acquired the modern meaning we know today, based not only on the epistemological principle of the degrees of belief that one can grant to a proposition but also on the mathematical calculation of the possible outcomes of a given situation. This transformation, as Hacking has shown as far as the philosophical and scientific history of the notion is concerned, is based on the emergence—from this moment on, in different fields of knowledge and of economic, medical, commercial, and mathematical practices—of a modern notion of evidence (Hacking, 1975). But it also has visible consequences for the history of literary forms. One can indeed think that the promotion of several forms of literary realism during the first third of the eighteenth century, especially in narrative genres, is linked to the same transformation: the verisimilitude of fictions is no longer exclusively related to the different epistemological criteria that were previously involved in its evaluation, but can now also be related to the fact that a fiction recounts what is most likely to happen materially, in the order of probabilities.

In this matter, beneath the often-celebrated emergence of the modern principle of autonomy for literary fictions, held to be less and less constrained to conform to moral, social, and religious imperatives from the eighteenth century onward, one can distinguish two quite different phenomena. At one end of the spectrum of genres, the alleviation (very relative in some cases) of the requirement of moral and religious utility that weighed on Renaissance and classical fictions opens in the eighteenth century a brilliant career for fantastic tales and the eccentric anti-novel (Swift, Sterne), whose free fantasy it unleashes. On the other hand, the development of realistic narration, from Fielding to Dickens and from Stendhal to Zola, shows that this new freedom is also the sign of a transformation of the type of knowledge that one can expect from fictions: it is no longer only practical (ethical, social, psychological, religious) but becomes potentially propositional. One can henceforth expect certain fictions to entertain their public by proposing a credible and recognizable image of the world, i.e., by saying what is most likely to happen. They will then propose representations of probable facts, in the double modern sense of the term: epistemologically convincing and materially "provable"—always under the cover of a fictionality convention. Indeed, the critical formulation of this convention becomes necessary at the beginning of the nineteenth century, in the face of these nascent ambitions of realistic fiction.

From this new claim by fictions to propose a reliable representation of the present state of the world arises their capacity to speculate in an equally reliable way on its future states. Most of the ideological anticipation fictions characteristic of the eighteenth and first half of the nineteenth century are still based on the classical model of the utopia or the political or moral thought experiment, whether their vocation is critical, exhortative, or transformational. But next to these social or political projections, a new type of fiction projects a description of the world to come as it might result from our own, by a calculation that is a matter of material probability on the one hand, and of scientific speculation on the other.[4] It is thus partly from this type of speculation, based on the Laplacian idea that one can from the present state of a system not only know its previous states, but also predict its future states, that Jules Verne's science-fiction is born. With some notable exceptions (e.g., *Paris in the Twentieth Century*, written in 1864), Jules Verne's most famous novels do not take place in the future but in a "scientifically augmented" present, that is, in a version of the present world in which a currently possible scientific development will have taken place.[5]

While the first forms of scientific anticipation characteristic of the 1890s, notably in the work of Jules Verne, thus constitute a form of realism of the future, the increasingly clear divergence starting in the 1920s between scientific and natural descriptions of the world—notably with the advent of modern physics—gives a new function to literary, cinematographic, and soon televisual and graphic science fiction. Toward the end of the twentieth century, anticipation fictions have become the only means to invest by the imagination and to make intuitively conceivable future states of the world which are literally unrepresentable otherwise. It is thus the visionary function of fiction—its capacity to speculate freely about states of affairs never perceived, without limiting itself to what is possible in the present world—combined with its capacity to produce habitable worlds, which can today make credible the abstract and counter-intuitive hypotheses about the future produced by a new science, notably in the field of physics and quantum mechanics.

Thus, postmodern anticipation fictions now occupy a central place in the representations that we make of the future, in particular in their cinematographic and serial versions. They have in fact become inseparable from these representations, whether it be for the development of artificial intelligence, the occupation of space or the future biological evolution of species, as shown by the fact that popular science, while regularly denouncing the inaccuracy of these fictions, cannot avoid relying on them, just as it can only use the common language to articulate them. Ironically, it could be this widespread use of fiction in representations of the future that is now undermining the influence of scientific and political forecasts, notably in areas where the ability of the resulting predictions to modify behavior in the face of a predicted threat is of the utmost importance.[6] Regularly deplored by environmental activists, the relative lack of impact of these discourses, even on populations convinced of the reality of climate change, can thus be analyzed as a paradoxical effect of the success of anticipation fictions: by participating in the spectacularizing, and thus in the general fictionalizing of visions of the future, they contribute to emptying scientific discourses of their capacity to be believed, and to maintain the passivity of the "public" with regard to the threats they forecast (Ghosh, 2016).

It is in fact this effect that the experimentation carried out by the Red Team collective from 2019 proposes to reverse, insofar as it aims to reinvest literary fiction with a portion of the power of conviction usually attributed to serious (scientific, technological, military) discourse. Commissioning a team of fiction authors to sketch, in synergy with specialists in strategy and armament, a series of scenarios with a predictive vocation is not in itself a novel gesture, as has been said, especially if one considers that the main function of the experience would be reduced to an exercise in simulation/immersive projection, such as that regularly undertaken by armies as well as companies. More interesting is the decision to publish four of the six scenarios announced during the program, in the classic format of a book entitled *Ces guerres qui nous attendent* [Those Wars that Await Us] (2021). This public release, distinct from the simulation exercise intended for internal use, is in fact complementary to the latter, insofar as it aims to test, under real conditions this time, the credibility of literary fictions.

The Red Team Experiment: *Ces Guerres Qui Nous Attendent* (2021)

Why indeed publish these texts, which are a cross between artwork and technologico-strategic forecasts? Beyond the advertising value, and beyond their undeniable literary interest—the texts are well written, esthetically innovative, the settings are exciting, and the artwork well designed—their publication in book form allowed the measurement and more essentially the reinforcement of the credibility of the fictions created by artists, as compared to real projections (models, probability charts) on the one hand, and to computer-generated fictions on the other.

In this respect, the process differs, for instance, from the annual war games conducted by the Center for Strategic and International Studies for the United States Air Force in order to periodically adjust the forecasts on the probable outcomes of an open armed conflict between the United States and China over Taiwan.[7] In this case, while these simulations themselves benefit from good media coverage as soon as they are declassified, they do not lead to the publication of a book presented as a work of art by one or more authors; the game is classically used as a modeling device with an exclusively strategic vocation.[8] In this respect, *Ces Guerres qui nous attendent* is more akin to the genre of strategic anticipation novels, among which we can cite *2034: A Novel of the Next World War* published in 2021 by Elliot Ackerman and Admiral James Stavridis, advertised as "a tale of cautionary fiction" by its publishers. In the same way, the work of the Red Team in France is presented, if not as a finished work, at least as the scenaristic substratum of a collection of anticipation fictions produced by artists-authors.

The reading convention of the work is detailed in the set of texts that frame the publication: three introductory pieces and a back cover, to which one must add the website dedicated to the project.[9] First of all, there is a traditional fictionality pact. In an unsigned "Avertissement" ("Notice") both political and legal in content, the Ministry of the Armed Forces assumes responsibility for the "initiative" taken by the Red Team collective, but states unambiguously that "the characters and situations in these stories [are] purely fictitious"; it specifies, unsurprisingly, that "any resemblance to existing or former persons or situations is purely coincidental" (Red Team, 2021, 9). A second framing element is provided by a promotional "Preface" by the vice-president of Paris-Sciences et Lettres University (PSL) ("July 2019. Innovation headquarters of La Défense, Paris, France. The Ministry of the Armed Forces decides to form a special unit..."). It confirms the announcements of the back cover, which promises the public that, if what they are about to read thematically resembles the announcement of a Netflix series, it is in reality an experiment in anticipation with a real forecasting purpose: "this book, the result of a revolutionary undertaking, is a particularly informed geopolitical thriller, in which it is not forbidden to read our near future." Finally, at the threshold of the first scenario proposed, "The pirates of the P-Nation attack Kourou," a last, longer and much more well-informed text from Fabienne Casoli, the president of the Observatoire de Paris-PSL and an astrophysicist, takes stock of the scientific credibility of the technological innovations featured in the scenarios. Although some of them are impossible (the space elevator in this first scenario), and others still unlikely (interstellar space travel), that is not the point: "science fiction invites us to push back the limits of possibility, in order to explore the gap between the possible and the impossible, between the realistic and the imagined" (Red Team, 2021, 17).

The reading contract that emerges from this framework is thus clear: the propositional statements that follow are true neither in the present world nor in the near future, but the audience is nevertheless invited to take them seriously because they are likely to produce knowledge indirectly, just as in science "other discoveries" emerge from the "work of the imagination" on unrealizable factual objects (Red Team, 2021, 16). This learning is not only an ethical, emotional, or social knowing-how. It is indeed a knowing-that, a propositional knowledge of a particular kind: the statements that make up these scenarios are indirectly true insofar as they refer to objects belonging to a new paradigm, in which other similar objects may one day exist. They are not to be taken literally but considered as relevant examples of the products of this future paradigm; in this respect, the fictions that project them are, therefore, reliable predictions. Preparing psychologically civil society to deal politically with the kinds of conflicts imagined here could be the particular purpose of their public dissemination, but this requires that the proposed scenarios be themselves credible, in the double sense of subjectively convincing and objectively probable.

Has the program been fulfilled, then, when one has read the scripts? As for the fictional status of the texts, it is indeed apparent from the outset: we have access to the characters' thoughts, there are inner speeches, dialogues, and elements of narrative tension. The narrative and formal codes are those of anticipation science fiction: events placed in the very near future are told in the present or in the past, the projected universe is based on the current world but it is scientifically innovative, the narrative elements are presented in a non-linear way, in the form of a collage of fragments of different status (extracts from newspapers, interviews, technical and geostrategic analyses, official statements). The theme is at the crossroads of dystopian science fiction and contemporary geopolitical thriller: open conflict situations engage several parts of the world around a series of vital stakes for their survival, in the forefront of which are the threat represented by a new pirate nation born from the consequences of climate change and the migrations it has caused ("Scenario 2: Barbaresques 3.0"), the hacking of neural implants compromising the cooperation between the defense forces of an army, the balkanization of reality linked to the emergence of community spheres living alternative realities

("Scenario 3. Chronicle of a cultural death foretold"), or the polarization of the world into hyperfortresses and hyperclouds ("Scenario 4. The Sublime Gate opens again").

As for the plausibility of the whole work, it relies in particular on the insertion at the beginning of each scenario of "historical" summaries detailing the steps that have made it possible to go from the state of the world in 2019 to the very near future (a few decades) in which the scenario is set. This effect is further reinforced by the incompleteness and fragmentation of the work, which does not present itself as a full-fledged narrative: the scenarios are deliberately devoid of beginning, middle, and end, and do not present complete narrative arcs. They only offer readers the elements of a framework situation, inviting them to recognize a possibility of future development for the present world, but without exploiting them narratively. The device is thus much less immersive than that of the novel, without corresponding to that of the role-playing game or the various action video games. Readers have at their disposal the elements of a possible world, the existing power relations between the parties, the stakes of the conflict, and the conditions in which it could take place. They are thus invited to project themselves into it, but without being provided with characters to play or to identify with. The reading experience is thus neither ludic, nor indirect (by proxy) as in the case of a fiction, where we experience situations through the characters who live through them. *Ces guerres qui nous attendent* presents readers with a series of plausible threatening situations, both convincing and probable, which they can experience directly by cognitively projecting themselves into the future.

Now, all the danger situations represented constitute variants on what turns out to be the central node, both strategic and existential, of postmodern conflicts: a cyber-war whose stake is controlled by belligerents of reality's representations. This war is played out on different terrains, from manipulating neuronal networks in the human brain to taking control of satellites, via cyberspace and social, national, and international bubbles of more-or-less interconnected alternative reality. In all cases, the basic situation to face is one in which no institutional authority can control the circulation of information, or more importantly guarantee a reliable, stable, and shared access to a common reality. This ability is particularly essential from the perspective of an army, which has to manage not only populations but also its own internal chains of command. Thus, in 2045, Operation Omanyd (the reverse of Dynamo, the code name for the evacuation of Dunkirk in 1945) represented in Scenario 3, anticipates the difficulties that would be encountered in evacuating French nationals from the Grandisle (formerly Great Britain), in a context where populations live in "safe spheres" that give each community group access to a reality of its own. In this *novum*, we recognize the still-imaginary technological extension of the role actually played today by social networks in the fabrication of alternative realities, which in turn structure communities of users who only trust the statements they contain. How can an army manage populations that do not share the same reality space? Similarly, scenario 2 revolves around the hacking of a neural command system that prompts an officer to execute enemy orders from the outside, jeopardizing all the planned attack and defense operations (Red Team, 2021, 86).

Works of dystopian science fiction emanating from authors and artists from civil society, from Orwell's *Nineteen Eighty-Four* (1949) to Ray Bradbury's *Fahrenheit 451* (1953) or Philip K. Dick's *The Man in the High Castle* (1962), often focus on the fear of the totalitarian state, including when they are the fruit of industrialized production strategies, like those of streaming platforms. Here, on the contrary, the main threat around which these institutional scenarios are deployed is that of a balkanization of reality that would prevent any reliable sharing of information. Anarchy, the traditional adversary of public authorities, is thus succeeded by a form of *an-aletheia*, the impossibility of having common access to the truth, that directly threatens, beyond the operations themselves, the hierarchical articulation between political power, military forces, and civil society. The fourth chapter of scenario 3 is thus entitled "The Army of the Future. Responding to the challenge of a failed state," clearly reflecting the concerns of the ministry that commissioned the scenarios.

This is why the "Avertissement" that opens the work makes it a point to specify that the scenarios in question "do not reflect the official position of the Ministry of the Armed Forces, nor of the French government," and that "the authorization given to the diffusion of this publication does not, therefore, imply that the Ministry of the Armed Forces approves the opinions and situations imagined" (Red Team, 2021, 9). On this point, indeed, the disclaimer is not unnecessary: all the scenarios explicitly deal with France's involvement in the imagined conflicts, and its national interests are the central stakes. Scenario 1, which deals with the attack on a space elevator located in Kourou, French Guiana, by the P-Nation pirates, explicitly presents the geo-strategic situation of the French overseas territories, as do the three scenarios that follow. On the ideological level, obvious care is taken to ensure an equitable distribution of access to moral exemplarity between the belligerents, notably through the deployment of reported discourses that allow the expression of complex, nuanced, or valorized points of view ("Logbook of an anthropologist turned pirate 2041–2059" [53–69]; "Our real fuel is injustice. Interview with Ala N'Saadi" [97–113]). However, the conflict scenarios are organized from a point of view that is institutionally and politically that of France and its Western allies: thus, the phenomenon of climate migration is represented from the angle of the threat that the (admittedly legitimate) interests of migrants will present to historically sedentary continental populations that are geographically less vulnerable to rising water levels. The proximity between realistic fictional projections and real forecasts—the latter can be assumed to be included in the scenarios that have not been made public—is, therefore, undeniable, and reinforces the objective credibility of the whole.

It is in the light of this effect that we can interpret the very gesture of publishing these scenarios in the form of literary artwork. Intended for civil society, they appear to participate in a concerted effort to afford a new credibility to human literary fictions, which are victims on the one hand of their inability to convince civil society to act in the face of a threat, however announced, and on the other hand of the rising power of AI-engineered artificial worlds. Contrary to the virtual worlds, cyberspaces, secondary realities, and video-spaces that compete for the monopoly of the illusion of reality and are constantly likely to escape from the authority that produced them and from the function for which they are intended, literary fictions conceived, scripted, and illustrated by human beings are assignable to their authors and framed by a protocol of fictionality that endows them with a stable relationship with reality. Crafted by a consortium ideally composed of writers associated with scholars and experts working under the aegis of public authorities, they are likely to make predictions that are both subjectively convincing and objectively probable. Their statements can, therefore, be considered reliable and true, not literally ("this will happen") but paradigmatically ("something comparable to this, and likely to produce similar effects, will happen; it is advisable to prepare for it"). By participating in the epistemological rehabilitation of traditional fiction, the Red Team thus works toward a future in which the most threatened borders, and those that they think should be defended most determinedly, would be those between the real and the virtual, and between the true and the false.

Fictions of the Future, or How to "Put the Possible Back in Its Place"

Setting one's revelations in a too near future is not without risk, however, as any successful prophet knows. "I invite you to read this again in ten years," wrote C. Denis-Rémis confidently in the preface of the book, at the end of 2021 (11). A few weeks after its publication, on February 24, 2022, the surprise invasion of Ukraine by Russia, although announced for months by the United States and recognizable afterward as the logical extension of Vladimir Putin's foreign policy since 2002, had completely changed the order of the forecasts that it was reasonable to make in 2021. After one year of a brutal war of aggression in which analysts agree in recognizing a return to the military techniques and strategies specific to the conflicts of the twentieth century, it is thus the very form of future conflicts that has been retrospectively transformed by this actual sequence of events, as well as the globe's geopolitical balance. To the heralded arrival of post-modern cyber-conflicts whose main challenges would be the control of space, of communication networks and above all of the human brain, the real course of events has thus substituted a classic invasion war, whose outcome is currently determined on the ground by the number and efficiency of the traditional heavy armaments available to each of the belligerents, and by their skill in making use of them. As for the propaganda carried out by each of the belligerents for the control of the narrative, it evokes more the face-to-face characteristic of the Cold War between the Soviet bloc and the West in the 1950s, than the new multipolar cyber-manipulation of brains predicted by anticipation fiction.

Of course, this refutation inflicted by reality on fictional predictions does not jeopardize their reliability, in theory at least, just as a serious prediction can turn out to be inaccurate without being badly conceived or based on an erroneous calculation: the improbable is not impossible, in one case as in the other. On the other hand, this course of events allows us to specify the exact relationship between the credibility of fictional predictions and that of serious forecasts, by turning here to the reflections developed by Henri Bergson, from *Creative Evolution* (1907) to *The Creative Mind* (1934), on the relationship between art and nature respectively with the past, the present, and the future.

Bergson noted how unimaginable the outbreak of World War I had seemed to all who had lived through it until August 2, 1914. The event had only become possible, and therefore in retrospect probable, before seeming inevitable, on the very day of mobilization. The different states of our own consciousness, like the succession of worldly events, cannot be foretold because each of these states is radically new. To foresee them, we either project into the future past events, or rearrange them into a new composition. But no intelligence, Bergson affirms, can "foresee the simple, indivisible form, which gives to these quite abstract elements their concrete organization" in the future (Bergson, [1907] 1911, 21). That is why Bergson proposes considering each of the states of our conscience

As a moment in a history that is gradually unfolding: it is simple, and it cannot have been already perceived, since it concentrates in its indivisibility all that has been perceived and what the present is adding to it besides [...]. It is an original moment of a no less original history.

(21)

The way history unfolds, and even more the way works of art are created, serve to understand the way things happen in nature: there, the possible does not precede the real, contrary to what a tenacious illusion deceives us into believing. Just as "even with the knowledge of what explains it, no one, not even the artist, would have foreseen exactly what the portrait would be, for to predict it would have been to produce it before it was produced," so "we are continually creating ourselves" (21). The world in this respect thus functions like a work of art, insofar as it constantly generates new forms of itself, whose coming into existence allows us, in retrospect, to explain the organization that produced them: in both cases, "backwards over the course of time a constant remodeling of the past by the present, of the cause by the effect, is being carried out" (Bergson, [1934] 1946, 85).

In Bergson's analysis of possibility as a product of reality rather than its antecedent, the work of art is thus used as an analogy: the artist's activity sheds light on how successive states of the world, like those of our consciousness, can be understood as a continuous creation. The same analogy, taken in the other direction, can in return shed light on the way fictional predictions function in relation to serious predictions on the one hand, and to the productions of artificial intelligence on the other. Like them, literary fictions produce their images by reorganizing already known elements according to laws that are also known, but by virtue of a configuration that becomes unique and, therefore, uniquely significant, that the artist himself could not foresee: the one that is adopted by the final work. Conversely, applications for the creation of discursive (or plastic) contents based on the recombination of supplied data, such as Chat GPT, are not capable of signifying innovation insofar as they do not produce any new data, and do not conceive of a fundamentally new organization for those they use. Serious predictions, on the other hand, are bound to respect the current state of things, and its proven possibilities of organization; both convincing and probable, they are, however, not innovative insofar as they can only describe the future as the range of possible future states of a current system.

That is why the nature of the practical propositional knowledge we can hope to get from literary fictions is clearly highlighted by the case of anticipation fictions. The latter will always be less credible than serious descriptions of the world, and more limited than the products of artificial intelligence in the number of propositions they can contain as well as in the combinations they can propose between them. In return, the literary work is like the real event: singular, surpassable, and finite. Its final form cannot be entirely foreseen, because of the particular combination of human intentionality and random processes that determine it; it does not actualize a possible that would precede it, but explains in its very realization the sequence of processes that produced it. The model of the work of art allows us to "put the possible back in its place" (Bergson, [1934] 1946, 85) by showing by analogy how the real is freely created as it happens; in return the model of the event, whose occurrence leads us to reconfigure a posteriori our understanding of the system that made it possible, sheds light on how credible fiction of the future work. Insofar as the latter leads us to modify our behaviour in anticipation of future situations in which it allows us to project ourselves, because it makes them probable, it undoubtedly has a direct influence on our future.

This reconfiguring function is certainly not specific to modern and postmodern anticipation fiction. In this respect, it follows on from the classical utopias and dystopias that invite the audience they address to think differently about the world, and thus to act in order to contribute to bringing about or avoiding the advent of the desirable or formidable systems they present to the imagination. Moreover, the fiction of the future shares this function with all works carrying an exhortative discourse, whether they are about the future or not. But the anticipation fictions specific to the Anthropocene give a different dimension to this function: the structure of the threat (biological, military, terrorist, political, climatic) is co-extensive to the genre, and gives it its narrative dynamics.

The definition they give of this threat, and the implicit idea of the subject that is submitted to it is, therefore, particularly important; it is decisive not only for the meaning of the work but also for its pragmatic ambition. In the example we mentioned here of the Red Team productions in France, the outlook intended by the fictional program is that of the conflicts to come among humanity itself. *Ces Guerres qui nous attendent* is part of a generic continuum that goes from the ancient epic poems to Star Wars and to contemporary dystopian war fictions, where the state of conflict, which occupies the whole work and directs its narrative program, is understood implicitly as the disruption of a lost state of peace that must be recovered. The program of the work, as a fiction of anticipation, is conservative insofar as its effects aim at the preservation of a capitalocene status quo: the nation' integrity, populations' security, geo-political management of the climate change consequences, energy resources preservation, protection of borders between the true and the false, defense against the progress of a technology that would allow intrusions in mental processes, etc. The future itself is thus understood as a threat—certainly due to human actions' consequences—which darkens the horizon of the present for a subject implicitly conceived as masculine, sedentary, and anchored in a Western capitalist economy.

This defensive outlook sharply contrasts with the prospective and proactive perspective that anticipation fictions have been adopting for the last thirty years, centered on the fate of the eco-system formed by the planet and all its inhabitants rather than on that of humanity itself, whose only solution to the ruin of its primary habitat would be to escape to another space. Based on the recognition of mankind's responsibility in the irreversible degradation of this eco-system, these alternative fictions engage societies not to protect themselves against the consequences by trying to escape from them or to defend themselves against the conflicts that they will generate, but rather to face them by inventing new ways of "staying with the trouble," as suggested by the title of Donna Haraway's recent book (2016). As in all the productions of the collection "Experimental futures,"[10] the scenarios that Haraway sketches there, between essay and literary creation, are inspired by the alternative science-fiction of Alice Sheldon, Joanna Russ, Samuel Delany, and Ursula Le Guin's later writings. They aim at substituting for the apotropaic logic of the male science fiction resulting from the cold war the transformative power of a feminist science fictional thought, which would give its full sway back to the literary imagination.[11] That is what Ada Palmer's work also does, although it does not belong to the near future fictions (the action of the trilogy "Terra Ignota" is situated in 2454) but to an innovative form of futuristic counterfactual. Bypassing the ravages of the world's industrialization, Ada Palmer retrospectively grafts onto the utopian thought of the eighteenth century her fictional projection of a future that could have been more favorable for humanity. There, mankind would have renounced its traditional structures of prediction and of collective control (religion, nation-state), and replaced them by statistical forecasting, a Leibnitzian tool for determining the best of all possible worlds, and acting accordingly.

To the aspiration to leave and abandon present world irremediably damaged by the passage of time, as the only logical perspective for fictions of anticipation characteristic of the Capitalocene, these fictions of ecological future substitute the project to stay, and to learn how to live in the world to come by investing this present time with meaning, images, and actions aimed at promoting this future. They contribute to establishing a new relationship, both reflective and prospective, of fiction to the time which it configures, and to the public for which it is intended. By relying on the capacity of fictions to be epistemologically innovative as well as believable, these new writings of the future propose to replace credibility with trust in fictions.

Notes

1 The exhortative effect is not, of course, specific to fictions of anticipation, not is it only intended for the reader. But the modelling effect, optional in the case of works set in the present or in the past, is implicitly inseparable from fictions situated in the future.

2 My translation.

3 On the various aspects of the relationship between science fiction and anticipation fiction, see for instance Latham (2014), and the various issues of the online French journal *Res Futurae*, from 2012 to 2022.

4 Besides, all fictional representations are deeply marked, after the "taming of chance" in the nineteenth century, by the transfer of statistical thinking from mathematics and physics to the moral and social sciences, and in particular by their application to reflections on history (Hacking, 1990). On this point, we refer to Jacques Bouveresse's essential analyses in *L'Homme Probable* (1993). He shows the importance of the new scientific reflections on chance for Robert Musil's thinking on human development, and the challenge they represented in the 1930s for a heroic individualism that was then on the way out. Bouveresse sheds light in particular on the shift this implied, in the vocation of literature, from the "possible man" that writers were entrusted to imagine, to the "probable man," the average man, who was most likely to happen.

5 On Jules Verne's relation to science, see Serres et al. (2004).

6 During the recent pandemic, for instance, the unprecedented influx of data and projections on health risks provided via different and competing media (television, social networks, streaming fictions, and docufictions) contributed to weakening the institutional and scientific monopoly of prescription in health matters, and to the emergence of conspiratorial discourses and scenarios. In the debates that accompanied this phenomenon, an important role was played by the public's fictional habits and practices, which contributed to blurring boundaries between reliable and unreliable predictions.

7 These war games commonly oppose a "Blue Team" representing the United States to a "Red Team" representing China.

8 On the difference between recent French and American approaches to wargaming, see Yann Malard (2021); also Matthew B. Caffrey (2019).

9 https://redteamdefense.org/
10 "Experimental futures technological lives, scientific arts, anthropological voices," a series edited by Michael M. J. Fischer and Joseph Dumit for Duke University Press.
11 On literary cyberfeminism, see, for instance, Larue (2018).

Works Cited

Ackerman, Elliot, and James Stavridis. 2021. *2034: A Novel of the Next World War*. New York: Penguin Press.

Bergson, Henri. (1907) 1983. *Creative Evolution*. Translated by Arthur Mitchell. 2nd ed. Lanham, MD: University Press of America.

Bergson, Henri. (1934) 1946. *The Creative Mind: An Introduction to Metaphysics*. Translated by Mabelle Louise Andison. New York: Citadel Press.

Bouveresse, Jacques. 1993. *L'homme probable. Robert Musil, le hasard, la moyenne et l'escargot de l'histoire*. Paris: Editions de l'Eclat.

Caffrey, Matthew B. 2019. *On Wargaming: How Wargames Have Shaped History and How They May Shape the Future*. Newport: U.S. Naval War College (NWC), Newport papers.

Cave, Terence. 2017. *Thinking with Literature: Towards a Cognitive Criticism*. Oxford: Oxford University Press.

Currie, Gregory. 1990. *The Nature of Fiction*. Cambridge: Cambridge University Press.

Currie, Gregory. 2020. *Imagining and Knowing: The Shape of Fiction*. Oxford: Oxford University Press.

Daston, Lorraine. 1995. *Classical Probability in the Enlightenment*: Princeton, NJ: Princeton University Press.

Daston, Lorraine. 2000. "Probability and Evidence." In *The Cambridge History of Seventeenth-Century Philosophy*, edited by Daniel Garber and Michael Ayers, 1108–44. Cambridge, NY: Cambridge University Press.

Engel, Pascal. 2013. "Trois conceptions de la connaissance littéraire: cognitive, affective, pratique." *Philosophiques* 40, no. 1: 121–38.

Ghosh, Amitav. 2016. *The Great Derangement. Climate Change and the Unthinkable*. Oxford: Penguin Books.

Haraway, Donna. 2016. *Staying with the Trouble: Making Kin in the Chthulucene*. Durham, NC: Duke University Press.

Hobbes, Thomas. (1640) 1889. *The Elements of Law, Natural and Politic*. London: Routledge.

Kukkonen, Karin. 2019. *Probability Designs: Literature and Predictive Processing*. New York: Oxford University Press.

Larue, Ïan [Anne]. 2018. *Libère-toi cyborg! Le pouvoir transformateur de la science fiction féministe*. Paris: Cambourakis.

Latham, Rob, ed. 2014. *The Oxford Handbook of Science Fiction*. New York: Oxford University Press.

Lavocat, Françoise. 2016. *Fait et fiction. Pour une frontière*. Poétique. Paris: Seuil.

Lewis, David. 1990. "What Experience Teaches." In *Mind and Cognition: A Reader*, edited by William G. Lycan, 262–90. Cambridge, MA: Blackwell.

Malard, Yann. 2021. "Jeux de guerre: vers un nouvel essor." In *Idées de la guerre et guerre des idées, revue de la défense nationale*, edited by Centre des hautes études militaires, 351–67. Paris: CHEM.

Nussbaum, Martha. 1990. *Love's Knowledge*. New York: Oxford University Press.

Origgi, Gloria. 2008. *Qu'est-ce que la confiance?* Paris: Vrin.

Palmer, Ada. 2016. *Too Like the Lightning*. Terre Ignota series, book 1. New York: Tor Books/MacMillan.

Palmer, Ada. 2017a. *Seven Surrenders*. Terra Ignota series, book 2. New York: Tor Books/MacMillan.

Palmer, Ada. 2017b. *The Will to Battle*. Terra Ignota series, book 3. New York: Tor Books/MacMillan.

Palma, Ada. 2021. *Perhaps the Stars*. Terra Ignota series, book 4. New York: Tor Books/MacMillan.

Red Team collective. 2021. *Ces guerres qui nous attendent*. Paris: Equateurs/Humensis.

Renauld, Marion. 2014. *Philosophie de la fiction*. Rennes: Presses Universitaires de Rennes.

Ryle, Gilbert. (1949) 2002. "Knowing How and Knowing That." In *The Concept of Mind*, 27–71. Chicago, IL: University of Chicago Press.

Serres, Michel et al. 2004. *Jules Verne, de la science à l'imaginaire*. Paris: Larousse.

24

DYSTOPIAN FICTIONS
AND CONTEMPORARY FEARS

Jean-Paul Engélibert

Why has dystopia become a major genre since the beginning of the twenty-first century, so much so that it sometimes seems that all the great novels of today are dystopian? Among many examples, we can cite Margaret Atwood's *The Testaments*, Booker Prize 2019, or Cormac McCarthy's *The Road*, Pulitzer Prize for fiction 2007. Kazuo Ishiguro published *Never Let Me Go* in 2005 and received the Nobel Prize for Literature in 2017. In France, Antoine Volodine was honored with the Medicis Prize in 2014 for his novel *Terminus Radieux*. How is this rise linked to the question of belief? Rarely asked as such, the latter question is nevertheless central to the emergence and evolution of dystopia as a literary genre. Whatever the definition given and the date of its appearance in the history of literature, the very existence of dystopia is based on the idea of a close relationship between the imaginary society described in the fiction and the one in which the author and the reader live. Dystopia can be understood as a satirical painting of present-day society, an anticipation of what it may become, a warning against certain of its tendencies or a denunciation of a historical dynamic: all these modes of reading presuppose the common belief that fiction represents real society and constitutes a pertinent description of its functioning. It also presupposes an axiology: in order to recognize a dystopia as such, it is necessary to believe in the values that the society described flouts, fights against, or despises. Finally, these two conditions for reading imply a third: the idea that reality could join the dystopian fiction if the dynamics at work in the present are not effectively combated. Thus, if the question of belief is implied by the study of dystopia, it is in at least three distinct ways: in a sense that could be called heuristic, relating to the historical relevance of the dystopia, or its capacity to express contemporary socio-political problems; in an ethico-political sense, relating to the values attached to the society described, or arising in the opposition of the reader's moral values and those that dominate the fictional society, and in a properly historical sense, linked to the warning role accorded to fictions that are supposed to identify evil and contribute to awakening consciences so that the threats that they describe do not come true. In a letter to Julian Symons on February 4, 1949, Orwell puts the point precisely about *Nineteen Eighty-Four*: he did not think that what he imagined would necessarily happen, but that "something resembling it *could* arrive" and that "totalitarianism, *if not fought against*, could triumph anywhere" (Orwell, 1970, 564; emphasis in original). In giving us a few formulas, he clearly indicated the cognitive ambition of dystopia, its moral and political meaning and its commitment to history.

In order to delimit the object of this chapter, we will only consider dystopia as a literary genre. This allows us to set aside the anthropological approach of Gregory Claeys, who makes it a fundamental

311   DOI: 10.4324/9781003119456-27

element of the human psyche: "as a psychological state, dystopia may also be conceived to be humanity's starting point," he writes at the beginning of his *Natural History* of dystopia (Claeys, 2017, 9). According to this theory, dystopia can be found in biblical visions of the Apocalypse, in myths and medieval representations of hell, to which Claeys devotes a long chapter of his book (Claeys, 2017, 58–109). On the contrary, we will argue here that reserving the word "dystopia" for a particular type of literary fiction makes it more intelligible as a genre, and that it is from this methodological choice that we can best historicize the concept. We will therefore follow, at least provisionally, the widely accepted definition given by Lyman Tower Sargent:

> A non-existent society described in considerable detail and normally located in time and space that the author intended a contemporaneous reader to view as considerably worse than the society in which that reader lived.
>
> *(Sargent, 2016)*

This definition follows his definition of the positive utopia, which he also spells *eutopia*:

> Utopia: A non-existent society described in considerable detail and normally located in time and space. In standard usage utopia is used both as defined here and as an equivalent for eutopia (…). Eutopia or positive utopia: A non-existent society described in considerable detail and normally located in time and space that the author intended a contemporaneous reader to view as considerably better than the society in which that reader lived.
>
> *(Sargent, 2016)*

It should be noted that this definition makes the interpretation of dystopia dependent on the author's intention and its reception by the reader. But it is less a question of rehabilitating the notion of intention than of insisting on the fact that the author and the reader to whom they address themselves—and who are not implied readers, but historically situated readers—live in the same world and share its fundamental values. Later readers, living in a transformed society whose lifestyles, values, or beliefs have changed, might not identify as dystopian what was spontaneously understood as such when the text was written. This definition makes dystopia a profoundly historical genre, whose very identification is relative to history: readers of a dystopia cannot ignore the fact that they are historically situated, since their reading always leads them back to their own context if they are reading contemporary fiction, and to the text's original context if they are reading past fiction. This gives a twist to the question of belief: readers always refer to the common beliefs (ethical, political, religious, etc.) of their time in order to put them into perspective.

In fact, the very birth of the genre expresses its relationship to history. The history of dystopia can be traced back to *Utopia* itself. More's book is constructed in two symmetrical parts, and it is in contrast with the catastrophic picture of an England ravaged by misery that the island of Utopia appears as the place of a just and good social organization. It is a dystopian England that constitutes the society imagined by More as a utopia. Darko Suvin notes that *Utopia*

> Fuses the permanent though sometimes primitive folk longings for a life of abundance and peace with a high-minded intellectual construct of perfect [...] human relations known from antiquity on: it translates the Land of Cockayne and the Earthly Paradise into the language of the philosophical dialogue on the ideal state and of Renaissance discovery-literature as reinterpreted by More's unique blend of medieval collectivism and Christian humanism.
>
> *(Suvin, 1979, 92)*

The utopian genre was born from the amalgamation of these various historical, religious, philosophical, and literary traditions at a particular moment in history: the emergence of capitalism and what is now called early modernity. *Utopia* constantly refers readers back to it and requires them to take a reflective look at their own situation in history. Utopia and dystopia can thus be considered the most historical of all literary genres, as Suvin puts it: "This is not a defect but a strength of utopian horizons and artefacts: born in history, inciding on history, they laicize eternity and demand to be judged in and by history" (Suvin, 2003, 190).

This is why, after a few necessary definitions, we will approach the question of dystopia from the angle of history, as an expression of specific fears and, perhaps, hopes, born of specific historical conjunctures. First, we will see that dystopia as a genre engages the question of belief because it relies on processes of estrangement, as it has often been pointed out: it does not require the reader's literal credence, but rather a critical and skeptical reading, which proceeds by comparing the fictional world with the real world experienced by the reader. In the words of Keith Booker,

> The principal literary strategy of dystopian literature [is] defamiliarization: by focusing their critiques of society on imaginatively distant settings, dystopian fictions provide fresh perspectives on problematic social and political practices that might otherwise be taken for granted or considered natural and inevitable.
>
> *(Booker, 1994, 3–4)*

Although conceptually it can be traced back to Thomas More, dystopia as a genre only really appeared in the nineteenth century in France and England. Its skepticism is rooted in a history dominated by the ideology of progress, then in the twentieth century by communism and the disillusionment of the Soviet experience. Finally, we will observe the evolution of the genre in the twenty-first century under the effect of neoliberal hegemony and globalization. We will use the notion of regime of historicity proposed by François Hartog (2015), which allows us to understand how these phenomena are linked to horizons of expectation, that is, to the hopes and fears of people who, as much as the facts, are part of history, in each historical period.

From the French Revolution to the collapse of the USSR, the belief in progress accompanied the rise of industry and the transformation of societies that oriented themselves to the future. This is what Hartog calls the modern regime of historicity. Since the end of the twentieth century, this faith in the future has disappeared and we live in a present without perspective and with little hope: presentism, the feeling of a present that does not learn from the past nor project itself into the future, has supplanted the modern regime. One knows Fredric Jameson's famous statement that it is now easier to imagine the end of the world than to imagine the end of capitalism (Jameson, 2003).

Dystopia and Belief

Origins and Definitions

The first use of the word "dystopia" in English for the literary genre we know today is generally attributed to Glenn Negley and J. Max Patrick who say, "The *Mundus Alter et Idem* is utopia in the sense of nowhere; but it is the opposite of eutopia the ideal society: it is a dystopia, if it is permissible to coin a term" (Negley and Patrick, 1952, 248). Prior to this occurrence, the word sometimes appeared as early as the eighteenth century. It seems to have been coined by Henry Lewis Younge in his *Utopia or Apollo's Golden Days* in 1747 spelled as "dustopia" and used as a clear negative contrast to utopia (Sargent, 2010, 4). In 1782, Baptist Noel Turner (1739–1826) used the form "dys-topia" with the first three letters in Greek (Turner, 1782, 170). Apart from these early uses, the first notable use of the word was by John Stuart Mill, who used the adjective "dys-topian" in the House of Commons on March 12, 1868, to describe British policy in Ireland:

> I may, as one who, like many of my counterparts, has been accused of being a Utopian, congratulate the Government on having joined that good company. It is perhaps too flattering to call them utopians, they should rather be called dys-topians, or cacotopians. What is commonly called utopian is something too good to be practicable, but what they seem to favor is too bad to be practicable.
>
> *(Mill, 1965–1991, vol. 28, 248)[1]*

Theoretical efforts to define dystopia began in the 1950s and have multiplied since. Gregory Claeys points to a pioneering article by George Woodcock on Zamyatin, Huxley, and Orwell, in which the author locates a decisive turning point for utopia in 1914, since from that date onward the threats of the future seem to equal its promises (Woodcock, 1956). There were many studies in the 1960s and 1970s. Chad Walsh sees "anti-utopia" or "inverted utopia" becoming the dominant type of utopia in the twentieth century after having emerged in the nineteenth as a "satirical fringe" of utopia (Walsh, 1962, 12). A few years later, Mark Hillegas traces the history of the dystopia to Wells's *The Time Machine* (1895), which he presents as "the first well-executed, imaginatively coherent picture of a future worse than the present" and notes its influence on later writers such as Forster and Huxley (Hillegas, 1967, 99). Northrop Frye distinguishes "the straight utopia" from "the utopian satire or parody" which reverses the ideal state "in terms of slavery, tyranny, or anarchy" (Frye, 1967, 25–49).

While there have been many efforts to define and describe dystopia as a genre, the theoretical discussion of its processes has focused on the concept of estrangement proposed by Darko Suvin, which remains central today to understanding its textual functioning (Suvin, 1979).

Dystopia and Estrangement

The dystopia, like the utopia from which it derives, represents an imaginary society, different from that of the reader, situated in another point of space or time, and which is only intelligible because it refers, implicitly or explicitly, to the latter. Just as More's *Utopia* is interpreted in relation to Henry VIII's England, of which it is like an inverted image, all dystopias refer to the real world of the reader, who would otherwise have no point of comparison from which to judge them. This is how it makes sense, and this is also what makes it interesting in literary terms: the reader is led to estimate the gap between the imaginary world and the world in which they live, to interpret the former according to what they know about the latter, and this cognitive and evaluative activity, based on an implicit or explicit axiology, presupposing a comparison that is carried out on all levels of the narrative, represents a large part of the interest of dystopias. For the comparative activity works both ways: if the utopian (or dystopian) novelty can only be understood in relation to the known world, the latter in turn is informed in a new way by the world of fiction.

Corin Braga details the processes by which authors create these imaginary worlds: selection, extrapolation, inversion and projection (Braga, 2018, 123). The writer of a utopia selects the positive features of the world of reference, takes them to their limit and projects them into the utopian city where they are isolated and therefore more significant, denser, and more meaningful. The utopian world is thus "lightened," simplified: it does not include all the complexities and ambivalences of the world of reference. In the case of a dystopia, the positive elements of reality are inverted into negative elements and then projected into an equally simplified time-space, the meaning of which appears by comparison with the reader's world.

This is why we can consider with Darko Suvin that utopia and dystopia fundamentally belong to the estranged genres, as opposed to the naturalistic genres (Suvin, 1979, 53). While the realist novel, which has dominated the literary scene since the eighteenth century, seeks above all to reproduce the reader's empirical world, by means of a plausible space-time, a recognizable, even familiar social universe, and characters who are individualized but refer to known social types, the estranged genres seek to shed light on social relations by means of a radically different spatio-temporal setting and new human relationships. As Suvin writes, quoting Ernst Bloch, "the real function of estrangement is—and must be—the provision of a shocking and distancing mirror above the all too familiar reality" (Suvin, 1979, 54). In this sense, dystopia is akin to the ancient topos of the *mundus inversus*. Like it, it reverses salient aspects of the author's world and thus signals the axiological inversion that prevails in it. The reader is led to take a critical look at his own world, not so much because the imaginary world presented to him is "worse" than his own, but because it is different and thus prompts comparison.

Utopia and dystopia then belong to a particular type of narrative which does not require the literal credence of the reader. On the contrary, it relies on what Suvin terms "cognitive estrangement" (Suvin, 1979, 7). Estrangement is essential, but the adjective makes it clear that the distancing assumed by utopia is different from that produced by mythic or fantasy narratives, which involve fixed and supernaturally or magically determined human relationships. Utopian or dystopian distancing is a matter of rational thought. It isolates elements of the empirical world and poses them as social problems arising from a specific context and to be examined in that same context. It does not presuppose the reader's belief in supernatural entities or ahistorical causalities, but requires the effort of a rational, historically, and politically situated critical examination. Suvin's major theoretical reference, along with Ernst Bloch, is Bertolt Brecht: estrangement translates the Brechtian *Verfremdung*. Just as the spectators of Brechtian theatre know that they are attending a performance, the readers of dystopia know that they are reading a fiction, and they are led to relate it to the concrete world whose relations it illuminates. In this respect, dystopia poses a theoretical problem that the classical utopia did not: appearing as a genre after the rise of the realist novel, it was immediately blended with it and took on its essential features. Thus Orwell, wanting to characterize *Nineteen Eighty-Four* in a letter to Francis Henson on February 4, 1949, a few years before the word "dystopia" became commonplace, referred to it as a "Utopia in the form of a novel" (Orwell, 1970, 536). In dystopia, utopia and the realism inherent in the novel are combined: plausible space-time, details that bear a "reality effect" (Barthes, 1989, 141–48), characters described as ordinary people in the fictional world and not as exceptional beings. The disturbance caused by dystopia is, therefore, potentially greater than in the case of utopia: dystopia plays proportionally much more on the credibility of the fiction. Following Darko Suvin, who calls the ideas about the social world that dominate the author's and reader's society the "intertext" (Suvin, 2010, 239) of fiction, we can say that dystopia plays on possible confusions between this intertext and its own text, both referring to "some strategically central tendencies of the author's empirical world." In other words, "dystopia traffics between text and the reader's encyclopedia about reality" (Suvin, 2010, 239).

Dystopia as Critical Fiction

Nevertheless, dystopias have often been understood as pessimistic, even reactionary or nihilistic fiction, describing a bleak future and predicting inevitable catastrophes. Thus, in an early essay on *Nineteen Eighty-Four*, Gaylord LeRoy worries that Orwell's novel, like *Brave New World* a quarter century earlier, offers "no mitigation of the terrors it is designed to inspire" and presents "no practical alternative to its fearful vision of a pneumatic utopia." He writes that the books of Huxley and Orwell tend "to strengthen the belief, now becoming so widespread, that nothing can be done to salvage modern man from the mounting crisis of the times" and fears that, failing to explore ways of resisting these trends, they become complicit in what they denounce by giving in to "pessimism which constitutes so conspicuous a trend in contemporary thought" (Le Roy, 1950, 136–37).

This is why a major critical effort has been devoted to distinguishing between fictions that are indeed nihilistic or reactionary (which we will call anti-utopias) and those that, in depicting bleak futures, retain a utopian impulse (to which we will reserve the name of dystopias, according to a now well-established usage). In 1975, Lyman Tower Sargent considered that the word "anti-utopia" "should be reserved for that large class of works, both fictional and expository, which are directed against Utopia and utopian thought" (Sargent, 1975, 138). Dystopia, on the other hand, is not written against utopia, but preserves the desire for a better society and the belief in the possibility of its realization, even though it represents an imaginary world worse than the reader's. Tom Moylan has taken up and developed this distinction. He notably coined the term "critical dystopia" to label the fictions which "resist the anti-utopian subversion of Utopia that can occur within dystopian narrative," some of them opening out to "minimal utopian possibilities that are perhaps not even prefiguratively available," while "others offer new utopian trajectories against a seemingly overwhelming world system that is striving to achieve its historical goal of total external and internal exploitation of humanity and nature" (Moylan, 2000, 105). For him, critical dystopias emerge in the 1980s as a reaction to the "temptation of despair" (Moylan, 2000, 186) of that decade; these include Kim Stanley Robinson's *Gold Coast* (1988), Marge Piercy's *He, She and It* (1991), and Octavia Butler's *Parables* (1993, 1998).

Tom Moylan's work is valuable because it establishes this distinction in the structure of texts by showing that dystopias always include a narrative and a counter-narrative: the narrative of power and that of the narrator or the character who opposes it or simply becomes aware of its reality (Moylan, 2000, 156). It is this opposition that makes it possible for the reader to evaluate the fictional world, as they have the relay of one or more characters in the fiction. The contradiction can be resolved in two ways, which Moylan calls "open," or epic, and "closed," or mythic: open if the contradiction is maintained, that is if the dystopia "retains a utopian commitment at the core of its pessimistic presentation," closed if it "abandons the textual ambiguity of dystopian narrative for the absolutism of an anti-utopian stance." Dystopia "identifies a site for an alternative position in some enclave or other marker of difference, or in some way in its content or form manages to establish an estranged relationship with the historical situation that does not capitulate." Anti-utopia "produces a social paradigm that remains static because no serious challenge or change is desired or seen as possible" (Moylan, 2000, 157). The example of *Nineteen Eighty-Four* is again convincing here. Depending on which reading one chooses, Winston's disavowal and his final rallying to Big Brother show that any revolt is futile and ends up crushed, or on the contrary, the very fact that this mediocre civil servant undertook to fight against the regime shows that rebellion is possible under the most difficult conditions: Tom Moylan admits that the "Newspeak Appendix" supposes a "possible Other Place—one of present, satirical, critique, if not future, utopian opposition" (Moylan, 2000, 162). Obviously, the appendix prevents the narrative from closing. The latter interpretation makes the novel not a desperate fable, but a paradoxical expression of political hope, according to a humanistic and optimistic reading that is perhaps easier to sustain today.

If dystopia is thus defined by its critical function, the fact remains that this function has manifested itself in several ways in the history of the genre—a history that we must now address.

From Progress to Presentism

Dystopia and Prophecy

When Western societies started projecting themselves massively into the future, with the emergence of the modern regime of historicity in the second half of the eighteenth century (Hartog, 2015), literature invented forms of anticipation. The first utopia set in the future preceded the French Revolution by a short time. In *L'An 2440, Rêve s'il en fut jamais*, first published in 1771, Louis-Sébastien Mercier imagines France in the twenty-fifth century as a constitutional monarchy where tolerance, concord, and virtue reign. In 1799, for the reprinting of his book, he wrote: "I am reprinting [...] a dream that announced and prepared the French revolution, [...] a prediction that embraced all possible changes. [...] I am therefore the true prophet of the revolution" (qtd in Trousson, 1999, 165). This is what seems today to be the most striking feature of *L'An 2440*: not in the sense that its predictions would have come true, but in the sense that projecting the utopia into the future changed its interpretation for the next two centuries. The prosperous and peaceful constitutional monarchy that Mercier imagined was based on an idea of progress and the indefinite perfectibility of man typical of the Enlightenment. The book's epigraph is borrowed from Leibniz: "the present is big with the future." As the future can be predicted by learning from history, through the experience of the past, utopia becomes a rational assumption about the future of civilization. It is no longer just a thought experiment about lateral possibilities; when the better world is no longer situated on an island, facing ours like a distorting mirror, but in the future, then it does not simply reflect ours, it follows and extends it. It is the product of our history; the utopian claims not to invent anything, but to deduce what cannot fail to happen. In Mercier's book, changes do not occur in time, but through time, which is the medium of man's perfectibility. Society transforms gradually, without a hitch: utopia is, therefore, no longer frozen in an eternal perfection, it transforms slowly and continuously without ever completing its journey toward perfection. The year 2440 is, therefore, not considered to have reached an ideal but a stage on the indefinite path of progress. By the same token, utopia can claim to be not the chimera, or the compensatory fiction, that an author opposes to the reality of his time, but the image of history in progress or the objective to be reached.

Thus, utopia secularizes millenarian teleology. Here, the better world that is to be achieved is not the product of Providence but of human history. By assuming a prophetic function, utopia changes its status; it is no longer merely a work of imagination, but it fulfils a mission of anticipation. If history fulfils the truth of the novel, as Mercier claimed in 1799, literature becomes a secular gospel and prepares the events it announces. The status of the author changes with that of the genre: the utopian becomes a seer, taking on a messianic function. The whole of the nineteenth century understood utopia in this way. Wells's novel *A Modern Utopia*, published in 1905, can be seen as a culmination of this tradition. In it, Wells imagines a planet similar to Earth, but where a world government combines progress with political stability: utopia is perfected over time. This novel, which has the appearance of a philosophical dialogue, is also a prefiguration of the future of humanity.

But by playing on this identification of fiction with prophecy, the utopians at the same time opened up the possibility of denouncing historical trends and inventing, with the dystopia, a modern version of the prophecy of doom. Apocalyptic visions were also secularized, as evidenced by Jean-Baptiste Cousin de Grainville's prose epic *Le Dernier Homme* (*The Last Man*) in 1805, the first modern secular apocalypse (Cousin de Grainville, 2003). Visions of progress are reversed into threats of catastrophe and the promise of democracy into a warning of the reign of money and technology. In *Le Monde tel qu'il sera* (*The World as It Shall Be*) by Émile Souvestre, the former disciple of Saint-Simon, a newly married couple from 1845 are magically transported to the year 3000, where the "genius of progress" presents them with a society where economic interest and egoism have supplanted love and solidarity. Back home, overwhelmed by this revelation, the two young people see in their dreams the world destroyed by a vengeful God who condemns men for believing themselves to be the "masters of the world" (Souvestre, 2004). Dystopias condemning progress multiplied in the second half of the nineteenth century, leading to the genre we know in the twentieth century. In France, following Souvestre, these included Jules Verne with *Paris au XXe siècle* written in 1864, Maurice Spronck, *L'An 330 de la République*, published in 1894 and Daniel Halévy, *L'Histoire de quatre ans, 1997–2001*, published in 1903. The dystopia conquers England with Edward Bulwer-Lytton, *The Coming Race*, in 1871, and H. G. Wells, *The Time Machine*, in 1895.

Progress is the explicit target of E. M. Forster's 1909 short story "The Machine Stops," which tells of the climax and subsequent collapse of mechanical civilization in the distant future. In this future world, all human tasks have been delegated to the Machine, which Forster ironically spells with a capital letter, and idle human beings live confined and alone in a room they have no need to leave. After the hero of the story reveals that it is possible to live differently, a series of reforms harden the regime to stifle any desire for change. One of them establishes the religion of the Machine. Believers worship it, consult its instructions, the "Book of the Machine," like a bible, regard its instruments as saints whom they can ask to intercede for them with the Machine and a "minimal faith," called "non-denominational mechanism" (Forster, 1988, 137), is imposed on the whole population. Already controlling all dimensions of practical life, the Machine imposes itself as a divine entity. These reforms are not enforced by a revolution, nor by an authoritarian "Central Committee." Rather, they are the result of an overall process or of anonymous, unoriginated forces which are all the more powerful.

> Rather did [the Central Committee] yield to some invincible pressure, which came no one knew whither, and which, when gratified, was succeeded by some new pressure, equally invincible. To such a state of affairs it is convenient to give the name of progress. No one confessed the Machine was out of hand. Year by year it was served with increased efficiency and decreased intelligence. The better a man knew his own duties upon it, the less he understood the duties of his neighbor, and in all the world there was not one who understood the monster as a whole. [...] But Humanity, in its desire for comfort, had overreached itself. It had exploited the riches of nature too far. Quietly and complacently, it was sinking into decadence, and progress had come to mean the progress of the Machine.
>
> *(Forster, 1988, 138)*

The novella described the age of the Machine up to its peak. It then precipitates its decline. Without transition or explanation, at the precise moment when the Machine has thus been divinized, which is also the moment when human beings have completely renounced the experience of the world, it "stops." The allegorical character of the story is thus confirmed: the perfection of the Machine coincides with its irrefutability, it consists in its indisputable authority rather than in its flawless functioning. This authority is accomplished when humanity has "sunk" (Forster, 1988, 138), the loss of the world being both cause and effect of the delegation of life to the Machine. The Machine has become the soul of the world, since men and women have given up theirs to it. The first signs of its cessation are "curious gasping sighs that disfigure the symphonies" (Forster, 1988, 139) it broadcasts. The music of the world, once a sign of its harmony, is running out of steam. Soon afterward, "a blight" descends on the atmosphere, its luminosity decreases and the air becomes "foul" (Forster, 1988, 142). Finally, the communications system ceases to function and "the world, as they understood it, ended" (Forster, 1988, 142). The city collapses and, before dying, the hero has just enough time to whisper to his mother that men and women are hiding on the surface, waiting for civilization to die out, and will be the successors of humanity.

Forster thus imagined an ironic utopia, a satire of the mechanical civilization he saw developing at the beginning of the twentieth century. Wells claimed, at the beginning of *A Modern Utopia*, to be writing a utopia that was "not static, but kinetic" (Wells, 1905). Responding to history, utopia was no longer conceived of as the description of a city that was always identical to itself, but as a "transitional phase" in a process of continuous improvement. Progress, Forster replied, is only an illusion: it is only the progress of the Machine, that is, the progress of the dispossession of humanity. Human beings enslave themselves to the machine and take for progress what enslaves them more and more.

From the October Revolution to Neoliberal Hegemony

In the twentieth century, after the First World War and the Soviet revolution, utopia gradually aroused more fear than desire. Dystopia, or anti-utopia in the terminology of Lyman Tower Sargent, produced its most striking works: *We* (Zamyatin, 1921), *Brave New World* (1932), *Nineteen Eighty-Four* (1949), written against totalitarianisms. We remember the epigraph of *Brave New World*, borrowed by Huxley from Nicolas Berdiaev and quoted in French:

> Les utopies apparaissent comme bien plus réalisables qu'on ne le croyait autrefois. Et nous nous trouvons actuellement devant une question bien autrement angoissante : comment éviter leur réalisation définitive ? … Les utopies sont réalisables. La vie marche vers les utopies. Et peut-être un siècle nouveau commence-t-il, un siècle où les intellectuels et la classe cultivée rêveront aux moyens d'éviter les utopies et de retourner à une société non utopique moins « parfaite » et plus libre.
>
> *(Nicolas Berdiaev, cited in Huxley, 1998)*

This fear dominated the dystopia of the twentieth century all the more because the future seemed predictable. This future, a simple extrapolation of the present, was that of the modern regime of historicity to which we can no longer adhere since the collapse of revolutionary promises and the victory of the ultra-liberals in the 1980s which gave birth to a new world order. However, assigning utopia to the future by linking it to progress also meant reducing it to the regime of forecasting or prospective. As the philosopher Miguel Abensour has clearly seen, utopia risked losing what characterizes it: "the search for what is different" (Abensour, 2013, 238). If utopia only anticipates the future, it is no longer an opening toward an elsewhere, but a simple implementation of the tendencies of the present. It loses its capacity to challenge the order of the present in the name of an otherness, since the otherness it offers is no more than the development of certain trends of the present. Conversely, dystopia loses its virtue of warning and functioning as an "emergency brake" and is reduced to being no more than the demobilizing forecast of an inevitable catastrophe (the idea of revolution as "emergency brake" is proposed in Walter Benjamin's preparatory notes to *On the Concept of History* [see Löwy, 2019]).

In this respect, "presentism," which according to François Hartog has succeeded the modern regime of historicity, perhaps offers the advantage of an uncertain future. Indeed, it frees us from progress and its indexation on the future. We no longer see history as a future-oriented process over which human action has control. We stand in an interminable present that absorbs the past and the future: the former is no longer the bearer of lessons, and the latter, if it no longer represents a hope, is no longer announced as something we already know or can easily forecast, but is open to uncertainty. Presentism, by making any orientation in history more complex, preserves the future from being already written. Utopia can then recover the charge of otherness that its confinement within the limits of progress caused it to lose; dystopia no longer risks announcing an inescapable destiny: it gains a critical function that appears perhaps more clearly than ever. It is defined as a warning or prophecy of doom, formulated precisely so that it does not come true. In this sense, it only prophesies a terrifying future in order to assert the need to fight the forces that could lead to it. This is precisely the virtue that Tom Moylan recognizes in what he calls "critical dystopias."

These fictions "revive the dystopian strategy to map, warn and hope" (Moylan, 2000, 196). In a historical conjuncture—ours—that can be considered anti-utopian, they expose the full horror of the present moment.

Yet in the midst of their pessimistic forays, they refuse to allow the utopian tendency to be overshadowed by its anti-utopian nemesis. They therefore adopt a militant stance that is informed and empowered by a utopian horizon that appears in the text—or at least shimmers just beyond its pages.

(Moylan, 2000, 196)

Thus, after the end of the Cold War and the collapse of the USSR, other threats became more visible: overpopulation, climate disruption, mass extinction of wild species, pandemics, technological risks, etc.

The public and critical success of fictions such as Margaret Atwood's *MaddAddam* trilogy, Kazuo Ishiguro's *Never Let Me Go* (2005), Alain Damasio's *Les Furtifs* (2019) in France, and many others throughout the world, not to mention cinema, undoubtedly show the intensity of these fears. The number of works is also eloquent: Corin Braga's survey of twentieth- and twenty-first-century dystopias and anti-utopias alone takes up 150 pages of his book (Braga, 2018, 387–468, 561–621).

Among the most noted dystopias of the twenty-first century, the *MaddAddam* trilogy (2003, 2009, 2013) has the interest of forming a sharp satire of its time by describing a near future: all the fictional elements extrapolate from existing technical achievements, under study or at least possible in the current state of knowledge. However, this work, which begins as a very dark dystopia, evolves into a utopia and ends with the formation of a peaceful and happy community. The first volume describes a violently unequal and anti-democratic society where the wealth of the privileged leads to ecological devastation. A mad scientist spreads a virus that leads to the near extermination of human beings, while at the same time manufacturing genetically engineered creatures that are outwardly similar to humans but absolutely non-violent. The horizon of the fiction seems to be reduced to the destruction of humanity and its replacement by these post-human animals. But the next two volumes are devoted to the development of a new civilization in which they cohabit with the rare human survivors, forming a mixed culture, each species evolving in contact with the other: a social life is reborn, rites are established, alliances are forged, the need to educate children arises and, at the end of the trilogy, a young boy undertakes to write the history of the community. A "critical dystopia" in Moylan's terms, *MaddAddam* preserves the hope of a better life in a future world.

On the contrary, among other recent successes of the genre, Cormac McCarthy's *The Road* (2006) depicts a world of ashes, devastated by fires, probably after a nuclear war, where all animals and plants are dead. Rare human survivors wander the ruins in search of food. Cannibalism has become commonplace. Complete extinction seems inevitable. This dense, metaphysical novel is written entirely against hope. After the hero, a ten-year-old boy, wakes up from a dream whose content he does not want to reveal, his father tells him: "When your dreams are of some world that never was or of some world that never will be and you are happy again then you will have given up [...] And you can't give up" (McCarthy, 2006, 160). Here, hope is an illusion, and the disturbance caused by the imaginary must not awaken it. What allows one to live is no longer anything but the energy of despair.

Conclusion

Dystopia has a complex relationship with the fears and hopes of its readers, who are transported to imaginary worlds, different from their own, often worse, sometimes apocalyptic, in order to open up the distance of a critical view of their own world. This is its heuristic virtue: it expresses contemporary socio-political problems through satire. It presupposes at least the implicit recognition of values shared by the author and the reader, values opposed to the society described by the fiction, but carried by the characters or implied by their desires or ambitions. It, therefore, necessarily has an ethical and political significance: situated in history, it requires each reader to situate it in its original context and to recontextualize the reader's own world. It thus obliges a rational and critical reading, forbidding the escape into myth or fancy. Sometimes confused with forecasting or prophecy, because it is generally situated in the future, it has more the sense of a warning, warning against what might happen if the tendencies it brings to light are not effectively countered. From its birth as a genre in the nineteenth century to the present day, it has developed and colonized the novel to the point of occupying vast territories, asserting itself against successive dominant ideologies. As Fredric Jameson writes of utopia, it projects itself into the future in order to make the present appear, by contrast, as history (foreign and therefore analyzable), but also, paradoxically, to show the future as unknowable, unforeseeable, neither programmed nor programmable, and therefore open (Jameson, 2005, 288). Surprisingly, perhaps, for those who believe in its pessimism, dystopia always implies freedom.

Note

1 For further information on this point, see Claeys (2017, 273).

Works Cited

Abensour, Miguel. 2013. *L'homme est un animal utopique*. Utopiques II. Paris: Sens & Tonka.

Barthes, Roland. 1989. "The Reality Effect." In *The Rustle of Language*, translated by Richard Howard, 141–48. Berkeley: University of California Press.

Booker, M. Keith. 1994. *Dystopian Literature. A Theory and Research Guide*. Westport/London: Greenwood.

Braga, Corin. 2018. *Pour une morphologie du genre utopique*. Paris: Classiques Garnier.

Claeys, Gregory. 2017. *Dystopia: A Natural History*. Oxford: Oxford University Press.

Cousin de Grainville, Jean-Baptiste. 2003. *The Last Man*. Translated by I. F. Clarke. Middletown, CT: Wesleyan University Press.

Forster, Edward Morgan. 1988. "The Machine Stops." In *Collected Short Stories*, 109–46. Harmondsworth: Penguin.

Frye, Northrop. 1967. "Varieties of Literary Utopia." In *Utopias and Utopian Thought*, edited by Frank E. Manuel, 25–49. Boston, MA: Beacon Press.

Hartog, François. 2015. *Regimes of Historicity: Presentism and Experiences of Time*. Translated by Saskia Brown. New York: Columbia University Press.

Hillegas, Mark. 1967. *The Future as Nightmare: H.G. Wells and the Anti-Utopians*. Carbondale: Southern Illinois University Press.

Huxley, Aldous. 1998. *Brave New World*. New York: Perennial Classics.

Jameson, Fredric. 2003. "Future City." *New Left Review* 21 (May-June): 65–79. https://newleftreview.org/issues/ii21/articles/fredric-jameson-future-city.

Jameson, Fredric. 2005. *Archaeologies of the Future: The Desire Called Utopia and Other Science Fiction*. London and New York: Verso.

Le Roy, Gaylord. 1950. "A.F. 632 to 1984." *College English* 12, no. 3 (December): 135–38. Doi: 10.2307/372526.

Löwy, Michaël. 2019. *La révolution est le frein d'urgence*. Paris: L'Eclat.

McCarthy, Cormac. 2006. *The Road*. London: Picador.

Mill, John Stuart. 1965–91. *Collected Works of John Stuart Mill*. Edited by J. M. Robson. Vol. 28. London: Routledge and Kegan Paul.

Moylan, Tom. 2000. *Scraps of the Untainted Sky*. Boulder, CO: Westview Press.

Negley, Glenn and J. Max Patrick. 1952. The Quest for Utopia. New York: Henry Schuman.

Orwell, George. 1970. *In Front of your Nose, 1945–1950*. Vol. 4 of *The Collected Essays, Journalism and Letters of George Orwell*. Harmondsworth: Penguin Books.

Sargent, Lyman Tower. 1975. "Utopia–The Problem of Definition." *Extrapolation* 16, no. 2 (Spring): 137–48.

Sargent, Lyman Tower. 2010. *Utopianism. A Very Short Introduction*. Oxford: Oxford University Press.

Sargent, Lyman Tower. 2016. "Utopian Literature in English: An Annotated Bibliography from 1516 to the Present." University Park, PA: Penn State Libraries Open Publishing. https://openpublishing.psu.edu/utopia/content/definitions.

Souvestre, Émile. 2004. *The World as It Shall Be*. Translated by I. F. Clarke and M. Clarke. Middletown, CT: Wesleyan University Press.

Suvin, Darko. 1979. *Metamorphoses of Science Fiction. On the Poetics and History of a Literary Genre*. New Haven, CT and London: Yale University Press.

Suvin, Darko. 2003. "Theses on Dystopia 2001." In *Dark Horizons: Science Fiction and the Dystopian Imagination*, edited by Raffaela Baccolini and Tom Moylan, 187–202. New York and London: Routledge.

Suvin, Darko. 2010. *Defined by a Hollow: Essays on Utopia, Science Fiction and Political Epistemology*. Bern: Peter Lang.

Trousson, Raymond. 1999. *Voyages aux pays de nulle part*. Bruxelles: Éditions de l'université de Bruxelles.

Turner, Baptist Noel. 1782. Candid Suggestions in Eight Letters to Soame Jenyns, Esq., on the Respective Subjects of his Disquisitions, Lately Published, with Some Remarks on the Answerer of his Seventh Disquisition, Respecting the Principles of Mr. Locke. London: W. Harrod.

Walsh, Chad. 1962. *From Utopia to Nightmare*. London: Geoffrey Bles.

Wells, Herbert George. 1905. *A Modern Utopia*. E-book. https://library.uniteddiversity.coop/More_Books_and_Reports/H_G_Wells-A_Modern_Utopia.pdf.

Woodcock, George. 1956. "Utopias in Negative." *Sewanee Review* 64, no. 1 (January–March): 81–97.

25

FICTION, BELIEF, AND CLIMATE CHANGE

Paratexts, Skeptics, and Objects of Care

Erin James

To begin to unpack the fraught and polarized relationship between fiction, belief, and climate change, it helps to look at how fictional texts on both sides of the divide (those who are skeptical of climate change and those who accept it as a real frame) contextualize their relationship to climate science. On one side of the debate, we find the *2040 A.D.: Climate Change Edition* of *McSweeney's* magazine (2019), which pairs ten writers with a specialized policy expert from the National Resources Defense Council (NRDC). The special issue leans into the magazine's left-leaning bona fides; an independent nonprofit publishing company based in San Francisco, *McSweeney's* advertises on its website that their commitment to "our environment" includes "carbon offsets commensurate with our estimate of the impact of the printing, shipping, and travel necessary to publish our books and magazines" and an examination of "every business decision through a lens of sustainability" (Boas et al., n.d.). As the special issue's publicity blurb makes clear, each story, modeling a possible version of the year 2040, grapples with a different environmental threat to imagine "what the world might look like if the dire warnings issued by the *Special Report on Global Warming of 1.5°C* were to come true" (McSweeney's, 2019). The magazine issue, in other words, uses fiction to explore the "tangible, day-to-day implications" of the "cataclysmic scientific projections" of the United Nations' Intergovernmental Panel on Climate Change (IPCC). In her introduction to the collection, NRDC Chief Program Officer Susan Casey-Lefkowitz positions fiction as a necessary component of climate modeling:

> Scientists consistently confirm what we can plainly see with our own eyes: climate change is happening all around us, right now, in the form of altered weather patterns, rising seas, and skyrocketing summer temperatures. Their computerized models suggest how it might evolve in the near future, under certain conditions, and those models are crucial to our understanding of the issue.
>
> *(11–12)*

Still, she argues, "human beings are storytelling animals. Data can persuade, but it takes stories to move us" (11–12). For Casey-Lefkowitz and the editors of *McSweeney's*, fiction is a necessary tool in the mitigation project of scientific organizations like the IPCC. She argues that the special issue is "a collection where fiction's already considerable power is fortified by science," and states unequivocally that writers like those featured in *2040 A.D.*—"those of us who imagine things for a living, or as a calling"—are "indispensable partners" in "a goal that they share with climate advocates: moving people to think and act differently" (12–13).

DOI: 10.4324/9781003119456-28

The resulting collaborations of fiction writers and NRDC representatives take many forms in the special issue, running the gamut from speculative realism to more adventurous representations of possible futures. Herold, the narrator-protagonist of Tommy Orange's "New Jesus," begins his story by lamenting that his niece, upon visiting the San Francisco Bay Area from the mountains, "couldn't understand that we just walk on water now" (67). As Herold explains, he is among the "sea-level dwellers … the coastal flooded" who cannot afford to just "get up and go": "We got used to it," he says, "got used to the storms and floods and the heat, got used to knowing the end of the world had arrived finally not with a bang but a whimper, or a series of minor disasters" (67–68). The narrator of Asja Bakíc's "1740" occupies a more fantastic future, in which she can relieve the tedium of her over-heated life in a climate-altered Zagreb, Croatia, with time travel. In this narrator's world, "humans aren't quite an extinct species from the distant past, but they are endangered by their efforts to survive it at all costs" (111). Her life consists of "mostly loung[ing] on the patio" and reading fiction to "make the days shorter," all in view of the local garbage dump that has replaced the beloved cherry blossom trees that her father tended when she was a child. "No one bothers to cover the garbage anymore," she explains, "because the water carries it off regardless" (112). Yet, despite being endangered in this possible future, not all humans have learned the lesson that climate change can teach us. When given the chance to travel back in time and solve the climate crisis—back to 1964, when Yugoslav communists announce the economic reforms that will open their society to market economy and capitalism—the narrator opts instead for the "debauched age" of Louis XV's France (127). "We're in for some sweet cherry picking" she says devastatingly at the story's close, in a brutal echo of the real-world broader public's contemporary unwillingness to forgo decadence and convenience to mitigate the worst effects of the climate crisis (129).

Notably for a discussion of fiction and belief, the projections upon which the *McSweeney's* short stories take inspiration are themselves fictions, in that they imagine for us the possible worlds of our future. Scientific understanding of climate change, after all, is based upon speculation. The imagined futures of the IPCC's reports and the possible worlds that they conjure are well-informed and as scientifically accurate as possible, no doubt. But they remain just that: imaginations of what the future *could* be if the average global temperature rises 1°C. Or 1.5°C. Or 2°C. The language that these scientists use to explain their modeling makes this speculation clear. In an annex on methodology in their 2022 report, the IPCC stresses the importance of imaginations of possible futures to their work. They define scenarios as "descriptions of alternative future developments" and state, unequivocally, that these representations provide a "central tool" in analyzing the "wicked problem" of anthropogenic climate change (1870). In particular, imagined scenarios are vital to mitigating the worst effects of climate change, or "explor[ing] pathways towards long-term climate goals." In the same annex, the IPCC explains that they use a wide variety of models to do this work. Some models can forecast, or make "projections of how futures may evolve," while others can "backcast," or produce "projections of a future that meets a predefined goal" (1853). Still additional models explore "what-if" questions, such as the impact of new technologies.

Novelist Jonathan Franzen (2019) makes the connection between scenario modeling and fiction explicit when he likens his own writing process to that of IPCC scientists. To project the rise in global temperature, he writes, the scientists "take a host of variables and run them through supercomputers to generate, say, ten thousand different simulations for the coming century, in order to make a 'best' prediction." As a fiction writer, he, too, models:

> I run various future scenarios through my brain, apply the constraints of human psychology and political reality, take note of the relentless rise in global energy consumption … and count the scenarios in which collective action averts catastrophe.

Franzen and the IPCC come to different conclusions; while the IPCC maintains hope that they can use scenarios to "inform society" and established "desirable futures," Franzen ultimately is pessimistic about the limitations of human psychology: "I can run ten thousand scenarios through my model, and in not one of them do I see the two-degree target being met." But the core methodology—scenarios, models, predictions, imagined possible futures informed by current data—is shared. Indeed, we can understand both the climatologists of the IPCC and fiction writers like the *McSweeney's* contributors as drawing upon make-believe to make belief. While the former group uses scientific tools and predictions to imagine a range of possible futures, the latter use imagined events and people to bring alive those possible (likely?) speculative futures for their readers, all the while stressing the accuracy of their project in its cover blurbs and introduction.

But what if you're a reader who believes that climate change *itself* is a fiction? How might an introduction that stresses a fictional story's fidelity to "accurate" climate models move you? Indeed, why would you even look to a text like the *McSweeney's* special issue, which uses fiction to—in your mind—"prove" a fiction?

Such a reader might be much more interested in a text that lies on the other side of the climate divide, like Michael Crichton's infamous novel of climate skepticism, *State of Fear* (2004). Crichton's novel is a thinly veiled fictionalization of the dominant arguments of American climate skeptics, foremost among them that global warming is a money-making hoax that the country's financial and political elite lord over the country (and, by extension, the world). The basic plot of *State of Fear* replicates the climate divide that I sketch out above. Nicholas Drake, head of the National Environmental Resource Fund (NERF—an obvious counterpoint to the real-life NRDC) is a scientist who conspires with eco-terrorists to produce "natural" disasters as a money-making scheme. Their collaborations include, among other dastardly deeds, calving of a giant Antarctic iceberg to raise worldwide sea levels and using giant cavitators to cause a Pacific tide wave. As water rushes in (or up), so do donations to NERF from an alarmed public. The novel's hero is John Kenner, a jet-setting MIT professor turned federal agent determined to expose Drake and NERF—and thus, the scientific arguments for climate change more broadly—for the frauds that they are. Caught in the middle is NERF lawyer Peter Evans, who over the course of the novel is persuaded by Kenner's vehement and persistent sermonizing about the so-called climate crisis.

The characters in *State of Fear* and the short stories in *2040 A.D.* inhabit different fictional worlds. In the former, Drake—and, by extension, his fellow climate "scientists"—are the baddies, actively working to catastrophically raise the seas for their own gains. In the latter, characters such as Herold slowly have become acclimatized to literally walking on water and now must deal with the mundanities of their new climate-altered reality. It is thus all the more striking that Crichton makes a similar move to Casey-Lefkowitz and the editors of *McSweeney's*, stressing the relationship between his novel's fiction and reality. Crichton makes clear in the novel's declaration that, although it is a "work of fiction … references to real people, institutions, and organizations that are documented in footnotes are accurate" (2004, n.p.). Like the *McSweeney's* special issue, the packaging matter of *State of Fear* de-emphasizes the narrative's fictionality. But rather than confirming or bringing to life climate models, *State of Fear* presents Crichton as a truth-teller who can wisely guide his readers out of the labyrinth of climatological falsities. As he states in the final bullet of his "Author's Message," "everybody has an agenda. Except me" (630). The subtext to this sentence is, of course, believe *me*.

And believe him people do. Crichton's influence on the culture of skepticism in the US is also notable in a discussion of fiction and belief: upon publication of *State of Fear*, he was invited by then-Chief of Staff Karl Rove to consult with then-President George W. Bush and served as a witness in 2005 Senate hearing on "The Role of Science in Environmental Policy-Making." Crichton was also an invited speaker for organizations such as the American Enterprise Institute and won the American

Association of Petroleum Geologists' (APG) 2006 Journalism Award. Indeed, Crichton's fictional work plays such a strong role in the rebuttal of climate change science in America that literary critic George Handley states the author "may very well be the Rachel Carson" of climate skepticism, while also noting, dryly, "the obvious: fiction is not normally considered journalism, nor is the APG normally invested in literary awards" (Handley, 2019, 156).[1]

Depending on what side of the climate change divide you sit on, fiction is either evidence of the reality of climate change and a powerful tool by which to grapple with possible futures, or a vital tool in exposing the fabrication of climate change. Unsurprisingly, these two conversations remain largely separate. They draw from a separate corpus of primary texts and come to separate conclusions about the factuality of climate change and its causes. Yet, surprisingly, they share a common tendency to package fictional representations of climate change within supporting material that stresses factuality, accuracy, and truth-telling.

I push on this tension in this essay, paying particular attention to the possible effects that climate change fiction stands to have on self-identified climate skeptics. Pairing environmental humanities scholarship on the conventions of the emerging genre of cli-fi—especially those related to the packaging of a text, or its *paratexts*—with empirical research into the identity and beliefs of real-world climate skeptics and cognitive research on the ways in which narratives can impact readers, I argue that discussions of what cli-fi *is* and what it can *do* are thus far limited by assumptions of audience. In short, the paratextual positioning of cli-fi such as we see in the *McSweeney's* special issue does not account for the fundamental leap of logic baked into climate skepticism: if climate scenarios are themselves speculative, how can fidelity to this fiction in a second fictional story illuminate reality? Indeed, do paratexts that de-emphasize the fictionality of cli-fi get in the way of reaching a broader audience, and in particular an audience that is most in need of thinking and acting differently? How might different narrative resources, or even different uses of the same paratextual resources, better speak to skeptical readers and help move them toward pro-environmental behaviors? In considering these questions, I open up the analysis of cli-fi, and conceptualizations of what this genre is, to consider multiple paths to move diverse sets of readers in their beliefs about climate change.

Climate Change, Fiction, and Paratexts of Non-Fictionality

Narratologist Gérard Genette defines paratexts as elements which "surround and prolong" a narrative, such as the author's name, a title, a preface, an appendix, a book cover, illustrations, and interviews with the author (1991, 261). The paratext, he notes, is "the means by which a text makes a book of itself and proposes itself as such to its readers, and more generally to the public." Paratexts also establish fundamental expectations for readers. As he explains, a pragmatic characteristic of the paratext is the "*illocutionary force* of its message" (268; emphasis in original). As such, a paratext may impart "authorial and/or editorial *intention*": "this is the cardinal function of most prefaces," he writes, "and it is still that of the generic indication placed on certain covers or title pages" (emphasis in original). Genette argues that a generic indicator like "autobiography, history, memoirs" signals to readers "a more constraining contractual value ('I undertake to tell the truth') than others," such as a novel or an essay. As the examples above illustrate, paratexts are also intimately linked to marketing in that they are tools by which authors, editors, and publishers appeal to target audiences and tell those audiences how to engage with a text.

Genette's theorizing of paratexts is fundamental to my understanding of the emerging genre of cli-fi—both in terms of the ways in which cli-fi texts tend to identify themselves as such and establish specific expectations for readers. The August 19, 2019, issue of *High Country News* (*HCN*) is a third example of the paratexts of cli-fi in action. As Brian Calvert's "Editor's Note" explains, the issue is a "departure from our usual rigorous, fact-based journalism, and a foray into the world of imagination."

The authors featured in the special issue draw upon the *Fourth National Climate Assessment* and use its climate projections to "imagine what the West would look like 50 years from the release of the report." Calvert makes clear that these fictional stories are an attempt to combat the storytelling efforts of "slimeball" fossil fuel company lobbyists, such as those from the Global Climate Coalition that, in 1992, claimed that adding more carbon dioxide to the atmosphere would improve crop yields and end world hunger. "Thirty years later," Calvert writes, "we are still fighting stories with facts, and the results have been underwhelming." Thus, the time has come, he insists, to fight malicious stories of climate denial with productive and scientifically sound stories of speculative futures; "hardcore readers" can find more information on the relevant science in the issue's citations page. As with the narratives of the *McSweeney's* collection, the stories collected in the special issue of *HCN* aim to "inspire further exploration of the national climate assessment." Calvert closes his note with an argument commonly made by writers and scholars of cli-fi: "Our chance to change the future is now, but we'll need a better story first." The paratexts of the special issues of *McSweeney's* and *HCN* thus share two characteristics: they foreground the accuracy of their fictions by drawing an intimate link between the stories and cutting-edge scientific projections, and they position the stories as educational tools that can move readers to think and act differently in the real world.

We see the same two characteristics of cli-fi paratexts in yet another collection of short stories, *Everything Change: An Anthology of Climate Fiction* (2016). In his introduction to the anthology, cli-fi author Kim Stanley Robinson states that cli-fi narratives have a "fidelity to the real" and concern themselves with "events in the coming decades" (ix–x). Because of its allegiance to accuracy, cli-fi is "in effect the realism of our time" (x). The fact that cli-fi is so prescriptive—so "obviously meant to warn us"—is a "good thing," he writes:

> We decide what to do based on the stories that we tell ourselves, so we very much need to be telling stories about our responses to climate change and the associated massive problems bearing down on us and our descendants.
>
> *(xi, x)*

The production of the anthology, as editors Manjana Milkoreit, Meredith Martinez, and Joey Eschrich articulate in a second introduction, bears out Robinson's point about the educational nature of accurate fictional models of possible futures. Responding to a short story contest organized by Arizona State University's Imagination and Climate Futures Initiative, the judging panel that assembled the anthology included experts on sustainability, conservation, geology, and climate modeling. The contest's submission instructions tasked writers with imagining "how climate change will play out" in stories that "reflect current scientific knowledge about future climate change" (xiv, xv). As with the *McSweeney's* and *HCN* stories, the goal of the collection is to "inspire readers" and "facilitate conversations about the futures we want and how to create them" (xviii, xiv).

Ironically, in positing these questions, these writers and editors tend to de-emphasize the fictionality of cli-fi texts by foregrounding the scientific accuracy of the narrative's imagined worlds in their paratexts and emphasizing the narrative's possible real-world effects. Except that, with cli-fi, the constraining contractual value of the paratext is not truth, as it is with Genette's example genres of autobiography or memoir, but scenario accuracy—an imagination of the near-future loyal to cutting-edge climate science. Scholars of cli-fi tend to double down on the importance of paratexts to the genre by emphasizing the educational and reformist authorial intent of many cli-fi texts. Indeed, in many ways the intent of the text is a prime mechanism by which critics yoke together the various styles and textures of climate change fiction—a range we see easily in my discussion of "New Jesus" and "1740" above, and in novels as diverse as Jeff VanderMeer's weird fiction (*Annihilation*, 2014) and Barbara Kingsolver's realism (*The Poisonwood Bible*, 1998). Matthew Schneider-Mayerson, for example, argues cli-fi narratives not only "bear witness" but also "agitate and inspire apathetic and complicit readers" (2017, 309). And Antonia Mehnert defines climate change fiction as narratives that "explicitly engage with anthropogenic climate change" (2016, 38). While she warns against the risk that overly preachy cli-fi texts may alienate readers, she admits that many highlight the "didactic impulses" of their authors. Furthermore, she notes, the reputation of the genre to change the beliefs of readers is bolstered by "numerous newspaper articles" that conjure the "persuasive power of literature as well as its interventionist, educational and political power" (228). Cli-fi narratives are thus "seen as the last resort to communicate the urgency of environmental crisis and prompt action." Likewise, Bill McKibben, in his introduction to an early cli-fi short story collection, warns that "science can only take us so far" (2011, 3). "The scientists have done their job," he decries, "they've issued every possible warning, flashed every red light." Now is the time for the artists—and especially fiction writers, such as those that appear in the pages that follow—to "help us understand what things *feel* like" (emphasis in original). Although he admits that "the job of writers is not to push us in some particular direction" but simply to "illuminate," it is clear that this illumination should spotlight a less destructive future: he states that "one task ... of our letters in this emergency is to help provide that sense of what life might be like in the world past fossil fuel" (4). The label "cli-fi" thus makes the same two promises that we see in the paratexts above: that a text will not only be scientifically sound, according to climatological scenarios, but also offer readers some instruction for how to live better in the real world in which they read. We might be so bold as to think of the *genre* of cli-fi—the designation of a text as such—as itself a powerful paratext that communicates an authorial intent of bearing witness to agitate and inspire.

Yet the success of Crichton's novel and the persuasiveness of its paratexts illustrate the risks of these generic markers. Indeed, Crichton's novel is insistent in its use of paratexts to emphasize the validity of its fictional representation of dodgy science and climate conspiracies and his own trustworthiness as a guide to "real" knowledge. An epigraphical quote from George Orwell—"Within any important issue, there are always aspects no one wishes to discuss"—sets the political and ethical stakes for the novel (2004, x). An "Author's Message" at the end of the text picks up these stakes, noting that "a novel such as *State of Fear*, in which so many divergent views are expressed, may lead the reader to wonder where, exactly, the author stands on these issues" (625). Crichton makes his stance unequivocally clear in a six-page bullet list of conclusions that position climate change as a power grab of the political and financial elite. "I conclude that most environmental 'principles'," he writes, "have the effect of preserving the economic advantages of the West and thus constitute modern imperialism toward the developing world" (627). The novel is rounded out by a thirty-one-page bibliography and two appendices, one of which outlines "Why Politicized Science Is Dangerous" by drawing similarities between the embrace of climate change by "leading scientists, politicians, and celebrities around the world" and the disastrous interest in the science of eugenics at the turn of the twentieth century (631).

It is thus no wonder that *State of Fear* was celebrated by critics and reviewers for its truth-telling in a series of reviews that are also excerpted as paratexts in the paperback edition's cover matter: The *Wall Street Journal* declared the novel "The Da Vinci code with real facts" and "every bit as informative as it is entertaining," while *The Los Angeles Times* affirmed that Crichton "specializes in cutting-edge science fused with suspense" and is "a master of plausible and frightening scenarios of science unloosed in the hands of the unscrupulous and the obsessed" (Crichton, 2004, n.p.). American Senator James Inhofe, perhaps the American political elite's most notorious climate denier, even uses a lengthy fictional excerpt from *State of Fear* in an appendix to his own non-fictional book, *The Greatest Hoax: How the Global Warming Conspiracy Threatens Your Future* (2012). As Handley notes, the popularity of *State of Fear* is "evidence of the powerful impact a narrative can have on attitudes and behavior" (2019, 156). It is also evidence on the powerful impact a narrative can have on belief, as it asks of readers: whom do you believe? *What* do you believe?

In the cli-fi collections and *State of Fear*, respectively, we see a common tendency to package fictional representations of climate change within didactic paratexts that stress factuality, accuracy, and truth-telling. In the former, paratexts that de-emphasize a narrative's fictionality work to foster belief in climate change scenarios, while in the latter the same type of paratext works to deny that climate change *is* a reality. In other words, while the former encourages readers to believe in the validity of their fiction, the latter demands that readers believe in the invalidity of a fiction—*the* fiction of climate change—within which the narrative exists. Same narrative resources, different results.

This begs the question: what contribution might fictional texts that draw attention to their own fictionality make to beliefs about climate change? How might texts that underscore their make-believe—that do not pledge overt allegiance to accurate climatological science—stand to shift the attitudes, values, and behaviors of readers? What aspects of these fictional texts, if not their scientific accuracy, make them especially relevant to discussions of climate change and belief? And *why* should we turn to such texts?

Climate Skepticism, Emotions, and Objects of Care

We might answer the question of "why" via two paths, the first of which draws upon empirical research into the beliefs and attitudes of climate skeptics. In "Climate Change Skepticism as an Emotional Copy Strategy," sociologists Kristin Haltinner and Dilshani Sarathchandra note that, while the percentage of the US public skeptical of climate change is relatively small when compared to those expressing concern, it remains a significant portion of the population, ranging between 19% and 28% in the past decade (2018, 3). Citing sociological research from the past three decades, Haltinner and Sarathchandra explain that this "comparatively high" level of climate skepticism in the US, as opposed to other developed countries such as Germany, Australia, and Britain, is driven by an "active and well-funded disinformation campaign aimed at critiquing scientific understanding of the problem and discrediting climate scientists" that originates with, among others, the influential Koch brothers and the executives of oil megacorporation ExxonMobil (3). Using the same strategies of critique and discreditation that we see at work in the paratexts and fictional narrative of *State of Fear*, this disinformation campaign speaks especially loudly to specific members of the American public. As Haltinner and Sarathchandra explain, ample research shows that skepticism in the US "has explicated political orientation, race, gender, and religion as consistent individual-level predictors of attitudes towards climate change," and that American skeptics tend to be "politically right-leaning, white, male, and evangelical" (1).

Haltinner and Sarathchandra make clear that climate skepticism is not a homogenous category. Drawing upon the Monitor/Blunter-style scale, a popular diagnostic tool that psychologists use to evaluate information avoidance as a behavioral trait, they define "monitors" as those who "seek out threats and information about threats," and "blunters" as those who "try to avoid or distract themselves from uncomfortable information" (4). The latter category, they argue, is especially relevant to debates about climate change and belief because of the heightened emotions of many climate skeptics. Their own research suggests that "strong emotions such as fear may drive climate change skepticism and denial among some adherents" (1). Indeed, perhaps counterintuitively, they find that climate change skepticism and denial is, "at least in some cases, a form of exaggerated ostrich effect, whereby adherents are so driven to avoid learning about a specific problem" that they "actively seek to construct an alternative, safer narrative" (1). Importantly for considerations of fiction and belief, the more palatable stories that skeptics seek out tend to be the stuff of fiction: as Haltinner and Sarathchandra argue, "fear-driven 'blunters' may not only ignore information that perpetuates their anxiety," but go as far as to seek out "conspiracy theor[ies], which can provide psychological comfort by curbing fear and increasing perceived agency" (6). As such, efforts to make climatological science accessible to blunters may end up having adverse effects by ramping up the anxiety that tips into skepticism and denial. If done without attention to the impacts of fear, Haltinner and Sarathchandra state, "these efforts may actually have a negative effect on motivating change."

Given the role that fear and anxiety can play in driving climate skepticism and denial, Haltinner and Sarathchandra argue that "communication on climate change must attend to scholarship on emotion" (6). They are especially interested in worry and dread—two emotions often expressed in a series of thirty-three interviews and 1,000 surveys they conducted with self-declared climate change skeptics in the US Pacific Northwest, a region with an unusually large population of climate skeptics. Haltinner and Sarathchandra, in collaboration with affect specialist Jennifer Ladino, argue that "while worry and dread are themselves closely correlated, they seem to feel and function differently than fear and anxiety" (Haltinner, Ladino and Sarathchandra, 2021, 3). The skeptics they interviewed and surveyed did not tend to express a "chronic fear of environmental doom." But they did express worry and dread, especially about "objects of care," or "the people, places, and species that climate change impacts."

Haltinner, Ladino, and Sarathchandra borrow the phrase "objects of care" from Wang et al. (2018), who themselves use it to refer to "objects of affection, or a thing to be protected" from the worst effects of anthropogenic climate change (26). In their work on the ways in which emotions about climate change can predict pro-environmental policy support, Wang et al., write that objects of care can be important "connectors" that "make the issue of climate change seem relevant to the individual" (26). Haltinner, Ladino, and Sarathchandra, in turn, combine this idea with their empirical data of climate skepticism and emotions to posit a new definition of worry as *"an affective state that directs anxious feelings toward particular objects of care without succumbing to the pitfalls of fear"* (2021, 3; emphasis in original). Their research shows that, even though skeptics might not think of threats to specific people, places, and species in terms of anthropogenic climate change, their concern and worry for these objects is one rich path toward pro-environmental behavior and policy. They thus recommend that climate change communication does not focus on making science accessible to move skeptics to think and act differently, but instead tap into skeptics' pre-existing emotions about objects of care that open up conversations about pollution reduction, deforestation prevention, and investment in renewable energy. "Such efforts may not change skeptics' perspectives *about* climate change," they warn (7, my emphasis). But supporting skeptics as they engage with worry over the objects for which they care will help to mitigate climate change in the long run.

This research into the emotions of skeptics has pressing implications for climate change fiction, and especially the ways in which cli-fi texts are packaged by their paratexts. Rather than moving skeptics to reform their beliefs about climate change and thus engage more responsibly with the environments in which they read, I understand this empirical sociological research as suggesting that paratexts that stress a fictional story's scientific accuracy and didactically prescribe alternate behaviors based upon that warning may very well backfire for readers who are not already convinced of the validity of climate change. In other words, while these paratexts might prime a reader who already believes in climate change to act or think differently, climate skeptics stand to find them unpersuasive at best, and illogical at worst. The generic label of "cli-fi," and the introductions and marketing blurbs that tout its potential to encourage pro-environmental behaviors and beliefs in the real world, thus stands to turn off readers most in need of its insight.

The second path by which we might answer the questions of why we should turn to the texts that buck the paratextual trends of cli-fi begins in cognitive narrative theory. Cognitive narrative scholars such as Lisa Zunshine and Suzanne Keen have long argued that the process of narrative interpretation is deeply emotional—that readers, in addition to tracking the events that happen in a story, must also grapple with what it feels like for characters to experience these events. In *Why We Read Fiction* (2006), Zunshine argues that the simulation of the experiences and mental states of characters plays an important social function in human societies, in that it allows narrative interpreters to try on the emotions of others in safe, offline contexts. She thus sees fictional narratives as educational tools that help readers (and listeners and viewers) develop the mind-reading skills that everyday social interaction requires, as they permit readers to project themselves into other experiencing consciousnesses. Suzanne Keen, in her work theorizing narrative empathy, states clearly that "there is no question ... that readers feel empathy with (and sympathy for) fictional characters and other aspects of fictional works" (2007, vii). Although Keen is unpersuaded by claims that overstate the connection between narrative empathy and real-life altruism—what she calls the "empathy-altruism hypothesis"—she maintains that "readers' and authors' empathy certainly contributes to the emotional resonance of fiction, its success in the marketplace, and its character-improving reputation." This cognitive work helps to explain why fiction plays such a vital role in human life. Fiction, it argues, not only entertains but also helps us access experiences other than our own and thus understand better what it is like to live in the world.

Fiction's status as such is vital to the process of emotional contagion that cognitive narrative scholars such as Zunshine and Keen see as an essential part of the reading process. In *Empathy and the Novel* (2007), Keen builds to a robust theory of narrative empathy that accounts for situations in which readers try on the emotions of a narrative's characters. A key tenet of her theory is that "*readers' perception of a text's fictionality plays a role in subsequent empathetic response, by releasing readers from the obligations of self-perception through skepticism and suspicion*" (88, emphasis in original). Keen's theory suggests that readers find a certain emotional freedom in stories that signal their own fictionality—that by making clear their status as make believe, fictional narratives permit, or even encourage, readers to be emotionally adventurous.

Keen's theory helps to explain a favorite argument of many scholars of cli-fi: that fictional stories that represent future climate scenarios, via their immersive properties, can transport interpreters to alternate worlds in which they can access experiences they would otherwise not know. Yet, Keen's theory—and the emphasis in cognitive narrative studies on fiction, in particular—also exposes a problem with the paratexts that tend to surround cli-fi. Paratexts such as those that we see explicitly in the special issues of *McSweeney's* and *High Country News*, and additional, implicit paratexts of didactic authorial intent that often accompany a text's positioning as "cli-fi," do the opposite of what Keen's theory foregrounds. By emphasizing a narrative's fidelity to accurate scientific modeling—by *de*-emphasizing its fictionality to stress its connection to what *could* happen or is likely *to* happen— the paratexts of climate change fiction tend to task readers with embracing future realities instead of suspending disbelief. As such, they stand to inhibit a reader's empathy for the narrative's characters by lessening their perception of the story's fictionality. I see empirical research into the emotions of climate skeptics as suggesting that this dampening effect may be even more true for this group of readers. Keen's theory also helps to explain why a text such as Crichton's novel would be so appealing to skeptical readers. As Haltinner and Sarathchandra argue, climate skepticism is often a form of an exaggerated ostrich effect, in which advocates seek psychological comfort in alternative, "safer" narratives. We might understand *State of Fear*'s paratexts of non-fictionality as *suppressing* the emotional freedom and adventurousness of skeptical readers, and thereby promoting adherence to an already-familiar conspiracy theory of climate hoax.

Yet another component of Keen's theory of narrative empathy suggests a promising point of connection with climate skeptics. Keen is cautious of overly optimistic claims that, as Martha Nussbaum puts it, narratives can "transport us, while remaining ourselves, into the life of another, revealing similarities but also profound differences between the life and thought of that other and myself and making them comprehensible, or at least more nearly comprehensible" (Nussbaum, 1997, 111). Nussbaum's work is a particularly rich example of the empathy-altruism hypothesis, as it argues that narrative-inspired empathy can be an especially powerful way for readers to imaginatively overcome differences of gender, religion, race, sexuality, and class, and thus be kinder to people who express these identities in the real world. Keen is dubious, in that she finds the claim that reading fiction makes you a better person in the real world "inconclusive at best and nearly always exaggerated in favor of the beneficial effects of … reading" (2007, vii). Yet, given the empirical evidence of narrative empathy, she is unwilling to completely forgo the idea that reading about an experience in fiction can help a reader understand that experience. In her analysis of postcolonial literature and narrative empathy, Keen defines bridge characters as a member of an in-group who helps interpreters cross a significant barrier of difference, or access emotions and experiences that would otherwise be unavailable. As an example, she offers up Haitian-American writer Edwidge Danticat's short stories that foster empathy among white readers for non-white characters through her use of bridge characters: "literate, creative children and teenagers whose very bookishness or eloquence invites a book-reader on the other end of the narrative transaction into the storyworld" (2015, 353). Bridge characters, for Keen, are important mechanisms for pushing readers beyond of their own identities and imaginatively participating in the emotional experiences of others. By ushering readers into the world of a fictional text, bridge characters can serve as a conduit to a previously unavailable experience.

As with bridge characters, I argue, so too with objects of care in climate change fiction. Indeed, I contend that we productively read objects of care in cli-fi stories as potential bridges to pro-environmental behavior, especially for readers who may not identify readily with fictional characters who express actively their belief in climate change, nor with the editors, writers, and scholars who articulate similar beliefs in the paratexts that surround cli-fi. This effect of barrier crossing may be heightened in cli-fi texts that declare, loudly, their own fictionality. Such a text would not only invite skeptical readers into the pro-environmental behaviors in a storyworld but also allow them the imaginative room to try on the emotions and beliefs that underlie such behavior.

Caring for Fictional Objects

Ned Beauman's *Venomous Lumpsucker* (2022) is one example of such a text. The novel's protagonist, Karin Resaint, undergoes a significant change of heart. Initially, she finds it "easy not to care" about the mass extinction that defines her world—tens of thousands of species each and every year—because "the arguments against it were so feeble" (106). After all, in this speculative, post-2°C temperature rise, post-COVID-24 2030s, "the vast majority of animals on earth were extremely parochial parasites," and "nobody gave a shit about any of those." But then Resaint meets *Adelognathus marginatum*, a rare parasitoid wasp that lays its eggs in a specific species of small, stripy spider before coaxing it to build an unusually shaped web exactly suited to the needs of the wasp and devouring the spider. Resaint comes across the *marginatum* while on assignment for the agricultural company Kalynove AgroProduct in Western Ukraine. The company wants to replace 1.2 million hectares of sunflowers with a genetically modified strain of that plant that would starve out the wasp; Resaint, as an expert in cognition, is in town to assess the intelligence of the *marginatum* and the other species the replacement threatens. Her motivation is more financial than ethical: in Resaint's world, the newly formed World Commission on Species Extinction (WCSE) demands that companies and nations proposing actions that would annihilate a species must first spend an "extinction credit" that "could buy you bulldozing rights to any species on earth" (24). But credits do not cover any species certified as intelligent by Resaint and her cognitivist peers. Resaint's job thus sits at the center of a burgeoning extinction industry in which multinational companies whittle away at the WCSE via allowances, indulgences, exceptions, and delays. Resaint is not much moved by the stakes of her work until the potential eradication of the *marginatum* stays with her "like a papercut that won't stop bleeding" (112).

The *marginatum* is a gateway species for Resaint. At first, she is indifferent to the mass extinctions of her world's hyper-capitalist Anthropocene. But, on a dime, she cares. The transition is abrupt and baffling for her: the novel's narrator notes that, "to go from caring about this not at all to caring about it more than anything was like being turned inside out" (116). The *marginatum* reforms Resaint, such that she feels "awed by how evolution had not only wound its way toward this weird, snaggly marginal way of life—so many options and you choose *this one?*—but held on to it, continued to sharpen and perfect it, until it was no longer marginal but in fact a triumph" (117 emphasis in original). Indeed, the *marginatum* primes Resaint for her eventual relationship to the *Cyclopterus venenatur*, the titular venomous lumpsucker, a "bumpy, grayish fish" with a "toadlike face," "bulging eyes," and a "fat upper lip" (20). The lumpsucker is not a glamourous nor charismatic species; as another character quips, they are "ugly little fucker[s], with a nasty bite" (26). But they *are* intelligent—one of the most intelligent creatures on the planet, Resaint finds—and she grows fond enough of them that "she would be delighted to see them again" (4). Her quest to see the lumpsuckers again forms the backbone of Beauman's raucous ride of a cli-fi novel. Readers follow her as she travels the globe to save the unpleasant little fish that, "if it were a human being … would sweat from the forehead all the time and yet have a shockingly cold handshake" (20).

One productive way to read Resaint is as a reformed climate skeptic who shifts into pro-environmental behaviors via her relationship to an object of care. If not an outright denier of anthropogenic climate change and its accompanying mass extinction prior to her encounter with the *marginatum*, she certainly is apathetic in her response to the crisis. Prior to the *marginatum*, Resaint has trouble getting to grips with the accelerated pace of extinction in her world: the narrator notes that the "statistics about species dying out were not news to her … she worked in the extinction industry, after all" (116). And yet the *marginatum* is the object that localizes the crisis for Resaint. She moves from knowing that "ten thousand species a year" are dying out—"about a hundred times the rate that would be expected in the absence of human activity"—to worrying about "ten thousand *marginatum*. Probably gone too soon." Indeed, "the statistics were not new to her, but the force of them was." And importantly, her dominant emotional response to this new perspective is not grief, nor fear, but "puzzlement and incredulity." She now understands that "a single extinction was an unspeakable tragedy; and many thousands of them were happening a year; and nobody was really doing anything about it, *including her*" (116; emphasis in original). Resaint is not converted to pro-environmental behavior by accurate predictions of extinctions that could happen, nor by new and vivid fictional representations of those predictions. Instead, her activism is driven by pre-existing sense of awe for the process of evolution itself. Resaint finds the extinction of the *marginatum*—that most specialized of species—so hard to accept "not because of the probability that it could all just peter out after a quadrillion rounds, but because of the improbability that it should ever happen in the first place" (112). It is this awe for the processes of life, not scientific facts about the threats it faces, that lies at the root of her epiphany.

Resaint's emotional arc represents the exact transition that the paratexts of the special issues of *McSweeney's* and *High Country News* promise, in that she is moved to think and act differently about the climate crisis. Yet in Beauman's novel, this shift does not come about because of scientific data or any sense of fidelity to climatological science, but from her deep sense of care and worry for one particular species, precisely as empirical sociological research into the emotions and beliefs of climate skeptics predicts. Resaint's story thus offers us a powerful model of how this shift might role out in the real world.

And yet Beauman's novel also says: not so fast, and not so easy. Before encountering Resaint's epiphanic conversion, readers must grapple with the novel's opening "Author's Note":

> This novel is set in the near future. However, to minimize any need for mental arithmetic on the reader's part, sums of money are presented as if the euro has retained its 2022 value with no inflation. This is the sole respect in which the story deviates from how things will actually unfold.

The novel makes the note's facetiousness almost immediately clear, as Resaint's world clearly is fantastic. Robotic ships harness the wind in "unstraightforward ways, like a tennis ball backspinning off a racket" (6). Food has become so over-processed and unflavored that potatoes, carrots, beets, and apples are "distinguishable only by color, not by taste," and Inzidernil, a drug that removes an eater's "evaluative response" is doing big business (51, 53). Britain, in a post-Brexit joke, is known only as the "Hermit Kingdom." Even the book's title belies the authenticity of the note: on the Earth in which we read, there is no such thing as a venomous lumpsucker, and thus the presence of this creature demands a certain amount of mental arithmetic from readers. (Nor, for that matter, is there any such species on Earth as the *Adelognathus marginatum*.) The note—which Anthony Cummings, in his review of the novel, reads as a "twinkling deadpan" and "mischievous intelligence" typical of Beauman's work—thus functions more as a nod toward rambunctious satire than realism. It cues readers to enter into the novel with a sense of play and fun. Things won't *really* be this way, it signals. But come along for the ride nonetheless.

Venomous Lumpsucker provides us with an alternate example of how cli-fi might use specific narrative resources such as the paratext, and to whom it might speak. Unlike the short story collections with which I begin this essay, Beauman's novel refuses to package its scientific accuracy in paratexts that stress the reality of climate change. The novel's storyworld is faithful to the latest models of real-world climate crisis, in that such scenarios predict an extinction rate at one hundred times a baseline rate (Ceballos et al., 2015). Yet, by accentuating the fictionality of its storyworld in an opening paratext, it makes efforts to side-step feelings of anxiety and fear that such a scenario might otherwise produce. *Venomous Lumpsucker*'s tongue-and-cheek "Author's Note" tells us, clearly, not to take this book too seriously. This is *make-believe*, it says: go with it. In its representation of a skeptic moved to adopt pro-environmental behaviors because of her attachment to an object of care, it also suggests that, perhaps, there are multiple paths to inspiring readers in the creation of healthier and more just futures, and that some readers might find some paths more welcoming than others. Indeed, our understanding of climate change, fiction, and belief would benefit from diversifying our notion of cli-fi texts, their narrative resources, and their potential readers.

Note

1 By connecting Crichton and Carson, Handley emphasizes the influence that both writers had on American politics and environmental policy—Crichton via his work on climate skepticism and Carson via her testimony to Congress on the dangers of pesticide pollution on June 4, 1963. Unlike Crichton, Carson's testimony does not originate in fiction but in her non-fiction book *Silent Spring* (1962). Yet, literature scholars, myself included, highlight the seminal role that the book's opening short, fictional narrative, "A Fable for Tomorrow," played in its popularity. For more, see my discussion of "Fable" in *The Storyworld Accord* (James, 2015, 216–18).

Works Cited

Beauman, Ned. 2022. *Venomous Lumpsucker*. New York: Soho.
Boas, Natasha, Carol Davis, Brian Dice, Dave Eggers, Hilary Kivitz, Jordan Kurland, Caterine Fake, Gina Pell, Nion McEvoy, Isabel Duffy-Pinner, Jeremy Radcliffe, Jed Repko, and Vendela Vida. n.d. "McSweeney's: About Us." https://www.mcsweeneys.net/pages/about-us. Accessed February 22, 2023.

Boyle, Claire, and Dave Eggers, eds. 2019. "2040 A.D.: Climate Fiction Edition." Special issue, *McSweeney's* 58.

Calvert, Brian. August 19, 2019. "Editor's Note: The Case for Speculative Journalism." *High Country News.* https://www.hcn.org/issues/51.14/editors-note-the-case-for-speculative-journalism.

Casey-Lefkowitz, Susan. 2019. "Introduction." In "2040 A.D.: Climate Fiction Edition." *McSweeney's* 58: 8–14.

Ceballos, Gerardo, Paul R. Ehrlich, Anthony D. Barnosky, Andrés García, Robert M. Pringle, and Todd M. Palmer. 2015. "Accelerated Modern Human-Induced Species Losses: Entering the Sixth Mass Extinction." *Science Advances* 1, no. 5: e1400253.

Crichton, Michael. 2004. *State of Fear.* New York: Avon Books.

Cummings, Anthony. 2022. "Venomous Lumpsucker by Ned Beauman Review: Mischievous Meaning-of-Life Satire." *The Guardian*, July 17. https://www.theguardian.com/books/2022/jul/17/venomous-lumpsucker-by-ned-beauman-review-mischievous-meaning-of-life-satire.

Franzen, Jonathan. 2019. "What If We Stopped Pretending?" *The New Yorker*, September 8. https://www.newyorker.com/culture/cultural-comment/what-if-we-stopped-pretending.

Genette, Gérard. 1991. "Introduction to the Paratext." *New Literary History* 22, no. 2 (Spring): 261–72.

Haltinner, Kristin, Jennifer Ladino, and Dilshani Sarathchandra. 2021. "Feeling Skeptical: Worry, Dread, and Support for Environmental Policy Among Climate Skeptics." *Emotion, Space, and Society* 39: 100790.

Haltinner, Kristin, and Dilshani Sarathchandra. 2018. "Climate Change Skepticism as a Psychological Coping Strategy." *Sociology Compass* 12, no. 6: e12586.

Handley, George B. 2019. "Climate Scepticism and Christian Conservatism in the United States." In *Climate Change Scepticism: A Transnational Ecocritical Approach*, edited by Greg Garrard, Axel Goodbody, George B. Handley and Stephanie Posthumus, 133–74. London: Bloomsbury Academic.

Inhofe, James. 2012. *The Greatest Hoax: How the Global Warming Conspiracy Threatens Your Future.* Chicago, IL: WND Books.

IPCC. 2022. "Annex III: Scenarios and Modelling Methods." In *IPCC, 2022: Climate Change 2022: Mitigation of Climate Change. Contribution of Working Group III to the Sixth Assessment Report of the Intergovernmental Panel on Climate Change*, edited by P. R. Shukla, J. Skea, R. Slade and A. Al Khourdajie, et al., 1843–1908. Cambridge and New York: Cambridge University Press. Doi: 10.1017/9781009157926.

James, Erin. 2015. *The Storyworld Accord: Econarratology and Postcolonial Narratives.* Lincoln: University of Nebraska Press.

Keen, Suzanne. 2007. *Empathy and the Novel.* Oxford: Oxford University Press.

Keen, Suzanne. 2015. "Human Rights Discourse and the Universals of Cognition and Emotion." *Oxford Handbook of Cognitive Literary Criticism*, edited by Lisa Zunshine, 347–65. Oxford: Oxford University Press.

McKibben, Bill. 2011. "Introduction." In *I'm with the Bears: Short Stories from a Damaged Planet*, edited by Mark Martin, 1–5. New York: Verso.

McSweeney's Publishing, 2019. Summary for "2040 AD: Climate Fiction Edition." Special issue, *McSweeney's Quarterly Concern* 58. Cited in WorldCat. https://www.worldcat.org/title/2040-ad/oclc/1129099802.

Mehnert, Antonia. 2016. *Climate Change Fictions: Representations of Global Warming in American Literature.* London: Palgrave Macmillan.

Mikoreit, Manjana, Meredith Martinez, and Joey Eschrich. 2016. "Editor's Introduction." In *Everything Change: An Anthology of Climate Fiction*, edited by Manjana Mikoreit, Meredith Martinez and Joey Eschrich, xiii–xviii. Tucson: Arizona State University Press.

Nussbaum, Martha. 1997. *Cultivating Humanity: A Classical Defense of Reform in Liberal Education.* Cambridge, MA: Harvard University Press.

Robinson, Kim Stanley. 2016. "Foreword." *Everything Change: An Anthology of Climate Fiction*, edited by Manjana Mikoreit, Meredith Martinez, and Joey Eschrich, ix–xii. Tucson: Arizona State University.

Schneider-Mayerson, Matthew. 2017. "Climate Change Fiction." In *American Literature in Transition, 2000–2010*, edited by Rachel Greenwald Smith, 309–21. Cambridge: Cambridge University Press.

Wang, Susie, Zoe Leviston, Mark Hurlstone, Carmen Lawrence, and Iain Walker. 2018. "Emotions Predict Policy Support: Why it Matters How People Feel About Climate Change." *Global Environmental Change* 50: 25–40.

Zunshine, Lisa. 2006. *Why We Read Fiction: Theory of Mind and the Novel.* Columbus: Ohio State University Press.

PART III

Fiction and Religious Belief

26
GREEK MYTHOLOGY
Discourse, Belief, and Ritual Action

Claude Calame

My own fatherland is not without fame.
It is Sparta, and my father is Tyndareus. There is
a certain story that Zeus flew as a bird to my mother
Leda, taking the form of a swan.
Through deceit he shared her bed, pretending
to be pursued by an eagle, if the story is true.
I was named Helen, and the misfortunes that I suffered
I will now tell …[1]

These are the words spoken by Helen in the prologue of Euripides's tragedy about her abduction by Paris, the Trojan hero who had been summoned to judge the beauty contest between the goddesses Athena, Hera, and Aphrodite. These words were recited by a masked actor in front of the Athenian public gathered at the end of the fifth century BC in the sanctuary-theater dedicated to the god Dionysus Eleuthereus, on the occasion of the musical competition for the performance of tragedies that accompanied the ritual celebration of the Great Dionysia. Helen refers to a narrative that is not "clear" (*saphés*, translated above by the word "true"), which one cannot trust, and which explicitly contradicts the account that presents Helen as the daughter of Tyndareus, the king of Sparta. Or rather, it is a narrative which, like that of the birth of Heracles or Theseus, effectively attributes a double origin, divine and mortal, to the great heroic figure in question. In this case, are we dealing with a myth?

In fact, this "narrative" is twice referred to as a *lógos* in the passage cited above (verses 18 and 21, translated above as "story"). Furthermore, Euripides chose to present the specific version of Helen's abduction that results in her being absent from the war between the Greeks and the Trojans. In this version, during the crossing to Troy, Helen is kidnapped by Hermes and transported to Egypt to the court of King Proteus, while only her *eídolon*, her image, is present throughout the ten-year war. This account, created by the poet Stesichorus, has the effect of exonerating Helen from being the cause of the conflict between Achaeans and Trojans. Plato relates in the *Phaedrus* (243a) that Stesichorus, wishing to avoid being blinded as Homer was, decided not to speak ill of Helen, whereas several protagonists of the *Iliad*, including deities, accuse her of causing the Trojan War. He, therefore, composed a palinode (responding to one of his own earlier poems), and the first line of the new poem

DOI: 10.4324/9781003119456-30

announces: "This is not the real narrative" (*ouk étumos lógos hoûtos*; fr. 192 Page-Davies). Address-ing Helen directly, the poet adds: "You did not go up on the well assembled ships, you did not pass under the walls of Troy." In a new poem, he thus created a new version of the narrative of the abduc-tion of the young heroine, a fiction in the etymological meaning of the term: that of manufacture and creation, and in this case, poetic creation.

On this subject, the title of Paul Veyne's monograph of 1983, *Les Grecs ont-ils cru à leurs mythes?*, is misleading in two respects (despite the undeniable qualities of this work of criticism). Veyne argues that, for the Greeks, these myths represent "genuine historical traditions," that is, mythical traditions that are considered as being true, even though they present fantastical events (1983, 69–72). The first problem with this is that the Greeks did not know myths in the modern sense of the term (to which I shall return), but rather produced many heroic narratives relating to the past of their cities, featuring the presence and actions of the gods. The second problem is that, when the plausibility of these narra-tives was called into question, a poet would modify and recreate them according to a reality principle, adapting them to a new historical and cultural situation, and taking account of all the shared encyclo-pedic knowledge, perceptions, and beliefs of their new audience.

Narrative Fiction, Religion, and Beliefs

Let us therefore first address the question of belief, and since we are dealing with narratives featuring divine figures in particular, let us consider beliefs in the domain of what we have come to conceive as religion.

In fact, going back as far as the evolutionary anthropology of the eighteenth century, the concept of belief has been the basis for the very concept of religion. This was already the case for Edward Burnett Tylor, who, for the purposes of his study of "primitive culture" and in particular the religions of "low races" (those that have not yet reached the level of "civilization"), proposed that a "minimum definition of Religion" (with a capital letter) consists in "the belief in Spiritual Beings" ([1871] 1913: I:383). Tylor included these beliefs in the category of animism, and considered that this "minimum of religion" and first form of "Spiritualistic" philosophy—as opposed to "Materialistic" philosophy—is "the groundwork of the Philosophy of Religion" ([1871] 1913, 1:384–85).

Émile Durkheim was the first to attempt a sociological definition of religion. In his view, religion corresponds to a series of collective representations and practices that confer on objects a sacred dimension:

> Religious phenomena fall into two basic categories: beliefs and rites. The first are states of opinion and consist of representations; the second are particular modes of action. Between these two categories of phenomena lies all that separates thinking from doing.
>
> *([1912] 1995, 34)[2]*

For our purposes, the two essential points here are the association of belief with the idea of repre-sentation and the combination of belief of a religious order with practice considered as ritual. I shall return to this shortly. Whether or not Durkheim's definition of religion is applicable in our case, the two dimensions that it identifies correspond to the two meanings of the term "belief": belief as a content that corresponds to a representation (in our case, a narrative fiction), and belief as an act that is provoked by the plausibility of the representation in question (thus belonging to the domain of pragmatics).[3]

It might seem to be useful at this point, having considered definitions of religion, to propose a preliminary, and equally instrumental, definition of narrative fiction, but I shall defer this until I come to the conclusion of my discussion of Greek myths and beliefs. For the moment, let us adopt the distinction proposed by Françoise Lavocat when considering how beliefs are implied by fictions, implicitly understood here as narrative fictions: on the one hand, there is belief as an immersion which results in some degree of adhesion to the possible world constructed by the fictional discourse; on the other hand, there are the effects of this belief, of this credence through immersion, including the fact of the mental construction of another possible world, as a "projection of oneself in different possible worlds" (2016, 226).

Nevertheless, although the (mental? cognitive?) process of immersion can refer to a process of "feigning," in the sense of "make-believe," the "feigning" involved in the process of reception of narrative fiction cannot be considered as being purely ludic: fiction is not, then, a "shared ludic feint," as Jean-Marie Schaeffer concludes at the end of his long examination of the subject (2010, 138–39), but rather a practical process (which is also oriented toward action) through which we make-believe in a possible world.[4] For the undeniable effect of aesthetic satisfaction that fiction provokes, especially when its form is poetic, is also combined with a pragmatic effect leading to action, and this is especially the case when narrative fiction, of the sort labelled as myth in the modern sense of the term, is connected, through the poetic form of its discursive realization—for instance, as tragic performance at the Great Dionysia—with the ritual practice entailed in the Durkheimian concept of religion (however modern and Eurocentric that concept may be).

Myths: Between Fable and Religion

As for the modern sense of "myth," we are once again forced to undertake an effort of transcultural translation when making use of a definition derived from early anthropology, notably the field of the history of religions: this is the concept of the myth as a "narrative featuring supernatural beings, imaginary actions, collective fantasies, etc.," according to the first meaning of "myth" presented by the *Dictionnaire Larousse*,[5] or alternatively, according to the more precise definition offered by the *Encyclopaedia Britannica*, it is:

A symbolic narrative, usually of unknown origin and at least partly traditional, that ostensibly relates actual events and that is especially associated with religious belief. It is distinguished from symbolic behavior (cult, ritual) and symbolic places or objects (temples, icons). Myths are specific accounts of gods or superhuman beings involved in extraordinary events or circumstances in a time that is unspecified but which is understood as existing apart from ordinary human experience.[6]

At this point it is worth revisiting one of the key stages of anthropological thought. We should recall that, in the comparison undertaken by the Jesuit Father Joseph-François Lafitau between the "customs of the Amerindian savages" and the "customs of early times," the myths of the ancient world play a special role. These myths are viewed as "ridiculous fables" that are shrouded in "thick darkness" (1724, I:94–95)—especially the myths of the Greeks, such as Prometheus's journey to Heaven to steal fire or the creation of men and women by Deucalion and Pyrrha; as such they are considered to have contributed to corrupting an original Religion, of the sort that was later instituted by the emergence of Christianity. On the other hand, in *La scienza nuova prima* published one year after the work of Lafitau, Giambattista Vico ([1725] 1931, 145–73) presented the fables of the earliest poets as attempts to represent the forces of nature in human form, and thus to identify them through language; this, argues Vico, is what the Greeks did with the figures of Jupiter and Hercules [*sic!*], who were thus used to establish a "civil truth." And this was particularly the case of the "Homeric fables."

Myth thus came to be conceived as narrative, and more precisely fantastical narrative, with the "myths" of ancient Greece serving as the archetype. These myths are then conceived as together constituting a "mythology," which Jean-Pierre Vernant describes as "a set of narratives about gods and heroes, that is to say, the two types of characters to whom ancient cities addressed cults" (1981, 472). The historian of religions Jan Bremmer describes myths even more broadly as "traditional tales relevant to society" (1987, 7), with the proviso that, in the case of Greek myths, the supernatural presence of gods and heroes is indicative of a religion that is strongly anchored in society.[7]

In any case, we can observe that these different conceptions of myths-as-narratives raise two questions: the first question concerns the fictional, or indeed fictitious status of these narratives that form part of a cultural tradition, with particular reference to the type of reception that they elicit, such as an attitude of belief; the second question concerns the relationship that these definitions establish with the domain of what we commonly refer to as religion, in its Durkheimian dual conception as both a system of beliefs in supernatural beings and a set of ritual practices.

On a purely operative basis, with a view to examining the sort of belief elicited by the narrative fictions that we commonly conceive as myth, we could, therefore, adopt the overarching instrumental definition proposed by Bruce Lincoln (2012, 75–76), who argues that a religion can be identified by four distinctive manifestations: a discourse whose subject matter and status transcend the human, the temporal, and the contingent; a set of practices whose purpose is to construct an autonomous world with its own protagonists; a community whose members construct their identity by reference to this discourse and these practices; and an institution that regulates this discourse, these practices, and this community. This modern conception of religion, when applied to a transcendence that takes the form of supernatural beings, leads us once again to human practices identified as rituals and to forms of discourse that we now refer to as myths. Religion, or rather religions, can thus be understood in anthropological terms as historical-cultural and socio-cultural realities that are both flexible and shifting.[8]

Back to Indigenous Categories: *Mûthos* and *Lógos*

On this question, it is essential to return briefly to indigenous categories and the way in which they were originally used. This matter has been addressed repeatedly, starting with the lexical and semantic problem. In the case of "myth," we have borrowed from the Greek language a term that did not have the same meanings in its original uses. From as early as Homeric poetry, the term *mûthos* referred to a developed speech, a speech expressed with arguments, that is to say, a speech uttered in order to convince. To this end, the person who uttered the *mûthos* could refer to a heroic narrative as an example to support their demonstration; that narrative could be referred to as a *lógos*, which is the term used by Helen to designate the story of her divine birth, which she also presents as being implausible. In Plato's dialogues, *mûthos* (now referring to heroic narrative) could be used in the service of *lógos*, that is, in the service of discursive demonstration. This is notably the case of the version of the Prometheus myth that Plato adapts to his particular purpose in the *Protagoras* (Calame, 2012a).

It is significant that Plato in particular uses the verb *muthol@geîn*, which obviously combines both *mûthos* and *lógos*. We should recall here the verses of the *Odyssey* (XII, 447–54) in which Odysseus reaches the end of his long narrative, related in the first person, of his return from Troy to eventually arrive in Phaeacia, where he is received at the court of King Alcinous; Odysseus then uses the verb *muthologeúein* to refer to his narrative of his earlier stay with the nymph Calypso. However, in the *Republic*, Socrates speaks of the narratives to be used for the education of future citizens, arguing that the founders of the city must be familiar with the models used by poets to deliver their narratives (*muthol@geîn*, 379a). Significantly, the same verb is used again when speaking, not of the *mûthoi* and *lógoi* about gods, demons, heroes, and those who are in Hades, but about narratives about humans. Poets (*poietaí*) and historians (*logopoioí*, 392a)—note that both these terms are based on the verb *poieîn*, "to make"—must avoid singing and relating (*muthologeîn*, 392b) the happiness of men without respect for the principle of justice.

As I argued in a chapter in the collection *La fiction change-t-elle le monde?* (Calame, 2023), a central idea here is that of poetic crafting, which also, through the verb *pláttein*, brings us back to the etymological sense of fiction as manufacture, crafting. At the beginning of the same long development of the *Republic*, Socrates states that the education of future citizens is to be based on gymnastics and music: the exercises of the gymnasium for the body, and the arts of the Muses for the soul. The concept of music includes that of narratives (*lógoi*, 376e), and among these *lógoi* it is important to distinguish between truth and lie. Paradoxically, both types of narrative have their place in the education of citizens. Children are to be the main recipients of *mûthoi* (377a), as, even though these are falsehoods on the whole, they nevertheless present some truth. Indeed, young people are subjected to an education that "crafts" or "shapes" them, and so it is appropriate to leave an imprint (*túpos*, 379b) on them. It is, therefore, necessary to exercise control over those crafted stories (*múthous plasthéntas*), and consequently over those who fabricate stories (*muthopoioî*): good narratives should be kept, the others should be rejected. The criterion for judging between them is a moral one. For example, such immoral narratives as those composed by the poet Hesiod recounting the castration of Ouranos and the acts of anthropophagi committed by his son Cronos on his own children should be passed over in silence.[9]

The Fictional Charm of "Archaeology"

Let us turn now from the question of the creation of the Greek narrative fictions that we call myths, and their educational uses, to the question of their pragmatic status. For this, we must also take into account the aesthetic and intellectual attitude that they elicit. Maintaining our focus on the indigenous use of these terms, our enquiry leads us to Thucydides, who is wrongly considered to be the founder of history as writing of history. At the end of the "archaeological" prelude to his history of the Peloponnesian War, Thucydides acknowledges that his research on ancient times (*palaiá*; 1, 20, 1) is based on testimonies in which it is not always easy to trust (*pisteûsai*). Indeed, the historian relies on the accounts (*légousi*; 1, 9, 2) of poets such as Homer for events such as King Minos of Crete's conquest of the Cyclades in the Aegean Sea, Agamemnon leading the Greek army to the Trojan War, and the domination of the Peloponnese by its eponymous hero Pelops. As for the credibility (*pisteúein*; 1, 9, 3) that should be attributed to these *lógoi*, it is necessary to take into account their poetic effect: Homer, as a poet, undoubtedly adorned (*kosmêsai*; 1, 10, 3) those narratives in order to magnify the reported heroic acts. Thucydides therefore concludes, with regard to those events from ancient times, that caution and research are required, since human beings are so predisposed to accept local oral traditions, such as the Athenian tradition regarding the murder of the tyrant Hipparchus by Harmodius and Aristogeiton.

According to Thucydides, the discourse of the historian, based on an evaluation of evidence and testimonies, is more trustworthy than the embellishments used not only by poets, but also by the logographers themselves, that is, the composers of narratives who are eager to seduce their public through a charming "fictional" mode.[10] In Thucydides's clear examination of past events, which is also a way of anticipating the future because of the constancy of human "nature," the principle of utility takes precedence and makes the work into "a possession forever" (1, 22, 4). As for these acts of the past, whatever the form of the narrative that conveys them, and whatever effects of fictionality or charm may be present, they are always designated—by Thucydides, Herodotus, and later by the rhetorician Isocrates—as *tà archaîa* ("the facts of origins"), *tà palaiá* ("things of the old times"), or even *tà patrôia* ("deeds of the forefathers").

These actions of the past are not "myths," but they correspond to "archaeologies." Poets recreate them in accordance with both the circumstances of the ritual performance of their songs and the political and cultural conjuncture that determines the configuration of a particular narrative, which must be exemplary, if only by antinomy. Historians integrate these "archeological" enquiries into their investigations with the same concern for exemplarity. When Thucydides considers an account of the first domination of one ruler over the Aegean Sea, by King Minos, he sees it as a narrative anticipating the contemporary domination of the Athenians over that same sea, which was also one of the causes of the Peloponnesian War. In this respect, the historicity of the reported actions (*erga;* 1, 21, 2) is never questioned, and although the modern distinction between fact and fiction is useful here, the essential difference lies in the aesthetic criterion mentioned above, since poets tend to magnify and embellish the "facts" when they sing them and logographers are less concerned with the truth (*alethésteron*; 1, 21, 1) than with adorning their narratives with charm. Consequently, the appropriate attitude is a certain degree of caution (*ou pisteúon*): distrust rather than either belief or disbelief.

Back to Referential Fiction, via Pragmatics

Returning now from our anthropological engagement with apparently fictional phenomena from another culture to a critical engagement with our own modern concepts, we can make three different, but complementary, observations.

First of all, from the point of view of the theory of possible worlds and its operative applicability to the field of narrative fiction, we should note once again that the fictional narrative cannot be evaluated according to the parameters of modal logic organizing possible worlds, as formulated by Saul Kripke. But in this respect, the solution reaffirmed by Thomas Pavel in the "unpublished afterword" to the new 2017 French edition of *Fictional Worlds*, titled *L'Univers de la fiction* (2017, 248–52; but see also in this work 97–108) would not be adequate to an understanding of the narrative settings of Greek myths. Pavel's conception involves considering the worlds of literary fiction as worlds offering two levels of reality: one level corresponding to the "really real" world, and the other corresponding to a "salient" world. At the moment of reading, the "salient" world is substituted for the "really real" world. The reader is permitted, not so much through reference but rather through an interplay of inferences, to participate, or at least adhere to both real worlds and fictional ones.

However, there is a constant back and forth movement—for example, in the dramatic staging of the specific version of the "myth" of Helen's abduction presented by Euripides in the corresponding tragedy—between the dramatized action taking place in the time of heroes and, not the real world, but the representations and practices manifested for the spectators through the poet's creative language. These poetic interferences between heroic narrative action and the current political, religious, and cultural world with its values, representations, and practices can particularly be observed in the songs of the chorus; its different voices are by turns emotional, interpretative, and ritually performative. It is, therefore, not a matter of inference, but of reference through the intermediary of a world that is undoubtedly a possible world, but one that is narrativized and firmly anchored in a real world made of practices and representations, whose meanings are developed by the poet, at the same time as eliciting both aesthetic and affective emotion (see Calame, 2020).

As far as religion is concerned, including both the world of belief that it implies and the ritual practices that support that belief, this interplay of poetic and fictional creation of a referential order is particularly evident in the verses that conclude the final sung intervention of the chorus, which is made up of Helen's followers and companions (verses 1497–1511). The young women directly address the Dioscuri, the sons of Tyndareus, to call for their intervention. The chorus asks the two deified heroes to accompany their sister on her voyage back to Sparta, just as sailors would call for the protection of Zeus through the two deified heroes. And, returning again to the represented heroic action, the Dioscuri are also called upon to wash Helen of the "dishonor of a barbarian bed" (verses

1506–07), even though the heroine never saw the walls of Ilium, a Troy that, for Athenian spectators of the fifth century, belonged to historical reality.

Furthermore, the construction of a fiction in a particular narrative configuration produces something that we could designate as a possible world, but more specifically it is a semantic universe of an extraordinary poetic richness. Staying with Euripides's *Helen* and the interventions of the chorus, the song marking the conclusion of the tragedy evokes the "Phoenician ship of Sidon" (verse, 1451) which will carry Helen, who has found her husband Menelaus in Egypt, on her return journey to Sparta. The chorus members metonymically address the "oar, dear mother of noisy strokes" (verses, 1452–53). The oar, addressed in the second person, becomes the leader of the "beautiful choruses" of dolphins (verse, 1454) which swim around the ship, while Galene, the daughter of Pontus, the incarnation of calm seas, asks the sailors, in direct speech, to spread the sails to bring Helen back home safely. The young chorus members, therefore, not only make the return of Helen to Sparta into a choral dance, but also project onto this metaphorical dance the choreographic song that they are performing.[11] The double metaphor allows the poetic world of the tragedy (which we can call a possible world) to coincide with the actual world of the ritual practice of the choral group, and this process occurs *hic et nunc* in the presence of the spectators ritually assembled in the sanctuary-theater of Dionysus Eleuthereus, at the foot of the Acropolis of Athens at the end of the fifth century.

Ultimately, when we speak of the relation between the possible world of fiction and the real world, both through poetic utterance and the procedures of invocations in the second person, we are speaking of pragmatics. From this point of view, a crucial role is played by the conclusion of the tragedy, which draws a connection between the dramatization of the narrative fiction and the founding of a ritual tradition: the narrative unfolding of the representation, which elicits belief, leads back to ritual practice, thus combining the two components of religion according to Durkheim's operative definition. Indeed, the ritual invitation by the choral group of Helen's companions proves to be effective, since the Dioscuri ultimately appear on stage to provide the plot of the tragedy with its practical conclusion (verses, 1661–69):

I address my sister.
Sail on with your husband, you will have a favorable wind.
We two, your savior brothers,
Will escort you, astride the waves, to your homeland.
When you reach you destination, you will have reached the end of your life.
You will be invoked as a goddess and with the Dioscuri
You will participate in the libations and the gifts of hospitality
From mortal men. Zeus himself wishes it so.

The Dioscuri then continue their founding of the rite by an act of naming: the small island off the coast of Attica which received Helen when the god Hermes removed her from the hands of Paris, who was taking her to Troy, will henceforth bear the name of the heroine. As for Menelaus, the rediscovered husband, his destiny is to reach the islands of the Blessed. For him too, the Dioscuri foresee both heroization and divinization, corresponding to the important cult in Sparta devoted to both husband and wife, on the site of Therapne.[12]

This narrative and dramatic conclusion performs an etiological function, since it makes the cult in Sparta honoring Helen, who was heroized then deified, into the end of the narrative plot developed in the tragedy. From the point of view of the construction of the dramatized narrative, the concluding verses that Euripides places in the mouths of the Dioscuri make the spatio-temporal framework of the narrative fiction (Egypt, then Sparta at the time of the heroes of the Trojan War) coincide with the time and space inhabited by the spectators ritually participating in the performance of Euripides's tragedy: Attica at the end of the fifth century BCE.[13] In this foundational etiological conclusion, from a pragmatic perspective, an essential role is played by the enunciative postures adopted first by the group of Helen's followers in their choral song, and then by the Dioscuri themselves, her brothers; for this conclusion corresponds both to the denouement of the dramatized plot that revolves around the choral group, and to the practical realization of the fictional world that the dramatized narration deploys. Belief is maintained both by the poetic dramatization of the heroic action and by the foundational act that connects it to ritual practices. Furthermore, it has been shown that, in the sung parts of Attic tragedy in particular, the interpretative modality of the choral voice can be linked to the voice of a poet who, as in the case of Pindar, is generally very enunciatively present in the different forms of "lyric" poetry (see Calame, 2019), from which tragedy is partly derived.

The pragmatics of narrative fiction, as manifested in Greek tragedy, therefore develops on three different levels: in the narrative deployment of the dramatized mimetic action, which leads, in the case discussed here, to the foundation of ritual practices; in the semantic configuration of a "possible world" as a complex poetic reality; and by means of the enunciative modalities that carry out the deployment of the dramatized action. This pragmatics obviously has a practical dimension, but also a symbolic, aesthetic, and emotional dimension. This triple poetic development is thus a matter of narrative logic, of metaphorical-semantic configuration, and of the enunciative modalities of the spoken and sung word; it turns that which appears to us as a myth into a poetic fiction (in the etymological sense of these two terms), and also into both a referential and pragmatic fiction.

This is especially the case since the tragedies of Aeschylus, Sophocles, and Euripides constituted ritualized musical performances, carried out in the sanctuary-theater dedicated to Dionysus Eleuthereus, during the ritual festival of the Great Dionysia. In this respect, they were the object of an implicit pragmatic "pact" on the part of the public for whom they were intended, who were participants in the worship of a god, which we could consider to be of a religious order.[14]

Through a mimetic poetics, in the Aristotelian sense of these two words, and through a sung and danced performance, the process of poetic creation makes the narrative fiction into a ritual act pertaining both to religion, as understood in its operative definition, and to the regime of belief that establishes it—in this case a regime of a polytheistic order (Calame, forthcoming). The dynamics of referential fiction at work in Attic tragedy contribute to reshaping and sustaining this regime of belief, while inscribing it in a politically and religiously active cultural memory.[15]

Translated from the French by Sam Ferguson.

Notes

1 Euripides, *Helen*, vv. 16–23. Except where indicated otherwise, all citations from works not originally in English are our own translations.

2 See also the earlier article of 1899, where Durkheim proposes the following definition of the phenomena that he designates as religious: "The phenomena that we call religious consist of obligatory beliefs, connected to defined practices that relate to objects given in these beliefs" (1899, 21). On the various attempts that have been made at defining religion by anthropologists and historians of religion, see the useful collection provided by Meylan (2019).

3 For the immediate purposes of finding a purely operative definition, I will leave aside conceptions of religion inspired by cognitivist research, or even by neuroscience, which are based on the concept of the contagion of counter-intuitive ideas, and which are also strongly Christianocentric.

4 In this regard, our present reflections contradict the statement that concludes Schaeffer's study, arguing that fictional representations are distinguished by a contract of ludic feigning: "Indeed, this contract invites us to isolate the representations that it frames from the background network of beliefs that delimit our vision of reality, and to construct the fictional universe as a world closed on itself" (2005, 35).

5 https://www.larousse.fr/dictionnaires/francais/mythe/53630

6 https://www.britannica.com/topic/myth, entry written by Richard G.A. Buxton, Kees W. Bolle, and Jonathan Z. Smith.

7 Bremmer later proposed a slightly different formulation: "performances of traditional plots relevant to society" (2021, 67–68).

8 These various reflections on the elusive concept of religion will be developed in a future study. As for Greek religion, see in particular the synoptic monograph by Bremmer (2021).

9 See the extended commentary of Giovanni Cerri on this important passage (2015, 37–55).

10 I have previously proposed to use the term "fictional" to translate the term *muthôdes*, as used by Thucydides 1, 21, 1 and 1, 22, 4; see Calame (2011, 64–66), including the numerous references in these pages concerning the use of the terms *tà archaîa* and *tà palaiá*.

11 I am referring here to the process of "choral projection" described by Albert Henrichs in his excellent studies of the chorus in Attic tragedy, as well as to the polyphonic combination of three voices that can be found in the choral songs composed by the tragic poets; on this, see the references in my 2017 study, 93–111.

12 On the subject of the dual cult honoring Helen in Sparta, the heroic honors celebrated at the Platanistas, and her likely worship as a deity at Therapne, see the comprehensive and critical account by Edmunds (2016, 164–73, 174–85).

13 On the fictional and mimetic reference to both the dramatic action represented and the ritual performed *hic et nunc*, in the case of the conclusion to Aeschylus's *Oresteia*, through the transformation of the Erinyes into the Eumenides by Athena's will, see Calame (2017, 117–24).

14 See Calame (2017: 65–88) on the Great Dionysia, and Lejeune (1975) 1996 on the concept of a reading pact.

15 On the concept of "referential fiction," see the study by Calame (2010), with apologies for the number of bibliographical self-references.

Works Cited

Bremmer, Jan. 1987. "What Is a Greek Myth?" In *Interpretations of Greek Mythology*, edited by Jan Bremmer, 1–9. London: Croom Helm.

Bremmer, Jan. 2021. *Greek Religion*. 2nd ed. Cambridge: Cambridge University Press.

Calame, Claude. 2010. "La pragmatique poétique des mythes grecs: fiction référentielle et performance rituelle." In *Fiction et cultures*, edited by Françoise Lavocat and Anne Duprat, 33–56. Paris: Lucie, SFLGC.

Calame, Claude. 2011. *Mythe et histoire dans l'antiquité grecque: la création symbolique d'une colonie*. 2nd ed. Paris: Les Belles Lettres.

Calame, Claude. 2012a. "The Pragmatics of 'Myth' in Plato's Dialogues: The Story of Prometheus in the *Protagoras*." In *Plato and Myth: Studies in the Use and Status of Platonic Myths*, edited by Catherine Collobert, Pierre Destrée and Francisco J. Gonzalez, 127–43. Leiden: Brill.

Calame, Claude. 2012b. "Vraisemblance référentielle, nécessité narrative, poétique de la vue: l'historiographie grecque classique entre factuel et fictif." *Annales: histoire, sciences sociales* 67: 81–101.

Calame, Claude. 2015. *Qu'est-ce que la mythologie grecque?* Paris: Gallimard.

Calame, Claude. 2017. *La tragédie chorale: poésie grecque et rituel musical*. Paris: Les Belles Lettres.

Calame, Claude. 2019. "Greek Lyric Poetry, a Non-Existent Genre?" In *Greek Lyric. Oxford Readings in Classical Studies*, edited by Ian Rutherford, 33–60. Oxford: Oxford University Press.

Calame, Claude, 2020. "Narratology and the Test of Greek Myths: The Poetic Birth of a Colonial City." In *Contemporary French and Francophone Narratology*, edited by John Pier, 172–200. Columbus: The Ohio State University Press.

Calame, Claude. 2023. "Poetic Forms of Narrative and Pragmatic Fiction: Poiein—Plattein—Prattein." In *Can Fiction Change the World?* edited by Alison James, Akihiro Kubo and Françoise Lavocat, 17–30. Oxford: Legenda.

Calame, Claude. Forthcoming. "Pour une pragmatique de la fiction impossible: mythes grecs et mimésis." In *Impossible Fictions*, proceedings of conference at the University of Chicago, March 2022. Fabula.org.

Cerri, Giovanni. 2015. *La poétique de Platon*. Translated by Myrto Gondicas. Paris: Les Belles Lettres.

Durkheim, Émile. 1899. "De la définition des phénomènes religieux." *Année sociologique* 2: 1–28.

Durkheim, Émile. (1912) 1995. *The Elementary Forms or Religious Life*. Translated by Karen E. Fields. New York: Free Press.

Edmunds, Lowell. 2016. *Stealing Helen: The Myth of the Abducted Wife in Comparative Perspective*. Princeton, NJ: Princeton University Press.

Lafitau, Joseph-François. 1724. *Mœurs des sauvages amériquains comparées aux mœurs des premiers temps*. Paris: Saugrain Hochereau.

Lavocat, Françoise. 2010a. "Les genres de la fiction: état des lieux et propositions." In *La théorie littéraire des mondes possibles*, edited by Françoise Lavocat, 15–51. Paris: CNRS.

Lavocat, Françoise, ed. 2010b. *La théorie littéraire des mondes possibles*. Poétique. Paris: CNRS.

Lavocat, Françoise. 2016. *Fait et fiction: pour une frontière*. Poétique. Paris: Seuil.

Lavocat, Françoise, and Anne Duprat, eds. 2010. *Fiction et cultures*. Paris: Lucie éditions, SFLGC.

Lejeune, Philippe. 1996. *Le pacte autobiographique*. 2nd ed. Paris: Seuil.

Lincoln, Bruce. 2012. *Gods and Demons, Priests and Scholars: Critical Exploration in the History of Religions*. Chicago, IL: University of Chicago Press.

Meylan, Nicolas. 2019. *Qu'est-ce que la religion? Onze auteurs, onze définitions*. Geneva: Labor et Fides.

Pavel, Thomas. 2017. *Univers de la fiction*. 2nd French ed. Paris: Seuil. First published as *Fictional Worlds* Cambridge, MA: Harvard University Press, 1986.

Schaeffer, Jean-Marie. 2005. "Quelles vérités pour quelles fictions?" *L'Homme* 175–176 (July–September): 19–36.

Schaeffer, Jean-Marie. 2010. *Why Fiction?* Translated by Dorrit Cohn. Lincoln: University of Nebraska Press.

Tylor, Edward B. (1871) 1913. *Primitive Culture: Researches into the Development of Mythology, Philosophy, Religion, Language, Art, and Custom*. London: John Murray.

Vernant, Jean-Pierre. 1981. "Grèce: le problème mythologique." In *Dictionnaire des mythologies*, edited by Yves Bonnefoy, 1:471–75. Paris: Larousse.

Veyne, Paul. 1983. *Les Grecs ont-ils cru à leurs mythes?* Paris: Seuil.

Vico, Giambattista. (1725) 1931. *La scienza nuova prima*. Edited by Fausto Nicolini. Bari: Laterza.

27

FICTION AND BELIEF

Approaching Medieval Latin Christendom

Julie Orlemanski

Fictions invite their audiences to respond to events recounted—to feel, to visualize, to infer, to speculate. These responses have long been understood as the outcome of a certain kind of belief, belief that may be qualified or partial but that is nonetheless powerful. Such "make-believe" occupies an unstable place alongside other forms of believing, like religious faith or general convictions about what counts as true. How is it that readers can entertain fiction's provisional assertions? The present chapter considers the relations of fiction and belief in the literary cultures of medieval Latin Christendom, including the various literatures in the vernacular (or the regional language of spoken discourse) that gradually developed alongside Latin writing. In many modern literary histories, the medieval period has served as an archaic predecessor to the emergence of fiction-properly-so-called. According to these accounts, the Middle Ages lacked a fully formed idea or practice of fiction. By contrast, the present chapter argues that sophisticated and contested models of fictionality were in circulation in the Middle Ages, models that operated in close relation to authenticated discourses like historiography or religious doctrine while being demarcated from them. Mine is a broad, even promiscuous, understanding of medieval fiction, grounded on the assumption that fiction-making in any period takes place at the interface between language's fundamental capacity to portray the nonactual and the regularizations of that capacity in specific discursive contexts.

Before turning to my overarching arguments below, I begin with a specific example—a medieval reflection on the unstable calibrations of fiction, belief, and religious truth. In his *Speculum caritatis* ("Mirror of Charity," completed in the early 1140s), the Cistercian monk, and later abbot, Aelred of Rievaulx recounts a long conversation he had with a novice in the monastic order. At the time, Aelred was a novice-master, in charge of guiding new Cistercian recruits into the rigors of monastic life. The novice approaches Aelred with a concern: before his entry into the monastery, "when he was still in the secular condition and way of life," he felt his love for God more intensely and more often than he does now.[1] Why should that be, since he now lives the devout life of a monk?

Crucially for the interests of the present chapter, Aelred seeks to instruct the junior monk by comparing the impassioned piety he used to feel to experiences of literary fiction. As Aelred explains, no one should evaluate love according to "momentary affection" (*momentaneum ... affectum*), a point that he illustrates with an example:

Sometimes in tragedies or in vain songs [*in tragoediis uanisue carminibus*], someone [*quisquam*] is portrayed [*fingitur*] as persecuted, whose loveable handsomeness, marvelous courage,

349

DOI: 10.4324/9781003119456-31

or gracious disposition have been extolled. If a person hearing these things being sung [*haec...
canuntur audiens*] or listening to them being recited [*cernens... recitentur*] is moved [*mouea-
tur*] by some emotion [*affectu*], even to the point of weeping [*ad expressionem lacrymarum*],
would it not be terribly absurd on the basis of this worthless devotion [*uanissima pietate*] to
make an inference about the quality of his love, that he should love some fabulous being,
whomsoever it is [*fabulosum illum nescio quem*]—a being for whose rescue he would not pay
a small fraction of his possessions, even if all these events were taking place before his very
eyes [*uere prae oculis*]?

(II.17.50; 198–99)

Aelred sketches a listener who reacts passionately to the misadventures of a narrative "someone," a
fabulous entity devised and formed (*fingitur*) in a literary text. Although the listener may be driven to
tears, such a character has only a partial claim on the listener's ontological commitments. After all,
it would be absurd to imagine the listener materially helping this *fabulosum*, no matter how vivid the
narrative events may seem. Aelred's point, as he goes on to make explicit, is that back in the man's
secular life, punctuated as it was with sporadic devotional enthusiasm—God too was treated like a
fictional character. Emotions may have been catalyzed and tears shed, but to think of these as true
measures of love is preposterous.

In a sign that Aelred's comparison of fiction and devotion has hit its mark, the novice responds
with penitent acknowledgement, and he echoes the account in terms of his own literary experience:

At these words the novice blushed and, with his head bowed and his eyes fixed on the ground,
he said: "Truly so, very truly so. For also in fables [*fabulis*] that are popularly made up [*uulgo...
finguntur*] about that Arthur, whoever he is [*de nescio quo ... Arthuro*], I remember I was sometimes moved to the point of shedding tears."

(II.17.51; 199)

With this confession, the novice updates Aelred's terminology of classical poetry (*tragoediae* and
carmina) by mapping it onto the genre of chivalric romance, "fables ... popularly made up about a
certain Arthur." As this account suggests, the novice brings with him into the monastery a literary
sensibility that has been shaped outside of it and that influences his rhetorical, narrative, and affective
expectations. Indeed, the novice continues his confession by connecting his experience of romances
directly to that of devotional utterance:

I am not just a little ashamed of my vanity, that if those things that are read with piety about
the Lord, or chanted, or, of course, said publicly in sermons [*de Domino pie leguntur, uel
cantantur, uel certe publico sermone dicuntur*] should be able to wring a tear from me, then I
immediately congratulate myself on my holiness.

(II.17.51; 199)

In a calculus of tears, religious and non-religious texts, sermons and fables, operate similarly for the
novice. Classical poetry, courtly romance, and devotional speech all have the power to move their
audiences to powerful but ephemeral emotions. Against such indistinguishable rushes of feeling,
Aelred is concerned to separate out what he presents as love's true expression—committed action,
exemplified by the monk's lifelong commitment to asceticism and obedience.

One subtle concern of Aelred's account is the ontological status of the entities to which these
several kinds of texts refer. Aelred sets up an ironic contrast between the plenitude of God's reality

and the unreality of the figures in fictional narratives—"some fabulous being, whosoever he is [*fabulosum nescio quem*]" and "that Arthur, whoever he is [*de nescio quo ... Arthuro*]." Readers have recognized echoes of Augustine's *Confessions* throughout the *Speculum caritatis* and, in this part of the text, of Augustine's reflections on the allure of classical spectacle and literature specifically. Barbara Newman briefly notes the source for Aelred's phrase "nescio quis" (Newman, 2003, 361, n.23)—an idiom used to express uncertainty about a particular entity, as in "I know not who" or "somebody, a certain person" (Lewis and Short, *nescio*). In the *Confessions*, the phrase occurs in a passage where Augustine recalls how greatly he preferred reading poetry to learning the rules of grammar. Coming to know Latin, he acknowledges,

> was better than the poetry I was later forced to learn about the wanderings of some legendary fellow named Aeneas [*Aeneae nescio cuius errores*], forgetful of my own wanderings, and to weep over the death of a Dido who took her own life from love. In reading this, O God my life, I myself was meanwhile dying in my alienation from you, and my miserable condition brought no tear to my eyes.
>
> *(I.xiii.20; Augustine, 1992, 15)*

Here, again, is the weighing of tears. Here again is the effort to adjudicate literary sensibilities and ontological commitments as they extend across the boundary of a conversion—from paganism to Christianity in Augustine's case, from secular to monastic life for the novice. Like Augustine, Aelred qualifies the narrative protagonist with the phrase "nescio quis," set in ironic contrast with God's ontological plenitude. In this way, "nescio quis" emerges in Aelred's intertextual use of it as something like a term of art, one that links Aeneas, Dido, Arthur, and all the "fabulous" persons that incite a kind of literary belief. We might even take the phrase as a point of contact between Aelred and present-day scholarly conversations about the role of proper names in fiction, conversations that range from literary history, about the "nobodies" of novelistic character (Gallagher, 1994), to the philosophy of language, wondering after names that do and do not refer (for an overview, Freitag, 2019). The palpable emotions that these names help catalyze, according to Aelred, demand second-order evaluation. It is at a distance from the moment of impassioned reception that God can be reliably distinguished from literary phantasm, and "momentary affection" separated out from real love.

This short passage from Aelred's *Speculum caritatis* suggests that the medieval monastery could be an environment of literary innovation, where different narrative and rhetorical sensibilities clashed and fused and where lines between fiction and belief were drawn and redrawn. Indeed, Aelred's treatise meant to intervene in such negotiations. Because Cistercians required novices to be at least fifteen years of age to join the order (rather than joining as children, as was common in other forms of monasticism), many new monks had already received a schoolroom introduction to classical Latin poetry, not to mention a taste for the burgeoning vernacular literary culture of the courts (Tahkokallio, 2008). This was true of Aelred himself, who spent his boyhood at the court of King David of Scotland. It is perhaps then no surprise that Cistercian monasteries were lively settings for experiments with fiction, evident in the order's special relationship to the erotic poetry of the Song of Songs (Orlemanski, 2021), its role in gathering and disseminating didactic stories (McGuire, 2002), and its cultivation of techniques for imaginative immersion and visionary contemplation (Newman, 2005). While Aelred's *Speculum caritatis* could be cited as evidence of medieval Christianity's antagonism toward fiction, that would be to ignore the complexity and ambivalence of the encounter. Aelred acknowledges the specificity of fiction and its power, and the dialogue he has composed draws on techniques of fiction-writing in an effort to domesticate literature's outsized emotional force and its cultural prominence.

In the remainder of this essay, I attend to some of the theoretical and historiographic issues that arise in approaching fiction and belief in medieval Latin Christendom. My recommendation is for a broad, but not unbounded, idea of fictionality. Following consideration of grounding methodological issues, I turn my attention to three topics central to the study of medieval fictionality: to the limits of literary-theoretical vocabularies, to the genres against which fiction was defined, and to the varied scales of medieval fictions.

Theoretical and Historiographic Groundwork

Theorists and scholars have often defined fiction in terms of the realist novel, by identifying the emergence of fictionality with the novel's distinctive practice of referring to nonactual people with regular-sounding names (e.g., Gallagher, 2006; Paige, 2011). Even when explicit accounts of the "rise of fictionality" are absent, realist novels tend to provide the key examples and case studies for theorizing fiction (e.g., Cohn, 1999). As Eva von Contzen and Stefan Tilg point out, "relatively few studies […] deal with the premodern period" (Contzen and Tilg, 2020, 91). What model of fiction should be used to study nonmodern literary cultures, which stand apart from the consolidated norms of novelistic narrative?

The matter becomes more urgent when we recognize that histories of fiction—tracing fictionality as idea and as literary mode across time—are often told as narratives of epistemic progress. Modernity, so the story goes, brings with it more sophisticated distinctions between fact and fiction. Zones of mixed referential truth, of legend and lore, are gradually rationalized, and literary authors both participate in and offer consolations for the course of disenchantment. On this account, fiction requires a certain civilizational coordination of rationality and imagination, disbelief and belief. Yet, there are conceptual and political reasons to reject this progressive, periodizing narrative (Orlemanski, 2019). As postcolonial thinkers have shown, at least since the stadial histories of the Enlightenment, claims for the uniqueness of modern circumstances have functioned to locate what is nonmodern outside the purview of a whole range of concepts—the individual, rationality, reflexivity, the political sphere, and historical consciousness, among others (see, e.g., Chakrabarty, 2000). Meanwhile, ideologies of secularism and disenchantment recount modernity's emergence from a supposedly credulous past, sometimes played by the Middle Ages, sometimes by non-Western, "nonmodern" cultures where "enchantment" has continued its reign.[2] Such entanglements between fiction and disenchantment are neither superficial nor accidental because both notions have historically involved judgments about the organization of belief and its proper limits.

"Belief," of course, has a double meaning in present-day parlance. It is, on the one hand, the mental conviction that something is true, pertinent to any apprehension of reality. On the other hand, it also designates religious faith, or trust in a transcendent being or order. These two senses are closely entwined in modernity's double narrative of secularism and disenchantment, or of religion's compartmentalization alongside the ascendance of scientific rationality. They are also closely linked in post-medieval accounts of medieval fiction. In the memorable words of playwright Ben Jonson (d. 1637), medieval romances were "Abortives of the fabulous, dark cloister,/Sent out to poison courts and infest manners" (*The New Inn* I.vi.127–28; Jonson, 1984, 90). The Scottish novelist Tobias Smollett, in the 1748 preface to *The Adventures of Roderick Random*, remarks of the Middle Ages that

> when the minds of men were debauched by the imposition of priestcraft to the most absurd pitch of credulity, the authors of romance arose, and losing sight of probability, filled their performances with the most monstrous hyperboles … and the world actually began to be infected

with the spirit of knight-errantry, when Cervantes, by an inimitable piece of ridicule, reformed the taste of mankind.

(Smollett, [1748] 1824, x–xi)

In Smollett's sketch, the effects of "priestcraft" reached beyond benighted doctrine to general credulity, moving from religious belief to all beliefs. The disposition ultimately infected reality, "the world," with the absurd contents of fiction—just as Jonson's "fabulous, dark cloisters" "poisoned" and "infested" the rest. According to Smollett, it is the novel that comes to the rescue.

A similar conception of the Middle Ages takes on specific forms in the Renaissance, the eighteenth century, the nineteenth, and the twentieth, and it modulates across national and confessional boundaries as well. In its broad outlines, however, it has been long-lived and attaches not just to the genre of romance. It is evident, for instance, in Johan Huizinga's influential 1919 study, *The Autumn of the Middle Ages*, in which he characterizes medieval allegory as evidence for "a sort of magic idealism" that medieval people shared with "every primitive mind": "Here the ties that bind the Middle Ages to a very remote cultural past are very clearly displayed" (Huizinga, 1924, 186 and 199; see Breen, 2021, 16–20). As Katharine Breen has recently remarked, Huizinga's alteritism is representative of "the anti-Catholic vein typical of many early-twentieth-century northern European medievalists" (Breen, 2021, 17). Medieval allegory, for them, is the reflex of a religious worldview that retarded cognition itself. For scholars wary of such civilizational exclusions, it may be preferable to keep open the possibility that ritual and fiction, belief and the willing suspension of disbelief, may assume surprising or unforeseen relations in cultures different from our own.

This critical historiography nonetheless leaves us with many questions. If we step back from a novelistic or secularist conception of fictionality, what is the alternative? How might literary fiction in medieval Latin Christendom be conceived? After all, norms of semantic unearnestness do vary across milieux, and writing what is known not to be known as true can entail metaphysical, gnoseological, institutional, and rhetorical considerations that differ from place to place and epoch to epoch. Should a biblical play ever count as fiction? A devotional meditation? A narrative poem about historical events? If, analytically, we want to avoid the panfictionalism that tends to drain the category of its significance (by claiming that all representations, or all narratives, are fiction), then how are such lines to be drawn? The strategy that I adopt in the remainder of the chapter is to approach these queries with a pared-down and to some degree *unfinished* notion of fiction—simply, that fictions refer unearnestly, presenting nonactual states of affairs, and that they are recognized to do so, by at least someone.[3] Such an encompassing definition acts a bit like a trawling net, gathering many specimens for consideration and comparison. Some that wind up in the net might need to be thrown back in the sea; others will turn out to be surprisingly relevant as we seek to understand what was at stake in the period's semantic demarcations and narrative inventions.

Medieval Terminology and Its Limits

Medieval thinkers had numerous models for identifying and explaining fictionality. For the most part, these models were elaborated in Latin commentaries, prologues, and grammatical and rhetorical treatises, the transmission of which was closely tied to institutions like the grammar school, the monastery, and the university. In this body of writing, a number of important formulations on fictionality were cited and recited over the course of the Middle Ages. Yet, in practice, these several models operated in unsystematized relation to one another, and they rarely treated new literary productions, much less fictions in the vernacular, such as courtly romance. Such factors point to the limits of explicit, 'emic' categories to account for the Middle Ages' heterogeneous practices of writing what was known not to be known as true.

353

One important medieval paradigm for theorizing fiction came from the fourth-century theologian and former rhetorician Lactantius, who influentially defined poetry in terms of its deviation from true events:

It is the office of the poet [*officium poetae*] to transfer [*traducat*] things that have really occurred [*ea quae gesta sunt vere*] into other appearances [*in alias species*] and with oblique figures [*obliquis figurationibus*] to turn them about with a certain elegance [*cum decore aliquo conversa*].[4]

According to this explanation, poets transform actual situations so that they appear otherwise. As Nicolette Zeeman has shown, the process that Lactantius describes is similar to the tropic "turn" that rhetorical figures give to the literal sense—a parallel that makes good on the common etymological root of *fictio* and *figura* (Zeeman, 1996). Lactantius' statement became a commonplace of medieval discussions of poetry, appearing almost verbatim in the writings of numerous encyclopedists and commentators. Lactantius' model, we might notice, presumes a complex topology of belief. It was originally part of a euhemeristic text intended to promote Christianity to elite audiences in the Roman Empire. The pagan gods are unfit for belief, Lactantius argues, but poetry does not solicit belief in them. People who think poets are liars are wrong, he explains, because they "do not know what the measure of poetic license is (*poeticae licentiae modus*), how far it is permitted to proceed by fictionalizing (*quousque progredi fingendo liceat*)."[5] As Lactantius' formulation circulated in the Christian Middle Ages, it both authorized fiction's existence and suggested the possibility of identifying truthful traces within such fabulations. It supported practices of mythography and rationalizing commentary, even as it identified the poet with departures from the truth.

Another widely available theory, drawn from Ciceronian rhetorical manuals, was the threefold rhetorical classification of narratives according to their degree of truthfulness, as *fabula*, *argumentum*, or *historia*—"the oldest and most constant generic taxonomy in the Middle Ages" (Copeland and Sluiter, 2009, 42).[6] *Fabula* is neither true nor verisimilar, *argumentum* is fictional but narrated according to the conventions of accepted reality, and *historia* tells of actual occurrences (Mehtonen, 1996). The triad is notable for escaping the binary definition of fiction against truth and instead collocating together criteria of vericonditionality and plausibility. Verisimilitude concerns, of course, what is believable. In his commentary on Cicero's *De inventione*, shortly after the introduction of the triad, Thierry of Chartres (d. *c.* 1150) remarks,

Those things which usually appear in reality are those things through which the appearance of truth, that is verisimilitude, is usually present in narration. These are eight in number, that is, the seven circumstances and an eighth, belief [*opinio*], without which the others are worth little. For if one will have presented circumstances in the narration that are not believable to the audience, there is no plausibility.

(Translation in Copeland and Sluiter, 2009, 433, commenting on De inventione 1.21.29)

Despite the evident importance of verisimilitude to this narrative taxonomy, the genre of plausible fiction, *argumentum*, received relatively little comment in medieval literary culture. Both *fabula* and *historia* were elaborated extensively on their own, but *argumentum* and its realism were not. If discussed at all, it was just to save it out as a valorized category of narrative, with *fabula* made to bear the suspect qualities of frivolity and deceit. This is the case, for instance, in the categorization of biblical parables as *argumenta* in Thomas of Chobham's *Summa de arte praedicandi* (see translation in Copeland and Sluiter, 2009, 617).

Ideas of allegorical integument likewise constituted an important model of fictionality. According to Macrobius' influential *Commentary on the Dream of Scipio* (*c.* 400), the only kind of fabulous narrative (*narratio fabulosa*) with a valid role to play in philosophy was one that hid truths "beneath a modest veil of allegory" (Macrobius, 1952, 85). The treatise further explains that Nature, because she seeks to conceal her mysteries from those who are unworthy, prefers "to have her secrets handled by more prudent individuals through fabulous narratives" (Macrobius, 1952, 86). Bernard of Chartres (d. after 1124), in his commentary on the *Timaeus*, seems to have been the first medieval thinker to use the term *integumentum*, meaning "veil" or "covering," to characterize a text's fictional elements (Wetherbee, 2008, 132). Bernard's student William of Conches (c. 1080–c. 1154) then adopted the term and extended its significance in commentaries on Plato, Macrobius, Boethius, and other authors. The model of truth wrapped in poetic fiction was important not only to medieval scholarship but also to literary production. The twelfth-century intellectual and poet Bernardus Silvestris composed an original allegory about the creation of the universe, entitled the *Cosmographia*, that put this model into practice. A few decades later, Alan of Lille wrote a pair of allegories under the influence of the *Cosmographia*, the *Plaint of Nature* and *Anticlaudianus*. Bernardus' and Alain's works were soon regarded as masterpieces and became established as models for subsequent Latin and vernacular literature.

There are more paradigms to include in the catalogue of fiction's meta-discourse in the Middle Ages. For instance, Hermann the German's Latin translation of the Arabic commentary on Aristotle's *Poetics* by Ibn Rushd (known in the Latin West as *Averroes*, d. 1198) survives in over twenty manuscripts and was excerpted and discussed in numerous others (Zeeman, 1990, 222ff). Another possibility for theorizing fictionality was the idea of the licensed lie. In his *Soliloquies*, Augustine distinguished between a truly deceptive act (*fallax*) and a merely false one (*mendax*), with the latter reserved for mimetic activity (II.11.19). This distinction encouraged thinkers to acknowledge playful lying (*mendacium iocosum*) as its own type of activity, authorized by the poetic license to lie and make up (*licentia mentiendi et fingendi*) (Mehtonen, 1996, 18). Such license dovetailed with Horace's *Ars poetica*, where the Roman poet discusses the artistic permission (*veniam*, line 11) granted to poets and painters "to dare anything" (*quidlibet audendi*, line 10). And this list of metafictional vocabulary could be extended.

These medieval accounts of *poetria, res ficta, figmenta, fabula, argumentum, integumentum,* and poetic *licentia* are attractive rebuttals to charges of premodern conceptual naiveté. Semantic distinctions between proper and poetic signification, divisions of fictional genres on the basis of verisimilitude, and awareness that hermeneutic premises affect the operations of reference all testify to the Middle Ages' sophisticated accounts of fictionality (though none, of course, correspond precisely to the present-day paradigm of prose fiction). However, the *severalness* of these contemporary theories also suggests their partialness, or the failure of any one of them to be a governing account of fictionality, constitutive of or sufficient to the varied instances of medieval literary fiction. This partialness resonates with Zygmunt G. Barański's contention that in the Middle Ages literary texts were perceived less as exemplars of singular genres than as "storehouses of examples with which to illustrate *every kind* of textual characteristic": "No single category could even begin to suggest the full character of a work" (1995, 30). Thus, for example, an influential thirteenth-century commentary on Ovid's *Metamorphoses* announces (quite unexceptionally) that the poem is narrated in the full panoply of referential modes: *historia, argumentum, fabula,* and *comedia* (Gillespie, 2008, 198). Similarly, the *Epistle to Can Grande della Scala* (an influential Latin letter interpreting Dante Alighieri's *Divine Comedy*, perhaps by Dante himself) posits that the "form or manner of treatment" in the *Comedy* is "poetic, fictive, descriptive, digressive, and figurative; and further, it is definitive, analytical, probative, refutative, and exemplificative."[7] This emphasis on the copiousness of literary works, rather than their specification, answered to manuscript culture's habits of intensive, reiterative reading. Lacking the mechanisms of standardization and genre consolidation that eventually developed in the mass-market book trade, medieval readers privileged instead the semantic plenitude of texts, containing both truth and fiction. These contents were distinguishable, but were so *within* a larger work.

The plurality of fiction's medieval theorizations and these paradigms' uneven circulation beyond academic settings suggest why modern scholars still need a flexible, "etic" definition of fiction, one that may not have an exact parallel in the period itself (although the widely used term *fabula* may come close). The activities of metafictional commentary and literary creativity were not in lockstep. As Aelred's dialogue illustrates, medieval individuals moved among literary contexts and reflected on the claims that different literary representations made on them, even without a stable vocabulary to taxonomize that experience. Part of the interest of premodern literary cultures for a comparative poetics of fiction lies in the fact that narratives tend not to come presorted into tidy macro-genres of fiction and nonfiction. Nonetheless, both writers and audiences show interest in semantic categorization and the special kinds of meaning produced by language exempt from truthful reference.

Fiction versus What?

Audiences recognize fictions by distinguishing them from truthful discourses and from idioms referring to, or directly affecting, real states of affairs. The activity of distinction suggests that the category of fiction is *relational*—a point also elegantly expressed in Wolfgang Iser's claim that fiction is "an act of boundary crossing which, nonetheless, keeps in view what has been overstepped" (1993, xiv–xv). There were numerous truthful discourses that could be invoked and then put in abeyance to create medieval fictions—discourses like history, philosophy, legal testimony, mystical vision, prophecy, the efficacious performance of a sacrament, and everyday empirical statements. Each of these modes of truth-bearing speech had a distinctive claim to actuality; each invited different forms of ontological commitment and belief. All such claims, in turn, had the potential to be suspended, and the heterogeneous results can arguably be grouped together as fiction.

This observation troubles the centrality of the modern diacritical pairing of *fact and fiction*, which relies, as Katharine Eisaman Maus has observed, on the "silent equation of truth with the world of ordinary experience" (2020, 249). Indeed, Monika Fludernik's recent thesis on the "*rise of factuality*" helps us recognize that fiction's contrarious bond with the fact belongs to a historically particular discursive regime. As part of her critique of "rise of fictionality" narratives, Fludernik observes in counterpoint that

> What is notable for the early modern period is not its invention of fictionality but its invention of genres that provide descriptions of the real world (rather than following time-honored authority). This trend occurs in response to the public's craving for factuality[,]

an appetite stoked by the print publication of scientific endeavors, geographic discoveries, historiography, and proto-journalistic reports (Fludernik, 2018, 83). It was only with this "institutionalization of factuality" that fiction "attained its peculiar connotation as an entirely separate realm opposed to factual discourse" (84). Thus, "rather than observing a rise of fictionality," Fludernik continues, "one should therefore postulate a *rise of factuality*" (84, emphasis original). Fludernik's alternative narrative grapples with an important episode of literary-historical change, as pseudofactual novels and realist novels were popularized and fiction became intimately linked to factuality, with which it competed and to which it responded. Her historical narrative account has the advantage of not blotting out other and earlier models of fiction-making, many of which persisted long past factuality's rise and continue into the present, helping to generate fiction's ongoing heterogeneity. To borrow a distinction from Eve Sedgwick (who used it to temper claims for modernity's novelty within the history of sexuality), we can recognize the fact-fiction pair as "an important *intervening* model" without assuming it is a fully "*supervening*" one—which is to say, it was a momentous but not a totalizing shift (Sedgwick, 1990, 47).

Fludernik's comments on the historical specificity of factuality also help to foreground the changing lineaments of discourses of knowledge and truth. Michelle Karnes, in her insightful recent study of medieval marvels, draws attention to the special significance of possibility, rather than factuality, within medieval philosophies of nature. As Karnes shows, natural philosophers hold that "nature, as a concept, includes what might be as well as what is" (2022, 85). These philosophers often reason *secundum imaginationem*, by "entertain[ing] hypotheticals, often stemming from suppositions about God's absolute power" (86). Within natural philosophy, marvels are "nonimpossibilities," which "represent nature's highest creative potential" (83). As Karnes tracks the circulation of marvels across philosophical treatises, travelogues, and romance narratives, the categories of medieval fiction and medieval science assume new, surprising proximity, thanks to the common ground of possibility and language's role in expounding it.

In answering the question "fiction versus what?" medieval writers most often drew contrasts between fabular stories and the truth claims of historiography. One reason for this lay in the entangled genealogies of the genres of romance and history. The close proximity of the genres meant that history writers often felt the need to distinguish and defend their epistemic authority against the charge of fictionalizing (see, inter alia, Green, 2002; Morse, 1991; Spiegel, 1984). Yet, even apart from the close relationship between romance and history, authors often invoked history (rather than any other model of truthful discourse) to set their own compositions apart. Take, for instance, the *Ecbasis captivi*, an anonymous poem dating to the eleventh century that is the oldest surviving beast epic from medieval Europe. Populated with talking animals, it could hardly be mistaken for history. As Isidore of Seville wrote in his influential *Etymologies* (early seventh century),

> Poets named "fables" [*fabula*] from "speaking" [*fari*] because they are not actual events that took place, but were only invented in words. They are presented with the intention that the conversation of imaginary dumb animals among themselves may be recognized as a certain image of the life of humans.
>
> *(I.xl.5; Isidore, 2006, 66)*

Despite this straightforwardness, the poet of the *Ecbasis captivi* remarks rather elaborately on his eschewing of historiographical standards:

> The custom prevailed in the time of our fathers
> That no one dared to describe any deeds he might wish,
> Unless the writer himself had definitely heard
> Or had been an eye-witness to what was to be set down in writing.
> Thus the page vouched, under witness, for the certainty of the event.
> If I offer a mere fable [*raram ... fabellam*], I will undo that practice.
> I confess my guilt: I present a fictitious work [*mendosam ... cartam*].
> Nevertheless there are many useful [*utilia*] things to be recorded in it[.]
>
> *(Ecbasis, 1964, lines 34–41)*

The poet invokes a standard of historiographic truth that could not plausibly have been attached to his narrative. His confession stems less from the real need for semantic disambiguation than to open a space for the playful articulation of what the poem's value might be. Perhaps because of the wide dissemination of the "*histora, argumentum, fabula*" distinction, and perhaps because the truth claims of secular historiography had lower stakes than those of theology or the Bible, many poets found it a conducive genre for marking their own fabular departures.

Nonetheless, some fictions did relate themselves, and distinguish themselves, from sacred text, ritual, and history. In lay religious drama, the extra-liturgical status of biblical plays and the artificed quality of dramatized miracles foregrounded issues of fictionality. These performances portrayed events understood to be divinely sanctioned and historically real, but to the extent that they were reenacted outside the clerical bounds of church rite, they could also be understood as fictions. Jesus, then, was not crucified on the streets of York. The eucharistic wafer bled by stagecraft, not divine miracle. Biblical plays also included invented, extra-biblical characters as well as episodes and speech that referred to the present-day world of the later Middle Ages. Indeed, specific plays seem to thematize or contest their own fictionality. The *Croxton Play of the Sacrament* is a particularly complex example. The play's central character is a Jewish merchant named Jonathas, fixated on what he calls the "conceit," or trick, of the Eucharist. The ritualistic transformation of bread and wine into the body and blood of Christ is a lie, he thinks, and he sets out to prove it. Indeed, the difficulty of believing properly in the Eucharist was a preoccupation of medieval Christianity, and in the later Middle Ages, miracle stories proliferated recounting how skeptics witnessed visible, tangible evidence of sacramental change. The play's main purpose would seem to be to dramatize one such miracle, as supernatural proof of divine power. Yet, the performance necessarily simulates (rather than sacramentally or miraculously reenacting) the transformation of bread into Christ's body. The play thus relies on theatrical effects to create, if not fake miracles, then fictional ones. That fiction nonetheless gives rise to the enactment of religious and civic unity at the play's end, as the play's bishop leads a procession with the Eucharistic wafer through the assembled crowd of actors and spectators. As Sarah Beckwith remarks of the play, "The line between liturgy, church, and theater is a line that needs to be drawn and redrawn" (1992, 77).

The *Croxton Play* and medieval religious theater more broadly illustrate the complex ways that fictions may be defined against events and discourses that they simultaneously imitate and approach, like sacrament, miracle, prophecy, and sacred history. Meanwhile, the unstable relationship between religious drama and liturgical rite indicates not a fixed and settled role for dramatic fiction but an experimental practice, one that excepted itself from certain modes of belief while laying claim to others.

Scales of Fiction

At what scale does the category of fiction apply, to the whole work or to component parts? Modern philosophers have tended to make fictionality's unit the propositional statement, while the twenty-first-century literary marketplace tends to sort entire genres by whether they count as fiction or nonfiction. Referentiality, this suggests, can be stabilized at various levels. For a comparative poetics of fiction, a particularly promising development within recent theoretical work has been the establishment of what has been called a "rhetorical" approach to fictionality. This approach sees fictionality as a fundamental mode of discourse, defined by the signaled communication of invented contents. Fictionality, on this account, exceeds the bounds of uniformly narrative genres and instead pops up within a wide array of communicative situations, often embedded as a discrete but identifiable element within everyday speech and writing (Zetterberg Gjerlevsen, 2016; also see Nielsen, Phelan, and Walsh, 2015; Walsh, 2007). While the rhetorical approach shares with analytic philosophy a concern with discursive units smaller than whole texts, it departs from philosophy in concentrating less on language's securing of logical and scientific truth and more on its pragmatic power to communicate. Accordingly, context matters greatly. This framework thus pluralizes what counts as fictional, allowing not only a wider array of present-day contexts to matter but also a broader spectrum of textual history.

The rhetorical approach to fictionality resembles some of the ways that readers in medieval Latin Christendom understood the semantic variation characteristic of poetic and literary discourse. For instance, the preacher, theologian, schoolmaster, and poet Alan of Lille, in his allegory the *Plaint of Nature*, has Nature define the work of poets as follows:

> Poets often join historical events [*hystoriales eventus*] to their own playful fabulations [*ioculationibus fabulosis*] by a sort of elegant stitching, in order that from the artful conjoining of these diverse materials a more elegant narrative pattern [*narrationis elegantior picture*] may emerge.
>
> *(Prose 8.18; Alan of Lille, 2013, 101)*

Poetry, according to this conceit, is the discourse that quilts together history and fable. Such combination and variation is recognized by the rhetorical approach to fictionality as well. In general, late antique and medieval readers seem to have paid close attention to the referential dappling of poetic narratives, as if trying to find the seams of poets' "artful conjoining." An influential instance is Servius' commentary on Virgil's *Aeneid* (early fifth century), which begins by defining the nature (*qualitas*) of the poem in these terms:

> It has divine and human characters and contains both truth and fiction [*veris cum fictis*], for it is obvious that Aeneas did come to Italy, but it is certainly made-up [*compositum*] that Venus spoke to Jove or that Mercury was sent.
>
> *(Servii grammatici, I.4)*

As the commentary continues, Servius often parses true and fictional elements: certain events "have been fashioned in opposition to this history [*contra hanc historiam ficta sunt*]" and in such a way as to show that Virgil "has done so not through ignorance but according to poetic art [*per artem poeticam*]" (I.267). And history is not the only truthful discourse joined to fable; Virgil also "mingles poetic fictions with philosophy [*Miscet philosophiae figmenta poetica*]" (VI.719).[8] Servius' commentary, beyond its considerable direct influence, is also broadly representative of the genre of grammatical *scholia* that continued to be written during the Middle Ages.

From a certain angle, then, medieval commentators were exercising something like the rhetorical approach to the study of fiction, noting when, and inferring why, authors switched into a fictional mode. In their "Ten Theses about Fictionality" (a pithy articulation of some of the main tenets of the "rhetorical" school), Henrik Skov Nielsen, James Phelan, and Richard Walsh offer the following as thesis #2: "Even as fictive discourse is a clear alternative to nonfictive discourse, the two are closely interrelated in continuous exchange, and so are the ways in which we engage with them" (64). Grammatical commentaries are interested in both the distinction and the interrelation of these referential modes. They pursue this interest by atomizing existing texts, marking figural from literal language and identifying and analyzing other departures from truthful discourse.

That such understandings of poetic mixture were available to vernacular writers as well is clear from both their narrative practices and the moments of self-commentary in their works. A particularly well-known instance occurs in the *Roman de Brut* by the twelfth-century Norman poet Wace. The poet claims that the adventures of Arthur are "not all lies, not all truth, neither total folly nor total wisdom" (*Ne tut mençunge, ne tut veir, / Ne tut folie ne tut saveir*). Nonetheless, Wace continues, storytellers (*cunteür*) and inventors of fables (*fableür*) have recounted them in such a fashion as to make everything appear fictional (*tut unt fait fable sembler*) (lines 9793–98). This self-reflexive remark draws attention to the interaction between the local mingling of truth and untruth and how it "all" (*tut*) ultimately appears (*sembler*) as *fable*. Such statements about the internal semantic differentiation of fabular narratives might help us think anew about other dappled representations, as in the self-consciously artful or playful inclusion of extra-biblical characters in biblical drama.

One of the affordances of the "rhetorical" school of fiction studies is its distinction between, on the one hand, the macro-genre of literary fiction and, on the other, fictionality as a widespread mode—with analytical attention falling on the latter, broader set of communicative acts. At the same time, the dynamic interchange between smaller and larger units of what counts as fiction was of interest in the Middle Ages (as the commentary tradition attests), and it remains of interest today. This dynamic interchange stems from the kind of thing that fiction is—something with properties generated from the complex interaction of component elements, rather than the simple sum of parts. Nearly all readers of fiction face situations in which apparently real entities and truthful statements appear within fictional works, and theorists disagree about what referential status those entities and statements have. Gérard Genette, for instance, argues that "every borrowing" from extratextual reality "is transformed into an element of fiction, like Napoleon in *War and Peace* or Rouen in *Madame Bovary*" (Genette, 1993, 26). By contrast, Françoise Lavocat argues for fiction's referential hybridity, mixing real and unreal elements: "no fiction is an autonomous and homogenous world within which everything is fiction" (Lavocat, 2020, 71; see also Lavocat, 2016, 402–12). As she writes, fictions "go well beyond the real world in the variety of ontological species they admit into them," yet, at the same time, the really existent beings they portray "are not deactivated by their proximity to fictional entities" (72). Lavocat's emphasis on referential heterogeneity is amenable to the ways premodern fictions often work, less to invent entirely separate worlds than to stage partial departures. As we have seen, some narrative episodes struck readers as more fictional than others. It remains an open question how essentially different this is from modern genres like the realist novel or historical fiction, which mingle accurate portrayals of lived environments, historical events, and social systems alongside fictive characters and events.

In studying medieval fiction, scholars will continue to investigate how medieval readers negotiated between local semantic and referential distinctions and the overall imaginative experience of recounted events. To what degree did the operators of fictionality lie in genre, and when did fiction's apprehension vary intra-textually, across episodes or passages? Historically specific perceptions about textual wholeness and fixity, correlated in part with practices of textual transmission, are important for reconstructing medieval literary experience. The pan-European circulation of brief narratives like *exempla* suggests how often small textual units traveled apart from the larger rhetorical contexts in which these stories came to be embedded.[9] Manuscript transmission instilled sensitivity to the fact that texts are partible and changeable, a quality designated by Paul Zumthor as *mouvance*, "an incessant vibration and a fundamental instability" [*une incessante vibration et une instabilité fondamentale*] characteristic of works "before the age of the book" [*avant l'âge du livre*] (Zumthor, 1972, 507). How manuscript transmission redounded on practices of imaginative writing remains to be studied further. In the meantime, it is evident that medieval writers and readers recognized and relished fiction's possibilities for inspiring complex experiences of disbelief, belief, and make-believe.

Notes

1 *Speculum caritatis* II.17.41; English translation quoted from Aelred (1990, 193). Latin quotations are drawn from Aelred (1971). Henceforth, I provide citations parenthetically, first to the textual divisions of the *Speculum caritatis*, then the page number of the translation. Note that I have silently altered the translation at numerous points.

2 For discussions of this dynamic with respect to the Middle Ages, see Davis (2008) and Justice (2008).

3 I understand texts to "refer" to fictive entities as well as real ones, which differs from the narrow sense of reference common in analytic philosophy (following Gottlob Frege), according to which only really existent entities can be referred to. For a lucid justification, see Ryan (1984, 122–23).

4 *Divinae Institutiones* I.11; *Patrologia Latina* 6: 171B; translation adapted from Lactantius (1955, 48).

5 *Divinae Institutiones* I.11; *Patrologia Latina* 6: 171B; translation adapted from Lactantius (1955, 48).

6 See *Rhetorica ad Herennium* 1.8.12-13 and *De inventione* 1.19.27.

7 Translation from Minnis and Scott (1988, 460).

8 For discussion see Zeeman (1996).

9 The *Thesaurus exemplorum medii aevi* is a database that makes this narrative diffusion apprehensible; see https://eadh.org/projects/thesaurus-exemplorum-medii-aevi-thema.

Works Cited

Aelred of Rievaulx. 1971. *Opera Omnia*. Vol. 1. Edited by A. Hoste and C. H. Talbot. Corpus Christianorum. Turnhout: Brepols.

Aelred of Rievaulx. 1990. *The Mirror of Charity*. Translated by Elizabeth Connor. Kalamazoo, MI: Cistercian Publications.

Alan of Lille. 2013. *Literary Works*. Translated by Winthrop Wetherbee. Cambridge, MA: Harvard University Press.

Augustine. 1992. *Confessions*. Translated by Henry Chadwick. Oxford: Oxford University Press.

Barański, Zygmunt G. 1995. "'Tres Enim Sunt Manerie Dicendi…': Some Observations on Medieval Literature, 'Genre,' and Dante." *The Italianist* 15, supplement 2.

Beckwith, Sarah. 1992. "Ritual, Church and Theatre: Medieval Dramas of the Sacramental Body." In *Culture and History, 1350–1600: Essays on English Communities, Identities and Writing*, edited by David Aers, 65–89. Detroit: Wayne State Univ. Press.

Breen, Katharine. 2021. *Machines of the Mind: Personification in Medieval Literature*. Chicago, IL: University of Chicago Press.

Chakrabarty, Dipesh. 2000. *Provincializing Europe: Postcolonial Thought and Historical Difference*. Princeton, NJ: Princeton University Press.

Cohn, Dorrit. 1999. *The Distinction of Fiction*. Baltimore, MD: Johns Hopkins University Press.

Contzen, Eva von, and Stefan Tilg. 2020. "Fictionality Before Fictionality? Historicizing a Modern Concept." In *Travelling Concepts: New Fictionality Studies*, edited by Monika Fludernik and Henrik Skov Nielsen, 91–113. Berlin: Peter Lang.

Copeland, Rita, and Ineke Sluiter. 2009. *Medieval Grammar and Rhetoric: Language Arts and Literary Theory, AD 300–1475*. Oxford: Oxford University Press.

Davis, Kathleen. 2008. *Periodization and Sovereignty: How Ideas of Feudalism and Secularization Govern the Politics of Time*. Philadelphia, PA: Univeristy of Pennsylvania Press.

Ecbasis Cuiusdam Captivi Per Tropologiam—Escape of a Certain Captive Told in a Figurative Manner: An Eleventh-Century Latin Beast Epic. 1964. Translated by Edwin H. Zeydel. UNC Studies in the Germanic Languages and Literatures. Chapel Hill: University of North Carolina Press.

Fludernik, Monika. 2018. "The Fiction of the Rise of Fictionality." *Poetics Today* 39, no. 1: 67–92.

Freitag, Wolfgang. 2019. "Reference in Philosophy." In *Narrative Factuality: A Handbook*, edited by Monika Fludernik and Marie-Laure Ryan, 245–66. Berlin: Gruyter.

Gallagher, Catherine. 1994. *Nobody's Story: The Vanishing Acts of Women Writers in the Marketplace, 1670–1820*. Berkeley: University of California Press.

Gallagher, Catherine. 2006. "The Rise of Fictionality." In *The Novel* vol. 1, *History, Geography, and Culture*, edited by Franco Moretti, 336–63. Princeton, NJ: Princeton University Press.

Genette, Gérard. 1993. *Fiction and Diction*. Translated by Catherine Porter. Ithaca, NY: Cornell University Press.

Gillespie, Vincent. 2008. "The Study of Classical Authors: From the Twelfth Century to *c*. 1450." *The Cambridge History of Literary Criticism, Vol. 2, The Middle Ages*, edited by Alastair Minnis and Ian Johnson, 145–235. Cambridge: Cambridge University Press.

Green, D. H. 2002. *The Beginnings of Medieval Romance: Fact and Fiction, 1150–1220*. Cambridge: Cambridge University Press.

Huizinga, Johan. 1924. *The Waning of the Middle Ages: A Study of the Forms of Life, Thought and Art in France and the Netherlands in the XIVth and XVth Centuries*. Translated by Frederik Jan Hopman. London: E. Arnold & Co.

Iser, Wolfgang. 1993. *The Fictive and the Imaginary: Charting Literary Anthropology*. Baltimore: Johns Hopkins University Press.

Isidore of Seville. 2006. *The Etymologies of Isidore of Seville*. Translated by Stephen Barney, W. J. Lewis, J. A. Beach and Oliver Berghof. Cambridge: Cambridge University Press.

Jonson, Ben. 1984. *The New Inn*. Edited by Michael Hattaway. Manchester: Manchester University Press.

Justice, Steven. 2008. "Did the Middle Ages Believe in Their Miracles?" *Representations* 103, no. 1: 1–29.

Karnes, Michelle. 2022. *Medieval Marvels and Fictions in the Latin West and Islamic World*. Chicago: University of Chicago Press.

Lactantius. 1955. *Divine Institutes, Books I–VII*. Translated by Mary Francis McDonald. Washington, DC: Catholic University of America Press.

Lavocat, Françoise. 2016. *Fait et fiction: pour une frontière*. Poétique. Paris: Seuil.

Lavocat, Françoise. 2020. "The Frontiers between Fact and Fiction in the Light of Tridimensional Comparatism." In *Travelling Concepts: New Fictionality Studies*, edited by Monika Fludernik and Henrik Skov Nielsen, 69–90. Berlin: Peter Lang.

Lewis, Charlton T. Lewis, and Charles Short. "Nescio." In *A Latin Dictionary*. http://www.perseus.tufts.edu/hopper/text?doc=Perseus:text:1999.04.0059:entry=nescio

Macrobius. 1952. *Commentary on the Dream of Scipio*. Translated by by W. H. Stahl. New York: Columbia University Press.

Maus, Katharine Eisaman. 2020. "Fake News." *New Literary History* 51, no. 1: 249–252.

McGuire, Brian Patrick. 2002. *Friendship and Faith: Cistercian Men, Women, and Their Stories, 1100–1250*. Aldershot: Ashgate.

Mehtonen, Päivi. 1996. *Old Concepts and New Poetics: Historia, Argumentum, and Fabula in the Twelfth- and Early Thirteenth-Century Latin Poetics of Fiction*. Helsinki: Finnish Society of Sciences and Letters.

Minnis, A. J., and A. B. Scott, with D. Wallace. 1988. *Medieval Literary Theory and Criticism c.1100-c.1375: The Commentary Tradition*. Revised ed. Oxford: Oxford University Press.

Morse, Ruth. 1991. *Truth and Convention in the Middle Ages: Rhetoric, Representation and Reality*. Cambridge: Cambridge University Press.

Newman, Barbara. 2003. *God and the Goddesses: Vision, Poetry, and Belief in the Middle Ages*. Philadelphia, PA: University of Pennsylvania Press.

Newman, Barbara. 2005. "What Did It Mean to Say 'I Saw'? The Clash between Theory and Practice in Medieval Visionary Culture." *Speculum* 80: 1–43.

Orlemanski, Julie. 2019. "Who Has Fiction? Modernity, Fictionality, and the Middle Ages." *New Literary History* 50, no. 2: 145–70.

Orlemanski, Julie. 2021. "Literary Persons and Medieval Fiction in Bernard of Clairvaux's Sermons on the Song of Songs." *Representations* 153: 29–50.

Paige, Nicholas D. 2011. *Before Fiction: The Ancien Régime of the Novel*. Philadelphia, PA: University of Pennsylvania Press.

Ryan, Marie-Laure. 1984. "Fiction as a Logical, Ontological, and Illocutionary Issue." *Style* 18: 121–39.

Sedgwick, Eve Kosofsky. 1990. *The Epistemology of the Closet*. Berkeley: University of California Press.

Servius. 1881. *Servii grammatici qui feruntur in vergilii carmina commentarii*. Edited by Georgius Thilo and Hermannus Hagen. Leipzig: B.G. Teubner.

Skov Nielsen, Henrik, James Phelan, and Richard Walsh. 2015. "Ten Theses about Fictionality." *Narrative* 23, no. 1: 61–73.

Smollett, Tobias. (1748) 1824. *The Adventures of Roderick Random*. London: T. Davison, Whitefriars.

Spiegel, Gabrielle M. 1984. "Forging the Past: The Language of Historical Truth in the Middle Ages." *The History Teacher* 17, no. 2: 267–83.

Tahkokallio, Jaakko. 2008. "Fables of King Arthur: Aelred of Rievaulx and Secular Pastimes." *Mirator* 9, no. 1: 19–36. http://www.glossa.fi/mirator/index_fi.html

Walsh, Richard. 2007. *The Rhetoric of Fictionality*. Columbus: The Ohio State University Press.

Wetherbee, Winthrop. 2008. "From Late Antiquity to the Twelfth Century." In *The Cambridge History of Literary Criticism, Vol. 2, The Middle Ages*, edited by Alastair Minnis and Ian Johnson, 99–144. Cambridge: Cambridge University Press.

Zeeman, Nicolette. 1990. "Alterations of Language." *Paragraph* 13, no. 2: 217–28.

Zeeman, Nicolette. 1996. "The Schools Give a License to Poets." In *Criticism and Dissent in the Middle Ages*, edited by Rita Copeland, 151–80. Cambridge: Cambridge University Press.

Zetterberg Gjerlevsen, Simona. 2016. "Fictionality." *The Living Handbook of Narratology*. https://www-archiv.fdm.uni-hamburg.de/lhn/node/138.html.

Zumthor, Paul. 1972. *Essai de poétique médiévale*. Paris. Seuil.

28

LITERARY FICTIONS, "FABLES," AND UNBELIEF IN THE WEST

Nicolas Correard

In the memoirs left at his death in 1696, Father Paul Beurrier testifies that he had listened to the last confession of a doctor named Basin, who told him that the Christian religion is "the greatest of all the fables ever contrived" and the Bible "the most ancient of all romances [*romans*]." "Your Bible is a true romance," he would have declared, "full of a thousand tall tales," and what is more, "badly written" ones (Adam, 1964, 116–17).[1] Beurrier was Blaise Pascal's personal confessor, and we might suspect some exaggeration, typical from the apologists warning against looming "atheism."[2] These statements cannot be taken at face value. Yet, they may reflect some reality. Indeed, the comparison between the Bible and *romans* (the French term covering both romances and novels), and more generally the reduction of religious creeds to some kind of fiction, played a central role in irreligious discourses. While scholarship on early modern unbelief has long discussed the notions of "beliefs," "creeds," and "faith," as well as their antonyms—incredulity, disbelief, and unbelief, all notions that should be manipulated with care—the other side of the comparison ("fables," *romans*, fiction) has been quite neglected, as if it sounded all too familiar, a part of the common rhetoric of irreligion (alleged or real). However, this comparison may be a complex mental construction that owes much to a rich culture of literary fictions.

A connection is missing here between literary studies and the history of ideas. Philosophers, historians, or even literary critics who sought expressions of unbelief in early modern European history have looked for explicit statements in religious polemics, philosophical treatises, or everyday writings. Inquisitorial registers have been searched from top to bottom, yielding rich information about the existence of many types and degrees of unbelief, that are not encompassed neither by ancient classifications of heresies, nor by the single, modern notion of "atheism" (i.e., the positive assertion that there are no gods). The variety and complexity of irreligious thoughts is staggering, especially if we start from the Renaissance on (Addante, 2010; Berriot, 1984), if we consider high and low culture as being interpenetrated (Barbierato, 2012; Ginzburg, 1976), and if we take into account the vast corpus of clandestine philosophical manuscripts which has recently been rediscovered (Paganini, 2005). These studies have measured the breadth and depth of early modern religious skepticism, but they were not interested in the development of a rich culture of literary fiction at the time. Despite some brilliant exceptions (Cavaillé, 2013), this is also the case of reference works (Foucault, 2010; Israel, 2001; Minois, 1999; Mori, 2021) or recent collective publications (Cavaillé, 2017; Hunter and Wooton, 1992; Staquet, 2013). On the other side, classical studies on the "rise of the novel" have mainly followed the pattern drawn by Georg Lukács who echoes Max Weber's theses about the "disenchantment" of the world, i.e., the process of secularization triggered by Renaissance and religious reformations. In his *Theory*

363   DOI: 10.4324/9781003119456-32

of the Novel (1916), Lukács famously suggested that new stories of the quest of an individual hero in a secularized world, progressively replacing epics, provided a "reenchantment" of the world, after beliefs in the agency of gods in human affairs had been abandoned (Lukács, 1974). This authoritative view underpins many accounts of the modern rise of the novel, such as Ian Watt's *The Rise of the Novel* (1957). Other recent studies, for instance, on the success of fairy tales in a "post-critical" era (Sermain, 2005), also suggest that literary fictions filled the void left by declining creeds in the supernatural.

We will consider the reverse thesis: that the development of a modern culture and conscience of fiction was a driving force in the emergence of religious unbelief. By culture, we mean a combination of knowledge, practices, and habits. Why "modern"? Despite persisting doubts about the status of these texts, ancient and medieval readers enjoyed Apuleius's *Golden Ass* or chivalric romances *as* fiction—we should not depict them as more naïve than they were. Yet, early modern Europe was unquestionably characterized by the development of an extraordinary diversity of competing universes of fiction (including some in which Christian beliefs would find little space), and by an unprecedented effort to understand what fiction is (Lavocat, 2004). This process paralleled the development of a much more pluralistic universe of religious creeds, and a more distanced relationship to religious beliefs for many. Lucien Febvre's much discussed contention that Renaissance "mentalities" lacked the "tools" to doubt the reality of God's agency in the human world (Febvre, 1982) has been widely discredited (see Wirth, 1977). But what if literary fictions, precisely, had provided the right "mental tools" to understand traditional beliefs in a different way?

A quick reminder is here necessary about the relationship between fiction and belief on a more theoretical level. As studies of fiction have shown, fiction requires some kind of belief, some "suspension of disbelief" at least, to enable ludic immersion, but the involvement of the reader in the universe set by a novel, for instance, may be quite different from the non-ludic commitment of believers holding certain metaphysical representations as true, despite the lack of positive knowledge or the impossibility of checking such kind of "truths."[3] Coleridge's formula bespeaks the romantic desire to reenchant the world, but it obliterates the fact that the immersion in a literary fiction also requires some suspension of belief (Walton, 1991, 35–43). A predecessor of Kendall Walton, David Hume, defined fiction as a kind of weak belief, at the end of the period we will consider. The distinction is according to Hume a matter of degree, not of nature (*An Enquiry Concerning Human Understanding*, 1748, V, ii, 11–13): "the sentiment of belief is nothing but a conception more intense and steady than what attends the mere fictions of the imagination" (Hume, 1999, 126).

The playful make-belief of an artistic game is indeed quite different from the firm, intimate conviction of a passionate believer—some people being eventually ready to lose their lives and waste others' for their beliefs, while the passion for literary or cinematographic characters rarely bears such results. Religious zeal remained a major force involved in most political conflicts in early modern Europe. Of course, religious beliefs are generally not as "hard" as they seem, they are more plastic or adaptable, and they rarely determine behaviors only by themselves, as some philosophers started to note at the end of the seventeenth century (we might think of Pierre Bayle's *Pensées sur la comète*, 1683). They also include doubt (without which belief would be only simple faith), and deliberate choice (it was already the case in a context of the diversification of beliefs and confessions following the religious reformations, even though the latitude of choice depended a lot on social and territorial situations). They also relied on a permanent social and individual negotiation about which beliefs were admissible. Many people wavered between orthodoxies and heterodoxies (both plurals). But what was the contribution that the experience of fiction, of reading novels notably (a practice shared by a growing number of people), brought to this more and more relativistic universe of religious creeds? Did it have a weakening effect on "strong" beliefs?

The specific contribution of some type of irreligious fictions—or fictions of unbelief, if we may label them—has always been neglected by historians of ideas, while they add much complexity to the usual accounts of the rise of unbelief as a consequence of growing philosophical and scientific rationalism. After pointing at their existence and their influence, we will considerer the crux of the matter: the comparison of the Scriptures with fictions. Of what kind? Interestingly, various models were compared, from ancient myths and allegories to Aesop's fables, medieval romances, and verisimilar novels. Finally, the modern experience of fiction, particularly through Quixotic novels and fairy tales, provided some new, accurate insights into the psychology of religious beliefs: they helped understand the desire and need to believe.

Into the Fabric of Modern Unbelief: The Critical Use of Fiction

Humanist intellectuals generally despised chivalric romance, but their growing use of fiction, particularly the type inspired by the notoriously irreligious Greek satirist Lucian of Samosata, is emblematic of their critical attitude toward given beliefs. The kind of irony displayed by Lucian toward ancient beliefs found new applications as soon as he was rediscovered and imitated.

Known as the "Batavian Lucian" because he had supervised the translations of the Greek satirist's works when he did not translate them himself, Erasmus often contrasted gullible characters and incredulous ones in his dialogues. Ogyges, the pilgrim who tells all the miracles he thinks he has witnessed, is thus set against Menedemes, his sarcastic listener, in "The Pilgrimage." In "The Exorcist," another dialogue of the *Colloquies* by Erasmus (1519), the incredulous narrator warns the reader against a fake ghost story, of which the victim was a poor priest who thought himself an exorcist (Erasmus, 1999). Lucianic irony was thus applied to the hottest topics of the Reformation (cult of the saints, demonological beliefs …). Training the readers' critical sense by playing on beliefs meant inventing a new mental attitude, which was not easily accepted. Where would it stop? It is no wonder that Luther or Calvin, no less aggressive than Catholic authorities, treated Erasmus and other new "Lucianists" as "atheists" of the worst kind, luring the reader into believing that "religions have been forged in men's brains" (Calvin, 1984, 141). Blending laughter with serious matters seemed disrespectful; blending literary fiction with the sacred was dangerous. Religious representations belonged to an entirely different realm for theologians: they could be true or false, without any space in between. Introducing fiction into the game could allow more flexibility, and question the very nature of belief.

Playful fictionalization of religious creeds was not new. Writing around 1350, Boccaccio staged cunning clerics who exploited beliefs in the reality of the supernatural. The case of Ferondo is telling: this rich but uncultivated peasant is tricked by a clever abbot into believing that he is dead and has awakened in Purgatory (*Decameron*, III, 8). While the abbot enjoys his wife, the sequestrated Ferondo is tormented by a witty guard (a monk he takes for a soul), who listens to his anxious questions about whether he may come back to life, whether bodies eat or not in Purgatory, where exactly this place is located, etc. (Boccaccio, 1998, 300–02). The monk's ironical answers enhance both the gullibility of a simple mind and the absurdity of what was taught about Purgatory, a creed elevated to the status of dogma by the Church in the thirteenth century, mainly on the authority of Thomas Aquinas (Le Goff, 1991). The novella ends with the resurrected Ferondo brought back to life, so happy to raise a child, actually fathered by the abbot, that he vows a cult to Saint Benedict, while the villagers believe in a miracle. Boccaccio anticipated the political theses that Machiavelli later draws from his reading of Roman history (*Discorsi*, II, 2; III, 1), i.e., that religious creeds are a powerful tool for scaring and manipulating people—efficient fictions. Boccaccio inspired Chaucer or the author of *Lazarillo de Tormes* (1554), and he was read by a much larger audience than Machiavelli until the eighteenth century.

The resources of narrative fiction could be used in more complex ways. The anonymous Spanish author of the *Crotalón*, a work left in manuscript form in the middle of the sixteenth century, staged a talking rooster who wakens the poor Mycilo up at night, in order to communicate devastating revelations about clerics and theologians, notably. At first, the animal speaking triggers the incredulity of Mycilo, before he is convinced by the rooster, in a rather ironical tone, that he should really believe that this miracle-like event is happening (Crotalón, 1990, 99–103). The point of the author is of course to activate the reader's incredulity toward some generally admitted fictions. When Rabelais's narrative asks the reader to believe in the "strange nativity" of Gargantua out of the left ear of Gargamelle (*Gargantua*, Chapter 5), alluding to a doubtful and rather recent dogma of the Catholic world (the virginal conception of Christ through the words of the archangel Gabriel), he pokes fun at credulous ears. But in this case, it is the (drunken) narrator Alcofrybas Nasier who uses evangelical mottos like "*charitas omnia credit*" in order to test the reader's resistance, a device that ironically stages religious rhetoric as playful make-believe (Rabelais, 1994, 39). Incredulity does not mean unbelief: Rabelais felt deeply Christian. When he initiated a new literary practice, biblical parody, by recounting in chapter 1 of *Pantagruel* the genealogy of his hero back to Adam—which includes Giant Hurtaly's quaint intervention in the story of the Flood, riding astride Noah's ark (Rabelais, 1994, 307)—it is not to discredit *Genesis*, but maybe to poke fun at a literal reading of it. As we will see below, doubts about the authenticity of Scriptures were already numerous in the wake of Erasmus's philological work, and they were expressed by erudite and iconoclastic intellectuals such as Cornelius Agrippa and Sebastian Franck (Bietenholz, 2009, 13–68). Rabelais probably conceived the Bible as a kind of Christian mythology—that is to say, *a good one*—that his own comical epic, new Pantagruelic mythology was to emulate. But this was a revolutionary attitude, clearly heterodox by the standards of most Catholics or Protestant thinkers of the time.

And there were much more radical fictions of unbelief, which challenged fundamental Christian creeds. Leon Battista Alberti's *Momus*, written around 1450, or the anonymous *Cymbalum mundi* (attributed to Des Périers), published in France in 1537 before being severely repressed (only three copies survived at the time), are two cases of complex, enigmatic fictions which let themselves deciphered only by trained, humanistic readers. They call into question the existence of a divine providence (Correard in James, Kubo, and Lavocat, 2023, 69–84; McClure, 2018); they deride religious attitudes as an effect of fear, ignorance, or manipulation, echoing Epicurean theses about creeds as figments, *figmenta* (Alberti, 2019, 26–31); they attack the figures of gods "descending" among men as an intellectual imposture, alluding to Christ (see Mothu, 2017). Alberti's Book IV of *Momus* even includes a whole etiology of why people need religious beliefs (equated to fictional representations) in order to make sense of their ordinary experience.

Precisely, the comprehension of such works, crafted by humanistic expertise in allegory out of the necessity to bypass censorship, requires interpretative effort. This is what makes them very different from the first explicitly irreligious statements of the time, such as Noël Journet's, which exposed the inauthenticity of the Old Testament, applying the notion of "fables" to many precise *loci* (see Berriot, 1978, 243). Journet was burnt at the stake in 1582 in Metz. It is also what sets them apart from the first philosophical treatises of unbelief, which dealt with fiction in a different, negative way. As soon as they started to "square everything down to the level of reason," as Gabriel Naudé proposed (Naudé, 1623, 64; see Pintard, 1983, 446), philosophers who submitted religious beliefs to a rational and critical scrutiny tried to find the way *out* of (religious) fictions: the times of Merlin and the "magic romances" had passed (Naudé, 1625, 440). We can observe this shift in the pivotal, clandestine *Theophrastus redivivus*, written anonymously in the milieu of the French *libertins érudits* (recent research points to Guy Patin). A vast compendium written in Latin around 1660, it rehearses arguments against religious beliefs. The speaker pretends he writes to help apologists understand and refute these claims. In reality, he lays out a radical option, unfolding from the very first premise: "everything that can be formed and conceived in the understanding without coming from the senses is but a fiction [*figmentum*]" (*Theophrastus Redivivus*, 1981, 1: 139). Typically, the immortality of the soul, Paradise, Hell are *figmenta*, imaginary creations. Angels, demons, and gods are also figments. This staunch rationalism does not leave room for a positive conception of fiction: the wise ones will just avoid "feigning fictions" (*falsa fingendo*) (*Theophrastus Redivivus*, 1981, 1: 44–45). Should we hence draw the conclusion that a clear opposition between the philosophical/rational/natural on the one side and the religious/irrational/imaginary on the other was then established, entailing a rejection of fiction as a vector of (wrong) beliefs?

The history of ideas offers many complexities, especially when it intersects with literary history. *Theophrastus redivivus* enjoyed some success among a reduced audience, in the shadows. But Cyrano de Bergerac's *États et Empires de la Lune et du Soleil* (1657–1662) were published, widely read and imitated. This fiction of a journey toward the moon and the sun is subtle, complex, and burlesque. Obviously, it derides miracles and develops a fully irreligious, poetic, and materialistic cosmology, as we can judge by modern editions that have been reconstructed from several manuscripts. This was already the case with the first editions, even though they omitted the most daring passages. One of these stages a character named the *"jeune fils de l'hôte,"* who develops in brief (and in plain French), what *Theophrastus redivivus* develops at fastidious length (and in abstruse Latin). He states: "that there is a God, as far as I am concerned I deny it, plainly" (Cyrano, 2004, 155). Cyrano puts him at a good distance, somewhere in the reversed world of the moon, with the narrator pretending to be relieved when some Devil carries this blasphemer away (a clear allusion to the threat of censorship). Another key section is set in a fake Paradise, where the narrator meets Enoch and Elijah, supposedly "ascended" to heaven. *Genesis* and the Books of the Prophets become the object of a kind of parody very different from that of Rabelais: a truly destructive one, which reduces the sacred text to a "tale of a tub" (*fariboles*), and the serpent that tempted Eve to a vulgar phallic image (Cyrano, 2004, 45). Fiction was not merely a more prudent way to express unbelief than direct philosophical discourse. It reached a larger audience. And it was a sharper tool, a most accurate one to penetrate into the fabric of creeds.

There were indeed Christian utopias in the wake of Thomas More, but the genre became a massive channel for the (literary) expression of unbelief at the eve of the Enlightenment. The idea that deist, or even atheist, societies were possible, a problem discussed by philosophers like Pierre Bayle, took shape in various imaginary travels. The French Huguenots in exile, such as Gabriel Foigny, Denis Veiras, and Simon Tyssot de Patot, imagined alternate, tolerant societies, where cults are reduced to a minimal state. These societies are often presented as the results of a complex history, going back to the time when imposture raged: such is the story of the impostor Stroukaras (so similar to Christ) who passed for the son of the Sun by staging false miracles in Veiras's *Histoire des Sévarambes* (1677), while the good legislator Sevarias, who replaced him, also resorted to fiction in order to educate his people—deism being finally presented as a kind of necessary fiction. You cannot really tell the people that there is no god, a wise character named Scromegas explains at the very end of the Book (Veiras in Racault, 2020, 423–27). After Machiavelli and the *libertins érudits*, these authors still clung to the idea that the wise ones should not only accept some religious fictions but promote them in order to maintain morality and social cohesion.

Others were more radical, such as the author of the anonymous *République des philosophes, ou Histoire des Ajaoiens* (maybe Fontenelle), or Tyssot de Patot in his *Aventures de Jacques Massé* (1714). In this "Spinozist novel," as it is often presented (Israel, 2001, 591–98)—a much too reductive category—the character traveling through the world suffers many blows of fortune but meets several wise people who help him detach from his early beliefs and understand that there is no God accountable for evils. An ironical and fully atheistic Gascon tells him in captivity in Algiers an "irrelevant and ridiculous tale" (Tyssot de Patot, 1710, 476): a gardener got angry at his bees, killed them all, felt guilty, then sent his own son transformed into a bee in order to resurrect some of them—at least, that is what the wasps force the remaining bees to believe, according to the tale. Just a bad fiction. Can one believe in it? The crucial recognition came to Massé when he himself had to dupe his comrades in order to boost their morale in a savage and hostile country: "I invented some fictions on the go, which, though hastily patched up, did have the expected effect" (Tyssot de Patot, 1710, 108; see Delon's analysis, 1980). Some fictions do not have to be verisimilar, or well contrived, in order to be believed. They just need to feed hope. And this is what authors of anti-Christian utopias wanted to provide too, though by different means, with their counter-fictions.

What Kind of Fiction Is the Bible?

Some types of literary fiction fuelled unbelief, while unbelief explains the vogue for some types of fiction. Yet, the relationship between rationalization of the supernatural and the growing appetite for literary fictions is not binary. It was affected by the change in the ways sacred texts were read, as we have seen from the examples of Cyrano and Tyssot de Patot. How common was it to compare the Bible to a *roman* and to deem its contents fictions? What words were actually used? "Fable," the more common, is extraordinarily polysemic, for instance. From its very start with Lorenzo Valla, humanistic—that is to say philological, critical—exegesis unsettled not only the authority of the Church but also the authority of biblical texts. It reached some decisive stage after 1650, when the combined work of Spinoza, Father Richard Simon (author of the landmark *Histoire critique du vieux Testament*, 1685), and others made historical comprehension the crux of exegesis, proposing scrutiny, doubts and difficulties everywhere, instead of the simple meditation of the words of God. This process entailed frequent comparison with various kinds of fiction, a tendency to read the Scriptures with the same eyes literature is read, and finally the possibility of applying aesthetic criteria to judge it.

This evolution was facilitated by the most sincerely Christian and accurate translator of the Bible in the early sixteenth century: Erasmus, frequently pleading for a non-literalist understanding of the Scriptures. Were they not endowed by a sacred message (the Revelation), biblical tales would be perfectly comparable to Homer's fictions, *fabulae*: the creation of man out of mud, the temptation of Eve, Loth's daughter, the story of Samson are examples given in "*Sileni Alcibiadis*" in *Adagia* (Erasmus, 1992, 34: 262–65), which echo Erasmus's philological works on the Scriptures. The parallel with Aesop's fables alone would deserve a whole chapter. There is hardly a more burlesque, derisory comparison—conflating the highest type of text with the lowest one, that is, comical and secular apologues of the "Hunchback" fabulist—but it was underpinned by the idea that many biblical episodes should be conceived as fictional envelopes for a sacred wisdom. On July 6, 1547, Calvin had supervised the execution of Jacques Gruet, a blasphemer who called into doubt the veracity of *Genesis*, calling Christ a "*fantasticus*" (a raving madman), whose stories and parables "have less meaning than Aesop's fables" (see Berriot, 1977, 598). The comparison then returns in the writings of the most determined critics of the established religion. Giulio Cesare Vanini drew the parallel between Scriptures and Aesop's fables in his *Amphitheatrum* (1615), which had a notable influence after he was executed in 1617 (Vanini, 2010, 444). So was Thomas Aikenhead, a Scottish student executed in 1697: he compared theology to "poeticall fictions" and "called the Old Testament Ezra's fables, in profane allusion to Esop's fables," according to the proceedings of the trial (Graham, 2008, 103).

Most interesting is the elaboration of this parallel in the *Colloquium heptaplomeres* attributed to Jean Bodin (c. 1590). In this long, complex dialogue between seven characters standing for various creeds, supposed to have taken place in Venice, the voices of Senamy the sceptic and Torralba, the partisan of natural (deist) religion, stand out as stronger, but it is largely Salomon the Hebrew and Octavius, a convert to Islam, who cast doubt on the Christian readings of the Bible upheld by Coroni, the Catholic host, Friedrich, the Lutheran, and Curtius, the Calvinist. Long sections are devoted to biblical episodes such as the Fall, reinforcing Salomon's contention, supported by a millenary tradition of Jewish *kaballah*, that it should be read as a "beautiful and divine allegory" (Bodin, 1984, 480). While the obscurity of Scriptures is suspected by Senamy of being a device of impostors, Salomon proposes a more charitable interpretation at the beginning of Book III: exactly as Aesop' s tales bear some wisdom under the envelope of fiction, Scriptures help believers improve themselves. Thus, a Father told his sons, before dying, that a treasure was buried under the vineyard: they ploughed and dug the ground incessantly, so that the vines yielded more fruits than ever (Bodin, 1984, 120). In this Aesopic fable ("The Farmer and his Sons," fable 42 in the Perry index), which sounds so biblical,[4] *there is no treasure* to be found, precisely. It is an image of the Scriptures as an allegorical text which hides no Revelation (no divine message properly speaking), but triggers some hermeneutical activity which is still worth it, for it helps cultivate human wisdom. The author of *Colloquium heptaplomeres* had drawn his own conclusion from Erasmus's transfer of the allegorical method to reading the Bible (Freed, 1991). "There is a great danger to use allegory to explain the mysteries of Scriptures, lest things that really happened would degenerate [*sic*] into fables," reacts the character of Friedrich (Bodin, 1984, 123).

Indeed, we should recall that for orthodox exegetes, as much as for average believers, the Bible was no allegorical book of wisdom, but the historical narrative of events that happened from the Creation to Salvation (the Book of Revelation by John standing apart), told by God himself or by his inspired scribes. It was no sacred fable, to put it in other words, because these two notions would constitute an oxymoron. Revelation was truth, while "fable" (i.e., myth) was the realm of ancient poets and priests. But a dangerous paradox loomed since the Italian *Quattrocento*, with the promotion of the *prisca theologia*. Christian humanists justified their interest in Pagan mythology by allegorical readings: the religion of the ancients was made of poetical fictions enveloping profane wisdom. But the ancients also had a forefeeling of the Revelation to come, they added: Jupiter is an intuition of the supreme God; Hercules or Mercury an anticipation of Christ, etc. This had been a commonplace since Pierre Bersuire's *Ovidius moralizatus* and Boccaccio's *De genealogia deorum*. A major displacement happened in the seventeenth and eighteenth centuries. Without really erasing the Machiavellian idea that political leaders like Moses (the Numa of the Hebrews) plotted fictions in order to manipulate their people, the allegorical reading, both charitable and reductive as it is, became central in religious criticism. Actually, it perfectly matched the political theses of religions as institutions set by *legislatores*: all cults "are ridiculous and vain things, invented by those who had an interest in introducing them, and then confirmed by blind and popular custom," states Orasius, the mouthpiece of La Mothe Le Vayer in his dialogue "De la Divinité" (1636). But the wise ones, he adds, did approve, because "this fiction is useful to repress the vicious ones" (La Mothe Le Vayer, 1988, 329). Interestingly, Le Vayer uses the French word "*fiction*" (what is feigned, from *fingere*), more abstract but also more suggestive of a manipulation than "fable."

Comparative mythology encouraged this comprehension. It led Pierre Bayle, in his famous and very widely read *Dictionnaire historique et critique* (1695), to liken the Christian story of Noah to other similar mythologies of the Flood, or that of Jonah to other narratives where characters are swallowed by a whale (Bayle, 1740, 2: 852–53). As Julie Boch showed, commenting on Bayle's works, "*fable*" had become an all-encompassing model to understand the religious phenomenon (Boch, 2002, 364–412). The erudite scholar Nicolas Fréret, a member of the *Académie des inscriptions*, resorted to his extensive learning in oriental languages and religions to establish the origin of biblical narratives in Semitic mythology. His most scathing criticism of Christian narratives took the form of a fiction of a letter that the philosopher Thrasybule would have addressed to a smart woman, Leucippe, in the third century AD. Less a device for concealing heterodoxy than a device for vulgarizing unbelief (in the way Fontenelle or Algarotti vulgarized abstruse scientific matters by addressing women), fiction still operates as a lever for decentering the reader's point of view, asking for an effort of the imagination to understand the imaginative nature of belief. How can we understand the Lord's goodness, or even "divinity," "providence"? As "visions," as the depictions of poets, explains Thrasybule (Fréret in Mothu and Mori, 2010, 65–66). We can see the result of this movement with Thomas Paine, who in *The Age of Reason* (1794) elaborates at length the idea that "the theory of what is called the Christian church sprung out of the tail of the heathen mythology" ("theory" standing for "theology") (Paine, 1995, 669). The tale of Christ is compared to that of other heroes such as Orpheus and Hercules, God's damning Satan to Jupiter's banishing the Giants, etc. The "Christian mythologists," as they are called all along, had worked well, but along predictable paths.

Not all critics would grant this reading. In one of the first full-fledged atheist treatises (which remained almost unknown before Voltaire published scraps of it), the *Mémoires* of Bishop Meslier (1664–1729), the modern *"Christicoles"* are accused of extracting "allegorical" and "mystical" meaning from the vain fictions of the ancients (Meslier, 1972, 1: 330). Biblical exegesis was now plagued by the usual reproof about allegory: that it was not meant by the author but applied by readers to give more meaning to a text than it really carried. Centuries of error on the case of Homer had been freshly demonstrated in the "Quarrel of Homer," led by Anne Dacier, who delegitimized, on behalf of philological accuracy, excessive allegorical readings. D'Holbach's *Le Christianisme dévoilé* reduces the whole Bible to "fantastical stories," which at best can be taken as "a pack of fables and allegories" (unfortunately this is not the case, according to him, with the theological constructions that the doctors of the Church grafted on it) (D'Holbach, 1998, 1: 59).

Meanwhile, the comparison to *romans*—that is to say, to the rising genre of the time—had become more and more frequent, eliciting the general notion of "fable" in a different sense. "Fables" are collective mythologies, their origins unaccountable, their rationale fuzzy (they can explain the origin of everything, they justified religious cults for the ancients and provided material to poets); novels have precise authors (even anonymous ones), they are designed, they serve an aesthetic purpose, i.e., they have to seduce their readers by enchanting their imagination with other worlds. What is more, early eighteenth-century novels often pretended to be "true" stories, real memoirs: their hiding their fictionality (in a ludic way) was one of their best enticements (Paige, 2011). The experience of this pseudo-factual regime of the novel could fit, or fuel suspicious readings of sacred texts, increasingly understood as not only *confused* but intentionally *contrived*, captivating the imagination of uncritical readers. The polemical exegesis of the Bible by Enlightenment philosophers would not only assess the problematic authorship of sacred texts but also pay more attention to the *way* they were written, to their composition and style. "There are in Scripture Stories that do exceed the Fables of Poets, and to a captious Reader sound like Gargantua or Bevis," joked the English deist Charles Blount, alluding to Rabelais and the medieval romances of Bevis of Hampton, in a letter gathered in the *Oracles of Reason* (Blount, 1693, 3). Fréret dedicates a whole chapter of his *Examen critique* to underline the *"traits si romanesques"* ("obvious novelistic features") in the book of Tobias, especially in the story of Sarah whose suitors died one by one in their wedding nights, before Tobias expelled the demon and married her (Fréret, 1728, 214). Now attributed to César Chesneau Du Marsais, a leading grammarian, the clandestine treatise *Examen de la religion* submits the Bible to devastating rhetoric and stylistic analyses: the Christian religion is "wholly metaphoric"; it is plagued by ridiculous contradictions, as if men wanted to "have God play in a comedy lasting more than four thousand years" (Du Marsais, 1998, 171).

The most radical opponents of Christianity were also the most prone to this type of explanation. The leading figure of the school of French materialists after 1750, baronet d'Holbach, thus attacked the status of the Gospels as historical testimonies, a very different target than the Old Testament. "Nothing like this happened. The Gospels are but an oriental romance [*roman oriental*], disgusting for any man of taste," he writes in the preface of his *Histoire critique de Jésus-Christ*, a close, erudite, and hostile scrutiny. Why? Because "the critic can find no relationship between facts, circumstances do not match, and there is no uniformity in the narratives" (D'Holbach, 1999, 2: 655). In order to rationalize some episodes, he rewrites them in the style of contemporary novels, for instance to account for the Angel Gabriel's visitation to the Virgin. What kind of "conception" happened then? The "rabbinic tale" might be better understood, jokes d'Holbach, if we imagine that Gabriel was just a gallant. He would start thus: *"Hello, my dear Mary, you are so adorable! such charms! such graces!"* (D'Holbach, 1999, 2: 672–73). The discourse runs on a full page, written with the light touch of contemporary *libertinage* (we might think of a pastiche of Hamilton, Marivaux or Crébillon).

The feelings of scandal, disgust, or disdain sometimes expressed by d'Holbach show how unbelief had also become a matter of taste, and how the aesthetic norms of neo-classicism played against the Bible. Father Simon already noted inconsistencies, repetitions (*hysteron proteron*), poor literary organization, and lack of decorum (Schwartzbach, 2011). Most of the critics of the Bible understood the Old Testament as a kind of epic of the Hebrews, but their distaste grew accordingly. Voltaire, of course, offered the most comprehensive synthesis of the grievances. Oriented as it was, his reading of the Bible was most detailed. Opposing the argument of fictionality to Dom Calmet's desperate attempt at restoring a literal reading of the Scriptures (*Commentaire littéral sur tous les livres de l'Ancien et du Nouveau Testament*, 1707–1716, 23 vol.), he also dismissed allegorical reading. The article "Fable" in the *Dictionnaire philosophique* states that "it goes with ancient fables exactly as with modern tales: some are morally instructive, some pleasant; others are just insipid." The preceding article, "Ezequiel," concluded with the idea that if the prophet's visions may eventually be interpreted as "ingenious fictions," as some voices claimed (using the allegorical argument as a last resort), they were not worth Homer, Virgil, or Horace (Voltaire, 2008, 188–89]. Neither instructive, nor pleasant: "insipid" in a word. As a literary critic, Voltaire could spare some episodes: dramatic shifts (*"peripeties"*), recognitions, final outcome, emotion, the story of Joseph, more moving than Homer's *Odysseus*, lacks nothing of what makes great literature (Voltaire, 2008, 249–52).

But he was generally dismissive. In his *Tractatus* (1670), Spinoza had grounded the hypothesis that the prophet Esdras (and not Moses) might be the real author of the Pentateuch, reinforcing a commonplace of anti-Christian rhetoric about "Esdras' fables." Voltaire deepens the parallel. Esdras wrote a "romance," but one not worth the "History of the Knights of the Round Table and the Twelve Pears of Charlemagne": "in what ridiculous romance could we bear to hear of a man changing all the waters into blood by a flourish of his rod?," he asked in his *Examen important de Milord Bolingbroke* (1767). "Is this the story of Gargantua? Is this the story of God's people?" (about Joshua's victory on the Amorites). "Our Gulliver has similar fables, but not such contradictions," he goes on about the huge number of soldiers in Salomon's army (Voltaire, 1968–2022, 62: 187, 196, 200). And he went further in *La Bible enfin expliquée* (1776), underlining parallels between Balaam's ass and literary prosopopoeia; Jonas's adventures in the whale and Ariosto's burlesque epics; the Saba kingdom and utopical narratives (Voltaire, 1968–2022, 79A(I): 254, 480–81, 397). By the multiplication of examples, and the systematical aspect of the comparisons, we can better assess how "modern tales" had become the standard to which the Scriptures were (unfavorably) compared. And we can feel that Voltaire's paradoxical fascination with the Scriptures shares something with his ambivalent judgment on Shakespeare, a genius, but barbaric and so often absurd according to the 1734 *Lettres philosophiques* (which revealed the Bard to Europe).

Toward the Subjectivity of Belief: Experiments in Quixotic Novels, Fairy Tales, and Psychological Fictions

"Religion is true; or it is false. If it is just a vain fiction, then it is sixty years lost, if you want, for a good man, a Carthusian or a loner; they risk nothing else. But if it is grounded on truth […]" (La Bruyère, 1995, 586). The statement, at the end of La Bruyère's *Caractères* (1688), addresses the *"esprits forts"* and reads as a variation on Pascal's gambit: there is nothing to lose if religion is just fiction; if it is no fiction, there is everything to win or to lose (depending on whether one believed or not). Between truth and error, a third notion had crept in, which could eventually lead to the exoneration of religious "fables": their reduction to a literary pastime. Enlightenment philosophers were more prone to underline the noxiousness of religious fictions, linked to passionate zeal, obstinacy and eventually violent behavior, contrasted with the harmlessness of pure fiction. The notion of "enthousiast," as portrayed by Shaftesbury in his *Characteristics of Men* (1711), summed it all up; in French, *enthousiaste* tended to replace the notion of *"visionnaire"* (visionary mind), so often used by seventeenth-century sceptics about religious minds. The latter insisted more on the power of imagination and on the cogency of representations which cause behavior, the former on the effect. Novelistic writing offered a new glimpse into the subjective experience of belief, and helped understand *why* non-existent entities, supernatural scenarios, and explanations beyond reason were so alluring and persistent. Even the most obtuse rationalists could understand that qualifying religious representations as "false," "fake," or plotted fell short of explaining their success. They were something more. Literary fictions were understood, precisely, to offer a small-scale experience—just a bit softer or weaker, to borrow David Hume's concept of fiction—of the great thrill that religions provided to believers.

The beginnings of the historical apprehension of the Bible met the beginnings of literary history at this point. Two decades after Father Pierre Daniel Huet had issued his famous thesis *De l'origine des romans* (published as a preface to Segrais's *Zaïde* in 1670), which tied the craze for fiction to a deep anthropological need and raised the idea that the first *romans* came from the Orient, two short *Essays* published in London by a certain "L. P." (sometimes attributed to the free thinker John Toland), applied the same ideas to sacred texts. Oriental peoples such as the Persians, the Assyrians, and the Hebrews had their folktales; no wonder the Talmud is filled with "fables." The Arabs went further, with their descriptions of imaginary paradise and their love for similes. Then they contaminated Spain and Provence with the taste for giants, erring knights and enchanted castles, disseminating the "seeds of fiction." Thus, the Scriptures, "altogether mysterious, allegorical and enigmatical," are equated with chivalric romances, and degenerate philosophy, i.e., theology, with "romantick hypotheses" (*Two Essays,* 1695, 30, 33, 39). With the same anti-Semitic overtone, Voltaire too suggested that the religious stories of monotheism all originated in some gross "Arabic" taste (Voltaire, 1968–2022, 79A(I): 151). That the psychology of belief pointed to the power of imagination was also at the very center of the famous essay by Fontenelle, *De l'origine des fables* (1684). "A heap of chimeras, fancies, absurdities," that is what "fable" (and religion, incidentally) is about for Fontenelle. Primitive people experienced the power of fiction without being able to recognize it, taking stories for history: "The fables of the Greeks were not like our romances [*romans*], which are given to us as such, not as history" (Fontenelle, 1989, 3: 187). Fontenelle also takes aim at Arabic stories and at certain Christian legends. The difference is not in nature, but in pragmatics: some fictions are given as what they are (literature), others as stories to be believed in, supposedly true. The distinction was crucial in the ongoing "pyrrhonian crisis" of the writing of history, that Fontenelle pondered, i.e., the suspicion that some historical events which had long seemed unquestionable were actually based on unreliable, fabulous "chronicles" (disguised romances).

As we can see, the unbeliever is not necessarily a hardcore rationalist who lacks imagination, or who refuses to indulge in childish, sensual, or fantastic fancies (as the great narrative of unbelief goes, describing unbelievers as tied to the mast of reason in order to resist the enchanting songs of religious fables). He might be a skilled, highly qualified reader of novels, who experienced *more* fictions than uneducated people did. This is the portrait of Fontenelle, a literary-minded contributor to the *Mercure galant* and a novelist himself, before he became a leading philosopher of the Enlightenment. This is also the portrait of the free thinker Lord Bolingbroke. In his *Letters on the Study and Use of History* (1752), he distinguished between *Amadis of Gaul*, loaded with "a thread of absurdities," but which "lay no claim to belief," and falsely historical fables inherited from tradition (Bolingbroke, 1844, 2: 212). In his no less scandalous *Letter Occasioned by one of Archbishop Tillotson's Sermons*, he explains the writing of Pentateuch by the "enthusiasm of poetry." Believing would be Quixotic.

> We may laugh at Don Quixote, as long as we please, for reading romances till he believed them
> to be true histories, and for quoting archbishop Turpin with great solemnity; but when we speak
> of the Pentateuch, as of an authentic history, are we much less mad than he was?
>
> *(Bolingbroke, 1844, 3: 20)*

The popularity of *Don Quixote* throughout Europe mattered from this point of view, all the more that the vocabulary of belief is omnipresent in Cervantes's fiction, and it was a striking feature that seventeenth-century readers and imitators made even more salient. The most widely read English imitation before 1700 was not a novel properly speaking, but a mock epic by Samuel Butler, indeed a fiction entitled *Hudibras* (1663–1678), written just after the English civil wars. In order to satirize fanatics, Butler staged a religious Quixote, a knight-errant of Presbyterian confession, intoxicated by reading an explosive blend of Scriptures and romances. Devotion stands as the ultimate passion. Half-hypocritical and half-crazy, Hudibras believes he acts in a Christian epic, charging most of the people he meets in the English countryside as "infidels." Hudibras will finish "enchanted" in a masquerade, believing himself the victim of Spirits and hobgoblins, without abjuring his faith (Butler, 1967, III, iii).

As the border between the miraculous and the marvellous was put to scrutiny, another parallel was frequently drawn between religious creeds and fairy tales, which emerged as a distinct literary genre during the seventeenth century. After having demolished any attempt at founding current beliefs about demons and spirits on the Scriptures, Thomas Hobbes famously suggested that the real spirits contributing to the "Kingdom of Darkness" (i.e., the very place we live in) were clerical ones, who strove to establish the power of churches on such beliefs as Hell or Purgatory. Thus was the Catholic Church a "Kingdome of Fairies," which "have no existence but in the fancies of ignorant people, rising from the traditions of old wives, or old poets" (*Leviathan*, IV, chapter 47; Hobbes, 2012, 5: 1122). These wicked "fairies" are strangely equated with ghosts, that Henry VIII "exorcised" (5: 1118–24). Hobbes wanted his discourse to remain admissible by his English audience, but his duplicity is made obvious by the end of the chapter, which calls for some generalization to other churches. In the Latin version of the *Leviathan*, he mentions the source of this two-page long comparison with the fairies paying a cult to Oberon (the Pope): *Huon de Bordeaux*, the most fantastic of all chivalric romances, which had already inspired Shakespeare's *Midsummer Night's Dream* (Hobbes, 2012, 5: 1119).

Institutional creeds could thus be destabilized by their comparison or assimilation to strange, old or new, but obviously fictional (literary) ones. A masterpiece in this respect is the *Comte de Gabalis* (1670) by Henri de Montfaucon (known as "abbé de Villars"), which enjoyed considerable success: reedited more than ten times in France before 1800, it was translated thrice in English, twice in Italian, and German. It may be read as a satire on the "secret sciences" put in the mouth of a Quixotic believer, who expands on Paracelsus's original conceptions of the role of elementary spirits (Sylphs, Hobgoblins, Nymphs, and Salamanders), which account for all kinds of inexplicable phenomena in the world. The narrator (his auditor) opposes some "difficulties" in a skeptical, Lucianic tone, pushing Gabalis further in his passionate plea, which hastily blends Christian beliefs with his own, apocryphal ones: quoting the Fathers, Gabalis sketches alternate explanations for the Fall or Noah's Ark, before explaining supernatural ways of making children with spirits (Montfaucon, 2022, 215–39). The book was forbidden: the real butt of the satire, maybe, was not Paracelsus's quaint theory of *Geistmensch*, alchemy or magic, but Christian theology, easily embedded in Gabalis's farrago. The parallel between orthodox creeds and occult spiritism would thus inspire, in the same vein, the lengthy *Lettres cabalistiques* by Boyer d'Argens (1737–1738), a fictional enquiry into the origins of religious beliefs (Boyer d'Argens, 2017).

Samuel Butler and Montfaucon de Villars had another common source of inspiration: the Rosicrucian affair, which had shown how a bunch of sophisticated German humanists, led by the genial Johann Valentin Andreae, had more or less intentionally created a new, artificial or fake (if we admit that there are authentic ones) religious creed centered on the character of Christian Rosenkreutz. *Fama fraternitatis* (1614), the first book of a series of Rosicrucian manifestos, reads like a novel, depicting him as an inspired scholar who had traveled through the Orient, met the wise Brahmins in India and Muslim mystics in Damas, and returned with an esoteric and alchemical philosophy destined to reform Christianity, which only the chosen ones would understand (Gorceix, 1998). Blending the story of Apollonius of Tiana with that of modern religious prophets (Luther), Paracelsus's millenari-anism and occult theosophy with sound Christian morals, Andreae had composed a perfect religious fiction—the type of an "oriental romance," to use d'Holbach's word—that he afterward exposed as a pure hoax, in a Lucianic tone, in his *Menippus* (1617). Too late. This Frankenstein-like experiment in creating a new spiritual narrative had succeeded beyond hope—precisely because it met the expectations of the public. Despite the fact that the fraud had been detected (it was a "*fabuleux roman*" according to some [Naudé, 1623, 91]), it inspired the creation of real Rosicrucian societies a century later, exerting a strong influence in the Age of Enlightenment (Yates, 2001). The case would of course fuel conspiracy theories applied to the writing of the Gospels: if such a forgery had almost succeeded in creating a new religion in an age of reason, some wondered, what would have happened a thousand years ago? Many more would have believed, maybe.

The publication of the *Arabian Nights* by Antoine Galland (1704) oriented biblical criticism to-ward an even more fruitful path, following the argument of the oriental origin. The comparison is repeatedly made by Emilie Du Châtelet in her ruthless *Examens de la Bible*, for example, about the Book of Esther: is it canonical? Is it an allegory? No, it reads like the *Arabian Nights* (Du Châtelet, 2011, 487). "Does the Holy Spirit entirely belong to the Orient?," asked Du Marsais about biblical allegories that degenerate into obscurities (Du Marsais, 1998, 163). Voltaire reached the summit of this irony with the writing of *The White Bull* (*Le Taureau blanc*), a philosophical tale that mixes bibli-cal parody with the style of the *Arabian Nights* and Ovid's *Metamorphoses*. The result is a hotchpot, which can produce strange effects on the reader: it is both indigestible and pleasant by its very ab-surdities (a quality often attributed to fairy tales). Still, the main character, beautiful Amaside, com-plains to the serpent (who becomes the confidant) that verisimilar stories would be more palatable than a dream-like narrative, after the serpent had told her episodes of the Old Testament (Voltaire, 1994, 763). Taste changes according to time, and Voltaire had a limited appetite for fairy tales, a wan-ing genre by 1750, that he parodied along with the Bible.

Robert Challe had confronted his reader with a similar dilemma (Moureau, 1986). A polymath, traveler, and major novelist for his *Illustres Françaises* (1713), he has been identified as the author of the clandestine treatise *Difficultés sur la religion* (1710), an attack on "*religions factices*" (which carries a more open meaning than "factitious" in English: "fake," or "artificial," "fabricated," or "fictitious religions"): "what are the books of these fabricated religions if not facts out of the bounds of nature, of custom and reason, and consequently fables or romances?" (Challe, 2000, 123). The treatise underlines the extravagant nature of such episodes as the Fall:

> Could you find in fables or romances something more burlesque than the temptation of Eve? This serpent was the most clever of all animals, he spoke, he was condemned to eat the ground and to walk on his chest: this is so grotesque.
>
> *(Challe, 2000, 316)*

A distinction is made: "fables" are closer to fairy tales because of the supernatural events, while romances can be more verisimilar without being true, easily provoking belief: such are the medieval romance of Jean de Paris and the Gospels (Challe, 2000, 161–62, 344]. Challe knew it from his own practice of the verisimilar, psychological novel, as exemplified by the *Illustres Françaises*. Some critics remain puzzled by the non-congruence between the philosophical treatise and the fiction: addressed to a wide audience, the *Illustres Françaises* stage no irreligious content—not even one seductive cleric, surprisingly—as if the two genres belonged to different realms (Goldzink, 2001). Yet, imagination and illusion are driving forces for the lovers of the *Illustres françaises*: Des Frans, the main character, construes a wrong image of Sylvie out of passionate and jealous zeal. Challe is also the author of a sequel of *Don Quixote* (*Continuation de l'admirable histoire de Don Quichotte,*

1713), and he probably drew from his frequentation of Cervantes's masterpiece a strong sense of the power of imagination, when it is possessed by a desire to believe.

Early modern novels, typically under the French form of *roman d'analyse* dedicated to the psychology of passion, had largely nurtured the parallel between profane love and religious zeal. While Honoré d'Urfé could discreetly celebrate Catholicity through the passions of his pastoral lovers, thanks to the neo-Platonist scheme governing his pseudo-druidic Gaul (*Astrée*, 1607–1627), Prévost's Des Grieux would venerate Manon Lescaut *instead* of God (*Manon Lescaut*, 1731), and libertine novelists would stage clerical pornography so as to point to the link between sexual arousal and religious excitation (for instance, Boyer d'Argens in *Thérèse philosophe*, 1748). Ordinary fictions could, therefore, contribute to giving secularized insights into religious feelings as irrational impulses. The case could be made about the English deist and novelist Charles Gildon (Nowka in Crowe, 2019, 177–97). But more than anyone, Christoph Martin Wieland gathered all these threads together. Known as the "German Voltaire," he had a noticeably different profile than his French counterpart and model: the son of a Lutheran minister, he experienced *Schwärmerei* (which can be conceived both as religious piety and a more general disposition of the mind to enthusiasm), before he turned to the *Aufklärung*, the opposite pole of Germanic culture in the eighteenth century. Writing his first great novel, *Don Sylvio von Rosalva* (1764), he keeps constantly in mind the parallel between the love for fairy tales, that his Quixotic character experiences everywhere, and religious zeal, so that the work, as much as *Gabalis*, can be read as a satire on superstition. Only the experience of real love will cure the hero. But the reading of an absurd fairy tale designed by a benevolent and wise master (Biribinker's tale) will be a turning point, helping him distance himself from his early beliefs (Wieland, 2001, 326–408).

Later on, Wieland rewrote the lives of the false philosopher Peregrinus, the object of Lucian's harsh satire (*Peregrinus*, 1791), and of Apollonius, the Pagan magus whose life had been told by Philostratus (*Agathodämon*, 1792). The result will be two oriental romances *and* philosophical fictions at the same time. In Wieland's "secret history" of Peregrinus, we learn that the character had experienced the illusions and disillusions of love with the same fervor he later experiences for religion. Placing the real locus of beliefs in the desiring imagination, Wieland makes his character the victim of another type of fiction: that of the fake prophet Kerinthus, who embodies the spirit of early Christian communities. When Peregrinus himself becomes a religious leader, it is as a "honest enthusiast," well aware by his own experience that people want to be fooled (Wieland, 1791, 2: 421). A similar experience, more or less, happens to Wieland's alternate version of Apollonius, who passes from the status of a young, Quixotic *schwärmer* to that of a wise religious leader, ready to give people the fictions they need, "goodhearted prejudices and errors rich in wonders" (Wieland, 1966, 549). But the prophet of the Christians, he reckons, has been more efficient because more universal and radical in his promises. At the threshold of romanticism, the passion for literary fiction had led Wieland to conceive the religious enthusiasm of his youth in a philosophical, but still sympathetic way, quite different from the French philosophers' full rejection: as responding to an existential need for fiction.

Conclusion: Literary Fictions as Quasi Beliefs

Are we entitled, therefore, to think that proliferating experiments in ludic, literary make-believe games encouraged their readers to conceptualize religious beliefs as *being made* by men; God or the Virgin as Dulcinea-like figments; Jesus as the fascinating hero of an archaic epic; the saints of the hagiography as kinds of djinns? Many historical phenomena accounting for the rise of unbelief were certainly independent from the birth and rise of a modern culture of fiction: the scrutinizing of the authenticity of the Scriptures; confronting various creeds through comparative religions; submitting the tenets of Christian metaphysics to philosophical discussion; expelling the supernatural from the realm of modern physics. But there was an interaction with literary history. Our survey has been limited to some kinds of fiction, while the inquiry may be extended to theatrical fictions, which could offer a model to help understand the social interactions at play in religious behaviors (the role of feigning more particularly). And it is limited in time, while the case of contemporary novelists, such as Salman Rushdie or Orhan Pamuk, shows that the crossings of fiction and unbelief remain a burning issue.

Kendall Walton has described the emotions procured by fictions as quasi-emotions, that we never *really* take for real when we experience them, but which nevertheless give us a hint at, if not a knowledge of, the emotions felt outside of fiction (Walton, 1991, 244–89). We may extend the idea: fictional representations do not beget beliefs as such, but let us experience quasi beliefs. From Renaissance Lucianic fictions to modern novelists of the eighteenth century, authors were conscious that they could manipulate their readers into embracing small-scale beliefs before encouraging them to distance themselves, thus providing a better understanding of beliefs—the big ones, strongly defended by some institutions or other people. A critical understanding, but eventually a sympathetic one as well. While these authors particularly meant to do so, we may even generalize the thesis to other kinds of fictional make-believe, even those that did not particularly deal with religious matters or were not created to puzzle their reader. Didn't novels, more generally speaking, contribute to accustoming the mind to adopting and abandoning different universes of fictions, different kinds of representations or sets of values?

We may object that Christian writers of the same period constantly opposed fictions of belief to the ones we reviewed. But a detailed survey would probably show that these also stemmed from the author's own skepticism. Milton produced *Paradise Lost* in the middle of religious turmoil. He was inclined to Arianism (believing that Jesus was a man, not a god-made man), and his rewriting would not have been possible if the authenticity of *Genesis* had not become a problem. That poetic justice was so prevalent in eighteenth-century British novels (in stark contrast with French ones) is probably an admission that the traditional doctrine of providence had become difficult to believe (Reeves, 2020). Beliefs started to use modern novelistic forms because they were threatened, in addition, by disaffection in favor of other types of secularized fictions. Now they avowedly needed literary fictions.

Notes

1 Translations into English are mine unless otherwise indicated.
2 The notion was widely used in Christian apologetics of the time, with a rather broad meaning: negating the existence of god(s), but negating the Creation of the world, the immortality of the soul, the existence of Heaven and Hell, the existence of a divine Providence, or the divinity of Jesus would also be labeled "atheistic" by most Catholic or Reformed theologians and authorities.
3 We do not deal in this chapter with the ritual side of religions, but with representations. Whatever anthropology tells us about the primacy of behaviors over beliefs in the religious experience, early modern Christianity offers a particular case: it was extremely concerned with legitimate representations, and with the boundaries dividing right and wrong creeds (shifting, of course, according to confession, or even between individuals).
4 See the parable of the two sons (*Matt*, 21: 28–32).

Works Cited

Adam, Antoine, ed. 1964. *Les libertins au XVIIe siècle.* Paris: Buchet/Chastel.
Addante, Lucca. 2010. *Eretici e libertini nel cinquecento.* Bari: Laterza.
Alberti, Leon Battista. 2019. *Momvs/Momus.* Edited by Paolo d'Alessandro and Francesco Furlan. Paris: Les Belles Lettres.
Barbierato, Federico. 2012. *The Inquisitor in the Hat Shop: Inquisition, Forbidden Books and Unbelief in Early Modern Venice.* Farnham: Ashgate Publishing.
Bayle, Pierre. 1740. *Dictionnaire historique et critique.* 5th ed. Amsterdam: P. Des Maizeaux.
Berriot, François. 1977. "Un procès d'athéisme à Geneve: l'affaire Gruet 1547–1550." *Bulletin de la société française d'histoire du protestantisme* 125 (October, November, December): 577–592.

Berriot, François. 1978. "Hétérodoxie religieuse et utopie politique dans les 'erreurs estranges' de Noël Journet (1582)." *Bulletin de la société de l'histoire du protestantisme français (1903–2015)* 124 (April, May, June): 236–48.

Berriot, François. 1984. *Athéismes et athéistes au XVIᵉ siècle en France.* Paris: Les Éditions du Cerf.

Bietenholz, Peter G. 2009. *Encounters with a Radical Erasmus. Erasmus' Work as a Source of Radical Thought in Early Modern Europe.* Toronto: Toronto University Press.

Blount, Charles, et al. 1693. *The Oracles of Reason.* London.

Bodin, Jean. 1984. *Colloque entre sept sçavans.* Edited by François Berriot. Geneva: Droz.

Boccaccio, Giovanni. 1998. *Decameron.* Edited by Vittore Branca. Milan: Mondadori.

Boch, Julie. 2002. *Les dieux désenchantés. La fable dans la pensée française de Huet à Voltaire (1680–1760).* Paris: H. Champion.

Bolingbroke, Henry St. John, Viscount. 1844. *Works.* London: G. Bohn.

Boyer d'Argens, Jean-Baptiste. 2017. *Lettres cabalistiques.* Edited by Jacques Marx. Paris: H. Champion.

Butler, Samuel. 1967. *Hudibras.* Edited by John Wilders. Oxford: The Clarendon Press.

Calvin, Jean. 1984. *Des scandales.* Edited by Olivier Fatio. Geneva: Droz.

Cavaille, Jean-Pierre. 2013. *Les Déniaisés. Irréligion et libertinage au début de l'époque moderne.* Paris: Classiques Garnier.

Cavaillé, Jean-Pierre, ed. 2017. *Libertinage, athéisme et incrédulité.* 2 vols. *Littératures classiques*, no. 92, issue 1/2.

Challe, Robert. 2000. *Difficultés sur la religion proposées au Père Malebranche.* Edited by Frédéric Deloffre and François Moureau. Geneva: Droz.

El crotalón. 1990. Edited by Asunción Rallo. Madrid: Cátedra.

Crowe, Nicholas J., ed. 2019. *The Ways of Fiction: New Essays on the Literary Cultures of the Eighteenth Century.* Newcastle upon Tyne: Cambridge Scholars Publishing.

Cyrano de Bergerac, Savinien. 2004. *Les états et empires de la lune et du soleil.* Edited by Madeleine Alcover. Paris: Classiques Garnier.

Delon, Michel. 1980. "Tyssot de patot et le recours à la fiction." *Revue d'histoire littéraire de la France* 80ᵉ année, no. 5 (September–October): 707–19.

D'Holbach, Paul Thiry (baronet). 1998–1999. *Œuvres philosophiques.* Edited by Jean-Pierre Jackson. 2 vols. Paris: Alive.

Du Châtelet, Émilie. 2011. *Examens de la Bible.* Edited by Bertram Eugene Schwartzbach. Paris: H. Champion.

Du Marsais, César Chesneau. 1998. *Examen de la religion.* Edited by Gianluca Mori. Oxford: Voltaire Foundation.

Erasmus, Desiderius. 1992. *Adages: II vii 1 to III iii 100.* In *Collected Works of Erasmus.* Vol. 34. Translated by R. A. B. Mynors. Toronto: University of Toronto Press.

Erasmus, Desiderius. 1999. *Collected Works of Erasmus.* Vols. 39–40. Edited and translated by Craig R. Thompson. Toronto: University of Toronto Press.

Febvre, Lucien. (1946) 1982. *The Problem of Unbelief in the Sixteenth Century.* Translated by Beatrice Gottlieb. Cambridge, MA: Harvard University Press.

Fontenelle, Bernard (de). 1989. *Œuvres complètes.* Vol. 3. Edited by Alain Niderst. Paris: Fayard.

Foucault, Didier. 2010. *Histoire du libertinage.* Paris: Perrin.

Freed, Marianne T. 1991. "L'allégorie dans Érasme et *Le colloque des sept scavans* de Jean Bodin, et quelques vues divergentes." *Moreana* 28, no. 106/107 (July): 165–78.

Fréret, Nicolas. 1768. *Examen critique des apologistes de la religion chrétienne.* [no place, no editor]

Ginzburg, Carlo. 1976. *Il formaggio e i vermi. Il cosmo di un mugnaio del '500.* Turin: Einaudi.

Goldzink, Jean. 2001. "Des *Difficultés sur la religion* aux *Illustres françaises*: écarts et interpretations." *Revue d'histoire littéraire de la France* 101e Année, no. 2 (March–April): 313–26.

Gorceix, Bernard, ed. 1998. *La Bible des Rose-Croix: traduction et commentaire des trois premiers écrits rosicruciens.* Paris: Presses Universitaires de France.

Graham, Michael F. 2008. *The Blasphemies of Thomas Aikenhead. Boundaries of Belief on the Eve of the Enlightenment.* Edinburgh: Edinburgh University Press.

Hazard, Paul. (1961) 2013. *La crise de la conscience européenne, 1680–1730.* Paris: Le Livre de Poche.

Hobbes, Thomas. 2012. *Leviathan: The English and Latin Texts* (ii). Vol. 5 of *The Clarendon Edition of the Works of Thomas Hobbes.* Oxford: Oxford University Press.

Hume, David. 1999. *An Enquiry Concerning Human Understanding.* Edited by Tom L. Beauchamp. Oxford Philosophical Texts. Oxford: Oxford University Press.

Hunter, Michael, and David Wooton, eds. 1992. *Atheism from the Reformation to the Enlightenment.* Oxford: Clarendon Press.

Israel, Jonathan. 2001. *Radical Enlightenment. Philosophy and the Making of Modernity 1650–1750.* Oxford: Oxford University Press.

James, Alison, Akihiro Kubo, and Françoise Lavocat, ed. 2023. *Can Fiction Change the World?* Cambridge: Legenda.

La Bruyère. 1995. *Les caractères.* Edited by Emmanuel Bury. Paris: Librairie Générale Française.La Mothe Le Vayer, François. 1988. *Dialogues faits à l'imitation des anciens.* Paris: Fayard.

Lavocat, Françoise, ed. 2004. *Usages et théories de la fiction. Le débat contemporain à l'épreuve des textes anciens (XVIe–XVIIIe siècles).* Rennes: Presses Universitaires de France.

Le Goff, Jacques. 1991. *La naissance du purgatoire.* Paris: Gallimard.

Lukács, Georg. 1974. *Theory of the Novel.* Cambridge, MA: MIT Press.

McClure, George. 2018. *Doubting the Divine in Early Modern Europe. The Revival of Momus, the Agnostic God.* Cambridge: Cambridge University Press.

Meslier, Jean. 1972. *Œuvres de Jean Meslier.* Edited by Jean Duprun, Roland Desné and Albert Soboul. Paris: Anthropos.Minois, Georges. 1999. *Histoire de l'athéisme.* Paris: Fayard.

Montfaucon de Villars, Henri. 2022. *Le comte de Gabalis ou entretiens sur les sciences secrètes.* Edited by Didier Kahn. Paris: H. Champion.

Mori, Gianluca. 2021. *Early Modern Atheism from Spinoza to d'Holbach.* Oxford: Voltaire Foundation.

Mothu, Alain. 2017. "La satire de la *Révélation* dans le *Cymbalum mundi.*" *Revue de l'Histoire des religions* 234, no. 3: 457–83.

Mothu, Alain. 2022. "Deux 'jeunes éventés': Geoffroy Vallée et Noël Journet." *Les dossiers du Grihl*, Hors-série no. 3. https://journals.openedition.org/dossiersgrihl/2083.

Mothu, Alain, and Gianluca Mori. 2010. *Philosophes sans Dieu. Textes athées clandestins du XVIIIe siècle.* Paris: H. Champion.

Moureau, François. 1986. "Robert Challe et le roman de la religion." *Revue de l'histoire des religions* 203, no. 2 (April–June): 185–94.

Naudé, Gabriel. 1623. *Instructions à la France sur la vérité de l'histoire des frères de la Roze-Croix.* Paris: Julliot.

Paganini, Gianni. 2005. *Les philosophies clandestines à l'âge classique.* Paris: Presses universitaires de France.

Paige, Nicholas. 2011. *Before Fiction. The Ancien Régime of the Novel.* Philadelphia: University of Pennsylvania Press.

Paine, Thomas. 1995. *Thomas Paine: Collected Writings.* Edited by Eric Foner. New York: Library of America.

Pintard, René. 1983. *Le libertinage érudit dans la première moitié du XVIIe siecle.* Geneva: Slatkine.

Rabelais, François. 1994. *Les cinq livres.* Edited by Gérard Defaux. Paris: Librairie Générale Française.

Racault, Jean-Michel, ed. 2020. *Trois récits utopiques classiques.* La Réunion: Presses Universitaires Indianocéaniques.

Reeves, James Bryant. 2020. *Godless Fictions in the Eighteenth Century. A History of Literary Atheism.* Cambridge: Cambridge University Press.

Robichaud, Denis. 2013. "Renaissance and Reformation." In *The Oxford Handbook of Atheism*, edited by Stephen Bullivant and Michael Ruse, 179–94. Oxford: Oxford University Press.

Schwartzbach, Bertram E. 2011. "Reason and the Bible in the So-Called Age of Reason." *Huntington Library Quarterly* 74, no. 3 (September): 437–70.

Sermain, Jean-Paul. 2005. *Le conte de fées du classicisme aux Lumières.* Paris: Desjonquères.Theophrastus redivivus. 1981–1982. Edited by Guido Canziani and Gianni Paganini. 2 vols. Florence: La nuova Italia.

Two Essays in a Letter from Oxford to a Nobleman in London. 1695. London: R. Baldwin.

Tyssot de Patot, Simon. 1710 [or 1714–1717]. *Voyages et aventures de Jacques Massé.* Bordeaux: J. L'Aveugle [La Haye].Vanini, Guilio Cesare. 2010. *Tutte le opere.* Milan: Bompiani.

Voltaire. 1968–2022. *Œuvres complètes.* 205 vols. Oxford: Voltaire Foundation.

Voltaire. 1994. *Romans et contes en vers et en prose.* Edited by Édouard Guitton. Paris: Librairie Générale française.

Voltaire. 2008. *Dictionnaire philosophique.* Edited by Raymond Naves and Olivier Ferret. Paris: Classiques Garnier.

Walton, Kendall. 1991. *Mimesis as Make-Believe. On the Foundations of the Representational Arts.* Cambridge, MA: Harvard University Press.

Wieland, Christoph Martin. 1791. *Geheime Geschichte des Philosophen Peregrinus Proteus.* 2 vols. Leipzig: Göschen.

Wieland, Christoph Martin. 1966. *Werke.* Edited by Fritz Martini and Reinhard Döhl. 2 vols. Munich: Carl Hanser.

Wieland, Christoph Martin. 2001. *Die Abenteuer des Don Sylvio von Rosalvo.* Stuttgart: Reclam.

Wirth, Jean. 1977. "'Libertins' et 'Epicuriens': aspects de l'irréligion au XVIe siècle." *Bibliothèque d'Humanisme et renaissance* 39: 601–27.

Yates, Frances. 2001. *The Rosicrucian Enlightenment.* London: Routledge Paperbacks.

29

SAINTS, BETWEEN FAITH, BELIEF, AND FICTION

Barbara Selmeci Castioni

On the fringe of theology, the lives of the saints in the Middle Ages were mainly used for spiritual recreation (De Certeau, [1975] 2002, 322). Even though a host of imaginary saints were invented, for various cultic and political purposes, as early as late antiquity (Busin, 2018), and apart from the special case of facetious hagiography (Merceron, 1997) hagiography in the Middle Ages did not fall within the realm of fiction, in the sense that the writing of saints' lives could not be identified with a shared ludic feint linked to an aesthetic pleasure (Schaeffer, 2010). Hagiography was above all intended to perpetuate the memory of exceptional men and women who embodied the values of the Christian faith in a heroic manner, and around whom a set of beliefs and devotional practices were built. From the nineteenth century onward, as the gap between the church and state opened by the French Revolution widened, literature acquired a new autonomy that allowed it to treat the saint in the same way as other fictional characters (Bonord, 2011; Dunn-Lardeau, 1999; Narr-Leute, 2010). In the interval between the Middle Ages and the modern age, however, the cult of the saints and its representations were profoundly shaken by the Reformation, but also by the reaction of the Catholic Church. The authenticity of the saint became a cornerstone of the debate on sanctity, and the ontological status of the saint then evolved in a zone of tension between truth and fiction. In this context, the encounter between sanctity and literary fiction constitutes a singular moment in the relationship between faith, belief, and fiction, especially in seventeenth-century France. Indeed, at that time, the Edict of Nantes guaranteed a certain number of rights to Protestants in a France that remained predominantly Catholic. From being a sacred figure, belonging exclusively to the field of Christian spirituality, the saint also became, in a France divided between two denominations and two distinct relationships to sanctity, a paper character who began to survey the territories, which were also shifting, of literary fiction, operating in the process an original way of putting beliefs into play (Lavocat, 2016, 224).

The Saint in the Aftermath of the Reformation, an Ontology in Motion

Christian sanctity, as we know, underwent profound upheavals in the sixteenth century. It was not sanctity itself that was threatened, but the practices associated with the cult of the saints, which Protestants considered excessive and erroneous. They denounced the lack of a biblical foundation for the cult of the saints and emphasized that it distracted the faithful from veneration, which should above all be turned toward God and Christ. Critics converge in denouncing the invocation of saints,

379

DOI: 10.4324/9781003119456-33

their powers of intercession and protection, and of course the dubious authenticity of countless relics and the devotional practices associated with them. Calvin's *Treatise on Relics* was a runaway success (ten editions in fifty years and multiple translations), bringing to the attention of the faithful a profoundly ironic critique of the external marks of sanctity: "instead of observing their lives in order to imitate their examples, it [the world] directed all its attention to the preservation and admiration of their bones, shirts, sashes, caps, and other similar trash" (Calvin, [1543] 1854, 218). By vigorously denouncing the cult of relics, the Protestants indirectly cast doubt on the authenticity of many saints, especially the saints of the early centuries, whose historicity became suspect due to lack of sufficient documentation. The Reformation did not, however, put a definitive end to a centuries-old cult, and the attachment to the cult of the saints continued, among Catholics of course, but sometimes in a clandestine manner within the Protestant Church itself (Krumenacker, 2010). However, the virulence of the Reformed attacks on the cult of saints forced the Roman Church to react. At the end of the Council of Trent, it forcefully reaffirmed the legitimacy of the cult of the saints by a decree "on the invocation, veneration, and relics of the saints, and on sacred images" (1563) (Fabre, 2013). However, it quickly put in place strategies to better control the content and forms of worship. Canonizations were henceforth supervised by the Sacred Congregation of Rites, founded in 1588, and the Catholic Church began a profound revision of the liturgical calendar in the light of the emerging modern historiography. The *Roman Martyrology* of Cardinal Baronius (1584), intended for all the Christian churches, was the first official martyrology based on historiographical requirements. The publication of the *Acta sanctorum* by the Bollandists (67 volumes), from 1643 onward, represents the most extensive editorial undertaking to revise the lives of saints (Godding et al., 2007).

The confessional controversies surrounding the cult of the saints, as well as the revision of the liturgical calendar undertaken by the Catholic Church, certainly affect, albeit to different extents, the beliefs attached to the saints, as well as the way in which their lives are represented, whether in writing or visually. One of the most emblematic examples of the troubled state of hagiography at this time is the dispute over the origin of the Carmelites. According to the tradition, still widely shared in the seventeenth century, the Carmelite Order was founded by the prophet Elijah himself. However, despite their prudence, the Bollandists' research into the various saints of the Carmelite Order (Saint Cyril, Saint Berthold, Saint Albert) led them to refute this origin, which gave rise to an intense controversy, to the point of being brought before the Inquisition and the Pope (Godding et al., 2007, 105–08). Another example, which is particularly interesting with regard to the relationship between sanctity, literature, and fiction, is the life of Saint Paulinus, Bishop of Nola (353–451). While the historicity of his life is not disputed, the legendary episode of his captivity (he is said to have offered himself in captivity to the Vandals in exchange for the captive son of a widow) gave rise to controversy within the Catholic Church in the seventeenth century. Recounted by Gregory the Great, the episode is still accepted by Baronius and occupies a prominent place in the *Flos sanctorum*, a collection of saints' lives by Father Ribadeneira, published in Spain from 1599, translated into French in 1608 and republished many times until the middle of the eighteenth century. But in 1662, the Jesuit Pierre-François Chifflet, a collaborator of the first Bollandists, began to point out certain inconsistencies. He was followed twenty years later by Jean-Baptiste Le Brun des Marettes, who was close to the Jansenist milieu and who relegated the contentious episode to the margins of the narrative in a "Dissertation on the captivity of S. Paulinus." In the 1701 edition of Adrien Baillet's *Vies des saints*, the episode is refuted. As we can see, the polemics were ongoing, and first of all in scholarly circles. If they only affected religious practices and beliefs at a later stage, their effects on the writing of the lives of the saints were more immediate. In the case of Saint Paulinus of Nola, should his life be represented from the end of the seventeenth century onward without mentioning this episode around which the belief in his sanctity was built? Contested by scholars, does this pivotal episode in the life of the saint become a matter of fiction?

In 1686, Perrault dedicated a heroic poem to Saint Paulinus of Nola. In a dedicatory epistle to Bossuet, he defends the historicity of the episode of the captivity with a surprising vehemence: he challenges the criticism of those who claim "that this story was pure fiction" ("que cette Histoire estoit une fiction toute pure") while claiming for the poet the right to "the freedom to adorn his Work with all the pleasant incidents that his genius can provide, without fear of being denied" ("la liberté d'orner son Ouvrage de tous les incidens agreables, que son genie luy peut fournir, sans craindre d'estre dementi," Perrault, 1686, n.p.). These words of Perrault are representative not only of the tensions that permeate the field of hagiography but of the tensions that underlie historiography in general at the end of the seventeenth century. At this time, historiography is indeed still largely imbued with a rhetorical conception that gives pride of place to ornament and verisimilitude, while claiming to be distinct from fiction (Guion, 2010). The representation of the saint, in this particular case, also offers an original point of view on the Quarrel of the Ancients and Moderns, which critics have long considered as a dispute between antiquarian conservatives and minds prefiguring the Enlightenment. From this point of view, one might have expected Perrault, the future leader of the Moderns, to approach the life of Saint Paulinus with a more critical attitude. But Perrault, probably because he wished for the advent of a Christian art, clings here to tradition, despite the progress of a critical historiography. Thus, the episode of the captivity of Saint Paulinus, situated at the end of the seventeenth century in a gray zone between belief and fiction, hagiography, historiography, and literature, shows how a Modern can remain, as Norman (2011) has shown, below the progress of knowledge. In a configuration where the beliefs of the Catholic Church are predominant, but those of the Reformed tolerated, where the cult of the saints is both criticized and reaffirmed, where Catholics as well as Protestants can experience and show different forms of attachment or rejection toward the saint, this hero of the Christian faith finds himself in a very singular situation, exposed simultaneously to a plurality of belief regimes.

The Weave of Fiction and Truth

This period of hagiographic upheaval also coincided with profound changes in the premodern literary field (Jouhaud, 2000; Viala, 1985). Literary fiction in France then experienced a boom, driven by the printing press, of course, but also by the importance of French as a vernacular language (opposed to Latin), as well as by humanism, which made it possible to revisit a certain number of ancient works and treatises, foremost among which Aristotle's *Poetics* contributed to an in-depth remodeling of the literature. Like hagiography, literary fictions were then the subject of important debates, which concern their moral utility, their forms or their conditions of production and reception. It was in this doubly polemical context that a new literary production emerged, as a result of the encounter between traditional hagiography and literary fiction.

In the Middle Ages, hagiographic texts (*vita*, miracle or mystery play) were mainly consumed in devotional contexts. Despite the banning of mystery plays in Paris in 1548, similar plays continued to be performed in the provinces in devotional contexts. At the same time, another institutional dramatic practice developed: hagiographic plays performed in colleges.

Nevertheless, the rise of the printing press changed the modes of consumption of hagiographic literature from the sixteenth century onward, making it a commercial product as well (Bledniak, 1994). Thus, the hagiographic collections elaborated in the Middle Ages in order to be articulated to the liturgical calendar can be fragmented by the printers and, consequently, the narratives are detached from the religious temporality that governed their reception. Moreover, the lives of the saints were distributed on a larger scale and entered the private sphere, where they now rubbed shoulders with secular literature. And if, at the end of the Council of Trent, the church regained control of hagiographic productions, the saint seemed to pursue his quest for freedom by investing, in parallel, a new space: the literary field. Nearly one hundred works in France during the seventeenth century display in this sense multiple phenomena of formal hybridization between hagiography and secular literary genres. The main genres concerned are tragedy, novel, and epic. The saints become the main or secondary characters in novels, dramas, and poems which look less like traditional hagiographic forms than like new forms of literary fiction. These mixed works are thus distinguished from traditional hagiography by their formal hybridity and their worldly destination (favored by printing, but also by the evolution of the worldly theater which knows a vogue for martyrological subjects in the seventeenth century), two elements that allow the saint to move also outside the liturgical or cultic context that traditionally defines the modalities of his reception.

The authors of these mixed works are nevertheless in a delicate position, and move along a tightrope between fact and fiction, respect and challenge of beliefs. They are careful to emphasize the historicity of the saints whose lives they represent, and they avoid anything that might seem contrary to orthodoxy (even though orthodoxy, in the case of hagiography, is in flux). This is why, in the introductory texts, they readily refer to various authorities (the Fathers of the church and the Tridentine reformers of hagiography), but also to more questionable hagiographers (notably Ribadeneira) who nevertheless enjoyed a certain authority. At the same time, however, novelists, playwrights, and poets also often specify the poetic "ornaments" they add to their sources. This attitude pursues a double objective: to confer religious legitimacy on their production while at the same time allowing for creative freedom within the text.

Corneille's play *Polyeucte martyr*, performed during the 1641–1642 season at the Théâtre du Marais and printed the following year, is probably one of the most representative examples of the challenges of this production. Corneille takes care, in an introductory text (*Abrégé du martyre de Polyeucte*), to distinguish between "fictions" and "truth" ("fictions" and "vérité"). He specifies what he draws from historical sources (Metaphraste and Surius): the life of Polyeucte, an Armenian soldier converted to Christianity who undergoes martyrdom despite the pleas of his father-in-law and his wife. Then he emphasizes what is his invention:

> The dream of Pauline, the love of Severus, the effective baptism of Polyeucte, the sacrifice for the victory of the emperor, the dignity of Felix [...], the death of Nearchus, the conversion of Felix and Pauline, are inventions and embellishments of theater.
>
> (Le songe de Pauline, l'amour de Sévère, le baptême effectif de Polyeucte, le sacrifice pour la victoire de l'empereur, la dignité de Félix [...], la mort de Néarque, la conversion de Félix et Pauline, sont des inventions et des embellissements de théâtre.)
>
> *Corneille, [1643] 1980, 978*

The playwright relies on an "ingenious weaving of fiction with truth" ("ingénieuse tissure des fictions avec la verité") to achieve new effects on his audience. Corneille not only renews the traditional representation of sanctity by weaving a plot around the saint that gives pride of place to earthly attachments, but also, by bringing the subject onto the professional stage, he changes the conditions of reception for hagiographic figures. Corneille's play is not isolated, however, but is part of a vogue for martyrdom theatre which, in the middle of the seventeenth century, contributed to the renewal of dramatic writing (Teulade, 2012).

Between Faith, Belief, and Fiction: Multiplied Regimes of Adhesion

These particular hagiographic fictions are thus challenges to premodern poetics, but also to the traditional modalities of the representation of the saint. Aware of their potential effects on beliefs, Corneille theorizes in this sense the modes of adherence that the faithful must show to characters taken from the Bible and to those taken from the lives of the saints, the latter being the only ones that an author is entitled to mix with fiction:

> We owe only a pious belief in the lives of the Saints, and we have the same right to what we take from them to bring to the Theatre, as we have to what we borrow from other Stories. But we owe a Christian and indispensable faith to all that is in the Bible, which leaves us no liberty to change anything in it.[1]

The distinction between "belief" and "faith" suggests that there is only one permissible cognitive posture in relation to biblical figures, total adherence, while the reader is only indebted to a lower and variable type of adherence to the saint, who is henceforth considered in the same way as other historical figures. Corneille here follows the principles of the Catholic Church as redefined by the Tridentine Reformation which distinguishes different levels of worship: the cult of *latria* for the figures of the Trinity, and the cult of *dulia* for the saints (*dulia* coming from the Greek word meaning "servant"). In fact, while the believer owes God a cult of adoration, he must address the saints only with respect and homage, because the saints are only the servants of God and intermediaries between God and men. The cult of *dulia* is, therefore, a cult of a lower degree. What the church tries to regulate by this distinction is the correctness of the inner disposition of the faithful, which must be different according to whether he is addressing God or the saints. This is also what Corneille tries to grasp, by calling on his reader/spectator to distinguish different types of adherence, depending on whether the authors are portraying figures from the Bible or from hagiography.

However, Corneille's insistence on the "pious" character of the belief that the faithful owe to the saint, as opposed to the "indispensable faith" that they owe to biblical figures, suggests that the modalities of adherence to the saint are not self-evident. The epithet "pious," which produces an apparent tautology in relation to "belief," points to a malaise probably associated with the changing ontological and cultic status of the saints in the seventeenth century. Perhaps even more than the Protestant attacks on the cult of the saints, it was the revision of the liturgical calendar by the Catholic Church that may have contributed in spite of itself to the shaking of beliefs as they were traditionally associated with the saints. By making the historicity of the saint a new condition of belief, the Catholic Church invited the faithful to question their relationship to institutional sanctity. Did the saints they believe in exist? If their existence is uncertain, what about their protective powers? Why continue to offer a cult to figures whose existence and powers are questionable? The example of the Carmelites mentioned above shows how difficult it is to see the foundations of a belief refuted. Perrault's attitude toward the captivity of Saint Paulinus of Nola is of the same order: Perrault is a scholar, but when erudition undermines a founding episode of a belief, he refuses to take it into consideration.

Affectively attached to their patron saints and/or more generally to the will of the church which continued to support the cult of the saints, many faithful probably continued to believe, while being conscious that their belief rested henceforth on fragile bases. The relation of Catholics to sanctity in the seventeenth century can be seen here in the light of the psychoanalytic concepts of *Verleugnung* (denial) and splitting: after a belief has been refuted, the subject who wants to preserve his belief consciously refuses to accept its refutation and adopts a cleaved attitude. In this case, he "knows well" that the evidence of sanctity is compromised, "but nevertheless" he wants to continue to believe in it—to use the terms of the famous expression analyzed by Octave Mannoni ([1964] 2022). Such a posture of belief can also evoke that of the Greeks toward their deities, as defined by Paul Veyne, that is, a critical posture that does not constitute a brake either on beliefs or on ritual practices (Veyne, 1983).

In a France divided between two confessions that were at the same time sisters and rivals, the revision of the liturgical calendar may have contributed to undermining the regime of belief that united the faithful to the saints until the sixteenth century. Yet, at the same time, the church continued to encourage this belief by organizing, regulating, and promoting the cult of the saints. Subjected, as it were, to a paradoxical injunction, the faithful did probably not abandon their belief, but this belief became the object of multiple questionings and opened to new supports. In this context, the new alliance of fiction and hagiography presents itself precisely as a new support for a troubled, maybe split belief, a support that is both rich and problematic. The authors of texts that mix hagiography and literary fiction in fact try to channel, for different purposes, a double libidinal impulse: the desire for sanctity and the desire for fiction.

From the Religious Figure to the Hero of Fiction: Issues and Difficulties

The encounter between sanctity and literary fiction in seventeenth-century France is, therefore, neither accidental nor gratuitous. The authors who chose the figure of the saint as a literary character had different aims, which varied according to their position in the literary and social fields. Some ecclesiastics, foremost among them Jean-Pierre Camus, the bishop novelist (Robic-de-Baecque, 1999), quickly grasped the benefits of a skillful mixture between hagiography and literary fiction. It was above all a question of capturing the seductive power of secular literature and putting it to use in the service of edification, in the hope of winning back the faithful who would now prefer to go to the theatre rather than to the church, or who were maybe less interested in devotional texts than by the novels in vogue which put in scene the thwarted loves of characters of high moral quality, without excluding however some libertine characters. For their part, the authors of secular literary fictions, whose success was growing but whose moral legitimacy was still suspect, also perceived the advantages of making an exemplary figure such as the saint a herald of modern poetic forms. All of them tried to take advantage of this simultaneous reconfiguration of the hagiographic and literary domains in order to create new effects based on an unprecedent construction of sanctity for a public that had become familiar with these religious figures through the cult of the saints. At a time when literature was still deeply involved in the moral edification of the reader, but was already in search of autonomy, and when the Catholic Church needed to win back the hearts of some of the faithful after the turmoil of the sixteenth century, the saint appeared to be a very interesting character for both secular and religious authors. Sanctity and literary fiction are thus, in a way, in a relationship of mutual necessity.

But making the saint a character in a novel, tragedy or epic is not self-evident. Indeed, as a literary character, the saint does not completely meet the criteria which, in the prism of Aristotelian poetics, define the fictional hero: "a man who is not eminently good and just, yet whose misfortune is brought about not by vice or depravity, but by some error or frailty" (Aristotle, *Poetics*, Part XIII), a definition which was widely taken up and commented on in the sixteenth and seventeenth centuries. As a religious and exemplary figure, who heroically embodies the imitation of Christ, the saint does not in fact arouse the same reactions from the public as a character with flaws and exposed to misfortune. On the other hand, the saint's death is not the result of a fault he has committed, nor does it constitute a misfortune: on the contrary, the day of the saint's death becomes the day of his feast because it consecrates his true birth in God in the eyes of the church. Corneille bitterly noted this tension between the hieratic nature of the saint and the dynamic construction of the fictional character when he lamented the failure of his second and last hagiographic tragedy, *Théodore vierge et martyre*: "a virgin and martyr on a theater is nothing else than a terminal statue which has neither legs nor arms, and consequently no action" ("une vierge et martyre sur un théâtre n'est autre chose qu'un terme qui n'a ni jambes ni bras, et par consequent point d'action," Corneille, [1646], 1980, 272).

The management of this hieratic dimension of the saint undoubtedly represents one of the major challenges for seventeenth-century authors seeking to mix hagiography and literary fiction. Human feelings are indeed problematic elements in the lives of the saints: their portrayal pushes authors to explore a dimension of the hero—his inner self—that the church strives to control, in contrast to literary fictions that make the analysis of feelings and passions their favorite domain. The authors of hagiographic fictions explore several paths in this direction. The most common option is to divide the story by shifting the sentimental conflicts to the characters around the saint. This is why, for example, Corneille invents the love of Severus, former suitor of Pauline, wife of Polyeucte. This choice preserves the religious dignity of the saint by showing him only slightly affected by earthly love. The novel offers more latitude in this respect. This is the case, for example, in *Agatonphile ou les Martyrs siciliens* (1620) by Jean-Pierre Camus, who invents from a few lines of the *Roman Martyrology* a novel of almost 800 pages which gives pride of place to the earthly affections of the future saints. La Fontaine goes even further in the exploration of the saint's feelings. In *La Captivité de saint Malc*, a poem published in 1673, La Fontaine recounts the life of Saint Malc, a fourth-century Syrian monk who was captured and married by force. The poet depicts the holy man struggling against the carnal temptation he experiences with a wife who is "saintly, it is true, but charming" ("sainte, il est vrai, mais charmante," La Fontaine 1958 [1673], 53). While preserving the hermit's chastity, but through a skillful use of preterition and various processes of suggestion, La Fontaine offers the reader's imagination the surprising superposition of two a priori antithetical domains: sanctity and voluptuousness.

But the hagiographic tradition also contains figures who were not always perfectly virtuous, on the contrary. In this sense, the category of penitent saints has a certain potential for fictional literature. An interesting example can be found in a novel entitled *La Courtisane solitaire* (1622), written by a certain Jehan Lourdelot, an author from Dijon. Lourdelot interweaves a wealth of novelistic material with the lives of several saints, some of whom led reprehensible lives before undergoing a sincere penance that enabled them to attain sanctity. This is the case of Saint James, a hermit in Palestine in the sixth century who, according to legend, buried himself in a tomb to atone for the rape and murder of a young girl. As a reward for his penance, he received the gift of miracles. In *La Courtisane solitaire*, not only does the story stop before the miracles are performed, but above all, in order to explain the hermit's criminal act, the author of the novel chooses a particular figure from a secular register to designate James. The future saint is in fact described several times as a satyr (Lourdelot, 1622, 173–77), an interesting comparison on several levels. First, it brings the figure of the holy man back to a bestial representation that makes it possible to question the devastating power of human passions from a quasi-physiological point of view (and no longer solely through the prism of diabolic temptation). Moreover, the comparison is interesting on an ontological level as well. Both the holy man and the satyr are double beings (half-man, half-animal on the one hand, half-man, half-sacred figure on the other) whose referentiality, at the turn of the sixteenth and seventeenth centuries, is the subject of various questions. Until the beginning of the seventeenth century, doubts remained as to the possible existence of the satyr, whose ambivalent ontological status was expressed in literature by an oscillation between allegory, novel, and fairy (Lavocat, 2007). In a similar dynamic, until the Reformation, the referentiality of the saint, whether proven or doubtful, was less important than the powers attributed to him. In the seventeenth century, however, his historicity became a central issue in hagiography, on which the maintenance of religious belief depended. The metamorphosis of the holy man into a satyr, brought about by literary fiction, thus contributed to making visible the turmoil that belief in sanctity was undergoing at the time.

The Recognition of the Saint as an Aesthetic Game

This troubled religious belief is at the heart of the texts which mix sanctity and fiction, amplified by a specific play on the recognition of the saint. As Thomas Pavel shows in his contribution to this volume, recognition is one of the main elements, with plausibility, that enable the reader/spectators to believe in a fictional character: readers/spectators recognize the aspects of human existence present in the story.[2] The modalities of recognition that support belief in the fictional character are in a tense relationship with those that govern the recognition of the saint as a religious figure and object of worship. The belief of the faithful in the saint is in fact conditioned by his recognition as a religious figure. What Henry Phillips points out about the visual image also applies to traditional hagiography:

> The image is a stimulus to a reverent attitude, having no other virtue than […] to produce by its likeness the memory of the original. Questions naturally arose concerning the precise measure of that "resemblance." What is certain is that they must contain nothing which is either distracting or unorthodox.
>
> *(Phillips, 1997, 48)*

An excerpt from the dialogue between the Chevalier and the Abbé about a tapestry depicting Saint Stephen in Perrault's *Le Parallèle* shows the confusion that can be caused by an image of sanctity that is not sufficiently recognizable and that thwarts the viewer's expectations.

THE CHEVALIER

When the piece of tapestry in which the martyrdom of this Saint is represented was brought to Saint Estienne du Mont, the Connoisseurs were quite pleased, but the little people of the parish were not at all. I found myself near a good Bourgeois who had in his hours a small Image of Saint Estienne on Velin. The Saint was planted upright on his two knees with a crimson red Dalmatic, bordered all around with a golden net, he had his arms extended, and held in one of his hands a large palm of a beautiful green Emerald. "Here is a Saint Estienne," he said, speaking to two of his neighbors, "there is not a child who does not recognize him. And, my God, why don't the painters paint like that?"

THE ABBE

There are many pretended Connoisseurs in Paris, who would explain themselves like this good Bourgeois if they were not afraid of being mocked. Generally what is the finest and wittiest in all the Arts, has the gift of displeasing the common people.[3]

Perrault stages the confusion caused by a representation that does not allow the faithful to recognize the saint at the first sight (Selmeci Castioni, 2015). Two models of representation are in competition here: on the one hand, the tapestry model, an aesthetic representation implicitly situated on the side of the Moderns, and on the other, the small image on vellum, presented as archaic but immediately recognizable. In the eyes of the people and bourgeois, only this second representation is legitimate. The saint is recognizable by a hieratic posture and specific attributes which conform to traditional representations. In terms of reception, this representation is presented as potentially unanimous across different social classes, since the Parisian so-called connoisseur would be tempted to adhere to the same hagiographic model as the people if he did not fear the reprobation of his peers.

The modern representation of sanctity, on the other hand, can only be guessed at in contrast to the archaic representation of the saint. Perrault refrains from describing it and leaves it to the reader's imagination. But this modern representation is valued by the abbot, Perrault's representative in *Le Parallèle*. The confrontation of these two models thus generates a shift in the recognition of the saint from the religious and cultic sphere to the domains of aesthetics.

This shift from the religious to the aesthetic is precisely one of the main characteristics of literary hagiographic fictions in the seventeenth century, and is not without consequence for the belief that the faithful owe to the saint. Conventional signs of the divine such as the palm fade away and are replaced by embellishments which, considered solely from the perspective of edification, are not at all necessary. Likewise, the love of Severus does not help to reinforce the sanctity of Polyeucte. Corneille goes even further in *Théodore vierge et martyre*: the saint does not die on the scaffold as a testimony to her faith but is stabbed to death by Marcelle, a character invented by Corneille, who murders Théodore to avenge her daughter, Flavie, who died of grief because the man she loved was in love with Théodore. This scene is also depicted in the frontispiece of the play, which however no longer offers any support to the recognition of Théodore as a saint. None of the traditional attributes of the saint's iconography (the exchange of clothes in the brothel or the martyrdom palms) are used, and nothing allows the reader of Corneille's play to recognize the saint on the frontispiece (Selmeci Castioni, 2017).

In spite of their allegedly historical framework, the fictions that mixed hagiography and literature in the seventeenth century played at momentarily veiling the sanctity of the character, perhaps as a compensation for the difficulties of subjecting the saint's inner self to an in-depth analysis. In contrast to authors who do not hesitate to call saints figures not (yet) recognized as such (Le Brun, 2003), some hagiographic fictions elide the qualifier of saint in the text. Moreover, the tension between the concealment and the unveiling of the saint's identity is particularly strong in the portraits and galleries of imaginary paintings staged in these works. For example, in Perrault's poem about saint Paulinus of Nola, there is an episode in which a character named Euric leads Paulinus through a gallery in the palace of Prince Trasimond, to whom Paulinus is held captive. The two characters observe statues representing mythological characters and then paintings depicting moderner subjects. This is a totally imaginary episode in terms of the legend. A doubly fictitious episode in fact, because Perrault inserts it into the heart of the episode of the captivity of Saint Paulinus, also considered fictitious by scholars. The statues include Atalanta, Adonis, Narcissus, and the "old father Silene" ("vieux père Silene," Perrault, 1686, 42)—another satyr, but who does not function here as a mirror revealing the criminal face of the saint, but rather as a figure representing ancient (and morally dubious) art which, in this imaginary gallery, invites the readers to question their own relationship to art through the eyes of the saint. After considering the ancient statues, Paulinus and his guide turn to the paintings. One of them represent Trasimund's opposition to the burning and sacking of Rome. One other shows the charity of a bishop of Nola who is none other than Paulinus! The poem features the saint looking at his own image and taking part in the process of his own recognition. This scene of the poem thematizes the transition from ancient to modern art, a modern Christian art as Perrault defends it. The saint here embodies no particular Christian virtues, but Perrault's aesthetic ideas.

In these fictions, the recognition of the saint becomes an aesthetic game that momentarily relegates the religious dimension of the text to second place. Religious edification remains on the authors' horizon, and an author like Lourdelot justifies the mixture he makes between fiction and religion by defending his edifying intention: "I have covered the virtuous deeds of these Saints with amorous and courting words, in order to make them insensibly loved and imitated by those who would otherwise abhor the mere telling of them" ("J'ay couvert de paroles amoureuses & courtisanes les vertueuses actions de [c]esSaincts, à fin de les faire insensiblement gouster & imiter par ceux qui autrement en abhorreroient le seul récit," Lourdelot, 1622, n.p.). But the religious dimension must now be combined with a new dimension, that functions as a major condition for the advent of fiction: aesthetic satisfaction, in other words pleasure (Schaeffer, 2010, 301). Pleasure for the audience, but also pleasure for the author, independently of the success or failure of the book. The author of *La Courtisane solitaire* explicitly admits this: "I will always have this that I enjoyed it" ("j'aurai toujours cela que d'y avoir pris plaisir"; Lourdelot, 1622, n.p.).

The encounter between hagiography and literary fiction in seventeenth-century France is revealing in several respects. On the literary level, it tests the rules of the poetic art of tragedy and epic, and accompanies the birth of the modern novel; it forces authors to think about the place of their authority to the point of putting them in competition with the supreme authority, that of God, outlining behind the writer the silhouette of the demiurge; it revisits the Aristotelian division of the respective tasks of the historian and the poet in matters of truth and verisimilitude; it accelerates the constitution of a public whose judgement now has the value of an ethical and aesthetic verdict (Merlin, 1994, 35–112). On the hagiographic level, this encounter experiences the belief in the saint and leads this religious figure along the path of secularization. But, in fact, at the same time, authors are attempting to take advantage of the modalities of belief reserved for fiction in order to consolidate—or remotivate—the "pious belief" that the faithful are supposed to have in the saint.

While maintaining fiction within the orb of religious edification, the metamorphosis of the saint into a fictional character in the seventeenth century contributes to the exploration of the autonomy of literature and the specific pleasure associated with fiction. By attempting to create a new literary space in which, through a series of ludic and aesthetic operations, the saint should be recognizable both as a human being and as a religious figure, these particular fictions remain nevertheless on the fringe both of the evolution of modern literature and of critical hagiography. But in the aftermath of the Wars of Religion and before the proclaimed triumph of Reason, this particular weave of belief and fiction briefly pursues an original dream of coincidence between immanence and transcendence presence in the world and spiritual elevation.

Notes

1 "Nous ne devons qu'une croyance pieuse à la vie des Saints, et nous avons le même droit sur ce que nous en tirons pour le porter sur le Théâtre, que sur ce que nous empruntons des autres Histoires. Mais nous devons une foi Chrétienne et indispensable à tout ce qui est dans la Bible, qui ne nous laisse aucune liberté d'y rien changer," Corneille, *Examen* de Polyeucte ([1643] 1980, 979).

2 See Chapter 5 of the present volume.

3 Le Chevalier

> [...] Quand on porta à Saint Estienne du Mont la piece de tapisserie où le martyre de ce Saint est representé, les Connoisseurs en furent assez contens, mais le menu peuple de la Paroisse ne le fut point du tout. Je me trouvay auprés d'un bon Bourgeois qui avoit dans ses heures une petite Image de saint Estienne sur du Velin. Le Saint estoit planté bien droit sur ses deux genoux avec une Dalmatique rouge cramoisi, bordée tout alentour d'un filet d'or, il avoit les bras étendus, & tenoit dans l'une de ses mains une grande palme d'un beau verd Emeraude. Voila un saint Estienne, disoit-il, en parlant à deux de ses voisines, il n'y a pas d'enfant qui ne le reconnoisse. Et, mon dieu, que Messieurs les Peintres ne peignent-ils comme cela.

L'Abbé

> Il y a bien de pretendus Connoisseurs à Paris, qui s'expliqueroient comme ce bon Bourgeois s'ils ne craignoient d'estre raillez. Generalement ce qui est de plus fin & de plus spirituel dans tous les Arts, a le don de déplaire au commun du monde.

(Perrault, [1688–1697] 1979, 70)

Works Cited

Aristotle. [c.335 BCE]. 1922. *Poetics*. Translated by S. H. Butcher. London: MacMillan and Co. http://classics.mit.edu//Aristotle/poetics.html.

Baillet, Adrien. 1704. *Les vies des saints composees sur ce qui nous en est reste de plus authentique*. Paris: Jean de Nully.

Bledniak, Sonia. 1994. "L'hagiographie imprimée: œuvres en français, 1476–1550". In *Hagiographies. Histoire internationale de la littérature hagiographique latine et vernaculaire en Occident des origines* à 1550, edited by Guy Philippart, 1: 359–405. Turnhout: Brepols.

Bonord, Aude. 2011. *Les "hagiographes de la main gauche": variations de la vie de saints au XXe siècle*. Paris: Classiques Garnier.

Busin, Aude. 2018. "L'hagiographie fictive: origines et développement d'un genre litteraire dans l'antiquité tardive." *Problèmes d'histoire des religions* no. 25: 39–49. https://digistore.bib.ulb.ac.be/2020/i9782800416373_f.pdf.

Calvin, John. (1543) 1854. *A Treatise on Relics*. Edinburgh: Johnstone and Hunter.

Camus, Jean-Pierre. 1620. *Agatonphile ou les martyrs siciliens*. Paris: Chappelet.

Certeau, Michel de. (1975) 2002. "Une variante: l'édification hagio-graphique." In *L'écriture de l'histoire*, 316–35. Paris: Gallimard.

Chifflet, Pierre-François. 1662. *Paulinus Illustratus*. Divione: Chavance.

Corneille, Pierre. (1643) 1980. "Polyeucte." In *Pierre Corneille: Œuvres complètes*, edited by Georges Couton, 1: 973–1050. Paris: Gallimard.

Corneille, Pierre. (1646) 1984. *Théodore vierge et martyre*. In *Pierre Corneille: Œuvres complètes*, edited by Georges Couton, 1: 267–343. Paris: Gallimard.

Dunn-Lardeau, Brenda. 1999. *Le saint fictif. L'hagiographie médiévale dans la littérature contemporaine*. Paris: Champion.

Fabre, Pierre-Antoine, 2013. *Décréter l'image? La XXVe Session du Concile de Trente*. Paris: Les Belles Lettres.

Godding, Robert, Joassart, Bernard, Lequeux, Xavier, De Vriendt, François, and van der Straeten, Joseph. 2007. *Bollandistes. Saints et légendes. Quatre siècles de recherche*. Bruxelles: Société des Bollandistes.

Guion, Béatrice. 2010. "Comment écrire l'histoire: l'*ars historica* à l'âge classique." *Dix-septième siècle*, 246: 9–25. https://doi.org/10.3917/dss.101.0009.

Jouhaud, Christian. 2000. *Les pouvoirs de la littérature. Histoire d'un paradoxe*. Paris: Gallimard.

Krumenacker, Yves. 2010. "Sainteté catholique et sainteté protestante (XVIe–XVIIe siècles)." 21e congres international des sciences historiques. Amsterdam. https://shs.hal.science/file/index/docid/528313/filename/SaintetA_.pdf.

La Fontaine, Jean de. (1673) 1958. "La captivite de saint Malc." In *Œuvres diverses*, edited by Pierre Clarac, 47–61. Paris: Gallimard.

Lavocat, Françoise. 2007. "De l'allégorie à la fiction: le personnage du satyre." In *La fabrique du personnage*, edited by Françoise Lavocat, Claude Murcia and Régis Salado, 185–98. Paris: Champion.

Lavocat, Françoise. 2016. *Fait et fiction: pour une frontière*. Poétique. Paris: Seuil.

Le Brun des Marettes, Jean-Baptiste. 1686. *La vie de saint Paulin de Nole*. Paris: Jean Couterot and Louis Guérin.

Le Brun, Jacques. 2003. "La sainteté à l'époque classique et le problème de l'autorisation." In *Confessionnal Sanctity (c. 1500–c.1800)*, edited by J. Beyer et al., 149–62. Mainz: Philipp von Zaberne.

Lourdelot, Jehan. 1622. *La courtisane solitaire*. Lyon: Vincent de Coeursilly.

Mannoni, Octave. (1964) 2022. *Je sais bien mais quand même…* Paris: Seuil.

Merceron, Jacques E. 1997. "Prélude aux Sermons joyeux. L'équivoque hagiographique et la sanctification facétieuse du XIIIe au XVe siècle." *Le Moyen Âge,* 103: 527–544.

Merlin, Hélène. 1994. *Littérature et public en France au XVIIe siècle*. Paris: Les Belles-Lettres.

Narr-Leute, Sabine. 2010. *Die Legende als Kunstform. Victor Hugo, Gustave Flaubert, Emile Zola*. Paderborn: Wilhelm Fink.

Norman, Larry F. 2011. *The Shock of the Ancient: Literature & History in Early Modern France*. Chicago, IL: University of Chicago Press.

Perrault, Charles. 1686. *Saint Paulin, évesque de Nole*. Paris: Jean-Baptiste Coignard.

Perrault, Charles. (1688–1697) 1979. *Le parallele des anciens et des modernes*. Genève: Slatkine Reprints.

Phillips, Henry. 1997. *Church and Culture in Seventeenth-Century France*. Cambridge: University Press.

Robic-de-Baecque, Sylvie. 1999. *Le salut par l'excès. Jean-Pierre Camus (1584–1652), la poétique d'un évêque romancier.* Paris: Honoré Champion.

Schaeffer, Jean-Marie. 2010. *Why Fiction?* Translated by Dorrit Cohn. Lincoln: University of Nebraska Press.

Selmeci Castioni, Barbara. 2015. "'Voilà un Saint Étienne…, il n'y a pas d'enfant qui ne le reconnoisse!' L'imagerie de la sainteté chez Charles Perrault: entre spiritualité, poétique et esthétique." In *Légende(s). Lire et écrire des vies de saints (XVIIe–XIXe/XXe siecles)*, edited by Sophie Houdard, Marion de Lencquesaing and Didier Philippot. Les Dossiers de Grihl, 9-1. https://doi.org/10.4000/dossiersgrihl.6381.

Selmeci Castioni, Barbara. 2017. "Déjouer le saint. Le devenir de l'image du saint dans le théâtre religieux en France au XVIIe siècle, à l'interstice du théâtralisable et du théâtralisé." In *Fabula-LhT*, n°19 (October). *Les Conditions du théâtre: le théâtralisable et le théâtralisé*, Romain Bionda (dir.). https://www.fabula.org/lht/19/selmecicastioni.html.

Teulade, Anne. 2012. *Le saint mis en scène. Un personnage paradoxal*. Paris: Cerf.

Viala, Alain. 1985. *Naissance de l'écrivain. Sociologie de la littérature à l'âge classique*. Paris: Éditions de Minuit.

Veyne, Paul. 1983. *Les Grecs ont-ils cru a leurs mythes? Essai sur l'imagination constituante*. Paris: Seuil.

30

THE ROLE OF FICTION IN BUDDHIST HAGIOGRAPHY

The Case of Shinran

Markus Rüsch

Introduction

At first glance, the hagiography genre may not be directly connected to fiction. If followers of a religious tradition believe in an eminent figure of their denomination, the so-called facts about this figure's life are unquestionable. However, we must distinguish between an individual's faith and the information that led someone to their faith. Religious faith is often characterized by being based on points that cannot be verified as facts. One such example is miracles. Although one approach lies in trying to prove such phenomena using natural science, the more common way includes irrational elements that go beyond human knowledge into one's own concept of past events. The third way of integrating inexplicable points involves conceiving them as mere metaphors. For example, purple clouds (*shiun* 紫雲) often appear in hagiographies at the time of the death of an eminent Buddhist practitioner. The first method would try to clarify under what scientific conditions clouds appear purple. The second approach acknowledges that people in former times may have seen a phenomenon they conceived as purple clouds, but this perception is not accessible to most of us today. In the third case, purple clouds stand in no relation to a phenomenon and are simply a sign of the good birth of the person who died. The first and second approaches are unsuitable for discussing fiction because their only interest lies in clarifying the purple clouds' relation to facts. Although fiction does not mean to think of the world only in metaphors, the third approach illustrates that the focus on facts as such is problematic in the context of religious faith. Wittgenstein described this relationship between faith and facts as follows:

> The historical accounts of the Gospels might, in the historical sense, be demonstrably false, & yet belief would lose nothing through this: but not because it has to do with "universal truths of reason [allgemeine Vernunftwahrheiten]"! rather, because historical proof [der historische Beweis] (the historical proof-game) is irrelevant to belief.
>
> *(1998, 37–38)*[1]

This quote illustrates that a significant part of faith relies on fiction. Needless to say, there is a difference between religious *faith* and secular *belief,* because the former represents the fundament of one's life. One way to divide these two types of relationship to fiction is to see whether understanding them is connected to an idea about salvation or to a doctrinal system. There can be no *formal* difference

DOI: 10.4324/9781003119456-34

390

in a fictional book that allows for a distinction between religious and secular content. Otherwise, we would have to be able to limit the group of readers whose ideas of salvation, for example, make the decisive difference in the religious meaning of the book. We can read the story of Jesus as a fantasy novel and Goethe's *Faust* as a guidebook for human liberation.[2] The main question is whether there is a soteriological or other "religious" background. For example, we can treat the *New Testament* as holy scripture because there is a doctrinal environment called Christianity. Even though not every text can be called "sacred," there is no intrinsic reason that a text cannot be simply secular. Only the use gives the text this quality.

This also applies to the hagiographic genre. I understand hagiography as one type within the genre of biography. Therefore, while every hagiography also is a biography, not every biography belongs to the group of hagiographies. What is the criterion that gives a biography a hagiographic quality? There cannot be any *absolute* reason within the text that distinguishes a hagiography from a biography. However, the text can provide us with means that enable us to have good *arguments* for calling the text either hagiography or biography. These include signs such as stylistic norms that a distinct group or society associates with a genre. The purpose of this chapter lies in clarifying some of these arguments for calling a text a hagiography. If we speak about "hagiographies," we are automatically within a religious framework because the concept of the holy (*hagion*) has meaning only in a religious context. Unless we define the book itself as sacred, we must presume that the narrative's topic is connected to the problem of the holy. The easiest way to locate that element is to look at how the narrator presents a figure, mostly the protagonist, as someone the reader should conceive as a saint.

However, what is the role of fiction in hagiography? Many hagiographies are not about deities that might have lived aeons of years ago, but about people conceived as human beings that once lived on this earth. Considering that religious institutions mostly return to the founder of their tradition, the idea that this person actually existed is essential for them. Therefore, one condition of many hagiographies is that the previous existence of the central figure must be given as a possibility, even if this question may be irrelevant for certain believers. This is why many authors are forced to link their narrative with elements that let the reader believe they are reading a "true" story. If we understand hagiography as a genre that tries to persuade a reader to gain faith in an eminent figure and we follow the statement by Wittgenstein, these elements of so-called historical facts should be of little interest in the context of research on hagiography. However, much secondary literature, as well as the writings themselves, tends to highlight the question of historical adequacy. Consequently, although the function of *fiction* within hagiography has been mostly neglected, it lies much more at this genre's centre.

We can also observe this dichotomy of contrary approaches to hagiography—namely, texts that aim to be as nonfictional as possible, and those that attempt the opposite—in the development of Shinran biographies after Japan's modernization in the nineteenth century. There were two diverging trends in writing new biographies on Shinran. One group of biographies emphasized the emotional parts of Shinran. In contrast, another group tried to write his life story while focusing on points regarded as established facts. One prominent example for the first group is *The Human Shinran* (*Ningen Shinran* 人間親鸞, 1922) written by Ishimaru Gohei, and for the second, Murata Tsutomu's *The True Biography of Shinran: A Historical Critique* (*Shinran shinden: shiteki hihyō* 親鸞真傳：史的批評, 1896).

To address this issue, it is necessary to define what "fiction" means in the context of hagiography. The easiest way is to distinguish fiction from fact. We can define as "facts" what a society or a group accepts as specific truth at a distinct time. In writing the history of a saint, the authorities of a religious group have a crucial influence on what are considered to be the facts about this figure. To some extent, they have even more impact on the "historical proof-game" than independent historians. Therefore, in the following, biographies authorized by the head temple should serve as the source for facts in the above-mentioned meaning. To that end, any discussion of fiction in hagiographies must focus on parts of the narrative that are not covered by official biographies.

In my understanding of fiction, I follow the remarks of Käte Hamburger. She detaches the concept from its relation to the facts by emphasizing that it is not the as-if structure but the as-structure that is decisive. In the case of fiction, understood in the second meaning, a book's content can produce a semblance of reality regardless of how unreal the story is. My point is that we should focus on the as-structure of a hagiography to analyze the book's "non-reality or fiction," which a reader can enter without caring about reality while being existentially involved (Hamburger, 1968, 55). I want to connect these two aspects of fiction. We need Hamburger's approach to emphasize that fiction is not the antagonist of "fact" nor equal to "lie." Although fiction is, in Hamburger's understanding, not-reality, it is simultaneously something that is fundamentally connected with our factual world in the sense that it appears to be the factual world. Facts in the meaning of accepted knowledge by society play a crucial function within the book, since those parts help the reader perceive the story as connected with their reality. According to Hamburger, however, fiction is neither the impression that something factually happened nor a perfect deception ("as-if"), but content that satisfies the reader in their thinking of it as reality.

In my chapter, I will answer the question of the role of fiction in hagiography using the example of an author who does not belong to a distinct sect. Although some points refer to (Japanese) Buddhism in particular, the basal parts of my argument try to be a general suggestion of tools for the analysis of hagiographies. My guiding question will be: How does the narrator include historical events or actual locations with parts the reader can identify as fictional? Why does hagiography require fiction? For example, I will focus on the Japanese priest Shinran 親鸞 (1173–1263) and a biography of him written by Satō Yōjirō 佐藤洋二郎 (b. 1949) in 2014. The advantage of using a recently published book is that the development of writing history and the heterogenization of authors—which did not begin with Japan's modernization, but significantly earlier—support more extensive use of fictional elements and allow a more precise identification of them. To identify fictional parts of a book, we must have a clear idea of what is understood as historical fact, and this problem can be much more easily solved if we do not have to discuss what the discourse on historiography was at a distinct time.

Hagiography in Buddhism

Records of the lives of eminent monks play an essential role in the history of Buddhism. This already applies to the biographies of Śākyamuni's life (and his former lives). This text is called *Jātaka* ("[Stories] concerning the lives"), and the first sculptures depicting stories from the *Jātaka* can be found around the second century BC. The Pali version includes 547 stories.[3] The crucial role of biography is also grounded in the fact that some critical experiences in one's spiritual development and the connection between teacher and disciple are closely intertwined with the doctrinal standpoint. We can observe this tendency, for example, in Buddhist lineages—supposedly most prominent in the Zen Buddhist context, where a teacher can trace back the transmission of the teachings to the masters in China (*hōmyaku* 法脈, "Dharma line"). But we can also find this in other sects, such as the Jōdoshin School (*jōdo shinshū* 浄土真宗) of Shinran, where lists verify that an abbot is the official successor of Shinran (*ketsumyaku* 血脈, "bloodline").[4]

Equally, we can find hagiographies in all sects of Japanese Buddhism. The most important ones are about the sects' founders, but eminent figures who contributed to the development of the sect in a doctrinal or institutional sense are also revered through hagiography. Shinran represents a figure in Japanese Buddhism who has often become an object of biographic writing.[5] This applies not only to pre-modern biographies but also to modern and contemporary hagiographies. The difference between pre-modern and modern or contemporary works does not lie mainly at the genre level. The crucial difference, if any, may be that the types of authors have become more heterogeneous, and writing the history of a priest or monk has become less limited to the clerical class. Therefore, we can observe a rapid increase in secular writers beginning in the first quarter of the twentieth century, although hagiographies approved by religious authorities remained the central source for each type of writer. This is a very useful reference for discussing the role of fiction in hagiography due to its influence on the public discourse about the facts of a priest's life.

General Introduction to Shinran

Shinran is the founder of the Jōdoshin sect, which has the highest number of followers in Japan.[6] He spread the so-called Pure Land teachings (*jōdokyō* 浄土教) and was the disciple of the monk Hōnen 法然 (1133–1212), who is today treated as the founder of the Jōdo sect (*jōdoshū* 浄土宗). The most crucial idea in Shinran's thinking is that the Buddha Amida 阿弥陀 (in Sanskrit Amitâbha ("Buddha of Limitless Light") or Amitâyus ("Buddha of Limitless Life")—the creator of the Pure Land—can save any human regardless of their ability to conduct practices. One crucial detail in the context of hagiography lies in Shinran's rejection of the veneration of individuals and a specific type of saints. However, this does not imply that he negated worship of eminent monks.[7] His emphasis lies in criticizing the idea that human beings are capable of saving themselves or others by their own power. Notably, this profoundly influences what the term "holy" must mean in the context of Jōdoshin Buddhism. For example, a Jōdoshin Buddhist saint is not someone who gained awakening. To claim to have reached such a state would merely express one's delusion. Consequently, a Jōdoshin Buddhist saint still has qualities such as "greed, anger, and nescience" (*tonjinchi* 貪瞋癡), which are the so-called three poisons (*sandoku* 三毒) in Buddhism. Noteworthy, since there is not only one possible interpretation of Jōdoshin Buddhism, the above-mentioned points are only understandings shared by many scholars and believers. The interpretation that, in contrast, a Jōdoshin Buddhist saint is someone who realizes the Pure Land on this earth is even conceivable. Therefore, a deeper analysis of hagiographies demands a clarification of the interpreter's understanding of Jōdoshin Buddhism.

The apparent similarities between Shinran's and Luther's teachings even led to the conception of Shinran as the founder of the Protestant version of Buddhism. One example is the fact that Luther developed the concept of clerical marriage, and another is the shift from legalism to justification by faith alone (*sola fide*). Shinran also married, and the crucial factor was not that he lived together with a woman but that he did it without hiding. Moreover, he criticized the idea that a human being must accumulate merits (*kudoku* 功徳) to gain salvation. He instead emphasized that the origin of birth in the Pure Land is faith alone (*yuishin* 唯信).[8] This not only gave rise to interreligious and inter-theological research, but also took shape in the rhetoric of Shinran biographies, especially from the late Meiji (1868–1912) to the Taishō Period (1912–1926). In this context, most prominent are the biographies by Ishimaru Gohei (1886–1969) and Kurata Hyakuzō (1891–1943).

Concerning the history of biographies on Shinran, two elements are essential for understanding its development. The first is the influence of memorials of Shinran's death. Although the community remembers the death of its founder every year, anniversaries every fifty years are of particular importance. This fact not only influenced the ceremonies but was also a reason for creating new biographies. This applies specifically to 1662, 1862, 1912, 1962, and 2012. For example, between 2010 and 2012 alone, seven new biographies on Shinran were written, and this number does not include reprints or commentaries of the standardized biographies.

The second remarkable element is the so-called Shinran-Boom around the Taishō Period. This was a period of popularization of Shinran, when Shinran was no longer discussed solely in the context of the Jōdoshin community but also by people who were not affiliated with this institution. Most prominent in this context are Kurata Hyakuzō and his drama *The Priest and His Disciple* (*Shukke to sono deshi* 出家とその弟子, first published in 1916). The increasing number of secular writers of Shinran biographies has influenced the topics discussed in the discourse concerning Shinran's life. However, this does not necessarily imply a secularization of biographies on Shinran. Instead, this was an occasion to contextualize Shinran's holiness in a new manner, which also had an important influence on doctrinal studies. If there is any crucial difference in biographies after the pre-modern era, it lies mainly in the internalization of religion, and this was a supportive circumstance for making more use of fiction. I discuss this point below in more detail, but my main argument is that faith and fiction share the point that the reason why they become meaningful for their subjects (the believer or reader) does not lie in their being factually true or false. They are *connected* to factuality but not dependent.

Development of Hagiographies on Shinran: Fiction and Nonfiction

The oldest hagiography on Shinran we know today—*The Story of the Saint Shinran* (*Shinran shōnin goinnen* 親鸞聖人御因縁)—was written in 1288. Currently, the newest is *The Ignorant Bald-headed Shinran: A Novel* (*Shōsetsu gutoku Shinran* 小説愚禿親鸞), which was written by Asuka Ryōko 飛鳥涼子 and published in 2016. If we define "fiction," as suggested above, as content not covered by the authorized version of Shinran's biography, most pre-modern works on Shinran are nonfiction. Notably, we could also define fiction as information that could not be verified—as, for example, direct speech or detailed information about Shinran's experiences. We could call those parts effective "signposts of fictionality" in Dorrit Cohn's sense.[9] In this case, there would be a considerably higher number of pre-modern fictional works, including the earliest hagiographies. If we were to follow this definition, we would have to differentiate precisely between fictional and nonfictional parts within one hagiography. Then, fictionality would have no binary quality but be a question of graduation. The assumption of the existence of an authorized version does not mean that only one official version of Shinran's life existed, because each rival denomination within Jōdoshin Buddhism claimed that its version was true.[10] However, the type of narration can be called nonfictional, and therefore, even within Jōdoshin Buddhism, a variety of discourses coexist that partly contradict each other. The authors of hagiographies can be divided into three types:

- priests, monks, or other associated members of a religious institution.
- writers who received direct instruction or were commissioned by a religious institution.
- mostly independent writers.

The proportion of authors belonging to the second and, especially, to the third type, increased at the end of the nineteenth century. Simultaneously, the number of fictional works within the genre of hagiography increased. However, although the proportion of books by authors from the first category and those from the second and third may seem to be an argument for the rising importance of fictional hagiography in Japan, one should not forget that the official version of Shinran's biography written by Kakunyo (see below) remains the principal source for most readers. There are several reprints and commentaries of the authorized version of one head temple. Therefore, we can say that today, it is more challenging to write a new nonfictional than a fictional hagiography. As a result, we can observe a much higher amount of fiction than nonfiction in the field of hagiography since Japan's modernization.

It is necessary to distinguish between the first and third types and also to introduce the second type that lies in the middle position. These authors aim to create an image of the saint that is as close to the so-called facts as possible. Although they do not simply reproduce nonfictional hagiographies, their objective is to draw an image of the saint that is arguably the historical truth. One prominent example is the book *Shinran* written by Itsuki Hiroyuki (b. 1932), published in six volumes between 2010 and

2014. The length of this hagiography alone reveals that he could not rely solely on the official versions of Shinran's biography. However, he emphasized in interviews that he took classes on Jōdoshin Buddhism at Ryukoku University, which is the university that belongs to the Jōdoshin head temple Honganji 本願寺. Such statements are significant for the discourse on Itsuki since the reader obtains essential information on the author's intention to write his book, which is to write a biography that relies on official sources to a significant extent.

In contrast, authors of the third type focus on a particular message—for example, the problem of suffering or the similarities between Shinran's Buddhism and Christianity—that they want to convey to the reader. This message may be intertwined with the historicity of the protagonist, but their primary interest lies in discussing a particular problem, whether ethical or religious. An example of the third type is the hagiography written by Satō Yōjirō.

The Role of Fiction in *No Blame for the Past*

Satō Yōjirō's book on Shinran, entitled *No Blame for the Past* (*Kiō wa togamezu* 既往は咎めず), was published in 2014.[11] Most of Satō's works do not focus on religious content. However, there are exceptions, such as a work on Japanese shrines (*Deities in Silence, Chinmoku no kamigami* 沈黙の神々, [2008] 2005) and a treatise on the monk Ippen (*The Saint Ippen and His Pilgrimage, Ippen shōnin to yugyō no tabi* 一遍上人と遊行の旅, cowritten with Ueda Kaoru 上田薫, 2016). Therefore, in light of Satō's present œuvre, he could hardly be described as an author with religious motivation in the sense of official theology, and is principally considered a novelist.

To discuss the fictional aspects of Satō's biography, we must define what is nonfictional in this context. In the case of Shinran, there is a hagiography that we can call the standard version: *Illustrated Biography of the Saint of Honganji* (*Honganji shōnin denne* 本願寺聖人伝絵, below: *The Saint of Honganji*). Shinran's grandson Kakunyo 覚如 (1270–1351) compiled this work in the late thirteenth century. It is a comparatively short biography that begins with Shinran's years of study and ends with his death and the erection of his mausoleum. The importance of this biography is that it is the object of the essential Jōdoshin Buddhist ceremony called Hōonkō 報恩講 ("Meeting in Return for [Shinran's] Kindness [to Spread the Teachings]"). Such significance in the ritual context is central to discussing its importance for the community. Although there are also other biographies used in Jōdoshin Buddhist rituals, especially in different denominations, their significance does not compare to the leading role of *The Saint of Honganji*. Due to its ritual function and the fact that it was compiled shortly after Shinran's death, this hagiography is, for a significant part, considered a record of the facts of Shinran's life. Therefore, it can serve as the prototype for a modern nonfictional hagiography on Shinran.

The text is divided into fifteen parts (see Table 30.1). On the right, I have indicated each part's function in persuading the reader to conceive of Shinran as a saint.

Although an analysis of how Kakunyo designed the hagiography would provide exciting insights into the creation of a saint's image, I want to focus on Satō's book and use the table above to identify its nonfictional parts.

Regarding the question of fiction, a critical difference between the two hagiographies is that Satō uses footnotes to clarify the historical background of some events within the book. This rhetorical figure has a crucial impact on the type of reading since the reader recognizes that the annotated parts of the book are connected to nonfiction, regardless of whether the intradiegetic sections are fiction. Satō thereby shows that his concept of writing a biography about Shinran relies, to some extent, on nonfictional elements. From the perspective of research on hagiographies, this reveals an aspect that we can often observe in this genre: the author tries to construct a connection between the world of the saint and the reader. One simple, effective method of reaching this goal lies in emphasizing that the

Table 30.1 The sections of *The Saint of Honganji* and their functions

1	ORDINATION AND STUDY	The background of Shinran
2	ENTERING THE YOSHIMIZU-GROUP (I.E. THE GROUP OF HIS PRINCIPAL TEACHER)	The background of Shinran
3	DREAM IN THE HALL ROKKAKUDŌ	Shinran's religious standpoint
4	VISION OF REN'I (A DISCIPLE)	People's view on Shinran
5	RECEIVING THE SCRIPTURE SENJAKU HONGAN NENBUTSUSHŪ (THE MAIN SCRIPTURE OF SHINRAN'S PRINCIPAL TEACHER)	The background of Shinran
6	THE DISPUTE ON FAITH AND PRACTICE	Shinran's standpoint concerning the teachings
7	DISPUTE ON FAITH	Shinran's standpoint concerning the teachings
8	VISION OF NYŪSAI	People's view on Shinran
9	EXILE OF TEACHER AND DISCIPLE	Only biographical data
10	DISTRIBUTION OF THE TEACHINGS IN INADA	Creating a community
11	SALVATION OF BENNEN (A MOUNTAIN PRIEST)	Creating a community
12	PREACHING OF A GHOST IN HAKONE	A deity's view on Shinran
13	PREACHING OF A GHOST IN KUMANO	A deity's view on Shinran
14	DYING IN KYOTO	Only biographical data
15	ERECTION OF THE MAUSOLEUM	Continuity of the community

saint and the reader share the same realm of living through a connection within history. However, this is an empirical and not a theoretical observation. For a believer, the hagiography of an utterly fictional figure could also be meaningful in terms of faith. The need to place the saint within history mostly results from the influence of religious institutions. Another practical and often-observed method of giving a hagiography a nonfictional frame is the appearance of well-known historical figures. In the case of Shinran and Satō's book, this means his principal teacher Hōnen, his first teacher Jien 慈円 (1155–1225), the father of his first wife, Kujō Kanezane 九条兼実 (1149–1207), and many more.

One significant difference in Satō's biography is that it covers only a short span of Shinran's life. This characteristic appears (with some exceptions) only after Japan's modernization at the end of the nineteenth century. The story begins on the boat that brings Shinran to his place of exile and ends with his decision to leave this place some years after the remitting of the banishment. This span corresponds only to part nine (and one sentence in part ten) of *The Saint of Honganji*, which, moreover, is one of the shorter sections. Kakunyo wrote at the end of this section and the beginning of the following:[12]

[In the second fire year of the rabbit's year (1207)], as an offender, the saint [Gen]kū received the [secular] name Fujii no Motohiko and was banished to Hata in Tosa Province. The saint [Shin]ran received the [secular] name Fujii no Yoshizane and was dismissed to Kokufu in Echigo Province. I skip the cases of other disciples who were banished or sentenced to death here. During the realm of the emperor (his personal name was Morinari and his official name Sado no in), in the second gold year of the ram's year [1211], on the seventh day of the middle part of the rat's month [the eleventh month], the Minister Okazaki no Chūnagon no Norimitsu gave imperial permission [to lift the banishment]. As mentioned above, the saint answered the emperor using the character "bald head." The Imperial Majesty was moved [by his answer], and the courtier appreciated it very much. Although the banishment was lifted, [the saint] remained in this province for a while to introduce the teachings to the people [of Echigo].

From Echigo Province, the saint (Shinran) reached Hitachi Province and found a quiet place to live in the village of Inada in the Kasama district.

This shows that the biography deals only with about five years of Shinran's ninety-year life. However, the author uses several analepses as metadiegetic narratives to inform the reader of some prominent points in Shinran's thinking and the book's focus. Satō's story can be divided into the parts as shown below (see Table 30.2). The figure that follows the table illustrates the narrative time relative to the page range. The analepses are parts where Shinran remembers his past (see Figure 30.1).

Most of the intradiegetic part and essential sections in the metadiegetic part belong to what the reader can identify as fiction, since they do not simply retell well-known stories about Shinran and use direct speech extensively. Therefore, Satō refers only to the fundamental elements of Shinran's biography as nonfiction, but he uses the essential book's passages to clarify his image of Shinran's "holy" features.

One prominent attraction of the extensive use of fiction is that the reader gets insight into Shinran's inner thoughts, which are another signpost of fictionality and essential to explaining his motives. This is even more important if there are only a few autobiographical sources, as in the case of Shinran. In contrast, the hagiography written by Shinran's grandson tells the reader about Shinran's standpoint in most cases via the following two methods, which differ from Satō's way of convincing by fiction: *The Saint of Honganji* uses debates on doctrinal issues (parts six and seven) and descriptions of figures impressed by Shinran. Although letting the reader approach Shinran's standpoint through the appreciation of other people is a feature shared by most hagiographies, the crucial difference in the modern case is that other people also participate in Shinran's development toward a figure that satisfies the conditions of a saint. *The Saint of Honganji* instead refers to other people's views on Shinran to verify his special status. As a result, these references become less fictional than the cases of comparable rhetorical figures in Satō's book. Therefore, the extensive use of fiction in Satō's book serves as a type of discourse to persuade the reader that Shinran should be conceived as a Jōdoshin Buddhist saint. Here, fiction tends to be a less result-oriented but more a process-oriented type of persuasion.

Table 30.2 The sections of *No Blame for the Past*

Topic		Main content	Number of pages (minus the number of pages of the metadiegetic part)
On a boat to the place of exile (Echigo)			50 (−11)
Shinran's origin	Analepsis	↑	1
An episode from "yesterday"	Analepsis	Shinran's struggles	3
Life with wife and child	Analepsis	↓	5
Years of study	Analepsis		2
Arrival in Echigo		↑	111 (−89)
The day before setting off for Echigo	Analepsis	Exemplification of the	1
The time when Shinran first met his wife	Analepsis	book's main topic:	17
Last years of study	Analepsis	The role of women in	29
Meeting with a woman in the night	Analepsis	Buddhist practice	24*
The debate about Shinran's marriage	Analepsis	↓	18
Life in Echigo			50*
Scene at a seaside			5
Scene at a seaside (four years later)			24
Remarriage of Shinran			18
Death of Shinran's teacher			7
Remitting of the banishment, decision to go to east Japan			5

*Parts that refer to the book title.

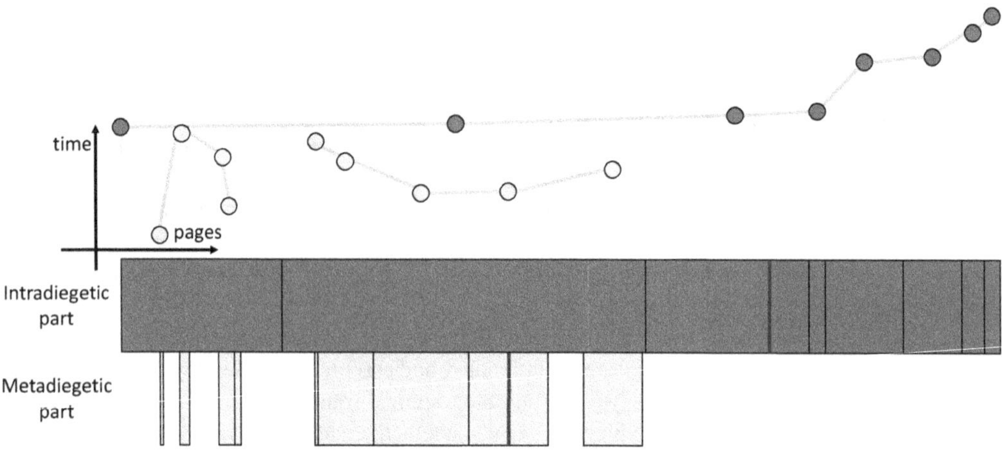

Figure 30.1   The narrative structure of *No Blame for the Past.*

The following section provides an example of the mechanism in Satō's book that intertwines fiction and nonfiction, thereby giving an insight into the central elements of Shinran's teachings, which are the elements that define the text as hagiography. In a central passage within the book that refers to its title, Satō writes:

[Shinran:] "There is the saying 'No Blame for the Past.' [It means that] there is no meaning in caring for one's family line or past. Even if one repents mistakes or other things that have been done, it cannot be helped now."

[The woman:] "What kind of mistakes may I have made? If that were true, I want to go to the mountain—even only once—to perform practices. Why do you think you could reject someone only because she is a woman? The monks that do sinful deeds [day by day] can go up to the mountain, but for any woman, it is impossible. What is the reason for this? Does being a woman imply that one violates the precepts?"

Her way of speaking was soft, but her words touched Shinran's heart powerfully. In front of this woman, whose age was not so different to his own, he felt that she made much more progress in practising.

She was also well-educated. More than anyone else, she relied on Buddha's power. She honestly confessed her past as well as her natural dispositions. Instead, she was a person with a clear heart. If she were not a woman, without a doubt, she would have become an outstanding monk.

(2014, 119)

Later, Shinran reflects on this experience: "If I would not have been able to meet this woman, I think I would not have married Tamahi, even if Kujō Kanezane and the saint Hōnen encouraged me to do so" (Satō, 2014, 200). For Satō, the question of clerical marriage and the problem of women's and laypeople's salvation is the book's central topic. Therefore, the quoted part is central to clarifying Shinran's standpoint on this question. The second quote, which includes a meeting with a woman when he was young, his marriage to Tamahi, and the encouragement of two well-known historical figures, deals with information that can be considered nonfiction. Although these parts do not appear in *The Saint of Honganji*, they are all part of a historiographical discourse on Shinran's biography.

However, the critical function in terms of religious faith—and, therefore, the leading interest for a hagiographic analysis—involves the episode quoted before, which is part of the section "Meeting with a woman in the night." The direct quotations, the description of Shinran's inner thoughts, and the portrayal of a woman about whom nothing more is known than she may have existed are clear signposts for readers that they are reading fiction. The doctrinal question raised in this paragraph is why the Buddhist path is limited to a small group of ordained men even if they expended no effort in religious practice and violate precepts. At the same time, the question follows as to why the path remains blocked for women who carry out the demanded practices. This problem becomes even more evident in the case of the woman who "would have become an outstanding monk" if she had been a man.

The fact that "her words touched Shinran's heart powerfully" illustrates that this an urgent problem in his understanding of Buddhist teachings. Shinran solves the problem of women's salvation by developing an understanding of the Pure Land teachings that guarantees unconditioned salvation, which implies that salvation does not depend on any practice. Therefore, he does not react to the problem by searching for a way that allows women to gain salvation through practice, but he doubts the effectiveness of practice for salvation. The woman in Satō's book serves only as a prototype for human beings and the problem of dealing with their unchangeable past (of this and former lives).

Notably, fiction in *No Blame for the Past* also serves to provide the reader with a vital image of the era in which Shinran lived. Therefore, in general, the mix of nonfictional and fictional elements enables the author to provide the reader with knowledge that is not limited to objective information. This is an aspect that hagiographies share with historical novels. In this chapter, it is impossible to go deeper into this point. Still, one crucial difference between these two genres is that a historical novel's primary purpose is to provide the reader with a vital image of history and, sometimes, highlight an issue of, for example, society or politics that is also meaningful for the reader's present.

In contrast, hagiographies share the quality of being directed toward faith. This approach of merging nonfictional and fictional elements with a focus on religious questions provides the reader with unverifiable but convincing information. This method is essential since, as quoted from Wittgenstein at the beginning, "historical proof (the historical proof-game) is irrelevant to belief." Therefore, a reader may mainly be influenced in terms of faith by scenes that are very rich in detail and give a vivid impression of Shinran's living conditions. Although the historical novel uses similar tools, the purpose is to provide the reader with a distinct image of historical events without being limited to proofing in the sense of historical scholarship. We can call fiction—which is the type of information that allows no historical proof-game—the essential element in a hagiography because it is a significant condition for a reader to conceive the book's content as something that has meaning for their faith. To refer to the above-quoted parts, for example, it is quite unlikely that someone would lose their faith if Shinran were not dismissed to Echigo Province in "the second fire year of the rabbit's year," but to Echizen Province in the dragon's year. On the contrary, the part in Satō's book where Shinran begins to doubt whether the type of Buddhist practice that excludes women is the right one is central to get an insight into Shinran's understanding of the Buddhist path.

Conclusion: The Function of Fiction in Hagiography

The objective of this chapter was to clarify, using one Japanese hagiography as an example, (a) the central issue of hagiography in general, (b) the reference values for analysis, and (c) the primary role of fiction in enabling the reader faith-centered access to the book.

a If we use the term "hagiography" instead of "biography," we presuppose that the story is about someone whom a particular group of people say is a saint. Since the notion of "saint" is not an objective value that could be fully clarified by historiography or any other method, hagiographies necessarily touch on the realm of faith or belief. Therefore, we need something different from just historical information as a reference to leave the historical proof-game.

b   These are primarily a doctrinal context and a nonfiction *framework*. The first is necessary to define the term "saint" because, for example, a Christian saint must meet different conditions than a Buddhist saint if we define this term generally as someone who reaches a distinct religious goal. The nonfiction framework is not necessary for hagiographies in general, but only for an analysis of fiction, and it is not at the book's *core*. Hagiographies with no nonfiction framework are very rare. One reason is that many hagiographies were also written to legitimate a religious school's authority, and this objective is based on the assumption that the saint once factually existed. However, in Buddhism, we can still find examples that have at least a very small nonfiction framework. These are, for example, the so-called biographies [on people] who received birth [in the Pure Land] (jp. *ōjōden* 往生伝). These texts are collections of shorter biographies which are for the most part about people who are unknown, whereas a factual framework as described above is nearly not given.

c   The points considered facts are the basis for dividing the nonfictional and fictional parts of the text. If we were to draw a simplified structure of a hagiography, we could say that the nonfiction framework shows that the saint and the reader share the same world, and the fictional content gives the author the space to express doctrine they consider crucial to understanding central issues of particular religious teaching through distinct narrative points.[13] Therefore, fictional parts of the book are essential for determining whether an author wants to write a hagiography or simply a fictional biography or historical novel. If we can identify a specific religious message in these fictional parts, we have good arguments to say we are analyzing a hagiography. Further, they are necessary for the reader to connect with the story on the level of faith rather than through a historical proof-game.

In history, we can observe different ways of expressing fiction within hagiography, and the hagiographic tools differ depending on historical knowledge and most of all on the level of freedom of writing and its economic conditions. For example, the political or religious environment may make it difficult to write about intimate contacts between a monk and a woman, or the development of printing may not allow long sections with a slow pace of narration or to reach a general public. However, fiction as such is a constant element in this genre, because the objective of hagiography is not to provide the reader with information about a person but to let them believe in that person. There are numerous ways by which someone develops their faith, and in the case of text-based contacts with a religion, doctrinal treatises and hagiographies may be the most prominent. In both cases, distinct biographical or other historical information is not at the core of the reader's interest—in that case, the reader would choose an encyclopaedia or similar book. Since hagiographies are narratives about a person's life, the fictional parts that cannot be included in reference books are central to developing faith.

In modern hagiography, the possibility of fiction arises due to the development of historical studies and the emergence of authors who do not belong to a religious community. Therefore, fiction is a familiar element that did not appear in modern Japan initially, but the proportion of fictional elements has increased until today. Although *The Saint of Honganji* has many parts that should be called fictional, the details of each scene in *No Blame for the Past* have a far more significant proportion of fictional elements. Another difference is Satō's focus on a specific problem within Shinran's teachings. Although it serves as a representative example of the overall thoughts of Shinran, the book's focus of interest is much more limited than in *The Saint of Honganji*. This increases the impact of its detailed descriptions because the narrator can use the slower pace of the narrative solely for one doctrinal question.

To conclude, an analysis of hagiographies with a focus on their fictional elements is the most direct way to connect the narrative with questions of faith. From the standpoint of a reader, the existence of fiction in connection with religious questions within the narrative is the very condition that can form their religious belief in the saint described and the corresponding doctrinal concepts, because a biography without fiction would affect them only on the level of historical knowledge.

Notes

1 See Wittgenstein (1994, 72–73) for original German.
2 See, for example, Bruno Petzold who compared Mahāyāna Buddhism with Goethe's pantheism (Petzold, 1982) or Dieter Strauss who explicitly discusses the question of salvation in Goethe's *Faust* (Strauss, 2018).
3 For a detailed analysis, see Foucher (1955).
4 In Jōdoshin Buddhism, these are called "illustrated family trees" (*ekeizu* 絵系図) (Shinkō no zōkeiteki hyōgen kenkyūiinkai, 1988, 114–79).
5 See a detailed list of Shinran biographies in Rüsch (2019, 516–28).
6 Bunkachō (2022, 72–73).
7 In the context of Pure Land Buddhism, there is a hagiographic genre called "Biographies [on people who gained] birth [in the Pure Land]" (*ōjōden* 往生伝). While most of them still emphasize the achievement of birth as the result of extraordinary practice, there emerged in the Jōdoshin context a genre that thematized the salvation of ordinary people who were not able to conduct any practice but were able to receive true faith in Amida which results in the assurance of birth in the Pure Land. This type of hagiography has the name "Biographies on wondrously excellent people" (*myōkōninden* 妙好人伝).
8 Examples of monographs that deal with the relationship between Shinran and Luther are Oguro (1985) and Katō (1987).
9 See Cohn (1990), where Cohn argues for identifying "fiction-specific signals," which are characteristic parts *within* texts (776), and emphasizes the difference between "matter" and "manner" in a historical novel (788). For him, the manner of the text is the basis for arguing whether it is fiction, which corresponds to the approach in this chapter.
10 The institutional reason for this phenomenon lies in the fact that most hagiographies see their climax—or at least a central part in the development of the narrative—in the founding of the temple that later becomes the head-temple of a Jōdoshin Buddhist denomination.
11 First, the novel was published in the journal *Seiron* 正論 from 2010 to 2012.
12 Kakunyo (2016, 93–94).
13 Another argument for nonfictional elements is that to believe in something presupposes that one can at least think of the possibility of its existence. Therefore, even if an author writes an episode about Shinran that is highly convincing in terms of faith, the reader could not accept this point—supposedly not even on the level of faith—if it stands in contradiction to the central elements of Shinran's nonfictional biography.

Works Cited

Asuka Ryōko 飛鳥涼子. *Shōsetsu Gutoku Shinran* 小説愚禿親鸞. Osaka: Fūeisha.
Bunkachō 文化庁. 2022. *Shūkyō Nenkan* 宗教年鑑. Tokyo: Bunkachō. https://www.bunka.go.jp/tokei_hakusho_shuppan/hakusho_nenjihokokus o/shukyo_nenkan/pdf/r04nenkan.pdf.
Cohn, Dorrit. 1990. "Signposts of Fictionality: A Narratological Perspective." *Poetics Today* 11, no. 4 (Winter): 775–804.
Foucher, Alfred. 1955. *Les vies anterieures de Bouddha: d'apres les textes et les monuments de l'Inde.* Paris: Presses universitaires de France.
Hamburger, Käte. 1968. *Die Logik der Dichtung.* Stuttgart: Ernst Klett.
Ishimaru, Gohei 石丸梧平. 1922. *Ningen Shinran* 人間親鸞. Tokyo: Zōkyō shoin.
Itsuki, Hiroyuki 五木寛之. 2010–2014. *Shinran* 親鸞. Six volumes. Tokyo: Kōdansha.
Kakunyo 覺如. 2016. "Shinran Shōnin Denne (Godenshō)" 親鸞聖人伝絵（御伝鈔）. In *Jōdo Shinshū Seiten Zensho* 浄土真宗聖典全書, vol. 4, edited by Jōdo Shinshū honganjiha sōgō kenkyūjo 浄土真宗本願寺派総合研究所, 71–108. Kyoto: Honganji shuppan.
Katō, Chiken 加藤智見. 1987. *Shinran to Rutā: Shinkō No Shūkyōgakuteki Kōsatsu* 親鸞とルター：信仰の宗教学的考察. Tokyo: Waseda daigaku shuppanbu.

Kurata, Hyakuzō 倉田百三. 2003. *Shukke to Sono Deshi* 出家とその弟子. Tokyo: Shinchōsha.

Murata, Tsutomu 村田勤. 1896. *Shinran Shinden: Shiteki Hihyō* 親鸞真傳：史的批評. Tokyo: Kyōbunkan.

Oguro, Tatsuo. 1985. *Der Rettungsgedanke bei Shinran und Luther: Eine Religionsvergleichende Untersuchung.* Hildesheim, New York: Olms.

Petzold, Bruno. 1982. *Goethe und der Mahayana Buddhismus.* Edited by Joseph P. Strelka. Vienna: Octopus.

Rüsch, Markus. 2019. *Argumente des Heiligen: Rhetorische Mittel und narrative Strukturen in Hagiographien am Beispiel des japanischen Mönchs Shinran.* Munich: Iudicium.

Satō, Yōjirō 佐藤洋二郎. 2014. *Kiō wa togamezu* 既往は咎めず. Tokyo: Shōhakusha.

Shinkō no zōkeiteki hyōgen kenkyūiinkai 信仰の造形的表現研究委員会, ed. 1988. *Bokie, Ekeizu, Gensei Shōnin eden* 慕帰絵 絵系図 源誓上人絵伝 (Shinshū jūhō shuei 真宗重宝聚英, vol. 10). Kyoto: Dōhōsha shuppan.

Strauss, Dieter. 2018. *Wir sind Faust: Teufelspakt und Erlösung bei Goethe, Thomas Mann und Klaus Mann.* Berlin: Peter Lang.

Unknown author. 2011. "Shinran Shōnin Goinnen" 親鸞聖人御因縁. In *Taikei Shinshū Shiryō Denkihen* 大系真宗史料伝記編, vol. 1, edited by Shinshū shiryō kankōkai真宗史料刊行会, 5–39. Kyoto: Hōzōkan.

Wittgenstein, Ludwig. 1994. *Vermischte Bemerkungen.* Werkausgabe, vol. 8. Frankfurt a.M.: Suhrkamp.

Wittgenstein, Ludwig. 1998. *Culture and Value: A Selection from the Posthumous Remains.* Oxford: Blackwell.

31

FICTION AND BELIEF IN ANCIENT AND EARLY MEDIEVAL INDIA

Isabelle Ratié

In memory of Marie-Claude Porcher

India is home to many religions. They include Hinduism, whose followers constitute a majority of the Indian population. Yet, Hinduism is by no means the sole Indian creed—first, because what we nowadays designate as the Hindu religion results from the complex history of different—and often rival—movements,[1] but also because it is on the Indian subcontinent that Buddhism arose and developed into diverse traditions before spreading throughout Asia. And if Buddhism constituted a prominent part of the Indian religious and intellectual landscape for over 1,500 years, Jainism, which is just as ancient, is still thriving in India. Not to mention less famous religions that have altogether disappeared (such as Ājīvikism), Islam and Sikhism have also come to play a considerable role in India's spiritual, political, and intellectual history, although in a period that is beyond the scope of this essay (concerned with the first millennium CE and the first two centuries of the second millennium). Recent studies have emphasized how the competition between these numerous religious movements and their attempts to establish the superiority of their doctrines in debates with champions of rival faiths led to the emergence of a philosophical field where theoretical discourse rested on reason and experience rather than scriptural authority, since no interreligious dialogue was possible without such a relatively neutral ground (e.g., Eltschinger and Ratié, 2023, 48–61). But what of the relationship of these religious movements with other types of discourses—discourses involving fiction? The Indian civilization has produced an extraordinary wealth of fictional works: tales of all kinds, epics, ornate poems, novels, theatrical plays. The ambivalent relationship of religions with fiction (their mistrust of its constitutive "make-believe," but also their interest for its power to spread or strengthen beliefs) has often been highlighted;[2] yet studies on fiction and belief rarely take account of the Indian context. The present chapter is in no way an exhaustive analysis of the relationship between fiction and belief in India; its only ambition is to show that this relationship is far richer than is usually assumed, and to provide a glimpse of the subtle ways in which Indian thinkers have understood it.

What Can Be Called Fiction in India?

The lines between legends, myths, historical or biographical narratives often seem blurry in ancient and medieval India, as evidenced by the use of the word *itihāsa* (sometimes rendered as "narrative

403

DOI: 10.4324/9781003119456-35

of the way things were" [see e.g., Pollock, 2003, 58ff.]) not merely to designate what we now label as historical accounts, but also legends from the epics of the *Mahābhārata* and *Rāmāyaṇa*. And the fictional status of Indian religious narratives may sometimes seem particularly ambiguous, as in the case of Buddhist Jātakas, i.e., stories that, despite sharing many a fanciful feature with ordinary tales, achieve a (multi-)biographical status inasmuch as they claim to depict past lives of the historical figure of the Buddha. Yet one should not conclude from this that the difference between fact and fiction was utterly unknown or ignored in premodern India. Just as in the West, it was certainly toyed with, transgressed and contested, but it wasn't nonexistent. Thus, the distinction between a biographical or historical account and an "invented story" (*kathā*), for instance, was explicitly made by a number of Indian authors, who (like Bhāmaha in the seventh century CE) understood the first as narrating what actually happened (*vṛtta*) or had been perceived (*upalabdha*) while defining the second as a work of imagination (*kalpanā*) (Warder, 1972, 181–87), the word *kathā* being also used more generally to characterize a discourse depicting a state of affairs having no correspondence with reality. And poets (*kavi*)—whose works, generically named *kāvya*, may be composed in prose or verse and include theatrical compositions—were expected to create or transform stories through a faculty called *pratibhā*—something like their "creative insight," which is akin to the European understanding of "imagination" at least inasmuch as it includes, as the great philosopher and poetician Abhinavagupta (tenth–eleventh century CE) puts it, the ability "to create something never [experienced] before" (*Dhvanyālokalocana*, 1.6, 92).[3] Fiction will therefore be broadly understood here as the narration of a state of affairs known to be either invented or at least substantially transformed by the poet's imagination. Admittedly, the ability to invent stories was not considered to be the defining feature of poetry by most Indian poeticians, who rather understood the characteristic of poetry as the power of a poet's language to make us enjoy *rasa*, the essence (literally, the "sap" or "juice") of human emotions.[4] But not to mention that the opinion of these theoreticians (who belonged to an elite mostly concerned with ornate poetry) may not have been that of many a story-teller with less claims to refinement, even poeticians admitted that story-telling is a crucial aspect of poetry's power to make us relish *rasa*. One of the most influential among them, Ānandavardhana (ninth century CE), thus explained that a poet, even when using an already well-known story as a basis for his work, should not hesitate to eliminate any element of the plot that may prove an impediment to aesthetic enjoyment or to add a story of his own, "for it is not at all a poet's business to bring about a mere chronicle of events as they happened, since it is history (*itihāsa*) that accomplishes this" (*Dhvanyāloka*, 336).[5]

The Didactic Function of Indian Religious Fictions

What makes literary works[6] involving such fictions specifically Buddhist, or Jain, etc., is frequently the fact that they present characters embodying the virtues deemed cardinal by this or that religion—which is why, for example, telling and hearing stories (*kathā*) are, respectively, integral parts of the lives of Jain monks and laymen, and are considered a kind of study in its own right: in Jainism, story-telling clearly has, as Nalini Balbir has put it, an "ideological status" (Balbir, 1994, 223). Studies of narratives in South Asian religious traditions, particularly Buddhist and Jain, have multiplied in recent decades,[7] highlighting how these sources can be as helpful as non-narrative, "systematic" ones when it comes to understanding religious doctrines (Collins, 1998, 121ff.), since stories obviously played a key didactic role and helped spread moral teachings (Appleton, 2014, 192).

This is not to say that in such narratives the hero is perfect from the start; rather, many of them focus on the evolution through which the main protagonist, gradually becoming disillusioned with mundane existence, ends up realizing how embracing a specific religion is the only way to salvation. Thus in the second century BC, the Buddhist poet Aśvaghoṣa authored a lengthy poem, *Handsome*

Nanda (*Saundarananda*), telling the story (which he did not invent but greatly expanded [Covill, 2007, 16–17]) of a young hero named Nanda who is deeply in love with his attractive wife and happily absorbed in his new marital life, but gets unwillingly ordained as a Buddhist monk, progressively abandons any interest for beauty in all of its manifestations while studying the Buddha's teachings, and eventually reaches liberation. The end of the work explains that the poem is not meant to bring about pleasure but only peace in its readers, poetry being like "honey" with which one mixes "a bitter medicine"—i.e., the Buddha's teachings. The assertion is particularly striking given that throughout the poem the hero struggles to free himself from the fascination for beauty that rivets him to the *saṃsāra*, the beginningless cycle of transmigration and pain. The poetic beauty that Aśvaghoṣa presents in conclusion as a mere didactic tool in the service of his religion certainly includes the elegance of his Sanskrit verses, but also the story itself, with its many twists and turns and its erotic atmosphere. He thus forces his readers to consider in hindsight how the whole plot was nothing but a potent soteriological device: he was only trying to convey the truth "in the guise of poetry," and all the "entertaining" aspects of his poem should be discarded (*Saundarananda* 18.63–64; see Covill, 2007, 363). This ambivalent view of poetry (as a charming and, therefore, potentially deceiving force, but also as capable of tricking readers into learning difficult truths) haunts later Indian works, particularly those of poeticians, who often discuss whether the legitimate goal of poetry is "pleasure" (*prīti*) or "instruction" (*vyutpatti/vyutpādana*).[8] Abhinavagupta remarks, for instance (possibly echoing an earlier, lost work of Bhaṭṭa Nāyaka), that while scriptures teach as a master (i.e., by providing injunctions and prohibitions) and history (*itihāsa*) teaches as a friend (i.e., by offering advice/examples?), poetry teaches as a loving wife (i.e., by charming) (*Dhvanālokalocana*, 40).[9]

This soteriological function of stories is particularly obvious in allegorical plays. Aśvaghoṣa may already have authored a Buddhist one[10] but the first fully preserved work of this kind is a Vaiṣṇava eleventh-century drama, *The Rise of Wisdom Moon* (*Prabodhacandrodaya*) by Kṛṣṇamiśra (see Kapstein, 2009). It tells the story of a power struggle between noble families, but while doing so, it also depicts the efforts of a soul to attain the final understanding of universal nonduality as defined in the Brahmanical (Vaiṣṇava-leaning) tradition of Advaita Vedānta. That the story is to be grasped as happening on both the concrete plane and its symbolic counterpart is made explicit through constant reminders of this double status, such as the characters' names all corresponding to abstract notions (Intuition, Ignorance, Illusion, Lust, etc.).[11] Although allegorical plays never reached the status of a distinct genre in the treatises of poeticians, *The Rise of Wisdom Moon* was often imitated, sometimes by members of rival movements (notably Śaiva and Jain ones [Kapstein, 2009, xliv–xlv; Keith, 1924, 251–56])[12] who used the format so as to praise their own doctrines; and at least ten commentaries were composed on it, which has been taken as an indication that it was often used for didactic purposes (Kapstein 2009, xliv–xlv). Allegorical fictions were not limited to theater either, and were also found, for example, in tales and novels in the Jaina tradition (Osier, 1994).

One may wonder, however, what precise didactic function such works were expected to fulfill: were they exoteric instruments of conversion, or esoteric works only meant to be read by fellow practitioners? Were they designed to spread the doctrine, or to offer those who had already adopted it a deeper understanding of it? It seems that one function or the other may have prevailed depending on the allegorical work. Thus Jean-Pierre Osier, while analyzing Jain allegorical poems, has pointed out that plays such as Kṛṣṇamiśra's undoubtedly had "propaganda" as their goal and were obviously meant to reach out beyond the religious circle to which the author belonged, whereas Jain allegorical poems, the main function of which may have been to enliven the numerous (and often fastidious) lists of concepts that followers were to learn (Osier, 1994, 276), were certainly written for a readership of initiates (Osier, 1994, 284).

Fictionalizing Religious Conflicts: Jayanta the Spin Doctor?

So fiction was certainly seen in India as a means of spreading and strengthening religious beliefs. And its "ideological status" (to borrow again Nalini Balbir's words) also had to do, of course, with political power, if only because, in order to make a living, poets mostly relied on the generosity of royal families and court dignitaries—and were sometimes dignitaries themselves. The ninth-century play by the Brahmanical philosopher Jayanta, *Much Ado about Religion* (*Āgamaḍambara*), remarkably illustrates this intimate relationship of religion, political power, and story-telling in medieval India. The play is about the dissensions between rival religious movements (Buddhism, Jainism, Brahmanical orthodoxy, as well as Śaiva and Vaiṣṇava currents variously deviating from this orthodoxy) in the kingdom of Kashmir. It has sometimes been read as an irenic appeal to oecumenism, because in the final act Dhairyarāśi, the wise character who eventually manages to appease these dissensions, asserts that all religions are basically to be tolerated provided that they do not go against public decency.[13] Yet, Jayanta's fierce satire does nothing to hide the prejudices of its Brahmanical author (Buddhist monks are presented as hypocritical gluttons, Jain philosophers, as idiots who torture themselves with asceticism, etc.), and surely the happy ending did not make the audience forget about its ferocious jokes. Besides, a key feature in the play's plot happens to be an event that actually took place in Kashmir, and in which Jayanta himself was directly involved: as a minister/adviser (*amātya*) of King Śaṅkaravarman, he was instrumental in banishing from Kashmir the sect of the Black Blankets (*nīlāmbara*), so called because—as explained in the play—their religious practice included copulating under a blanket in public places. The drama repeatedly reminds the audience of Jayanta's role in this affair (Acts II and III; see Dezsö, 2005, 123, 131–33) while making numerous references to the actual king and royal family members. And by defining the acceptable religions as those that do not offend public decency, the so-called irenic conclusion of the play legitimizes this religious ban. Jayanta thus intertwines fiction and reality in a "Dokumentarspiel" (Wezler, 1976, 340) weaving together fictional elements with real characters (including himself, even though he does not directly appear on the stage and is only talked about by other characters), and it is hard not to suspect that he thus fictionalizes historical events so as to suit his own political and religious agenda, using the theatrical stage to alter the spectators' beliefs as to what really happened.

Sadly no preserved independent source can tell us whether the play had any impact of this kind. At any rate, there is also much in the play that should make us wary of just seeing Jayanta as a spin doctor exploiting fiction in order to justify the king's (and his own) politics—to start with, the prologue, which shows as a character the stage manager in the throes of despair. The metaleptic presence of the stage manager and other actors playing themselves at the outset of the representation is a common feature of classical Indian plays; playwrights often took advantage of the prologue to extol the merits of the show about to be performed and defend its novelties (Dezsö, 2007, 92–93). In and of itself, the stage manager's proclaimed wish to relinquish his trade and become a renunciate is not surprising either: a similar claim is found in the prologue of earlier Sanskrit plays that also deal with religious matters, such as Harṣa's seventh-century *How the Nāgas Were Pleased* (*Nāgānanda*), which tells the Buddhist story of a prince's self-sacrifice to save serpentine beings (*nāgas*) from being sacrificed to Garuḍa (a bird-like, snake-killing Hindu divinity) (see Skilton, 2008). But whereas in the latter case, the stage manager is led to abandon all worldly concerns by the holy atmosphere of the play about to be performed, in *Much Ado about Religion*, what makes him wish to leave the world is the fact that he was burdened with the impossible task of putting on Jayanta's new play, a bizarre work that obviously transgresses the revered rules laid out in treatises of dramaturgy! The prologue, in which Jayanta seems to be making fun of himself before joking at the expense of others, thus warns the audience from the beginning that, if the play is "not worldly" (it is about religion, and it does contain several lengthy philosophical debates), it is not to be taken too seriously either. Csaba Dezsö (2007) has rightly pointed out that in many respects it can be said to belong to the category of plays whose dominant *rasa* is "the appeased" (i.e., the goal of which is to make us relish the emotion that arises from spiritual detachment)[14] as it is defined in treatises on theater. Yet from the prologue its humor is in stark contrast with the seriousness of plays seen as belonging to this category, such as *How the Nāgas Were Pleased*, and it rather brings to mind the genre of farces (*prahasana*), in which "the favourite victims of satire ... are *yogin*s and other saintly characters" (Warder, 1972, 132)[15]—although such farces are supposed to have very different formal features (their length, number of acts, etc.). Despite this farcical dimension, Jayanta's unclassifiable work cannot be labeled anti-religious either, as he clearly upheld a certain orthodox view of the Brahmanical religion (that of the Nyāya, in defense of which he has also written a major philosophical treatise, *A Cluster of Flowers of the Nyāya* [*Nyāyamañjarī*]), and his sarcasms are not aimed at all religious movements with the same force. Yet even orthodox religious attitudes are made fun of at times (albeit in a rather benevolent way, and while refraining from targeting his own movement).[16] In fact, as the play's title indicates (*Āgamaḍambara* literally means something like *The Cacophony of Scriptures*), he seems at least as interested in showing how laughable the fuss sometimes made about religious matters is as in justifying his political choices. Besides, the reason why he presents his own play as transgressing established dramatic rules is that it mixes poetry with theoretical debates, but also, possibly, that it combines fiction and historical facts in an unprecedented way (Dezsö, 2007, 117–23): Abhinavagupta's explicit condemnation of plays representing contemporary real events in his work on theater (*Abhinavabhāratī*, vol. II, 413)[17] postdates Jayanta, but this could have already been seen as a breach of custom in Jayanta's time.[18] The prologue highlights this departure from tradition, thus drawing attention to the very border between fact and fiction that Jayanta is about to cross. It also reminds the audience that the dramatist could not but carefully avoid incurring the king's displeasure: when the assistant asks the stage manager whether he fears some "threat from the king" if he goes on with the show, the latter replies "with a smile" that it is not the case (*Āgamaḍambara*, 34–35).

On the whole, *Much Ado about Religion* therefore seems to be less about defending King Śaṅkaravarman's religious politics by making fiction pass for historical reality than about creating a playful space where it is acceptable to laugh about the most serious matters, precisely because they are fictionalized—and advertised as such. And there is ample additional evidence that in India, fiction, even when bearing on religious matters, was not only used to strengthen religious beliefs.

Religious Competition, Irony, and the Art of (re-)Telling Stories

Thus, some of these stories are built so as to produce a kind of satirical echo of sacred texts. It is the case of the *Tales of the Vetāla*, a collection of twenty-five stories found in several famous Indian larger works. Its most elaborated version has survived in the eleventh-century work by Somadeva (who belonged to a Brahmanical tradition), the *Ocean of Story* (*Kathāsaritsāgara*), a huge collection of tales linked through a complex structure of embedded narratives (see Tawney, 1926). In the *Tales of the Vetāla*, a young, courageous king finds himself alone at night, having to move a corpse through a terrifying cremation ground while a spirit (*vetāla*) inhabiting the corpse being carried on the king's shoulders tells him stories. At the end of each tale, the *vetāla* presents the king with a riddle, adding that his head will be shattered if he fails to solve it correctly. This delightfully scary narrative frame efficiently ties the stories together with its suspenseful thread, but it is also a transparent reference (see e.g., Renou, 1963, 19) to theologico-ritualistic riddling contests (*brahmodya*) recorded in the ancient Vedic corpus of the *Brāhmaṇa*s, where discussants were threatened with having their head shattered (see Witzel, 1987). This venerable tradition of the *brahmodya* is displaced, however, in a setting that is utterly impure from a Vedic viewpoint: a cremation ground full of foul substances and dreadful spirits. By doing so, Somadeva was certainly not trying to subvert the Vedic religion, and in many regards the stories told by the *vetāla* illustrate the socio-religious duty (*dharma*) as understood in the Brahmanical perspective. But the contrast between the dialogue's Vedic echoes and its strikingly unvedic environment adds much piquancy to the narration, and is in fact characteristic of the entire work's tone, which Louis Renou has aptly described as "imperceptibly tinged with irony" (Renou, 1963, 20).[19]

In Somadeva's case, such religious references seem to be put in the service of story-telling, rather than having any particular ideological function—after all, even the gods love nothing more than a good story, as the very beginning of the *Ocean of Story* makes clear (according to it, the entire collection of narratives ultimately owes its existence to the goddess Pārvatī's whim to hear a great and unheard-of tale). But fictions can also become something of a religious battlefield in India, albeit one where humor is never absent.

This is true of farces, whose authors seemed to enjoy nothing more than laughing about self-proclaimed *guru*s and saints.[20] Lee Siegel has suggested that the social function of such plays was "to prevent religion from becoming all too absolutely hallowed" (Siegel, 1987, 188–89). One could object that many of them took aim at specific movements (most often Buddhist and esoteric Śaiva currents) rather than mocking religion in general. As seen above with respect to Jayanta's play, these two endeavors were not necessarily incompatible, but it is reasonable to assume that in many cases those laughed at were targeted first and foremost so as to please another religious group. The religious battlefield extended far beyond theatrical farces, however, and was not just about inventing stories to make fun of other religions: it was also about *appropriating* other religions' stories.

Thus, some Jain authors have claimed to rewrite the two great (and Brahmanical) Indian epics, the *Mahābhārata* and *Rāmāyaṇa*.[21] This "Jainization" of the epics[22] certainly had some political motivations: epic rewritings were often a way of legitimizing a local royal dynasty, and religious movements probably saw in this an opportunity to attract a king's favors (Brocquet, 2010; Chojnacki, 2018, 185–88; Thapar, 2000, 660–66).[23] In some cases, it may also have been an attempt to show how Jain minority views were not irreconcilable with the Brahmanical, dominant lore (Chojnacki, 2018). But some of these works emphatically exposed the inconsistencies and improbabilities of the Brahmanical ones (thus according to a Jain version of the *Rāmāyaṇa*, the demon Rāvaṇa owes his name "Ten Necks" to the fact that his nine-pearled necklace reflects his head rather than to his actually possessing ten heads). Instead of expounding the criticism in a conceptual form, however, they offered rival *stories* and built a "counter-tradition" of tales and myths (Jaini, 1993),[24] thus seemingly acknowledging that only fiction can effectively counterbalance the power of fiction.

It has also been suggested that *Kapphiṇa's Triumph* (*Kapphiṇābhyudaya*), a ninth-century ornate poem by Śivasvāmin that tells the story of king Kapphiṇa's conversion to Buddhism, can in fact be read, thanks to a series of refined stylistic devices that allow for several different, simultaneous meanings (*śleṣa*), as depicting at a deeper level the hero's conversion to Śaivism (Yokochi, 2012). That the poem may tell two different stories at once is no rarity in South Asian literature,[25] and if Yuko Yokochi's hypothesis can be substantiated by further research,[26] Śivasvāmin's poem could turn out to be one striking manifestation of the "inclusivistic" strategy often adopted by Indian religions, that is, their claim to make room for other religious movements, the better to present them as inferior forms of their own doctrines and practices.[27] Śivasvāmin may have used the ambiguities of his highly refined poetry to present the Buddhist story of Kapphiṇa as narrating, at a more profound level and only for those enlightened enough to see it, the triumph of Śaivism.

As far as this religious competition in the story-telling arena is concerned, another fascinating Jain work (which may have belonged to a genre of which very few exemplars have survived [Osier and Balbir, 2004, 19]) is Haribhadra's eight-century *Ballad of the Rogues* (*Dhuttakkhāṇa*; see Osier and Balbir, 2004; Upadhye, 1944). Thieves, unable to earn a living during heavy monsoon rains, pass the time together by playing a game: each participant must tell a story that the others must establish to be authentic by appealing to the authority of the Brahmanical epics and Purāṇas (collections of myths)—and whoever fails must pay for everybody's meal. Each rogue tells an outlandish story; yet, the revered Brahmanical narratives invariably lend credence to the thieves' tall tales (why should the crook Mūladeva not have been actually chased by an elephant inside a pot where he had sought refuge, if the four social classes were able to emerge from the single body of the creator god Brahmā? And so forth). By showing how Brahmanical stories can be used to confirm the most ludicrous reports, the text highlights their implausibility and forces its readers to wonder why they have blindly trusted them so far. Jean-Pierre Osier has pointed out that Haribhadra's work is less satirical than ironical in that it does not targets persons (which would go against the Jain ethics of non-violence), and that, rather than being used to propagate beliefs, it is meant *to instill doubt* (Osier, 2005, 321–23).

Fiction and Doubt

The latter point is of interest, all the more since Françoise Lavocat has recently argued that what religions both fear and covet about fiction might be, rather than its ability to strengthen belief, its power to make us doubt (Lavocat, 2016, 219–72)—and there is much in South Asian literature to support this hypothesis. Thus, the tenth-century *Way to Liberation* (*Mokṣopāya*) and a later, much-expanded version of it that is known today as the *Yogavāsiṣṭha*[28] defend an uncompromising idealism according to which the entire phenomenal world pertains to the realm of cosmic illusion (*māyā*), the only reality being an eternal, single consciousness, and in these texts interweaving tales with theoretical reflections, fictions have the crucial function of shattering their readers' certainties as to the reality of what they perceive. One way of achieving this is to show the fictional characters themselves no longer knowing if they should trust their senses or if they are trapped in a dream (Hanneder, 2006, 115–16) as in the story of king Lavaṇa, who dreamt, in what seemed like a life-long experience, that he was an untouchable living in another country—and upon awakening, got to meet his "dream-family" (Doniger O'Flaherty, 1984, 134–35; Hanneder, 2008, 94; Hulin, 1987, 39–63). The character of Lavaṇa is, by the way, presented as the grand-son of Hariścandra, whose story also involves a dream that was experienced by the dreamer as lasting twelve years when it "really" lasted no longer than the night.[29] These stories, "genuine narratives of metaphysical fiction" (Hulin, 1987, 26), force their readers to acknowledge how easily they accept the reality of their dreams *as long as they are dreaming*—and thus powerfully question their reasons for assuming that what they take to be real now is actually so (see Hanneder, 2008).

Indian stories have many ways of thus blurring the distinction between dream and reality, even on the theatrical stage. The play *Vāsavadattā in a dream* (*Svapnavāsavadatta*)[30], for instance, has as its centerpiece a dialogue that is *simultaneously* dreamt and real, as king Udayana, dreaming of his beloved queen Vāsavadattā (whom he wrongly believes to be dead), talks to her in his sleep while she is actually present in the room and answers him; the king wakes up as she disappears, left in excruciating doubt as to whether the experience "really" took place. The spectators know that it *both* did and did not, and their knowledge is almost as disconcerting as the king's doubt, as it rids them of the comfortable confidence that an experience must be either real or unreal. Incidentally, it is no coincidence that immediately before this scene, the king's fool has mistaken a garland on the floor for a snake,[31] such a mistake being a stock example in philosophical treatises that discuss the mechanism of illusion, particularly in Vedāntic works according to which the whole empirical world is illusory.

Stories within Stories, Dreams within Dreams, Plays within Plays

Another characteristic of the *Way to Liberation* and its later versions is their keen interest in the phenomenon of the "dream within a dream," that is, what happens when one dreams, wakes up, and then realizes that this so-called wakeful state was in fact another dream—an experience understood by Indian authors to have occurred because one shorter dream became embedded in another, larger one. These texts are replete with allusions to such nested dreams[32] and present the passages from one dream to another as all occurring within "the great dream called the wakeful state" (*Mokṣopāya* 6.76.3; cf. 6.29.40). Thus, a monk daydreams that he is a *bon vivant* layman called Jīvaṭa, who dreams that he is a Brahmin, who dreams that he is a prince, etc. (see Doniger O'Flaherty, 1984, 206–09; Hulin, 1987, 121–34). And one cannot but draw a parallel here with the pan-Indian technique of embedded narratives, where one smaller story is narrated by one of the characters of a larger story, which is itself embedded in an even larger story, etc.; the *Way to Liberation* makes great use of it. Both structures tend to make the larger element (the longer story or dream) appear as the real one as opposed to the embedded fiction, since a dream is deemed unreal in relation to the other state in the midst of which it occurs, and a story is taken to be fiction in relation to the larger story in which its narration takes place. Both of them also involve an inescapable effect of metaphysical vertigo: at some point the larger, "real" narrative turns out to be another fiction since it is in fact embedded in an even larger story, just as, in a dream within a dream, we awaken to a reality that eventually turns out to be just another dream. And what prevents us from suspecting a possible *regressus ad infinitum* here? Indian philosophical systems according to which the empirical world, far from existing outside consciousness, is ultimately nothing but internal aspects taken on by consciousness, have often invoked this phenomenon of nested dreams to establish their idealism. This is the case in the Buddhist idealistic tradition of Yogācāra (Eltschinger and Ratié, 2023, 120) but also in Śaiva nondualism. In his philosophical works, Abhinavagupta—one of the foremost proponents of Śaiva nondualism—examines at length the nature of experience in embedded dreams (Ratié, 2011, 651–55) and his commentator Bhāskarakaṇṭha, who has also authored a commentary on the *Way to Liberation*, quotes the latter while explaining Abhinavagupta's analysis of dreams (*Bhāskarī*, vol. II, 268, quoting *Mokṣopāya* 4.1.11). Abhinavagupta also describes the *saṃsāra* as a fiction or an invented story (*kathā*) while comparing everyday errors occurring within it (such as confusing a piece of mother-of-pearl with silver) with dreams within a dream (*Īśvarapratyabhijñāvivṛtivimarśinī*, vol. III, 153; see Ratié, 2011, 651). And interestingly, he makes use of the same analogy of nested dreams in his work on theater, as he explains the device of the "play within a play," i.e., the fact that the characters of some dramas become the actors and spectators of a theatrical representation that is part of the plot.

The latter device, often presented as an invention of the European Baroque age (e.g., Forestier, 1996; Nelson, 1971) with some ancient Greek antecedents (see e.g. Ringer, 1998), is known in Sanskrit as "mock play" (*nāṭyāyita*) or "embryo play" (*garbhāṅka*), and constitutes an important feature of classical Indian theater (Bansat-Boudon, 1992, 350–54, 377–84, 1995; Jackson, 1898; Lockwood and Bhat, 1995; Porcher, 1986). Indian playwrights used it so as to present reflections on their own art,[33] but they probably also wished to take advantage of its metaphysical implications, as it hints at the unsettling fluidity of personal identity (Porcher, 1986; Shulman, 1997) by having real actors play the roles of characters who themselves are playing roles, and who most often impersonate in the embedded play characters that are "real" in the larger drama! Thus, watching the identity of the different characters dissolve and take on new shapes, we seem to be invited to witness the most mysterious metamorphoses of *saṃsāra* (the *Treatise on Theater* repeatedly compares the actor taking on a role with a transmigrating soul adopting a new body [see Cuneo and Ganser, 2022, 207–09]). Besides, Sanskrit metadramas are usually shown being watched by characters who fail to understand (or forget) that what is happening on the stage *is just a play*: just as Don Quixote attacks puppets (*Don Quixote* 2.1.26), in Bhavabhūti's play (*Uttararāmacarita*, act VII), Rāma, watching a representation about his wife's ordeal, addresses her character and must be reminded by his brother that this is only theater; in Harṣa's play, the queen watching her own love story played on the stage must be told again and again that "it is just a show" (*Priyadarśikā*, act III, 35 and 41); in Rājaśekhara's, the demon Rāvaṇa must be stopped by his minister from killing the actor playing his enemy Rāma, etc. (*Bālarāmāyaṇa*, act III; see also Dezsö, 2007, 115–17). The nested plays thus put the real spectators in the position of watching fake spectators watching a fake show, and being deluded into taking the show for reality. This, as was noted long ago, has the effect of "making the drama itself more realistic" (Jackson, 1898, 246). The larger play seems more real, because, as Abhinavagupta already points out, we only ever consider an experience to be a dream, or a theatrical fiction, in relation to (*tadapekṣa*) what we take to be reality: it is the mock spectators' gaze on the mock play that makes the latter appear as a play, and it appears thus in contrast with the mock spectators' reality.[34] That Abhinavagupta compares nested dreams and nested plays probably has to do with the fact that he takes as an example of the latter a lost drama (*Vāsavadattānāṭyadhārā*) by Subandhu whose main character, Vāsavadattā, happens to be, as seen above, tightly connected with dreams and the transgression of reality's boundaries,[35] but the analogy should also be read in accordance with what Abhinavagupta says of nested dreams in his philosophical works—namely, that upon awakening from a dream, we discard our past experience as fictitious and assume that the present one is real, whereas in fact, nothing assures us that we are not about to awaken from a "larger" dream. As Baroque metatheater, the Indian play within a play suggests the world's theatricality by inducing the doubt that what we take to be real might well be a cosmic show—an idea all the more appealing to Abhinavagupta since the religious tradition to which he belongs, Śaiva nondualism, sees Śiva as the author, director, spectator, and actor of the *theatrum mundi*.[36] In turn, this theatricalization of the world can be seen as echoing the nested structure of Vālmīki's great epic, the *Rāmāyaṇa*, and the contagion of fiction to reality with which its end seems to threaten us:[37] as noted by Jorge Luis Borges, its last part shows the hero, Rāma, listening to his sons narrating Vālmīki's work (*Rāmāyaṇa* 7.85),[38] of which he is but a character, thus making the story "monstruously embrace itself" (like that of *Don Quixote*, again)[39] and as a result, producing in its readers the anxiety that they too "might be fictitious" (Borges, 1952, 209–11).

On the Distinction between Believing and Enjoying Make-Believe

Indian plays within plays show spectators failing to enjoy the beauty of the show because they lose sight of the fact that it is not real. The point is of importance: from the Indian perspective, *it is not because we believe in fiction that we enjoy it*. If it were the case, we would ruin the representation by jumping on the stage, as do Rāvaṇa and Quixote; and by showing these spectators' blind faith in the reality of what they are perceiving, metatheater also has us reflect on the judgment of existence that we tacitly pass on all the objects of our ordinary perceptions. Perceiving, in our everyday lives, includes the silent acknowledgement that what we perceive actually exists, but this is not how we apprehend fiction when we understand it to be fiction. Admittedly, Indian aestheticians depict the mind of those watching a play as undergoing a process that is somewhat similar to Coleridge's "suspension of disbelief." Abhinavagupta rather describes it, however, as the enduring tension resulting from a double and simultaneous negation (*nihnava*): when we watch a play, being aware of the various theatrical conventions (costume, make-up, etc.), we apprehend what we see on the stage as not being the actor himself; while doing so, however, we also deny the fictional character's reality, as the same theatrical conventions (including things "not to be found in ordinary life" such as the space delimited by the stage) make it impossible for us to assume that the character's image superimposed onto the actor is real (*Abhinavabhāratī*, vol. I, 282; see Gnoli, 1985, 65–66). The spectator's consciousness, incapable of fully "resting" in the belief of either entity's existence, must leave what it sees on the stage floating in this ontological limbo—neither fully existing, nor completely nonexistent—that constitutes the very space of fiction. Of course, we can only enjoy the story that we are told if it presents human emotions with which we can in some way relate, otherwise there cannot be any "sympathetic response" (*hṛdayasaṃvāda*) and "emotional identification" (*tanmayībhāva*), and therefore no aesthetic pleasure. But the sympathetic response itself cannot occur if the story is apprehended as happening to a particular individual (be it the spectator him-/herself or someone else): it has to be grasped in a "generalized" or "universalized" way (*sādhāraṇīkṛta*) without which there can be no distancing from one's narrow concerns, no detachment from the preoccupations of ordinary existence, and therefore no aesthetic pleasure[40] (this is why, as mentioned above, Abhinavagupta proscribes representing contemporary events on the stage). Fiction is not enjoyable because it would imitate the particularities of life so perfectly that we might be fooled into confusing it with reality; on the contrary, it can only be enjoyed provided that the awareness that it is fiction does not altogether disappear.

Fiction and Playfulness

This paradox of fiction—the fact that we enjoy it if we can be "drawn" into the story while remaining aware that it is *just a story*—is subsumed by Śaiva nondualist authors under that of the playfulness (*krīḍā*) that characterizes any consciousness according to them:[41] conscious beings are not only able to make objects manifest (a capacity named *prakāśa*, literally "light" or "illumination") but also *to playfully ignore what they know*. There is something profoundly mysterious about this ability; what could be more difficult for consciousness—the self-manifest source of all phenomena—than obscuring its own self-evident nature? And yet it is also the most familiar of all powers, one that even children constantly experience while roleplaying, along with its constitutive joy or relishing (*camatkāra*), and one that remains present in the lives of adults whenever they enjoy a theatrical play or a novel, or simply when they let themselves be distracted and choose not to pay attention to their environment. This wondrous ability of consciousness to ignore its own knowledge, which might remind some readers of Jean-Marie Schaeffer's "shared ludic feint" (Schaeffer, 2010, 138–39) is a fundamental expression of the innermost core of consciousness in the Śaiva nondualistic phenomenology, i.e. what they name *vimarśa*—an untranslatable term that designates the fact that consciousness does not just passively manifests a given but actively and freely apprehends itself as being *x* or *y* (see Ratié, 2011, 158–62). This freedom or autonomy (*svātantrya*) of consciousness is obvious in imagination, understood as the ability to picture at will creatures that have never been perceived by anybody (as a "five-trunked, four-tusked elephant running in the sky"), and the Śaiva nondualists defend, against various Brahmanical authors, the thesis that such *ficta* do not result from the mechanical assembling of mnemonic impressions left by previous perceptions, and that there is always a genuine creativity in imagination.[42] But they also call attention to this freedom in perceptual experiences, showing how perception is never just the passive reflection of an external datum, and involves the *choice* to pay attention or to be distracted, to focus on this or that aspect of the sensory material, to present itself in turn as the subject and object of the perception, etc. While thus creating and enjoying fiction, what we relish, according to these authors, is the essential dynamism of the universal consciousness, the god Śiva, who creates the phenomenal universe by playfully manifesting himself in its countless forms. In this perspective, fiction is a soteriological tool, not because it would illustrate rightful conducts or induce belief in those who doubt, but rather, because it reminds us of the absolute freedom of consciousness (a freedom that is the very essence of God) to present itself as this or that definite form while retaining its infinite plasticity, and to enjoy its own make-believe.

By Way of a Conclusion

Indian religions have used stories in many ways. They have exploited the pleasure induced by fiction to help propagate the "bitter medicine," in Aśvaghoṣa's words, of their moral and soteriological teachings. They have also weaponized story-telling in various ways against other religious groups, fictionalizing historical religious dissensions, satirizing the religious conducts of their rivals, rewriting their stories, ironically using their myths to justify the most extravagant reports, inventing all kinds of counter-stories. Most importantly perhaps, they have exploited the power of fiction to make us *doubt*—to question our implicit acceptance that what we perceive must be real, notably by having recourse to nested structures in collections of tales and in theatrical plays, and thus suggesting that the phenomenal world is a mental projection comparable to dreams. Such practices are evidently (and as seen above, often explicitly) connected with idealistic systems developed both in Buddhist and Hindu circles. This idealistic tendency to blur the distinction between reality and fiction in India is undeniable, and has had echoes in global popular culture in recent times: in online games and Hollywood movies, one commonly designates a digital representation acting as a proxy for a person in a virtual environment by using the word "avatar" (from the Sanskrit noun *avatāra*, "descent," which designates the partial, perceptible forms sometimes used by the god Viṣṇu to manifest himself in the empirical world that he vastly transcends); one discusses the influence on *The Matrix* of a flimsily defined Buddhist Yogācāra idealism,[43] etc. But the cliché of a mystical India that would be from time immemorial convinced that the *saṃsāra* is a mere fiction, and that would use fiction itself to propagate its denial of the world's reality, should not be left unquestioned. First, because idealism was never a matter of consensus in India: many influential currents of thought (Brahmanical, but also Buddhist and Jain) staunchly defended the idea that the world exists independently of consciousness, and the idealistic traditions had to constantly respond to their scathing criticisms.[44] Besides, these traditions themselves defended a fundamental distinction between two levels of truth (*satya*)—one conventional, relative or superficial (*saṃvṛtisatya*), and the other, absolute, or valid in the ultimate sense (*paramārthasatya*); and they argued that as long as one has not fully "awakened" to a higher reality, the criteria commonly used to distinguish reality from illusion (the permanence of a phenomenon, its apprehension by more than one subject, etc.) must remain valid. Moreover, even the idealistic traditions that used fiction so as to induce the suspicion that the empirical world itself is a fiction were keen on maintaining a clear distinction between error (as an inadvertent confusion) and fiction (as a playful pretense): even if, as in Śaiva nondualism, they considered that ultimately, all inadvertent confusions have their root in Śiva's playful manifestation of himself in the infinitely varied forms of the universe, they also made a point of highlighting how fiction can only be enjoyed *if we do not quite believe in it*, i.e., if we remain aware that it is unreal, and if we nonetheless playfully choose to ignore this awareness of ours. In Śaiva nondualism, it is this playfulness without which fiction can neither be created nor relished that is in fact the ultimate reality, and enjoying the most mundane fictions is, in this respect, experiencing for a fleeting moment one's identity with the divine.

Finally, it might be worth noting that while India's idealistic movements tend to equate the empirical world with a fiction, this does not necessarily lead to a "radical depreciation" of the world as in the Baroque *theatrum mundi* (see e.g., Lavocat, 2016, 393). Śaiva nondualist authors, including Abhinavagupta, make the point that if phenomena are mere *appearances* taken on by consciousness, they are not to be discarded as *illusions*: precisely because they are manifestations of the ultimate consciousness' creative freedom, they are real, and the awareness of their beauty is to be cultivated. In such a system, imagination, understood as the ability to produce and appreciate fiction, is not condemned as a pernicious means of deception: it is rather presented as a possible soteriological path, provided that it is exercised while focusing on the fundamental creativity that it involves.[45]

Notes

1 The common use of the word "Hindu" is late (although it is not a sheer product of nineteenth-century colonialism as is sometimes claimed: see e.g. Chojnacki, 2011; Lorenzen, 2009). As far as ancient and medieval India is concerned, the term "Brahmanism" is often preferred so as to designate movements that, despite their wide divergences, shared a belief in the scriptural authority of a body of texts (first and foremost the Veda, of which Brahmans were the guardians) as well as the acceptance of a specific socio-religious order. Yet, what is termed "Hinduism" today also includes many traditions of that period that deviated to various

degrees from (and sometimes simply contradicted) Brahmanical orthodoxy thus defined. On the problematic use of the "Hindu" label and the underlying assumption of a monolithic religious identity, see e.g., Thapar (1996).

2 See (also for further bibliographical references) Lavocat (2016, 219–72).

3 Cf. Ingalls et al. (1990, 120). On *pratibhā* and its relationship with imagination see Shulman, 2008 (on imagination see also below, n. 42).

4 On this fundamental notion in Indian aesthetics and for further references see Cuneo (2015); Gnoli (1985); Masson and Patwardhan (1969; Pollock (2016).

5 Cf. Ingalls et al. (1990, 436).

6 See Hahn (2010) for a glimpse of the considerable diversity of genres to which Buddhist fictional works for instance belong.

7 See e.g., the references in Appleton (2014, 191, n. 1).

8 On this debate see e.g. Bansat-Boudon (1992, 104–07) and Pollock (2016, 31–34).

9 See e.g. Cuneo (2015, 77), Dezsö (2007, 104), Ganser (2021, 174) and Pollock (2016, 31–34).

10 On the fragments (discovered in Turfan) of a play ascribed to Aśvaghoṣa, and on the debate as to whether they belonged to a work that was entirely allegorical or not, see Steiner (2018) and Tieken (2010).

11 On the fact that the symbolic plane does not cancel the concrete one, see Osier (1994, 271). The ninth-century Jaina writer Siddharṣi describes his use of allegory as a form of comparison (*upamā/upamiti*), see Balbir (1994, 259).

12 The play also had a Persian version composed in the circle of the Moghol prince Dara Shikoh (see Kapstein, 2009, xlvi–xlvii).

13 Wezler (1976) already challenges this irenic reading.

14 On this specific *rasa*, see e.g. Masson and Patwardhan (1969).

15 The seventh-century *Mattavilāsa* in particular (see Unni, 1974) was certainly influential on Jayanta.

16 The young hero, Saṅkarṣaṇa, thus keeps getting carried away in his eagerness to defend the principles of the tradition to which he belongs, the Mīmāṃsā, which claims to represent the core of Brahmanical orthodoxy. In Act III, for example, he must momentarily join forces with a representative of the Śaiva Siddhānta (a tradition that sees Śiva as the highest divinity and that, while close to Brahmanical orthodoxy, significantly deviates from it in several respects) so as to defeat a materialist (Cārvāka) who denies basic tenets of the Vedic tradition, such as the existence of an enduring soul or any afterlife. In the course of this debate, the Śaiva demonstrates at length, against the materialist, the existence of a creator god—a demonstration that must be terribly embarrassing for a representative of the Mīmāṃsā, which staunchly denied the existence of such a god (see e.g. Eltschinger and Ratié, 2023, chapter 8). The presence on the stage of the hero having to silently witness this excoriating criticism of one of the main principles of his own tradition must have been very amusing to the audience (Jayanta himself belonged to the Nyāya, a theistic Brahmanical tradition).

17 See Bansat-Boudon (1992, 128, n. 212); Dezsö (2007, 121); Gnoli (1968, 64, n. 1).

18 Some theoreticians of theater did tolerate that a court poet may sing the deeds of his king (Dezsö, 2007, 117), but I know of no other classical Indian play in which contemporary events involving the dramatist himself are so conspicuously prominent in the plot.

19 "ombrées d'une imperceptible ironie."

20 See above, n. 15.

21 Vimalasūri (third century) and Raviṣeṇa (seventh century) have composed Jain versions of the *Rāmāyaṇa*; Jain rewritings of the *Mahābhārata* include Devaprabha's and Amaracandra's (thirteenth century) as well as Śubhacandra's (sixteenth century) (see Chojnacki, 2018; Clines, 2022; Jaini, 1993; Osier and Balbir, 2004, 20–25).

22 Some of these works combine the *Mahābhārata* stories with those of Jain religious leaders (*tīrthaṅkara*s).

23 Cf. Pollock (2006, 356–63).

24 Cf. Osier and Balbir (2004, 23) ("mythologie contre mythologie").

25 Cf. for instance Sandhyākaranandin's *Rāmacarita*, which can be read as simultaneously telling both the *Rāmāyaṇa*'s plot and a narrative of king Rāmapāla's retaking of East Bengal in the eleventh century (see Brocquet, 2010). On simultaneous narration in Indian sources, see Bronner 2010.

26 It is at least certain that Canto 19 in its entirety can be read in two distinct languages (Sanskrit and Prakrit), as demonstrated in Hahn (2007 and 2012), but whether it is a praise of the Buddha in both cases or not remains unclear for now (no complete translation has been published to date owing to the poem's reconditeness).

27 On such inclusivistic strategies, see e.g., Hacker (1957) and Halbfass (1988, 403–18).

28 On the distinction between *Mokṣopāya* and *Yogavāsiṣṭha*, which we owe to Walter Slaje's groundbreaking studies, see e.g., Hanneder (2006, 1–68).

29 The story, sometimes alluded to as "Hariścandra's night" (Ratié, 2021, 155–156), is not without affinities with the ninth-century Chinese tale by Shen Jiji (mentioned in Lavocat, 2016, 257, 393) of a discontented scholar who experiences in a dream, while his meal is being cooked, a fifty-year long brilliant career.

30 *Svapnavāsavadatta* (see Kale, 1945) is ascribed to Bhāsa, although this attribution is contested and his dates are uncertain (see e.g. Bansat-Boudon ed., 2006, 1181–92).

31 See Kale (1945, 42–44); cf. Bansat-Boudon ed. (2006, 1260).

32 See e.g. *Mokṣopāya* 3.4.77, 6.63.49, 6.65.31, 6.71.9.

33 Contrary to Baroque works, which tend to avoid technical terms (see Forestier, 1996, 224 on this "metalinguistic silence"), Indian plays within plays make great use of them (see, for instance, Bansat-Boudon, 1992).

34 *Abhinavabhāratī*, chapter 22, 48–49, vol. III, 172; cf. Bansat-Boudon (1992, 379).

35 Besides *Svapnavāsavadattā* (a preserved play also centering on Vāsavadattā, as mentioned above), see, among other sources, Subandhu's own poem *Vāsavadattā*, translated in Gray (1913).

36 See e.g., Bansat-Boudon (2004, 35–61, 144–45, 211–18, 273–75), Cuneo and Ganser (2022, 253–62), Ratié (2011, 559–60), Törzsök (2016). One striking difference with European Baroque theater is the fact that Śiva, both transcendent and immanent to the universe, is considered the actor *par excellence*, whereas the Christian God's transcendence prevents him from assuming the actor's function (cf. e.g. Forestier, 1996, 41).

37 At least two famous cases of plays within plays, the *Uttararāmacarita* and *Bālarāmāyaṇa*, are explicitly based on it.

38 See Goldman and Sutherland Goldman (2022, 840–41).

39 That *Don Quixote* is one of the few Western literary works translated into Sanskrit could be seen as meaningful in this respect, were it not for the fact that the translation was requested by an American collector (see Zadoo and Shastri, [1935–1936] 2019).

40 On the different stages of aesthetic pleasure see e.g. Bansat-Boudon (2004, 89–123) and Gnoli (1985).

41 On this playfulness, see Ratié (2011, 558–62, 2017, 450–52).

42 On the Indian philosophical controversy on the nature of imagination and the Śaiva nondualists' position, see Ratié (2010, 2017, 444–45).

43 See e.g. (with much caution) Ford (2000).

44 See e.g. Eltschinger and Ratié (2023, chapter 2).

45 See Ratié (2011, chapter 9 and 2010).

Works Cited

Prakrit and Sanskrit sources

Abhinavagupta. 1926–1964. *Abhinavabhāratī*. In *Nāṭyaśāstra with the Commentary of Abhinavagupta*, edited by Manavalli Ramakrishna Kavi. 4 vols. Baroda: Oriental Institute.

Abhinavagupta. 1938–1943. *Īśvarapratyabhijñāvivṛtivimarśinī*, edited by Madhusudan Kaul Shastri. 3 vols. Srinagar: Kashmir Series of Texts and Studies.

Abhinavagupta. 1940. *Dhvanyālokalocana*. In *Dhvanyāloka of Ānandavardhana*, edited by Pattābhirāma Śāstrī. Benares: Kashi sanskrit series 135.

Anonymus Casmiriensis. 2011–2019. *Mokṣopāya. Historisch-Kritische Gesamtausgabe*, edited by Jürgen Hanneder et al. 6 vols. Wiesbaden: Otto Harrassowitz Verlag.

Aśvaghoṣa. 1928. *Saundarananda*, edited by E. H. Johnston. London: Oxford University Press/Humphrey Milford.

Bhāskarakaṇṭha. [1938] 1986. "Bhāskarī." In *Īśvarapratyabhijñāvimarśinī of Abhinavagupta, Doctrine of Divine Recognition*, vols. I–II: *Sanskrit Text with the Commentary Bhāskarī*, edited by K. A. S. Iyer and K. C. Pandey. Delhi: Motilal Banarsidass.

Bhavabhūti. 1982. *Uttararāmacarita*. See Kale.

Haribhadra. 1944. [*Dhuṭṭakhāṇa*] *Dhūrtākhyāna. With an Elaborate Critical Essay by A.N. Upādhye*, edited by Vijaya Muni. Bombay: Bharatiya Vidya Bhavan.

Harṣa. 1977. *Priyadarśikā*. See Kale.

Harṣa. 2008. *Nāgānanda*. See Skilton.

Jayanta. 1959. *Nyāyamañjarī*, edited by K. S. Varadacharya. 2 vols. Mysore: Oriental Research Institute.

Jayanta. 2005. *Āgamaḍambara*. See Dezsö.

Kṛṣṇamiśra. 2009. *Prabodhacandrodaya*. See Kapstein.

Rājaśekhara. 1995. *Bālarāmāyaṇa*, edited by Bhāskarācārya Tripāṭhī. Delhi: Nag Publishers.

Śivasvāmin. 2007. *Kapphiṇābhyudaya or Kapphiṇa's Triumph: A Ninth Century Kashmiri Buddhist Poem*, edited by Michael Hahn. Kyoto: Ryukoku University Studies in Buddhist Culture.

Somadeva. 1930. *Kathāsaritsāgara*, edited by Pandit Durgāprasād and Kāśināth Pāndurang Parab. Revised edition. Bombay: Nirnaya Sagar Press.

Secondary Sources : Translations and Studies

Appleton, Naomi. 2014. *Narrating Karma and Rebirth. Buddhist and Jain Multi-Life Stories*. Cambridge, NY: Cambridge University Press.

Balbir, Nalini. 1994. "Formes et terminologie du narratif jaina ancien." In *Genres littéraires en Inde*, edited by Nalini Balbir, 223–61. Paris: Presses de la Sorbonne Nouvelle.

Bansat-Boudon, Lyne. 1992. *Poétique du théâtre indien. Lectures du Nāṭyaśāstra*. Paris: École Française d'Extrême-Orient.

Bansat-Boudon, Lyne. 1995. "Abhinavagupta, Exegete and Connoisseur of Theatrical Practice: An Essay on the 'nāṭyāyita.'" *Indo-Iranian Journal* 38: 149–65.

Bansat-Boudon, Lyne. 2004. *Pourquoi le théâtre? La réponse indienne*. Paris: Mille et Une Nuits.

Bansat-Boudon, Lyne, ed. 2006. *Théâtre de l'Inde ancienne*. Paris: Gallimard, Pléiade.

Borges, Jorge Luis. [1952] 2013. *Inquisiciones. Otras inquisiciones*. Buenos Aires: Debolsillo.

Brocquet, Sylvain. 2010. *La geste de Rāma: poème à double sens de Sandhyākaranandin*. Pondicherry: Institut Français de Pondichéry/École Française d'Extrême-Orient.

Bronner, Yigal. 2010. *Extreme Poetry. The South Asian Movement of Simultaneous Narration*. New York: Columbia University Press.

Chojnacki, Christine. 2011. "Shifting Communities in Early Jain Prabandha Literature: Sectarian Attitudes and Emergent Identities." *Studies in History* 27: 197–219.

Chojnacki, Christine. 2018. "Summarizing or Adapting the Great Indian Epic? Jain Mahābhārata's Epitomes from the Thirteenth Century." In *The Gift of Knowledge: Patterns of Patronage in Jainism*, edited by Christine Chojnacki and Basile Leclère, 165–95. Bangalore: Sapna Book House.

Clines, Gregory M. 2022. *Jain Rāmāyaṇa Narratives. Moral Vision and Literary Innovation*. London/New York: Routledge.

Collins, Steven, 1998. *Nirvana and Other Buddhist Felicities. Utopias of the Pali Imaginaire*. Cambridge: Cambridge University Press.

Covill, Linda. 2007. *Handsome Nanda by Aśvaghoṣa*. Clay Sanskrit Library. New York: New York University Press.

Cuneo, Daniele. 2015. "Rasa: Abhinavagupta on the Purpose(s) of Art." In *The Natyashastra and the Body in Performance: Essays on Indian Theories of Dance and Drama*, edited by Sreenath Nair, 72–88. New York: McFarland.

Cuneo, Daniele, and Elisa Ganser. 2022. "The Emotional and Aesthetic Experience of the Actor. Diderot's *Paradoxe sur le comédien* in Sanskrit Dramaturgy." In *'Verità e Bellezza.' Essays in Honour of Raffaele Torella*, edited by Francesco Sferra and Vincenzo Vergiani, 193–272. Naples: UniorPress.

Dezsö, Csaba. 2005. *Much Ado About Religion by Bhaṭṭa Jayanta*. New York: New York University Press, Clay Sanskrit Library.

Dezsö, Csaba. 2007. "A Curious Play (*kim api rūpakam*): Bhaṭṭa Jayanta's *Āgamaḍambara* in the Light of Classical Indian Dramaturgy." In *Indian Languages and Texts Through the Ages. Essays of Hungarian Indologists in Honor of Prof. Csaba Töttössy*, edited by Csaba Dezsö, 87–145. New Delhi: Manohar.

Doniger O'Flaherty, Wendy. 1984. *Dreams, Illusion and Other Realities*. Chicago, IL: The University of Chicago Press.

Eltschinger, Vincent, and Isabelle Ratié. 2023. *Qu'est-ce que la philosophie indienne?* Paris: Gallimard, Folio Essais.

Ford, James L. 2000. "Buddhism, Christianity, and The Matrix: The Dialectic of Myth-Making in Contemporary Cinema." *Journal of Religion & Film* 4 no. 2: 1–13.

Forestier, Georges. 1996. *Le théâtre dans le théâtre sur la scène française du XVIIᵉ siècle*. Geneva: Librairie Droz.

Ganser, Elisa. 2021. *Theatre and Its Other. Abhinavagupta on Dance and Dramatic Acting*. Leiden/Boston: Brill.

Gnoli, Raniero. 1985. *The Aesthetic Experience According to Abhinavagupta*. [Rome: ISMEO, 1956. Enlarged edition.] Varanasi: Chowkhamba.

Goldman, Robert P., and Sally J. Sutherland Goldman. 2022. *The Rāmāyaṇa of Vālmīki. The Complete English Translation*. Princeton, NJ: Princeton University Press.

Gray, Louis H. 1913. *Vāsavadattā. A Sanskrit Romance by Subandhu*. New York: Columbia University Press.

Hacker, Paul. 1957. "Religiöse Toleranz und Intoleranz im Hinduismus." *Saeculum* 8: 167–79.

Hahn, Michael. 2010. "The Buddhist Contribution to the Indian Belles Lettres." *Acta Orientalia Academiae Scientiarum Hungaricae* 63: 455–71.

Hahn, Michael. 2012. "Der *Bhāṣāśleṣa* – eine Besonderheit kaschmirischer Dichter und Poetiker?" In *Highland Philology*, edited by Roland Steiner, 77–106. Halle: Universitätsverlag Halle-Wittenberg.

Halbfass, Wilhelm. 1988. *India and Europe. An Essay in Understanding*. Albany: State University of New York Press.

Hanneder, Jürgen. 2006. *Studies on the Mokṣopāya*. Wiesbaden: Harrasowitz Verlag.

Hanneder, Jürgen. 2008. "Dreams and Other States of Consciousness in the *Mokṣopāya*." In *The Indian Night. Sleep and Dreams in Indian Culture*, edited by Claudine Bautze-Picron, 64–99. New Delhi: Rūpa & Co.

Hulin, Michel. 1987. *Sept récits initiatiques tirés du Yogavasistha*. Paris: Berg International.

Ingalls, Daniels H. H., Jeffrey Moussaieff Masson, and M. V. Patwardhan. 1990. *The Dhvanyāloka of Ānandavardhana with the Locana of Abhinavagupta*. Cambridge, MA: Harvard University Press.

Jackson, Williams. 1898. "Certain Dramatic Elements in Sanskrit Plays, with Parallels in the English Drama." *American Journal of Philology* 19: 241–54.

Jaini, Padmanabh S. 1993. "Jaina Purāṇas: A Purāṇic Counter Tradition." In *Purāṇa Perennis*, edited by Wendy Doniger, 209–49, 284–93. Albany: State University of New York Press.

Kale, M. R. 1945. *Svapnavāsavadatta of Bhāsa*. Bombay: Nava Bharat Prakashan Sanstha.

Kale, M. R. 1977 [1928]. *Priyadarśikā of Śrīharṣadeva*. Delhi: Motilal Banarsidass.

Kale, M. R. 1982 [1934]. *The Uttararāmacharita of Bhavabhūti*. Delhi: Motilal Banarsidass.

Kapstein, Matthew. 2009. *The Rise of Wisdom Moon by Kṛṣṇamiśra*. New York: New York University Press, Clay Sanskrit Library.

Keith, A. Berriedale. 1924. *The Sanskrit Drama in its Origin, Development, Theory and Practice*. Oxford: Oxford University Press.

Lavocat, Françoise. 2016. *Fait et fiction: pour une frontière*. Poétique. Paris: Seuil.

Lockwood, Michael, and A. Vishnu Bhat. 1995. *Metatheater and Sanskrit Drama*. New Delhi: Munshiram Manoharlal.

Lorenzen, David N. 2009. *Who Invented Hinduism? Essays on Religion in History*. Delhi: Yoda Press.

Masson, J. L., and M. V. Patwardhan. 1969. *Śāntarasa and Abhinavagupta's Philosophy of Aesthetics*. Poona: Bhandarkar Oriental Research Institute.

Nelson, Robert J. 1971. *Play Within a Play. The Dramatist's Conception of His Art: Shakespeare to Anouilh*. New York: Da Capo Press.

Osier, Jean-Pierre. 1994. "Essai de définition du genre allégorique en Inde." In *Genres littéraires en Inde*, edited by Nalini Balbir, 263–86. Paris: Presses de la Sorbonne Nouvelle.

Osier, Jean-Pierre. 2005. *Les jaïna critiques de la mythologie hindoue*. Paris: Cerf.

Osier, Jean-Pierre, and Nalini Balbir. 2004. *Haribhadra. Ballade des coquins*. Paris: GF Flammarion.

Pollock, Sheldon. 2003. "Sanskrit Literary Culture from the Inside Out." In *Literary Cultures in History. Reconstructions from South Asia*, edited by Sheldon Pollock, 39–130. Berkeley: University of California Press.

Pollock, Sheldon. 2006. *The Language of the Gods in the World of Men. Sanskrit, Power, and Culture in Pre-Modern India*. Berkeley/Los Angeles: University of California Press.

Pollock, Sheldon. 2016. *A Rasa Reader. Classical Indian Aesthetics*. New York: Columbia University Press.

Porcher, Marie-Claude. 1986. "Un exemple indien de théâtre dans le théâtre." *Poétique* 67: 335–48.

Ratié, Isabelle. 2010. "'A Five-Trunked, Four-Tusked Elephant Is Running in the Sky': How Free Is Imagination According to Utpaladeva and Abhinavagupta?" *Études asiatiques/Asiatische Studien* 64: 341–85.

Ratié, Isabelle. 2011. *Le soi et l'autre. Identité, différence et altérité dans la philosophie de la Pratyabhijñā*. Leiden/Boston: Brill.

Ratié, Isabelle. 2017. "Utpaladeva and Abhinavagupta on the Freedom of Consciousness." In *The Oxford Handbook of Indian Philosophy*, edited by Jonardon Ganeri, 437–68. Oxford: Oxford University Press.

Ratié, Isabelle. 2021. *Utpaladeva on the Power of Action. A First Edition, Annotated Translation and Study of Īśvarapratyabhijñāvivṛti, Chapter 2.1*. Cambridge, MA: Harvard University Press.

Renou, Louis. 1963. *Contes du vampire traduits du sanskrit et annotés*. Paris: Gallimard.

Ringer, Mark. 1998. *Electra and the Empty Urn. Metatheater and Role Playing in Sophocles*. Chapel Hill and London: The University of North Carolina Press.

Schaeffer, Jean-Marie. 2010. *Why Fiction?* Translated by Dorrit Cohn. Lincoln: University of Nebraska Press.

Shulman, David. 1997. "Embracing the Subject: Harṣa's Play Within a Play." *Journal of Indian Philosophy* 25: 69–89.

Shulman, David. 2008. "Illumination, Imagination, Creativity: Rājaśekhara, Kuntaka, and Jagannātha on *pratibhā*." *Journal of Indian Philosophy* 36: 481–505.

Siegel, Lee. 1987. *Laughing Matters. Comic Tradition in India*. Delhi: Motilal Banarsidass.

Skilton, Andrew. 2008. *How the Nagas Were Pleased by Harsha & The Shattered Thighs by Bhasa*. New York: New York University Press, Clay Sanskrit Library.

Steiner, Roland. 2018. "Die Schauspiele des Dichters Aśvaghoṣa." In *Festschrift für Jens-Uwe Hartmann zum 65. Geburtstag*, edited by Oliver von Criegern, Gudrun Melzer and Johannes Schneider, 489–500. Vienna: Arbeitskreis für tibetische und buddhistische Studien Universität Wien.

Tawney, C.H. 1924–1928. *The Ocean of Story*. 10 vols. London: Chas J. Sawyer Ltd.

Thapar, Romila. 1996. "The Tyranny of Labels." *Social Scientist* 24, no. 9–10: 3–23.

Thapar, Romila. 2000. *Cultural Pasts. Essays in Early Indian History*. Oxford: Oxford University Press.

Tieken, Herman. 2010. "Aśvaghoṣa and the History of Allegorical Literature in India." In *From Turfan to Ajanta. Festschrift for Dieter Schlingloff on the Occasion of his Eightieth Birthday*, edited by Eli Franco and Monika Zin, 993–97. Bhairahawa: Lumbini International Research Institute.

Törzsök, Judit. 2016. "Theatre, Acting and the Image of the Actor in Abhinavagupta's Tantric Sources." In *Around Abhinavagupta. Aspects of the Intellectual History of Kashmir from the Ninth to the Eleventh Century*, edited by Eli Franco and Isabelle Ratié, 451–94. Berlin: Lit Verlag [2nd ed. Delhi: Dev, 2022.]

Unni, N. P. 1974. *Mattavilāsa Prahasana of Mahendravikramavarman*. Trivandrum: College Book House.

Upādhye, A. N. 1944. See Haribhadra, *Dhūrtākhyāna*.

Warder, A. K. 1972. *Indian Kāvya Literature*, vol. I: *Literary Criticism*. Delhi: Motilal Banarsidass.

Wezler, Albrecht. 1976. "Zur Proklamation religiös-weltanschaulicher Toleranz bei dem indischen Philosophen Jayantabhaṭṭa." *Saeculum* 27: 329–47.

Witzel, Michael. 1987. "The Case of the Shattered Head." *Studien zur Indologie und Iranistik* 13–14: 363–415.

Yokochi, Yuko. 2012. "Triumph of Buddhism or Śaivism? A study in the Ninth-Century Kashmirian Poem *Kapphiṇābhyudaya*." *Journal of Indian and Buddhist Studies* 60, no. 3: 29–36.

Zadoo, Jagaddhar, and Nityanand Shastri. 2019. *Ḍān Kvikṣoṭaḥ: Don Quixote (Chapters I.2, I.3, I.8, I.10, I.16, I.17, I.18 & I.23) By Miguel de Cervantes Saavedra, Translated from English into Sanskrit*. Introduced and edited by Dragomir Dimitrov. Pune: Pune Indological Series.

32

FICTION, RELIGION, AND PREMODERN ARAB-ISLAMIC LITERATURE (EIGHTH– EIGHTEENTH CENTURIES)

Aboubakr Chraïbi

Between the seventh and eighth centuries, Islam spread from the Arabian Peninsula throughout the Near East and beyond: east to Persia and India, and west to the Maghreb and Spain. Islam carries a major book, the Koran, that relates events concerning the Prophet Muhammad (d. 630), as well as ancient stories about Adam, Moses, Solomon, the Seven Sleepers, etc. The narrative occupies a significant place in it. In fact, the Koran develops, as an extension of the Judeo-Christian traditions, a new history of the world as decided by God and dictated by the angel Gabriel to Muhammad. The Koran is essential to the Muslim religion and to its understanding. It is equally essential, politically, to the first two Arab dynasties, Umayyad (seventh and eighth centuries) and Abbasid (eighth–thirteenth centuries), whose legitimacy it upheld. These two dynasties were from the same family as the Prophet and, like him, originated from Mecca, and as such were his heirs. They, therefore, imposed and valued the Koran throughout the Muslim world as a unique object of divine origin of which they were in a way the guardians. At the same time, in this already-rich Near East, the valorization of the Koran, a text rapidly fixed in written form in the Arabic language—and the dynasties that carried it, who also spoke Arabic—contributed to the promotion of a new culture in this language, which thus came to be superposed on those already existing. The way was open to the transformation and assimilation of older cultures, and not the least, already present in these vast territories, such as the Berbers, Byzantines, Copts, Greeks, Jews, Persians, and Syriacs. The turning point came in the middle of the eighth century, when texts other than the Koran began to be composed and adapted into Arabic: lexicons and works of grammar, advice to the prince and collections of poems, but also narrative texts, which recount the wars of the pre-Islamic tribes, the life of the Prophet or the creation of the world, and various texts adapted from other languages. How to identify in this production the works of fiction? The jinn' quarrel with Solomon or the story of the seven young men who sleep for three centuries and then wake up (The Seven Sleepers), is it fiction or history? For which audience?

In an article titled "Prohibiting the Pilgrimage: Politics and Fiction in Mâlikî 'Fatwâs,' " Jocelyn Hendrickson (2016, 212) discusses how Muslim theologians in the fifteenth century inserted a fictional story into their legal text in order to convince people not to make the pilgrimage. More specifically, they added a debate between the jinn of the East and the jinn of the West in which each group of jinn explains its method for deterring believers from the straight path. For modern readers, this is fiction combined with a religious text. But was it fiction for the readers of the time? It is not clear that it was. As Robert G. Hoyland writes (2006, 39): "We may be unjustified in drawing too rigid a

419

DOI: 10.4324/9781003119456-36

line between 'Fables and Legends' [...] and 'History' [...]." To reduce this type of ambiguity, we will operate on the principle that a premodern Arab-Islamic literary work is fiction if it is presented as such when it is produced—in the preface, for example—and/or when it is received as such by its first commentators. Using this definition as our starting point, we see that such works are rare, especially those that present themselves as fiction, for ideological reasons, as Youssef Seddik and Alison Rice stress (2011, 186): "The entire Arab-Islamic tradition of writing has suffered, as a dogma, from this incapacity [facing the Koran] for the humans we are to create fiction through language."

A first question arises: how was the act of creation conceived? In pre-Islamic times, every poet (shâ'ir) was accompanied by a jinn (Tâbi') who inspired him. We understand this well: it is in a way his muse. But when the poet thinks he is inventing imaginary characters or places, it does not happen at all as he thinks: these characters and these places do exist. They are inspired to him by his jinn. It is not really a question of creation nor of fiction, but of *another reality*. After the arrival of the Koran and Islam, these jinn, former deities of Arabia, became competitors of the Koranic god who inspired the Prophet (via his angel Gabriel). They were downgraded, even demonized. There is only one reality, one narrative, one God (creator of this reality, author of this narrative): perhaps this is how we can understand the limited space left by the Koran for a work of fiction, seen as the creation, through the human, by a competing instance of a competing reality. Therefore, from a dissident or oppositional point of view, the act of "creating" could be regarded as an act of liberation from the grip of the one God, carrying with it the possibility of unveiling a history other than that of the Koran. We thus come to a second question: what is the history reported by the Koran? It corresponds to biblical history augmented by specifically Islamic data:

1   A space that includes Earth, Heaven, Paradise, and Hell;
2   A Time that is eternity;
3   Ancient prophets and saints: humans elected by God who can serve as intermediaries with the rest of humanity;
4   Muhammad: the last prophet, who brings with him the ultimate word of God, the Koran;
5   Biblical creatures: Angels, Demons, anthropomorphized, like the Devil (Iblîs), permanent temptor of humans;
6   Arab creatures, the jinn: ancient divinities, downgraded, anthropomorphized, who can be good or bad;
7   Humans (descendants of Adam): born, die and then resurrect to find themselves in Paradise or Hell according to the judgment of God;
8   Objects (stone, tree, river, cloud, wind ...) and animals (spider, dove, wolf, camel ...): can speak, only by the will of God or by the prayers that each one can address to him;
9   Any imaginable action (instantaneous transport, metamorphosis, communication with the dead, reading of the mind or the future, resurrection...): is possible by the will of God or by the prayers that each one can address to him.
10 A central character always and everywhere present: God Almighty, who decides the history and fate of all things, including humans, from their birth to their death, resurrection, and entry into Paradise or Hell.

As we can see, almost all fictions are conceivable as long as they are placed in the space and time of Islam, submitted to the divine will, and presented as a reality that extends the Koranic history. Premodern Arab culture has thus created a gigantic mass of narratives, in fact unassumed fictions. But they have been identified outside Islam as fictions. This is what the *Thousand and One Tales, Stories and Arab Legends* translated by René Basset tell us, even if its material comes essentially from very serious premodern Arab authors (Basset, 2005). At the same time, almost no narrative is acceptable to Islam if it offers an alternative history. Safeguarding the uniqueness of the Koranic viewpoint was important to the first two dynasties of Islam, as has been said, because the "power" of the Koran guaranteed theirs. Taken together, these two constraints meant that there was a huge amount of freedom to create (unassumed) fictions, and very little to free these fictions from divine control: the main creator of everything, and thus also author of everything, was God and him alone. Basically, both the political and the religious understood that "official" History is so fragile that any narrative that escaped the divine could also escape them.

In this sense we can say that the Koran, the founding book of Islam, inspired a standard that was inappropriate to imitate, except to claim to be an author like God. The Koran became inimitable, even from a formal or stylistic point of view. However, what made Islam successful and increased the power of the first two dynasties—i.e., their expansion toward neighboring civilizations in the seventh and eighth centuries and the necessary promotion of the Arabic language—is also at the origin of the arrival of new texts, in the Arab culture, through translation.

Kalîla and Dimna (Eighth Century) and the Waters of Consolation (Twelfth Century)
One of the first works of fiction in Arabic was *Kalîla and Dimna* (or *Kalîlah and Dimnah*), which dates from the mid-eighth century (ANE 614–615). The book is an adaptation by a Persian man of letters named Ibn al-Muqaffa' (d. ca. 756) of a work in Middle Persian that itself came from the Sanskrit and was known in India as the *Panchatantra*. It is a collection of animal fables presented explicitly as fiction meant to provide its readers with a political education—what today we would call a "mirror for princes." No word that can be translated as "fiction" is used in *Kalîla and Dimna*. The book is presented in such a way that we understand that it is clearly fiction (*Kalîlah and Dimnah*, 2022, 23):

> This book is a work of parables and stories composed by the people of India [...] In order to make their intentions comprehensible, scholars of every nation and tongue have employed a variety of devices [...] One device was to put eloquent and elegant language into the mouths of animals and birds. This enabled them to accomplish a number of things: they found a way to speak indirectly and to communicate through implications.

The book was hugely successful and translated into some forty languages (Gruendler et al., 2020, 243). Translations of the Arabic text of *Kalîla and Dimna* (*Kalîlah and Dimnah,* 2022, xxxii) were made as early as the eleventh century into Greek (c. 1080), Hebrew (twelfth century), Spanish (1251), and Latin (from Hebrew, c. 1275), and spread to most European languages and then to the world (ANE 615): "By virtue of its international distribution, *Kalîla wa-Dimna* belongs to the most widespread texts of world literature, and many of its fables became part of the European repertoire of moral tales." However, the Arabic version is notable for its introductions, in which the religions are the subject of a stimulating debate (*Kalîlah and Dimnah*, 2022, 43):

> Religion communities were many and diverse, and their adherents fell into three groups: those who inherited their religion from their forefathers, those who had been forced by fear to adopt their religion, and those who sought worldly pleasures, status, and prosperity through their religion. Each group claimed that their religion provided true guidance and that all who thought otherwise were in error [...] It became clear to me that their responses and arguments were arbitrary and tendentious.

The author of this analysis, Barzawayh the Physician, ends up taking the position that all religions are equal (Chraïbi, 2007, 212–13) and that they agree on the separation between good and evil, the most important to follow (*Kalîlah and Dimnah,* 2022, 49): "I decided to limit myself to deeds universally regarded as righteous and on which all religions concur." He also proposes as an ideal form of religion for the most convinced believers: asceticism and renunciation of the earthly world. This religious ideal also implies the rejection of the material world of humans and their power to devote themselves entirely to the divine (Chraïbi, 2006, 81–84; *Kalîlah and Dimnah,* 2022, 59). We are not far from a mystical vision of religion.

Kalîla and Dimna, therefore, introduced at least two new concepts to the Arab-Islamic world in the eighth century: the first, an ideological one, rejects a conflict between the different beliefs and instead seeks to join them around a shared moral code, or an even greater spirituality; the second, which relates to its posterity, is literary. *Kalîla and Dimna* successfully promoted fiction as a literary genre worthy of academic interest, as Rina Drory writes (1994, 158): "Its dual status in the Arabic literary system, of representing alien poetic norms, yet being a recognized and highly appreciated literary work, made this book a perfect emblem for promoting new literary initiatives."

One of the most influential works that followed *Kalîla and Dimna* was *Waters of Consolation for the Ruler during the Hostility of Subjects* (*Sulwân al-mutâ' fî 'udwân al-atbâ'*), which is also a mirror for princes. It was written in the twelfth century by an Arab man of letters, Ibn Zafar, for Arabic-speaking readers (Bellino, 2015, 103–04). Robert Irwin (1992, 41) notes Ibn Zafar was inspired first by *Kalîla and Dimna*: "The most popular and influential imitation of *Kalîla wa-Dimna* was produced in the twelfth century, by Ibn Zafar, a Sicilian Arab who had lived for some time in Syria." But at the same time, Ibn Zafar creates an original work. In terms of content, he combines historical anecdotes and animal fables (Bellino, 2015, 109): "Juxtaposing different types of narratives, Ibn Zafar introduced into his work a sophisticated device of cross-references and frames, which allowed him to switch from the historical to the fictional plan seamlessly." Ibn Zafar also deviates from *Kalîla and Dimna* when it comes to religion, putting forward a creed that is clearly centered around Islam. However, within Islam, as in *Kalîla and Dimna*, he prioritizes a greater spirituality and asceticism.

As Robert Irwin (1992, 44) and Francesca Bellino (2015, 110) underscore, from the very beginning of the long version of his work, Ibn Zafar unambiguously depends on the authority of the major religious figures of Islam: "In the Preface of the first redaction, Ibn Zafar quoted two animal fables [...] respectively on the authority of the Prophet's cousin 'Ali b. Abî Tālib and his companion Nu'mân b. Bashîr." He takes the same approach in the body of the work. He begins each of the five chapters that comprise the work with Koranic verses along with sayings and actions attributed to the Prophet (Bellino, 2015, 108). A closer examination of the themes chosen by Ibn Zafar reveals that all the chapters except for chapter 2 display a mystical sensibility. The theme of chapter 1 is "Trust in God" (Bellino, 2015, 105), while the theme of chapter 3 is "Patience" (*sabr*): "[...] the cardinal virtue in mysticism" (EI 2nd ed. *sabr*); likewise, for the theme of chapter 4, the "ridâ [is] literally 'the fact of being pleased or contented; contentment, approval' [...] a term found in Şūfī mysticism and also in early Islamic history" (EI 2nd ed. *ridâ*). Chapter 5, the final chapter, is devoted to "zuhd: the material and spiritual asceticism facilitating closer association with the divine" (Gobillot, 2012).

Kalîla and Dimna, the first work of fiction in Arabic, offered in the eighth century a universalist vision that brings the different religions into alignment while giving priority to renunciation. Ibn Zafar's twelfth-century *Waters of Consolation*, the main work *Kalîla and Dimna* inspired, is embedded firmly in Islam. However, Ibn Zafar chose a more spiritual Islam that leads to asceticism and direct contact with God.

An interesting observation: the fables of *Kalîla and Dimna* were sometimes used by "History" but also by the religious discourse, particularly in what are known as the *hadîth*: the actions and sayings attributed to Muhammad, the Prophet of Islam. These fables then underwent a transformation—a sort of "defictionalization"—to erase their unrealistic dimension and incorporate them into a historic process (Chraïbi, 2007, 216, 220–23).

Thus, in *Kalîla and Dimna* (mid-eighth century), a rat tells a tortoise, in *The Rat's Story* (*Kalîlah and Dimnah*, 2022, 192–205), how a man seized the gold coins that the rat had inside his burrow. The rat then loses its strength and all its friends abandon him. The first idea put forward by this fable is that, as the rat says (*Kalîlah and Dimnah,* 2022, 199): "I see that only money can guarantee followers, helpers, kinfolk, and friends. Only money can guarantee intelligence and strength." However, a little later in the text, this conclusion is qualified by the wiser turtle, who considers personal qualities more important than external wealth (*Kalîlah and Dimnah,* 2022, 205):

> Don't grieve over your lack of wealth. A man of valor is honored without wealth, just as a lion is feared even when at rest. A rich man without valor is scorned despite his wealth, as a dog is scorned even if he wears a jeweled collar [...] The wise man doesn't rejoice over an abundance of wealth or grieve over its loss.

However, *The Rat's Story*, and more precisely its central theme (the man who seizes the gold that a rat had in its burrow), is transformed and told a century later (mid-ninth century) as a true story, in religious texts that concern the deeds of the Prophet of Islam (Chraïbi, 2007, 220):

> Al-Miqdâd ibn al-Aswad, who was at a place called Buqay' al-Khabjaba, seized the gold possessed by a rat and came to show it to the Prophet. The Prophet asked him whether he had taken the gold from inside or outside the rat's burrow. Al-Miqdâd explained that he took it from outside the burrow. The Prophet then says that this gold is lawful, that he can keep it all without having to pay anything.

This story is quoted several times in Sunni Islamic law about "found objects" by a Muslim, what is lawful to keep or return, and whether or not a tax should be paid on it (Chraïbi, 2007, 220–23).

In fact, the animal fable has been defictionalized and transformed into a religious text, a prophetic tradition, firstly thanks to the change of perspective, and to the narration of the story not by the rat, who possessed the gold, but by the man who takes the gold from him. The rat is now mute. Then, details were added on the identity of this man, on his listener (the Prophet), on the time and the place, so as to anchor the whole in a collective memory of the origins: that of the foundation of Islam. The new version, presented as a *Hadîth,* can also serve as an example, a model, just as the fable claimed to serve as a model. But the *Hadîth,* a historical account conceived under the benevolent gaze of God by the Prophet and intended for believers, has set out to ethically disqualify the fable, a fiction fashioned by men. In the fable, the gold was taken from inside the rat's burrow, which is condemnable from the Islamic point of view. It is no longer wealth or poverty that is the subject of this new, more "official" version, but the separation between licit and illicit wealth, and probably also, in the same way, the separation between two textual categories. It should be noted that an eleventh-century Andalusian scholar, Ibn Hazm, questioned the authenticity of this prophetic tradition (Chraïbi, 2007, 221).

It should also be noted that there was a more radical attempt in the tenth century: the complete defictionalization of the book of *Kalîla and Dimna* undertaken by a certain Abû 'Abd Allâh al-Yamanî (Chraïbi, 2008, 29–33). He composed a new work in which he reproduced only the lessons of wisdom contained in *Kalîla and Dimna* as well as analogous Arabic poems, more interesting in his opinion than the original prose. He voluntarily suppressed all the narrative part where, for example, the animals speak, this being identified by Abû 'Abd Allâh as pure delirium. This work does not seem to have had much success.

The Thousand and One Nights (Ninth–Nineteenth Centuries)

The *Thousand and One Nights,* or *Alf layla wa-layla,* is undoubtedly one of the most influential premodern Arabic works and, therefore, merits special attention here. In the tenth century, the era of the

423

first commentators, the *Thousand and One Nights*, whose frame tale is of Persian origin, was cited alongside *Kalîla and Dimna* as a work of fiction by Ibn al-Nadîm, a Baghdadian bookseller of the tenth century (Chraïbi, 2016, 23–24). The term used by Ibn al-Nadîm to designate fiction is *khurâfa*. But this term has a long history and a double meaning. It was used in the early days of Islam, at the beginning of the seventh century, to mock the religion advocated by Muhammad and his belief in resurrection, by means of a poem that has become famous (Chraïbi, 2016, 28–29):

Life then death then resurrection / This is a fabular tale (i.e. *khurâfa*), O my good mother.

The attack on Islam is violent, for moreover *kurâfa* is not a neutral term, which can be identified simply with "fiction"; it can be likened by its root (*kh-r-f*) to the rambling of a senile old man. In response to this attack, in the ninth century, many Muslim scholars explained that the Prophet himself said (Chraïbi, 2016, 32): "Khurâfa is true," adding that Khurâfa is actually the name of a person, a Bedouin, to whom various adventures among the jinn happened, admittedly very astonishing, but absolutely true. There was a process of personification of the fiction (Chraïbi, 2015). We then find ourselves with two meanings attached to khurâfa: an ancient meaning which refers to a fabular tale, and a more recent meaning which applies to a character who would have according to Islamic tradition really existed. Of course, through this doubling, what is sought to be legitimized, contrary to what Rina Drory proposes, is not fiction but religion itself, and more precisely the phenomenon of the resurrection. This is an excellent example where within Islam it has proved difficult, in the face of certain critics, to convince of a real difference between, on the one hand, fiction and, on the other hand, the religious history of the world.

Regarding the *Thousand and One Nights*, they have been systematically qualified by the different authors as *khurâfa* or its plural *khurâfât*, without any ambiguity, in the sense of fiction. One could even say that they have been recognized as "The archetypal book of khurâfât" (Chraïbi, 2016, 23). At the same time, when we read the introductions to different versions of the *Thousand and One Nights* that have come down to us (Burton, Haddawy), we see that the *Nights* itself is presented as a collection of edifying historical tales (Chraïbi, 2022, 31–33). Here we will take the point of view of the commentators, who since the beginning considered the *Nights* a work of fiction and to this day continue to view it as such.

The *Thousand and One Nights* poses an interesting equation from the point of view of religion. As the *Arabian Nights Encyclopedia* (ANE 688) writes, "Religion is omnipresent in the *Arabian Nights*. The majority of stories are set in a Muslim environment." But despite its overt Muslim nature, the *Nights* enjoyed great success in non-Muslim countries (Marzolph, 2004, xxiii): "No other work of fiction of non-Western origin has had a greater impact on Western culture than the *Arabian Nights*." What is it about the portrayal of Islam in the *Nights* that has enabled the work to circulate so fluidly outside of Islam? It is difficult to respond by studying all the stories of the *Nights* and the works that are dedicated to it because the topic is too broad (ANE 745–82). Here we will limit ourselves to examining the first stories and a few iconic characters such as the angel of death and the devout man.

The *Thousand and One Nights* is made up of a frame tale, "The Story of Shahriyâr and His Brother" (ANE 370), which represents its "signature" (Sallis, 1999, 87) and which inserts a variable set of stories told by Shahrazâd to King Shahriyâr to stop him from continuing to massacre the young women of the kingdom. These key characters function as foils for each other: the king is bad and Shahrazâd is good. However, both characters are based on a religious essence that draws on Islam.

As a reference we will take one of the most authoritative versions of the *Nights*, which was translated into English by Husain Haddawy (1990) and is readily available. In this version, the king cites a passage from the Koran to justify his violent behavior (Chraïbi, 2022, 48). He interprets the founding text of Islam as it suits him so he can massacre women. However, the population rebels and prays to God to save it from the king. Shahrazâd then arrives to defend the population like an extension of the divine will to help the people (Chraïbi, 2022, 52). Through the two characters, two religious sensibilities are brought into opposition: that of the king, who relies on an abusive interpretation of the Koranic text, and the superior one—Shahrazâd's—that draws its legitimacy from a direct relationship with God. The idea of an omnipotent god (the final recourse against injustice) is shared with other religions. It is the basis of Shahrazâd's independence from the king power, which is marked here by a misogynistic and unjust interpretation of the Koran, and probably contributed to Shahrazâd's success outside Islam. In sum, two forms of compliance with Islam appear from the start of the frame tale: (1) a first form, which is more material and depicted negatively, is accomplished through the texts, and (2) a second, more spiritual form that is portrayed positively is accomplished through a direct relationship with God.

What is the situation with the material inserted into the frame tale? The first story told by Shahrazâd, "The Story of the Trader and the Jinnî" (ANE 419), follows the same scenario as a story from the late ninth century attributed to the Prophet of Islam (Chraïbi, 2016, 37–39). This is noteworthy in and of itself as Shahrazâd and the Prophet say similar things. In addition, in both cases, the stories that are told help save lives; this gives Shahrazâd's first stories a lifesaving function, just like the religious text. Within "The Story of the Trader and the Jinnî" we can discern other hallmarks of religion: (1) the trader prays, (2) the trader takes an oath in God's name and abides by it, and (3) the trader's good behavior entitles him to a happy ending. The Islam of the *Nights* is manifested here based on a nearly universal blueprint of "perform a good deed => receive a reward." This helps to promulgate the stories.

Daniel Beaumont has pointed out other, deeper connections between this first story and religion. Indeed, "The Story of the Trader and the Jinnî" may evoke "the story of Tamar, Er, Onan, and Judah in Genesis 38" (Beaumont, 1998, 121, 125–29). As for the first story that buys the trader's life, "The First Shaykh's Story" (ANE 376), Beaumont (1998, 121–25) writes that it "takes up and revises the story of Abraham in Genesis 11–25." The *Nights* may, therefore, also be understood through a potent Islamic—and more broadly biblical—religious intertext.

Generally speaking, one of the most present biblical characters in the *Thousand and One Nights* is undoubtedly Solomon (ANE 706): "In the *Arabian Nights* there are several stories in which Solomon plays an indirect but important role." He appears in the second story told by Shahrazâd, "The Story of the Fisherman and the Jinnî" (ANE 183): Solomon is the one who can control the jinn and punish them for disobedience by imprisoning them in jars. This is what we find in this story but also in another story of the *Thousand and One Nights*: "The City of Brass," which uses several historic figures of Islam to make the motif of the jinn imprisoned by Solomon the central theme (ANE 146) of an initiatory voyage:

> The story is thus, ultimately, the account of a journey to hell, or to the realm of the dead. Richard van Leeuwen (1998) relates the story's metaphorical structure to its narrative structure. [...] In this way, *The City of Brass* corresponds to the literary topos of the labyrinthine space containing the choice between good and evil.

What might at first glance seem strictly Islamic deploys a legacy and issues that touch a very broad audience.

In "The Second Qalandar's Tale" (ANE 338), we encounter the notable case of a character from the *Thousand and One Nights* who dedicates his youth to studying the Koran and its different interpretations and specializes in calligraphy and the religious sciences. He is a *faqîh*—that is, a jurist. He represents official Islam, the one learned in schools. However, "the life he lives is nothing but a series of catastrophes" (Chraïbi, 2019, 103). More specifically (Chraïbi, 2019, 109):

> The education he received in the usual religious sciences is of no help to him. It is even a burden. It creates false illusions and leads him into inextricable situations where, far from saving

or helping anyone, he becomes responsible for the death of two young women. These misfortunes cease only when he renounces […] the world, chooses a fringe mystical path, and decides to make himself a qalandar.

As in the frame tale, in "The Second Qalandar's Tale," Islam is manifested most positively in a spiritual and direct relationship with the divine.

Commentary on the angel of death and the character of the devout man in the *Nights* has reached similar conclusions (Chraïbi, 2017, 76–85). Politics joins with the religious in this case as the character of the king plays an important role (ANE 104). The angel of death, in the form of a beggar, punishes the king and puts himself at the disposal of the devout man (Chraïbi, 2017, 81):

The story is constructed on a distinct opposition: on the one hand, the king, wealth, arrogance, false power, and hell, and on the other, the devout man, modesty, poverty, true power, and heaven. […] While the king is required to submit to the angel who denies him the slightest extension, the devout man makes the angel obey him and gets what he wants from him. The new hierarchy […] places the devout man above the celestial being, who himself is above kings.

The perfect model of the Muslim is provided in the *Nights* by the figure of al-Khadir—the "Green Man" (ANE 615)—who pertains to mystical Islam: detachment from this world, direct relationship with God, and acquisition of great privileges.

Laboratory/Speculative Fiction and "Exercises in Style"

A number of thinkers in the premodern Arab world who had a theory to defend invented fictions that brought their speculations to life like a laboratory experiment. Philosophical fiction is a part of this genre. The question that arises here is, which Islam were they advancing? *The Epistle of Forgiveness* (*Risâlat al-Ghufrân*) by al-Maʿarrî (d. 1058) is a monument of the genre that derives both from speculative, or laboratory, fiction and the exercise in style, and of which there is now a complete translation (Schoeler and van Gelder, 2016). Suzanne Stetkevych Pinckney (2016, 3) has summarized its focus:

He [Ibn al-Qārih, a grammarian] thereby insinuates a challenge to the religious beliefs of al-Maʿarrî, who expressed in his poetry ideas considered heretical by many. Al-Maʿarrî takes up this challenge in his response, *Risâlat al-Ghufrân* [*The Epistle of Forgiveness*], by presenting a tour de force of his own extraordinary learning, and further by offering an imaginary and derisive depiction of Ibn al-Qârih in the Islamic afterworld. There, Ibn al-Qârih is repeatedly taken by surprise at the mercy of the Almighty, as he discovers in the heavenly garden poets and men of letters that he himself had condemned as unbelievers. Hence the title of al-Maʿarrî's epistle and its abiding message: that man should not presume to limit God's mercy.

The text conveys the message "talk to the organ grinder, not the monkey"—in other words, a direct relationship with God is better than a relationship through his creatures. This is very similar to the lesson of the *Thousand and One Nights*, and it is also quite common in the mystical way, which also takes refuge in a direct spirituality. Such phenomena can be explained by the fact that Arab scholars and thinkers can enjoy greater freedom if they are not under the power of those who want to impose, sometimes by force, their own interpretation of what God expects of us.

The second work that deserves special attention is the one by Ibn Tufayl (d. 1185), *Treatise of the Alive, Son of the Awake* (*Risâlat Hayy ibn Yaqzân*), which brings us into the realm of utopia (Regnier,

2018), but it is a utopia that once again gives priority to personal discovery of God and precisely the mystical path (Lauri, 2013, 24):

> He [a feral child called Hayy ibn Yaqzân] lives on a desert island, fostered by a gazelle. Completely alone, he manages to attain the highest knowledge of the physical and metaphysical world, as understood by Aristotelian philosophy, by himself, through observation of animals, nature, and celestial bodies, until he reaches the ecstatic state of contemplation of the Intelligibles and mystical union with the True Being.

Critics saw in this tale a possible source of inspiration for both Thomas More's *Utopia* (Regnier, 2018, 42–45) and Daniel Defoe's *Robinson Crusoe* (Lauri, 2013, 25). It can also be associated, in a wider sense, with the myth of the wild child (Picherot, 2017).

There is one more genre of fiction worthy of examination that is both prestigious in the premodern Arab world and relatively limited at the international level: *Impostures* (*Maqâmât*). This landmark work by al-Harîrî (d. 1122) is now easy to find in English (Cooperson, 2021). The *Impostures* it contains form forty-nine variations on the same scenario: an encounter between two characters. The first one, who is named Abû Zayd, is extraordinarily eloquent and changes his appearance each time:

> He changes appearance at will, showing a new face on every occasion, an actor taking on various roles: now a blind man, now a lame one, a decrepit old man, a jurist, a hemiplegic, a shrewd litigant, a preacher, a seller of charms.
>
> *(Kilito, 2021, xii)*

His goal is to trick people so that, most often, he can extract money from them. However, he is always ultimately recognized by the second character.

With this work we enter the universe of what Raymond Queneau called *Exercises in Style*. As Kilito writes (2021, xiii):

> The palindrome in particular is a device much favored by al-Ḥarīrī. For example, one poem by Abû Zayd reads the same from beginning to end as it does from end to beginning: even when read backward the content remains consistent.

While the protagonist's behavior often contradicts the religious precepts—"he has engaged in repugnant activities, lied, stolen, swindled" (Kilito, 2021, xv)—in the fiftieth and final *imposture* he ultimately becomes a good Muslim. The Islam he chooses is also marked by strong spirituality, the renunciation of the world, and a direct relationship with God (Kilito, 2021, xvi): "He is now leading the life of an ascetic. […] the reality of Abû Zayd's repentance and of his total detachment from the trappings of the world is confirmed. […] His interlocutor this time around is God."

In the premodern era, assumed fictions are rare for political and religious reasons. From the religious perspective, God being the creator of all things, he is the invisible author of each narrative, which must fit into the history of the world as suggested by the Koran and which it is, therefore, not appropriate to imitate or compete with. From the political point of view, the first two Arab-Muslim dynasties, from the same family as the Prophet, wanted the Koranic model, which justified their legitimacy and privileges, to remain unique and not to suffer any competition. Thus, the first fictions appeared with the expansion of Islam to neighboring cultures and the adaptation of foreign works of fiction into Arabic, like the animal fables, some of which, however, have undergone a process of defictionalization to be better integrated into the official history. Other fictions followed, more local. But they had to fit into Islam, and its overall history of the world, where there are several possible intermediaries between God and humans, some attested in the Koran, such as prophets and saints, others newly imposed, such as theologians and rulers. Among these different possibilities, fiction, by virtue of its status, was free to choose what it wanted. However premodern Arab-Islamic fiction seems to prioritize most often the direct relationship with God. This may be explained by the doubt that these fictions express toward the justice of humans, their teachings, and interpretations. This may explain, perhaps, the success outside of Islam of fictions such as *Treatise of the Alive, Son of the Awake* and the *Thousand and One Nights*.

Abbreviations

ANE = Marzolph, Ulrich, and Richard van Leeuwen. 2004. *Arabian Nights Encyclopedia.* Santa Barbara: ABC-CLIO.

EI 2nd ed. *ridâ* = *Encyclopaedia of Islam*. 2nd ed. *Glossary and Index of Terms*. Edited by: P.J. Bearman et al.

EI 2nd ed. *sabr* = *Encyclopaedia of Islam*. 2nd ed. *Glossary and Index of Terms*. Edited by: P.J. Bearman et al.

Works Cited

Basset, René, trans. (1924–1926) 2005. *Les mille et un contes, récits et légendes arabes*. 2 vols. Paris: Corti.
Beaumont, Daniel. 1998. "'Peut-on…': Intertextual Relations in The *Arabian Nights* and Genesis." *Comparative Literature* 50: 120–35.
Bellino, Francesca. 2015. "Animal Fables in The 'Sulwân al-Mutâ'' by Ibn Zafar al-Siqillî." *Quaderni di studi arabi* 10: 103–22.
Burton, Richard, trans. 1885–1888a. *The Book of The Thousand Nights and a Night*. 10 vol. London: The Burton Club.
Burton, Richard, trans. 1885–1888b. *Supplemental Nights to the Book of Thousand Nights and a Night*. 6 vol. The Burton Club.
Chraïbi, Aboubakr. 2006. "L'homme dans le puits et l'homme dans l'arbre." *Journal asiatique* 294, no. 1: 81–89.
Chraïbi, Aboubakr. 2007. "Fiction, religion et observations sur les rongeurs: la souris aux pièces d'or." In *Classer les récits. Théories et pratiques*, edited by Aboubakr Chraïbi, 211–31. Paris: L'Harmattan.
Chraïbi, Aboubakr. 2008. *Les mille et une nuits: histoire du texte et classification des contes*. Paris: L'Harmattan.
Chraïbi, Aboubakr. 2015. "Personnification, enchâssement, étonnement et littérature arabe médiane." *Cahiers de recherches médiévales et humanistes* 29: 23–42. https://doi.org/10.4000/crm.13771.
Chraïbi, Aboubakr. 2016. "Introduction." In *Arabic Manuscripts of the Thousand and One Nights*, edited by Aboubakr Chraïbi, 15–64. Paris: Espaces&signes.
Chraïbi, Aboubakr. 2017. "Cinq super-héros de l'Islam ou le rêve de science et éternité." *Diogène* 257: 67–88.
Chraïbi, Aboubakr. 2019. "Quatre personnages éduqués du début des *Mille et une nuits*." In *Savants, amants, poètes et fous: séances offertes à Katia Zakharia*, edited by Catherine Pinon, 85–112. Beirut and Damascus: Presses de l'Institut Francais du Proche-Orient.
Chraïbi, Aboubakr. 2022. "Histoire plurielle des *Mille et une nuits*." *Journal asiatique* 310, no. 1: 27–53.
Cooperson, Michael, trans. 2021. *Impostures, by al-Harîrî*. Foreword by Abdelfattah Kilito. New York: New York University Press.
Drory, Rina. 1994. "Three Attempts to Legitimize Fiction in Classical Arabic Literature." *Jerusalem Studies in Arabic and Islam* 18: 146–64. http://dx.doi.org/10.1163/1573-3912_ei2glos_SIM_gi_03989
Gobillot, Geneviève. 2012. "Zuhd." In *Encyclopaedia of Islam*, 2nd ed., edited by P. Bearman, Th. Bianquis, C.E. Bosworth, E. van Donzel, W.P. Heinrichs. http://dx.doi.org/10.1163/1573-3912_islam_SIM_8201. First published online: 2012. First print edition: ISBN: 9789004161214.
Gruendler, Beatrice et al. 2020. "An Interim Report on the Editorial and Analytical Work of the AnonymClassic Project." *Medieval Worlds* no. 11: 241–79.
Haddawy, Husain, trans. 1990. *The Arabian Nights*. New York: W.W. Norton.
Hendrickson, Jocelyn. 2016. "Prohibiting the Pilgrimage: Politics and Fiction in Mālikī Fatwās.'" *Islamic Law and Society* 23, no. 3: 161–238.

Hoyland, Robert G. 2006. "History, Fiction and Authorship in the First Centuries of Islam." In *Writing and Representation in Medieval Islam*, edited by Julia Bray, 16–46. London: Routledge.

Ibn al-Muqaffa'. 2022. *Kalîlah and Dimnah: Fables of Virtue and Vice*. Edited by Beatrice Gruendler and Michael Fishbein. Translated by Michael Fishbein and James E. Montgomery. New York: New York University Press.

Irwin, Robert. 1992. "The Arabic Beast Fable." *Journal of the Warburg and Courtauld Institutes* 55: 36–50.

Kilito, Abdelfattah. 2021. "Foreword." In *Impostures,* edited by al-Harîrî, translated by Michael Cooperson, x–xvi. New York: New York University Press.

Lauri, Marco. 2013. "Utopias in the Islamic Middle Ages: Ibn Ṭufayl and Ibn al-Nafîs." *Utopian Studies* 24, no. 1: 23–40.

Marzolph, Ulrich. 2004. "Introduction." In *Arabian Nights Encyclopedia*, edited by Ulrich Marzolph and Richard van Leeuwen, xxiii–xxvii. Santa Barbara: ABC-CLIO.

Marzolph, Ulrich, and Richard van Leeuwen. 2004. *Arabian Nights Encyclopedia*. Santa Barbara: ABC-CLIO.

Picherot, Émilie. 2017. "L'éducation par l'expérience d'Ibn Tufayl à Gracián." In *Enfants sauvages. Représentations et saviors*, edited by Mathilde Lévêque and Déborah Lévy-Bertherat, 193–212. Paris: Hermann, https://doi.org/10.3917/herm.leveq.2017.01.0193.

Regnier, Daniel. 2018. "Utopia's Moorish Inspiration: Thomas More's Reading of Ibn Ṭufayl." *Renaissance and Reformation / Renaissance et Réforme* 41, no. 3 (Summer): 17–45. "ridâ." In *Encyclopaedia of Islam*, Second Edition, Glossary and Index of Terms, edited by P. J. Bearman, Th. Banquis, C. E. Bowworth, E. van Donzel, W. P. Heinrichs Bowworth. http://dx.doi.org/10.1163/1573-3912_ei2glos_SIM_gi_03901. First published online: 2012. First print edition: ISBN: 97890041444484. "sabr." In *Encyclopaedia of Islam*, Second Edition, Glossary and Index of Terms, edited by P. J. Bearman, Th. Banquis, C. E. Bowworth, E. van Donzel, W. P. Heinrichs Bowworth. http://dx.doi.org/10.1163/1573-3912_ei2glos_SIM_gi_03989. First published online: 2012. First print edition: ISBN: 97890041444484.

Sallis, Eva. 1999. *Sheherazade Through the Looking Glass: The Metamorphosis of the Thousand and One Nights*. Richmond, Surrey: Curzon.

Schoeler, Gregor, and Geert Jan van Gelder, trans. 2016. *The Epistle of Forgiveness by Abû al-'Alâ' al-Ma'arrî*. Vol. 1 and 2. New York: New York University Press.

Seddik, Youssef, and Alison Rice. 2011. "The Nowhere of Prose and Fiction." *Religion & Literature* 43, no. 1 (Spring): 185–90.

Stetkevych, Suzanne Pinckney. 2016. "The Snake in the Tree in Abû al-'Alâ' al-Ma'arrî's 'Epistle of Forgiveness': Critical Essay and Translation." *Journal of Arabic Literature* 45: 1–80.

Van Leeuwen, Richard. 1998. "Referentialiteit en metafoor in 'Het verhaal van de Koperen Stad.'" *Tijdschrift voor Literatuurwetenschap* 3, no. 2: 125–35.

33

FICTION AGAINST BELIEF AND BELIEF IN FICTION IN MODERN AND CONTEMPORARY ARABIC LITERATURE

Ève de Dampierre-Noiray

The connections between fiction and belief in the Arab-Islamic World, and more precisely in the Arab-Islamic literary field during modern and contemporary times, raise issues which are different from those in the classical period, mainly because of the entry of European models into the Arab cultural landscape. Whatever events we may take as the starting point of cultural modernity in the Arab world—Napoleon's expedition to Egypt (1798–1801), the Tunisian Reformist movement, etc.—this cultural modernity is mainly linked to the *Nahda* movement, that takes its roots in Egyptian history and the dismemberment of the Ottoman Empire. As a transversal movement of Arab cultural renaissance, the *Nahda* is also based on a set of contacts with the West and its cultural and literary practices. The ambiguity of European influence on literature and the arts is a particularity of this period, which Heidi Toelle and Katia Zakharia analyze in terms of duality between "the two sides [*les deux faces*] of the Nahda: *ihyâ'* and *iqtibâs*," i.e., revitalizing the literary heritage (*ihyâ*) and lighting one's fire at someone else's fires (*iqtibâs*)—in other words, taking inspiration from European works (Toelle and Zakharia, 2003, 200). According to a more evolutionary conception of literature, whose teleological dimension is questionable, Kadhim Jihad Hassan considers that despite the presence of significant narrative and novelistic material before the *Nahda*, the contact with the West has been a necessary factor in the emergence of modern Arab fiction: thanks to this contact, "the passion for narrative" could "regain its rights and get close the modern conception of the novel" (Jihad Hassan, 2006, 14, my translation). In fact, studies of Arab literary modernity often stress the link between cultural reconfiguration and the rise of fiction:

> The beginnings of a fictional tradition in modern Arabic literature are part of the wider process of revival and cultural assimilation known in Arabic as al-Nahdah. This process involved a creative fusion of two separate forces. One is the rediscovery of the treasures of the Arabic literary heritage and the emergence there from of a "neo-classical" movement. The other is the translation of works of European fiction into Arabic, their adaptation and imitation, and the eventual appearance of an indigenous tradition of modern Arabic fiction.
>
> *(Badawi, 1993, 180)*

The idea of a literary and novelistic revival under the influence of the West is recurrent in many studies of Arab modern literature (see also Badawi, 195; Hallaq and Toelle, 2007, 193) and show that the

DOI: 10.4324/9781003119456-37

430

association of fiction and modernity is both a reality and a Western-inflected critical commonplace (sometimes deeply rooted in the works produced by Arab critics). This is why we shall take it as a starting point.

In order to give a rough sense of the relationships between fiction and belief with respect to culture, literature, and, to a lesser extent, religion, in the modern and contemporary period, one needs a varied set of angles. If we take as a starting point the apparent incompatibility between the notions of fiction and belief, or an investigation into the ways fictional texts affect our beliefs, we should be aware of our Western use of the word, and try to compare it to a Middle-Eastern, or more Arab-centered, approach—where fictional elements are contained in various literary forms coming from different traditions. We must also bear in mind how impossible it is to properly decenter the approach, since studies on Arab-Islamic literatures have mainly been produced in other—dominant—languages such as French and English (Jacquemond, 2014, 13). Indeed, Badawi's *Cambridge History of Modern Arabic Literature* is a good example of the ways the Western notion of fiction is applied to a non-Western literature in order to highlight its proper evolution.

Furthermore, the identification of conflicting relationships between fiction and belief is mainly found in reception studies of contemporary Arabic literature in the West which have proliferated in recent decades (see, for example, Daoud, 2006; Jacquemond and Abdelsalam, 2021; Leonhardt-Santini, 2006; Mardam-Bey, 1999; Sapiro, 2008), showing that this tension is not specific to the act of creative writing. Finally, even if we start from simple questions and hypotheses on the articulation between religion and fiction (namely: how religious figures may become fictional characters; how religious institutions have been suspicious of fictions or condemned them as blasphemous), one should wonder whether our focus will be on what religious text says on fiction (for example, the use of fiction in a theological context), or on the ways fiction can discuss and represent religious issues or beliefs. The former question, surely important, will not be addressed here (see "Theology and Literature in Islam" in Bencheikh, 1994, 398–414); the latter, which belongs to representation studies and what we can call "imagology" will be briefly broached at the end of the chapter. It would obviously take too long to present the main aspects of the representation of belief in modern and contemporary fiction (for general issues related to "The Faith of Islam Modern Arabic Fiction," see Le Gassick, 1988). This is why I shall only give a few examples of the way—in this case, humorous evocations, close to satire and caricature—hyper-contemporary literature can refer to religious themes or the image of God.

This study will mainly focus on the kinds of complementarity, conflicts, or rivalry between fiction and belief and their specificity in modern and contemporary literature.

What Name and Status for Fiction?

A quick survey of the terms used to refer to fiction in Arab literature studies, written either in Arabic or other languages, shows that fiction became at the same time a body of texts in its own right as well as an object of study and an interpretative issue. This is most obvious in recent works belonging to Translation studies or Sociology of Literature, where a category such as fiction is relevant. For example, a whole section of the *HTLF* (*History of Translation in French Language*, 2019) is dedicated to "prose fictions" (HTLF, 745–848), and part of its purpose is to explore which literary genres are translated from non-European literatures. The category of "novelistic fiction" is central in Richard Jacquemond's works, whether he deals with the "translation flows" from and to Arabic (Jacquemond, 2014, 9) or studies the Egyptian literary field and the status of twentieth-century Arab writers as *Conscience of the Nation* (Jacquemond, 2008, 88). The notion of "fiction," in its English meaning (i.e. *creative writing, novel, narrative prose*) or its French meaning (more abstract: *imaginary, not referring to the real world,* and more recently associated with the genre of the novel, novelistic fiction and prose fiction), is a possible way into the literature for this field. It is also considered as relevant in particular fields such as pedagogy or research. To take just one example, the case of French teaching examinations is significant: a few years ago, the notion of *fiction* would not have been a key concept, whereas it is now in the heart of specific academic programs and syllabuses for teaching examinations in France such as CAPES and Agrégation—milestones in the career of high school or university teachers).[1]

On the other hand, a category such as *Arabic Fiction* is hardly in use in the Arab-centered handbooks or dictionaries until recent decades. For example, whereas J. Bencheikh's *Dictionary of Arab and Maghrebian French-speaking Literatures* (*Dictionnaires des littératures arabe et maghrébine francophone*, 1994) provides an index with entries such as *qissa* (narrative) or *riwaya* (novel), the word "fiction" does not turn up. The same is true for Toelle and Zakharia's survey *À la découverte de la littérature arabe* (To the Discovery of Arabic Literature), despite the presence of a 150-page chapter on Modern and Contemporary literature and a glossary of Arabic notions and categories: the concept of *fiction* doesn't belong. It appears in Badawi's index (1993), but only combined with other notions (such as "socialist realism," "translation," "novel" or "short story") and not as an autonomous notion (556). In a more recent *History of Modern Arab Literature* (2007), the entry "fiction" appears and has thirty-five references: the notion seems to be an issue, although it refers to a component or an ingredient of a literary text, rather than to a genre as such (Hallaq and Toelle, 2007, 751). However, its frequent mention underlines how the birth of *Arab fiction* is a turning point in literary history, as is shown by the existence, since 2007, of a literary prize specifically dedicated to works of fiction, the IPAF (International Prize for Arabic Fiction).

The spread of the term as an academic field and the frequent use of its subgenres and derivatives (خيال علمي: science fiction; خيال ذاتي: autofiction; خيال نفسي: psychological fiction, etc.) by literary critics of the Arab field, especially in online papers (see Hilali Bacar, 2019; Almaiman, 2018, website *Orient XXI*) is obvious. But we notice that, whereas the latter categories unambiguously refer to specific genres or subgenres, the term خيال /*khiyal* used alone doesn't refer to a genre (*fiction*) but to a faculty, a component: imagination, fantasy, fancy. "Fiction" does not merge with the literary forms that may contain it, such as رواية /*riwâya* (novel) or قصة /*qissa* (narrative). The evolution of the term *khayal* from the sense of *fictional component* to the literary form itself did not occur as it did in French or Japanese usage.

Moreover, one can be struck by a somehow negative connotation that the word still carries, as opposed to what is real, documented, thus serious—according to a standard that strangely recalls Drory's statement about premodern literature ("Such a strict and powerful literary model [i.e. a model of prose "which is designed to create the impression of 'actual' reality"] would not permit the introduction into classical Arabic prose, certainly not into its canonized genres, of any kind of fiction *that declares itself to be such*": Drory, 1994, 147, my italics). Such a mistrust toward fiction, considered as pure illusion or invention—and even suspected, when it comes from Western authors, of complicity with Orientalism—can be found in Alexandrian writer Edwar Al-Kharrat's poetical essay on his native city which becomes a diatribe against foreign writers and their fictions fancying the East—and particularly against their skewed use of religion in fiction (see de Dampierre-Noiray, 2014, 38–49). But it also may be related to Jacquemond's statements about a few Egyptian writers whose novels, dealing with events and characters too remote from reality, seem to exclude them from the national literary canon: for example, Nabil Naum's fictions, imbued with irrationality and dreams (Jacquemond, 2008, 110, 228).

The ambiguous status of fiction, always suspected of lies or complicity in lies, may explain why several studies try to evaluate the very possibility of fiction—to be understood here as a literary genre—and its subgenres. In different ways, historians and theorists of literature (either Western or Middle Eastern) have looked into the specificity of the Arabic context as a land on which fiction and fictional forms may grow (or not). The aforementioned academic syllabus, as well as Jacquemond's works on the Egyptian literary field (2003) or even an academic work on a genre such as Letellier's *Penser le fantastique en contexte arabe* (2012), an inquiry into the possibility that formal artifacts and freedom of imagination may exist in an "Arab context" that she calls "a space where thinking takes place in Arabic" (Letellier, 2012, 26, my translation), are good examples of investigations that take this Arab-Islamic background—where language itself is inseparable from truth—as a starting point. This primacy of truth can be understood from an endogenous perspective—language and revealed truth are inseparable (see, for example, Blachère, 1970, 178; Lenoir, 2008, 304; or the entry *lugha* [language] in *Encyclopédie de l'Islam* [1913])—but also from an exogenous perspective, where literature seems to be only intended for revealing or depicting another type of truth that is historical and social.

This brief survey on terminology reveals a first paradox: fiction seems to emerge and develop as a literary genre at the very moment where its genuine fictional essence is questioned or limited in an Arab context, and where its legitimacy is contested, as we will see.

Fiction, Morals, Belief: Primary Antagonisms

Various studies on the genesis of fiction make visible its articulation with moral and religious conceptions. If we first go back to some narrative or discursive forms among premodern Arab literary tradition which include one or more elements that can be identified as embryonic "modern fiction," the tension with morals or beliefs appears. Embryonic is here to be understood in a double meaning: first, because the influence and importation of Western models inevitably orientate literary theory through an evolutive perspective, second, because any investigation on the genesis of fiction leads to former literary genres made of fictional patterns, pieces, or nuclei. This tension is obvious in genres as different as the *sîra* or the *maqâma*. According to Jean-Patrick Guillaume (in Bencheikh, 1994, 357), the *sîra* (which refers to popular chivalry or adventure narrative centered on a character, and nowadays to biography) is, "along with the *Thousand and One Nights*, the almost unique representative of the fictional narrative in premodern Arabic literature." As for the genre of the *maqâma*, whose definition remains unstable (Toelle and Zakharia, 2003, 363), its short narratives also include some elements of fiction. But in both cases, although their respective aesthetics and uses are different, these forms run up against a modern conception of *fiction* where elements such as exemplarity or moral and edifying intentions are not always key. Indeed, the evolution of a literary form such as the *sîra*, which can be seen as an epic genre, an heir of which could be modern fiction, shows that, after being "ostracised by religious circles and official scholars" (Bencheikh, 1994, 359), it started falling into disuse and being replaced by other narrative models imitating Western novels or even TV fictions (Bencheikh, 1994, 257). Fiction seems to be allowed to exist or survive only when it is conditioned to moral or, later, ideological conceptions. (See, for example, Jacquemond's analysis of the official expectations for the Cairo Prize for literary creation [Jacquemond, 2003, 127], or my study on Najîb Mahfûz's novel *Miramar* as a political allegory [de Dampierre-Noiray, 2014, 193–95]).

A different perspective on the rise of fiction also reveals how it can confront religion, not as an institution but as a set of beliefs. In his introduction to Hallaq and Toelle's *Histoire de la littérature arabe moderne* (History of Modern Arabic Literature, 2007), Yves Gonzales-Quijano reviews some of the cornerstones of modern literary production and mentions the publication in 1855 of "the first— and huge—fiction book in modern times, *al-Sâq 'ala al-Sâq* [*Leg over Leg or the Turtle in the Tree*] by Fâris al-Shidyâq." As he then reviews different "Arab fictions," a footnote speaks out against a common belief about the genesis of fiction. Gonzales-Quijano indeed reminds us how difficult it is to give a date of birth to Arabic novel and how skewed such an attempt is, based as it is on "a purely Western, if not European categorization of the novel, ignoring the existence of specific forms for Arabic prose fiction—that do exist." However interesting such a critique of a theoretical preconception, the second part of the footnote, about the emergence of authorship, is also significant:

Their appearance [that of "terms such as author and writer"] in the Arab culture at that time, through various names, is an undeniable proof of a revolution in the symbolic field: the emergence of a new body of mediators, specialists of the Word.

(Hallaq and Toelle, 2007, 98; my translation)

As a specialist in the word, the writer becomes, as implied by the capital letter, God's potential competitor. But this commonplace of literary creation is particularly interesting in the case of fiction: as *creative* writing, it is here compared to a Promethean gesture that can generate other beliefs, directly challenging the divine. The commonplace of human creation as *hybris* sheds effective light on the competition between fiction and belief in an Islamic context. On one hand, because fiction (which semantics refers us to illusion, falsehood, imagination) can be seen as the climax of a process of creation, or creative gesture. On the other hand, and above all, because this rivalry between the author, i.e., a human creator, and God, which is precisely a frequent topic of fiction literature (think, for example, of the myth of Frankenstein, from Mary Shelley to Iraki novelist Ahmad Saadawi's *Frankenstein in Baghdad* (2013) is itself exacerbated in an Islamic context. Indeed, the divine lies not only in the performative word (*fiat lux*) but in the language itself, uncreated word of God revealing the Quran in a single and *a priori* untranslatable language (see Diagne, 2022, 135–57).

Such an issue—the divine nature of the word, even more specific in Arab-Islamic context where language itself is sacred, holy text itself—is pervasive in the history of Arabic-speaking literature, and we shall come back to it. But what appears in the meantime is the paradoxical evolution of modern fiction, at the same time emancipated from morals and religion and creating—or subject to—new forms of belief.

Fiction as a "Truthful Discourse"

Among the new terms referring to the writer, the word *kâtib* is often mentioned as a mark of these changes. The section title "From the *adîb* to the *katîb*: the new status of the writer" (Hallaq and Toelle, 2007, 371), as well as the analyses of the ways the term's meaning slowly shifted from a meaning, i.e., "secretary" to another "writer" (101) accurately complete, in the more recent works, earlier studies on the evolution of the concept of *adab* from a moral and social meaning to its modern and contemporary sense, i.e., "literature." However, we will see that this terminology remains ambiguous in some cases, as shown by Richard Jacquemond's works on the status of Egyptian writers in contemporary literature.

The first stage of this evolution is significant, since it shows a separation process between the texts which belong to *adab*, a set of practical, moral, and social rules, and those which belong to *'ilm*, religious sciences. The teachings of Islam had thus a very limited role in the sphere of the *adab*, even before the notion became emancipated from its moral sense and purpose. In its further evolution, *adab* refers to a time of what C. Pellat calls "High literature" (*Belles lettres*), time in which "a true literature" started to be promoted (in Bencheikh, 1994, 13). Therefore, in spite of the important gap between premodern *adab* and the contemporary notion of *adab*, as "literature," "creative writing" or "fiction" (see also Hallaq and Toelle, 364–68; Toelle and Zakharia, 100–01), a look over the stages of its evolution clearly outlines the secularization process which has led to fiction.

At the beginning of the twentieth century, the normative dimension of literature disappears in favor of a more European conception of writing, where artistic creation is key. Yet, this transformation, as described on the back cover of A. Badawi's work, generates an ambiguous conception of literature.

With the spread of secular education, printing and journalism, a new reading public emerged. Against the background of the disintegration of the Ottoman Empire, the rise of nationalism, and the conflict between Islam and increasing Westernization, the traditional conception of literature as a display of verbal skill was replaced by the view that literature should reflect and indeed change social and political reality.

(Badawi, 1993)

If the idea that fiction's rise was always limited by a burden of "speech" and "didactical purpose" imposed on it (Hallaq and Toelle, 2007, 193) is indeed a commonplace in the history of modern Arabic literature, this overview of Badawi's book shows that this burden, although different, doesn't really disappear. As mentioned in the quote, literature's new task should be to "reflect and change social and political reality," so that its secularization only generates a change of paradigm. This change of paradigm is one of Richard Jacquemond's focuses in his analysis of the legitimacy of modern fiction in post-1952 Egypt, where he points to "the rejection of 'escapist literature' and of literature written under the banner of 'art for art's sake' in favor of 'realism' and 'commitment.' "

Though the ideologies might have changed, the way of thinking has remained the same. A preference for didacticism can alos be found in the debates on the novel's legitimacy that accompanied the form's emergence at the turn of the twentieth century, and which were resolved through the paradox of realism—that fiction could seek, and attain, legitimacy by claiming to correspond to reality. Indeed, "it was by presenting itself as moral or didactic, and not as fiction, or as being as far removed from fiction as possible, that the novel attempted to gain admittance to Arabic literature."

(Jacquemond, 2008, 25, also quoting Deheuvels, 1996)

The paradox that Jacquemond states about the "hegemony of the realist paradigm" in Egyptian twentieth century novelistic fiction which always has to "present and legitimate itself as a form of truthful discourse" (Jacquemond, 2008, 88) seems to be relevant for the whole of modern Arabic literature. But this statement also invites us to draw an analogy between this paradoxical status of contemporary fiction, always subject to a social and political task, and its lack of legitimacy in premodern literature. Before fiction achieved the status of a literary genre, its purpose was mainly discussed and questioned: fiction could only exist through a continuous exchange of topics with religious texts. In modern and contemporary literature, that has mainly been defined as the era of the rise of narrative fiction, its ambivalent relationship with truth—a political or ideological truth—and with a set of beliefs, remains. Moreover, in the age of decolonization and independence, where national identity is a constant issue for fiction, this "truthful discourse" still dominates. Truth has been partly emancipated from religious dogma and practices, but thereafter refers to a social and political discourse, possibly including opposition or support to the regime. The close and constant relationship between novelists and national history is made evident by the way textbooks and introductions to Arab literature are organized (see, for example, Jihad Hassan, 2006; Tomiche, 1993). Oddly enough, the role of fiction writers is not so much to be artists or creators but the "conscience of the nation" (Jacquemond, 2008). Even female writers are not spared from this necessary political positioning, as Iman Mersal states in her investigative narrative *In the Footsteps of Enayat Al-Zayyat* (2019), where Enayat's invisibility as a novelist is explained by the "doxa" that dominates essays on Arab literature "the female writer is involved in national causes, women's liberation depends on the liberation of the country" (Mersal, 2019, 234).

A Need for Fiction?

This paradoxical status of fiction, while often analyzed from the point of view of creation, also affects the reception of this literature. Just as, far from claiming the elaboration of unreal or unrealistic worlds, novelistic fiction had to give voice to a social and political mission of the writers, in the same way, fiction's impossibility to be a shelter from reality or a place of escape is sometimes perceived as inherent to its Arab-Islamic environment. Egyptian writer Alaa al-Aswani addresses a similar paradoxal understanding of fiction in the preface to his collection of short stories نيران صديقة/*Friendly Fires* (2004) where he takes an amused look at the reader's obsession with realism. The preface thus starts with the story of the arrival of cinema in Egypt, and the first projection which took place in Alexandria in 1896, in front of an enthusiastic audience. Yet, the audience's "great enjoyment" is suddenly disturbed, he explains, by an "unexpected difficulty."

> In this state of deep emotion the audience experienced the events completely from the within, imagining that what they were looking at was real. They were frightened by the sight of a stormy sea with big waves, and if a fast train appeared on the screen churning out thick smoke, many of them would scream in horror and rush out of the room.
>
> *(Al-Aswani, 2004, 10; my translation)*

This deliberately naive description serves as a starting point for questioning the reception of fictional literature in Egypt and the possible acceptance of imagination and art. The representation of the Egyptian audience as a savage people frightened by mere images serves here as a very casual rewriting of a familiar account of the impossible suspension of disbelief. But beyond this introductory anecdote, the entire preface claims a need for fiction, as well as a right to fiction. Over fifteen years later, this right to fiction is still to be claimed, if we are to believe Abdelsalam and Jacquemond's observation about Arab literature's reception in France

> the dominant mode of reception remains ethnologizing and overpoliticized. The Arab writer is received as an Arab rather than as a writer. He is first of all a witness and therefore an informant, and ideally an engaged witness.
>
> *(Abdelsalam and Jacquemond, 2021, 16; my translation)*

This analysis highlights the link between the need for fiction, mentioned by Aswani with respect to Egyptian readers, and the right to fiction, for writers who may wish to escape from "the injunction to take a stand on Islam, terrorism, dictatorship, the condition of Arab and Muslim women, etc." (Abdelsalam and Jacquemond, 2021, 16). This claim is made obvious by another scene staged in Aswani's preface. In that comic scene, yet presented as a real-life and serious episode, the author has to write an official denial of his protagonist's eccentric and suspicious opinions. He thus does so, in front of the censorship office employee, but he mentions at the bottom of the page: "this disavowal is written at the request of the Book Office's reading committee" (Al-Aswani, 2004, 20). Al-Aswani's choice of comical staging is interesting. Far from being a purely theoretical paratext, the preface uses narrative and humorous devices in order to warn its reader about the necessity of fiction.

In a different register, French Algerian writer, Mohamed Kacimi's essay *L'Orient après l'amour* (*The Orient after Love*, 2008) offers another example of how a conception of belief can be staged in its relationship to fiction—within what can be called a "creative non-fiction" book. Although the text ("Language of God and language of the I") is not a preface, it assumes the function of a poetical prologue. Kacimi evokes the two languages of his childhood in Algiers, the Arabic of his origins and the French discovered and learned at school: a very topical situation, but one that he pictures in a sort of scenography that represents a struggle between the language of submission to God and that of creative freedom.

> At the beginning of the Word, of the imaginary, at the beginning of the Arabic language is God. […]

> Night and day, the world, my world, the world of my childhood, was given over to incanta-
> tion, the incessant chanting of the Koranic word. [...] How could I read, dream, without coming
> face to face with the Lord? [...]
>
> As a child, I was prisoner of a language that could only provide access to hell or heaven. I
> was far, very far from the words that had been given to me. What place could they offer me,
> when they were in charge of eternity? [...]
>
> So I used this language without ever taking my eyes off the sky. I could not speak with it,
> for through it, the beyond was haranguing me. [...]
>
> A strange multicoloured alphabet ran along the walls of the classroom. The teacher, a native
> of the village, presented it to us as follows: "Here are the letters of the French language, there
> are 26 of them. As you can see, each one is written on its own, detached from the others. They
> don't have solidarity, unlike our language." [...] I fell in love with the solitude of these letters.
> They vibrated, they lived on their own. A.E.I.O.U. Each vowel, finally visible, had its own
> colour and seemed to escape God and the tribe.

From that day on, my long transhumance toward another imaginary world began.

> I did not leave a mother tongue, but a divine language. The French language has become for
> me the native language of the I, the language of the painful emergence of the Ego. It is not a
> question of bilingualism, nor is it a question of being torn apart. The distribution is clear. To my
> original language I give the beyond and the sky; to the French language, I give desire, doubt,
> flesh. In it, I was born as an individual.
>
> To write in French is to forget the gaze of God and the tribe, to invent my illusory but vital
> margin, my intimate space [...]. It is to deny dogma in order to celebrate any transgression.
>
> *(Kacimi, 2008, 15–21; my translation)*

We know that the question of the language of writing, and of the relationship between the writer
and his or her mother tongue, is central to postcolonial literature. In the Arab-Islamic context, where
postcolonial issues are complexified by the specific link between the language and the divine, it is
a major concern for essays or interviews of writers such as the French Tunisian Albert Memmi, the
Palestinian American Edward Said, the Moroccans Abdelkebir Khatibi and Abdelfattah Kilito, the
Lebanese writer Hoda Barakat, the Algerians Kamel Daoud, Iraki Sinan Antoonm and many others,
whose views and perceptions of Arabic language may be completely different. Kacimi's tale here
goes against the common representation of emancipation through language and creation. Arabic becomes, by virtue of its inherent relationship to God, an oppressive and dominating language, whereas
the colonial language, which is usually described as a means of occupation and cultural amnesia
inflicted on the Arab space, becomes the means of liberation. This introductory text makes visible a
linguistic dichotomy that seriously affects religious belief and the omnipresence of God in language;
one might ask what this has to do with the problem of fiction. On the one hand, the idea of a linguistic
duality is slightly biased, since the Arabic language referred to here is classical Arabic, thus not a
spoken language. That language of God is remote from the mother tongue, strictly speaking—likely
Algerian dialect in which he used to speak with his family in everyday life, and to express the child's
thoughts and emotions. This autobiographical essay is therefore to be read as an autofiction, or at
least a fictionalized staging, rather than as a pure testimony. Yet, the fiction that occurs here and in
the whole passage, where reality is stylized and spectacular episodes are told (the pupils of the kuttab
had to "drink their lesson," i.e., ink and water in order to "purify" themselves), seems to allow the
distancing of the divine territory and power that block creative writing. On the other hand, it is indeed
a matter of creation: writing in the first person is here related to *invention, illusion,* and *transgression,*

which alone are able to liberate the writer from God's invasive presence in the language. Ultimately, fiction also lies in the imaginary staging of a shared world, where languages become almost characters: French is colorful, independent, individualistic, and reckless; Arabic is dependent but also intransigent and supportive. As we saw, the bipolarity itself, because it is caricatured, is fictionalized.

Poetry and Parody: Distancing Belief

The generic instability of these texts is interesting: although they are not fiction properly speaking, they seem to react against both the realism and the religious tradition concerning the world. These examples show how literature can question truth and belief, either within a fictional framework, or by inserting a *moment of fiction* or fantasy in a nonfiction context. As it happens in Al-Aswani's preface, or to a lesser extent in Kacimi's prologue, the staging of a relationship between belief and truth often creates a situational comedy or poetical images. Alongside theoretical and critical texts that attempt to describe and define the specificities of fiction in an Arab context, and on the other side, novelistic literature which, in the wake of Taha Hussein's *Al Ayyam* (1926–1967), carries a heavy critique of religious and popular beliefs, we can therefore conclude this approach by mentioning some examples where the distancing of both belief and fiction seems to rely on poetical and humorous processes.

As a response to the prohibition of figurative representation in Islam, and perhaps in the wake of Marjane Satrapi's drawing of God with human features (his face merges with that of Marx) and as a character of the cartoon *Persepolis*, Adulrahman Khallouf's poetry often plays with the presence of the revealed truths and that of God in Syrians' everyday life. In his poem "Winter lesson" (*Happiness is a bee that stings me on the hip* /الفرح نحلَةٌ تلسعني على خاصِرتي, 2022), he stages God as a member of the family, all at once deaf old man, superhero, and a rival for maternal love:

And when the TV news starts
he [my father] commands us to laugh low voices
because walls have ears.
My mother puts the tray on the floor in the centre of the room
imploring God in a loud voice
to wipe Israel off the face of the earth
and I imagine that God is a hard-of-hearing old man
I dream of killing all our enemies
and supplanting God in my mother's heart
As we dine, the fire whispers in the oil stove
"No one knows what tomorrow will bring".
Once satisfied, my father curses this life
my mother agrees with him
most of the time.

(Khallouf, 2022, 45; my translation)

In a comparable perspective, the representation of God as an irrational being leads, in Kamel Daoud's short story *The Arab and the Vast Country of Ô* [L'Arabe et le vaste pays de l'Ô] to a comic sketch of his relationship with his creatures and the absurdity of what they take as law.

Imagine you are God. You have just finished creating the world in the form of a convoluted biography. You've already divided up the tasks, the kingdoms, and the scents, the doses of gravity, and discovered that the game would be even more fun if you added absurd rules, unnatural limits, prohibitions contrary to the laws you've written into it. The kind of rules that force the creature to dance on one leg, lick its ears and walk on the tip of its nose to understand the meaning of your work and the purpose of your journey around yourself. […]

All roads lead to you, and you, you only dream of one road that will allow you to escape from boredom, to meet someone else by making him from scratch, and to strike up a conversation with a human being that must learn your language by only contemplating you.

(Daoud, 2015, 124–25; my translation)

Here, belief becomes, in a way, fiction, as suggested by this staging of a fanciful divine law resulting in a quasi-comical scenography of the creature. The final image is a nod to the idea, mentioned above, that God and the Arabic language are inseparable—a nod that is all the more effective given that Daoud writes in French. The absurdity of contradictory divine laws is reflected in another way in Iman Mersal's prose poems, which underline with humor and self-mockery the absurdity of immigrants' perseverance in their beliefs. The *Alternative Geography* (بديلة جُغْرَافيا) where they find themselves makes it even more difficult for them to fulfil their duties as believers:

The mummy did not choose to emigrate, but those who lined up at consulates and built houses in other countries dream of returning home when they are corpses. "You must take us there", they write in the wills they leave around their children's necks, as if death was an uncomplete identity that could only be fulfilled inside the family vault.

[…]

The accent does not die, but the foreigners, like good gravediggers, post the names of their dead relatives on the fridge door so as not to call them by mistake.

In order to write a successful letter to the family, the immigrant will have to respect six rules and only six:
– choose a moment when he does not miss them;
– turn his back to the street, because the walls are more neutral;
– distribute greetings with precision;
– remember all the metaphors he learned as a child […].
– repeat "God be praised" abundantly so that they are reassured of his faith.

(Mersal, 2006, 13; my translation)

New rules, imposed by life abroad, are added to the first ones that compose the believer's duties (to which refers the derogatory return of the corpse to Islamic land, or the formula "God be praised," *Al-hamdolillah*), at the very moment when life abroad, as desired from the country of origins, turns out to be a mirage, a fiction.

A study of the representation of religion and beliefs in twenty-first-century Arab fiction and creative non-fiction, although of high relevance, cannot be outlined or synthesized here. But these few examples of twenty-first-century literature should capture our attention for several reasons. First, fiction and belief are represented and questioned by a set of devices that have something to do with fiction, even in other literary genres. Secondly, the autobiographical episode that puts belief at a distance seems to be transformed for poetic or comic purpose—or both. At last, these scenes make visible how immigration, which means changing location and language, could be a third term in the relationship between fiction (as a writing practice and process, as well as a need of imagination) and belief—but this chapter remains to be written.

Note

1 See, for example, the site Aracapag, aimed at candidates for these examinations: https://aracapag.hypotheses.org/

Works Cited

Abdelsalam, Mahmoud, and Richard Jacquemond. 2021. *Les flux de traduction arabe-français depuis 2010 (Littérature moderne et contemporaine)*. Paris: LEILA Research Project; Iremmo. https://iremmo.org/wp-content/uploads/2022/05/Flux-de-traduction-arabe-francais_etude-LEILA_24-03-22.pdf.

Al-Aswani, Alaa. (2004) 2009. *J'aurais voulu être égyptien* (*Nîrân Sadîqa* / نيران صديقة). Arles: Actes sud.

Al-Kharrât, Edwâr. 1994. اسكندرياتي مدينتي القدسية الحوشية / *Iskindariyyatî madînatî al-qudsiyyat al-hûshiyyat* (*My Alexandria, My Holy Tawny City*). Cairo: Dâr al-matâbi' wa-l-mustaqbal.

Allen, Roger. 2000. *An Introduction to Arabic Literature*. Cambridge: Cambridge University Press.

Almaiman, Salwa. 2018. "L'arabie saoudite découvre la science-fiction." *Orient XXI*. https://orientxxi.info/lu-vu-entendu/l-arabie-saoudite-decouvre-la-science-fiction, 2222.

Aracapag. 2002. "La fiction et son statut dans la littérature arabe contemporaine". https://aracapag.hypotheses.org/305.

Badawi, Mahmoud Mustafa. 1993. "History of Modern Arab Literature." In *The Cambridge History of Modern Arabic Literature*. Cambridge: Cambridge University Press.

Barakat, Hoda. 2019. "'Je veux bien respecter les textes sacres, mais la langue ne peut pas etre sacrée': entretien avec Christophe Ayad." *Le Monde*, July 25, 2019.

Bencheikh, Jamel-Eddine. 1994. "Théologie et littérature en Islam." In *Dictionnaire des littératures arabe et maghrébine francophone*, edited by Jamel-Eddine Bencheikh, 398–414. Paris: PUF.

Blachère, Régis. 1966. *Histoire de la littérature arabe*. Paris: Maisonneuve.

Boidin, Carole, Ève de Dampierre-Noiray, and Émilie Picherot. 2014. "Les littératures arabes: quelle place dans la littérature comparée?" In *Orientalisme et comparatisme*, edited by Yves Clavaron, *Émilie Picherot and Zoé Schweitzer*, 69–90. Saint-Étienne: Presses universitaires de Saint-Étienne.

de Dampierre-Noiray, Ève. 2007. "Durrell-al-kharrat : un combat pour le monopole poétique d'Alexandrie ?" In *Alexandria ad europam, Études alexandrines* n°14, edited by Sophie Basch and Jean-Yves Empereur, 179–88. Cairo: IFAO.

de Dampierre-Noiray, Ève. 2014. *De l'Égypte à la fiction. Récits arabes et européens du XXème siecle*. Paris: Classiques Garnier.

de Dampierre-Noiray, Ève. 2017. "'Mahfûz,' and 'Riwâya et Roman Naturaliste'." In *Dictionnaire des naturalismes*, edited by Colette Becker and Pierre Dufief, 592, 829. Paris: Champion.

Daoud, Mohamed. 2006. "Le monde arabe dans l'imaginaire occidental: traduction et interculturalité." *Insaniyat*, 32–33: 87–95.

Daoud, Kamel. 2015. *L'arabe et le vaste pays de Ô* in *La preface du nègre et autres nouvelles*. Arles: Actes sud.

Daoud, Kamel. 2018. *La masterclasse de Kamel Daoud*. France Culture, June 18.

Deheuvels, Luc-Willy. 1996. "Mythe, raison et imaginaire dans la littérature égyptienne contemporaine. Un *Extrait du Hadith* 'Isa Ibn Hisham de Muhammad al-Muwaylihi." *Peuples méditerrannéens* 77: 10–11.

Diagne, Souleymane Bachir. 2022. *De langue à langue. L'hospitalité de la traduction*. Paris: Albin Michel.

Drory, Rina. 1994. "Three Attempts to Legitimize Fiction in Classical Arabic Literature." *Jerusalem Studies in Arabic and Islam* 18: 146–64.

Encyclopaedia of Islam (=*EI*) online. 2012. Second Edition. Edited by P.J. Bearman et al. Consulted online on December 5, 2022. https://referenceworks.brillonline.com/entries/encyclopedie-de-l-islam/

Guillaume, Jean-Patrick. 1994. "Sîra." In *Dictionnaire des littératures arabe et maghrébine francophone*, edited by Jamel-Eddine Bencheikh, 357–59. Paris: PUF.

Hafez, Sabry. 1993. *The Genesis of Arabic Narrative Discourse. A Study in the Sociology of Modern Arabic Literature*. London: Saqy Books.

Hallaq, Boutros, and Heidi Toelle. 2007. *Histoire de la littérature arabe moderne*. Arles: Actes sud.

Hilali Bacar, Darouèche. 2019. *Des autofictions arabes*. Lyon: Presses Universitaires de Lyon.

HTLF – Histoire des traductions en langue française. XXème siècle. 2019. Edited by Banoun, Bernard, Yves Chevrel, Isabelle Poulin. Lagrasse: Verdier.

Hussein, Taha. 1947. *Le livre des jours* (*Al-Ayyâm* /الأيام). Translated by Jean Lecerf (part 1, 1927) and Gaston Wiet (part 2, 1939). Paris: Gallimard.

Hussein, Taha. 1992. *La traversée intérieure (Al-Ayyâm /الأيام)*. Translated by Guy Rocheblave (part 3, 1967). Paris: Gallimard.

Issa, Rana. 2022. *The Modern Arabic Bible Translation, Dissemination and Literary Impact.* Edinburgh: Edinburgh University Press.

Jacquemond, Richard. 2003. *Entre scribes et écrivains. Le champ littéraire dans l'Égypte contemporaine.* Arles: Actes Sud.

Jacquemond, Richard. 2008. *Conscience of the Nation* (first published in 2003 by Actes Sud in French as *Entre scribes et écrivains. Le champ littéraire dans lÉgypte contemporaine*). Translated by David Tresilian. Cairo and New York: The American University Press.

Jacquemond, Richard. 2014. "Les flux de traduction de et vers l'arabe." *Bibliodiversity, Journal of Publishing in Globalization* (February): 11–17.

Jihad Hassan, Kadhim. 2006. *Le roman arabe (1834–2004)*. Arles: Actes Sud.

Kacimi, Mohamed. 2008. *L'Orient après l'amour*. Arles: Actes Sud.

Khallouf, Abdulrahman. 2022. الفرح نحلةٌ تلسعني على خاصِرتي / *Le bonheur est une abeille qui me pique à la hanche*. Translated by Eve de Dampierre-Noiray and Abdulrahman Khallouf. Thonon-les-Bains: Alidades.

Kilito, Abdelfattah. 2013. *Je parle toutes les langues mais en arabe*. Arles: Actes sud.

Le Gassick, Trevor. 1988. "The Faith of Islam in Modern Arabic Fiction." *Religion & Literature* 20, no. 1: 97–109.

Lenoir, Frédéric. 2008. *Petit traité d'histoire des religions*. Paris: Plon.

Leonhardt Santini, Maud. 2006. *Paris, librairie arabe*. Marseille: Parenthèses.

Letellier, Bénédicte. 2012. *Penser le fantastique en contexte arabe*. Paris: Classiques Garnier.

Mardam-Bey, Farouq, 1999. "*La réception en France de la littérature arabe.*" In *The Translation of Contemporary Arabic Literature in Europe, Cuadernos de la escuela de traductores de Toledo*, n° 2: 7–13.

Mehrez, Samia. 2005. *Egyptian Writers Between History and Fiction: Essays on Nagiub Mahfouz, Sonallah Ibrahim, and Gamal al-Ghitani.* Cairo; New York: The American University in Cairo Press.

Memmi, Albert. 1957. *Portrait du colonisé*. Paris: Buchet-Chastel, Corrêa.

Mersal, Iman. 2006. بديلة جُغْرَافيا / *Jûghrâfiâ Badîla (Alternative Geography)*. Cairo: Dar Sharqiyat.

Mersal, Iman. 2019. في أثر عنايات الزيات / *Fî Athar 'Inayât Al-Zayât (In the Footsteps of Enayat Al-Zayyat)*. Cairo: Kutub Khan.

Phillips, Christina. 2021. *Religion in the Egyptian Novel*. Edinburgh: Edinburgh University Press.

Salim, Samah. 2021. *Popular Fiction, Translation and the Nahda in Egypt*. Cham, Switzerland: Palgrave Macmillan.

Sapiro, Gisèle, 2008. *Translatio. Le marché de la traduction en France à l'heure de la mondialisation*. Paris: CNRS Editions.

Satrapi, Marjane. 2000. *Persepolis*. Vol. 1. Paris: L'Association.

Toelle, Heidi, and Katia Zakharia. 2003. *À la découverte de la littérature arabe*. Paris: Flammarion.

Tomiche, Nadia. 1993. *La littérature arabe contemporaine: roman-nouvelle-théâtre*. Paris: Maisonneuve & Larose.

34

ON JEWISH FICTION AND BELIEF

Duplicity, Parables, Confession

Sarah Hammerschlag

Belief

I come at the subject of fiction and belief as a scholar of religion and literature, which means that for me to ask the question of the role of belief in fiction is also to consider it in relation to the role of belief in religion. Within the field most of us have long accepted that the term "religion" itself cannot be separated from its Latin etymology, and indeed from the phenomenon of colonization, by which it was exported onto other nations, culminating in the nineteenth century with the project to create a taxonomy of world religions, which, to quote Tomoko Masuzawa, entailed the assertion of a "common universal core of all religions, high and low" from fetishism to modern Christianity (Masuzawa, 2000, 247). This taxonomy, evident from Hegel's lectures on the philosophy of religion in 1832 to Max Muller's Gifford lectures in 1888, bequeathed to the field a structure that would dominate its textbooks and thus its teaching through most of the twentieth century, one that inevitably ranked protestant Christianity as the highest form of religion for the purity of its spiritual essence and rational core, and a vocabulary by which the world's other religions would have to subsequently define their history, essence, and value.

It perhaps goes without saying that the concepts of belief and faith were thus fundamental to religion's definition after the eighteenth century, after Hegel, as the act of comparison between traditions became crucial to the study of religion, remaining the case into the twentieth century even for those scholars who attempted to push back against it by centering practice or ritual.[1] As Donald Lopez describes in his entry on belief for the 1998 edition of *Critical Terms for Religious Studies*, "belief" has become the most common term to define religion to one another, even as it is a term so multifarious and complex that it often requires another term to pair with it, to which it "stands in a relation of weakness or strength," a function that changes depending on the word with which it is paired, whether that other term is doubt, knowledge, or faith (Lopez, 1998, 22). However, as one of the strongest markers of an ideology produced by the history of Christianity, it has come to be synonymous, at least within the context of religious encounters, as "an interior assent to certain truths" (31). Yet the assertion of such a claim, Lopez concludes, only has traction, power, valence when uttered in a contestatory context, as an agonistic affirmation. In other words, it involves, at the very least, the stipulation of some other, to whose unbelief it stands in contrast.

It is not much of a stretch from here to imagine how Judaism has itself been implicated at almost every historical turn in the perpetuation of faith as a Christian ideal. This has continued even outside

DOI: 10.4324/9781003119456-38

"

of strictly religious contexts, for example, in the renaissance of Pauline thinking in the first decades of the twenty-first century, most prominently in Alain Badiou's championing of the figure of Paul in *Saint Paul: The Foundation of Universalism* ([1997] 2003). Even in Badiou's thought, in a reading which reduces the event of Christ to a fable, the procedure of linking truth to an event, the belief in which creates the conditions for overcoming communitarianism, Judaism must be conjured as the very form of legalism, particularism, and communitarianism to be overcome.[2]

Badiou was not the only person in the late 1990s and aughts thinking about Paul. A bevy of texts from the likes of Slavoj Žižek, Simon Critchley, John D. Caputo, Giorgio Agamben, and Ward Blanton turned to the figure of Paul as read through Martin Heidegger, Walter Benjamin, or Jacob Taubes. While belief was not at the center of all of these accounts, faith or a stance of relation toward the future often was. One legacy of this moment is the lingering impact of "political theology," a term associated first and foremost with Karl Schmitt, but on which the Pauline discourse had a powerful effect, by allowing for the language of religion to re-enter political theory, not by means of dogmatic commitment but by the examination of religious structures as crucial to political discourse.

I have argued elsewhere both that this resurgence of interest in Paul was something of a backlash against what was construed as the Jewishness of a certain turn to alterity and difference associated with the thought of Levinas, Blanchot, and Derrida (Hammerschlag, 2013), and that many of the attempts to resuscitate Paul to provide "a conception of the present as a time of 'now' " failed to adequately consider how unearthing the theological traces of secular modernity involves digging up the surrounding sediment as well (Benjamin, 1969, 263). Given that Paul's own notion of faith was constructed in contrast to Jewish law, his concept of the circumcision of the heart in contrast to the Jewish circumcision of the flesh, any attempt to resuscitate these Pauline forms will inevitably entail a resuscitation of their denigrated other. Badiou's own 2005 text *Circonstances III* and *Polemics* with its distinction between virtual and authentic Jews, and its attack on the SIT complex (Shoah, Israel, Tradition) is a case in point.[3]

I rehearse all of these here in order to suggest that the relationship between Jewish fiction and the concept of belief cannot be described exclusively from structures internal to Judaism—as if any tradition can mark out a clear distinction between internal and external influence—but rather must be analyzed in a dialogical relationship with the Christian tradition and its legacies, even when the concept is being employed beyond the boundaries of religion properly understood. Moreover, to get at the relationship between belief and fiction, particularly in the modern Jewish tradition, one must consider how Judaism appears through the prism of Christianity. It is certainly the case that Jewish literature has long reflected that gaze.

Operation Shylock: A Confession

In and of itself Jewish fiction is a category too diffuse to define and could include anything from the *mashal*, the form of the parable already evident in the Hebrew Bible, to the modern diasporic or Israeli novel. Instead of trying to track the role of belief in all of these forms, I will focus on a single novel by the American author Philip Roth: *Operation Shylock: A Confession* (1993), which itself reflects on various forms of Jewish literature while indeed revealing how Jewish fiction is refracted through a Christian gaze. It will be important first, to consider the stakes of using Philip Roth as our representative.

Philip Roth is both an exemplary figure of modern Jewish diasporic literature and one of its more reluctant representatives. In 1962, very early on in his career after the publication of *Goodbye, Columbus*, he famously appeared on a panel at Yeshiva University on "artistic conscience," during which he was denounced for his story "Defender of the Faith" because of its unflattering representation of Jews. The moderator went as far as asking Roth if he would have written the same story had he been living in Nazi Germany.[4] Seven years later when *Portnoy's Complaint* was published, Gershom Scholem, the towering scholar of Jewish Mysticism, responding to review of it in *Haaretz,* described it as the book "for which all antisemites have been praying" (Bailey, 2021, 314). In response to both these episodes, Roth himself expressed his reluctance at being read as a Jewish writer, even as he recognized the notoriety as productive to his career. "The Luckiest break I could ever have had," he wrote in *The Facts*, "I was branded" (Roth, 2008, 409). In the following decades, his name nonetheless became synonymous with a canon of American Jewish Literature, which included Bernard Malamud—a friend and influence, arguably the subject of Roth's own work (*The Ghost Writer*), Henry Roth—also suspected to be a model for E.I. Lonoff—Saul Bellow and Cynthia Ozick, among others. In 2014, in something of a reversal, he was given an honorary degree by another great New York Jewish Educational institution: the Jewish Theological Seminary, at which time he too seemed also to reverse his own stance, perhaps with some irony, declaring, "I welcome the honor. Who takes Jews more seriously than J.T.S and what writer takes Jews more seriously than I do?" (Thurman, 2014).

His own ambivalence (or duplicity) might at the same time be what makes Roth exemplary of the category of Jewish literature. Its peculiarity as a subgenre is itself put into relief when represented by Roth. This is the case on one level because of the awkward fit of "Jewish literature" with the concept of a national literature. The idea of national literature was largely an outgrowth of the German Romantics, particularly Johann Gottfried von Herder and the Schlegel brothers who emphasized the role of language as the medium of national consciousness (Perkins, 1991, 1; Wisse, 2000, 5). It was indeed Herder's concept of nationhood that helped solidify the trope of the Jews in the nineteenth century as the rootless people par excellence (Arendt, 2007, 14–15). Cultural Zionism and its concomitant renaissance of Hebrew and Hebrew letters was then the reply. Jews too could meet Herder's criteria by cultivating their language and their land. S.Y. Agnon's 1966 Nobel Prize represents the fulfillment of that promise. Roth himself subscribed to this definition of national literature when he said in response to a rabbi's query at the JTS ceremony in 2014 as to whether he liked to be called a Jewish writer, "I prefer to be called an American writer. A writer is defined by his language" (Thurman, 2014). And yet, as a diaspora tradition, Jews have written in languages ranging from Russian, Polish, French, Arabic, German, Yiddish, and Ladino to Hebrew, and Jewish Literature has been widely recognized as a canon that encompasses multiple languages and nationalities, diasporic consciousness as well as Israeli national consciousness. This conflict between the diasporic and the Israeli, the Hebrew and the English is itself dramatized by *Operation Shylock.* The book, which follows Roth on a trip to Israel as he meets a doppelganger who is using his likeness to Roth to become something of an inverse Theodor Herzl, advocating for the return of Jews from Palestine to the diaspora, contends in its very conceit with the question of what counts as authentically Jewish and on what indeed is the right form of national consciousness for the Jewish people. Like Herzl, Roth's double is, however, more concerned with countering anti-Semitism than he is with national consciousness, thus suggesting that the two are in fact deeply intertwined. Indeed, there is no modern Jewish national consciousness without the specter of the Christian gaze. There is also the suggestion in the novel through the figure of doubling that as a consequence of this gaze, Jewishness is always already inauthentic, formed by a certain duplicity.

The anxiety surrounding representation is reflected in the novel, but it is equally present in Roth's own encounters with the Jewish community. It is what the goyim will think of the Jews that had Roth's angry Jewish readers so terrified. While this dynamic has certainly been intensified since assimilation, it is represented in Jewish literature going back to the Middle Ages and arguably to the Talmud (Schaefer, 2009). The Coen brothers in their most obviously Jewish film, *A Serious Man* (2009)— equally subject to criticism for its unflattering portrayal of a Minneapolis Jewish community—went so far as to include a disclaimer in the film's credits: "No Jews were harmed in the making of this motion picture."

Roth's novel includes a similar amendment. A note to the reader, not unlike the legal disclaimer often found at the end of novels, appears at the end of the work. It begins, "the book is a work of fiction," and ends "the confession is false" (Roth, 1993, 399). There is much to be said about this note and its relationship to the title: *Operation Shylock, A Confession.* In fact, with these two bookends, the novel is already raising the question of Jewish fiction's relation to the Christian gaze. In much of Roth's work, he is captivated by the relationship between fiction as a genre, an imitative narrative art, and its alternative definition as deceit, deception, dissimulation, pretense, but perhaps nowhere is this more explicitly a theme than in *Operation Shylock*. It is at work at every level of the novel from its outermost sheaves to its innermost core.

Let's begin thus with the title: *Operation Shylock: A Confession.* Leaving aside for the moment its reference to the infamous character of Shakespeare's *The Merchant of Venice*, to focus on the subtitle, we must first consider the status of confession as itself a Christian form, deriving from the injunction in the Gospel of James (5: 16) to "confess your sins to one another and pray for one another." It developed into a literary genre by means of Augustine's own *Confessions* in the late fourth century and was codified as a sacrament of penance in 1215 by the Lateran council. Its proximity in the title to the name of Shylock already initiates a subversion, one carried out most clearly in the final note. While the note carries the standard language, "the names, characters, places and incidents [represented here] either are products of the author's imagination or are used fictitiously. Any resemblance to actual events or locales or persons, living or dead is entirely coincidental," the concluding lines, "this confession is false," subvert its very function. On the face of it, the book has the trappings of autobiography—its main character, after all, is the writer Philip Roth, who did indeed travel to Israel in January 1988 to interview the Israeli writer Aharon Appelfeld. The note might refer then to itself, rendering the legal disclaimer a contradiction, or it might refer to the larger work, given the subtitle, and thus render the whole book a false confession. In which case, its fictional status is set up as a falsification of Christian confession.

As Augustine's work sets up and the very practice of penance entails, the truth of confession is a consequence of God's vision, his seeing into the heart. God is its guarantor. In which case, false confession would be a form of self-deception, for which attunement to God's will and goodness is the cure. But in Roth's work, the closest we come to such a guarantor is a Mossad agent named Smilesburger, who recruits Roth to serve as an Israeli agent. He seems to see all, but says himself that he does not represent the good, and in a play on Exodus 3:14, when describing how he will explain his actions before a court of judgment that would rightly see the Palestinian cause on the side of the good, he says, "I do what I do because I do what I do … I did what I did because I did what I did" (351).

If the falseness of the confession refers only to the note, a possibility that would indeed follow from the epilogue, which Roth informs us was itself only appended to the book after it had been written as nonfiction because Roth was counselled by Smilesburger to include it in order to protect himself from the Israeli police, then the account in the novel is true, but the category of fiction is serving as a means of deception. Additionally, while the concluding note to readers establishes the book as fiction, its preface does the opposite, avowing that

> The book is as accurate an account as I am able to give of actual occurrences that I lived through during my middle fifties and that culminated, early in 1988, in my agreeing to undertake an intelligence-gathering operation for Israel's foreign intelligence service Mossad.
>
> *(13)*

Thus, at its most exterior layer, on the edges of the two covers, the book has already begun to play with the nature of fiction and link it to the book's status as Jewish novel. It has already set itself up as deceptive, as a counter-genre to the Christian form, even as it resists resolving on which layer the deception takes place.

Inside this frame, in its narrative presentation, the novel opens with Roth, while recovering from a psychotic break brought on by a prescription for Halcion, receiving news from his cousin of an imposter, a double traveling around Israel preaching diasporism, that is to say, making an appeal to Jews to return to their European homeland, to save the Jewish race from destruction. This dual set of circumstances determines from the outset the stymying of belief, the reader's as well as Roth's, both because Roth, by virtue of the break, has lost confidence in his own hold on reality and because the event itself seems so unbelievable. It also establishes the theme of doubling and duplicity—both internal and external—that runs through the novel, not only by means of Roth's encounters with a man who claims also to be named Philip Roth and who shares an uncanny resemblance to the author, but also by setting up diasporism as the negative image of Zionism, and the fake Roth as an anti-Herzl. At the same time the subplot of the novel concerns another account of doubling—the historical trial of John Ivan Demjanjuk, accused of being Treblinka's Ivan the Terrible, but who had been living out his life as an autoworker in Ohio. While the action of the novel takes place before the trial's conclusion, Roth wrote the book after it had been discovered through Soviet intelligence that Ivan the Terrible's surname was in fact Marchenko, not Demjanjuk, but before the conclusion of the appeal, thus before Demjanjuk, whom multiple witnesses swore was in fact the engineer of the gas chambers at Treblinka (Marchenko's uncanny double)—was nonetheless sentenced to prison for complicity in the death of 900 Jews murdered at a different camp in Sobibor, Poland. The hearing, as seen through Roth's eyes, is a trial of witnessing itself, of our limited capacity to attest to the truth, a fact that fiction itself reveals, as "the dramatization of conflicting points of view and the ironic uses of contradictory testimony," Roth says in the novel following Henry James (294). Fiction then is set up as the opposite of the attestation of belief, the opposite of the principle that Paul taught in his epistles, if we accept Badiou's interpretation—a witnessing that secures my identity with the universal through the declaration of a shared but singular truth.

Again and again throughout the novel, doubt, duplicity, and deceit appear and reappear, often linked indeed to certain tropes of Jewishness and through Roth's explicit association of these stereotypes with Jews, Judaism, and Jewish fiction. The play on Shakespeare's notorious moneylending character from *The Merchant of Venice* redoubles the effect. The term "Shylock," which, as a consequence of Shakespeare's character, came to refer to Jewish moneylending as an exploitative practice, alludes to the ways in which Judaism and Zionism have been shaped in a dialectic of response and counter-response to Christian anti-Judaism and anti-Semitism. In employing the trope for the title, Roth, not so subtly, suggests that Zionism is a revenge project. Within the novel, it is in the character of George Ziad, his Palestinian friend from graduate school, who voices this view most clearly, suggesting furthermore that the pound of flesh extracted for the revenge of the Holocaust is Palestinian flesh.

> *Because this state* ... has *forfeited* its moral identity ... The state of Israel has drawn the last of its moral credit out of the bank of the dead six million—this is what they have done by breaking the hands of Arab children.

(135)

There are two other references to the Shakespeare character in the novel. The first is in the voice of a Mossad agent, posing as a book dealer, who describes the term as the figure of the Jew in the Christian imagination, "the embodiment [for the Christian] of the Jew in the way Uncle Sam embodies for them the spirit of the United States." The second is as a reference to the one chapter of the book entitled "Operation Shylock," which Roth himself claims in the book to have excluded from the novel because of its top-secret content (274). Thus, as a title, it is itself already a substitution, a double, standing in for the real story, the true intrigue, that Roth excludes because Mossad forbid him from publishing it. The one thing, thus, that the novel does not describe is the mission itself, and yet its title serves as the title of the novel. This itself might feel like a sleight of hand.

Jewish Fiction

While the book certainly deals with multiple facets of Jewish life and politics in the twentieth century, I chose Roth as a representative to discuss Jewish fiction and belief not to suggest that his *Operation Shylock* is the most Jewish of stories or the most focused on belief—one might consider Isaac Basheva Singer and his gullible "Gimpel" for that honor, with its meditation on the relation between gullibility, religious faith, and creative imagination, or S.Y. Agnon's *In the Heart of the Seas*, with its pilgrims' naïve hopes for the land of Israel—but because, like much of Roth's work, it focuses on the complexity of the category of fiction, and includes its own reflection on that category by means of its plot, which purports to be nonfiction, but also because the nonfictional pretext for the novel is itself a meditation on Jewish fiction: Roth was asked by *The New York Times* to interview the Israeli author of Holocaust fiction, Aharon Appelfeld in Israel—an interview subsequently published in the newspaper on February 28 of that year. Indeed, sections of the interview as they were published in the newspaper appear in the novel itself. In the section reproduced word-for-word, Appelfeld formulates his own relation to perhaps the most iconic Jewish fiction writer of the modern era, Franz Kafka. Appelfeld describes both the influence and the contrast here.

> Kafka emerges from an inner world and tries to get some grip on reality, and I came from a world of detailed, empirical reality, the camps and the forest. My real world was far beyond the power of imagination, and my task as an artist was not to develop my imagination but to restrain it, and even then it seemed impossible to me, because everything was so unbelievable that one seemed oneself to be fictional.
>
> *(Roth, 1988, 56)*

These words of Appelfeld allow us to unpack the nature of two strands of Jewish fiction, one as ancient as Judaism, and the other born of Jewish suffering in the twentieth century. In both cases, belief and the dynamics of representation are equally at stake, as Appelfeld suggests, although in opposing ways.

The Parable

The first of these is the parable, of which Franz Kafka is the modern master. Unlike the narratives of origin recorded in Genesis, or the accounts of the covenant in Exodus, Deuteronomy, and Leviticus, the mashal, the ancient Hebrew term for the Jewish parable, is a form of narrative whose function depends upon its fictionality. It is also a form that appears across the tradition, in the Bible, rabbinic literature, medieval philosophical sources, Hasidic tales and among the modern masters of Jewish fiction, Franz Kafka, S.Y. Agnon, and most recently Etgar Keret. As David Stern notes in *Parables in Midrash* (1991), what distinguishes the mashal, as a subgenre of the fable, a form that can be found among almost every culture, is the use of an imaginary, clearly fictional and narrated event and its parallel to a "real" situation. Commonly in the rabbinic context, the form is used to explain God's actions by comparing him to a king. The figure of the king is used, for example, to explain why the Jewish people suffer, to provide an account of why God allowed the temple to be destroyed and the Jews to go into exile. God is thus like a king and father who loves but must also sometimes punish his beloved children. As Stern points out, the form invites interpretation, as well as the impulse to see the narrative as disclosive. One might assume thus that these rabbinic parables provide a bridge to a truth that cannot otherwise be expressed, given the mysterious nature of the divine. If such were the case, then this fiction would be intimately tied to belief as the parable would provide accessible means by which to imagine the unimaginable. Stern points out, however, that such reasoning is itself a consequence of the Greek and the Christian traditions. It is the Septuagint that originally renders mashal as *parabole*, a term with its own philosophical history. Among Aristotle and other Greek rhetoricians, parables served as means of philosophical demonstration. This history and the subsequent Christian interpretation of scripture, particularly the impulse toward allegorical reading, has thus skewed, he suggests, the interpretation of how the mashal functioned in rabbinic literature. Stern describes it instead as a rhetorical device, a means of persuasion. One feature that the rabbinic mashal shares with its modern iteration is its resistance to complete transparency. "The mashal's effectiveness in persuading its audience of the truth of its message lies in its refusing to state that message explicitly, thereby making the audience deduce it for themselves" (Stern, 9). In the rabbinic literature these stories are often put in the service of an exegetical argument, providing a parallel that justifies an interpretation of scripture and serving as a link between biblical passages. If belief is at issue here, it is in the interpreter's solicitation of his audience's credulity. He persuades by inviting further reflection and multiplying connections.

Gilah Safran Naveh argues in *Biblical Parables and Their Modern Re-creations* (2000) that belief becomes more crucial to the Hasidic iteration of the form. For Eastern European Jews in the eighteenth and nineteenth centuries, living in diaspora and facing already the forces of modernity, persecution from their Christian neighbors, and the danger of disillusionment, the exegetical function of the parable is subordinated to its utility as an invocation of faith. "We suggest," she writes, "that the modern narrative moves the listener from 'why we say,' to 'how ought we believe' " (Naveh, 108).

In both cases, the rabbinic and the Hasidic, there is, nonetheless, a certain duplicity encapsulated by the form, both because of the distance between the "real situation" and its parallel and because of the form's resistance to purely dogmatic principles, or credo. It paves the way for a certain uneasy coexistence between belief and unbelief, indeed for the playing out of an ironic dimension in Jewish literature. Take, for example, this tale about messianic faith from the town of Chelm:

It was once rumored that the Messiah was about to appear. So the Chelmites, fearing that he might bypass their town, engaged a watchman, who was to be on the lookout for the divine guest and welcome him if he should happen along.

The watchman in the meantime thought to himself that his weekly salary of ten gulden was mighty little with which to support a wife and children, and so he applied to the town elders for an increase.

The rabbi turned down his request. "True enough," he argued, "that ten gulden a week is an inadequate salary. But one must take into account that this is a permanent job."

(Howe, 1973, 626)

This story among many about the foolish people of Chelm, a genre that emerged in Yiddish literature in the late nineteenth century and became popular in the early twentieth, reveals a folkloric shift toward a tongue-in-cheek attitude about genuine faith, one represented as well in other Yiddish literature of the time, perhaps most famously in Shalom Aleichem's *Tevye the Dairyman* where ritual and belief itself are subordinated to the concerns of economic and political good fortune (Aleichem, 1996; Von Bernuth, 2016).

In Kafka's parables this ironic dimension grows dark, although without losing its humor. In tales such as "Eine Kaiserliche Botschaft [An Imperial Message]," he reintroduces the figure of the king, or Kaiser, whose actions don't serve any longer to explain the divine, so much as to render the theological inaccessible to meaning. In addition, Kafka makes some classical biblical stories themselves the subject of parabolic thinking in retellings of the story of Babel, Abraham, and the revelation at Mt. Sinai. While they are devoid of elucidating explanation and function without explicit parallels, they manage nonetheless to retain the lure of interpretation, and thus the aroma of belief, in the thrall they solicit toward meaning, as well as the sense that we should read them as somehow reflections on a current reality. Walter Benjamin famously described this dynamic: they unfold, he said, but not like a paper that can be made flat and smooth so that one has the meaning "on the palm of his hand" (Benjamin, 1969, 122). Kafka's parables instead "unfold … the way a bud turns into a blossom" (122). They attract but do not disclose. While they seem to have lost their doctrine, they can nonetheless "be told for clarification" (122).

It is Roth himself who first raises the possibility of reading his own novel/adventure in relation to Kafka and Kafka's parables. For he compares the news he receives of his imposter to "The Imperial Message," writing, "As for the messengers bearing the news of my Jerusalem counterself, they too couldn't have been more grossly emblematic of the dreaming's immediate, personal ramifications," and he compares those messengers themselves, Appelfeld and his cousin Apter, to Kafka's *Metamorphosis*, continuing, "[t]he much praised transfigurations concocted by Franz Kafka pale beside the unthinkable metamorphoses perpetrated by the Third Reich" (29). That Kafka is a significant referent for Roth is perhaps a given. He taught the work of the Czech-Jewish writer during the 1960s and 1970s in courses at University of Pennsylvania, and wrote an essay which is itself a counterfactual biography of Kafka in the 1970s entitled, "I always wanted you to admire my fasting; or Looking at Kafka" which imagines Kafka as an émigré to New Jersey. When Kafka's name appears again in *Operation Shylock*, it is when Roth suggests that Appelfeld's writing invites the comparison. What follows is Appelfeld's formulation of the relationship between Holocaust fiction and Kafka's work. The suggestion is not only that the terror depicted in Kafka seems to foreshadow the Holocaust, but also that the relation between fiction and truth between these two writers represents a fundamental shift in Jewish literature. If Appelfeld's quote is the centerpiece of the interview, it is also a provocation for the reader to understand how Roth sees himself in relation to this dichotomy. It is followed only a few paragraphs later by another meditation on fiction as a certain kind of deception in the person of his cousin Apter, also a survivor, whose stories about his daily happenings Roth "thinks of as fiction that, like so much of fiction, provides the storyteller with the lie through which to expose an unspeakable truth" (58). Truth appears here but not as realizable. Like Freud's unconscious, it can only come to the surface already disguised, transformed, making itself known but retaining its unspeakable quality. In the novel Kafka is the iconic figure representing this parabolic dynamic for both Appelfeld and for Roth. If Roth asks Appelfeld about his relation to Kafka, we must also assume that the question pertains to the novel we are reading as well. The other references to Kafka and the parabolic form are more oblique in the text, but they are strewn throughout. At one point Roth finds himself like K, taken hold of by two plain clothed men who drag him into a classroom. Here Kafka's *Trial* merges both with the beit midrash of Roth's youth, memorialized famously in "The Conversion of the Jews" (Roth, 1959, 137–48), and with Kafka's parable "Abraham," in which he imagines an Abraham for whom the test of faith is not whether to sacrifice his own son but an Abraham who stands to be honored as the first of the class, when he is in fact the last, an Abraham parable which is itself about doubling, about the possibility of mistaking oneself for the one truly called (Kafka, 1961, 41). Like this Abraham, Roth too "arrives like an eager student" (Roth, 1993, 311) only to find himself in front of a verse from Genesis, one that Roth in the book cannot in fact decipher, but which serves as the epigraph of the book itself in Hebrew and translated, "So Jacob was left alone and a man wrestled with him until darkness" (Genesis, 32: 24). The epigraph itself suggests that the theme of doubling, the story of the imposter—also the story of Jacob and Esau—is one that goes back all the way to Genesis. The agent Smilesburger might be taken himself for the angel, who in verbally wrestling with Roth also chooses Roth to serve as a representative of his people on a Mossad mission.

There is a sense in which the biblical story, rather than being deciphered through a parable, serves as a parabolic referent for Roth's own novel.

Holocaust Fiction

Kafka appears in Appelfeld's quote as a point of contrast with the form of Holocaust fiction. And just as the novel invites us to consider its relation to Kafka and his parables, it also invites us to consider its relation to Holocaust fiction. What Appelfeld says about Holocaust fiction is equally a meditation on the relationship between fiction and belief. The world itself, Appelfeld says, became stranger, more nightmarish than Kafka's imaginative descriptions. Its horrors, as many survivors and commentators suggest, were beyond representation. Certainly, the literary genre that the Shoah itself most clearly provoked was memoir or testimony, and indeed the most widely proliferated form of its representation; Elie Wiesel's *Night*, Primo Levi's *Survival in Auschwitz* [*If This Is a Man*], Jean Amery's *At the Mind's Limits* are attempts at testimony, attempts which reflect on the limit of that form. This limit to the power of representation has been a major topic of literary and philosophical reflection over the last forty-five years, by Maurice Blanchot in *The Writing of the Disaster*, Giorgio Agamben in *Remnants of Auschwitz*, and Jean-Francois Lyotard in *The Differend*, among others. And there are those texts such as Georges Perec's *W, or the Memory of Childhood*, by a member of what Susan Suleiman has called the 1.5 generation, child survivors with a belated relationship to the event, which binds a meditation on testimony to a fiction, in a double-sided work (Suleiman, 2002). All of these aforementioned meditations raise the question of the relationship between memory, belief, and testimony when faced with unspeakable horror. Holocaust fiction adds the question of the imagination as well.

For some writers whose works invite the categorization of fiction, or artistic representation, the term "Holocaust fiction" has been treated as something of a dangerous oxymoron. Elie Wiesel wrote that "A novel about Auschwitz is not a novel, or else it is not about Auschwitz" (Wiesel, 1975, 315). Art Spiegelman protested the categorization of *Maus* as fiction by *The New York Times*, writing that he shuddered "to think how David Duke would respond to seeing a carefully researched work based on my father's life in Hitler's Europe and in the death camps classified as fiction." Claude Lanzmann said in an interview that "the truth kills the possibility of fiction" (Horowitz, 1997, 7). Even Appelfeld himself asked, "horror and art. Can they co-exist?" (Appelfeld, 1988, 83). One confronts here in the category of Holocaust fiction a range of resistances. The relation between fiction and falsehood provokes the fear that allying the two only gives fodder to Holocaust deniers and Historical revisionists. The idea of art as aesthetic, a celebration of beauty, and an affirmation of human creativity as generative is an idea that the Holocaust belies, thus Adorno's famous phrase "To write poetry after Auschwitz is barbaric," and Blanchot's final lines from his 1973 story *La Folie du jour*, "A story? No stories, never again" (Adorno, 1967, 19; Blanchot, 1999, 199). The suggestion from both Adorno and Blanchot is that the world rendered absurd and horrific by Auschwitz can no longer be made to make sense by narrative form, affirmed by art. Finally, there is the crisis of witnessing itself, the notion from Primo Levi's *Drowned and the Saved* that those who had truly witnessed were those who touched bottom, those who would not survive to tell. Fiction would thus be a double betrayal of that truth, as though the imagination could conjure what there were no witnesses to document. And yet, as Sara Horowitz writes in *Voicing the Void*, it is exactly the way that literature "foregrounds its own rhetoricity ... explored not as a transparent medium through which one comes to see reality but as implicated in the reality we see, as shaping our limited and fragile knowledge" that makes Holocaust fiction an important category for Holocaust Studies, even as it is disquieting for exactly this capacity (Horowitz, 1997, 17). For the capacity of language to shape our reality, to change our perceptions, was itself harnessed toward the persecution of the Jews. Horowitz thus cites George Steiner on the frightening way that in the enactment of the Final solution "words lost their original meaning and acquired nightmarish definitions. *Jude, Pole, Russe* came to mean two-legged lice, putrid vermin, which good Aryans must squash as a party manual said, 'like roaches on a dirty shelf'" (Steiner, 1969, 142 in Horowitz, 1997, 19). What is clear, Horowitz suggests, is that Holocaust fiction does raise to the fore the question of belief. Frequently in critical discussions of the genre, "[q]uestions of morality and 'authenticity' displace discussions of literary technique and narrative strategy" (Horowitz, 1997, 16). Here too the specter of the Christian gaze is not far removed from the debates. One can hear in Spiegelman's, Lanzmann's and Steiner's anxiety a fear about how the language and representation of the atrocity can in fact be turned against its victims, whether by raising the question of verifiability, once the atrocity is treated as that which transcends representation, or by calling into question language itself as a reliable medium.

For Appelfeld, as his interview with Roth suggests, fiction was instrumental to allowing him the ability to voice the surreal quality of his own experiences. Eventually Appelfeld, who escaped a detainment camp and spent the war as a boy roaming the Ukrainian countryside, sleeping in the forest, subsisting on scraps from the time he was eight until he found a haven with the Red Army, too wrote a memoir, *The Story of a Life* (1999), but long after Roth published *Operation Shylock* and as Adam Kirsch points out, it is the most meager and sparse of his books (Kirsch, 2020). Fiction served Appelfeld as a means to recreate the world that the Nazis destroyed and to overcome the impasse that his own suffering and loss created. It is in his interview with Roth that he is most explicit about this dynamic, particularly in regards to the work "Tzili," which tells the story of a child surviving in the wilderness under Nazi occupation, but from a girl's perspective.

> The reality of the Holocaust surpassed any imagination. If I remained true to the facts, no one would believe me. But the moment I chose a girl, a little older than I was at the time, I removed "the story of my life" from the mighty grip of memory and gave it over to the creative laboratory. There one needs a causal explanation, a thread to tie things together.
>
> *(Roth, 1988)*

Ironically, thus, the imagination here becomes the constraint on believability when reality is "unbelievable, inexplicable, out of all proportion."

Conclusions

Once we recognize that Roth's work contains within itself a meditation on fiction and belief, then it becomes clear that one aim of the novel is to find another form of modern Jewish experience that is not traditionalist, nor Zionist, nor that of the survivor. We can see, then, that in all this layering of realism and delusion, myth and history, the novel develops its own form of the uncanny. It is neither the uncanny of Kafka, nor of Appelfeld, but another version of Jewish fiction inflected by both, by the experience of having missed the horrors of the camps and finding oneself called into the drama of the Jewish state as the world's most visible manifestation of Jewishness, but one which also calls the goodness of that nationalist endeavor into question.

The metafictional and literary critical threads of the novel are woven together by the narrative development toward the Mossad mission for which Roth is sent by Smilesburger to Athens, the inclusion of which would make it something of a Zionist spy novel; yet, this is the part of the work that, according to Roth, has been removed, because of the threat it would present to him were it published. It is also this missing node which establishes the link between Jewish fiction and politics.

This missing chapter calls to mind the concept of "the misplaced middle" which Henry James himself described as that defining feature of fiction most fundamental to it, that the narrative itself seeks to hide.[5] Roth aligns this missing center itself with the act of politics, not only by leaving out of the novel the moment of political intervention in which Roth supposedly participated in a mission to infiltrate the PLO's secret Jewish base in Athens, but also by comparing this intervention to the act of writing fiction itself. Both are described as acts of improvisation, emerging from a "dense kernel, the compact core," and initiating a form of speculation, "guesswork morally speaking," a kind of daring, a mess from which an "*operation,* rounded, pointed, structured, yet projecting the illusion of having been as spontaneously generated, as coincidental, untidy and improbable as life" (346). Both are thus grounded in a deception. It is a version of both politics and fiction held together by means of that for which they are always already a foil, that is to say by and against a Christian political theology for which an Augustinian all-seeing God stands as confession's moral guarantor, and for which the singular allegiance to truth guides a radical transformation toward the universal. In contrast, Jewish fiction looks messy, duplicitous, ironic, but in the process it reveals the process of contestation that always already secretly undergirds the phenomenon of belief.

Notes

1 For the purposes of this essay, I will treat faith and belief as interchangeable, although one could make an argument for keeping them distinct. For a dynamic and relational description of both, one productively at odds with Badiou and Critchley's, see Furey (2017).

2 To see the connection between Badiou's writings on Paul and his assessment of Judaism, see the essays collected in *Circonstances 3: Portées du mot "Juif"* (2005) in which he distinguishes between "authentic" and "virtual" Jews, defining the former as those who embrace universalism and the later as those who set themselves apart as a people and want to guard their identity against possible usurpation. For more on this dynamic in Paul, see Hammerschlag (2010, 261–62).

3 See note 2 above.

4 Plenty has been written on this event, particularly since Roth's death. See, in particular, Zipperstein (2018).

5 For more on this concept in James, see Miller (1998, 94).

Works Cited

Adorno, Theodore. 1967. *Prisms*. Translated by Samuel and Shierry Weber. Cambridge, MA: MIT Press.

Agamben, Giorgio. 1999. *Remnants of Auschwitz: The Witness and the Archive*. Translated by Daniel Heller-Rosen. New York: Zone.

Agamben, Giorgio. 2005. *The Time that Remains: A Commentary on the Letter to the Romans*. Translated by Patricia Dailey. Stanford, CA: Stanford University Press.

Aleichem, Shalom. 1996. *Tevye the Dairyman and the Railroad Stories*. Translated by Hillel Halkin. New York: Schocken.

Alter, Robert. 2000. *Canon and Creativity*. New Haven, CT: Yale University Press.

Amery, Jean. 2009. *At the Mind's Limits*. Translated by Sidney and Stella Rosenfeld. Bloomington: Indiana University Press.

Appelfeld, Aharon. 1983. *Tzili: The Story of a Life*. Translated by Dalya Bilu. New York: Schocken.

Appelfeld, Aharon. 1988. "After the Holocaust." In *Writing and the Holocaust*, edited by Berel Lang, 83–92. New York: Holmes and Meyer.

Appelfeld, Aharon. 2004. *The Story of a Life*. Translated by Aloma Halter. New York, Schocken.

Appelfeld, Aharon. 2009. *Badenheim 1939*. Translated by Dalya Bilu. Boston: Godine Press.

Arendt, Hannah. 2007. "The Enlightenment and the Jewish Question." In *The Jewish Writings*, edited by Jerome Kohn and Ron H. Feldman, 3–18. New York: Schocken.

Badiou, Alain. 2003. *Saint Paul: The Foundation of Universalism*. Translated by Ray Brassier. Stanford, CA: Stanford University Press.

Badiou, Alain. 2005. *Circonstances 3: portees du mot "juif."* Paris: Lignes & Manifestos.

Badiou, Alain. 2006. *Polemics*. Translated by Steve Corcoran. London: Verso.

Bailey, Blake. 2021. *Philip Roth: The Biography*. New York: Norton.

Benjamin, Walter. 1969. *Illuminations*. Translated by Harry Zohn. New York: Schocken.

Blanchot, Maurice. 1980. *The Writing of the Disaster*. Translated by Ann Smock. Lincoln University of Nebraska.

Blanchot, Maurice. 1999. *The Station Hill Blanchot Reader.* Translated by Lydia Davis. Barrytown: Station Hill Press.

Blanton, Ward. 2014. *A Materialism for the Masses: Saint Paul and the Philosophy of Undying Life.* New York: Columbia University Press.

Caputo, John D., and Linda Martin Alcoff, eds. 2009. *St. Paul Among the Philosophers.* Bloomington: Indiana University Press.

Critchley, Simon. 2012. *Faith of the Faithless: Experiments in Political Theology.* London Verso.

Furey, Constance. 2017. *Poetic Relations: Intimacy and Faith in the English Reformation.* Chicago, IL: University of Chicago Press.

Hammerschlag, Sarah. 2010. *The Figural Jew: Politics and Identity in Postwar French Thought.* Chicago, IL: University of Chicago Press.

Hammerschlag, Sarah. 2013. "Bad Jews, Authentic Jews, Figural Jews: Badiou and the Politics of Exemplarity." In *Judaism, Liberalism & Political Theology*, edited by Randi Rashkover and Martin Kavka, 221–40. Bloomington: Indiana University Press.

Horowitz, Sara. 1997. *Voicing the Void: Muteness and Memory in Holocaust Fiction.* Albany: SUNY Press.

Howe, Irving, and Eliezer Greenberg, eds. 1973. *A Treasury of Yiddish Stories.* New York Schocken.

Kafka, Franz. 1961. *Parabeln und Paradoxe/Parables and Paradoxes.* New York: Schocken.

Kirsch, Adam. 2020. "Aharon Appelfeld's Legends of Home." *The New Yorker*, March 2, 2020.

Levi, Primo. 1988. *The Drowned and the Saved.* Translated by Raymond Rosenthal. New York Simon and Schuster.

Levi, Primo. 1996. *Survival in Auschwitz.* Translated by Stuart Woolf. New York: Collier.

Lopez, Donald. 1998. "Belief." In *Critical Terms for Religious Studies*, edited by Mark C. Taylor, 21–35. Chicago, IL: University of Chicago Press.

Lyotard, Jean-Francois. 1988. *The Differend: Phrases in Dispute.* Translated by Georges Van Den Abbeele. Minneapolis: University of Minnesota Press.

Masuzawa, Tomoko. 2000. "Troubles with Materiality: The Ghost of Fetishism in the Nineteenth Century." *Cambridge Studies in Society and History* 42, no. 2 (April): 242–67.

Miller, J. Hillis. 1998. *Reading Narrative.* Norman: University of Oklahoma Press.

Naveh, Gila Safran. 2000. *Biblical Parables and Their Modern Re-creations.* Albany: SUNY Press.

Perec, Georges. 2010. *W, Or the Memory of Childhood.* Translated by David Bellos. New York Verba Mundi.

Perkins, David. 1991. *Theoretical Issues in Literary History.* Cambridge, MA: Harvard University Press.

Roth, Philip. 1959. *Goodbye Columbus.* New York: Vintage.

Roth, Philip. 1988. "Walking the way of the Survivor; A Talk with Aharon Appelfeld." *The New York Times*, February 28, 1988.

Roth, Philip. (1988) 2008. "The Facts." In *Novels and Other Narratives 1986–1991*, 305–462. New York: Library of America.

Roth, Philip. 1993. *Operation Shylock: A Confession.* New York: Vintage.

Schaefer, Peter. 2009. *Jesus in the Talmud.* Princeton, NJ: Princeton University Press.

Steiner, George. 1969. *Language and Silence: Essays on Language, Literature and the Inhuman.* New York: Penguin.

Stern, David. 1991. *Parables in Midrash: Narrative and Exegesis in Rabbinic Literature.* Cambridge, MA: Harvard University Press.

Suleiman, Susan Rubin. 2002. "The 1.5 Generation: Thinking about Child Survivors and the Holocaust." *American Imago* 59, no. 3 (Fall): 277–95.

Thurman, Judith. 2014. "Philip Roth Is Good for the Jews." *The New Yorker*, May 28, 2014.

Von Bernuth, Ruth. 2016. *How the Wise Men Got to Chelm: The Life and Times of a Yiddish Folk Tradition.* New York: NYU Press.

Wiesel, Elie. 1975. "For Some Measure of Humility." *Sh'ma* 5, no. 100 (October): 314–16.

Wiesel, Elie. 1982. *Night.* New York: Bantam.

Wisse, Ruth. 2000. *The Modern Jewish Canon.* New York: The Free Press.

Zipperstein, Stephen. 2018. "Philip Roth's Forgotten Tape: The Beginnings of the Great American Writer." *Forward*, May 28, https://forward.com/culture/401928/philip-roths-forgotten-tape-the-beginnings-of-the-great-american-writer/.

Zizek, Slavoj. 2000. *The Fragile Absolute—or, Why Is the Christian Legacy Worth Fighting For?* London: Verso.

Zizek, Slavoj. 2003. *The Puppet and the Dwarf: The Perverse Core of Christianity.* Cambridge, MA: MIT Press.

35
RELIGIOUS USES OF FANTASY FICTION

Markus Altena Davidsen

Introduction

In early 2001, a chain email urged the citizens of New Zealand, Australia, Canada, and Great Britain to put down "Jedi" as their religious affiliation in the upcoming census. Part political protest, part practical joke, the email campaign was a massive success, helped along by generous media coverage by newspapers such as *The Guardian* and by the renewed interest in *Star Wars* following the release of *Star Wars Episode 1: The Phantom Menace* in 1999 (Porter, 2006, 96; Singler, 2014, 154). With more than 390,000 self-identified adherents, Jedi came out as the fourth most common religious affiliation in Great Britain, outscoring both Judaism and Buddhism. The largest concentration of Jedi proved to live in New Zealand, where they constituted almost 1.4% of the total population (Porter, 2006, 96–98; Possamai, 2005, 72–73)—in some university cities, close to 10%. In total, more than 500,000 Britons, New Zealanders, Australians, and Canadians claimed to be Jedi.

The "Jedi Census Phenomenon" was largely a prank. The vast majority of those who put down Jedi on the census form did not seriously practice a Force-based religion. But in the years preceding the Census Phenomenon, a very real, but much smaller, community of self-identified Jedi Realists— i.e., individuals who aim to live according to the Jedi philosophy—had emerged out of the online *Star Wars* role-playing community. The Jedi Census Phenomenon inspired some Jedi Realists to *actually* create the religion to which people in the census prank had jokingly claimed to belong. These individuals who refer to themselves as Jediists (rather than Jedi Realists) have developed creeds and rituals and have successfully applied for legal recognition of their faith—Jediism—in several countries (this story is told in detail in Davidsen, 2017a; see also Davidsen, 2016a; Singler, 2014).

After journalists had uncovered the real phenomena of Jedi Realism and Jediism, scholars of religion began to research these and similar groups and to theorize the religious use of fantasy fiction.[1] The two main pioneers were Adam Possamai and Carole Cusack, who carved out a new research field with their monographs *Religion and Popular Culture* (Possamai, 2005) and *Invented Religions* (Cusack, 2010) and who subsequently took the lead in charting the field with handbook and anthology projects (Cusack and Kosnáč, 2017; Possamai, 2012a; Sutcliffe and Cusack, 2013). Besides Jediism, religions based on fantasy fiction that have been studied over the last twenty years include the neo-pagan organization Church of All Worlds, which has taken its name and several ritual practices from Robert A. Heinlein's science fiction novel *Stranger in a Strange Land* (Cusack, 2010, Chapter

DOI: 10.4324/9781003119456-39

454

3, 2016a); Satanists and chaos magicians who invoke the monster gods from H.P. Lovecraft's horror cycle, the so-called Cthulhu Mythos (Gonce, 2003; Hanegraaff, 2007); and various self-identified pagan, Christian, and gnostic groups that draw on J.R.R. Tolkien's literary mythology and claim to communicate with the Valar, the lower gods of Tolkien's universe (Davidsen, 2012, 2014, 2017b).

Some reflections on how to refer to religions using fantasy fiction may be needed immediately. In my own work I use the term "fiction-based religion," which I have defined as "religion in which fictional texts are used as authoritative texts" (Davidsen, 2013, 384). Possamai prefers the term "hyper-real religion" which he, inspired by the French philosopher Jean Baudrillard, has defined as a "simulacrum of a religion created out of popular culture" (2005, 79). In practice, fiction-based religion and hyper-real religion refer to the same empirical phenomena and can be treated as synonyms. However, since *all* religions can be qualified as "hyper-real" in Baudrillard's sense, namely as simulacra (or imaginations) that have come to be treated as real, it may be confusing to use "hyper-real religion" to designate a certain class of religions, namely those based on fantasy fiction/popular culture (Davidsen, 2013, 381–84). The label fiction-based religion may serve us better if we want to distinguish analytically between religions that use fantasy fiction as authoritative texts, over and against conventional religions based on narratives claiming to tell of supernatural interventions in the actual world—such as the Christian Gospels that depict Jesus' incarnation, wonderworking, resurrection, and ascension as historical events (Davidsen, 2013, 384–88).[2]

Cusack's notion of invented religions refers to a different but overlapping set of phenomena than fiction-based/hyper-real religions, namely "those religions that announce their invented status" (2010, 1). For Cusack this category includes both fiction-based religions, such as Jediism and the Church of All Worlds, and parody religions, such as Discordianism and the Church of the Flying Spaghetti Monster. This is problematic for two reasons. First, fiction-based religions turn out *not* to announce their invented status but to be keen on presenting themselves as "real religions" (see Singler, 2014 and Davidsen, 2017a on Jediism in this respect). Second, according to a substantive definition of "religion" as beliefs and practices that assume the existence of supernatural agents (such as gods and angels), worlds (such as heaven and the astral plane), and/or processes (such as magic or the karma law) (cf. Davidsen and Van Rijn, 2020, 93), fiction-based religions are genuine religions because they make supernatural claims, whereas parody religions are no religions at all because they, by their very nature, make no such claims.[3] By the same token, fiction-based religions—such as Jediism, which assumes the existence of the Force in the actual world—may be contrasted to fandom, including the *Star Wars* fandom, which makes no such assumption. Based on a functional and broad (rather than a substantive and narrow) definition of religion, Michael Jindra (1994) has argued that fandom *is* religion, because fandom, like conventional religion, functions as a provider of community, myth, and meaning. A weakness of Jindra's approach, however, is that it obscures the crucial difference between (fiction-based) religion and fandom, namely that religion makes supernatural claims about the actual world whereas fandom does not (Davidsen, 2013, 388–90).[4]

In the rest of this chapter, I chart the various ways in which contemporary fantasy fiction has been read and used in religious ways. I begin by distinguishing four modes of religious use of fantasy fiction, which I label the binocular, mythopoeic, cosmological, and historical modes, respectively (Section "Four Modes of Religious Use of Fantasy Fiction"). After that, I discuss the various functions that fantasy fiction may have within religious traditions (Section "Fiction Based Religion in a Strict and a Loose Sense") and the strategies used to legitimize the religious use of fiction (Section "Legitimizing Religioius Use of Fantasy Fiction"). The final section takes up the question why only some fantasy fiction, but not all, lends itself to religious use (i.e., has "religious affordance"; Section "The Religious Affordance of Fantasy Fiction").

Four Modes of Religious Use of Fantasy Fiction

Adam Possamai originally defined hyper-real religion as a "simulacrum of a religion created out of popular culture *that provides inspiration for believers/consumers at a metaphorical level*" (2005, 79; my emphasis). It is very well possible, however, to believe quite literally (rather than metaphorically) in the supernatural entities depicted in fiction. Within Tolkien spirituality, for example, it is common to believe that Middle-earth is a real place and that the Elves and Valar really exist (Davidsen, 2012, 2014, 2017b). In response to me pointing out this fact (Davidsen, 2012, 201–02; cf. Possamai, 2012b, 19), Possamai adapted his definition of hyper-real religion. It now sounds: "A hyper-real religion is a simulacrum of a religion created out of, or in symbiosis with, commodified popular culture which provides inspiration at a metaphorical level *and/or is a source of belief for everyday life*" (Possamai, 2012b, 20; emphasis added).

Expanding the simple dichotomy between metaphorical inspiration and literal belief, I have suggested the existence of several distinct religious modes in which fantasy fiction (and conventional religious narratives, too) can be used (Davidsen, 2014, 137–43). In what follows, I discuss the four most prominent modes: the binocular, mythopoeic, cosmological, and historical modes. Each mode represents a distinct way of using fiction religiously and of rationalizing such use. Of the four modes, the binocular mode ascribes the lowest level of authority to the fantasy text in question, and the historical mode, the highest.

The Binocular Mode

Individuals and groups who use fantasy fiction in the binocular mode consider the characters, the storyline, and the religious elements of the text to be wholly fictional but are, nevertheless, moved to believe that religious entities (e.g., elves or magic) *very much like* those depicted in the fictional text exist in the real world.

A good example of the binocular mode is found in neo-paganism, a broad movement encompassing, among other branches, modern witchcraft (wicca), druidry, and heathenry/asatru. Neo-pagans aim to revive the religions of Europe's pre-Christian past, and for that reason consider Celtic, Germanic, Greek, and other ancient mythologies to constitute their authentic and authoritative text base. Neo-paganism is thus no fiction-based religion, but fantasy fiction nevertheless plays a crucial role in inspiring neo-pagan belief. Reflecting on the importance of fantasy for the very emergence of neo-paganism, Graham Harvey (2000) argued "that J.R.R. Tolkien's *Lord of the Rings* provided *metaphorical binoculars* through which the realm of Faerie became visible again" (emphasis added). In other words, it was after reading Tolkien and other fantasy novels that many to-be-pagans in the 1960s and 1970s first started asking themselves whether magic, elves, and a Faery Otherworld might exist also in the real world. These people did not believe that Tolkien wrote about real deities (if they did, they would have approached *The Lord of the Rings* in the cosmological mode—see below). But *The Lord of the Rings* inspired them to search for more authoritative myths and to go into the forest in the hope of experiencing the presence of real elves. For committed pagans, moreover, continued immersion in fantasy helps sustain a pagan worldview in which elves and magic are real (Harvey, 2006). For example, members of the Goddess movement find inspiration in Marion Zimmer Bradley's *The Mists of Avalon* (1983) and eco-oriented (British) pagans in Robert Holdstock's *Mythago Wood* series (e.g., 1984).

Fantasy (and horror) novels, movies, and role-playing games have also inspired individuals to self-identify as various non-human beings. Inspired by Tolkien's *The Lord of the Rings*, some individuals began to self-identify as Elves in the early 1970s (Davidsen, 2014, 238–44), and from the movement of self-identified Elves emerged in the 1990s the broader Otherkin movement, whose members may also self-identify as (were)wolves, dragons, and so on (Davidsen, 2014, 245–50). The Vampire community, whose members include both blood-drinking and psychic vampires, as well as human donors, constitutes the largest fiction-inspired identity movement. White Wolf's role-playing games *Vampire: The Masquerade* (1991), *Werewolf: The Apocalypse* (1992), and *Changeling: The Dreaming* (1995), were instrumental to the growth of the Otherkin and Vampire communities in the 1990s and later. As Lupa (2007, 50) explains,

> [T]he subject matter of the games led to the inevitable wonderings: "Well, what if this was real? What if there really were werewolves, and vampires, and faeries in our day and age?" Most players likely simply shrugged it off as a passing fancy. However, many Otherkin found that the flights of fancy could open up opportunities to discuss more serious approaches to the idea of nonhumans in a human world.

In other words: the role-playing games were approached in the binocular mode. While players recognized that the settings and story-worlds of the games were entirely fictional, the games became metaphorical binoculars that allowed players to appreciate their own "true" Otherkin identities—and prompted them to seek out authoritative, non-fictional sources that might explain and legitimize those identities (Davidsen, 2014, 250–52, 267–75; Laycock, 2012).

The Mythopoeic Mode

Individuals who use fantasy fiction in the mythopoeic mode consider the text in question to be an allegory that conveys real spiritual truths. It is important to note that not all allegorical readings are mythopoeic. Readers who interpret the One Ring in *The Lord of the Rings* as an allegorical reference to the atomic bomb—and thus interpret something supernatural as an allegory of something natural—approach the text in the fictional mode. A mythopoeic interpretation, by contrast, has a supernatural target domain for the allegory. An interpretation of Gandalf and Galadriel as allegorical references to the wiccan God and Goddess, for example, is mythopoeic. Fiction approached in the mythopoeic mode can be considered a viable basis for rituals and magical "work," as long as the text is understood properly with the right hermeneutic key. For example, wiccans may use depictions of Gandalf and Galadriel in ritual, while at the same time stressing that the supernatural entities with whom they really engage are the God and the Goddess.

Lovecraftian magic constitutes a fiction-based esoteric current entirely governed by the mythopoeic mode. Consider, for example, the use of H.P. Lovecraft in the Church of Satan. Michael Aquino wrote two Lovecraft-themed rituals for *The Satanic Rituals* (LaVey, 1972, 173–201), "The Ceremony of the Nine Angles" and "The Call to Cthulhu," together with an accompanying essay, "The Metaphysics of Lovecraft." Already prior to the publication of these rituals, LaVey had used Lovecraft-based incantations within the Church of Satan and the new rituals, too, were intended for actual use (Aquino, 1977). Even so, Cthulhu and the other Lovecraftian entities addressed in the rituals were not believed to exist in their own right but were understood merely as metaphorical references to Satan. Similarly, when influential British occultist Kenneth Grant integrated Lovecraftian themes into Aleister Crowley's system of ceremonial magic, he did so in the mythopoeic mode. Interpreting Lovecraft's stories through the lens of his own Qabalistic speculations, Grant identified, for example, Lovecraft's Yog-Sothoth (referred to in "The Dunwich Horror") with John Dee's demon Coronzon/Choronzon, whom Grant considered to be the guardian of the gateway of Daath (cf. Gonce, 2003, 102–11). Grant's mythopoeic interpretation of Lovecraft's mythos provided the theoretical rationale for the Lovecraftian magic of later groups such as the Esoteric Order of Dagon (Davidsen, forthcoming), Michael Bertiaux's Confraternity of Oblates of the Monastery of the Seven Rays (Gonce, 2003,

113–15), and the Dragon Rouge, especially its Polish "Magan" lodge (Wagenseil 2015). Chaos magicians working with Lovecraft's mythos in the tradition of Phil Hine's *Pseudonomicon* ([1994] 2004) also do so in the mythopoeic mode and have experimented with both possession and pathworking rituals (Gonce, 2003, 119; Hanegraaff, 2007, 104–06).

J.R.R. Tolkien's literary mythology, including *The Lord of the Rings* (1954–1955; paperback 1965) and *The Silmarillion* (1977), has been approached in the mythopoeic mode, too. Gareth Knight, for instance, included a Tolkien-themed pathworking ritual in his book *The Magical World of the Inklings* (1990), and declared, in a manner strikingly similar to Grant's take on Lovecraft, Tolkien's literary mythology to be a "mythopoeic creative work" (1990, 136) and "a fleshing out of Qabalistic doctrines" (1990, 114). Accordingly, Tolkien's mythology constituted, "from the magical point of view," a departure point for magical work as valid as any "'real' myth or legend" (Knight, 1990, 136). Similarly, a group within the North Carolina-based Fifth Way Mystery School, headed by Vincent Bridges, constructed a "High Elvish Working" in 1993 aiming to "explore the Truth beyond J.R.R. Tolkien's created Arda." The ritual circulated in print among pagans in the United States and New Zealand and was later published online (cf. Davidsen, 2014, 291–98). The two only fiction-based Tarot decks currently on the market, Terry Donaldson's *The Lord of the Rings Tarot Deck & Card Game* (1997; cf. Davidsen, 2014, 299–310) and Donald Tyson's *Necronomicon Tarot* (2007; cf. Cowan, 2012), are premised on a mythopoeic reading of Tolkien's and Lovecraft's fiction, respectively.

The Cosmological Mode

Using a piece of fantasy fiction in the cosmological mode entails treating it as a fictional story about supernatural agents, worlds, and/or processes that exist in the actual world in the way they are described in the text. In other words, where the mythopoeic mode is allegorical, the cosmological mode is literal. For example, members of the Tribunal of the Sidhe, Tië eldaliéva (The Elven Path), and Ilsalunté Valion (The Silver Ship of the Valar) consider Tolkien's Valar to exist quite as Tolkien described them. All three groups engage in ritual exchanges with these fictional entities, and Tië eldaliéva and Ilsalunté Valion have drawn up elaborate ritual calendars that dedicate each moon celebration to one of the Valar (Davidsen, 2017b). Members of Tië eldaliéva and Ilsalunté Valion also believe that the Blessed Realm, the abode of the Valar in Tolkien's mythology, exists on some spiritual plane, and they travel there to visit the Valar (and the Elves and Maiar) in ritual. The structure of these rituals is inspired by wiccan and neo-shamanic practices, but crucially the Valar are believed to be who Tolkien says they are (cosmological mode) and not just allegories for other deities (mythopoeic mode). Similarly, Jedi Realists and Jediists consider the storyline in *Star Wars* to be fictional, but nevertheless believe that the Force exists in our world (Davidsen, 2016a, 2017a). And even though members of the Jedi Community consider Yoda and Obi-Wan Kenobi to be fictional characters imagined by George Lucas, they quote and discuss the wisdom about the Force taught by these spiritual teachers. Indeed, Jediists and Jedi Realists enlist the authority of the *Star Wars* Jedi masters both when their own Force theology aligns with the Force theology in *Star Wars* (i.e., the Force is in itself good; the "dark side" refers to the instrumental and egoistic use of the Force and has no being of its own) and when they, inspired by the notion of yin and yang in Taoism, depart from the theology in *Star Wars* (i.e., by viewing the Force in dualistic terms and considering "balance in the Force" to require equal measures of the light side and the dark side). In terms of practice, Jedi Realists and Jediists alike mediate to "feel the Force," and Jediists, who more than the Jedi Realists see the Force as a providential power with a will and a plan for the world, may also pray to the Force.

Practitioners fully committed to using fantasy fiction in the cosmological mode are rare, but it is striking that many individuals oscillate between the mythopoeic and cosmological modes. In many cases, the cosmological mode governs ritual practice (which, even when experimental or playful, entails working with fictional entities and powers as if they were literally real), whereas individuals fall back on the more cautious mythopoeic stance when justifying the practice to themselves and others. We see this oscillation within the Jedi Community whose beliefs and rituals are taken right out of the *Star Wars* films (cosmological mode), but where members sometimes stress that the fictional Force in *Star Wars* (which Lucas created) refers only metaphorically to the *real* Force that they work with and which reveals itself in all the world's religions (mythopoeic mode; Davidsen, 2017a, 23–24). As a second example of oscillation between the mythopoeic and cosmological modes, one may consider the reception of Edward Bulwer-Lytton's fiction by Helena Petrovna (Madame) Blavatsky, co-founder of the Theosophical Society. The mythopoeic mode is at work in the passage of *The Secret Doctrine* where Blavatsky argues that Bulwer-Lytton's notion of Vril, mentioned in *The Coming Race* (1871), is a fictional reference to the real esoteric force known to the Atlanteans as mash-mak (1888, 563). But when she in a letter suggests that the Ascended Masters count the adept Zanoni, from Bulwer-Lytton's 1842 story of the same name, as one of their own, she slides into the cosmological mode (Strube, 2013, 65).[5]

The Historical Mode

As mentioned in the introduction, religious narratives proper (such as the Christian Gospels) have reference ambition, which is to say that these texts themselves *aim* to be read in the historical mode as (relatively) accurate accounts of supernatural interventions in actual history. This is so even if such texts are often *de facto* approached, especially in modern times, in the cosmological, mythopoeic, or fictional modes. Fantasy fiction, by contrast, lacks reference ambition by definition and, therefore, does not lend itself well to a historical reading. In fact, the historical use of fantasy fiction seems restricted to Tolkien spirituality, and even in this context it is a minority position. Ravenwolf Neurion, a proponent of the historical approach to Tolkien's mythology, has summed up his position as follows (spelling corrected):

> Here's what I honestly believe. Middle-earth and the core elements of Tolkien's Legendarium happened in real time on this physical world. After the flood (Days of Noah in the Bible, fall of Atlantis or fall of Númenor—all the same) there was [a] period of several centuries when Elves and magic still remained strong. [...] At that point we had the full blood and half elves (like Elrond) who entered hidden realms [...] We also have living people who existed through the ages right down to this present day who are of part Elf blood from people like Arwen and Aragorn's descendants and other part elves.
>
> *(Ravenwolf, 2005)*

It should be stressed that the majority of those engaged in Tolkien spirituality consider Ravenwolf's historical reading of Tolkien to be delusional and prefer to engage Tolkien's work in the mythopoeic or cosmological modes.

Fiction-Based Religion in a Strict and a Loose Sense: Fantasy Fiction as Core or Periphery in Religious Traditions

To get a grip on the different functions that fantasy fiction can play within religious traditions, it is useful to distinguish between fiction-based religion in a strict and in a loose sense. We have fiction-based religion in the strict sense when a particular corpus of a fantasy fiction serves as the narrative core of a religious tradition; when this is the case, the fantasy fiction in question will usually be approached in the cosmological or historical mode (Davidsen, 2012, 198). In Tië eldaliéva and Ilsaluntë

Valion, Tolkien's Legendarium constitutes such a narrative core. Members of these "Legendarium Reconstructionist" groups refer to *The Silmarillion* as "Our Bible," engage in meticulous Tolkien exegesis, and have crafted belief charters, ritual calendars, and magical correspondence tables that draw exclusively on Tolkien's mythology (Davidsen, 2014, 379–431, 2017b). They also tend to view other religions through a Tolkienesque lens, arguing, for example, that the gods and goddesses of the world's various pantheons are really the Valar appearing in different guises (Davidsen, 2017b, 27). (That is, they interpret Tolkien's stories in the cosmological mode and all other mythologies in the mythopoeic mode). Within the Jedi Community, we see the same, just with the *Star Wars* movies— and, for many Jedi Realists, also the novels and role-playing material from the so-called Expanded Universe—as the narrative core. It is *Star Wars* that provides the raison d'être for the Jedi Community and determines the core belief (in the Force), ritual (meditation to feel the Force), identity (as Jedi Knight), ethics (the Jedi Code), and social organization (with master and apprentices; Davidsen, 2017a). Jediists (and to a lesser extent Jedi Realists) may peruse new age, esoteric, Western Buddhist, and Christian literature for additional spiritual inspiration, but they do so within a *Star Wars* frame of reference where literature from other religious traditions is used to shed light on the deeper nature of the Force. In other words: the Legendarium Reconstructionist Tolkien groups and the Jedi Community show structural similarities to conventional religions, such as Judaism, Christianity, and Hinduism, that all, too, revolve around a more or less fixed narrative core. The only difference is that the Legendarium Reconstructionists and the Jedi Community have "adopted," as the narrative core of their tradition, somebody else's fantasy fiction.

By contrast, we may speak of fiction-based religion in a loose sense, when the fantasy fiction that inspires and sustains belief is used only as a secondary textual resource within a religious tradition that has another, non-fictional scriptural core. This is the case in various branches of neo-paganism that approach J.K. Rowling's *Harry Potter*, Terry Pratchett's *Discworld* series, and other works of fantasy in the binocular mode as stories pointing vaguely to the reality of magic. It is also the case for Christians who read C.S. Lewis's *The Lion, the Witch and the Wardrobe* in the mythopoeic mode, interpreting Aslan as a transfigured Christ (on Lewis: Stausberg, 2020, 327–36). In both cases, audiences place fantasy fiction in the periphery of a religious tradition that includes a narrative core read in the cosmological or historical modes—various pre-Christian mythologies in the case of neo-paganism, and the Gospels and more broadly the Bible in the case of Christianity. Secondary fantasy fiction interpreted in the light of primary religious narratives can either be "adopted" (Rowling and Pratchett did not intend to promote neo-paganism) or it can be written for this very purpose (Lewis intended the *Chronicles of Narnia* to introduce young people to Christianity). When fantasy fiction is written with the aim to convey a religious message, we may speak of "religious fantasy fiction." George Lucas, too, conceived of his *Star Wars* movies as religious fantasy fiction. In an interview with Bill Moyers, Lucas stated that he "put the Force into the movie in order to awaken a certain kind of spirituality in young people—more a belief in God than a belief in any particular religious system" (Moyers, 1999; cf. Davidsen, 2017a, 11). Like Lewis, Lucas intended his narratives to be consumed in the mythopoeic mode with the Force as a metaphor for God (and they often are); he did not want, nor foresee, that some people would go one step further, adopt a cosmological mode, and consider the Force in *Star Wars* to be a direct reference to a real Force in the actual world.[6]

In theosophy and ceremonial magic, as well as in their later offshoots, such as new age, Satanism, chaos magic, and wicca, we encounter a related dynamic. The textual core of these traditions is discursive rather than narrative, in the sense that the tradition-defining texts, such as Blavatsky's *The Secret Doctrine* (1888), Spangler's *Revelation: The Birth of a New Age* (1971), LaVey's *The Satanic Bible* (1969), Carroll's *Liber Null & Psychonaut* (1987), and Gardner's *Witchcraft Today* (1954), are of an argumentative kind. It seems that religious traditions such as these, which lack a narrative core, tend to go for the second best—a narrative periphery of fantasy fiction. Again, this fantasy fiction can be "adopted," as we have seen with theosophy adopting Bulwer-Lytton's fiction and Satanism and chaos magic adopting Lovecraft's Cthulhu Mythos. But religious leaders may also take the pen in their own hands and write religious fantasy fiction themselves. Some examples of theosophical, wiccan, and new age fiction of this religious-didactic sort written to complement more central non-narrative religious works include Dion Fortune's *The Sea Priestess* (1938), Gerald Gardner's *A Goddess Arrives* (Scire, 1939), and James Redfield's *The Celestine Prophecy* (1993).[7] Obviously, religious-didactic fiction may also be written by authors who do not have a leading role in a religious organization. One of the most sold and influential works of religious fantasy fiction is Paulo Coelho's new age fable *The Alchemist* (1993; cf. Stausberg, 2020, 628–36).

Legitimizing Religious Use of Fantasy Fiction

Of the various legitimation strategies employed to justify the religious use of fiction, the appeal to revelation is by far the most common. Already in *Isis Unveiled*, Blavatsky commented that Bulwer-Lytton's fiction "sounds more like the faithful echo of memory than the exuberant outflow of mere imagination" (1877, 285), and fifty years later, C. Nelson Stewart argued that Bulwer-Lytton's stories "Zicci" and "A Strange Story" were based on dreams of a sort which "we should now call 'astral experiences'" (1927, 17). In a similar way Kenneth Grant claimed that the *Necronomicon*, a forbidden grimoire featured in Lovecraft's fiction, in fact refers to secret lore existing in the Akashic Records which Lovecraft had unconsciously perused and worked into his tales.[8] It is for this reason, argued Grant, that Lovecraft's Mythos constitutes valid material for magical work (cf. Gonce, 2003, 102–11). Tolkien, too, has been claimed to have read the Akashic Records (Knight, 1990, 136), and Terry Donaldson, creator of *The Lord of the Rings Tarot Deck & Card Game*, has suggested that Tolkien channeled his entire work (cf. Davidsen, 2014, 307). Stephen Hoeller, the leader of the Los Angeles-based Ecclesia Gnostica, proposed that Tolkien had accessed what Henry Corbin has called the Imaginal Realm and that his narratives provide a gateway for others into this spiritual realm, an idea adopted by Tolkien-based groups such as Tië eldaliéva and Ilsaluntë Valion (Davidsen, 2014, 385, 424–25, 2017b, 25–26). Crucially, individuals involved in Lovecraftian magic and Tolkien spirituality find support for their legitimization efforts in Lovecraft's and Tolkien's letters, which contain evidence of the fervent dream lives of both authors and, in the case of Tolkien, of his experience of "reporting" or "recording" rather than "inventing" his secondary world (Davidsen, 2014, 372–74).

Practitioners of fiction-based religion committed to the cosmological or historical modes sometimes top off the appeal to revelation with additional legitimization strategies. Practitioners of Tolkien spirituality refer to their own experiences, induced by trance-work and pathworking, as proof of the existence of the Elves and the Valar, and members of the Tribunal of the Sidhe argue that Tolkien was an astral being who chose to be incarnated in human form to bring certain truths into this world, truths that he communicated in secret form through his fiction (Davidsen, 2014, 228). Other practitioners of Tolkien spirituality seek evidence for the historicity of Tolkien's narratives, for example, by comparing the coastline of Middle-earth with that of Europe before the Ice Age (Davidsen, 2014, 422). Members of the Jedi Community use an opposite strategy (Davidsen, 2017a, 23–24). Being somewhat embarrassed by the fact that they base their religion on a movie series, they do not frame George Lucas as a prophet but prefer to emphasize the similarities between the Force religion taught by Yoda and those religions they themselves deem authoritative (mainly Buddhism and Christianity). They also cite new age science publications that claim that quantum mechanics and other frontier fields of natural science have proven the ultimately spiritual nature of energy. The references to authoritative religion and authoritative science have the same function: to provide backing for Yoda's teachings about the Force from respected sources external to the *Star Wars* universe.

The Religious Affordance of Fantasy Fiction

Not all works of fantasy fiction lend themselves equally well to religious use. Religious communities and traditions have emerged from *Star Wars* and Tolkien's literary mythology, but Frank Herbert's *Dune* books have not moved anyone to emulate the religion of the Fremen, fans of James Cameron's *Avatar* do not worship Eywa, and the readers of George R.R. Martin's *A Song of Ice and Fire* series have not felt an urge to address the Seven, the Drowned God, or the Red God R'hllor in prayer. Why this difference? Drawing on narratology and theories of how religious narratives work, I have explored this question together with colleagues in a thematic issue of the journal *Religion* (see especially Davidsen, 2016b, and compare Cusack, 2016a; Feldt, 2016; Petersen, 2016). The general picture emerging from this work is that fantasy fiction has "religious affordance," i.e., affords religious use, if it features narrative religion that can be used as a model for religious belief and practice in the actual world, and if an aura of veracity is created around that narrative religion so that it becomes detachable from its fictional frame.

We have narrative religion when human-like characters discuss religious beliefs, engage in religious rituals, or have religious visions, but also when gods and angels appear explicitly as characters in the story. Features of narrative religion that seem to increase the religious affordance of fantasy fiction include the following:

- The protagonist is explicitly involved, and easy-to-emulate rituals, gestures, and sayings are present (such as the water-sharing ritual and the greeting "Thou Art God" in Heinlein's *Stranger in a Strange Land*; cf. Cusack, 2016a).
- An extraordinary identity is provided that can make one feel special (e.g., it is cool to be a Jedi Knight or an Elf).
- The narrative religion resonates with the audience's concerns and interests and provides a new language to speak of beliefs already held (this seems to be the great strength of the concept of "the Force" from *Star Wars*).
- The divine beings with whom humans or humanlike characters exchange are benign and responsive (note: the divine beings in Martin's *A Song of Ice and Fire* are not).
- The divine beings are of a spiritual nature, and therefore easy to "detach" from the fictional storyworld (note: *Avatar* has all of the above—an iconic greeting ["I see you"], an extraordinary identity one can metaphorically adopt [na'vi], a fashionable moral message [warning against greed and the environmental crisis], and a benign divine being [Eywa]. But Eywa is physical and undetachable from fictional Pandora, and presumable for that reason, no *Avatar*-based religion came off the ground, but see Davidsen, 2010).

Obvious intertextual loans from existing religious traditions limit religious use to the binocular and mythopoeic modes. This is the case with religious fiction, such as Lewis' *The Lion, the Witch and the Wardrobe*, which is *meant* to be read in the mythopoeic mode as a Christian allegory. The explicit loans from Islam in Herbert's *Dune* and the loans from both Islam and Hinduism in Robert Jordan's *Wheel of Time* series, too, seem to stand in the way of a cosmological/literal adoption of the religion of the Fremen or of the Aes sedai similar to the Jedi Community's adoption of the Force religion of the Jedi Knights from *Star Wars*.

The religious affordance of fantasy fiction can be enhanced if an aura of veracity is constructed around the narrative religion in the work in question. This can be done in three main ways. First, authoritative teacher figures may instruct less knowledgeable characters with whom the reader can identify on religious matters. Jesus serves this function vis-à-vis the disciples in the Christian Gospels, and Yoda serves it vis-à-vis Luke Skywalker in *Star Wars* (Davidsen, 2016b, 532–33). Second, the narrator may demonstrate that what the teacher figures preach is true, by presenting supernatural agents, places, and processes as straightforwardly real within the story-world (Davidsen, 2016b, 530–32). In Tolkien's literary mythology, we have an example of this when Eru and the Valar appear and act as characters in *The Silmarillion* (whereas they are only spoken of in *The Lord of the Rings*). Third, the author may endorse the narrative religion as true, worthy, and relevant in letters (such as Tolkien's letters on how his stories were seemingly revealed to him, discussed above) or in interviews (such as Lucas' interview with Moyers in which he said that he put the Force into the movies to make young people interested in God, also mentioned above; Davidsen, 2016b, 540–41). The author may also blur the distinction between himself and his text-internal narrator; Lovecraft does this when he draws on material from his own haunting dreams in the description of his narrator-protagonists' dream visions.

Conclusion

In this chapter, I have explored how fantasy fiction may be used religiously, how individuals legitimize their religious use of fantasy fiction, and why certain fantasy texts have greater religious affordance than others. A few general conclusions emerge. (1) An analytical distinction can be drawn between religious narratives and fantasy fiction: both genres include supernatural elements (narrative religion), but only religious narratives claim to speak of supernatural interventions in the actual world (they have reference ambition) whereas fantasy fiction is non-referential. (2) Because fantasy fiction is recognized as fiction, readers rarely consider the *storyline* of fantasy fiction to be actual history (though some do and read fantasy fiction in the historical mode). Even so, readers often take fantasy fiction to carry some religious truth. Readers may either take fantasy fiction to point to other, more authoritative and non-fictional religious sources (binocular mode), to present supernatural entities in transfigured form (mythopoeic mode), or to be fictional stories about supernatural beings and places that exist in the actual world (cosmological mode). (3) When fantasy fiction is used in the cosmological (or historical) modes, distinct communities and traditions may arise. The best examples of such fiction-based religions are the Jedi Community based on *Star Wars* and the spiritual Tolkien milieu based on Tolkien's Middle-earth saga. (4) Religious communities that base themselves on fiction experience a greater need to legitimize their beliefs than do members of more conventional religious groups, but the legitimization strategies employed are well known: it may be claimed that the fiction is in fact based on revelation (Lovecraftian magic; Tolkien spirituality), or that the religious teachings contained in the fictional text express perennial wisdom and/or are proved by science (Jedi Community). (5) Not all pieces of fantasy fiction have the same degree of religious affordance. An explicit and engaging narrative religion with benign and responsive divine exchange partners and an extraordinary identity enhances religious affordance, as does the endorsement of the truth and relevance of the narrative religion by the author, or by a narrator or teacher figure speaking on the author's behalf.

Notes

1 I use the term "fantasy"/"fantasy fiction" as shorthand for what might more precisely be labelled supernatural fiction, i.e., fiction that features supernatural agents, worlds, and/or processes within its story-world. I thus extend the category of fantasy to include portions of horror and science fiction.

2 Because religious narratives have what Torsten Pettersson (2005) calls reference ambition, they belong to the broader category of non-fiction. This is so, even if a contemporary reader may judge the supernatural claims put forward in such texts as implausible. By contrast, fictional texts, including fantasy fiction, are "nonreferential" (Cohn, 1999, 12) because they lack reference ambition; they do not tell of the actual world, but project a fictional world of their own making.

3 The reader may compare the argument here to Cusack's discussion of her own position in relation to those of Possamai and myself (Cusack, 2016b).

4   This is not the place to rehearse in detail the debates within the study of religion on how to properly define religion (substantively or functionally; stipulatively or prototypically), and on whether defining religion is desirable at all, or even possible. A reader interested in these debates may consult Platvoet and Molendijk (1999). Schilbrack (2017) provides a philosophical argument for the position adopted here, i.e., that religion can be defined and should be defined substantively and stipulatively.

5   Since this chapter focuses on contemporary religious uses of fantasy fiction, I mention Blavatsky's use of Bulwer-Lytton's fiction only briefly. For a fascinating discussion of this case, the reader may consult Frenschkowski (2021). A briefer discussion can be found in Davidsen (2014, 90–95).

6   Another example of a religious group drawing literal inspiration from a text that was meant to carry spiritual significance only metaphorically is Ernst Bernhardt's *Gralsbewegung* (Grail Movement) which was based largely on Richard Wagner's opera *Parsifal* (Gruber, 2009, 32–34).

7   See Gilhus and Mikaelsson (2013) for an overview of early theosophical fiction written with a religious-didactic aim. Cusack (2012, 166) mentions that George Ivanovich Gurdjieff aimed to convey the message of his "Work" with his fictional trilogy *Beelzebub's Tales to His Grandson* (1950), *Meetings with Remarkable Men* (1963), and *Life Is Real Only When 'I Am'* (1975).

8   According to theosophy and anthroposophy, the Akashic Records is a spiritual compendium which stores information on everything that has ever happened and will happen. It is believed to be located on a non-material plane.

Works Cited

Aquino, Michael A. 1977. "Lovecraftian Ritual." *Nyctalops* (May 1977): 13–15. Reprinted as appendix #74 in Michael A. Aquino. 2013. *The Church of Satan: Volume II – Appendixes*, 8th ed., 228–35. San Francisco.

Blavatsky, Helena P. 1877. *Isis Unveiled: A Master-Key to the Mysteries of Ancient and Modern Science and Theology*. New York and London: J. W. Bouton/Bernard Quaritch.

Blavatsky, Helena P. 1888. *The Secret Doctrine: The Synthesis of Science, Religion, and Philosophy, Vol. I – Cosmogenesis*. London: Theosophical Publishing Co.

Bradley, Marion Zimmer. 1983. *The Mists of Avalon*. New York: Alfred A. Knopf.

Bulwer-Lytton, Edward. 1871. *The Coming Race*. London: W. Blackwood and Sons.

Carroll, Peter J. 1987. *Liber Null & Psychonaut: An Introduction to Chaos Magic*. Boston and York Beach, ME: Weiser Books.

Coelho, Paulo. 1993. *The Alchemist*. London: Harper Collins.

Cohn, Dorrit. 1999. *The Distinction of Fiction*. Baltimore: The Johns Hopkins University Press.

Cowan, Douglas E. 2012. "Dealing a New Religion: Material Culture, Divination, and Hyper-Religious Innovation." In *Handbook of Hyper-Real Religions*, edited by Adam Possamai, 247–65. Leiden: Brill.

Cusack, Carole M. 2010. *Invented Religions: Imagination, Fiction and Faith*. Aldershot: Ashgate.

Cusack, Carole M. 2012. "Cognitive Narratology and the Study of New Religions." *The Alternative Spirituality and Religion Review* 3, no. 2: 154–71.

Cusack, Carole M. 2016a. "Fiction into Religion: Imagination, Other Worlds, and Play in the Formation of Community." *Religion* 46, no. 4: 575–90.

Cusack, Carole M. 2016b. "Invention in "New New" Religions." In *The Oxford Handbook of New Religious Movements*, Vol. 2, edited by James R. Lewis and Inga B. Tøllefsen, 237–47. New York and Oxford: Oxford University Press.

Cusack, Carole M., and Pavol Kosnáč, eds. 2017. *Fiction, Invention and Hyper-Reality: From Popular Culture to Religion*. In the *Routledge Inform Series on Minority Religions and Spiritual Movements*, Eileen Barker, series editor. Abingdon & New York: Routledge.

Davidsen, Markus. 2010. "Genfødt og blå: religiøsitet baseret på James Camerons film *Avatar*." In *Religion 2.0? Tendenser og trends i det nye årtusind*, edited by René Dybdal Pedersen, 50–55. Aarhus: Det Teologiske Fakultet, Aarhus Universitet. https://samtidsreligion.au.dk/religion-20-tendenser-og-trends-i-det-nye-aartusind.

Davidsen, Markus Altena. 2012. "The Spiritual Milieu Based on J.R.R. Tolkien's Literary Mythology." In *Handbook of Hyper-Real Religions*, edited by Adam Possamai, 185– 204. Leiden: Brill.

Davidsen, Markus Altena. 2013. "Fiction-Based Religion: Conceptualising a New Category Against History-based Religion and Fandom." *Religion and Culture: An Interdisciplinary Journal* 14, no. 4: 378–95.

Davidsen, Markus Altena. 2014. *The Spiritual Tolkien Milieu: A Study of Fiction-based Religion*. PhD dissertation, University of Leiden. A monograph based on the dissertation is under preparation and will be published with De Gruyter under the title *Tolkien Spirituality: Constructing Belief and Tradition in Fiction-based Religion*.

Davidsen, Markus Altena. 2016a. "From *Star Wars* to Jediism: The Emergence of Fiction-based Religion." In *Words: Religious Language Matters*, edited by Ernst van den Hemel and Asja Szafraniec, 376–89, 571–75. New York: Fordham University Press.

Davidsen, Markus Altena. 2016b. "The Religious Affordance of Fiction: A Semiotic Approach." In "Religion in Fiction." Special issue, *Religion* 46, no. 4: 521–49.

Davidsen, Markus Altena. 2017a. "The Jedi Community: History and Folklore of a Fiction-based Religion." *New Directions in Folklore* 15, no. 1/2: 7–49.

Davidsen, Markus Altena. 2017b. "The Elven Path and the Silver Ship of the Valar: Two Spiritual Groups Based on J. R. R. Tolkien's Legendarium," including two appendices, "Tië eldaliéva", by Rev. Michaele Alyras de Cygne and Calantirniel, and "Ilsaluntë Valion", by Gwineth. In *Fiction, Invention and Hyper-Reality: From Popular Culture to Religion*, edited by Carole M. Cusack and Pavol Kosnáč, 15–39. Abingdon and New York: Routledge.

Davidsen, Markus Altena. Forthcoming. "Esoteric Order of Dagon." In *Brill Dictionary of Contemporary Esotericism*, edited by in Egil Asprem. Leiden: Brill.

Davidsen, Markus Altena, and Bastiaan van Rijn. 2020. "Studying Religions as Narrative Cultures: Angel Experience Narratives in the Netherlands and Some Ideas for a Narrative Research Programme for the Study of Religion." In *Narrative Cultures and the Aesthetics of Religion: Storytelling—Imagination—Reception*, edited by Dirk Johannsen, Anja Kirsch and Jens Kreinath, 91–122. Leiden: Brill.

Feldt, Laura. 2016. "Contemporary Fantasy Fiction and Representations of Religion: Playing with Reality, Myth, and Magic in *His Dark Materials* and *Harry Potter*." *Religion* 46, no. 4: 550–74.

Fortune, Dion. 1938. *The Sea Priestess*. London: Society of the Inner Light.

Frenschkowski, Marco. 2021. "Magic and Literary Imagination in H. P. Blavatsky's Theosophy." In *Fictional Practice: Magic, Narration, and the Power of Imagination*, edited by Bernd-Christian Otto and Dirk Johannsen, 133–73. Leiden: Brill.

Gardner, Gerald B. 1954. *Witchcraft Today*. London: Rider & Co.

Gilhus, Ingvild Sælid, and Lisbeth Mikaelsson. 2013. "Theosophy and Popular Fiction." In *Handbook of the Theosophical Current*, edited by Olav Hammer and Mikael Rothstein, 453–72. Leiden: Brill.

Gonce, John Wisdom III. 2003. "Lovecraftian Magick – Sources and Heirs." In *The Necronomicon Files: The Truth Behind Lovecraft's Legend*, edited by Daniel Harms and John Wisdom Gonce III, 2nd ed., 85–126. Boston and York Beach, ME: Weiser Books.

Gruber, Bettina. 2009. "Literature and Religion: Features of a Systematic Comparison." *Journal of Religion in Europe* 2, no. 1: 21–36.

Hanegraaff, Wouter J. 2007. "Fiction in the Desert of the Real: Lovecraft's Cthulhu Mythos." "Esotericism and Fiction." Special issue. *Aries* 7, no. 1: 85–109.

Harvey, Graham. 2000. "Fantasy in the Study of Religions: Paganism as Observed and Enhanced by Terry Pratchett." *Diskus* (now *Journal of the British Association for the Study of Religion*) 6. http://jbasr.com/basr/diskus/diskus1-6/harvey-6.txt.

Harvey, Graham. 2006. "Discworld and Otherworld: The Imaginative Use of Fantasy Literature among Pagans." In *Popular Spiritualities: The Politics of Contemporary Enchantment*, edited by Lynn Hume and Kathleen McPhillips, 41–52. Aldershot and Burlington, VT: Ashgate.

Hine, Phil. (1994) 2004. *The Pseudonomicon.* 3rd revised ed. Tempe, AZ: The Original Falcon Press.

Holdstock, Robert. 1984. *Mythago Wood*. London: Victor Gollancz.

Jindra, Michael. 1994. "*Star Trek* Fandom as a Religious Phenomenon." *Sociology of Religion* 55, no. 1: 27–51.

Knight, Gareth [Basil Wilby]. 1990. *The Magical World of the Inklings*. Longmead: Element Books.

LaVey, Anton Szandor. 1969. *The Satanic Bible*. New York: Avon Books.

LaVey, Anton Szandor. 1972. *The Satanic Rituals: Companion to The Satanic Bible*. New York: Avon Books.

Laycock, Joseph. 2012. ""We Are Spirits of Another Sort": Ontological Rebellion and Religious Dimensions." *Nova Religio: The Journal of Alternative and Emergent Religions* 15, no. 3: 65–90.

Lupa. 2007. *A Field Guide to Otherkin*. Stafford: Megalithica Books.

McCormick, Debra. 2012. "The Sanctification of *Star Wars*: From Fans to Followers". In *Handbook of Hyperreal Religions*, edited by Adam Possamai, 165–84. Leiden: Brill.

Moyers, Bill. 1999. "Of Myth and Men: A Conversation between Bill Moyers and George Lucas about the Meaning of the Force and the True Theology of Star Wars." *Time*, April 26, 1999. http://content.time.com/time/subscriber/article/0,33009,990820-1,00.html.

Petersen, Anders Klostergaard. 2016. "The Difference Between Religious Narratives and Fictional Literature: A Matter of Degree Only." *Religion* 46, no. 4: 500–20.

Pettersson, Torsten. 2005. "Bibelns relation till verkligheten: En principiell jämförelse med sakprosan och skönlitteraturen." In *Litteraturen og det hellige: Urtekst – Intertekst – Kontekst*, edited by Ole Davidsen, 219–35. Aarhus: Aarhus University Press.

Platvoet, Jan G., and Arie L. Molendijk, eds. 1999. *The Pragmatics of Defining Religion: Contexts, Concepts and Contests*. Leiden, Boston and Köln: Brill.

Porter, Jennifer E. 2006. "'I Am a Jedi': *Star Wars* Fandom, Religious Belief and the 2001 Census." In *Finding the Force of the Star Wars Franchise: Fans, Merchandise and Critics*, edited by Matthew Wilhelm Kapell and John Shelton Lawrence, 95–112. New York: Peter Lang.

Possamai, Adam. 2005. *Religion and Popular Culture: A Hyper-Real Testament*. Brussels: P. I. E. Peter Lang.

Possamai, Adam. Ed. 2012a. *Handbook of Hyper-Real Religions*. Brill Handbooks on Contemporary Religion, edited by Carole M. Cusack and James R. Lewis, 5. Leiden: Brill.

Possamai, Adam. 2012b. "Yoda Goes to Glastonbury: An Introduction to Hyper-real Religions." In *Handbook of Hyper-real Religions*, edited by Adam Possamai, 1–21. Brill Handbooks on Contemporary Religion, series editors Carole M. Cusack and James R. Lewis. Leiden: Brill.

Ravenwolf. 2005. "Middle-Earth: Physical or Other Plane." Post #1646 in the Yahoo! Group Children of the Varda. Posted October 9, 2005. Accessed July 26, 2017.

Redfield, James. 1993. *The Celestine Prophecy: An Adventure*. Hoover, AL: Satori.

Schilbrack, Kevin. 2017. "A Realist Social Ontology of Religion." *Religion* 47, no. 2: 161–78.

Scire [Gardner, Gerald B.] 1939. *A Goddess Arrives*. London: Stockwell.

Singler, Beth. 2014. "'See Mom It Is Real': The UK Census, Jediism and Social Media." *Journal of Religion in Europe* 7, no. 2: 150–68.

Spangler, David. 1971. *Revelation: The Birth of a New Age*. The Findhorn Foundation.

Stausberg, Michael. 2020. *Die Heilsbringer: Eine Globalgeschichte der Religionen im 20. Jahrhundert*. Munich: C.H. Beck.

Stewart, C. Nelson. 1927. *Bulwer Lytton as Occultist*. London: Theosophical Publishing House.

Strube, Julian. 2013. *Vril: Eine okkulte Urkraft in Theosophie und esoterischem Neonazismus*. Munich: Wilhelm Fink.

Sutcliffe, Steven J., and Carole M. Cusack, eds. 2013. "Invented Religions: Creating New Religions through Fiction, Parody and Play." Special issue, *Culture and Religion: An Interdisciplinary Journal* 14, no. 4.

Tolkien, John Ronald Reuel. 1954–1955. *The Lord of the Rings*. London: George Allen & Unwin. Comprised of *The Fellowship of the Ring* (1954), second edition 1965 by Ballantine Books, *The Two Towers* (1954), second edition 1965 by Ballantine Books, and *The Return of the King* (1955), second edition 1965 by Ballantine Books.

Tolkien, John Ronald Reuel. 1977. *The Silmarillion*. Edited by Christopher Tolkien. London: George Allen & Unwin.

Wagenseil, Christoph. 2015. "Lovecraft Goes Magick: Cthulhus Ruf in Phantastik und (neuer) Religion." [Interview with Friedemann Rimbach-Sator]. *ReMid*. http://www.remid.de/blog/2015/07/lovecraft-goes-magick-cthulhus-ruf-in-phantastik-und-neuer-religion/.

36

FAKE CULTS, HYPER-REAL RELIGIONS, VIRTUAL BELIEFS AT THE CROSSROADS OF FICTION, THE SACRED, AND TECHNOLOGY

Lionel Obadia

Introduction

From an anthropological perspective, this chapter deals with the development of non-conformist forms of religion—or so-called ones—that result from recent metamorphoses in the collective cultural imagination. These religions fall into different conceptual categories, and at least four of them will be considered and discussed in this chapter: fake, fiction, parody, or invented religions. They are all forms of religious expression, according to a nowadays prominent religiocentric perspective that has turned mainstream in sociology and communication sciences, and they disclose a notable creativity that unfolds on the margins of official religious organizations or even in parallel with them. The contemporary debates on religious innovation also bring about other perspectives, all equally interesting, which nevertheless allow the same phenomena to be interpreted from different angles: as extensions of religions, derivations, or parallel developments of systems of beliefs. Through the presentation of some of these groups labelled as cults—the most prominent and most representative of this movement—we will take up the main lines of the debates surrounding their definition and describe what these cults illustrate in terms of religious creativity. However, the analysis cannot be reduced to *religious* creativity only. It is also a question of broader *cultural* creativity that will be brought to light here, by addressing the essential issue of the dependence of our analysis on the religious approach. From an anthropological perspective, the question of creativity will be brought to bear on the dynamics of the imaginary and the ontological status of fiction, by focusing on a dimension that is a common feature of these unconventional religions but rarely tackled in a central way in the existing scholarship: that of digital technologies.

Sacred Creativity in the Digital Area

This chapter addresses the issue of the development of non-conformist forms of religion with regard to the historical metamorphoses of collective imagination and in systems of belief in Western countries, i.e., in the context of ideological and technological modernity. Secularization processes are the usual suspects in the theories of recent religious change: they, however, mostly focus on political, sociological, and, to a certain extent, cultural factors in this process. Yet, the development of digital technologies and the advent of the Internet, AI, and other technologies have also brought about

467

DOI: 10.4324/9781003119456-40

profound transformations in beliefs and rituals, and in modes of communication and transmission. These transformations are often considered from the exclusive angle of the impact of the revolution on religions: religious symbols and messages circulate by means of electronic networks and anyone can "find god on the Internet" (Campbell, 2013). Hence, secularization and digitization are considered separately, as if technologies and beliefs, and by extension, technological and religious imaginaries, have undertaken singular trajectories and only occasionally and fortuitously intermingled and eventually met in the history of modernity. Yet, evidence of cross-fertilization between the two domains exists, and gives rise to systems of meaning and aesthetics that are continuously gaining visibility in contemporary societies: while the universes of belief are spanned by technologies and religions are inspired by them (Davis, 2015), the world of technologies is gradually more and more permeable to religious influences, especially in an oblique way (hypermodern technologies are *analogically* adorned with sacred, or transcendental, qualities) (Obadia, 2020; Stahl, 1995; Stolow, 2013).

Modernity and globalization are defined as key factors for the transformation of religions and the rise of new religions and new beliefs. Secularization and deinstitutionalization processes at once undermine the foundations of historical religions, offer new conditions and regimes of existence to traditions, and compel them to reshape alongside the new religious agencies and new modalities of appropriation of sacredness in what now is called an "open economy of the sacred" (Obadia, 2013). The theories aiming to account for these rapid changes are nonetheless quite complex since they are conceptualized with reference to different and sometimes contradictory approaches: secularization, which proclaims a decline of the sacred (Tschannen, 1992), is challenged by desecularization, according to which "God is back" (Berger, 1999), a sociology of individualization of religious beliefs and practices (Hervieu-Léger, 1993) which is disputed by a sociology of ethnic boundaries and separatism (Kepel, 1991), and the idea of a revival of religion (which proceeds from a return or a displacement of religion in society, and in any case, from a rearrangement of religious traditions) and, on the other hand, the invention of non-conformist religions. However, for all the scholars who have debated these issues, whatever the perspective or theory supported, these processes obviously prove the lively creativity of the sacred in the core of modern and globalized societies. The digital revolution, which is now a well-documented process, has brought about new behavior patterns, new attitudes to the world, and even genuine worldviews that mix the technological views of reality with ancient imaginaries (Davis, 2005). The most timely, controversial, and burning issue concerns the digital impact on the relationship of modern citizens to the world as it is mediated and biased by the distortion of information, fakes, and the creation of virtual universes that blur the lines between imagination and reality (van Doorn, Duivestein, and Pepping, 2021).

The media revolution, which came before the digital one, has enabled the cross-pollination of the film industry and leisure with popular culture to generate, after the "society of the spectacle" (theorized by Debord) and then the "culture of simulacra" (elaborated by Baudrillard), a new era of "fakes" that mimic not only reality but also authenticity (Chidester, 2005). This process is all the more palpable in the new modern and digital expressions of the sacred, flourishing quickly and blooming under many forms and directions, that partake of this (con)fusion between images of reality and lived reality, between authenticity and fiction, between the imaginary (in the realm of collective ideas) and the imagination (in the realm of fiction).

In the vast movement of reinvention of the sacred, the examples of hybridization between religion and fiction increase in number and surface each time more clearly in the frameworks of global culture. On the one hand, one can find what are now called "fictional religions," which are religions that exist only by means of fiction or fantasy: the Jedi religion in the *Star Wars* saga is a regularly cited example (Davidsen, 2017; Possamai, 2012). These are not to be confused with religious references in science fiction, divine allegories in the *Superman* movies or in *Interstellar* (2004) (Yazbek, 2020), or Buddhist allegories in *The Matrix* saga (Flannery-Dailey and Wagner, 2001). Science fiction narratives have been particularly creative and innovative in framing a series of fictional religions, i.e., imagined religions that are part of the fantasy universes: *Goa'uld* religion in the television series *Stargate SG-1*, Klingon religion in the *Star Trek* series.

Science fiction generates such a fascination that it is even possible to consider it in some ways as a religion *per se* (Kreuziger, 1986). On the other hand, another type of genuine relationship to the sacred can be observed in the forms that will be under consideration in this chapter: "fake" or "parody" religions that directly address the issue of fiction as a key factor in the modern transformations of beliefs. In fact, these movements, which number by dozens, manifest themselves in rather different forms but share common features, that this chapter will attempt to highlight. What is interesting is that these movements, some of which have existed for several decades, were virtually ignored by research in religious studies, social sciences of religion, and the humanities until they emerged into the cultural landscape of modern and globalized-connected societies. They surfaced on the occasion of surveys that revealed, for example, that more than 16,000 British citizens claimed to be members of the "Jedi religion"—albeit in the form of a prank, in order to divert the obligation to fit into a given religious taxonomy established by public administration for use in censuses (Davidsen, 2013). Since then, the research has developed quite quickly, but remains fairly limited to scholars specialized in the field (such as Carole Cusack, who has made it a privileged research object) or others who have shown a more intermittent interest in this and referred to non-conformist religions as a way to discuss more general theorical challenges, mainly the relationships of modern social actors to their media and technological environment (this is the case of Adam Possamai, who locates these objects in a broad sociology of mediatization and digitalization, and not just a sociology of cults [Possamai, 2018]). Fake cults are, therefore, research topics, but they have raised different perspectives and issues, depending on the area of disciplinary specialization, and they thus grant fiction relatively contrasting epistemological statuses, depending on whether it is considered a *duplication* of reality or a *diversion* of it. It is precisely these variations that we will examine under the different conceptual locutions forged in the theoretical debate: the lexical variety reflects the complexity of a field that is torn between different approaches.

Fields of Definitions and Problematics

Several concepts have been framed to grasp the relationship between religions and fictions. All of them are part of the same debate and echo each other, but each is worded in such a way as to bring out a different focus. It is both the noun and the adjective of the different expressions that should be subjected to analysis. First, the term "religion" is used alternately with "cult." If at first sight, the two may appear as semantic equivalents due to a certain number of common features (belief, symbols, and related social organization), they obviously refer to different repertoires. The notion of religion is used as a mirror of historical traditions, which are the object of a particular treatment: *mocked, inverted, transfigured,* religions passed through the prism of these fictional matrixes are images or models of religion that are necessarily out of step with reality, because they proceed from a diversion for the purposes of criticism or mockery. David Chidester evokes "fake religions" (2003), and he was followed in this line by Thomas Alberts (2008). Chidester has chosen to question the authenticity of these religions, framing the notion with the oxymoronic term "authentic fakes" and the logic of interplay between the two terms: new forms of religion borrow from repertoires that have nothing to do with religion (scientific and cultural fictions), while fictions are inspired by religious symbolism and values. His reflection follows on from his work on the ambivalent logics of popular culture, which is redefined in the light of the shift in reality generated by the hypermediatization of societies.

The expression "invented religions" has been proposed and defined by Carole Cusack and theorized in several of her publications (e.g., 2010). It epitomizes a certain relationship to reality as mediated by the narrative prism of fiction. In this sense, what interests Cusack is the way in which fiction operates as a matrix for the transfiguration of religion. Chidester (2003, 2005), however, associates the term "fake" with that of "fraud," which allows him to further generalize and to consider the question of fiction in religion from the point of view of a distortion of reality, whereas Cusack shifts the focus from "fake" to "imagination": these are two slightly different perspectives on cultural creativity when it takes religion as subject matter. Chidester examines the forms and meanings allocated to unconventional ways of thinking about religion, while Cusack (2010) is interested in the role of modern imaginary frameworks in religious innovation. For both scholars, literature and film play a key role in this regard. This approach has been championed by Adam Possamai who has understood these new cultural and religious realities as what he terms "hyperreal religions" (2012), which states that the media and technological ecosystem provides narratives and symbolic resources (drawn from science fiction) that infuse popular culture. As such, a hyperreal religion is anything but real since it is a simulacrum of a religion existing only in the media of popular culture (films, books, TV series, and so on). Markus Davidsen's approach combines and confronts both approaches: the key concept of his theory is that of *fiction-based religions* (2013), which associates the role of narrative and filmic fictions with that of visual and communicative technologies.[1] Davidsen distinguishes himself from other scholars in the field by the special place he assigns to fiction. According to him, this is not a diversion or transfiguration of religious institutions, but a source of creativity for religious dynamics. Other terms, whose authorship is difficult to trace, are also popularized on anonymous websites: for instance, "parody religion" and "mock religions" characterize the joking and sarcastic side of some of these "religions." Cusack (2018) suggests that "mock religion" is a sub-category of "invented" (or fiction-based or hyper-real) religions, and must exclusively be reserved for those that rely on this ironic dimension (such as the Church of the Flying Spaghetti Monster, hereafter CFSM). The quite comprehensive and apropos Wikipedia page (2023) devoted to the CFSM suggests, on the contrary, that we consider parody and mock religions as broad and inclusive categories. It is important to note that these reflections only concern the concept of religion so far. Another category, which is also in common use but which has not given rise to substantial developments, is that of "fake cults," that can be found in the descriptors of Internet pages and in some academic works (Obadia, 2015): it is sometimes related, at least for its adjectival part, to the issue of authenticity raised by Chidester.

The second facet of these hyphenated movements (fake-invented-hyperreal religions), regarding the noun, rather than the adjective, is just as interesting, if not more so. The term "cult," in addition to defining a minority—which is the first formal characteristic of these movements—is also associated with a negative stigma, that of a community in tension with the rest of society (which is the hallmark of the "cult"). Yet, these movements embody tensions between different ideological orientations. This is also the reason why the author of these lines advocates the concept of "fake cults," precisely to point out the subversive, if not secessionist, character of these movements. The idea of "fake" highlights the creative and productive character of the matrixes of fiction, and the concept of "cult" complements it with the seditious character of the intellectual positions assumed by the creators and followers or sympathizers of these movements. Obviously, the above-mentioned authors defend singular views, and their theories cannot be assimilated into each other. In addition, there are quite significant variations in the conceptual categories and theoretical angles favored, on the one hand, and each author strives to specify the intellectual perimeter of the theoretical expression he or she favors. But there are also cases that mobilize elements of fiction and raise questions about the use of the labels "cult" and "religion." For example, the Church of Scientology, founded by L. Ron Hubbard in 1953, a science fiction writer, has become the head of its own religion but is considered a dangerous cult by governments. Then there is a multitude of references to religion in literary and cinematic fiction (but also in electronic games, see Campbell and Grieve, 2014; Servais, 2020), which is precisely what the concepts of fiction-based religion and hyperreal religion capture. Leaving aside the presence of the classical or reinvented religious in fiction for aesthetic or narrative purposes, however, it is another modality that is examined here: the reference to religion in fictions that is established in the mode of intentional shift.

Some Case Studies

A rather large number of empirical cases feed a reflection that is developing, and each conceptual category is more or less associated with a movement or a group that embodies its type. Rather than repeating the list of religions or cults and their associated categories, we shall retain, for the purposes of analysis, only a subset of them, a series of case studies chosen not by virtue of their similarities but, on the contrary, by virtue of their distinctive particularities: Discordianism, the Church of Subgenius, the Church of the Flying Spaghetti Monster and Kopimism are movements that are widely quoted because they are highly visible. Each one has its own singularity, but taken together, they can fall into several categories, and it is precisely for this reason that they are interesting for questioning the interplay between fictional effects and reality games. After briefly presenting the cases selected for this chapter, which I cannot develop fully (the reader will turn to the authors who have examined each of them in greater detail), I will begin on this basis a fundamental reflection on what they reveal about the relationship between fiction and religion.

The first case is "Discordianism," allegedly (and maybe really) the first to be created among the fake or invented cults, and often said to be "a prank religion." It was invented in 1963 by two college students, Kerry Thornley and Greg Hill, who wrote a *Principia Discordia* setting out all the basic propositions in order to establish a cult to the Goddess of strife, discord, and sacred chaos. Carole Cusack has devoted a significant part of her research to this case, underscoring on one occasion its status as a mock religion (Cusack, 2010). If Discordianism resembles a Neo-pagan religion (with an emphasis on references to ancient mythologies), it is a parody religion inspired by "chaos magic" (an early twentieth-century magical movement). The two founders wanted to create a "religion of chaos—of causing maximum cognitive confusion in order to spark actual creative thinking outside the narrow confines of dogma" in their own words. The second case of interest is *the Church of Subgenius*. Founded in 1979, by Ivan Stang (born Douglas St. Clair Smith) and Philo Drummond (born Steve Wilcox), the movement is often regarded as a parody of religion in general, with elements of fundamentalist Christianity, Zen, Scientology, New Age cults, pop-psychology, and motivational sales techniques. According to the Church of Subgenius (hereafter CoS) God is named "JHV1," salesmen are "prophets," and the church a sort of "enterprise" of the sacred, whose main figure is J. R. "Bob" Dobbs, a smiling face with a pipe who epitomizes the post-war baby-boomer but is depicted as "world avatar." The Cos is a reference in the field of "parody religions" (Cusack, 2010; Kirby, 2012) since it is a mix between capitalistic and religious ideologies (both of which are mocked). A third and equally famous case is the CFSM, or Pastafarianism. Founded in 2005 by Bobby Henderson, a student of science in Oregon, it was established in opposition to the anti-Darwinian teaching of Intelligent Design in public schools in the United States. Henderson wanted to point explicitly to the illogical causalities of religions when they attempt to erode the foundation of science. He designed a god-like creature made of meatballs and pasta and a specific pantheon where humans were rewarded after life with beer and striptease. This satire of religions echoes the context of conflict between atheist and confessional groups over education in the USA. Strangely, the CFSM received recognition as "religion" by followers who wanted to challenge the rules of state recognition for religions. In Poland, a CFSM follower successfully forced the government to accept him wearing a colander on his head for his passport photo (Obadia, 2015). The fourth case is Jediism, inspired by the fictional narrative of the cinematographic saga *Star Wars*, and is named and framed after the fictional religion of the Jedi as described in the movies. Early websites dedicated to bringing up a belief system from the *Star Wars* films were "The Jedi Religion and regulations" and "Jediism." These websites cited the Jedi code, consisting of twenty-one maxims, as the starting point for a "real Jedi" belief system. The real-world Jediism movement has no leader or central structure. It offers an interesting case for a discussion on fiction (Davidsen, 2017). A fifth case is Dudeism. Dudeism is a religion or lifestyle inspired by "The Dude," the protagonist 1998 film *The Big Lebowski*. Dudeism's stated primary objective is to promote a modern form of Chinese Taoism, blended with concepts from the ancient Greek philosopher Epicurus (341–270 BCE) and presented in a style as personified by the character of Jeffrey "The Dude" Lebowski, a fictional character portrayed by Jeff Bridges in the film. Dudeism is sometimes regarded as a mock religion but its founder and many adherents take the underlying philosophy seriously (Benjamin, 2015). A sixth case, also regularly quoted in the list of these fiction/fake/invented religions is the Missionary Church of Kopimism, aka Kopimism. This "congregation of file sharers" who believe that copying information is a sacred virtue was founded in Sweden in 2010 by Isak Gerson, a philosophy student, and Gustav Nip (John, 2013). The church, based in Sweden, was officially recognized by the Legal, Financial, and Administrative Services Agency as a religious community in January 2012, after three attempts. Their key symbol is a ying-yang image including the Crtl-C and Crtl-V acronyms. The Missionary Church was criticized by some Swedish media as devoid of religion, but championed by others as a truly original initiative (Kirby and McIntyre, 2017).

A last and seventh case, this one far less cited, is the "Church of kek" or "Pepe the Frog" movement. The "Pepe the Frog" religion was created by American artist and cartoonist Matt Furie in 2005. Its usage as an Internet meme came from his comic *Boy's Club #1*. As it is the case for *Kopimism*, "Pepe the Frog" has benefited from the electronic ecosystem of Internet communication, especially social networks like Twitter and Facebook. One of the mottos of the Kek church, the sentence "feels good man!" (a truly annoying one, according to the founder of the movement), has become an Internet meme. It even became a symbol of "coolness" around the global and gave birth to its own narrative: the name "kek" means "LOL" (laugh out loud) in Korean, and a country *kekland* has been imagined (Ellis, 2010).

The list is, of course, far from limited to these case studies and there are many other examples that could join the ever-extending group of fictions labelled as "churches," "cults," or "religions." Regardless of their diversity, they all have in common that they raise awareness of the role of fiction in the dynamics of religious creativity as well as in the conception of new frameworks of fiction.

The Role of Fiction: Mirror or Ricochet of Reality?

The relationship between religion and fiction, which is being reexamined today, is unremitting throughout history in the *longue durée*: religion is in some way a producer of fiction (it creates universes of meaning and imaginary worlds through narratives and aesthetic representations), but it obviously sets up frameworks in particular terms because they are entirely centered around the norm of the *sacred*. What the new religions presented above highlight is rather the reinvention of fictional frameworks and collective imaginations, and in particular the impact of new technologies on the transformations they are subjected to. The emphasis is placed here on fictions with religious content (which are not exactly nor entirely "religious fictions") that are quickly developing in the context of heavy digitization. Technological environments are often seen as a facilitators or accelerators for creativity, but one theoretical question arises: is technology responsible (and to what extent?) for such changes or must they be attributed to other (social, cultural, or political) conditions? In order to isolate the role of technology in the process of creation of these new, false, or invented religions, it would be necessary to examine information on such movements *before* the digital revolution; nevertheless, in historical works focused on recent periods (Stolow, 2013) or on a longer duration (Debray, 2001), there is an obvious concomitance between communication technologies (first graphic and oral, then to textual and hypertextual) and religions, which have adapted to these changing environments.

Scholars who have addressed the issues have pointed out that the technologies have also been re-shaped by the transformations that have affected societies and religions, and the adaptative logics of religions so as to ensure the preservation and dissemination of their salvation messages and sacred symbols. It, therefore, seems obvious that the rise of information and communication technologies must have had an impact on these movements, in one way or another, by providing religions the opportunity to spread (Subgenius, Discordianism), and in some cases, allowing them to exist as natively digital creations (CFSM, Church of kek). Some are even directly inspired by the aesthetics and references of computer science (Kopimism).

It would be a mistake, however, to consider that all invented or imagined religions are dependent on media or digital technologies. There are some examples (which do not exactly form a subcategory of invented religions) that show that the relationship between the imagination and the world of practices is more complex than a simple separation (real versus invented) or a process of one (fake religion) being engendered by the other (social conditions and digital technologies). In some cases, invented religions, which originate in literary, television, and cinema fictions or that are fictional duplicates of social, ideological, and cultural realities, can be embodied in attitudes, practices, and social dynamics: this is the case of the CFSM, which is now materialized in costumes worn by followers, street marches, statues, art exhibitions, festivals and symbols present in the social world by means of urban art, for example. The epistemological circle moves here from reality to fiction, and then returns from fiction to reality: the CFSM started as a purely digital fiction and materialized in social life, a process that in turn gave higher visibility to the digital facet of the church (Obadia, 2015).

Taking up the issue of invented religions, Wadsworth and Črnič (2021) observed an identical process in Slovenia with the birth and the progress in social and political spaces of a "Zombie Church" (the *Zombie Church of the Blissful Ringing*, hereafter ZCBR), which is a quite original (to say the least!) mix between (gore) fiction and (institutionalized) religion; the ZCBR serves has subversive force against the government (Wadsworth, and Črnič, 2021) While the CFSM symbolized a struggle between the progressive wing of scientists and the conservative wing of religions in the United States, the ZCBR was born in a context of political instability and became an instrument of resistance and protest. These two examples of the "repatriation" of invented religions from abstraction to the materiality of social reality (in this case of a political nature) prove that it is also necessary to consider the unexpected effects of fiction on reality, even though irony purportedly prevents us from considering scholars as such.

The humor and ironic character of fake religions indeed preclude them from being taken seriously and maintain them in the realm of pure fiction. This is the criticism that Bekkering (2016) addresses to Cusack (2010) regarding the Church of Subgenious, because Cusack regards irony as a surface "masquerade" that does not prevent the church from possessing all the symbolic and morphological elements necessary to figure out a religion. Bekkering brings irony to the forefront of the analysis and shows that it is structuring and not secondary to the analysis. Irony not only plays a psychic and social role in adapting to reality, therefore infusing modern popular culture (Declercq, 2020), but also creates the conditions for new cultural expressions, and by extension religious and spiritual ones, which are relayed by the highly mediatized society. Popular modern culture thus partakes in a reconfiguration of the actors' systems of representation and action, which is tinged with irony and simulacra, and it is, therefore, normal that it now appears as an essential ingredient of the reconfiguration and bricolage logics of modernity, whether in the field of culture or of religion (Kirby, 2012). In this respect, it is important to note that the role of play in all senses of the word, be it "theater" or "game", should not be underestimated: Davidsen observed in Jediism the passage from "role-playing" (mimicry) to "religion" (in practice) (2016). In this regard, there is a potential embodiment of fiction in reality; a similar shift from fiction and irony to material and social reality is occurring in the CFSM after its having been a purely digital "cult" (Obadia, 2015).

Religious Creativity and New Technologies—Again?

This idea that religion is a way of "playing" with reality is far from new, in fact. It was first expressed by Johannes Huizinga ([1938] 1950), for whom culture is of ludic origin. And as early as the beginning of the 1980s, Kliever (1981) developed a theory of Fictive Religion based on two elements, "Rhetoric" and "Play," and she considered side by side the importance of "word games" and "playful games." More recently, Laycock recalled the debate on play in religion, and tackled the issue of humor in fake religions: for him, the ironic and comical characters of parodic or fictional cults should not be considered a derivation of religion but a means of reconnecting to it. They create a distance on the one hand but bring us back to religion on the other: in this sense, humor operates a grand tour of the imagination that returns us to the very reality of religion, questioning its deep nature (2013). In analyzing the role of humor in religious creativity in a slightly different way, Scott Simpson (2018) assumes that laughter and humor have played a crucial role in yielding invented religions throughout history, albeit under particular conditions, even if the processes are similar in ancient and modern times. Simpson exposes a series of inventions in religion (such as Pherecydes of Syros who rearranged Greek mythology and its pantheon in a strange way in the sixth century BCE, or more recently William Blake's very personal and mosaic mythopoeia and the four divine entities or "Zoas" who were dwelling in an imaginary pantheon [Simpson, 2011, 98]). Are fake cults or invented religions hence *really* modern or do they replay in modernity a scenario that has already been played out? The question will not be entirely resolved in this chapter; however, it is interesting to underscore the fact that the wholesale invention of cults and religion in the realm of fantasy is one of the hallmarks of modernity, in contrast with the ancient times that saw invention *within* cults and religion.

In 2012, Cusack opens up other perspectives and attempts to bring together Robert Bellah's social and mental evolutionism, which considers religious inventions in the very long term (followed in this perspective by the sociologist Yves Lambert [1999]), and Johannes Huizinga's game theory, in order to describe aspects of playful narrativity. If Lambert makes modernity the main matrix for the transformation of religion, Cusack draws a distinction between "new religious movements" and "invented religions," according to whether or not they recognize a background in tradition and stick to a repertoire of authenticity. Accordingly, the ever-increasing number of members of this "family" of religious and fictional hybrids is evidence of the creativity of and in religion, which is simply assuming new forms in modernity (2012). Still, this analysis remains faithful to a religiocentric bias: Cusack indeed proposes that the analysis depart from a core religious perspective and ends up at the margins of religion, and since invented religions cannot be anything else than extensions—but in the realm of imagination—of existing religions. A similar proposition is supported, but in a slightly broader perspective, by Teemu Taira who suggests in addition to examine not only the fields of definition but also the social uses of the category of religion, and in particular the instrumental uses of the category by invented religions (Taira, 2013). This is also the criticism made by Davidsen in his critique of the Cusack's notion of "religion" (Davidsen, 2011).

The cases cited and many others show that there is an ongoing debate on the qualification "religion," which engages a fundamental discussion on the nature of these movements but also on their genealogy and the factors or contexts which saw them come into being. Are they religious in their form, or in their functions? due to their mimetic correspondence with their model or their reverse mimesis (anti-religions)? Rather than asking whether invented/fake religions are religions or not, it is legitimate to ask to what extent a definition of these subversive, alternative, or imaginary expressions remains *dependent on* a religious norm. Possamai's view that media and digital technologies facilitate and accelerate this transformation opens an intellectual path to considering the imaginary developments of these religions that are not really religions per se but are similar to them. This line of reflection paves the way to a world of imitation, simulation, and cultural artifice where religions are not only reinvented but also properly invented. This engages a displacement of the focus for the core of religious systems to their margins and helps us to distance ourselves from the religiocentrism of mainstream analyses. After all, the interest of anthropologists does not really lie in the resemblances of the above-mentioned movements and cults to historical religions, but rather in the transfiguration of religions in the realm of imagination.

As for the technologies of information and communication, they have undoubtedly favored original forms of belief system that sometimes bear the name of "church" or "religion" but which are mimetic variants of them, in most cases in a parodic mode. There is, however, a desire to distinguish these cults from religions; what precisely characterizes their position in the social and imaginary space is that they are opposed to religions by the play of contrasts and similarities. Thus, in terms of their nature, they are counter-religions (they are counter-models) and in many cases anti-religions. It is (again) to Chidester that we owe a subtle analysis of the way in which fake or invented religions circulate on the Internet and then become above all "virtual religions" which from then on nourish an intense discussion as to the labels of which they are the object. For Chidester, there is an ambiguity in the designations of these "religions" which can be "cults" when they are stigmatized by traditional religions, while the Internet offers a space for negotiation between authenticity and falsity, virtuality and reality, novelty and tradition—making these fake religions "real fakes" (Chidester, 2003). Finally, what more can be said on the role of new technologies in this regard? It is a fairly common truism in the information and communication sciences to point out that Internet technologies have made it possible to liberate creativity (when the conditions of political control allow it). But is it enough to point out the role (however complex and essential) of technologies and in particular of the Internet? A distinction must be made from the outset between the fake cults that could exist offline and that, like established religions, have appropriated the new communication tools but were previously familiar with other media (press, literature, etc.), and others that, although in a minority position and in a position of contestation of the religious order, spread out a large part of their activity in the digital world. Thus, if we examine all the relationships that "fake" or "invented" or "fictional" religions have with "real" or "authentic" religions, a whole set of complex relationships unfolds: pure invention, simple mimicry or replication, inverted mimicry, translation through the prism of humor, political messages underlying the symbolism of these cults. But the same cults, which can also be described as pseudo- or para-cults, produce reality effects by materializing in the form of actual beliefs and behaviors, which blur the already-porous border between fiction and reality.

Note

1 See Markus Davidsen's contribution to the present volume.

Works Cited

Alberts, Thomas. 2008. "Virtually Real: Fake Religions and Problems of Authenticity in Religion." *Culture and Religion* 9, no. 2: 125–39.

Aupers, Stef. 2002. "The Revenge of the Machines: On Modernity, Digital Technology and Animism." *Asian Journal of Social Science* 30, no. 2: 199–220.

Bekkering, Denis J. 2016. "Fake Religions, Politics and Ironic Fandom: The Church of the SubGenius, *Zontar* and American Televangelism. *Culture and Religion* 17, no. 2: 129–47.

Benjamin, Oliver. 2015. *The Tao of the Dude: Awesome Insights of Deep Dudes from Lao Tzu to Lebowski.* CreateSpace Independent Publishing Platform, Abide University Press.

Berger, Peter L., ed. 1999. *The Desecularization of the* World, *Resurgent Religion and* World *Politics*. Grand Rapids, MI: Eerdmans.

Campbell, Heidi A. 2013. *Digital Religion. Understanding Religious Practice in New Media Worlds*. Abingdon and New York: Routledge.
Campbell, Heidi, and Gregory Price Grieve, eds. 2014. *Playing with Religion in Digital Games*. Bloomington: Indiana University Press.
Chidester, David. 2003. "Fake Religion: Ordeals of Authenticity in the Study of Religion." *Journal for the Study of Religion* 16, no. 2: 71–97.
Chidester, David. 2005. *Authentic Fakes. Religion and American Popular Culture*. Berkeley: University of California Press.
Cusack, Carole M. 2010. *Invented Religions: Imagination, Fiction, and Faith*. Farnham: Ashgate.
Cusack, Carole M. 2013. "Play, Narrative and the Creation of Religion: Extending the Theoretical Base of 'Invented Religions.'" *Culture and Religion* 14, no. 4: 362–77.
Cusack, Carole M. 2018. "Mock Religions." In *Encyclopedia of Latin American Religions*, edited by Henri Gooren. Cham: Springer. online: https://link.springer.com/referenceworkentry/10.1007/978-3-319-08956-0_559-1
Davis, E. 2015. *TechGnosis. Myth, Magic & Mysticism in the Age of Information*. Berkeley: North Atlantic Books.
Davidsen, Markus A. 2011. "Review of Invented Religions: Imagination, Fiction and Faith (2010), by Carole M. Cusack." *Literature & Aesthetics: Journal of the Sydney Society of Literature and Aesthetics* 21, no. 1: 259–26.
Davidsen, Markus A. 2013. "Fiction-Based Religion: Conceptualising a New Category Against History-Based Religion and Fandom." *Culture and Religion: An Interdisciplinary Journal* 14, no. 4: 378–95.
Davidsen, Markus. 2016. "Fiction and Religion: How Narratives About the Supernatural Inspire Religious Belief: Introducing the Thematic Issue." *Religion* 46, no. 4: 489–99.
Davidsen, Markus A. 2017. "The Jedi Community: History and Folklore of a Fiction-Based Religion." In "The Folk Awakens: Star Wars and Folkloristics," edited by John E. Price. Bloomington, IN: IUScholarWorks Journals. Special issue, *New Directions in Folklore* 15, nos. 1–2: 7–49.
Debray, Régis. 2001. *Dieu, un itineraire*. Paris: Odile Jacob.
Declercq, Dieter. 2020. "Irony, Disruption and Moral Imperfection." *Ethical Theory and Moral Practice* 23, no. 3: 545–59.
Ellis, Emma Grey. 2010. "Witches, Frog-Gods, and the Deepening Schism of Internet Religions." *WIRED*, April 3. https://www.wired.com/story/witchblr-kek-online-occultism/
Flannery-Dailey, Frances, and Rachel L. Wagner. 2001. "Wake up! Gnosticism and Buddhism in *The Matrix*." *Journal of Religion & Film* 5, no. 2 (October): article 4. https://digitalcommons.unomaha.edu/jrf/vol5/iss2/4.
Hervieu-Léger, Danièle. 1993. *La religion pour memoire*. Paris: Le Cerf.
Huizinga, Johan. 1950. *Homo Ludens: A Study of the Play Element in Culture*. Boston, MA: Beacon Press.
John, Nicholas A. 2013. "Sharing and Web 2.0: The Emergence of a Keyword." *New Media & Society* 15, no. 2: 167–82.
Kepel, G. 1991. *La revanche de Dieu: chretiens, juifs et musulmans a la reconquete du monde*. Paris: Seuil.
Kirby, Danielle L. 2012. "Occultural Bricolage and Popular Culture: Remix and Art in Discordianism, the Church of the SubGenius, and the Temple of Psychick Youth." In *Handbook of Hyper-Real Religions*, edited by Adam Possamai, 37–57. Leiden: Brill.
Kirby, Danielle L., and Elisha H. McIntyre. 2017. "Kopimism and Media Devotion: Piracy, Activism, Art and Critique as Religious Practice." In *Fiction, Invention and Hyper-Reality*, edited by Carole M. Cusack and Pavol Kosnáč, 227–39. Abingdon and New York: Routledge.
Kliever, Lonnie D. (1981). "Fictive Religion: Rhetoric and Play." *Journal of the American Academy of Religion* 49, no. 4: 657–669.
Kreuziger, Frederick A. 1986. *The Religion of Science Fiction*. Bowling Green, OH: Bowling Green State University Popular Press.
Lambert, Yves. 1999. "Religion in Modernity as a New Axial Age: Secularization or New Religious Forms?" *Sociology of Religion* 60, no. 3: 303–333.
Laycock, Joseph. P. 2013. "Laughing Matters: 'Parody Religions' and the Command to Compare." *Bulletin for the Study of Religion* 42, no. 3: 19–26.
Obadia, Lionel. 2013. *La marchandisation de Dieu. Économies religieuses*. Paris: CNRS.
Obadia, Lionel. 2015. "When Virtuality Shapes Social Reality: Fake Cults and the Church of the Flying Spaghetti Monster." *Heidelberg Journal of Religions on the Internet* 8: 115–28. https://heiup.uni-heidelberg.de/journals/index.php/religions/article/view/20327
Obadia, Lionel. 2020. "Moral and Financial Economics of 'Digital Magic.' Explorations of an Opening Field." *Social Compass* 67, no. 1: 1–19.
Possamai, Adam, ed. 2012. *Handbook of Hyper-Real Religions*. Leiden: Brill.

Possamai, Adam. 2018. *The I-zation of Society, Religion, and Neoliberal Post-Secularism*. Singapore: Palgrave Macmillan.

Servais Olivier. 2020. *Dans la peau des gamers. anthropologie d'une guilde de "world of warcraft."* Continent digital. Paris: Karthala.

Simpson, Scott. 2011. "Joke Religions: Make-Believe in the Sandbox of the Gods." *Ex Nihilo* 2, no. 6: 91–118.

Stahl, William A. 1995. "Venerating the Black Box: Magic in Media Discourse on Technology." *Science, Technology, & Human Values* 20, no. 2: 234–58.

Stolow, Jeremy, ed. 2013. *Deus in Machina: Religion, Technology, and the Things in Between*. New York: Fordham University Press.

Taira, Teemu. 2013. "The Category of 'Invented Religion': A New Opportunity for Studying Discourses on 'Religion.'" *Culture and Religion* 14, no. 4: 477–93.

Tschannen, Olivier. 1992. *Les théories de la sécularisation*. Geneva: Droz.

van Doorn, Menno, Sander Duivestein, and Thijs Pepping. 2021. *Real Fake: Playing with Reality in the Age of AI, Deepfakes and the Metaverse*. Groningen: Ludibrium Publishers.

Wadsworth, Nancy D., and Aleš Črnič. 2021. "Invented Religion, the Awakened Polis, and Sacred Disestablishment: The Case of Slovenia's 'Zombie Church.'" *Politics and Religion* 14, no. 3: 526–51.

Wikipedia. 2023. "Flying Spaghetti Monster." Wikimedia Foundation. Last modified March 11, 2023, 03:30. https://en.wikipedia.org/wiki/Flying_Spaghetti_Monster.

Yazbek, Elie. 2020. ed. "Science Fiction and Religion." Special issue, *Journal for Religion, Film and Media* 6, no. 1. https://jrfm.eu/index.php/ojs_jrfm/issue/view/10/9

York, Michael. 1999. "Invented Culture/Invented Religion: The Fictional Origins of Contemporary Paganism." *Nova Religio: The Journal of Alternative and Emergent Religions* 3, no. 1: 135–46.

INDEX

Note: **Bold** page numbers refer to tables; *italic* page numbers refer to figures and page numbers followed by "n" denote endnotes.

Climate Change Edition of *McSweeney* (magazine) 323
climatological: scenarios 328; science 329, 330, 333
Clues, Myths, and the Historical Method (Ginzburg) 249
Coady, C.A.J. 135n14
Coelho, Paulo: *The Alchemist* 461
Coetzee, J.M.: *Boyhood, Youth, Summertime* 78
cognitive/cognitivism 55, 104; adaptations 96; attitude 2; bias 89–90; dissonance 89, 95; fictions 3–4; immersion 104; investments 2; literary 90; modelization 204, 205; narrative scholars 330–1; predisposition 92; processes 160; psychologists 88; psychology 95–6; sciences 2, 4
Cohen, Sacha Baron: *Borat!* 197; *Da Ali G Show* 197
Cohn, Dorrit 104, 401n9
Coleridge, Samuel Taylor 1, 3, 28–9, 31–6, 37n3, 38n9, 38n10, 38n13, 45, 54, 196, 210; *Biographia Literaria* 18; definition of poetic faith 3; on dramatic illusion 28–30; personal theology 37; "suspension of disbelief" 1, 3, 7, 18, 28–38, 41, 54, 199, 203, 210, 283, 353, 364
collaborative fictional immersion 217
collective belief worlds (Lewis) 4
collective imaginations 467, 472
Collins, Steven 169
Collins, Suzanne: *The Hunger Games* 163, 275
Colloquies (Erasmus) 365
colonization 72–3, 442
The Coming Race (Bulwer-Lytton) 318
Commentary on the Dream of Scipio (Macrobius) 355
Comment on écrit l'histoire? (Veyne) 102
commitment 4, 6, 21, 28, 120, 132, 246, 250, 275, 281, 283, 284, 323, 350, 435
common sense 238, 289
communication 263; acts **259**; of beliefs in nonfiction 21; mode of 209–10; signaling invention in 260; strategies 258, 283; technologies 472–3; tracks of 80, 81, 84
communitarianism 443
Comolli, Jean-Louis 210
Compagnon, Antoine 210
comparative mythology 369
Comte de Gabalis (Montfaucon de Villars) 373
conditioning, evaluative 175–6
Confessions (Augustine) 351
The Confidence-Man (Melville) 236, 237, 241, 244
confirmation bias 226
conflicted belief 88
Confucius 141
Conrad, Joseph 294, 297n4; fictional discourse 291–2; *Heart of Darkness* 290–3
consciousness 307; ability of 412
constitutional monarchy 317
consumers 23, 28, 180, 220, 221, 230, 232n23, 233n27

contemporary literature: Arabic literature 431; communication strategy and/or political commitment 281–3; fantasy references, political context 278–81; fiction and 202, 249, 250, 254, 275–8; fiction and propaganda 283–4; novels 9, 252, 370, 376; populism 236; revisionism 127; romantic comedies 173
Cook, Christopher 162
Corneille, Pierre 102, 383–5, 387; *Polyeucte martyr* 382
Corriveau, Kathleen H. 188, 190
Cortazar, Julio: *Libro de Manuel* 105
Cosmos: A Spacetime Odyssey (series) 19
Council of Trent 380–2
counterconditioning 179, 180; evaluative 180; opportunities for 180
counter-immersive effects 217
counter-stereotype exposure 180
Cousin de Grainville, Jean-Baptiste: *Le Dernier Homme (The Last Man)* 317
Craven, Wes 278
creative: expression 296n2; nonfiction 22; writing 90, 437–8
Creative Evolution (Bergson) 307
The Creative Mind (Bergson) 307
credibility 89; of fictions 300, 301
credit: description of 248–50; economies 3; giving 252; notion of 250; novel about 241–4; seeking 250–2; social imagery of 249
credulity, description of 236–8
creeds 363–8, 373
Crichton, Michael 9, 326, 331, 334n1; *State of Fear* 325, 328–9
Critchley, Simon 443, 452n1
critical dystopias 316, 319, 320
critical hagiography 388
Critical Terms for Religious Studies (Lopez) 442
critics converge 379–80
Crnic, Aleš 473
Croce, Michel 223–4, 232n23
Cromwell, Thomas 128
cross-checking 209–10
Crowley, Aleister 457
Croxton Play of the Sacrament (Sebastien) 358
Cthulhu Mythos 455, 461
cults, symbolism of 475
cultural/culture: assets 220; contexts 93; creativity 467; knowledge 289; modernity 430; prominence 351; of simulacra 468; specificity 289; translation, politics of 289
Cummings, Anthony 334
Currie, Gregory 19, 25n13, 38n14, 61n5, 134n3
Cusack, Carole 454, 455, 463n3, 464n6, 464n7, 469–71, 473–4
Cutrufelli, Maria Rosa 253
cyber-war 305
Cyrano de Bergerac, Savinien de: *États et Empires de la Lune et du Soleil* 367

media: communication 282–3; conversation, popularization of 280–1; coverage 454; environment 221; images of conflict 260; mass 283; revolution 468; technologies 474

medieval: allegory 353; circulation in 349; collectivism 312; commentators 359; conception of 353; course of 353; fantasy 284; fiction/fictionality 352, 355, 360, 381; heterogeneous practices 353; interest in 360; reflection 349; sophisticated accounts of fictionality 355; theorizations 356

medieval India: believing and enjoying make-believe 411–12; description of 403; fiction 403–4, 406–7, 409, 412; religious competition 407–9; religious fictions 404–5

medieval Latin Christendom 349; fiction and belief in 352; literary fiction in 353; readers in 359

Mehnert, Antonia 328

Mélenchon, Jean-Luc 278

Melville, Herman 8, 97, 236–46; *The Confidence-Man* 236, 237, 241, 244; *Moby Dick* 20, 21

Memmi, Albert 437

memory, psychology of 132

Mendelsohn, Daniel: *The Lost* 106

mental evolutionism 474

mental states, attribution of 94

The Merchant of Venice (Shakespeare) 445, 446

Mercier, Hugo 93, 317

Mersal, Iman: *Alternative Geography* 439; *In the Footsteps of Enayat Al-Zayyat* 435

meta-fictional reflection 244

Metahistory (White) 102

metaleptic effects 214

The Metamorphosis (Kafka) 449

Michael, Archangel 72

Michael Kohlhaas (Kleist) 72

Michelet, Jules 102

Middle Ages *see* medieval

Middlemarch (Eliot) 16, 18

Milkoreit, Manjana 327

millenarian teleology 317

Mill, John Stuart 314

Mimesis as Make-Believe (Walton) 41, 61n4

mimetic 46; dimension 49; immersion 47; poetics 346

mindreading, cognitive illusion of 94

mirror box 251, 254n6

Missionary Church of Kopimism 472

Mister Johnson (Cary) 290, 292, 293

Mitchell, Chris J. 176

Moby Dick (Melville) 20, 21

mock religions 470

model system 120–1

modern/modernity 352; advent of 239; aesthetics 30; culture, development of 364; definition of 468; forms in 474; hallmarks of 474; history of 468; unbelief 365–8

A Modern Utopia (Wells) 317, 318

Modiano, Patrick: *Dora Bruder* 108

Modleski, Tania 266–7, 272n22

Molendijk, Arie L. 464n4

Momus (Alberti) 366

The Monk (Lewis) 35

Monsjou, Elizabeth van 146

Montfaucon de Villars, Henri: *Comte de Gabalis* 373

moral: exemplarity 306; panic 209, 211; teachings 404

More, Thomas 313, 367, 427; *Utopia* 314

Morris, Edmund: *Dutch* 20

Morris, Heather: *The Tattooist of Auschwitz* 107

Moscow Art Theater 199

Mossad mission 445–6, 449, 451

motor resonance 45

Moyers, Bill 460

Moylan, Tom 316, 320

Mukerji, Nikil 223, 232n22

Muller, Max 442

multi-media franchises 46

al-Muqaffa, Ibn: *Kalîla and Dimna* 421–3

Murata, Tsutomu: *The True Biography of Shinran* 391

Murdoch, Iris 254

Murray, Janet 45

Musil, Robert 309n4; *The Man without Qualities* 299

Muslim 259, 291, 373, 419, 423, 424, 427; *see also* religious/religions

mûthos 101, 342–3

mutual agreement 43

Mutual Belief Principle (MBP) (Walton) 4

mutual trust 242–3

mystery genres 165, 168, 170n9, 381

My Struggle (Knausgaard) 78

mythical traditions 340

mythopoeic interpretation 457, 458

myths/mythology 67, 339, 341–4, 403–4; counter-tradition of 408; Helen's abduction 344

Nabokov, Vladimir 85; *Lolita* 17

al-Nadîm, Ibn 424

Nahda movement 430

Napoleon 44, 360

Narrative Factuality (Ryan) 6

narrative/narration 188–9; audience 80; character 77, 85; communication 79, 80; comprehension 23; default macro-genre of 80; elements of 79; features of 160–1; fictional 189, 346, 365; fundamental distinction between 187; and history 101, 103; persuasion 178, 179; realistic 188; religious 187–9, 404; representations 101; as rhetoric 79–80; techniques 47, 110; theoretical legitimacy of 102; theory 82; unreliable 76, 77, 79, 81, 84, 85

narratological scholarship 103

National Incident-Based Reporting System (NIBRS) 147

National Resources Defense Council (NRDC) 323, 324

World Trade Center (movie) 267
wornout mythical explanations 3
worship, content and forms of 380; *see also* religion, religious
W, or the Memory of Childhood (Perec) 450
writers/writing 289, 296n2; European conception of 434; of generic fiction 82; history and fiction 111; language of 437; literary 108, 296n2; nonfictional 296n2; nonliterary 296n2; postcolonial 290; protocols 110; resources of 111; techniques and belief 110
The Writing of the Disaster (Blanchot) 450
Wu Ming 255n15

Year Zero (game) 198
Younge, Henry Lewis: *Utopia or Apollo's Golden Days* 313

Zafar, Ibn: *Waters of Consolation for the Ruler during the Hostility of Subjects* 421–3
Zakharia, Katia 430, 432
Zayd, Abû 427
Zeeman, Nicolette 354
Zelenski, Volodymyr 283
Zetterberg-Nielsen, Henrik *see* Nielsen, Henrik Skov
Zeus 344–5
Žižek, Slavoj 443; *Sociology through the Projector* 267
Zionism 444, 446
Zoller, Fredrick 269
Zombie Church of the Blissful Ringing (ZCBR) 473
Zumthor, Paul 360
Zunshine, Lisa 2, 330; *The Secret Life of Literature* 96; *Why We Read Fiction* 331